THE MODERN LIBRARY

of the World's Best Books

>>

THE BEST-KNOWN
NOVELS OF GEORGE ELIOT

>>

The publishers will be pleased to send, upon request, an illustrated folder setting forth the purpose and scope of THE MODERN LIBRARY, *and listing each volume in the series. Every reader of books will find titles he has been looking for, handsomely printed, in unabridged editions, and at an unusually low price.*

>>>

THE BEST-KNOWN
NOVELS OF GEORGE ELIOT

ADAM BEDE

THE MILL ON THE FLOSS

SILAS MARNER

ROMOLA

THE MODERN LIBRARY

NEW YORK

THE MODERN LIBRARY

is published by RANDOM HOUSE, INC.

BENNETT CERF • DONALD S. KLOPFER

Manufactured in the United States of America by H. Wolff

GEORGE ELIOT

MARY ANN EVANS CROSS

(1819-1880)

A Note on the Author

It is noteworthy that George Eliot's very first literary venture was a translation from the German of a Life of Jesus. Such an undertaking, in view of her later development as a thinker and novelist, throws light upon the influences of her early youth and her subsequent heterodox way of life. Born Mary Ann Evans in Warwickshire, she was brought up in the severest tradition of religious training. It was not until her family moved to Coventry in 1841 that she became aware of the daring world of thought that existed beyond her family circle. A transformation was wrought in her; rebellion carried her forthwith into the then-flourishing rationalist movement. What she knew of the evangelical point of view stood her in good stead when she wrote her first work of fiction, *Scenes of Clerical Life*. Because she was acutely aware of a strong prejudice against women as writers, she assumed a male pseudonym.

After the death of her father, George Eliot became an assistant editor of the *Westminster Review*. Then she met George Henry Lewes, journalist and author of the famous biography of Goethe. Under his influence her genius as a novelist came into full flower. With him she traveled to Germany and there studied philosophy, the first fruits of which were translations from the works of Feuerbach and Spinoza.

In 1859, *Adam Bede* was published and George Eliot was acclaimed as one of the great novelists of her time. There followed in rapid succession *The Mill on the Floss, Silas Marner, Romola* and *Felix Holt*. A drama in blank verse, *The Spanish Gypsy*, was enthusiastically received, and, in 1874, a volume of verse, *The Legend of Jubal and Other Poems*, appeared. *Middlemarch* was written in 1872, and *Daniel Deronda* in 1876. The death of George Lewes, in 1878, virtually ended her artistic career. Two years before her own death on December 22, 1880, she was married to J. W. Cross. At that time her reputation had spread far beyond the insular limits of Britain and had become world-wide. Today there is a growing revival of enthusiasm for all her novels.

CONTENTS

ADAM BEDE

CONTENTS

★

BOOK ONE

BOOK TWO

BOOK THREE

3

CONTENTS

BOOK FOUR

BOOK FIVE

BOOK SIX

BOOK ONE

★

CHAPTER I

THE WORKSHOP

WITH a single drop of ink for a mirror, the Egyptian sorcerer undertakes to reveal to any chance comer far-reaching visions of the past. This is what I undertake to do for you, reader. With this drop of ink at the end of my pen, I will show you the roomy workshop of Mr. Jonathan Burge, carpenter and builder, in the village of Hayslope, as it appeared on the eighteenth of June, in the year of our Lord 1799.

The afternoon sun was warm on the five workmen there, busy upon doors and window-frames and wainscoting. A scent of pine-wood from a tent-like pile of planks outside the open door mingled itself with the scent of the elder-bushes which were spreading their summer snow close to the open window opposite; the slanting sunbeams shone through the transparent shavings that flew before the steady plane, and lit up the fine grain of the oak panelling which stood propped against the wall. On a heap of those soft shavings a rough grey shepherd-dog had made himself a pleasant bed, and was lying with his nose between his forepaws, occasionally wrinkling his brows to cast a glance at the tallest of the five workmen, who was carving a shield in the centre of a wooden mantelpiece. It was to this workman that the strong barytone belonged which was heard above the sound of plane and hammer singing—

> "Awake, my soul, and with the sun
> Thy daily stage of duty run;
> Shake off dull sloth . . ."

Here some measurement was to be taken which required more concentrated attention, and the sonorous voice subsided into a low whistle; but it presently broke out again with renewed vigour—

> "Let all thy converse be sincere,
> Thy conscience as the noonday clear."

Such a voice could only come from a broad chest, and the broad chest belonged to a large-boned muscular man nearly six feet high, with a back so flat and a head so well poised that when he drew himself up to take a more distant survey of his work, he had the air of a soldier standing at ease. The sleeve rolled up above the elbow showed an arm that was likely to win the prize for feats of strength; yet the long supple hand, with its

5

broad finger-tips, looked ready for works of skill. In his tall stalwartness
Adam Bede was a Saxon, and justified his name; but the jet-black hair,
made the more noticeable by its contrast with the light paper cap, and
the keen glance of the dark eyes that shone from under strongly marked,
prominent and mobile eyebrows, indicated a mixture of Celtic blood. The
face was large and roughly hewn, and when in repose had no other beauty
than such as belongs to an expression of good-humoured honest intelligence.

It is clear at a glance that the next workman is Adam's brother. He is
nearly as tall; he has the same type of features, the same hue of hair and
complexion; but the strength of the family likeness seems only to render
more conspicuous the remarkable difference of expression both in form
and face. Seth's broad shoulders have a slight stoop; his eyes are grey;
his eyebrows have less prominence and more repose than his brother's;
and his glance, instead of being keen, is confiding and benignant. He has
thrown off his paper cap, and you see that his hair is not thick and
straight, like Adam's, but thin and wavy, allowing you to discern the
exact contour of a coronal arch that predominates very decidedly over
the brow.

The idle tramps always felt sure they could get a copper from Seth;
they scarcely ever spoke to Adam.

The concert of the tools and Adam's voice was at last broken by Seth,
who, lifting the door at which he had been working intently, placed it
against the wall, and said—

"There! I've finished my door to-day, anyhow."

The workmen all looked up; Jim Salt, a burly red-haired man, known
as Sandy Jim, paused from his planing, and Adam said to Seth, with a
sharp glance of surprise—

"What! dost think thee'st finished the door?"

"Ay, sure," said Seth, with answering surprise; "what's awanting
to't?"

A loud roar of laughter from the other three workmen made Seth look
round confusedly. Adam did not join in the laughter, but there was a
slight smile on his face as he said, in a gentler tone than before—

"Why, thee'st forgot the panels."

The laughter burst out afresh as Seth clapped his hands to his head,
and coloured over brow and crown.

"Hoorray!" shouted a small lithe fellow, called Wiry Ben, running forward and seizing the door. "We'll hang up th' door at fur end o' th' shop
an' write on't 'Seth Bede, the Methody, his work.' Here, Jim, lend's hould
o' th' red-pot."

"Nonsense!" said Adam. "Let it alone, Ben Cranage. You'll mayhap
be making such a slip yourself some day; you'll laugh o' th' other side o'
your mouth then."

"Catch me at it, Adam. It'll be a good while afore my head's full o'
th' Methodies," said Ben.

"Nay, but it's often full o' drink and that's worse."

Ben, however, had now got the "red-pot" in his hand, and was about to begin writing his inscription, making, by way of preliminary, an imaginary S in the air.

"Let it alone, will you?" Adam called out, laying down his tools, striding up to Ben, and seizing his right shoulder. "Let it alone, or I'll shake the soul out o' your body."

Ben shook in Adam's iron grasp, but, like a plucky small man as he was, he didn't mean to give in. With his left hand he snatched the brush from his powerless right, and made a movement as if he would perform the feat of writing with his left. In a moment Adam turned him round, seized his other shoulder, and, pushing him along, pinned him against the wall. But now Seth spoke.

"Let be, Addy, let be. Ben will be joking. Why, he's i' the right to laugh at me—I canna help laughing at myself."

"I shan't loose him, till he promises to let the door alone," said Adam.

"Come, Ben, lad," said Seth, in a persuasive tone, "don't let's have a quarrel about it. You know Adam will have his way. You may's well try to turn a waggon in a narrow lane. Say you'll leave the door alone, and make an end on't."

"I binna frighted at Adam," said Ben, "but I donna mind sayin' as I'll let 't alone at your askin', Seth."

"Come, that's wise of you, Ben," said Adam, laughing and relaxing his grasp.

They all returned to their work now; but Wiry Ben, having had the worst in the bodily contest, was bent on retrieving that humiliation by a success in sarcasm.

"Which was ye thinkin' on, Seth," he began—"the pretty parson's face or her sarmunt, when ye forgot the panels?"

"Come and hear her, Ben," said Seth, good-humouredly; "she's going to preach on the Green to-night; happin ye'd get something to think on yourself, then, instead o' those wicked songs you're so fond on. Ye might get religion, and that 'ud be the best day's earnings y' ever made."

"All i' good time for that, Seth; I'll think about that when I'm agoin' to settle i' life; bachelors doesn't want such heavy earnin's. Happen I shall do the coortin' an' the religion both together, as ye do, Seth; but ye wouldna ha' me get converted an' chop in atween ye an' the pretty preacher, an' carry her aff?"

"No fear o' that, Ben; she's neither for you nor for me to win, I doubt. Only you come and hear her, and you won't speak lightly on her again."

"Well, I'n half a mind t' ha' a look at her to-night, if there isn't good company at th' Holly Bush. What'll she take for her text? Happen ye can tell me, Seth, if so be as I shouldna come up i' time for't. Will 't be, —What come ye out for to see? A prophetess? Yea, I say unto you, and more than a prophetess—a uncommon pretty young woman."

"Come, Ben," said Adam, rather sternly, "you let the words o' the Bible alone; you're going too far now."

"What! are *ye* a-turnin' roun', Adam? I thought ye war dead again'
th' women preachin', a while agoo?"

"Nay, I'm not turnin' noway. I said nought about the women preachin'; I said, You let the Bible alone: you've got a jest-book, han't you, as
you're rare and proud on? Keep your dirty fingers to that."

"Why, y' are gettin' as big a saint as Seth. Y' are goin' to th' preachin'
to-night, I should think. Ye'll do finely t' lead the singin'. But I don'
know what Parson Irwine 'ull say at his gran' favright Adam Bede a-
turnin' Methody."

"Never do you bother yourself about me, Ben. I'm not a-goin' to turn
Methodist any more nor you are—though it's like enough you'll turn to
something worse. Mester Irwine's got more sense nor to meddle wi' people's doing as they like in religion. That's between themselves and God,
as he's said to me many a time."

"Ay, ay; but he's none so fond o' your dissenters, for all that."

"Maybe; I'm none so fond o' Josh Tod's thick ale, but I don't hinder
you from making a fool o' yourself wi't."

There was a laugh at this thrust of Adam's, but Seth said, very seriously,

"Nay, nay, Addy, thee mustna say as anybody's religion's like thick
ale. Thee dostna believe but what the dissenters and the Methodists
have got the root o' the matter as well as the church folks."

"Nay, Seth, lad; I'm not for laughing at no man's religion. Let 'em
follow their consciences, that's all. Only I think it 'ud be better if their
consciences 'ud let 'em stay quiet i' the church—there's a deal to be learnt
there. And there's such a thing as being over-speritial; we must have
something besides Gospel i' this world. Look at the canals, an' th' aque-
ducs, an' th' coal-pit engines, and Arkwright's mills there at Cromford;
a man must learn summat beside Gospel to make them things, I reckon.
But t' hear some o' them preachers, you'd think as a man must be doing
nothing all's life but shutting's eyes and looking what's a-going on inside
him. I know a man must have the love o' God in his soul, and the Bible's
God's word. But what does the Bible say? Why, it says as God put his
sperrit into the workman as built the tabernacle, to make him do all the
carved work and things as wanted a nice hand. And this is my way o'
looking at it: there's the sperrit o' God in all things and all times—week-
days as well as Sunday—and i' the great works and inventions, and i'
the figuring and the mechanics. And God helps us with our headpieces
and our hands as well as with our souls; and if a man does bits o' jobs
out o' working hours—builds a oven for 's wife to save her from going
to the bakehouse, or scrats at his bit o' garden and makes two potatoes
grow instead o' one, he's doing more good, and he's just as near to God,
as if he was running after some preacher and a-praying and a-groaning."

"Well done, Adam!" said Sandy Jim, who had paused from his planing to shift his planks while Adam was speaking; "that's the best sarmunt
I've heared this long while. By th' same token, my wife's been a-plaguin'
on me to build her a oven this twelvemont."

"There's reason in what thee say'st, Adam," observed Seth, gravely. "But thee know'st thyself as it's hearing the preachers thee find'st so much fault with as has turned many an idle fellow into an industrious un. It's the preacher as empties th' alehouse; and if a man gets religion, he'll do his work none the worse for that."

"On'y he'll lave the panels out o' th' doors sometimes, eh, Seth?" said Wiry Ben.

"Ah, Ben, you've got a joke again' me as 'll last you your life. But it isna religion as was i' fault there; it was Seth Bede, as was allays a wool-gathering chap, and religion hasna cured him, the more's the pity."

"Ne'er heed me, Seth," said Wiry Ben, "y' are a downright good-hearted chap, panels or no panels; an' ye donna set up your bristles at every bit o' fun, like some o' your kin, as is mayhap cliverer."

"Seth, lad," said Adam, taking no notice of the sarcasm against himself, "tbee mustna take me unkind. I wasna driving at thee in what I said just now. Some 's got one way o' looking at things and some 's got another."

"Nay, nay, Addy, thee mean'st me no unkindness," said Seth, "I know that well enough. Thee't like thy dog Gyp—thee bark'st at me sometimes, but thee allays lick'st my hand after."

All hands worked on in silence for some minutes, until the church clock began to strike six. Before the first stroke had died away, Sandy Jim had loosed his plane and was reaching his jacket; Wiry Ben had left a screw half driven in, and thrown his screwdriver into his tool-basket; Mum Taft, who, true to his name, had kept silence throughout the previous conversation, had flung down his hammer as he was in the act of lifting it; and Seth, too, had straightened his back, and was putting out his hand towards his paper cap. Adam alone had gone on with his work as if nothing had happened. But observing the cessation of the tools, he looked up, and said, in a tone of indignation,

"Look there, now! I can't abide to see men throw away their tools i' that way, the minute the clock begins to strike, as if they took no pleasure i' their work, and was afraid o' doing a stroke too much."

Seth looked a little conscious, and began to be slower in his preparations for going, but Mum Taft broke silence, and said,

"Ay, ay, Adam lad, ye talk like a young un. When y' are six-an'-forty like me, istid o' six-an'-twenty, ye wonna be so flush o' workin' for nought."

"Nonsense," said Adam, still wrathful; "what's age got to do with it, I wonder? Ye arena getting stiff yet, I reckon. I hate to see a man's arms drop down as if he was shot, before the clock's fairly struck, just as if he'd never a bit o' pride and delight in 's work. The very grindstone 'ull go on turning a bit after you loose it."

"Bodderation, Adam!" exclaimed Wiry Ben. "Lave a chap aloon, will 'ee? Ye war a-finding faut wi' preachers a while agoo—y' are fond enough o' preachin' yoursen. Ye may like work better nor play, but I like play better nor work; that'll 'commodate ye—it laves ye th' more to do."

With this exit speech, which he considered effective, Wiry Ben shouldered his basket and left the workshop, quickly followed by Mum Taft
and Sandy Jim. Seth lingered, and looked wistfully at Adam, as if he
expected him to say something.

"Shalt go home before thee go'st to the preaching?" Adam asked,
looking up.

"Nay; I've got my hat and things at Will Maskery's. I shan't be home
before going for ten. I'll happen see Dinah Morris safe home, if she's
willing. There's nobody comes with her from Poyser's, thee know'st."

"Then I'll tell mother not to look for thee," said Adam.

"Thee artna going to Poyser's thyself to-night?" said Seth, rather
timidly, as he turned to leave the workshop.

"Nay, I'm going to th' school."

Hitherto Gyp had kept his comfortable bed, only lifting up his head
and watching Adam more closely as he noticed the other workmen departing. But no sooner did Adam put his ruler in his pocket, and begin
to twist his apron round his waist, than Gyp ran forward and looked up
in his master's face with patient expectation. If Gyp had had a tail he
would doubtless have wagged it, but being destitute of that vehicle for
his emotions, he was like many other worthy personages, destined to
appear more phlegmatic than nature had made him.

"What, art ready for the basket, eh, Gyp?" said Adam, with the same
gentle modulation of voice as when he spoke to Seth.

Gyp jumped and gave a short bark, as much as to say, "Of course."
Poor fellow, he had not a great range of expression.

The basket was the one which on workdays held Adam's and Seth's
dinner; and no official, walking in procession, could look more resolutely
unconscious of all acquaintances than Gyp with his basket, trotting at
his master's heels.

On leaving the workshop Adam locked the door, took the key out, and
carried it to the house on the other side of the woodyard. It was a low
house, with smooth grey thatch and buff walls, looking pleasant and
mellow in the evening light. The leaded windows were bright and speckless, and the door-stone was as clean as a white boulder at ebb tide. On
the door-stone stood a clean old woman, in a dark-striped linen gown,
a red kerchief, and a linen cap, talking to some speckled fowls which
appeared to have been drawn towards her by an illusory expectation of
cold potatoes or barley. The old woman's sight seemed to be dim, for
she did not recognise Adam till he said,

"Here's the key, Dolly; lay it down for me in the house, will you?"

"Ay, sure; but wunna ye come in, Adam? Miss Mary's i' th' house,
an' Mester Burge 'ull be back anon; he'd be glad t' ha' ye to supper
wi'm, I'll be's warrand."

"No, Dolly, thank you; I'm off home. Good-evening."

Adam hastened with long strides, Gyp close to his heels, out of the
workyard, and along the highroad leading away from the village and
down to the valley. As he reached the foot of the slope, an elderly horse-

man, with his portmanteau strapped behind him, stopped his horse when
Adam had passed him, and turned round to have another long look at
the stalwart workman in paper cap, leather breeches, and dark-blue
worsted stockings.

Adam, unconscious of the admiration he was exciting, presently struck
across the fields, and now broke out into the tune which had all day long
been running in his head:—

> "Let all thy converse be sincere,
> Thy conscience as the noonday clear;
> For God's all-seeing eye surveys
> Thy secret thoughts, thy works and ways."

CHAPTER II

THE PREACHING

ABOUT a quarter to seven there was an unusual appearance of excitement in the village of Hayslope, and through the whole length of its little
street, from the Donnithorne Arms to the churchyard gate, the inhabitants had evidently been drawn out of their houses by something more
than the pleasure of lounging in the evening sunshine. The Donnithorne
Arms stood at the entrance of the village, and a small farmyard and
stackyard which flanked it, indicating that there was a pretty take of
land attached to the inn, gave the traveller a promise of good feed for
himself and his horse, which might well console him for the ignorance
in which the weatherbeaten sign left him as to the heraldic bearings of
that ancient family, the Donnithornes. Mr. Casson, the landlord, had
been for some time standing at the door with his hands in his pockets,
balancing himself on his heels and toes, and looking towards a piece of
unenclosed ground, with a maple in the middle of it, which he knew
to be the destination of certain grave-looking men and women whom he
had observed passing at intervals.

Mr. Casson's person was by no means of that common type which can
be allowed to pass without description. On a front view it appeared to
consist principally of two spheres, bearing about the same relation to
each other as the earth and the moon: that is to say, the lower sphere
might be said, at a rough guess, to be thirteen times larger than the
upper, which naturally performed the function of a mere satellite and
tributary. But here the resemblance ceased, for Mr. Casson's head was
not at all a melancholy-looking satellite, nor was it a "spotty globe,"
as Milton has irreverently called the moon; on the contrary, no head
and face could look more sleek and healthy, and its expression, which
was chiefly confined to a pair of round and ruddy cheeks, the slight knot
and interruptions forming the nose and eyes being scarcely worth mention, was one of jolly contentment, only tempered by that sense of personal dignity which usually made itself felt in his attitude and bearing.

This sense of dignity could hardly be considered excessive in a man who had been butler to "the family" for fifteen years, and who, in his present high position, was necessarily very much in contact with his inferiors. How to reconcile his dignity with the satisfaction of his curiosity by walking towards the Green, was the problem that Mr. Casson had been revolving in his mind for the last five minutes; but when he had partly solved it by taking his hands out of his pockets, and thrusting them into the armholes of his waistcoat, by throwing his head on one side, and providing himself with an air of contemptuous indifference to whatever might fall under his notice, his thoughts were diverted by the approach of the horseman whom we lately saw pausing to have another look at our friend Adam, and who now pulled up at the door of the Donnithorne Arms.

"Take off the bridle and give him a drink, 'ostler," said the traveller to the lad in a smock-frock, who had come out of the yard at the sound of the horse's hoofs.

"Why, what's up in your pretty village, landlord?" he continued, getting down. "There seems to be quite a stir."

"It's a Methodis preaching, sir; it's been gev hout as a young woman's a-going to preach on the Green," answered Mr. Casson, in a treble and wheezy voice, with a slightly mincing accent. "Will you please to step in, sir, an' tek somethink?"

"No, I must be getting on to Rosseter. I only want a drink for my horse. And what does your parson say, I wonder, to a young woman preaching just under his nose?"

"Parson Irwine, sir, doesn't live here; he lives at Brox'on, over the hill there The parsonage here's a tumble-down place, sir, not fit for gentry to live in. He comes here to preach of a Sunday afternoon, sir, an' puts up his hoss here. It's a grey cob, sir, an' he sets great store by 't. He's allays put up his hoss here, sir, iver since before I hed the Donnithorne Arms. I'm not this countryman, you may tell by my tongue, sir. They're cur'ous talkers i' this country, sir; the gentry's hard work to understand 'em. I was brought hup among the gentry, sir, an' got the turn o' their tongue when I was a bye. Why, what do you think the folks here says for 'hevn't you?'—the gentry, you know, says, 'hevn't you'—well, the people about here says 'hanna yey?' It's what they call the dileck as is spoke hereabout, sir. That's what I've heard Squire Donn'.thorne say many a time; it's the dileck, says he."

"Ay, ay," said the stranger, smiling. "I know it very well. But you've not got many Methodists about here, surely—in this agricultural spot? I should have thought there would hardly be such a thing as a Methodist to be found about here. You're all farmers, aren't you? The Methodists can seldom lay much hold on *them*."

"Why, sir, there's a pretty lot o' workmen round about, sir. There's a Mester Burge as owns the timber-yard over there, he underteks a good bit o' building an' repairs. An' there's the Stone-Pits not far off There's plenty o' emply i' this countryside, sir. An' there's a fine batch o' Methodisses at Treddles'on—that's the market-town about three mile off—you'll maybe ha' come through it, sir. There's pretty nigh a score of 'em on the Green now, as come from there. That's where our people gets it from, though there's only two men of 'em in all Hayslope: that's Will Maskery, the wheelwright, and Seth Bede, a young man as works at the carpenterin'."

"The preacher comes from Treddleston, then, does she?"

"Nay, sir, she comes out o' Stonyshire, pretty nigh thirty mile off. But she's a-visitin' hereabout at Mester Poyser's at the Hall Farm— it's them barns an' big walnut-trees, right away to the left, sir. She's own niece to Poyser's wife, an' they'll be fine an' vexed at her for making a fool of herself i' that way. But I've heard as there's no holding these Methodisses when the maggit's once got i' their head: many of 'em goes stark starin' mad wi' their religion. Though this young woman's quiet enough to look at, by what I can make out; I've not seen her myself."

"Well, I wish I had time to wait and see her, but I must get on. I've been out of my way for the last twenty minutes, to have a look at that place in the valley. It's Squire Donnithorne's, I suppose?"

"Yes, sir, that's Donnithorne Chase, that is. Fine hoaks there, isn't there, sir? I should know what it is, sir, for I've lived butler there a-going i' fifteen year. It's Captain Donnithorne as is th' heir, sir—Squire Donnithorne's grandson. He'll be comin' of hage this 'ay-'arvest, sir, an' we shall hev fine doin's. He owns all the land about here, sir, Squire Donnithorne does."

"Well, it's a pretty spot, whoever may own it," said the traveller, mounting his horse; "and one meets some fine strapping fellows about too. I met as fine a young fellow as ever I saw in my life, about half an hour ago, before I came up the hill—a carpenter, a tall broad-shouldered fellow with black hair and black eyes, marching along like a soldier. We want such fellows as he to lick the French."

"Ay, sir, that's Adam Bede, that is, I'll be bound—Thias Bede's son —everybody knows him hereabout. He's an uncommon clever stiddy fellow, an' wonderful strong. Lord bless you, sir—if you'll hexcuse me for saying so—he can walk forty miles a-day, an' lift a matter o' sixty ston'. He's an uncommon favourite wi' the gentry, sir: Captain Donnithorne and Parson Irwine meks a fine fuss wi' him. But he's a little lifted up an' peppery-like."

"Well, good evening to you, landlord; I must get on."

"Your servant, sir; good evenin'."

The traveller put his horse into a quick walk up the village, but when he approached the Green, the beauty of the view that lay on his right hand, the singular contrast presented by the groups of villagers with the knot of Methodists near the maple, and perhaps yet more, curiosity to see the young female preacher, proved too much for his anxiety to get to the end of his journey, and he paused.

The Green lay at the extremity of the village, and from it the road branched off in two directions, one leading farther up the hill by the church, and the other winding gently down towards the valley. On the one side of the Green that led towards the church, the broken line of thatched cottages was continued nearly to the churchyard gate; but on the opposite, northwestern side, there was nothing to obstruct the view of gently-swelling meadow, and wooded valley, and dark masses of distant hill. That rich undulating district of Loamshire to which Hayslope belonged, lies close to a grim outskirt of Stonyshire, overlooked by its barren hills as a pretty blooming sister may sometimes be seen linked in the arm of a rugged, tall, swarthy brother; and in two or three hours' ride the traveller might exchange a bleak treeless region, intersected by lines of cold grey stone, for one where his road wound under the shelter of woods, or up swelling hills, muffled with hedgerows and long meadow-grass and thick corn; and where at every turn he came upon some fine old country-seat nestled in the valley or crowning the slope, some homestead with its long length of barn and its cluster of golden ricks, some grey steeple looking out from a pretty confusion of trees and thatch and dark-red tiles. It was just such a picture as this last that Hayslope Church had made to the traveller as he began to mount the gentle slope leading to its pleasant uplands, and now from his station near the Green he had before him in one view nearly all the other typical features of this pleasant land. High up against the horizon were the huge conical masses of hill, like giant mounds intended to fortify this region of corn and grass against the keen and hungry winds of the north; not distant enough to be clothed in purple mystery, but with sombre greenish sides visibly speckled with sheep, whose motion was only revealed by memory, not detected by sight; wooed from day to day by the changing hours, but responding with no change in themselves— left for ever grim and sullen after the flush of morning, the winged gleams of the April noonday, the parting crimson glory of the ripening summer sun. And directly below them the eye rested on a more advanced line of hanging woods, divided by bright patches of pasture or furrowed crops, and not yet deepened into the uniform leafy curtains of high summer, but still showing the warm tints of the young oak and the tender green of the ash and lime. Then came the valley, where the woods grew thicker, as if they had rolled down and hurried together from the patches left smooth on the slope, that they might take the better care of the tall mansion which lifted its parapets and sent its faint blue summer smoke among them. Doubtless there was a large sweep of park and a broad glassy pool in front of that mansion, but the swelling slope of meadow would not let our traveller see them from the village green. He saw instead a foreground which was just as lovely—the level sunlight lying like transparent gold among the gently-curving stems of the feathered grass and the tall red sorrel, and the white umbels of the hemlocks lining the bushy hedgerows. It was that moment in summer when the sound of the scythe being whetted makes us cast more lingering looks at the flower-sprinkled tresses of the meadows.

He might have seen other beauties in the landscape if he had turned a little in his saddle and looked eastward, beyond Jonathan Burge's pasture and woodyard towards the green cornfields and walnut-trees of the Hall Farm; but apparently there was more interest for him in the living groups close at hand. Every generation in the village was there, from old "Feyther Taft" in his brown worsted night-cap, who was bent nearly double, but seemed tough enough to keep on his legs a long while, leaning on his short stick, down to the babies with their little round heads lolling forward in quilted linen caps. Now and then there was a new arrival; perhaps a slouching labourer, who, having eaten his supper, came out to look at the unusual scene with a slow bovine gaze, willing to hear what any one had to say in explanation of it, but by no means excited enough to ask a question. But all took care not to join the Methodists on the Green, and identify themselves in that way with the expectant audience, for there was not one of them that would not have disclaimed the imputation of having come out to hear the "preacher-woman,"—they had only come out to see "what war a-goin' on, like." The men were chiefly gathered in the neighbourhood of the blacksmith's shop. But do not imagine them gathered in a knot. Villagers never swarm: a whisper is unknown among them, and they seem almost as incapable of an undertone as a cow or a stag. Your true rustic turns his back on his interlocutor, throwing a question over his shoulder as if he meant to run away from the answer, and walking a step or two farther off when the interest of the dialogue culminates. So the group in the vicinity of the blacksmith's door was by no means a close one, and formed no screen in front of Chad Cranage, the blacksmith himself, who stood with his black brawny arms folded, leaning against the doorpost, and occasionally sending forth a bellowing laugh at his own jokes, giving them a marked preference over the sarcasms of Wiry Ben, who had renounced the pleasures of the Holly Bush for the sake of seeing life under a new form. But both styles of wit were treated with equal contempt by Mr. Joshua Rann. Mr. Rann's leathern apron and subdued griminess can leave no one in any doubt that he is the village shoemaker; the thrusting out of his chin and stomach, and the twirling of his thumbs, are more subtle indications, intended to prepare unwary strangers for the discovery that they are in the presence of the parish clerk. "Old Joshway," as he is irreverently called by his neighbours, is in a state of simmering indignation; but he has not yet opened his lips except to say, in a resounding bass undertone, like the tuning of a violoncello, "Sehon, King of the Amorites: for His mercy endureth for ever; and Og the King of Basan: for His mercy endureth for ever,"—a quotation which may seem to have slight bearing on the present occasion, but, as with every other anomaly, adequate knowledge will show it to be a natural sequence. Mr. Rann was inwardly maintaining the dignity of the Church in the face of this scandalous irruption of Methodism, and as that dignity was bound up with his own sonorous utterance of the responses, his argument naturally suggested a quotation from the psalm he had read the last Sunday afternoon.

The stronger curiosity of the women had drawn them quite to the edge of the Green, where they could examine more closely the Quaker-like costume and odd deportment of the female Methodists. Underneath the maple there was a small cart which had been brought from the wheel-wright's to serve as a pulpit, and round this a couple of benches and a few chairs had been placed. Some of the Methodists were resting on these, with their eyes closed, as if wrapt in prayer or meditation. Others chose to continue standing, and had turned their faces towards the vil-lagers with a look of melancholy compassion, which was highly amusing to Bessy Cranage, the blacksmith's buxom daughter, known to her neighbours as Chad's Bess, who wondered "why the folks war a-makin' faces a that'ns." Chad's Bess was the object of peculiar compassion, because her hair, being turned back under a cap which was set at the top of her head, exposed to view an ornament of which she was much prouder than of her red cheeks, namely, a pair of large round earrings with false garnets in them, ornaments condemned not only by the Meth-odists, but by her own cousin and namesake Timothy's Bess, who, with much cousinly feeling, often wished "them earrings" might come to good.

Timothy's Bess, though retaining her maiden appellation among her familiars, had long been the wife of Sandy Jim, and possessed a handsome set of matronly jewels, of which it is enough to mention the heavy baby she was rocking in her arms, and the sturdy fellow of five in knee-breeches and red legs, who had a rusty milk-can round his neck by way of drum, and was very carefully avoided by Chad's small ter-rier. This young olive-branch, notorious under the name of Timothy's Bess's Ben, being of an inquiring disposition, unchecked by any false modesty, had advanced beyond the group of women and children, and was walking round the Methodists, looking up in their faces with his mouth wide open, and beating his stick against the milk-can by way of musical accompaniment. But one of the elderly women bending down to take him by the shoulder, with an air of grave remonstrance, Tim-othy's Bess's Ben first kicked out vigorously, then took to his heels and sought refuge behind his father's legs.

"Ye gallows young dog," said Sandy Jim, with some paternal pride, "if ye donna keep that stick quiet, I'll tek it from ye. What d'ye mane by kickin' foulks?"

"Here! gie him here to me, Jim," said Chad Cranage; "I'll tie him up an' shoe him as I do th' hosses. Well, Mester Casson," he continued, as that personage sauntered up towards the group of men, "how are ye t' naight? Are ye coom t' help groon? They say folks allays groon when they're hearkenin' to th' Methodys, as if they war bad i' th' inside. I mane to groon as loud as your cow did th' other naight, an' then the praicher 'ull think I'm i' th' raight way."

"I'd advise you not to be up to no nonsense, Chad," said Mr. Casson, with some dignity; "Poyser wouldn't like to hear as his wife's niece was treated any ways disrespectful, for all he mayn't be fond of her taking on herself to preach."

"Ay, an' she's a pleasant-looked un too," said Wiry Ben. "I'll stick up for the pretty women preachin'; I know they'd persuade me over a deal sooner nor th' ugly men. I shouldna wonder if I turn Methody afore the night's out, an' begin to coort the preacher, like Seth Bede."

"Why, Seth's looking rather too high, I should think," said Mr. Casson. "This woman's kin wouldn't like her to demean herself to a common carpenter."

"Tchu!" said Ben, with a long treble intonation, "what's folk's kin got to do wi't?—Not a chip. Poyser's wife may turn her nose up an' forget bygones, but this Dinah Morris, they tell me, 's poor as iver she was—works at a mill, an's much ado to keep hersen. A strappin' young carpenter as is a ready-made Methody, like Seth, wouldna be a bad match for her. Why, Poysers make as big a fuss wi' Adam Bede as if he war a nevvy o' their own."

"Idle talk! idle talk!" said Mr. Joshua Rann. "Adam an' Seth's two men; you wunna fit them two wi' the same last."

"Maybe," said Wiry Ben, contemptuously, "but Seth's the lad for me, though he war a Methody twice o'er. I'm fair beat wi' Seth, for I've been teazin' him iver sin' we've been workin' together, an' he bears me no more malice nor a lamb. An' he's a stout-hearted feller too, for when we saw the old tree all a-fire a-comin' across the fields one night, an' we thought as it war a boguy, Seth made no more ado, but he up to't as bold as a constable. Why, there he comes out o' Will Maskery's; an' there's Will hisself, lookin' as meek as if he couldna knock a nail o' the head for fear o' hurtin 't. An' there's the pretty preacher-woman! My eye, she's got her bonnet off. I mun go a bit nearer."

Several of the men followed Ben's lead, and the traveller pushed his horse on to the Green, as Dinah walked rather quickly, and in advance of her companions, towards the cart under the maple-tree. While she was near Seth's tall figure, she looked short, but when she had mounted the cart, and was away from all comparison, she seemed above the middle height of woman, though in reality she did not exceed it—an effect which was due to the slimness of her figure, and the simple line of her black stuff dress. The stranger was struck with surprise as he saw her approach and mount the cart—surprise, not so much at the feminine delicacy of her appearance, as at the total absence of self-consciousness in her demeanour. He had made up his mind to see her advance with a measured step, and a demure solemnity of countenance; he had felt sure that her face would be mantled with a smile of conscious saintship, or else charged with denunciatory bitterness. He knew but two types of Methodist—the ecstatic and the bilious. But Dinah walked as simply as if she were going to market, and seemed as unconscious of her outward appearance as a little boy: there was no blush, no tremulousness, which said, "I know you think me a pretty woman, too young to preach"; no casting up or down of the eyelids, no compression of the lips, no attitude of the arms, that said, "But you must think of me as a saint." She held no book in her ungloved hands, but let them hang down lightly crossed before her, as she stood and turned her grey eyes on the people. There was no keenness in the eyes; they seemed rather to be shedding love than making observations; they had the liquid look which tells that the mind is full of what it has to give out, rather than impressed by external objects. She stood with her left hand towards the descending sun, and leafy boughs screened her from its rays; but in this sober light the delicate colouring of her face seemed to gather a calm vividness, like flowers at evening. It was a small oval face, of a uniform transparent whiteness, with an egg-like line of cheek and chin, a full but firm mouth, a delicate nostril, and a low perpendicular brow, surmounted by a rising arch of parting between smooth locks of pale reddish hair. The hair was drawn straight back behind the ears, and covered, except for an inch or two, above the brow, by a net Quaker cap. The eyebrows, of the same colour as the hair, were perfectly horizontal and firmly pencilled; the eyelashes, though no darker, were long and abundant; nothing was left blurred or unfinished. It was one of those faces that make one think of white flowers with light touches of colour on their pure petals. The eyes had no peculiar beauty, beyond that of expression; they looked so simple, so candid, so gravely loving, that no accusing scowl, no light sneer could help melting away before their glance. Joshua Rann gave a long cough, as if he were clearing his throat in order to come to a new understanding with himself; Chad Cranage lifted up his leather skull-cap and scratched his head; and Wiry Ben wondered how Seth had the pluck to think of courting her.

"A sweet woman," the stranger said to himself, "but surely nature never meant her for a preacher."

Perhaps he was one of those who think that nature has theatrical properties, and, with the consideration of facilitating art and psychology, "makes up" her characters, so that there may be no mistake about them. But Dinah began to speak.

"Dear friends," she said, in a clear but not loud voice, "let us pray for a blessing."

She closed her eyes, and hanging her head down a little, continued in the same moderate tone, as if speaking to some one quite near her:—

"Saviour of sinners! when a poor woman, laden with sins, went out to the well to draw water, she found Thee sitting at the well. She knew Thee not; she had not sought Thee; her mind was dark; her life was unholy. But thou didst speak to her, Thou didst teach her, Thou didst show her that her life lay open before Thee, and yet Thou wast ready to give her that blessing which she had never sought. Jesus! Thou art in the midst of us, and Thou knowest all men: if there is any here like that poor woman—if their minds are dark, their lives unholy—if they have come out not seeking Thee, not desiring to be taught; deal with them according to the free mercy which Thou didst show to her. Speak to them, Lord; open their ears to my message; bring their sins to their minds, and make them thirst for that salvation which Thou art ready to give.

"Lord! Thou art with Thy people still: they see Thee in the night-watches, and their hearts burn within them as Thou talkest with them by the way. And Thou art near to those who have not known Thee: open their eyes that they may see Thee—see Thee weeping over them, and saying 'Ye will not come unto me that ye might have life'—see Thee hanging on the cross and saying, 'Father, forgive them, for they know not what they do'—see Thee as Thou wilt come again in Thy glory to judge them at the last. Amen."

Dinah opened her eyes again and paused, looking at the group of villagers, who were now gathered rather more closely on her right hand

"Dear friends," she began, raising her voice a little, "you have all of you been to church, and I think you must have heard the clergyman read these words: 'The spirit of the Lord is upon me, because he hath anointed me to preach the gospel to the poor.' Jesus Christ spoke those words—he said he came *to preach the Gospel to the poor;* I don't know whether you ever thought about those words much; but I will tell you when I remember first hearing them. It was on just such a sort of evening as this, when I was a little girl, and my aunt as brought me up, took me to hear a good man preach out of doors, just as we are here. I remember his face well: he was a very old man, and had very long white hair; his voice was very soft and beautiful, not like any voice I had ever heard before. I was a little girl, and scarcely knew anything, and this old man seemed to me such a different sort of a man from anybody I had ever seen before, that I thought he had perhaps come down from the sky to preach to us, and I said, 'Aunt, will he go back to the sky to-night, like the picture in the Bible?'

"That man of God was Mr. Wesley, who spent his life in doing what our blessed Lord did—preaching the Gospel to the poor—and he entered into his rest eight years ago. I came to know more about him years after, but I was a foolish thoughtless child then, and I remembered only one thing he told us in his sermon. He told us as 'Gospel' meant 'good news.' The Gospel, you know, is what the Bible tells us about God.

"Think of that now! Jesus Christ did really come down from heaven, as I, like a silly child, thought Mr. Wesley did; and what He came down for, was to tell good news about God to the poor. Why, you an' me, dear friends, are poor. We have been brought up in poor cottages, and have been reared on oat-cake, and lived coarse; and we haven't been to school much, nor read books, and we don't know much about anything but what happens just around us. We are just the sort of people that want to hear good news. For when anybody's well off, they don't much mind about hearing news from distant parts; but if a poor man or woman's in trouble and has hard work to make out a living, they like to have a letter to tell 'em they've got a friend as will help 'em. To be sure, we can't help knowing something about God, even if we've never heard the Gospel, the good news that our Saviour brought us. For we know everything comes from God: don't you say almost every day, 'This and that will happen, please God'; and 'We shall begin to cut the grass soon, please God to send us a little more sunshine?' We know very well we are altogether in the hands of God: we didn't bring ourselves into the world, we can't keep ourselves alive while we're sleeping; the day- light, and the wind, and the corn, and the cows to give us milk—every- thing we have comes from God. And he gave us our souls, and put love between parents and children, and husband and wife. But is that as much as we want to know about God? We see he is great and mighty, and can do what he will: we are lost, as if we was struggling in great waters, when we try to think of him.

"But perhaps doubts come into your mind like this: Can God take much notice of us poor people? Perhaps he only made the world for the great and the wise and the rich. It doesn't cost him much to give us our little handful of victual and bit of clothing; but how do we know he cares for us any more than we care for the worms and things in the garden, so as we rear our carrots and onions? Will God take care of us when we die? and has he any comfort for us when we are lame and sick and helpless? Perhaps, too, he is angry with us; else why does the blight come, and the bad harvests, and the fever, and all sorts of pain and trouble? For our life is full of trouble, and if God sends us good, he seems to send bad too. How is it? how is it?

"Ah! dear friends, we are in sad want of good news about God; and what does other good news signify if we haven't that? For everything else comes to an end, and when we die we leave it all. But God lasts when everything else is gone. What shall we do if He is not our friend?"

Then Dinah told how the good news had been brought, and how the mind of God towards the poor had been made manifest in the life of Jesus, dwelling on its lowliness and its acts of mercy.

"So you see, dear friends," she went on, "Jesus spent his time almost all in doing good to poor people; he preached out of doors to them, and he made friends of poor workmen, and taught them and took pains with them. Not but what he did good to the rich too, for he was full of love to all men, only he saw the poor were more in want of his help. So he cured the lame and the sick and the blind, and he worked miracles, to feed the hungry, because, he said, he was sorry for them; and he was very kind to the little children, and comforted those who had lost their friends; and he spoke very tenderly to poor sinners that were sorry for their sins.

"Ah! wouldn't you love such a man if you saw him—if he was here in this village? What a kind heart he must have! What a friend he would be to go to in trouble! How pleasant it must be to be taught by him.

"Well, dear friends, who *was* this man? Was he only a good man—a very good man, and no more—like our dear Mr. Wesley, who has been taken from us? . . . He was the Son of God—'in the image of the Father,' the Bible says; that means, just like God, who is the beginning and end of all things—the God we want to know about. So then, all the love that Jesus showed to the poor is the same love that God has for us. We can understand what Jesus felt, because he came in a body like ours, and spoke words such as we speak to each other. We were afraid to think what God was before—the God who made the world and the sky and the thunder and lightning. We could never see him; we could only see the things he had made; and some of these things was very terrible, so as we might well tremble when we thought of him. But our blessed Saviour has showed us what God is in a way us poor ignorant people can understand; he has showed us what God's heart is, what are his feelings towards us.

"But let us see a little more about what Jesus came on earth for. Another time he said, 'I came to seek and save that which was lost'; and another time, 'I came not to call the righteous but sinners to repentance.'

"The *lost!* . . . *Sinners!* . . . Ah, dear friends, does that mean you and me?"

Hitherto the traveller had been chained to the spot against his will by the charm of Dinah's mellow treble tones, which had a variety of modulation like that of a fine instrument touched with the unconscious skill of musical instinct. The simple things she said seemed like novelties, as a melody strikes us with a new feeling when we hear it sung by the pure voice of a boyish chorister; the quiet depth of conviction with which she spoke seemed in itself an evidence for the truth of her message. He saw that she had thoroughly arrested her hearers. The villagers had pressed nearer to her, and there was no longer anything but grave attention on all faces. She spoke slowly, though quite fluently, often pausing after a question, or before any transition of ideas. There was no change of attitude, no gesture; the effect of her speech was produced entirely by the inflections of her voice, and when she came to the question, "Will God take care of us when we die?" she uttered it in such a tone of plaintive appeal that the tears came into some of the hardest eyes. The stranger had ceased to doubt, as he had done at the first glance, that she could fix the attention of her rougher hearers, but still he wondered whether she could have that power of rousing their more violent emotions, which must surely be a necessary seal of her vocation as a Methodist preacher, until she came to the words, "Lost!—Sinners!" when there was a great change in her voice and manner. She had made a long pause before the exclamation, and the pause seemed to be filled by agitating thoughts that showed themselves in her features. Her pale face became paler; the circles under her eyes deepened, as they do when tears half gather without falling; and the mild loving eyes took an expression of appalled pity, as if she had suddenly discerned a destroying angel hovering over the heads of the people. Her voice became deep and muffled, but there was still no gesture. Nothing could be less like the ordinary type of the Ranter than Dinah. She was not preaching as she heard others preach, but speaking directly from her own emotions, and under the inspiration of her own simple faith.

But now she had entered into a new current of feeling. Her manner became less calm, her utterance more rapid and agitated, as she tried to bring home to the people their guilt, their wilful darkness, their state of disobedience to God—as she dwelt on the hatefulness of sin, the Divine holiness, and the sufferings of the Saviour, by which a way had been opened for their salvation. At last it seemed as if, in her yearning desire to reclaim the lost sheep, she could not be satisfied by addressing her hearers as a body. She appealed first to one and then to another, beseeching them with tears to turn to God while there was yet time; painting to them the desolation of their souls, lost in sin, feeding on the husks of this miserable world, far away from God their Father; and then the love of the Saviour, who was waiting and watching for their return.

There was many a responsive sigh and groan from her fellow Methodists, but the village mind does not easily take fire, and a little smouldering vague anxiety, that might easily die out again, was the utmost effect Dinah's preaching had wrought in them at present. Yet no one had retired, except the children and old "Feyther Taft," who being too deaf to catch many words, had some time ago gone back to his inglenook. Wiry Ben was feeling very uncomfortable, and almost wishing he had not come to hear Dinah; he thought what she said would haunt him somehow. Yet he couldn't help liking to look at her and listen to her, though he dreaded every moment that she would fix her eyes on him, and address him in particular. She had already addressed Sandy Jim, who was now holding the baby to relieve his wife, and the big softhearted man had rubbed away some tears with his fist, with a confused intention of being a better fellow, going less to the Holly Bush down by the Stone-Pits, and cleaning himself more regularly of a Sunday.

In front of Sandy Jim stood Chad's Bess, who had shown an unwonted quietude and fixity of attention ever since Dinah had begun to speak. Not that the matter of the discourse had arrested her at once, for she was lost in a puzzling speculation as to what pleasure and satisfaction there could be in life to a young woman who wore a cap like Dinah's. Giving up this inquiry in despair, she took to studying Dinah's nose, eyes, mouth, and hair, and wondering whether it was better to have such a sort of pale face as that, or fat red cheeks and round black eyes like her own. But gradually the influence of the general gravity told upon her, and she became conscious of what Dinah was saying. The gentle tones, the loving persuasion, did not touch her, but when the more severe appeals came she began to be frightened. Poor Bessy had always been considered a naughty girl; she was conscious of it; if it was necessary to be very good, it was clear she must be in a bad way. She couldn't find her places at church as Sally Rann could; she had often been tittering when she "curcheyed" to Mr. Irwine; and these religious deficiencies were accompanied by a corresponding slackness in the minor morals, for Bessy belonged unquestionably to that unsoaped, lazy class of femi‑ nine characters with whom you may venture to "eat an egg, an apple, or a nut." All this she was generally conscious of, and hitherto had not been greatly ashamed of it. But now she began to feel very much as if the constable had come to take her up and carry her before the justice for some undefined offence. She had a terrified sense that God, whom she had always thought was very far off, was very near to her, and that Jesus was close by looking at her, though she could not see him. For Dinah had that belief in visible manifestations of Jesus, which is com‑ mon among the Methodists, and she communicated it irresistibly to her hearers; she made them feel that he was among them bodily, and might at any moment show himself to them in some way that would strike anguish and penitence into their hearts.

"See!" she exclaimed, turning to the left, with her eyes fixed on a point above the heads of the people—"see where our blessed Lord stands and weeps, and stretches out his arms towards you. Hear what he says: 'How often would I have gathered you as a hen gathereth her chickens under her wings, and ye would not!' . . . and ye would not," she re‑ peated, in a tone of pleading reproach, turning her eyes on the people again. "See the print of the nails on his dear hands and feet. It is your sins that made them! Ah, how pale and worn he looks! He has gone through all that great agony in the garden, when his soul was exceed‑ ingly sorrowful even unto death, and the great drops of sweat fell like blood to the ground. They spat upon him and buffeted him, they scourged him, they mocked him, they laid the heavy cross on his bruised shoul‑ ders. Then they nailed him up. Ah! what pain! His lips are parched with thirst, and they mock him still in this great agony; yet with those parched lips he prays for them, 'Father, forgive them, for they know not what they do.' Then a horror of great darkness fell upon him, and he felt what sinners feel when they are for ever shut out from God. That was the last drop in the cup of bitterness. 'My God, my God!' he cries, 'why hast Thou forsaken me?'

"All this he bore for you! For you—and you never think of him; for you—and you turn your backs on him; you don't care what he has gone through for you. Yet he is not weary of toiling for you: he has risen from the dead, he is praying for you at the right hand of God—'Father, forgive them, for they know not what they do.' And he is upon this earth too; he is among us; he is there close to you now; I see his wounded body and his look of love."

Here Dinah turned to Bessy Cranage, whose bonny youth and evident vanity had touched her with pity.

"Poor child! poor child! He is beseeching you, and you don't listen to him. You think of ear-rings and fine gowns and caps, and you never think of the Saviour who died to save your precious soul. Your cheeks will be shrivelled one day, your hair will be grey, your poor body will be thin and tottering! Then you will begin to feel that your soul is not saved; then you will have to stand before God dressed in your sins, in your evil tempers and vain thoughts. And Jesus, who stands ready to help you now, won't help you then: because you won't have him to be your Saviour, he will be your judge. Now he looks at you with love and mercy, and says, 'Come to me that you may have life'; then he will turn away from you, and say, 'Depart from me into everlasting fire!' "

Poor Bessy's wide-open black eyes began to fill with tears, her great red cheeks and lips became quite pale, and her face was distorted like a little child's before a burst of crying.

"Ah! poor blind child!" Dinah went on, "think if it should happen to you as it once happened to a servant of God in the days of her vanity. *She* thought of her lace caps, and saved all her money to buy 'em; she thought nothing about how she might get a clean heart and a right spirit, she only wanted to have better lace than other girls. And one day when she put her new cap on and looked in the glass, she saw a bleeding Face crowned with thorns. That face is looking at you now," —here Dinah pointed to a spot close in front of Bessy.—"Ah! tear off those follies! cast them away from you, as if they were stinging adders. They *are* stinging you—they are poisoning your soul—they are dragging you down into a dark bottomless pit, where you will sink for ever, and for ever, and for ever, further away from light and God."

Bessy could bear it no longer: a great terror was upon her, and wrenching her earrings from her ears, she threw them down before her, sobbing aloud. Her father, Chad, frightened lest he should be "laid hold on" too, this impression on the rebellious Bess striking him as nothing less than a miracle, walked hastily away, and began to work at his anvil by way of reassuring himself. "Folks mun ha' hoss-shoes, praichin' or no praichin': the devil canna lay hould o' me for that," he muttered to himself.

But now Dinah began to tell of the joys that were in store for the penitent, and to describe in her simple way the divine peace and love with which the soul of the believer is filled—how the sense of God's love turns poverty into riches, and satisfies the soul, so that no uneasy desire vexes it, no fear alarms it: how, at last, the very temptation to sin is extinguished, and heaven is begun upon earth, because no cloud passes between the soul and God, who is its eternal sun.

"Dear friends," she said at last, "brothers and sisters, whom I love as those for whom my Lord has died, believe me I know what this great blessedness is; and because I know it, I want you to have it too. I am poor, like you: I have to get my living with my hands; but no lord nor lady can be so happy as me, if they haven't got the love of God in their souls. Think what it is—not to hate anything but sin; to be full of love to every creature; to be frightened at nothing; to be sure that all things will turn to good; not to mind pain, because it is our Father's will; to know that nothing—no, not if the earth was to be burnt up, or the waters come and drown us—nothing could part us from God who loves us, and who fills our souls with peace and joy, because we are sure that whatever he wills is holy, just, and good.

"Dear friends, come and take this blessedness; it is offered to you; it is the good news that Jesus came to preach to the poor. It is not like the riches of this world, so that the more one gets the less the rest can have. God is without end; his love is without end—

> 'Its streams the whole creation reach,
> So plenteous is the store;
> Enough for all, enough for each,
> Enough for evermore.' "

Dinah had been speaking at least an hour, and the reddening light of the parting day seemed to give a solemn emphasis to her closing words. The stranger, who had been interested in the course of her sermon, as if it had been the development of a drama—for there is this sort of fascination in all sincere unpremeditated eloquence, which opens to one the inward drama of the speaker's emotions—now turned his horse aside, and pursued his way, while Dinah said, "Let us sing a little, dear friends"; and as he was still winding down the slope, the voices of the Methodists reached him, rising and falling in that strange blending of exultation and sadness which belongs to the cadence of a hymn.

CHAPTER III

AFTER THE PREACHING

In less than an hour from that time Seth Bede was walking by Dinah's side along the hedgerow-path that skirted the pastures and green corn-fields which lay between the village and the Hall Farm. Dinah had taken off her little Quaker bonnet again, and was holding it in her hands that she might have a freer enjoyment of the cool evening twilight, and Seth could see the expression of her face quite clearly as he walked by her side, timidly revolving something he wanted to say to her. It was an expression of unconscious placid gravity—of absorption in thoughts that had no connection with the present moment or with her own personality: an expression that is most of all discouraging to a lover. Her very walk was discouraging: it had that quiet elasticity that asks for no support. Seth felt this dimly; he said to himself, "She's too good and holy for any man, let alone me," and the words he had been summoning rushed back again before they had reached his lips. But another thought gave him courage: "There's no man could love her better, and leave her freer to follow the Lord's work." They had been silent for many minutes now, since they had done talking about Bessy Cranage; Dinah seemed almost to have forgotten Seth's presence, and her pace was becoming so much quicker, that the sense of their being only a few minutes' walk from the yard-gates of the Hall Farm at last gave Seth courage to speak.

"You've quite made up your mind to go back to Snowfield o' Saturday, Dinah?"

"Yes," said Dinah, quietly. "I'm called there. It was borne in upon my mind while I was meditating on Sunday night, as sister Allen, who's in a decline, is in need of me. I saw her as plain as we see that bit of thin white cloud, lifting up her poor thin hand and beckoning to me. And this morning when I opened the Bible for direction, the first words my eyes fell on were, 'And after we had seen the vision, immediately we endeavoured to go into Macedonia.' If it wasn't for that clear showing of the Lord's will I should be loth to go, for my heart yearns over my aunt and her little ones, and that poor wandering lamb Hetty Sorrel. I've been much drawn out in prayer for her of late, and I look on it as a token that there may be mercy in store for her."

"God grant it," said Seth. "For I doubt Adam's heart is so set on her, he'll never turn to anybody else; and yet it 'ud go to my heart if he was to marry her, for I canna think as she'd make him happy. It's a deep mystery—the way the heart of man turns to one woman out of all the rest he's seen i' the world, and makes it easier for him to work seven years for *her*, like Jacob did for Rachel, sooner than have any other woman for th' asking. I often think of them words, 'And Jacob served seven years for Rachel; and they seemed to him but a few days for the love he had for her.' I know those words 'ud come true with me, Dinah, if so be you'd give me hope as I might win you after seven years was over. I know you think a husband 'ud be taking up too much o' your thoughts, because St. Paul says, 'She that's married careth for the things of the world how she may please her husband'; and may happen you'll think me over-bold to speak to you about it again, after what you told me o' your mind last Saturday. But I've been thinking it over again by night and by day, and I've prayed not to be blinded by my own desires, to think what's only good for me must be good for you too. And it seems to me there's more texts for your marrying than ever you can find against it. For St. Paul says as plain as can be in another place, 'I will that the younger women marry, bear children, guide the house, give none occasion to the adversary to speak reproachfully'; and then 'two are better than one'; and that holds good with marriage as well as with other things. For we should be o' one heart and o' one mind, Dinah. We both serve the same Master, and are striving after the same gifts; and I'd never be the husband to make a claim on you as could interfere with your doing the work God has fitted you for. I'd make a shift, and fend indoor and out, to give you more liberty—more than you can have now, for you've got to get your own living now, and I'm strong enough to work for us both."

When Seth had once begun to urge his suit, he went on earnestly, and almost hurriedly, lest Dinah should speak some decisive word before he had poured forth all the arguments he had prepared. His cheeks became flushed as he went on, his mild grey eyes filled with tears, and his voice trembled as he spoke the last sentence. They had reached one of those very narrow passes between two tall stones, which performed the office of a stile in Loamshire, and Dinah paused as she turned towards Seth and said, in her tender but calm treble notes—

"Seth Bede, I thank you for your love towards me, and if I could think of any man as more than a Christian brother, I think it would be you. But my heart is not free to marry. That is good for other women, and it is a great and a blessed thing to be a wife and mother; but 'as God has distributed to every man, as the Lord hath called every man, so let him walk.' God has called me to minister to others, not to have any joys or sorrows of my own, but to rejoice with them that do rejoice, and to weep with those that weep. He has called me to speak his word, and he has greatly owned my work. It could only be on a very clear showing that I could leave the brethren and sisters at Snowfield, who are favoured with very little of this world's good; where the trees are few, so that a child might count them, and there's very hard living for the poor in the winter. It has been given me to help, to comfort, and strengthen the little flock there, and to call in many wanderers; and my soul is filled with these things from my rising up till my lying down. My life is too short, and God's work is too great for me to think of making a home for myself in this world. I've not turned a deaf ear to your words, Seth, for when I saw as your love was given to me, I thought it might be a leading of Providence for me to change my way of life, and that we should be fellow-helpers; and I spread the matter before the Lord. But whenever I tried to fix my mind on marriage, and our living together, other thoughts always came in—the times when I've prayed by the sick and dying, and the happy hours I've had preaching, when my heart was filled with love, and the Word was given to me abundantly. And when I've opened the Bible for direction, I've always lighted on some clear word to tell me where my work lay. I believe what you say, Seth, that you would try to be a help and not a hindrance to my work; but I see that our marriage is not God's will—he draws my heart another way. I desire to live and die without husband or children. I seem to have no room in my soul for wants and fears of my own, it has pleased God to fill my heart so full with the wants and sufferings of his poor people."

Seth was unable to reply, and they walked on in silence. At last, as they were nearly at the yard-gate, he said—

"Well, Dinah, I must seek for strength to bear it, and to endure as seeing Him who is invisible. But I feel now how weak my faith is. It seems as if, when you are gone, I could never joy in anything any more. I think it's something passing the love of women as I feel for you, for I could be content without your marrying me if I could go and live at Snowfield, and be near you. I trusted as the strong love God had given me towards you was a leading for us both; but it seems it was only meant for my trial. Perhaps I feel more for you than I ought to feel for any creature, for I often can't help saying of you what the hymn says,—

'In darkest shades if she appear,
My dawning is begun;

She is my soul's bright morning-star,
And she my rising sun.'

That may be wrong, and I am to be taught better. But you wouldn't be displeased with me if things turned out so as I could leave this country and go to live at Snowfield?"

"No, Seth; but I counsel you to wait patiently, and not lightly to leave your own country and kindred. Do nothing without the Lord's clear bidding. It's a bleak and barren country there, not like this land of Goshen you've been used to. We mustn't be in a hurry to fix and choose our own lot; we must wait to be guided."

"But you'd let me write you a letter, Dinah, if there was anything I wanted to tell you?"

"Yes, sure; let me know if you're in any trouble. You'll be continually in my prayers."

They had now reached the yard-gate, and Seth said, "I won't go in, Dinah; so farewell." He paused and hesitated after she had given him her hand, and then said, "There's no knowing but what you may see things different after a while. There may be a new leading."

"Let us leave that, Seth. It's good to live only a moment at a time, as I've read in one of Mr. Wesley's books. It isn't for you and me to lay plans; we've nothing to do but to obey and to trust. Farewell."

Dinah pressed his hand with rather a sad look in her loving eyes, and then passed through the gate, while Seth turned away to walk lingeringly home. But instead of taking the direct road, he chose to turn back along the fields through which he and Dinah had already passed; and I think his blue linen handkerchief was very wet with tears long before he had made up his mind that it was time for him to set his face steadily homewards. He was but three-and-twenty, and had only just learned what it is to love—to love with that adoration which a young man gives to a woman whom he feels to be greater and better than himself. Love of this sort is hardly distinguishable from religious feeling. What deep and worthy love is so? whether of woman or child, or art or music. Our caresses, our tender words, our still rapture under the influence of autumn sunsets, or pillared vistas, or calm majestic statues, or Beethoven symphonies, all bring with them the consciousness that they are mere waves and ripples in an unfathomable ocean of love and beauty; our emotion in its keenest moment passes from expression into silence, our love at its highest flood rushes beyond its object, and loses itself in the sense of divine mystery. And this blessed gift of venerating love has been given to too many humble craftsmen since the world began, for us to feel any surprise that it should have existed in the soul of a Methodist carpenter half a century ago, while there was yet a lingering after-glow from the time when Wesley and his fellow-labourer fed on the hips and haws of the Cornwall hedges, after exhausting limbs and lungs in carrying a divine message to the poor.

That after-glow has long faded away; and the picture we are apt to make of Methodism in our imagination is not an amphitheatre of green hills, or the deep shade of broad-leavèd sycamores, where a crowd of rough men and weary-hearted women drank in a faith which was a rudimentary culture, which linked their thoughts with the past, lifted their imagination above the sordid details of their own narrow lives, and suffused their souls with the sense of a pitying, loving, infinite Presence, sweet as summer to the houseless needy. It is too possible that to some of my readers Methodism may mean nothing more than low-pitched gables up dingy streets, sleek grocers, sponging preachers, and hypocritical jargon—elements which are regarded as an exhaustive analysis of Methodism in many fashionable quarters.

That would be a pity; for I cannot pretend that Seth and Dinah were anything else than Methodists—not indeed of that modern type which reads quarterly reviews and attends in chapels with pillared porticoes; but of a very old-fashioned kind. They believed in present miracles, in instantaneous conversions, in revelations by dreams and visions; they drew lots, and sought for Divine guidance by opening the Bible at hazard, having a literal way of interpreting the Scriptures, which is not at all sanctioned by approved commentators; and it is impossible for me to represent their diction as correct, or their instruction as liberal. Still —if I have read religious history aright—faith, hope, and charity have not always been found in a direct ratio with a sensibility to the three concords; and it is possible, thank Heaven! to have very erroneous theories and very sublime feelings. The raw bacon which clumsy Molly spares from her own scanty store, that she may carry it to her neighbour's child to "stop the fits," may be a piteously inefficacious remedy; but the generous stirring of neighbourly kindness that prompted the deed has a beneficent radiation that is not lost.

Considering these things, we can hardly think Dinah and Seth beneath our sympathy, accustomed as we may be to weep over the loftier sorrows of heroines in satin boots and crinoline, and of heroes riding fiery horses, themselves ridden by still more fiery passions.

Poor Seth! he was never on horseback in his life except once, when he was a little lad, and Mr. Jonathan Burge took him up behind, telling him to "hold on tight"; and instead of bursting out into wild accusing apostrophes to God and destiny, he is resolving, as he now walks homeward under the solemn starlight, to repress his sadness, to be less bent on having his own will, and to live more for others, as Dinah does.

CHAPTER IV

HOME AND ITS SORROWS

A GREEN valley with a brook running through it, full almost to overflowing with the late rains; overhung by low stooping willows. Across this brook a plank is thrown, and over this plank Adam Bede is passing with his undoubting step, followed close by Gyp with the basket; evidently making his way to the thatched house, with a stack of timber by the side of it, about twenty yards up the opposite slope.

The door of the house is open, and an elderly woman is looking out; but she is not placidly contemplating the evening sunshine; she has been watching with dim eyes the gradually enlarging speck which for the last few minutes she has been quite sure is her darling son Adam. Lisbeth Bede loves her son with the love of a woman to whom her first-born has come late in life. She is an anxious, spare, yet vigorous old woman, clean as a snow-drop. Her grey hair is turned neatly back under a pure linen cap with a black band round it; her broad chest is covered with a buff neckerchief, and below this you see a sort of short bed-gown made of blue-checkered linen, tied round the waist and descending to the hips, from whence there is a considerable length of linsey-wolsey petticoat. For Lisbeth is tall, and in other points too there is a strong likeness between her and her son Adam. Her dark eyes are somewhat dim now—perhaps from too much crying—but her broadly-marked eye-brows are still black, her teeth are sound, and as she stands knitting rapidly and unconsciously with her work-hardened hands, she has as firmly-upright an attitude as when she is carrying a pail of water on her head from the spring. There is the same type of frame and the same keen activity of temperament in mother and son, but it was not from her that Adam got his well-filled brow and his expression of large-hearted intelligence.

Family likeness has often a deep sadness in it. Nature, that great tragic dramatist, knit us together by bone and muscle, and divides us by the subtler web of our brains; blends yearning and repulsion; and ties us by our heartstrings to the beings that jar us at every movement. We hear a voice with the very cadence of our own uttering the thoughts we despise; we see eyes—ah! so like our mother's—averted from us in cold alienation; and our last darling child startles us with the air and gestures of the sister we parted from in bitterness long years ago. The father to whom we owe our best heritage—the mechanical instinct, the keen sensibility to harmony, the unconscious skill of the modelling hand —galls us, and puts us to shame by his daily errors; the long-lost mother, whose face we begin to see in the glass as our own wrinkles come, once fretted our young souls with her anxious humours and irrational persistence.

It is such a fond anxious mother's voice that you hear, as Lisbeth says,

"Well, my lad, it's gone seven by th' clock. Thee't allays stay till the last child's born. Thee wants thy supper, I'll warrand. Where's Seth? gone arter some o's chapellin', I reckon?"

"Ay, ay, Seth's at no harm, mother, thee mayst be sure. But where's father?" said Adam quickly, as he entered the house and glanced into the room on the left hand, which was used as a workshop. "Hasn't he done the coffin for Tholer? There's the stuff standing just as I left it this morning."

"Done the coffin?" said Lisbeth, following him, and knitting unin-terruptedly, though she looked at her son very anxiously. "Eh, my lad, he went aff to Treddles'on this forenoon, an's niver come back. I doubt he's got to th' 'Waggin Overthrow' again."

A deep flush of anger passed rapidly over Adam's face. He said noth-ing, but threw off his jacket, and began to roll up his shirt-sleeves again.

"What art goin' to do, Adam?" said the mother, with a tone and look of alarm. "Thee wouldstna go to work again, wi'out ha'in thy bit o' supper?"

Adam, too angry to speak, walked into the workshop. But his mother threw down her knitting, and, hurrying after him, took hold of his arm, and said in a tone of plaintive remonstrance—

"Nay, my lad, my lad, thee munna go wi'out thy supper; there's the taters wi' the gravy in 'em, just as thee lik'st 'em. I saved 'em o' purpose for thee. Come an' ha' thy supper, come."

"Let be!" said Adam impetuously, shaking her off, and seizing one of the planks that stood against the wall. "It's fine talking about having supper when here's a coffin promised to be ready at Brox'on by seven o'clock to-morrow morning, and ought to ha' been there now, and not a nail struck yet. My throat's too full to swallow victuals."

"Why, thee canstna get the coffin ready," said Lisbeth. "Thee't work thyself to death. It 'ud take thee all night to do't."

"What signifies how long it takes me? Isn't the coffin promised? Can they bury the man without a coffin? I'd work my right hand off sooner than deceive people with lies i' that way. It makes me mad to think on't. I shall overrun these doings before long. I've stood enough of 'em."

Poor Lisbeth did not hear this threat for the first time, and if she had been wise she would have gone away quietly, and said nothing for the next hour. But one of the lessons a woman most rarely learns, is never to talk to an angry or a drunken man. Lisbeth sat down on the chopping bench and began to cry, and by the time she had cried enough to make her voice very piteous, she burst out into words.

"Nay, my lad, my lad, thee wouldstna go away an' break thy mother's heart, an' leave thy feyther to ruin. Thee wouldstna ha' 'em carry me to th' churchyard, an' thee not to follow me. I shanna rest i' my grave if I donna see thee at th' last; an how's they to let thee know as I'm a-dyin', if thee't gone a-workin' i' distant parts, an' Seth belike gone arter thee, and thy feyther not able to hold a pen for's hand shakin', besides not knowin' where thee art? Thee mun forgie thy feyther—thee munna be so bitter again' him. He was a good feyther to thee afore he took to th' drink. He's a clever workman, an' taught thee thy trade, remember, an's niver gen me a blow nor so much as an ill word—no, not even in 's drink. Thee wouldstna ha 'm go to workhus—thy own feyther—an' him as was a fine-growed man an' handy at everythin' amost as thee art thysen, five-an'-twenty 'ear ago, when thee wast a baby at the breast."

Lisbeth's voice became louder, and choked with sobs: a sort of wail, the most irritating of all sounds where real sorrows are to be borne, and real work to be done. Adam broke in impatiently.

"Now, mother, don't cry and talk so. Haven't I got enough to vex me without that? What's th' use o' telling me things as I only think too much on every day? If I didna think on 'em why should I do as I do, for the sake o' keeping things together here? But I hate to be talking where it's no use: I like to keep my breath for doing instead o' talking."

"I know thee dost things as nobody else 'ud do, my lad. But thee't allays so hard upo' thy feyther, Adam. Thee think'st nothing too much to do for Seth: thee snapp'st me up if iver I find faut wi' th' lad. But thee's so angered wi' thy feyther, more nor wi' anybody else."

"That's better than speaking soft, and letting things go the wrong way, I reckon, isn't it? If I wasn't sharp with him, he'd sell every bit o' stuff i' th' yard, and spend it on drink. I know there's a duty to be done by my father, but it isn't my duty to encourage him in running headlong to ruin. And what has Seth got to do with it? The lad does no harm as I know of. But leave me alone, mother, and let me get on with the work."

Lisbeth dared not say any more; but she got up and called Gyp, thinking to console herself somewhat for Adam's refusal of the supper she had spread out in the loving expectation of looking at him while he ate it, by feeding Adam's dog with extra liberality. But Gyp was watching his master with wrinkled brow and ears erect, puzzled at this unusual course of things; and though he glanced at Lisbeth when she called him, and moved his forepaws uneasily, well knowing that she was inviting him to supper, he was in a divided state of mind, and remained seated on his haunches, again fixing his eyes anxiously on his master. Adam noticed Gyp's mental conflict, and though his anger had made him less tender than usual to his mother, it did not prevent him from caring as much as usual for his dog. We are apt to be kinder to the brutes that love us than to the women that love us. Is it because the brutes are dumb?

"Go, Gyp; go, lad!" Adam said, in a tone of encouraging command; and Gyp, apparently satisfied that duty and pleasure were one, followed Lisbeth into the house-place.

But no sooner had he licked up his supper than he went back to his master, while Lisbeth sat down alone to cry over her knitting. Women who are never bitter and resentful are often the most querulous; and if Solomon was as wise as he is reputed to be, I feel sure that when he compared a contentious woman to a continual dropping on a very rainy day, he had not a vixen in his eye—a fury with long nails, acrid and selfish. Depend upon it, he meant a good creature, who had no joy but in the happiness of the loved ones whom she contributed to make uncomfortable, putting by all the tid-bits for them, and spending nothing on herself. Such a woman as Lisbeth for example—at once patient and complaining, self-renouncing and exacting, brooding the livelong day over what happened yesterday, and what is likely to happen to-morrow, and crying very readily both at the good and the evil. But a certain awe mingled itself with her idolatrous love of Adam, and when he said, "Leave me alone," she was always silenced.

So the hours passed, to the loud ticking of the old day-clock and the sound of Adam's tools. At last he called for a light and a draught of water (beer was a thing only to be drunk on holidays), and Lisbeth ventured to say as she took it in, "Thy supper stans ready for thee, when thee lik'st."

"Donna thee sit up, mother," said Adam, in a gentle tone. He had worked off his anger now, and whenever he wished to be especially kind to his mother, he fell into his strongest native accent and dialect, with which at other times his speech was less deeply tinged. "I'll see to father when he comes home; maybe he wonna come at all to-night. I shall be easier if thee't i' bed."

"Nay, I'll bide till Seth comes. He wonna be long now, I reckon."

It was then past nine by the clock, which was always in advance of the day, and before it had struck ten the latch was lifted and Seth entered. He had heard the sound of the tools as he was approaching.

"Why, mother," he said, "how is it as father's working so late?"

"It's none o' thy feyther as is a-workin'—thee might know that well anoof if thy head warna full o' chapellin'—it's thy brother as does iverything, for there's niver nobody else i' th' way to do nothin'."

Lisbeth was going on, for she was not at all afraid of Seth, and usually poured into his ears all the querulousness which was repressed by her awe of Adam. Seth had never in his life spoken a harsh word to his mother, and timid people always wreak their peevishness on the gentle. But Seth, with an anxious look, had passed into the workshop and said—

"Addy, how's this? What! father's forgot the coffin?"

"Ay, lad, th' old tale; but I shall get it done," said Adam, looking up, and casting one of his bright keen glances at his brother. "Why, what's the matter with thee? Thee't in trouble."

Seth's eyes were red, and there was a look of deep depression on his mild face.

"Yes, Addy, but it's what must be borne, and can't be helped. Why, thee'st never been to the school, then?"

"School? no; that screw can wait," said Adam, hammering away again.

"Let me take my turn now, and do thee go to bed," said Seth.

"No, lad, I'd rather go on, now I'm in harness. Thee't help me to carry it to Brox'on when it's done. I'll call thee up at sunrise. Go and eat thy supper, and shut the door, so as I mayn't hear mother's talk."

Seth knew that Adam always meant what he said, and was not to be persuaded into meaning anything else. So he turned, with rather a heavy heart, into the house-place.

"Adam's niver touched a bit o' victual sin' home he's come," said Lisbeth. "I reckon thee'st hed thy supper at some o' thy Methody folks."

"Nay, mother," said Seth, "I've had no supper yet."

"Come, then," said Lisbeth, "but donna thee ate the taters for Adam 'ull happen ate 'em if I leave 'em stannin'. He loves a bit o' taters an'

gravy. But he's been so sore an' angered, he wouldn't ate 'em, for all I'd
putten 'em by o' purpose for him. An' he's been a-threatenin' to go away
again," she went on, whimpering, "an' I'm fast sure he'll go some
dawnin' afore I'm up, an' niver let me know aforehand, an' he'll niver
come back again when once he's gone. An' I'd better niver ha' had a son,
as is like no other body's son for the deftness an' th' handiness, an' so
looked on by th' grit folks, an' tall an' upright like a poplar tree, an' me
to be parted from him, an' niver see 'm no more."

"Come, mother, donna grieve thyself in vain," said Seth, in a soothing voice. "Thee'st not half so good reason to think as Adam 'ull go
away as to think he'll stay with thee. He may say such a thing when he's
in wrath—and he's got excuse for being wrathful sometimes—but his
heart 'ud never let him go. Think how he's stood by us all when it's been
none so easy—paying his savings to free me from going for a soldier,
an' turnin' his earnins into wood for father, when he's got plenty o'
uses for his money, and many a young man like him 'ud ha' been married
and settled before now. He'll never turn round and knock down his own
work, and forsake them as it's been the labour of his life to stand by."

"Donna talk to me about's marr'in'," said Lisbeth, crying afresh.
"He's set's heart on that Hetty Sorrel, as 'ull niver save a penny, an' 'ull
toss up her head at's old mother. An' to think as he might ha' Mary
Burge, an' be took partners, an' be a big man wi' workmen under him,
like Mester Burge—Dolly's told me so o'er an' o'er again—if it warna
as he's set's heart on that bit of a wench, as is o' no more use nor the
gillyflower on the wall. An' he so wise at bookin' and figurin', an' not
to know no better nor that!"

"But, mother, thee know'st we canna love just where other folks 'ud
have us. There's nobody but God can control the heart of man. I could
ha' wished myself as Adam could ha' made another choice, but I wouldn't
reproach him for what he can't help. And I'm not sure but what he tries
to o'ercome it. But it's a matter as he doesn't like to be spoke to about,
and I can only pray to the Lord to bless and direct him."

"Ay, thee't allays ready enough at prayin', but I donna see as thee
gets much wi' thy prayin'. Thee wotna get double earnins o' this side
Yule. Th' Methodys 'll niver make thee half the man thy brother is, for
all they're a-makin' a preacher on thee."

"It's partly truth thee speak'st there, mother," said Seth, mildly;
"Adam's far before me, an's done more for me than I can ever do for
him. God distributes talents to every man according as He sees good. But
thee mustna undervally prayer. Prayer mayna bring money, but it brings
us what no money can buy—a power to keep from sin, and be content
with God's will, whatever He may please to send. If thee wouldst pray
to God to help thee, and trust in His goodness, thee wouldstna be so
uneasy about things."

"Unaisy? I'm i' th' right on't to be unaisy. It's well seen on *thee* what
it is niver to be unaisy. Thee't gi' away all thy earnins, an' niver be
unaisy as thee'st nothin' laid up again' a rainy day. If Adam had been as

aisy as thee, he'd niver ha' had no money to pay for thee. Take no thought for the morrow—take no thought—that's what thee't allays sayin'; an' what comes on't? Why, as Adam has to take thought for thee."

"Those are the words o' the Bible, mother," said Seth. "They don't mean as we should be idle. They mean we shouldn't be over anxious and worreting ourselves about what'll happen to-morrow, but do our duty, and leave the rest to God's will."

"Ay, ay, that's the way wi' thee: thee allays makes a peck o' thy own words out o' a pint o' the Bible's. I donna see how thee't to know as 'take no thought for the morrow' means all that. An' when the Bible's such a big book, an' thee canst read all thro't, an' ha' the pick o' the texes, I canna think why thee dostna pick better words as donna mean so much more nor they say. Adam doesna pick a that'n; I can understan' the tex as he's allays a-sayin', 'God helps them as helps theirsens.' "

"Nay, mother," said Seth, "that's no text o' the Bible. It comes out of a book as Adam picked up at the stall at Treddles'on. It was wrote by a knowing man, but over-worldly, I doubt. However, that sayin's partly true; for the Bible tells us we must be workers together with God."

"Well, how'm I to know? It sounds like a tex. But what's th' matter wi' th' lad? Thee't hardly atin' a bit o' supper. Dostna mean to ha' no more nor that bit o' oat-cake? An' thee lookst as white as a flick o' new bacon. What's th' matter wi' thee?"

"Nothing to mind about, mother; I'm not hungry. I'll just look in at Adam again, and see if he'll let me go on with the coffin."

"Ha' a drop o' warm broth?" said Lisbeth, whose motherly feeling now got the better of her "nattering" habit. "I'll set two-three sticks a-light in a minute."

"Nay, mother, thank thee; thee't very good," said Seth, gratefully; and encouraged by this touch of tenderness, he went on: "Let me pray a bit with thee for father, and Adam, and all of us—it'll comfort thee, happen, more than thee thinkst."

"Well, I've nothin' to say again' it."

Lisbeth, though disposed always to take the negative side in her conversations with Seth had a vague sense that there was some comfort and safety in the fact of his piety, and that it somehow relieved her from the trouble of any spiritual transactions on her own behalf.

So the mother and son knelt down together, and Seth prayed for the poor wandering father, and for those who were sorrowing for him at home. And when he came to the petition that Adam might never be called to set up his tent in a far country, but that his mother might be cheered and comforted by his presence all the days of her pilgrimage, Lisbeth's ready tears flowed again, and she wept aloud.

When they rose from their knees, Seth went to Adam again, and said, "Wilt only lie down for an hour or two, and let me go on the while?"

"No, Seth, no. Make mother go to bed, and go thyself."

Meantime Lisbeth had dried her eyes, and now followed Seth, holding

something in her hands. It was the brown-and-yellow platter containing
the baked potatoes with the gravy in them and bits of meat which she
had cut and mixed among them. Those were dear times, when wheaten
bread and fresh meat were delicacies to working people. She set the dish
down rather timidly on the bench by Adam's side, and said, "Thee canst
pick a bit while thee't workin'. I'll bring thee another drop o' water."

"Ay, mother, do," said Adam, kindly; "I'm getting very thirsty."

In half an hour all was quiet; no sound was to be heard in the house
but the loud ticking of the old day-clock, and the ringing of Adam's
tools. The night was very still: when Adam opened the door to look out
at twelve o'clock, the only motion seemed to be in the glowing, twinkling
stars; every blade of grass was asleep.

Bodily haste and exertion usually leave our thoughts very much at
the mercy of our feelings and imagination; and it was so tonight with
Adam. While his muscles were working lustily, his mind seemed as passive as a spectator at a diorama: scenes of the sad past, and probably
sad future, floating before him, and giving place one to the other in swift
succession.

He saw how it would be to-morrow morning, when he had carried the
coffin to Broxton and was at home again, having his breakfast: his father
perhaps would come in, ashamed to meet his son's glance—would sit
down, looking older and more tottering than he had done the morning
before, and hang down his head, examining the floor-quarries; while Lisbeth would ask him how he supposed the coffin had been got ready, that
he had slinked off and left undone—for Lisbeth was always the first to
utter the word of reproach, although she cried at Adam's severity towards
his father.

"So it will go on, worsening and worsening," thought Adam; "there's
no slipping up-hill again, and no standing still when once you've begun
to slip down." And then the day came back to him when he was a little
fellow and used to run by his father's side, proud to be taken out to
work, and prouder still to hear his father boasting to his fellow-workmen
how "the little chap had an uncommon notion o' carpentering." What a
fine active fellow his father was then! When people asked Adam whose
little lad he was, he had a sense of distinction as he answered, "I'm
Thias Bede's lad"—he was quite sure everybody knew Thias Bede:
didn't he make the wonderful pigeon-house at Broxton parsonage? Those
were happy days, especially when Seth, who was three years the younger,
began to go out working too, and Adam began to be a teacher as well as
a learner. But then came the days of sadness, when Adam was someway
on in his teens, and Thias began to loiter at the public-houses, and Lisbeth began to cry at home, and to pour forth her plaints in the hearing
of her sons. Adam remembered well the night of shame and anguish
when he first saw his father quite wild and foolish, shouting a song out
fitfully among his drunken companions at the "Waggon Overthrown." He
had run away once when he was only eighteen, making his escape in the
morning twilight with a little blue bundle over his shoulder, and his

"mensuration book" in his pocket, and saying to himself very decidedly that he could bear the vexations of home no longer—he would go and seek his fortune, setting up his stick at the crossways and bending his steps the way it fell. But by the time he got to Stoniton, the thought of his mother and Seth, left behind to endure everything without him, became too importunate, and his resolution failed him. He came back the next day, but the misery and terror his mother had gone through in those two days had haunted her ever since.

"No!" Adam said to himself to-night, "that must never happen again. It 'ud make a poor balance when my doings are cast up at the last, if my poor old mother stood o' the wrong side. My back's broad enough and strong enough; I should be no better than a coward to go away and leave the troubles to be borne by them as aren't half so able. 'They that are strong ought to bear the infirmities of those that are weak, and not to please themselves.' There's a text wants no candle to show't; it shines by its own light. It's plain enough you get into the wrong road i' this life if you run after this and that only for the sake o' making things easy and pleasant to yourself. A pig may poke his nose into the trough and think o' nothing outside it; but if you've got a man's heart and soul in you, you can't be easy a-making your own bed an' leaving the rest to lie on the stones. Nay, nay, I'll never slip my neck out o' the yoke, and leave the load to be drawn by the weak uns. Father's a sore cross to me, an's likely to be for many a long year to come. What then? I've got th' health, and the limbs, and the sperrit to bear it."

At this moment a smart rap, as if with a willow wand, was given at the house door, and Gyp, instead of barking, as might have been expected, gave a loud howl. Adam, very much startled, went at once to the door and opened it. Nothing was there; all was still, as when he opened it an hour before; the leaves were motionless, and the light of the stars showed the placid fields on both sides of the brook quite empty of visible life. Adam walked round the house, and still saw nothing except a rat which darted into the woodshed as he passed. He went in again, wondering; the sound was so peculiar, that the moment he heard it, it called up the image of the willow wand striking the door. He could not help a little shudder, as he remembered how often his mother had told him of just such a sound coming as a sign when some one was dying. Adam was not a man to be gratuitously superstitious; but he had the blood of the peasant in him as well as of the artisan, and a peasant can no more help believing in a traditional superstition than a horse can help trembling when he sees a camel. Besides, he had that mental combination which is at once humble in the region of mystery, and keen in the region of knowledge: it was the depth of his reverence quite as much as his hard commonsense, which gave him his disinclination to doctrinal religion, and he often checked Seth's argumentative spiritualism by saying, "Eh, it's a big mystery; thee know'st but little about it." And so it happened that Adam was at once penetrating and credulous. If a new building had fallen down and he had been told that this was a divine judgment, he would have said, "May be; but the bearing o' the roof and walls wasn't right, else it wouldn't ha' come down"; yet he believed in dreams and prognostics, and to his dying day he bated his breath a little when he told the story of the stroke with the willow wand. I tell it as he told it, not attempting to reduce it to its natural elements: in our eagerness to explain impressions, we often lose our hold of the sympathy that comprehends them.

But he had the best antidote against imaginative dread in the necessity for getting on with the coffin, and for the next ten minutes his hammer was ringing so uninterruptedly, that other sounds, if there were any, might well be overpowered. A pause came, however, when he had to take up his ruler, and now again came the strange rap, and again Gyp howled. Adam was at the door without the loss of a moment; but again all was still, and the starlight showed there was nothing but the dew-laden grass in front of the cottage.

Adam for a moment thought uncomfortably about his father; but of late years he had never come home at dark hours from Treddleston, and there was every reason for believing that he was then sleeping off his drunkenness at the "Waggon Overthrown." Besides, to Adam, the conception of the future was so inseparable from the painful image of his father, that the fear of any fatal accident to him was excluded by the deeply infixed fear of his continual degradation. The next thought that occurred to him was one that made him slip off his shoes and tread lightly up stairs, to listen at the bedroom doors. But both Seth and his mother were breathing regularly.

Adam came down and set to work again, saying to himself, "I won't open the door again. It's no use staring about to catch sight of a sound. Maybe there's a world about us as we can't see, but th' ear's quicker than the eye, and catches a sound from't now and then. Some people think they get a sight on't too, but they're mostly folk whose eyes are not much use to 'em at anything else. For my part, I think it's better to see when your perpendicular's true, than to see a ghost."

Such thoughts as these are apt to grow stronger and stronger as daylight quenches the candles and the birds begin to sing. By the time the red sunlight shone on the brass nails that formed the initials on the lid of the coffin, any lingering foreboding from the sound of the willow wand was merged in satisfaction that the work was done and the promise redeemed. There was no need to call Seth, for he was already moving overhead, and presently came down stairs.

"Now, lad," said Adam, as Seth made his appearance, "the coffin's done, and we can take it over to Brox'on, and be back again before half after six. I'll take a mouthful o' oat-cake, and then we'll be off."

The coffin was soon propped on the tall shoulders of the two brothers, and they were making their way, followed close by Gyp, out of the little woodyard into the lane at the back of the house. It was but about a mile and a half to Broxton over the opposite slope, and their road wound very pleasantly along lanes and across fields, where the pale woodbines and the dog-roses were scenting the hedgerows, and the birds were twittering and trilling in the tall leafy boughs of oak and elm. It was a strangely mingled picture—the fresh youth of the summer morning, with its Eden-like peace and loveliness, the stalwart strength of the two brothers in their rusty working clothes, and the long coffin on their shoulders. They paused for the last time before a small farmhouse outside the village of Broxton. By six o'clock the task was done, the coffin nailed down, and Adam and Seth were on their way home. They chose a shorter way homeward, which would take them across the fields and the brook in front of the house. Adam had not mentioned to Seth what had happened in the night, but he still retained sufficient impression from it himself to say—

"Seth, lad, if father isn't come home by the time we've had our breakfast, I think it'll be as well for thee to go over to Treddles'on and look after him, and thee canst get me the brass wire I want. Never mind about losing an hour at thy work; we can make that up. What dost say?"

"I'm willing," said Seth. "But see what clouds have gathered since we set out. I'm thinking we shall have more rain. It'll be a sore time for th' haymaking if the meadows are flooded again. The brook's fine and full now: another day's rain 'ud cover the plank, and we should have to go round by the road."

They were coming across the valley now, and had entered the pasture through which the brook ran.

"Why, what's that sticking against the willow?" continued Seth, beginning to walk faster. Adam's heart rose to his mouth: the vague anxiety about his father was changed into a great dread. He made no answer to Seth, but ran forward, preceded by Gyp, who began to bark uneasily; and in two moments he was at the bridge.

This was what the omen meant, then! And the grey-haired father, of whom he had thought with a sort of hardness a few hours ago, as certain to live to be a thorn in his side, was perhaps even then struggling with that watery death! This was the first thought that flashed through Adam's conscience, before he had time to seize the coat and drag out the tall heavy body. Seth was already by his side, helping him, and when they had it on the bank, the two sons in the first moments knelt and looked with mute awe at the glazed eyes, forgetting that there was need for action—forgetting everything but that their father lay dead before them. Adam was the first to speak.

"I'll run to mother," he said, in a loud whisper. "I'll be back to thee in a minute."

Poor Lisbeth was busy preparing her sons' breakfast, and their porridge was already steaming on the fire. Her kitchen always looked the pink of cleanliness, but this morning she was more than usually bent on making her hearth and breakfast-table look comfortable and inviting.

"The lads 'ull be fine an' hungry," she said, half aloud, as she stirred the porridge. "It's a good step to Brox'on, an' it's hungry air o'er the hill—wi' that heavy coffin too. Eh! it's heavier now, wi' poor Bob Tholer

in't. Howiver, I've made a drap more porridge nor common this mornin'. The feyther 'ull happen come in arter a bit. Not as he'll ate much
porridge. He swallers six-penn'orth o' ale, an' saves a hap'orth o' porridge—that's his way o' layin' by money, as I've told him many a time,
an' am likely to tell him again afore the day's out. Eh! poor mon, he
takes it quiet enough; there's no denyin' that."

But now Lisbeth heard the heavy "thud" of a running footstep on
the turf, and, turning quickly towards the door, she saw Adam enter,
looking so pale and overwhelmed that she screamed aloud and rushed
towards him before he had time to speak.

"Hush, mother," Adam said, rather hoarsely, "don't be frightened.
Father's tumbled into the water. Belike we may bring him round again.
Seth and me are going to carry him in. Get a blanket and make it hot
at the fire."

In reality Adam was convinced that his father was dead, but he knew
there was no other way of repressing his mother's impetuous wailing
grief than by occupying her with some active task which had hope in it.

He ran back to Seth, and the two sons lifted the sad burden in heart-
stricken silence. The wide-open glazed eyes were grey, like Seth's, and
had once looked with mild pride on the boys before whom Thias had
lived to hang his head in shame. Seth's chief feeling was awe and distress
at this sudden snatching away of his father's soul; but Adam's mind
rushed back over the past in a flood of relenting and pity. When death,
the great Reconciler, has come, it is never our tenderness that we repent
of, but our severity.

CHAPTER V

THE RECTOR

BEFORE twelve o'clock there had been some heavy storms of rain, and
the water lay in deep gutters on the sides of the gravel-walks in the
garden of Broxton Parsonage; the great Provence roses had been cruelly
tossed by the wind and beaten by the rain, and all the delicate-stemmed
border flowers had been dashed down and stained with the wet soil. A
melancholy morning—because it was nearly time hay-harvest should
begin, and instead of that the meadows were likely to be flooded.

But people who have pleasant homes get in-door enjoyments that they
would never think of but for the rain. If it had not been a wet morning,
Mr. Irwine would not have been in the dining-room playing at chess with
his mother, and he loves both his mother and chess quite well enough to
pass some cloudy hours very easily by their help. Let me take you into
that dining-room, and show you the Rev. Adolphus Irwine, Rector of
Broxton, Vicar of Hayslope, and Vicar of Blythe, a pluralist at whom
the severest Church-reformer would have found it difficult to look sour.
We will enter very softly, and stand still in the open doorway, without

awaking the glossy-brown setter who is stretched across the hearth, with her two puppies beside her; or the pug, who is dozing, with his black muzzle aloft, like a sleepy president.

The room is a large and lofty one, with an ample mullioned oriel window at one end; the walls, you see, are new, and not yet painted; but the furniture, though originally of an expensive sort, is old and scanty, and there is no drapery about the window. The crimson cloth over the large dining-table is very threadbare, though it contrasts pleasantly enough with the dead hue of the plaster on the walls; but on this cloth there is a massive silver waiter with a decanter of water on it, of the same pattern as two larger ones that are propped up on the sideboard with a coat-of-arms conspicuous in their centre. You suspect at once that the inhabitants of this room have inherited more blood than wealth, and would not be surprised to find that Mr. Irwine had a finely-cut nostril and upper lip; but at present we can only see that he has a broad flat back and an abundance of powdered hair, all thrown backward and tied behind with a black ribbon—a bit of conservatism in costume which tells you that he is not a young man. He will perhaps turn round by-and-by, and in the mean time we can look at that stately old lady, his mother, a beautiful aged brunette, whose rich-toned complexion is well set off by the complex wrappings of pure white cambric and lace about her head and neck. She is as erect in her comely embonpoint as a statue of Ceres; and her dark face, with its delicate aquiline nose, firm proud mouth, and small intense black eye, is so keen and sarcastic in its expression that you instinctively substitute a pack of cards for the chess-men, and imagine her telling your fortune. The small brown hand with which she is lifting her queen is laden with pearls, diamonds, and turquoises; and a large black veil is very carefully adjusted over the crown of her cap, and falls in sharp contrast on the white folds about her neck. It must take a long time to dress that old lady in the morning! But it seems a law of nature that she should be dressed so: she is clearly one of those children of royalty who have never doubted their right divine, and never met with any one so absurd as to question it.

"There, Dauphin, tell me what that is!" says this magnificent old lady, as she deposits her queen very quietly and folds her arms. "I should be sorry to utter a word disagreeable to your feelings."

"Ah! you witch-mother, you sorceress! How is a Christian man to win a game off you? I should have sprinkled the board with holy water before we began. You've not won that game by fair means, now, so don't pretend it."

"Yes, yes, that's what the beaten have always said of great conquerors. But see, there's the sunshine falling on the board, to show you more clearly what a foolish move you made with that pawn. Come, shall I give you another chance?"

"No, mother, I shall leave you to your own conscience, now it's clearing up. We must go and plash up the mud a little, mustn't we, Juno?" This was addressed to the brown setter, who jumped up at the sound of the voices and laid her nose in an insinuating way on her master's leg. "But I must go up-stairs first and see Anne. I was called away to Tholer's funeral just when I was going before."

"It's no use, child; she can't speak to you. Kate says she has one of her worst headaches this morning."

"O, she likes me to go and see her just the same; she's never too ill to care about that."

If you know how much of human speech is mere purposeless impulse or habit, you will not wonder when I tell you that this identical objection had been made, and had received the same kind of answer, many hundred times in the course of the fifteen years that Mr. Irwine's sister Anne had been an invalid. Splendid old ladies, who take a long time to dress in the morning, have often slight sympathy with sickly daughters.

But while Mr. Irwine was still seated, leaning back in his chair and stroking Juno's head, the servant came to the door and said, "If you please, sir, Joshua Rann wishes to speak with you, if you're at liberty."

"Let him be shown in here," said Mrs. Irwine, taking up her knitting. "I always like to hear what Mr. Rann has got to say. His shoes will be dirty, but see that he wipes them, Carroll."

In two minutes Mr. Rann appeared at the door with very deferential bows, which, however, were far from conciliating Pug, who gave a sharp bark, and ran across the room to reconnoitre the stranger's legs; while the two puppies, regarding Mr. Rann's prominent calf and ribbed worsted stockings from a more sensuous point of view, plunged and growled over them in great enjoyment. Meantime, Mr. Irwine turned round his chair and said:

"Well, Joshua, anything the matter at Hayslope, that you've come over this damp morning? Sit down, sit down. Never mind the dogs; give them a friendly kick. Here, Pug, you rascal!"

It is very pleasant to see some men turn round; pleasant as a sudden rush of warm air in winter, or the flash of firelight in the chill dusk. Mr. Irwine was one of those men. He bore the same sort of resemblance to his mother that our loving memory of a friend's face often bears to the face itself: the lines were all more generous, the smile brighter, the expression heartier. If the outline had been less finely cut, his face might have been called jolly; but that was not the right word for its mixture of bonhommie and distinction.

"Thank your reverence," answered Mr. Rann, endeavouring to look unconcerned about his legs, but shaking them alternately to keep off the puppies; "I'll stand, if you please, as more becoming. I hope I see you and Mrs. Irwine well, an' Miss Irwine—an' Miss Anne, I hope's as well as usual."

"Yes, Joshua, thank you. You see how blooming my mother looks. She beats us younger people hollow. But what's the matter?"

"Why, sir, I had to come to Brox'on to deliver some work, and I thought it but right to call and let you know the goins-on as there's been i' the village, such as I hanna seen i' my time, and I've lived in it man and boy sixty year come St. Thomas, and collected th' Easter dues for Mr. Blick before your reverence come into the parish, and been at the ringin' o' every bell, and the diggin' o' every grave, and sung i' the quire long afore Bartle Massey came from nobody knows where, wi' his counter-singin' and fine anthems, as puts everybody out but himself— one takin' it up after another like sheep a-bleatin' i' th' fold. I know what belongs to bein' a parish clerk, and I know as I should be wantin' i' respect to your reverence, an' church, an' king, if I was t' allow such goins-on wi'out speakin'. I was took by surprise, an' knowed nothin' on it beforehand, an' I was so flustered, I was clean as if I'd lost my tools. I hanna slep more nor four hour this night as is past an' gone; an' then it was nothin' but nightmare, as tired me worse nor wakin'."

"Why, what in the world is the matter, Joshua? Have the thieves been at the church lead again?"

"Thieves! no, sir,—an' yet, as I may say, it *is* thieves, an' a-thievin' the church, too. It's the Methodisses as is like to get th' upper hand i' th' parish, if your reverence an' his honour, Squire Donnithorne, doesna think well to say the word an' forbid it. Not as I'm a-dictatin' to you, sir; I'm not forgettin' myself so far as to be wise above my betters. Howiver, whether I'm wise or no, that's neither here nor there, but what I've got to say I say—as the young Methodis woman, as is at Mester Poyser's, was a-preachin' an' a-prayin' on the Green last night, as sure as I'm a-stannin' afore your reverence now."

"Preaching on the Green!" said Mr. Irwine, looking surprised but quite serene. "What, that pale pretty young woman I've seen at Poyser's? I saw she was a Methodist, or Quaker, or something of that sort, by her dress, but I didn't know she was a preacher."

"It's a true word as I say, sir," rejoined Mr. Rann, compressing his mouth into a semicircular form, and pausing long enough to indicate three notes of exclamation. "She preached on the Green last night; an' she's laid hold of Chad's Bess, as the girl's been i' fits welly iver sin'."

"Well, Bessy Cranage is a hearty-looking lass; I daresay she'll come round again, Joshua. Did anybody else go into fits?"

"No, sir, I canna say as they did. But there's no knowin' what'll come, if we're t' have such preachins as that a-goin' on ivery week— there'll be no livin' i' th' village. For them Methodisses make folks believe as if they take a mug o' drink extry, an' make theirselves a bit comfortable, they'll have to go to hell for't as sure as they're born. I'm not a tipplin' man nor a drunkard—nobody can say it on me—but I like a extry quart at Easter or Christmas time, as is nat'ral when we're goin' the rounds a-singin', an' folks offer't you for nothin'; or when I'm a-collectin' the dues; an' I like a pint wi' my pipe, an' a neighbourly chat at Mester Casson's now an' then, for I was brought up i' the Church, thank God, an' ha' been a parish clerk this two-an' thirty year: I should know what the church religion is."

"Well, what's your advice, Joshua? What do you think should be done?"

"Well, your reverence, I'm not for takin' any measures again' the young woman. She's well enough if she'd let alone preachin'; an' I hear as she's a-goin' away back to her own country soon. She's Mr. Poyser's own niece, an' I donna wish to say what's anyways disrepectful o' th' family at th' Hall Farm, as I've measured for shoes, little an' big, welly iver sin' I've been a shoemaker. But there's that Will Maskery, sir, as is the rampageousest Methodis as can be, an' I make no doubt it was him as stirred up th' young woman to preach last night, an' he'll be a-bringin' other folks to preach from Treddles'on, if his comb isn't cut a bit; an' I think as he should be let know as he isna t' have the makin' an' mendin' o' church carts an' implemens, let alone stayin' i' that house an' yard as is Squire Donnithorne's."

"Well, but you say yourself, Joshua, that you never knew any one come to preach on the Green before; why should you think they'll come again? The Methodists don't come to preach in little villages like Hay-slope, where there's only a handful of labourers, too tired to listen to them. They might almost as well go and preach on the Binton Hills. Will Maskery is no preacher himself, I think."

"Nay, sir, he's no gift at stringin' the words together wi'out book; he'd be stuck fast like a cow i' wet clay. But he's got tongue enough to speak disrespectful about's neebors, for he said as I was a blind Pharisee; —a-usin' the Bible i' that way to find nicknames for folks as are his elders an' betters!—and what's worse, he's been heard to say very unbe-comin' words about your reverence; for I could bring them as 'ud swear as he called you a 'dumb dog,' an' a 'idle shepherd.' You'll forgi'e me for sayin' such things over again."

"Better not, better not, Joshua. Let evil words die as soon as they're spoken. Will Maskery might be a great deal worse fellow than he is. He used to be a wild drunken rascal, neglecting his work and beating his wife, they told me; now he's thrifty and decent, and he and his wife look comfortable together. If you can bring me any proof that he inter-feres with his neighbours, and creates any disturbance, I shall think it my duty as a clergyman and a magistrate to interfere. But it wouldn't become wise people, like you and me, to be making a fuss about trifles, as if we thought the Church was in danger because Will Maskery lets his tongue wag rather foolishly, or a young woman talks in a serious way to a handful of people on the Green. We must 'live and let live,' Joshua, in religion as well as in other things. You go on doing your duty, as parish clerk and sexton, as well as you've always done it, and making those capital thick boots for your neighbours, and things won't go far wrong in Hayslope, depend upon it."

"Your reverence is very good to say so; an' I'm sensable as, you not livin' i' the parish, there's more upo' my shoulders."

"To be sure; and you must mind and not lower the Church in people's eyes by seeming to be frightened about it for a little thing, Joshua. I shall trust to your good sense, now, to take no notice at all of what Will Maskery says, either about you or me. You and your neighbours can

go on taking your pot of beer soberly, when you've done your day's
work, like good churchmen; and if Will Maskery doesn't like to join
you, but to go to a prayer-meeting at Treddleston instead, let him; that's
no business of yours, so long as he doesn't hinder you from doing what
you like. And as to people saying a few idle words about us, we must not
mind that, any more than the old church-steeple minds the rooks cawing
about it. Will Maskery comes to church every Sunday afternoon, and
does his wheelwright's business steadily in the week-days, and as long
as he does that he must be let alone."

"Ah, sir, but when he comes to church, he sits an' shakes his head, an'
looks as sour an' as coxy when we're a-singin', as I should like to fetch
him a rap across the jowl—God forgi'e me—an' Mrs. Irwine, an' your
reverence, too, for speakin' so afore you. An' he said as our Christmas
singin' was no better nor the cracklin' o' thorns under a pot."

"Well, he's got a bad ear for music, Joshua. When people have wooden
heads, you know, it can't be helped. He won't bring the other people
in Hayslope round to his opinion, while you go on singing as well as
you do."

"Yes, sir, but it turns a man's stomach t' hear the Scripture misused i'
that way. I know as much o' the words o' the Bible as he does, an' could
say the Psalms right through i' my sleep if you was to pinch me; but I
know better nor to take 'em to say my own say wi'. I might as well take
the Sacriment-cup home and use it at meals."

"That's a very sensible remark of yours, Joshua; but, as I said before——"

While Mr. Irwine was speaking, the sound of a booted step, and the
clink of a spur, were heard on the stone floor of the entrance-hall, and
Joshua Rann moved hastily aside from the doorway to make room for
some one who paused there, and said, in a ringing tenor voice,

"Godson Arthur;—may he come in?"

"Come in, come in, godson!" Mrs. Irwine answered, in a deep half-
masculine tone which belongs to the vigorous old woman, and there
entered a young gentleman in a riding-dress, with his right arm in a
sling; whereupon followed that pleasant confusion of laughing interjections, and hand-shakings, and "How are you's?" mingled with joyous
short barks and wagging of tails on the part of the canine members of
the family, which tells that the visitor is on the best terms with the
visited. The young gentleman was Arthur Donnithorne, known in Hayslope, variously, as "the young squire," "the heir," and "the captain."
He was only a captain in the Loamshire Militia; but to the Hayslope
tenants he was more intensely a captain than all the young gentlemen of
the same rank in his Majesty's regulars—he outshone them as the planet
Jupiter outshines the Milky Way. If you want to know more particularly
how he looked, call to your remembrance some tawny-whiskered, brown-
locked, clear-complexioned young Englishman whom you have met with
in a foreign town, and been proud of as a fellow-countryman—well-
washed, high-bred, white-handed, yet looking as if he could deliver well

from the left shoulder, and floor his man: I will not be so much of a
tailor as to trouble your imagination with the difference of costume, and
insist on the striped waistcoat, long-tailed coat, and low top-boots.

Turning round to take a chair, Captain Donnithorne said, "But don't
let me interrupt Joshua's business—he has something to say."

"Humbly begging your honour's pardon," said Joshua, bowing low,
"there was one thing I had to say to his reverence as other things had
drove out o' my head."

"Out with it, Joshua, quickly!" said Mr. Irwine.

"Belike, sir, you havena heard as Thias Bede's dead—drowned this
morning, or more like overnight, i' the Willow Brook, again' the bridge
right i' front o' the house."

"Ah!" exclaimed both the gentlemen at once, as if they were a good
deal interested in the information.

"An' Seth Bede's been to me this morning to say he wished me to tell
your reverence as his brother Adam begged of you particular t' allow
his father's grave to be dug by the White Thorn, because his mother's set
her heart on it, on account of a dream as she had; an' they'd ha' come
theirselves to ask you, but they've so much to see after with the crowner,
an' that; an' their mother's took on so, an' wants 'em to make sure o' the
spot for fear somebody else should take it. An' if your reverence sees
well and good, I'll send my boy to tell 'em as soon as I get home; an'
that's why I make bold to trouble you wi' it, his honour being present."

"To be sure, Joshua, to be sure, they shall have it. I'll ride round to
Adam myself, and see him. Send your boy, however, to say they shall
have the grave, lest anything should happen to detain me. And now,
good morning, Joshua; go into the kitchen and have some ale."

"Poor old Thias!" said Mr. Irwine, when Joshua was gone. "I'm
afraid the drink helped the brook to drown him. I should have been
glad for the load to have been taken off my friend Adam's shoulders in a
less painful way. That fine fellow has been propping up his father from
ruin for the last five or six years."

"He's a regular trump, is Adam," said Captain Donnithorne. "When
I was a little fellow, and Adam was a strapping lad of fifteen, and taught
me carpentering, I used to think if ever I was a rich sultan, I would
make Adam my grand-vizier. And I believe now, he would bear the exaltation as well as any poor wise man in an Eastern story. If ever I live
to be a large-acred man instead of a poor devil with a mortgaged allowance of pocket-money, I'll have Adam for my right-hand. He shall
manage my woods for me, for he seems to have a better notion of those
things than any man I ever met with; and I know he would make twice
the money of them that my grandfather does, with that miserable old
Satchell to manage, who understands no more about timber than an old
carp. I've mentioned the subject to my grandfather once or twice, but
for some reason or other he has a dislike to Adam, and *I* can do nothing.
But come, your reverence, are you for a ride with me? It's splendid out
of doors now. We can go to Adam's together. if you like; but I want to

call at the Hall Farm on my way, to look at the whelps Poyser is keep‧ing for me."

"You must stay and have lunch first, Arthur," said Mrs. Irwine. "It's nearly two. Carroll will bring it in directly."

"I want to go to the Hall Farm too," said Mr. Irwine, "to have another look at the little Methodist who is staying there. Joshua tells me she was preaching on the Green last night."

"O, by Jove!" said Captain Donnithorne, laughing. "Why, she looks as quiet as a mouse. There's something rather striking about her, though. I positively felt quite bashful the first time I saw her: she was sitting stooping over her sewing in the sunshine outside the house, when I rode up and called out, without noticing that she was a stranger, 'Is Martin Poyser at home?' I declare, when she got up and looked at me, and just said, 'He's in the house, I believe: I'll go and call him,' I felt quite ashamed of having spoken so abruptly to her. She looked like St. Catherine in a Quaker dress. It's a type of face one rarely sees among our common people."

"I should like to see the young woman, Dauphin," said Mrs. Irwine. "Make her come here on some pretext or other."

"I don't know how I can manage that, mother; it will hardly do for me to patronise a Methodist preacher, even if she would consent to be patronised by an idle shepherd, as Will Maskery calls me. You should have come in a little sooner, Arthur, to hear Joshua's denunciation of his neighbour Will Maskery. The old fellow wants me to excommunicate the wheelwright, and then deliver him over to the civil arm—that is to say, to your grandfather—to be turned out of house and yard. If I chose to interfere in this business, now, I might get up as pretty a story of hatred and persecution as the Methodists need desire to publish in the next number of their magazine. It wouldn't take me much trouble to persuade Chad Cranage and half a dozen other bull-headed fellows, that they would be doing an acceptable service to the Church by hunting Will Maskery out of the village with rope-ends and pitchforks; and then, when I had furnished them with half a sovereign to get gloriously drunk after their exertions, I should have put the climax to as pretty a farce as any of my brother clergy have set going in their parishes for the last thirty years."

"It is really insolent of the man, though, to call you an 'idle shepherd,' and a 'dumb dog,'" said Mrs. Irwine: "I should be inclined to check him a little there. You are too easy-tempered, Dauphin."

"Why, mother, you don't think it would be a good way of sustaining my dignity to set about vindicating myself from the aspersions of Will Maskery? Besides, I'm not so sure that they *are* aspersions. I *am* a lazy fellow, and get terribly heavy in my saddle; not to mention that I'm always spending more than I can afford in bricks and mortar, so that I get savage at a lame beggar when he asks me for sixpence. Those poor lean cobblers, who think they can help to regenerate mankind by setting out to preach in the morning twilight before they begin their day's work

may well have a poor opinion of me. But come, let us have our luncheon.
Isn't Kate coming to lunch?"

"Miss Irwine told Bridget to take her lunch up-stairs," said Carroll;
"she can't leave Miss Anne."

"O, very well. Tell Bridget to say I'll go up and see Miss Anne presently. You can use your right arm quite well, now, Arthur," Mr. Irwine
continued, observing that Captain Donnithorne had taken his arm out of
the sling.

"Yes, pretty well; but Godwin insists on my keeping it up constantly
for some time to come. I hope I shall be able to get away to the regiment,
though, in the beginning of August. It's a desperately dull business being
shut up at the Chase in the summer months, when one can neither hunt
nor shoot, so as to make one's self pleasantly sleepy in the evening. However, we are to astonish the echoes on the 30th of July. My grandfather
has given me *carte blanche* for once, and I promise you the entertainment shall be worthy of the occasion. The world will not see the grand
epoch of my majority twice. I think I shall have a lofty throne for you,
godmamma, or rather two, one on the lawn and another in the ball-
room, that you may sit and look down upon us like an Olympian goddess."

"I mean to bring out my best brocade, that I wore at your christening
twenty years ago," said Mrs. Irwine. "Ah, I think I shall see your poor
mother flitting about in her white dress, which looked to me almost like
a shroud that very day; and it *was* her shroud only three months after;
and your little cap and christening dress were buried with her too. She
had set her heart on that, sweet soul! Thank God you take after your
mother's family, Arthur. If you had been a puny, wiry, yellow baby, I
wouldn't have stood godmother to you. I should have been sure you
would turn out a Donnithorne. But you were such a broad-faced, broad-
chested, loud-screaming rascal, I knew you were every inch of you a
Tradgett."

"But you might have been a little too hasty there, mother," said Mr.
Irwine, smiling. "Don't you remember how it was with Juno's last pups?
One of them was the very image of its mother, but it had two or three of
its father's tricks notwithstanding. Nature is clever enough to cheat
even you, mother."

"Nonsense, child! Nature never makes a ferret in the shape of a
mastiff. You'll never persuade me that I can't tell what men are by their
outsides. If I don't like a man's looks, depend upon it I shall never like
him. I don't want to know people that look ugly and disagreeable, any
more than I want to taste dishes that look disagreeable. If they make me
shudder at the first glance, I say, take them away. An ugly, piggish, or
fishy eye, now, makes me feel quite ill; it's like a bad smell."

"Talking of eyes," said Captain Donnithorne, "that reminds me that
I've got a book I meant to bring you, godmamma. It came down in a
parcel from London the other day. I know you are fond of queer,
wizard-like stories. It's a volume of poems, 'Lyrical Ballads': most of

them seem to be twaddling stuff; but the first is in a different style—
'The Ancient Mariner' is the title. I can hardly make head or tail of it as
a story, but it's a strange, striking thing. I'll send it over to you; and
there are some other books that *you* may like to see, Irwine—pamphlets
about Antinomianism and Evangelicalism, whatever they may be. I can't
think what the fellow means by sending such things to me. I've written
to him, to desire that from henceforth he will send me no book or
pamphlet on anything that ends in *ism*."

"Well, I don't know that I'm very fond of *isms* myself; but I may as
well look at the pamphlets; they let one see what is going on. I've a little
matter to attend to, Arthur," continued Mr. Irwine, rising to leave the
room, "and then I shall be ready to set out with you."

The little matter that Mr. Irwine had to attend to took him up the
old stone staircase (part of the house was very old), and made him
pause before a door at which he knocked gently. "Come in," said a woman's voice, and he entered a room so darkened by blinds and curtains
that Miss Kate, the thin middle-aged lady standing by the bedside,
would not have had light enough for any other sort of work than the
knitting which lay on the little table near her. But at present she was
doing what required only the dimmest light—sponging the aching head
that lay on the pillow with fresh vinegar. It was a small face, that of the
poor sufferer; perhaps it had once been pretty, but now it was worn and
sallow. Miss Kate came towards ·her ·brother and whispered, "Don't
speak to her; she can't bear to be spoken to to-day." Anne's eyes were
closed, and her brow contracted as if from intense pain. Mr. Irwine went
to the bedside, and took up one of the delicate hands and kissed it; a
slight pressure from the small fingers told him that it was worth while to
have come up-stairs for the sake of doing that. He lingered a moment,
looking at her, and then turned away and left the room, treading very
gently—he had taken off his boots and put on slippers before he came
up-stairs. Whoever remembers how many things he has declined to do
ever for himself, rather than have the trouble of putting on or taking
off his boots, will not think this last detail insignificant.

And Mr. Irwine's sisters, as any person of family within ten miles of
Broxton could have testified, were such stupid, uninteresting women! It
was quite a pity handsome, clever Mrs. Irwine should have had such
commonplace daughters. That fine old lady herself was worth driving
ten miles to see, any day; her beauty, her well-preserved faculties, and
her old-fashioned dignity, made her a graceful subject for conversation
in turn with the King's health, the sweet new patterns in cotton dresses,
the news from Egypt, and Lord Dacey's lawsuit, which was fretting poor
Lady Dacey to death. But no one ever thought of mentioning the Miss
Irwines, except the poor people in Broxton village, who regarded them
as deep in the science of medicine, and spoke of them vaguely as "the
gentlefolks." If any one had asked old Job Dummilow who gave him his
flannel jacket, he would have answered, "the gentlefolks, last winter";
and widow Steene dwelt much on the virtues of the "stuff" the gentle-

folks gave her for her cough. Under this name, too, they were used with great effect as a means of taming refractory children, so that at the sight of poor Miss Anne's sallow face, several small urchins had a terrified sense that she was cognisant of all their worst misdemeanours, and knew the precise number of stones with which they had intended to hit farmer Britton's ducks. But for all who saw them through a less mythical medium, the Miss Irwines were quite superfluous existences; inartistic figures crowding the canvas of life without adequate effect. Miss Anne, indeed, if her chronic headaches could have been accounted for by a pathetic story of disappointed love, might have had some romantic interest attached to her; but no such story had either been known or invented concerning her, and the general impression was quite in accordance with the fact, that both the sisters were old maids for the prosaic reason that they had never received an eligible offer.

Nevertheless, to speak paradoxically, the existence of insignificant people has very important consequences in the world. It can be shown to affect the price of bread and the rate of wages, to call forth many evil tempers from the selfish, and many heroisms from the sympathetic, and, in other ways, to play no small part in the tragedy of life. And if that handsome, generous-blooded clergyman, the Rev. Adolphus Irwine, had not had these two hopelessly-maiden sisters, his lot would have been shaped quite differently: he would very likely have taken a comely wife in his youth, and now, when his hair was getting grey under the powder, would have had tall sons and blooming daughters—such possessions, in short, as men commonly think will repay them for all the labour they take under the sun. As it was—having with all his three livings no more than seven hundred a year, and seeing no way of keeping his splendid mother and his sickly sister, not to reckon a second sister, who was usually spoken of without any adjective, in such lady-like ease as became their birth and habits, and at the same time providing for a family of his own—he remained, you see, at the age of eight-and-forty, a bachelor, not making any merit of that renunciation, but saying laughingly, if any one alluded to it, that he made it an excuse for many indulgences which a wife would never have allowed him. And perhaps he was the only person in the world who did not think his sisters uninteresting and superfluous; for his was one of those large-hearted, sweet-blooded natures that never know a narrow or a grudging thought; epicurean, if you will, with no enthusiasm, no self-scourging sense of duty; but yet, as you have seen, of a sufficiently subtle moral fibre to have an unwearying tenderness for obscure and monotonous suffering. It was his large-hearted indulgence that made him ignore his mother's hardness towards her daughters, which was the more striking from its contrast with her doting fondness towards himself: he held it no virtue to frown at irremediable faults.

See the difference between the impression a man makes on you when you walk by his side in familiar talk, or look at him in his home, and the figure he makes when seen from a lofty historical level, or even in the eyes of a critical neighbour who thinks of him as an embodied system or opinion rather than as a man. Mr. Roe, the "travelling preacher" stationed at Treddleston, had included Mr. Irwine in a general statement concerning the Church clergy in the surrounding district, whom he described as men given up to the lusts of the flesh and the pride of life; hunting and shooting, and adorning their own houses; asking what shall we eat, and what shall we drink, and wherewithal shall we be clothed?—careless of dispensing the bread of life to their flocks, preaching at best but a carnal and soul-benumbing morality, and trafficking in the souls of men by receiving money for discharging the pastoral office in parishes where they did not so much as look on the faces of the people more than once a year. The ecclesiastical historian, too, looking into parliamentary reports of that period, finds honourable members zealous for the Church, and untainted with any sympathy for the "tribe of canting Methodists," making statements scarcely less melancholy than that of Mr. Roe. And it is impossible for me to say that Mr. Irwine was altogether belied by the generic classification assigned him. He really had no very lofty aims, no theological enthusiasm: if I were closely questioned, I should be obliged to confess that he felt no serious alarms about the souls of his parishioners, and would have thought it a mere loss of time to talk in a doctrinal and awakening manner to old "Feyther Taft," or even to Chad Cranage, the blacksmith. If he had been in the habit of speaking theoretically, he would perhaps have said that the only healthy form religion could take in such minds was that of certain dim but strong emotions, suffusing themselves as a hallowing influence over the family affections and neighbourly duties. He thought the custom of baptism more important than its doctrine, and that the religious benefits the peasant drew from the church where his fathers worshipped and the sacred piece of turf where they lay buried, were but slightly dependent on a clear understanding of the Liturgy or the sermon. Clearly the Rector was not what is called in these days an "earnest" man: he was fonder of church history than of divinity, and had much more insight into men's characters than interest in their opinions; he was neither laborious, nor obviously self-denying, nor very copious in almsgiving, and his theology, you perceive, was lax. His mental palate, indeed, was rather pagan, and found a savouriness in a quotation from Sophocles or Theocritus that was quite absent from any text in Isaiah or Amos. But if you feed your young setter on raw flesh, how can you wonder at its retaining a relish for uncooked partridge in after life? and Mr. Irwine's recollections of young enthusiasm and ambition were all associated with poetry and ethics that lay aloof from the Bible.

On the other hand, I must plead, for I have an affectionate partiality towards the Rector's memory, that he was not vindictive—and some philanthropists have been so; that he was not intolerant—and there is a rumour that some zealous theologians have not been altogether free from that blemish; that although he would probably have declined to give his body to be burned in any public cause, and was far from bestowing all his goods to feed the poor, he had that charity which has sometimes been lacking to very illustrious virtue—he was tender to other men's failings, and unwilling to impute evil. He was one of those men, and they are not the commonest, of whom we can know the best only by following them away from the market-place, the platform, and the pulpit, entering with them into their own homes, hearing the voice with which they speak to the young and aged about their own hearth-stone, and witnessing their thoughtful care for the everyday wants of everyday companions, who take all their kindness as a matter of course, and not as a subject for panegyric.

Such men, happily, have lived in times when great abuses flourished, and have sometimes even been the living representatives of the abuses. That is a thought which might comfort us a little under the opposite fact —that it is better sometimes *not* to follow great reformers of abuses beyond the threshold of their homes.

But whatever you may think of Mr. Irwine now, if you had met him that June afternoon riding on his grey cob, with his dogs running beside him—portly, upright, manly, with a good-natured smile on his finely-turned lips as he talked to his dashing young companion on the bay mare, you must have felt that, however ill he harmonised with sound theories of the clerical office, he somehow harmonised extremely well with that peaceful landscape.

See them in the bright sunlight, interrupted every now and then by rolling masses of cloud, ascending the slope from the Broxton side, where the tall gables and elms of the rectory predominate over the tiny white-washed church. They will soon be in the parish of Hayslope; the grey church-tower and village roofs lie before them to the left, and farther on, to the right, they can just see the chimneys of the Hall Farm.

CHAPTER VI

THE HALL FARM

EVIDENTLY that gate is never opened: for the long grass and the great hemlocks grow close against it; and if it were opened, it is so rusty, that the force necessary to turn it on its hinges would be likely to pull down the square stone-built pillars, to the detriment of the two stone lionesses which grin with a doubtful carnivorous affability above a coat-of-arms, surmounting each of the pillars. It would be easy enough, by the aid of the nicks in the stone pillars, to climb over the brick wall with its smooth stone coping; but by putting our eyes close to the rusty bars of the gate, we can see the house well enough, and all but the very corners of the grassy enclosure.

It is a very fine old place, of red brick, softened by a pale powdery lichen, which has dispersed itself with happy irregularity, so as to bring the red brick into terms of friendly companionship with the limestone ornaments surrounding the three gables, the windows, and the door-place.

But the windows are patched with wooden panes, and the door, I think, is like the gate—it is never opened: how it would groan and grate against the stone floor if it were! For it is a solid, heavy, handsome door, and must once have been in the habit of shutting with a sonorous bang be· hind a liveried lackey, who had just seen his master and mistress off the grounds in a carriage and pair.

But at present one might fancy the house in the early stage of a chancery suit, and that the fruit from that grand double row of walnut-trees on the right hand of the enclosure would fall and rot among the grass, if it were not that we heard the booming bark of dogs echoing from great buildings at the back. And now the half-weaned calves that have been sheltering themselves in a gorse-built hovel against the left-hand wall, come out and set up a silly answer to that terrible bark, doubtless supposing that it has reference to buckets of milk.

Yes, the house must be inhabited, and we will see by whom; for imagination is a licensed trespasser: it has no fear of dogs, but may climb over walls and peep in at windows with impunity. Put your face to one of the glass panes in the right-hand window: what do you see? A large open fireplace, with rusty dogs in it, and a bare boarded floor; at the far end, fleeces of wool stacked up; in the middle of the floor, some empty corn-bags. That is the furniture of the dining-room. And what through the left-hand window? Several clothes-horses, a pillion, a spinning-wheel, and an old box wide open, and stuffed full of coloured rags. At the edge of this box there lies a great wooden doll, which, so far as mutilation is concerned, bears a strong resemblance to the finest Greek sculpture, and especially in the total loss of its nose. Near it there is a little chair, and the butt-end of a boy's leather long-lashed whip.

The history of the house is plain now. It was once the residence of a country squire, whose family, probably dwindling down to mere spinster-hood, got merged in the more territorial name of Donnithorne. It was once the Hall; it is now the Hall Farm. Like the life in some coast-town that was once a watering-place, and is now a port, where the genteel streets are silent and grass-grown, and the docks and warehouses busy and resonant, the life at the Hall has changed its focus, and no longer radiates from the parlour, but from the kitchen and the farmyard.

Plenty of life there! though this is the drowsiest time of the year, just before hay-harvest; and it is the drowsiest time of the day too, for it is close upon three by the sun, and it is half-past three by Mrs. Poy-ser's handsome eight-day clock. But there is always a stronger sense of life when the sun is brilliant after rain; and now he is pouring down his beams, and making sparkles among the wet straw, and lighting up every patch of vivid green moss on the red tiles of the cow-shed, and turning even the muddy water that is hurrying along the channel to the drain into a mirror for the yellow-billed ducks, who are seizing the oppor· tunity of getting a drink with as much body in it as possible. There is quite a concert of noises: the great bull-dog, chained against the stables, is thrown into furious exasperation by the unwary approach of a cock too near the mouth of his kennel, and sends forth a thundering bark, which is answered by two fox-hounds shut up in the opposite cow-house; the old top-knotted hens, scratching with their chicks among the straw, set up a sympathetic croaking as the discomfited cock joins them; a sow with her brood, all very muddy as to the legs, and curled as to the tail, throws in some deep staccato notes; our friends the calves are bleating from the home croft; and, under all, a fine ear discerns the continuous hum of human voices.

For the great barn-doors are thrown wide open, and men are busy there mending the harness, under the superintendence of Mr. Goby the "whittaw," otherwise saddler, who entertains them with the latest Treddleston gossip. It is certainly rather an unfortunate day that Alick, the shepherd, has chosen for having the whittaws, since the morning turned out so wet; and Mrs. Poyser has spoken her mind pretty strongly as to the dirt which the extra number of men's shoes brought into the house at dinner-time. Indeed, she has not yet recovered her equanimity on the subject, though it is now nearly three hours since dinner, and the house-floor is perfectly clean again; as clean as everything else in that wonderful house-place, where the only chance of collecting a few grains of dust would be to climb on the salt-coffer, and put your finger on the high mantel-shelf on which the glittering brass candle-sticks are enjoying their summer sinecure; for at this time of year, of course, every one goes to bed while it is yet light, or at least light enough to discern the outline of objects after you have bruised your shins against them. Surely nowhere else could an oak clock-case and an oak table have got to such a polish by the hand: genuine "elbow polish," as Mrs. Poyser called it, for she thanked God she never had any of your varnished rubbish in her house. Hetty Sorrel often took the opportunity, when her aunt's back was turned, of looking at the pleasant reflection of herself in those polished surfaces, for the oak table was usually turned up like a screen, and was more for ornament than for use; and she could see herself sometimes in the great round pewter dishes that were ranged on the shelves above the long deal dinner-table, or in the hobs of the grate, which always shone like jasper.

Everything was looking at its brightest at this moment, for the sun shone right on the pewter dishes, and from their reflecting surfaces pleasant jets of light were thrown on mellow oak and bright brass;— and on a still pleasanter object than these; for some of the rays fell on Dinah's finely-moulded cheek, and lit up her pale red hair to auburn, as she bent over the heavy household linen which she was mending for her aunt. No scene could have been more peaceful, if Mrs. Poyser, who was ironing a few things that still remained from the Monday's wash, had not been making a frequent clinking with her iron, and moving to and fro whenever she wanted it to cool; carrying the keen glance of her blue-grey eye from the kitchen to the dairy, where Hetty was making up the butter, and from the dairy to the back-kitchen, where Nancy was taking the pies out of the oven. Do not suppose, however, that Mrs. Poyser was elderly or shrewish in her appearance; she was a good-looking woman, not more than eight-and-thirty, of fair complexion and sandy hair, well-shapen, light-footed: the most conspicuous article in her attire was an ample checkered linen apron, which almost covered her skirt; and nothing could be plainer or less noticeable than her cap and gown, for there was no weakness of which she was less tolerant than feminine vanity, and the preference of ornament to utility. The family likeness between her and her niece Dinah Morris, with the contrast between her keenness and Dinah's seraphic gentleness of expression, might have served a painter as an excellent suggestion for a Martha and Mary. Their eyes were just of the same colour, but a striking test of the difference in their operation was seen in the demeanour of Trip, the black-and-tan terrier, whenever that much-suspected dog unwarily exposed himself to the freezing arctic ray of Mrs. Poyser's glance. Her tongue was not less keen than her eye, and, whenever a damsel came within earshot, seemed to take up an unfinished lecture, as a barrel-organ takes up a tune, precisely at the point where it had left off.

The fact that it was churning-day was another reason why it was inconvenient to have the "whittaws," and why, consequently, Mrs. Poyser should scold Molly the house maid with unusual severity. To all appearance Molly had got through her after-dinner work in an exemplary manner, had "cleaned herself" with great despatch, and now came to ask, submissively, if she should sit down to her spinning till milking-time. But this blameless conduct, according to Mrs. Poyser, shrouded a secret indulgence of unbecoming wishes, which she now dragged forth and held up to Molly's view with cutting eloquence.

"Spinning, indeed! It isn't spinning as you'd be at, I'll be bound, and let you have your own way. I never knew your equals for gallowsness. To think of a gell o' your age wanting to go and sit with half-a-dozen men! I'd ha' been ashamed to let the words pass over my lips if I'd been you. And you, as have been here ever since last Michaelmas, and I hired you at Treddles'on stattits, without a bit o' character—as I say, you might be grateful to be hired in that way to a respectable place; and you knew no more o' what belongs to work when you come here than the mawkin i' the field. As poor a two-fisted thing as ever I saw, you know you was. Who taught you to scrub a floor, I should like to know? Why, you'd leave the dirt in heaps i' the corners—anybody'ud think you'd never been brought up among Christians. And as for spinning, why, you've wasted as much as your wage i' the flax you've spoiled learning to spin. And you've a right to feel that, and not to go about as gaping and as thoughtless as if you was beholding to nobody. Comb the wool for the whittaws, indeed! That's what you'd like to be doing, is it? That's the way with you—that's the road you'd all like to go, headlongs to ruin. You're never easy till you've got some sweetheart as is as big a fool as yourself: you think you'll be finely off when you're married, I

daresay, and have got a three-legged stool to sit on, and never a blanket
to cover you, and a bit o' oat-cake for your dinner, as three children are
a-snatching at."

"I'm sure I donna want t' go wi' the whittaws," said Molly, whimpering, and quite overcome by this Dantean picture of her future, "on'y
we allays used to comb the wool for 'n at Mester Ottley's; an' so I just
axed ye. I donna want to set eyes on the whittaws again; I wish I may
never stir if I do."

"Mr. Ottley's, indeed! It's fine talking o' what you did at Mr. Ottley's.
Your missis there might like her floors dirted wi' whittaws for what I
know. There's no knowing what people *wonna* like—such ways as I've
heard of! I never had a gell come into my house as seemed to know
what cleaning was; I think people live like pigs, for my part. And as
to that Betty as was dairymaid at Trent's before she come to me, she'd
ha' left the cheeses without turning from week's end to week's end, and
the dairy thralls, I might ha' wrote my name on 'em, when I come down-
stairs after my illness, as the doctor said it was inflammation—it was a
mercy I got well of it. And to think o' your knowing no better, Molly,
and been here a-going i' nine months, and not for want o' talking to,
neither—and what are you stanning there for, like a jack as is run down,
istead o' getting your wheel out? You're a rare un for sitting down to
your work a little while after it's time to put by."

"Munny, my iron's twite told; pease put it down to warm."

The small chirruping voice that uttered this request came from a little
sunny-haired girl between three and four, who, seated on a high chair at
the end of the ironing-table, was arduously clutching the handle of a
miniature iron with her tiny fat fist, and ironing rags with an assiduity
that required her to put her little red tongue out as far as anatomy
would allow.

"Cold, is it, my darling? Bless your sweet face!" said Mrs. Poyser, who
was remarkable for the facility with which she could relapse from her
official objurgatory tone to one of fondness or of friendly converse.
"Never mind! Mother's done her ironing now. She's going to put the
ironing things away."

"Munny, I tould 'ike to do into de barn to Tommy, to see de whit-
tawd."

"No, no, no; Totty 'ud get her feet wet," said Mrs. Poyser, carrying
away her iron. "Run into the dairy and see cousin Hetty make the
butter."

"I tould 'ike a bit o' plum-take," rejoined Totty, who seemed to be provided with several relays of requests; at the same time, taking the opportunity of her momentary leisure, to put her fingers into a bowl of
starch, and drag it down, so as to empty the contents with tolerable completeness on to the ironing-sheet.

"Did ever anybody see the like?" screamed Mrs. Poyser, running
towards the table when her eye had fallen on the blue stream. "The

child's allays i' mischief if your back's turned a minute. What shall I do to you, you naughty, naughty gell!"

Totty, however, had descended from her chair with great swiftness, and was already in retreat towards the dairy with a sort of waddling run, and an amount of fat on the nape of her neck, which made her look like the metamorphosis of a white sucking-pig.

The starch having been wiped up by Molly's help, and the ironing apparatus put by, Mrs. Poyser took up her knitting, which always lay ready at hand, and was the work she liked best, because she could carry it on automatically as she walked to and fro. But now she came and sat down opposite Dinah, whom she looked at in a meditative way, as she knitted her grey worsted stocking.

"You look th' image o' your aunt Judith, Dinah, when you sit a-sewing. I could almost fancy it was thirty years back, and I was a little gell at home, looking at Judith as she sat at her work, after she'd done th' house up; only it was a little cottage, father's was, and not a big rambling house as gets dirty i' one corner as fast as you clean it in another; but for all that, I could fancy you was your aunt Judith, only her hair was a deal darker than yours, and she was stouter and broader i' the shoulders. Judith and me allays hung together, though she had such queer ways, but your mother and her never could agree. Ah! your mother little thought as she'd have a daughter just cut out after the very pattern o' Judith, and leave her an orphan, too, for Judith to take on, and bring up with a spoon when *she* was in the graveyard at Stoniton. I allays said that o' Judith, as she'd bear a pound weight any day, to save anybody else carrying a ounce. And she was just the same from the first o' my remembering her; it made no difference in her, as I could see, when she took to the Methodists, only she talked a bit different, and wore a different sort o' cap; but she'd never in her life spent a penny on herself more than keeping herself decent."

"She was a blessed woman," said Dinah; "God had given her a loving, self-forgetting nature, and he perfected it by grace. And she was very fond of you too, aunt Rachel. I've often heard her talk of you in the same sort of way. When she had that bad illness, and I was only eleven years old, she used to say, 'You'll have a friend on earth in your aunt Rachel, if I'm taken from you; for she has a kind heart;' and I'm sure I've found it so."

"I don't know how, child; anybody 'ud be cunning to do anything for you, I think; you're like the birds o' th' air, and live nobody knows how. I'd ha' been glad to behave to you like a mother's sister, if you'd come and live i' this country, where there's some shelter and victual for man and beast, and folks don't live on the naked hills, like poultry a-scratching on a gravel bank. And then you might get married to some decent man, and there'd be plenty ready to have you, if you'd only leave off that preaching, as is ten times worse than anything your aunt Judith ever did. And even if you'd marry Seth Bede, as is a poor wool-gathering Methodist, and's never like to have a penny beforehand, I know your uncle 'ud help you with a pig, and very like a cow, for he's allays been good-natur'd to my kin, for all they're poor, and made 'em welcome to th' house; and 'ud do for you, I'll be bound, as much as ever he'd do for Hetty, though she's his own niece. And there's linen in the house as I could well spare you, for I've got lots o' sheeting and table-clothing, and towelling, as isn't made up. There's a piece o' sheeting I could give you as that squinting Kitty spun—she was a rare girl to spin, for all she squinted, and the children couldn't abide her; and, you know, the spinning's going on constant, and there's new linen wove twice as fast as th' old wears out. But where's the use o' talking, if ye wonna be per-suaded, and settle down like any other woman in her senses, istead o' wearing yourself out with walking and preaching, and giving away every penny you get, so as you've nothing saved against sickness; and all the things you've got i' the world, I verily believe, 'ud go into a bundle no bigger nor a double cheese. And all because you've got notions i' your head about religion more nor what's i' the Catechism and the Prayer-book."

"But not more than what's in the Bible, aunt," said Dinah.

"Yes, and the Bible too, for that matter," Mrs. Poyser rejoined, rather sharply; "else why shouldn't them as know best what's in the Bible—the parsons and people as have got nothing to do but learn it—do the same as you do? But, for the matter o' that, if everybody was to do like you, the world must come to a standstill; for if everybody tried to do without house and home, and with poor eating and drinking, and was allays talking as we must despise the things o' the world, as you say, I should like to know where the pick o' the stock, and the corn, and the best new-milk cheeses 'ud have to go. Everybody 'ud be wanting bread made o' tail ends, and everybody 'ud be running after everybody else to preach to 'em, istead o' bringing up their families, and laying by against a bad harvest. It stands to sense as that can't be the right religion."

"Nay, dear aunt, you never heard me say that all people are called to forsake their work and their families. It's quite right the land should be ploughed and sowed, and the precious corn stored, and the things of this life cared for, and right that people should rejoice in their families, and provide for them, so that this is done in the fear of the Lord, and that they are not unmindful of the soul's wants while they are caring for the body. We can all be servants of God wherever our lot is cast, but he gives us different sorts of work, according as he fits us for it and calls us to it. I can no more help spending my life in trying to do what I can for the souls of others, than you could help running if you heard little Totty crying at the other end of the house; the voice would go to your heart, you would think the dear child was in trouble or in danger, and you couldn't rest without running to help her and comfort her."

"Ah," said Mrs. Poyser, rising and walking towards the door, "I know it 'ud be just the same if I was to talk to you for hours. You'd make me

the same answer at th' end. I might as well talk to the running brook,
and tell it to stan' still."

The causeway outside the kitchen door was dry enough now for Mrs.
Poyser to stand there quite pleasantly and see what was going on in the
yard, the grey worsted stocking making a steady progress in her hands
all the while. But she had not been standing there more than five minutes
before she came in again, and said to Dinah, in rather a flurried, awe-
stricken tone,

"If there isn't Captain Donnithorne and Mr. Irwine a-coming into
the yard! I'll lay my life they're come to speak about your preaching on
the Green, Dinah; it's you must answer 'em, for I'm dumb. I've said
enough a'ready about your bringing such disgrace upo' your uncle's
family. I wouldn't ha' minded if you'd been Mr. Poyser's own niece—
folks must put up wi' their own kin, as they put up wi' their own noses
—it's their own flesh and blood. But to think of a niece o' mine being
cause o' my husband's being turned out of his farm, and me brought
him no fortin but my savins——"

"Nay, dear aunt Rachel," said Dinah gently, "you've no cause for
such fears. I've strong assurance that no evil will happen to you and my
uncle and the children from anything I've done. I didn't preach without
direction."

"Direction! I know very well what you mean by direction," said Mrs.
Poyser, knitting in a rapid and agitated manner. "When there's a bigger
maggot than usial in your head you call it 'direction'; and then nothing
can stir you—you look like the statty o' the outside o' Treddles'on
church, a-starin' and a-smilin' whether it's fair weather or foul. I hanna
common patience with you."

By this time the two gentlemen had reached the palings, and had got
down from their horses: it was plain they meant to come in. Mrs. Poyser
advanced to the door to meet them, curtsying low, and trembling between
anger with Dinah and anxiety to conduct herself with perfect propriety
on the occasion. For in those days the keenest of bucolic minds felt a
whispering awe at the sight of the gentry, such as of old men felt when
they stood on tip-toe to watch the gods passing by in tall human shape.

"Well, Mrs. Poyser, how are you after this stormy morning?" said
Mr. Irwine, with his stately cordiality. "Our feet are quite dry; we shall
not soil your beautiful floor."

"O, sir, don't mention it," said Mrs. Poyser. "Will you and the Captain please to walk into the parlour?"

"No, indeed, thank you, Mrs. Poyser," said the Captain, looking
eagerly round the kitchen, as if his eye were seeking something it could
not find. "I delight in your kitchen. I think it is the most charming room
I know. I should like every farmer's wife to come and look at it for a
pattern."

"O, you're pleased to say so, sir. Pray take a seat," said Mrs. Poyser,
relieved a little by this compliment and the Captain's evident good-

humour, but still glancing anxiously at Mr. Irwine, who, she saw, was looking at Dinah and advancing towards her.

"Poyser is not at home, is he?" said Captain Donnithorne, seating himself where he could see along the short passage to the open dairy-door.

"No, sir, he isn't; he's gone to Rosseter to see Mr. West, the factor, about the wool. But there's father i' the barn, sir, if he'd be of any use."

"No, thank you; I'll just look at the whelps and leave a message about them with your shepherd. I must come another day and see your husband; I want to have a consultation with him about horses. Do you know when he's likely to be at liberty?"

"Why, sir, you can hardly miss him, except it's o' Treddles'on market-day—that's of a Friday, you know. For if he's anywhere on the farm we can send for him in a minute. If we'd got rid o' the Scantlands we should have no outlying fields; and I should be glad of it, for if ever anything happens he's sure to be gone to the Scantlands. Things allays happen so contrairy, if they've a chance; and it's an unnat'ral thing to have one bit o' your farm in one county and all the rest in another."

"Ah, the Scantlands would go much better with Choyce's farm, especially as he wants dairy-land and you've got plenty. I think yours is the prettiest farm on the estate, though; and do you know, Mrs. Poyser, if I were going to marry and settle, I should be tempted to turn you out, and do up this fine old house, and turn farmer myself."

"O, sir," said Mrs. Poyser, rather alarmed, "you wouldn't like it at all. As for farming, it's putting money into your pocket wi' your right hand and fetching it out wi' your left. As fur as I can see, it's raising victual for other folks, and just getting a mouthful for yourself and your children as you go along. Not as you'd be like a poor man as wants to get his bread: you could afford to lose as much money as you liked i' farming; but it's poor fun losing money, I should think, though I understan' it's what the great folks i' London play at more than anything. For my husband heard at market as Lord Dacey's eldest son had lost thousands upo' thousands to the Prince o' Wales, and they said my lady was going to pawn her jewels to pay for him. But you know more about that than I do, sir. But, as for farming, sir, I canna think as you'd like it; and this house—the draughts in it are enough to cut you through, and it's my opinion the floors up-stairs are very rotten, and the rats i' the cellar are beyond anything."

"Why, that's a terrible picture, Mrs. Poyser. I think I should be doing you a service to turn you out of such a place. But there's no chance of that. I'm not likely to settle for the next twenty years, till I'm a stout gentleman of forty; and my grandfather would never consent to part with such good tenants as you."

"Well, sir, if he thinks so well o' Mr. Poyser for a tenant, I wish you could put in a word for him to allow us some new gates for the Five closes, for my husband's been asking and asking till he's tired, and to think o' what he's done for the farm, and's never had a penny allowed him, be the times bad or good. And as I've said to my husband often and often, I'm sure if the Captain had anything to do with it, it wouldn't be so. Not as I wish to speak disrespectful o' them as have got the power i' their hands, but it's more than flesh and blood 'ull bear sometimes, to be toiling and striving, and up early and down late, and hardly sleeping a wink when you lie down for thinking as the cheese may swell, or the cows may slip their calf, or the wheat may grow green again i' the sheaf —and after all, at th' end o' the year, it's like as if you'd been cooking a feast and had got the smell of it for your pains."

Mrs. Poyser, once launched into conversation, always sailed along without any check from her preliminary awe of the gentry. The confidence she felt in her own powers of exposition was a motive force that overcame all resistance.

"I'm afraid I should only do harm instead of good, if I were to speak about the gates, Mrs. Poyser," said the Captain, "though I assure you there's no man on the estate I would sooner say a word for than your husband. I know his farm is in better order than any other within ten miles of us; and as for the kitchen," he added, smiling, "I don't believe there's one in the kingdom to beat it. By the by, I've never seen your dairy: I must see your dairy, Mrs. Poyser."

"Indeed, sir, it's not fit for you to go in, for Hetty's in the middle o' making the butter, for the churning was thrown late, and I'm quite ashamed." This Mrs. Poyser said blushing, and believing that the Captain was really interested in her milk-pans, and would adjust his opinion of her to the appearance of her dairy.

"O, I've no doubt it's in capital order. Take me in," said the Captain, himself leading the way, while Mrs. Poyser followed.

CHAPTER VII

THE DAIRY

THE dairy was certainly worth looking at: it was a scene to sicken for with a sort of calenture in hot and dusty streets—such coolness, such purity, such fresh fragrance of new-pressed cheese, of firm butter, of wooden vessels perpetually bathed in pure water; such soft colouring of red earthenware and creamy surfaces, brown wood and polished tin, grey limestone and rich orange-red rust on the iron weights and hooks and hinges. But one gets only a confused notion of these details when they surround a distractingly pretty girl of seventeen, standing on little pattens and rounding her dimpled arm to lift a pound of butter out of the scale.

Hetty blushed a deep rose-colour when Captain Donnithorne entered the dairy and spoke to her; but it was not at all a distressed blush, for it was inwreathed with smiles and dimples, and with sparkles from under long curled dark eye-lashes; and while her aunt was discoursing to him about the limited amount of milk that was to be spared for butter and cheese so long as the calves were not all weaned, and a large quantity but inferior quality of milk yielded by the short-horn, which had been bought on experiment, together with other matters which must be interesting to a young gentleman who would one day be a landlord, Hetty tossed and patted her pound of butter with quite a self-possessed, coquettish air, slily conscious that no turn of her head was lost.

There are various orders of beauty, causing men to make fools of themselves in various styles, from the desperate to the sheepish; but there is one order of beauty which seems made to turn the heads not only of men, but of all intelligent mammals, even of women. It is a beauty like that of kittens, or very small downy ducks making gentle rippling noises with their soft bills, or babies just beginning to toddle and to engage in conscious mischief—a beauty with which you can never be angry, but that you feel ready to crush for inability to comprehend the state of mind into which it throws you. Hetty Sorrel's was that sort of beauty. Her aunt, Mrs. Poyser, who professed to despise all personal attractions, and intended to be the severest of mentors, continually gazed at Hetty's charms by the sly, fascinated in spite of herself; and after administering such a scolding as naturally flowed from her anxiety to do well by her husband's niece—who had no mother of her own to scold her, poor thing!—she would often confess to her husband, when they were safe out of hearing, that she firmly believed, "the naughtier the little huzzy behaved, the prettier she looked."

It is of little use for me to tell you that Hetty's cheek was like a rose-petal, that dimples played about her pouting lips, that her large dark eyes hid a soft roguishness under their long lashes, and that her curly hair, though all pushed back under her round cap while she was at work, stole back in dark delicate rings on her forehead, and about her white shell-like ears; it is of little use for me to say how lovely was the contour of her pink-and-white neckerchief, tucked into her low plum-coloured stuff boddice, or how the linen butter-making apron, with its bib, seemed a thing to be imitated in silk by duchesses, since it fell in such charming lines, or how her brown stockings and thick-soled buckle shoes lost all that clumsiness which they must certainly have had when empty of her foot and ankle;—of little use, unless you have seen a woman who affected you as Hetty affected her beholders, for otherwise, though you might conjure up the image of a lovely woman, she would not in the least resemble that distracting kitten-like maiden. I might mention all the divine charms of a bright spring day, but if you had never in your life utterly forgotten yourself in straining your eyes after the mounting lark, or in wandering through the still lanes when the fresh-opened blossoms fill them with a sacred silent beauty like that of fretted aisles, where would be the use of my descriptive catalogue? I could never make you know what I meant by a bright spring day. Hetty's was a spring-tide beauty; it was the beauty of young frisking things, round-limbed, gambolling, circumventing you by a false air of innocence—the innocence of a young star-browed calf, for example, that, being inclined for a promenade out of bounds, leads you a severe steeple-chase over hedge and ditch, and only comes to a stand in the middle of a bog.

And they are the prettiest attitudes and movements into which a pretty girl is thrown in making up butter—tossing movements that give a charming curve to the arm, and a sideward inclination of the round white neck; little patting and rolling movements with the palm of the hand, and nice adaptations and finishings which cannot at all be effected without a great play of the pouting mouth and the dark eyes. And then the butter itself seems to communicate a fresh charm—it is so pure, so sweet-scented; it is turned off the mould with such a beautiful firm surface, like marble in a pale yellow light! Moreover, Hetty was particularly clever at making up the butter; it was the one performance of hers that her aunt allowed to pass without severe criticism; so she handled it with all the grace that belongs to mastery.

"I hope you will be ready for a great holiday on the thirtieth of July, Mrs. Poyser," said Captain Donnithorne, when he had sufficiently admired the dairy, and given several improvised opinions on Swede turnips and short-horns. "You know what is to happen then, and I shall expect you to be one of the guests who come earliest and leave latest. Will you promise me your hand for two dances, Miss Hetty? If I don't get your promise now, I know I shall hardly have a chance, for all the smart young farmers will take care to secure you."

Hetty smiled and blushed, but before she could answer, Mrs. Poyser interposed, scandalised at the mere suggestion that the young squire could be excluded by any meaner partners.

"Indeed, sir, you are very kind to take that notice of her. And I'm sure, whenever you're pleased to dance with her, she'll be proud and thankful, if she stood still all the rest o' th' evening."

"O no, no, that would be too cruel to all the other young fellows who can dance. But you will promise me two dances, won't you?" the Captain continued, determined to make Hetty look at him and speak to him.

Hetty dropped the prettiest little curtsy, and stole a half-shy, half-coquettish glance at him as she said,

"Yes, thank you, sir."

"And you must bring all your children, you know, Mrs. Poyser; your little Totty, as well as the boys. I want all the youngest children on the estate to be there—all those who will be fine young men and women when I'm a bald old fellow."

"O dear sir, that 'ull be a long time first," said Mrs. Poyser, quite overcome at the young squire's speaking so lightly of himself, and thinking how her husband would be interested in hearing her recount this remarkable specimen of high-born humour. The Captain was thought to be "very full of his jokes," and was a great favourite throughout the estate on account of his free manners. Every tenant was quite sure things would be different when the reins got into his hands—there was to be a millennial abundance of new gates, allowances of lime, and returns of ten per cent.

"But where is Totty to-day?" he said. "I want to see her."

"Where *is* the little un, Hetty?" said Mrs. Poyser. "She came in here not long ago."

"I don't know. She went into the brewhouse to Nancy, I think."

The proud mother, unable to resist the temptation to show her Totty, passed at once into the back-kitchen, in search of her, not, however, without misgivings lest something should have happened to render her person and attire unfit for presentation.

"And do you carry the butter to market when you've made it?" said the Captain to Hetty, meanwhile.

"O no, sir; not when it's so heavy: I'm not strong enough to carry it. Alick takes it on horseback."

"No, I'm sure your pretty arms were never meant for such heavy weights. But you go out a-walk sometimes these pleasant evenings, don't you? Why don't you have a walk in the Chase sometimes, now it's so green and pleasant? I hardly ever see you anywhere except at home and at church."

"Aunt doesn't like me to go a-walking only when I'm going some where," said Hetty. "But I go through the Chase sometimes."

"And don't you ever go to see Mrs. Best, the housekeeper? I think I saw you once in the hounsekeeper's room."

"It isn't Mrs. Best, it's Mrs. Pomfret, the lady's-maid, as I go to see. She's teaching me tent-stitch and the lace-mending. I'm going to tea with her to-morrow afternoon."

The reason why there had been space for this *tête-à-tête* can only be known by looking into the back-kitchen, where Totty had been discovered rubbing a stray blue-bag against her nose, and in the same moment allowing some liberal indigo drops to fall on her afternoon pinafore. But now she appeared holding her mother's hand—the end of her round nose rather shiny from a recent and hurried application of soap and water.

"Here she is!" said the Captain, lifting her up and setting her on the low stone shelf. "Here's Totty! By the by, what's her other name? She wasn't christened Totty."

"O sir, we call her sadly out of her name. Charlotte's her christened name. It's a name i' Mr. Poyser's family: his grandmother was named Charlotte. But we began with calling her Lotty, and now it's got to Totty. To be sure it's more like a name for a dog than a Christian child."

"Totty's a capital name. Why, she looks like a Totty. Has she got a pocket on?" said the Captain, feeling in his own waistcoat pockets.

Totty immediately with great gravity lifted up her frock, and showed a tiny pink pocket at present in a state of collapse.

"It dot notin in it," she said, as she looked down at it very earnestly.

"No! what a pity! such a pretty pocket. Well, I think I've got some things in mine that will make a pretty jingle in it. Yes! I declare I've got five little round silver things, and hear what a pretty noise they make in Totty's pink pocket." Here he shook the pocket with the five six-pences in it, and Totty showed her teeth and wrinkled her nose in great glee; but, divining that there was nothing more to be got staying, she jumped off the shelf and ran away to jingle her pocket in the hearing of Nancy, while her mother called after her, "O for shame, you naughty gell! not to thank the Captain for what he's given you. I'm sure, sir, it's very kind of you! but she's spoiled shameful; her father won't have her said nay in anything, and there's no managing her. It's being the young-est, and th' only gell."

"O, she's a funny little fatty; I wouldn't have her different. But I must be going now, for I suppose the Rector is waiting for me."

With a "good-by," a bright glance, and a bow to Hetty, Arthur left the dairy. But he was mistaken in imagining himself waited for. The Rector had been so much interested in his conversation with Dinah, that he would not have chosen to close it earlier; and you shall hear now what they had been saying to each other.

CHAPTER VIII

A VOCATION

DINAH, who had risen when the gentlemen came in, but still kept hold of the sheet she was mending, curtsied respectfully when she saw Mr. Irwine looking at her and advancing towards her. He had never yet spoken to her, or stood face to face with her, and her first thought, as her eyes met his, was, "What a well-favoured countenance! O that the good seed might fall on that soil, for it would surely flourish." The agree-able impression must have been mutual, for Mr. Irwine bowed to her with a benignant deference, which would have been equally in place if she had been the most dignified lady of his acquaintance.

"You are only a visitor in this neighborhood, I think?" were his first words, as he seated himself opposite to her.

"No, sir, I come from Snowfield, in Stonyshire. But my aunt was very kind, wanting me to have rest from my work there, because I'd been ill, and she invited me to come and stay with her for a while."

"Ah, I remember Snowfield very well; I once had occasion to go there. It's a dreary bleak place. They were building a cotton-mill there; but that's many years ago now: I suppose the place is a good deal changed by the employment that mill must have brought."

"It *is* changed so far as the mill has brought people there, who get a livelihood for themselves by working in it, and make it better for the tradesfolks. I work in it myself, and have reason to be grateful, for thereby I have enough and to spare. But it's still a bleak place, as you say, sir—very different from this country."

"You have relations living there probably, so that you are attached to the place as your home?"

"I had an aunt there once; she brought me up, for I was an orphan. But she was taken away seven years ago, and I have no other kindred that I know of, besides my aunt Poyser, who is very good to me, and would have me come and live in this country, which to be sure is a good land, wherein they eat bread without scarceness. But I'm not free to leave Snowfield, where I was first planted, and have grown deep into it, like the small grass on the hill-top."

"Ah, I daresay you have many religious friends and companions there, you are a Methodist—a Wesleyan, I think?"

"Yes, my aunt at Snowfield belonged to the Society, and I have cause to be thankful for the privileges I have had thereby from my earliest childhood."

"And have you been long in the habit of preaching?—for I understand you preached at Hayslope last night."

"I first took to the work four years since, when I was twenty-one."

"Your Society sanctions women's preaching, then?"

"It doesn't forbid them, sir, when they've a clear call to the work, and when their ministry is owned by the conversion of sinners, and the strengthening of God's people. Mrs. Fletcher, as you may have heard about, was the first woman to preach in the Society, I believe, before she was married, when she was Miss Bosanquet; and Mr. Wesley approved of her undertaking the work. She had a great gift, and there are many others now living who are precious fellow-helpers in the work of the ministry. I understand there's been voices raised against it in the Society of late, but I cannot but think their counsel will come to nought. It isn't for men to make channels for God's Spirit, as they make channels for the water-courses, and say, 'Flow here, but flow not there.' "

"But don't you find some danger among your people—I don't mean to say that it is so with you, far from it—but don't you find sometimes that both men and women fancy themselves channels for God's Spirit, and are quite mistaken. so that they set about a work for which they are unfit, and bring holy things into contempt?"

"Doubtless it is so sometimes; for there have been evil-doers among us who have sought to deceive the brethren, and some there are who deceive their own selves. But we are not without discipline and correction to put a check upon these things. There's a very strict order kept among us, and the brethren and sisters watch for each other's souls as they that must give account. They don't go every one his own way and say, 'Am I my brother's keeper!' "

"But tell me—if I may ask, and I am really interested in knowing it —how you first came to think of preaching?"

"Indeed, sir, I didn't think of it at all—I'd been used from the time I was sixteen to talk to the little children and teach them, and sometimes I had had my heart enlarged to speak in class, and was much drawn out in prayer with the sick. But I had felt no call to preach; for when I'm not greatly wrought upon, I'm too much given to sit still and keep

by myself: it seems as if I could sit silent all day long with the thought
of God overflowing my soul—as the pebbles lie bathed in the Willow
Brook. For thoughts are so great—aren't they, sir? They seem to lie
upon us like a deep flood; and it's my besetment to forget where I am
and everything about me, and lose myself in thoughts that I could give
no account of, for I could neither make a beginning nor ending of them
in words. That was my way as long as I can remember; but sometimes
it seemed as if speech came to me without any will of my own, and words
were given to me that came out as the tears come, because our hearts
are full and we can't help it. And those were always times of great
blessing, though I had never thought it could be so with me before a
congregation of people. But, sir, we are led on, like the little children, by
a way that we know not. I was called to preach quite suddenly, and since
then I have never been left in doubt about the work that was laid upon
me."

"But tell me the circumstances—just how it was, the very day you
began to preach."

"It was one Sunday I walked with brother Marlowe, who was an aged
man, one of the local preachers, all the way to Hetton-Deeps—that's a
village where the people get their living by working in the lead-mines,
and where there's no church nor preacher, but they live like sheep without a shepherd. It's better than twelve miles from Snowfield, so we set out
early in the morning, for it was summer-time; and I had a wonderful
sense of the Divine love as we walked over the hills, where there's no
trees, you know, sir, as there is here, to make the sky look smaller, but
you see the heavens stretched out like a tent, and you feel the everlasting arms around you. But before we got to Hetton, brother Marlowe was
seized with a dizziness that made him afraid of falling, for he over-
worked himself sadly, at his years, in watching and praying, and walking so many miles to speak the Word, as well as carrying on his trade of
linen-weaving. And when we got to the village, the people were expecting
him, for he'd appointed the time and the place when he was there before,
and such of them as cared to hear the Word of Life were assembled on a
spot where the cottages was thickest, so as others might be drawn to
come. But he felt as he couldn't stand up to preach, and he was forced to
lie down in the first of the cottages we came to. So I went to tell the
people, thinking we'd go into one of the houses, and I would read and
pray with them. But as I passed along by the cottages and saw the aged
trembling women at the doors, and the hard looks of the men, who
seemed to have their eyes no more filled with the sight of the Sabbath
morning than if they had been dumb oxen that never looked up to the
sky, I felt a great movement in my soul, and I trembled as if I was
shaken by a strong spirit entering into my weak body. And I went to
where the little flock of people was gathered together, and stepped on
the low wall that was built against the green hill-side, and I spoke the
words that were given to me abundantly. And they all came round me

out of all the cottages, and many wept over their sins, and have since been joined to the Lord. That was the beginning of my preaching, sir, and I've preached ever since."

Dinah had let her work fall during this narrative, which she uttered in her usual simple way, but with that sincere, articulate, thrilling treble, by which she always mastered her audience. She stooped now to gather up her sewing, and then went on with it as before. Mr. Irwine was deeply interested. He said to himself, "He must be a miserable prig who would act the pedagogue here: one might as well go and lecture the trees for growing in their own shape."

"And you never feel any embarrassment from the sense of your youth —that you are a lovely young woman on whom men's eyes are fixed?" he said aloud.

"No, I've no room for such feelings, and I don't believe the people ever take notice about that. I think, sir, when God makes His presence felt through us, we are like the burning bush: Moses never took any heed what sort of bush it was—he only saw the brightness of the Lord. I've preached to as rough ignorant people as can be in the villages about Snowfield—men that looked very hard and wild: but they never said an uncivil word to me, and often thanked me kindly as they made way for me to pass through the midst of them."

"*That* I can believe—that I can well believe," said Mr. Irwine, emphatically. "And what did you think of your hearers last night, now? Did you find them quiet and attentive?"

"Very quiet, sir; but I saw no signs of any great work upon them, except in a young girl named Bessy Cranage, towards whom my heart yearned greatly, when my eyes first fell on her blooming youth, given up to folly and vanity. I had some private talk and prayer with her afterwards, and I trust her heart is touched. But I've noticed, that in these villages where the people lead a quiet life among the green pastures and the still waters, tilling the ground and tending the cattle, there's a strange deadness to the Word, as different as can be from the great towns, like Leeds, where I once went to visit a holy woman who preaches there. It's wonderful how rich is the harvest of souls up those high-walled streets, where you seemed to walk as in a prison-yard, and the ear is deafened with the sounds of worldly toil. I think maybe it is because the promise is sweeter when this life is so dark and weary, and the soul gets more hungry when the body is ill at ease."

"Why, yes, our farm-labourers are not easily roused. They take life almost as slowly as the sheep and cows. But we have some intelligent workmen about here. I daresay you know the Bedes; Seth Bede, by the by, is a Methodist."

"Yes, I know Seth well, and his brother Adam a little. Seth is a gracious young man—sincere and without offence; and Adam is like the patriarch Joseph, for his great skill and knowledge, and the kindness he shows to his brother and his parents."

"Perhaps you don't know the trouble that has just happened to them?

Their father, Matthias Bede, was drowned in the Willow Brook last night, not far from his own door. I'm going now to see Adam."

"Ah, their poor aged mother!" said Dinah, dropping her hands, and looking before her with pitying eyes, as if she saw the object of her sympathy. "She will mourn heavily; for Seth has told me she's of an anxious, troubled heart. I must go and see if I can give her any help."

As she rose and was beginning to fold up her work, Captain Donnithorne, having exhausted all plausible pretexts for remaining among the milk-pans, came out of the dairy, followed by Mrs. Poyser. Mr. Irwine now rose also, and, advancing towards Dinah, held out his hand, and said——

"Good-by. I hear you are going away soon; but this will not be the last visit you will pay your aunt—so we shall meet again, I hope."

His cordiality towards Dinah set all Mrs. Poyser's anxieties at rest, and her face was brighter than usual, as she said——

"I've never asked after Mrs. Irwine and the Miss Irwines, sir; I hope they're as well as usual."

"Yes, thank you, Mrs. Poyser, except that Miss Anne has one of her bad headaches to-day. By the by, we all liked that nice cream-cheese you sent us—my mother especially."

"I'm very glad, indeed, sir. It is but seldom I make one, but I remembered Mrs. Irwine was fond of 'em. Please to give my duty to her, and to Miss Kate and Miss Anne. They've never been to look at my poultry this long while, and I've got some beautiful speckled chickens, black and white, as Miss Kate might like to have some of amongst hers."

"Well, I'll tell her; she must come and see them. Good-by," said the Rector, mounting his horse.

"Just ride slowly on, Irwine," said Captain Donnithorne, mounting also. "I'll overtake you in three minutes. I'm only going to speak to the shepherd about the whelps. Good-by, Mrs. Poyser; tell your husband I shall come and have a long talk with him soon."

Mrs. Poyser curtsied duly, and watched the two horses until they had disappeared from the yard, amidst great excitement on the part of the pigs and the poultry, and under the furious indignation of the bull-dog, who performed a Pyrrhic dance, that every moment seemed to threaten the breaking of his chain. Mrs. Poyser delighted in this noisy exit; it was a fresh assurance to her that the farmyard was well guarded, and that no loiterers could enter unobserved; and it was not until the gate had closed behind the Captain that she turned into the kitchen again, where Dinah stood with her bonnet in her hand, waiting to speak to her aunt, before she set out for Lisbeth Bede's cottage.

Mrs. Poyser, however, though she noticed the bonnet, deferred remarking on it until she had disburdened herself of her surprise at Mr. Irwine's behaviour.

"Why, Mr. Irwine wasn't angry, then? What did he say to you, Dinah? Didn't he scold you for preaching?"

"No, he was not at all angry; he was very friendly to me. I was quite

drawn out to speak to him; I hardly know how, for I had always thought
of him as a worldly Sadducee. But his countenance is as pleasant as the
morning sunshine."

"Pleasant! and what else did y' expect to find him but pleasant?" said
Mrs. Poyser, impatiently, resuming her knitting. "I should think his
countenance *is* pleasant indeed! and him a gentleman born, and's got a
mother like a picter. You may go the country round, and not find such
another woman turned sixty-six. It's summat-like to see such a man as
that i' the desk of a Sunday! As I say to Poyser, it's like looking at a full
crop o' wheat, or a pasture with a fine dairy o' cows in it; it makes you
think the world's comfortable-like. But as for such creaturs as you
Methodisses run after, I'd as soon go to look at a lot o' bare-ribbed runts
on a common. Fine folks they are to tell you what's right, as look as if
they'd never tasted nothing better than bacon-sword and sour-cake i'
their lives. But what did Mr. Irwine say to you about that fool's trick
o' preaching on the Green?"

"He only said he'd heard of it; he didn't seem to feel any displeasure
about it. But, dear aunt, don't think any more about that. He told me
something that I'm sure will cause you sorrow, as it does me. Thias
Bede was drowned last night in the Willow Brook, and I'm thinking
that the aged mother will be greatly in need of comfort. Perhaps I can
be of use to her, so I have fetched my bonnet and am going to set out."

"Dear heart, dear heart! But you must have a cup o' tea first, child,"
said Mrs. Poyser, falling at once from the key of B with five sharps to
the frank and genial C. "The kettle's boiling—we'll have it ready in a
minute; and the young uns 'ull be in and wanting theirs directly. I'm
quite willing you should go and see th' old woman, for you're one as is
allays welcome in trouble, Methodist or no Methodist; but, for the matter o' that, it's the flesh and blood folks are made on as makes the difference. Some cheeses are made o' skimmed milk and some o' new milk,
and it's no matter what you call 'em, you may tell which is which by the
look and the smell. But as to Thias Bede, he's better out o' the way nor
in—God forgi' me for saying so—for he's done little this ten year but
make trouble for them as belonged to him; and I think it 'ud be well for
you to take a little bottle o' rum for th' old woman, for I daresay she's
got never a drop o' nothing to comfort her inside. Sit down, child, and be
easy, for you shan't stir out till you've had a cup o' tea, and so I tell
you."

During the latter part of this speech, Mrs. Poyser had been reaching
down the tea-things from the shelves, and was on her way towards the
pantry for the loaf (followed close by Totty, who had made her appearance on the rattling of the tea-cups), when Hetty came out of the dairy
relieving her tired arms by lifting them up, and clasping her hands at
the back of her head.

"Molly," she said, rather languidly, "just run out and get me a bunch
of dock-leaves: the butter's ready to pack up now."

"D'you hear what's happened, Hetty?" said her aunt.

"No; how should I hear anything?" was the answer, in a pettish tone.

"Not as you'd care much, I daresay, if you did hear; for you're too feather-headed to mind if everybody was dead, so as you could stay up-stairs a-dressing yourself for two hours by the clock. But anybody besides yourself 'ud mind about such things happening to them as think a deal more of you than you deserve. But Adam Bede and all his kin might be drownded for what you'd care—you'd be perking at the glass the next minute."

"Adam Bede—drownded?" said Hetty, letting her arms fall, and looking rather bewildered, but suspecting that her aunt was as usual exaggerating with a didactic purpose.

"No, my dear, no," said Dinah, kindly, for Mrs. Poyser had passed on to the pantry without deigning more precise information. "Not Adam. Adam's father, the old man, is drowned. He was drowned last night in the Willow Brook. Mr. Irwine has just told me about it."

"O, how dreadful!" said Hetty, looking serious, but not deeply affected; and as Molly now entered with the dock-leaves, she took them silently and returned to the dairy without asking further questions.

CHAPTER IX

HETTY'S WORLD

WHILE she adjusted the broad leaves that set off the pale fragrant butter as the primrose is set off by its nest of green, I am afraid Hetty was thinking a great deal more of the looks Captain Donnithorne had cast at her than of Adam and his troubles. Bright, admiring glances from a handsome young gentleman, with white hands, a gold chain, occasional regimentals, and wealth and grandeur immeasurable—those were the warm rays that set poor Hetty's heart vibrating, and playing its little foolish tunes over and over again. We do not hear that Memnon's statue gave forth its melody at all under the rushing of the mightiest wind, or in response to any other influence divine or human than certain short-lived sunbeams of morning; and we must learn to accommodate ourselves to the discovery that some of those cunningly-fashioned instruments called human souls have only a very limited range of music, and will not vibrate in the least under a touch that fills others with tremulous rapture or quivering agony.

Hetty was quite used to the thought that people liked to look at her. She was not blind to the fact that young Luke Britton of Broxton came to Hayslope Church on a Sunday afternoon on purpose that he might see her; and that he would have made much more decided advances if her uncle Poyser, thinking but lightly of a young man whose father's land was so foul as old Luke Britton's, had not forbidden her aunt to encourage him by any civilities. She was aware, too, that Mr. Craig, the gardener at the Chase, was over head and ears in love with her, and had lately made unmistakable avowals in luscious strawberries and hyperbolical peas. She knew still better, that Adam Bede—tall, upright, clever, brave Adam Bede—who carried such authority with all the people round about, and whom her uncle was always delighted to see of an evening, saying that "Adam knew a fine sight more o' the natur o' things than those as thought themselves his betters"—she knew that this Adam, who was often rather stern to other people, and not much given to run after the lasses, could be made to turn pale or red any day by a word or a look from her. Hetty's sphere of comparison was not large, but she couldn't help perceiving that Adam was "something like" a man; always knew what to say about things, could tell her uncle how to prop the hovel, and had mended the churn in no time; knew, with only looking at it, the value of the chestnut tree that was blown down, and why the damp came in the walls, and what they must do to stop the rats; and wrote a beautiful hand that you could read off, and could do figures in his head —a degree of accomplishment totally unknown among the richest farm- ers of that country-side. Not at all like that slouching Luke Britton, who, when she once walked with him all the way from Broxton to Hayslope, had only broken silence to remark that the grey goose had begun to lay. And as for Mr. Craig, the gardener, he was a sensible man enough, to be sure, but he was knock-kneed, and had a queer sort of sing-song in his talk; moreover, on the most charitable supposition, he must be far on the way to forty.

Hetty was quite certain her uncle wanted her to encourage Adam, and would be pleased for her to marry him. For those were times when there was no rigid demarcation of rank between the farmer and the respectable artisan, and on the home hearth, as well as in the public- house, they might be seen taking their jug of ale together; the farmer having a latent sense of capital, and of weight in parish affairs, which sustained him under his conspicuous inferiority in conversation. Martin Poyser was not a frequenter of public-houses, but he liked a friendly chat over his own home-brewed; and though it was pleasant to lay down the law to a stupid neighbour who had no notion how to make the best of his farm, it was also an agreeable variety to learn something from a clever fellow like Adam Bede. Accordingly, for the last three years—ever since he had superintended the building of the new barn—Adam had always been made welcome at the Hall Farm, specially of a winter evening, when the whole family, in patriarchal fashion, master and mistress, children and servants, were assembled in that glorious kitchen, at well- graduated distances from the blazing fire. And for the last two years, at least, Hetty had been in the habit of hearing her uncle say, "Adam Bede may be working for wage now, but he'll be a master-man some day, as sure as I sit in this chair. Mester Burge is in the right on't to want him to go partners and marry his daughter, if it's true what they say; the woman as marries him 'ull have a good take, be't Lady-day or Michael- mas,"—a remark which Mrs. Poyser always followed up with her cordial assent. "Ah," she would say, "it's all very fine having a ready-made rich

man, but may-happen he'll be a ready-made fool; and it's no use filling
your pocket full o' money if you've got a hole in the corner. It'll do you
no good to sit in a spring-cart o' your own, if you've got a soft to drive
you: he'll soon turn you over into the ditch. I allays said I'd never marry
a man as had got no brains; for where's the use of a woman having
brains of her own if she's tackled to a geck as everybody's a-laughing at?
She might as well dress herself fine to sit back'ards on a donkey."

These expressions, though figurative, sufficiently indicated the bent of
Mrs. Poyser's mind with regard to Adam; and though she and her husband might have viewed the subject differently if Hetty had been a
daughter of their own, it was clear that they would have welcomed the
match with Adam for a penniless niece. For what could Hetty have been
but a servant elsewhere, if her uncle had not taken her in and brought
her up as a domestic help to her aunt, whose health since the birth of
Totty had not been equal to more positive labour than the superintendence of servants and children? But Hetty had never given Adam any
steady encouragement. Even in the moments when she was most thoroughly conscious of his superiority to her other admirers, she had never
brought herself to think of accepting him. She liked to feel that this
strong, skilful, keen-eyed man was in her power, and would have been
indignant if he had shown the least sign of slipping from under the yoke
of her coquettish tyranny, and attaching himself to the gentle Mary
Burge, who would have been grateful enough for the most trifling notice
from him. "Mary Burge, indeed! such a sallow-faced girl: if she put on a
bit of pink ribbon, she looked as yellow as a crow-flower, and her hair
was as straight as a hank of cotton." And always when Adam stayed
away for several weeks from the Hall Farm, and otherwise made some
show of resistance to his passion as a foolish one, Hetty took care to entice him back into the net by little airs of meekness and timidity, as if
she were in trouble at his neglect. But as to marrying Adam, that was a
very different affair! There was nothing in the world to tempt her to do
that. Her cheeks never grew a shade deeper when his name was mentioned; she felt no thrill when she saw him passing along the causeway
by the window, or advancing towards her unexpectedly in the footpath
across the meadow; she felt nothing when his eyes rested on her, but the
cold triumph of knowing that he loved her, and would not care to look at
Mary Burge: he could no more stir in her the emotions that make the
sweet intoxication of young love, than the mere picture of a sun can stir
the spring sap in the subtle fibres of the plant. She saw him as he was—a
poor man, with old parents to keep, who would not be able, for a long
while to come, to give her even such luxuries as she shared in her uncle's
house. And Hetty's dreams were all of luxuries: to sit in a carpeted
parlour, and always wear white stockings: to have some large beautiful
earrings, such as were all the fashion; to have Nottingham lace round
the top of her gown, and something to make her handkerchief smell nice,
like Miss Lydia Donnithorne's when she drew it out at church; and not
to be obliged to get up early or be scolded by anybody. She thought, if

Adam had been rich and could have given her tnese things, she loved him well enough to marry him.

But for the last few weeks a new influence had come over Hetty—vague, atmospheric, shaping itself into no self-confessed hopes or prospects, but producing a pleasant narcotic effect, making her tread the ground and go about her work in a sort of dream, unconscious of weight or effort, and showing her all things through a soft, liquid veil, as if she were living not in this solid world of brick and stone, but in a beautiful world, such as the sun lights up for us in the waters. Hetty had become aware that Mr. Arthur Donnithorne would take a good deal of trouble for the chance of seeing her; that he always placed himself at church so as to have the fullest view of her both sitting and standing; that he was constantly finding reasons for calling at the Hall Farm, and always would contrive to say something for the sake of making her speak to him and look at him. The poor child no more conceived at present the idea that the young squire could ever be her lover, than a baker's pretty daughter in the crowd, whom a young emperor distinguishes by an imperial but admiring smile, conceives that she shall be made empress. But the baker's daughter goes home and dreams of the handsome young emperor, and perhaps weighs the flour amiss while she is thinking what a heavenly lot it must be to have him for a husband: and so poor Hetty had got a face and a presence haunting her waking and sleeping dreams; bright, soft glances had penetrated her, and suffused her life with a strange, happy languor. The eyes that shed those glances were really not half so fine as Adam's, which sometimes looked at her with a sad, beseeching tenderness; but they had found a ready medium in Hetty's little silly imagination, whereas Adam's could get no entrance through that atmosphere. For three weeks, at least, her inward life had consisted of little else than living through in memory the looks and words Arthur had directed towards her—of little else than recalling the sensations with which she heard his voice outside the house, and saw him enter, and became conscious that his eyes were fixed on her, and then became conscious that a tall figure, looking down on her with eyes that seemed to touch her, was coming nearer in clothes of beautiful texture, with an odour like that of a flower-garden borne on the evening breeze. Foolish thoughts! but all this happened, you must remember, nearly sixty years ago, and Hetty was quite uneducated—a simple farmer's girl, to whom a gentleman with a white hand was dazzling as an Olympian god. Until to-day, she had never looked farther into the future than to the next time Captain Donnithorne would come to the Farm, or the next Sunday when she should see him at church; but now she thought, perhaps he would try to meet her when she went to the Chase to-morrow—and if he should speak to her, and walk a little way, when nobody was by! That had never happened yet; and now her imagination, instead of retracing the past, was busy fashioning what would happen to-morrow—whereabout in the Chase she should see him coming towards her, how she should put her new rose-coloured ribbon on, which he had never seen, and what he would say to her to make her return his glance—a glance which she would be living through in her memory, over and over again, all the rest of the day.

In this state of mind, how could Hetty give any feeling to Adam's troubles, or think much about poor old Thias being drowned? Young souls, in such pleasant delirium as hers, are as unsympathetic as butterflies sipping nectar; they are isolated from all appeals by a barrier of dreams—by invisible looks and impalpable arms.

While Hetty's hands were busy packing up the butter, and her head filled with these pictures of the morrow, Arthur Donnithorne, riding by Mr. Irwine's side towards the valley of the Willow Brook, had also certain indistinct anticipations, running as an undercurrent in his mind while he was listening to Mr. Irwine's account of Dinah;—indistinct, yet strong enough to make him feel rather conscious when Mr. Irwine suddenly said,

"What fascinated you so in Mrs. Poyser's dairy, Arthur? Have you become an amateur of damp quarries and skimming-dishes?"

Arthur knew the Rector too well to suppose that a clever invention would be of any use, so he said, with his accustomed frankness,

"No, I went to look at the pretty butter-maker, Hetty Sorrel. She's a perfect Hebe; and if I were an artist, I would paint her. It's amazing what pretty girls one sees among the farmers' daughters, when the men are such clowns. That common round red face one sees sometimes in the men—all cheek and no features, like Martin Poyser's—comes out in the women of the family as the most charming phiz imaginable."

"Well, I have no objection to your contemplating Hetty in an artistic light, but I must not have you feeding her vanity, and filling her little noddle with the notion that she's a great beauty, attractive to fine gentlemen, or you will spoil her for a poor man's wife—honest Craig's, for example, whom I have seen bestowing soft glances on her. The little puss seems already to have airs enough to make a husband as miserable as it's a law of nature for a quiet man to be when he marries a beauty. Apropos of marrying, I hope our friend Adam will get settled, now the poor old man's gone. He will only have his mother to keep in future, and I've a notion that there's a kindness between him and that nice modest girl, Mary Burge, from something that fell from old Jonathan one day when I was talking to him. But when I mentioned the subject to Adam he looked uneasy, and turned the conversation. I suppose the love-making doesn't run smooth, or perhaps Adams hangs back till he's in a better position. He has independence of spirit enough for two men—rather an excess of pride, if anything."

"That would be a capital match for Adam. He would slip into old Burge's shoes, and make a fine thing of that building business, I'll answer for him. I should like to see him well settled in this parish; he would be ready then to act as my grand-vizier when I wanted one. We could plan no end of repairs and improvements together. I've never seen the girl, though, I think—at least I've never looked at her."

"Look at her next Sunday at church—she sits with her father on the left of the reading-desk. You needn't look quite so much at Hetty Sorrel then. When I've made up my mind that I can't afford to buy a tempting dog, I take no notice of him, because if he took a strong fancy to me, and looked lovingly at me, the struggle between arithmetic and inclination might become unpleasantly severe. I pique myself on my wisdom there, Arthur, and as an old fellow to whom wisdom has become cheap, I bestow it upon you."

"Thank you. It may stand me in good stead some day, though I don't know that I have any present use for it. Bless me! how the brook has overflowed. Suppose we have a canter, now we're at the bottom of the hill."

That is the great advantage of dialogue on horseback; it can be merged any minute into a trot or a canter, and one might have escaped from Socrates himself in the saddle. The two friends were free from the necessity of further conversation till they pulled up in the lane behind Adam's cottage.

CHAPTER X

DINAH VISITS LISBETH

At five o'clock Lisbeth came down-stairs with a large key in her hand: it was the key of the chamber where her husband lay dead. Throughout the day, except in her occasional outbursts of wailing grief, she had been in incessant movement, performing the initial duties to her dead with the awe and exactitude that belong to religious rites. She had brought out her little store of bleached linen, which she had for long years kept in reserve for this supreme use. It seemed but yesterday—that time so many mid-summers ago, when she had told Thias where this linen lay, that he might be sure and reach it out for her when *she* died, for she was the elder of the two. Then there had been work of cleansing to the strictest purity every object in the sacred chamber, and of removing from it every trace of common daily occupation. The small window which had hitherto freely let in the frosty moonlight or the warm summer sunrise on the working man's slumber, must now be darkened with a fair white sheet, for this was the sleep which is as sacred under the bare rafters as in ceiled houses. Lisbeth had even mended a long-neglected and unnoticeable rent in the checkered bit of bed-curtain; for the moments were few and precious now in which she would be able to do the smallest office of respect or love for the still corpse, to which in all her thoughts she attributed some consciousness. Our dead are never dead to us until we have forgotten them: they can be injured by us, they can be wounded; they know all our penitence, all our aching sense that their place is empty, all the kisses we bestow on the smallest relic of their presence.

And the aged peasant-woman most of all believes that her dead are conscious. Decent burial was what Lisbeth had been thinking of for herself through years of thrift, with an indistinct expectation that she should know when she was being carried to the churchyard, followed by her husband and her sons; and now she felt as if the greatest work of her life were to be done in seeing that Thias was buried decently before her —under the white throne, where once, in a dream, she had thought she lay in the coffin, yet all the while saw the sunshine above, and smelt the white blossoms that were so thick upon the thorn the Sunday she went to be churched after Adam was born.

But now she had done everything that could be done to-day in the chamber of death—had done it all herself, with some aid from her sons in lifting, for she would let no one be fetched to help her from the village, not being fond of female neighbours generally; and her favourite Dolly, the old housekeeper at Mr. Burge's, who had come to condole with her in the morning as soon as she heard of Thias's death, was too dim-sighted to be of much use. She had locked the door, and now held the key in her hand, as she threw herself wearily into a chair that stood out of its place in the middle of the house floor, where in ordinary times she would never have consented to sit. The kitchen had had none of her attention that day; it was soiled with the tread of muddy shoes, and untidy with clothes and other objects out of place. But what at another time would have been intolerable to Lisbeth's habits of order and cleanliness, seemed to her now just what should be: it was right that things should look strange and disordered and wretched, now the old man had come to his end in that sad way: the kitchen ought not to look as if nothing had happened. Adam, overcome with the agitations and exertions of the day after his night of hard work, had fallen asleep on a bench in the workshop; and Seth was in the back kitchen making a fire of sticks that he might get the kettle to boil, and persuade his mother to have a cup of tea, an indulgence which she rarely allowed herself.

There was no one in the kitchen when Lisbeth entered and threw herself into the chair. She looked round with blank eyes at the dirt and confusion on which the bright afternoon's sun shone dismally; it was all of a piece with the sad confusion of her mind—that confusion which belongs to the first hours of a sudden sorrow, when the poor human soul is like one who has been deposited sleeping among the ruins of a vast city, and wakes up in dreary amazement, not knowing whether it is the growing or the dying day—not knowing why and whence came this illimitable scene of desolation, or why he too finds himself desolate in the midst of it.

At another time Lisbeth's first thought would have been, "Where is Adam?" but the sudden death of her husband had restored him in these hours to that first place in her affections which he had held six-and-twenty years ago: she had forgotten his faults as we forget the sorrows of our departed childhood, and thought of nothing but the young husband's kindness and the old man's patience. Her eyes continued to wander blankly until Seth came in and began to remove some of the scattered things, and clear the small round deal table that he might set out his mother's tea upon it.

"What art goin' to do?" she said, rather peevishly.

"I want thee to have a cup of tea, mother," answered Seth, tenderly. "It'll do thee good; and I'll put two or three of these things away, and make the house look more comfortable."

"Comfortable! How canst talk o' ma'in' things comfortable? Let a-be, let a-be. There's no comfort for me no more," she went on, the tears coming when she began to speak, "now thy poor feyther's gone, as I'n washed for and mended, an' got's victual for him for thirty 'ear, an' him allays so pleased wi' iverything I done for him, an' used to be so handy an' do the jobs for me when I war ill an' cumbered wi' th' babby, an' made me the posset an' brought it up-stairs as proud as could be, an' carried the lad as war as heavy as two children for five mile an' ne'er grumbled, all the way to Warson Wake, 'cause I wanted to go an' see my sister, as war dead an' gone the very next Christmas as e'er come. An' him to be drownded in the brook as we passed o'er the day we war married an' come home together, an' he'd made them lots o' shelves for me to put my plates an' things on, an' showed 'em me as proud as could be, 'cause he know'd I should be pleased. An' he war to die an' me not to know, but to be a-sleeping i' my bed, as if I caredna nought about it. Eh! an' me to live to see that! An' us as war young folks once, an' thought we should do rarely when we war married. Let a-be, lad, let a-be! I wonna ha' no tay: I carena if I ne'er ate nor drink no more. When one o' th' bridge tumbles down, where's th' use o' the other stannin'? I may's well die, an' foller my old man. There's no knowin' but he'll want me."

Here Lisbeth broke from words into moans, swaying herself backwards and forwards on her chair. Seth, always timid in his behaviour towards his mother, from the sense that he had no influence over her, felt it was useless to attempt to persuade or soothe her, till this passion was past; so he contented himself with tending the back-kitchen fire, and folding up his father's clothes, which had been hanging out to dry since morning; afraid to move about in the room where his mother was, lest he should irritate her further.

But after Lisbeth had been rocking herself and moaning for some minutes, she suddenly paused, and said aloud to herself,

"I'll go an' see arter Adam, for I canna think where he's gotten; an' I want him to go up-stairs wi' me afore it's dark, for the minutes to look at the corpse is like the meltin' snow."

Seth overheard this, and coming into the kitchen again, as his mother rose from her chair, he said,

"Adam's asleep in the workshop, mother. Thee'dst better not wake him. He was o'erwrought with work and trouble."

"Wake him? Who's a-goin' to wake him? I shanna wake him wi'

lookin' at him. I hanna seen the lad this two hour—I'd welly forgot as he'd e'er growed up from a babby when's feyther carried him."

Adam was seated on a rough bench, his head supported by his arm, which rested from the shoulder to the elbow on the long planing-table in the middle of the workshop. It seemed as if he had sat down for a few minutes' rest, and had fallen asleep without slipping from his first attitude of sad, fatigued thought. His face, unwashed since yesterday, looked pallid and clammy; his hair was tossed shaggily about his forehead, and his closed eyes had the sunken look which follows upon watching and sorrow. His brow was knit, and his whole face had an expression of weariness and pain. Gyp was evidently uneasy, for he sat on his haunches resting his nose on his master's stretched-out leg, and dividing the time between licking the hand that hung listlessly down, and glancing with a listening air towards the door. The poor dog was hungry and restless, but would not leave his master, and was waiting impatiently for some change in the scene. It was owing to this feeling on Gyp's part, that when Lisbeth came into the workshop, and advanced towards Adam as noiselessly as she could, her intention not to awake him was immediately defeated; for Gyp's excitement was too great to find vent in anything short of a sharp bark, and in a moment Adam opened his eyes and saw his mother standing before him. It was not very unlike his dream, for his sleep had been little more than living through again, in a fevered delirious way, all that had happened since daybreak, and his mother with her fretful grief was present to him through it all. The chief difference between the reality and the vision was, that in his dream Hetty was continually coming before him in bodily presence—strangely mingling herself as an actor in scenes with which she had nothing to do. She was even by the Willow Brook; she made his mother angry by coming into the house; and he met her with her smart clothes quite wet through as he walked in the rain to Treddleston, to tell the coroner. But wherever Hetty came, his mother was sure to follow soon; and when he opened his eyes, it was not at all startling to see her standing near him.

"Eh, my lad, my lad!" Lisbeth burst out immediately, her wailing impulse returning, for grief in its freshness feels the need of associating its loss and its lament with every change of scene and incident, "the'st got nobody now but thy old mother to torment thee and be a burden to thee: thy poor feyther 'ull ne'er anger thee no more; an' thy mother may's well go arter him—the sooner the better—for I'm no good to nobody now. One old coat 'ull do to patch another, but it's good for nought else. Thee'dst like to ha' a wife to mend thy clothes an' get thy victual, better nor thy old mother. An' I shall be nought but cumber, a-sittin' i' th' chimney-corner." Adam winced and moved uneasily; he dreaded, of all things, to hear his mother speak of Hetty. "But if thy feyther had lived, he'd ne'er ha' wanted me to go to make room for another, for he could no more ha' done wi'out me nor one side o' the scissars can do wi'out th' other. Eh, we should ha' been both flung away together;

an' then I shouldna ha' seen this day, an' one buryin' 'ud ha' done for us both."

Here Lisbeth paused, but Adam sat in pained silence: he could not speak otherwise than tenderly to his mother to-day; but he could not help being irritated by this plaint. It was not possible for poor Lisbeth to know how it affected Adam, any more than it is possible for a wounded dog to know how his moans affect the nerves of his master. Like all complaining women, she complained in the expectation of being soothed, and when Adam said nothing, she was only prompted to complain more bitterly.

"I know thee couldst do better wi'out me, for thee couldst go where thee likedst, an' marry them as thee likedst. But I donna want to say thee nay, let thee bring home who thee wut; I'd ne'er open my lips to find faut, for when folks is old an' o' no use, they may think theirsens well off to get the bit an' the sup, though they'n to swallow ill words wi't. An' if thee'st set thy heart on a lass as'll bring thee nought and waste all, when thee mightst ha' them as 'ud make a man on thee, I'll say nought, now thy feyther's dead an' drownded, for I'm no better nor an old haft when the blade's gone."

Adam, unable to bear this any longer, rose silently from the bench, and walked out of the workshop into the kitchen. But Lisbeth followed him.

"Thee wutna go up-stairs an' see thy feyther, then? I'n done everythin' now, an' he'd like thee to go an' look at him, for he war allays so pleased when thee wast mild to him."

Adam turned round at once, and said, "Yes, mother; let us go up-stairs. Come, Seth, let us go together."

They went up-stairs, and for five minutes all was silence. Then the key was turned again, and there was a sound of footsteps on the stairs. But Adam did not come down again; he was too weary and worn out to encounter more of his mother's querulous grief, and he went to rest on his bed. Lisbeth no sooner entered the kitchen and sat down than she threw her apron over her head, and began to cry and moan, and rock herself as before. Seth thought, "She will be quieter by-and-by, now we have been up-stairs"; and he went into the back-kitchen again to tend his little fire, hoping that he should presently induce her to have some tea.

Lisbeth had been rocking herself in this way for more than five minutes, giving a low moan with every forward movement of her body, when she suddenly felt a hand placed gently on hers, and a sweet treble voice said to her, "Dear sister, the Lord has sent me to see if I can be a comfort to you."

Lisbeth paused, in a listening attitude, without removing her apron from her face. The voice was strange to her. Could it be her sister's spirit come back to her from the dead after all those years? She trembled, and dared not look.

Dinah, believing that this pause of wonder was in itself a relief for the sorrowing woman, said no more just yet, but quietly took off her bonnet, and then, motioning silence to Seth, who, on hearing her voice, had come in with a beating heart, laid one hand on the back of Lisbeth's chair, and leaned over her, that she might be aware of a friendly presence. Slowly Lisbeth drew down her apron, and timidly she opened her dim dark eyes. She saw nothing at first but a face—a pure, pale face, with loving grey eyes, and it was quite unknown to her. Her wonder increased; perhaps it *was* an angel. But in the same instant Dinah had laid her hand on Lisbeth's again, and the old woman looked down at it. It was a much smaller hand than her own, but it was not white and delicate, for Dinah had never worn a glove in her life, and her hand bore the traces of labour from her childhood upwards. Lisbeth looked earnestly at the hand for a moment, and then, fixing her eyes again on Dinah's face, said, with something of restored courage, but in a tone of surprise,

"Why, ye're a workin' woman!"

"Yes, I am Dinah Morris, and I work in the cotton-mill when I am at home."

"Ah!" said Lisbeth slowly, still wondering; "ye comed in so light, like the shadow on the wall, an' spoke i' my ear, as I thought ye might be a sperrit. Ye've got a'most the face o' one as is a-sittin' on the grave i' Adam's new Bible."

"I come from the Hall Farm now. You know Mrs. Poyser—she's my aunt, and she has heard of your great affliction, and is very sorry; and I'm come to see if I can be any help to you in your trouble; for I know your sons Adam and Seth, and I know you have no daughter; and when the clergyman told me how the hand of God was heavy upon you, my heart went out towards you, and I felt a command, to come and be to you in the place of a daughter in this grief, if you will let me."

"Ah! I know who y' are now; y' are a Methody, like Seth; he's tould me on you," said Lisbeth, fretfully, her overpowering sense of pain returning, now her wonder was gone. "Ye'll make it out as trouble's a good thing, like *he* allays does. But where's the use o' talkin' to me a-that'n? Ye canna make the smart less wi' talkin'. Ye'll ne'er make me believe as it's better for me not to ha' my old man die in's bed, if he must die, an' ha' the parson to pray by him, an' me to sit by him, an' tell him ne'er to mind th' ill words I've gi'en him sometimes when I war angered, an' to gi' him a bit an' a sup, as long as a bit an' a sup he'd swallow. But eh! to die i' the cold water, an' us close to him, an' ne'er to know; an' me a-sleepin', as if I ne'er belonged to him no more nor if he'd been a journeyman tramp from nobody knows where!"

Here Lisbeth began to cry and rock herself again; and Dinah said,

"Yes, dear friend, your affliction is great. It would be hardness of heart to say that your trouble was not heavy to bear. God didn't send me to you to make light of your sorrow, but to mourn with you, if you will let me. If you had a table spread for a feast, and was making merry with your friends, you would think it was kind to let me come and sit down and rejoice with you, because you'd think I should like to share those good things; but I should like better to share in your trouble and your labour, and it would seem harder to me if you denied me that. You won't send me away? You're not angry with me for coming?"

"Nay, nay; angered! who said I war angered? It war good on you to come. An' Seth, why donna ye get her some tay? Ye war in a hurry to get some for me, as had no need, but ye donna think o' gettin' 't for them as wants it. Sit ye down; sit ye down. I thank you kindly for comin', for it's little wage ye get by walkin' through the wet fields to see an old woman like me. . . . Nay, I'n got no daughter o' my own— ne'er had one—an' I warna sorry, for they're poor queechy things, gells is; I allays wanted to ha' lads, as could fend for theirsens. An' the lads 'ull be marryin'—I shall ha' daughters eno', an' too many. But now, do ye make the tay as ye like it for I'n got no taste i' my mouth this day —it's all one what I swaller—it's all got the taste o' sorrow wi't."

Dinah took care not to betray that she had had her tea, and accepted Lisbeth's invitation very readily, for the sake of persuading the old woman herself to take the food and drink she so much needed after a day of hard work and fasting.

Seth was so happy now Dinah was in the house that he could not help thinking her presence was worth purchasing with a life in which grief incessantly followed upon grief; but the next moment he reproached himself—it was almost as if he were rejoicing in his father's sad death. Nevertheless the joy of being with Dinah *would* triumph: it was like the influence of climate, which no resistance can overcome. And the feeling even suffused itself over his face so as to attract his mother's notice, while she was drinking her tea.

"Thee may'st well talk o' trouble bein' a good thing, Seth, for thee thriv'st on't. Thee look'st as if thee know'dst no more o' care an' cumber nor when thee wast a babby a-lyin' awake i' th' cradle. For thee'dst allays lie still wi' thy eyes open, an' Adam ne'er 'ud lie still a minute when he wakened. Thee wast allays like a bag o' meal as can ne'er be bruised—though, for the matter o' that, thy poor feyther war just such another. But *ye*'ve got the same look too" (here Lisbeth turned to Dinah). "I reckon it's wi' bein' a Methody. Not as I'm a-findin' faut wi' ye for't, for ye've no call to be frettin', an' somehow ye looken sorry too. Eh! well, if the Methodies are fond o' trouble, they're like to thrive: it's a pity they canna ha't all, an' take it away from them as donna like it. I could ha' gi'en 'em plenty; for when I'd gotten my old man I war worreted from morn till night; and now he's gone, I'd be glad for the worst o'er again."

"Yes," said Dinah, careful not to oppose any feeling of Lisbeth's, for her reliance, in her smallest words and deeds, on a divine guidance, always issued in that finest woman's tact which proceeds from acute and ready sympathy—"yes; I remember, too, when my dear aunt died, I longed for the sound of her bad cough in the nights, instead of the silence that came when she was gone. But now, dear friend, drink this other cup of tea and eat a little more."

"What!" said Lisbeth, taking the cup, and speaking in a less querulous tone, "had ye got no feyther and mother, then, as ye war so sorry about your aunt?"

"No, I never knew a father or mother; my aunt brought me up from a baby. She had no children, for she was never married, and she brought me up as tenderly as if I'd been her own child."

"Eh, she'd fine work wi' ye, I'll warrant, bringin' ye up from a babby, an' her a lone woman—it's ill bringin' up a cade lamb. But I daresay ye warna franzy, for ye look as if ye'd ne'er been angered i' your life. But what did ye do when your aunt died, an' why didna ye come to live i' this country, bein' as Mrs. Poyser's your aunt too?"

Dinah, seeing that Lisbeth's attention was attracted, told her the story of her early life—how she had been brought up to work hard, and what sort of place Snowfield was, and how many people had a hard life there —all the details that she thought likely to interest Lisbeth. The old woman listened, and forgot to be fretful, unconsciously subject to the soothing influence of Dinah's face and voice. After a while she was persuaded to let the kitchen be made tidy; for Dinah was bent on this, believing that the sense of order and quietude around her would help in disposing Lisbeth to join in the prayer she longed to pour forth at her side. Seth, meanwhile, went out to chop wood; for he surmised that Dinah would like to be left alone with his mother.

Lisbeth sat watching her as she moved about in her still quick way, and said at last, "Ye've got a notion o' cleanin' up. I wouldna mind ha'in ye for a daughter, for ye wouldna spend the lad's wage i' fine clothes an' waste. Ye're not like the lasses o' this countryside. I reckon folks is different at Snowfield from what they are here."

"They have a different sort of life, many of 'em," said Dinah; "they work at different things—some in the mill, and many in the mines, in the villages round about. But the heart of man is the same everywhere, and there are the children of this world and the children of light there as well as elsewhere. But we've many more Methodists there than in this country."

"Well, I didna know as the Methody women war like ye, for there's Will Maskery's wife, as they say's a big Methody, isna pleasant to look at, at all. I'd as lief look at a tooad. An' I'm thinkin' I wouldna mind if ye'd stay an' sleep here, for I should like to see ye i' th' house i' th' mornin'. But may-happen they'll be lookin' for ye at Mester Poyser's."

"No," said Dinah, "they don't expect me, and I should like to stay, if you'll let me."

"Well, there's room; I'n got my bed laid i' th' little room o'er the back kitchen, an' ye can lie beside me. I'd be glad to ha' ye wi' me to speak to i' th' night, for ye've got a nice way o' talkin'. It puts me i' the mind o' the swallows as was under the thack last 'ear, when they fust begun to sing low an' soft-like i' th' mornin'. Eh, but my old man war fond o' them birds! an' so war Adam, but they'n ne'er comed again this 'ear. Happen *they*'re dead too."

"There," said Dinah, "now the kitchen looks tidy, and now, dear
mother—for I'm your daughter to-night, you know—I should like you
to wash your face and have a clean cap on. Do you remember what
David did, when God took away his child from him? While the child
was yet alive he fasted and prayed to God to spare it, and he would
neither eat nor drink, but lay on the ground all night, beseeching God
for the child. But when he knew it was dead, he rose up from the ground
and washed and anointed himself, and changed his clothes, and ate and
drank; and when they asked him how it was that he seemed to have left
off grieving now the child was dead, he said, 'While the child was yet
alive, I fasted and wept; for I said, Who can tell whether God will be
gracious to me, that the child may live? But now he is dead, wherefore
should I fast? can I bring him back again? I shall go to him, but he shall
not return to me.' "

"Eh, that's a true word," said Lisbeth. "Yea, my old man wonna come
back to me, but I shall go to him—the sooner the better. Well, ye may
do as ye like wi' me: there's a clean cap i' that drawer, an' I'll go i'
the back-kitchen an' wash my face. An' Seth, thee mayst reach down
Adam's new Bible wi' th' picters in, an' she shall read us a chapter. Eh,
I like them words—'I shall go to him, but he wonna come back to me.' "

Dinah and Seth were both inwardly offering thanks for the greater
quietness of spirit that had come over Lisbeth. This was what Dinah
had been trying to bring about, through all her still sympathy and absence from exhortation. From her girlhood upwards she had had experience among the sick and the mourning, among minds hardened and
shrivelled through poverty and ignorance, and had gained the subtlest
perception of the mode in which they could best be touched, and softened into willingness to receive words of spiritual consolation or warning.
As Dinah expressed it, "she was never left to herself; but it was always
given her when to keep silence and when to speak." And do we not all
agree to call rapid thought and noble impulse by the name of inspiration? After our subtlest analysis of the mental process, we must still
say, as Dinah did, that our highest thoughts and our best deeds are all
given to us.

And so there was earnest prayer—there was faith, love, and hope
pouring itself forth that evening in the little kitchen. And poor aged
fretful Lisbeth, without grasping any distinct idea, without going through
any course of religious emotions, felt a vague sense of goodness and
love, and of something light lying underneath and beyond all this sorrowing life. She couldn't understand the sorrow; but, for these moments,
under the subduing influence of Dinah's spirit, she felt that she must
be patient and still.

CHAPTER XI

IT was but half-past four the next morning, when Dinah, tired of lying awake listening to the birds, and watching the growing light through the little window in the garret roof, rose and began to dress herself very quietly, lest she should disturb Lisbeth. But already some one else was astir in the house, and had gone down-stairs, preceded by Gyp. The dog's pattering step was a sure sign that it was Adam who went down; but Dinah was not aware of this, and she thought it was more likely to be Seth, for he had told her how Adam had stayed up working the night before. Seth, however, had only just awakened at the sound of the opening door. The exciting influence of the previous day, heightened at last by Dinah's unexpected presence, had not been counteracted by any bodily weariness, for he had not done his ordinary amount of hard work; and so when he went to bed, it was not till he had tired himself with hours of tossing wakefulness, that drowsiness came, and led on a heavier morning sleep than was usual with him.

But Adam had been refreshed by his long rest, and with his habitual impatience of mere passivity, he was eager to begin the new day, and subdue sadness by his strong will and strong arm. The white mist lay in the valley; it was going to be a bright, warm day, and he would start work again when he had had his breakfast.

"There's nothing but what's bearable as long as a man can work," he said to himself: "the natur o' things doesn't change, though it seems as if one's own life was nothing but change. The square o' four is sixteen, and you must lengthen your lever in proportion to your weight, is as true when a man's miserable as when he's happy; and the best o' working is, it gives you a grip hold o' things outside your own lot."

As he dashed the cold water over his head and face, he felt completely himself again, and with his black eyes as keen as ever, and his thick black hair all glistening with the fresh moisture, he went into the workshop to look out the wood for his father's coffin, intending that he and Seth should carry it with them to Jonathan Burge's, and have the coffin made by one of the workmen there, so that his mother might not see and hear the sad task going forward at home.

He had just gone into the workshop, when his quick ear detected a light rapid foot on the stairs—certainly not his mother's. He had been in bed and asleep when Dinah had come in, in the evening, and now he wondered whose step this could be. A foolish thought came, and moved him strangely. As if it could be Hetty! She was the last person likely to be in the house. And yet he felt reluctant to go and look, and have the clear proof that it was some one else. He stood leaning on a plank he

85

had taken hold of, listening to sounds which his imagination interpreted
for him so pleasantly, that the keen strong face became suffused with a
timid tenderness. The light footstep moved about the kitchen, followed
by the sound of the sweeping brush, hardly making so much noise as
the lightest breeze that chases the autumn leaves along the dusty path;
and Adam's imagination saw a dimpled face, with dark bright eyes and
roguish smiles, looking backward at this brush, and a rounded figure
just leaning a little to clasp the handle. A very foolish thought—it could
not be Hetty; but the only way of dismissing such nonsense from his
head was to go and see *who* it was, for his fancy only got nearer and
nearer to belief while he stood there listening. He loosed the plank, and
went to the kitchen door.

"How do you do, Adam Bede?" said Dinah, in her calm treble, pausing from her sweeping, and fixing her mild grave eyes upon him. "I trust
you feel rested and strengthened again to bear the burthen and heat of
the day."

It was like dreaming of the sunshine, and awaking in the moonlight.
Adam had seen Dinah several times, but always at the Hall Farm, where
he was not very vividly conscious of any woman's presence except
Hetty's, and he had only in the last day or two begun to suspect that
Seth was in love with her, so that his attention had not hitherto been
drawn towards her for his brother's sake. But now her slim figure, her
plain black gown, and her pale serene face, impressed him with all the
force that belongs to a reality contrasted with a preoccupying fancy.
For the first moment or two he made no answer, but looked at her with
the concentrated, examining glance which a man gives to an object in
which he has suddenly begun to be interested. Dinah, for the first time
in her life, felt a painful self-consciousness; there was something in the
dark penetrating glance of this strong man so different from the mildness and timidity of his brother Seth. A faint blush came, which deepened as she wondered at it. This blush recalled Adam from his forgetfulness.

"I was quite taken by surprise; it was very good of you to come and
see my mother in her trouble," he said, in a gentle grateful tone, for his
quick mind told him at once how she came to be there. "I hope my
mother was thankful to have you," he added, wondering rather anxiously
what had been Dinah's reception.

"Yes," said Dinah, resuming her work, "she seemed greatly comforted after a while, and she's had a good deal of rest in the night, by
times. She was fast asleep when I left her."

"Who was it took the news to the Hall Farm?" said Adam, his
thoughts reverting to some one there; he wondered whether *she* had
felt anything about it.

"It was Mr. Irwine, the clergyman, told me, and my aunt was grieved
for your mother when she heard it, and wanted me to come; and so is
my uncle, I'm sure, now he's heard it, but he was gone out to Rosseter all yesterday. They'll look for you there as soon as you've got time

to go, for there's nobody round that hearth but what's glad to see you."

Dinah, with her sympathetic divination, knew quite well that Adam was longing to hear if Hetty had said anything about their trouble; she was too rigorously truthful for benevolent invention, but she had contrived to say something in which Hetty was tacitly included. Love has a way of cheating itself consciously, like a child who plays at solitary hide-and-seek; it is pleased with assurances that it all the while disbelieves. Adam liked what Dinah had said so much that his mind was directly full of the next visit he should pay to the Hall Farm, when Hetty would perhaps behave more kindly to him than she had ever done before.

"But you won't be there yourself any longer?" he said to Dinah.

"No, I go back to Snowfield on Saturday, and I shall have to set out to Treddleston early, to be in time for the Oakbourne carrier. So I must go back to the farm to-night, that I may have the last day with my aunt and her children. But I can stay here all to-day, if your mother would like me; and her heart seemed inclined towards me last night."

"Ah, then, she's sure to want you to-day. If mother takes to people at the beginning, she's sure to get fond of 'em; but she's a strange way of not liking young women. Though, to be sure," Adam went on, smiling, "her not liking other young women is no reason why she shouldn't like you."

Hitherto Gyp had been assisting at this conversation in motionless silence, seated on his haunches, and alternately looking up in his master's face to watch its expression, and observing Dinah's movements about the kitchen. The kind smile with which Adam uttered the last words was apparently decisive with Gyp of the light in which the stranger was to be regarded, and as she turned round after putting aside her sweeping-brush, he trotted towards her, and put up his muzzle against her hand in a friendly way.

"You see Gyp bids you welcome," said Adam, "and he's very slow to welcome strangers."

"Poor dog!" said Dinah, patting the rough grey coat, "I've a strange feeling about the dumb things as if they wanted to speak, and it was a trouble to 'em because they couldn't. I can't help being sorry for the dogs always, though perhaps there's no need. But they may well have more in them than they know how to make us understand, for we can't say half what we feel, with all our words."

Seth came down now, and was pleased to find Adam talking with Dinah; he wanted Adam to know how much better she was than all other women. But after a few words of greeting, Adam drew him into the workshop to consult about the coffin, and Dinah went on with her cleaning.

By six o'clock they were all at breakfast with Lisbeth in a kitchen as clean as she could have made it herself. The window and door were open, and the morning air brought with it a mingled scent of southernwood, thyme, and sweetbriar from the patch of garden by the side of the cottage. Dinah did not sit down at first, but moved about, serving the others with the warm porridge and the toasted oat-cake, which she had got ready in the usual way, for she had asked Seth to tell her just what his mother gave them for breakfast. Lisbeth had been unusually silent since she came down-stairs, apparently requiring some time to adjust her ideas to a state of things in which she came down like a lady to find all the work done, and sat still to be waited on. Her new sensations seemed to exclude the remembrance of her grief. At last, after tasting the porridge, she broke silence:

"Ye might ha' made the parridge worse," she said to Dinah; "I can ate it wi'out it's turnin' my stomach. It might ha' been a trifle thicker an' no harm, an' I allays putten a sprig o' mint in mysen; but how's ye t' know that? The lads arena like to get folks as 'll make their parridge as I'n made it for 'em; it's well if they get onybody as 'll make parridge at all. But ye might do, wi' a bit o' showin'; for ye're a stirrin' body in a mornin', an' ye've a light heel, an' ye've cleaned th' house well enough for a ma'-shift."

"Makeshift, mother?" said Adam. "Why, I think the house looks beautiful. I don't know how it could look better."

"Thee dostna know?—nay; how's thee to know? Th' men ne'er know whether the floor's cleaned or cat-licked. But thee'lt know when thee gets thy parridge burnt, as it's like enough to be when I'n gi'en o'er makin' it. Thee'lt think thy mother war good for summat then."

"Dinah," said Seth, "do come and sit down now and have your breakfast. We're all served now."

"Ay, come an' sit ye down—do," said Lisbeth, "an' ate a morsel; ye'd need, arter bein' upo' your legs this hour an' half a'ready. Come, then," she added, in a tone of complaining affection, as Dinah sat down by her side, "I'll be loath for ye t' go, but ye canna stay much longer, I doubt. I could put up wi' ye i' th' house better nor wi' most folks."

"I'll stay till to-night if you're willing," said Dinah. "I'd stay longer, only I'm going back to Snowfield on Saturday, and I must be with my aunt to-morrow."

"Eh, I'd ne'er go back to that country. My old man come from that Stonyshire side, but he left it when he war a young un, an' i' the right on't too; for he said as there war no wood there, an' it 'ud ha' been a bad country for a carpenter."

"Ah," said Adam, "I remember father telling me when I was a little lad, that he made up his mind if ever he moved it should be south'ard. But I'm not so sure about it. Bartle Massey says—and he knows the South—as the northern men are a finer breed than the southern, harder-headed and stronger-bodied, and a deal taller. And then he says, in some o' those counties it's as flat as the back o' your hand, and you can see nothing of a distance, without climbing up the highest trees. I couldna abide that: I like to go to work by a road that'll take me up a bit of a hill, and see the fields for miles round me, and a bridge, or a town, or a bit of a steeple here and there. It makes you feel the world's a big place, and there's other men working in it with their heads and hands besides yourself."

"I like th' hills best," said Seth, "when the clouds are over your head, and you see the sun shining ever so far off, over the Loamford way, as I've often done o' late, on the stormy days: it seems to me as if that was heaven where there's always joy and sunshine, though this life's dark and cloudy."

"O, I love the Stonyshire side," said Dinah; "I shouldn't like to set my face towards the counties where they're rich in corn and cattle, and the ground so level and easy to tread; and to turn my back on the hills where the poor people have to live such a hard life, and the men spend their days in the mines away from the sunlight. It's very blessed on a bleak cold day, when the sky is hanging dark over the hill, to feel the love of God in one's soul, and carry it to the lonely, bare, stone houses where there's nothing else to give comfort."

"Eh!" said Lisbeth, "that's very well for ye to talk, as looks welly like the snowdrop-flowers as ha' lived for days an' days when I'n gethered 'em, wi' nothin' but a drop o' water an' a peep o' daylight; but th' hungry foulks had better leave th' hungry country. It makes less mouths for the scant cake. But," she went on, looking at Adam, "donna thee talk o' goin' south'ard or north'ard, an' leavin' thy feyther and mother i' the churchyard, an' goin' to a country as they know nothin' on. I'll ne'er rest i' my grave if I donna see thee i' the churchyard of a Sunday."

"Donna fear, mother," said Adam. "If I hadna made up my mind not to go, I should ha' been gone before now."

He had finished his breakfast now, and rose as he was speaking.

"What art goin' to do?" asked Lisbeth. "Set about thy feyther's coffin?"

"No, mother," said Adam; "we're going to take the wood to the village, and have it made there."

"Nay, my lad, nay," Lisbeth burst out in an eager, wailing tone; "thee wotna let nobody make thy feyther's coffin but thysen? Who'd make it so well? An' him as know'd what good work war, an's got a son as is th' head o' the village, an' all Treddles'on too, for cleverness."

"Very well, mother, if that's thy wish, I'll make the coffin at home; but I thought thee wouldstna like to hear the work going on."

"An' why shouldna I like 't? It's the right thing to be done. An' what's liking got to do wi't? It's choice o' mislikings is all I'n got i' this world. One morsel's as good as another when your mouth's out o' taste. Thee mun set about it now this mornin' fust thing. I wonna ha' nobody to touch the coffin but thee."

Adam's eyes met Seth's, which looked from Dinah to him rather wistfully.

"No, mother," he said, "I'll not consent but Seth shall have a hand in it too, if it's to be done at home. I'll go to the village this forenoon, because Mr. Burge 'ull want to see me; and Seth shall stay at home and begin the coffin. I can come back at noon, and then he can go."

"Nay, nay," persisted Lisbeth, beginning to cry, "I'n set my heart on't as thee shalt ma' thy feyther's coffin. Thee't so stiff an' masterful, thee't ne'er do as thy mother wants thee. Thee wast often angered wi' thy feyther when he war alive; thee must be the better to him, now he's gone. He'd ha' thought nothin' on't for Seth to ma's coffin."

"Say no more, Adam, say no more," said Seth, gently, though his voice told that he spoke with some effort; "mother's in the right. I'll go to work, and do thee stay at home."

He passed into the workshop immediately, followed by Adam; while Lisbeth, automatically obeying her old habits, began to put away the breakfast things, as if she did not mean Dinah to take her place any longer. Dinah said nothing, but presently used the opportunity of quietly joining the brothers in the workshop.

They had already got on their aprons and paper-caps, and Adam was standing with his left hand on Seth's shoulder, while he pointed with the hammer in his right to some boards which they were looking at. Their backs were turned towards the door by which Dinah entered, and she came in so gently that they were not aware of her presence till they heard her voice saying, "Seth Bede!" Seth started, and they both turned round. Dinah looked as if she did not see Adam, and fixed her eyes on Seth's face, saying with calm kindness,

"I won't say farewell. I shall see you again when you come from work. So as I'm at the farm before dark, it will be quite soon enough."

"Thank you, Dinah; I should like to walk home with you once more. It'll perhaps be the last time."

There was a little tremor in Seth's voice. Dinah put out her hand and said, "You'll have sweet peace in your mind to-day, Seth, for your tenderness and long-suffering towards your aged mother."

She turned round and left the workshop as quickly and quietly as she had entered it. Adam had been observing her closely all the while, but she had not looked at him. As soon as she was gone, he said,

"I don't wonder at thee for loving her, Seth. She's got a face like a lily."

Seth's soul rushed to his eyes and lips: he had never yet confessed his secret to Adam, but now he felt a delicious sense of disburthenment, as he answered,

"Ay, Addy, I do love her—too much, I doubt. But she doesna love me, lad, only as one child o' God loves another. She'll never love any man as a husband—that's my belief."

"Nay, lad, there's no telling; thee mustna lose heart. She's made out o' stuff with a finer grain than most o' the women; I can see that clear enough. But if she's better than they are in other things, I canna think she'll fall short of 'em in loving."

No more was said. Seth set out to the village, and Adam began his work on the coffin.

"God help the lad, and me too," he thought, as he lifted the board. "We're like enough to find life a tough job—hard work inside and out. It's a strange thing to think of a man as can lift a chair with his teeth, and walk fifty mile on end, trembling and turning hot and cold at only a look from one woman out of all the rest i' the world. It's a mystery we can give no account of; but no more we can of the sprouting o' the seed, for that matter."

CHAPTER XII

IN THE WOOD

THAT same Thursday morning, as Arthur Donnithorne was moving about in his dressing-room, seeing his well-looking British person reflected in the old-fashioned mirrors, and stared at, from a dingy olive-green piece of tapestry by Pharaoh's daughter and her maidens, who ought to have been minding the infant Moses, he was holding a discussion with himself, which, by the time his valet was tying the black silk sling over his shoulder, had issued in a distinct practical resolution.

"I mean to go to Eagledale and fish for a week or so," he said aloud. "I shall take you with me, Pym, and set off this morning; so be ready by half-past eleven."

The low whistle, which had assisted him in arriving at this resolution, here broke out into its loudest ringing tenor, and the corridor, as he hurried along it, echoed to his favourite song from the "Beggar's Opera," "When the heart of a man is oppressed with care." Not an heroic strain; nevertheless Arthur felt himself very heroic as he strode towards the stables to give his orders about the horses. His own approbation was necessary to him, and it was not an approbation to be enjoyed quite gratuitously; yet it must be won by a fair amount of merit. He had never yet forfeited that approbation, and he had considerable reliance on his own virtues. No young man could confess his faults more candidly; candour was one of his favorite virtues; and how can a man's candour be seen in all its lustre unless he has a few failings to talk of? But he had an agreeable confidence that his faults were all of a generous kind —impetuous, warm-blooded, leonine; never crawling, crafty, reptilian. It was not possible for Arthur Donnithorne to do anything mean, dastardly, or cruel. "No! I'm a devil of a fellow for getting myself into a hobble, but I always take care the load shall fall on my own shoulders." Unhappily there is no inherent poetical justice in hobbles, and they will sometimes obstinately refuse to inflict their worst consequences on the prime offender, in spite of his loudly-expressed wish. It was entirely owing to this deficiency in the scheme of things that Arthur had ever brought any one into trouble besides himself. He was nothing, if not good-natured; and all his pictures of the future, when he should come into the estate, were made up of a prosperous, contented tenantry,

adoring their landlord, who would be the model of an English gentleman—mansion in first-rate order, all elegance and high taste—jolly
housekeeping, finest stud in Loamshire—purse open to all public objects
—in short, everything as different as possible from what was now associated with the name of Donnithorne. And one of the first good actions
he would perform in that future should be to increase Irwine's income
for the vicarage of Hayslope, so that he might keep a carriage for his
mother and sisters. His hearty affection for the Rector dated from the
age of frocks and trousers. It was an affection partly filial, partly fraternal;—fraternal enough to make him like Irwine's company better
than that of most younger men, and filial enough to make him shrink
strongly from incurring Irwine's disapprobation.

    You perceive that Arthur Donnithorne was "a good fellow"—all his
college friends thought him such: he couldn't bear to see any one uncomfortable; he would have been sorry even in his angriest moods for
any harm to happen to his grandfather; and his aunt Lydia herself had
the benefit of that soft-heartedness which he bore towards the whole
sex. Whether he would have self-mastery enough to be always as harmless and purely beneficent as his good nature led him to desire, was a
question that no one had yet decided against him: he was but twenty-
one, you remember; and we don't inquire too closely into character in
the case of a handsome generous young fellow, who will have property
enough to support numerous peccadilloes—who, if he should unfortunately break a man's legs in his rash driving will be able to pension him
handsomely; or if he should happen to spoil a woman's existence for
her, will make it up to her with expensive *bon-bons*, packed up and
directed by his own hand. It would be ridiculous to be prying and analytic in such cases, as if one were inquiring into the character of a confidential clerk. We use round, general, gentlemanly epithets about a
young man of birth and fortune; and ladies, with that fine intuition
which is the distinguishing attribute of their sex, see at once that he is
"nice." The chances are that he will go through life without scandalising
any one; a seaworthy vessel that no one would refuse to insure. Ships,
certainly, are liable to casualties, which sometimes make terribly evident some flaw in their construction, that would never have been discov-
erable in smooth water; and many a "good fellow," through a disastrous
combination of circumstances, has undergone a like betrayal.

    But we have no fair ground for entertaining unfavourable auguries
concerning Arthur Donnithorne, who this morning proves himself capable of a prudent resolution founded on conscience. One thing is clear:
Nature has taken care that he shall never go far astray with perfect
comfort and satisfaction to himself; he will never get beyond that bor-
derland of sin, where he will be perpetually harassed by assaults from
the other side of the boundary. He will never be a courtier of Vice, and
wear her orders in his button-hole.

    It was about ten o'clock, and the sun was shining brilliantly; every-
thing was looking lovelier for the yesterday's rain. It is a pleasant thing

on such a morning to walk along the well-rolled gravel on one's way to the stables, meditating an excursion. But the scent of the stables, which, in a natural state of things, ought to be among the soothing influences of a man's life, always brought with it some irritation to Arthur. There was no having his own way in the stables; everything was managed in the stingiest fashion. His grandfather persisted in retaining as head groom an old dolt whom no sort of level could move out of his old habits, and who was allowed to hire a succession of raw Loamshire lads as his subordinates, one of whom had lately tested a new pair of shears by clipping an oblong patch on Arthur's bay mare. This state of things is naturally embittering; one can put up with annoyances in the house, but to have the stable made a scene of vexation and disgust, is a point beyond what human flesh and blood can be expected to endure long together without danger of misanthropy.

Old John's wooden, deep-wrinkled face was the first object that met Arthur's eyes as he entered the stable-yard, and it quite poisoned for him the bark of the two bloodhounds that kept watch there. He could never speak quite patiently to the old blockhead.

"You must have Meg saddled for me and brought to the door at half-past eleven, and I shall want Rattler saddled for Pym at the same time. Do you hear?"

"Yes, I hear, I hear, Cap'n," said old John, very deliberately, following the young master into the stable. John considered a young master as the natural enemy of an old servant, and young people in general as a poor contrivance for carrying on the world.

Arthur went in for the sake of patting Meg, declining as far as possible to see anything in the stables, lest he should lose his temper before breakfast. The pretty creature was in one of the inner stables, and turned her mild head as her master came beside her. Little Trot, a tiny spaniel, her inseparable companion in the stable, was comfortably curled up on her back.

"Well, Meg, my pretty girl," said Arthur, patting her neck, "we'll have a glorious canter this morning."

"Nay, your honour, I donna see as that can be," said John.

"Not be? Why not?"

"Why, she's got lamed."

"Lamed, confound you! what do you mean?"

"Why, th' lad took her too close to Dalton's hosses, an' one on 'em flung out at her, an' she's got her shank bruised o' the near foreleg."

The judicious historian abstains from narrating precisely what ensued. You understand that there was a great deal of strong language, mingled with soothing "who-ho's" while the leg was examined; that John stood by with quite as much emotion as if he had been a cunningly-carved crab-tree walking-stick, and that Arthur Donnithorne presently repassed the iron gates of the pleasure-ground without singing as he went.

He considered himself thoroughly disappointed and annoyed. There

was not another mount in the stable for himself and his servant besides
Meg and Rattler. It was vexatious; just when he wanted to get out of
the way for a week or two. It seemed culpable in Providence to allow
such a combination of circumstances. To be shut up at the Chase with
a broken arm, when every other fellow in his regiment was enjoying
himself at Windsor—shut up with his grandfather, who had the same
sort of affection for him as for his parchment deeds! And to be disgusted at every turn with the management of the house and the estate!
In such circumstances a man necessarily gets in an ill humour, and
works off the irritation by some excess or other. "Salkeld would have
drunk a bottle of port every day," he muttered to himself; "but I'm not
well seasoned enough for that. Well, since I can't go to Eagledale, I'll
have a gallop on Rattler to Norburne this morning, and lunch with
Gawaine."

Behind this explicit resolution there lay an implicit one. If he lunched
with Gawaine and lingered chatting, he should not reach the Chase
again till nearly five, when Hetty would be safe out of his sight in the
housekeeper's room; and when she set out to go home, it would be his
lazy time after dinner, so he should keep out of her way altogether. There
really would have been no harm in being kind to the little thing, and
it was worth dancing with a dozen ballroom belles only to look at Hetty
for half an hour. But perhaps he had better not take any more notice
of her; it might put notions into her head, as Irwine had hinted; though
Arthur, for his part, thought girls were not by any means so soft and
easily bruised; indeed, he had generally found them twice as cool and
cunning as he was himself. As for any real harm in Hetty's case, it was
out of the question: Arthur Donnithorne accepted his own bond for
himself with perfect confidence.

So the twelve o'clock sun saw him galloping towards Norburne; and
by good fortune Halsell Common lay in his road, and gave him some
fine leaps for Rattler. Nothing like "taking" a few bushes and ditches
for exorcising a demon; and it is really astonishing that the Centaurs,
with their immense advantages in this way, have left so bad a reputation in history.

After this, you will perhaps be surprised to hear, that although Gawaine was at home, the hand of the dial in the courtyard had scarcely
cleared the last stroke of three, when Arthur returned through the en-
trance-gates, got down from the panting Rattler, and went into the
house to take a hasty luncheon. But I believe there have been men since
his day who have ridden a long way to avoid a rencontre, and then galloped hastily back lest they should miss it. It is the favourite stratagem
of our passions to sham a retreat, and to turn sharp round upon us at
the moment we have made up our minds that the day is our own.

"The Cap'n's been ridin' the devil's own pace," said Dalton the coachman, whose person stood out in high relief as he smoked his pipe against
the stable wall, when John brought up Rattler.

"An' I wish he'd get the devil to do's grooming for'n," growled John.

"Ay; he'd hev a deal haimabler groom nor what he has now," observed Dalton; and the joke appeared to him so good, that, being left alone upon the scene, he continued at intervals to take his pipe from his mouth in order to wink at an imaginary audience, and shake luxuriously with a silent, ventral laughter; mentally rehearsing the dialogue from the beginning, that he might recite it with effect in the servants' hall.

When Arthur went up to his dressing-room again after luncheon, it was inevitable that the debate he had had with himself there earlier in the day should flash across his mind; but it was impossible for him now to dwell on the remembrance—impossible to recall the feelings and reflections which had been decisive with him then, any more than to recall the peculiar scent of the air that had freshened him when he first opened his window. The desire to see Hetty had rushed back like an ill-stemmed current; he was amazed himself at the force with which this trivial fancy seemed to grasp him: he was even rather tremulous as he brushed his hair—pooh! it was riding in that breakneck way. It was because he had made a serious affair of an idle matter, by thinking of it as if were of any consequence. He would amuse himself by seeing Hetty to-day, and get rid of the whole thing from his mind. It was all Irwine's fault. "If Irwine had said nothing, I shouldn't have thought half so much of Hetty as of Meg's lameness." However, it was just the sort of day for lolling in the Hermitage, and he would go and finish Dr. Moore's *Zeluco* there before dinner. The Hermitage stood in Fir-tree Grove—the way Hetty was sure to come in walking from the Hall Farm. So nothing could be simpler and more natural: meeting Hetty was a mere circumstance of his walk, not its object.

Arthur's shadow flitted rather faster among the sturdy oaks of the Chase than might have been expected from the shadow of a tired man on a warm afternoon, and it was still scarcely four o'clock when he stood before the tall narrow gate leading into the delicious labyrinthine wood which skirted one side of the Chase, and which was called Fir-tree Grove, not because the firs were many, but because they were few. It was a wood of beeches and limes, with here and there a light, silver-stemmed birch—just the sort of wood most haunted by the nymphs: you see their white sunlit limbs gleaming athwart the boughs, or peeping from behind the smooth-sweeping outline of a tall lime; you hear their soft liquid laughter—but if you look with a too curious sacrilegious eye, they vanish behind the silvery beeches, they make you believe that their voice was only a running brooklet, perhaps they metamorphose themselves into a tawny squirrel that scampers away and mocks you from the topmost bough. It was not a grove with measured grass or rolled gravel for you to tread upon, but with narrow, hollow-shaped, earthy paths, edged with faint dashes of delicate moss—paths which look as if they were made by the free-will of the trees and underwood, moving reverently aside to look at the tall queen of the white-footed nymphs.

It was along the broadest of these paths that Arthur Donnithorne passed, under an avenue of limes and beeches. It was a still afternoon— the golden light was lingering languidly among the upper boughs, only glancing down here and there on the purple pathway and its edge of faintly-sprinkled moss: an afternoon in which destiny disguises her cold awful face behind a hazy radiant veil, encloses us in warm downy wings, and poisons us with violet-scented breath. Arthur strolled along carelessly, with a book under his arm, but not looking on the ground as meditative men are apt to do; his eyes *would* fix themselves on the distant bend in the road, round which a little figure must surely appear before long. Ah! there she comes: first a bright patch of colour, like a tropic bird among the boughs, then a tripping figure, with a round hat on, and a small basket under her arm; then a deep-blushing, almost frightened, but bright-smiling girl, making her curtsy with a fluttered yet happy glance, as Arthur came up to her. If Arthur had had time to think at all, he would have thought it strange that he should feel fluttered too, be conscious of blushing too—in fact, look and feel as foolish as if he had been taken by surprise instead of meeting just what he expected. Poor things! It was a pity they were not in that golden age of childhood when they would have stood face to face, eyeing each other with timid liking, then given each other a little butterfly kiss, and toddled off to play together. Arthur would have gone home to his silk-curtained cot, and Hetty to her home-spun pillow, and both would have slept without dreams, and to-morrow would have been a life hardly conscious of a yesterday.

Arthur turned round and walked by Hetty's side without giving a reason. They were alone together for the first time. What an overpowering presence that first privacy is! He actually dared not look at this little buttermaker for the first minute or two. As for Hetty, her feet rested on a cloud, and she was borne along by warm zephyrs; she had forgotten her rose-coloured ribbons; she was no more conscious of her limbs than if her childish soul had passed into a water-lily resting on a liquid bed, and warmed by the midsummer sunbeams. It may seem a contradiction, but Arthur gathered a certain carelessness and confidence from his timidity: it was an entirely different state of mind from what he had expected in such a meeting with Hetty; and full as he was of vague feeling, there was room, in those moments of silence, for the thought that his previous debates and scruples were needless.

"You are quite right to choose this way of coming to the Chase," he said at last, looking down at Hetty, "it is so much prettier as well as shorter than coming by either of the lodges."

"Yes, sir," Hetty answered, with a tremulous, almost whispering voice. She didn't know one bit how to speak to a gentleman like Mr. Arthur, and her very vanity made her more coy of speech.

"Do you come every week to see Mrs. Pomfret?"

"Yes, sir, every Thursday, only when she's got to go out with Miss Donnithorne."

"And she's teaching you something, is she?"

"Yes, sir, the lace-mending as she learnt abroad, and the stocking mending—it looks just like the stocking, you can't tell it's been mended; and she teaches me cutting-out too."

"What, are *you* going to be a lady's-maid?"

"I should like to be one very much indeed." Hetty spoke more audibly now, but still rather tremulously; she thought, perhaps she seemed as stupid to Captain Donnithorne as Luke Britton did to her.

"I suppose Mrs. Pomfret always expects you at this time?"

"She expects me at four o'clock. I'm rather late to-day, because my aunt couldn't spare me; but the regular time is four, because that gives us time before Miss Donnithorne's bell rings."

"Ah, then, I must not keep you now, else I should like to show you the Hermitage. Did you ever see it?"

"No, sir."

"This is the walk where we turn up to it. But we must not go now. I'll show it you some other time, if you'd like to see it."

"Yes, please, sir."

"Do you always come back this way in the evening, or are you afraid to come so lonely a road?"

"O no, sir, it's never late; I always set out by eight o'clock, and it's so light now in the evening. My aunt would be angry with me if I didn't get home before nine."

"Perhaps Craig, the gardener, comes to take care of you?"

A deep blush overspread Hetty's face and neck. "I'm sure he doesn't; I'm sure he never did; I wouldn't let him; I don't like him," she said hastily, and the tears of vexation had come so fast, that before she had done speaking a bright drop rolled down her hot cheek. Then she felt ashamed to death that she was crying, and for one long instant her happiness was all gone. But in the next she felt an arm steal round her, and a gentle voice said,

"Why, Hetty, what makes you cry? I didn't mean to vex you. I wouldn't vex you for the world, you little blossom. Come, don't cry; look at me, else I shall think you won't forgive me."

Arthur had laid his hand on the soft arm that was nearest to him, and was stooping towards Hetty with a look of coaxing entreaty. Hetty lifted her long dewy lashes, and met the eyes that were bent towards her with a sweet, timid, beseeching look. What a space of time those three moments were, while their eyes met and his arms touched her! Love is such a simple thing when we have only one-and-twenty summers and a sweet girl of seventeen trembles under our glance, as if she were a bud first opening her heart with wondering rapture to the morning. Such young unfurrowed souls roll to meet each other like two velvet peaches that touch softly and are at rest; they mingle as easily as two brooklets that ask for nothing but to entwine themselves and ripple with ever-interlacing curves in the leafiest hiding-places. While Arthur gazed into Hetty's dark beseeching eyes, it made no

difference to him what sort of English she spoke; and even if hoops
and powder had been in fashion, he would very likely not have been
sensible just then that Hetty wanted those signs of high breeding.

But they started asunder with beating hearts: something had fallen
on the ground with a rattling noise; it was Hetty's basket; all her little
workwoman's matters were scattered on the path, some of them showing a capability of rolling to great lengths. There was much to be
done in picking up, and not a word was spoken; but when Arthur hung
the basket over her arm again, the poor child felt a strange difference
in his look and manner. He just pressed her hand, and said, with a look
and tone that were almost chilling to her,

"I have been hindering you; I must not keep you any longer now.
You will be expected at the house. Good-by."

Without waiting for her to speak, he turned away from her and hurried back towards the road that led to the Hermitage, leaving Hetty
to pursue her way in a strange dream, that seemed to have begun in
bewildering delight, and was now passing into contrarieties and sadness. Would he meet her again as she came home? Why had he spoken
almost as if he were displeased with her? and then run away so suddenly? She cried, hardly knowing why.

Arthur too was very uneasy, but his feelings were lit up for him by a
more distinct consciousness. He hurried to the Hermitage, which stood
in the heart of the wood, unlocked the door with a hasty wrench,
slammed it after him, pitched *Zeluco* into the most distant corner, and,
thrusting his right hand into his pocket, first walked four or five times
up and down the scanty length of the little room, and then seated himself on the ottoman in an uncomfortable stiff way, as we often do when
we wish not to abandon ourselves to feeling.

He was getting in love with Hetty—that was quite plain. He was
ready to pitch everything else—no matter where—for the sake of sur-
rendering himself to this delicious feeling which had just disclosed itself.
It was no use blinking the fact now—they would get too fond of each
other, if he went on taking notice of her—and what would come of
it? He should have to go away in a few weeks, and the poor little thing
would be miserable. He *must not* see her alone again; he must keep
out of her way. What a fool he was for coming back from Gawaine's!

He got up and threw open the windows, to let in the soft breath of
the afternoon, and the healthy scent of the firs that made a belt round
the Hermitage. The soft air did not help his resolutions, as he leaned out
and looked into the leafy distance. But he considered his resolution
sufficiently fixed: there was no need to debate with himself any longer.
He had made up his mind not to meet Hetty again; and now he might
give himself up to thinking how immensely agreeable it would be if
circumstances were different—how pleasant it would have been to meet
her this evening as she came back, and put his arm round her again
and look into her sweet face. He wondered if the dear little thing were
thinking of him too—twenty to one she was. How beautiful her eyes

were with the tear on their lashes! He would like to satisfy his soul for a day with looking at them, and he *must* see her again:—he must see her, simply to remove any false impression from her mind about his manner to her just now. He would behave in a quiet, kind way to her —just to prevent her from going home with her head full of wrong fancies. Yes, that would be the best thing to do after all.

It was a long while—more than an hour—before Arthur had brought his meditations to this point; but once arrived there, he could stay no longer at the Hermitage. The time must be filled up with movement until he should see Hetty again. And it was already late enough to go and dress for dinner, for his grandfather's dinner-hour was six.

CHAPTER XIII

EVENING IN THE WOOD

It happened that Mrs. Pomfret had had a slight quarrel with Mrs. Best, the housekeeper, on this Thursday morning—a fact which had two consequences highly convenient to Hetty. It caused Mrs. Pomfret to have tea sent up to her own room, and it inspired that exemplary lady's-maid with so lively a recollection of former passages in Mrs. Best's conduct, and of dialogues in which Mrs. Best had decidedly the inferiority as an interlocutor with Mrs. Pomfret, that Hetty required no more presence of mind than was demanded for using her needle, and throwing in an occasional "yes" or "no." She would have wanted to put on her hat earlier than usual; only she had told Captain Donnithorne that she usually set out about eight o'clock, and if he *should* go to the Grove again expecting to see her, and she should be gone! Would he come? Her little butterfly-soul fluttered incessantly between memory and dubious expectation. At last the minute-hand of the old-fashioned brazen-faced timepiece was on the last quarter to eight, and there was every reason for its being time to get ready for departure. Even Mrs. Pomfret's preoccupied mind did not prevent her from noticing what looked like a new flush of beauty in the little thing as she tied on her hat before the looking-glass.

"That child gets prettier and prettier every day, I do believe," was her inward comment. "The more's the pity. She'll get neither a place nor a husband any the sooner for it. Sober well-to-do men don't like such pretty wives. When I was a girl, I was more admired than if I had been so very pretty. However, she's reason to be grateful to me for teaching her something to get her bread with, better than farmhouse work. They always told me I was good-natured—and that's the truth, and to my hurt, too, else there's them in this house that wouldn't be here now to lord it over me in the housekeeper's room."

Hetty walked hastily across the short space of pleasure-ground which she had to traverse. dreading to meet Mr. Craig, to whom she could hardly have spoken civilly. How relieved she was when she had got safely under the oaks and among the fern of the Chase! Even then she was as ready to be startled as the deer that leaped away at her approach. She thought nothing of the evening light that lay gently in the grassy alleys between the fern, and made the beauty of their living green more visible than it had been in the overpowering flood of noon: she thought of nothing that was present. She only saw something that was possible: Mr. Arthur Donnithorne coming to meet her again along the Fir-tree Grove. That was the foreground of Hetty's picture; behind it lay a bright hazy something—days that were not to be as the other days of her life had been. It was as if she had been wooed by a river-god, who might any time take her to his wondrous halls below a watery heaven. There was no knowing what would come, since this strange entrancing delight had come. If a chest full of lace and satin and jewels had been sent her from some unknown source, how could she but have thought that her whole lot was going to change, and that to-morrow some still more bewildering joy would befall her? Hetty had never read a novel; if she had ever seen one, I think the words would have been too hard for her: how then could she find a shape for her expectations? They were as formless as the sweet languid odours of the garden at the Chase, which had floated past her as she walked by the gate.

She is at another gate now—that leading into Fir-tree Grove. She enters the wood, where it is already twilight, and at every step she takes, the fear at her heart becomes colder. If he should not come! O how dreary it was—the thought of going out at the other end of the wood, into the unsheltered road, without having seen him. She reaches the first turning towards the Hermitage, walking slowly—he is not there. She hates the leveret that runs across the path: she hates everything that is not what she longs for. She walks on, happy whenever she is coming to a bend in the road, for perhaps he is behind it. No. She is beginning to cry: her heart has swelled so, the tears stand in her eyes; she gives one great sob, while the corners of her mouth quiver, and the tears roll down.

She doesn't know that there is another turning to the Hermitage, that she is close against it, and that Arthur Donnithorne is only a few yards from her, full of one thought, and a thought of which she only is the object. He is going to see Hetty again: that is the longing which has been growing through the last three hours to a feverish thirst. Not, of course, to speak in the caressing way into which he had unguardedly fallen before dinner, but to set things right with her by a kindness which would have the air of friendly civility, and prevent her from running away with wrong notions about their mutual relation.

If Hetty had known he was there, she would not have cried; and it would have been better, for then Arthur would perhaps have behaved as wisely as he had intended. As it was, she started when he appeared at the end of the side-alley, and looked up at him with two great drops rolling down her cheeks. What else could he do but speak to her in a soft, soothing tone, as if she were a bright-eyed spaniel with a thorn in her foot?

"Has something frightened you, Hetty? Have you seen anything in the wood? Don't be frightened—I'll take care of you now."

Hetty was blushing so, she didn't know whether she was happy or miserable. To be crying again—what did gentlemen think of girls who cried in that way? She felt unable even to say "no," but could only look away from him, and wipe the tears from her cheek. Not before a great drop had fallen on her rose-coloured strings: she knew that quite well.

"Come, be cheerful again. Smile at me, and tell me what's the matter. Come, tell me."

Hetty turned her head towards him, whispered, "I thought you wouldn't come," and slowly got courage to lift her eyes to him. That look was too much: he must have had eyes of Egyptian granite not to look too lovingly in return.

"You little frightened bird! little tearful rose! silly pet! You won't cry again, now I'm with you, will you?"

Ah, he doesn't know in the least what he is saying. This is not what he meant to say. His arm is stealing round the waist again, it is tightening its clasp; he is bending his face nearer and nearer to the round cheek, his lips are meeting those pouting child-lips, and for a long moment time has vanished. He may be a shepherd in Arcadia for aught he knows, he may be the first youth kissing the first maiden, he may be Eros himself, sipping the lips of Psyche—it is all one.

There was no speaking for minutes after. They walked along with beating hearts till they came within sight of the gate at the end of the wood. Then they looked at each other, not quite as they had looked before, for in their eyes there was the memory of a kiss.

But already something bitter had begun to mingle itself with the fountain of sweets: already Arthur was uncomfortable. He took his arm from Hetty's waist, and said,

"Here we are, almost at the end of the Grove. I wonder how late it is," he added, pulling out his watch. "Twenty minutes past eight—but my watch is too fast. However, I'd better not go any farther now. Trot along quickly with your little feet, and get home safely. Good-by."

He took her hand, and looked at her half sadly, half with a constrained smile. Hetty's eyes seemed to beseech him not to go away yet; but he patted her cheek and said "Good-by" again. She was obliged to turn away from him, and go on.

As for Arthur, he rushed back through the wood, as if he wanted to put a wide space between himself and Hetty. He would not go to the Hermitage again; he remembered how he had debated with himself there before dinner, and it had all come to nothing—worse than nothing. He walked right on into the Chase, glad to get out of the Grove, which surely was haunted by his evil genius. Those beeches and smooth limes —there was something enervating in the very sight of them; but the strong knotted old oaks had no bending languor in them—the sight of them would give a man some energy. Arthur lost himself among the narrow openings in the fern, winding about without seeking any issue, till the twilight deepened almost to night under the great boughs, and the hare looked black as it darted across his path.

He was feeling much more strongly than he had done in the morning: it was as if his horse had wheeled round from a leap, and dared to dispute his mastery. He was dissatisfied with himself, irritated, mortified. He no sooner fixed his mind on the probable consequences of giving way to the emotions which had stolen over him to-day—of continuing to notice Hetty, of allowing himself any opportunity for such slight caresses as he had been betrayed into already—than he refused to believe such a future possible for himself. To flirt with Hetty was a very different affair from flirting with a pretty girl of his own station: that was understood to be an amusement on both sides; or, if it became serious, there was no obstacle to marriage. But this little thing would be spoken ill of directly, if she happened to be seen walking with him; and then those excellent people, the Poysers, to whom a good name was as precious as if they had the best blood in the land in their veins— he should hate himself if he made a scandal of that sort, on the estate that was to be his own some day, and among tenants by whom he liked, above all, to be respected. He could no more believe that he should so fall in his own esteem than that he should break both his legs and go on crutches all the rest of his life. He couldn't imagine himself in that position; it was too odious, too unlike him.

And even if no one knew anything about it, they might get too fond of each other, and then there could be nothing but the misery of parting, after all. No gentleman, out of a ballad, could marry a farmer's niece. There must be an end to the whole thing at once. It was too foolish.

And yet he had been so determined this morning, before he went to Gawaine's; and while he was there something had taken hold of him and made him gallop back. It seemed he couldn't quite depend on his own resolution, as he had thought he could: he almost wished his arm would get painful again, and then he should think of nothing but the comfort it would be to get rid of the pain. There was no knowing what impulse might seize him to-morrow, in this confounded place, where there was nothing to occupy him imperiously through the live-long day. What could he do to secure himself from any more of this folly?

There was but one resource. He would go and tell Irwine—tell him everything. The mere act of telling it would make it seem trivial; the temptation would vanish, as the charm of fond words vanishes when one repeats them to the indifferent. In every way it would help him, to tell Irwine. He would ride to Broxton Rectory the first thing after breakfast to-morrow.

Arthur had no sooner come to this determination than he began to think which of the paths would lead him home, and made as short a walk thither as he could. He felt sure he should sleep now: he had had enough to tire him, and there was no more need for him to think.

CHAPTER XIV

THE RETURN HOME

WHILE that parting in the wood was happening, there was a parting in the cottage too, and Lisbeth had stood with Adam at the door, straining her aged eyes to get the last glimpse of Seth and Dinah, as they mounted the opposite slope.

"Eh, I'm loath to see the last on her," she said to Adam, as they turned into the house again. "I'd ha' been willin' t' ha' her about me till I died and went to lie by my old man. She'd make it easier dyin'—she spakes so gentle an' moves about so still. I could be fast sure that pictur was drawed for her i' thy new Bible—th' angel a-sittin' on the big stone by the grave. Eh, I wouldna mind ha'in a daughter like that; but nobody ne'er marries them as is good for aught."

"Well, mother, I hope thee *wilt* have her for a daughter; for Seth's got a liking for her, and I hope she'll get a liking for Seth in time."

"Where's the use o' talkin' a-that'n? She caresna for Seth. She's goin' away twenty mile aff. How's she to get a likin' for him, I'd like to know? No more nor the cake 'ull come wi'out the leaven. Thy figurin' books might ha' tould thee better nor that, I should think, else thee mightst as well read the commin print, as Seth allays does."

"Nay, mother," said Adam, laughing, "the figures tell us a fine deal, and we couldn't go far without 'em, but they don't tell us about folks' feelings. It's a nicer job to calculate *them*. But Seth's as good-hearted a lad as ever handled a tool, and plenty o' sense, and good-looking too; and he's got the same way o' thinking as Dinah. He deserves to win her, though there's no denying she's a rare bit o' workmanship. You don't see such women turned off the wheel every day."

"Eh, thee't allays stick up for thy brother. Thee'st been just the same, e'er sin' ye war little uns together. Thee wart allays for halving iverything wi' him. But what's Seth got to do with marryin', as is on'y three-an'-twenty? He'd more need to learn an' lay by sixpence. An' as for his desarving her—she's two 'ear older nor Seth: she's pretty near as old as thee. But that's the way; folks mun allays choose by contrairies, as if they must be sorted like the pork—a bit o' good meat wi' a bit o' offal."

To the feminine mind in some of its moods, all things that might be, receive a temporary charm from comparison with what is; and since Adam did not want to marry Dinah himself, Lisbeth felt rather peevish on that score—as peevish as she would have been if he *had* wanted to marry her, and so shut himself out from Mary Burge and the partnership as effectually as by marrying Hetty.

It was more than half-past eight when Adam and his mother were talking in this way, so that when, about ten minutes later, Hetty reached the turning of the lane that led to the farmyard gate, she saw Dinah and Seth approaching it from the opposite direction, and waited for them to come up to her. They, too, like Hetty, had lingered a little in their walk, for Dinah was trying to speak words of comfort and strength to Seth in these parting moments. But when they saw Hetty, they paused and shook hands: Seth turned homewards, and Dinah came on alone.

"Seth Bede would have come and spoken to you, my dear," she said, as she reached Hetty, "but he's very full of trouble to-night."

Hetty answered with a dimpled smile, as if she did not quite know what had been said; and it made a strange contrast to see that sparkling self-engrossed loveliness looked at by Dinah's calm pitying face, with its open glance which told that her heart lived in no cherished secrets of its own, but in feelings which it longed to share with all the world. Hetty liked Dinah as well as she had ever liked any woman; how was it possible to feel otherwise towards one who always put in a kind word for her when her aunt was finding fault, and who was always ready to take Totty off her hands—little tiresome Totty, that was made such a pet of by every one, and that Hetty could see no interest in at all? Dinah had never said anything disapproving or reproachful to Hetty during her whole visit to the Hall Farm; she had talked to her a great deal in a serious way, but Hetty didn't mind that much, for she never listened: whatever Dinah might say, she almost always stroked Hetty's cheek after it, and wanted to do some mending for her. Dinah was a riddle to her; Hetty looked at her much in the same way as one might imagine a little perching bird that could only flutter from bough to bough, to look at the swoop of the swallow or the mounting of the lark; but she did not care to solve such riddles, any more than she cared to know what was meant by the pictures in the "Pilgrim's Progress," or in the old folio Bible that Marty and Tommy always plagued her about on a Sunday.

Dinah took her hand now and drew it under her own arm.

"You look very happy to-night, dear child," she said. "I shall think of you often when I'm at Snowfield, and see your face before me as it is now. It's a strange thing—sometimes when I'm quite alone, sitting in my room with my eyes closed, or walking over the hills, the people I've seen and known, if it's only been for a few days, are brought before me, and I hear their voices and see them look and move almost plainer than I ever did when they were really with me so as I could touch them. And then my heart is drawn out towards them, and I feel their lot as if it was my own, and I take comfort in spreading it before the Lord and resting in His love, on their behalf as well as my own. And so I feel sure you will come before me."

She paused a moment, but Hetty said nothing.

"It has been a very precious time to me," Dinah went on, "last night and to-day—seeing two such good sons as Adam and Seth Bede. They are so tender and thoughtful for their aged mother. And she has been telling me what Adam has done, for these many years, to help his father and his brother; it's wonderful what a spirit of wisdom and knowledge he has, and how he's ready to use it all in behalf of them that are feeble. And I'm sure he has a loving spirit too. I've noticed it often among my own people around Snowfield, that the strong, skilful men are often the gentlest to the women and children; and it's pretty to see 'em carrying the little babies as if they were no heavier than little birds. And the babies always seem to like the strong arm best. I feel sure it would be so with Adam Bede. Don't you think so, Hetty?"

"Yes," said Hetty, abstractedly, for her mind had been all the while in the wood, and she would have found it difficult to say what she was assenting to. Dinah saw she was not inclined to talk, but there would not have been time to say much more, for they were now at the yard-gate.

The still twilight, with its dying western red, and its few faint struggling stars, rested on the farmyard, where there was not a sound to be heard but the stamping of the cart-horses in the stable. It was about twenty minutes after sunset: the fowls were all gone to roost, and the bull-dog lay stretched on the straw outside his kennel, with the black-and-tan terrier by his side, when the falling-to of the gate disturbed them, and set them barking, like good officials, before they had any distinct knowledge of the reason.

The barking had its effect in the house, for, as Dinah and Hetty approached, the doorway was filled by a portly figure, with a ruddy black-eyed face, which bore in it the possibility of looking extremely acute, and occasionally contemptuous, on market-days, but had now a predominant after-supper expression of hearty good-nature. It is well known that great scholars who have shown the most pitiless acerbity in their criticism of other men's scholarship, have yet been of a relenting and indulgent temper in private life; and I have heard of a learned man meekly rocking the twins in the cradle with his left hand, while with his right he inflicted the most lacerating sarcasms on an opponent who had betrayed a brutal ignorance of Hebrew. Weaknesses and errors must be forgiven—alas! they are not alien to us—but the man who takes the wrong side on the momentous subject of the Hebrew points must be treated as the enemy of his race. There was the same sort of antithetic mixture in Martin Poyser: he was of so excellent a disposition that he had been kinder and more respectful than ever to his old father since he had made a deed of gift of all his property, and no man judged his neighbours more charitably on all personal matters; but for a farmer, like Luke Britton, for example, whose fallows were not well cleaned, who didn't know the rudiments of hedging and ditching, and showed but a small share of judgment in the purchase of winter stock, Martin Poyser was as hard and implacable as the north-east wind. Luke Britton could not make a remark, even on the weather, but Martin

Poyser detected in it a taint of that unsoundness and general ignorance which was palpable in all his farming operations. He hated to see the fellow lift the pewter pint to his mouth in the bar of the Royal George on market-day, and the mere sight of him on the other side of the road brought a severe and critical expression into his black eyes, as different as possible from the fatherly glance he bent on his two nieces as they approached the door. Mr. Poyser had smoked his evening pipe, and now held his hands in his pockets, as the only resource of a man who continues to sit up after the day's business is done.

"Why, lasses, ye'er rather late to-night," he said, when they reached the little gate leading into the causeway. "The mother's begun to fidget about you, an' she's got the little un ill. An' how did you leave the old woman Bede, Dinah? Is she much down about the old man? He'd been but a poor bargain to her this five year."

"She's been greatly distressed for the loss of him," said Dinah; "but she's seemed more comforted to-day. Her son Adam's been at home all day, working at his father's coffin, and she loves to have him at home. She's been talking about him to me almost all the day. She has a loving heart, though she's sorely given to fret and be fearful. I wish she had a surer trust to comfort her in her old age."

"Adam's sure enough," said Mr. Poyser, misunderstanding Dinah's wish. "There's no fear but he'll yield well i' the threshing. He's not one o' them as is all straw and no grain. I'll be bond for him any day, as he'll be a good son to the last. Did he say he'd be coming to see us soon? But come in, come in," he added, making way for them; "I hadn't need keep y' out any longer."

The tall buildings round the yard shut out a good deal of the sky, but the large window let in abundant light to show every corner of the house-place.

Mrs. Poyser, seated in the rocking-chair, which had been brought out of the "right-hand parlour," was trying to soothe Totty to sleep. But Totty was not disposed to sleep; and when her cousins entered, she raised herself up, and showed a pair of flushed cheeks, which looked fatter than ever now they were defined by the edge of her linen night-cap.

In the large wicker-bottomed arm-chair in the left-hand chimney-nook sat old Martin Poyser, a hale but shrunken and bleached image of his portly black-haired son—his head hanging forward a little, and his elbows pushed backward so as to allow the whole of his forearm to rest on the arm of the chair. His blue handkerchief was spread over his knees, as was usual in-doors, when it was not hanging over his head; and he sat watching what went forward with the quiet *outward* glance of healthy old age, which, disengaged from any interest in an inward drama, spies out pins upon the floor, follows one's minutest motions with an unexpected purposeless tenacity, watches the flickering of the flame or the sun-gleams on the wall, counts the quarries on the floor, watches even the hand of the clock, and pleases itself with detecting a, rhythm in the tick.

"What a time o' night this is to come home, Hetty," said Mrs. Poyser. "Look at the clock, do; why, it's going on for half-past nine, and I've sent the gells to bed this half-hour, and late enough too; when they've got to get up at half after four, and the mowers' bottles to fill, and the baking; and here's this blessed child wi' the fever for what I know, and as wakeful as if it was dinner-time, and nobody to help me to give her the physic but your uncle, and fine work there's been, and half of it spilt on her night-gown—it's well if she's swallowed more nor 'ull make her worse instead o' better. But folks as have no mind to be o' use have allays the luck to be out o' the road when there's anything to be done."

"I did set out before eight, aunt," said Hetty, in a pettish tone, with a slight toss of her head. "But this clock's so much before the clock at the Chase, there's no telling what time it'll be when I get here."

"What! you'd be wanting the clock set by gentle-folks's time, would you? an' sit up burnin' candle, an' lie a-bed wi' the sun a-bakin' you like a cowcumber i' the frame? The clock hasn't been put forrard for the first time to-day, I reckon."

The fact was, Hetty had really forgotten the difference of the clocks when she told Captain Donnithorne that she set out at eight, and this, with her lingering pace, had made her nearly half an hour later than usual. But here her aunt's attention was diverted from this tender subject by Totty, who, perceiving at length that the arrival of her cousins was not likely to bring anything satisfactory to her in particular, began to cry, "Munny, munny," in an explosive manner.

"Well, then, my pet, mother's got her, mother won't leave her; Totty be a good dilling, and go to sleep now," said Mrs. Poyser, leaning back and rocking the chair, while she tried to make Totty nestle against her. But Totty only cried louder, and said, "Don't yock!" So the mother, with that wondrous patience which love gives to the quickest temperament, sat up again, and pressed her cheek against the linen night-cap and kissed it, and forgot to scold Hetty any longer.

"Come, Hetty," said Martin Poyser, in a conciliatory tone, "go and get your supper i' the pantry, as the things are all put away; an' then you can come an' take the little un while your aunt undresses herself, for she won't lie down in bed without her mother. An' I reckon *you* could eat a bit, Dinah, for they don't keep much of a house down there."

"No, thank you, uncle," said Dinah; "I ate a good meal before I came away, for Mrs. Bede would make a kettle-cake for me."

"I don't want any supper," said Hetty, taking off her hat. "I can hold Totty now, if aunt wants me."

"Why, what nonsense that is to talk!" said Mrs. Poyser. "Do you think you can live wi'out eatin', an' nourish your inside wi' stickin' red ribbons on your head? Go an' get your supper this minute, child; there's a nice bit o' cold pudding i' the safe—just what you're fond of."

Hetty complied silently by going towards the pantry, and Mrs. Poyser went on speaking to Dinah.

"Sit down, my dear, an' look as if you knowed what it was to make yourself a bit comfortable i' the world. I warrant the old woman was glad to see you, since you stayed so long."

"She seemed to like having me there at last; but her sons say she doesn't like young women about her commonly; and I thought just at first she was almost angry with me for going."

"Eh, it's a poor look-out when th' ould foulks doesna like the young uns," said old Martin, bending his head down lower, and seeming to trace the pattern of the quarries with his eye.

"Ay, it's ill livin' in a hen-roost for them as doesn't like fleas," said Mrs. Poyser. "We've all had our turn at bein' young, I reckon, be't good luck or ill."

"But she must learn to 'commodate herself to young women," said Mr. Poyser, "for it isn't to be counted on as Adam and Seth 'ull keep bachelors for the next ten year to please their mother. That 'ud be unreasonable. It isn't right for old nor young nayther to make a bargain all o' their own side. What's good for one's good all round i' the long run. I'm no friend to young fellows a-marrying afore they know the difference atween a crab an' a apple; but they may wait o'er long."

"To be sure," said Mrs. Poyser; "if you go past your dinner-time, there'll be little relish o' your meat. You turn it o'er an' o'er wi' your fork, an' don't eat it after all. You find faut wi' your meat, an' the faut's all i' your own stomach."

Hetty now came back from the pantry, and said, "I can take Totty now, aunt, if you like."

"Come, Rachel," said Mr. Poyser, as his wife seemed to hesitate, seeing that Totty was at last nestling quietly, "thee'dst better let Hetty carry her up-stairs, while thee' tak'st thy things off. Thee't tired. It's time thee wast in bed. Thee't bring on the pain in thy side again."

"Well, she may hold her if the child 'ull go to her," said Mrs. Poyser.

Hetty went close to the rocking-chair, and stood without her usual smile, and without any attempt to entice Totty, simply waiting for her aunt to give the child into her hands.

"Wilt go to cousin Hetty, my dilling, while mother gets ready to go to bed? Then Totty shall go into mother's bed, and sleep there all night."

Before her mother had done speaking, Totty had given her answer in an unmistakable manner, by knitting her brow, setting her tiny teeth against her under-lip, and leaning forward to slap Hetty on the arm with her utmost force. Then, without speaking, she nestled to her mother again.

"Hey, hey," said Mr. Poyser, while Hattie stood without moving, "not go to cousin Hetty? That's like a babby: Totty's a little woman, an' not a babby."

"It's no use trying to persuade her," said Mrs. Poyser. "She allays takes against Hetty when she isn't well. Happen she'll go to Dinah."

Dinah, having taken off her bonnet and shawl, had hitherto kept quietly seated in the background, not liking to thrust herself between Hetty and what was considered Hetty's proper work. But now she came forward, and, putting out her arms, said, "Come, Totty, come and let Dinah carry her up-stairs along with mother: poor, poor mother! she's so tired—she wants to go to bed."

Totty turned her face towards Dinah, and looked at her an instant, then lifted herself up, put out her little arms, and let Dinah lift her from her mother's lap. Hetty turned away without any sign of ill-humour, and, taking her hat from the table, stood waiting with an air of indifference, to see if she should be told to do anything else.

"You may make the door fast now, Poyser; Alick's been come in this long while," said Mrs. Poyser, rising with an appearance of relief from her low chair. "Get me the matches down, Hetty, for I must have the rushlight burning i' my room. Come, father."

The heavy wooden bolts began to roll in the house doors, and old Martin prepared to move, by gathering up his blue handkerchief, and reaching his bright knobbed walnut-tree stick from the corner. Mrs. Poyser then led the way out of the kitchen, followed by the grandfather, and Dinah with Totty in her arms—all going to bed by twilight, like the birds. Mrs. Poyser, on her way, peeped into the room where her two boys lay, just to see their ruddy round cheeks on the pillow, and to hear for a moment their light regular breathing.

"Come, Hetty, get to bed," said Mr. Poyser, in a soothing tone, as he himself turned to go up-stairs. "You didna mean to be late, I'll be bound, but your aunt's been worried to-day. Good-night, my wench, good-night."

CHAPTER XV

THE TWO BED-CHAMBERS

HETTY and Dinah both slept in the second story, in rooms adjoining each other, meagrely-furnished rooms, with no blinds to shut out the light, which was now beginning to gather new strength from the rising of the moon—more than enough strength to enable Hetty to move about and undress with perfect comfort. She could see quite well the pegs in the old painted linen-press on which she hung her hat and gown; she could see the head of every pin on her red cloth pin-cushion; she could see a reflection of herself in the old-fashioned looking-glass, quite as distinct as was needful, considering that she had only to brush her hair and put on her night-cap. A queer old looking-glass! Hetty got into an ill temper with it almost every time she dressed. It had been considered a handsome glass in its day, and had probably been bought into the Poyser family a quarter of a century before, at a sale of genteel household furniture. Even now an auctioneer could say something for it: it had a great deal of tarnished gilding about it; it had a firm mahogany base, well supplied with drawers, which opened with a decided jerk, and sent the contents leaping out from the farthest corners, without giving you the trouble of reaching them; above all, it had a brass candle-socket on each side, which would give it an aristocratic air to the very last. But Hetty objected to it because it had numerous dim blotches sprinkled over the mirror, which no rubbing would remove, and because, instead of swinging backwards and forwards, it was fixed in an upright position, so that she could only get one good view of her head and neck, and that was to be had only by sitting down on a low chair before her dressing-table. And the dressing-table was no dressing-table at all, but a small old chest of drawers, the most awkward thing in the world to sit down before, for the big brass handles quite hurt her knees, and she couldn't get near the glass at all comfortably. But devout worshippers never allow inconveniences to prevent them from performing their religious rites, and Hetty this evening was more bent on her peculiar form of worship than usual.

Having taken off her gown and white kerchief, she drew a key from the large pocket that hung outside her petticoat, and, unlocking one of the lower drawers in the chest, reached from it two short bits of wax candle—secretly bought at Treddleston—and stuck them in the two brass sockets. Then she drew forth a bundle of matches, and lighted the candles; and last of all, a small red-framed shilling looking-glass, without blotches. It was into this small glass that she chose to look first after seating herself. She looked into it, smiling, and turning her head on one side, for a minute, then laid it down and took out her brush and comb from an upper drawer. She was going to let down her hair, and make herself look like that picture of a lady in Miss Lydia Donnithorne's dressing-room. It was soon done, and the dark hyacinthine curves fell on her neck. It was not heavy, massive, merely rippling hair, but soft and silken, running at every opportunity into delicate rings. But she pushed it all backward to look like the picture, and form a dark curtain, throwing into relief her round white neck. Then she put down her brush and comb, and looked at herself, folding her arms before her, still like the picture. Even the old mottled glass couldn't help sending back a lovely image, none the less lovely because Hetty's stays were not of white satin—such as I feel sure heroines must generally wear—but of a dark greenish cotton texture.

O yes! she was very pretty: Captain Donnithorne thought so. Prettier than anybody about Hayslope—prettier than any of the ladies she had ever seen visiting at the Chase—indeed it seemed fine ladies were rather old and ugly—and prettier than Miss Bacon, the miller's daughter, who was called the beauty of Treddleston. And Hetty looked at

herself to-night with quite a different sensation from what she had ever
felt before; there was an invisible spectator whose eye rested on her
like morning on the flowers. His soft voice was saying over and over
again those pretty things she had heard in the wood; his arm was round
her, and the delicate rose-scent of his hair was with her still. The vainest
woman is never thoroughly conscious of her own beauty till she is loved
by the man who sets her own passion vibrating in return.

But Hetty seemed to have made up her mind that something was
wanting, for she got up and reached an old black lace scarf out of the
linen-press, and a pair of large earrings out of the sacred drawer from
which she had taken her candles. It was an old scarf, full of rents,
but it would make a becoming border round her shoulders, and set off
the whiteness of her upper arm. And she would take out the little earrings she had in her ears—oh, how her aunt had scolded her for having
her ears bored!—and put in those large ones: they were but coloured
glass and gilding; but if you didn't know what they were made of, they
looked just as well as what the ladies wore. And so she sat down again,
with the large earrings in her ears, and the black lace scarf adjusted
round her shoulders. She looked down at her arms: no arms could be
prettier down to a little way below the elbow—they were white and
plump, and dimpled to match her cheeks; but towards the wrist, she
thought with vexation that they were coarsened by butter-making, and
other work that ladies never did.

Captain Donnithorne couldn't like her to go on doing work: he would
like to see her in nice clothes, and thin shoes and white stockings, perhaps with silk clocks to them; for he must love her very much—no one
else had ever put his arm round her and kissed her in that way. He
would want to marry her, and make a lady of her; she could hardly
dare to shape the thought—yet how else could it be? Marry her quite
secretly, as Mr. James, the Doctor's assistant, married the Doctor's
niece, and nobody ever found it out for a long while after, and then
it was of no use to be angry. The Doctor had told her aunt all about it
in Hetty's hearing. She didn't know how it would be, but it was quite
plain the old Squire could never be told anything about it, for Hetty
was ready to faint with awe and fright if she came across him at the
Chase. He might have been earth-born, for what she knew: it had never
entered her mind that he had been young like other men; he had always
been the old Squire at whom everybody was frightened. O, it was impossible to think how it would be! But Captain Donnithorne would
know; he was a great gentleman, and could have his way in everything,
and could buy everything he liked. And nothing could be as it had been
again: perhaps some day she should be a grand lady, and ride in her
coach, and dress for dinner in a brocaded silk, with feathers in her
hair, and her dress sweeping the ground, like Miss Lydia and Lady
Dacey, when she saw them going into the dining-room one evening,
as she peeped through the little round window in the lobby; only she
should not be old and ugly like Miss Lydia, or all the same thickness

like Lady Dacey, but very pretty, with her hair done in a great many different ways, and sometimes in a pink dress, and sometimes in a white one—she didn't know which she liked best; and Mary Burge and everybody would perhaps see her going out in her carriage—or rather, they would *hear* of it: it was impossible to imagine these things happening at Hayslope in sight of her aunt. At the thought of all this splendour, Hetty got up from her chair, and in doing so caught the little red-framed glass with the edge of her scarf, so that it fell with a bang on the floor; but she was too eagerly occupied with her vision to care about picking it up; and after a momentary start, began to pace with a pigeon-like stateliness backwards and forwards along her room, in her coloured stays and coloured skirt, and the old black lace scarf round her shoulders, and the great glass earrings in her ears.

How pretty the little puss looks in that odd dress! It would be the easiest folly in the world to fall in love with her: there is such a sweet baby-like roundness about her face and figure; the delicate dark rings of hair lie so charmingly about her ears and neck; her great dark eyes with their long eyelashes touch one so strangely, as if an imprisoned frisky sprite looked out of them.

Ah, what a prize the man gets who wins a sweet bride like Hetty! How the men envy him who come to the wedding breakfast, and see her hanging on his arm in her white lace and orange blossoms. The dear, young, round, soft, flexible thing! Her heart must be just as soft, her temper just as free from angles, her character just as pliant. If anything ever goes wrong, it must be the husband's fault there: he can make her what he likes—that is plain. And the lover himself thinks so too: the little darling is so fond of him, her little vanities are so bewitching, he wouldn't consent to her being a bit wiser; those kitten-like glances and movements are just what one wants to make one's heart a paradise. Every man under such circumstances is conscious of being a great physiognomist. Nature, he knows, has a language of her own, which she uses with strict veracity, and he considers himself an adept in the language. Nature has written out his bride's character for him in those exquisite lines of cheek and lip and chin, in those eyelids delicate as petals, in those long lashes curled like the stamen of a flower, in the dark liquid depths of those wonderful eyes. How she will dote on her children! She is almost a child herself, and the little pink round things will hang about her like florets round the central flower; and the husband will look on, smiling benignly, able, whenever he chooses, to withdraw into the sanctuary of his wisdom, towards which his sweet wife will look reverently, and never lift the curtain. It is a marriage such as they made in the golden age, when the men were all wise and majestic, and the women all lovely and loving.

It was very much in this way that our friend Adam Bede thought about Hetty; only he put his thoughts into different words. If ever she behaved with cold vanity towards him, he said to himself, it is only because she doesn't love me well enough; and he was sure that her love, whenever she gave it, would be the most precious thing a man could possess on earth. Before you despise Adam as deficient in penetration, pray ask yourself if you were ever predisposed to believe evil of any pretty woman—if you ever *could,* without hard head-breaking demonstration, believe evil of the *one* supremely pretty woman who has bewitched you. No: people who love downy peaches are apt not to think of the stone, and sometimes jar their teeth terribly against it.

Arthur Donnithorne, too, had the same sort of notion about Hetty, so far as he had thought of her nature at all. He felt sure she was a dear, affectionate, good little thing. The man who awakes the wondering tremulous passion of a young girl always thinks her affectionate; and if he chances to look forward to future years, probably imagines himself being virtuously tender to her, because the poor thing is so clingingly fond of him. God made these dear women so—and it is a convenient arrangement in case of sickness.

After all, I believe the wisest of us must be beguiled in this way sometimes, and must think both better and worse of people than they deserve. Nature has her language, and she is not unveracious; but we don't know all the intricacies of her syntax just yet, and in a hasty reading we may happen to extract the very opposite of her real meaning. Long dark eyelashes, now: what can be more exquisite? I find it impossible not to expect some depth of soul behind a deep grey eye with a long dark eyelash, in spite of an experience which has shown me that they may go along with deceit, peculation, and stupidity. But if, in the reaction of disgust, I have betaken myself to a fishy eye, there has been a surprising similarity of result. One begins to suspect at length that there is no direct correlation between eyelashes and morals; or else, that the eyelashes express the disposition of the fair one's grandmother, which is on the whole less important to us.

No eyelashes could be more beautiful than Hetty's; and now, while she walks with her pigeon-like stateliness along the room and looks down on her shoulders bordered by the old black lace, the dark fringe shows to perfection on her pink cheek. They are but dim ill-defined pictures that her narrow bit of an imagination can make of the future; but of every picture she is the central figure in fine clothes; Captain Donnithorne is very close to her, putting his arm round her, perhaps kissing her, and everybody else is admiring and envying her—especially Mary Burge, whose new print dress looks very contemptible by the side of Hetty's resplendent toilette. Does any sweet or sad memory mingle with this dream of the future—any loving thought of her second parents—of the children she had helped to tend—of any youthful companion, any pet animal, any relic of her own childhood even? Not one. There are some plants that have hardly any roots: you may tear them from their native nook of rock or wall, and just lay them over your ornamental flower-pot, and they blossom none the worse. Hetty could have cast all her past life behind her, and never cared to be reminded of it again. I think she had no feeling at all towards the old

house, and did not like the Jacob's Ladder and the long row of hollyhocks in the garden better than other flowers—perhaps not so well.
It was wonderful how little she seemed to care about waiting on her
uncle, who had been a good father to her: she hardly remembered to
reach him his pipe at the right time without being told, unless a visitor
happened to be there, who would have a better opportunity of seeing
her as she walked across the hearth. Hetty did not understand how anybody could be very fond of middle-aged people. And as for those tiresome children, Marty and Tommy and Totty, they had been the very
nuisance of her life—as bad as buzzing insects that will come teasing
you on a hot day when you want to be quiet. Marty, the eldest, was a
baby when she first came to the farm, for the children born before him
had died, and so Hetty had had them all three, one after the other,
toddling by her side in the meadow, or playing about her on wet days
in the half-empty rooms of the large old house. The boys were out of
hand now, but Totty was still a day-long plague, worse than either of
the others had been, because there was more fuss made about her. And
there was no end to the making and mending of clothes. Hetty would
have been glad to hear that she should never see a child again; they
were worse than the nasty little lambs that the shepherd was always
bringing in to be taken special care of in lambing time; for the lambs
were got rid of sooner or later. As for the young chickens and turkeys,
Hetty would have hated the very word "hatching," if her aunt had not
bribed her to attend to the young poultry by promising her the proceeds of one out of every brood. The round downy chicks peeping out
from under their mother's wing never touched Hetty with any pleasure;
that was not the sort of prettiness she cared about, but she did care about
the prettiness of the new things she would buy for herself at Treddleston
fair with the money they fetched. And yet she looked so dimpled, so
charming, as she stooped down to put the soaked bread under the hencoop, that you must have been a very acute personage indeed to suspect
her of that hardness. Molly, the housemaid, with a turn-up nose and a
protuberant jaw, was really a tender-hearted girl, and, as Mrs. Poyser
said, a jewel to look after the poultry; but her stolid face showed nothing
of this maternal delight, any more than a brown earthenware pitcher
will show the light of the lamp within it.

It is generally a feminine eye that first detects the moral deficiencies
hidden under the "dear deceit" of beauty: so it is not surprising that
Mrs. Poyser, with her keenness and abundant opportunity for observation, should have formed a tolerably fair estimate of what might be
expected from Hetty in the way of feeling, and in moments of indignation she had sometimes spoken with great openness on the subject to
her husband.

"She's no better than a peacock, as 'ud strut about on the wall, and
spread its tail when the sun shone if all the folk i' the parish was dying:
there's nothing seems to give her a turn i' th' inside, not even when we
thought Totty had tumbled into the pit. To think o' that dear cherub!

And we found her wi' her little shoes stuck i' the mud an' crying fit to break her heart by the far horse-pit. But Hetty niver minded it, I could see, though she's been at the nussin' o' the child ever since it was a babby. It's my belief her heart's as hard as a pebble."

"Nay, nay," said Mr. Poyser, "thee mustn't judge Hetty too hard. Them young gells are like th' unripe grain; they'll make a good meal by-and-by, but they're squashy as yet. Thee't see Hetty 'll be all right when she's got a good husband and children of her own."

"*I* don't want to be hard upo' the gell. She's got cliver fingers of her own, and can be useful enough when she likes, and I should miss her wi' the butter, for she's got a cool hand. An' let be what may, I'd strive to do my part by a niece o' yours, an' *that* I've done: for I've taught her everything as belongs to a house, an' I've told her her duty often enough, though, God knows, I've no breath to spare, an' that catchin' pain comes on dreadful by times. Wi' them three gells in the house I'd need have twice the strength, to keep 'em up to their work. It's like having roast-meat at three fires; as soon as you've basted one, another's burnin'."

Hetty stood sufficiently in awe of her aunt to be anxious to conceal from her so much of her vanity as could be hidden without too great a sacrifice. She could not resist spending her money in bits of finery which Mrs. Poyser disapproved; but she would have been ready to die with shame, vexation, and fright, if her aunt had this moment opened the door, and seen her with her bits of candle lighted, and strutting about decked in her scarf and earrings. To prevent such a surprise, she always bolted her door, and she had not forgotten to do so to-night. It was well: for there now came a light tap, and Hetty with a leaping heart, rushed to blow out the candles and throw them into the drawer. She dared not stay to take out her earrings, but she threw off her scarf, and let it fall on the floor, before the light tap came again. We shall know how it was that the light tap came, if we leave Hetty for a short time, and return to Dinah, at the moment when she had delivered Totty to her mother's arms, and was come up-stairs to her bedroom, adjoining Hetty's

Dinah delighted in her bedroom window. Being on the second story of that tall house, it gave her a wide view over the fields. The thickness of the wall formed a broad step about a yard below the window, where she could place her chair. And now the first thing she did, on entering her room, was to seat herself in this chair, and look out on the peaceful fields beyond which the large moon was rising, just above the hedgerow elms. She liked the pasture best where the milch cows were lying, and next to that the meadow where the grass was half mown, and lay in silvered sweeping lines. Her heart was very full, for there was to be only one more night on which she would look out on those fields for a long time to come; but she thought little of leaving the mere scene, for, to her, bleak Snowfield had just as many charms: she thought of all the dear people whom she had learned to care for among these

peaceful fields, and who would now have a place in her loving remembrance for ever. She thought of the struggles and the weariness that
might lie before them in the rest of their life's journey, when she
would be away from them, and know nothing of what was befalling
them; and the pressure of this thought soon became too strong for her
to enjoy the unresponding stillness of the moonlit fields. She closed her
eyes, that she might feel more intensely the presence of a Love and
Sympathy deeper and more tender than was breathed from the earth
and sky. That was often Dinah's mode of praying in solitude. Simply
to close her eyes, and to feel herself enclosed by the Divine Presence;
then gradually her fears, her yearning anxieties for others, melted away
like ice-crystals in a warm ocean. She had sat in this way perfectly still,
with her hands crossed on her lap, and the pale light resting on her
calm face, for at least ten minutes, when she was startled by a loud
sound, apparently of something falling in Hetty's room. But like all
sounds that fall on our ears in a state of abstraction, it had no distinct
character, but was simply loud and startling, so that she felt uncertain
whether she had interpreted it rightly. She rose and listened, but all
was quiet afterwards, and she reflected that Hetty might merely have
knocked something down in getting into bed. She began slowly to undress; but now, owing to the suggestions of this sound, her thoughts
became concentrated on Hetty: that sweet young thing, with life and
all its trials before her—the solemn daily duties of the wife and mother
—and her mind so unprepared for them all; bent merely on little foolish, selfish pleasures, like a child hugging its toys in the beginning of
a long toilsome journey, in which it will have to bear hunger and cold
and unsheltered darkness. Dinah felt a double care for Hetty, because
she shared Seth's anxious interest in his brother's lot, and she had not
come to the conclusion that Hetty did not love Adam well enough to
marry him. She saw too clearly the absence of any warm, self-devoting
love in Hetty's nature, to regard the coldness of her behaviour towards
Adam as any indication that he was not the man she would like to
have for a husband. And this blank in Hetty's nature, instead of exciting Dinah's dislike, only touched her with a deeper pity: the lovely
face and form affected her as beauty always affects a pure and tender
mind, free from selfish jealousies: it was an excellent, divine gift, that
gave a deeper pathos to the need, the sin, the sorrow with which it was
mingled, as the canker in a lily-white bud is more grievous to behold
than in a common pot-herb.

By the time Dinah had undressed and put on her night-gown, this
feeling about Hetty had gathered a painful intensity; her imagination
had created a thorny thicket of sin and sorrow, in which she saw the
poor thing struggling torn and bleeding, looking with tears for rescue
and finding none. It was in this way that Dinah's imagination and
sympathy acted and reacted habitually, each heightening the other. She
felt a deep longing to go now and pour into Hetty's ear all the words
of tender warning and appeal that rushed into her mind. But perhaps

Hetty was already asleep. Dinah put her ear to the partition, and heard still some slight noises, which convinced her that Hetty was not yet in bed. Still she hesitated; she was not quite certain of a divine direction; the voice that told her to go to Hetty seemed no stronger than the other voice which said that Hetty was weary, and that going to her now in an unseasonable moment would only tend to close her heart more obstinately. Dinah was not satisfied without a more unmistakable guidance than those inward voices. There was light enough for her, if she opened her Bible, for her to discern the text sufficiently to know what it would say to her. She knew the physiognomy of every page, and could tell on what book she opened, sometimes on what chapter, without seeing title or number. It was a small thick Bible, worn quite round at the edges. Dinah laid it sideways on the window ledge, where the light was strongest, and then opened it with her forefinger. The first words she looked at were those at the top of the left-hand page: "And they all wept sore, and fell on Paul's neck and kissed him." That was enough for Dinah; she had opened on that memorable parting at Ephesus, when Paul had felt bound to open his heart in a last exhortation and warning. She hesitated no longer, but, opening her own door gently, went and tapped at Hetty's. We know she had to tap twice, because Hetty had to put out her candles and throw off her black lace scarf; but after the second tap the door was opened immediately. Dinah said, "Will you let me come in, Hetty?" and Hetty, without speaking, for she was confused and vexed, opened the door wider and let her in.

What a strange contrast the two figures made! Visible enough in that mingled twilight and moonlight. Hetty, her cheeks flushed and her eyes glistening from her imaginary drama, her beautiful neck and arms bare, her hair hanging in a curly tangle down her back, and the baubles in her ears. Dinah, covered with her long white dress, her pale face full of subdued emotion, almost like a lovely corpse into which the soul has returned charged with sublimer secrets and a sublimer love. They were nearly of the same height; Dinah evidently a little the taller as she put her arm round Hetty's waist, and kissed her forehead.

"I knew you were not in bed, my dear," she said, in her sweet clear voice, which was irritating to Hetty, mingling with her own peevish vexation like music with jangling chains, "for I heard you moving; and I longed to speak to you again to-night, for it is the last but one that I shall be here, and we don't know what may happen to-morrow to keep us apart. Shall I sit down with you while you do up your hair?"

"O yes," said Hetty, hastily turning round and reaching the second chair in the room, glad that Dinah looked as if she did not notice her earrings.

Dinah sat down, and Hetty began to brush together her hair before twisting it up, doing it with that air of excessive indifference which belongs to confused self-consciousness. But the expression of Dinah's eyes gradually relieved her; they seemed unobservant of all details.

"Dear Hetty," she said, "it has been borne in upon my mind to-night

that you may some day be in trouble—trouble is appointed for us all
here below, and there comes a time when we need more comfort and
help than the things of this life can give. I want to tell you that if ever
you are in trouble, and need a friend that will always feel for you and
love you, you have got that friend in Dinah Morris at Snowfield; and
if you come to her, or send for her, she'll never forget this night and the
words she is speaking to you now. Will you remember it, Hetty?"

"Yes," said Hetty, rather frightened. "But why should you think I
shall be in trouble? Do you know of anything?"

Hetty had seated herself as she tied on her cap, and now Dinah leaned
forwards and took her hands as she answered—

"Because, dear, trouble comes to us all in this life: we set our hearts
on things which it isn't God's will for us to have, and then we go sorrowing; the people we love are taken from us, and we can joy in nothing
because they are not with us; sickness comes, and we faint under the
burden of our feeble bodies; we go astray and do wrong, and bring ourselves into trouble with our fellow-men. There is no man or woman born
into this world to whom some of these trials do not fall, and so I feel
that some of them must happen to you; and I desire for you, that while
you are young you should seek for strength from your Heavenly Father,
that you may have a support which will not fail you in the evil day."

Dinah paused and released Hetty's hands, that she might not hinder
her. Hetty sat quite still; she felt no response within herself to Dinah's
anxious affection; but Dinah's words, uttered with solemn pathetic distinctness, affected her with a chill fear. Her flush had died away almost
to paleness; she had the timidity of a luxurious pleasure-seeking nature,
which shrinks from the hint of pain. Dinah saw the effect, and her
tender anxious pleading became the more earnest, till Hetty, full of a
vague fear that something evil was some time to befall her, began to cry.

It is our habit to say that while the lower nature can never understand the higher, the higher nature commands a complete view of the
lower. But I think the higher nature has to learn this comprehension, as
we learn the art of vision, by a good deal of hard experience, often with
bruises and gashes incurred in taking things up by the wrong end, and
fancying our space wider than it is. Dinah had never seen Hetty affected
in this way before, and, with her usual benignant hopefulness, she
trusted it was the stirring of a divine impulse. She kissed the sobbing
thing, and began to cry with her for grateful joy. But Hetty was simply
in that excitable state of mind in which there is no calculating what turn
the feelings may take from one moment to another, and for the first
time she became irritated under Dinah's caress. She pushed her away
impatiently, and said, with a childish sobbing voice,—

"Don't talk to me so, Dinah. Why do you come to frighten me? I've
never done anything to you. Why can't you let me be?"

Poor Dinah felt a pang. She was too wise to persist, and only said
mildly. "Yes, my dear, you're tired; I won't hinder you any longer.
Make haste and get into bed. Good-night."

She went out of the room almost as quietly and quickly as if she had been a ghost; but once by the side of her own bed, she threw herself on her knees, and poured out in deep silence all the passionate pity that filled her heart.

As for Hetty, she was soon in the wood again—her waking dreams being merged in a sleeping life scarcely more fragmentary and confused.

CHAPTER XVI

LINKS

ARTHUR DONNITHORNE, you remember, is under an engagement with himself to go and see Mr. Irwine this Friday morning, and he is awake and dressing so early, that he determines to go before breakfast, instead of after. The Rector, he knows, breakfasts alone at half-past nine, the ladies of the family having a different breakfast hour; Arthur will have an early ride over the hill and breakfast with him. One can say everything best over a meal.

The progress of civilisation has made a breakfast or a dinner an easy and cheerful substitute for more troublesome and disagreeable ceremonies. We take a less gloomy view of our errors now our father confessor listens to us over his egg and coffee. We are more distinctly conscious that rude penances are out of the question for gentlemen in an enlightened age, and that mortal sin is not incompatible with an appetite for muffins. An assault on our pockets, which in more barbarous times would have been made in the brusque form of a pistol-shot, is quite a well-bred and smiling procedure now it has become a request for a loan thrown in as an easy parenthesis between the second and third glasses of claret.

Still, there was this advantage in the old rigid forms, that they committed you to the fulfilment of a resolution by some outward deed: when you have put your mouth to one end of a hole in a stone wall, and are aware that there is an expectant ear at the other end, you are more likely to say what you came out with the intention of saying, than if you were seated with your legs in an easy attitude under the mahogany, with a companion who will have no reason to be surprised if you have nothing particular to say.

However, Arthur Donnithorne, as he winds among the pleasant lanes on horseback in the morning sunshine, has a sincere determination to open his heart to the Rector, and the swirling sound of the scythe as he passes by the meadow is all the pleasanter to him because of this honest purpose. He is glad to see the promise of settled weather now, for getting in the hay, about which the farmers have been fearful; and there is something so healthful in the sharing of a joy that is general and not merely personal, that this thought about the hay-harvest reacts on his state of mind, and makes his resolution seem an easier matter. A man

about town might perhaps consider that these influences were not to
be felt out of a child's story-book; but when you are among the fields
and hedgerows, it is impossible to maintain a consistent superiority to
simple natural pleasures.

Arthur had passed the village of Hayslope, and was approaching the
Broxton side of the hill, when, at a turning in the road he saw a figure
about a hundred yards before him which it was impossible to mistake
for any one else than Adam Bede, even if there had been no grey,
tailless, shepherd-dog at his heels. He was striding along at his usual
rapid pace; and Arthur pushed on his horse to overtake him, for he
retained too much of his boyish feeling for Adam to miss an opportunity of chatting with him. I will not say that his love for that good
fellow did not owe some of its force to the love of patronage: our friend
Arthur liked to do everything that was handsome, and to have his
handsome deeds recognised.

Adam looked round as he heard the quickening clatter of the horse's
heels, and waited for the horseman, lifting his paper cap from his head
with a bright smile of recognition. Next to his own brother Seth, Adam
would have done more for Arthur Donnithorne than for any other
young man in the world. There was hardly anything he would not rather
have lost than the two-foot ruler which he always carried in his pocket;
it was Arthur's present, bought with his pocket-money when he was a
fair-haired lad of eleven, and when he had profited so well by Adam's
lessons in carpentering and turning, as to embarrass every female in
the house with gifts of superfluous thread-reels and round boxes. Adam
had quite a pride in the little squire in those early days, and the feeling
had only become slightly modified as the fair-haired lad had grown into
the whiskered young man. Adam, I confess, was very susceptible to
the influence of rank, and quite ready to give an extra amount of respect
to every one who had more advantages than himself, not being a philosopher, or a proletaire with democratic ideas, but simply a stout-limbed
clever carpenter with a large fund of reverence in his nature, which
inclined him to admit all established claims unless he saw very clear
grounds for questioning them. He had no theories about setting the
world to rights, but he saw there was a great deal of damage done by
building with ill-seasoned timber—by ignorant men in fine clothes making plans for outhouses and workshops and the like, without knowing
the bearings of things—by slovenly joiners' work, and by hasty contracts that could never be fulfilled without ruining somebody; and he
resolved, for his part, to set his face against such doings. On these
points he would have maintained his opinion against the largest landed
proprietor in Loamshire or Stonyshire either; but he felt that beyond
these it would be better for him to defer to people who were more knowing than himself. He saw as plainly as possible how ill the woods on the
estate were managed, and the shameful state of the farm-buildings; and
if old Squire Donnithorne had asked him the effect of this mismanage-
ment, he would have spoken his opinion without flinching, but the im-

pulse to a respectful demeanour towards a "gentleman" would have been strong within him all the while. The word "gentleman" had a spell for Adam, and, as he often said, he "couldn't abide a fellow who thought he made himself fine by being coxy to's betters." I must remind you again that Adam had the blood of the peasant in his veins, and that since he was in his prime half a century ago, you must expect some of his characteristics to be obsolete.

Towards the young squire this instinctive reverence of Adam's was assisted by boyish memories and personal regard; so you may imagine that he thought far more of Arthur's good qualities, and attached far more value to very slight actions of his, than if they had been the qualities and actions of a common workman like himself. He felt sure it would be a fine day for everybody about Hayslope when the young squire came into the estate—such a generous open-hearted disposition as he had, and an "uncommon" notion about improvements and repairs, considering he was only just coming of age. Thus there was both respect and affection in the smile with which he raised his paper cap as Arthur Donnithorne rode up.

"Well, Adam, how are you?" said Arthur, holding out his hand. He never shook hands with any of the farmers, and Adam felt the honour keenly. "I could swear to your back a long way off. It's just the same back, only broader, as when you used to carry me on it. Do you remember?"

"Ay, sir, I remember. It 'ud be a poor look-out if folks didn't remember what they did and said when they were lads. We should think no more about old friends than we do about new uns, then."

"You're going to Broxton, I suppose?" said Arthur, putting his horse on at a slow pace while Adam walked by his side. "Are you going to the Rectory?"

"No, sir, I'm going to see about Bradwell's barn. They're afraid of the roof pushing the walls out; and I'm going to see what can be done with it before we send the stuff and the workmen."

"Why, Burge trusts almost everything to you now, Adam, doesn't he? I should think he will make you his partner soon. He will if he's wise."

"Nay, sir, I don't see as he'd be much the better off for that. A foreman, if he's got a conscience, and delights in his work, will do his business as well as if he was a partner. I wouldn't give a penny for a man as 'ud drive a nail in slack because he didn't get extra pay for it."

"I know that, Adam; I know you work for him as well as if you were working for yourself. But you would have more power than you have now, and could turn the business to better account perhaps. The old man must give up his business some time, and he has no son; I suppose he'll want a son-in-law who can take to it. But he has rather grasping fingers of his own, I fancy: I daresay he wants a man who can put some money into the business. If I were not as poor as a rat, I would gladly invest some money in that way, for the sake of having you settled on the estate. I'm sure I should profit by it in the end. And perhaps I shall be better off in a year or two. I shall have a larger allowance now I'm of age; and when I've paid off a debt or two, I shall be able to look about me."

"You're very good to say so, sir, and I'm not unthankful. But"— Adam continued, in a decided tone—"I shouldn't like to make any offers to Mr. Burge, or t' have any made for me. I see no clear road to a partnership. If he should ever want to dispose of the business, that 'ud be a different matter. I should be glad of some money at a fair interest then, for I feel sure I could pay it off in time."

"Very well, Adam," said Arthur, remembering what Mr. Irwine had said about a probable hitch in the love-making between Adam and Mary Burge, "we'll say no more about it at present. When is your father to be buried?"

"On Sunday, sir; Mr. Irwine's coming earlier on purpose. I shall be glad when it's over, for I think my mother 'ull perhaps get easier then. It cuts one sadly to see the grief of old people; they've no way o' working it off; and the new spring brings no new shoots out on the withered tree."

"Ah, you've had a good deal of trouble and vexation in your life, Adam. I don't think you've ever been harebrained and light-hearted, like other youngsters. You've always had some care on your mind."

"Why, yes, sir; but that's nothing to make a fuss about. If we're men, and have men's feelings, I reckon we must have men's troubles. We can't be like the birds, as fly from their nest as soon as they've got their wings, and never know their kin when they see 'em, and get a fresh lot every year. I've had enough to be thankful for: I've allays had health and strength and brains to give me a delight in my work; and I count it a great thing as I've had Bartle Massey's night-school to go to. He's helped me to knowledge I could never ha' got by myself."

"What a rare fellow you are, Adam!" said Arthur, after a pause, in which he had looked musingly at the big fellow walking by his side. "I could hit out better than most men at Oxford, and yet I believe you would knock me into next week if I were to have a battle with you."

"God forbid I should ever do that, sir," said Adam, looking round at Arthur, and smiling. "I used to fight for fun; but I've never done that since I was the cause o' poor Gil Tranter being laid up for a fortnight. I'll never fight any man again, only when he behaves like a scoundrel. If you get hold of a chap that's got no shame nor conscience to stop him, you must try what you can do by bunging his eyes up."

Arthur did not laugh, for he was preoccupied with some thought that made him say presently,

"I should think now, Adam, you never have any struggles within yourself. I fancy you would master a wish that you had made up your mind it was not quite right to indulge, as easily as you would knock down a drunken fellow who was quarrelsome with you. I mean, you are never shilly-shally, first making up your mind that you won't do a thing, and then doing it after all?"

"Well," said Adam, slowly, after a moment's hesitation—"no. I don't remember ever being see-saw in that way, when I'd made my mind up, as you say, that a thing was wrong. It takes the taste out o' my mouth for things, when I know I should have a heavy conscience after 'em. I've seen pretty clear, ever since I could cast up a sum, as you can never do what's wrong without breeding sin and trouble more than you can ever see. It's like a bit o' bad workmanship—you never see th' end o' the mischief it'll do. And it's a poor look-out to come into the world to make your fellow-creatures worse off instead o' better. But there's a difference between the things folks call wrong. I'm not for making a sin of every little fool's trick, or bit o' nonsense anybody may be let into, like some o' them dissenters. And a man may have two minds whether it isn't worth while to get a bruise or two for the sake of a bit o' fun. But it isn't my way to be see-sawing about anything: I think my fault lies th' other way. When I've said a thing, if it's only to myself, it's hard for me to go back."

"Yes, that's just what I expected of you," said Arthur. "You've got an iron will, as well as an iron arm. But however strong a man's resolution may be, it costs him something to carry it out, now and then. We may determine not to gather any cherries, and keep our hands sturdily in our pockets, but we can't prevent our mouths from watering."

"That's true, sir; but there's nothing like settling with ourselves as there's a deal we must do without i' this life. It's no use looking on life as if it was Treddles'on fair, where folks only go to see shows and get fairings. If we do, we shall find it different. But where's the use o' me talking to you, sir? You know better than I do."

"I'm not so sure of that, Adam. You've had four or five years of experience more than I've had, and I think your life has been a better school to you than college has been to me."

"Why, sir, you seem to think o' college something like what Bartle Massey does. He says college mostly makes people like bladders—just good for nothing but t' hold the stuff as is poured into 'em. But he's got a tongue like a sharp blade, Bartle has: it never touches anything but it cuts. Here's the turning, sir. I must bid you good-morning, as you're going to the Rectory."

"Good-by, Adam, good-by."

Arthur gave his horse to the groom at the Rectory gate, and walked along the gravel towards the door which opened on the garden. He knew that the Rector always breakfasted in his study, and the study lay on the left hand of this door, opposite the dining-room. It was a small low room, belonging to the old part of the house—dark with the sombre covers of the books that lined the walls; yet it looked very cheery this morning as Arthur reached the open window. For the morning sun fell aslant on the great glass globe with gold fish in it, which stood on a scagliola pillar in front of the ready-spread bachelor breakfast-table, and by the side of this breakfast-table was a group which would have made any room enticing. In the crimson damask easy-chair sat Mr. Irwine, with that radiant freshness which he always had when he came from his morning toilette; his finely-formed plump white hand was playing along Juno's brown curly back; and close to Juno's tail, which was wagging with calm matronly pleasure, the two brown pups were rolling over each other in an ecstatic duet of worrying noises. On a cushion a little removed sat Pug, with the air of a maiden lady, who looked on these familiarities as animal weaknesses, which she made as little show as possible of observing. On the table, at Mr. Irwine's elbow, lay the first volume of the Foulis Æschylus, which Arthur knew well by sight; and the silver coffee-pot, which Carroll was bringing in, sent forth a fragrant steam which completed the delights of a bachelor breakfast.

"Hallo, Arthur, that's a good fellow! You're just in time," said Mr. Irwine, as Arthur paused and stepped in over the low window-sill. "Carroll, we shall want more coffee and eggs, and haven't you got some cold fowl for us to eat with that ham? Why, this is like old days, Arthur; you haven't been to breakfast with me these five years."

"It was a tempting morning for a ride before breakfast," said Arthur; "and I used to like breakfasting with you so when I was reading with you. My grandfather is always a few degrees colder at breakfast than at any other hour in the day. I think his morning bath doesn't agree with him."

Arthur was anxious not to imply that he came with any special purpose. He had no sooner found himself in Mr. Irwine's presence than the confidence which he had thought quite easy before, suddenly appeared the most difficult thing in the world to him, and at the very moment of shaking hands he saw his purpose in quite a new light. How could he make Irwine understand his position unless he told him those little scenes in the wood; and how could he tell them without looking like a fool? And then his weakness in coming back from Gawaine's, and doing the very opposite of what he intended! Irwine would think him a shilly-shally fellow ever after. However, it must come out in an unpremeditated way; the conversation might lead up to it.

"I like breakfast-time better than any other moment in the day," said Mr. Irwine. "No dust has settled on one's mind then, and it presents a clear mirror to the rays of things. I always have a favourite book by me at breakfast, and I enjoy the bits I pick up then so much, that regularly every morning it seems to me as if I should certainly become studious again. But presently Dent brings up a poor fellow who has killed a hare, and when I've got through my 'justicing,' as Carroll calls it, I'm inclined for a ride round the glebe, and on my way back I meet with the master of the workhouse, who has got a long story of a mutinous pauper to tell me; and so the day goes on, and I'm always the same lazy fellow before evening sets in. Besides, one wants the stimulus of sympathy, and I have never had that since poor D'Oyley left Treddleston. If you had stuck to your books well, you rascal, I should have had a pleasanter prospect before me. But scholarship doesn't run in your family blood."

"No indeed. It's well if I can remember a little inapplicable Latin to adorn my maiden speech in Parliament six or seven years hence. 'Cras ingens iterabimus æquor,' and a few shreds of that sort, will perhaps stick to me, and I shall arrange my opinions so as to introduce them. But I don't think a knowledge of the classics is a pressing want to a country gentleman; as far as I can see, he'd much better have a knowledge of manures. I've been reading your friend Arthur Young's books lately, and there is nothing I should like better than to carry out some of his ideas in putting the farmers on a better management of their land; and, as he says, making what was a wild country, all the same dark hue, bright and variegated with corn and cattle. My grandfather will never let me have any power while he lives; but there's nothing I should like better than to undertake the Stonyshire side of the estate— it's in a dismal condition—and set improvements on foot, and gallop about from one place to another and overlook them. I should like to know all the labourers, and see them touching their hats to me with a look of goodwill."

"Bravo, Arthur! a man who has no feeling for the classics couldn't make a better apology for coming into the world than by increasing the quantity of food to maintain scholars—and rectors who appreciate scholars. And whenever you enter on your career of model landlord may I be there to see. You'll want a portly rector to complete the picture, and take his tithe of all the respect and honour you get by your hard work. Only don't set your heart too strongly on the goodwill you are to get in consequence. I'm not sure that men are the fondest of those who try to be useful to them. You know Gawaine has got the curses of the whole neighbourhood upon him about that enclosure. You must make it quite clear to your mind which you are most bent upon, old boy—popularity or usefulness—else you may happen to miss both."

"O! Gawaine is harsh in his manners; he doesn't make himself personally agreeable to his tenants. I don't believe there's anything you can't prevail on people to do with kindness. For my part, I couldn't live in a neighbourhood where I was not respected and beloved; and it's very pleasant to go among the tenants here, they seem all so well inclined to me. I suppose it seems only the other day to them since I was a little lad, riding on a pony about as big as a sheep. And if fair allowances were made to them, and their buildings attended to, one could persuade them to farm on a better plan, stupid as they are."

"Then mind you fall in love in the right place, and don't get a wife who will drain your purse and make you niggardly in spite of yourself. My mother and I have a little discussion about you sometimes: she says, 'I'll never risk a single prophecy on Arthur until I see the woman he falls in love with.' She thinks your lady-love will rule you as the moon rules the tides. But I feel bound to stand up for you, as my pupil, you know; and I maintain that you're not of that watery quality. So mind you don't disgrace my judgment."

Arthur winced under this speech, for keen old Mrs. Irwine's opinion about him had the disagreeable effect of a sinister omen. This, to be sure, was only another reason for persevering in his intention, and get-ting an additional security against himself. Nevertheless, at this point in the conversation, he was conscious of increased disinclination to tell his story about Hetty. He was of an impressible nature, and lived a great deal in other people's opinions and feelings concerning himself; and the mere fact that he was in the presence of an intimate friend, who had not the slightest notion that he had had any such serious internal struggle as he came to confide, rather shook his own belief in the serious-ness of the struggle. It was not, after all, a thing to make a fuss about; and what could Irwine do for him that he could not do for himself? He would go to Eagledale in spite of Meg's lameness—go on Rattler, and let Pym follow as well as he could on the old hack. That was his thought as he sugared his coffee; but the next minute, as he was lifting the cup to his lips, he remembered how thoroughly he had made up his mind last night to tell Irwine. No! he would not be vacillating again—he *would* do what he had meant to do, this time. So it would be well not to let the personal tone of the conversation altogether drop. If they went to quite indifferent topics, his difficulty would be heightened. It had required no noticeable pause for this rush and rebound of feeling, before he answered,—

"But I think it is hardly an argument against a man's general strength of character, that he should be apt to be mastered by love. A fine constitution doesn't insure one against small-pox or any other of those inevitable diseases. A man may be very firm in other matters, and yet be under a sort of witchery from a woman."

"Yes; but there's this difference between love and small-pox, or be-witchment either—that if you detect the disease at an early stage and try change of air, there is every chance of complete escape, without any further development of symptoms. And there are certain alterative doses which a man may administer to himself by keeping unpleasant conse-quences before his mind: this gives you a sort of smoked glass through which you may look at the resplendent fair one and discern her true outline; though I'm afraid, by the by, the smoked glass is apt to be missing just at that moment it is most wanted. I daresay, now, even a man fortified with a knowledge of the classics might be lured into an imprudent marriage, in spite of the warning given him by the chorus in the Prometheus."

The smile that flitted across Arthur's face was a faint one, and instead of following Mr. Irwine's playful lead, he said, quite seriously—"Yes, that's the worst of it. It's a desperately vexatious thing, that after all one's reflections and quiet determinations, one should be ruled by moods that one can't calculate on beforehand. I don't think a man ought to be blamed so much if he is betrayed into doing things in that way, in spite of his resolutions."

"Ah, but the moods lie in his nature, my boy, just as much as his reflections did, and more. A man can never do anything at variance with his own nature. He carries within him the germ of his most exceptional action; and if we wise people make eminent fools of ourselves on any particular occasion, we must endure the legitimate conclusion that we carry a few grains of folly to our ounce of wisdom."

"Well, but one may be betrayed into doing things by a combination of circumstances, which one might never have done otherwise."

"Why, yes, a man can't very well steal a bank-note unless the bank-note lies within convenient reach; but he won't make us think him an honest man because he begins to howl at the bank-note for falling in his way."

"But surely you don't think a man who struggles against a temptation into which he falls at last, as bad as the man who never struggles at all?"

"No, certainly; I pity him in proportion to his struggles, for they foreshadow the inward suffering which is the worst form of Nemesis. Consequences are unpitying. Our deeds carry their terrible consequences, quite apart from any fluctuations that went before—consequences that are hardly ever confined to ourselves. And it is best to fix our minds on that certainty, instead of considering what may be the elements of excuse for us. But I never knew you so inclined for moral discussion, Arthur? Is it some danger of your own that you are considering in this philosophical, general way?"

In asking this question, Mr. Irwine pushed his plate away, threw himself back in his chair, and looked straight at Arthur. He really suspected that Arthur wanted to tell him something, and thought of smoothing the way for him by this direct question. But he was mistaken. Brought suddenly and involuntarily to the brink of confession, Arthur shrank back, and felt less disposed towards it than ever. The conversation had taken a more serious tone than he had intended—it would quite mislead Irwine—he would imagine there was a deep passion for Hetty, while there was no such thing. He was conscious of colouring, and was annoyed at his boyishness.

"O no, no danger," he said, as indifferently as he could. "I don't know that I am more liable to irresolution than other people; only there are little incidents now and then that set one speculating on what might happen in the future."

Was there a motive at work under this strange reluctance of Arthur's which had a sort of backstairs influence, not admitted to himself? Our mental business is carried on much in the same way as the business of the State: a great deal of hard work is done by agents who are not acknowledged. In a piece of machinery, too, I believe there is often a small unnoticeable wheel which has a great deal to do with the motion of the large obvious ones. Possibly there was some such unrecognised agent secretly busy in Arthur's mind at this moment—possibly it was the fear lest he might hereafter find the fact of having made a confession to the Rector a serious annoyance, in case he should *not* be able quite to carry out his good resolutions? I dare not assert that it was not so. The human soul is a very complex thing.

The idea of Hetty had just crossed Mr. Irwine's mind as he looked inquiringly at Arthur, but his disclaiming, indifferent answer confirmed the thought which had quickly followed—that there could be nothing serious in that direction. There was no probability that Arthur ever saw her except at church, and at her own home under the eye of Mrs. Poyser; and the hint he had given Arthur about her the other day had no more serious meaning than to prevent him from noticing her so as to rouse the little chit's vanity, and in this way perturb the rustic drama of her life. Arthur would soon join his regiment, and be far away: no, there could be no danger in that quarter, even if Arthur's character had not been a strong security against it. His honest, patronising pride in the goodwill and respect of everybody about him was a safeguard even against foolish romance, still more against a lower kind of folly. If there had been anything special on Arthur's mind in the previous conversation, it was clear he was not inclined to enter into details, and Mr. Irwine was too delicate to imply even a friendly curiosity. He perceived a change of subject would be welcome, and said—

"By the way, Arthur, at your colonel's birthday fête there were some transparencies that made a great effect in honour of Britannia, and Pitt, and the Loamshire Militia, and, above all, the 'generous youth,' the hero of the day. Don't you think you should get up something of the same sort to astonish our weak minds?"

The opportunity was gone. While Arthur was hesitating, the rope to which he might have clung had drifted away—he must trust now to his own swimming.

In ten minutes from that time, Mr. Irwine was called for on business, and Arthur, bidding him good-by, mounted his horse again with a sense of dissatisfaction, which he tried to quell by determining to set off for Eagledale without an hour's delay.

BOOK TWO

★

CHAPTER XVII

IN WHICH THE STORY PAUSES A LITTLE

"THIS Rector of Broxton is little better than a pagan!" I hear one of my readers exclaim. "How much more edifying it would have been if you had made him give Arthur some truly spiritual advice. You might have put into his mouth the most beautiful things—-quite as good as reading a sermon."

Certainly I could, if I held it the highest vocation of the novelist to represent things as they never have been and never will be. Then, of course, I might refashion life and character entirely after my own liking; I might select the most unexceptionable type of clergyman, and put my own admirable opinions into his mouth on all occasions. But it happens, on the contrary, that my strongest effort is to avoid any such arbitrary picture, and to give a faithful account of men and things as they have mirrored themselves in my mind. The mirror is doubtless defective; the outlines will sometimes be disturbed, the reflection faint or confused; but I feel as much bound to tell you as precisely as I can what that reflection is, as if I were in the witness-box narrating my experience on oath.

Sixty years ago—it is a long time, so no wonder things have changed —all clergymen were not zealous; indeed there is reason to believe that the number of zealous clergymen was small, and it is probable that if one among the small minority had owned the livings of Broxton and Hayslope in the year 1799, you would have liked him no better than you like Mr. Irwine. Ten to one, you would have thought him a tasteless, indiscreet, methodistical man. It is so very rarely that facts hit that nice medium required by our own enlightened opinions and refined taste! Perhaps you will say, "Do improve the facts a little, then; make them more accordant with those correct views which it is our privilege to possess. The world is not just what we like; do touch it up with a taste-ful pencil, and make believe it is not quite such a mixed, entangled affair. Let all people who hold unexceptionable opinions act unexceptionably. Let your most faulty characters always be on the wrong side, and your virtuous ones on the right. Then we shall see at a glance whom we are to condemn, and whom we are to approve. Then we shall be able to admire, without the slightest disturbance of our prepossessions: we shall hate and despise with that true ruminant relish which belongs to un-doubting confidence."

But, my good friend, what will you do then with your fellow-parishioner who opposes your husband in the vestry?—with your newly-appointed vicar, whose style of preaching you find painfully below that of his regretted predecessor?—with the honest servant who worries your soul with her one failing?—with your neighbour, Mrs. Green, who was really kind to you in your last illness, but has said several ill-natured things about you since your convalescence?—nay, with your excellent husband himself, who has other irritating habits besides that of not wiping his shoes? These fellow-mortals, every one, must be accepted as they are: you can neither straighten their noses, nor brighten their wit, nor rectify their dispositions; and it is these people—amongst whom your life is passed—that it is needful you should tolerate, pity, and love: it is these more or less ugly, stupid, inconsistent people, whose movements of goodness you should be able to admire—for whom you should cherish all possible hopes, all possible patience. And I would not, even if I had the choice, be the clever novelist who could create a world so much better than this, in which we get up in the morning to do our daily work, that you would be likely to turn a harder, colder eye on the dusty streets and the common green fields—on the real breathing men and women, who can be chilled by your indifference or injured by your prejudice; who can be cheered and helped onward by your fellow-feeling, your forbearance, your outspoken, brave justice.

So I am content to tell my simple story, without trying to make things seem better than they were; dreading nothing, indeed, but falsity, which, in spite of one's best efforts, there is reason to dread. Falsehood is so easy, truth so difficult. The pencil is conscious of a delightful facility in drawing a griffin—the longer the claws, and the larger the wings, the better; but that marvellous facility which we mistook for genius is apt to forsake us when we want to draw a real unexaggerated lion. Examine your words well, and you will find that even when you have no motive to be false, it is a very hard thing to say the exact truth, even about your own immediate feelings—much harder than to say something fine about them which is *not* the exact truth.

It is for this rare, precious quality of truthfulness that I delight in many Dutch paintings, which lofty-minded people despise. I find a source of delicious sympathy in these faithful pictures of a monotonous homely existence, which has been the fate of so many more among my fellow-mortals than a life of pomp or of absolute indigence, of tragic suffering or of world-stirring actions. I turn, without shrinking, from cloud-borne angels, from prophets, sibyls, and heroic warriors, to an old woman bending over her flower-pot, or eating her solitary dinner, while the noonday light, softened perhaps by a screen of leaves, falls on her mob-cap, and just touches the rim of her spinning-wheel, and her stone

jug, and all those cheap common things which are the precious necessaries of life to her;—or I turn to that village wedding, kept between
four brown walls, where an awkward bridegroom opens the dance with
a high-shouldered, broad-faced bride, while elderly and middle-aged
friends look on, with very irregular noses and lips, and probably with
quart-pots in their hands, but with an expression of unmistakable contentment and goodwill. "Foh!" says my idealistic friend, "what vulgar
details! What good is there in taking all these pains to give an exact
likeness of old women and clowns? What a low phase of life!—what
clumsy, ugly people!"

But bless us, things may be lovable that are not altogether handsome,
I hope? I am not at all sure that the majority of the human race have
not been ugly, and even among those "lords of their kind," the British,
squat figures, ill-shapen nostrils, and dingy complexions are not startling
exceptions. Yet there is a great deal of family love amongst us. I have a
friend or two whose class of features is such that the Apollo curl on the
summit of their brows would be decidedly trying; yet to my certain
knowledge tender hearts have beaten for them, and their miniatures—
flattering, but still not lovely—are kissed in secret by motherly lips. I
have seen many an excellent matron, who could never in her best days
have been handsome, and yet she had a packet of yellow love-letters in
a private drawer, and sweet children showered kisses on her sallow
cheeks. And I believe there have been plenty of young heroes, of middle
stature and feeble beards, who have felt quite sure they could never love
anything more insignificant than a Diana, and yet have found themselves
in middle life happily settled with a wife who waddles. Yes! thank God;
human feeling is like the mighty rivers that bless the earth: it does not
wait for beauty—it flows with resistless force and brings beauty with it.

All honour and reverence to the divine beauty of form! Let us cultivate it to the utmost in men, women, and children—in our gardens and
in our houses. But let us love that other beauty too, which lies in no
secret of proportion, but in the secret of deep human sympathy. Paint
us an angel, if you can, with a floating violet robe, and a face paled by
the celestial light; paint us yet oftener a Madonna, turning her mild
face upward and opening her arms to welcome the divine glory; but do
not impose on us any æsthetic rules which shall banish from the region
of Art those old women scraping carrots with their work-worn hands,
those heavy clowns taking holiday in a dingy pot-house, those rounded
backs and stupid weather-beaten faces that have bent over the spade
and done the rough work of the world—those homes with their tin
pans, their brown pitchers, their rough curs, and their clusters of onions.
In this world there are so many of these common coarse people, who have
no picturesque sentimental wretchedness! It is so needful we should remember their existence, else we may happen to leave them quite out
of our religion and philosophy, and frame lofty theories which only fit
a world of extremes. Therefore let Art always remind us of them; there-

fore let us always have men ready to give the loving pains of a life to
the faithful representing of commonplace things—men who see beauty
in these commonplace things, and delight in showing how kindly the
light of heaven falls on them. There are few prophets in the world; few
sublimely beautiful women; few heroes. I can't afford to give all my
love and reverence to such rarities: I want a great deal of those feelings
for my everyday fellow-men, especially for the few in the foreground of
the great multitude, whose faces I know, whose hands I touch, for whom
I have to make way with kindly courtesy. Neither are picturesque laz ·
zaroni or romantic criminals half so frequent as your common labourer,
who gets his own bread, and eats it vulgarly but creditably with his own
pocket-knife. It is more needful that I should have a fibre of sympathy
connecting me with that vulgar citizen who weighs out my sugar in a
vilely-assorted cravat and waistcoat, than with the handsomest rascal
in red scarf and green feathers;—more needful that my heart should
swell with loving admiration at some trait of gentle goodness in the
faulty people who sit at the same hearth with me, or in the clergyman
of my own parish, who is perhaps rather too corpulent, and in other
respects is not an Oberlin or a Tillotson, than at the deeds of heroes
whom I shall never know except by hearsay, or at the sublimest abstract
of all clerical graces that was ever conceived by an able novelist.

And so I come back to Mr. Irwine, with whom I desire you to be in
perfect charity, far as he may be from satisfying your demands on the
clerical character. Perhaps you think he was not—as he ought to have
been—a living demonstration of the benefits attached to a national
church? But I am not sure of that; at least I know that the people in
Broxton and Hayslope would have been very sorry to part with their
clergyman, and that most faces brightened at his approach; and until
it can be proved that hatred is a better thing for the soul than love, I
must believe that Mr. Irwine's influence in his parish was a more wholesome one than that of the zealous Mr. Ryde, who came there twenty
years afterwards, when Mr. Irwine had been gathered to his fathers. It
is true, Mr. Ryde insisted strongly on the doctrines of the Reformation,
visited his flock a great deal in their own homes, and was severe in rebuking the aberrations of the flesh—put a stop, indeed, to the Christmas
rounds of the church singers, as promoting drunkenness, and too light
handling of sacred things. But I gathered from Adam Bede, to whom I
talked of these matters in his old age, that few clergymen could be less
successful in winning the hearts of their parishioners than Mr. Ryde.
They learned a great many notions about doctrine from him, so that
almost every churchgoer under fifty began to distinguish as well between
the genuine gospel and what did not come precisely up to that standard,
as if he had been born and bred a Dissenter; and for some time after his
arrival there seemed to be quite a religious movment in that quiet rural
district. "But," said Adam, "I've seen pretty clear, ever since I was a
young un, as religion's something else besides notions. It isn't notions

sets people doing the right thing—it's feelings. It's the same with the
notions in religion as it is with math'matics,—a man may be able to
work problems straight off in's head as he sits by the fire and smokes his
pipe; but if he has to make a machine or a building, he must have a
will and a resolution, and love something else better than his own ease.
Somehow, the congregation began to fall off, and people began to speak
light o' Mr. Ryde. I believe he meant right at bottom; but, you see, he
was sourish-tempered, and was for beating down prices with the people
as worked for him; and his preaching wouldn't go down well with that
sauce. And he wanted to be like my lord judge i' the parish, punishing
folks for doing wrong; and he scolded 'em from the pulpit as if he'd
been a Ranter, and yet he couldn't abide the Dissenters, and was a deal
more set against 'em than Mr. Irwine was. And then he didn't keep
within his income, for he seemed to think at first go-off that six hundred
a-year was to make him as big a man as Mr. Donnithorne: that's a sore
mischief I've often seen with the poor curates jumping into a bit of a
living all of a sudden. Mr. Ryde was a deal thought on at a distance, I
believe, and he wrote books; but as for math'matics and the nature o'
things, he was as ignorant as a woman. He was very knowing about doctrines, and used to call 'em the bulwarks of the Reformation; but I've
always mistrusted that sort o' learning as leaves folks foolish and unreasonable about business. Now Mester Irwine was as different as could
be: as quick!—he understood what you meant in a minute; and he
knew all about building, and could see when you'd made a good job.
And he behaved as much like a gentleman to the farmers, and th' old
women and the labourers, as he did to the gentry. You never saw *him*
interfering and scolding, and trying to play th' emperor. Ah! he was a
fine man as ever you set eyes on; and so kind to's mother and sisters.
That poor sickly Miss Anne—he seemed to think more of her than of
anybody else in the world. There wasn't a soul in the parish had a word
to say against him; and his servants stayed with him till they were so
old and pottering, he had to hire other folks to do their work."

"Well," I said, "that was an excellent way of preaching in the week-
days; but I daresay, if your old friend Mr. Irwine were to come to life
again, and get into the pulpit next Sunday, you would be rather ashamed
that he didn't preach better after all your praise of him."

"Nay, nay," said Adam, broadening his chest and throwing himself
back in his chair, as if he were ready to meet all inferences, "nobody has
ever heard me say Mr. Irwine was much of a preacher. He didn't go into
deep speritial experience; and I know there's a deal in a man's inward
life as you can't measure by the square, and say, 'Do this and that'll
follow,' and, 'Do that and this'll follow.' There's things go on in the
soul, and times when feelings come into you like a rushing mighty wind,
as the Scripture says, and part your life in two a'most, so as you look
back on yourself as if you was somebody else. Those are things as you
can't bottle up in a 'do this' and 'do that'; and I'll go so far with the

strongest Methodist ever you'll find. That shows me there's deep speritial things in religion. You can't make much out wi' talking about it,
but you feel it. Mr. Irwine didn't go into those things: he preached short
moral sermons, and that was all. But then he acted pretty much up to
what he said; he didn't set up for being so different from other folks
one day, and then be as like 'em as two peas the next. And he made folks
love him and respect him, and that was better nor stirring up their gall
wi' being over-busy. Mrs. Poyser used to say—you know she would have
her word about everything—she said, Mr. Irwine was like a good meal o'
victual, you were the better for him without thinking on it, and Mr.
Ryde was like a dose o' physic, he gripped you and worreted you, and
after all he left you much the same."

"But didn't Mr. Ryde preach a great deal more about that spiritual
part of religion that you talk of, Adam? Couldn't you get more out of
his sermons than out of Mr. Irwine's?"

"Eh, I knowna. He preached a deal about doctrines. But I've seen
pretty clear ever since I was a young un, as religion's something else
besides doctrines and notions. I look at it as if the doctrines was like
finding names for your feelings, so as you can talk of 'em when you've
never known 'em, just as a man may talk o' tools when he knows their
names, though he's never so much as seen 'em, still less handled 'em.
I've heard a deal o' doctrine i' my time, for I used to go after the dissenting preachers along wi' Seth, when I was a lad o' seventeen, and got
puzzling myself a deal about th' Arminians and the Calvinists. The
Wesleyans, you know, are strong Arminians; and Seth, who could never
abide anything harsh, and was always for hoping the best, held fast by
the Wesleyans from the very first; but I thought I could pick a hole or
two in their notions, and I got disputing wi' one o' the class leaders
down at Treddles'on, and harassed him so, first o' this side and then o'
that, till at last he said, 'Young man, it's the devil making use o' your
pride and conceit as a weapon to war against the simplicity o' the truth.'
I couldn't help laughing then, but as I was going home, I thought the
man wasn't far wrong. I began to see as all this weighing and sifting
what this text means and that text means, and whether folks are saved
all by God's grace, or whether there goes an ounce o' their own will to 't,
was no part o' real religion at all. You may talk o' these things for hours
on end, and you'll only be all the more coxy and conceited for 't. So I
took to going nowhere but to church, and hearing nobody but Mr. Irwine, for he said nothing but what was good, and what you'd be the
wiser for remembering. And I found it better for my soul to be humble
before the mysteries o' God's dealings, and not be making a clatter about
what I could never understand. And they're poor foolish questions after
all; for what have we got either inside or outside of us but what comes
from God? If we've got a resolution to do right, He gave it us, I reckon,
first or last; but I see plain enough we shall never do it without a resolution, and that's enough for me."

Adam, you perceive, was a warm admirer, perhaps a partial judge, of Mr. Irwine, as, happily, some of us still are of the people we have known familiarly. Doubtless it will be despised as a weakness by that lofty order of minds who pant after the ideal, and are oppressed by a general sense that their emotions are of too exquisite a character to find fit objects among their everyday fellow-men. I have often been favoured with the confidence of these select natures, and find them to concur in the experience that great men are over-estimated and small men are insupportable; that if you would love a woman without ever looking back on your love as a folly, she must die while you are courting her; and if you would maintain the slightest belief in human heroism, you must never make a pilgrimage to see the hero. I confess I have often meanly shrunk from confessing to these accomplished and acute gentlemen what my own experience has been. I am afraid I have often smiled with hypocritical assent, and gratified them with an epigram on the fleeting nature of our illusions, which any one moderately acquainted with French literature can command at a moment's notice. Human converse, I think some wise man has remarked, is not rigidly sincere. But I herewith discharge my conscience, and declare, that I have had quite enthusiastic movements of admiration towards old gentlemen who spoke the worst English, who were occasionally fretful in their temper, and who had never moved in a higher sphere of influence than that of parish overseer; and that the way in which I have come to the conclusion that human nature is lovable—the way I have learnt something of its deep pathos, its sublime mysteries—has been by living a great deal among people more or less commonplace and vulgar, of whom you would perhaps hear nothing very surprising if you were to inquire about them in the neighbourhoods where they dwelt. Ten to one most of the small shopkeepers in their vicinity saw nothing at all in them. For I have observed this remarkable coincidence, that the select natures who pant after the ideal, and find nothing in pantaloons or petticoats great enough to command their reverence and love, are curiously in unison with the narrowest and pettiest. For example, I have often heard Mr. Gedge, the landlord of the Royal Oak, who used to turn a blood-shot eye on his neighbours in the village of Shepperton, sum up his opinion of the people in his own parish—and they were all the people he knew—in these emphatic words: "Ay, sir, I've said it often, and I'll say it again, they're a poor lot i' this parish—a poor lot, sir, big and little." I think he had a dim idea that if he could migrate to a distant parish, he might find neighbours worthy of him; and indeed he did subsequently transfer himself to the Saracen's Head, which was doing a thriving business in the back street of a neighbouring market-town. But, oddly enough, he has found the people up that back street of precisely the same stamp as the inhabitants of Shepperton—"a poor lot, sir, big and little, and them as comes for a go o' gin are no better than them as comes for a pint o' twopenny—a poor lot."

CHAPTER XVIII

CHURCH

"HETTY, Hetty, don't you know church begins at two, and it's gone half after one a'ready? Have you got nothing better to think on this good Sunday, as poor old Thias Bede's to be put into the ground, and him drownded i' the' dead o' the night, as it's enough to make one's back run cold, but you must be 'dizening yourself as if there was a wedding istid of a funeral?"

"Well, aunt," said Hetty, "I can't be ready so soon as everybody else, when I've got Totty's things to put on. And I'd ever such work to make her stand still."

Hetty was coming down-stairs, and Mrs. Poyser, in her plain bonnet and shawl, was standing below. If ever a girl looked as if she had been made of roses, that girl was Hetty in her Sunday hat and frock. For her hat was trimmed with pink, and her frock had pink spots, sprinkled on a white ground. There was nothing but pink and white about her, except in her dark hair and eyes and her little buckled shoes. Mrs. Poyser was provoked at herself, for she could hardly keep from smiling, as any mortal is inclined to do at the sight of pretty round things. So she turned without speaking, and joined the group outside the house door, followed by Hetty, whose heart was fluttering so at the thought of some one she expected to see at church, that she hardly felt the ground she trod on.

And now the little procession set off. Mr. Poyser was in his Sunday suit of drab, with a red-and-green waistcoat, and a green watch-ribbon having a large cornelian seal attached, pendant like a plumb-line from that promontory where his watch-pocket was situated; a silk handkerchief of a yellow tone round his neck; and excellent grey ribbed stockings, knitted by Mrs. Poyser's own hand, setting off the proportions of his leg. Mr. Poyser had no reason to be ashamed of his leg, and suspected that the growing abuse of top-boots and other fashions tending to disguise the nether limbs, had their origin in a pitiable degeneracy of the human calf. Still less had he reason to be ashamed of his round jolly face, which was good-humour itself as he said, "Come, Hetty—come, little uns!" and, giving his arm to his wife, led the way through the causeway gate into the yard.

The "little uns" addressed were Marty and Tommy, boys of nine and seven, in little fustian tailed coats and knee-breeches, relieved by rosy cheeks and black eyes; looking as much like their father as a very small elephant is like a very large one. Hetty walked between them, and behind came patient Molly, whose task it was to carry Totty through the yard, and over all the wet places on the road; for Totty, having speedily recovered from her threatened fever, had insisted on going to

church to-day, and especially on wearing her red-and-black necklace
outside her tippet. And there were many wet places for her to be carried
over this afternoon, for there had been heavy showers in the morning,
though now the clouds had rolled off and lay in towering silvery masses
on the horizon.

You might have known it was Sunday if you had only waked up in
the farmyard. The cocks and hens seemed to know it, and made only
crooning subdued noises; the very bull-dog looked less savage, as if he
would have been satisfied with a smaller bite than usual. The sunshine
seemed to call all things to rest and not to labour; it was asleep itself on
the moss-grown cow-shed; on the group of white ducks nestling together
with their bills tucked under their wings; on the old black sow stretched
languidly on the straw, while her largest young one found an excellent
spring-bed on his mother's fat ribs; on Alick, the shepherd, in his new
smock-frock, taking an uneasy siesta, half-sitting half-standing on the
granary steps. Alick was of opinion that church, like other luxuries, was
not to be indulged in often by a foreman who had the weather and the
ewes on his mind. "Church! nay—I'n gotten summat else to think on,"
was an answer which he often uttered in a tone of bitter significance that
silenced further question. I feel sure Alick meant no irreverence; indeed,
I know that his mind was not of a speculative, negative cast, and he
would on no account have missed going to church on Christmas Day,
Easter Sunday, and "Whissuntide." But he had a general impression
that public worship and religious ceremonies, like other non-productive
employments, were intended for people who had leisure.

"There's father a-standing at the yard-gate," said Martin Poyser. "I
reckon he wants to watch us down the field. It's wonderful what sight
he has, and him turned seventy-five."

"Ah, I often think it's wi' th' old folks as it is wi' the babbies," said
Mrs. Poyser; "they're satisfied wi' looking, no matter what they're
looking at. It's God A'mighty's way o' quietening 'em, I reckon, afore
they go to sleep."

Old Martin opened the gate as he saw the family procession approaching, and held it wide open, leaning on his stick—pleased to do this bit
of work; for, like all old men whose life has been spent in labour, he
liked to feel that he was still useful—that there was a better crop of
onions in the garden because he was by at the sowing—and that the
cows would be milked the better if he stayed at home on a Sunday afternoon to look on. He always went to church on Sacrament Sundays, but
not very regularly at other times; on wet Sundays, or whenever he had a
touch of rheumatism, he used to read the three first chapters of Genesis
instead.

"They'll ha' putten Thias Bede i' the ground afore ye get to the
churchyard," he said, as his son came up. "It 'ud ha' been better luck if
they'd ha' buried him i' the forenoon when the rain was fallin'; there's
no likelihoods of a drop now; an' the moon lies like a boat there, dost

see? That's a sure sign o' fair weather—there's a many as is false, but
that's sure."

"Ay, ay," said the son, "I'm in hopes it'll hold up now."

"Mind what the parson says, mind what the parson says, my lads,"
said Grandfather to the black-eyed youngsters in knee-breeches, conscious of a marble or two in their pockets, which they looked forward to
handling a little, secretly, during the sermon.

"Dood-by, dandad," said Totty. "Me doin to church. Me dot my net-
lace on. Dive me a peppermint."

Grandad, shaking with laughter at this "deep little wench," slowly
transferred his stick to his left hand, which held the gate open, and
slowly thrust his finger into the waistcoat pocket on which Totty had
fixed her eyes with a confident look of expectation.

And when they were all gone, the old man leaned on the gate again,
watching them across the lane along the Home Close, and through the
far gate, till they disappeared behind a bend in the hedge. For the
hedgerows in those days shut out one's view, even on the better-managed
farms; and this afternoon, the dogroses were tossing out their pink
wreaths, the nightshade was in its yellow and purple glory, the pale
honeysuckle grew out of reach, peeping high up out of a holly bush, and
over all an ash or a sycamore every now and then threw its shadow across
the path.

There were acquaintances at other gates who had to move aside and
let them pass: at the gate of the Home Close there was half the dairy
of cows standing one behind the other, extremely slow to understand
that their large bodies might be in the way; at the far gate there was
the mare holding her head over the bars, and beside her the liver-coloured
foal with its head towards its mother's flank, apparently still much embarrassed by its own straddling existence. The way lay entirely through
Mr. Poyser's own fields till they reached the main road leading to the
village, and he turned a keen eye on the stock and the crops as they
went along, while Mrs. Poyser was ready to supply a running commentary on them all. The woman who manages a dairy has a large share
in making the rent, so she may well be allowed to have her opinion on
stock and their "keep"—an exercise which strengthens her understanding so much that she finds herself able to give her husband advice on
most other subjects.

"There's that short-horned Sally," she said, as they entered the Home
Close, and she caught sight of the meek beast that lay chewing the cud,
and looking at her with a sleepy eye. "I begin to hate the sight o' the
cow; and I say now what I said three weeks ago, the sooner we get rid
of her the better, for there's that little yellow cow as doesn't give half
the milk, and yet I've twice as much butter from her."

"Why, thee't not like the women in general," said Mr. Poyser; "they
like the short-horns, as give such a lot o' milk. There's Chowne's wife
wants him to buy no other sort."

"What's it sinnify what Chowne's wife likes?—a poor soft thing, wi' no more head-piece nor a sparrow. She'd take a big cullender to strain her lard wi', and then wonder as the scratchins run through. I've seen enough of her to know as I'll niver take a servant from her house again —all hugger-mugger—and you'd niver know, when you went in, whether it was Monday or Friday, the wash draggin' on to th' end o' the week; and as for her cheese, I know well enough it rose like a loaf in a tin last year. And then she talks o' the weather bein' i' fault, as there's folks 'ud stand on their heads and then say the fault was i' their boots."

"Well, Chowne's been wanting to buy Sally, so we can get rid of her if thee lik'st," said Mr. Poyser, secretly proud of his wife's superior power of putting two and two together; indeed, on recent market-days he had more than once boasted of her discernment in this very matter of short-horns.

"Ay, them as choose a soft for a wife may's well buy up the short-horns, for if you get your head stuck in a bog your legs may's well go after it. Eh! talk o' legs, there's legs for you," Mrs. Poyser continued, as Totty, who had been set down now the road was dry, toddled on in front of her father and mother. "There's shapes! An' she's got such a long foot, she'll be her father's own child."

"Ay, she'll be well such a one as Hetty i' ten years' time, on'y she's got *thy* coloured eyes. I niver remember a blue eye i' my family; my mother had eyes as black as sloes, just like Hetty's."

"The child 'ull be none the worse for having summat as isn't like Hetty. An' I'm none for having her so over pretty. Though, for the matter o' that, there's people wi' light hair an' blue eyes as pretty as them wi' black. If Dinah had got a bit o' colour in her cheeks, an' didn't stick that Methodist cap on her head, enough to frighten the cows, folks 'ud think her as pretty as Hetty."

"Nay, nay," said Mr. Poyser, with rather a contemptuous emphasis, "thee dostna know the pints of a woman. The men 'ud niver run after Dinah as they would after Hetty."

"What care I what the men 'ud run after? It's well seen what choice the most of 'em know how to make, by the poor draggle-tails o' wives you see, like bits o' gauze ribbon, good for nothing when the colour's gone."

"Well, well, thee canstna say but what I knowed how to make a choice when I married thee," said Mr. Poyser, who usually settled little con-jugal disputes by a compliment of this sort; "and thee wast twice as buxom as Dinah ten years ago."

"I niver said as a woman had need to be ugly to make a good missis of a house. There's Chowne's wife ugly enough to turn the milk an' save the rennet, but she'll niver save nothing any other way. But as for Dinah, poor child, she's niver likely to be buxom as long as she'll make her dinner o' cake and water, for the sake o' giving to them as want. She provoked me past bearing sometimes; and, as I told her, she went clean again' the Scriptur', for that says, 'Love your neighbour as yourself'; 'but,' I said, 'if you loved your neighbour no better nor you do your-

self, Dinah, it's little enough you'd do for him. You'd be thinking he
might do well enough on a half-empty stomach.' Eh, I wonder where she
is this blessed Sunday!—sitting by that sick woman, I daresay, as
she'd set her heart on going to all of a sudden."

"Ah, it was a pity she should take such megrims into her head, when
she might ha' stayed wi' us all summer, and eaten twice as much as she
wanted, and it 'ud niver ha' been missed. She made no odds in th' house
at all, for she sat as still at her sewing as a bird on the nest, and was
uncommon nimble at running to fetch anything. If Hetty gets married,
theed'st like to ha' Dinah wi' thee constant."

"It's no use thinking o' that," said Mrs. Poyser. "You might as well
beckon to the flying swallow, as ask Dinah to come an' live here comfortable, like other folks. If anything could turn her, *I* should ha' turned
her, for I've talked to her for a hour on end, and scolded her too; for
she's my own sister's child, and it behoves me to do what I can for her.
But eh, poor thing, as soon as she'd said us 'good-by,' an' got into the
cart, an' looked back at me with her pale face, as is welly like her aunt
Judith come back from heaven, I begun to be frightened to think o' the
set-downs I'd given her; for it comes over you sometimes as if she'd a
way o' knowing the rights o' things more nor other folks have. But I'll
niver give in as that's 'cause she's a Methodist, no more nor a white
calf's white 'cause it eats out o' the same bucket wi' a black un."

"Nay," said Mr. Poyser, with as near an approach to a snarl as his
good-nature would allow; "I'n no opinion o' the Methodists. It's on'y
tradesfolks as turn Methodists; you niver knew a farmer bitten wi' them
maggots. There's maybe a workman now an' then, as isn't over clever
at's work, takes to preachin' an' that, like Seth Bede. But you see Adam,
as has got one o' the best head-pieces hereabout, knows better; he's a
good Churchman, else I'd never encourage him for a sweetheart for
Hetty."

"Why, goodness me," said Mrs. Poyser, who had looked back while
her husband was speaking, "look where Molly is with them lads. They're
the field's length behind us. How *could* you let 'em do so, Hetty? Anybody might as well set a pictur to watch the children as you. Run back,
and tell 'em to come on."

Mr. and Mrs. Poyser were now at the end of the second field, so they
set Totty on the top of one of the large stones forming the true Loamshire stile, and awaited the loiterers; Totty observing with complacency,
"Dey naughty, naughty boys—me dood."

The fact was that this Sunday walk through the fields was fraught
with great excitement to Marty and Tommy, who saw a perpetual drama
going on in the hedgerows, and could no more refrain from stopping
and peeping than if they had been a couple of spaniels or terriers. Marty
was quite sure he saw a yellowhammer on the boughs of the great ash,
and while he was peeping, he missed the sight of a white-throated stoat,
which had run across the path and was described with much fervour by
the junior Tommy. Then there was a little greenfinch, just fledged, flut-

tering along the ground, and it seemed quite possible to catch it, till it managed to flutter under the blackberry bush. Hetty could not be got to give any heed to these things, so Molly was called on for her ready sympathy, and peeped with open mouth wherever she was told, and said "Lawks!" whenever she was expected to wonder.

Molly hastened on with some alarm when Hetty had come back and called to them that her aunt was angry; but Marty ran on first, shouting, "We've found the speckled turkey's nest, mother!" with the instinctive confidence that people who bring good news are never in fault.

"Ah," said Mrs. Poyser, really forgetting all discipline in this pleasant surprise, "that's a good lad; why, where is it?"

"Down in ever such a hole, under the hedge. I saw it first, looking after the greenfinch, and she sat on th' nest."

"You didn't frighten her, I hope," said the mother, "else she'll forsake it."

"No, I went away as still as still, and whispered to Molly—didn't I, Molly?"

"Well, well, now come on," said Mrs. Poyser, "and walk before father and mother, and take your little sister by the hand. We must go straight on now. Good boys don't look after the birds of a Sunday."

"But, mother," said Marty, "you said you'd give half-a-crown to find the speckled turkey's nest. Mayn't I have the half crown put into my money-box?"

"We'll see about that, my lad, if you walk along now, like a good boy."

The father and mother exchanged a significant glance of amusement at their eldest-born's acuteness; but on Tommy's round face there was a cloud.

"Mother," he said, half crying, "Marty's got ever so much more money in his box nor I've got in mine."

"Munny, me want half-a-toun in my bots," said Totty.

"Hush, hush, hush," said Mrs. Poyser, "did ever anybody hear such naughty children? Nobody shall ever see their money-boxes any more, if they don't make haste and go on to church."

This dreadful threat had the desired effect, and through the two remaining fields the three pair of small legs trotted on without any serious interruption, notwithstanding a small pond full of tadpoles, alias "bullheads," which the lads looked at wistfully.

The damp hay that must be scattered and turned afresh to-morrow was not a cheering sight to Mr. Poyser, who during hay and corn harvest had often some mental struggles as to the benefits of a day of rest; but no temptation would have induced him to carry on any field-work, however early in the morning, on a Sunday; for had not Michael Holdsworth had a pair of oxen "sweltered" while he was ploughing on Good Friday? That was a demonstration that work on sacred days was a wicked thing; and with wickedness of any sort Martin Poyser was quite clear that he would have nothing to do, since money got by such means would never prosper.

"It a'most makes your fingers itch to be at the hay now the sun shines so," he observed, as they passed through the "Big Meadow." "But it's poor foolishness to think o' saving by going against your conscience. There's that Jim Wakefield, as they used to call 'Gentleman Wakefield,' used to do the same of a Sunday as o' week-days, and took no heed to right or wrong, as if there was nayther God nor Devil. An' what's he come to? Why, I saw him myself last market-day a-carrying a basket wi' oranges in't."

"Ah, to be sure," said Mrs. Poyser, emphatically, "you make but a poor trap to catch luck if you go and bait it wi' wickedness. The money as is got so's like to burn holes i' your pocket. I'd niver wish us to leave our lads a sixpence but what was got i' the rightful way. And as for the weather, there's One above makes it, and we must put up wi't: it's nothing of a plague to what the wenches are."

Notwithstanding the interruption in their walk, the excellent habit which Mrs. Poyser's clock had of taking time by the forelock, had secured their arrival at the village while it was still a quarter to two, though almost every one who meant to go to church was already within the churchyard gates. Those who stayed at home were chiefly mothers, like Timothy's Bess, who stood at her own door nursing her baby, and feeling as women feel in that position—that nothing else can be expected of them.

It was not entirely to see Thias Bede's funeral that the people were standing about the churchyard so long before service began; that was their common practice. The women, indeed, usually entered the church at once, and the farmers' wives talked in an under-tone to each other, over the tall pews, about their illnesses and the total failure of doctor's stuff, recommending dandelion-tea, and other home-made specifics, as far preferable—about the servants, and their growing exorbitance as to wages, whereas the quality of their services declined from year to year, and there was no girl nowadays to be trusted any further than you could see her—about the bad price Mr. Dingal, the Treddleston grocer, was giving for butter, and the reasonable doubts that might be held for his solvency, notwithstanding that Mrs. Dingal was a sensible woman, and they were all sorry for *her,* for she had very good kin. Meantime the men lingered outside, and hardly any of them except the singers, who had a humming and fragmentary rehearsal to go through, entered the church until Mr. Irwine was in the desk. They saw no reason for that premature entrance,—what could they do in church, if they were there before service began?—and they did not conceive that any power in the universe could take it ill of them if they stayed out and talked a little about "bus'ness."

Chad Cranage looks like quite a new acquaintance to-day, for he has got his clean Sunday face, which always makes his little grand-daughter cry at him as a stranger. But an experienced eye would have fixed on him at once as the village blacksmith, after seeing the humble deference with which the big saucy fellow took off his hat and stroked his hair to

the farmers; for Chad was accustomed to say that a working-man must
hold a candle to——a personage understood to be as black as he was
himself on week-days; by which evil-sounding rule of conduct he meant
what was, after all, rather virtuous than otherwise, namely, that men
who had horses to be shod must be treated with respect. Chad and the
rougher sort of workmen kept aloof from the grave under the white
thorn, where the burial was going forward; but Sandy Jim and several of
the farm-labourers made a group round it, and stood with their hats off,
as fellow-mourners with the mother and sons. Others held a midway
position, sometimes watching the group at the grave, sometimes listening
to the conversation of the farmers, who stood in a knot near the church
door, and were now joined by Martin Poyser, while his family passed
into the church. On the outside of this knot stood Mr. Casson, the landlord of the Donnithorne Arms, in his most striking attitude—that is to
say, with the forefinger of his right hand thrust between the buttons of
his waistcoat, his left hand in his breeches pocket, and his head very
much on one side; looking, on the whole, like an actor who has only a
monosyllabic part intrusted to him, but feels sure that the audience
discern his fitness for the leading business; curiously in contrast with old
Jonathan Burge, who held his hands behind him, and leaned forward
coughing asthmatically, with an inward scorn of all knowingness that
could not be turned into cash. The talk was in rather a lower tone than
usual to-day, hushed a little by the sound of Mr. Irwine's voice reading
the final prayers of the burial-service. They had all had their word of
pity for poor Thias, but now they had got upon the nearer subject of
their own grievances against Satchell, the Squire's bailiff, who played the
part of steward so far as it was not performed by old Mr. Donnithorne
himself, for that gentleman had the meanness to receive his own rents
and make bargains about his own timber. This subject of conversation
was an additional reason for not being loud, since Satchell himself might
presently be walking up the paved road to the church door. And soon
they became suddenly silent; for Mr. Irwine's voice had ceased, and the
group round the white thorn was dispersing itself towards the church.

They all moved aside, and stood with their hats off, while Mr. Irwine
passed. Adam and Seth were coming next, with their mother between
them; for Joshua Rann officiated as head sexton as well as clerk, and
was not yet ready to follow the rector into the vestry. But there was a
pause before the three mourners came on: Lisbeth had turned round to
look again towards the grave! Ah! there was nothing now but the brown
earth under the white thorn. Yet she cried less to-day than she had done
any day since her husband's death: along with all her grief there was
mixed an unusual sense of her own importance in having a "burial," and
in Mr. Irwine's reading a special service for her husband; and besides,
she knew the funeral psalm was going to be sung for him. She felt this
counter-excitement to her sorrow still more strongly as she walked with
her sons towards the church door, and saw the friendly sympathetic
nods of their fellow-parishioners.

The mother and sons passed into the church, and one by one the loiterers followed, though some still lingered without; the sight of Mr.
Donnithorne's carriage, which was winding slowly up the hill, perhaps
helping to make them feel that there was no need for haste.

But presently the sound of the bassoon and the key-bugles burst
forth; the evening hymn, which always opened the service, had begun,
and every one must now enter and take his place.

I cannot say that the interior of Hayslope Church was remarkable for
anything except for the grey age of its oaken pews—great square pews
mostly, ranged on each side of a narrow aisle. It was free, indeed, from
the modern blemish of galleries. The choir had two narrow pews to themselves in the middle of the right-hand row, so that it was a short process
for Joshua Rann to take his place among them as principal bass, and
return to his desk after the singing was over. The pulpit and desk, grey
and old as the pews, stood on one side of the arch leading into the chancel, which also had its grey square pews for Mr. Donnithorne's family
and servants. Yet I assure you these grey pews, with the buff-washed
walls, gave a very pleasing tone to this shabby interior, and agreed extremely well with the ruddy faces and bright waistcoats. And there were
liberal touches of crimson toward the chancel, for the pulpit and Mr.
Donnithorne's own pew had handsome crimson cloth cushions; and, to
close the vista, there was a crimson altar-cloth, embroidered with golden
rays by Miss Lydia's own hand.

But even without the crimson cloth, the effect must have been warm
and cheering when Mr. Irwine was in the desk, looking benignly round
on that simple congregation—on the hardy old men, with bent knees
and shoulders, perhaps, but with vigour left for much hedge-clipping and
thatching; on the tall stalwart frames and roughly-cut bronzed faces of
the stone-cutters and carpenters; on the half-dozen well-to-do farmers,
with their apple-cheeked families; and on the clean old women; mostly
farm-labourers' wives, with their bit of snow-white cap-border under
their black bonnets, and with their withered arms, bare from the elbow,
folded passively over their chests. For none of the old people held books
—why should they? not one of them could read. But they knew a few
"good words" by heart, and their withered lips now and then moved
silently, following the service without any very clear comprehension indeed, but with a simple faith in its efficacy to ward off harm and bring
blessing. And now all faces were visible, for all were standing up—the
little children on the seats peeping over the edge of the grey pews, while
good Bishop Ken's evening hymn was being sung to one of those lively
psalm-tunes which died out with the last generation of rectors and choral
parish-clerks. Melodies die out, like the pipe of Pan, with the ears that
love them and listen for them. Adam was not in his usual place among
the singers to-day, for he sat with his mother and Seth, and he noticed
with surprise that Bartle Massey was absent too: all the more agreeable
for Mr. Joshua Rann, who gave out his bass notes with unusual com-

placency, and threw an extra ray of severity into the glances he sent over his spectacles at the recusant Will Maskery.

I beseech you to imagine Mr. Irwine looking round on this scene, in his ample white surplice, that became him so well, with his powdered hair thrown back, his rich brown complexion, and his finely-cut nostril and upper lip; for there was a certain virtue in that benignant yet keen countenance, as there is in all human faces from which a generous soul beams out. And over all streamed the delicious June sunshine through the old windows, with their desultory patches of yellow, red, and blue, that threw pleasant touches of colour on the opposite wall.

I think, as Mr. Irwine looked round to-day, his eyes rested an instant longer than usual on the square pew occupied by Martin Poyser and his family. And there was another pair of dark eyes that found it impossible not to wander thither, and rest on that round pink-and-white figure. But Hetty was at that moment quite careless of any glances—she was absorbed in the thought that Arthur Donnithorne would soon be coming into church, for the carriage must surely be at the church gate by this time. She had never seen him since she parted with him in the wood on Thursday evening, and oh! how long the time had seemed! Things had gone on just the same as ever since that evening; the wonders that had happened then had brought no changes after them; they were already like a dream. When she heard the church door swinging, her heart beat so, she dared not look up. She felt that her aunt was curtsying; she curtsied herself. That must be old Mr. Donnithorne—he always came first, the wrinkled small old man, peering round with short-sighted glances at the bowing and curtsying congregation; then she knew Miss Lydia was passing, and though Hetty liked so much to look at her fashionable little coal-scuttle bonnet, with the wreath of small roses round it, she didn't mind it to-day. But there were no more curtsies—no, he was not come; she felt sure there was nothing else passing the pew door but the housekeeper's black bonnet, and the lady-maid's beautiful straw that had once been Miss Lydia's, and then the powdered heads of the butler and footman. No, he was not there; yet she would look now—she might be mistaken—for, after all, she had not looked. So she lifted up her eyelids and glanced timidly at the cushioned pew in the chancel: —there was no one but old Mr. Donnithorne rubbing his spectacles with his white handkerchief, and Miss Lydia opening the large gilt-edged prayer-book. The chill disappointment was too hard to bear: she felt herself turning pale, her lips trembling; she was ready to cry. Oh, what *should* she do? Everybody would know the reason; they would know she was crying because Arthur was not there. And Mr. Craig, with the wonderful hot-house plant in his button-hole, was staring at her, she knew. It was dreadfully long before the General Confession began, so that she could kneel down. Two great drops *would* fall then, but no one saw them except good-natured Molly, for her aunt and uncle knelt with their backs towards her. Molly, unable to imagine any cause for tears in church except faintness, of which she had a vague traditional knowledge, drew out of her pocket a queer little flat blue smelling-bottle, and after much labour in pulling the cork out, thrust the narrow neck against Hetty's nostrils. "It donna smell," she whispered, thinking this was a great advantage which old salts had over fresh ones: they did you good without biting your nose. Hetty pushed it away peevishly; but this little flash of temper did what the salts could not have done—it roused her to wipe away the traces of her tears, and try with all her might not to shed any more. Hetty had a certain strength in her vain little nature: she would have borne anything rather than be laughed at, or pointed at with any other feeling than admiration; she would have pressed her own nails into her tender flesh rather than people should know a secret she did not want them to know.

What fluctuations there were in her busy thoughts and feelings, while Mr. Irwine was pronouncing the solemn "Absolution" in her deaf ears, and through all the tones of petition that followed! Anger lay very close to disappointment, and soon won the victory over the conjectures her small ingenuity could devise to account for Arthur's absence on the supposition that he really wanted to come, really wanted to see her again. And by the time she rose from her knees mechanically, because all the rest were rising, the colour had returned to her cheeks even with a heightened glow, for she was framing little indignant speeches to herself, saying she hated Arthur for giving her this pain—she would like him to suffer too. Yet while this selfish tumult was going on in her soul, her eyes were bent down on her prayer-book, and the eyelids with their dark fringe looked as lovely as ever. Adam Bede thought so, as he glanced at her for a moment on rising from his knees.

But Adam's thoughts of Hetty did not deafen him to the service; they rather blended with all the other deep feelings for which the church service was a channel to him this afternoon, as a certain consciousness of our entire past and our imagined future blends itself with all our moments of keen sensibility. And to Adam the church service was the best channel he could have found for his mingled regret, yearning, and resignation; its interchange of beseeching cries for help, with outbursts of faith and praise—its recurrent responses and the familiar rhythm of its collects, seemed to speak for him as no other form of worship could have done; as, to those early Christians who had worshipped from their childhood upward in catacombs, the torchlight and shadows must have seemed nearer the Divine presence than the heathenish daylight of the streets. The secret of our emotions never lies in the bare object, but in its subtle relations to our own past: no wonder the secret escapes the unsympathising observer, who might as well put on his spectacles to discern odours.

But there was one reason why even a chance comer would have found the service in Hayslope Church more impressive than in most other village nooks in the kingdom—a reason of which I am sure you have not the slightest suspicion. It was the reading of our friend Joshua Rann.

Where that good shoemaker got his notion of reading from, remained a mystery even to his most intimate acquaintances. I believe, after all, he got it chiefly from Nature, who had poured some of her music into this honest conceited soul, as she had been known to do into other narrow souls before his. She had given him, at least, a fine bass voice and a musical ear; but I cannot positively say whether these alone had sufficed to inspire him with the rich chant in which he delivered the responses. The way he rolled from a rich deep forte into a melancholy cadence, subsiding, at the end of the last word, into a sort of faint resonance, like the lingering vibrations of a fine violoncello, I can compare to nothing for its strong calm melancholy but the rush and cadence of the wind among the autumn boughs. This may seem a strange mode of speaking about the reading of a parish-clerk—a man in rusty spectacles, with stubbly hair, a large occiput, and a prominent crown. But that is Nature's way: she will allow a gentleman of splendid physiognomy and poetic aspirations to sing woefully out of tune, and not give him the slightest hint of it; and takes care that some narrow-browed fellow, trolling a ballad in the corner of a pot-house, shall be as true to his intervals as a bird.

Joshua himself was less proud of his reading than of his singing, and it was always with a sense of heightened importance that he passed from the desk to the choir. Still more to-day: it was a special occasion; for an old man, familiar to all the parish, had died a sad death—not in his bed, a circumstance the most painful to the mind of the peasant—and now the funeral psalm was to be sung in memory of his sudden departure. Moreover, Bartle Massey was not at church, and Joshua's importance in the choir suffered no eclipse. It was a solemn minor strain they sang. The old psalm-tunes have many a wail among them, and the words——

> "Thou sweep'st us off as with a flood;
> We vanish hence like dreams"—

seemed to have a closer application than usual, in the death of poor Thias. The mother and sons listened, each with peculiar feelings. Lisbeth had a vague belief that the psalm was doing her husband good; it was part of that decent burial which she would have thought it a greater wrong to withhold from him than to have caused him many unhappy days while he was living. The more there was said about her husband, the more there was done for him, surely the safer he would be. It was poor Lisbeth's blind way of feeling that human love and pity are a ground of faith in some other love. Seth, who was easily touched, shed tears, and tried to recall, as he had done continually since his father's death, all that he had heard of the possibility that a single moment of consciousness at the last might be a moment of pardon and reconcilement; for was it not written in the very psalm they were singing, that the divine dealings were not measured and circumscribed by time? Adam had never been unable to join in a psalm before. He had known plenty of trouble and vexation since he had been a lad; but this was the first sorrow that had hemmed in his voice, and strangely enough it was sorrow because the chief source of his past trouble and vexation was for ever gone out of his reach. He had not been able to press his father's hand before their parting, and say, "Father, you know it was all right between us; I never forgot what I owed you when I was a lad; you forgive me if I have been too hot and hasty now and then!" Adam thought but little to-day of the hard work and the earnings he had spent on his father: his thoughts ran constantly on what the old man's feelings had been in moments of humiliation, when he had held down his head before the rebukes of his son. When our indignation is borne in submissive silence, we are apt to feel twinges of doubt afterwards as to our own generosity, if not justice; how much more when the object of our anger has gone into everlasting silence, and we have seen his face for the last time in the meekness of death!

"Ah, I was always too hard," Adam said to himself. "It's a sore fault in me as I'm so hot and out o' patience with people when they do wrong, and my heart gets shut up against 'em, so as I can't bring myself to forgive 'em. I see clear enough there's more pride nor love in my soul, for I could sooner make a thousand strokes with th' hammer for my father than bring myself to say a kind word to him. And there went plenty o' pride and temper to the strokes, as the devil *will* be having his finger in what we call our duties as well as our sins. Mayhap the best thing I ever did in my life was only doing what was easiest for myself. It's allays been easier for me to work nor to sit still, but the real tough job for me 'ud be to master my own will and temper, and go right against my own pride. It seems to me now, if I was to find father at home to-night, I should behave different; but there's no knowing—perhaps nothing 'ud be a lesson to us if it didn't come too late. It's well we should feel as life's a reckoning we can't make twice over; there's no real making amends in this world, any more nor you can mend a wrong subtraction by doing your addition right."

This was the key-note to which Adam's thoughts had perpetually returned since his father's death, and the solemn wail of the funeral psalm was only an influence that brought back the old thoughts with stronger emphasis. So was the sermon, which Mr. Irwine had chosen with reference to Thias's funeral. It spoke briefly and simply of the words, "In the midst of life we are in death"—how the present moment is all we can call our own for works of mercy, of righteous dealing, and of family tenderness. All very old truths—but what we thought the oldest truth becomes the most startling to us in the week when we have looked on the dead face of one who has made a part of our own lives. For when men want to impress us with the effect of a new and wonderfully vivid light, do they not let it fall on the most familiar objects, that we may measure its intensity by remembering the former dimness?

Then came the moment of the final blessing, when the forever sublime words, "The peace of God, which passeth all understanding," seemed to blend with the calm afternoon sunshine that fell on the bowed heads of the congregation; and then the quiet rising, the mothers tying on the bonnets of the little maidens who had slept through the sermon, the fathers collecting the prayer-books, until all streamed out through the old archway into the green churchyard, and began their neighbourly talk, their simple civilities, and their invitations to tea; for on a Sunday every one was ready to receive a guest—it was the day when all must be in their best clothes and their best humour.

Mr. and Mrs. Poyser paused a minute at the church gate: they were waiting for Adam to come up, not being contented to go away without saying a kind word to the widow and her sons.

"Well, Mrs. Bede," said Mrs. Poyser, as they walked on together, "you must keep up your heart; husbands and wives must be content when they've lived to rear their children and see one another's hair grey."

"Ay, ay," said Mr. Poyser; "they wonna have long to wait for one another then, anyhow. And ye've got two o' the strapping'st sons in the country; and well you may, for I remember poor Thias as fine a broad-shouldered fellow as need to be; and as for you, Mrs. Bede, why you're straighter i' the back nor half the young women now."

"Eh," said Lisbeth, "it's poor luck for the platter to wear well when it's broke i' two. The sooner I'm laid under the thorn the better. I'm no good to nobody now."

Adam never took notice of his mother's little unjust plaints; but Seth said, "Nay, mother, thee mustna say so. Thy sons 'ull never get another mother."

"That's true, lad, that's true," said Mr. Poyser; "and it's wrong on us to give way to grief, Mrs. Bede; for it's like the children cryin' when the fathers and mothers take things from 'em. There's One above knows better nor us."

"Ah," said Mrs. Poyser, "an' it's poor work allays settin' the dead above the livin'. We shall all on us be dead some time, I reckon—it 'ud be better if folks 'ud make much on us beforehand, istid o' beginnin' when we're gone. It's but little good you'll do a-watering the last year's crop."

"Well, Adam," said Mr. Poyser, feeling that his wife's words were, as usual, rather incisive than soothing, and that it would be well to change the subject, "you'll come and see us again now, I hope. I hanna had a talk with you this long while, and the missis here wants you to see what can be done with her best spinning-wheel, for it's got broke, and it'll be a nice job to mend it—there'll want a bit o' turning. You'll come as soon as you can now, will you?"

Mr. Poyser paused and looked round while he was speaking, as if to see where Hetty was; for the children were running on before. Hetty was not without a companion, and she had, besides, more pink and white about her than ever; for she held in her hand the wonderful pink-and-white hot-house plant, with a very long name—a Scotch name, she supposed, since people said Mr. Craig the gardener was Scotch. Adam took the opportunity of looking round too; and I am sure you will not require of him that he should feel any vexation in observing a pouting

expression on Hetty's face as she listened to the gardener's small-talk.
Yet in her secret heart she was glad to have him by her side, for she would
perhaps learn from him how it was Arthur had not come to church. Not
that she cared to ask him the question, but she hoped the information
would be given spontaneously; for Mr. Craig, like a superior man, was
very fond of giving information.

Mr. Craig was never aware that his conversation and advances were
received coldly, for to shift one's point of view beyond certain limits is
impossible to the most liberal and expansive mind; we are none of us
aware of the impressions we produce on Brazilian monkeys of feeble
understanding—it is possible they see hardly anything in us. Moreover,
Mr. Craig was a man of sober passions, and was already in his tenth
year of hesitation as to the relative advantages of matrimony and
bachelorhood. It is true that, now and then, when he had been a little
heated by an extra glass of grog, he had been heard to say of Hetty that
the "lass was well enough," and that "a man might do worse"; but on
convivial occasions men are apt to express themselves strongly.

Martin Poyser held Mr. Craig in honour, as a man who "knew his
business," and who had great lights concerning soils and compost; but
he was less of a favourite with Mrs. Poyser, who had more than once
said in confidence to her husband, "You're mighty fond o' Craig; but
for my part, I think he's welly like a cock as thinks the sun's rose o'
purpose to hear him crow." For the rest, Mr. Craig was an estimable
gardener, and was not without reasons for having a high opinion of himself. He had also high shoulders and high cheek-bones, and hung his head
forward a little, as he walked along with his hands in his breeches
pockets. I think it was his pedigree only that had the advantage of being
Scotch, and not his "bringing up"; for except that he had a stronger
burr in his accent, his speech differed little from that of the Loamshire
people about him. But a gardener is Scotch, as a French teacher is
Parisian.

"Well, Mr. Poyser," he said, before the good slow farmer had time to
speak, "ye'll not be carrying your hay to-morrow, I'm thinking: the glass
sticks at 'change,' and ye may rely upo' my word as we'll ha' more
downfall afore twenty-four hours is past. Ye see that darkish blue cloud
there upo' the 'rizon—ye know what I mean by the 'rizon, where the
land and sky seems to meet?"

"Ay, ay, I see the cloud," said Mr. Poyser, " 'rizon or no 'rizon. It's
right o'er Mike Holdsworth's fallow, and a foul fallow it is."

"Well, you mark my words, as that cloud 'ull spread o'er the sky
pretty nigh as quick as you'd spread a tarpaulin over one o' your hay-
ricks. It's a great thing to ha' studied the look o' the clouds. Lord bless
you! th' met'orological almanecks can learn me nothing, but there's a
pretty sight o' things I could let *them* up to, if they'd just come to me.
And how are *you*, Mrs. Poyser?—thinking o' getherin' the red currants
soon, I reckon. You'd a deal better gether 'em afore they're o'er-ripe,
wi' such weather as we've got to look forward to. How do ye do, Mistress

Bede?" Mr. Craig continued, without a pause, nodding by the way to Adam and Seth. "I hope y' enjoyed them spinach and gooseberries as I sent Chester with th' other day. If ye want vegetables while ye're in trouble, ye know where to come to. It's well known I'm not giving other folks' things away; for when I've supplied the house, the garden's my own spekilation, and it isna every man th' old Squire could get as 'ud be equil to the undertaking, let alone asking whether he'd be willing. I've got to run my calkilation fine, I can tell you, to make sure o' getting back the money as I pay the Squire. I should like to see some o' them fellows as make the almanecks looking as far before their noses as I've got to do every year as comes."

"They look pretty fur, though," said Mr. Poyser, turning his head on one side, and speaking in rather a subdued reverential tone. "Why, what could come truer nor that pictur o' the cock wi' the big spurs, as has got its head knocked down wi' th' anchor, an' th' firin', an' th' ships behind? Why, that pictur was made afore Christmas, and yit it's come as true as th' Bible. Why, th' cock's France, an' th' anchor's Nelson—an' they told us that beforehand."

"Pee—ee-eh!" said Mr. Craig. "A man doesna want to see fur to know as th' English 'ull beat the French. Why, I know upo' good authority as it's a big Frenchman as reaches five foot high, an' they live upo' spoon-meat mostly. I knew a man as his father had a particular knowledge o' the French. I should like to know what them grasshoppers are to do against such fine fellows as our young Captain Arthur. Why, it 'ud astonish a Frenchman only to look at him; his arm's thicker nor a Frenchman's body, I'll be bound, for they pinch theirsells in wi' stays; and it's easy enough, for they've got nothing i' their insides."

"Where *is* the Captain, as he wasna at church to-day?" said Adam. "I was talking to him o' Friday, and he said nothing about his going away."

"Oh, he's only gone to Eagledale for a bit o' fishing; I reckon he'll be back again afore many days are o'er, for he's to be at all th' arranging and preparing o' things for the comin' o' age o' the thirtieth o' July. But he's fond o' getting away for a bit, now and then. Him and th' old Squire fit one another like frost and flowers."

Mr. Craig smiled and winked slowly as he made this last observation, but the subject was not developed farther, for now they had reached the turning in the road where Adam and his companions must say "good-by." The gardener, too, would have had to turn off in the same direction if he had not accepted Mr. Poyser's invitation to tea. Mrs. Poyser duly seconded the invitation, for she would have held it a deep disgrace not to make her neighbours welcome to her house: personal likes and dislikes must not interfere with that sacred custom. Moreover, Mr. Craig had always been full of civilities to the family at the Hall Farm, and Mrs. Poyser was scrupulous in declaring that she had "nothing to say again' him, on'y it was a pity he couldna be hatched o'er again, an' hatched different."

So Adam and Seth, with their mother between them, wound their way down to the valley and up again to the old house, where a saddened memory had taken place of a long, long anxiety—where Adam would never have to ask again as he entered, "Where's father?"

And the other family party, with Mr. Craig for company, went back to the pleasant bright house-place at the Hall Farm—all with quiet minds, except Hetty, who knew now where Arthur was gone, but was only the more puzzled and uneasy. For it appeared that his absence was quite voluntary; he need not have gone—he would not have gone if he had wanted to see her. She had a sickening sense that no lot could ever be pleasant to her again if her Thursday night's vision was not to be fulfilled; and in this moment of chill, bare, wintry disappointment and doubt, she looked towards the possibility of being with Arthur again, of meeting his loving glance, and hearing his soft words, with that eager yearning which one may call the "growing pain" of passion.

CHAPTER XIX

ADAM ON A WORKING DAY

NOTWITHSTANDING Mr. Craig's prophecy, the dark-blue cloud dispersed itself without having produced the threatened consequences. "The weather," as he observed the next morning—"the weather, you see, 's a ticklish thing, an' a fool 'ull hit on't sometimes when a wise man misses; that's why the almanecks get so much credit. It's one o' them chancy things as fools thrive on."

This unreasonable behaviour of the weather, however, could displease no one else in Hayslope besides Mr. Craig. All hands were to be out in the meadows this morning as soon as the dew had risen; the wives and daughters did double work in every farmhouse, that the maids might give their help in tossing the hay; and when Adam was marching along the lanes, with his basket of tools over his shoulder, he caught the sound of jocose talk and ringing laughter from behind the hedges. The jocose talk of haymakers is best at a distance; like those clumsy bells round the cows' necks, it has rather a coarse sound when it comes close, and may even grate on your ears painfully; but heard from far off, it mingles very prettily with the other joyous sounds of nature. Men's muscles move better when their souls are making merry music, though their merriment is of a poor blundering sort, not at all like the merriment of birds.

And perhaps there is no time in a summer's day more cheering, than when the warmth of the sun is just beginning to triumph over the freshness of the morning—when there is just a lingering hint of early coolness to keep off languor under the delicious influence of warmth. The reason Adam was walking along the lanes at this time was because his work for the rest of the day lay at a country house about three miles off, which was being put in repair for the son of a neighbouring squire; and he had been busy since early morning with the packing of panels, doors, and chimney-pieces, in a waggon which was now gone on before him, while Jonathan Burge himself had ridden to the spot on horseback, to await its arrival and direct the workmen.

This little walk was a rest to Adam, and he was unconsciously under the charm of the moment. It was summer morning in his heart, and he saw Hetty in the sunshine: a sunshine without glare—with slanting rays that tremble between the delicate shadows of the leaves. He thought, yesterday, when he put out his hand to her as they came out of church, that there was a touch of melancholy kindness in her face, such as he had not seen before, and he took it as a sign that she had some sympathy with his family trouble. Poor fellow! that touch of melancholy came from quite another source; but how was he to know? We look at the one little woman's face we love, as we look at the face of our mother earth, and see all sorts of answers to our own yearnings. It was impossible for Adam not to feel that what had happened in the last week had brought the prospect of marriage nearer to him. Hitherto he had felt keenly the danger that some other man might step in and get possession of Hetty's heart and hand, while he himself was still in a position that made him shrink from asking her to accept him. Even if he had had a strong hope that she was fond of him—and his hope was far from being strong—he had been too heavily burthened with other claims to provide a home for himself and Hetty—a home such as he could expect her to be content with after the comfort and plenty of the Farm. Like all strong natures, Adam had confidence in his ability to achieve something in the future; he felt sure he should some day, if he lived, be able to maintain a family, and make a good broad path for himself; but he had too cool a head not to estimate to the full the obstacles that were to be overcome. And the time would be so long! And there was Hetty, like a bright-cheeked apple hanging over the orchard wall, within sight of everybody, and everybody must long for her! To be sure, if she loved him very much, she would be content to wait for him; but *did* she love him? His hopes had never risen so high that he had dared to ask her. He was clear-sighted enough to be aware that her uncle and aunt would have looked kindly on his suit, and indeed without this encouragement he would never have persevered in going to the Farm; but it was impossible to come to any but fluctuating conclusions about Hetty's feelings. She was like a kitten, and had the same distractingly pretty looks, that meant nothing, for everybody that came near her.

But now he could not help saying to himself that the heaviest part of his burden was removed, and that even before the end of another year his circumstances might be brought into a shape that would allow him to think of marrying. It would always be a hard struggle with his mother, he knew: she would be jealous of any wife he might choose, and she had set her mind especially against Hetty—perhaps for no other reason than that she suspected Hetty to be the woman he *had* chosen. It would never do, he feared, for his mother to live in the same house with him when he was married; and yet how hard she would think it if he asked her to leave him! Yes, there was a great deal of pain to be gone through with his mother, but it was a case in which he must make her feel that his will was strong—it would be better for her in the end. For himself, he would have liked that they should all live together till Seth was married, and they might have built a bit themselves to the old house, and made more room. He did not like "to part wi' th' lad": they had hardly ever been separated for more than a day since they were born.

But Adam had no sooner caught his imagination leaping forward in this way—making arrangements for an uncertain future—than he checked himself. "A pretty building I'm making, without either bricks or timber. I'm up in the garret a'ready, and haven't so much as dug the foundation." Whenever Adam was strongly convinced of any proposition, it took the form of a principle in his mind: it was knowledge to be acted on, as much as the knowledge that damp will cause rust. Perhaps here lay the secret of the hardness he had accused himself of: he had too little fellow-feeling with the weakness that errs in spite of foreseen consequences. Without this fellow-feeling, how are we to get enough patience and charity towards our stumbling, falling companions in the long and changeful journey? And there is but one way in which a strong determined soul can learn it—by getting his heart-strings bound round the weak and erring, so that he must share not only the outward consequence of their error, but their inward suffering. That is a long and hard lesson, and Adam had at present only learned the alphabet of it in his father's sudden death, which, by annihilating in an instant all that had stimulated his indignation, had sent a sudden rush of thought and memory over what had claimed his pity and tenderness.

But it was Adam's strength, not its correlative hardness, that influenced his meditations this morning. He had long made up his mind that it would be wrong as well as foolish for him to marry a blooming young girl, so long as he had no other prospect than that of growing poverty with a growing family. And his savings had been so constantly drawn upon (besides the terrible sweep of paying for Seth's substitute in the militia), that he had not enough money beforehand to furnish even a small cottage, and keep something in reserve against a rainy day. He had good hope that he should be "firmer on his legs" by-and-by; but he could not be satisfied with a vague confidence in his arm and brain; he must have definite plans, and set about them at once. The partnership with Jonathan Burge was not to be thought of at present—there were things implicitly tacked to it that he could not accept; but Adam thought that he and Seth might carry on a little business for themselves in addition to their journeyman's work, by buying a small stock of superior wood and making articles of household furniture, for which Adam had no end of contrivances. Seth might gain more by working at separate jobs under Adam's direction than by his journeyman's work, and Adam, in his over-hours, could do all the "nice" work, that required peculiar skill. The money gained in this way, with the good wages he received as foreman, would soon enable them to get beforehand with the world. so sparingly as they would all live now. No sooner had this little plan shaped itself in his mind than he began to be busy with exact calculations about the wood to be bought, and the particular article of furniture that should be undertaken first—a kitchen cupboard of his own contrivance, with such an ingenious arrangement of sliding-doors and bolts, such convenient nooks for stowing household provender, and such a symmetrical result to the eye, that every good housewife would be in raptures with it, and fall through all the gradations of melancholy longing till her husband promised to buy it for her. Adam pictured to himself Mrs. Poyser examining it with her keen eye, and trying in vain to find out a deficiency; and, of course, close to Mrs. Poyser stood Hetty, and Adam was again beguiled from calculations and contrivances into dreams and hopes. Yes, he would go and see her this evening—it was so long since he had been at the Hall Farm. He would have liked to go to the night-school, to see why Bartle Massey had not been at church yesterday, for he feared his old friend was ill; but, unless he could manage both visits, this last must be put off till to-morrow—the desire to be near Hetty, and to speak to her again, was too strong.

As he made up his mind to this, he was coming very near to the end of his walk, within the sound of the hammers at work on the refitting of the old house. The sound of tools to a clever workman who loves his work is like the tentative sounds of the orchestra to the violinist who has to bear his part in the overture: the strong fibres begin their accustomed thrill, and what was a moment before joy, vexation, or ambition, begins its change into energy. All passion becomes strength when it has an outlet from the narrow limits of our personal lot in the labour of our right arm, the cunning of our right hand, or the still, creative activity of our thought. Look at Adam through the rest of the day, as he stands on the scaffolding with the two-foot ruler in his hand, whistling low while he considers how a difficulty about a floor-joist or a window-frame is to be overcome; or as he pushes one of the younger workmen aside, and takes his place in upheaving a weight of timber, saying, "Let alone, lad! thee'st got too much gristle i' thy bones yet"; or as he fixes his keen black eyes on the motions of a workman on the other side of the room, and warns him that his distances are not right. Look at this broad-shouldered man with the bare muscular arms, and the thick firm black hair tossed about like trodden meadow-grass whenever he takes off his paper cap, and with the strong barytone voice bursting every now and then into loud and solemn psalm-tunes, as if seeking an outlet for superfluous strength, yet presently checking himself, apparently crossed by some thought which jars with the singing. Perhaps, if you had not been already in the secret, you might not have guessed what sad memories, what warm affection, what tender fluttering hopes, had their home in this athletic body with the broken finger-nails—in this rough man, who knew no better lyrics than he could find in the Old and New Versions and an occasional hymn; who knew the smallest possible amount of profane history; and for whom the motion and shape of the earth, the course of the sun, and the changes of the seasons, lay in the region of mystery just made visible by fragmentary knowledge. It had cost Adam a great deal of trouble, and work in over-hours, to know what he knew over and above the secrets of his handicraft, and that acquaintance with mechanics and figures, and the nature of the materials he worked with, which was made easy to him by inborn inherited faculty—to get the mastery of his pen, and write a plain hand, to spell without any other mistakes than must in fairness be attributed to the unreasonable character of orthography rather than to any deficiency in the speller, and, moreover, to learn his musical notes and part-singing. Besides all this, he had read his Bible, including the apocryphal books; "Poor Richard's Almanac," Taylor's "Holy Living and Dying," "The Pilgrim's Progress," with Bunyan's Life and "Holy War," a great deal of Bailey's Dictionary, "Valentine and Orson," and part of a "History of Babylon," which Bartle Massey had lent him. He might have had many more books from Bartle Massey, but he had no time for reading "the common print," as Lisbeth called it, so busy as he was with figures in all the leisure moments which he did not fill up with extra carpentry.

Adam, you perceive, was by no means a marvellous man, nor, properly speaking, a genius, yet I will not pretend that his was an ordinary character among workmen; and it would not be at all a safe conclusion that the next best man you may happen to see with a basket of tools over his shoulder and a paper cap on his head has the strong conscience and the strong sense, the blended susceptibility and self-command, of our friend Adam. He was not an average man. Yet such men as he are reared here and there in every generation of our peasant artisans—with an inheritance of affections nurtured by a simple family life of common need and common industry, and an inheritance of faculties trained in skilful courageous labour: they make their way upward, rarely as geniuses, most commonly as painstaking honest men, with the skill and conscience to do well the tasks that lie before them. Their lives have no discernible echo beyond the neighbourhood where they dwelt, but you are almost sure to find there some good piece of road, some building, some application of mineral produce, some improvement in farming practice, some reform of parish abuses, with which their names are associated by one or two generations after them. Their employers were the richer for them, the work of their hands has worn well, and the work of their brains has guided well the hands of other men. They went about in their youth in flannel or paper caps, in coats black with coal-dust or streaked with lime and red paint; in old age their white hairs are seen in a place of honour at church and at market, and they tell their well-dressed sons and daughters seated round the bright hearth on winter evenings, how pleased they were when they first earned their twopence a-day. Others there are who die poor, and never put off the workman's coat on week-days: they have not had the art of getting rich; but they are men of trust, and when they die before the work is all out of them, it is as if some main screw had got loose in a machine; the master who employed them says, "Where shall I find their like?"

CHAPTER XX

ADAM VISITS THE HALL FARM

ADAM came back from his work in the empty waggon; that was why he had changed his clothes, and was ready to set out to the Hall Farm when it still wanted a quarter to seven. "What's thee got thy Sunday cloose on for?" said Lisbeth, complainingly, as he came down-stairs. "Thee artna goin' to th' school i' thy best coat?"

"No, mother," said Adam, quietly. "I'm going to the Hall Farm, but mayhap I may go to the school after, so thee mustna wonder if I'm a bit late. Seth 'ull be at home in half an hour—he's only gone to the village; so thee wutna mind."

"Eh, an' what's thee got thy best cloose on for to go to th' Hall Farm? The Poyser folks see'd thee in 'em yesterday, I warrand. What dost mean by turnin' worki'day into Sunday a-that'n? It's poor keepin' company wi' folks as donna like to see thee i' thy workin' jacket."

"Good-by, mother, I can't stay," said Adam, putting on his hat and going out.

But he had no sooner gone a few paces beyond the door than Lisbeth became uneasy at the thought that she had vexed him. Of course, the secret of her objection to the best clothes was her suspicion that they were put on for Hetty's sake; but deeper than all her peevishness lay the need that her son should love her. She hurried after him, and laid hold of his arm before he had got halfway down to the brook, and said, "Nay, my lad, thee wutna go away angered wi' thy mother, an' her got nought to do but to sit by hersen an' think on thee?"

"Nay, nay, mother," said Adam, gravely, and standing still while he put his arm on her shoulder, "I'm not angered. But I wish, for thy own sake, thee'dst be more contented to let me do what I've made up my mind to do. I'll never be no other than a good son to thee as long as we live. But a man has other feelings besides what he owes to's father and mother; and thee oughtna want to rule over me body and soul. And thee must make up thy mind, as I'll not give way to thee where I've a right to do what I like. So let us have no more words about it."

"Eh," said Lisbeth, not willing to show that she felt the real bearing of Adam's words, "an' who likes to see thee i' thy best cloose better nor thy mother? An' when thee'st got thy face washed as clean as the smooth white pibble, an' thy hair combed so nice, and thy eyes a-sparklin'—what else is there as thy old mother should like to look at half so well? An' thee sh't put on thy Sunday cloose when thee lik'st for me—I'll ne'er plague thee no moor about'n."

"Well, well; good-by, mother," said Adam, kissing her, and hurrying away. He saw there was no other means of putting an end to the dialogue. Lisbeth stood still on the spot, shading her eyes and looking after him till he was quite out of sight. She felt to the full all the meaning that had lain in Adam's words, and, as she lost sight of him and turned back slowly into the house, she said aloud to herself—for it was her way to speak her thoughts aloud in the long days when her husband and sons were at their work—"Eh, he'll be tellin' me as he's goin' to bring her home one o' these days; an' she'll be missis o'er me, and I mun look on, belike, while she uses the blue-edged platters, and breaks 'em, mayhap, though there's ne'er been one broke sin' my old man an' me bought 'em at the fair twenty 'ear come next Whissuntide. Eh!" she went on, still louder, as she caught up her knitting from the table, "but she'll ne'er knit the lads' stockins, nor foot 'em nayther, while I live; an' when I'm gone, he'll bethink him as nobody 'ull ne'er fit's leg an' foot as his old mother did. She'll know nothin' o' narrowin' an' heelin', I warrand, an' she'll make a long toe as he canna get's boot on. That's what comes o' marr'in' young wenches. I war gone thirty, an' th' feyther too, afore we war married; an' young enough too. She'll be a poor dratchell by then *she's* thirty, a-marr'in' a-that'n, afore her teeth's all come."

Adam walked so fast that he was at the yard gate before seven. Martin Poyser and the grandfather were not yet come in from the meadow: every one was in the meadow, even to the black-and-tan terrier—no one kept watch in the yard but the bull-dog; and when Adam reached the house-door, which stood wide open, he saw there was no one in the bright clean house-place. But he guessed where Mrs. Poyser and some one else would be, quite within hearing; so he knocked on the door and said in his strong voice, "Mrs. Poyser within?"

"Come in, Mr. Bede, come in," Mrs. Poyser called out from the dairy. She always gave Adam this title when she received him in her own house. "You may come into the dairy if you will, for I canna justly leave the cheese."

Adam walked into the dairy, where Mrs. Poyser and Nancy were crushing the first evening cheese.

"Why, you might think you war come to a dead-house," said Mrs. Poyser, as he stood in the open doorway; "they're all i' the meadow; but Martin's sure to be in afore long, for they're leaving the hay cocked to-night, ready for carrying first thing to-morrow. I've been forced t have Nancy in, upo' 'count as Hetty must gether the red currents to-night; the fruit allays ripens so contrary, just when every hand's wanted. An' there's no trustin' the children to gether it, for they put more into their own mouths nor into the basket; you might as well set the wasps to gether the fruit."

Adam longed to say he would go into the garden till Mr. Poyser came in, but he was not quite courageous enough, so he said, "I could be looking at your spinning-wheel, then, and see what wants doing to it Perhaps it stands in the house, where I can find it?"

"No, I've put it away in the right-hand parlour; but let it be till I can fetch it and show it you. I'd be glad now, if you'd go into the garden, and tell Hetty to send Totty in. The child 'ull run in if she's told, an' I know Hetty's lettin' her eat too many currans. I'll be much obliged to you, Mr. Bede, if you'll go and send her in; an' there's the York and Lankester roses beautiful in the garden now—you'll like to see 'em. But you'd like a drink o' whey first, p'r'aps; I know you're fond o' whey, as most folks is when they hanna got to crush it out."

"Thank you, Mrs. Poyser," said Adam; "a drink o' whey's allays a treat to me. I'd rather have it than beer any day."

"Ay, ay," said Mrs. Poyser, reaching a small white basin that stood on the shelf, and dipping it into the whey-tub, "the smell o' bread's sweet t' everybody but the baker. The Miss Irwines allays say, 'O Mrs. Poyser, I envy you your dairy; and I envy you your chickens; and what a beautiful thing a farmhouse is, to be sure!' An' I say, 'Yes; a farmhouse is a fine thing for them as look on, an' don't know the liftin', an' the stannin', an' the worritin' o' th' inside, as belongs to't.' "

"Why, Mrs. Poyser, you wouldn't like to live anywhere else but in a farmhouse, so well as you manage it," said Adam, taking the basin; "and there can be nothing to look at pleasanter nor a fine milch cow, standing up to 'ts knees in pasture, and the new milk frothing in the pail, and the fresh butter ready for market, and the calves, and the poultry. Here's to your health, and may you allays have strength to look after your own dairy, and set a pattern t' all the farmers' wives in the country."

Mrs. Poyser was not to be caught in the weakness of smiling at a compliment, but a quiet complacency overspread her face like a stealing sunbeam, and gave a milder glance than usual to her blue-grey eyes, as she looked at Adam drinking the whey. Ah! I think I taste that whey now—with a flavour so delicate that one can hardly distinguish it from an odour, and with that soft gliding warmth that fills one's imagination with a still, happy dreaminess. And the light music of the dropping whey is in my ears, mingling with the twittering of a bird outside the wire network window—the window overlooking the garden, and shaded by tall Gueldres roses.

"Have a little more, Mr. Bede?" said Mrs. Poyser, as Adam set down the basin.

"No, thank you; I'll go into the garden now, and send in the little lass."

"Ay, do; and tell her to come to her mother in the dairy."

Adam walked round by the rick-yard, at present empty of ricks, to the little wooden gate leading into the garden—once the well-tended kitchen-garden of a manor-house; now, but for the handsome brick wall with stone coping that ran along one side of it, a true farmhouse garden, with hardy perennial flowers, unpruned fruit-trees, and kitchen vegetables growing together in careless, half-neglected abundance. In that leafy, flowery, bushy time, to look for any one in this garden was like playing at "hide-and-seek." There were the tall hollyhocks beginning to

flower, and dazzle the eye with their pink, white, and yellow; there were
the syringas and Gueldres roses, all large and disorderly for want of trimming; there were leafy walls of scarlet beans and late peas; there was a
row of bushy filberts in one direction, and in another a huge apple-tree
making a barren circle under its low-spreading boughs. But what signified a barren patch or two? The garden was so large. There was always a superfluity of broad beans—it took nine or ten of Adam's strides
to get to the end of the uncut grass walk that ran by the side of them;
and as for other vegetables, there was so much more room than was
necessary for them, that in the rotation of crops a large flourishing bed
of groundsel was of yearly occurrence on one spot or other. The very rose-
trees, at which Adam stopped to pluck one, looked as if they grew wild;
they were all huddled together in bushy masses, now flaunting with wide
open petals, almost all of them of the streaked pink-and-white kind,
which doubtless dated from the union of the houses of York and Lan-
caster. Adam was wise enough to choose a compact Provence rose that
peeped out half-smothered by its flaunting scentless neighbours, and
held it in his hand—he thought he should be more at ease holding something in his hand—as he walked on to the far end of the garden, where he
remembered there was the largest row of currant-trees, not far off from
the great yew-tree arbour.

But he had not gone many steps beyond the roses, when he heard the
shaking of a bough, and a boy's voice saying,

"Now, then, Totty, hold out your pinny—there's a duck."

The voice came from the boughs of a tall cherry-tree, where Adam
had no difficulty in discerning a small blue-pinafored figure perched in
a commodious position where the fruit was thickest. Doubtless Totty
was below, behind the screen of peas. Yes—with her bonnet hanging
down her back, and her fat face, dreadfully smeared with red juice,
turned up towards the cherry-tree, while she held her little round hole of
a mouth and her red-stained pinafore to receive the promised downfall. I
am sorry to say, more than half the cherries that fell were hard and yellow instead of juicy and red; but Totty spent no time in useless regrets,
and she was already sucking the third juiciest when Adam said, "There
now, Totty, you've got your cherries. Run into the house with 'em to
mother—she wants you—she's in the dairy. Run in this minute—there's
a good little girl."

He lifted her up in his strong arms and kissed her as he spoke, a
ceremony which Totty regarded as a tiresome interruption to cherry-
eating; and when he set her down she trotted off quite silently towards
the house, sucking her cherries as she went along.

"Tommy, my lad, take care you're not shot for a little thieving bird,"
said Adam, as he walked on towards the currant-trees.

He could see there was a large basket at the end of the row: Hetty
would not be far off, and Adam already felt as if she were looking at
him. Yet when he turned the corner she was standing with her back
towards him, and stooping to gather the low-hanging fruit. Strange that

she had not heard him coming! perhaps it was because she was making the leaves rustle. She started when she became conscious that some one was near—started so violently that she dropped the basin with the currants in it, and then, when she saw it was Adam, she turned from pale to deep red. That blush made his heart beat with a new happiness. Hetty had never blushed at seeing him before.

"I frightened you," he said, with a delicious sense that it didn't signify what he said, since Hetty seemed to feel as much as he did; "let *me* pick the currants up."

That was soon done, for they had only fallen in a tangled mass on the grass-plot, and Adam, as he rose and gave her the basin again, looked straight into her eyes with the subdued tenderness that belongs to the first moments of hopeful love.

Hetty did not turn away her eyes; her blush had subsided, and she met his glance with a quiet sadness, which contented Adam, because it was so unlike anything he had seen in her before.

"There's not many more currants to get," she said; "I shall soon ha' done now."

"I'll help you," said Adam; and he fetched the large basket, which was nearly full of currants, and set it close to them.

Not a word more was spoken as they gathered the currants. Adam's heart was too full to speak, and he thought Hetty knew all that was in it. She was not indifferent to his presence after all; she had blushed when she saw him, and then there was that touch of sadness about her which must surely mean love, since it was the opposite of her usual manner, which had often impressed him as indifference. And he could glance at her continually as she bent over the fruit, while the level evening sunbeams stole through the thick apple-tree boughs, and rested on her round cheek and neck as if they too were in love with her. It was to Adam the time that a man can least forget in after-life,—the time when he believes that the first woman he has ever loved betrays by a slight something—a word, a tone, a glance, the quivering of a lip or an eyelid —that she is at least beginning to love him in return. The sign is so slight, it is scarcely perceptible to the ear or eye—he could describe it to no one—it is a mere feather-touch, yet it seems to have changed his whole being, to have merged an uneasy yearning into a delicious unconsciousness of everything but the present moment. So much of our early gladness vanishes utterly from our memory: we can never recall the joy with which we laid our heads on our mother's bosom or rode on our father's back in childhood; doubtless that joy is wrought up into our nature, as the sunlight of long-past mornings is wrought up in the soft mellowness of the apricot; but it is gone for ever from our imagination, and we can only *believe* in the joy of childhood. But the first glad moment in our first love is a vision which returns to us to the last, and brings with it a thrill of feeling intense and special as the recurrent sensation of a sweet odour breathed in a far-off hour of happiness. It is a memory that gives a more exquisite touch to tenderness, that feeds the madness of jealousy, and adds the last keenness to the agony of despair.

Hetty bending over the red bunches, the level rays piercing the screen of apple-tree boughs, the length of bushy garden beyond, his own emotion as he looked at her and believed that she was thinking of him, and that there was no need for them to talk—Adam remembered it all to the last moment of his life.

And Hetty? You know quite well that Adam was mistaken about her. Like many other men, he thought the signs of love for another were signs of love towards himself. When Adam was approaching unseen by her, she was absorbed as usual in thinking and wondering about Arthur's possible return: the sound of any man's footstep would have affected her just in the same way—she would have *felt* it might be Arthur before she had time to see, and the blood that forsook her cheek in the agitation of that momentary feeling would have rushed back again at the sight of any one else as much as at the sight of Adam. He was not wrong in thinking that a change had come over Hetty: the anxieties and fears of a first passion, with which she was trembling, had become stronger than vanity, had given her for the first time that sense of helpless dependence on another's feeling which awakens the clinging deprecating womanhood even in the shallowest girl that can ever experience it, and creates in her a sensibility to kindness which found her quite hard before. For the first time Hetty felt that there was something soothing to her in Adam's timid yet manly tenderness: she wanted to be treated lovingly—O, it was very hard to bear this blank of absence, silence, apparent indifference, after those moments of glowing love! She was not afraid that Adam would tease her with love-making and flattering speeches like her other admirers: he had always been so reserved to her: she could enjoy without any fear the sense that this strong brave man loved her, and was near her. It never entered into her mind that Adam was pitiable too—that Adam, too, must suffer one day.

Hetty, we know, was not the first woman that had behaved more gently to the man who loved her in vain, because she had herself begun to love another. It was a very old story; but Adam knew nothing about it, so he drank in the sweet delusion.

"That'll do," said Hetty, after a little while. "Aunt wants me to leave some on the trees. I'll take 'em in now."

"It's very well I came to carry the basket," said Adam, "for it 'ud ha' been too heavy for your little arms."

"No; I could ha' carried it with both hands."

"O, I daresay," said Adam, smiling, "and been as long getting into the house as a little ant carrying a caterpillar. Have you ever seen those tiny fellows carrying things four times as big as themselves?"

"No," said Hetty, indifferently, not caring to know the difficulties of ant-life.

"O, I used to watch 'em often when I was a lad. But now, you see, I can carry the basket with one arm, as if it was an empty nutshell, and give you th' other arm to lean on. Won't you? Such big arms as mine were made for little arms like yours to lean on."

Hetty smiled faintly, and put her arm within his. Adam looked down at her, but her eyes were turned dreamily towards another corner of the garden.

"Have you ever been to Eagledale?" she said, as they walked slowly along.

"Yes," said Adam, pleased to have her ask a question about himself; "ten years ago, when I was a lad, I went with father to see about some work there. It's a wonderful sight—rocks and caves such as you never saw in your life. I never had a right notion o' rocks till I went there."

"How long did it take you to get there?"

"Why, it took us the best part o' two days' walking. But it's nothing of a day's journey for anybody as has got a first-rate nag. The Captain 'ud get there in nine or ten hours, I'll be bound, he's such a rider. And I shouldn't wonder if he's back again to-morrow; he's too active to rest long in that lonely place, all by himself, for there's nothing but a bit of a inn i' that part where he's gone to fish. I wish he'd got th' estate in his hands; that 'ud be the right thing for him, for it 'ud give him plenty to do, and he'd do 't well too, for all he's so young; he's got better notions o' things than many a man twice his age. He spoke very handsome to me th' other day about lending me money to set up i' business; and if things came round that way, I'd rather be beholding to him nor to any man i' the world."

Poor Adam was led on to speak about Arthur because he thought Hetty would be pleased to know that the young squire was so ready to befriend him; the fact entered into his future prospects, which he would like to seem promising in her eyes. And it was true that Hetty listened with an interest which brought a new light into her eyes and a half smile upon her lips.

"How pretty the roses are now!" Adam continued, pausing to look at them. "See! I stole the prettiest, but I didna mean to keep it myself. I think these as are all pink, and have got a finer sort o' green leaves, are prettier than the striped uns, don't you?"

He set down the basket, and took the rose from his button-hole.

"It smells very sweet," he said; "those striped uns have no smell. Stick it in your frock, and then you can put it in water after. It 'ud be a pity to let it fade."

Hetty took the rose, smiling as she did so at the pleasant thought that Arthur could so soon get back if he liked. There was a flash of hope and happiness in her mind, and with a sudden impulse of gaiety she did what she had very often done before—stuck the rose in her hair a little above the left ear. The tender admiration in Adam's face was slightly shadowed by reluctant disapproval. Hetty's love of finery was just the thing that would most provoke his mother, and he himself disliked it as much as it was possible for him to dislike anything that belonged to her.

"Ah," he said, "that's like the ladies in the pictures at the Chase;

they've mostly got flowers or feathers or gold things i' their hair, but somehow I don't like to see 'em: they allays put me i' mind o' the painted women outside the shows at Treddles'on fair. What can a woman have to set her off better than her own hair, when it curls so, like yours? If a woman's young and pretty, I think you can see her good looks all the better for her being plain dressed. Why, Dinah Morris looks very nice, for all she wears such a plain cap and gown. It seems to me as a woman's face doesna want flowers; it's almost like a flower itself. I'm sure yours is."

"O, very well," said Hetty, with a little playful pout, taking the rose out of her hair. "I'll put one o' Dinah's caps on when we go in, and you'll see if I look better in it. She left one behind, so I can take the pattern."

"Nay, nay, I don't want you to wear a Methodist cap like Dinah's. I daresay it's a very ugly cap, and I used to think when I saw her here, as it was nonsense for her to dress different t' other people; but I never rightly noticed her till she came to see mother last week, and then I thought the cap seemed to fit her face somehow as th' acorn cup fits th' acorn, and I shouldn't like to see her so well without it. But you've got another sort o' face; I'd have you just as you are now, without anything t' interfere with your own looks. It's like when a man's singing a good tune, you don't want t' hear bells tinkling and interfering wi' the sound."

He took her arm and put it within his again, looking down on her fondly. He was afraid she should think he had lectured her; imagining, as we are apt to do, that she had perceived all the thoughts he had only half expressed. And the thing he dreaded most was lest any cloud should come over this evening's happiness. For the world he would not have spoken of his love to Hetty yet, till this commencing kindness towards him should have grown into unmistakable love. In his imagination he saw long years of his future life stretching before him, blest with the right to call Hetty his own: he could be content with very little at present. So he took up the basket of currants once more, and they went on towards the house.

The scene had quite changed in the half hour that Adam had been in the garden. The yard was full of life now: Marty was letting the screaming geese through the gate, and wickedly provoking the gander by hissing at him; the granary door was groaning on its hinges as Alick shut it, after dealing out the corn; the horses were being led out to watering, amidst much barking of all three dogs, and many "whups" from Tim the ploughman, as if the heavy animals who held down their meek, intelligent heads, and lifted their shaggy feet so deliberately, were likely to rush wildly in every direction but the right. Everybody was come back from the meadow; and when Hetty and Adam entered the house-place, Mr. Poyser was seated in the three-cornered chair, and the grandfather in the large arm-chair opposite, looking on with pleasant expectation while the supper was being laid on the oak table. Mrs. Poyser had laid the cloth herself—a cloth made of homespun linen, with a shining checkered pattern on it, and of an agreeable whitey-brown hue, such as all sensible housewives like to see—none of your bleached "shop-rag" that would wear into holes in no time, but good homespun that would last for two generations. The cold veal, the fresh lettuces, and the stuffed chine, might well look temping to hungry men who had dined at half-past twelve o'clock. On the large deal table against the wall there were bright pewter plates and spoons and cans, ready for Alick and his companions; for the master and servants ate their supper not far off each other; which was all the pleasanter, because if a remark about to-morrow morning's work occurred to Mr. Poyser, Alick was at hand to hear it.

"Well, Adam, I'm glad to see ye," said Mr. Poyser. "What! ye've been helping Hetty to gether the currans, eh? Come, sit ye down, sit ye down. Why, it's pretty near a three-week since y' had your supper with us; and the missis has got one of her rare stuffed chines. I'm glad ye're come."

"Hetty," said Mrs. Poyser, as she looked into the basket of currants to see if the fruit was fine, "run up-stairs, and send Molly down. She's putting Totty to bed, and I want her to draw th' ale, for Nancy's busy yet i' the dairy. You can see to the child. But whativer did you let her run away from you along wi' Tommy for, and stuff herself wi' fruit as she can't eat a bit o' good victual?"

This was said in a lower tone than usual, while her husband was talking to Adam; for Mrs. Poyser was strict in adherence to her own rules of propriety, and she considered that a young girl was not to be treated sharply in the presence of a respectable man who was courting her. That would not be fair-play: every woman was young in her turn, and had her chances of matrimony, which it was a point of honour for other women not to spoil—just as one market-woman who has sold her own eggs must not try to balk another of a customer.

Hetty made haste to run away up-stairs, not easily finding an answer to her aunt's question, and Mrs. Poyser went out to see after Marty and Tommy, and bring them in to supper.

Soon they were all seated—the two rosy lads, one on each side, by the pale mother, a place being left for Hetty between Adam and her uncle. Alick too was come in, and was seated in his far corner, eating cold broad beans out of a large dish with his pocketknife, and finding a flavour in them which he would not have exchanged for the finest pine-apple.

"What a time that gell is drawing th' ale, to be sure," said Mrs. Poyser, when she was dispensing her slices of stuffed chine. "I think she sets the jug under and forgets to turn the tap, as there's nothing you can't believe o' them wenches: they'll set the empty kettle o' the fire, and then come an hour after to see if the water boils."

"She's drawin' for the men too," said Mr. Poyser. "Thee shouldst ha' told her to bring our jug up first."

"Told her?" said Mrs. Poyser: "yes, I might spend all the wind i' my body, an' take the bellows too, if I was to tell them gells everything as their own sharpness wonna tell 'em. Mr. Bede, will you take some

vinegar with your lettuce? Ay, you're i' the right not. It spoils the flavour
o' the chine, to my thinking. It's poor eating where the flavour o' the
meat lies i' the cruets. There's folks as make bad butter, and trusten to
the salt t' hide it."

Mrs. Poyser's attention was here diverted by the appearance of Molly,
carrying a large jug, two small mugs, and four drinking-cans, all full of
ale or small beer—an interesting example of the prehensile power
possessed by the human hand. Poor Molly's mouth was rather wider open
than usual, as she walked along with her eyes fixed on the double cluster
of vessels in her hands, quite innocent of the expression in her mistress's
eye.

"Molly, I niver knew your equils— to think o' your poor mother as
is a widow, an' I took you wi' as good as no character, an' the times an'
times I've told you" . . . .

Molly had not seen the lightning, and the thunder shook her nerves
the more for the want of that preparation. With a vague alarmed sense
that she must somehow comport herself differently, she hastened her
step a little towards the far deal table, where she might set down her
cans—caught her foot in her apron, which had become untied, and fell
with a crash and a splash into a pool of beer; whereupon a tittering
explosion from Marty and Tommy, and a serious "Ello!" from Mr.
Poyser, who saw his draught of ale unpleasantly deferred.

"There you go!" resumed Mrs. Poyser, in a cutting tone, as she rose
and went towards the cupboard while Molly began dolefully to pick up
the fragments of pottery. "It's what I told you 'ud come, over and over
again; and there's your month's wage gone, and more, to pay for that
jug as I've had i' the house this ten year, and nothing ever happened
to't before; but the crockery you've broke sin' here in th' house you've
been 'ud made a parson swear—God forgi' me for saying so; an' if it had
been boiling wort out o' the copper, it 'ud ha' been the same, and you'd
ha' been scalded, and very like lamed for life, as there's no knowing but
what you will be some day if you go on; for anybody 'ud think you'd got
the St. Vitus's Dance, to see the things you've throwed down. It's a pity
but what the bits was stacked up for you to see, though it's neither seeing nor hearing as 'ull make much odds to you—anybody 'ud think you
war case-hardened."

Poor Molly's tears were dropping fast by this time, and in her desperation at the lively movement of the beer-stream towards Alick's legs, she
was converting her apron into a mop, while Mrs. Poyser, opening the
cupboard, turned a blighting eye upon her.

"Ah," she went on, "you'll do no good wi' crying an' making more wet
to wipe up. It's all your own wilfulness, as I tell you, for there's nobody
no call to break anything if they'll only go the right way to work. But
wooden folks had need ha' wooden things t' handle. And here must I take
the brown-and-white jug, as it's niver been used three times this year,
and go down i' the cellar myself, and belike catch my death, and be laid
up wi' inflammation" . . . .

Mrs. Poyser had turned round from the cupboard with the brown-and-white jug in her hand, when she caught sight of something at the other end of the kitchen; perhaps it was because she was already trembling and nervous that the apparition had so strong an effect on her; perhaps jug-breaking, like other crimes, has a contagious influence. However it was she stared and started like a ghost-seer, and the precious brown-and-white jug fell to the ground, parting for ever with its spout and handle.

"Did ever anybody see the like?" she said, with a suddenly-lowered tone, after a moment's bewildered glance round the room. "The jugs are bewitched, *I* think. It's them nasty glazed handles—they slip o'er the finger like a snail."

"Why, thee'st let thy own whip fly i' thy face," said her husband, who had now joined in the laugh of the young ones.

"It's all very fine to look on and grin," rejoined Mrs. Poyser; "but there's times when the crockery seems alive, an' flies out o' your hand like a bird. It's like the glass, sometimes, 'ull crack as it stands. What is to be broke *will* be broke, for I never dropped a thing i' my life for want o' holding it, else I should never ha' kept the crockery all these 'ears as 1 bought at my own wedding. And Hetty, are you mad? Whativer do you mean by coming down i' that way, and making one think as there's a ghost a-walking i' th' house?"

A new outbreak of laughter, while Mrs. Poyser was speaking, was caused, less by her sudden conversion to a fatalistic view of jug-breaking, than by that strange appearance of Hetty, which had startled her aunt. The little minx had found a black gown of her aunt's, and pinned it close round her neck to look like Dinah's, had made her hair as flat as she could, and had tied on one of Dinah's high-crowned borderless net-caps. The thought of Dinah's pale grave face and mild grey eyes, which the sight of the gown and cap brought with it, made it a laughable surprise enough to see them replaced by Hetty's round rosy cheeks and coquettish dark eyes. The boys got off their chairs and jumped round her, clapping their hands, and even Alick gave a low ventral laugh as he looked up from his beans. Under cover of the noise, Mrs. Poyser went into the back kitchen to send Nancy into the cellar with the great pewter measure, which had some chance of being free from bewitchment.

"Why, Hetty, lass, are ye turned Methodist?" said Mr. Poyser, with that comfortable slow enjoyment of a laugh which one only sees in stout people. "You must pull your face a deal longer before you'll do for one; mustna she, Adam? How come you to put them things on, eh?"

"Adam said he liked Dinah's cap and gown better nor my clothes," said Hetty, sitting down demurely. "He says folks look better in ugly clothes."

"Nay, nay," said Adam, looking at her admiringly; "I only said they seemed to suit Dinah. But if I'd said you'd look pretty in 'em, I should ha' said nothing but what was true."

"Why, thee thought'st Hetty war a ghost, didstna?" said Mr. Poyser to his wife, who now came back and took her seat again. "Thee look'dst as scared as scared."

"It little sinnifies how I looked," said Mrs. Poyser; "looks 'ull mend no jugs, nor laughing neither, as I see. Mr. Bede, I'm sorry you've to wait so long for your ale, but it's coming in a minute. Make yourself at home wi' th' cold potatoes: I know you like 'em. Tommy, I'll send you to bed this minute, if you don't give over laughing. What is there to laugh at, I should like to know? I'd sooner cry nor laugh at the sight o' that poor thing's cap; and there's them as 'ud be better if they could make theirselves like her i' more ways nor putting on her cap. It little becomes anybody i' this house to make fun o' my sister's child, an' her just gone away from us, as it went to my heart to part wi' her: an' I know one thing, as if trouble was to come, an' I was to be laid up i' my bed, an' the children was to die—as there's no knowing but what they will—an' the murrain was to come among the cattle again, an' everything went to rack an' ruin—I say we might be glad to get sight o' Dinah's cap again, wi' her own face under it, border or no border. For she's one o' them things as look the brightest on a rainy day, and loves you the best when you're most i' need on't."

Mrs. Poyser, you perceive, was aware that nothing would be so likely to expel the comic as the terrible. Tommy, who was of a susceptible disposition, and very fond of his mother, and who had, besides, eaten so many cherries as to have his feelings less under command than usual, was so affected by the dreadful picture she had made of the possible future, that he began to cry; and the good-natured father, indulgent to all weaknesses but those of negligent farmers, said to Hetty,

"You'd better take the things off again, my lass; it hurts your aunt to see 'em."

Hetty went up-stairs again, and the arrival of the ale made an agreeable diversion; for Adam had to give his opinion of the new tap, which could not be otherwise than complimentary to Mrs. Poyser; and then followed a discussion on the secrets of good brewing, the folly of stinginess in "hopping," and the doubtful economy of a farmer's making his own malt. Mrs. Poyser had so many opportunities of expressing herself with weight on these subjects, that by the time supper was ended, the ale-jug refilled, and Mr. Poyser's pipe alight, she was once more in high good-humour, and ready, at Adam's request, to fetch the broken spinning-wheel for his inspection.

"Ah," said Adam, looking at it carefully, "here's a nice bit o' turning wanted. It's a pretty wheel. I must have it up at the turning-shop in the village, and do it there, for I've no convenience for turning at home. If you'll send it to Mr. Burge's shop i' the morning, I'll get it done for you by Wednesday. I've been turning it over in my mind," he continued, looking at Mr. Poyser, "to make a bit more convenence at home for nice jobs o' cabinet-making. I've always done a deal at such little things in odd hours, and they're profitable, for there's more workmanship nor material in 'em. I look for me and Seth to get a little business for our-selves i' that way, for I know a man at Rosseter as 'ull take as many things as we should make, besides what we could get orders for round about."

Mr. Poyser entered with interest into a project which seemed a step towards Adam's becoming a "master-man"; and Mrs. Poyser gave her approbation to the scheme of the movable kitchen cupboard, which was to be capable of containing grocery, pickles, crockery, and house-linen, in the utmost compactness, without confusion. Hetty, once more in her own dress, with her neckerchief pushed a little backwards on this warm evening, was seated picking currants near the window, where Adam could see her quite well. And so the time passed pleasantly till Adam got up to go. He was pressed to come again soon, but not to stay longer, for at this busy time sensible people would not run the risk of being sleepy at five o'clock in the morning.

"I shall take a step farther," said Adam, "and go on to see Mester Massey, for he wasn't at church yesterday, and I've not seen him for a week past. I've never hardly known him to miss church before."

"Ay," said Mr. Poyser, "we've heared nothing about him, for it's the boys' hollodays now, so we can give you no account."

"But you'll niver think o' going there at this hour o' th' night?" said Mrs. Poyser, folding up her knitting.

"Oh, Mester Massey sits up late," said Adam. "An' the night-school's not over yet. Some o' the men don't come till late—they've got so far to walk. And Bartle himself's never in bed till it's gone eleven."

"I wouldna have him to live wi' me, then," said Mrs. Poyser, "a-drop-ping candle-grease about, as you're like to tumble down o' the floor the first thing i' the morning."

"Ay, eleven o'clock's late—it's late," said old Martin. "I ne'er sot up so i' my life, not to say as it warna a marr'in', or a christenin', or a wake, or th' harvest supper. Eleven o'clock's late."

"Why, I sit up till after twelve often," said Adam, laughing, "but it isn't t' eat and drink extry, it's to work extry. Good-night, Mrs. Poyser; good-night, Hetty."

Hetty could only smile and not shake hands, for hers were dyed and damp with currant juice; but all the rest gave a hearty shake to the large palm that was held out to them, and said, "Come again, come again!"

"Ay, think o' that now," said Mr. Poyser, when Adam was out on the causeway. "Sitting up till past twelve to do extry work! Ye'll not find many men o' six-an'-twenty as 'ull do to put i' the shafts wi' him. If you can catch Adam for a husband, Hetty, you'll ride i' your own spring-cart some day, I'll be your warrant."

Hetty was moving across the kitchen with the currants, so her uncle did not see the little toss of the head with which she answered him. To ride in a spring-cart seemed a very miserable lot indeed to her now.

CHAPTER XXI

THE NIGHT-SCHOOL AND THE SCHOOLMASTER

BARTLE MASSEY'S was one of a few scattered houses on the edge of a common, which was divided by the road to Treddleston. Adam reached it in a quarter of an hour after leaving the Hall Farm; and when he had his hand on the doorlatch, he could see, through the curtainless window, that there were eight or nine heads bending over the desks, lighted by thin dips.

When he entered, a reading lesson was going forward, and Bartle Massey merely nodded, leaving him to take his place where he pleased. He had not come for the sake of a lesson to-night, and his mind was too full of personal matters, too full of the last two hours he had passed in Hetty's presence, for him to amuse himself with a book till school was over; so he sat down in a corner, and looked on with an absent mind. It was a sort of scene which Adam had beheld almost weekly for years; he knew by heart every arabesque flourish in the framed specimen of Bartle Massey's handwriting which hung over the schoolmaster's head, by way of keeping a lofty ideal before the minds of his pupils; he knew the backs of all the books on the shelf running along the whitewashed wall above the pegs for the slates; he knew exactly how many grains were gone out of the ear of Indian-corn that hung from one of the rafters; he had long ago exhausted the resources of his imagination in trying to think how the bunch of leathery sea-weed had looked and grown in its native element; and from the place where he sat, he could make nothing of the old map of England that hung against the opposite wall, for age had turned it of a fine yellow brown, something like that of a well-seasoned meerschaum. The drama that was going on was almost as familiar as the scene, nevertheless habit had not made him indifferent to it, and even in his present self-absorbed mood, Adam felt a momentary stirring of the old fellow-feeling, as he looked at the rough men painfully holding pen or pencil with their cramped hands, or humbly labouring through their reading lesson.

The reading class now seated on the form in front of the schoolmaster's desk, consisted of the three most backward pupils. Adam would have known it only by seeing Bartle Massey's face as he looked over his spectacles, which he had shifted to the ridge of his nose, not requiring them for present purposes. The face wore its mildest expression: the grizzled bushy eyebrows had taken their more acute angle of compassionate kindness, and the mouth, habitually compressed with a pout of the lower lip, was relaxed so as to be ready to speak a helpful word or syllable in a moment. This gentle expression was the more interesting because the schoolmaster's nose, an irregular aquiline twisted a little on one side, had rather a formidable character; and his brow, moreover, had that peculiar tension which always impresses one as a sign of a keen, impatient temperament: the blue veins stood out like cords under the transparent yellow skin, and this intimidating brow was softened by no tendency to baldness, for the grey bristly hair, cut down to about an inch in length, stood round it in as close ranks as ever.

"Nay, Bill, nay," Bartle was saying in a kind tone, as he nodded to Adam, "begin that again, and then perhaps, it'll come to you what d, r, y, spells. It's the same lesson you read last week, you know."

"Bill" was a sturdy fellow, aged four-and-twenty, an excellent stone-sawyer, who could get as good wages as any man in the trade of his years; but he found a reading lesson in words of one syllable a harder matter to deal with than the hardest stone he had ever had to saw. The letters, he complained, were so "uncommon alike, there was no tellin' 'em one from another," the sawyer's business not being concerned with minute differences such as exist between a letter with its tail turned up and a letter with its tail turned down. But Bill had a firm determination that he would learn to read, founded chiefly on two reasons: first, that Tom Hazelow, his cousin, could read anything "right off," whether it was print or writing, and Tom had sent him a letter from twenty miles off, saying how he was prospering in the world, and had got an over-looker's place; secondly, that Sam Phillips, who sawed with him, had learned to read when he was turned twenty; and what could be done by a little fellow like Sam Phillips, Bill considered, could be done by himself, seeing that he could pound Sam into wet clay if circumstances required it. So here he was, pointing his big finger towards three words at once, and turning his head on one side that he might keep better hold with his eye of the one word which was to be discriminated out of the group. The amount of knowledge Bartle Massey must possess was some-thing so dim and vast that Bill's imagination recoiled before it: he would hardly have ventured to deny that the schoolmaster might have some-thing to do in bringing about the regular return of daylight and the changes in the weather.

The man seated next to Bill was of a very different type: he was a Methodist brickmaker, who, after spending thirty years of his life in perfect satisfaction with his ignorance, had lately "got religion," and along with it the desire to read the Bible. But with him, too, learning was a heavy business, and on his way out to-night he had offered as usual a special prayer for help, seeing that he had undertaken this hard task with a single eye to the nourishment of his soul—that he might have a greater abundance of texts and hymns wherewith to banish evil mem-ories and the temptations of old habit; or, in brief language, the devil. For the brickmaker had been a notorious poacher, and was suspected, though there was no good evidence against him, of being the man who had shot a neighbouring gamekeeper in the leg. However that might be, it is certain that shortly after the accident referred to, which was coin-cident with the arrival of an awakening Methodist preacher at Treddle-ston, a great change had been observed in the brickmaker; and though he was still known in the neighbourhood by his old sobriquet of "Brimstone," there was nothing he held in so much horror as any further transactions with that evil-smelling element. He was a broad-chested fellow, with a fervid temperament, which helped him better in imbibing religious ideas than in the dry process of acquiring the mere human knowledge of the alphabet. Indeed, he had been already a little shaken in his resolution by a brother Methodist, who assured him that the letter was a mere obstruction to the Spirit, and expressed a fear that Brimstone was too eager for the knowledge that puffeth up.

The third beginner was a much more promising pupil. He was a tall but thin and wiry man, nearly as old as Brimstone, with a very pale face, and hands stained a deep blue. He was a dyer, who in the course of dipping homespun wool and old women's petticoats, had got fired with the ambition to learn a great deal more about the strange secrets of colour. He had already a high reputation in the district for his dyes, and he was bent on discovering some method by which he could reduce the expense of crimsons and scarlets. The druggist at Treddleston had given him a notion that he might save himself a great deal of labour and expense if he could learn to read, and so he had begun to give his spare hours to the night-school, resolving that his "little chap" should lose no time in coming to Mr. Massey's day-school as soon as he was old enough.

It was touching to see these three big men, with the marks of their hard labour about them, anxiously bending over the worn books, and painfully making out, "The grass is green," "The sticks are dry," "The corn is ripe"—a very hard lesson to pass to after columns of single words all alike except in the first letter. It was almost as if three rough animals were making humble efforts to learn how they might become human. And it touched the tenderest fibre in Bartle Massey's nature, for such full-grown children as these were the only pupils for whom he had no severe epithets, and no impatient tones. He was not gifted with an imperturbable temper, and on music-nights it was apparent that patience could never be an easy virtue to him; but this evening, as he glances over his spectacles at Bill Downes, the sawyer, who is turning his head on one side with a desperate sense of blankness before the letters d, r, y, his eyes shed their mildest and most encouraging light.

After the reading class, two youths, between sixteen and nineteen, came up with imaginary bills of parcels, which they had been writing out on their slates, and were now required to calculate "off-hand"—a test which they stood with such imperfect success that Bartle Massey, whose eyes had been glaring at them ominously through his spectacles for some minutes, at length burst out in a bitter, high-pitched tone, pausing between every sentence to rap the floor with a knobbed stick which rested between his legs.

"Now, you see, you don't do this thing a bit better than you did a fortnight ago; and I'll tell you what's the reason. You want to learn accounts; that's well and good. But you think all you need do to learn accounts is to come to me and do sums for an hour or so, two or three times a week; and no sooner do you get your caps on and turn out of doors again, than you sweep the whole thing clean out of your mind. You go whistling about, and take no more care what you're thinking of than if your heads were gutters for any rubbish to swill through that happened to be in the way; and if you get a good notion in 'em, it's pretty soon washed out again. You think knowledge is to be got cheap—you'll come and pay Bartle Massey sixpence a week, and he'll make you clever at figures without your taking any trouble. But knowledge isn't to be got with paying sixpence, let me tell you: if you're to know figures, you must turn 'em over in your own heads, and keep your thoughts fixed on 'em. There's nothing you can't turn into a sum, for there's nothing but what's got number in it—even a fool. You may say to yourselves, 'I'm one fool, and Jack's another; if my fool's head weighed four pound, and Jack's three pound three ounces and three quarters, how many pennyweights heavier would my head be than Jack's?' A man that had got his heart in learning figures would make sums for himself, and work 'em in his head: when he sat at his shoemaking, he'd count his stitches by fives, and then put a price on his stitches, say half a farthing, and then see how much money he could get in an hour; and then ask himself how much money he'd get in a day at that rate; and then how much ten workmen would get working three, or twenty, or a hundred years at that rate—and all the while his needle would be going just as fast as if he left his head empty for the devil to dance in. But the long and the short of it is—I'll have nobody in my night-school that doesn't strive to learn what he comes to learn, as hard as if he was striving to get out of a dark hole into broad daylight. I'll send no man away because he's stupid: if Billy Taft, the idiot, wanted to learn anything, I'd not refuse to teach him. But I'll not throw away good knowledge on people who think they can get it by the sixpenn'orth, and carry it away with 'em as they would an ounce of snuff. So never come to me again, if you can't show that you've been working with your own heads, instead of thinking you can pay for mine to work for you. That's the last word I've got to say to you."

With this final sentence, Bartle Massey gave a sharper rap than ever with his knobbed stick, and the discomfited lads got up to go with a sulky look. The other pupils had happily only their writing-books to show, in various stages of progress from pot-hooks to round text; and mere pen-strokes, however perverse, were less exasperating to Bartle than false arithmetic. He was a little more severe than usual on Jacob Storey's Z's, of which poor Jacob had written a pageful, all with their tops turned the wrong way, with a puzzled sense that they were not right "somehow." But he observed in apology, that it was a letter you never wanted hardly, and he thought it had only been put there "to finish off th' alphabet, like, though ampus-and (&) would ha' done as well, for what he could see."

At last the pupils had all taken their hats and said their "Good-nights," and Adam, knowing his old master's habits, rose and said, "Shall I put the candles out, Mr. Massey?"

"Yes, my boy, yes, all but this, which I'll carry into the house; and just lock the outer door, now you're near it," said Bartle, getting his stick in the fitting angle to help him in descending from his stool. He was no sooner on the ground than it became obvious why the stick was necessary—the left leg was much shorter than the right. But the schoolmaster was so active with his lameness, that it was hardly thought of as a misfortune; and if you had seen him make his way along the schoolroom floor, and up the step into his kitchen, you would perhaps have understood why the naughty boys sometimes felt that his pace might be indefinitely quickened, and that he and his stick might overtake them even in their swiftest run.

The moment he appeared at the kitchen door with the candle in his hand, a faint whimpering began in the chimney-corner, and a brown-and-tan-coloured bitch, of that wise-looking breed with short legs and long body, known to an unmechanical generation as turn-spits, came creeping along the floor, wagging her tail, and hesitating at every other step, as if her affections were painfully divided between the hamper in the chimney-corner and the master, whom she could not leave without a greeting.

"Well, Vixen, well then, how are the babbies?" said the schoolmaster, making haste towards the chimney-corner, and holding the candle over the low hamper, where two extremely blind puppies lifted up their heads towards the light, from a nest of flannel and wool. Vixen could not even see her master look at them without painful excitement: she got into the hamper and got out again the next moment, and behaved with true feminine folly, though looking all the while as wise as a dwarf with a large old-fashioned head and body on the most abbreviated legs.

"Why, you've got a family, I see, Mr. Massey?" said Adam, smiling, as he came into the kitchen. "How's that? I thought it was against the law here."

"Law? What's the use o' law when a man's once such a fool as to let a woman into his house?" said Bartle, turning away from the hamper with some bitterness. He always called Vixen a woman, and seemed to have lost all consciousness that he was using a figure of speech. "If I'd known Vixen was a woman, I'd never have held the boys from drowning her; but when I'd got her into my hand, I was forced to take to her. And now you see what she's brought me to—the sly, hypocritical wench"—Bartle spoke these last works in a rasping tone of reproach, and looked at Vixen, who poked down her head and turned up her eyes towards him with a keen sense of opprobrium—"and contrived to be brought to bed on a Sunday at church-time. I've wished again and again I'd been a bloody-minded man, that I could have strangled the mother and the brats with one cord."

"I'm glad it was no worse a cause kept you from church," said Adam. "I was afraid you must be ill for the first time i' your life. And I was particularly sorry not to have you at church yesterday."

"Ah, my boy, I know why, I know why," said Bartle, kindly, going up to Adam, and raising his hand up to the shoulder that was almost on a level with his own head. "You've had a rough bit o' road to get over since I saw you—a rough bit o' road. But I'm in hopes there are better times coming for you. I've got some news to tell you. But I must get my supper first, for I'm hungry, I'm hungry. Sit down, sit down."

Bartle went into his little pantry, and brought out an excellent home-baked loaf; for it was his one extravagance in these dear times to eat bread once a day instead of oat-cake; and he justified it by observing, that what a schoolmaster wanted was brains, and oat-cake ran too much to bone instead of brains. Then came a piece of cheese and a quart jug with a crown of foam upon it. He placed them all on the round deal table which stood against his large arm-chair in the chimney-corner, with Vixen's hamper on one side of it, and a window-shelf with a few books piled up in it on the other. The table was as clean as if Vixen had been an excellent housewife in a checkered apron; so was the quarry floor; and the old carved oaken press, table, and chairs, which in these days would be bought at a high price in aristocratic houses, though, in that period of spider-legs and inlaid cupids, Bartle had got them for an old song, were as free from dust as things could be at the end of a summer's day.

"Now, then, my boy, draw up, draw up. We'll not talk about business till we've had our supper. No man can be wise on an empty stomach. But," said Bartle, rising from his chair again, "I must give Vixen her supper too, confound her! though she'll do nothing with it but nourish those unnecessary babbies. That's the way with these women, they've got no head-pieces to nourish, and so their food all runs either to fat or to brats."

He brought out of the pantry a dish of scraps, which Vixen at once fixed her eyes on, and jumped out of her hamper to lick up with the utmost despatch.

"I've had my supper, Mr. Massey," said Adam, "so I'll look on while you eat yours. I've been at the Hall Farm, and they always have their supper betimes, you know: they don't keep your late hours."

"I know little about their hours," said Bartle, dryly, cutting his bread and not shrinking from the crust. "It's a house I seldom go into, though I'm fond of the boys, and Martin Poyser's a good fellow. There's too many women in the house for me: I hate the sound of women's voices; they're always either a-buzz or a-squeak—always either a-buzz or a-squeak. Mrs. Poyser keeps at the top o' the talk like a fife; and as for the young lasses, I'd as soon look at water-grubs—I know what they'll turn to—stinging gnats, stinging gnats. Here, take some ale, my boy: it's been drawn for you—it's been drawn for you."

"Nay, Mr. Massey," said Adam, who took his old friend's whim more seriously than usual to-night, "don't be so hard on the creaturs God has made to be companions for us. A working man 'ud be badly off without a wife to see to th' house and the victual, and make things clean and comfortable."

"Nonsense! It's the silliest lie a sensible man like you ever believed, to say a woman makes a house comfortable. It's a story got up, because the women are there, and something must be found for 'em to do. I tell you there isn't a thing under the sun that needs to be done at all, but what a man can do better than a woman, unless it's bearing children, and they do that in a poor make-shift way; it had better ha' been left to the men—it had better ha' been left to the men. I tell you, a woman 'ull bake you a pie every week of her life, and never come to see that the hotter th' oven the shorter the time. I tell you, a woman 'ull make your porridge every day for twenty years, and never think of measuring the proportion between the meal and the milk—a little more or less, she'll think, doesn't signify: the porridge *will* be awk'ard now and then: if it's wrong, it's summat in the meal, or it's summat in the milk, or it's summat in the water. Look at me! I make my own bread, and there's no difference between one batch and another from year's end to year's end; but if I'd got any other woman besides Vixen in the house, I must pray to the Lord every baking to give me patience if the bread turned out heavy. And as for cleanliness, my house is cleaner than any house on the Common, though the half of 'em swarm with women. Will Baker's lad comes to help me in a morning, and we get as much cleaning done in one hour without any fuss, as a woman 'ud get done in three, and all the while be sending buckets o' water after your ankles, and let the fender and the fire-irons stand in the middle o' the floor half the day, for you to break your shins against 'em. Don't tell me about God having made such creatures to be companions for us! I don't say but He might make Eve to be a companion to Adam in Paradise—there was no cooking to be spoilt there, and no other woman to cackle with and make mischief; though you see what mischief she did as soon as she'd an opportunity. But it's an impious, unscriptural opinion to say a woman's a blessing to a man now; you might as well say adders and wasps, and foxes and wild beasts, are a blessing, when they're only the evils that belong to this state o' probation, which it's lawful for a man to keep as clear of as he can in this life, hoping to get quit of 'em for ever in another—hoping to get quit of 'em for ever in another."

Bartle had become so excited and angry in the course of his invective that he had forgotten his supper, and only used the knife for the purpose of rapping the table with the haft. But towards the close, the raps became so sharp and frequent, and his voice so quarrelsome, that Vixen felt it incumbent on her to jump out of the hamper and bark vaguely.

"Quiet, Vixen!" snarled Bartle, turning round upon her. "You're like the rest o' the women—always putting in *your* word before you know why."

Vixen returned to her hamper again in humiliation, and her master continued his supper in a silence which Adam did not choose to interrupt; he knew the old man would be in a better humour when he had had his supper and lighted his pipe. Adam was used to hear him talk in this way, but had never learned so much of Bartle's past life as to know whether his view of married comfort was founded on experience. On that point Bartle was mute; and it was even a secret where he had lived previous to the twenty years in which, happily for the peasants and artisans of this neighbourhood, he had been settled among them as their only schoolmaster. If anything like a question was ventured on this subject, Bartle always replied, "Oh, I've seen many places—I've been a deal in the south"—and the Loamshire men would as soon have thought of asking for a particular town in Africa as in "the south."

"Now then, my boy," said Bartle, at last, when he had poured out his second mug of ale and lighted his pipe—"now then, we'll have a little talk. But tell me first, have you heard any particular news to-day?"

"No," said Adam, "not as I remember."

"Ah, they'll keep it close, they'll keep it close, I daresay. But I found it out by chance; and it's news that may concern you, Adam, else I'm a man that don't know a superficial square foot from a solid."

Here Bartle gave a series of fierce and rapid puffs, looking earnestly the while at Adam. Your impatient loquacious man has never any notion of keeping his pipe alight by gentle measured puffs; he is always letting it go nearly out, and then punishing it for that negligence. At last he said,

"Satchell's got a paralytic stroke. I found it out from the lad they sent to Treddleston for the doctor, before seven o'clock this morning. He's a good way beyond sixty, you know; it's much if he get's over it."

"Well," said Adam, "I daresay there'd be more rejoicing than sorrow in the parish at his being laid up. He's been a selfish, tale-bearing, mischievous fellow; but, after all, there's nobody he's done so much harm to as to th' old Squire. Though it's the Squire himself as is to blame —making a stupid fellow like that sort o' man-of-all-work, just to save th' expense of having a proper steward to look after th' estate. And he's lost more by ill-management o' the woods, I'll be bound, than 'ud pay for two stewards. If he's laid on the shelf, it's to be hoped he'll make way for a better man, but I don't see how it's like to make any difference to me."

"But I see it, but I see it," said Bartle; "and others besides me. The Captain's coming of age now—you know that as well as I do—and it's to be expected he'll have a little more voice in things. And I know, and you know too, what 'ud be the Captain's wish about the woods, if there was a fair opportunity for making a change. He's said in plenty of people's hearing that he'd make you manager of the woods to-morrow, if he'd the power. Why, Carroll, Mr. Irwine's butler, heard him say so to the parson not many days ago. Carroll looked in when we were smoking our pipes o' Saturday night at Casson's, and he told us about it; and whenever anybody says a good word for you, the parson's ready to back it, that I'll answer for. It was pretty well talked over, I can tell you, at Casson's, and one and another had their fling at you: for if donkeys set to work to sing, you're pretty sure what the tune 'll be."

"Why, did they talk it over before Mr. Burge?" said Adam; "or wasn't he there o' Saturday?"

"O, he went away before Carroll came; and Casson—he's always for setting other folks right, you know—would have it Burge was the man to have the management of the woods. 'A substantial man,' says he, 'with pretty near sixty years' experience o' timber: it 'ud be all very well for Adam Bede to act under him, but it isn't to be supposed the Squire 'ud appoint a young fellow like Adam, when there's his elders and betters at hand!' But I said, 'That's a pretty notion o' yours, Casson. Why, Burge is the man to buy timber; would you put the woods into his hands, and let him make his own bargains? I think you don't leave your customers to score their own drink, do you? And as for age, what that's worth depends on the quality o' the liquor. It's pretty well known who's the backbone of Jonathan Burge's business.' "

"I thank you for your good word, Mr. Massey," said Adam. "But, for all that, Casson was partly i' the right for once. There's not much likelihood that th' old Squire 'ud ever consent t' employ me: I offended him about two years ago, and he's never forgiven me."

"Why, how was that? You never told me about it," said Bartle.

"O, it was a bit o' nonsense. I'd made a frame for a screen for Miss Lyddy—she's allays making something with her worsted-work, you know—and she'd given me particular orders about this screen, and there was as much talking and measuring as if we'd been planning a house. However, it was a nice bit o' work, and I liked doing it for her. But, you know, those little friggling things take a deal o' time. I only worked at it in over-hours—often late at night—and I had to go to Treddleston over an' over again, about little bits o' brass nails and such gear; and I turned the little knobs and the legs, and carved th' open work, after a pattern, as nice as could be. And I was uncommon pleased with it when it was done. And when I took it home, Miss Lyddy sent for me to bring it into her drawing-room, so as she might give me directions about fastening on the work—very fine needlework, Jacob and Rachel a-kissing one another among the sheep, like a picture—and th' old Squire was sitting there, for he mostly sits with her. Well, she was mighty pleased with the screen, and then she wanted to know what pay she was to give me. I didn't speak at random—you know it's not my way; I'd calculated pretty close, though I hadn't made out a bill, and I said, 'One pound thirteen.' That was paying for the mater'als and paying me, but none too much, for my work. Th' old Squire looked up at this, and peered in his way at the screen, and said, 'One pound thirteen for a gimcrack like that! Lydia, my dear, if you must spend money on these things, why don't you get them at Rosseter, instead of paying double price for clumsy work here? Such things are not work for a carpenter like Adam. Give him a guinea, and no more.' Well, Miss Lyddy, I reckon, believed what he told her, and she's not over-fond o' parting with the money herself—she's not a bad woman at bottom, but she's been brought up under his thumb; so she began fidgeting with her purse, and turned as red as her ribbon. But I made a bow, and said, 'No, thank you, madam; I'll make you a present o' the screen, if you please. I've charged a regular price for my work, and I know it's done well; and I know, begging his honour's pardon, that you couldn't get such a screen at Rosseter under two guineas. I'm willing to give you my work—it's been done in my own time, and nobody's got anything to do with it but me; but if I'm paid, I can't take a smaller price than I asked, because that 'ud be like saying, I'd asked more than was just. With your leave, madam, I'll bid you good-morning.' I made my bow and went out before she'd time to say any more, for she stood with the purse in her hand, looking almost foolish. I didn't mean to be disrespectful, and I spoke as polite as I could; but I can give in to no man, if he wants to make it out as I'm trying t' overreach him. And in the evening the footman brought me the one pound thirteen wrapped in paper. But since then I've seen pretty clear as th' old Squire can't abide me."

"That's likely enough, that's likely enough," said Bartle, meditatively. "The only way to bring him round would be to show him what was for his own interest, and that the Captain may do—that the Captain may do."

"Nay, I don't know," said Adam; "the Squire's 'cute enough, but it takes something else besides 'cuteness to make folks see what'll be their interest in the long run. It takes some conscience and belief in right and wrong, I see that pretty clear. You'd hardly ever bring round th' old Squire to believe he'd gain as much in a straightfor'ard way as by tricks and turns. And, besides, I've not much mind to work under him: I don't want to quarrel with any gentleman, more particular an old gentleman turned eighty, and I know we couldn't agree long. If the Captain was master o' th' estate, it 'ud be different: he's got a conscience and a will to do right, and I'd sooner work for him nor for any man living."

"Well, well, my boy, if good luck knocks at your door, don't you put your head out at window and tell it to be gone about its business, that's all. You must learn to deal with odd and even in life, as well as in figures. I tell you now, as I told you ten year ago, when you pommelled young Mike Holdsworth for wanting to pass a bad shilling, before you knew whether he was in jest or earnest—you're over-hasty and proud, and apt to set your teeth against folks that don't square to your notions. It's no harm for *me* to be a bit fiery and stiff-backed: I'm an old schoolmaster, and shall never want to get on to a higher perch. But where's the use of all the time I've spent in teaching you writing and mapping and mensuration, if you're not to get for'ard in the world, and show folks there's some advantage in having a head on your shoulders, instead of a turnip? Do you mean to go on turning up your nose at every opportunity, because it's got a bit of a smell about it that nobody finds out but yourself? It's as foolish as that notion o' yours that a wife is to make a working man comfortable. Stuff and nonsense!—stuff and nonsense! Leave that to fools that never got beyond a sum in simple addition. Simple addition enough! Add one fool to another fool, and in six years' time six fools more—they're all of the same denomination, big and little's nothing to do with the sum!"

During this rather heated exhortation to coolness and discretion the pipe had gone out, and Bartle gave the climax to his speech by striking a light furiously, after which he puffed with fierce resolution, fixing his eye still on Adam, who was trying not to laugh.

"There's a good deal o' sense in what you say, Mr. Massey," Adam began, as soon as he felt quite serious, "as there always is. But you'll give in that it's no business o' mine to be building on chances that may never happen. What I've got to do is to work as well as I can with the tools and mater'als I've got in my hands. If a good chance comes to me, I'll think o' what you've been saying; but till then, I've got nothing to do but to trust to my own hands and my own head-piece. I'm turning over a little plan for Seth and me to go into the cabinet-making a bit by ourselves, and win a extra pound or two in that way. But it's getting late now—it'll be pretty near eleven before I'm at home, and mother may happen to lie awake; she's more fidgety nor usual now. So I'll bid you good-night."

"Well, well, we'll go to the gate with you—it's a fine night," said Bartle, taking up his stick. Vixen was at once on her legs, and without further words the three walked out into the starlight, by the side of Bartle's potato-beds, to the little gate.

"Come to the music o' Friday night, if you can, my boy," said the old man, as he closed the gate after Adam, and leaned against it.

"Ay, ay," said Adam, striding along towards the streak of pale road. He was the only object moving on the wide common. The two grey donkeys, just visible in front of the gorse bushes, stood as still as lime-stone images—as still as the grey-thatched roof of the mud cottage a little farther on. Bartle kept his eye on the moving figure till it passed into the darkness, while Vixen, in a state of divided affection, had twice run back to the house to bestow a parenthetic lick on her puppies.

"Ay, ay," muttered the schoolmaster, as Adam disappeared; "there you go, stalking along—stalking along; but you wouldn't have been what you are if you hadn't had a bit of old lame Bartle inside you. The strongest calf must have something to suck at. There's plenty of these big, lumbering fellows 'ud never have known their A B C, if it hadn't been for Bartle Massey. Well, well, Vixen, you foolish wench, what is it, what is it? I must go in, must I? Ay, ay, I'm never to have a will o' my own, any more. And those pups, what do you think I'm to do with 'em, when they're twice as big as you?—for I'm pretty sure the father was that hulking bull-terrier of Will Baker's—wasn't he now, eh, you sly hussy?" (Here Vixen tucked her tail between her legs, and ran forward into the house. Subjects are sometimes broached which a well-bred female will ignore.)

"But where's the use of talking to a woman with babbies?" continued Bartle: "she's got no conscience—no conscience; it's all run to milk."

BOOK THREE

★

CHAPTER XXII

GOING TO THE BIRTHDAY FEAST

THE thirtieth of July was come, and it was one of those half-dozen warm days which sometimes occur in the middle of a rainy English summer. No rain had fallen for the last three or four days, and the weather was perfect for that time of the year: there was less dust than usual on the dark-green hedgerows, and on the wild camomile that starred the roadside, yet the grass was dry enough for the little children to roll on it, and there was no cloud but a long dash of light, downy ripple, high, high up in the far-off blue sky. Perfect weather for an out-door July merrymaking, yet surely not the best time of year to be born in. Nature seems to make a hot pause just then—all the loveliest flowers are gone; the sweet time of early growth and vague hopes is past; and yet the time of harvest and ingathering is not come, and we tremble at the possible storms that may ruin the precious fruit in the moment of its ripeness. The woods are all one dark monotonous green; the waggon-loads of hay no longer creep along the lanes, scattering their sweet-smelling fragments on the blackberry branches; the pastures are often a little tanned, yet the corn has not got its last splendour of red and gold; the lambs and calves have lost all traces of their innocent frisky prettiness, and have become stupid young sheep and cows. But it is a time of leisure on the farm—that pause between hay and corn harvest, and so the farmers and labourers in Hayslope and Broxton thought the Captain did well to come of age just then, when they could give their undivided minds to the flavour of the great cask of ale which had been brewed the autumn after "the heir" was born, and was to be tapped on his twenty-first birthday. The air had been merry with the ringing of church-bells very early this morning, and every one had made haste to get through the needful work before twelve, when it would be time to think of getting ready to go to the Chase.

The mid-day sun was streaming into Hetty's bed-chamber, and there was no blind to temper the heat with which it fell on her head as she looked at herself in the old speckled glass. Still, that was the only glass she had in which she could see her neck and arms, for the small hanging glass she had fetched out of the next room—the room that had been Dinah's—would show her nothing below her little chin, and that beautiful bit of neck where the roundness of her cheek melted into another roundness shadowed by dark delicate curls. And to-day she thought more than usual about her neck and arms; for at the dance this eve-ning she was not to wear any neckerchiefs, and she had been busy yes-terday with her spotted pink-and-white frock, that she might make the sleeves either long or short at will. She was dressed now just as she was to be in the evening, with a tucker made of "real" lace, which her aunt had lent her for this unparalleled occasion, but with no orna-ments besides; she had even taken out her small round earrings which she wore every day. But there was something more to be done, appar-ently, before she put on her neckerchief and long sleeves, which she was to wear in the day-time, for now she unlocked the drawer that held her private treasures. It is more than a month since we saw her unlock that drawer before, and now it holds new treasures, so much more pre-cious than the old ones that these are thrust into the corner. Hetty would not care to put the large coloured glass earrings into her ears now; for see! she has got a beautiful pair of gold and pearls and garnet, lying snugly in a pretty little box lined with white satin. O, the delight of taking out that little box and looking at the earrings! Do not reason about it, my philosophical reader, and say that Hetty, being very pretty, must have known that it did not signify whether she had on any ornaments or not; and that, moreover, to look at earrings which she could not possibly wear out of her bed-room could hardly be a sat-isfaction, the essence of vanity being a reference to the impressions produced on others; you will never understand women's natures if you are so excessively rational. Try rather to divest yourself of all your rational prejudices, as much as if you were studying the psychology of a canary bird, and only watch the movements of this pretty round creature as she turns her head on one side with an unconscious smile at the earrings nestled in the little box. Ah, you think, it is for the sake of the person who has given them to her, and her thoughts are gone back now to the moment when they were put into her hands. No; else why should she have cared to have earrings rather than anything else? and I know that she had longed for earrings from among all the orna-ments she could imagine.

"Little, little ears!" Arthur had said, pretending to pinch them one evening, as Hetty sat beside him on the grass without her hat. "I wish I had some pretty earrings!" she said in a moment, almost before she knew what she was saying—the wish lay so close to her lips, it *would* flutter past them at the slightest breath. And the next day—it was only last week—Arthur had ridden over to Rosseter on purpose to buy them. That little wish so naïvely uttered, seemed to him the prettiest bit of childishness; he had never heard anything like it before; and he had wrapped the box up in a great many covers, that he might see Hetty unwrapping it with growing curiosity, till at last her eyes flashed back their new delight into his.

No, she was not thinking most of the giver when she smiled at the earrings, for now she is taking them out of the box, not to press them to her lips, but to fasten them in her ears,—only for one moment, to see how pretty they look, as she peeps at them in the glass against the wall, with first one position of the head and then another, like a listening bird. It is impossible to be wise on the subject of earrings as one looks at her; what should those delicate pearls and crystals be made for, if not for such ears? One cannot even find fault with the tiny round hole which they leave when they are taken out; perhaps water-nixies, and such lovely things without souls, have these little round holes in their ears by nature, ready to hang jewels in. And Hetty must be one of them: it is too painful to think that she is a woman, with a woman's destiny before her—a woman spinning in young ignorance a light web of folly and vain hopes which may one day close round her and press upon her, a rancorous poisoned garment, changing all at once her fluttering, trivial butterfly sensations into a life of deep human anguish.

But she cannot keep in the earrings long, else she may make her uncle and aunt wait. She puts them quickly into the box again, and shuts them up. Some day she will be able to wear any earrings she likes, and already she lives in an invisible world of brilliant costumes, shimmering gauze, soft satin, and velvet, such as the lady's-maid at the Chase has shown her in Miss Lydia's wardrobe: she feels the bracelets on her arms, and treads on a soft carpet in front of a tall mirror. But she has one thing in the drawer which she can venture to wear to-day, because she can hang it on the chain of dark-brown berries which she has been used to wear on grand days, with a tiny flat scent-bottle at the end of it tucked inside her frock; and she *must* put on her brown berries—her neck would look so unfinished without it. Hetty was not quite as fond of the locket as of the earrings, though it was a handsome large locket, with enamelled flowers at the back and a beautiful gold border round the glass, which showed a light brown, slightly waving lock, forming a background for two little dark rings. She must keep it under her clothes, and no one would see it. But Hetty had another passion; only a little less strong than her love of finery; and that other passion made her like to wear the locket even hidden in her bosom. She would always have worn it, if she had dared to encounter her aunt's questions about a ribbon round her neck. So now she slipped it on along her chain of dark-brown berries, and snapped the chain round her neck. It was not a very long chain, only allowing the locket to hang a little way below the edge of her frock. And now she had nothing to do but to put on her long sleeves, her new white gauze neckerchief, and her straw hat trimmed with white to-day instead of the pink, which had become rather faded under the July sun. That hat made the drop of bitterness in Hetty's cup to-day, for it was not quite new—everybody would see that it was a little tanned against the white ribbon—and Mary Burge, she felt sure, would have a new hat or bonnet on. She looked for consolation at her fine white cotton stockings: they really were very nice indeed, and she had given almost all her spare money for them.

Hetty's dream of the future could not make her insensible to triumph in the present: to be sure, Captain Donnithorne loved her so, that he would never care about looking at other people, but then those other people didn't know how he loved her, and she was not satisfied to appear shabby and insignificant in their eyes even for a short space.

The whole party was assembled in the house-place when Hetty went down, all of course in their Sunday clothes; and the bells had been ringing so this morning in honour of the Captain's twenty-first birthday, and the work had all been got done so early, that Marty and Tommy were not quite easy in their minds until their mother had assured them that going to church was not part of the day's festivities. Mr. Poyser had once suggested that the house should be shut up, and left to take care of itself; "for," said he, "there's no danger of anybody's breaking in—everybody'll be at the Chase, thieves an' all. If we lock th' house up, all the men can go: it's a day they wonna see twice i' their lives." But Mrs. Poyser answered with great decision: "I never left th' house to take care of itself since I was a missis, and I never will. There's been ill-looking tramps enoo' about the place this last week, to carry off every ham an' every spoon we'n got; and they all collogue together, them tramps, as it's a mercy they hanna come and pisoned the dogs and murdered us all in our beds aforewe knowed, some Friday night when we'n got the money in th' house to pay the men. And it's like enough the tramps know where we're going as well as we do oursens; for if old Harry wants any work done, you may be sure he'll find the means."

"Nonsense about murdering us in our beds," said Mr. Poyser; "I've got a gun i' our room, hanna I? and thee'st got ears as 'ud find it out if a mouse was gnawing the bacon. Howiver, if thee wouldstna be easy, Alick can stay at home i' the forepart o' the day, and Tim can come back tow'rds five o'clock, and let Alick have his turn. They may let Growler loose if anybody offers to do mischief, and there's Alick's dog, too, ready enough to set his tooth in a tramp if Alick gives him a wink."

Mrs. Poyser accepted this compromise, but thought it advisable to bar and bolt to the utmost; and now, at the last moment before starting, Nancy, the dairymaid, was closing the shutters of the house-place, although the window, lying under the immediate observation of Alick and the dogs, might have been supposed the least likely to be selected for a burglarious attempt.

The covered cart, without springs, was standing ready to carry the whole family except the men-servants: Mr. Poyser and the grandfather sat on the seat in front, and within there was room for all the women and children; the fuller the cart the better, because then the jolting would not hurt so much, and Nancy's broad person and thick arms were an excellent cushion to be pitched on. But Mr. Poyser drove at no more than a walking pace, that there might be as little risk of jolting as possible on this warm day; and there was time to exchange greetings and remarks with the foot-passengers who were going the same way, specking the paths between the green meadows and the golden corn-fields with bits of movable bright colour—a scarlet waistcoat to match the poppies that nodded a little too thickly among the corn, or a dark-blue neckerchief with ends flaunting across a bran-new white smock-frock. All Broxton and all Hayslope were to be at the Chase, and make merry there in honour of "th' heir"; and the old men and women, who had never been so far down this side of the hill for the last twenty years, were being brought from Broxton and Hayslope in one of the farmers' waggons, at Mr. Irwine's suggestion. The church-bells had struck up again now—a last tune, before the ringers came down the hill to have their share of the festival; and before the bells had finished, other music was heard approaching, so that even Old Brown, the sober horse that was drawing Mr. Poyser's cart, began to prick up his ears. It was the band of the Benefit Club, which had mustered in all its glory; that is to say, in bright-blue scarfs and blue favours, and carry-ing its banner with the motto, "Let brotherly love continue," encircling a picture of a stone-pit.

The carts, of course, were not to enter the Chase. Every one must get down at the lodges, and the vehicles must be sent back.

"Why, the Chase is like a fair a'ready," said Mrs. Poyser, as she got down from the cart, and saw the groups scattered under the great oaks, and the boys running about in the hot sunshine to survey the tall poles surmounted by the fluttering garments that were to be the prizes of the successful climbers. "I should ha' thought there wasna so many people i' the two parishes. Mercy on us! how hot it is out o' the shade! Come here, Totty, else your little face 'ull be burnt to a scratchin'! They might ha' cooked the dinners i' that open space, an' saved the fires. I shall go to Mrs. Best's room an' sit down."

"Stop a bit, stop a bit," said Mr. Poyser. "There's th' waggin coming wi' th' old folks in't; it'll be such a sight as wonna come o'er again, to see 'em get down an' walk along all together. You remember some on 'em i' their prime, eh, father?"

"Ay, ay," said old Martin, walking slowly under the shade of the lodge porch, from which he could see the aged party descend. "I remem-ber Jacob Taft walking fifty mile after the Scotch raybels, when they turned back from Stoniton."

He felt himself quite a youngster, with a long life before him, as he saw the Hayslope patriarch, old Feyther Taft, descend from the waggon and walk towards him, in his brown nightcap, and leaning on his two sticks.

"Well, Mester Taft," shouted old Martin, at the utmost stretch of his voice,—for though he knew the old man was stone deaf, he could not omit the propriety of a greeting,—"you're hearty yet. You can enjoy yoursen to-day, for-all you're ninety an' better."

"Your sarvant, mesters, your sarvant," said Feyther Taft in a treble tone, perceiving that he was in company.

The aged group, under care of sons or daughters, themselves worn

and grey, passed on along the least-winding carriage-road towards the
house, where a special table was prepared for them; while the Poyser
party wisely struck across the grass under the shade of the great trees,
but not out of view of the house-front, with its sloping lawn and flower-
beds, or of the pretty striped marquee at the edge of the lawn, standing
at right angles with two larger marquees on each side of the open green
space where the games were to be played. The house would have been
nothing but a plain square mansion of Queen Anne's time, but for the
remnant of an old abbey to which it was united at one end, in much
the same way as one may sometimes see a new farmhouse rising high
and prim at the end of older and lower farm-offices. The fine old remnant stood a little backward and under the shadow of tall beeches, but
the sun was now on the taller and more advanced front, the blinds were
all down, and the house seemed asleep in the hot mid-day: it made
Hetty quite sad to look at it: Arthur must be somewhere in the back
rooms, with the grand company, where he could not possibly know that
she was come, and she should not see him for a long, long while—not
till after dinner, when they said he was to come up and make a speech.

But Hetty was wrong in part of her conjecture. No grand company
was come except the Irwines, for whom the carriage had been sent early,
and Arthur was at that moment not in a back room, but walking with
the Rector into the broad stone cloisters of the old abbey, where the
long tables were laid for all the cottage tenants and the farm-servants.
A very handsome young Briton he looked to-day, in high spirits and a
bright-blue frock-coat, the highest mode—his arm no longer in a sling.
So open-looking and candid, too; but candid people have their secrets,
and secrets leave no lines in young faces.

"Upon my word," he said, as they entered the cool cloisters, "I think
the cottagers have the best of it: these cloisters make a delightful dining-
room on a hot day. That was capital advice of yours, Irwine, about the
dinners—to let them be as orderly and comfortable as possible, and only
for the tenants: especially as I had only a limited sum after all; for
though my grandfather talked of a *carte blanche,* he couldn't make up
his mind to trust me, when it came to the point."

"Never mind, you'll give more pleasure in this quiet way," said Mr.
Irwine. "In this sort of thing people are constantly confounding liberality with riot and disorder. It sounds very grand to say that so many
sheep and oxen were roasted whole, and everybody ate who liked to
come; but in the end it generally happens that no one has had an enjoy-
able meal. If the people get a good dinner and a moderate quantity of
ale in the middle of the day, they'll be able to enjoy the games as the
day cools. You can't hinder some of them from getting too much towards
evening, but drunkenness and darkness go better together than drunkenness and daylight."

"Well, I hope there won't be much of it. I've kept the Treddleston
people away, by having a feast for them in the town; and I've got Casson and Adam Bede, and some other good fellows, to look to the giving

out of ale in the booths, and to take care things don't go too far. Come, let us go up above now, and see the dinner-tables for the large tenants."

They went up the stone staircase leading simply to the long gallery above the cloisters, a gallery where all the dusty worthless old pictures had been banished for the last three generations—mouldy portraits of Queen Elizabeth and her ladies, General Monk with his eye knocked out, Daniel very much in the dark among the lions, and Julius Cæsar on horseback, with a high nose and laurel crown, holding his Commentaries in his hand.

"What a capital thing it is that they saved this piece of the old abbey," said Arthur. "If I'm ever master here, I shall do up the gallery in first-rate style: we've got no room in the house a third as large as this. That second table is for the farmers' wives and children: Mrs. Best said it would be more comfortable for the mothers and children to be by themselves. I was determined to have the children, and make a regular family thing of it. I shall be 'the old squire' to those little lads and lasses some day, and they'll tell their children what a much finer young fellow I was than my own son. There's a table for the women and children below as well. But you will see them all—you will come up with me after dinner, I hope?"

"Yes, to be sure," said Mr. Irwine. "I wouldn't miss your maiden speech to the tenantry."

"And there will be something else you'll like to hear," said Arthur. "Let us go into the library and I'll tell you all about it while my grandfather is in the drawing-room with the ladies. Something that will surprise you," he continued, as they sat down. "My grandfather has come round after all."

"What, about Adam?"

"Yes; I should have ridden over to tell you about it, only I was so busy. You know I told you I had quite given up arguing the matter with him—I thought it was hopeless; but yesterday morning he asked me to come in here to him before I went out, and astonished me by saying that he had decided on all the new arrangements he should make in consequence of old Satchell being obliged to lay by work, and that he intended to employ Adam in superintending the woods at a salary of a guinea a-week, and the use of a pony to be kept here. I believe the secret of it is, he saw from the first it would be a profitable plan, but he had some particular dislike of Adam to get over—and besides, the fact that I propose a thing is generally a reason with him for rejecting it. There's the most curious contradiction in my grandfather: I know he means to leave me all the money he has saved, and he is likely enough to have cut off poor aunt Lydia, who has been a slave to him all her life, with only five hundred a-year, for the sake of giving me all the more; and yet I sometimes think he positively hates me because I'm his heir. I believe if I were to break my neck, he would feel it the greatest misfortune that could befall him, and yet it seems a pleasure to him to make my life a series of petty annoyances."

"Ah, my boy, it is not only woman's love that is ἀπέρωτος ἔρως, as old Æschylus calls it. There's plenty of 'unloving love' in the world of a masculine kind. But tell me about Adam. Has he accepted the post? I don't see that it can be much more profitable than his present work, though, to be sure, it will leave him a good deal of time on his own hands."

"Well, I felt some doubt about it when I spoke to him, and he seemed to hesitate at first. His objection was, that he thought he should not be able to satisfy my grandfather. But I begged him as a personal favour to me not to let any reason prevent him from accepting the place, if he really liked the employment, and would not be giving up anything that was more profitable to him. And he assured me he should like it of all things;—it would be a great step forward for him in business, and it would enable him to do what he had long wished to do—to give up working for Burge. He says he shall have plenty of time to superintend a little business of his own, which he and Seth will carry on, and will perhaps be able to enlarge by degrees. So he has agreed at last, and I have arranged that he shall dine with the large tenants to-day; and I mean to announce the appointment to them, and ask them to drink Adam's health. It's a little drama I've got up in honour of my friend Adam. He's a fine fellow, and I like the opportunity of letting people know that I think so."

"A drama in which friend Arthur piques himself on having a pretty part to play," said Mr. Irwine, smiling. But when he saw Arthur colour, he went on relentingly, "My part, you know, is always that of the old Fogy who sees nothing to admire in the young folks. I don't like to admit that I'm proud of my pupil when he does graceful things. But I must play the amiable old gentleman for once, and second your toast in honour of Adam. Has your grandfather yielded on the other point too, and agreed to have a respectable man as steward?"

"O no," said Arthur, rising from his chair with an air of impatience, and walking along the room with his hands in his pockets. "He's got some project or other about letting the Chase Farm, and bargaining for a supply of milk and butter for the house. But I ask no questions about it—it makes me too angry. I believe he means to do all the business himself, and have nothing in the shape of a steward. It's amazing what energy he has, though."

"Well, we'll go to the ladies now," said Mr. Irwine, rising too. "I want to tell my mother what a splendid throne you've prepared for her under the marquee."

"Yes, and we must be going to luncheon too," said Arthur. "It must be two o'clock, for there is the gong beginning to sound for the tenants' dinners."

CHAPTER XXIII

DINNER-TIME

WHEN Adam heard that he was to dine up-stairs with the large tenants, he felt rather uncomfortable at the idea of being exalted in this way above his mother and Seth, who were to dine in the cloisters below. But Mr. Mills, the butler, assured him that Captain Donnithorne had given particular orders about it, and would be very angry if Adam was not there.

Adam nodded, and went up to Seth, who was standing a few yards off. "Seth, lad," he said, "the Captain has sent to say I'm to dine up-stairs—he wishes it particular, Mr. Mills says, so I suppose it 'ud be behaving ill for me not to go. But I don't like sitting up above thee and mother, as if I was better than my own flesh and blood. Thee't not take it unkind, I hope?"

"Nay, nay, lad," said Seth, "thy honour's our honour; and if thee get'st respect, thee'st won it by thy deserts. The further I see thee above me, the better, so long as thee feel'st like a brother to me. It's because o' thy being appointed over the woods, and it's nothing but what's right. That's a place o' trust, and thee't above a common workman now."

"Ay," said Adam, "but nobody knows a word about it yet. I haven't given notice to Mr. Burge about leaving him, and I don't like to tell anybody else about it before he knows, for he'll be a good bit hurt, I doubt. People 'ull be wondering to see me there, and they'll like enough be guessing the reason, and asking questions, for there's been so much talk up and down about my having the place, this last three weeks."

"Well, thee canst say thee wast ordered to come without being told the reason. That's the truth. And mother 'ull be fine and joyful about it. Let's go and tell her."

Adam was not the only guest invited to come up-stairs on other grounds than the amount he contributed to the rent-roll. There were other people in the two parishes who derived dignity from their functions rather than from their pocket, and of these Bartle Massey was one. His lame walk was rather slower than usual on this warm day, so Adam lingered behind when the bell rang for dinner, that he might walk up with his old friend; for he was a little too shy to join the Poyser party on this public occasion. Opportunities of getting to Hetty's side would be sure to turn up in the course of the day, and Adam contented himself with that, for he disliked any risk of being "joked" about Hetty;—the big, outspoken, fearless man was very shy and diffident as to his love-making.

"Well, Mester Massey," said Adam, as Bartle came up, "I'm going to dine up-stairs with you to-day: the Captain's sent me orders."

"Ah!" said Bartle, pausing, with one hand on his back. "Then there's something in the wind—there's something in the wind. Have you heard anything about what the old Squire means to do?"

"Why, yes," said Adam; "I'll tell you what I know, because I believe you can keep a still tongue in your head if you like; and I hope you'll not let drop a word till it's common talk, for I've particular reasons against its being known."

"Trust to me, my boy, trust to me. I've got no wife to worm it out of me and then run out and cackle it in everybody's hearing. If you trust a man, let him be a bachelor—let him be a bachelor."

"Well, then, it was so far settled yesterday, that I'm to take the management o' the woods. The Captain sent for me, t' offer it me, when I was seeing to the poles and things here, and I've agreed to 't. But if anybody asks any questions up-stairs, just you take no notice, and turn the talk to something else, and I'll be obliged to you. Now, let us go on, for we're pretty nigh the last, I think."

"I know what to do, never fear," said Bartle, moving on. "The news will be good sauce to my dinner. Ay, ay, my boy, you'll get on. I'll back you for an eye at measuring, and a head-piece for figures, against any man in this county; and you've had good teaching—you've had good teaching."

When they got up-stairs, the question which Arthur had left unsettled, as to who was to be president, and who vice, was still under discussion, so that Adam's entrance passed without remark.

"It stands to sense," Mr. Casson was saying, "as old Mr. Poyser, as is th' oldest man i' the room, should sit at top o' the table. I wasn't butler fifteen year without learning the rights and the wrongs about dinner."

"Nay, nay," said old Martin, "I'n gi'en up to my son; I'm no tenant now: let my son take my place. Th' ould foulks ha' had their turn: they mun make way for the young uns."

"I should ha' thought the biggest tenant had the best right, more nor th' oldest," said Luke Britton, who was not fond of the critical Mr. Poyser; "there's Mester Holdsworth has more land nor anybody else on th' estate."

"Well," said Mr. Poyser, "suppose we say the man wi' the foulest land shall sit at top; then whoever gets th' honour, there'll be no envying on him."

"Eh, here's Mester Massey," said Mr. Craig, who, being a neutral in the dispute, had no interest but in conciliation; "the schoolmaster ought to be able to tell you what's right. Who's to sit at top o' the table, Mr. Massey?"

"Why, the broadest man," said Bartle; "and then he won't take up other folks' room; and the next broadest must sit at bottom."

This happy mode of settling the dispute produced much laughter—a smaller joke would have sufficed for that. Mr. Casson, however, did not feel it compatible with his dignity and superior knowledge to join in the laugh, until it turned out that he was fixed on as the second broadest man. Martin Poyser, the younger, as the broadest, was to be president, and Mr. Casson, as next broadest, was to be vice.

Owing to this arrangement, Adam, being, of course, at the bottom of the table, fell under the immediate observation of Mr. Casson, who, too much occupied with the question of precedence, had not hitherto noticed his entrance. Mr. Casson, we have seen, considered Adam "rather lifted up and peppery-like": he thought the gentry made more fuss about this young carpenter than was necessary; they made no fuss about Mr. Casson, although he had been an excellent butler for fifteen years.

"Well, Mr. Bede, you're one o' them as mounts hup'ards apace," he said, when Adam sat down. "You've niver dined here before, as I remember."

"No, Mr. Casson," said Adam, in his strong voice, that could be heard along the table; "I've never dined here before, but I come by Captain Donnithorne's wish, and I hope it's not disagreeable to anybody here."

"Nay, nay," said several voices at once, "we're glad ye're come. Who's got anything to say again' it?"

"And ye'll sing us 'Over the hills and far away,' after dinner, wonna ye?" said Mr. Chowne. "That's a song I'm uncommon fond on."

"Peeh!" said Mr. Craig; "it's not to be named by side o' the Scotch tunes. I've never cared about singing myself; I've had something better to do. A man that's got the names and the natur o'plants in's head isna likely to keep a hollow place t' hold tunes in. But a second cousin o' mine, a drovier, was a rare hand at remembering the Scotch tunes. He'd got nothing else to think on."

"The Scotch tunes!" said Bartle Massey, contemptuously; "I've heard enough o' the Scotch tunes to last me while I live. They're fit for nothing but to frighten the birds with—that's to say, the English birds, for the Scotch birds may sing Scotch for what I know. Give the lads a bagpipe instead of a rattle, and I'll answer for it the corn 'll be safe."

"Yes, there's folks as find a pleasure in undervallying what they know but little about," said Mr. Craig.

"Why, the Scotch tunes are just like a scolding, nagging woman," Bartle went on, without deigning to notice Mr. Craig's remark. "They go on with the same thing over and over again, and never come to a reasonable end. Anybody 'd think the Scotch tunes had always been asking a question of somebody as deaf as old Taft, and had never got an answer yet."

Adam minded the less about sitting by Mr. Casson, because this position enabled him to see Hetty, who was not far off him at the next table. Hetty, however, had not even noticed his presence yet, for she was giving angry attention to Totty, who insisted on drawing up her feet on to the bench in antique fashion, and thereby threatened to make dusty marks on Hetty's pink-and-white frock. No sooner were the little fat legs pushed down than up they came again, for Totty's eyes were too busy in staring at the large dishes to see where the plum-pudding was, for her to retain any consciousness of her legs. Hetty got quite out of patience, and at last, with a frown and pout, and gathering tears, she said,

"O dear, aunt, I wish you'd speak to Totty; she keeps putting her legs up so, and messing my frock."

"What's the matter wi' the child? She can niver please you," said the mother. "Let her come by the side o' me, then: *I* can put up wi' her."

Adam was looking at Hetty, and saw the frown and pout, and the dark eyes seeming to grow larger with pettish half-gathered tears. Quiet Mary Burge, who sat near enough to see that Hetty was cross, and that Adam's eyes were fixed on her, thought that so sensible a man as Adam must be reflecting on the small value of beauty in a woman whose temper was bad. Mary was a good girl, not given to indulge in evil feelings, but she said to herself, that, since Hetty had a bad temper, it was better Adam should know it. And it was quite true, that if Hetty had been plain she would have looked very ugly and unamiable at that moment, and no one's moral judgment upon her would have been in the least beguiled. But really there was something quite charming in her pettishness: it looked so much more like innocent distress than ill-humour; and the severe Adam felt no movement of disapprobation; he only felt a sort of amused pity, as if he had seen a kitten setting up its back, or a little bird with its feathers ruffled. He could not gather what was vexing her, but it was impossible to him to feel otherwise than that she was the prettiest thing in the world, and that if he could have his way, nothing should ever vex her any more. And presently, when Totty was gone, she caught his eye, and her face broke into one of its brightest smiles, as she nodded to him. It was a bit of flirtation: she knew Mary Burge was looking at them. But the smile was like wine to Adam.

CHAPTER XXIV

THE HEALTH-DRINKING

WHEN the dinner was over, and the first draughts from the great cask of birthday ale were brought up, room was made for the broad Mr. Poyser at the side of the table, and two chairs were placed at the head. It had been settled very definitely what Mr. Poyser was to do when the young Squire should appear, and for the last five minutes he had been in a state of abstraction, with his eyes fixed on the dark picture opposite, and his hands busy with the loose cash and other articles in his breeches pockets.

When the young Squire entered, with Mr. Irwine by his side, every one stood up, and this moment of homage was very agreeable to Arthur. He liked to feel his own importance, and besides that, he cared a great deal for the goodwill of these people: he was fond of thinking that they had a hearty, special regard for him. The pleasure he felt was in his face as he said,

"My grandfather and I hope all our friends here have enjoyed their dinner, and find my birthday ale good. Mr. Irwine and I are come to taste it with you, and I'm sure we shall all like anything the better that the Rector shares with us."

All eyes were now turned on Mr. Poyser, who, with his hands still busy in his pockets, began with the deliberateness of a slow-striking clock. "Captain, my neighbours have put it upo' me to speak for 'em to-day, for where folks think pretty much alike, one spokesman's as good as a score. And though we've may happen got contrairy ways o' thinking about a many things—one man lays down his land one way, an' another another—an' I'll not take it upon me to speak to no man's farming, but my own—this I'll say, as we're all o' one mind about our young Squire. We've pretty nigh all on us known you when you war a little un, an' we've niver known anything on you but what was good an' honorable. You speak fair an' y' act fair, an' we're joyful when we look forrard to your being our landlord, for we b'lieve you mean to do right by everybody, an' 'ull make no man's bread bitter to him if you can help it. That's what I mean, an' that's what we all mean; and when a man's said what he means, he'd better stop, for th' ale 'ull be none the better for stannin'. An' I'll not say how we like th' ale yet, for we couldna well taste till we'd drunk your health in it; but the dinner was good, an' if there's anybody hasna enjoyed it, it must be the fault of his own inside. An' as for the Rector's company, it's well known as that's welcome t' all the parish wherever he may be; an' I hope, an' we all hope, as he'll live to see us old folks, an' our children grown to men an' women, an' your honor a family man. I've no more to say as concerns the present time, an' so we'll drink our young Squire's health—three times three."

Hereupon a glorious shouting, a rapping, a jingling, a clattering, and a shouting, with plentiful *da capo*, pleasanter than a strain of sublimest music in the ears that receive such a tribute for the first time. Arthur had felt a twinge of conscience during Mr. Poyser's speech, but it was too feeble to nullify the pleasure he felt in being praised. Did he not deserve what was said of him on the whole? If there was something in his conduct that Poyser wouldn't have liked if he had known it, why, no man's conduct will bear too close an inspection; and Poyser was not likely to know it; and, after all, what had he done? Gone a little too far, perhaps, in flirtation, but another man in his place would have acted much worse; and no harm could come—no harm *should* come, for the next time he was alone with Hetty, he would explain to her that she must not think seriously of him or of what had passed. It was necessary to Arthur, you perceive, to be sat-

isfied with himself: uncomfortable thoughts must be got rid of by good
intentions for the future, which can be formed so rapidly, that he had
time to be uncomfortable and to become easy again before Mr. Poyser's slow speech was finished, and when it was time for him to speak
he was quite light-hearted.

"I thank you all, my good friends and neighbours," Arthur said,
"for the good opinion of me, and the kind feelings towards me which
Mr. Poyser has been expressing on your behalf and on his own, and it
will always be my heartiest wish to deserve them. In the course of things
we may expect that, if I live, I shall one day or other be your landlord;
indeed it is on the ground of that expectation that my grandfather has
wished me to celebrate this day and to come among you now; and I
look forward to this position, not merely as one of power and pleasure
for myself, but as a means of benefiting my neighbours. It hardly becomes so young a man as I am, to talk much about farming to you,
who are most of you so much older, and are men of experience; still, I
have interested myself a good deal in such matters, and learned as
much about them as my opportunities have allowed; and when the
course of events shall place the estate in my hands, it will be my first
desire to afford my tenants all the encouragement a landlord can give
them, in improving their land, and trying to bring about a better practice of husbandry. It will be my wish to be looked on by all my deserving
tenants as their best friend, and nothing would make me so happy as
to be able to respect every man on the estate, and to be respected by
him in return. It is not my place at present to enter into particulars;
I only meet your good hopes concerning me by telling you that my own
hopes correspond to them—that what you expect from me I desire to
fulfil; and I am quite of Mr. Poyser's opinion, that when a man has
said what he means, he had better stop. But the pleasure I feel in
having my own health drunk by you would not be perfect if we did
not drink the health of my grandfather, who has filled the place of
both parents to me. I will say no more, until you have joined me in
drinking his health on a day when he has wished me to appear among
you as the future representative of his name and family."

Perhaps there was no one present except Mr. Irwine who thoroughly
understood and approved Arthur's graceful mode of proposing his
grandfather's health. The farmers thought the young Squire knew
well enough that they hated the old Squire, and Mrs. Poyser said,
"he'd better not ha' stirred a kettle o' sour broth." The bucolic mind
does not readily apprehend the refinements of good taste. But the toast
could not be rejected, and when it had been drunk, Arthur said,

"I thank you, both for my grandfather and myself; and now there
is one more thing I wish to tell you, that you may share my pleasure
about it, as I hope and believe you will. I think there can be no man
here who has not a respect, and some of you, I am sure, have a very high
regard, for my friend Adam Bede. It is well known to every one in this
neighbourhood that there is no man whose word can be more depended

on than his; that whatever he undertakes to do, he does well, and is as careful for the interests of those who employ him as for his own. I'm proud to say that I was very fond of Adam when I was a little boy, and I have never lost my old feeling for him—I think that shows that I know a good fellow when I find him. It has long been my wish that he should have the management of the woods on the estate, which happen to be very valuable; not only because I think so highly of his character, but because he has the knowledge and the skill which fit him for the place. And I am happy to tell you that it is my grandfather's wish too, and it is now settled that Adam shall manage the woods—a change which I am sure will be very much for the advantage of the estate; and I hope you will by-and-by join me in drinking to his health, and in wishing him all the prosperity in life that he deserves. But there is a still older friend of mine than Adam Bede present, and I need not tell you that it is Mr. Irwine. I'm sure you will agree with me that we must drink no other person's health until we have drunk his. I know you have all reason to love him, but no one of his parishioners has so much reason as I. Come, charge your glasses, and let us drink to our excellent Rector —three times three!"

This toast was drunk with all the enthusiasm that was wanting to the last, and it certainly was the most picturesque moment in the scene when Mr. Irwine got up to speak, and all the faces in the room were turned towards him. The superior refinement of his face was much more striking than that of Arthur's when seen in comparison with the people round them. Arthur's was a much commoner British face, and the splendour of his new-fashioned clothes was more akin to the young farmer's taste in costume than Mr. Irwine's powder, and the well-brushed but well-worn black, which seemed to be his chosen suit for great occasions; for he had the mysterious secret of never wearing a new-looking coat.

"This is not the first time, by a great many," he said, "that I have had to thank my parishioners for giving me tokens of their goodwill, but neighbourly kindness is among those things that are the more precious the older they get. Indeed, our pleasant meeting to-day is a proof that when what is good comes of age and is likely to live, there is reason for rejoicing, and the relation between us as clergyman and parishioners came of age two years ago, for it is three-and-twenty years since I first came among you, and I see some tall fine-looking young men here, as well as some blooming young women, that were far from looking as pleasantly at me when I christened them, as I am happy to see them looking now. But I'm sure you will not wonder when I say, that among all those young men, the one in whom I have the strongest interest is my friend Mr. Arthur Donnithorne, for whom you have just expressed your regard. I had the pleasure of being his tutor for several years, and have naturally had opportunities of knowing him intimately which cannot have occurred to any one else who is present; and I have some pride as well as pleasure in assuring you that I share your high hopes concerning him, and your confidence in his possession of those qualities which will make him an excellent landlord when the time shall come for him to take that important position among you. We feel alike on most matters on which a man who is getting towards fifty can feel in common with a young man of one-and-twenty, and he has just been expressing a feeling which I share very heartily, and I would not willingly omit the opportunity of saying so. That feeling is his value and respect for Adam Bede. People in a high station are of course more thought of and talked about, and have their virtues more praised, than those whose lives are passed in humble everyday work; but every sensible man knows how necessary that humble everyday work is, and how important it is to us that it should be done well. And I agree with my friend Mr. Arthur Donnithorne in feeling that when a man whose duty lies in that sort of work shows a character which would make him an example in any station, his merit should be acknowledged. He is one of those to whom honour is due, and his friends should delight to honour him. I know Adam Bede well—I know what he is as a workman, and what he has been as a son and brother—and I am saying the simplest truth when I say that I respect him as much as I respect any man living. But I am not speaking to you about a stranger; some of you are his intimate friends, and I believe there is not one here who does not know enough of him to join heartily in drinking his health."

As Mr. Irwine paused, Arthur jumped up, and, filling his glass, said, "A bumper to Adam Bede, and may he live to have sons as faithful and clever as himself!"

No hearer, not even Bartle Massey, was so delighted with this toast as Mr. Poyser: "tough work" as his first speech had been, he would have started up to make another if he had not known the extreme irregularity of such a course. As it was, he found an outlet for his feeling in drinking his ale unusually fast, and setting down his glass with a swing of his arm and a determined rap. If Jonathan Burge and a few others felt less comfortable on the occasion, they tried their best to look contented, and so the toast was drunk with a goodwill apparently unanimous.

Adam was rather paler than usual when he got up to thank his friends. He was a good deal moved by this public tribute—very naturally, for he was in the presence of all his little world, and it was uniting to do him honour. But he felt no shyness about speaking, not being troubled with small vanity or lack of words; he looked neither awkward nor embarrassed, but stood in his usual firm upright attitude, with his head thrown a little backward and his hands perfectly still, in that rough dignity which is peculiar to intelligent, well-built workmen, who are never wondering what is their business in the world.

"I'm quite taken by surprise," he said. "I didn't expect anything o' this sort, for it's a good deal more than my wages. But I've the more reason to be grateful to you, Captain, and to you, Mr. Irwine, and to all my friends here, who've drunk my health and wished me well. It 'ud be nonsense for me to be saying, I don't at all deserve th' opinion you have of me; that 'ud be poor thanks to you, to say that you've known me all these years, and yet haven't sense enough to find out a great deal o' the truth about me. You think, if I undertake to do a bit o' work, I'll do it well, be my pay big or little—and that's true. I'd be ashamed to stand before you here if it wasna true. But it seems to me, that's a man's plain duty, and nothing to be conceited about, and it's pretty clear to me as I've never done more than my duty; for let us do what we will, it's only making use o' the sperrit and the powers that ha' been given to us. And so this kindness o' yours, I'm sure, is no debt you owe me, but a free gift, and as such I accept it and am thankful. And as to this new employment I've taken in hand, I'll only say that I took it at Captain Donnithorne's desire, and that I'll try to fulfil his expectations. I'd wish for no better lot than to work for him, and to know that while I was getting my own bread I was taking care of his int'rests. For I believe he's one o' those gentlemen as wishes to do the right thing, and to leave the world a bit better than he found it, which it's my belief every man may do, whether he's gentle or simple, whether he sets a good bit o' work going and finds the money, or whether he does the work with his own hands. There's no occasion for me to say any more about what I feel towards him: I hope to show it through the rest o' my life in my actions."

There were various opinions about Adam's speech: some of the women whispered that he didn't show himself thankful enough, and seemed to speak as proud as could be; but most of the men were of opinion that nobody could speak more straight-for'ard, and that Adam was as fine a chap as need be. While such observations were being buzzed about, mingled with wonderings as to what the old Squire meant to do for a bailiff, and whether he was going to have a steward, the two gentlemen had risen, and were walking round to the table where the wives and children sat. There was none of the strong ale here, of course, but wine and dessert—sparkling gooseberry for the young ones, and some good sherry for the mothers. Mrs. Poyser was at the head of this table, and Totty was now seated in her lap, bending her small nose deep down into a wine-glass in search of the nuts floating there.

"How do you do, Mrs. Poyser?" said Arthur. "Weren't you pleased to hear your husband make such a good speech to-day?"

"O, sir, the men are mostly so tongue-tied—you're forced partly to guess what they mean, as you do wi' the dumb creaturs."

"What! you think you could have made it better for him?" said Mr. Irwine, laughing.

"Well, sir, when I want to say anything, I can mostly find words to say it in, thank God. Not as I'm a-finding faut wi' my husband, for if he's a man o' few words, what he says he'll stand to."

"I'm sure I never saw a prettier party than this," Arthur said, looking round at the apple-cheeked children. "My aunt and the Miss Irwines will come up and see you presently. They were afraid of the noise of the toasts, but it would be a shame for them not to see you at the table."

He walked on, speaking to the mothers and patting the children, while Mr. Irwine satisfied himself with standing still, and nodding at a distance, that no one's attention might be disturbed from the young Squire, the hero of the day. Arthur did not venture to stop near Hetty, but merely bowed to her as he passed along the opposite side. The foolish child felt her heart swelling with discontent; for what woman was ever satisfied with apparent neglect, even when she knows it to be the mask of love? Hetty thought this was going to be the most miserable day she had had for a long while; a moment of chill daylight and reality came across her dream: Arthur, who had seemed so near to her only a few hours before, was separated from her, as the hero of a great procession is separated from a small outsider in the crowd.

CHAPTER XXV

THE GAMES

THE great dance was not to begin until eight o'clock; but for any lads and lasses who liked to dance on the shady grass before them, there was music always at hand; for was not the band of the Benefit Club capable of playing excellent jigs, reels, and hornpipes? And, besides this, there was a grand band hired from Rosseter, who, with their wonderful wind-instruments and puffed-out cheeks, were themselves a delightful show to the small boys and girls. To say nothing of Joshua Rann's fiddle, which, by an act of generous forethought, he had provided himself with, in case any one should be of sufficiently pure taste to prefer dancing to a solo on that instrument.

Meantime, when the sun had moved off the great open space in front of the house, the games began. They were of course well-soaped poles to be climbed by the boys and youths, races to be run by the old women, races to be run in sacks, heavy weights to be lifted by the strong men, and a long list of challenges to such ambitious attempts as that of walking as many yards as possible on one leg—feats in which it was generally remarked that Wiry Ben, being "the lissom'st, springest fellow i' the country," was sure to be pre-eminent. To crown all, there was to be a donkey-race—that sublimest of all races, conducted on the grand socialistic idea of everybody encouraging everybody else's donkey, and the sorriest donkey winning.

And soon after four o'clock, splendid old Mrs. Irwine, in her damask satin and jewels and black lace, was led out by Arthur, followed by the whole family party, to her raised seat under the striped marquee, where she was to give out the prizes to the victors. Staid, formal Miss Lydia had requested to resign that queenly office to the royal old lady, and Arthur was pleased with this opportunity of gratifying his godmother's taste for stateliness. Old Mr. Donnithorne, the delicately clean, finely scented, withered old man, led out Miss Irwine, with his air of punctilious, acid politeness; Mr. Gawaine brought Miss Lydia, looking neutral and stiff in an elegant peach-blossom silk; and Mr. Irwine came last with his pale sister Anne. No other friend of the family, besides Mr. Gawaine, was invited to-day; there was to be a grand dinner for the neighbouring gentry on the morrow, but to-day all the forces were required for the entertainment of the tenants.

There was a sunk fence in front of the marquee, dividing the lawn from the park, but a temporary bridge had been made for the passage of the victors, and the groups of people standing, or seated here and there on benches, stretched on each side of the open space from the white marquees up to the sunk fence.

"Upon my word it's a pretty sight," said the old lady, in her deep voice, when she was seated, and looked round on the bright scene with its dark-green background; "and it's the last fête-day I'm likely to see, unless you make haste and get married, Arthur. But take care you get a charming bride, else I would rather die without seeing her."

"You're so terribly fastidious, godmother," said Arthur, "I'm afraid I should never satisfy you with my choice."

"Well, I won't forgive you if she's not handsome. I can't be put off with amiability, which is always the excuse people are making for the existence of plain people. And she must not be silly; that will never do. because you'll want managing, and a silly woman can't manage you. Who is that tall young man, Dauphin, with the mild face? There, standing without his hat, and taking such care of that tall old woman by the side of him—his mother, of course. I like to see that."

"What, don't you know him, mother?" said Mr. Irwine. "That's Seth Bede, Adam's brother—a Methodist, but a very good fellow. Poor Seth has looked rather down-hearted of late; I thought it was because of his father's dying in that sad way; but Joshua Rann tells me he wanted to marry that sweet little Methodist preacher who was here about a month ago, and I suppose she refused him."

"Ah, I remember hearing about her: but there are no end of people here that I don't know, for they're grown up and altered so since I used to go about."

"What excellent sight you have!" said old Mr. Donnithorne, who was holding a double glass up to his eyes, "to see the expression of that young man's face so far off. His face is nothing but a pale blurred spot to me. But I fancy I have the advantage of you when we come to look close. I can read small print without spectacles."

"Ah, my dear sir, you began with being very near-sighted, and those near-sighted eyes always wear the best. I want very strong spectacles to read with, but then I think my eyes get better and better for things at a distance. I suppose if I could live another fifty years, I should be blind to everything that wasn't out of other people's sight, like a man who stands in a well, and sees nothing but the stars."

"See," said Arthur, "the old women are ready to set out on their race now. Which do you bet on, Gawaine?"

"The long-legged one, unless they're going to have several heats, and then the little wiry one may win."

"There are the Poysers, mother, not far off on the right hand," said Miss Irwine. "Mrs. Poyser is looking at you. Do take notice of her."

"To be sure I will," said the old lady, giving a gracious bow to Mrs. Poyser. "A woman who sends me such excellent cream-cheese is not to be neglected. Bless me! what a fat child that is she is holding on her knee! But who is that pretty girl with dark eyes?"

"That is Hetty Sorrel," said Miss Lydia Donnithorne, "Martin Poyser's niece—a very likely young person, and well-looking too. My maid has taught her fine needlework, and she has mended some lace of mine very respectably indeed—very respectably."

"Why, she has lived with the Poysers six or seven years, mother; you must have seen her," said Miss Irwine.

"No, I've never seen her, child; at least not as she is now," said Mrs. Irwine, continuing to look at Hetty. "Well-looking, indeed! She's a perfect beauty! I've never seen anything so pretty since my young days. What a pity such beauty as that should be thrown away among the farmers, when it's wanted so terribly among the good families without fortune! I daresay, now, she'll marry a man who would have thought her just as pretty if she had had round eyes and red hair."

Arthur dared not turn his eyes towards Hetty while Mrs. Irwine was speaking of her. He feigned not to hear, and to be occupied with something on the opposite side. But he saw her plainly enough without looking; saw her in heightened beauty, because he heard her beauty praised—for other men's opinion, you know, was like a native climate to Arthur's feelings: it was the air on which they thrived the best, and grew strong. Yes! she *was* enough to turn any man's head: any man in his place would have done and felt the same. And to give her up after all, as he was determined to do, would be an act that he should always look back upon with pride.

"No, mother," said Mr. Irwine, replying to her last words; "I can't agree with you there. The common people are not quite so stupid as you imagine. The commonest man, who has his ounce of sense and feeling, is conscious of the difference between a lovely, delicate woman, and a coarse one. Even a dog feels a difference in their presence. The man may be no better able than the dog to explain the influence the more refined beauty has on him, but he feels it."

"Bless me, Dauphin, what does an old bachelor like you know about it?"

"O, that is one of the matters in which old bachelors are wiser than married men, because they have time for more general contemplation. Your fine critic of women must never shackle his judgment by calling one woman his own. But, as an example of what I was saying, that pretty Methodist preacher I mentioned just now, told me that she had preached to the roughest miners, and had never been treated with anything but the utmost respect and kindness by them. The reason is—though she doesn't know it—that there's so much tenderness, refinement, and purity about her. Such a woman as that brings with her 'airs from heaven' that the coarsest fellow is not insensible to."

"Here's a delicate bit of womanhood, or girlhood, coming to receive a prize, I suppose," said Mr. Gawaine. "She must be one of the racers in the sacks, who had set off before we came."

The "bit of womanhood" was our old acquaintance Bessy Cranage, otherwise Chad's Bess, whose large red cheeks and blowsy person had undergone an exaggeration of colour, which, if she had happened to be a heavenly body, would have made her sublime. Bessy, I am sorry to say, had taken to her earrings again since Dinah's departure, and was otherwise decked out in such small finery as she could muster. Any one who could have looked into poor Bessy's heart would have seen a striking resemblance between her little hopes and anxieties and Hetty's. The advantage, perhaps, would have been on Bessy's side in the matter of feeling. But then, you see, they were so very different outside! You would have been inclined to box Bessy's ears, and you would have longed to kiss Hetty.

Bessy had been tempted to run the arduous race, partly from mere hoidenish gaiety, partly because of the prize. Some one had said there were to be cloaks and other nice clothes for prizes, and she approached the marquee, fanning herself with her handkerchief, but with exultation sparkling in her round eyes.

"Here is the prize for the first sack-race," said Miss Lydia, taking a large parcel from the table where the prizes were laid, and giving it to Mrs. Irwine before Bessy came up; "an excellent grogram gown and a piece of flannel."

"You didn't think the winner was to be so young, I suppose, aunt?" said Arthur. "Couldn't you find something else for this girl, and save that grim-looking gown for one of the older women?"

"I have bought nothing but what is useful and substantial," said Miss Lydia, adjusting her own lace; "and I should not think of encouraging a love of finery in young women of that class. I have a scarlet cloak, but that is for the old woman who wins."

This speech of Miss Lydia's produced rather a mocking expression in Mrs. Irwine's face as she looked at Arthur, while Bessy came up and dropped a series of curtsies.

"This is Bessy Cranage, mother," said Mr. Irwine, kindly, "Chad Cranage's daughter. You remember Chad Cranage, the blacksmith?"

"Yes, to be sure," said Mrs. Irwine. "Well, Bessy, here is your prize—excellent warm things for winter. I'm sure you have had hard work to win them this warm day."

Bessy's lip fell as she saw the ugly, heavy gown,—which felt so hot and disagreeable, too, on this July day, and was such a great ugly thing to carry. She dropped her curtsies again, without looking up, and with a growing tremulousness about the corners of her mouth, and then turned away.

"Poor girl," said Arthur; "I think she's disappointed. I wish it had been something more to her taste."

"She's a bold-looking young person," observed Miss Lydia. "Not at all one I should like to encourage."

Arthur silently resolved that he would make Bessy a present of money before the day was over, that she might buy something more to her mind; but she, not aware of the consolation in store for her, turned out of the open space, where she was visible from the marquee, and throwing down the odious bundle under a tree, began to cry—very much tittered at the while by the small boys. In this situation she was descried by her discreet matronly cousin, who lost no time in coming up, having just given the baby into her husband's charge.

"What's the matter wi' ye?" said Bess the matron, taking up the bundle and examining it. "Ye'n sweltered yoursen, I reckon, running that fool's race. An' here, they'n gi'en you lots o' good grogram and flannel, as should ha' been gi'en by good rights to them as had the sense to keep away from such foolery. Ye might spare me a bit o' this grogram to make clothes for the lad—ye war ne'er ill-natured, Bess; I ne'er said that on ye."

"Ye may take it all, for what I care," said Bess the maiden with a pettish movement, beginning to wipe away her tears and recover herself.

"Well, I could do wi't, if so be ye want to get rid on't," said the disinterested cousin, walking quickly away with the bundle, lest Chad's Bess should change her mind.

But that bonny-cheeked lass was blest with an elasticity of spirits that secured her from any rankling grief; and by the time the grand climax of the donkey-race came on, her disappointment was entirely lost in the delightful excitement of attempting to stimulate the last donkey by hisses, while the boys applied the argument of sticks. But the strength of the donkey mind lies in adopting a course inversely as the arguments urged, which, well considered, requires as great a mental force as the direct sequence; and the present donkey proved the first-rate order of his intelligence by coming to a dead standstill just when the blows were thickest. Great was the shouting of the crowd, radiant the grinning of Bill Downes, the stone-sawyer and the fortunate rider of this superior beast, which stood calm and stiff-legged in the midst of its triumph.

Arthur himself had provided the prizes for the men, and Bill was made happy with a splendid pocket-knife, supplied with blades and gimlets enough to make a man at home on a desert island. He had hardly returned from the marquee with the prize in his hand, when it began to be understood that Wiry Ben proposed to amuse the company, before the gentry went to dinner, with an impromptu and gratuitous performance—namely, a hornpipe, the main idea of which was doubtless borrowed; but this was to be developed by the dancer in so peculiar and complex a manner that no one could deny him the praise of originality. Wiry Ben's pride in his dancing—an accomplishment productive of great effect at the yearly Wake—had needed only slightly elevating by an extra quantity of good ale, to convince him that the gentry would be very much struck with his performance of the horn-pipe; and he had been decidedly encouraged in this idea by Joshua Rann, who observed that it was nothing but right to do something to please the young Squire, in return for what he had done for them. You will be the less surprised at this opinion in so grave a personage when you learn that Ben had requested Mr. Rann to accompany him on the fiddle, and Joshua felt quite sure that though there might not be much in the dancing, the music would make up for it. Adam Bede, who was present in one of the large marquees, where the plan was being dis-cussed, told Ben he had better not make a fool of himself—a remark which at once fixed Ben's determination: he was not going to let any-thing alone because Adam Bede turned up his nose at it.

"What's this, what's this?" said old Mr. Donnithorne. "Is it some-thing you've arranged, Arthur? Here's the clerk coming with his fiddle, and a smart fellow with a nosegay in his button-hole."

"No," said Arthur; "I know nothing about it. By Jove, he's going to dance! It's one of the carpenters—I forget his name at this moment."

"It's Ben Cranage—Wiry Ben, they call him," said Mr. Irwine; "rather a loose fish, I think. Anne, my dear, I see that fiddle-scraping is too much for you: you're getting tired. Let me take you in now, that you may rest till dinner."

Miss Anne rose assentingly, and the good brother took her away, while Joshua's preliminary scrapings burst into the "White Cockade," from which he intended to pass to a variety of tunes, by a series of transitions which his good ear really taught him to execute with some skill. It would have been an exasperating fact to him, if he had known it, that the general attention was too thoroughly absorbed by Ben's dancing for any one to give much heed to the music.

Have you ever seen a real English rustic perform a solo dance? Perhaps you have only seen a ballet rustic, smiling like a merry coun-tryman in crockery, with graceful turns of the haunch and insinuating movements of the head. That is as much like the real thing as the "Bird Waltz" is like the song of birds. Wiry Ben never smiled: he looked as serious as a dancing monkey—as serious as if he had been an experi-mental philosopher ascertaining in his own person the amout of shak-ing and the varieties of angularity that could be given to the human limbs.

To make amends for the abundant laughter in the striped marquee, Arthur clapped his hands continually and cried "Bravo!" But Ben had one admirer whose eyes followed his movements with a fervid gravity that equalled his own. It was Martin Poyser, who was seated on a bench, with Tommy between his legs.

"What dost think o' that?" he said to his wife. "He goes as pat to
the music as if he was made o' clockwork. I used to be a pretty good
un at dancing myself when I was lighter, but I could niver ha' hit it
just to th' hair like that."

"It's little matter what his limbs are, to my thinking," returned
Mrs. Poyser. "He's empty enough i' the upper story, or he'd niver come
jigging an' stamping i' that way, like a mad grasshopper, for the gentry
to look at him. They're fit to die wi' laughing, I can see."

"Well, well, so much the better, it amuses 'em," said Mr. Poyser, who
did not easily take an irritable view of things. "But they're going away
now, t' have their dinner, I reckon. We'll move about a bit, shall we? and
see what Adam Bede's doing. He's got to look after the drinking and
things: I doubt he hasna had much fun."

CHAPTER XXVI

THE DANCE

ARTHUR had chosen the entrance-hall for the ball-room: very wisely, for
no other room could have been so airy, or would have had the advantage
of the wide doors opening into the garden, as well as a ready entrance
into the other rooms. To be sure, a stone floor was not the pleasantest
to dance on, but then, most of the dancers had known what it was to
enjoy a Christmas dance on kitchen quarries. It was one of those en-
trance-halls which make the surrounding rooms look like closets—with
stucco angels, trumpets, and flower-wreaths on the lofty ceiling, and
great medallions of miscellaneous heroes on the walls, alternating with
statues in niches. Just the sort of place to be ornamented well with
green boughs, and Mr. Craig had been proud to show his taste and his
hot-house plants on the occasion. The broad steps of the stone staircase
were covered with cushions to serve as seats for the children, who were
to stay till half-past nine with the servant-maids, to see the dancing;
and as this dance was to be confined to the chief tenants, there was
abundant room for every one. The lights were charmingly disposed
in coloured-paper lamps, high up among the green boughs, and the
farmers' wives and daughters, as they peeped in, believed no scene
could be more splendid; they knew now quite well in what sort of rooms
the king and queen lived, and their thoughts glanced with some pity
towards cousins and acquaintances who had not this fine opportunity of
knowing how things went on in the great world. The lamps were already
lit, though the sun had not long set, and there was that calm light out
of doors in which we seem to see all objects more distinctly than in the
broad day.

It was a pretty scene outside the house: the farmers and their families were moving about the lawn, among the flowers and shrubs, or along
the broad straight road leading from the east front, where a carpet of

mossy grass spread on each side, studded here and there with a dark
flat-boughed cedar, or a grand pyramidal fir sweeping the ground with
its branches, all tipped with a fringe of paler green. The group of cottagers in the park were gradually diminishing, the young ones being
attracted towards the lights that were beginning to gleam from the
windows of the gallery in the abbey, which was to be their dancing-
room, and some of the sober elder ones thinking it time to go home
quietly. One of these was Lisbeth Bede, and Seth went with her—not
from filial attention only, for his conscience would not let him join in
dancing. It had been rather a melancholy day to Seth: Dinah had never
been more constantly present with him than in this scene, where everything was so unlike her. He saw her all the more vividly after looking
at the thoughtless faces and gay-coloured dresses of the young women
—just as one feels the beauty and the greatness of a pictured Madonna
the more, when it has been for a moment screened from us by a vulgar
head in a bonnet. But this presence of Dinah in his mind only helped him
to bear the better with his mother's mood, which had been becoming
more and more querulous for the last hour. Poor Lisbeth was suffering
from a strange conflict of feelings. Her joy and pride in the honour paid
to her darling son Adam was beginning to be worsted in the conflict
with the jealousy and fretfulness which had revived when Adam came
to tell her that Captain Donnithorne desired him to join the dancers in
the hall. Adam was getting more and more out of her reach; she wished
all the old troubles back again, for then it mattered more to Adam what
his mother said and did.

"Eh, it's fine talkin' o' dancin'," she said, "an' thy feyther not a five
week in's grave. An' I wish I war there too, istid o' bein' left to take up
merrier folks's room above ground."

"Nay, don't look at it i' that way, mother," said Adam, who was determined to be gentle to her to-day. "I don't mean to dance—I shall
only look on. And since the Captain wishes me to be there, it 'ud look
as if I thought I knew better than him to say as I'd rather not stay.
And thee know'st how he's behaved to me to-day."

"Eh, thee't do as thee lik'st, for thy old mother's got no right t' hinder thee. She's nought but th' old husk, and thee'st slipped away from
her, like the ripe nut."

"Well, mother," said Adam, "I'll go and tell the Captain as it hurts
thy feelings for me to stay, and I'd rather go home upo' that account:
he won't take it ill then, I daresay, and I'm willing." He said this with
some effort, for he really longed to be near Hetty this evening.

"Nay, nay, I wonna ha' thee do that—the young Squire 'ull be angered. Go an' do what thee 't ordered to do, an' me and Seth 'ull go
whome. I know it's a grit honour for thee to be so looked on—an' who's
to be prouder on it nor thy mother? Hadna she the cumber o' rearin'
thee an' doin' for thee all these 'ears?"

"Well, good-by, then, mother—good-by, lad—remember Gyp when
you get home," said Adam, turning away towards the gate of the pleas-

ure-grounds, where he hoped he might be able to join the Poysers, for he had been so occupied throughout the afternoon that he had had no time to speak to Hetty. His eye soon detected a distant group, which he knew to be the right one, returning to the house along the broad gravel road, and he hastened on to meet them.

"Why, Adam, I'm glad to get sight on y' again," said Mr. Poyser, who was carrying Totty on his arm. "You're going t' have a bit o' fun, I hope, now your work's all done. And here's Hetty has promised no end o' partners, an' I've just been askin' her if she's agreed to dance wi' you, an' she says no."

"Well, I didn't think o' dancing to-night," said Adam, already tempted to change his mind, as he looked at Hetty.

"Nonsense!" said Mr. Poyser. "Why, everybody's goin' to dance to-night, all but th' old Squire and Mrs. Irwine. Mrs. Best's been tellin' us as Miss Lyddy and Miss Irwine 'ull dance, an' the young Squire 'ull pick my wife for his first partner, t' open the ball: so she'll be forced to dance, though she's laid by even sin' the Christmas afore the little un was born. You canna for shame stand still, Adam, an' you a fine young fellow, and can dance as well as anybody."

"Nay, nay," said Mrs. Poyser, "it 'ud be unbecomin'. I know the dancin's nonsense; but if you stick at everything because it's nonsense, you wanna go far i' this life. When your broth's ready-made for you, you mun swallow the thickenin', or else let the broth alone."

"Then if Hetty 'ull dance with me," said Adam, yielding either to Mrs. Poyser's argument or to something else, "I'll dance whichever dance she's free."

"I've got no partner for the fourth dance," said Hetty; "I'll dance that with you, if you like."

"Ah," said Mr. Poyser, "but you mun dance the first dance, Adam, else it'll look partic'ler. There's plenty o' nice partners to pick an' choose from, an' it's hard for the gells when the men stan' by and don't ask 'em."

Adam felt the justice of Mr. Poyser's observation: it would not do for him to dance with no one besides Hetty; and remembering that Jonathan Burge had some reason to feel hurt to-day, he resolved to ask Miss Mary to dance with him the first dance, if she had no other partner.

"There's the big clock strikin' eight," said Mr. Poyser; "we must make haste in now, else the Squire and the ladies 'ull be in afore us, an' that wouldna look well."

When they had entered the hall, and the three children under Molly's charge had been seated on the stairs, the folding-doors of the drawing-room were thrown open, and Arthur entered in his regimentals, leading Mrs. Irwine to a carpet-covered dais ornamented with hot-house plants, where she and Miss Anne were to be seated with old Mr. Donnithorne, that they might look on at the dancing, like the kings and queens in the plays. Arthur had put on his uniform to please the tenants, he said,

who thought as much of his militia dignity as if it had been an elevation to the premiership. He had not the least objection to gratify them
in that way: his uniform was very advantageous to his figure.

The old Squire, before sitting down, walked round the hall to greet
the tenants and make polite speeches to the wives: he was always polite;
but the farmers had found out, after long puzzling, that this polish was
one of the signs of hardness. It was observed that he gave his most
elaborate civility to Mrs. Poyser to-night, inquiring particularly about
her health, recommending her to strengthen herself with cold water
as he did, and avoid all drugs. Mrs. Poyser curtsied and thanked him
with great self-command, but when he had passed on, she whispered to
her husband, "I'll lay my life he's brewin' some nasty turn against us.
Old Harry doesna wag his tail so for nothin'." Mr. Poyser had no time
to answer, for now Arthur came up and said, "Mrs. Poyser, I'm come to
request the favour of your hand for the first dance; and, Mr. Poyser,
you must let me take you to my aunt, for she claims you as her partner."

The wife's pale cheek flushed with a nervous sense of unwonted
honour as Arthur led her to the top of the room; but Mr. Poyser, to
whom an extra glass had restored his youthful confidence in his good
looks and good dancing, walked along with them quite proudly, secretly
flattering himself that Miss Lydia had never had a partner in _her_ life
who could life her off the ground as he would. In order to balance the
honours given to the two parishes, Miss Irwine danced with Luke Britton, the largest Broxton farmer, and Mr. Gawaine led out Mrs. Britton.
Mr. Irwine, after seating his sister Anne, had gone to the abbey gallery,
as he had agreed with Arthur beforehand, to see how the merriment of
the cottagers was prospering. Meanwhile, all the less distinguished couples had taken their places: Hetty was led out by the inevitable Mr.
Craig, and Mary Burge by Adam; and now the music struck up, and
the glorious country-dance, best of all dances, began.

Pity it was not a boarded floor! Then the rhythmic stamping of the
thick shoes would have been better than any drums. That merry stamping, that gracious nodding of the head, that waving bestowal of the
hand—where can we see them now? That simple dancing of well-cov-
ered matrons, laying aside for an hour the cares of house and dairy,
remembering but not affecting youth, not jealous but proud of the young
maidens by their side—that holiday sprightliness of portly husbands
paying little compliments to their wives, as if their courting days were
come again—those lads and lasses a little confused and awkward with
their partners, having nothing to say—it would be a pleasant variety
to see all that sometimes, instead of low dresses and large skirts, and
scanning glances exploring costumes, and languid men in lackered boots
smiling with double meaning.

There was but one thing to mar Martin Poyser's pleasure in this
dance: it was, that he was always in close contact with Luke Britton,
that slovenly farmer. He thought of throwing a little glazed coldness

into his eyes in the crossing of hands; but then, as Miss Irwine was opposite to him instead of the offensive Luke, he might freeze the wrong person. So he gave his face up to hilarity, unchilled by moral judgments.

How Hetty's heart beat as Arthur approached her! He had hardly looked at her to-day: now he *must* take her hand. Would he press it? would he look at her? She thought she would cry if he gave her no sign of feeling. Now he was there—he had taken her hand—yes, he was pressing it. Hetty turned pale as she looked up at him for an instant and met his eyes, before the dance carried him away. That pale look came upon Arthur like the beginning of a dull pain, which clung to him, though he must dance and smile and joke all the same. Hetty would look so, when he told her what he had to tell her; and he should never be able to bear it—he should be a fool and give way again. Hetty's look did not really mean so much as he thought: it was only the sign of a struggle between the desire for him to notice her, and the dread lest she should betray the desire to others. But Hetty's face had a language that transcended her feelings. There are faces which nature charges with a meaning and pathos not belonging to the single human soul that flutters beneath them, but speaking the joys and sorrows of foregone generations—eyes that tell of deep love which doubtless had been and is somewhere, but not paired with these eyes—perhaps paired with pale eyes that can say nothing; just as a national language may be instinct with poetry unfelt by the lips that use it. That look of Hetty's oppressed Arthur with a dread which yet had something of a terrible, unconfessed delight in it, that she loved him too well. There was a hard task before him, for at that moment he felt he would have given up three years of his youth for the happiness of abandoning himself without remorse to his passion for Hetty.

These were the incongruous thoughts in his mind, as he led Mrs. Poyser, who was panting with fatigue, and secretly resolving that neither judge nor jury should force her to dance another dance, to take a quiet rest in the dining-room, where supper was laid out for the guests to come and take it as they chose.

"I've desired Hetty to remember as she's got to dance wi' you, sir," said the good innocent woman; "for she's so thoughtless, she'd be like enough to go an' engage herself for ivery dance. So I told her not to promise too many."

"Thank you, Mrs. Poyser," said Arthur, not without a twinge. "Now, sit down in this comfortable chair, and here is Mills ready to give you what you would like best."

He hurried away to seek another matronly partner, for due honour must be paid to the married women before he asked any of the young ones; and the country-dances, and the stamping, and the gracious nodding, and the waving of the hands, went on joyously.

At last the time had come for the fourth dance—longed for by the strong, grave Adam, as if he had been a delicate-handed youth of eighteen; for we are all very much alike when we are in our first love; and

Adam had hardly ever touched Hetty's hand for more than a transient greeting—had never danced with her but once before. His eyes had followed her eagerly to-night in spite of himself, and had taken in deeper draughts of love. He thought she behaved so prettily, so quietly; she did not seem to be flirting at all, she smiled less than usual; there was almost a sweet sadness about her. "God bless her!" he said inwardly; "I'd make her life a happy un, if a strong arm to work for her, and a heart to love her, could do it."

And then there stole over him delicious thoughts of coming home from work, and drawing Hetty to his side, and feeling her cheek softly pressed against his, till he forgot where he was, and the music and the tread of feet might have been the falling of rain and the roaring of the wind, for what he knew.

But now the third dance was ended, and he might go up to her and claim her hand. She was at the far end of the hall near the staircase, whispering with Molly, who had just given the sleeping Totty into her arms, before running to fetch shawls and bonnets from the landing. Mrs. Poyser had taken the two boys away into the dining-room to give them some cake before they went home in the cart with grandfather, and Molly was to follow as fast as possible.

"Let me hold her," said Adam, as Molly turned up-stairs: "the children are so heavy when they're asleep."

Hetty was glad of the relief, for to hold Totty in her arms, standing, was not at all a pleasant variety to her. But this second transfer had the unfortunate effect of rousing Totty, who was not behind any child of her age in peevishness at an unseasonable awaking. While Hetty was in the act of placing her in Adam's arms, and had not yet withdrawn her own, Totty opened her eyes, and forthwith fought out with her left fist at Adam's arm, and with her right caught at the string of brown beads round Hetty's neck. The locket leaped out from her frock, and the next moment the string was broken, and Hetty, helpless, saw beads and locket scattered wide on the floor.

"My locket, my locket!" she said, in a loud frightened whisper to Adam; "never mind the beads."

Adam had already seen where the locket fell, for it had attracted his glance as it leaped out of her frock. It had fallen on the raised wooden dais where the band sat, not on the stone floor; and as Adam picked it up, he saw the glass with the dark and light locks of hair under it. It had fallen that side upwards, so the glass was not broken. He turned it over on his hand, and saw the enamelled gold back.

"It isn't hurt," he said, as he held it towards Hetty, who was unable to take it because both her hands were occupied with Totty.

"O, it doesn't matter, I don't mind about it," said Hetty, who had been paled and was now red.

"Not matter?" said Adam, gravely. "You seemed very frightened about it. I'll hold it till you're ready to take it," he added, quietly closing his hand over it, that she might not think he wanted to look at it again.

By this time Molly had come with bonnet and shawl, and as soon as
she had taken Totty, Adam placed the locket in Hetty's hand. She took
it with an air of indifference, and put it in her pocket; in her heart vexed
and angry with Adam, because he had seen it, but determined now that
she would show no more signs of agitation.

"See," she said, "they're taking their places to dance; let us go."

Adam assented silently. A puzzled alarm had taken possession of him.
Had Hetty a lover he didn't know of?—for none of her relations, he
was sure, would give her a locket like that; and none of her admirers,
with whom he was acquainted, was in the position of an accepted lover,
as the giver of that locket must be. Adam was lost in the utter impossibility of finding any person for his fears to alight on: he could only feel
with a terrible pang that there was something in Hetty's life unknown
to him; that while he had been rocking himself in the hope that she
would come to love him, she was already loving another. The pleasure
of the dance with Hetty was gone; his eyes, when they rested on her,
had an uneasy questioning expression in them; he could think of nothing
to say to her; and she, too, was out of temper and disinclined to speak.
They were both glad when the dance was ended.

Adam was determined to stay no longer; no one wanted him, and no
one would notice if he slipped away. As soon as he got out of doors,
he began to walk at his habitual rapid pace, hurrying along without
knowing why, busy with the painful thought that the memory of this
day, so full of honour and promise to him, was poisoned for ever. Suddenly, when he was far on through the Chase, he stopped, startled by
a flash of reviving hope. After all, he might be a fool, making a great
misery out of a trifle. Hetty, fond of finery as she was, might have bought
the thing herself. It looked too expensive for that—it looked like the
things on white satin in the great jeweller's shop at Rosseter. But Adam
had very imperfect notions of the value of such things, and he thought
it could certainly not cost more than a guinea. Perhaps Hetty had had as
much as that in Christmas boxes, and there was no knowing but she
might have been childish enough to spend it in that way; she was such
a young thing, and she couldn't help loving finery! But then, why had
she been so frightened about it at first, and changed colour so, and afterwards pretended not to care? Oh, that was because she was ashamed of
his seeing that she had such a smart thing—she was conscious that it
was wrong for her to spend her money on it, and she knew that Adam
disapproved of finery. It was a proof she cared about what he liked and
disliked. She must have thought from his silence and gravity afterwards that he was very much displeased with her, that he was inclined
to be harsh and severe towards her foibles. And as he walked on more
quietly, chewing the cud of this new hope, his only uneasiness was that
he had behaved in a way which might chill Hetty's feelings towards
him. For this last view of the matter *must* be the true one. How could
Hetty have an accepted lover, quite unknown to him? She was never
away from her uncle's house for more than a day; she could have no

acquaintances that did not come there, and no intimacies unknown to
her uncle and aunt. It would be folly to believe that the locket was
given to her by a lover. The little ring of dark hair he felt sure was
her own; he could form no guess about the light hair under it, for he
had not seen it very distinctly. It might be a bit of her father's or
mother's, who had died when she was a child, and she would naturally
put a bit of her own along with it.

And so Adam went to bed comforted, having woven for himself an
ingenious web of probabilities—the surest screen a wise man can place
between himself and the truth. His last waking thoughts melted into a
dream that he was with Hetty again at the Hall Farm, and that he was
asking her to forgive him for being so cold and silent.

And while he was dreaming this, Arthur was leading Hetty to the
dance, and saying to her in low hurried tones, "I shall be in the wood
the day after to-morrow at seven; come as early as you can." And
Hetty's foolish joys and hopes, which had flown away for a little space,
scared by a mere nothing, now all came fluttering back, unconscious
of the real peril. She was happy for the first time this long day, and
wished that dance would last for hours. Arthur wished it too; it was
the last weakness he meant to indulge in; and a man never lies with
more delicious languor under the influence of a passion, than when he
has persuaded himself that he shall subdue it to-morrow.

But Mrs. Poyser's wishes were quite the reverse of this, for her mind
was filled with dreary forebodings as to the retardation of to-morrow
morning's cheese in consequence of these late hours. Now that Hetty
had done her duty and danced one dance with the young Squire, Mr.
Poyser must go out and see if the cart was come back to fetch them,
for it was half-past ten o'clock, and notwithstanding a mild suggestion
on his part that it would be bad manners for them to be the first to
go, Mrs. Poyser was resolute on the point, "manners or no manners."

"What! going already, Mrs. Poyser?" said old Mr. Donnithorne, as
she came to curtsy and take leave; "I thought we should not part with
any of our guests till eleven: Mrs. Irwine and I, who are elderly people,
think of sitting out the dance till then."

"O, your honour, it's all right and proper for gentlefolks to stay up by
candle-light—they've got no cheese on their minds. We're late enough
as it is, an' there's no lettin' the cows know as they mustn't want to be
milked so early to-morrow mornin'. So, if you'll please t' excuse us, we'll
take our leave."

"Eh!" she said to her husband, as they set off in the cart, "I'd sooner
ha' brewin' day and washin' day together than one o' these pleasurin'
days. There's no work so tirin' as danglin' about an' starin' an' not
rightly knowin' what you're goin' to do next; and keepin' your face i'
smilin' order like a grocer o' market-day for fear people shouldna think
you civil enough. An' you've nothing to show for't when it's done, if it
isn't a yallow face wi' eatin' things as disagree."

"Nay, nay," said Mr. Poyser, who was in his merriest mood, and

felt that he had had a great day, "a bit o' pleasuring's good for thee sometimes. An' thee danc'st as well as any of 'em, for I'll back thee against
all the wives i' the parish for a light foot an' ankle. An' it was a great
honour for the young Squire to ask thee first—I reckon it was because
I sat at th' head o' the table an' made the speech. An' Hetty too—
she never had such a partner before—a fine young gentleman in reg'-
mentals. It'll serve you to talk on, Hetty, when you're an old woman—
how you danced wi' th' young Squire the day he come o' age."

BOOK FOUR

★

CHAPTER XXVII

A CRISIS

It was beyond the middle of August—nearly three weeks after th-
birthday feast. The reaping of the wheat had begun in our north mid-
land county of Loamshire, but the harvest was likely still to be retarded
by the heavy rains, which were causing inundations and much damage
throughout the country. From this last trouble the Broxton and Hayslope farmers, on their pleasant uplands, and in their brook-watered
valleys, had not suffered, and as I cannot pretend that they were such
exceptional farmers as to love the general good better than their own,
you will infer that they were not in very low spirits about the rapid rise
in the price of bread, so long as there was hope of gathering in their
own corn undamaged; and occasional days of sunshine and drying winds
flattered this hope.

The eighteenth of August was one of these days, when the sunshine
looked brighter in all eyes for the gloom that went before. Grand masses
of clouds were hurried across the blue, and the great round hills behind
the Chase seemed alive with their flying shadows; the sun was hidden
for a moment, and then shone out warm again like a recovered joy;
the leaves, still green, were tossed off the hedgerow trees by the wind;
around the farmhouses there was a sound of clapping doors; the apples
fell in the orchards; and the stray horses on the green sides of the lanes
and on the common had their manes blown about their faces. And yet
the wind seemed only part of the general gladness because the sun was
shining. A merry day for the children, who ran and shouted to see if
they could top the wind with their voices; and the grown-up people,
too, were in good spirits, inclined to believe in yet finer days, when the
winds had fallen. If only the corn were not ripe enough to be blown
out of the husk and scattered as untimely seed!

And yet a day on which a blighting sorrow may fall upon a man-
For if it be true that Nature at certain moments seems charged with a
presentiment of one individual lot, must it not also be true that she seems
unmindful, unconscious of another? For there is no hour that has not
its births of gladness and despair, no morning brightness that does not
bring new sickness to desolation as well as new forces to genius and
love. There are so many of us, and our lots are so different: what won-

der that Nature's mood is often in harsh contrast with the great crisis of our lives? We are children of a large family, and must learn, as such children do, not to expect that our hurts will be made much of —to be content with little nurture and caressing, and help each other the more.

It was a busy day with Adam, who of late had done almost double work; for he was continuing to act as foreman for Jonathan Burge, until some satisfactory person could be found to supply his place, and Jonathan was slow to find that person. But he had done the extra work cheerfully, for his hopes were buoyant again about Hetty. Every time she had seen him since the birthday, she had seemed to make an effort to behave all the more kindly to him, that she might make him understand she had forgiven his silence and coldness during the dance. He had never mentioned the locket to her again; too happy that she smiled at him—still happier because he observed in her a more subdued air, something that he interpreted as the growth of womanly tenderness and seriousness. "Ah!" he thought, again and again, "she's only seventeen; she'll be thoughtful enough after a while. And her aunt allays says how clever she is at the work. She'll make a wife as mother'll have no occasion to grumble at, after all." To be sure, he had only seen her at home twice since the birthday; for one Sunday, when he was intending to go from church to the Hall Farm, Hetty had joined the party of upper servants from the Chase, and had gone home with them—almost as if she were inclined to encourage Mr. Craig. "She's takin' too much likin' to them folks i' the housekeeper's room," Mrs. Poyser remarked. "For my part, I never was over-fond o' gentlefolks's servants—they're mostly like the fine ladies' fat dogs, nayther good for barking nor butcher's meat, but on'y for show." And another evening she was gone to Treddleston to buy some things; though, to his great surprise, as he was returning home, he saw her at a distance getting over a stile quite out of the Treddleston road. But, when he hastened to her, she was very kind, and asked him to go in again when he had taken her to the yard gate. She had gone a little farther into the fields after coming from Treddleston, because she didn't want to go in, she said: it was so nice to be out of doors, and her aunt always made such a fuss about it if she wanted to go out. "O, do come with me!" she said, as he was going to shake hands with her at the gate, and he could not resist that. So he went in, and Mrs. Poyser was contented with only a slight remark on Hetty's being later than was expected; while Hetty, who had looked out of spirits when he met her, smiled and talked, and waited on them all with unusual promptitude.

That was the last time he had seen her; but he meant to make leisure for going to the Farm to-morrow. To-day, he knew, was her day for going to the Chase to sew with the lady's-maid, so he would get as much work done as possible this evening, that the next might be clear.

One piece of work that Adam was superintending was some slight repairs at the Chase Farm, which had been hitherto occupied by Satchell, as bailiff, but which it was now rumoured that the old Squire was going to let to a smart man in top-boots, who had been seen to ride over it one day. Nothing but the desire to get a tenant could account for the Squire's undertaking repairs, though the Saturday-evening party at Mr. Casson's agreed over their pipes that no man in his senses would take the Chase Farm unless there was a bit more ploughland laid to it. However that might be, the repairs were ordered to be executed with all despatch; and Adam, acting for Mr. Burge, was carrying out the order with his usual energy. But to-day, having been occupied elsewhere, he had not been able to arrive at the Chase Farm till late in the afternoon; and he then discovered that some old roofing which he had calculated on preserving, had given way. There was clearly no good to be done with this part of the building without pulling it all down; and Adam immediately saw in his mind a plan for building it up again, so as to make the most convenient of cow-sheds and calf-pens, with a hovel for implements; and all without any great expense for materials. So, when the workmen were gone, he sat down, took out his pocket-book, and busied himself with sketching a plan, and making a specification of the expenses, that he might show it to Burge the next morning, and set him on persuading the Squire to consent. To "make a good job" of anything, however small, was always a pleasure to Adam; and he sat on a block, with his book resting on a planing-table, whistling low every now and then, and turning his head on one side with a just perceptible smile of gratification—of pride, too, for if Adam loved a bit of good work, he loved also to think, "I did it!" And I believe the only people who are free from that weakness are those who have no work to call their own. It was nearly seven before he had finished and put on his jacket again; and on giving a last look round, he observed that Seth, who had been working here to-day, had left his basket of tools behind him. "Why, th' lad's forgot his tools," thought Adam, "and he's got to work up at the shop to-morrow. There never was such a chap for wool-gathering; he'd leave his head behind him, if it was loose. However, it's lucky I've seen 'em; I'll carry 'em home."

The buildings of the Chase Farm lay at one extremity of the Chase, at about ten minutes' walking distance from the Abbey. Adam had come thither on his pony, intending to ride to the stables, and put up his nag on the way home. At the stables he encountered Mr. Craig, who had come to look at the Captain's new horse, on which he was to ride away the day after to-morrow; and Mr. Craig detained him to tell him how all the servants were to collect at the gate of the courtyard to wish the young Squire luck as he rode out; so that, by the time Adam had got into the Chase, and was striding along with the basket of tools over his shoulder, the sun was on the point of setting, and was sending level crimson rays among the great trunks of the old oaks, and touching every bare patch of ground with a transient glory, that made it look like a jewel dropt upon the grass. The wind had fallen now, and there was only enough breeze to stir the delicate-stemmed leaves. Any one who had been sitting in the house all day would have been glad to walk now; but Adam had been quite enough in the open air to wish to shorten his way home; and he bethought himself that he might do so by striking across the Chase and going through the Grove, where he had never been for years. He hurried on across the Chase, stalking along the narrow paths between the fern, with Gyp at his heels, not lingering to watch the magnificent changes of the light—hardly once thinking of it—yet feeling its presence in a certain calm happy awe which mingled itself with his busy working-day thoughts. How could he help feeling it? The very deer felt it, and were more timid.

Presently Adam's thoughts recurred to what Mr. Craig had said about Arthur Donnithorne, and pictured his going away, and the changes that might take place before he came back: then they travelled back affectionately over the old scenes of boyish companionship, and dwelt on Arthur's good qualities, which Adam had a pride in, as we all have in the virtues of the superior who honours us. A nature like Adam's, with a great need of love and reverence in it, depends for so much of its happiness on what it can believe and feel about others! And he had no ideal world of dead heroes; he knew little of the life of men in the past; he must find the beings to whom he could cling with loving admiration among those who came within speech of him. These pleasant thoughts about Arthur brought a milder expression than usual into his keen rough face: perhaps they were the reason why, when he opened the old green gate leading into the Grove, he paused to pat Gyp, and say a kind word to him.

After that pause, he strode on again along the broad winding path through the Grove. What grand beeches! Adam delighted in a fine tree of all things; as the fisherman's sight is keenest on the sea, so Adam's perceptions were more at home with trees than with other objects. He kept them in his memory, as a painter does, with all the flecks and knots in their bark, all the curves and angles of their boughs: and had often calculated the height and contents of a trunk to a nicety, as he stood looking at it. No wonder that, notwithstanding his desire to get on, he could not help pausing to look at a curious large beech which he had seen standing before him at a turning in the road, and convince himself that it was not two trees wedded together, but only one. For the rest of his life he remembered that moment when he was calmly examining the beech, as a man remembers his last glimpse of the home where his youth was passed, before the road turned, and he saw it no more. The beech stood at the last turning before the Grove ended in an archway of boughs that let in the eastern light; and as Adam stepped away from the tree to continue his walk, his eyes fell on two figures about twenty yards before him.

He remained as motionless as a statue, and turned almost as pale. The two figures were standing opposite to each other, with clasped hands, about to part; and while they were bending to kiss, Gyp, who had been running among the brushwood, came out, caught sight of them, and gave a sharp bark. They separated with a start—one hurried through the gate out of the Grove, and the other, turning round, walked slowly, with a sort of saunter, towards Adam, who still stood transfixed and pale, clutching tighter the stick with which he held the basket of tools over his shoulder, and looking at the approaching figure with eyes in which amazement was fast turning to fierceness.

Arthur Donnithorne looked flushed and excited; he had tried to make unpleasant feelings more bearable by drinking a little more wine than usual at dinner to-day, and was still enough under its flattering influence to think more lightly of this unwished-for rencounter with Adam than he would otherwise have done. After all, Adam was the best person who could have happened to see him and Hetty together: he was a sensible fellow, and would not babble about it to other people. Arthur felt confident that he could laugh the thing off, and explain it away. And so he sauntered forward with elaborate carelessness—his flushed face, his evening dress of fine cloth and fine linen, his hands half thrust into his waistcoat pockets, all shone upon by the strange evening light which the light clouds had caught up even to the zenith, and were now shedding down between the topmost branches above him.

Adam was still motionless, looking at him as he came up. He understood it all now—the locket, and everything else that had been doubtful to him: a terrible scorching light showed him the hidden letters that changed the meaning of the past. If he had moved a muscle, he must inevitably have sprung upon Arthur like a tiger; and in the conflicting emotions that filled those long moments, he had told himself that he would not give loose to passion, he would only speak the right thing. He stood as if petrified by an unseen force, but the force was his own strong will.

"Well, Adam," said Arthur, "you've been looking at the fine old beeches, eh? They're not to be come near by the hatchet, though; this is a sacred grove. I overtook pretty little Hetty Sorrel as I was coming to my den—the Hermitage, there. She ought not to come home this way so late. So I took care of her to the gate, and asked for a kiss for my pains. But I must get back now, for this road is confounded damp. Good-night, Adam: I shall see you tomorrow—to say good-by, you know."

Arthur was too much preoccupied with the part he was playing himself to be thoroughly aware of the expression in Adam's face. He did not look directly at Adam, but glanced carelessly round at the trees, and then lifted up one foot to look at the sole of his boot. He cared to say no more; he had thrown quite dust enough into honest Adam's eyes; and as he spoke the last words, he walked on.

"Stop a bit, sir," said Adam, in a hard peremptory voice, without turning round. "I've got a word to say to you."

Arthur paused in surprise. Susceptible persons are more affected by a change of tone than by unexpected words, and Arthur had the susceptibility of a nature at once affectionate and vain. He was still more surprised when he saw that Adam had not moved, but stood with his back to him, as if summoning him to return. What did he mean? He was going to make a serious business of this affair. Arthur felt his temper rising. A patronising disposition always has its meaner side, and in the confusion of his irritation and alarm there entered the feeling that a man to whom he had shown so much favour as Adam, was not in a position to criticise his conduct. And yet he was dominated, as one who feels himself in the wrong always is, by the man whose good opinion he cares for. In spite of pride and temper, there was as much deprecation as anger in his voice when he said,

"What do you mean, Adam?"

"I mean, sir," answered Adam, in the same harsh voice, still without turning round,—"I mean, sir, that you don't deceive me by your light words. This is not the first time you've met Hetty Sorrel in this grove, and this is not the first time you've kissed her."

Arthur felt a startled uncertainty how far Adam was speaking from knowledge, and how far from mere inference. And this uncertainty, which prevented him from contriving a prudent answer, heightened his irritation. He said in a high sharp tone,

"Well, sir, what then?"

"Why, then, instead of acting like th' upright, honourable man we've all believed you to be, you've been acting the part of a selfish, light-minded scoundrel. You know, as well as I do, what it's to lead to, when a gentleman like you kisses and makes love to a young woman like Hetty, and gives her presents as she's frightened for other folks to see. And I say it again, you're acting the part of a selfish, light-minded scoundrel, though it cuts me to th' heart to say so, and I'd rather ha' lost my right hand."

"Let me tell you, Adam," said Arthur, bridling his growing anger, and trying to recur to his careless tone, "you're not only devilishly impertinent, but you're talking nonsense. Every pretty girl is not such a fool as you, to suppose that when a gentleman admires her beauty and pays her a little attention, he must mean something particular. Every man likes to flirt with a pretty girl, and every pretty girl likes to be flirted with. The wider the distance between them the less harm there is, for then she's not likely to deceive herself."

"I don't know what you mean by flirting," said Adam, "but if you mean behaving to a woman as if you loved her, and yet not loving her all the while, I say that's not th' action of an honest man, and what isn't honest does come t' harm. I'm not a fool, and you're not a fool, and you know better than what you're saying. You know it couldn't be made public as you've behaved to Hetty as y' have done without her losing her character, and bringing shame and trouble on her and her relations. What if you meant nothing by your kissing and your presents? Other folks won't believe as you've meant nothing; and don't tell me about her not deceiving herself. I tell you as you've filled her mind so with the thought of you as it'll mayhap poison her life; and she'll never love another man as 'ud make her a good husband."

Arthur had felt a sudden relief while Adam was speaking; he perceived that Adam had no positive knowledge of the past, and that there was no irrevocable damage done by this evening's unfortunate rencontre. Adam could still be deceived. The candid Arthur had brought himself into a position in which successful lying was his only hope. The hope allayed his anger a little.

"Well, Adam," he said, in a tone of friendly concession, "you're perhaps right. Perhaps I've gone a little too far in taking notice of the pretty little thing, and stealing a kiss now and then. You're such a grave, steady fellow, you don't understand the temptation to such trifling. I'm sure I wouldn't bring any trouble or annoyance on her and the good Poysers on any account if I could help it. But I think you look a little too seriously at it. You know I'm going away immediately, so I shan't make any more mistakes of the kind. But let us say good-night,"— Arthur here turned round to walk on,—"and talk no more about the matter. The whole thing will soon be forgotten."

"No, by God!" Adam burst out with rage that could be controlled no longer, throwing down the basket of tools, and striding forward till he was right in front of Arthur. All his jealousy and sense of personal injury, which he had been hitherto trying to keep under, had leaped up and mastered him. What man of us, in the first moments of a sharp agony, could ever feel that the fellow-man who has been the medium of inflicting it, did not mean to hurt us? In our instinctive rebellion against pain, we are children again, and demand an active will to wreak our vengeance on. Adam at this moment could only feel that he had been robbed of Hetty—robbed treacherously by the man in whom he had trusted; and he stood close in front of Arthur, with fierce eyes glaring at him, with pale lips and clenched hands, the hard tones in which he had hitherto been constraining himself to express no more than a just indignation, giving way to a deep agitated voice that seemed to shake him as he spoke.

"No, it'll not soon be forgot, as you've come in between her and me, when she might ha' loved me—it'll not soon be forgot as you've robbed me o' my happiness, while I thought you was my best friend, and a noble-minded man, as I was proud to work for. And you've been kissing her, and meaning nothing, have you? And I never kissed her i' my life —but I'd ha' worked hard for years for the right to kiss her. And you make light of it. You think little o' doing what may damage other folks, so as you get your bit o' trifling, as means nothing. I throw back your favours, for you're not the man I took you for. I'll never count you my friend any more. I'd rather you'd act as my enemy, and fight me where I stand—it's all th' amends you can make me."

Poor Adam, possessed by rage that could find no other vent, began to throw off his coat and his cap, too blind with passion to notice the change that had taken place in Arthur while he was speaking. Arthur's lips were now as pale as Adam's; his heart was beating violently. The discovery that Adam loved Hetty, was a shock which made him for the moment see himself in the light of Adam's indignation, and regard Adam's suffering as not merely a consequence, but an element of his error. The words of hatred and contempt—the first he had ever heard in his life—seemed like scorching missiles that were making ineffaceable scars on him. All screening, self-excuse, which rarely falls quite away while others respect us, forsook him for an instant, and he stood face to face with the first great irrevocable evil he had ever committed. He was only twenty-one—and three months ago—nay, much later—he had thought proudly that no man should ever be able to reproach him justly. His first impulse, if there had been time for it, would perhaps have been to utter words of propitiation; but Adam had no sooner thrown off his coat and cap, than he became aware that Arthur was standing pale and motionless, with his hands still thrust in his waistcoat pockets.

"What!" he said, "won't you fight me like a man? You know I won't strike you while you stand so."

"Go away, Adam," said Arthur, "I don't want to fight you."

"No," said Adam, bitterly; "you don't want to fight me,—you think I'm a common man, as you can injure without answering for it."

"I never meant to injure you," said Arthur, with returning anger. "I didn't know you loved her."

"But you've made her love *you*," said Adam. "You're a double-faced man—I'll never believe a word you say again."

"Go away, I tell you," said Arthur, angrily, "or we shall both repent."

"No," said Adam, with a convulsed voice, "I swear I won't go away without fighting you. Do you want provoking any more? I tell you you're a coward and a scoundrel, and I despise you."

The colour had all rushed back to Arthur's face: in a moment his right hand was clenched, and dealt a blow like lightning, which sent Adam staggering backward. His blood was as thoroughly up as Adam's now, and the two men, forgetting the emotions that had gone before, fought with the instinctive fierceness of panthers in the deepening twilight darkened by the trees. The delicate-handed gentleman was a match for the workman in everything but strength, and Arthur's skill enabled him to protract the struggle for some long moments. But between unarmed men the battle is to the strong, where the strong is no blunderer, and Arthur must sink under a well-planted blow of Adam's, as a steel rod is broken by an iron bar. The blow soon came, and Arthur fell, his head lying concealed in a tuft of fern, so that Adam could only discern his darkly-clad body.

He stood still in the dim light waiting for Arthur to rise.

The blow had been given now, towards which he had been straining all the force of nerve and muscle—and what was the good of it? What had he done by fighting? Only satisfied his own passion, only wreaked his own vengeance. He had not rescued Hetty, not changed the past—

there it was just as it had been, and he sickened at the vanity of his own rage.

But why did not Arthur rise? He was perfectly motionless, and the time seemed long to Adam. . . . Good God! had the blow been too much for him? Adam shuddered at the thought of his own strength, as with the oncoming of this dread he knelt down by Arthur's side and lifted his head from among the fern. There was no sign of life: the eyes and teeth were set. The horror that rushed over Adam completely mastered him, and forced upon him its own belief. He could feel nothing but that death was in Arthur's face, and that he was helpless before it. He made not a single movement, but knelt like an image of despair gazing at an image of death.

CHAPTER XXVIII

A DILEMMA

It was only a few minutes measured by the clock—though Adam always thought it had been a long while—before he perceived a gleam of consciousness in Arthur's face and a slight shiver through his frame. The intense joy that flooded his soul brought back some of the old affection with it.

"Do you feel any pain, sir?" he said, tenderly, loosening Arthur's cravat.

Arthur turned his eyes on Adam with a vague stare which gave way to a slightly startled motion as if from the shock of returning memory. But he only shivered again and said nothing.

"Do you feel any hurt, sir?" Adam said again, with a trembling in his voice.

Arthur put his hand up to his waistcoat buttons, and when Adam had unbuttoned it, he took a longer breath. "Lay my head down," he said, faintly, "and get me some water if you can."

Adam laid the head down gently on the fern again, and emptying the tools out of the flag-basket, hurried through the trees to the edge of the Grove bordering on the Chase, where a brook ran below the bank.

When he returned with his basket leaking, but still half full, Arthur looked at him with a more thoroughly reawakened consciousness.

"Can you drink a drop out o' your hand, sir?" said Adam, kneeling down again to lift up Arthur's head.

"No," said Arthur, "dip my cravat in and souse it on my head."

The water seemed to do him some good, for he presently raised himself a little higher, resting on Adam's arm.

"Do you feel any hurt inside, sir?" Adam asked again.

"No—no hurt," said Arthur, still faintly, "but rather done up."

After a while he said, "I suppose I fainted away when you knocked me down."

"Yes, sir, thank God," said Adam. "I thought it was worse."

"What! you thought you'd done for me, eh? come, help me on my legs."

"I feel terribly shaky and dizzy," Arthur said, as he stood leaning on Adam's arm; "that blow of yours must have come against me like a battering-ram. I don't think I can walk alone."

"Lean on me, sir; I'll get you along," said Adam. "Or, will you sit down a bit longer, on my coat here? and I'll prop y' up. You'll perhaps be better in a minute or two."

"No," said Arthur. "I'll go to the Hermitage—I think I've got some brandy there. There's a short road to it a little further on, near the gate. If you'll just help me on."

They walked slowly, with frequent pauses, but without speaking again. In both of them, the concentration in the present which had attended the first moments of Arthur's revival, had now given way to a vivid recollection of the previous scene. It was nearly dark in the narrow path among the trees, but within the circle of fir-trees round the Hermitage there was room for the growing moonlight to enter in at the windows. Their steps were noiseless on the thick carpet of fir-needles, and the outward stillness seemed to heighten their inward consciousness, as Arthur took the key out of his pocket and placed it in Adam's hand, for him to open the door. Adam had not known before that Arthur had furnished the old Hermitage and made it a retreat for himself, and it was a surprise to him when he opened the door to see a snug room with all the signs of frequent habitation.

Arthur loosed Adam's arm and threw himself on the ottoman. "You'll see my hunting-bottle somewhere," he said. "A leather case with a bottle and glass in."

Adam was not long in finding the case. "There's very little brandy in it, sir," he said, turning it downwards over the glass, as he held it before the window, "hardly this little glassful."

"Well, give me that," said Arthur, with the peevishness of physical depression. When he had taken some sips, Adam said, "Hadn't I better run to th' house, sir, and get some more brandy? I can be there and back pretty soon. It'll be a stiff walk home for you, if you don't have something to revive you."

"Yes—go. But don't say I'm ill. Ask for my man Pym, and tell him to get it from Mills, and not to say I'm at the Hermitage. Get some water too."

Adam was relieved to have an active task—both of them were relieved to be apart from each other for a short time. But Adam's swift pace could not still the eager pain of thinking—of living again with concentrated suffering through the last wretched hour, and looking out from it over all the new, sad future.

Arthur lay still for some minutes after Adam was gone, but presently he rose feebly from the ottoman and peered about slowly in the broken moonlight, seeking something. It was a short bit of wax candle that stood amongst a confusion of writing and drawing materials. There was more searching for the means of lighting the candle, and when that was done, he went cautiously round the room as if wishing to assure himself of the presence or absence of something. At last he had found a slight thing, which he put first in his pocket, and then, on a second thought, took out again, and thrust deep down into a waste-paper basket. It was a woman's little pink silk neckerchief. He set the candle on the table and threw himself down on the ottoman again, exhausted with the effort.

When Adam came back with his supplies, his entrance awoke Arthur from a doze.

"That's right," Arthur said; "I'm tremendously in want of some brandy-vigour."

"I'm glad to see you've got a light, sir," said Adam. "I've been thinking I'd better have asked for a lanthorn."

"No, no; the candle will last long enough—I shall soon be up to walking home now."

"I can't go before I've seen you safe home, sir," said Adam, hesitatingly.

"No: it will be better for you to stay—sit down."

Adam sat down, and they remained opposite to each other in uneasy silence, while Arthur slowly drank brandy-and-water, with visibly renovating effect. He began to lie in a more voluntary position, and looked as if he were less overpowered by bodily sensations. Adam was keenly alive to these indications, and as his anxiety about Arthur's condition began to be allayed, he felt more of that impatience which every one knows who has had his just indignation suspended by the physical state of the culprit. Yet there was one thing on his mind to be done before he could recur to remonstrance: it was to confess what had been unjust in his own words. Perhaps he longed all the more to make this confession, that his indignation might be free again; and as he saw the signs of returning ease in Arthur, the words again and again came to his lips and went back, checked by the thought that it would be better to leave everything till to-morrow. As long as they were silent they did not look at each other, and a foreboding came across Adam that if they began to speak as though they remembered the past—if they looked at each with full recognition—they must take fire again. So they sat in silence till the bit of wax candle flickered low in the socket; the silence all the while becoming more irksome to Adam. Arthur had just poured out some more brandy-and-water, and he threw one arm behind his head and drew up one leg in an attitude of recovered ease, which was an irresistible temptation to Adam to speak what was on his mind.

"You begin to feel more yourself again, sir," he said, as the candle went out, and they were half-hidden from each other in the faint moonlight.

"Yes: I don't feel good for much—very lazy, and not inclined to move; but I'll go home when I've taken this dose."

There was a slight pause before Adam said,

"My temper got the better of me, and I said things as wasn't true. I'd no right to speak as if you'd known you was doing me an injury: you'd no grounds for knowing it; I've always kept what I felt for her as secret as I could."

He paused again before he went on.

"And perhaps I judged you too harsh—I'm apt to be harsh; and you may have acted out o' thoughtlessness more than I should ha' believed was possible for a man with a heart and a conscience. We're not all put together alike, and we may misjudge one another. God knows, it's all the joy I could have now, to think the best of you."

Arthur wanted to go home without saying any more—he was too painfully embarrassed in mind, as well as too weak in body, to wish for any further explanation to-night. And yet it was a relief to him that Adam reopened the subject in a way the least difficult for him to answer. Arthur was in the wretched position of an open, generous man, who has committed an error which makes deception seem a necessity. The native impulse to give truth in return for truth, to meet trust with frank confession, must be suppressed, and duty was become a question of tactics. His deed was reacting upon him—was already governing him tyrannously, and forcing him into a course that jarred with his habitual feelings. The only aim that seemed admissible to him now was to deceive Adam to the utmost: to make Adam think better of him than he deserved. And when he heard the words of honest retraction—when he heard the sad appeal with which Adam ended—he was obliged to rejoice in the remains of ignorant confidence it implied. He did not answer immediately, for he had to be judicious, and not truthful.

"Say no more about our anger, Adam," he said, at last, very languidly, for the labour of speech was unwelcome to him; "I forgive your momentary injustice—it was quite natural, with the exaggerated notions you had in your mind. We shall be none the worse friends in future, I hope, because we've fought: you had the best of it, and that was as it should be, for I believe I've been most in the wrong of the two. Come, let us shake hands."

Arthur held out his hand, but Adam sat still.

"I don't like to say 'No' to that, sir," he said, "but I can't shake hands till it's clear what we mean by't. I was wrong when I spoke as if you'd done me an injury knowingly, but I wasn't wrong in what I said before, about your behaviour t' Hetty, and I can't shake hands with you as if I held you my friend the same as ever, till you've cleared that up better."

Arthur swallowed his pride and resentment as he drew back his hand. He was silent for some moments, and then said, as indifferently as he could,

"I don't know what you mean by clearing up, Adam. I've told you already that you think too seriously of a little flirtation. But if you are right in supposing there is any danger in it—I'm going away on Saturday, and there will be an end of it. As for the pain it has given you, I'm heartily sorry for it. I can say no more."

Adam said nothing, but rose from his chair, and stood with his face towards one of the windows, as if looking at the blackness of the moonlit fir-trees; but he was in reality conscious of nothing but the conflict within him. It was of no use now—his resolution not to speak till to-morrow: he must speak there and then. But it was several minutes before he turned round and stepped nearer to Arthur, standing and looking down on him as he lay.

"It'll be better for me to speak plain," he said, with evident effort, "though it's hard work. You see, sir, this isn't a trifle to me, whatever it may be to you. I'm none o' them men as can go making love first to one woman and then t' another, and don't think it much odds which of 'em I take. What I feel for Hetty's a different sort o' love, such as I believe nobody can know much about but them as feel it, and God as has given it to 'em. She's more nor everything else to me, all but my conscience and my good name. And if it's true what you've been saying all along—and if it's only been trifling and flirting as you call it, as'll be put an end to by your going away—why, then, I'd wait, and hope her heart 'ud turn to me after all. I'm loath to think you'd speak false to me, and I'll believe your word, however things may look."

"You would be wronging Hetty more than me not to believe it," said Arthur, almost violently, starting up from the ottoman, and moving away. But he threw himself into a chair again directly, saying more feebly, "You seem to forget that, in suspecting me, you are casting imputations upon her."

"Nay, sir," Adam said, in a calmer voice, as if he were half relieved —for he was too straightforward to make a distinction between a direct falsehood and an indirect one—"Nay, sir, things don't lie level between Hetty and you. You're acting with your eyes open, whatever you may do; but how do you know what's been in her mind? She's all but a child —as any man with a conscience in him ought to feel bound to take care on. And whatever you may think, I know you've disturbed her mind. I know she's been fixing her heart on you; for there's a many things clear to me now as I didn't understand before. But you seem to make light o' what *she* may feel—you don't think o' that."

"Good God, Adam, let me alone!" Arthur burst out impetuously; "I feel it enough without your worrying me."

He was aware of his indiscretion as soon as the words had escaped him.

"Well, then, if you feel it," Adam rejoined, eagerly; "if you feel as you may ha' put false notions into her mind, and made her believe as you loved her, when all the while you meant nothing, I've this demand to make of you;—I'm not speaking for myself, but for her. I ask you t' undeceive her before you go away. Y'aren't going away for ever; and if you leave her behind with a notion in her head o' your feeling about her the same as she feels about you, she'll be hankering after you, and the mischief may get worse. It may be a smart to her now, but it'll save her pain i' th' end. I ask you to write a letter—you may trust to my seeing

as she get it: tell her the truth, and take blame to yourself for behaving
as you'd no right to do to a young woman as isn't your equal. I speak
plain, sir. But I can't speak any other way. There's nobody can take
care o' Hetty in this thing but me."

"I can do what I think needful in the matter," said Arthur, more and
more irritated by mingled distress and perplexity, "without giving
promises to you. I shall take what measures I think proper."

"No," said Adam, in an abrupt decided tone, "that won't do. I must
know what ground I'm treading on. I must be safe as you've put an end
to what ought never to ha' been begun. I don't forget what's owing to
you as a gentleman; but in this thing we're man and man, and I can't
give up."

There was no answer for some moments. Then Arthur said, "I'll see
you to-morrow. I can bear no more now; I'm ill." He rose as he spoke,
and reached his cap, as if intending to go.

"You won't see her again!" Adam exclaimed, with a flash of recurring
anger and suspicion, moving towards the door and placing his back
against it. "Either tell me she can never be my wife—tell me you've been
lying—or else promise me what I've said."

Adam uttering this alternative, stood like a terrible fate before Arthur,
who had moved forward a step or two, and now stopped, shaken, sick in
mind and body. It seemed long to both of them—that inward struggle
of Arthur's—before he said, feebly, "I promise; let me go."

Adam moved away from the door and opened it, but when Arthur
reached the step, he stopped again and leaned against the door-post.

"You're not well enough to walk alone, sir," said Adam. "Take my
arm again."

Arthur made no answer, and presently walked on, Adam following.
But, after a few steps, he stood still again, and said coldly, "I believe
I must trouble you. It's getting late now, and there may be an alarm
set up about me at home."

Adam gave his arm, and they walked on without uttering a word, till
they came to where the basket of tools lay.

"I must pick up the tools, sir," Adam said. "They're my brother's. I
doubt they'll be rusted. If you'll please to wait a minute."

Arthur stood still without speaking, and no other word passed between them till they were at the side entrance, where he hoped to get
in without being seen by any one. He said then, "Thank you; I needn't
trouble you any further."

"What time will it be conven'ent for me to see you to-morrow, sir?"
said Adam.

"You may send me word that you're here at five o'clock," said Arthur; "not before."

"Good-night, sir," said Adam. But he heard no reply; Arthur had
turned into the house.

CHAPTER XXIX

THE NEXT MORNING

ARTHUR did not pass a sleepless night; he slept long and well. For sleep comes to the perplexed—if the perplexed are only weary enough. But at seven he rang his bell and astonished Pym by declaring he was going to get up, and must have breakfast brought to him at eight.

"And see that my mare is saddled at half-past eight, and tell my grandfather when he's down that I'm better this morning, and am gone for a ride."

He had been awake an hour, and could rest in bed no longer. In bed our yesterdays are too oppressive: if a man can only get up, though it be but to whistle or to smoke, he has a present which offers some resistance to the past—sensations which assert themselves against tyrannous memories. And if there were such a thing as taking averages of feeling, it would certainly be found that in the hunting and shooting seasons regret, self-reproach, and mortified pride, weigh lighter on country gentlemen than in late spring and summer. Arthur felt that he should be more of a man on horseback. Even the presence of Pym, waiting on him with the usual deference, was a reassurance to him after the scenes of yesterday. For, with Arthur's sensitiveness to opinion, the loss of Adam's respect was a shock to his self-contentment which suffused his imagination with the sense that he had sunk in all eyes; as a sudden shock of fear from some real peril makes a nervous woman afraid even to step, because all her perceptions are suffused with a sense of danger.

Arthur's, as you know, was a loving nature. Deeds of kindness were as easy to him as a bad habit: they were the common issue of his weakness and good qualities, of his egoism and his sympathy. He didn't like to witness pain, and he liked to have grateful eyes beaming on him as the giver of pleasure. When he was a lad of seven, he one day kicked down an old gardener's pitcher of broth, from no motive but a kicking impulse, not reflecting that it was the old man's dinner; but on learning that sad fact, he took his favourite pencil-case and a silver-hafted knife out of his pocket and offered them as compensation. He had been the same Arthur ever since, trying to make all offences forgotten in benefits. If there were any bitterness in his nature, it could only show itself against the man who refused to be conciliated by him. And perhaps the time was come for some of that bitterness to rise. At the first moment, Arthur had felt pure distress and self-reproach at discovering that Adam's happiness was involved in his relation to Hetty: if there had been a possibility of making Adam tenfold amends—if deeds of gift, or any other deeds, could have restored Adam's contentment and regard for him as a benefactor, Arthur would not only have executed them without hesitation, but would have felt bound all the more closely to

Adam, and would never have been weary of making retribution. But Adam could receive no amends; his suffering could not be cancelled; his respect and affection could not be recovered by any prompt deeds of atonement. He stood like an immovable obstacle against which no pressure could avail; an embodiment of what Arthur most shrank from believing in—the irrevocableness of his own wrong-doing. The words of scorn, the refusal to shake hands, the mastery asserted over him in their last conversation in the Hermitage—above all, the sense of having been knocked down, to which a man does not very well reconcile himself, even under the most heroic circumstances—pressed on him with a galling pain which was stronger than compunction. Arthur would so gladly have persuaded himself that he had done no harm! And if no one had told him the contrary, he could have persuaded himself so much better. Nemesis can seldom forge a sword for herself out of our consciences—out of the suffering we feel in the suffering we may have caused: there is rarely metal enough there to make an effective weapon. Our moral sense learns the manners of good society, and smiles when others smile; but when some rude person gives rough names to our actions, she is apt to take part against us. And so it was with Arthur: Adam's judgment of him, Adam's grating words disturbed his self-soothing arguments.

Not that Arthur had been at ease before Adam's discovery. Struggles and resolves had transformed themselves into compunction and anxiety. He was distressed for Hetty's sake, and distressed for his own, that he must leave her behind. He had always, both in making and breaking resolutions, looked beyond his passion, and seen that it must speedily end in separation; but his nature was too ardent and tender for him not to suffer at this parting; and on Hetty's account he was filled with uneasiness. He had found out the dream in which she was living—that she was to be a lady in silks and satins; and when he had first talked to her about his going away, she had asked him tremblingly to let her go with him and be married. It was his painful knowledge of this which had given the most exasperating sting to Adam's reproaches. He had said no word with the purpose of deceiving her, her vision was all spun by her own childish fancy; but he was obliged to confess to himself that it was spun half out of his own actions. And to increase the mischief, on this last evening he had not dared to hint the truth to Hetty: he had been obliged to soothe her with tender, hopeful words, lest he should throw her into violent distress. He felt the situation acutely; felt the sorrow of the dear thing in the present, and thought with a darker anxiety of the tenacity which her feelings might have in the future. That was the one sharp point which pressed against him; every other he could evade by hopeful self-persuasion. The whole thing had been secret; the Poysers had not the shadow of a suspicion. No one, except Adam, knew anything of what had passed—no one else was likely to know; for Arthur had impressed upon Hetty that it would be fatal to betray, by word or look, that there had been the least intimacy between them; and

Adam, who knew half their secret, would rather help them to keep it than betray it. It was an unfortunate business altogether, but there was no use in making it worse than it was, by imaginary exaggerations and forebodings of evil that might never come. The temporary sadness for Hetty was the worst consequence: he resolutely turned away his eyes from any bad consequence that was not demonstrably inevitable. But—but Hetty might have had the trouble in some other way if not in this. And perhaps hereafter he might be able to do a great deal for her, and make up to her for all the tears she would shed about him. She would owe the advantage of his care for her in future years to the sorrow she had incurred now. *So* good comes out of evil. Such is the beautiful arrangement of things!

Are you inclined to ask whether this can be the same Arthur who, two months ago, had that freshness of feeling, that delicate honour which shrinks from wounding even a sentiment, and does not contemplate any more positive offence as possible for it?—who thought that his own self-respect was a higher tribunal than any external opinion? The same, I assure you, only under different conditions. Our deeds determine us, as much as we determine our deeds; and until we know what has been or will be the peculiar combination of outward with inward facts, which constitutes a man's critical actions, it will be better not to think ourselves wise about his character. There is a terrible coercion in our deeds which may first turn the honest man into a deceiver, and then reconcile him to the change; for this reason—that the second wrong presents itself to him in the guise of the only practicable right. The action which before commission has been seen with that blended commonsense and fresh untarnished feeling which is the healthy eye of the soul, is looked at afterwards with the lens of apologetic ingenuity, through which all things that men call beautiful and ugly are seen to be made up of textures very much alike. Europe adjusts itself to a *fait accompli,* and so does an individual character—until the placid adjustment is disturbed by a convulsive retribution.

No man can escape this vitiating effect of an offence against his own sentiment of right, and the effect was the stronger in Arthur because of that very need of self-respect which, while his conscience was still at ease, was one of his best safeguards. Self-accusation was too painful to him—he could not face it. He must persuade himself that he had not been very much to blame; he began even to pity himself for the necessity he was under of deceiving Adam: it was a course so opposed to the honesty of his own nature. But then, it was the only right thing to do.

Well, whatever had been amiss in him, he was miserable enough in consequence: miserable about Hetty: miserable about this letter he had promised to write, and that seemed at one moment to be a gross barbarity, at another perhaps the greatest kindness he could do to her. And across all this reflection would dart every now and then a sudden impulse of passionate defiance towards all consequences: he would carry Hetty away, and all other considerations might go to . . .

In this state of mind the four walls of his room made an intolerable prison to him; they seemed to hem in and press down upon him all the crowd of contradictory thoughts and conflicting feelings, some of which would fly away in the open air. He had only an hour or two to make up his mind in, and he must get clear and calm. Once on Meg's back, in the fresh air of that fine morning, he should be more master of the situation.

The pretty creature arched her bay neck in the sunshine, and pawed the gravel, and trembled with pleasure when her master stroked her nose, and patted her, and talked to her even in a more caressing tone than usual. He loved her the better because she knew nothing of his secrets. But Meg was quite as well acquainted with her master's mental state as many others of her sex with the mental condition of the nice young gentlemen towards whom their hearts are in a state of fluttering expectation.

Arthur cantered for five miles beyond the Chase, till he was at the foot of a hill where there were no hedges or trees to hem in the road. Then he threw the bridle on Meg's neck, and prepared to make up his mind.

Hetty knew that their meeting yesterday must be the last before Arthur went away; there was no possibility of their contriving another without exciting suspicion; and she was like a frightened child, unable to think of anything, only able to cry at the mention of parting, and then put her face up to have the tears kissed away. He *could* do nothing but comfort her, and lull her into dreaming on. A letter would be a dreadfully abrupt way of awakening her! Yet there was truth in what Adam said—that it would save her from a lengthened delusion, which might be worse than a sharp immediate pain. And it was the only way of satisfying Adam, who *must* be satisfied, for more reasons than one. If he could have seen her again! But that was impossible; there was such a thorny hedge of hindrances between them, and an imprudence would be fatal. And yet, if he *could* see her again, what good would it do? Only cause him to suffer more from the sight of her distress and the remembrance of it. Away from him, she was surrounded by all the motives to self-control.

A sudden dread here fell like a shadow across his imagination—the dread lest she should do something violent in her grief; and close upon that dread came another, which deepened the shadow. But he shook them off with the force of youth and hope. What was the ground for painting the future in that dark way? It was just as likely to be the reverse. Arthur told himself, he did not deserve that things should turn out badly—he had never meant beforehand to do anything his conscience disapproved —he had been led on by circumstances. There was a sort of implicit confidence in thim that he was really such a good fellow at bottom, Providence would not treat him harshly.

At all events, he couldn't help what would come now: all he could do was to take what seemed the best course at the present moment. And he persuaded himself that that course was to make the way open between Adam and Hetty. Her heart might really turn to Adam, as he said, after a while; and in that case there would have been no great harm done, since it was still Adam's ardent wish to make her his wife. To be sure, Adam was deceived—deceived in a way that Arthur would have resented as a deep wrong if it had been practised on himself. That was a reflection that marred the consoling prospect. Arthur's cheeks even burned in mingled shame and irritation at the thought. But what could a man do in such a dilemma? He was bound in honour to say no word that could injure Hetty: his first duty was to guard *her*. He would never have told or acted a lie on his own account. Good God! what a miserable fool he was to have brought himself into such a dilemma; and yet, if ever a man had excuses, he had. (Pity that consequences are determined not by excuses but by actions!)

Well, the letter must be written; it was the only means that promised a solution of the difficulty. The tears came into Arthur's eyes as he thought of Hetty reading it; but it would be almost as hard for him to write it: he was not doing anything easy to himself; and this last thought helped him to arrive at a conclusion. He could never deliberately have taken a step which inflicted pain on another and left him at ease. Even a movement of jealousy at the thought of giving up Hetty to Adam, went to convince him that he was making a sacrifice.

When once he had come to this conclusion, he turned Meg round, and set off home again in a canter. The letter should be written the first thing, and the rest of the day would be filled up with other business: he should have no time to look behind him. Happily Irwine and Gawaine were coming to dinner, and by twelve o'clock the next day he should have left the Chase miles behind him. There was some security in this constant occupation against an uncontrollable impulse seizing him to rush to Hetty, and thrust into her hand some mad proposition that would undo everything. Faster and faster went the sensitive Meg, at every slight sign from her rider, till the canter had passed into a swift gallop.

"I thought they said th' young mester war took ill last night," said sour old John, the groom, at dinner-time in the servants' hall. "He's been ridin' fit to split the mare i' two this forenoon."

"That's happen one o' the symptoms, John," said the facetious coachman.

"Then I wish he war let blood for 't, that's all," said John, grimly.

Adam had been early at the Chase to know how Arthur was, and had been relieved from all anxiety about the effects of his blow by learning that he was gone out for a ride. At five o'clock he was punctually there again, and sent up word of his arrival. In a few minutes Pym came down with a letter in his hand, and gave it to Adam, saying that the Captain was too busy to see him, and had written everything he had to say. The letter was directed to Adam, but he went out of doors again before opening it. It contained a sealed enclosure directed to Hetty. On the inside of the cover Adam read:—

"In the enclosed letter I have written everything you wish. I leave it to you to decide whether you will be doing best to deliver it to Hetty or to return it to me.

Ask yourself once more whether you are not taking a measure which may pain her more than mere silence.

"There is no need for our seeing each other again now. We shall meet with better feelings some months hence.   A.D."

"Perhaps he's i' th' right on 't not to see me," thought Adam. "It's no use meeting to say more hard words, and it's no use meeting to shake hands and say we're friends again. We're not friends, an' it's better not to pretend it. I know forgiveness is a man's duty, but, to my thinking, that can only mean as you're to give up all thoughts o' taking revenge: it can never mean as you're t' have your old feelings back again, for that's not possible. He's not the same man to me, and I can't *feel* the same towards him. God help me! I don't know whether I feel the same towards anybody: I seem as if I'd been measuring my work from a false line, and had got it all to measure over again."

But the question about delivering the letter to Hetty soon absorbed Adam's thoughts. Arthur had procured some relief to himself by throwing the decision on Adam with a warning; and Adam, who was not given to hesitation, hesitated here. He determined to feel his way—to ascertain as well as he could what was Hetty's state of mind before he decided on delivering the letter.

CHAPTER XXX

THE DELIVERY OF THE LETTER

THE next Sunday Adam joined the Poysers on their way out of church, hoping for an invitation to go home with them. He had the letter in his pocket, and was anxious to have an opportunity of talking to Hetty alone. He could not see her face at church, for she had changed her seat, and when he came up to her to shake hands, her manner was doubtful and constrained. He expected this, for it was the first time she had met him since she had been aware that he had seen her with Arthur in the Grove.

"Come, you'll go with us, Adam," Mr. Poyser said when they reached the turning; and as soon as they were in the fields Adam ventured to offer his arm to Hetty. The children soon gave them an opportunity of lingering behind a little, and then Adam said,

"Will you contrive for me to walk out in the garden a bit with you this evening, if it keeps fine, Hetty? I've something partic'lar to talk to you about."

Hetty said, "Very well." She was really as anxious as Adam was that she should have some private talk with him: she wondered what he thought of her and Arthur: he must have seen them kissing, she knew, but she had no conception of the scene that had taken place between Arthur and Adam. Her first feeling had been that Adam would be very angry with her, and perhaps would tell her aunt and uncle; but it never entered her mind that he would dare to say anything to Captain Donnithorne. It was a relief to her that he behaved so kindly to her to-day, and wanted to speak to *her* alone; for she had trembled when she found he was going home with them lest he should mean "to tell." But, now he wanted to talk to her by herself, she should learn what he thought, and what he meant to do. She felt a certain confidence that she could persuade him not to do anything she did not want him to do; she could perhaps even make him believe that she didn't care for Arthur; and as long as Adam thought there was any hope of her having him, he would do just what she liked, she knew. Besides, she *must* go on seeming to encourage Adam, lest her uncle and aunt should be angry, and suspect her of having some secret lover.

Hetty's little brain was busy with this combination, as she hung on Adam's arm, and said "yes" or "no" to some slight observations of his about the many hawthorn-berries there would be for the birds this next winter, and the low-hanging clouds that would hardly hold up till morning. And when they rejoined her aunt and uncle, she could pursue her thoughts without interruption, for Mr. Poyser held that though a young man might have liked to have the woman he was courting on his arm, he would nevertheless be glad of a little reasonable talk about business the while; and, for his own part, he was curious to hear the most recent news about the Chase Farm. So, through the rest of the walk, he claimed Adam's conversation for himself; and Hetty laid her small plots, and imagined her little scenes of cunning blandishment, as she walked along by the hedgerows on honest Adam's arm, quite as well as if she had been an elegantly clad coquette alone in her boudoir. For if a country beauty in clumsy shoes be only shallow-hearted enough, it is astonishing how closely her mental processes may resemble those of a lady in society and crinoline, who applies her refined intellect to the problem of committing indiscretions without compromising herself. Perhaps the resemblance was not much the less because Hetty felt very unhappy all the while. The parting with Arthur was a double pain to her; mingling with the tumult of passion and vanity, there was a dim undefined fear that the future might shape itself in some way quite unlike her dream. She clung to the comforting hopeful words Arthur had uttered in their last meeting —"I shall come again at Christmas, and then we will see what can be done." She clung to the belief that he was so fond of her, he would never be happy without her; and she still hugged her secret—that a great gentleman loved her—with gratified pride, as a superiority over all the girls she knew. But the uncertainty of the future, the possibilities to which she could give no shape, began to press upon her like the invisible weight of air; she was alone on her little island of dreams, and all around her was the dark unknown water where Arthur was gone. She could gather no elation of spirits now by looking forward, but only by looking backward to build confidence on past words and caresses. But occasionally, since Thursday evening, her dim anxieties had been almost

lost behind the more definite fear that Adam might betray what he
knew to her uncle and aunt, and his sudden proposition to talk with her
alone had set her thoughts to work in a new way. She was eager not to
lose this evening's opportunity; and after tea, when the boys were going
into the garden, and Totty begged to go with them, Hetty said, with an
alacrity that surprised Mrs. Poyser—

"I'll go with her, aunt."

It did not seem at all surprising that Adam said he would go too; and
soon he and Hetty were left alone together on the walk by the filbert-
trees, while the boys were busy elsewhere gathering the large unripe nuts
to play at "cob-nut" with, and Totty was watching them with a puppy-
like air of contemplation. It was but a short time—hardly two months
—since Adam had had his mind filled with delicious hopes, as he stood
by Hetty's side in this garden. The remembrance of that scene had often
been with him since Thursday evening: the sunlight through the apple-
tree boughs, the red bunches, Hetty's sweet blush. It came importunately
now, on this sad evening, with the low-hanging clouds; but he tried to
suppress it, lest some emotion should impel him to say more than was
needful for Hetty's sake.

"After what I saw on Thursday night, Hetty," he began, "you won't
think me too free in what I'm going to say. If you was being courted by
any man as 'ud make you his wife, and I'd known you was fond of him,
and meant to have him, I should have no right to speak a word to you
about it; but when I see you're being made love to by a gentleman as can
never marry you, and doesna think o' marrying you, I feel bound t'
interfere for you. I can't speak about it to them as are i' the place o' your
parents, for that might bring worse trouble than's needful."

Adam's words relieved one of Hetty's fears, but they also carried a
meaning which sickened her with a strengthened foreboding. She was
pale and trembling, and yet she would have angrily contradicted Adam,
if she had dared to betray her feelings. But she was silent.

"You're so young, you know, Hetty," he went on, almost tenderly,
"and y' haven't seen much o' what goes on in the world. It's right for me
to do what I can to save you from getting into trouble for want o' your
knowing where you're being led to. If anybody besides me knew what I
know about your meeting a gentleman, and having fine presents from
him, they'd speak light on you, and you'd lose your character. And besides that, you'll have to suffer in your feelings, wi' giving your love to
a man as can never marry you, so as he might take care of you all your
life."

Adam paused, and looked at Hetty, who was plucking the leaves from
the filbert-trees, and tearing them up in her hand. Her little plans and
preconcerted speeches had all forsaken her, like an ill-learnt lesson, under
the terrible agitation produced by Adam's words. There was a cruel force
in their calm certainty which threatened to grapple and crush her flimsy
hopes and fancies. She wanted to resist them—she wanted to throw
them off with an angry contradiction; but the determination to conceal

what she felt still governed her. It was nothing more than a blind prompting now, for she was unable to calculate the effect of her words.

"You've no right to say as I love him," she said, faintly, but impetuously, plucking another rough leaf and tearing it up. She was very beautiful in her paleness and agitation, with her dark childish eyes dilated,
and her breath shorter than usual. Adam's heart yearned over her as he
looked at her. Ah, if he could but comfort her, and soothe her, and save
her from this pain; if he had but some sort of strength that would enable
him to rescue her poor troubled mind, as he would have rescued her
body in the face of all danger!

"I doubt it must be so, Hetty," he said, tenderly; "for I canna believe
you'd let any man kiss you by yourselves, and give you a gold box with
his hair, and go a-walkin i' the Grove to meet him, if you didna love
him. I'm not blaming you, for I know it 'ud begin by little and little,
till at last you'd not be able to throw it off. It's him I blame for stealing
your love i' that way, when he knew he could never make you the right
amends. He's been trifling with you, and making a plaything of you, and
caring nothing about you as a man ought to care."

"Yes, he does care for me; I know better nor you," Hetty burst out.
Everything was forgotten but the pain and anger she felt at Adam's
words.

"Nay, Hetty," said Adam, "if he'd cared for you rightly he'd never
ha' behaved so. He told me himself he meant nothing by his kissing and
presents, and he wanted to make me believe as you thought light of 'em
too. But I know better nor that. I can't help thinking as you've been
trusting to his loving you well enough to marry you, for all he's a gentleman. And that's why I must speak to you about it, Hetty,—for fear you
should be deceiving yourself. It's never entered his head the thought o'
marrying you."

"How do you know? How durst you say so?" said Hetty, pausing in
her walk and trembling. The terrible decision of Adam's tone shook her
with fear. She had no presence of mind left for the reflection that Arthur
would have his reasons for not telling the truth to Adam. Her words and
look were enough to determine Adam: he must give her the letter.

"Perhaps you can't believe me, Hetty; because you think too well of
him—because you think he loves you better than he does. But I've got
a letter i' my pocket, as he wrote himself for me to give you. I've not read
the letter, but he says he's told you the truth in it. But before I give you
the letter, consider, Hetty, and don't let it take too much hold on you.
It wouldna ha' been good for you if he'd wanted to do such a mad thing
as marry you: it 'ud ha' led to no happiness i' th' end."

Hetty said nothing: she felt a revival of hope at the mention of a
letter which Adam had not read. There would be something quite different from what he thought.

Adam took out the letter, but he held it in his hand still, while he
said, in a tone of tender entreaty——

"Don't you bear me ill-will, Hetty, because I'm the means o' bringing you this pain. God knows I'd ha' borne a good deal worse for the sake o' sparing it you. And think—there's nobody but me knows about this; and I'll take care of you as if I was your brother. You're the same as ever to me, for I don't believe you've done any wrong knowingly."

Hetty laid her hand on the letter, but Adam did not loose it till he had done speaking. She took no notice of what he said—she had not listened; but when he loosed the letter, she put it into her pocket, without opening it, and then began to walk more quickly, as if she wanted to go in.

"You're in the right not to read it just yet," said Adam. "Read it when you're by yourself. But stay out a little bit longer, and let us call the children: you look so white and ill; your aunt may take notice of it."

Hetty heard the warning. It recalled to her the necessity of rallying her native powers of concealment, which had half given way under the shock of Adam's words. And she had the letter in her pocket: she was sure there was comfort in that letter, in spite of Adam. She ran to find Totty, and soon reappeared with recovered colour, leading Totty, who was making a sour face, because she had been obliged to throw away an unripe apple that she had set her small teeth in.

"Hegh, Totty," said Adam, "come and ride on my shoulder—ever so high—you'll touch the tops o' the trees."

What little child ever refused to be comforted by that glorious sense of being seized strongly and swung upward? I don't believe Ganymede cried when the eagle carried him away, and perhaps deposited him on Jove's shoulder at the end. Totty smiled down complacently from her secure height, and pleasant was the sight to the mother's eyes, as she stood at the house door and saw Adam coming with his small burthen.

"Bless your sweet face, my pet," she said, the mother's strong love filling her keen eyes with mildness, as Totty leaned forward and put out her arms. She had no eyes for Hetty at that moment, and only said, without looking at her, "You go and draw some ale, Hetty: the gells are both at the cheese."

After the ale had been drawn and her uncle's pipe lighted, there was Totty to be taken to bed, and brought down again in her nightgown, because she would cry instead of going to sleep. Then there was supper to be got ready, and Hetty must be continually in the way to give help. Adam stayed till he knew Mrs. Poyser expected him to go, engaging her and her husband in talk as constantly as he could, for the sake of leaving Hetty more at ease. He lingered, because he wanted to see her safely through that evening, and he was delighted to find how much self-command she showed. He knew she had not had time to read the letter, but he did not know she was buoyed up by a secret hope that the letter would contradict everything he had said. It was hard work for him to leave her—hard to think that he should not know for days how she was bearing her trouble. But he must go at last, and all he could do was to press her hand gently as he said "Good-by," and hope she would take that as a sign that if his love could ever be a refuge for her, it was there the same as ever. How busy his thoughts were, as he walked home, in devising pitying excuses for her folly; in referring all her weakness to the sweet lovingness of her nature; in blaming Arthur, with less and less inclination to admit that *his* conduct might be extenuated too! His exasperation at Hetty's suffering—and also at the sense that she was possibly thrust for ever out of his own reach—deafened him to any plea for the miscalled friend who had wrought this misery. Adam was a clearsighted, fair-minded man—a fine fellow, indeed, morally as well as physically. But if Aristides the Just was ever in love and jealous, he was at that moment not perfectly magnanimous. And I cannot pretend that Adam, in these painful days, felt nothing but righteous indignation and loving pity. He was bitterly jealous; and in proportion as his love made him indulgent in his judgment of Hetty, the bitterness found a vent in his feeling towards Arthur.

"Her head was allays likely to be turned," he thought, "when a gentleman, with his fine manners, and fine clothes, and his white hands, and that way o' talking gentlefolks have, came about her, making up to her in a bold way, as a man couldn't do that was only her equal; and it's much if she'll ever like a common man now." He could not help drawing his own hands out of his pockets, and looking at them—at the hard palms and the broken finger-nails. "I'm a roughish fellow, altogether: I don't know, now I come to think on't, that there is much for a woman to like about me; and yet I might ha' got another wife easy enough, if I hadn't set my heart on her. But it's little matter what other women think about me, if she can't love me. She might ha' loved me, perhaps, as likely as any other man—there's nobody hereabouts as I'm afraid of, if *he* hadn't come between us; but now I shall belike be hateful to her because I'm so different to him. And yet there's no telling—she may turn round the other way, when she finds he's made light of her all the while. She may come to feel the vally of a man as 'ud be thankful to be bound to her all his life. But I must put up with it whichever way it is—I've only to be thankful it's been no worse: I am not th' only man that's got to do without much happiness i' this life. There's many a good bit o' work done with a sad heart. It's God's will, and that's enough for us: we shouldn't know better how things ought to be than He does, I reckon, if we was to spend our lives i' puzzling. But it 'ud ha' gone near to spoil my work for me, if I'd seen her brought to sorrow and shame, and through the man as I've always been proud to think on. Since I've been spared that, I've no right to grumble. When a man's got his limbs whole, he can bear a smart cut or two."

As Adam was getting over a stile at this point in his reflections, he perceived a man walking along the field before him. He knew it was Seth, returning from an evening preaching, and made haste to overtake him.

"I thought thee'dst be at home before me," he said, as Seth turned round to wait for him, "for I'm later than usual to-night."

"Well, I'm later too, for I got into talk, after meeting, with John

Barnes, who has lately professed himself in a state of perfection, and I'd
a question to ask him about his experience. It's one o' them subjects
that lead you further than y' expect—they don't lie along the straight
road."

They walked along together in silence two or three minutes. Adam
was not inclined to enter into the subtleties of religious experience, but
he *was* inclined to interchange a word or two of brotherly affection and
confidence with Seth. That was a rare impulse in him, much as the
brothers loved each other. They hardly ever spoke of personal matters,
or uttered more than an allusion to their family troubles. Adam was by
nature reserved in all matters of feeling, and Seth felt a certain timidity
towards his more practical brother.

"Seth, lad," Adam said, putting his arm on his brother's shoulder,
"hast heard anything from Dinah Morris since she went away?"

"Yes," said Seth. "She told me I might write her word after a while,
how we went on, and how mother bore up under her trouble. So I wrote
her a fortnight ago, and told her about thee having a new employment,
and how mother was more contented; and last Wednesday, when I called
at the post at Treddles'on I found a letter from her. I think thee'dst perhaps like to read it; but I didna say anything about it, because thee'st
seemed so full of other things. It's quite easy t' read—she writes wonderful for a woman."

Seth had drawn the letter from his pocket and held it out to Adam,
who said, as he took it,

"Aye, lad, I've got a tough load to carry just now—thee mustna take
it ill if I'm a bit silent and crustier nor usual. Trouble doesna make me
care the less for thee. I know we shall stick together to the last."

"I take nought ill o' thee, Adam: I know well enough what it means
if thee't a bit short wi' me now and then."

"There's mother opening the door to look out for us," said Adam, as
they mounted the slope. "She's been sitting i' the dark as usual. Well,
Gyp, well! art glad to see me?"

Lisbeth went in again quickly and lighted a candle, for she had heard
the welcome rustling of footsteps on the grass, before Gyp's joyful bark.

"Eh, my lads! th' hours war ne'er so long sin' I war born as they'n
been this blessed Sunday night. What can ye both ha' been doin' till
this time?"

"Thee shouldstna sit i' the dark, mother," said Adam; "that makes
the time seem longer."

"Eh, what am I to do wi' burnin' candle of a Sunday, when there's
on'y me, an' it's sin to do a bit o' knittin'? The daylight's long enough
for me to stare i' th' booke as I canna read. It 'ud be a fine way o'
shortenin' the time, to make it waste the good candle. But which on
you's for ha'in' supper? Ye mun ayther be clemmed or full, I should
think, seein' what time o' night it is."

"I'm hungry, mother," said Seth, seating himself at the little table,
which had been spread ever since it was light.

"I've had my supper," said Adam. "Here, Gyp," he added, taking some cold potato from the table, and rubbing the rough grey head that looked up towards him.

"Thee needstna be gi'in th' dog," said Lispeth: "I'n fed him well a'ready. I'm not likely to forget him, I reckon, when he's all o' thee I can get sight on."

"Come, then, Gyp," said Adam, "we'll go to bed. Good-night, mother; I'm very tired."

"What ails him, dost know?" Lisbeth said to Seth, when Adam was gone up-stairs. "He's like as if he was struck for death this day or two —he's so cast down. I found him i' the shop this forenoon, arter thee wast gone, a-sittin' an' doin' nothin'—not so much as a booke afore him."

"He's a deal o' work upon him just now, mother," said Seth, "and I think he's a bit troubled in his mind. Don't you take notice of it, because it hurts him when you do. Be as kind to him as you can, mother, and don't say anything to vex him."

"Eh, what dost talk o' vexin' him? an' what am I like to be but kind? I'll ma' him a kettle-cake for breakfast i' the mornin'."

Adam, meanwhile, was reading Dinah's letter by the light of his dip candle.

"DEAR BROTHER SETH,—Your letter lay three days beyond my knowing of it at the Post, for I had not money enough by me to pay the carriage, this being a time of great need and sickness here, with the rains that have fallen, as if the windows of heaven were opened again; and to lay by money, from day to day, in such a time, when there are so many in present need of all things, would be a want of trust like the laying up of the manna. I speak of this, because I would not have you think me slow to answer, or that I had small joy in your rejoicing at the worldly good that has befallen your brother Adam. The honour and love you bear him is nothing but meet, for God has given him great gifts, and he uses them as the patriarch Joseph did, who, when he was exalted to a place of power and trust, yet yearned with tenderness towards his parents and his younger brother.

"My heart is knit to your aged mother since it was granted me to be near her in the day of trouble. Speak to her of me, and tell her I often bear her in my thoughts at evening time, when I am sitting in the dim light as I did with her, and we held one another's hands, and I spoke the words of comfort that were given to me. Ah, that is a blessed time, isn't it, Seth, when the outward light is fading, and the body is a little wearied with its work and its labour. Then the inward light shines the brighter, and we have a deeper sense of resting on the Divine strength. I sit on my chair in the dark room and close my eyes, and it is as if I was out of the body and could feel no want for evermore. For then, the very hardship, and the sorrow, and the blindness, and the sin I have beheld and been ready to weep over,—yea, all the anguish of the children of men, which sometimes wraps me round like sudden darkness—I can bear with a willing pain, as if I was sharing the Redeemer's cross. For I feel it, I feel it—infinite love is suffering too—yea, in the fulness of knowledge it suffers, it yearns, it mourns; and that is a blind self-seeking which wants to be freed from the sorrow wherewith the whole creation groaneth and travaileth. Surely it is not true blessedness to be free from sorrow, while there is sorrow and sin in the world: sorrow is then a part of love, and love does not seek to throw it off. It is not the spirit only that tells me this—I see it in the whole work and word of the gospel. Is there not pleading in heaven? Is not the Man of Sorrows there in that crucified body wherewith he ascended? And is He not one with the Infinite Love itself—as our love is one with our sorrow?

"These thoughts have been much borne in on me of late, and I have seen with new clearness the meaning of those words, 'If any man loves me, let him take up my cross.' I have heard this enlarged on as if it meant the troubles and persecutions we bring on ourselves by confessing Jesus. But surely that is a narrow thought. The true cross of the Redeemer was the sin and sorrow of this world—*that* was what lay on his heart—and that is the cross we shall share with him, that is the cup we must drink of with him, if we would have any part in that Divine Love which is one with his sorrow.

"In my outward lot, which you ask about, I have all things and abound. I have had constant work in the mill, though some of the other hands have been turned off for a time; and my body is greatly strengthened, so that I feel little weariness after long walking and speaking. What you say about staying in your own country with your mother and brother shows me that you have a true guidance: your lot is appointed there by a clear showing, and to seek a greater blessing elsewhere would be like laying a false offering on the altar and expecting the fire from heaven to kindle it. My work and my joy are here among the hills, and I sometimes think I cling too much to my life among the people here, and should be rebellious if I was called away.

"I was thankful for your tidings about the dear friends at the Hall Farm; for though I sent them a letter, by my aunt's desire, after I came back from my sojourn among them, I have had no word from them. My aunt has not the pen of a ready writer, and the work of the house is sufficient for the day, for she is weak in body. My heart cleaves to her and her children as the nearest of all to me in the flesh; yea, and to all in that house. I am carried away to them continually in my sleep, and often in the midst of work, and even of speech, the thought of them is borne in on me as if they were in need and trouble, which yet is dark to me. There may be some leading here; but I wait to be taught. You say they are all well.

"We shall see each other again in the body, I trust,—though, it may be, not for a long while; for the brethren and sisters at Leeds are desirous to have me for a short space among them, when I have a door opened me again to leave Snowfield.

"Farewell, dear Brother—and not yet farewell. For those children of God whom it has been granted to see each other face to face and to hold communion together and to feel the same spirit working in both, can nevermore be sundered, though the hills may lie between. For their souls are enlarged for evermore by that union, and they bear one another about in their thoughts continually as it were a new strength.—Your faithful Sister and fellow-worker in Christ,

DINAH MORRIS."

"I have not skill to write the words so small as you do, and my pen moves slow. And so I am straitened, and say but little of what is in my mind. Greet your mother for me with a kiss. She asked me to kiss her twice when we parted."

Adam had refolded the letter, and was sitting meditatively with his head resting on his arm at the head of the bed, when Seth came up-stairs.

"Hast read the letter?" said Seth.

"Yes," said Adam. "I don't know what I should ha' thought of her and her letter if I'd never seen her: I daresay I should ha' thought a preaching woman hateful. But she's one as makes everything seem right she says and does, and I seemed to see her and hear her speaking when I read the letter. It's wonderful how I remember her looks and her voice. She'd make thee rare and happy, Seth; she's just the woman for thee."

"It's no use thinking o' that," said Seth, despondingly. "She's spoke so firm, and she's not the woman to say one thing and mean another."

"Nay, but her feelings may grow different. A woman may get to love by degrees—the best fire doesna flare up the soonest. I'd have thee go and see her by-and-by: I'd make it conven'ent for thee to be away three or four days, and it 'ud be no walk for thee—only between twenty and thirty mile."

"I should like to see her again, whether or no, if she wouldna be displeased with me for going," said Seth.

"She'll be none displeased," said Adam, emphatically, getting up and throwing off his coat. "It might be a great happiness to us all, if she'd have thee, for mother took to her so wonderful, and seemed so contented to be with her."

"Ay," said Seth, rather timidly, "and Dinah's fond o' Hetty too; she thinks a deal about her."

Adam made no reply to that, and no other word but "good-night" passed between them.

CHAPTER XXXI

IN HETTY'S BED-CHAMBER

It was no longer light enough to go to bed without a candle, even in Mrs. Poyser's early household, and Hetty carried one with her as she went up at last to her bedroom soon after Adam was gone, and bolted the door behind her.

Now she would read her letter. It must—it must have comfort in it. How was Adam to know the truth? It was always likely he should say what he did say.

She set down the candle, and took out the letter. It had a faint scent of roses, which made her feel as if Arthur were close to her. She put it to her lips, and a rush of remembered sensations for a moment or two swept away all fear. But her heart began to flutter strangely, and her hands to tremble as she broke the seal. She read slowly; it was not easy for her to read a gentleman's handwriting, though Arthur had taken pains to write plainly.

"Dearest Hetty,—I have spoken truly when I have said that I loved you, and I shall never forget our love. I shall be your true friend as long as life lasts, and I hope to prove this to you in many ways. If I say anything to pain you in this letter, do not believe it is for want of love and tenderness towards you, for there is nothing I would not do for you, if I knew it to be really for your happiness. I cannot bear to think of my little Hetty shedding tears when I am not there to kiss them away; and if I followed only my own inclinations, I should be with her at this moment instead of writing. It is very hard for me to part from her—harder still for me to write words which may seem unkind, though they spring from the truest kindness.

"Dear, dear Hetty, sweet as our love has been to me, sweet as it would be to me for you to love me always, I feel that it would have been better for us both if we had never had that happiness, and that it is my duty to ask you to love me and care for me as little as you can. The fault has all been mine, for though I have been unable to resist the longing to be near you, I have felt all the while that your affection for me might cause you grief. I ought to have resisted my feelings. I should have done so, if I had been a better fellow than I am; but now, since the past cannot be altered, I am bound to save you from any evil that I have power to prevent. And I feel it would be a great evil for you if your affections continued so fixed on me that you could think of no other man who might be able to make you happier by his love than I ever can, and if you continued to look towards something in the future which cannot possibly happen. For, dear Hetty, if I were to do what you one day spoke of, and make you my wife, I should do what you yourself would come to feel was for your misery instead of your welfare. I know you can never be happy except by marrying a man in your own station; and if I were to marry you now, I should only be adding to any wrong I have done, besides offending against my duty in the other relations of life. You know nothing, dear Hetty, of the world in which I must always live, and you would soon begin to dislike me, because there would be so little in which we should be alike.

"And since I cannot marry you, we must part—we must try not to feel like lovers any more. I am miserable while I say this, but nothing else can be. Be angry with me, my sweet one, I deserve it; but do not believe that I shall not always care for you—always be grateful to you—always remember my Hetty; and if any trouble should come that we do not now foresee, trust in me to do everything that lies in my power.

"I have told you where you are to direct a letter to, if you want to write, but I put it down below lest you should have forgotten. Do not write unless there is something I can really do for you; for, dear Hetty, we must try to think of each other as little as we can. Forgive me, and try to forget everything about me, except that I shall be, as long as I live, your affectionate friend,

ARTHUR DONNITHORNE."

Slowly Hetty had read this letter; and when she looked up from it there was the reflection of a blanched face in the old dim glass—a white marble face with rounded childish forms, but with something sadder than a child's pain in it. Hetty did not see the face—she saw nothing—she only felt that she was cold and sick and trembling. The letter shook and rustled in her hand. She laid it down. It was a horrible sensation—this cold and trembling: it swept away the very ideas that produced it, and Hetty got up to reach a warm cloak from her clothes-press, wrapped it round her, and sat as if she were thinking of nothing but getting warm. Presently she took up the letter with a firmer hand, and began to read it through again. The tears came this time—great rushing tears, that blinded her and blotched the paper. She felt nothing but that Arthur was cruel—cruel to write so, cruel not to marry her. Reasons why he could not marry her had no existence for her mind; how could she believe in any misery that could come to her from the fulfilment of all she had been longing for and dreaming of? She had not the ideas that could make up the notion of that misery.

As she threw down the letter again, she caught sight of her face in the glass; it was reddened now, and wet with tears; it was almost like a companion that she might complain to—that would pity her. She leaned forward on her elbows, and looked into those dark overflooding eyes, and at that quivering mouth, and saw how the tears came thicker and thicker, and how the mouth became convulsed with sobs.

The shattering of all her little dream-world, the crushing blow on her new-born passion, afflicted her pleasure-craving nature with an overpowering pain that annihilated all impulse to resistance, and suspended her anger. She sat sobbing till the candle went out, and then, wearied, aching, stupefied with crying, threw herself on the bed without undressing, and went to sleep.

There was a feeble dawn in the room when Hetty awoke, a little after four o'clock, with a sense of dull misery, the cause of which broke upon her gradually, as she began to discern the objects round her in the dim light. And then came the frightening thought that she had to conceal her misery, as well as to bear it, in this dreary daylight that was coming. She could lie no longer: she got up and went towards the table: there lay the letter; she opened her treasure-drawer: there lay the earrings and the locket—the signs of all her short happiness—the signs of the life-long dreariness that was to follow it. Looking at the little trinkets which she had once eyed and fingered so fondly as the earnest of her future paradise of finery, she lived back in the moments when they had been given to her with such tender caresses, such strangely pretty words, such glowing looks which filled her with a bewildering delicious surprise—they were so much sweeter than she had thought anything could be. And the Arthur who had spoken to her and looked at her in this way, who was present with her now—whose arm she felt round her, his cheek against hers, his very breath upon her—was the cruel, cruel Arthur who had written that letter:—that letter which she snatched and crushed and then opened again, that she might read it once more. The half-benumbed mental condition which was the effect of the last night's violent crying, made it necessary for her to look again and see if her wretched thoughts were actually true—if the letter was really so cruel. She had to hold it close to the window, else she could not have read it by the faint light. Yes! it was worse—it was more cruel. She crushed it up again in her anger. She hated the writer of that letter—hated him for the very reason that she hung upon him with all her love—all the girlish passion and vanity that made up her love.

She had no tears this morning. She had wept them all away last night, and now she felt that dry-eyed morning misery, which is worse than the first shock, because it has the future in it as well as the present. Every morning to come, as far as her imagination could stretch, she would have to get up and feel that the day would have no joy for her. For there is no despair so absolute as that which comes with the first moments of our first great sorrow, when we have not yet known what it is to have suffered and be healed, to have despaired and to have recovered hope. As Hetty began languidly to take off the clothes she had worn all the night, that she might wash herself and brush her hair, she had the sickening sense that her life would go on in this way: she should always be doing things she had no pleasure in, getting up to the old tasks of work, seeing people she cared nothing about, going to church, and to Treddleston, and to tea with Mrs. Best, and carrying no happy thought with her. For her short poisonous delights had spoiled for ever all the little joys that had once made the sweetness of her life—the new frock ready for Treddleston fair, the party at Mr. Britton's at Broxton Wake, the beaux that she would say "No" to for a long while, and the prospect of the wedding that was to come at last when she would have a silk gown and a great many clothes all at once. These things were all flat and dreary to her now: everything would be a weariness: and she would carry about for ever a hopeless thirst and longing.

She paused in the midst of her languid undressing, and leaned against the dark old clothes-press. Her neck and arms were bare, her hair hung down in delicate rings; and they were just as beautiful as they were that night two months ago, when she walked up and down this bed-chamber glowing with vanity and hope. She was not thinking of her neck and arms now; even her own beauty was indifferent to her. Her eyes wandered sadly over the dull old chamber, and then looked out vacantly towards the growing dawn. Did a remembrance of Dinah come across her mind? —of her foreboding words, which had made her angry?—of Dinah's affectionate entreaty to think of her as a friend in trouble? No, the impression had been too slight to recur. Any affection or comfort Dinah could have given her would have been as indifferent to Hetty this morning as everything else was except her bruised passion. She was only thinking she could never stay here and go on with the old life—she could better bear something quite new than sinking back into the old everyday round. She would like to run away that very morning, and never see any of the old faces again. But Hetty's was not a nature to face difficulties —to dare to loose her hold on the familiar, and rush blindly on some unknown condition. Hers was a luxurious and vain nature, not a passionate one; and if she were ever to take any violent measure, she must be urged to it by the desperation of terror. There was not much room for her thoughts to travel in the narrow circle of her imagination, and she soon fixed on the one thing she would do to get away from her old life: she would ask her uncle to let her go to be a lady's-maid. Miss Lydia's maid would help her to get a situation, if she knew Hetty had her uncle's leave.

When she had thought of this, she fastened up her hair and began to wash: it seemed more possible to her to go down-stairs and try to behave as usual. She would ask her uncle this very day. On Hetty's blooming health it would take a great deal of such mental suffering as hers to leave any deep impress; and when she was dressed as neatly as usual in her working-dress, with her hair tucked up under her little cap, an indifferent observer would have been more struck with the young roundness of her cheek and neck, and the darkness of her eyes and eyelashes, than with any signs of sadness about her. But when she took up the crushed letter and put it in her drawer, that she might lock it out of sight, hard smarting tears, having no relief in them as the great drops had that fell last night, forced their way into her eyes. She wiped them away quickly: she must not cry in the day-time: nobody should find out how miserable she was, nobody should know she was disappointed about anything; and the thought that the eyes of her aunt and uncle would be upon her, gave her the self-command which often accompanies a great dread. For Hetty looked out from her secret misery towards the possibility of their ever knowing what had happened, as the sick and weary prisoner might think of the possible pillory. They would think her conduct shameful; and shame was torture. That was poor little Hetty's conscience.

So she locked up her drawer and went away to her early work.

In the evening, when Mr. Poyser was smoking his pipe, and his good-nature was therefore at its superlative moment, Hetty seized the opportunity of her aunt's absence to say,

"Uncle, I wish you'd let me go for a lady's-maid."

Mr. Poyser took the pipe from his mouth, and looked at Hetty in mild surprise for some moments. She was sewing, and went on with her work industriously.

"Why, what's put that into your head, my wench?" he said at last, after he had given one conservative puff.

"I should like it—I should like it better than farm-work."

"Nay, nay; you fancy so because you donna know it, my wench. It wouldn't be half so good for your health, nor for your luck i' life. I'd like you to stay wi' us till you've got a good husband: you're my own niece, and I wouldn't have you go to service, though it was a gentleman's house, as long as I've got a home for you."

Mr. Poyser paused, and puffed away at his pipe.

"I like the needlework," said Hetty, "and I should get good wages."

"Has your aunt been a bit sharp wi' you?" said Mr. Poyser, not noticing Hetty's further argument. "You mustna mind that, my wench—she does it for your good. She wishes you well; an' there isn't many aunts as are no kin to you 'ud ha' done by you as she has."

"No, it isn't my aunt," said Hetty, "but I should like the work better."

"It was all very well for you to learn the work a bit—an' I gev my consent to that fast enough, sin' Mrs. Pomfret was willing to teach you. For if anything was t' happen, it's well to know how to turn your hand to different sorts o' things. But I niver meant you to go to service, my wench; my family's ate their own bread and cheese as fur back as anybody knows, hanna they, father? You wouldna like your grandchild to take wage?"

"Na-a-y," said old Martin, with an elongation of the word, meant to make it bitter as well as negative, while he leaned forward and looked down on the floor. "But the wench takes arter her mother. I'd hard work t' hould *her* in, an' she married i' spite o' me—a feller wi' on'y two head o' stock when there should ha' been ten on's farm—she might well die o' th' inflammation afore she war thirty."

It was seldom that the old man made so long a speech; but his son's question had fallen like a bit of dry fuel on the embers of a long unextinguished resentment, which had always made the grandfather more indifferent to Hetty than to his son's children. Her mother's fortune had been spent by that good-for-nought Sorrel, and Hetty had Sorrel's blood in her veins.

"Poor thing, poor thing!" said Martin the younger, who was sorry to have provoked this retrospective harshness. "She'd but bad luck. But Hetty's got as good a chance o' getting a solid, sober husband as any gell i' this country."

After throwing out this pregnant hint, Mr. Poyser recurred to his pipe and his silence, looking at Hetty to see if she did not give some sign of having renounced her ill-advised wish. But instead of that, Hetty, in spite of herself, began to cry, half out of ill-temper at the denial, half out of the day's repressed sadness.

"Hegh, hegh!" said Mr. Poyser, meaning to check her playfully, "don't let's have any crying. Crying's for them as ha' got no home, not for them as want to get rid o' one. What dost think?" he continued to his wife, who now came back into the house-place, knitting with fierce rapidity, as if that movement were a necessary function, like the twittering of a crab's antennæ.

"Think?—why, I think we shall have the fowl stole before we are much older, wi' that gell forgetting to lock the pens up o' nights. What's the matter, now, Hetty? What are you crying at?"

"Why, she's been wanting to go for a lady's-maid," said Mr. Poyser. "I tell her we can do better for her nor that."

"I thought she'd got some maggot in her head, she's gone about wi' her mouth buttoned up so all day. It's all wi' going so among them servants at the Chase, as we war fools for letting her. She thinks it 'ud be a finer life than being wi' them as are akin to her, and ha' brought her up sin' she war no bigger nor Marty. She thinks there's nothing belongs to being a lady's-maid but wearing finer clothes nor she was born to, I'll be bound. It's what rag she can get to stick on her as she's thinking on from morning till night; as I often ask her if she wouldn't like to be the mawkin i' the field, for then she'd be made o' rags inside and out. I'll never gi' my consent to her going for a lady's-maid, while she's got good friends to take care on her till she's married to somebody better nor o' them valets, as is neither a common man nor a gentleman, an' must live on the fat o' the land, an's like enough to stick his hands under his coat tails and expect his wife to work for him."

"Ay, ay," said Mr. Poyser, "we must have a better husband for her nor that, and there's better at hand. Come, my wench, give over crying, and get to bed. I'll do better for you nor letting you go for a lady's-maid. Let's hear no more on't."

When Hetty was gone up-stairs he said,

"I canna make it out as she should want to go away, for I thought she'd got a mind t' Adam Bede. She's looked like it o' late."

"Eh, there's no knowing what she's got a liking to, for things take no more hold on her than if she was a dried pea. I believe that gell, Molly —as is aggravatin' enough, for the matter o' that—but I believe she'd care more about leaving us and the children, for all she's been here but a year come Michaelmas, nor Hetty would. But she's got this notion o' being a lady's-maid wi' going among them servants—we might ha' known what it 'ud lead to when we let her go to learn the fine work. But I'll put a stop to it pretty quick."

"Thee'dst be sorry to part wi' her, if it wasn't for her good," said Mr. Poyser. "She's useful to thee i' the work."

"Sorry? yes; I'm fonder on her nor she deserves—a little hard-hearted hussy, wanting to leave us i' that way. I can't ha' had her about me these seven year, I reckon, and done for her, and taught her everything, wi'out caring about her. An' here I'm having linen spun, an' thinking all the while it'll make sheeting and table-clothing for her when she's married, an' she'll live i' the parish wi' us, and never go out of our sights—like a fool as I am for thinking aught about her, as is no better nor a cherry wi' a hard stone inside it."

"Nay, nay, thee mustna make so much of a trifle," said Mr. Poyser, soothingly. "She's fond on us, I'll be bound; but she's young, an' gets things in her head as she can't rightly give account on. Them young fillies 'ull run away often wi'out knowing why."

Her uncle's answers, however, had another effect on Hetty besides that of disappointing her and making her cry. She knew quite well whom he had in his mind in his allusions to marriage, and to a sober, solid husband; and when she was in her bedroom again, the possibility of her marrying Adam presented itself to her in a new light. In a mind where no strong sympathies are at work, where there is no supreme sense of right to which the agitated nature can cling and steady itself to quiet endurance, one of the first results of sorrow is a desperate vague clutching after any deed that will change the actual condition. Poor Hetty's vision of consequences, at no time more than a narrow fantastic calculation of her own probable pleasures and pains, was now quite shut out by reckless irritation under present suffering, and she was ready for one of those convulsive, motiveless actions by which wretched men and women leap from a temporary sorrow into a life-long misery.

Why should she not marry Adam? She did not care what she did, so that it made some change in her life. She felt confident that he would still want to marry her, and any further thought about Adam's happiness in the matter had never yet visited her.

"Strange!" perhaps you will say, "this rush of impulse towards a course that might have seemed the most repugnant to her present state of mind, and in only the second night of her sadness!"

Yes, the actions of a little trivial soul like Hetty's, struggling amidst the serious, sad destinies of a human being, *are* strange. So are the motions of a little vessel without ballast tossed about on a stormy sea. How pretty it looked with its particoloured sail in the sunlight, moored in the quiet bay!

"Let that man bear the loss who loosed it from its moorings."

But that will not save the vessel—the pretty thing that might have been a lasting joy.

CHAPTER XXXII

MRS. POYSER "HAS HER SAY OUT"

THE next Saturday evening there was much excited discussion at the Donnithorne Arms concerning an incident which had occurred that very day—no less than a second appearance of the smart man in top-boots, said by some to be a mere farmer in treaty for the Chase Farm, by others to be the future steward; but by Mr. Casson himself, the personal witness to the stranger's visit, pronounced contemptuously to be nothing better than a bailiff, such as Satchell had been before him. No one had thought of denying Mr. Casson's testimony to the fact that he had seen the stranger, nevertheless he proffered various corroborating circumstances.

"I see him myself," he said; "I see him coming along by the Crab-tree meadow on a bald-faced hoss. I'd just been t' hev a pint—it was half after ten i' the forenoon, when I hev my pint as reg'lar as the clock—and I says to Knowles, as druv up with his waggon, 'You'll get a bit o' barley to-day, Knowles,' I says, 'if you look about you'; and then I went round by the rick-yard, and towart the Treddles'on road; and just as I come up by the big ash-tree, I see the man i' top-boots coming along on a bald-faced hoss—I wish I may never stir if I didn't. And I stood still till he come up, and I says, 'Good-morning, sir,' I says, for I wanted to hear the turn of his tongue, as I might know whether he was a this-country-man; so I says, 'Good-morning, sir: it'll 'old hup for the barley this morning, I think. There'll be a bit got hin, if we've good-luck.' And he says, 'Eh, ye may be raight, there's noo tallin',' he says; and I knowed by that"—here Mr. Casson gave a wink—"as he didn't come from a hundred mile off. I daresay he'd think me a hodd talker, as you Loamshire folks allays does hany one as talks the right language."

"The right language!" said Bartle Massey, contemptuously. "You're about as near the right language as a pig's squeaking is like a tune played on a key-bugle."

"Well, I don't know," answered Mr. Casson, with an angry smile. "I should think a man as has lived among the gentry from a b'y, is likely to know what's the right language pretty nigh as well as a schoolmaster."

"Ay, ay, man," said Bartle, with a tone of sarcastic consolation, "you talk the right language for *you*. When Mike Holdsworth's goat says ba-a-a, it's all right—it 'ud be unnatural for it to make any other noise."

The rest of the party being Loamshire men, Mr. Casson had the laugh strongly against him, and wisely fell back on the previous question, which, far from being exhausted in a single evening, was renewed in the churchyard, before service, the next day, with the fresh interest conferred on all news when there is a fresh person to hear it; and that fresh hearer was Martin Poyser, who, as his wife said, "never went boozin' with that set at Casson's, a-sittin' soakin'-in drink, and looking as wise as a lot o' cod-fish wi' red faces."

It was probably owing to the conversation she had had with her husband on their way from church, concerning this problematic stranger, that Mrs. Poyser's thoughts immediately reverted to him when, a day or two afterwards, as she was standing at the house door with her knitting, in that eager leisure which came to her when the afternoon cleaning was done, she saw the old Squire enter the yard on his black pony, followed by John the groom. She always cited it afterwards as a case of prevision, which really had something more in it than her own remarkable penetration, that the moment she set eyes on the Squire, she said to herself, "I shouldna wonder if he's come about that man as is a-going to take the Chase Farm, wanting Poyser to do something for him without pay. But Poyser's a fool if he does."

Something unwonted must clearly be in the wind, for the old Squire's visits to his tenantry were rare; and though Mrs. Poyser had during the last twelvemonth recited many imaginary speeches, meaning even more than met the ear, which she was quite determined to make to him the next time he appeared within the gates of the Hall Farm, the speeches had always remained imaginary.

"Good-day, Mrs. Poyser," said the old Squire, peering at her with his short-sighted eyes—a mode of looking at her which, as Mrs. Poyser observed, "allays aggravated her: it was as if you was a insect, and he was going to dab his finger-nail on you."

However, she said, "Your servant, sir," and curtsied with an air of perfect deference as she advanced towards him: she was not the woman to misbehave towards her betters, and fly in the face of the catechism, without severe provocation.

"Is your husband at home, Mrs. Poyser?"

"Yes, sir; he's only i' the rick-yard. I'll send for him in a minute, if you'll please to get down and step in."

"Thank you; I will do so. I want to consult him about a little matter; but you are quite as much concerned in it, if not more. I must have your opinion too."

"Hetty, run and tell your uncle to come in," said Mrs. Poyser, as they entered the house, and the old gentleman bowed low in answer to Hetty's curtsy; while Totty, conscious of a pinafore stained with goose-

berry jam, stood hiding her face against the clock, and peeping round
furtively.

"What a fine old kitchen this is!" said Mr. Donnithorne, looking
round admiringly. He always spoke in the same deliberate, well-chis-
elled, polite way, whether his words were sugary or venomous. "And you
keep it so exquisitely clean, Mrs. Poyser. I like these premises, do you
know, beyond any on the estate."

"Well, sir, since you're fond of 'em, I should be glad if you'd let a
bit o' repairs be done to 'em, for the boarding's i' that state, as we're
like to be eaten up wi' rats and mice; and the cellar, you may stan' up
to your knees i' water in't, if you like to go down; but perhaps you'd
rather believe my words. Won't you please to sit down, sir?"

"Not yet; I must see your dairy. I have not seen it for years, and I
hear on all hands about your fine cheese and butter," said the Squire,
looking politely unconscious that there could be any question on which
he and Mrs. Poyser might happen to disagree. "I think I see the door
open, there: you must not be surprised if I cast a covetous eye on your
cream and butter. I don't expect that Mrs. Satchell's cream and butter
will bear comparison with yours."

"I can't say, sir, I'm sure. It's seldom I see other folks's butter, though
there's some on it as one's no need to see—the smell's enough."

"Ah, now this I like," said Mr. Donnithorne, looking round at the
damp temple of cleanliness, but keeping near the door. "I'm sure I should
like my breakfast better if I knew the butter and cream came from this
dairy. Thank you, that really is a pleasant sight. Unfortunately, my
slight tendency to rheumatism makes me afraid of damp: I'll sit down
in your comfortable kitchen. Ah, Poyser, how do you do? In the midst
of business, I see, as usual. I've been looking at your wife's beautiful
dairy—the best manager in the parish, is she not?"

Mr. Poyser had just entered in shirt-sleeves and open waistcoat, with
a face a shade redder than usual, from the exertion of "pitching." As
he stood, red, rotund, and radiant, before the small, wiry, cool, old
gentleman, he looked like a prize apple by the side of a withered crab.

"Will you please to take this chair, sir?" he said, lifting his father's
arm-chair forward a little: "you'll find it easy."

"No, thank you, I never sit in easy-chairs," said the old gentleman,
seating himself on a small chair near the door. "Do you know, Mrs.
Poyser—sit down, pray, both of you—I've been far from contented,
for some time, with Mrs. Satchell's dairy management. I think she has
not a good method, as you have."

"Indeed, sir, I can't speak to that," said Mrs. Poyser, in a hard voice,
rolling and unrolling her knitting, and looking icily out of the window,
as she continued to stand opposite the Squire. Poyser might sit down if
he liked, she thought: *she* wasn't going to sit down, as if she'd give in to
any such smooth-tongued palaver. Mr. Poyser, who looked and felt
the reverse of icy, did sit down in his three-cornered chair.

"And now, Poyser, as Satchell is laid up, I am intending to let the Chase Farm to a respectable tenant. I'm tired of having a farm on my own hands—nothing is made the best of in such cases, as you know. A satisfactory bailiff is hard to find; and I think you and I, Poyser, and your excellent wife here, can enter into a little arrangement in consequence, which will be to our mutual advantage."

"Oh," said Mr. Poyser, with a good-natured blankness of imagination as to the nature of the arrangement.

"If I'm called upon to speak, sir," said Mrs. Poyser, after glancing at her husband with a pity at his softness, "you know better than me; but I don't see what the Chase Farm is t' us—we've cumber enough wi' our own farm. Not but what I'm glad to hear o' anybody respectable coming into the parish: there's some as ha' been brought in as hasn't been looked on i' that character."

"You're likely to find Mr. Thurle an excellent neighbour, I assure you: such a one as you will feel glad to have accommodated by the little plan I'm going to mention; especially as I hope you will find it as much to your own advantage as his."

"Indeed, sir, if it's anything t' our advantage, it'll be the first offer o' the sort I've heared on. It's them as take advantage that get advantage i' this world, *I* think: folks have to wait long enough afore it's brought to 'em."

"The fact is, Poyser," said the Squire, ignoring Mrs. Poyser's theory of worldly prosperity, "there is too much dairy land, and too little plough land, on the Chase Farm, to suit Thurle's purpose—indeed, he will only take the farm on condition of some change in it: his wife, it appears, is not a very clever dairy-woman like yours. Now, the plan I'm thinking of is to effect a little exchange. If you were to have the Hollow Pastures, you might increase your dairy, which must be so profitable under your wife's management; and I should request you, Mrs. Poyser, to supply my house with milk, cream, and butter at the market prices. On the other hand, Poyser, you might let Thurle have the lower and upper ridges, which really, with our wet seasons, would be a good riddance for you. There is much less risk in dairy land than corn land."

Mr. Poyser was leaning forward, with his elbows on his knees, his head on one side, and his mouth screwed up—apparently absorbed in making the tips of his fingers meet so as to represent with perfect accuracy the ribs of a ship. He was much too acute a man not to see through the whole business, and to foresee perfectly what would be his wife's view of the subject; but he disliked giving unpleasant answers: unless it was on a point of farming practice, he would rather give up than have a quarrel, any day; and, after all, it mattered more to his wife than to him. So after a few moments' silence, he looked up at her and said mildly, "What dost say?"

Mrs. Poyser had had her eyes fixed on her husband with cold severity during his silence, but now she turned away her head with a toss, looked

icily at the opposite roof of the cow-shed, and spearing her knitting together with the loose pin, held it firmly between her clasped hands.

"Say? Why, I say you may do as you like about giving up any o'
your corn land afore your lease is up, which it won't be for a year come
next Michaelmas, but I'll not consent to take more dairy work into my
hands, either for love or money; and there's nayther love nor money
here, as I can see, on'y other folks's love o' theirselves, and the money
as is to go into other folks's pockets. I know there's them as is born t'
own the land, and them as is born to sweat on't"—here Mrs. Poyser
paused to gasp a little—"and I know it's christened folks's duty to
submit to their betters as fur as flesh and blood 'ull bear it; but I'll
not make a martyr o' myself, and wear myself to skin and bone, and
worret myself as if I was a churn wi' butter a-coming in't, for no landlord in England, not if he was King George himself."

"No, no, my dear Mrs. Poyser, certainly not," said the Squire, still
confident in his own powers of persuasion, "you must not overwork
yourself; but don't you think your work will rather be lessened than
increased in this way? There is so much milk required at the Abbey,
that you will have little increase of cheese and butter making from the
addition to your dairy; and I believe selling milk is the most profitable
way of disposing of dairy produce, is it not?"

"Ay, that's true," said Mr. Poyser, unable to repress an opinion on
a question of farming profits, and forgetting that it was not in this
case a purely abstract question.

"I daresay," said Mrs. Poyser bitterly, turning her head halfway
towards her husband, and looking at the vacant arm-chair—"I daresay
it's true for men as sit i' th' chimney-corner and make believe as everything's cut wi' ins an' outs to fit int' everything else. If you could make
a pudding wi' thinking o' the batter, it 'ud be easy getting dinner. How
do I know whether the milk 'ull be wanted constant? What's to make
me sure as the house won't be put o' board wage afore we're many
months older, and then I may have to lie awake o' nights wi' twenty
gallons o' milk on my mind—and Dingall 'ull take no more butter, let
alone paying for it; and we must fat pigs till we're obliged to beg the
butcher on our knees to buy 'em, and lose half of 'em wi' the measles.
And there's the fetching and carrying, as 'ud be welly half a day's
work for a man an' hoss—*that's* to be took out o' the profits, I reckon?
But there's folks 'ud hold a sieve under the pump and expect to carry
away the water."

"That difficulty—about the fetching and carrying—you will not have,
Mrs. Poyser," said the Squire, who thought that this entrance into particulars indicated a distant inclination to compromise on Mrs. Poyser's
part—"Bethell will do that regularly with the cart and pony."

"O, sir, begging your pardon, I've never been used t' having gentlefolks's servants coming about my back places, a-making love to both
the gells at once, and keeping 'em with their hands on their hips listening to all manner o' gossip when they should be down on their knees

a-scouring. If we're to go to ruin, it shanna be wi' having our back kitchen turned into a public."

"Well, Poyser," said the Squire, shifting his tactics, and looking as if he thought Mrs. Poyser had suddenly withdrawn from the proceedings and left the room, "you can turn the Hollows into feeding-land. I can easily make another arrangement about supplying my house. And I shall not forget your readiness to accommodate your landlord as well as a neighbour. I know you will be glad to have your lease renewed for three years, when the present one expires; otherwise, I daresay Thurle, who is a man of some capital, would be glad to take both the farms, as they could be worked so well together. But I don't want to part with an old tenant like you."

To be thrust out of the discussion in this way would have been enough to compel Mrs. Poyser's exasperation, even without the final threat. Her husband, really alarmed at the possibility of their leaving the old place where he had been bred and born—for he believed the old Squire had small spite enough for anything—was beginning a mild remonstrance explanatory of the inconvenience he should find in having to buy and sell more stock, with—

"Well, sir, I think as it's ruther hard" . . . when Mrs. Poyser burst in with the desperate determination to have her say out this once, though it were to rain notices to quit, and the only shelter were the workhouse.

"Then, sir, if I may speak—as, for all I'm a woman, and there's folks as thinks a woman's fool enough to stan' by an' look on while the men sign her soul away, I've a right to speak, for I make one quarter o' the rent, and save another quarter—I say, if Mr. Thurle's so ready to take the farms under you, it's a pity but what he should take this, and see if he likes to live in a house wi' all the plagues o' Egypt in't— wi' the cellar full o' water, and frogs and toads hoppin' up the steps by dozens—and the floors rotten, and the rats and mice gnawing every bit o' cheese, and runnin' over our heads as we lie i' bed till we expect 'em to eat us up alive—as it's a mercy they hanna eat the children long ago. I should like to see if there's another tenant besides Poyser as 'ud put up wi' never having a bit o' repairs done till a place tumbles down —and not then, on'y wi' begging and praying, and having to pay half— and being strung up wi' the rent as it's much if he gets enough out o' the land to pay, for all he's put his own money into the ground before-hand. See if you'll get a stranger to lead such a life here as that: a mag-got must be born i' the rotten cheese to like it, I reckon. You may run away from my words, sir," continued Mrs. Poyser, following the old Squire beyond the door—for after the first moments of stunned sur-prise he had got up, and, waving his hands towards her with a smile, had walked out towards his pony. But it was impossible for him to get away immediately, for John was walking the pony up and down the yard, and was some distance from the causeway when his master beckoned.

"You may run away from my words, sir, and you may go spinnin'

underhand ways o' doing us a mischief, for you've got Old Harry to
your friend, though nobody else is, but I tell you for once as we're not
dumb creaturs to be abused and made money on by them as ha' got
the lash i' their hands, for want o' knowing how t' undo the tackle. An'
if I'm th' only one as speaks my mind, there's plenty o' the same way
o' thinking i' this parish and the next to 't, for your name's no better
than a brimstone match in everybody's nose—if it isna two-three old
folks as you think o' saving your soul by giving 'em a bit o' flannel and
a drop o' porridge. An' you may be right i' thinking it'll take but little
to save your soul, for it'll be the smallest savin' y' iver made, wi' all
your scrapin'."

There are occasions on which two servant-girls and a waggoner may
be a formidable audience, and as the Squire rode away on his black
pony, even the gift of short-sightedness did not prevent him from
being aware that Molly and Nancy and Tim were grinning not far
from him. Perhaps he suspected that sour old John was grinning behind
him—which was also the fact. Meanwhile the bull-dog, the black-and-
tan terrier, Alick's sheep-dog, and the gander hissing at a safe distance
from the pony's heels, carried out the idea of Mrs. Poyser's solo in an
impressive quartette.

Mrs. Poyser, however, had no sooner seen the pony move off than she
turned round, gave the two hilarious damsels a look which drove them
back into the kitchen, and, unspearing her knitting, began to knit again
with her usual rapidity, as she reëntered the house.

"Thee'st done it now," said Mr. Poyser, a little alarmed and uneasy,
but not without some triumphant amusement at his wife's outbreak.

"Yes, I know I've done it," said Mrs. Poyser; "but I've had my say
out, and I shall be th' easier for't all my life. There's no pleasure i'
living, if you're to be corked up for ever, and only dribble your mind
out by the sly, like a leaky barrel. I shan't repent saying what I think,
if I live to be as old as th' old Squire; and there's little likelihoods—for
it seems as if them as aren't wanted here are th' only folks as aren't
wanted i' th' other world."

"But thee wutna like moving from th' old place, this Michaelmas
twelvemonth," said Mr. Poyser, "and going into a strange parish, where
thee know'st nobody. It'll be hard upon us both, and upo' father too."

"Eh, it's no use worreting; there's plenty o' things may happen
between this and Michaelmas twelvemonth. The Captain may be master
afore then, for what we know," said Mrs. Poyser, inclined to take an
unusually hopeful view of an embarrassment which had been brought
about by her own merit, and not by other people's fault.

"*I'm* none for worreting," said Mr. Poyser, rising from his three-
cornered chair, and walking slowly towards the door; "but I should be
loath to leave th' old place, and the parish where I was bred and born,
and father afore me. We should leave our roots behind us, I doubt, and
niver thrive again."

CHAPTER XXXIII

MORE LINKS

THE barley was all carried at last, and the harvest suppers went by without waiting for the dismal black crop of beans. The apples and nuts were gathered and stored; the scent of whey departed from the farmhouses, and the scent of brewing came in its stead. The woods behind the Chase, and all the hedgerow trees, took on a solemn splendour under the dark low-hanging skies. Michaelmas was come, with its fragrant basketfuls of purple damsons, and its paler purple daisies, and its lads and lasses leaving or seeking service, and winding along between the yellow hedges, with their bundles under their arms. But though Michaelmas was come, Mr. Thurle, that desirable tenant, did not come to the Chase Farm, and the old Squire, after all, had been obliged to put in a new bailiff. It was known throughout the two parishes that the Squire's plan had been frustrated because the Poysers had refused to be "put upon," and Mrs. Poyser's outbreak was discussed in all the farmhouses with a zest which was only heightened by frequent repetition. The news that "Bony" was come back from Egypt was comparatively insipid, and the repulse of the French in Italy was nothing to Mrs. Poyser's repulse of the old Squire. Mr. Irwine had heard a version of it in every parishioner's house, with the one exception of the Chase. But since he had always, with marvellous skill, avoided any quarrel with Mr. Donnithorne, he could not allow himself the pleasure of laughing at the old gentleman's discomfiture with any one besides his mother, who declared that if she were rich she should like to allow Mrs. Poyser a pension for life, and wanted to invite her to the parsonage, that she might hear an account of the scene from Mrs. Poyser's own lips.

"No, no, mother," said Mr. Irwine; "it was a little bit of irregular justice on Mrs. Poyser's part, but a magistrate like me must not countenance irregular justice. There must be no report spread that I have taken notice of the quarrel, else I shall lose the little good influence I have over the old man."

"Well, I like that woman even better than her cream-cheeses," said Mrs. Irwine. "She has the spirit of three men, with that pale face of hers; and she says such sharp things too."

"Sharp! yes, her tongue is like a new-set razor. She's quite original in her talk, too; one of those untaught wits that help to stock a country with proverbs. I told you that capital thing I heard her say about Craig—that he was like a cock who thought the sun had risen to hear him crow. Now that's an Æsop fable in a sentence."

"But it will be a bad business if the old gentleman turns them out of the farm next Michaelmas, eh?" said Mrs. Irwine.

"O, that must not be; and Poyser is such a good tenant, that Donnithorne is likely to think twice, and digest his spleen rather than turn him out. But if he should give them notice at Lady Day, Arthur and I must move heaven and earth to mollify him. Such old parishioners as they are must not go."

"Ah, there's no knowing what may happen before Lady Day," said Mrs. Irwine. "It struck me on Arthur's birthday that the old man was a little shaken: he's eighty-three, you know. It's really an unconscionable age. It's only women who have a right to live as long as that."

"When they've got old-bachelor sons who would be forlorn without them," said Mr. Irwine, laughing, and kissing his mother's hand.

Mrs. Poyser, too, met her husband's occasional forebodings of a notice to quit with "There's no knowing what may happen before Lady Day":—one of those undeniable general propositions which are usually intended to convey a particular meaning very far from undeniable. But it is really too hard upon human nature that it should be held a criminal offence to imagine the death even of the king when he is turned eighty-three. It is not to be believed that any but the dullest Britons can be good subjects under that hard condition.

Apart from this foreboding, things went on much as usual in the Poyser household. Mrs. Poyser thought she noticed a surprising improvement in Hetty. To be sure, the girl got "closer tempered, and sometimes she seemed as if there'd be no drawing a word from her with cart-ropes"; but she thought much less about her dress, and went after the work quite eagerly, without any telling. And it was wonderful how she never wanted to go out now—indeed, could hardly be persuaded to go; and she bore her aunt's putting a stop to her weekly lesson in fine-work at the Chase, without the least grumbling or pouting. It must be, after all, that she had set her heart on Adam at last, and her sudden freak of wanting to be a lady's-maid must have been caused by some little pique or misunderstanding between them, which had passed by. For whenever Adam came to the Hall Farm, Hetty seemed to be in better spirits, and to talk more than at other times, though she was almost sullen when Mr. Craig or any other admirer happened to pay a visit there.

Adam himself watched her at first with trembling anxiety, which gave way to surprise and delicious hope. Five days after delivering Arthur's letter, he had ventured to go to the Hall Farm again—not without dread lest the sight of him might be painful to her. She was not in the house-place when he entered, and he sat talking to Mr. and Mrs. Poyser for a few minutes with a heavy fear on his heart that they might presently tell him Hetty was ill. But by-and-by there came a light step that he knew, and when Mrs. Poyser said, "Come, Hetty, where have you been?" Adam was obliged to turn round, though he was afraid to see the changed look there must be in her face. He almost started when he saw her smiling as if she were pleased to see him—looking the same as ever at a first glance, only that she had her cap on, which he had

never seen her in before when he came of an evening. Still, when he
looked at her again and again as she moved about or sat at her work,
there was a change: the cheeks were as pink as ever, and she smiled
as much as she had ever done of late, but there was something different
in her eyes, in the expression of her face, in all her movements, Adam
thought—something harder, older, less child-like. "Poor thing!" he said
to himself, "that's allays likely. It's because she's had her first heartache. But she's got a spirit to bear up under it. Thank God for that."

As the weeks went by, and he saw her always looking pleased to see
him—turning up her lovely face towards him as if she meant him to
understand that she was glad for him to come—and going about her
work in the same equable way, making no sign of sorrow, he began to
believe that her feelings towards Arthur must have been much slighter
than he had imagined in his first indignation and alarm, and that she
had been able to think of her girlish fancy that Arthur was in love with
her and would marry her, as a folly of which she was timely cured.
And it perhaps was, as he had sometimes in his more cheerful moments
hoped it would be—her heart was really turning with all the more
warmth towards the man she knew to have a serious love for her.

Possibly you think that Adam was not at all sagacious in his interpretations, and that it was altogether extremely unbecoming in a sensible
man to behave as he did—falling in love with a girl who really had
nothing more than her beauty to recommend her, attributing imaginary
virtues to her, and even condescending to cleave to her after she had
fallen in love with another man, waiting for her kind looks as a patient
trembling dog waits for his master's eye to be turned upon him. But in
so complex a thing as human nature, we must consider, it is hard to
find rules without exceptions. Of course, I know that, as a rule, sensible
men fall in love with the most sensible women of their acquaintance,
see through all the pretty deceits of coquettish beauty, never imagine
themselves loved when they are not loved, cease loving on all proper
occasions, and marry the woman most fitted for them in every respect
—indeed, so as to compel the approbation of all the maiden ladies in
their neighbourhood. But even to this rule an exception will occur now
and then in the lapse of centuries, and my friend Adam was one. For
my own part, however, I respect him none the less: nay, I think the
deep love he has for that sweet, rounded, blossom-like, dark-eyed Hetty,
of whose inward self he was really very ignorant, came out of the
very strength of his nature, and not out of any inconsistent weakness.
Is it any weakness, pray, to be wrought on by exquisite music?—to feel
its wondrous harmonies searching the subtlest windings of your soul,
the delicate fibres of life where no memory can penetrate, and binding
together your whole being past and present in one unspeakable vibration: melting you in one moment with all the tenderness, all the love
that has been scattered through the toilsome years, concentrating in
one emotion of heroic courage or resignation all the hard-learnt lessons
of self-renouncing sympathy, blending your present joy with past sor-

row, and your present sorrow with all your past joy? If not, then neither
is it a weakness to be so wrought upon by the exquisite curves of a
woman's cheek and neck and arms, by the liquid depths of her beseeching eyes, or the sweet childish pout of her lips. For the beauty of a
lovely woman is like music: what can one say more? Beauty has an
expression beyond and far above the one woman's soul that it clothes,
as the words of genius have a wider meaning than the thought that
prompted them: it is more than a woman's love that moves us in a
woman's eyes—it seems to be a far-off mighty love that has come near
to us, and made speech for itself there; the rounded neck, the dimpled
arm, move us by something more than their prettiness—by their close
kinship with all we have known of tenderness and peace. The noblest
nature sees the most of this *impersonal* expression in beauty (it is needless to say that there are gentlemen with whiskers dyed and undyed
who see none of it whatever), and for this reason, the noblest nature is
often the most blinded to the character of the one woman's soul that
the beauty clothes. Whence, I fear, the tragedy of human life is likely
to continue for a long time to come, in spite of mental philosophers
who are ready with the best receipts for avoiding all mistakes of the
kind.

Our good Adam had no fine words into which he could put his feeling
for Hetty: he could not disguise mystery in this way with the appearance of knowledge; he called his love frankly a mystery, as you have
heard him. He only knew that the sight and memory of her moved him
deeply, touching the spring of all love and tenderness, all faith and
courage within him. How could he imagine narrowness, selfishness, hardness in her? He created the mind he believed in out of his own, which
was large, unselfish, tender.

The hopes he felt about Hetty softened a little his feeling towards
Arthur. Surely his attentions to Hetty must have been of a slight kind;
they were altogether wrong, and such as no man in Arthur's position
ought to have allowed himself, but they must have had an air of playfulness about them, which had probably blinded him to their danger,
and had prevented him from laying any strong hold on Hetty's heart.
As the new promise of happiness rose for Adam, his indignation and
jealousy began to die out: Hetty was not made unhappy; he almost
believed that she liked him best; and the thought sometimes crossed
his mind that the friendship which had once seemed dead for ever
might revive in the days to come, and he would not have to say "good-
by" to the grand old woods, but would like them better because they
were Arthur's. For this new promise of happiness, following so quickly
on the shock of pain, had an intoxicating effect on the sober Adam, who
had all his life been used to much hardship and moderate hope. Was
he really going to have an easy lot after all? It seemed so; for at the
beginning of November, Jonathan Burge, finding it impossible to replace Adam, had at last made up his mind to offer him a share in the
business, without further condition than that he should continue to

give his energies to it, and renounce all thought of having a separate business of his own. Son-in-law or no son-in-law, Adam had made himself too necessary to be parted with, and his headwork was so much more important to Burge than his skill in handicraft, that his having the management of the woods made little difference in the value of his services; and as to the bargains about the Squire's timber, it would be easy to call in a third person. Adam saw here an opening into a broadening path of prosperous work, such as he had thought of with ambitious longing ever since he was a lad: he might come to build a bridge, or a town-hall, or a factory, for he had always said to himself that Jonathan Burge's building business was like an acorn, which might be the mother of a great tree. So he gave his hand to Burge on that bargain, and went home with his mind full of happy visions, in which (my refined reader will perhaps be shocked when I say it) the image of Hetty hovered and smiled over plans for seasoning timber at a trifling expense, calculations as to the cheapening of bricks per thousand by water-carriage, and a favourite scheme for the strengthening of roofs and walls with a peculiar form of iron girder. What then? Adam's enthusiasm lay in these things; and our love is inwrought in our enthusiasm as electricity is inwrought in the air, exalting its power by a subtle presence.

Adam would be able to take a separate house now, and provide for his mother in the old one; his prospects would justify his marrying very soon, and if Dinah consented to have Seth, their mother would perhaps be more contented to live apart from Adam. But he told himself that he would not be hasty—he would not try Hetty's feeling for him until it had had time to grow strong and firm. However, to-morrow, after church, he would go to the Hall Farm and tell them the news. Mr. Poyser, he knew, would like it better than a five-pound note, and he should see if Hetty's eyes brightened at it. The months would be short with all he had to fill his mind, and this foolish eagerness which had come over him of late must not hurry him into any premature words. Yet when he got home and told his mother the good news, and ate his supper, while she sat by almost crying for joy, and wanting him to eat twice as much as usual because of his good-luck, he could not help preparing her gently for the coming change, by talking of the old house being too small for them all to go on living in it always.

CHAPTER XXXIV

THE BETROTHAL

It was a dry Sunday, and really a pleasant day for the 2d of November. There was no sunshine, but the clouds were high, and the wind was so still that the yellow leaves which fluttered down from the hedgerow elms must have fallen from pure decay. Nevertheless, Mrs. Poyser did not go to church, for she had taken a cold too serious to be neglected;

only two winters ago she had been laid up for weeks with a cold; and since his wife did not go to church, Mr. Poyser considered that on the whole it would be as well for him to stay away too and "keep her company." He could perhaps have given no precise form to the reasons that determined this conclusion; but it is well known to all experienced minds that our firmest convictions are often dependent on subtle impressions for which words are quite too coarse a medium. However it was, no one from the Poyser family went to church that afternoon except Hetty and the boys; yet Adam was bold enough to join them after church, and said that he would walk home with them, though all the way through the village he appeared to be chiefly occupied with Marty and Tommy, telling them about the squirrels in Binton Coppice, and promising to take them there some day. But when they came to the fields he said to the boys, "Now, then, which is the stoutest walker? Him as gets to th' home-gate first shall be the first to go with me to Binton Coppice on the donkey. But Tommy must have the start up to the next stile, because he's the smallest."

Adam had never behaved so much like a determined lover before. As soon as the boys had both set off, he looked down at Hetty, and said, "Won't you hang on my arm, Hetty?" in a pleading tone, as if he had already asked her and she had refused. Hetty looked up at him smilingly and put her round arm through his in a moment. It was nothing to her—putting her arm through Adam's; but she knew he cared a great deal about having her arm through his, and she wished him to care. Her heart beat no faster, and she looked at the half-bare hedgerows and the ploughed field with the same sense of oppressive dulness as before. But Adam scarcely felt that he was walking; he thought Hetty must know that he was pressing her arm a little—a very little; words rushed to his lips that he dared not utter—that he had made up his mind not to utter yet; and so he was silent for the length of that field. The calm patience with which he had once waited for Hetty's love, content only with her presence and the thought of the future, had forsaken him since that terrible shock nearly three months ago. The agitations of jealousy had given a new restlessness to his passion—had made fear and uncertainty too hard almost to bear. But though he might not speak to Hetty of his love, he would tell her about his new prospects, and see if she would be pleased. So when he was enough master of himself to talk, he said—

"I'm going to tell your uncle some news that'll surprise him, Hetty; and I think he'll be glad to hear it too."

"What's that?" Hetty said, indifferently.

"Why, Mr. Burge offered me a share in his business, and I'm going to take it."

There was a change in Hetty's face, certainly not produced by any agreeable impression from this news. In fact she felt a momentary annoyance and alarm; for she had so often heard it hinted by her uncle that Adam might have Mary Burge and a share in the business any

day if he liked, that she associated the two objects now, and the thought
immediately occurred that perhaps Adam had given her up because of
what had happened lately, and had turned towards Mary Burge. With
that thought, and before she had time to remember any reasons why
it could not be true, came a new sense of forsakenness and disappointment: the one thing—the one person—her mind had rested on in all its
dull weariness, had slipped away from her, and peevish misery filled her
eyes with tears. She was looking on the ground, but Adam saw her face,
saw the tears, and before he had finished saying, "Hetty, dear Hetty,
what are you crying for?" his eager rapid thought had flown through
all the causes conceivable to him, and at last alighted on half the true
one. Hetty thought he was going to marry Mary Burge—she didn't like
him to marry—perhaps she didn't like him to marry any one but herself? All caution was swept away—all reason for it was gone, and Adam
could feel nothing but trembling joy. He leaned towards her and took
her hand, as he said—

"I could afford to be married now, Hetty—I could make a wife comfortable; but I shall never want to be married if you won't have me."

Hetty looked up at him, and smiled through her tears as she had done
to Arthur that first evening in the wood, when she had thought he was
not coming, and yet he came. It was a feebler relief, a feebler triumph
she felt now, but the great dark eyes and the sweet lips were as beautiful
as ever, perhaps more beautiful, for there was a more luxuriant womanliness about Hetty of late. Adam could hardly believe in the happiness
of that moment. His right hand held her left, and he pressed her arm
close against his heart as he leaned down towards her.

"Do you really love me, Hetty? Will you be my own wife, to love and
take care of as long as I live?"

Hetty did not speak, but Adam's face was very close to hers, and she
put up her round cheek against his, like a kitten. She wanted to be
caressed—she wanted to feel as if Arthur were with her again.

Adam cared for no words after that, and they hardly spoke through
the rest of the walk. He only said, "I may tell your uncle and aunt,
mayn't I, Hetty?" and she said, "Yes."

The red fire-light on the hearth at the Hall Farm shone on joyful
faces that evening, when Hetty was gone up-stairs and Adam took the
opportunity of telling Mr. and Mrs. Poyser and the grandfather that
he saw his way to maintaining a wife now, and that Hetty had consented
to have him.

"I hope you have no objections against me for her husband," said
Adam; "I'm a poor man as yet, but she shall want nothing as I can
work for."

"Objections?" said Mr. Poyser, while the grandfather leaned forward
and brought out his long "Nay, nay." "What objections can we ha' to
you, lad? Never mind your being poorish as yet; there's money in your
head-piece as there's money i' the sown field, but it must ha' time.
You'n got enough to begin on, and we can do a deal tow'rt the bit o'

furniture you'll want. Thee'st got feathers and linen to spare—plenty, eh?"

This question was of course addressed to Mrs. Poyser, who was wrapped up in a warm shawl, and was too hoarse to speak with her usual facility. At first she only nodded emphatically, but she was presently unable to resist the temptation to be more explicit.

"It 'ud be a poor tale if I hadna feathers and linen," she said, hoarsely, "when I never sell a fowl but what's plucked, and the wheel's a-going every day o' the week."

"Come, my wench," said Mr. Poyser, when Hetty came down, "come and kiss us, and let us wish you luck."

Hetty went very quietly and kissed the big good-natured man.

"There!" he said, patting her on the back, "go and kiss your aunt and your grandfather. I'm as wishful t' have you settled well as if you was my own daughter; and so's your aunt, I'll be bound, for she's done by you this seven 'ear, Hetty, as if you'd been her own. Come, come, now," he went on, becoming jocose, as soon as Hetty had kissed her aunt and the old man, "Adam wants a kiss too, I'll warrant, and he's a right to one now."

Hetty turned away, smiling, towards her empty chair.

"Come, Adam, then, take one," persisted Mr. Poyser, "else y' arena half a man."

Adam got up, blushing like a small maiden—great strong fellow as he was—and, putting his arm round Hetty, stooped down and gently kissed her lips.

It was a pretty scene in the red fire-light: for there were no candles; why should there be, when the fire was so bright, and was reflected from all the pewter and the polished oak? No one wanted to work on a Sunday evening. Even Hetty felt something like contentment in the midst of all this love. Adam's attachment to her, Adam's caress, stirred no passion in her, were no longer enough to satisfy her vanity; but they were the best her life offered her now—they promised her some change.

There was a great deal of discussion before Adam went away, about the possibility of his finding a house that would do for him to settle in. No house was empty except the one next to Will Maskery's in the village, and that was too small for Adam now. Mr. Poyser insisted that the best plan would be for Seth and his mother to move, and leave Adam in the old home, which might be enlarged after a while, for there was plenty of space in the woodyard and garden; but Adam objected to turning his mother out.

"Well, well," said Mr. Poyser at last, "we needna fix everything to-night. We must take time to consider. You canna think o' getting married afore Easter. I'm not for long courtships, but there must be a bit o' time to make things comfortable."

"Ay, to be sure," said Mrs. Poyser, in a hoarse whisper; "Christian folks can't be married like cuckoos, I reckon."

"I'm a bit daunted, though," said Mr. Poyser, "when I think as we may have notice to quit, and belike be forced to take a farm twenty mile off."

"Eh," said the old man, staring at the floor, and lifting his hands up and down, while his arms rested on the elbows of his chair, "it's a poor tale if I mun leave th' ould spot, an' be buried in a strange parish. An' you'll happen ha' double rates to pay," he added, looking up at his son.

"Well, thee mustna fret beforehand, father," said Martin the younger. "Happen the Captain 'ull come home and make our peace wi' th' old Squire. I build upo' that, for I know the Captain 'll see folks righted if he can."

CHAPTER XXXV

THE HIDDEN DREAD

It was a busy time for Adam—the time between the beginning of November and the beginning of February, and he could see little of Hetty, except on Sundays. But a happy time, nevertheless; for it was taking him nearer and nearer to March, when they were to be married; and all the little preparations for their new housekeeping marked the progress towards the longed-for day. Two new rooms had been "run up" to the old house, for his mother and Seth were to live with them after all. Lisbeth had cried so piteously at the thought of leaving Adam, that he had gone to Hetty and asked her if, for the love of him, she would put up with his mother's ways, and consent to live with her. To his great delight, Hetty said, "Yes; I'd as soon she lived with us as not." Hetty's mind was oppressed at that moment with a worse difficulty than poor Lisbeth's ways, she could not care about them. So Adam was consoled for the disappointment he had felt when Seth had come back from his visit to Snowfield and said "it was no use—Dinah's heart wasna turned towards marrying." For when he told his mother that Hetty was willing they should all live together, and there was no more need of them to think of parting, she said, in a more contented tone than he had heard her speak in since it had been settled that he was to be married, "Eh, my lad, I'll be as still as th' ould tabby, an' ne'er want to do aught but th' offal work, as *she* wonna like t' do. An' then, we needna part the platters an' things, as ha' stood on the shelf together sin' afore thee wast born."

There was only one cloud that now and then came across Adam's sunshine: Hetty seemed unhappy sometimes. But to all his anxious, tender questions, she replied with an assurance that she was quite contented and wished nothing different; and the next time he saw her she was more lively than usual. It might be that she was a little overdone with work and anxiety now, for soon after Christmas Mrs. Poyser had taken another cold, which had brought on inflammation, and this illness had confined her to her room all through January. Hetty had to manage everything down-stairs, and half supply Molly's place too, while that good damsel waited on her mistress; and she seemed to throw herself so entirely into her new functions, working with a grave steadiness which was new in her, that Mr. Poyser often told Adam she was wanting to show him what a good housekeeper he would have; but he "doubted the lass was o'erdoing it—she must have a bit o' rest when her aunt could come down-stairs."

This desirable event of Mrs. Poyser's coming down-stairs happened in the early part of February, when some mild weather thawed the last patch of snow on the Binton Hills. On one of these days, soon after her aunt came down, Hetty went to Treddleston to buy some of the wedding things which were wanting, and which Mrs. Poyser had scolded her for neglecting, observing that she supposed "it was because they were not for th' outside, else she'd ha' bought 'em fast enough."

It was about ten o'clock when Hetty set off, and the slight hoar-frost that had whitened the hedges in the early morning had disappeared as the sun mounted the cloudless sky. Bright February days have a stronger charm of hope about them than any other days in the year. One likes to pause in the mild rays of the sun, and look over the gates at the patient plough-horses turning at the end of the furrow, and think that the beautiful year is all before one. The birds seem to feel just the same: their notes are as clear as the clear air. There are no leaves on the trees and hedgerows, but how green all the grassy fields are! and the dark purplish brown of the ploughed earth and of the bare branches is beautiful too. What a glad world this looks like, as one drives or rides along the valleys and over the hills! I have often thought so when, in foreign countries, where the fields and woods have looked to me like our English Loamshire—the rich land tilled with just as much care, the woods rolling down the gentle slopes to the green meadows—I have come on something by the roadside which has reminded me that I am not in Loamshire: an image of a great agony—the agony of the Cross. It has stood perhaps by the clustering apple-blossoms, or in the broad sunshine by the cornfield, or at a turning by the wood where a clear brook was gurgling below; and surely, if there came a traveller to this world who knew nothing of the story of man's life upon it, this image of agony would seem to him strangely out of place in the midst of this joyous nature. He would not know that hidden behind the apple-blossoms, or among the golden corn, or under the shrouding boughs of the wood, there might be a human heart beating heavily with anguish; perhaps a young blooming girl, not knowing where to turn for refuge from swift-advancing shame; understanding no more of this life of ours than a foolish lost lamb wandering farther and farther in the nightfall on the lonely heath; yet tasting the bitterest of life's bitterness.

Such things are sometimes hidden among the sunny fields and behind

he blossoming orchards; and the sound of the gurgling brook, if you
ame close to one spot behind a small bush, would be mingled for your
ar with a despairing human sob. No wonder man's religion has much
orrow in it: no wonder he needs a Suffering God.

Hetty, in her red cloak and warm bonnet, with her basket in her
and, is turning towards a gate by the side of the Treddleston road,
)ut not that she may have a more lingering enjoyment of the sunshine,
nd think with hope of the long unfolding year. She hardly knows that
he sun is shining; and for weeks, now, when she has hoped at all, it
las been for something at which she herself trembles and shudders. She
•nly wants to be out of the highroad, that she may walk slowly, and
lot care how her face looks, as she dwells on wretched thoughts; and
hrough this gate she can get into a field-path behind the wide thick
ledgerows. Her great dark eyes wander blankly over the fields like the
:yes of one who is desolate, homeless, unloved, not the promised bride
)f a brave, tender man. But there are no tears in them: her tears were
ll wept away in the weary night, before she went to sleep. At the next
tile the pathway branches off: there are two roads before her—one
dong by the hedgerow, which will by-and-by lead her into the road
igain; the other across the fields, which will take her much farther out
)f the way into the Scantlands, low shrouded pastures where she will
ee nobody. She chooses this, and begins to walk a little faster, as if she
lad suddenly thought of an object towards which it was worth while to
lasten. Soon she is in the Scantlands, where the grassy land slopes grad-
lally downwards, and she leaves the level ground to follow the slope.
'arther on there is a clump of trees on the low ground, and she is mak-
ng her way towards it. No, it is not a clump of trees, but a dark
hrouded pool, so full with the wintry rains that the under boughs
)f the elder-bushes lie low beneath the water. She sits down on the
grassy bank, against the stooping stem of the great oak that hangs over
he dark pool. She has thought of this pool often in the nights of the
nonth that has just gone by, and now at last she comes to see it. She
:lasps her hands round her knees and leans forward, and looks earnestly
lt it, as if trying to guess what sort of bed it would make for her young
ound limbs.

No, she has not courage to jump into that cold watery bed, and if
.he had, they might find her—they might find out why she had drowned
lerself. There is but one thing left to her: she must go away, go where
hey can't find her.

After the first on-coming of her great dread, some weeks after her
)etrothal to Adam, she had waited and waited, in the blind vague hope
hat something would happen to set her free from her terror; but she
:ould wait no longer. All the force of her nature had been concentrated
)n the one effort of concealment, and she had shrunk with irresistible
lread from every course that could tend towards a betrayal of her mis-
•rable secret. Whenever the thought of writing to Arthur had occurred
:o her, she had rejected it: he could do nothing for her that would shelter

her from discovery and scorn among the relatives and neighbours wh
once more made all her world, now her airy dream had vanished. He
imagination no longer saw happiness with Arthur, for he could d
nothing that would satisfy or soothe her pride. No, something els
would happen—something *must* happen—to set her free from this dread
In young, childish, ignorant souls there is constantly this blind trust i
some unshapen chance: it is as hard to a boy or girl to believe that
great wretchedness will actually befall them, as to believe that they wil
die.

But now necessity was pressing hard upon her—now the time of he
marriage was close at hand—she could no longer rest in this blind trus
She must run away; she must hide herself where no familiar eyes coul
detect her; and *then* the terror of wandering out into the world, c
which she knew nothing, made the possibility of going to Arthur
thought which brought some comfort with it. She felt so helpless now
so unable to fashion the future for herself, that the prospect of throw
ing herself on him had a relief in it which was stronger than her prid
As she sat by the pool, and shuddered at the dark cold water, the hop
that he would receive her tenderly—that he would care for her an
think for her—was like a sense of lulling warmth, that made her for th
moment indifferent to everything else; and she began now to think c
nothing but the scheme by which she should get away.

She had a letter from Dinah lately, full of kind words about the com
ing marriage, which she had heard of from Seth; and when Hetty ha
read this letter aloud to her uncle, he had said, "I wish Dinah 'ud com
again now, for she'd be a comfort to your aunt when you're gone. Wha
do you think, my wench, o' going to see her as soon as you can b
spared, and persuading her to come back wi' you? You might happe
persuade her wi' telling her as her aunt wants her, for all she writes c
not being able to come." Hetty had not liked the thought of going t
Snowfield, and felt no longing to see Dinah, so she only said, "It's s
far off, uncle." But now she thought this proposed visit would serve as
pretext for going away. She would tell her aunt when she got home agai
that she should like the change of going to Snowfield for a week or te
days. And then, when she got to Stoniton, where nobody knew her, sh
would ask for the coach that would take her on the way to Windso
Arthur was at Windsor, and she would go to him.

As soon as Hetty had determined on this scheme, she rose from th
grassy bank of the pool, took up her basket, and went on her way t
Treddleston, for she must buy the wedding things she had come out fo
though she would never want them. She must be careful not to rais
any suspicion that she was going to run away.

Mrs. Poyser was quite agreeably surprised that Hetty wished to g
and see Dinah, and try to bring her back to stay over the wedding. Th
sooner she went the better, since the weather was pleasant now; an
Adam, when he came in the evening, said, if Hetty could set off to-mo

row, he would make time to go with her to Treddleston, and see her safe into the Stoniton coach.

"I wish I could go with you and take care of you, Hetty," he said, the next morning, leaning in at the coach door; "but you won't stay much beyond a week—the time'll seem long."

He was looking at her fondly, and his strong hand held hers in its grasp. Hetty felt a sense of protection in his presence—she was used to it now: if she could have had the past undone, and known no other love than her quiet liking for Adam! The tears rose as she gave him the last look.

"God bless her for loving me," said Adam, as he went on his way to work again, with Gyp at his heels.

But Hetty's tears were not for Adam—not for the anguish that would come upon him when he found she was gone from him for ever. They were for the misery of her own lot, which took her away from this brave tender man who offered up his whole life to her, and threw her, a poor helpless suppliant, on the man who would think it a misfortune that she was obliged to cling to him.

At three o'clock that day, when Hetty was on the coach that was to take her, they said, to Leicester—part of the long, long way to Windsor —she felt dimly that she might be travelling all this weary journey towards the beginning of new misery.

Yet Arthur was at Windsor; he would surely not be angry with her. If he did not mind about her as he used to do, he had promised to be good to her.

BOOK FIVE

★

CHAPTER XXXVI

THE JOURNEY IN HOPE

A LONG lonely journey, with sadness in the heart; away from the familiar to the strange: that is a hard and dreary thing even to the rich, the strong, the instructed: a hard thing, even when we are called by duty, not urged by dread.

What was it then to Hetty? With her poor narrow thoughts, no longer melting into vague hopes, but pressed upon by the chill of definite fear; repeating again and again the same small round of memories—shaping again and again the same childish, doubtful images of what was to come—seeing nothing in this wide world but the little history of her own pleasures and pains; with so little money in her pocket, and the way so long and difficult. Unless she could afford always to go in the coaches—and she felt sure she could not, for the journey to Stoniton was more expensive than she had expected—it was plain that she must trust to carriers' carts or slow waggons; and what a time it would be before she could get to the end of her journey! The burly old coachman from Oakbourne, seeing such a pretty young woman among the outside passengers, had invited her to come and sit beside him; and feeling that it became him as a man and a coachman to open the dialogue with a joke, he applied himself as soon as they were off the stones to the elaboration of one suitable in all respects. After many cuts with his whip and glances at Hetty out of the corner of his eye, he lifted his lips above the edge of his wrapper and said,

"He's pretty nigh six foot, I'll be bound, isna he, now?"

"Who?" said Hetty, rather startled.

"Why, the sweetheart as you've left behind, or else him as you're goin' arter—which is it?"

Hetty felt her face flushing and then turning pale. She thought this coachman must know something about her. He must know Adam, and might tell him where she was gone, for it is difficult to country people to believe that those who make a figure in their own parish are not known everywhere else, and it was equally difficult to Hetty to understand that chance words could happen to apply closely to her circumstances. She was too frightened to speak.

"Hegh, hegh!" said the coachman, seeing that his joke was not so gratifying as he had expected, "you munna take it too ser'ous; if he's behaved ill, get another. Such a pretty lass as you can get a sweetheart any day."

Hetty's fear was allayed by-and-by, when she found that the coach-man made no further allusion to her personal concerns; but it still had the effect of preventing her from asking him what were the places on the road to Windsor. She told him she was only going a little way out of Stoniton, and when she got down at the inn where the coach stopped, she hastened away with her basket to another part of the town. When she had formed her plan of going to Windsor, she had not foreseen any difficulties except that of getting away; and after she had overcome this by proposing the visit to Dinah, her thoughts flew to the meeting with Arthur, and the question how he would behave to her—not resting on any probable incidents of the journey. She was too entirely ignorant of travelling to imagine any of its details, and with all her store of money—her three guineas—in her pocket, she thought herself amply provided. It was not until she found how much it cost her to get to Stoniton that she began to be alarmed about the journey, and then, for the first time, she felt her ignorance as to the places that must be passed on her way. Oppressed with this new alarm, she walked along the grim Stoniton streets, and at last turned into a shabby little inn, where she hoped to get a cheap lodging for the night. Here she asked the landlord if he could tell her what places she must go to, to get to Windsor.

"Well, I can't rightly say. Windsor must be pretty nigh London, for it's where the king lives," was the answer. "Anyhow, you'd best go t' Ashby next—that's south'ard. But there's as many places from here to London as there's houses in Stoniton, by what I can make out. I've never been no traveller myself. But how comes a lone young woman like you, to be thinking o' taking such a journey as that?"

"I'm going to my brother—he's a soldier at Windsor," said Hetty, frightened at the landlord's questioning look. "I can't afford to go by the coach; do you think there's a cart goes toward Ashby in the morning?"

"Yes, there may be carts if anybody knowed where they started from; but you might run over the town before you found out. You'd best set off and walk, and trust to summat overtaking you."

Every word sank like lead on Hetty's spirits; she saw the journey stretch bit by bit before her now; even to get to Ashby seemed a hard thing: it might take the day, for what she knew, and that was nothing to the rest of the journey. But it must be done—she must get to Arthur: oh, how she yearned to be again with somebody who would care for her! She who had never got up in the morning without the certainty of seeing familiar faces, people on whom she had an acknowledged claim; whose farthest journey had been to Rosseter on the pillion with her uncle; whose thoughts had always been taking holiday in dreams of pleasure, because all the business of her life was managed for her:—this kitten-like Hetty, who till a few months ago had never felt any other grief than that of envying Mary Burge a new ribbon, or being girded at by

her aunt for neglecting Totty, must now make her toilsome way in
loneliness, her peaceful home left behind for ever, and nothing but a
tremulous hope of distant refuge before her. Now for the first time, as
she lay down to-night in the strange hard bed, she felt that her home
had been a happy one, that her uncle had been very good to her, that
her quiet lot at Hayslope among the things and people she knew, with
her little pride in her one best gown and bonnet, and nothing to hide
from any one, was what she would like to wake up to as a reality, and
find that all the feverish life she had known besides was a short nightmare. She thought of all she had left behind with yearning regret for her
own sake: her own misery filled her heart: there was no room in it for
other people's sorrow. And yet, before the cruel letter, Arthur had been
so tender and loving: the memory of that had still a charm for her
though it was no more than a soothing draught that just made pain
bearable. For Hetty could conceive no other existence for herself in
future than a hidden one, and a hidden life, even with love, would have
had no delights for her; still less a life mingled with shame. She knew no
romances, and had only a feeble share in the feelings which are the
source of romance, so that well-read ladies may find it difficult to understand her state of mind. She was too ignorant of everything beyond the
simple notions and habits in which she had been brought up, to have
any more definite idea of her probable future than that Arthur would
take care of her somehow, and shelter her from anger and scorn. He
would not marry her and make her a lady; and apart from that she
could think of nothing he could give towards which she looked with
longing and ambition.

The next morning she rose early, and taking only some milk and
bread for her breakfast, set out to walk on the road towards Ashby,
under a leaden-coloured sky, with a narrowing streak of yellow, like a
departing hope, on the edge of the horizon. Now in her faintness of
heart at the length and difficulty of her journey, she was most of all
afraid of spending her money, and becoming so destitute that she would
have to ask people's charity; for Hetty had the pride not only of a
proud nature but of a proud class—the class that pays the most poor-
rates, and most shudders at the idea of profiting by a poor-rate. It had
not yet occurred to her that she might get money for her locket and
earrings which she carried with her, and she applied all her small
arithmetic and knowledge of prices to calculating how many meals and
how many rides were contained in her two guineas, and the odd shillings,
which had a melancholy look, as if they were the pale ashes of the other
bright-flaming coin.

For the first few miles out of Stoniton she walked on bravely, always
fixing on some tree or gate or projecting bush at the most distant
visible point in the road as a goal, and feeling a faint joy when she had
reached it. But when she came to the fourth milestone, the first she
had happened to notice among the long grass by the roadside, and read
that she was still only four miles beyond Stoniton, her courage sank.

he had come only this little way, and yet felt tired, and almost hungry
again in the keen morning air; for though Hetty was accustomed to
much movement and exertion in-doors, she was not used to long walks,
which produce quite a different sort of fatigue from that of household
activity. As she was looking at the milestone she felt some drops falling
on her face—it was beginning to rain. Here was a new trouble which
had not entered into her sad thoughts before; and quite weighed down
by this sudden addition to her burden, she sat down on the step of a
stile and began to sob hysterically. The beginning of hardship is like
the first taste of bitter food—it seems for a moment unbearable; yet, if
there is nothing else to satisfy our hunger, we take another bite and
find it possible to go on. When Hetty recovered from her burst of weeping, she rallied her fainting courage: it was raining, and she must try
to get on to a village where she might find rest and shelter. Presently,
as she walked on wearily, she heard the rumbling of heavy wheels
behind her; a covered waggon was coming, creeping slowly along with
a slouching driver cracking his whip beside the horses. She waited for
it, thinking that if the waggoner were not a very sour-looking man, she
would ask him to take her up. As the waggon approached her, the driver
had fallen behind, but there was something in the front of the big
vehicle which encouraged her. At any previous moment in her life she
would not have noticed it; but now, the new susceptibility that suffering had awakened in her caused this object to impress her strongly. It
was only a small white-and-liver-coloured spaniel which sat on the
front ledge of the waggon, with large timid eyes, and an incessant
trembling in the body, such as you may have seen in some of these small
creatures. Hetty cared little for animals, as you know, but at this moment she felt as if the helpless timid creature had some fellowship with
her, and without being quite aware of the reason, she was less doubtful
about speaking to the driver, who now came forward—a large ruddy
man, with a sack over his shoulders by way of scarf or mantle.

"Could you take me up in your waggon, if you're going towards
Ashby?" said Hetty. "I'll pay you for it."

"Aw," said the big fellow, with that slowly-dawning smile which belongs to heavy faces, "I can take y' up fawst enough wi'out bein' paid
for't if you dooant mind lyin' a bit closish a-top o' the wool-packs. Where
do you coom from? and what do you want at Ashby?"

"I come from Stoniton. I'm going a long way—to Windsor."

"What! arter some service, or what?"

"Going to my brother—he's a soldier there."

"Well, I'm going no furder nor Leicester—and fur enough too—but
I'll take you, if you dooant mind being a bit long on the road. Th'
hosses wooant feel *your* weight no more nor they feel the little doog
here, as I puck up on the road a fortni't agoo. He war lost, I b'lieve,
an's been all of a tremble iver sin'. Come, gi' us your basket, an' come
behind and let me put y' in."

To lie on the wool-packs, with a cranny left between the curtains of

the awning to let in the air, was luxury to Hetty now, and she half slep
away the hours till the driver came to ask her if she wanted to get dow
and have "some victual"; he himself was going to eat his dinner at th
"public." Late at night they reached Leicester, and so this second da
of Hetty's journey was past. She had spent no money except what sh
had paid for food, but she felt that this slow journey would be intol
erable for her another day, and in the morning she found her way to :
coach-office to ask about the road to Windsor, and see if it would cos
too much to go part of the distance by coach again. Yes! the distanc
was too great—the coaches were too dear—she must give them up; bu
the elderly clerk at the office, touched by her pretty anxious face, wrot
down for her the names of the chief places she must pass through. Thi
was the only comfort she got in Leicester, for the men stared at her a
she went along the street, and for the first time in her life Hetty wishe
no one would look at her. She set out walking again; but this day sh
was fortunate, for she was soon overtaken by a carrier's cart which car
ried her to Hinckley, and by the help of a return chaise, with a drunke
postilion,—who frightened her by driving like Jehu the son of Nimshi
and shouting hilarious remarks at her, twisting himself backwards o
his saddle,—she was before night in the heart of woody Warwickshire
but still almost a hundred miles from Windsor, they told her. O what
large world it was, and what hard work for her to find her way in it
She went by mistake to Stratford-on-Avon, finding Stratford set dow
in her list of places, and then she was told she had come a long wa
out of the right road. It was not till the fifth day that she got to Ston
Stratford. That seems but a slight journey as you look at the map, o
remember your own pleasant travels to and from the meadowy banks o
the Avon. But how wearily long it was to Hetty! It seemed to her as i
this country of flat fields and hedgerows, and dotted houses, and vil
lages, and market-towns—all so much alike to her indifferent eyes—
must have no end, and she must go on wandering among them for ever
waiting tired at toll-gates for some cart to come, and then finding th
cart went only a little way—a very little way—to the miller's a mile o
perhaps; and she hated going into the public-houses, where she mus
go to get food and ask questions, because there were always men loung
ing there, who stared at her and joked her rudely. Her body was ver
weary too with these days of new fatigue and anxiety; they had mad
her look more pale and worn than all the time of hidden dread she ha
gone through at home. When at last she reached Stony Stratford, he
impatience and weariness had become too strong for her economic
caution; she determined to take the coach for the rest of the way
though it should cost her all her remaining money. She would nee
nothing at Windsor but to find Arthur. When she had paid the fare fo
the last coach, she had only a shilling; and as she got down at th
sign of the Green Man in Windsor at twelve o'clock in the middle o
the seventh day, hungry and faint, the coachman came up, and begge
her to "remember him." She put her hand in her pocket, and took ou

he shilling, but the tears came with the sense of exhaustion and the hought that she was giving away her last means of getting food, which he really required before she could go in search of Arthur. As she held ut the shilling, she lifted up her dark tear-filled eyes to the coachman's ace and said, "Can you give me back sixpence?"

"No, no," he said gruffly, "never mind—put the shilling up again."

The landlord of the Green Man had stood near enough to witness this cene, and he was a man whose abundant feeding served to keep his ood-nature, as well as his person, in high condition. And that lovely earful face of Hetty's would have found out the sensitive fibre in most 1en.

"Come, young woman, come in," he said, "and have a drop o' some-hing; you're pretty well knocked up: I can see that."

He took her into the bar and said to his wife, "Here, missis, take this oung woman into the parlour; she's a little overcome,"—for Hetty's ars were falling fast. They were merely hysterical tears: she thought he had no reason for weeping now, and was vexed that she was too reak and tired to help it. She was at Windsor at last, not far from rthur.

She looked with eager, hungry eyes at the bread and meat and beer hat the landlady brought her, and for some minutes she forgot every-hing else in the delicious sensations of satisfying hunger and recover-1g from exhaustion. The landlady sat opposite to her as she ate, and ooked at her earnestly. No wonder: Hetty had thrown off her bonnet, nd her curls had fallen down: her face was all the more touching in its outh and beauty because of its weary look; and the good woman's eyes resently wandered to her figure, which in her hurried dressing on her ourney she had taken no pains to conceal; moreover, the stranger's eye etects what the familiar unsuspecting eye leaves unnoticed.

"Why, you're not very fit for travelling," she said, glancing while she poke at Hetty's ringless hand. "Have you come far?"

"Yes," said Hetty, roused by this question to exert more self-com-1and, and feeling the better for the food she had taken. "I've come a ood long way, and it's very tiring. But I'm better now. Could you tell 1e which way to go to this place?" Here Hetty took from her pocket a it of paper: it was the end of Arthur's letter on which he had written is address.

While she was speaking, the landlord had come in, and had begun to ook at her as earnestly as his wife had done. He took up the piece of aper which Hetty handed across the table, and read the address.

"Why, what do you want at this house?" he said. It is in the nature f innkeepers, and all men who have no pressing business of their own, o ask as many questions as possible before giving information.

"I want to see a gentleman as is there," said Hetty.

"But there's no gentleman there," returned the landlord. "It's shut p—been shut up this fortnight. What gentleman is it you want? Per-aps I can let you know where to find him."

"It's Captain Donnithorne," said Hetty, tremulously, her heart beginning to beat painfully at this disappointment of her hope that she should find Arthur at once.

"Captain Donnithorne? Stop a bit," said the landlord, slowly. "Was he in the Loamshire Militia? A tall young officer with a fairish skin and reddish whiskers—and had a servant by the name o' Pym?"

"O yes," said Hetty; "you know him—where is he?"

"A fine sight o' miles away from here: the Loamshire Militia's gone to Ireland; it's been gone this fortnight."

"Look there! she's fainting," said the landlady, hastening to support Hetty, who had lost her miserable consciousness and looked like a beautiful corpse. They carried her to the sofa and loosened her dress.

"Here's a bad business, I suspect," said the landlord, as he brought in some water.

"Ah, it's plain enough what sort of business it is," said the wife. "She's not a common flaunting dratchell, I can see that. She looks like a respectable country girl, and she comes from a good way off, to judge by her tongue. She talks something like that ostler we had that come from the north: he was as honest a fellow as we ever had about the house—they're all honest folks in the north."

"I never saw a prettier young woman in my life," said the husband. "She's like a pictur in a shop-winder. It goes to one's 'eart to look at her."

"It 'ud have been a good deal better for her if she'd been uglier and had more conduct," said the landlady, who on any charitable construction must have been supposed to have more "conduct" than beauty. "But she's coming to again. Fetch a drop more water."

CHAPTER XXXVII

THE JOURNEY IN DESPAIR

HETTY was too ill through the rest of that day for any questions to be addressed to her—too ill even to think with any distinctness of the evils that were to come. She only felt that all her hope was crushed, and that instead of having found a refuge she had only reached the borders of a new wilderness where no goal lay before her. The sensations of bodily sickness, in a comfortable bed, and with the tendance of the good-natured landlady, made a sort of respite for her; such respite as there is in the faint weariness which obliges a man to throw himself on the sand, instead of toiling onward under the scorching sun.

But when sleep and rest had brought back the strength necessary for the keenness of mental suffering,—when she lay the next morning looking at the growing light which was like a cruel taskmaster returning to urge from her a fresh round of hated hopeless labour,—she began to think what course she must take, to remember that all her money was

one, to look at the prospect of further wandering among strangers
with the new clearness shed on it by the experience of her journey to
Windsor. But which way could she turn? It was impossible for her to
enter into any service, even if she could obtain it: there was nothing but
immediate beggary before her. She thought of a young woman who had
been found against the church wall at Hayslope one Sunday, nearly
dead with cold and hunger—a tiny infant in her arms: the woman was
rescued and taken to the parish. "The parish!" You can perhaps hardly
understand the effect of that word on a mind like Hetty's, brought up
among people who were somewhat hard in their feelings even towards
poverty, who lived among the fields, and had little pity for want and
rags as a cruel inevitable fate such as they sometimes seem in cities,
but held them a mark of idleness and vice—and it was idleness and vice
that brought burthens on the parish. To Hetty the "parish" was next
to the prison in obloquy; and to ask anything of strangers—to beg—
lay in the same far-off hideous region of intolerable shame that Hetty
had all her life thought it impossible she could ever come near. But
now the remembrance of that wretched woman whom she had seen herself, on her way from church, being carried into Joshua Rann's, came
back upon her with the new terrible sense that there was very little
now to divide *her* from the same lot. And the dread of bodily hardship
mingled with the dread of shame; for Hetty had the luxurious nature
of a round, soft-coated pet animal.

How she yearned to be back in her safe home again, cherished and
cared for as she had always been! Her aunt's scolding about trifles
would have been music to her ears now: she longed for it: she used to
fear it in a time when she had only trifles to hide. Could she be the
same Hetty that used to make up the butter in the dairy with the
gueldres roses peeping in at the window—she, a runaway whom her
friends would not open their doors to again, lying in this strange bed,
with the knowledge that she had no money to pay for what she received, and must offer those strangers some of the clothes in her basket?
It was then she thought of her locket and earrings, and seeing her pocket
lie near, she reached it and spread the contents on the bed before her.
There were the locket and earrings in the little velvet-lined boxes, and
with them there was a beautiful silver thimble which Adam had bought
her, the words "Remember me" making the ornament of the border; a
steel purse, with her one shilling in it, and a small red-leather case fastening with a strap. Those beautiful little earrings with their delicate
pearls and garnet, that she had tried in her ears with such longing in
the bright sunshine on the 30th of July! She had no longing to put
them in her ears now: her head with its dark rings of hair lay back
languidly on the pillow, and the sadness that rested about her brow
and eyes was something too hard for regretful memory. Yet she put her
hands up to her ears: it was because there were some thin gold rings in
them, which were also worth a little money. Yes, she could surely get
some money for her ornaments: those Arthur had given her must have

cost a great deal of money. The landlord and landlady had been goo
to her; perhaps they would help her to get the money for these things.

But this money would not keep her long: what should she do whe
it was gone? Where should she go? The horrible thought of want an
beggary drove her once to think she would go back to her uncle an
aunt, and ask them to forgive her and have pity on her. But she shran
from that idea again, as she might have shrunk from scorching metal
she could never endure that shame before her uncle and aunt, befor
Mary Burge, and the servants at the Chase, and the people at Broxtor
and everybody who knew her. They should never know what had hap
pened to her. What *could* she do? She would go away from Windsor—
travel again as she had done the last week, and get among the fla
green fields with the high hedges round them, where nobody could se
her or know her; and there, perhaps, when there was nothing else sh
could do, she should get courage to drown herself in some pond like tha
in the Scantlands. Yes, she would get away from Windsor as soon a
possible: she didn't like these people at the inn to know about her, t
know that she had come to look for Captain Donnithorne: she mus
think of some reason to tell them why she had asked for him.

With this thought she began to put the things back into her pocke
meaning to get up and dress before the landlady came to her. She ha
her hand on the red-leather case, when it occurred to her that ther
might be something in this case which she had forgotten—somethin
worth selling; for without knowing what she should do with her lif
she craved the means of living as long as possible; and when we desi
eagerly to find something, we are apt to search for it in hopeless place
No, there was nothing but common needles and pins, and dried tulip
petals between the paper leaves where she had written down her litt
money-accounts. But on one of these leaves there was a name, which
often as she had seen it before, now flashed on Hetty's mind like
newly-discovered message. The name was *Dinah Morris, Snowfiel*
There was a text above it, written, as well as the name, by Dinah's ow
hand with a little pencil, one evening that they were sitting together an
Hetty happened to have the red case lying open before her. Hetty di
not read the text now: she was only arrested by the name. Now, for th
first time she remembered without indifference the affectionate kindne
Dinah had shown her, and those words of Dinah in the bed-chamber—
that Hetty must think of her as a friend in trouble. Suppose she wer
to go to Dinah, and ask her to help her? Dinah did not think abou
things as other people did: she was a mystery to Hetty, but Hetty kne
she was always kind. She couldn't imagine Dinah's face turning awa
from her in dark reproof or scorn, Dinah's voice willingly speaking i
of her, or rejoicing in her misery, as a punishment. Dinah did not seer
to belong to that world of Hetty's whose glance she dreaded like scorch
ing fire. But even to her Hetty shrank from beseeching and confession
she could not prevail on herself to say, "I will go to Dinah"; she onl
thought of that as a possible alternative, if she had not courage for deat

The good landlady was amazed when she saw Hetty come downstairs soon after herself, neatly dressed, and looking resolutely self-possessed. Hetty told her she was quite well this morning; she had only been very tired and overcome with her journey, for she had come a long way to ask about her brother who had run away, and they thought he was gone for a soldier, and Captain Donnithorne might know, for he had been very kind to her brother once. It was a lame story, and the landlady looked doubtfully at Hetty as she told it; but there was a resolute air of self-reliance about her this morning, so different from the helpless prostration of yesterday, that the landlady hardly knew how to make a remark that might seem like prying into other people's affairs. She only invited her to sit down to breakfast with them, and in the course of it Hetty brought out her earrings and locket, and asked the landlord if he could help her to get money for them: her journey, she said, had cost her much more than she expected, and now she had no money to get back to her friends, which she wanted to do at once.

It was not the first time the landlady had seen the ornaments, for she had examined the contents of Hetty's pocket yesterday, and she and her husband had discussed the fact of a country girl having these beautiful things, with a stronger conviction than ever that Hetty had been miserably deluded by the fine young officer.

"Well," said the landlord, when Hetty had spread the precious trifles before him, "we might take 'em to the jeweller's shop, for there's one not far off; but Lord bless you, they wouldn't give you a quarter o' what the things are worth. And you wouldn't like to part with 'em?" he added, looking at her inquiringly.

"O, I don't mind," said Hetty, hastily, "so as I can get money to go back."

"And they might think the things were stolen as you wanted to sell 'em," he went on; "for it isn't usual for a young woman like you to have fine jew'llery like that."

The blood rushed to Hetty's face with anger. "I belong to respectable folks," she said; "I'm not a thief."

"No, that you aren't, I'll be bound," said the landlady; "and you'd do to call to say that," looking indignantly at her husband. "The things were gev to her: that's plain enough to be seen."

"I didn't mean as I thought so," said the husband, apologetically, "but I said it was what the jeweller might think, and so he wouldn't be offering much money for 'em."

"Well," said the wife, "suppose you were to advance some money on the things yourself, and then if she liked to redeem 'em when she got home, she could. But if we heard nothing from her after two months, we might do as we liked with 'em."

I will not say that in this accommodating proposition the landlady had no regard whatever to the possible reward of her good-nature in the ultimate possession of the locket and earrings: indeed, the effect they would have in that case on the mind of the grocer's wife had presented itself with remarkable vividness to her rapid imagination. The landlord took up the ornaments and pushed out his lips in a meditative manner. He wished Hetty well, doubtless; but pray how many of your well wishers would decline to make a little gain out of you? Your landlady is sincerely affected at parting with you, respects you highly, and will really rejoice if any one else is generous to you; but at the same time she hands you a bill by which she gains as high a percentage as possible.

"How much money do you want to get home with, young woman?" said the well-wisher, at length.

"Three guineas," answered Hetty, fixing on the sum she set out with, for want of any other standard, and afraid of asking too much.

"Well, I've no objections to advance you three guineas," said the landlord; "and if you like to send it me back and get the jewellery again you can, you know: the Green Man isn't going to run away."

"O, yes, I'll be very glad if you'll give me that," said Hetty, relieved at the thought that she would not have to go to the jeweller's, and be stared at and questioned.

"But if you want the things again, you'll write before long," said the landlady, "because when two months are up, we shall make up our minds as you don't want 'em."

"Yes," said Hetty, indifferently.

The husband and wife were equally content with this arrangement. The husband thought, if the ornaments were not redeemed, he could make a good thing of it by taking them to London and selling them: the wife thought she would coax the good man into letting her keep them. And they were accommodating Hetty, poor thing:—a pretty respectable looking young woman, apparently in a sad case. They declined to take anything for her food and bed: she was quite welcome. And at eleven o'clock Hetty said "Good-by" to them, with the same quiet, resolute air she had worn all the morning, mounting the coach that was to take her twenty miles back along the way she had come.

There is a strength of self-possession which is the sign that the last hope has departed. Despair no more leans on others than perfect contentment, and in despair pride ceases to be counteracted by the sense of dependence.

Hetty felt that no one could deliver her from the evils that would make life hateful to her; and no one, she said to herself, should ever know her misery and humiliation. No; she would not confess even to Dinah: she would wander out of sight, and drown herself where her body would never be found, and no one should know what had become of her.

When she got off this coach, she began to walk again, and take cheap rides in carts, and get cheap meals, going on and on without distinct purpose, yet strangely, by some fascination, taking the way she had come, though she was determined not to go back to her own country. Perhaps it was because she had fixed her mind on the grassy Warwick shire fields, with the bushy tree-studded hedgerows that made a hiding face even in this leafless season. She went more slowly than she came, often getting over the stiles, and sitting for hours under the hedgerows, looking before her with blank, beautiful eyes; fancying herself at the edge of a hidden pool, low down, like that in the Scantlands; wondering if it were very painful to be drowned, and if there would be anything worse after death than what she dreaded in life. Religious doctrines had taken no hold on Hetty's mind: she was one of those numerous people who have had godfathers and godmothers, learned their catechism, been confirmed, and gone to church every Sunday, and yet, for any practical result of strength in life, or trust in death, have never appropriated a single Christian idea or Christian feeling. You would misunderstand her thoughts during these wretched days, if you imagined that they were influenced either by religious fears or religious hopes.

She chose to go to Stratford-on-Avon again, where she had gone before by mistake; for she remembered some grassy fields on her former way towards it—fields among which she thought she might find just the sort of pool she had in her mind. Yet she took care of her money still; she carried her basket: death seemed still a long way off, and life was so strong in her! She craved food and rest—she hastened towards them at the very moment she was picturing to herself the bank from which she would leap towards death. It was already five days since she had left Windsor, for she had wandered about, always avoiding speech or questioning looks, and recovering her air of proud self-dependence whenever she was under observation, choosing her decent lodging at night, and dressing herself neatly in the morning, and setting off on her way steadily, or remaining under shelter if it rained, as if she had a happy life to cherish.

And yet, even in her most self-conscious moments, the face was sadly different from that which had smiled at itself in the old specked glass, or smiled at others when they glanced at it admiringly. A hard and even fierce look had come in the eyes, though their lashes were as long as ever, and they had all their dark brightness. And the cheek was never dimpled with smiles now. It was the same rounded, pouting, childish prettiness, but with all love and belief in love departed from it—the sadder for its beauty, like that wondrous Medusa-face, with the passionate, passionless lips.

At last she was among the fields she had been dreaming of, on a long narrow pathway leading towards a wood. If there should be a pool in that wood! It would be better hidden than one in the fields. No, it was not a wood, only a wild brake, where there had once been gravel-pits, leaving mounds and hollows studded with brushwood and small trees. She roamed up and down, thinking there was perhaps a pool in every hollow before she came to it, till her limbs were weary, and she sat down to rest. The afternoon was far advanced, and the leaden sky was darkening, as if the sun were setting behind it. After a little while Hetty started up again, feeling that darkness would soon come on; and she must put off finding the pool till to-morrow, and make her way to some

shelter for the night. She had quite lost her way in the fields, and migh
as well go in one direction as another, for aught she knew. She walke
through field after field, and no village, no house was in sight; but *ther*
at the corner of this pasture, there was a break in the hedges; the lan
seemed to dip down a little, and two trees leaned towards each othe
across the opening. Hetty's heart gave a great beat as she thought ther
must be a pool there. She walked towards it heavily over the tufte
grass, with pale lips and a sense of trembling: it was as if the thin
were come in spite of herself, instead of being the object of her search.

There it was, black under the darkening sky: no motion, no soun
near. She set down her basket, and then sank down herself on the gras
trembling. The pool had its wintry depth now: by the time it got sha
low, as she remembered the pools did at Hayslope, in the summer, n
one could find out that it was her body. But then there was her baske
—she must hide that too: she must throw it into the water—make
heavy with stones first, and then throw it in. She got up to look abou
for stones, and soon brought five or six, which she laid down beside he
basket, and then sat down again. There was no need to hurry—there wa
all the night to drown herself in. She sat leaning her elbow on tl
basket. She was weary, hungry. There were some buns in her basket-
three, which she had supplied herself with at the place where she at
her dinner. She took them out now, and ate them eagerly, and then sa
still again, looking at the pool. The soothed sensation that came ove
her from the satisfaction of her hunger, and this fixed dreamy attitud
brought on drowsiness, and presently her head sank down on her knee
She was fast asleep.

When she awoke it was deep night, and she felt chill. She was frigh
ened at this darkness—frightened at the long night before her. If sl
could but throw herself into the water! No, not yet. She began to wa
about that she might get warm again, as if she would have more res
lution then. O how long the time was in that darkness! The brigl
hearth and the warmth and the voices of home,—the secure uprising ar
lying down,—the familiar fields, the familiar people, the Sundays ar
holidays with their simple joys of dress and feasting,—all the sweets
her young life rushed before her now, and she seemed to be stretchir
her arms towards them across a great gulf. She set her teeth when sl
thought of Arthur: she cursed him, without knowing what her cursir
would do: she wished he too might know desolation, and cold, and a li
of shame that he dared not end by death.

The horror of this cold, and darkness, and solitude—out of all huma
reach—became greater every long minute: it was almost as if she we
dead already, and knew that she was dead, and longed to get back
life again. But no: she was alive still; she had not taken the dreadf
leap. She felt a strange contradictory wretchedness and exultatio:
wretchedness, that she did not dare to face death; exultation, that sl
was still in life—that she might yet know light and warmth again. S!
walked backwards and forwards to warm herself, beginning to disce

something of the objects around her, as her eyes became accustomed
to the night: the darker line of the hedge, the rapid motion of some
living creature—perhaps a field-mouse—rushing across the grass. She
no longer felt as if the darkness hedged her in: she thought she could
walk back across the field, and get over the stile; and then, in the very
next field, she thought she remembered there was a hovel of furze near a
sheepfold. If she could get into that hovel, she would be warmer; she
could pass the night there, for that was what Alick did at Hayslope in
lambing-time. The thought of this hovel brought the energy of a new
hope: she took up her basket and walked across the field, but it was
some time before she got in the right direction for the stile. The exercise
and the occupation of finding the stile were a stimulus to her, however,
and lightened the horror of the darkness and solitude. There were sheep
in the next field, and she startled a group as she set down her basket
and got over the stile; and the sound of their movement comforted her,
for it assured her that her impression was right: this *was* the field where
she had seen the hovel, for it was the field where the sheep were. Right
on along the path, and she would get to it. She reached the opposite
gate, and felt her way along its rails, and the rails of the sheepfold, till
her hand encountered the pricking of the gorsy wall. Delicious sensation! She had found the shelter: she groped her way, touching the
prickly gorse, to the door and pushed it open. It was an ill-smelling
close place, but warm, and there was straw on the ground: Hetty sank
down on the straw with a sense of escape. Tears came—she had never
shed tears before since she left Windsor—tears and sobs of hysterical
joy that she had still hold of life, that she was still on the familiar
earth, with the sheep near her. The very consciousness of her own
limbs was a delight to her: she turned up her sleeves, and kissed her
arms with the passionate love of life. Soon warmth and weariness lulled
her in the midst of her sobs, and she fell continually into dozing, fancying herself at the brink of the pool again—fancying that she had jumped
into the water, and then awaking with a start, and wondering where
she was. But at last deep dreamless sleep came; her head, guarded by
her bonnet, found a pillow against the gorsy wall; and the poor soul,
driven to and fro between two equal terrors, found the one relief that
was possible to it—the relief of unconsciousness.

Alas! that relief seems to end the moment it has begun. It seemed
to Hetty as if those dozing dreams had only passed into another dream
—that she was in the hovel, and her aunt was standing over her with a
candle in her hand. She trembled under her aunt's glance, and opened
her eyes. There was no candle, but there was light in the hovel—the
light of early morning through the open door. And there was a face
looking down on her; but it was an unknown face, belonging to an
elderly man in a smock-frock.

"Why, what do you do here, young woman?" the man said roughly.

Hetty trembled still worse under this real fear and shame than she
had done in her momentary dream under her aunt's glance. She felt

that she was like a beggar already—found sleeping in that place. But in spite of her trembling, she was so eager to account to the man for her presence here, that she found words at once.

"I lost my way," she said. "I'm travelling—north'ard, and I got away from the road into the fields, and was overtaken by the dark. Will you tell me the way to the nearest village?"

She got up as she was speaking, and put her hands to her bonnet to adjust it, and then laid hold of her basket.

The man looked at her with a slow bovine gaze, without giving her any answer, for some seconds. Then he turned away and walked towards the door of the hovel, but it was not till he got there that he stood still, and, turning his shoulder half round towards her, said,

"Aw, I can show you the way to Norton, if you like. But what do you do gettin' out o' the highroad?" he added, with a tone of gruff reproof. "Y'ull be gettin' into mischief, if you dooant mind."

"Yes," said Hetty, "I won't do it again. I'll keep in the road, if you'll be so good as show me how to get to it."

"Why dooant you keep where there's finger-poasses an' folks to ax the way on?" the man said, still more gruffly. "Anybody 'ud think you was a wild woman, an' look at yer."

Hetty was frightened at this gruff old man, and still more at this last suggestion that she looked like a wild woman. As she followed him out of the hovel she thought she would give him a sixpence for telling her the way, and then he would not suppose she was wild. As he stopped to point out the road to her, she put her hand in her pocket to get the sixpence ready, and when he was turning away, without saying good-morning, she held it out to him and said, "Thank you; will you please to take something for your trouble?"

He looked slowly at the sixpence, and then said, "I want none o your money. You'd better take care on't, else you'll get it stool from yer, if you go trapesin' about the fields like a mad woman a-that-way."

The man left her without further speech, and Hetty held on her way. Another day had risen, and she must wander on. It was no use to think of drowning herself—she could not do it, at least while she had money left to buy food, and strength to journey on. But the incident on her waking this morning heightened her dread of that time when her money would be all gone; she would have to sell her basket and clothes then, and she would really look like a beggar or a wild woman, as the man had said. The passionate joy in life she had felt in the night, after escaping from the brink of the black cold death in the pool, was gone now. Life now, by the morning light, with the impression of that man's hard wondering look at her, was as full of dread as death:—it was worse; it was a dread to which she felt chained, from which she shrank and shrank as she did from the black pool, and yet could find no refuge from it.

She took out her money from her purse, and looked at it; she had still two-and-twenty shillings; it would serve her for many days more, or it would help her to get on faster to Stonyshire, within reach o

Dinah. The thought of Dinah urged itself more strongly now, since the experience of the night had driven her shuddering imagination away from the pool. If it had been only going to Dinah—if nobody besides Dinah would ever know—Hetty could have made up her mind to go to her. The soft voice, the pitying eyes, would have drawn her. But afterwards the other people must know, and she could no more rush on that shame than she could rush on death.

She must wander on and on, and wait for a lower depth of despair to give her courage. Perhaps death would come to her, for she was getting less and less able to bear the day's weariness. And yet—such is the strange action of our souls, drawing us by a lurking desire towards the very ends we dread—Hetty, when she set out again from Norton, asked the straightest road northward towards Stonyshire, and kept it all that day.

Poor wandering Hetty, with the rounded childish face, and the hard unloving despairing soul looking out of it—with the narrow heart and narrow thoughts, no room in them for any sorrows but her own, and tasting that sorrow with the more intense bitterness! My heart bleeds for her as I see her toiling along on her weary feet, or seated in a cart, with her eyes fixed vacantly on the road before her, never thinking or caring whither it tends, till hunger comes and makes her desire that a village may be near.

What will be the end?   the end of her objectless wandering, apart from all love, caring for human beings only through her pride, clinging to life only as the hunted wounded brute clings to it?

God preserve you and me from being the beginners of such misery!

CHAPTER XXXVIII

THE QUEST

THE first ten days after Hetty's departure passed as quietly as any other days with the family at the Hall Farm, and with Adam at his daily work. They had expected Hetty to stay away a week or ten days at least, perhaps a little longer if Dinah came back with her, because there might then be something to detain them at Snowfield. But when a fortnight had passed they began to feel a little surprise that Hetty did not return; she must surely have found it pleasanter to be with Dinah than any one could have supposed. Adam, for his part, was getting very impatient to see her, and he resolved that, if she did not appear the next day (Saturday), he would set out on Sunday morning to fetch her. There was no coach on a Sunday; but by setting out before it was light, and perhaps getting a lift in a cart by the way, he would arrive pretty early at Snowfield, and bring back Hetty the next day—Dinah too, if she were coming. It was quite time Hetty came home, and he would afford to lose his Monday for the sake of bringing her.

His project was quite approved at the Farm when he went there on Saturday evening. Mrs. Poyser desired him emphatically not to come back without Hetty, for she had been quite too long away, considering the things she had to get ready by the middle of March, and a week was surely enough for any one to go out for their health. As for Dinah, Mrs. Poyser had small hope of their bringing her, unless they could make her believe the folks at Hayslope were twice as miserable as the folks at Snowfield. "Though," said Mrs. Poyser, by way of conclusion, "you might tell her she's got but one aunt left, and *she's* wasted pretty nigh to a shadder; and we shall p'rhaps all be gone twenty mile further off her next Michaelmas, and shall die o' broken hearts among strange folks, and leave the children fatherless and motherless."

"Nay, nay," said Mr. Poyser, who certainly had the air of a man perfectly heart-whole, "it isna so bad as that. Thee't looking rarely now, and getting flesh every day. But I'd be glad for Dinah t' come, for she'd help thee wi' the little uns: they took t' her wonderful."

So at daybreak, on Sunday, Adam set off. Seth went with him the first mile or two, for the thought of Snowfield, and the possibility that Dinah might come again, made him restless, and the walk with Adam in the cold morning air, both in their best clothes, helped to give him a sense of Sunday calm. It was the last morning in February, with a low grey sky, and a slight hoarfrost on the green border of the road and on the black hedges. They heard the gurgling of the full brooklet hurrying down the hill, and the faint twittering of the early birds. For they walked in silence, though with a pleased sense of companionship.

"Good-by, lad," said Adam, laying his hand on Seth's shoulder, and looking at him affectionately as they were about to part, "I wish thee wast going all the way wi' me, and as happy as I am."

"I'm content, Addy, I'm content," said Seth, cheerfully. "I'll be an old bachelor, belike, and make a fuss wi' thy children."

They turned away from each other, and Seth walked leisurely homeward, mentally repeating one of his favourite hymns—he was very fond of hymns:—

> "Dark and cheerless is the morn
>   Unaccompanied by thee:
> Joyless is the day's return
>   Till thy mercy's beams I see:
> Till thou inward light impart,
> Glad my eyes and warm my heart.
>
> Visit, then, this soul of mine,
>   Pierce the gloom of sin and grief,—
> Fill me, Radiancy Divine,
>   Scatter all my unbelief.
> More and more thyself display,
> Shining to the perfect day."

Adam walked much faster, and any one coming along the Oakbourne road at sunrise that morning must have had a pleasant sight in this tall broad-chested man, striding along with a carriage as upright and firm as any soldier's, glancing with keen glad eyes at the dark-blue hills as they began to show themselves on his way. Seldom in Adam's life had his face been so free from any cloud of anxiety as it was this morning; and this freedom from care, as is usual with constructive practical minds like his, made him all the more observant of the objects round him, and all the more ready to gather suggestions from them towards his own favourite plans and ingenious contrivances. His happy love—the knowledge that his steps were carrying him nearer and nearer to Hetty, who was so soon to be his—was to his thoughts what the sweet morning air was to his sensations: it gave him a consciousness of wellbeing that made activity delightful. Every now and then there was a rush of more intense feeling towards her, which chased away other images than Hetty; and along with that would come a wondering thankfulness that all this happiness was given to him—that this life of ours had such sweetness in it. For Adam had a devout mind, though he was perhaps rather impatient of devout words; and his tenderness lay very close to his reverence, so that the one could hardly be stirred without the other. But after feeling had welled up and poured itself out in this way, busy thought would come back with the greater vigour; and this morning it was intent on schemes by which the roads might be improved that were so imperfect all through the country, and on picturing all the benefits that might come from the exertions of a single country gentleman, if he would set himself to getting the roads made good in his own district.

It seemed a very short walk. the ten miles to Oakbourne, that pretty town within sight of the blue hills, where he breakfasted. After this, the country grew barer and barer: no more rolling woods, no more wide-branching trees near frequent homesteads, no more bushy hedgerows; but grey stone walls intersecting the meagre pastures, and dismal wide-scattered grey stone houses on broken lands where mines had been and were no longer. "A hungry land," said Adam to himself. "I'd rather go south'ard, where they say it's as flat as a table, than come to live here; though if Dinah likes to live in a country where she can be the most comfort to folks, she's i' the right to live o' this side; for she must look as if she'd come straight from heaven, like th' angels in the desert, to strengthen them as ha' got nothing t' eat." And when at last he came in sight of Snowfield, he thought it looked like a town that was "fellow to the country," though the stream through the valley where the great mill stood gave a pleasant greenness to the lower field. The town lay, grim, stony, and unsheltered, up the side of a steep hill, and Adam did not go forward to it at present, for Seth had told him where to find Dinah. It was at a thatched cottage outside the town, a little way from the mill—an old cottage, standing sideways towards the road, with a little bit of potato-ground before it. Here Dinah lodged with an elderly couple; and if she and Hetty happened to be out, Adam could learn where they were gone, or when they would be home again. Dinah might be out on some preaching errand, and perhaps she would have left

Hetty at home. Adam could not help hoping this, and as he recognised the cottage by the roadside before him, there shone out in his face that involuntary smile which belongs to the expectation of a near joy.

He hurried his step along the narrow causeway, and rapped at the door. It was opened by a very clean old woman, with a slow palsied shake of the head.

"Is Dinah Morris at home?" said Adam.

"Eh? . . . no," said the old woman, looking up at this tall stranger with a wonder that made her slower of speech than usual. "Will ye please to come in?" she added, retiring from the door, as if recollecting herself. "Why, ye're brother to the young man as come afore, arena ye?"

"Yes," said Adam, entering. "That was Seth Bede. I'm his brother Adam. He told me to give his respects to you and your good master."

"Ay, the same t' him: he was a gracious young man. An' ye feature him, on'y ye're darker. Sit ye down i' th' arm-chair. My man isna come home from meeting."

Adam sat down patiently, not liking to hurry the shaking old woman with questions, but looking eagerly towards the narrow twisting stairs in one corner, for he thought it was possible Hetty might have heard his voice, and would come down them.

"So you're come to see Dinah Morris?" said the old woman, standing opposite to him. "An' you didna know she was away from home, then?"

"No," said Adam, "but I thought it likely she might be away, seeing as it's Sunday. But the other young woman—is she at home, or gone along with Dinah?"

The old woman looked at Adam with a bewildered air.

"Gone along wi' her?" she said. "Eh, Dinah's gone to Leeds, a big town ye may ha' heared on, where there's a many o' the Lord's people. She's been gone sin' Friday was a fortnight: they sent her the money for her journey. You may see her room here," she went on, opening a door, and not noticing the effect of her words on Adam. He rose and followed her, and darted an eager glance into the little room, with its narrow bed, the portrait of Wesley on the wall, and the few books lying on the large Bible. He had had an irrational hope that Hetty might be there. He could not speak in the first moment after seeing that the room was empty; an undefined fear had seized him—something had happened to Hetty on the journey. Still the old woman was so slow of speech and apprehension, that Hetty might be at Snowfield after all.

"It's a pity ye didna know," she said. "Have ye come from your own country o' purpose to see her?"

"But Hetty—Hetty Sorrel," said Adam, abruptly; "where is *she?*"

"I know nobody by that name," said the old woman, wonderingly. "Is it anybody ye've heared on at Snowfield?"

"Did there come no young woman here—very young and pretty—Friday was a fortnight, to see Dinah Morris?"

"Nay; I'n seen no young woman."

"Think; are you quite sure? A girl, eighteen years old, with dark eyes and dark curly hair, and a red cloak on, and a basket on her arm? You couldn't forget her if you saw her."

"Nay; Friday was a fortnight—it was the day as Dinah went away —there come nobody. There's ne'er been nobody asking for her till you come, for the folks about know as she's gone. Eh dear, eh dear, is there summat the matter?"

The old woman had seen the ghastly look of fear in Adam's face. But he was not stunned or confounded; he was thinking eagerly where he could inquire about Hetty.

"Yes; a young woman started from our country to see Dinah, Friday was a fortnight. I came to fetch her back. I'm afraid something has happened to her. I can't stop. Good-by."

He hastened out of the cottage, and the old woman followed him to the gate, watching him sadly with her shaking head, as he almost ran towards the town. He was going to inquire at the place where the Oakbourne coach stopped.

No! no young woman like Hetty had been seen there. Had any accident happened to the coach a fortnight ago? No. And there was no coach to take him back to Oakbourne that day. Well, he would walk: he couldn't stay here, in wretched inaction. But the innkeeper, seeing that Adam was in great anxiety, and entering into this new incident with the eagerness of a man who passes a great deal of time with his hands in his pockets looking into an obstinately monotonous street, offered to take him back to Oakbourne in his own "taxed cart" this very evening. It was not five o'clock; there was plenty of time for Adam to take a meal, and yet to get to Oakbourne before ten o'clock. The innkeeper declared that he really wanted to go to Oakbourne, and might as well go to-night; he should have all Monday before him then. Adam, after making an ineffectual attempt to eat, put the food in his pocket, and, drinking a draught of ale, declared himself ready to set off. As they approached the cottage, it occurred to him that he would do well to learn from the old woman where Dinah was to be found in Leeds: if there was trouble at the Hall Farm—he only half admitted the foreboding that there would be—the Poysers might like to send for Dinah. But Dinah had not left any address, and the old woman, whose memory for names was infirm, could not recall the name of the "blessed woman" who was Dinah's chief friend in the Society at Leeds.

During that long, long journey in the taxed cart, there was time for all the conjectures of importunate fear and struggling hope. In the very first shock of discovering that Hetty had not been to Snowfield, the thought of Arthur had darted through Adam like a sharp pang: but he tried for some time to ward off its return by busying himself with modes of accounting for the alarming fact, quite apart from that intolerable thought. Some accident had happened. Hetty had, by some strange chance, got into a wrong vehicle from Oakbourne: she had been taken ill, and did not want to frighten them by letting them know. But this frail fence of vague improbabilities was soon hurled down by a rush of

distinct agonising fears. Hetty had been deceiving herself in thinking
that she could love and marry him: she had been loving Arthur all the
while: and now, in her desperation at the nearness of their marriage, she
had run away. And she was gone to *him*. The old indignation and
jealousy rose again, and prompted the suspicion that Arthur had been
dealing falsely—had written to Hetty—had tempted her to come to him
—being unwilling, after all, that she should belong to another man besides himself. Perhaps the whole thing had been contrived by him, and
he had given her directions how to follow him to Ireland: for Adam
knew that Arthur had been gone thither three weeks ago, having recently learnt it at the Chase. Every sad look of Hetty's, since she had
been engaged to Adam, returned upon him now with all the exaggeration of painful retrospect. He had been foolishly sanguine and confident.
The poor thing hadn't perhaps known her own mind for a long while;
had thought that she could forget Arthur; had been momentarily drawn
towards the man who offered her a protecting faithful love. He couldn't
bear to blame her: she never meant to cause him this dreadful pain.
The blame lay with that man who had selfishly played with her heart—
had perhaps even deliberately lured her away.

At Oakbourne, the ostler at the Royal Oak remembered such a young
woman as Adam described getting out of the Treddleston coach more
than a fortnight ago—wasn't likely to forget such a pretty lass as that
in a hurry—was sure she had not gone on by the Buxton coach that
went through Snowfield, but had lost sight of her while he went away
with the horses, and had never set eyes on her again. Adam then went
straight to the house from which the Stoniton coach started: Stoniton
was the most obvious place for Hetty to go to first, whatever might be
her destination, for she would hardly venture on any but the chief coach-
roads. She had been noticed here too, and was remembered to have sat
on the box by the coachman; but the coachman could not be seen, for
another man had been driving on that road in his stead the last three or
four days: he could probably be seen at Stoniton, through inquiry at
the inn where the coach put up. So the anxious, heart-stricken Adam
must of necessity wait and try to rest till morning—nay, till eleven
o'clock, when the coach started.

At Stoniton another delay occurred, for the old coachman who had
driven Hetty would not be in the town again till night. When he did
come he remembered Hetty well, and remembered his own joke addressed to her, quoting it many times to Adam, and observing with
equal frequency that he thought there was something more than common, because Hetty had not laughed when he joked her. But he declared, as the people had done at the inn, that he had lost sight of Hetty
directly she got down. Part of the next morning was consumed in inquiries at every house in the town from which a coach started—(all in
vain; for you know Hetty did not start from Stoniton by coach, but on
foot in the grey morning)—and then in walking out to the first toll-gates
on the different lines of road, in the forlorn hope of finding some recol-

lection of her there. No, she was not to be traced any farther; and the next hard task for Adam was to go home, and carry the wretched tidings to the Hall Farm. As to what he should do beyond that, he had come to two distinct resolutions amidst the tumult of thought and feeling which was going on within him while he went to and fro. He would not mention what he knew of Arthur Donnithorne's behaviour to Hetty till there was a clear necessity for it: it was still possible Hetty might come back, and the disclosure might be an injury or an offence to her. And as soon as he had been home, and done what was necessary there to prepare for his further absence, he would start off to Ireland: if he found no trace of Hetty on the road, he would go straight to Arthur Donnithorne, and make himself certain how far he was acquainted with her movements. Several times the thought occurred to him that he would consult Mr. Irwine; but that would be useless unless he told him all, and so betrayed the secret about Arthur. It seems strange that Adam, in the incessant occupation of his mind about Hetty, should never have alighted on the probability that she had gone to Windsor, ignorant that Arthur was no longer there. Perhaps the reason was, that he could not conceive Hetty's throwing herself on Arthur uncalled; he imagined no cause that could have driven her to such a step, after that letter written in August. There were but two alternatives in his mind: either Arthur had written to her again and enticed her away, or she had simply fled from her approaching marriage with himself, because she found, after all, she could not love him well enough, and yet was afraid of her friends' anger if she retracted.

With this last determination on his mind, of going straight to Arthur, the thought that he had spent two days in inquiries which had proved to be almost useless, was torturing to Adam; and yet, since he would not tell the Poysers his conviction as to where Hetty was gone, or his intention to follow her thither, he must be able to say to them that he had traced her as far as possible.

It was after twelve o'clock on Tuesday night when Adam reached Treddleston; and, unwilling to disturb his mother and Seth, and also to encounter their questions at that hour, he threw himself without undressing on a bed at the "Waggon Overthrown," and slept hard from pure weariness. Not more than four hours, however; for before five o'clock he set out on his way home in the faint morning twilight. He always kept a key of the workshop door in his pocket, so that he could let himself in; and he wished to enter without awaking his mother, for he was anxious to avoid telling her the new trouble himself by seeing Seth first, and asking him to tell her when it should be necessary. He walked gently along the yard, and turned the key gently in the door; but, as he expected, Gyp, who lay in the workshop, gave a sharp bark. It subsided when he saw Adam, holding up his finger at him to impose silence; and in his dumb, tail-less joy he must content himself with rubbing his body against his master's legs.

Adam was too heart-sick to take notice of Gyp's fondling. He threw himself on the bench, and stared dully at the wood and the signs of work around him, wondering if he should ever come to feel pleasure in them again; while Gyp, dimly aware that there was something wrong with his master, laid his rough grey head on Adam's knee, and wrinkled his brows to look up at him. Hitherto, since Sunday afternoon, Adam had been constantly among strange people and in strange places, having no associations with the details of his daily life; and now that by the light of this new morning he was come back to his home, and surrounded by the familiar objects that seemed for ever robbed of their charm, the reality—the hard, inevitable reality—of his troubles pressed upon him with a new weight. Right before him was an unfinished chest of drawers, which he had been making in spare moments for Hetty's use, when his home should be hers.

Seth had not heard Adam's entrance, but he had been roused by Gyp's bark, and Adam heard him moving about in the room above, dressing himself. Seth's first thoughts were about his brother: he would come home to-day, surely, for the business would be wanting him sadly by to-morrow, but it was pleasant to think he had had a longer holiday than he had expected. And would Dinah come too? Seth felt that that was the greatest happiness he could look forward to for himself, though he had no hope left that she would ever love him well enough to marry him; but he had often said to himself, it was better to be Dinah's friend and brother than any other woman's husband. If he could but be always near her, instead of living so far off!

He came down-stairs and opened the inner door leading from the kitchen into the workshop, intending to let out Gyp; but he stood still in the doorway, smitten with a sudden shock at the sight of Adam seated listlessly on the bench, pale, unwashed, with sunken blank eyes, almost like a drunkard in the morning. But Seth felt in an instant what the marks meant: not drunkenness, but some great calamity. Adam looked up at him without speaking, and Seth moved forward towards the bench, himself trembling so that speech did not come readily.

"God have mercy on us, Addy," he said, in a low voice, sitting down on the bench beside Adam, "what is it?"

Adam was unable to speak: the strong man, accustomed to suppress the signs of sorrow, had felt his heart swell like a child's at this first approach of sympathy. He fell on Seth's neck and sobbed.

Seth was prepared for the worst now, for, even in his recollections of their boyhood, Adam had never sobbed before.

"Is it death, Adam? Is she dead?" he asked, in a low tone, when Adam raised his head and was recovering himself.

"No, lad; but she's gone—gone away from us. She's never been to Snowfield. Dinah's been gone to Leeds ever since last Friday was a fortnight, the very day Hetty set out. I can't find out where she went after she got to Stoniton."

Seth was silent from utter astonishment: he knew nothing that could suggest to him a reason for Hetty's going away.

"Hast any notion what she's done it for?" he said, at last.

"She can't ha' loved me: she didn't like our marriage when it came nigh—that must be it," said Adam. He had determined to mention no further reason.

"I hear mother stirring," said Seth. "Must we tell her?"

"No, not yet," said Adam, rising from the bench, and pushing the hair from his face, as if he wanted to rouse himself. "I can't have her told yet; and I must set out on another journey directly, after I've been to the village and th' Hall Farm. I can't tell thee where I'm going, and thee must say to her I'm gone on business as nobody is to know anything about. I'll go and wash myself now." Adam moved towards the door of the workshop, but after a step or two he turned round, and meeting Seth's eyes with a calm sad glance, he said, "I must take all the money out o' the tin box, lad; but if anything happens to me, all the rest 'll be thine, to take care o' mother with."

Seth was pale and trembling: he felt there was some terrible secret under all this. "Brother," he said, faintly—he never called Adam "brother" except in solemn moments—"I don't believe you'll do anything as you can't ask God's blessing on."

"Nay, lad," said Adam, "don't be afraid. I'm for doing nought but what's a man's duty."

The thought that if he betrayed his trouble to his mother, she would only distress him by words, half of blundering affection, half of irrepressible triumph that Hetty proved as unfit to be his wife as she had always foreseen, brought back some of his habitual firmness and self-command. He had felt ill on his journey home—he told her when she came down,—had stayed all night at Treddleston for that reason; and a bad headache, that still hung about him this morning, accounted for his paleness and heavy eyes.

He determined to go to the village, in the first place; attend to his business for an hour, and give notice to Burge of his being obliged to go on a journey, which he must beg him not to mention to any one; for he wished to avoid going to the Hall Farm near breakfast-time, when the children and servants would be in the house-place, and there must be exclamations in their hearing about his having returned without Hetty. He waited until the clock struck nine before he left the work-yard at the village, and set off, through the fields, towards the Farm. It was an immense relief to him, as he came near the Home Close, to see Mr. Poyser advancing towards him, for this would spare him the pain of going to the house. Mr. Poyser was walking briskly this March morning, with a sense of Spring business on his mind: he was going to cast the master's eye on the shoeing of a new cart-horse, carrying his spud as a useful companion by the way. His surprise was great when he caught sight of Adam, but he was not a man given to presentiments of evil.

"Why, Adam, lad, is't you? Have ye been all this time away, and not brought the lasses back, after all? Where are they?"

"No, I've not brought 'em," said Adam, turning round, to indicate that he wished to walk back with Mr. Poyser.

"Why," said Martin, looking with sharper attention at Adam, "ye look bad. Is there anything happened?"

"Yes," said Adam, heavily. "A sad thing's happened. I didna find Hetty at Snowfield."

Mr. Poyser's good-natured face showed signs of troubled astonishment. "Not find her? What's happened to her?" he said, his thoughts flying at once to bodily accident.

"That I can't tell, whether anything's happened to her. She never went to Snowfield—she took the coach to Stoniton, but I can't learn nothing of her after she got down from the Stoniton coach."

"Why, you donna mean she's run away?" said Martin, standing still, so puzzled and bewildered that the fact did not yet make itself felt as a trouble by him.

"She must ha' done," said Adam. "She didn't like our marriage when it came to the point—that must be it. She'd mistook her feelings."

Martin was silent for a minute or two, looking on the ground, and rooting up the grass with his spud, without knowing what he was doing. His usual slowness was always trebled when the subject of speech was painful. At last he looked up, right in Adam's face, saying,

"Then she didna deserve t' ha' ye, my lad. An' I feel i' fault myself, for she was my niece, and I was allays hot for her marr'ing ye. There's no amends I can make ye, lad—the more's the pity: it's a sad cut-up for ye, I doubt."

Adam could say nothing; and Mr. Poyser, after pursuing his walk for a little while, went on:—

"I'll be bound she's gone after trying to get a lady's-maid place, for she'd got that in her head half a year ago, and wanted me to gi' my consent. But I'd thought better on her," he added, shaking his head slowly and sadly—"I'd thought better on her, nor to look for this, after she'd gi'en her word, an' everything been got ready."

Adam had the strongest motives for encouraging this supposition in Mr. Poyser, and he even tried to believe that it might possibly be true. He had no warrant for the *certainty* that she was gone to Arthur.

"It was better it should be so," he said, as quietly as he could, "if she felt she couldn't like me for a husband. Better run away before than repent after. I hope you won't look harshly on her if she comes back, as she may do if she finds it hard to get on away from home."

"I canna look on her as I've done before," said Martin, decisively. "She's acted bad by you, and by all of us. But I'll not turn my back on her: she's but a young un, and it's the first harm I've knowed on her It'll be a hard job for me to tell her aunt. Why didna Dinah come back wi' ye?—she'd ha' helped to pacify her aunt a bit."

"Dinah wasn't at Snowfield. She's been gone to Leeds this fortnight; and I couldn't learn from th' old woman any direction where she is at Leeds, else I should ha' brought it you."

"She'd a deal better be staying wi' her own kin," said Mr. Poyser, indignantly, "than going preaching among strange folks a-that'n."

"I must leave you now, Mr. Poyser," said Adam, "for I've a deal to see to."

"Ay, you'd best be after your business, and I must tell the missis when I go home. It's a hard job."

"But," said Adam, "I beg particular, you'll keep what's happened quiet for a week or two. I've not told my mother yet, and there's no knowing how things may turn out."

"Ay, ay; least said, soonest mended. We'n no need to say why the match is broke off, an' we may hear of her after a bit. Shake hands wi' me, lad: I wish I could make thee amends."

There was something in Martin Poyser's throat at that moment which caused him to bring out those scanty words in rather a broken fashion. Yet Adam knew what they meant all the better; and the two honest men grasped each other's hard hands in mutual understanding.

There was nothing now to hinder Adam from setting off. He had told Seth to go to the Chase, and leave a message for the Squire, saying that Adam Bede had been obliged to start off suddenly on a journey,—and to say as much, and no more, to any one else who made inquiries about him. If the Poysers learned that he was gone away again, Adam knew they would infer that he was gone in search of Hetty.

He had intended to go right on his way from the Hall Farm; but now the impulse which had frequently visited him before—to go to Mr. Irwine, and make a confidant of him—recurred with the new force which belongs to a last opportunity. He was about to start on a long journey— a difficult one—by sea—and no soul would know where he was gone. If anything happened to him? or, if he absolutely needed help in any matter concerning Hetty? Mr. Irwine was to be trusted; and the feeling which made Adam shrink from telling anything which was *her* secret, must give way before the need there was that she should have some one else besides himself, who would be prepared to defend her in the worst extremity. Towards Arthur, even though he might have incurred no new guilt, Adam felt that he was not bound to keep silence when Hetty's interest called on him to speak.

"I must do it," said Adam, when these thoughts, which had spread themselves through hours of his sad journeying, now rushed upon him in an instant, like a wave that had been slowly gathering; "it's the right thing. I can't stand alone in this way any longer."

CHAPTER XXXIX

THE TIDINGS

ADAM turned his face towards Broxton and walked with his swiftest stride, looking at his watch with the fear that Mr. Irwine might be gone

out—hunting, perhaps. The fear and haste together produced a state of
strong excitement before he reached the Rectory gate; and outside it he
saw the deep marks of a recent hoof on the gravel.

But the hoofs were turned towards the gate, not away from it; and
though there was a horse against the stable door, it was not Mr. Irwine's:
it had evidently had a journey this morning, and must belong to some one
who had come on business. Mr. Irwine was at home, then; but Adam
could hardly find breath and calmness to tell Carroll that he wanted to
speak to the Rector. The double suffering of certain and uncertain sorrow
had begun to shake the strong man. The butler looked at him wonderingly, as he threw himself on a bench in the passage and stared absently
at the clock on the opposite wall: the master had somebody with him,
he said, but he heard the study door open—the stranger seemed to be
coming out, and as Adam was in a hurry, he would let the master know
at once.

Adam sat looking at the clock: the minute-hand was hurrying along
the last five minutes to ten, with a loud hard indifferent tick, and Adam
watched the movement and listened to the sound as if he had had some
reason for doing so. In our times of bitter suffering, there are almost
always these pauses, when our consciousness is benumbed to everything
but some trivial perception or sensation. It is as if semi-idiocy came to
give us rest from the memory and the dread which refused to leave us in
our sleep.

Carroll, coming back, recalled Adam to the sense of his burthen. He
was to go into the study immediately. "I can't think what that strange
person's come about," the butler added, from mere incontinence of remark, as he preceded Adam to the door, "he's gone i' the dining-room.
And master looks unaccountable—as if he was frightened." Adam took
no notice of the words: he could not care about other people's business.
But when he entered the study and looked in Mr. Irwine's face, he felt
in an instant that there was a new expression in it, strangely different
from the warm friendliness it had always worn for him before. A letter
lay open on the table, and Mr. Irwine's hand was on it; but the changed
glance he cast on Adam could not be owing entirely to preoccupation
with some disagreeable business, for he was looking eagerly towards the
door, as if Adam's entrance were a matter of poignant anxiety to him.

"You want to speak to me, Adam," he said, in that low constrainedly
quiet tone which a man uses when he is determined to suppress agitation. "Sit down here." He pointed to a chair just opposite to him, at no
more than a yard's distance from his own, and Adam sat down with a
sense that this cold manner of Mr. Irwine's gave an additional unexpected difficulty to his disclosure. But when Adam had made up his
mind to a measure, he was not the man to renounce it for any but
imperative reasons.

"I come to you, sir," he said, "as the gentleman I look up to most of
anybody. I've something very painful to tell you—something as it'll pain

you to hear, as well as me to tell. But if I speak o' the wrong other people have done, you'll see I didn't speak till I'd good reason."

Mr. Irwine nodded slowly, and Adam went on rather tremulously.

"You was t' ha' married me and Hetty Sorrel, you know, sir, o' the fifteenth o' this month. I thought she loved me, and I was th' happiest man i' the parish. But a dreadful blow's come upon me."

Mr. Irwine started up from his chair, as if involuntarily, but then, determined to control himself, walked to the window and looked out.

"She's gone away, sir, and we don't know where. She said she was going to Snowfield o' Friday was a fortnight, and I went last Sunday to fetch her back; but she'd never been there, and she took the coach to Stoniton, and beyond that I can't trace her. But now I'm going a long journey to look for her, and I can't trust t' anybody but you where I'm going."

Mr. Irwine came back from the window and sat down.

"Have you no idea of the reason why she went away?" he said.

"It's plain enough she didn't want to marry me, sir," said Adam. "She didn't like it when it came so near. But that isn't all, I doubt. There's something else I must tell you, sir. There's somebody else concerned besides me."

A gleam of something—it was almost like relief or joy-—came across the eager anxiety of Mr. Irwine's face at that moment. Adam was looking on the ground, and paused a little: the next words were hard to speak. But when he went on, he lifted up his head and looked straight at Mr. Irwine. He would do the thing he had resolved to do, without flinching.

"You know who's the man I've reckoned my greatest friend," he said, "and used to be proud to think as I should pass my life i' working for him, and had felt so ever since we were lads" . . . .

Mr. Irwine, as if all self-control had forsaken him, grasped Adam's arm, which lay on the table, and, clutching it tightly like a man in pain, said, with pale lips and a low hurried voice,

"No, Adam, no—don't say it, for God's sake!"

Adam, surprised at the violence of Mr. Irwine's feeling, repented of the words that had passed his lips, and sat in distressed silence. The grasp on his arm gradually relaxed, and Mr. Irwine threw himself back in his chair, saying, "Go on—I must know it."

"That man played with Hetty's feelings, and behaved to her as he'd no right to do to a girl in her station o' life—made her presents, and used to go and meet her out a-walking: I found it out only two days before he went away—found him a-kissing her as they were parting in the Grove. There'd been nothing said between me and Hetty then, though I'd loved her for a long while, and she knew it. But I reproached him with his wrong actions, and words and blows passed between us; and he said solemnly to me, after that, as it had been all nonsense, and no more than a bit o' flirting. But I made him write a letter to tell Hetty he'd meant nothing; for I saw clear enough, sir, by several things as I hadn't understood at the time, as he'd got hold of her heart, and I thought she'd belike go on thinking of him, and never come to love another man as wanted to marry her. And I gave her the letter, and she seemed to bear it all after a while better than I'd expected . . . and she behaved kinder and kinder to me . . . I daresay she didn't know her own feelings then, poor thing, and they came back upon her when it was too late . . . I don't want to blame her . . . I can't think as she meant to deceive me. But I was encouraged to think she loved me, and —you know the rest, sir. But it's on my mind as he's been false to me, and 'ticed her away, and she's gone to him—and I'm going now to see; for I can never go to work again till I know what's become of her."

During Adam's narrative, Mr. Irwine had had time to recover his self-mastery in spite of the painful thoughts that crowded upon him. It was a bitter remembrance to him now—that morning when Arthur breakfasted with him, and seemed as if he were on the verge of a confession. It was plain enough *now* what he had wanted to confess. And if their words had taken another turn . . . if he himself had been less fastidious about intruding on another man's secrets . . . it was cruel to think how thin a film had shut out rescue from all this guilt and misery. He saw the whole history now by that terrible illumination which the present sheds back upon the past. But every other feeling as it rushed upon him was thrown into abeyance by pity, deep respectful pity, for the man who sat before him,—already so bruised, going forth with sad blind resignedness to an unreal sorrow, while a real one was close upon him, too far beyond the range of common trial for him ever to have feared it. His own agitation was quelled by a certain awe that comes over us in the presence of a great anguish; for the anguish he must inflict on Adam was already present to him. Again he put his hand on the arm that lay on the table, but very gently this time, as he said solemnly,

"Adam, my dear friend, you have had some hard trials in your life. You can bear sorrow manfully, as well as act manfully: God requires both tasks at our hands. And there is a heavier sorrow coming upon you than any you have yet known. But you are not guilty—you have not the worst of all sorrows. God help him who has!"

The two pale faces looked at each other; in Adam's there was trembling suspense, in Mr. Irwine's hesitating, shrinking pity. But he went on.

"I have had news of Hetty this morning. She is not gone to *him*. She is in Stonyshire—at Stoniton."

Adam started up from his chair, as if he thought he could have leaped to her that moment. But Mr. Irwine laid hold of his arm again, and said, persuasively, "Wait, Adam, wait." So he sat down.

"She is in a very unhappy position—one which will make it worse for you to find her, my poor friend, than to have lost her for ever."

Adam's lips moved tremulously, but no sound came. They moved again, and he whispered, "Tell me."

"She has been arrested . . . she is in prison."

It was as if an insulting blow had brought back the spirit of resistance into Adam. The blood rushed to his face, and he said, loudly and sharply, "For what?"

"For a great crime—the murder of her child."

"It *can't be!*" Adam almost shouted, starting up from his chair, and making a stride towards the door; but he turned round again, setting his back against the book-case, and looking fiercely at Mr. Irwine. "It isn't possible. She never had a child. She can't be guilty. *Who* says it?"

"God grant she may be innocent, Adam. We can still hope she is."

"But who says she is guilty?" said Adam, violently. "Tell me everything."

"Here is a letter from the magistrate before whom she was taken, and the constable who arrested her is in the dining-room. She will not confess her name or where she comes from; but I fear, I fear, there can be no doubt it is Hetty. The description of her person corresponds, only that she is said to look very pale and ill. She had a small red-leather pocket-book in her pocket with two names written in it—one at the beginning, 'Hetty Sorrel, Hayslope,' and the other near the end, 'Dinah Morris, Snowfield.' She will not say which is her own name—she denies everything, and will answer no questions; and application has been made to me, as a magistrate, that I may take measures for identifying her, for it was thought probable that the name which stands first is her own name."

"But what proof have they got against her, if it *is* Hetty?" said Adam, still violently, with an effort that seemed to shake his whole frame. "I'll not believe it. It couldn't ha' been, and none of us know it."

"Terrible proof that she was under the temptation to commit the crime; but we have room to hope that she did not really commit it. Try and read that letter, Adam."

Adam took the letter between his shaking hands, and tried to fix his eyes steadily on it. Mr. Irwine meanwhile went out to give some orders. When he came back, Adam's eyes were still on the first page—he couldn't read—he could not put the words together, and make out what they meant. He threw it down at last, and clenched his fist.

"It's *his* doing," he said; "if there's been any crime, it's at his door, not at hers. *He* taught her to deceive—*he* deceived me first. Let 'em put *him* on his trial—let him stand in court beside her, and I'll tell 'em how he got hold of her heart, and 'ticed her t' evil, and then lied to me. Is *he* to go free, while they lay all the punishment on her . . . so weak and young?"

The image called up by these last words gave a new direction to poor Adam's maddened feelings. He was silent, looking at the corner of the room as if he saw something there. Then he burst out again, in a tone of appealing anguish,

"I *can't* bear it . . . O God, it's too hard to lay upon me—it's too hard to think she's wicked."

Mr. Irwine had sat down again in silence: he was too wise to utter soothing words at present, and indeed the sight of Adam before him, with that look of sudden age which sometimes comes over a young face in moments of terrible emotion—the hard bloodless look of the skin, the deep lines about the quivering mouth, the furrows in the brow—the sight of this strong firm man shattered by the invisible stroke of sorrow, moved him so deeply that speech was not easy. Adam stood motionless, with his eyes vacantly fixed in this way for a minute or two; in that short space he was living through all his love again.

"She can't ha' done it," he said, still without moving his eyes, as if he were only talking to himself: "it was fear made her hide it . . . I forgive her for deceiving me . . . I forgive thee, Hetty . . . thee wast deceived too . . . it's gone hard wi' thee, my poor Hetty . . . but they'll never make me believe it."

He was silent again for a few moments, and then he said, with fierce abruptness,

"I'll go to him—I'll bring him back—I'll make him go and look at her in her misery—he shall look at her till he can't forget it—it shall follow him night and day—as long as he lives it shall follow him—he shan't escape wi' lies this time—I'll fetch him, I'll drag him myself."

In the act of going towards the door, Adam paused automatically and looked about for his hat, quite unconscious where he was, or who was present with him. Mr. Irwine had followed him, and now took him by the arm, saying, in a quiet but decided tone,

"No, Adam, no; I'm sure you will wish to stay and see what good can be done for her, instead of going on a useless errand of vengeance. The punishment will surely fall without your aid. Besides, he is no longer in Ireland: he must be on his way home—or would be, long before you arrived; for his grandfather, I know, wrote for him to come at least ten days ago. I want you now to go with me to Stoniton. I have ordered a horse for you to ride with us, as soon as you can compose yourself."

While Mr. Irwine was speaking, Adam recovered his consciousness of the actual scene: he rubbed his hair off his forehead and listened.

"Remember," Mr. Irwine went on, "there are others to think of, and act for, besides yourself, Adam: there are Hetty's friends, the good Poysers, on whom this stroke will fall more heavily than I can bear to think. I expect it from your strength of mind, Adam—from your sense of duty to God and man—that you will try to act as long as action can be of any use."

In reality, Mr. Irwine proposed this journey to Stoniton for Adam's own sake. Movement, with some object before him, was the best means of counteracting the violence of suffering in these first hours.

"You *will* go with me to Stoniton, Adam?" he said again, after a moment's pause. "We have to see if it is really Hetty who is there, you know."

"Yes, sir," said Adam, "I'll do what you think right. But the folks at th' Hall Farm?"

"I wish them not to know till I return to tell them myself. I shall have ascertained things then which I am uncertain about now, and I shall return as soon as possible. Come now, the horses are ready."

CHAPTER XL

THE BITTER WATERS SPREAD

MR. IRWINE returned from Stoniton in a post-chaise that night, and the first words Carroll said to him, as he entered the house, were, that Squire Donnithorne was dead—found dead in his bed at ten o'clock that morning—and that Mrs. Irwine desired him to say she should be awake when Mr. Irwine came home, and she begged him not to go to bed without seeing her.

"Well, Dauphin," Mrs. Irwine said, as her son entered her room, "you're come at last. So the old gentleman's fidgetiness and low spirits, which made him send for Arthur in that sudden way, really meant something. I suppose Carroll has told you that Donnithorne was found dead in his bed this morning. You will believe my prognostications another time, though I daresay I shan't live to prognosticate anything but my own death."

"What have they done about Arthur?" said Mr. Irwine. "Sent a messenger to await him at Liverpool?"

"Yes, Ralph was gone before the news was brought to us. Dear Arthur, I shall live now to see him master at the Chase, and making good times on the estate, like a generous-hearted fellow as he is. He'll be as happy as a king now."

Mr. Irwine could not help giving a slight groan: he was worn with anxiety and exertion, and his mother's light words were almost intolerable.

"What are you so dismal about, Dauphin? Is there any bad news? Or are you thinking of the danger for Arthur in crossing that frightful Irish Channel at this time of year?"

"No, mother, I'm not thinking of that; but I'm not prepared to rejoice just now."

"You've been worried by this law business that you've been to Stoniton about. What in the world is it, that you can't tell me?"

"You will know by-and-by, mother. It would not be right for me to tell you at present. Good-night: you'll sleep now you have no longer anything to listen for."

Mr. Irwine gave up his intention of sending a letter to meet Arthur, since it would not now hasten his return: the news of his grandfather's death would bring him as soon as he could possibly come. He could go to bed now and get some needful rest, before the time came for the morning's heavy duty of carrying his sickening news to the Hall Farm and to Adam's home.

Adam himself was not come back from Stoniton, for though he shrank
from seeing Hetty, he could not bear to go to a distance from her again.

"It's no use, sir," he said to the Rector—"it's no use for me to go
back. I can't go to work again while she's here; and I couldn't bear the
sight o' things and folks round home. I'll take a bit of a room here,
where I can see the prison walls, and perhaps I shall get, in time, to
bear seeing *her*."

Adam had not been shaken in his belief that Hetty was innocent of
the crime she was charged with, for Mr. Irwine, feeling that the belief in
her guilt would be a crushing addition to Adam's load, had kept from
him the facts which left no hope in his own mind. There was not any
reason for thrusting the whole burthen on Adam at once, and Mr. Irwine,
at parting, only said, "If the evidence should tell too strongly against
her, Adam, we may still hope for a pardon. Her youth and other circumstances will be a plea for her."

"Ah, and it's right people should know how she was tempted into the
wrong way," said Adam, with bitter earnestness. "It's right they should
know it was a fine gentleman made love to her, and turned her head wi'
notions. You'll remember, sir, you've promised to tell my mother, and
Seth, and the people at the Farm, who it was as led her wrong, else
they'll think harder of her than she deserves. You'll be doing her a
hurt by sparing him, and I hold him the guiltiest before God, let her ha'
done what she may. If you spare him, I'll expose him!"

"I think your demand is just, Adam," said Mr. Irwine, "but when you
are calmer, you will judge Arthur more mercifully. I say nothing now,
only that his punishment is in other hands than ours."

Mr. Irwine felt it hard upon him that he should have to tell of Arthur's sad part in the story of sin and sorrow—he who cared for Arthur
with fatherly affection—who had cared for him with fatherly pride.
But he saw clearly that the secret must be known before long, even apart
from Adam's determination, since it was scarcely to be supposed that
Hetty would persist to the end in her obstinate silence. He made up his
mind to withhold nothing from the Poysers, but to tell them the worst
at once, for there was no time to rob the tidings of their suddenness.
Hetty's trial must come on at the Lent assizes, and they were to be held
at Stoniton the next week. It was scarcely to be hoped that Martin
Poyser could escape the pain of being called as a witness, and it was
better he should know everything as long beforehand as possible.

Before ten o'clock on Thursday morning the home at the Hall Farm
was a house of mourning for a misfortune felt to be worse than death.
The sense of family dishonour was too keen even in the kind-hearted
Martin Poyser the younger, to leave room for any compassion towards
Hetty. He and his father were simple-minded farmers, proud of their
untarnished character, proud that they came of a family which had held
up its head and paid its way as far back as its name was in the parish
register; and Hetty had brought disgrace on them all—disgrace that
could never be wiped out. That was the all-conquering feeling in the

mind both of father and son—the scorching sense of disgrace, which neutralised all other sensibility; and Mr. Irwine was struck with surprise to observe that Mrs. Poyser was less severe than her husband. We are often startled by the severity of mild people on exceptional occasions; the reason is, that mild people are most liable to be under the yoke of traditional impressions.

"I'm willing to pay any money as is wanted towards trying to bring her off," said Martin the younger when Mr. Irwine was gone, while the old grandfather was crying in the opposite chair, "but I'll not go nigh her, nor ever see her again, by my own will. She's made our bread bitter to us for all our lives to come, an' we shall ne'er hold up our heads i' this parish nor i' any other. The parson talks o' folks pitying us: it's poor amends pity 'ull make us."

"Pity?" said the grandfather, sharply. "I ne'er wanted folks's pity i' *my* life afore . . . an' I mun begin to be looked down on now, an' me turned seventy-two last St. Thomas's, an' all th' under-bearers and pall-bearers as I'n picked for my funeral are i' this parish and the next to 't. . . . It's o' no use now . . . I mun be ta'en to the grave by strangers."

"Don't fret so, father," said Mrs. Poyser, who had spoken very little, being almost overawed by her husband's unusual hardness and decision. "You'll have your children wi' you; an' there's the lads and the little un 'ull grow up in a new parish as well as i' th' old un."

"Ah, there's no staying i' this country for us now," said Mr. Poyser, and the hard tears trickled slowly down his round cheeks. "We thought it 'ud be bad luck if the old Squire gave us notice this Lady Day, but I must gi' notice myself now, an' see if there can anybody be got to come an' take to the crops as I'n put i' the ground; for I wonna stay upo' that man's land a day longer nor I'm forced to't. An' me, as thought him such a good upright young man, as I should be glad when he come to be our landlord. I'll ne'er lift my hat to him again, nor sit i' the same church wi' him . . . a man as has brought shame on respectable folks . . . an' pretended to be such a friend t' everybody. . . . Poor Adam there . . . a fine friend he's been t' Adam, making speeches an' talking so fine, an' all the while poisoning the lad's life, as it's much if he can stay i' this country any more nor we can."

"An' you t' ha' to go into court and own you're akin t' her," said the old man. "Why, they'll cast it up to the little un, as isn't four 'ear old, some day—they'll cast it up t' her as she'd a cousin tried at 'sizes for murder."

"It'll be their own wickedness, then," said Mrs. Poyser, with a sob in her voice. "But there's One above 'ull take care o' the innicent child, else it's but little truth they tell us at church. It'll be harder nor ever to die an' leave the little uns, an' nobody to be a mother to 'em."

"We'd better ha' sent for Dinah, if we'd known where she is," said Mr. Poyser; "but Adam said she'd left no direction where she'd be at Leeds."

"Why, she'd be wi' that woman as was a friend t' her aunt Judith," said Mrs. Poyser, comforted a little by this suggestion of her husband's. "I've often heard Dinah talk of her, but I can't remember what name she called her by. But there's Seth Bede; he's like enough to know, for she's a preaching woman as the Methodists think a deal on."

"I'll send to Seth," said Mr. Poyser. "I'll send Alick to tell him to come, or else to send us word o' the woman's name, an' thee canst write a letter ready to send off to Treddles'on as soon as we can make out a direction."

"It's poor work writing letters when you want folks to come to you i' trouble," said Mrs. Poyser. "Happen it'll be ever so long on the road, an' never reach her at last."

Before Alick arrived with the message, Lisbeth's thoughts too had already flown to Dinah, and she had said to Seth,

"Eh, there's no comfort for us i' this world any more, wi'out thee couldst get Dinah Morris to come to us, as she did when my old man died. I'd like her to come in an' take me by th' hand again, an' talk to me: she'd tell me the rights on't, belike—she'd happen know some good i' all this trouble an' heartbreak comin' upo' that poor lad, as ne'er done a bit o' wrong in's life, but war better nor anybody else's son, pick the country round. Eh, my lad . . . Adam, my poor lad!"

"Thee wouldstna like me to leave thee, to go and fetch Dinah?" said Seth, as his mother sobbed, and rocked herself to and fro.

"Fetch her?" said Lisbeth, looking up, and pausing from her grief, like a crying child, who hears some promise of consolation. "Why, what place is't she's at, do they say?"

"It's a good way off, mother—Leeds, a big town. But I could be back in three days, if thee couldst spare me."

"Nay, nay, I canna spare thee. Thee must go an' see thy brother, an' bring me word what he's a-doin'. Mester Irwine said he'd come an' tell me, but I canna make out so well what it means when he tells me. Thee must go thysen, sin' Adam wonna let me go to him. Write a letter to Dinah, canstna? Thee't fond enough o' writin' when nobody wants thee."

"I'm not sure where she'd be i' that big town," said Seth. "If I'd gone myself, I could ha' found out by asking the members o' the Society. But perhaps, if I put Sarah Williamson, Methodist preacher, Leeds, o' th' outside, it might get to her; for most like she'd be wi' Sarah Williamson."

Alick came now with the message, and Seth, finding that Mrs. Poyser was writing to Dinah, gave up the intention of writing himself; but he went to the Hall Farm to tell them all he could suggest about the address of the letter, and warn them that there might be some delay in the delivery, from his not knowing an exact direction.

On leaving Lisbeth, Mr. Irwine had gone to Jonathan Burge, who had also a claim to be acquainted with what was likely to keep Adam away from business for some time; and before six o'clock that evening there were few people in Broxton and Hayslope who had not heard the sad news. Mr. Irwine had not mentioned Arthur's name to Burge, and yet the story of his conduct towards Hetty, with all the dark shadows cast upon it by its terrible consequences, was presently as well known as that his grandfather was dead, and that he was come into the estate. For Martin Poyser felt no motive to keep silence towards the one or two neighbours who ventured to come and shake him sorrowfully by the hand on the first day of his trouble; and Carroll, who kept his ears open to all that passed at the Rectory, had framed an inferential version of the story, and found early opportunities of communicating it.

One of these neighbours who came to Martin Poyser and shook him by the hand without speaking for some minutes, was Bartle Massey. He had shut up his school, and was on his way to the Rectory, where he arrived about half-past seven in the evening, and, sending his duty to Mr. Irwine, begged pardon for troubling him at that hour, but had something particular on his mind. He was shown into the study, where Mr. Irwine soon joined him.

"Well, Bartle?" said Mr. Irwine, putting out his hand. That was not his usual way of saluting the schoolmaster, but trouble makes us treat all who feel with us very much alike. "Sit down."

"You know what I'm come about as well as I do, sir, I daresay," said Bartle.

"You wish to know the truth about the sad news that has reached you . . . about Hetty Sorrel?"

"Nay, sir, what I wish to know is about Adam Bede. I understand you left him at Stoniton, and I beg the favour of you to tell me what's the state of the poor lad's mind, and what he means to do. For as for that bit o' pink-and-white they've taken the trouble to put in jail, I don't value her a rotten nut—not a rotten nut—only for the harm or good that may come out of her to an honest man—a lad I've set such store by—trusted to, that he'd make my bit o' knowledge go a good way in the world. . . . Why, sir, he's the only scholar I've had in this stupid country that ever had the will or the head-piece for mathematics. If he hadn't had so much hard work to do, poor fellow, he might have gone into the higher branches, and then this might never have happened—might never have happened."

Bartle was heated by the exertion of walking fast in an agitated frame of mind, and was not able to check himself on this first occasion of venting his feelings. But he paused now to rub his moist forehead, and probably his moist eyes also.

"You'll excuse me, sir," he said, when this pause had given him time to reflect, "for running on in this way about my own feelings, like that foolish dog of mine, howling in a storm, when there's nobody wants to listen to me. I came to hear you speak, not to talk myself; if you'll take the trouble to tell me what the poor lad's doing."

"Don't put yourself under any restraint, Bartle," said Mr. Irwine. "The fact is, I'm very much in the same condition as you just now; I've a great deal that's painful on my mind, and I find it hard work to be quite silent about my own feelings and only attend to others. I share your concern for Adam, though he is not the only one whose sufferings I care for in this affair. He intends to remain at Stoniton till after the trial: it will come on probably a week to-morrow. He has taken a room there, and I encouraged him to do so, because I think it better he should be away from his own home at present; and, poor fellow, he still believes Hetty is innocent—he wants to summon up courage to see her if he can; he is unwilling to leave the spot where she is."

"Do you think the creatur's guilty, then?" said Bartle. "Do you think they'll hang her?"

"I'm afraid it will go hard with her: the evidence is very strong. And one bad symptom is that she denies everything—denies that she has had a child, in the face of the most positive evidence. I saw her myself, and she was obstinately silent to me; she shrank up like a frightened animal when she saw me. I was never so shocked in my life as at the change in her. But I trust that, in the worst case, we may obtain a pardon for the sake of the innocent who are involved."

"Stuff and nonsense!" said Bartle, forgetting in his irritation to whom he was speaking—"I beg your pardon, sir, I mean it's stuff and nonsense for the innocent to care about her being hanged. For my own part, I think the sooner such women are put out o' the world the better; and the men that help 'em to do mischief had better go along with 'em for that matter. What good will you do by keeping such vermin alive? eating the victual that 'ud feed rational beings. But if Adam's fool enough to care about it, I don't want him to suffer more than's needful. . . . Is he very much cut up, poor fellow?" Bartle added, taking out his spectacles and putting them on, as if they would assist his imagination.

"Yes, I'm afraid the grief cuts very deep," said Mr. Irwine. "He looks terribly shattered, and a certain violence came over him now and then yesterday, which made me wish I could have remained near him. But I shall go to Stoniton again to-morrow, and I have confidence enough in the strength of Adam's principle to trust that he will be able to endure the worst without being driven to anything rash."

Mr. Irwine, who was involuntarily uttering his own thoughts rather than addressing Bartle Massey in the last sentence, had in his mind the possibility that the spirit of vengeance towards Arthur, which was the form Adam's anguish was continually taking, might make him seek an encounter that was likely to end more fatally than the one in the Grove. This possibility heightened the anxiety with which he looked forward to Arthur's arrival. But Bartle thought Mr. Irwine was referring to suicide, and his face wore a new alarm.

"I'll tell you what I have in my head, sir," he said, "and I hope you'll approve of it. I'm going to shut up my school: if the scholars come, they must go back again, that's all: and I shall go to Stoniton and look after Adam till this business is over. I'll pretend I'm come to look on at the assizes; he can't object to that. What do you think about it, sir?"

"Well," said Mr. Irwine, rather hesitatingly, "there would be some real advantages in that . . . and I honour you for your friendship towards him, Bartle. But . . . you must be careful what you say to him, you know. I'm afraid you have too little fellow-feeling in what you consider his weakness about Hetty."

"Trust to me, sir—trust to me. I know what you mean. I've been a fool myself in my time, but that's between you and me. I shan't thrust myself on him—only keep my eye on him, and see that he gets some good food, and put in a word here and there."

"Then," said Mr. Irwine, reassured a little as to Bartle's discretion, "I think you'll be doing a good deed; and it will be well for you to let Adam's mother and brother know that you're going."

"Yes, sir, yes," said Bartle, rising, and taking off his spectacles, "I'll do that, I'll do that; though the mother's a whimpering thing—I don't like to come within earshot of her; however, she's a straight-backed, clean woman, none of your slatterns. I wish you good-by, sir, and thank you for the time you've spared me. You're everybody's friend in this business—everybody's friend. It's a heavy weight you've got on your shoulders."

"Good-by, Bartle, till we meet at Stoniton, as I daresay we shall."

Bartle hurried away from the Rectory, evading Carroll's conversational advances, and saying in an exasperated tone to Vixen, whose short legs pattered beside him on the gravel,

"Now, I shall be obliged to take you with me, you good-for-nothing woman. You'd go fretting yourself to death if I left you—you know you would, and perhaps get snapped up by some tramp; and you'll be running into bad company, I expect, putting your nose in every hole and corner where you've no business! but if you do anything disgraceful, I'll disown you—mind that, madam, mind that!"

CHAPTER XLI

THE EVE OF THE TRIAL

AN upper room in a dull Stoniton street, with two beds in it—one laid on the floor. It is ten o'clock on Thursday night, and the dark wall opposite the window shuts out the moonlight that might have struggled with the light of the one dip candle by which Bartle Massey is pretending to read, while he is really looking over his spectacles at Adam Bede, seated near the dark window.

You would hardly have known it was Adam without being told. His face has got thinner this last week: he has the sunken eyes, the neglected beard of a man just risen from a sick-bed. His heavy black hair hangs over his forehead, and there is no active impulse in him which inclines him to push it off, that he may be more awake to what is around him. He has one arm over the back of the chair, and he seems to be looking down at his clasped hands. He is roused by a knock at the door.

"There he is," said Bartle Massey, rising hastily and unfastening
the door. It was Mr. Irwine.

Adam rose from his chair with instinctive respect, as Mr. Irwine approached him and took his hand.

"I'm late, Adam," he said, sitting down on the chair which Bartle
placed for him; "but I was later in setting off from Broxton than I
intended to be, and I have been incessantly occupied since I arrived. I
have done everything now, however—everything that.can be done to-
night, at least. Let us all sit down."

Adam took his chair again mechanically, and Bartle, for whom there
was no chair remaining, sat on the bed in the background.

"Have you seen her, sir?" said Adam, tremulously.

"Yes, Adam; I and the chaplain have both been with her this evening."

"Did you ask her, sir . . . did you say anything about me?"

"Yes," said Mr. Irwine, with some hesitation, "I spoke of you. I said
you wished to see her before the trial, if she consented."

As Mr. Irwine paused, Adam looked at him with eager, questioning
eyes.

"You know she shrinks from seeing any one, Adam. It is not only you
—some fatal influence seems to have shut up her heart against her
fellow-creatures. She has scarcely said anything more than 'No,' either
to me or the chaplain. Three or four days ago, before you were mentioned to her, when I asked her if there was any one of her family whom
she would like to see—to whom she could open her mind, she said,
with a violent shudder, 'Tell them not to come near me—I won't see
any of them.' "

Adam's head was hanging down again, and he did not speak. There
was silence for a few minutes, and then Mr. Irwine said,

"I don't like to advise you against your own feelings, Adam, if they
now urge you strongly to go and see her to-morrow morning, even without her consent. It is just possible, notwithstanding appearances to the
contrary, that the interview might affect her favourably. But I grieve to
say I have scarcely any hope of that. She didn't seem agitated when I
mentioned your name; she only said 'No,' in the same cold, obstinate
way as usual. And if the meeting had no good effect on her, it would be
pure, useless suffering for you—severe suffering, I fear. She is very much
changed" . . .

Adam started up from his chair, and seized his hat which lay on the
table. But he stood still then, and looked at Mr. Irwine, as if he had a
question to ask, which it was yet difficult to utter. Bartle Massey rose
quietly, turned the key in the door, and put it in his pocket.

"Is he come back?" said Adam at last.

"No, he is not," said Mr. Irwine, quietly. "Lay down your hat, Adam,
unless you like to walk out with me for a little fresh air. I fear you have
not been out again to-day."

"You needn't deceive me, sir," said Adam, looking hard at Mr. Irwine, and speaking in a tone of angry suspicion. "You needn't be afraid of me. I only want justice. I want him to feel what she feels. It's his work . . . she was a child as it 'ud ha' gone t' anybody's heart to look at . . . I don't care what she's done . . . it was him brought her to it. And he shall know it . . . he shall feel it . . . if there's a just God, he shall feel what it is t' ha' brought a child like her to sin and misery" . . .

"I'm not deceiving you, Adam," said Mr. Irwine. "Arthur Donnithorne is not come back—was not come back when I left. I have left a letter for him: he will know all as soon as he arrives."

"But you don't mind about it," said Adam, indignantly. "You think it doesn't matter as she lies there in shame and misery, and he knows nothing about it—he suffers nothing."

"Adam, he *will* know—he *will* suffer, long and bitterly. He has a heart and a conscience: I can't be entirely deceived in his character. I am convinced—I am sure he didn't fall under temptation without a struggle. He may be weak, but he is not callous, not coldly selfish. I am persuaded that this will be a shock of which he will feel the effects all his life. Why do you crave vengeance in this way? No amount of torture that you could inflict on *him* could benefit *her.*"

"No—O God, no," Adam groaned out, sinking on his chair again; "but then, that's the deepest curse of all . . . that's what makes the blackness of it . . . *it can never be undone.* My poor Hetty . . . she can never be my sweet Hetty again . . . the prettiest thing God had made—smiling up at me . . . I thought she loved me . . . and was good" . . .

Adam's voice had been gradually sinking into a hoarse undertone, as if he were only talking to himself; but now he said abruptly, looking at Mr. Irwine,

"But she isn't as guilty as they say? You don't think she is, sir? She can't ha' done it."

"That perhaps can never be known with certainty, Adam," Mr. Irwine answered, gently. "In these cases we sometimes form our judgment on what seems to us strong evidence, and yet, for want of knowing some small fact, our judgment is wrong. But suppose the worst: you have no right to say that the guilt of her crime lies with him, and that he ought to bear the punishment. It is not for us men to apportion the shares of moral guilt and retribution. We find it impossible to avoid mistakes even in determining who has committed a single criminal act, and the problem how far a man is to be held responsible for the unforeseen consequences of his own deed, is one that might well make us tremble to look into it. The evil consequences that may lie folded in a single act of selfish indulgence, is a thought so awful that it ought surely to awaken some feeling less presumptuous than a rash desire to punish. You have a mind that can understand this fully, Adam, when you are calm. Don't suppose I can't enter into the anguish that drives you into this state of revengeful hatred; but think of this: if you were to obey your passion—for it *is* passion, and you deceive yourself in calling it justice—it might be with you precisely as it has been with Arthur; nay, worse; your passion might lead you yourself into a horrible crime."

"No—not worse," said Adam, bitterly; "I don't believe it's worse—I'd sooner do it—I'd sooner do a wickedness as I could suffer for by myself, than ha' brought *her* to do wickedness and then stand by and see 'em punish her while they let me alone; and all for a bit o' pleasure, as, if he'd had a man's heart in him, he'd ha' cut his hand off sooner than he'd ha' taken it. What if he didn't foresee what's happened? He foresaw enough: he'd no right to expect anything but harm and shame to her. And then he wanted to smooth it off wi' lies. No—there's plenty o' things folks are hanged for, not half so hateful as that: let a man do what he will, if he knows he's to bear the punishment himself, he isn't half so bad as a mean selfish coward as makes things easy t' himself, and knows all the while the punishment 'll fall on somebody else."

"There again you partly deceive yourself, Adam. There is no sort of wrong deed of which a man can bear the punishment alone; you can't isolate yourself, and say that the evil which is in you shall not spread. Men's lives are as thoroughly blended with each other as the air they breathe: evil spreads as necessarily as disease. I know, I feel the terrible extent of suffering this sin of Arthur's has caused to others; but so does every sin cause suffering to others besides those who commit it. An act of vengeance on your part against Arthur would simply be another evil added to those we are suffering under: you could not bear the punishment alone; you would entail the worst sorrows on every one who loves you. You would have committed an act of blind fury, that would leave all the present evils just as they were, and add worse evils to them. You may tell me that you meditate no fatal act of vengeance: but the feeling in your mind is what gives birth to such actions, and as long as you indulge it, as long as you do not see that to fix your mind on Arthur's punishment is revenge, and not justice, you are in danger of being led on to the commission of some great wrong. Remember what you told me about your feelings after you had given that blow to Arthur in the Grove."

Adam was silent: the last words had called up a vivid image of the past, and Mr. Irwine left him to his thoughts, while he spoke to Bartle Massey about old Donnithorne's funeral and other matters of an indifferent kind. But at length Adam turned round and said, in a more subdued tone,

"I've not asked about 'em at th' Hall Farm, sir. Is Mr. Poyser coming?"

"He is come; he is in Stoniton to-night. But I could not advise him to see you, Adam. His own mind is in a very perturbed state, and it is best he should not see you till you are calmer."

"Is Dinah Morris come to 'em, sir? Seth said they'd sent for her."

"No. Mr. Poyser tells me she was not come when he left. They're afraid the letter has not reached her. It seems they had no exact address."

Adam sat ruminating a little while, and then said,

"I wonder if Dinah 'ud ha' gone to see her. But perhaps the Poyser's would ha' been sorely against it, since they won't come nigh her themselves. But I think she would, for the Methodists are great folks for going into the prisons; and Seth said he thought she would. She'd a very tender way with her, Dinah had; I wonder if she could ha' done any good. You never saw her, sir, did you?"

"Yes, I did: I had a conversation with her—she pleased me a good deal. And now you mention it, I wish she would come; for it is possible that a gentle, mild woman like her might move Hetty to open her heart. The jail chaplain is rather harsh in his manner."

"But it's o' no use if she doesn't come," said Adam, sadly.

"If I'd thought of it earlier, I would have taken some measures for finding her out," said Mr. Irwine, "but it's too late now, I fear. . . . Well, Adam, I must go now. Try to get some rest to-night. God bless you. I'll see you early to-morrow morning."

CHAPTER XLII

THE MORNING OF THE TRIAL

At one o'clock the next day, Adam was alone in his dull upper room; his watch lay before him on the table, as if he were counting the long minutes. He had no knowledge of what was likely to be said by the witnesses on the trial, for he had shrunk from all the particulars connected with Hetty's arrest and accusation. This brave active man, who would have hastened towards any danger or toil to rescue Hetty from an apprehended wrong or misfortune, felt himself powerless to contemplate irremediable evil and suffering. The susceptibility which would have been an impelling force where there was any possibility of action, became helpless anguish when he was obliged to be passive, or else sought an active outlet in the thought of inflicting justice on Arthur. Energetic natures, strong for all strenuous deeds, will often rush away from a hopeless sufferer, as if they were hard-hearted. It is the overmastering sense of pain that drives them. They shrink by an ungovernable instinct, as they would shrink from laceration. Adam had brought himself to think of seeing Hetty, if she would consent to see him, because he thought the meeting might possibly be a good to her—might help to melt away this terrible hardness they told him of. If she saw he bore her no ill-will for what she had done to him, she might open her heart to him. But this resolution had been an immense effort; he trembled at the thought of seeing her changed face, as a timid woman trembles at the thought of the surgeon's knife; and he chose now to bear the long hours of suspense, rather than encounter what seemed to him the more intolerable agony of witnessing her trial.

Deep, unspeakable suffering may well be called a baptism, a regeneration, the initiation into a new state. The yearning memories, the bitter regret, the agonised sympathy, the struggling appeals to the Invisible Right—all the intense emotions which had filled the days and nights of the past week, and were compressing themselves again like an eager crowd into the hours of this single morning, made Adam look back on all the previous years as if they had been a dim sleepy existence, and he had only now awakened to full consciousness. It seemed to him as if he had always before thought it a light thing that men should suffer; as if all that he had himself endured and called sorrow before, was only a moment's stroke that had never left a bruise. Doubtless a great anguish may do the work of years, and we may come out from that baptism with a soul full of new awe and new pity.

"O God," Adam groaned, as he leaned on the table, and looked blankly at the face of the watch, "and men have suffered like this before . . . and poor helpless young things have suffered like her. . . . Such a little while ago looking so happy and so pretty . . . kissing 'em all, her grandfather and all of 'em, and they wishing her luck. . . . O my poor, poor Hetty . . . dost think on it now?"

Adam started and looked round towards the door. Vixen had begun to whimper, and there was a sound of a stick and a lame walk on the stairs. It was Bartle Massey come back. Could it be all over?

Bartle entered quietly, and, going up to Adam, grasped his hand and said, "I'm just come to look at you, my boy, for the folks are gone out of court for a bit."

Adam's heart beat so violently, he was unable to speak—he could only return the pressure of his friend's hand; and Bartle, drawing up the other chair, came and sat in front of him, taking off his hat and his spectacles.

"That's a thing never happened to me before," he observed—"to go out o' door with my spectacles on. I clean forgot to take 'em off."

The old man made this trivial remark, thinking it better not to respond at all to Adam's agitation: he would gather in an indirect way, that there was nothing decisive to communicate at present.

"And now," he said, rising again, "I must see to your having a bit of the loaf, and some of that wine Mr. Irwine sent this morning. He'll be angry with me if you don't have it. Come, now," he went on, bringing forward the bottle and the loaf, and pouring some wine into a cup, "I must have a bit and a sup myself. Drink a drop with me, my lad—drink with me."

Adam pushed the cup gently away, and said, entreatingly, "Tell me about it, Mr. Massey—tell me all about it. Was she there? Have they begun?"

"Yes, my boy, yes—it's taken all the time since I first went; but they're slow, they're slow; and there's the counsel they've got for her puts a spoke in the wheel whenever he can, and makes a deal to do with cross-examining the witnesses, and quarrelling with the other lawyers. That's all he can do for the money they give him; and it's a big sum —it's a big sum. But he's a 'cute fellow, with an eye that 'ud pick the needles out of the hay in no time. If a man had got no feelings, it 'ud be as good as a demonstration to listen to what goes on in court; but a tender heart makes one stupid. I'd have given up figures for ever only to have had some good news to bring to you, my poor lad."

"But does it seem to be going against her?" said Adam. "Tell me what they've said. I must know it now—I must know what they have to bring against her."

"Why, the chief evidence yet has been the doctors; all but Martin Poyser—poor Martin. Everybody in court felt for him—it was like one sob, the sound they made when he came down again. The worst was, when they told him to look at the prisoner at the bar. It was hard work, poor fellow—it was hard work. Adam, my boy, the blow falls heavily on him as well as you: you must help poor Martin; you must show courage. Drink some wine now, and show me you mean to bear it like a man."

Bartle had made the right sort of appeal. Adam, with an air of quiet obedience, took up the cup, and drank a little.

"Tell me how *she* looked," he said, presently.

"Frightened, very frightened, when they first brought her in; it was the first sight of the crowd and the judge, poor creatur. And there's a lot o' foolish women in fine clothes, with gewgaws all up their arms and feathers on their heads, sitting near the judge: they've dressed themselves out in that way, one 'ud think, to be scarecrows and warnings against any man ever meddling with a woman again; they put up their glasses, and stared and whispered. But after that she stood like a white image, staring down at her hands, and seeming neither to hear nor see anything. And she's as white as a sheet. She didn't speak when they asked her if she'd plead 'guilty' or 'not guilty,' and they pled 'not guilty' for her. But when she heard her uncle's name, there seemed to go a shiver right through her; and when they told him to look at her, she hung her head down, and cowered, and hid her face in her hands. He'd much ado to speak, poor man, his voice trembled so. And the counsellors,—who look as hard as nails mostly,—I saw, spared him as much as they could. Mr. Irwine put himself near him, and went with him out o' court. Ah, it's a great thing in a man's life to be able to stand by a neighbour, and uphold him in such trouble as that."

"God bless him, and you too, Mr. Massey," said Adam, in a low voice, laying his hand on Bartle's arm.

"Ay, ay, he's good metal: he gives the right ring when you try him, our parson does. A man o' sense—says no more than's needful. He's not one of those that think they can comfort you with chattering, as if folks who stand by and look on knew a deal better what the trouble was than those who have to bear it. I've had to do with such folks in my time—in the south, when I was in trouble myself. Mr. Irwine is to be a witness himself, by-and-by, on her side, you know, to speak to her character and bringing up."

"But the other evidence . . . does it go hard against her?" said Adam. "What do you think, Mr. Massey? Tell me the truth."

"Yes, my lad, yes: the truth is the best thing to tell. It must come at last. The doctor's evidence is heavy on her—is heavy. But she's gone on denying she's had a child from first to last: these poor silly women-things —they've not the sense to know it's no use denying what's proved. It'll make against her with the jury, I doubt, her being so obstinate: they may be less for recommending her to mercy, if the verdict's against her. But Mr. Irwine 'll leave no stone unturned with the judge—you may rely upon that, Adam."

"Is there nobody to stand by her, and seem to care for her, in the court?" said Adam.

"There's the chaplain o' the jail sits near her, but he's a sharp ferrety-faced man—another sort o' flesh and blood to Mr. Irwine. They say the jail chaplains are mostly the fag-end o' the clergy."

"There's one man as ought to be there," said Adam, bitterly. Presently he drew himself up, and looked fixedly out of the window, apparently turning over some new idea in his mind.

"Mr. Massey," he said at last, pushing the hair off his forehead, "I'll go back with you. I'll go into court. It's cowardly of me to keep away. I'll stand by her—I'll own her—for all she's been deceitful. They oughtn't to cast her off—her own flesh and blood. We hand folks over to God's mercy, and show none ourselves. I used to be hard sometimes: I'll never be hard again. I'll go, Mr. Massey—I'll go with you."

There was a decision in Adam's manner which would have prevented Bartle from opposing him, even if he had wished to do so. He only said,

"Take a bit, then, and another sup, Adam, for the love of me. See, I must stop and eat a morsel. Now, you take some."

Nerved by an active resolution, Adam took a morsel of bread, and drank some wine. He was haggard and unshaven, as he had been yesterday, but he stood upright again, and looked more like the Adam Bede of former days.

CHAPTER XLIII

THE VERDICT

THE place fitted up that day as court of justice was a grand old hall, now destroyed by fire. The mid-day light that fell on the close pavement of human heads, was shed through a line of high pointed windows, variegated with the mellow tints of old painted glass. Grim dusty armour hung in high relief in front of the dark oaken gallery at the farther end; and under the broad arch of the great mullioned window opposite was spread a curtain of old tapestry, covered with dim melancholy figures, like a dozing indistinct dream of the past. It was a place that through the rest of the year was haunted with the shadowy memories of old kings and queens, unhappy, discrowned, imprisoned; but to-day all those shadows had fled, and not a soul in the vast hall felt the presence of any but a living sorrow, which was quivering in warm hearts.

But that sorrow seemed to have made itself feebly felt hitherto, now when Adam Bede's tall figure was suddenly seen, being ushered to the side of the prisoner's dock. In the broad sunlight of the great hall, among the sleek shaven faces of other men, the marks of suffering in his face were startling even to Mr. Irwine, who had last seen him in the dim light of his small room; and the neighbours from Hayslope who were present, and who told Hetty Sorrel's story by their firesides in their old age, never forgot to say how it moved them when Adam Bede, poor fellow, taller by the head than most of the people round him, came into court, and took his place by her side. But Hetty did not see him. She was standing in the same position Bartle Massey had described, her hands crossed over each other, and her eyes fixed on them. Adam had not dared to look at her in the first moments, but at last, when the attention of the court was withdrawn by the proceedings, he turned his face towards her with a resolution not to shrink.

Why did they say she was so changed? In the corpse we love, it is the *likeness* we see—it is the likeness, which makes itself felt the more keenly because something else *was* and *is not*. There they were—the sweet face and neck, with the dark tendrils of hair, the long dark lashes, the rounded cheek and the pouting lips: pale and thin—yes—but like Hetty, and only Hetty. Others thought she looked as if some demon had cast a blighting glance upon her, withered up the woman's soul in her, and left only a hard despairing obstinacy. But the mother's yearning, that completest type of the life in another life which is the essence of real human love, feels the presence of the cherished child even in the debased, degraded man; and to Adam, this pale hard-looking culprit was the Hetty who had smiled at him in the garden under the apple-tree boughs —she was that Hetty's corpse, which he had trembled to look at the first time, and then was unwilling to turn away his eyes from.

But presently he heard something that compelled him to listen, and made the sense of sight less absorbing. A woman was in the witness-box, a middle-aged woman, who spoke in a firm distinct voice. She said, "My name is Sarah Stone. I am a widow, and keep a small shop licensed to sell tobacco, snuff, and tea, in Church Lane, Stoniton. The prisoner at the bar is the same young woman who came, looking ill and tired, with a basket on her arm, and asked for a lodging at my house on Saturday evening, the 27th of February. She had taken the house for a public, because there was a figure against the door. And when I said I didn't take in lodgers, the prisoner began to cry, and said she was too tired to go anywhere else, and she only wanted a bed for one night. And her prettiness, and her condition, and something respectable about her clothes and looks, and the trouble she seemed to be in, made me as I couldn't find my heart to send her away at once. I asked her to sit down. and gave her some tea, and asked her where she was going, and where

her friends were. She said she was going home to her friends: they were
farming folks a good way off, and she'd had a long journey that had cost
her more money than she expected, so as she'd hardly any money left
in her pocket, and was afraid of going where it would cost her much.
She had been obliged to sell most of the things out of her basket; but
she'd thankfully give a shilling for a bed. I saw no reason why I shouldn't
take the young woman in for the night. I had only one room, but there
were two beds in it, and I told her she might stay with me. I thought
she'd been led wrong, and got into trouble, but if she was going to her
friends, it would be a good work to keep her out of further harm."

The witness then stated that in the night a child was born, and she
identified the baby-clothes then shown to her as those in which she had
herself dressed the child.

"Those are the clothes. I made them myself, and had kept them by
me ever since my last child was born. I took a deal of trouble both for
the child and the mother. I couldn't help taking to the little thing and
being anxious about it. I didn't send for a doctor, for there seemed no
need. I told the mother in the day-time she must tell me the name of her
friends, and where they lived, and let me write to them. She said, by-
and-by she would write herself, but not to-day. She would have no nay,
but she would get up and be dressed, in spite of everything I could say.
She said she felt quite strong enough; and it was wonderful what spirit
she showed. But I wasn't quite easy what I should do about her, and
towards evening I made up my mind I'd go, after Meeting was over,
and speak to our minister about it. I left the house about half-past eight
o'clock. I didn't go out at the shop door, but at the back door, which
opens into a narrow alley. I've only got the ground floor of the house,
and the kitchen and bedroom both look into the alley. I left the prisoner
sitting up by the fire in the kitchen with the baby on her lap. She hadn't
cried or seemed low at all, as she did the night before. I thought she
had a strange look with her eyes, and she got a bit flushed towards evening. I was afraid of the fever, and I thought I'd call and ask an acquaintance of mine, an experienced woman, to come back with me when I
went out. It was a very dark night. I didn't fasten the door behind me:
there was no lock: it was a latch with a bolt inside, and when there was
nobody in the house I always went out at the shop door. But I thought
there was no danger in leaving it unfastened that little while. I was
longer than I meant to be, for I had to wait for the woman that came
back with me. It was an hour and a half before we got back, and when
we went in, the candle was standing burning just as I left it, but the
prisoner and the baby were both gone. She'd taken her cloak and bonnet,
but she'd left the basket and the things in it. . . . I was dreadful frightened, and angry with her for going. I didn't go to give information,
because I'd no thought she meant to do any harm, and I knew she had
money in her pocket to buy her food and lodging. I didn't like to set
the constable after her, for she'd a right to go from me if she liked."

The effect of this evidence on Adam was electrical; it gave him new force. Hetty could not be guilty of the crime—her heart must have clung to her baby—else why should she have taken it with her? She might have left it behind. The little creature had died naturally, and then she had hidden it: babies were so liable to death—and there might be the strongest suspicions without any proof of guilt. His mind was so occupied with imaginary arguments against such suspicions, that he could not listen to the cross-examination by Hetty's counsel, who tried, without result, to elicit evidence that the prisoner had shown some movements of maternal affection towards the child. The whole time this witness was being examined, Hetty had stood as motionless as before: no word seemed to arrest her ear. But the sound of the next witness's voice touched a chord that was still sensitive; she gave a start and a frightened look towards him, but immediately turned away her head and looked down at her hands as before. This witness was a man, a rough peasant. He said:

"My name is John Olding. I am a labourer, and live at Tedd's Hole, two miles out of Stoniton. A week last Monday, towards one o'clock in the afternoon, I was going towards Hetton Coppice, and about a quarter of a mile from the coppice I saw the prisoner, in a red cloak, sitting under a bit of a haystack not far off the stile. She got up when she saw me, and seemed as if she'd be walking on the other way. It was a regular road through the fields, and nothing very uncommon to see a young woman there, but I took notice of her because she looked white and scared. I should have thought she was a beggar-woman, only for her good clothes. I thought she looked a bit crazy, but it was no business of mine. I stood and looked back after her, but she went right on while she was in sight. I had to go to the other side of the coppice to look after some stakes. There's a road right through it, and bits of openings here and there, where the trees have been cut down, and some of 'em not carried away. I didn't go straight along the road, but turned off towards the middle, and took a shorter way towards the spot I wanted to get to. I hadn't got far out of the road into one of the open places, before I heard a strange cry. I thought it didn't come from any animal I knew, but I wasn't for stopping to look about just then. But it went on, and seemed so strange to me in that place, I couldn't help stopping to look. I began to think I might make some money of it, if it was a new thing. But I had hard work to tell which way it came from, and for a good while I kept looking up at the boughs. And then I thought it came from the ground; and there was a lot of timber-choppings lying about, and loose pieces of turf, and a trunk or two. And I looked about among them, but could find nothing; and at last the cry stopped. So I was for giving it up, and I went on about my business. But when I came back the same way pretty nigh an hour after, I couldn't help laying down my stakes to have another look. And just as I was stooping and laying down the stakes, I saw something odd and round and whitish lying on the ground under a nut-bush by the side of me. And I stooped down on hands and knees to pick it up. And I saw it was a little baby's hand."

At these words a thrill ran through the court. Hetty was visibly trembling: now, for the first time, she seemed to be listening to what a witness said.

"There was a lot of timber-choppings put together just where the ground went hollow, like, under the bush, and the hand came out from among them. But there was a hole left in one place, and I could see down it, and see the child's head; and I made haste and did away the turf and the choppings, and took out the child. It had got comfortable clothes on, but its body was cold, and I thought it must be dead. I made haste back with it out of the wood, and took it home to my wife. She said it was dead, and I'd better take it to the parish and tell the constable. And I said, 'I'll lay my life it's that young woman's child as I met going to the coppice.' But she seemed to be gone clean out of sight. And I took the child on to Hetton parish and told the constable, and we went on to Justice Hardy. And then we went looking after the young woman till dark at night, and we went and gave information at Stoniton, as they might stop her. And the next morning, another constable came to me, to go with him to the spot where I found the child. And when we got there, there was the prisoner a-sitting against the bush where I found the child; and she cried out when she saw us, but she never offered to move. She'd got a big piece of bread on her lap."

Adam had given a faint groan of despair while this witness was speaking. He had hidden his face on his arm, which rested on the boarding in front of him. It was the supreme moment of his suffering: Hetty was guilty: and he was silently calling to God for help. He heard no more of the evidence, and was unconscious when the case for the prosecution had closed—unconscious that Mr. Irwine was in the witness-box, telling of Hetty's unblemished character in her own parish, and of the virtuous habits in which she had been brought up. This testimony could have no influence on the verdict, but it was given as part of that plea for mercy which her own counsel would have made if he had been allowed to speak for her—a favour not granted to criminals in those stern times.

At last Adam lifted up his head, for there was a general movement round him. The judge had addressed the jury, and they were retiring. The decisive moment was not far off. Adam felt a shuddering horror that would not let him look at Hetty, but she had long relapsed into her blank hard indifference. All eyes were strained to look at her, but she stood like a statue of dull despair.

There was a mingled rustling, whispering, and low buzzing throughout the court during this interval. The desire to listen was suspended, and every one had some feeling or opinion to express in under-tones. Adam sat looking blankly before him, but he did not see the objects that were right in front of his eyes—the counsel and attorneys talking with an air of cool business, and Mr. Irwine in low earnest conversation with the judge: did not see Mr. Irwine sit down again in agitation, and shake his head mournfully when somebody whispered to him. The inward action was too intense for Adam to take-in outward objects until some strong sensation roused him.

It was not very long, hardly more than a quarter of an hour, before the knock which told that the jury had come to their decision, fell as a signal for silence on every ear. It is sublime—that sudden pause of a great multitude, which tells that one soul moves in them all. Deeper and deeper the silence seemed to become, like the deepening night, while the jurymen's names were called over, and the prisoner was made to hold up her hand, and the jury were asked for their verdict.

"Guilty."

It was the verdict every one expected, but there was a sigh of disappointment from some hearts, that it was followed by no recommendation to mercy. Still the sympathy of the court was not with the prisoner: the unnaturalness of her crime stood out the more harshly by the side of her hard immovability and obstinate silence. Even the verdict, to distant eyes, had not appeared to move her; but those who were near saw her trembling.

The stillness was less intense until the judge put on his black cap, and the chaplain in his canonicals was observed behind him. Then it deepened again, before the crier had had time to command silence. If any sound were heard, it must have been the sound of beating hearts. The judge spoke:

"Hester Sorrel." . . .

The blood rushed to Hetty's face, and then fled back again, as she looked up at the judge, and kept her wide-open eyes fixed on him, as if fascinated by fear. Adam had not yet turned towards her: there was a deep horror, like a great gulf, between them. But at the words—"and then to be hanged by the neck till you be dead," a piercing shriek rang through the hall. It was Hetty's shriek. Adam started to his feet and stretched out his arms towards her; but the arms could not reach her: she had fallen down in a fainting-fit, and was carried out of court.

CHAPTER XLIV

ARTHUR'S RETURN

WHEN Arthur Donnithorne landed at Liverpool, and read the letter from his aunt Lydia, briefly announcing his grandfather's death, his first feeling was, "Poor grandfather! I wish I could have got to him to be with him when he died. He might have felt or wished something at the last that I shall never know now. It was a lonely death."

It is impossible to say that his grief was deeper than that. Pity and softened memory took place of the old antagonism, and in his busy thoughts about the future, as the chaise carried him rapidly along towards the home where he was now to be master, there was a continually recurring effort to remember anything by which he could show a regard for his grandfather's wishes, without counteracting his own cherished aims for the good of the tenants and the estate. But it is not in human

natu——only in human pretence—for a young man like Arthur, with a
fine constitution and fine spirits, thinking well of himself, believing that
others think well of him, and having a very ardent intention to give
them more and more reason for that good opinion,—it is not possible
for such a young man, just coming into a splendid estate through the
death of a very old man whom he was not fond of, to feel anything very
different from exultant joy. *Now* his real life was beginning; now he
would have room and opportunity for action, and he would use them.
He would show the Loamshire people what a fine country gentleman
was; he would not exchange that career for any other under the sun.
He felt himself riding over the hills in the breezy autumn days, looking
after favourite plans of drainage and enclosure; then admired on sombre mornings as the best rider on the best horse in the hunt; spoken
well of on market-days as a first-rate landlord; by-and-by making
speeches at election dinners, and showing a wonderful knowledge of agri-
culture; the patron of new ploughs and drills, the severe upbraider of
negligent landowners, and withal a jolly fellow that everybody must
like,—happy faces greeting him everywhere on his own estate, and the
neighbouring families on the best terms with him. The Irwines should
dine with him every week, and have their own carriage to come in, for
in some very delicate way that Arthur would devise, the lay-impropria-
tor of the Hayslope tithes would insist on paying a couple of hundreds
more to the Vicar; and his aunt should be as comfortable as possible,
and go on living at the Chase, if she liked, in spite of her old-maidish
ways,—at least until he was married; and that event lay in the indistinct background, for Arthur had not yet seen the woman who would
play the lady-wife to the first-rate country gentleman.

These were Arthur's chief thoughts, so far as a man's thoughts
through hours of travelling can be compressed into a few sentences,
which are only like the list of names telling you what are the scenes in
a long, long panorama, full of colour, of detail, and of life. The happy
faces Arthur saw greeting him were not pale abstractions, but real ruddy
faces, long familiar to him: Martin Poyser was there—the whole Poyser
family.

What—Hetty?

Yes; for Arthur was at ease about Hetty: not quite at ease about the
past, for a certain burning of the ears would come whenever he thought
of the scenes with Adam last August,—but at ease about her present lot.
Mr. Irwine, who had been a regular correspondent, telling him all the
news about the old places and people, had sent him word nearly three
months ago that Adam Bede was not to marry Mary Burge, as he had
thought, but pretty Hetty Sorrel. Martin Poyser and Adam himself had
both told Mr. Irwine all about it;—that Adam had been deeply in love
with Hetty these two years, and that now it was agreed they were to be
married in March. That stalwart rogue Adam was more susceptible
than the Rector had thought; it was really quite an idyllic love affair;
and if it had not been too long to tell in a letter, he would have liked to

describe to Arthur the blushing looks and the simple strong words with which the fine honest fellow told his secret. He knew Arthur would like to hear that Adam had this sort of happiness in prospect.

Yes, indeed! Arthur felt there was not air enough in the room to satisfy his renovated life, when he had read that passage in the letter. He threw up the windows, he rushed out of doors into the December air, and greeted every one who spoke to him with an eager gaiety, as if there had been news of a fresh Nelson victory. For the first time that day since he had come to Windsor, he was in true boyish spirits: the load that had been pressing upon him was gone; the haunting fear had vanished. He thought he could conquer his bitterness towards Adam now —could offer him his hand, and ask to be his friend again, in spite of that painful memory which would still make his ears burn. He had been knocked down, and he had been forced to tell a lie: such things make a scar, do what we will. But if Adam were the same again as in the old days, Arthur wished to be the same too, and to have Adam mixed up with his business and his future, as he had always desired before that accursed meeting in August. Nay, he would do a great deal more for Adam than he should otherwise have done, when he came into the estate; Hetty's husband had a special claim on him—Hetty herself should feel that any pain she had suffered through Arthur in the past, was compensated to her a hundredfold. For really she could not have felt much, since she had so soon made up her mind to marry Adam.

You perceive clearly what sort of picture Adam and Hetty made in the panorama of Arthur's thoughts on his journey homeward. It was March now; they were soon to be married: perhaps they were already married. And *now* it was actually in his power to do a great deal for them. Sweet—sweet little Hetty! The little puss hadn't cared for him half as much as he cared for her; for he was a great fool about her still —was almost afraid of seeing her—indeed, had not cared much to look at any other woman since he parted from her. That little figure coming towards him in the Grove, those dark-fringed childish eyes, the lovely lips put up to kiss him—that picture had got no fainter with the lapse of months. And she would look just the same. It was impossible to think how he could meet her: he should certainly tremble. Strange, how long this sort of influence lasts; for he was certainly not in love with Hetty now: he had been earnestly desiring, for months, that she should marry Adam, and there was nothing that contributed more to his happiness in these moments than the thought of their marriage. It was the exaggerating effect of imagination that made his heart still beat a little more quickly at the thought of her. When he saw the little thing again as she really was, as Adam's wife, at work quite prosaically in her new home, he should perhaps wonder at the possibility of his past feelings. Thank heaven it had turned out so well! He should have plenty of affairs and interests to fill his life now, and not be in danger of playing the fool again.

Pleasant the crack of the postboy's whip! Pleasant the sense of being

hurried along in swift ease through English scenes, so like those round
his own home, only not quite so charming. Here was a market-town—
very much like Treddleston—where the arms of the neighbouring lord
of the manor were borne on the sign of the principal inn: then mere
fields and hedges, their vicinity to a market-town carrying an agreeable
suggestion of high rent, till the land began to assume a trimmer look,
the woods were more frequent, and at length a white or red mansion
looked down from a moderate eminence, or allowed him to be aware of
its parapet and chimneys among the dense-looking masses of oaks and
elms—masses reddened now with early buds. And close at hand came
the village: the small church, with its red-tiled roof, looking humble
even among the faded half-timbered houses; the old green grave-stones
with nettles round them; nothing fresh and bright but the children, opening round eyes at the swift post-chaise; nothing noisy and busy but
the gaping curs of mysterious pedigree. What a much prettier village
Hayslope was! And it should not be neglected like this place: vigorous
repairs should go on everywhere among farm-buildings and cottages,
and travellers in post-chaises, coming along the Rosseter road, should
do nothing but admire as they went. And Adam Bede should superintend all the repairs, for he had a share in Burge's business now, and, if
he liked, Arthur would put some money into the concern, and buy the
old man out in another year or two. That was an ugly fault in Arthur's
life, that affair of last summer; but the future should make amends.
Many men would have retained a feeling of vindictiveness towards
Adam; but *he* would not—he would resolutely overcome all littleness of
that kind, for he had certainly been very much in the wrong; and though
Adam had been harsh and violent, and had thrust on him a painful
dilemma, the poor fellow was in love, and had real provocation. No;
Arthur had not an evil feeling in his mind towards any human being:
he was happy, and would make every one else happy that came within
his reach.

And here was dear old Hayslope at last, sleeping on the hill like a
quiet old place as it was, in the late afternoon sunlight; and opposite
to it the great shoulders of the Binton Hills, below them the purplish
blackness of the hanging woods, and at last the pale front of the Abbey,
looking out from among the oaks of the Chase, as if anxious for the
heir's return. "Poor grandfather! and he lies dead there. *He* was a young
fellow once, coming into the estate, and making his plans. So the world
goes round! Aunt Lydia must feel very desolate, poor thing; but she
shall be indulged as much as she indulges her fat Fido."

The wheels of Arthur's chaise had been anxiously listened for at the
Chase, for to-day was Friday, and the funeral had already been deferred
two days. Before it drew up on the gravel of the courtyard, all the
servants in the house were assembled to receive him with a grave, decent
welcome, befitting a house of death. A month ago, perhaps, it would
have been difficult for them to have maintained a suitable sadness in

their faces, when Mr. Arthur was come to take possession; but the hearts of the head-servants were heavy that day for another cause than the death of the old Squire, and more than one of them was longing to be twenty miles away, as Mr. Craig was, knowing what was to become of Hetty Sorrel—pretty Hetty Sorrel—whom they used to see every week. They had the partisanship of household servants who like their places, and were not inclined to go the full length of the severe indignation felt against him by the farming tenants, but rather to make excuses for him; nevertheless, the upper servants, who had been on terms of neighbourly intercourse with the Poysers for many years, could not help feeling that the longed-for event of the young Squire's coming into the estate had been robbed of all its pleasantness.

To Arthur it was nothing surprising that the servants looked grave and sad: he himself was very much touched on seeing them all again, and feeling that he was in a new relation to them. It was that sort of pathetic emotion which has more pleasure than pain in it—which is perhaps one of the most delicious of all states to a good-natured man, conscious of the power to satisfy his good-nature. His heart swelled agreeably as he said,

"Well, Mills, how is my aunt?"

But now Mr. Bygate, the lawyer, who had been in the house ever since the death, came forward to give deferential greetings and answer all questions, and Arthur walked with him towards the library, where his aunt Lydia was expecting him. Aunt Lydia was the only person in the house who knew nothing about Hetty: her sorrow as a maiden daughter was unmixed with any other thoughts than those of anxiety about funeral arrangements and her own future lot; and, after the manner of women, she mourned for the father who had made her life important, all the more because she had a secret sense that there was little mourning for him in other hearts.

But Arthur kissed her tearful face more tenderly than he had ever done in his life before.

"Dear aunt," he said affectionately, as he held her hand, "*your* loss is the greatest of all, but you must tell me how to try and make it up to you all the rest of your life."

"It was so sudden and so dreadful, Arthur," poor Miss Lydia began, pouring out her little plaints; and Arthur sat down to listen with impatient patience. When a pause came, he said,

"Now, aunt, I'll leave you for a quarter of an hour just to go to my room, and then I shall come and give full attention to everything.

"My room is all ready for me, I suppose, Mills?" he said to the butler, who seemed to be lingering uneasily about the entrance-hall.

"Yes, sir, and there are letters for you; they are all laid on the writing-table in your dressing-room."

On entering the small anteroom which was called a dressing-room, but which Arthur really used only to lounge and write in, he just cast his eyes on the writing-table, and saw that there were several letters and packets lying there; but he was in the uncomfortable dusty condition of a man who has had a long hurried journey, and he must really refresh himself by attending to his toilette a little, before he read his letters. Pym was there, making everything ready for him; and soon, with a delightful freshness about him, as if he were prepared to begin a new day, he went back into his dressing-room to open his letters. The level rays of the low afternoon sun entered directly at the window, and as Arthur seated himself in his velvet chair with their pleasant warmth upon him, he was conscious of that quiet well-being which perhaps you and I have felt on a sunny afternoon, when, in our brightest youth and health, life has opened a new vista for us, and long to-morrows of activity have stretched before us like a lovely plain which there was no need for hurrying to look at, because it was all our own.

The top letter was placed with its address upwards: it was in Mr. Irwine's handwriting, Arthur saw at once; and below the address was written, "To be delivered as soon as he arrives." Nothing could have been less surprising to him than a letter from Mr. Irwine at that moment: of course there was something he wished Arthur to know earlier than it was possible for them to see each other. At such a time as that it was quite natural that Irwine should have something pressing to say. Arthur broke the seal with an agreeable anticipation of soon seeing the writer.

"I send this letter to meet you on your arrival, Arthur, because I may then be at Stoniton, whither I am called by the most painful duty it has ever been given me to perform; and it is right that you should know what I have to tell you without delay.

"I will not attempt to add by one word of reproach to the retribution that is now falling on you; any other words that I could write at this moment must be weak and unmeaning by the side of those in which I must tell you the simple fact.

"Hetty Sorrel is in prison, and will be tried on Friday for the crime of child-murder." . . .

Arthur read no more. He started up from his chair, and stood for a single minute with a sense of violent convulsion in his whole frame, as if the life were going out of him with horrible throbs; but the next minute he had rushed out of the room, still clutching the letter—he was hurrying along the corridor, and down the stairs into the hall. Mills was still there, but Arthur did not see him, as he passed like a hunted man across the hall and out along the gravel. The butler hurried out after him as fast as his elderly limbs could run: he guessed, he knew, where the young Squire was going.

When Mills got to the stables, a horse was being saddled, and Arthur was forcing himself to read the remaining words of the letter. He thrust it into his pocket as the horse was led up to him, and at that moment caught sight of Mills's anxious face in front of him.

"Tell them I'm gone—gone to Stoniton," he said, in a muffled tone of agitation—sprang into the saddle, and set off at a gallop.

CHAPTER XLV

NEAR sunset that evening an elderly gentleman was standing with his back against the smaller entrance-door of Stoniton jail, saying a few last words to the departing chaplain. The chaplain walked away, but the elderly gentleman stood still, looking down on the pavement, and stroking his chin with a ruminating air, when he was roused by a sweet clear woman's voice, saying,

"Can I get into the prison, if you please?"

He turned his head, and looked fixedly at the speaker for a few moments without answering.

"I have seen you before," he said, at last. "Do you remember preaching on the village green at Hayslope in Loamshire?"

"Yes, sir, surely. Are you the gentleman that stayed to listen on horseback?"

"Yes. Why do you want to go into the prison?"

"I want to go to Hetty Sorrel, the young woman who has been condemned to death—and to stay with her, if I may be permitted. Have you power in the prison, sir?"

"Yes; I am a magistrate, and can get admittance for you. But you know this criminal, Hetty Sorrel?"

"Yes, we are kin: my own aunt married her uncle, Martin Poyser. But I was away at Leeds, and didn't know of this great trouble in time to get here before to-day. I entreat you, sir, for the love of our heavenly Father, to let me go to her and stay with her."

"How did you know she was condemned to death, if you are only just come from Leeds?"

"I have seen my uncle since the trial, sir. He is gone back to his home now, and the poor sinner is forsaken of all. I beseech you to get leave for me to be with her."

"What! have you courage to stay all night in the prison? She is very sullen, and will scarcely make answer when she is spoken to."

"O, sir, it may please God to open her heart still. Don't let us delay."

"Come, then," said the elderly gentleman, ringing and gaining admission; "I know you have a key to unlock hearts."

Dinah mechanically took off her bonnet and shawl as soon as they were within the prison court, from the habit she had of throwing them off when she preached or prayed, or visited the sick; and when they entered the jailer's room, she laid them down on a chair unthinkingly. There was no agitation visible in her, but a deep concentrated calmness, as if, even when she was speaking, her soul was in prayer reposing on an unseen support.

After speaking to the jailer, the magistrate turned to her and said,

"The turnkey will take you to the prisoner's cell, and leave you there for the night, if you desire it; but you can't have a light during the night—it is contrary to rules. My name is Colonel Townley: if I can help you in anything, ask the jailer for my address, and come to me. I take some interest in this Hetty Sorrel, for the sake of that fine fellow, Adam Bede: I happened to see him at Hayslope the same evening I heard you preach, and recognised him in court to-day, ill as he looked."

"Ah, sir, can you tell me anything about him? Can you tell me where he lodges? For my poor uncle was too much weighed down with trouble to remember."

"Close by here. I inquired all about him of Mr. Irwine. He lodges over a tinman's shop, in the street on the right hand as you entered the prison. There is an old schoolmaster with him. Now, good-by: I wish you success."

"Farewell, sir. I am grateful to you."

As Dinah crossed the prison court with the turnkey, the solemn evening light seemed to make the walls higher than they were by day, and the sweet pale face in the cap was more than ever like a white flower on this background of gloom. The turnkey looked askance at her all the while, but never spoke: he somehow felt that the sound of his own rude voice would be grating just then. He struck a light as they entered the dark corridor leading to the condemned cell, and then said in his most civil tone, "It'll be pretty nigh dark in the cell a'ready; but I can stop with my light a bit, if you like."

"Nay, friend, thank you," said Dinah. "I wish to go in alone."

"As you like," said the jailer, turning the harsh key in the lock, and opening the door wide enough to admit Dinah. A jet of light from his lantern fell on the opposite corner of the cell, where Hetty was sitting on her straw pallet with her face buried in her knees. It seemed as if she were asleep, and yet the grating of the lock would have been likely to waken her.

The door closed again, and the only light in the cell was that of the evening sky, through the small high grating—enough to discern human faces by. Dinah stood still for a minute, hesitating to speak, because Hetty might be asleep; and looking at the motionless heap with a yearning heart. Then she said, softly,

"Hetty!"

There was a slight movement perceptible in Hetty's frame—a start such as might have been produced by a feeble electrical shock; but she did not look up. Dinah spoke again, in a tone made stronger by irrepressible emotion:

"Hetty . . . it's Dinah."

Again there was a slight, startled movement through Hetty's frame, and, without uncovering her face, she raised her head a little, as if listening.

"Hetty . . . Dinah is come to you."

After a moment's pause, Hetty lifted her head slowly and timidly from her knees, and raised her eyes. The two pale faces were looking at each other: one with a wild hard despair in it, the other full of sad, yearning love. Dinah unconsciously opened her arms and stretched them out.

"Don't you know me, Hetty? Don't you remember Dinah? Did you think I wouldn't come to you in trouble?"

Hetty kept her eyes fixed on Dinah's face,—at first like an animal that gazes, and gazes, and keeps aloof.

"I'm come to be with you, Hetty—not to leave you—to stay with you —to be your sister to the last."

Slowly, while Dinah was speaking, Hetty rose, took a step forward, and was clasped in Dinah's arms.

They stood so a long while, for neither of them felt the impulse to move apart again. Hetty, without any distinct thought of it, hung on this something that was come to clasp her now, while she was sinking helpless in a dark gulf; and Dinah felt a deep joy in the first sign that her love was welcomed by the wretched lost one. The light got fainter as they stood, and when at last they sat down on the straw pallet together, their faces had become indistinct.

Not a word was spoken. Dinah waited, hoping for a spontaneous word from Hetty; but she sat in the same dull despair, only clutching the hand that held hers, and leaning her cheek against Dinah's. It was the human contact she clung to, but she was not the less sinking into the dark gulf.

Dinah began to doubt whether Hetty was conscious who it was that sat beside her. She thought suffering and fear might have driven the poor sinner out of her mind. But it was borne in upon her, as she afterwards said, that she must not hurry God's work: we are over-hasty to speak—as if God did not manifest himself by our silent feeling, and make his love felt through ours. She did not know how long they sat in that way, but it got darker and darker, till there was only a pale patch of light on the opposite wall: all the rest was darkness. But she felt the Divine presence more and more,—nay, as if she herself were a part of it, and it was the Divine pity that was beating in her heart, and was willing the rescue of this helpless one. At last she was prompted to speak, and find out how far Hetty was conscious of the present.

"Hetty," she said, gently, "do you know who it is that sits by your side?"

"Yes," Hetty answered slowly, "it's Dinah."

"And do you remember the time when we were at the Hall Farm together, and that night when I told you to be sure and think of me as a friend in trouble?"

"Yes," said Hetty. Then, after a pause, she added, "But you can do nothing for me. You can't make 'em do anything. They'll hang me o' Monday—it's Friday now."

As Hetty said the last words, she clung closer to Dinah, shuddering.

"No, Hetty, I can't save you from that death. But isn't the suffering less hard when you have somebody with you, that feels for you—that you can speak to, and say what's in your heart? . . . Yes, Hetty: you lean on me: you are glad to have me with you."

"You won't leave me, Dinah? You'll keep close to me?"

"No, Hetty, I won't leave you. I'll stay with you to the last. . . . But, Hetty, there is some one else in this cell besides me, some one close to you."

Hetty said, in a frightened whisper, "Who?"

"Some one who has been with you through all your hours of sin and trouble—who has known every thought you have had—has seen where you went, where you lay down and rose up again, and all the deeds you have tried to hide in darkness. And on Monday, when I can't follow you,—when my arms can't reach you,—when death has parted us,— He who is with us now, and knows all, will be with you then. It makes no difference—whether we live or die, we are in the presence of God."

"Oh, Dinah, won't nobody do anything for me? *Will* they hang me for certain? . . . I wouldn't mind if they'd let me live."

"My poor Hetty, death is very dreadful to you. I know it's dreadful. But if you had a friend to take care of you after death—in that other world—some one whose love is greater than mine—who can do everything? . . . If God our Father was your friend, and was willing to save you from sin and suffering, so as you should neither know wicked feelings nor pain again? If you could believe he loved you and would help you, as you believe I love you and will help you, it wouldn't be so hard to die on Monday, would it?"

"But I can't know anything about it," Hetty said, with sullen sadness.

"Because, Hetty, you are shutting up your soul against him, by trying to hide the truth. God's love and mercy can overcome all things —our ignorance, and weakness, and all the burthen of our past wickedness—all things but our wilful sin; sin that we cling to, and will not give up. You believe in my love and pity for you, Hetty; but if you had not let me come near you, if you wouldn't have looked at me or spoken to me, you'd have shut me out from helping you: I couldn't have made you feel my love; I couldn't have told you what I felt for you. Don't shut God's love out in that way, by clinging to sin. . . . He can't bless you while you have one falsehood in your soul; his pardoning mercy can't reach you until you open your heart to him, and say, 'I have done this great wickedness; O God, save me, make me pure from sin.' While you cling to one sin and will not part with it, it must drag you down to misery after death, as it has dragged you to misery here in this world, my poor, poor Hetty. It is sin that brings dread, and darkness, and despair: there is light and blessedness for us as soon as we cast it off: God enters our souls then, and teaches us, and brings us strength and peace. Cast it off now, Hetty—now: confess the wickedness you have done—the sin you have been guilty of against your heavenly Father. Let us kneel down together, for we are in the presence of God."

Hetty obeyed Dinah's movement, and sank on her knees. They still held each other's hands, and there was long silence. Then Dinah said, "Hetty, we are before God: he is waiting for you to tell the truth."

Still there was silence. At last Hetty spoke, in a tone of beseeching, "Dinah . . . help me . . . I can't feel anything like you . . . my heart is hard."

Dinah held the clinging hand, and all her soul went forth in her voice:

"Jesus, thou present Saviour! Thou hast known the depths of all sorrow: thou hast entered that black darkness where God is not, and hast uttered the cry of the forsaken. Come, Lord, and gather of the fruits of thy travail and thy pleading: stretch forth thy hand, thou who art mighty to save to the uttermost, and rescue this lost one. She is clothed round with thick darkness: the fetters of her sin are upon her, and she cannot stir to come to thee: she can only feel her heart is hard, and she is helpless. She cries to me, thy weak creature. . . . Saviour! it is a blind cry to thee. Hear it! Pierce the darkness! Look upon her with thy face of love and sorrow that thou didst turn on him who denied thee; and melt her hard heart.

"See, Lord,—I bring her, as they of old brought the sick and helpless, and thou didst heal them: I bear her on my arms and carry her before thee. Fear and trembling have taken hold on her; but she trembles only at the pain and death of the body: breathe upon her thy life-giving Spirit, and put a new fear within her—the fear of her sin. Make her dread to keep the accursed thing within her soul: make her feel the presence of the living God, who beholds all the past, to whom the darkness is as noonday; who is waiting now, at the eleventh hour, for her to turn to him, and confess her sin, and cry for mercy—now, before the night of death comes, and the moment of pardon is for ever fled, like yesterday that returneth not.

"Saviour! it is yet time—time to snatch this poor soul from everlasting darkness. I believe—I believe in thy infinite love. What is *my* love or *my* pleading? It is quenched in thine. I can only clasp her in my weak arms, and urge her with my weak pity. Thou—thou wilt breathe on the dead soul, and it shall arise from the unanswering sleep of death.

"Yea, Lord, I see thee, coming through the darkness, coming, like the morning, with healing on thy wings. The marks of thy agony are upon thee—I see, I see thou art able and willing to save—thou wilt not let her perish for ever.

"Come, mighty Saviour! let the dead hear thy voice; let the eyes of the blind be opened: let her see that God encompasses her; let her tremble at nothing but at the sin that cuts her off from him. Melt the hard heart; unseal the closed lips: make her cry with her whole soul, 'Father, I have sinned.' . . ."

"Dinah," Hetty sobbed out, throwing her arms round Dinah's neck, "I will speak . . . I will tell . . . I won't hide it any more."

But the tears and sobs were too violent. Dinah raised her gently from her knees, and seated her on the pallet again, sitting down by her side. It was a long time before the convulsed throat was quiet, and even then they sat some time in stillness and darkness, holding each other's hands. At last Hetty whispered,

"I did do it, Dinah . . . I buried it in the wood . . . the little baby . . . and it cried . . . I heard it cry . . . ever such a way off . . . all night . . . and I went back because it cried."

She paused, and then spoke hurriedly in a louder pleading tone.

"But I thought perhaps it wouldn't die—there might somebody find it. I didn't kill it—I didn't kill it myself. I put it down there and covered it up, and when I came back it was gone. . . . It was because I was so very miserable, Dinah. . . . I didn't know where to go . . . and I tried to kill myself before, and I couldn't. O, I tried so to drown myself in the pool, and I couldn't. I went to Windsor—I ran away—did you know? I went to find him, as he might take care of me; and he was gone; and then I didn't know what to do. I daredn't go back home again —I couldn't bear it. I couldn't have bore to look at anybody, for they'd have scorned me. I thought o' you sometimes, and thought I'd come to you, for I didn't think you'd be cross with me, and cry shame on me: I thought I could tell you. But then the other folks 'ud come to know it at last, and I couldn't bear that. It was partly thinking o' you made me come toward Stoniton; and, besides, I was so frightened at going wandering about till I was a beggar-woman, and had nothing; and sometimes it seemed as if I must go back to the Farm sooner than that. O, it was so dreadful, Dinah . . . I was so miserable . . . I wished I'd never been born into this world. I should never like to go into the green fields again—I hated 'em so in my misery."

Hetty paused again, as if the sense of the past were too strong upon her for words.

"And then I got to Stoniton, and I began to feel frightened that night, because I was so near home. And then the little baby was born, when I didn't expect it; and the thought came into my mind that I might get rid of it, and go home again. The thought came all of a sudden, as I was lying in the bed, and it got stronger and stronger . . . I longed so to go back again . . . I couldn't bear being so lonely, and coming to beg for want. And it gave me strength and resolution to get up and dress myself. I felt I must do it . . . I didn't know how . . . I thought I'd find a pool, if I could, like that other, in the corner of the field, in the dark. And when the woman went out, I felt as if I was strong enough to do anything. . . . I thought I should get rid of all my misery. and go back home, and never let 'em know why I ran away. I put on my bonnet and shawl, and went out into the dark street, with the baby under my cloak; and I walked fast till I got into a street a good way off. and there was a public, and I got some warm stuff to drink and some bread. And I walked on and on, and I hardly felt the ground I trod on; and it got lighter, for there came the moon—O, Dinah, it frightened me when it first looked at me out o' the clouds—it never looked so before; and I turned out of the road into the fields, for I was afraid o' meeting anybody with the moon shining on me. And I came to a haystack, where I thought I could lie down and keep myself warm all night. There was a place cut into it, where I could make me a bed; and I lay comfortable, and the baby was warm against me; and I must have gone to sleep for a good while, for when I woke it was morning, but not very light, and the baby was crying. And I saw a wood a little way off . . . I thought there'd perhaps be a ditch or a pond there . . . and it was so early I thought I could hide the child there, and get a long way off before folks was up. And then I thought I'd go home—I'd get rides in carts and go home, and tell 'em I'd been to try and see for a place, and couldn't get one. I longed so for it, Dinah, I longed to be safe at home. I don't know how I felt about the baby. I seemed to hate it—it was like a heavy weight hanging round my neck; and yet its crying went through me, and I daredn't look at its little hands and face. But I went on to the wood, and I walked about; there was no water". . . .

Hetty shuddered. She was silent for some moments, and when she began again, it was in a whisper.

"I came to a place where there was lots of chips and turf, and I sat down on the trunk of a tree to think what I should do. And all of a sudden I saw a hole under the nut-tree, like a little grave. And it darted into me like lightning—I'd lay the baby there, and cover it with the grass and the chips. I couldn't kill it any other way. And I'd done it in a minute; and, O, it cried so, Dinah—I *couldn't* cover it quite up—I thought perhaps somebody 'ud come and take care of it, and then it wouldn't die. And I made haste out of the wood, but I could hear it crying all the while; and when I got out into the fields, it was as if I was held fast—I couldn't go away, for all I wanted so to go. And I sat against the haystack to watch if anybody 'ud come: I was very hungry, and I'd only a bit of bread left; but I couldn't go away. And after ever such a while—hours and hours—the man came—him in a smock-frock, and he looked at me so, I was frightened, and I made haste and went on.

"I thought he was going to the wood, and would perhaps find the baby. And I went right on, till I came to a village, a long way off from the wood; and I was very sick, and faint, and hungry. I got something to eat there, and bought a loaf. But I was frightened to stay. I heard the baby crying, and thought the other folks heard it too,—and I went on. But I was so tired, and it was getting towards dark. And at last, by the roadside there was a barn—ever such a way off any house—like the barn in Abbot's Close; and I thought I could go in there and hide myself among the hay and straw, and nobody 'ud be likely to come. I went in, and it was half full o' trusses of straw, and there was some hay, too. And I made myself a bed, ever so far behind, where nobody could find me; and I was so tired and weak, I went to sleep. . . . But oh, the baby's crying kept waking me; and I thought that man as looked at me so was come and laying hold of me. But I must have slept a long while at last, though I didn't know; for when I got up and went out of the barn, I didn't know whether it was night or morning. But it was morning, for it kept getting lighter; and I turned back the way I'd come. I couldn't help it, Dinah; it was the baby's crying made me go: and yet I was frightened to death. I thought that man in the smock-frock 'ud see me, and know I put the baby there. But I went on, for all that: I'd left off thinking about going home—it had gone out o' my mind. I saw nothing but that place in the wood where I'd buried the baby . . . I see it now. O Dinah! shall I allays see it?''

Hetty clung round Dinah, and shuddered again. The silence seemed long before she went on.

"I met nobody, for it was very early, and I got into the wood. . . . I knew the way to the place . . . the place against the nut-tree; and I could hear it crying at every step. . . . I thought it was alive. . . . I don't know whether I was frightened or glad. . . . I don't know what I felt. I only know I was in the wood, and heard the cry. I don't know what I felt till I saw the baby was gone. And when I'd put it there, I thought I should like somebody to find it, and save it from dying; but when I saw it was gone, I was struck like a stone, with fear. I never thought o' stirring, I felt so weak. I knew I couldn't run away, and everybody as saw me 'ud know about the baby. My heart went like a stone: I couldn't wish or try for anything; it seemed like as if I should stay there for ever, and nothing 'ud ever change. But they came and took me away."

Hetty was silent, but she shuddered again, as if there were still something behind; and Dinah waited, for her heart was so full, that tears must come before words. At last Hetty burst out, with a sob,

"Dinah, do you think God will take away that crying and the place in the wood, now I've told everything?"

"Let us pray, poor sinner: let us fall on our knees again, and pray to the God of all mercy."

CHAPTER XLVI

THE HOURS OF SUSPENSE

On Sunday morning, when the church bells in Stoniton were ringing for morning service, Bartle Massey re-entered Adam's room, after a short absence, and said,

"Adam, here's a visitor wants to see you."

Adam was seated with his back towards the door, but he started up and turned round instantly, with a flushed face and an eager look. His face was even thinner and more worn than we have seen it before, but he was washed and shaven this Sunday morning.

"Is it any news?" he said.

"Keep yourself quiet, my lad," said Bartle; "keep quiet. It's not what you're thinking of: it's the young Methodist woman come from the prison. She's at the bottom o' the stairs, and wants to know if you think well to see her, for she has something to say to you about that poor castaway; but she wouldn't come in without your leave, she said. She thought you'd perhaps like to go out and speak to her. These preaching women are not so back'ard commonly," Bartle muttered to himself.

"Ask her to come in," said Adam.

He was standing with his face towards the door, and as Dinah entered, lifting up her mild grey eyes towards him, she saw at once the great change that had come since the day when she had looked up at the tall man in the cottage. There was a trembling in her clear voice as she put her hand into his, and said,

"Be comforted, Adam Bede: the Lord has not forsaken her."

"Bless you for coming to her," Adam said. "Mr. Massey brought me word yesterday as you was come."

They could neither of them say any more just yet, but stood before each other in silence; and Bartle Massey, too, who had put on his spectacles, seemed transfixed, examining Dinah's face. But he recovered himself first, and said, "Sit down, young woman, sit down," placing the chair for her, and retiring to his old seat on the bed.

"Thank you, friend; I won't sit down," said Dinah, "for I must hasten back: she entreated me not to stay long away. What I came for, Adam Bede, was to pray you to go and see the poor sinner, and bid her farewell. She desires to ask your forgiveness, and it is meet you should see her to-day, rather than in the early morning, when the time will be short."

Adam stood trembling, and at last sank down on his chair again.

"It won't be," he said: "it'll be put off—there'll perhaps come a pardon. Mr. Irwine said there was hope; he said, I needn't quite give it up."

"That's a blessed thought to me," said Dinah, her eyes filling with tears. "It's a fearful thing hurrying her soul away so fast.

"But let what will be," she added, presently, "you will surely come, and let her speak the words that are in her heart. Although her poor soul is very dark, and discerns little beyond the things of the flesh, she is no longer hard: she is contrite—she has confessed all to me. The pride of her heart has given way, and she leans on me for help, and desires to be taught. This fills me with trust; for I cannot but think that the brethren sometimes err in measuring the Divine love by the sinner's knowledge. She is going to write a letter to the friends at the Hall Farm for me to give them when she is gone; and when I told her you were here, she said, 'I should like to say good-by to Adam, and ask him to forgive me.' You will come, Adam?—perhaps you will even now come back with me."

"I can't," Adam said: "I can't say good-by, while there's any hope.

I'm listening, and listening—I can think o' nothing but that. It can't be as she'll die that shameful death—I can't bring my mind to it."

He got up from his chair again, and looked away out of the window, while Dinah stood with compassionate patience. In a minute or two he turned round and said,

"I *will* come, Dinah . . . to-morrow morning . . . if it must be. I may have more strength to bear it, if I know it *must* be. Tell her, I forgive her; tell her I will come—at the very last."

"I will not urge you against the voice of your own heart," said Dinah. "I must hasten back to her, for it is wonderful how she clings now, and was not willing to let me out of her sight. She used never to make any return to my affection before, but now tribulation has opened her heart. Farewell, Adam: our heavenly Father comfort you, and strengthen you to bear all things." Dinah put out her hand, and Adam pressed it in silence.

Bartle Massey was getting up to lift the stiff latch of the door for her, but before he could reach it, she had said, gently, "Farewell, friend," and was gone, with her light step, down the stairs.

"Well," said Bartle, taking off his spectacles, and putting them into his pocket, "if there must be women to make trouble in the world, it's but fair there should be women to be comforters under it; and she's one —she's one. It's a pity she's a Methodist; but there's no getting a woman without some foolishness or other."

Adam never went to bed that night: the excitement of suspense, heightening with every hour that brought him nearer the fatal moment, was too great; and in spite of his entreaties, in spite of his promises that he would be perfectly quiet, the schoolmaster watched too.

"What does it matter to me, lad?" Bartle said: "a night's sleep more or less? I shall sleep long enough, by-and-by, underground. Let me keep thee company in trouble while I can."

It was a long dreary night in that small chamber. Adam would sometimes get up, and tread backwards and forwards along the short space from wall to wall; then he would sit down and hide his face, and no sound would be heard but the ticking of the watch on the table, or the falling of a cinder from the fire which the schoolmaster carefully tended. Sometimes he would burst out into vehement speech.

"If I could ha' done anything to save her—if my bearing anything would ha' done any good . . . but t' have to sit still, and know it, and do nothing . . . it's hard for a man to bear . . . and to think o' what might ha' been now, if it hadn't been for *him*. . . . O God, it's the very day we should ha' been married."

"Ay, my lad," said Bartle, tenderly, "it's heavy—it's heavy. But you must remember this: when you thought of marrying her, you'd a notion she'd got another sort of a nature inside her. You didn't think she could have got hardened in that little while to do what she's done."

"I know—I know that," said Adam. "I thought she was loving and tender-hearted, and wouldn't tell a lie, or act deceitful. How could I think any other way? And if he'd never come near her, and I'd married her, and been loving to her, and took care of her, she might never ha' done anything bad. What would it ha' signified—my having a bit o' trouble with her? It 'ud ha' been nothing to this."

"There's no knowing, my lad—there's no knowing what might have come. The smart's bad for you to bear now: you must have time—you must have time. But I've that opinion of you, that you'll rise above it all, and be a man again; and there may good come out of this that we don't see."

"Good come out of it!" said Adam, passionately. "That doesn't alter th' evil: *her* ruin can't be undone. I hate that talk o' people, as if there was a way o' making amends for everything. They'd more need be brought to see as the wrong they do can never be altered. When a man's spoiled his fellow-creatur's life, he's no right to comfort himself with thinking good may come out of it: somebody else's good doesn't alter her shame and misery."

"Well, lad, well," said Bartle, in a gentle tone, strangely in contrast with his usual peremptoriness and impatience of contradiction, "it's likely enough I talk foolishness: I'm an old fellow, and it's a good many years since I was in trouble myself. It's easy finding reasons why other folks should be patient."

"Mr. Massey," said Adam, penitently, "I'm very hot and hasty. I owe you something different; but you mustn't take it ill of me."

"Not I, lad—not I."

So the night wore on in agitation, till the chill dawn and the growing light brought the tremulous quiet that comes on the brink of despair. There would soon be no more suspense.

"Let us go to the prison now, Mr. Massey," said Adam, when he saw the hand of his watch at six. "If there's any news come, we shall hear about it."

The people were astir already, moving rapidly, in one direction, through the streets. Adam tried not to think where they were going, as they hurried past him in that short space between his lodging and the prison gates. He was thankful when the gates shut him in from seeing those eager people.

No; there was no news come—no pardon—no reprieve.

Adam lingered in the court half an hour, before he could bring himself to send to Dinah that he was come. But a voice caught his ear: he could not shut out the words.

"The cart is to set off at half-past seven."

It must be said—the last good-by: there was no help.

In ten minutes from that time, Adam was at the door of the cell. Dinah had sent him word that she could not come to him, she could not leave Hetty one moment; but Hetty was prepared for the meeting.

He could not see her when he entered, for agitation deadened his senses, and the dim cell was almost dark to him. He stood a moment after the door closed behind him, trembling and stupefied.

But he began to see through the dimness—to see the dark eyes lifted up to him once more, but with no smile in them. O God, how sad they looked! The last time they had met his was when he parted from her with his heart full of joyous, hopeful love, and they looked out with a tearful smile from a pink, dimpled, childish face. The face was marble now; the sweet lips were pallid and half-open, and quivering; the dimples were all gone—all but one, that never went; and the eyes—O! the worst of all was the likeness they had to Hetty's. They were Hetty's eyes looking at him with that mournful gaze, as if she had come back to him from the dead to tell him of her misery.

She was clinging close to Dinah; her cheek was against Dinah's. It seemed as if her last faint strength and hope lay in that contact; and the pitying love that shone out from Dinah's face looked like a visible pledge of the Invisible Mercy.

When the sad eyes met—when Hetty and Adam looked at each other, she felt the change in *him* too, and it seemed to strike her with fresh fear. It was the first time she had seen any being whose face seemed to reflect the change in herself: Adam was a new image of the dreadful past and the dreadful present. She trembled more as she looked at him.

"Speak to him, Hetty," Dinah said; "tell him what is in your heart."

Hetty obeyed her, like a little child.

"Adam . . . I'm very sorry . . . I behaved very wrong to you . . . will you forgive me . . . before I die?"

Adam answered with a half-sob: "Yes, I forgive thee, Hetty: I forgave thee long ago."

It had seemed to Adam as if his brain would burst with the anguish of meeting Hetty's eyes in the first moments; but the sound of her voice uttering these penitent words touched a chord which had been less strained: there was a sense of relief from what was becoming unbearable, and the rare tears came—they had never come before, since he had hung on Seth's neck in the beginning of his sorrow.

Hetty made an involuntary movement towards him; some of the love that she had once lived in the midst of was come near her again. She kept hold of Dinah's hand, but she went up to Adam and said, timidly,

"Will you kiss me again, Adam, for all I've been so wicked?"

Adam took the blanched wasted hand she put out to him, and they gave each other the solemn unspeakable kiss of a lifelong parting.

"And tell him," Hetty said, in rather a stronger voice, "tell him . . . for there's nobody else to tell him . . . as I went after him and couldn't find him . . . and I hated him and cursed him once . . . but Dinah says, I should forgive him . . . and I try . . . for else God won't forgive me."

There was a noise at the door of the cell now—the key was being turned in the lock, and when the door opened, Adam saw indistinctly that there were several faces there: he was too agitated to see more—even to see that Mr. Irwine's face was one of them. He felt that the last preparations were beginning, and he could stay no longer. Room was silently made for him to depart, and he went to his chamber in loneliness, leaving Bartle Massey to watch and see the end.

CHAPTER XLVII

THE LAST MOMENT

IT was a sight that some people remembered better even than their own sorrows—the sight in that grey clear morning, when the fatal cart with the two young women in it was described by the waiting watching multitude, cleaving its way towards the hideous symbol of a deliberately inflicted sudden death.

All Stoniton had heard of Dinah Morris, the young Methodist woman who had brought the obstinate criminal to confess, and there was as much eagerness to see her as to see the wretched Hetty.

But Dinah was hardly conscious of the multitude. When Hetty had caught sight of the vast crowd in the distance, she had clutched Dinah convulsively.

"Close your eyes, Hetty," Dinah said, "and let us pray without ceasing to God."

And in a low voice, as the cart went slowly along through the midst of the gazing crowd, she poured forth her soul with the wrestling intensity of a last pleading, for the trembling creature that clung to her and clutched her as the only visible sign of love and pity.

Dinah did not know that the crowd was silent, gazing at her with a sort of awe—she did not even know how near they were to the fatal spot, when the cart stopped, and she shrank appalled at a loud shout hideous to her ear, like a vast yell of demons. Hetty's shriek mingled with the sound, and they clasped each other in mutual horror.

But it was not a shout of execration—not a yell of exultant cruelty.

It was a shout of sudden excitement at the appearance of a horseman cleaving the crowd at full gallop. The horse is hot and distressed, but answers to the desperate spurring; the rider looks as if his eyes were glazed by madness, and he saw nothing but what was unseen by others. See, he has something in his hand—he is holding it up as if it were a signal.

The Sheriff knows him: it is Arthur Donnithorne, carrying in his hand a hard-won release from death.

CHAPTER XLVIII

ANOTHER MEETING IN THE WOOD

THE next day, at evening, two men were walking from opposite points towards the same scene, drawn thither by common memory. The scene was the Grove by Donnithorne Chase: you know who the men were.

The old Squire's funeral had taken place that morning, the will had been read, and now in the first breathing-space, Arthur Donnithorne had come out for a lonely walk, that he might look fixedly at the new future before him, and confirm himself in a sad resolution. He thought he could do that best in the Grove.

Adam, too, had come from Stoniton on Monday evening, and to-day he had not left home, except to go to the family at the Hall Farm, and tell them everything that Mr. Irwine had left untold. He had agreed with the Poysers that he would follow them to their new neighbourhood, wherever that might be; for he meant to give up the management of the woods, and, as soon as it was practicable, he would wind up his business with Jonathan Burge, and settle with his mother and Seth in a home within reach of the friends to whom he felt bound by a mutual sorrow.

"Seth and me are sure to find work," he said. "A man that's got our trade at his finger ends is at home everywhere; and we must make a new start. My mother won't stand in the way, for she's told me, since I came home, she'd made up her mind to being buried in another parish, if I wished it, and if I'd be more comfortable elsewhere. It's wonderful how quiet she's been ever since I came back. It seems as if the very greatness o' the trouble had quieted and calmed her. We shall all be better in a new country; though there's some I shall be loth to leave behind. But I won't part from you and yours, if I can help it, Mr. Poyser. Trouble's made us kin."

"Ay, lad," said Martin. "We'll go out o' hearing o' that man's name. But I doubt we shall ne'er go far enough for folks not to find out as we've got them belonging to us as are transported o'er the seas, and were like to be hanged. We shall have that flyin' up in our faces, and our children's after us."

That was a long visit to the Hall Farm, and drew too strongly on Adam's energies for him to think of seeing others, or re-entering on his old occupations till the morrow. "But to-morrow," he said to himself, "I'll go to work again. I shall learn to like it again some time, maybe; and it's right, whether I like it or not."

This evening was the last he would allow to be absorbed by sorrow: suspense was gone now, and he must bear the unalterable. He was resolved not to see Arthur Donnithorne again, if it were possible to avoid him. He had no message to deliver from Hetty now, for Hetty had seen Arthur; and Adam distrusted himself: he had learned to dread the violence of his own feeling. That word of Mr. Irwine's—that he must remember what he had felt after giving the last blow to Arthur in the Grove—had remained with him.

These thoughts about Arthur, like all thoughts that are charged with strong feeling, were continually recurring, and they always called up the image of the Grove—of that spot under the overarching boughs

where he had caught sight of the two bending figures, and had been possessed by sudden rage.

"I'll go and see it again to-night for the last time," he said; "it'll
do me good; it'll make me feel over again what I felt when I'd knocked
him down. I felt what poor empty work it was, as soon as I'd done it,
before I began to think he might be dead."

In this way it happened that Arthur and Adam were walking towards
the same spot at the same time.

Adam had on his working-dress again, now,—for he had thrown off
the other with a sense of relief as soon as he came home; and if he had
had the basket of tools over his shoulder, he might have been taken,
with his pale wasted face, for the spectre of the Adam Bede who entered
the Grove on that August evening eight months ago. But he had no
basket of tools, and he was not walking with the old erectness, looking
keenly round him; his hands were thrust in his side pockets, and his
eyes rested chiefly on the ground. He had not long entered the Grove,
and now he paused before a beech. He knew that tree well; it was the
boundary mark of his youth—the sign, to him, of the time when some
of his earliest, strongest feelings had left him. He felt sure they would
never return. And yet, at this moment, there was a stirring of affection
at the remembrance of that Arthur Donnithorne whom he had believed
in before he had come up to this beech eight months ago. It was affection for the dead; *that* Arthur existed no longer.

He was disturbed by the sound of approaching footsteps, but the beech
stood at a turning in the road, and he could not see who was coming,
until the tall slim figure in deep mourning suddenly stood before him
at only two yards' distance. They both started, and looked at each
other in silence. Often, in the last fortnight, Adam had imagined himself as close to Arthur as this, assailing him with words that should be
as harrowing as the voice of remorse, forcing upon him a just share in
the misery he had caused; and often, too, he had told himself that such
a meeting had better not be. But in imagining the meeting he had always
seen Arthur, as he had met him on that evening in the Grove, florid,
careless, light of speech; and the figure before him touched him with
the signs of suffering. Adam knew what suffering was—he could not
lay a cruel finger on a bruised man. He felt no impulse that he needed
to resist: silence was more just than reproach. Arthur was the first to
speak.

"Adam," he said, quietly, "it may be a good thing that we have met
here, for I wished to see you. I should have asked to see you to-morrow."

He paused, but Adam said nothing.

"I know it is painful to you to meet me," Arthur went on, "but it
is not likely to happen again for years to come."

"No, sir," said Adam, coldly, "that was what I meant to write to you
to-morrow, as it would be better all dealings should be at an end between us, and somebody else put in my place."

Arthur felt the answer keenly, and it was not without an effort that he spoke again.

"It was partly on that subject I wished to speak to you. I don't want to lessen your indignation against me, or ask you to do anything for my sake. I only wish to ask you if you will help me to lessen the evil consequences of the past, which is unchangeable. I don't mean consequences to myself but to others. It is but little I can do, I know. I know the worst consequences will remain; but something may be done, and you can help me. Will you listen to me patiently?"

"Yes, sir," said Adam, after some hesitation; "I'll hear what it is. If I can help to mend anything, I will. Anger 'ull mend nothing, I know. We've had enough o' that."

"I was going to the Hermitage," said Arthur. "Will you go there with me and sit down? We can talk better there."

The Hermitage had never been entered since they left it together, for Arthur had locked up the key in his desk. And now, when he opened the door, there was the candle burnt out in the socket; there was the chair in the same place where Adam remembered sitting; there was the waste-paper basket full of scraps, and deep down in it, Arthur felt in an instant, there was the little pink silk handkerchief. It would have been painful to enter this place if their previous thoughts had been less painful.

They sat down opposite each other in the old places, and Arthur said, "I'm going away, Adam; I'm going into the army."

Poor Arthur felt that Adam ought to be affected by this announcement—ought to have a movement of sympathy towards him. But Adam's lips remained firmly closed, and the expression of his face unchanged.

"What I want to say to you," Arthur continued, "is this: one of my reasons for going away is, that no one else may leave Hayslope—may leave their home on my account. I would do anything, there is no sacrifice I would not make, to prevent any further injury to others through my—through what has happened."

Arthur's words had precisely the opposite effect to that he had anticipated. Adam thought he perceived in them that notion of compensation for irretrievable wrong, that self-soothing attempt to make evil bear the same fruits as good, which most of all roused his indignation. He was as strongly impelled to look painful facts right in the face as Arthur was to turn away his eyes from them. Moreover, he had the wakeful suspicious pride of a poor man in the presence of a rich man. He felt his old severity returning as he said,

"The time's past for that, sir. A man should make sacrifices to keep clear of doing a wrong; sacrifices won't undo it when it's done. When people's feelings have got a deadly wound, they can't be cured with favours."

"Favours!" said Arthur, passionately; "no; how can you suppose I meant that? But the Poysers—Mr. Irwine tells me the Poysers mean to leave the place where they have lived so many years—for generations

Don't you see, as Mr. Irwine does, that if they could be persuaded to overcome the feeling that drives them away, it would be much better for them in the end to remain on the old spot, among the friends and neighbours who know them?"

"That's true," said Adam, coldly. "But then, sir, folk's feelings are not so easily overcome. It'll be hard for Martin Poyser to go to a strange place, among strange faces, when he's been bred up on the Hall Farm, and his father before him; but then it 'ud be harder for a man with his feelings to stay. I don't see how the thing's to be made any other than hard. There's a sort o' damage, sir, that can't be made up for."

Arthur was silent some moments. In spite of other feelings, dominant in him this evening, his pride winced under Adam's mode of treating him. Wasn't he himself suffering? Was not he too obliged to renounce his most cherished hopes? It was now as it had been eight months ago —Adam was forcing Arthur to feel more intensely the irrevocableness of his own wrong-doing: he was presenting the sort of resistance that was the most irritating to Arthur's eager, ardent nature. But his anger was subdued by the same influence that had subdued Adam's when they first confronted each other—by the marks of suffering in a long familiar face. The momentary struggle ended in the feeling that he could bear a great deal from Adam, to whom he had been the occasion of bearing so much; but there was a touch of pleading, boyish vexation in his tone as he said,

"But people may make injuries worse by unreasonable conduct—by giving way to anger and satisfying that for the moment, instead of thinking what will be the effect in the future.

"If I were going to stay here and act as landlord," he added, presently, with still more eagerness—"if I were careless about what I've done— what I've been the cause of, you would have some excuse, Adam, for going away and encouraging others to go. You would have some excuse then for trying to make the evil worse. But when I tell you I'm going away for years—when you know what that means for me, how it cuts off every plan of happiness I've ever formed—it is impossible for a sensible man like you to believe that there is any real ground for the Poysers refusing to remain. I know their feeling about disgrace,—Mr. Irwine has told me all; but he is of opinion that they might be persuaded out of this idea that they are disgraced in the eyes of their neighbours, and that they can't remain on my estate, if you would join him in his efforts, —if you would stay yourself, and go on managing the old woods."

Arthur paused a moment, and then added, pleadingly, "You know that's a good work to do for the sake of other people, besides the owner. And you don't know but that they may have a better owner soon, whom you will like to work for. If I die, my cousin Tradgett will have the estate, and take my name. He is a good fellow."

Adam could not help being moved: it was impossible for him not to feel that this was the voice of the honest, warm-hearted Arthur whom he had loved and been proud of in old days; but nearer memories would not be thrust away. He was silent; yet Arthur saw an answer in his face that induced him to go on, with growing earnestness.

"And then, if you would talk to the Poysers—if you would talk the matter over with Mr. Irwine—he means to see you to-morrow—and then if you'd join your arguments to his to prevail on them not to go . . . I know, of course, that they would not accept any favour from me: I mean nothing of that kind: but I'm sure they would suffer less in the end. Irwine thinks so too; and Mr. Irwine is to have the chief authority on the estate—he has consented to undertake that. They will really be under no man but one whom they respect and like. It would be the same with you, Adam; and it could be nothing but a desire to give me worse pain that could incline you to go."

Arthur was silent again for a little while, and then said, with some agitation in his voice,

"I wouldn't act so towards you, I know. If you were in my place and I in yours, I should try to help you to do the best."

Adam made a hasty movement on his chair, and looked on the ground. Arthur went on:

"Perhaps you've never done anything you've had bitterly to repent of in your life, Adam; if you had, you would be more generous. You would know then that it's worse for me than for you."

Arthur rose from his seat with the last words, and went to one of the windows, looking out and turning his back on Adam, as he continued, passionately,

"Haven't *I* loved her too? Didn't I see her yesterday? Shan't I carry the thought of her about with me as much as you will? And don't you think you would suffer more if you'd been in fault?"

There was silence for several minutes, for the struggle in Adam's mind was not easily decided. Facile natures, whose emotions have little permanence, can hardly understand how much inward resistance he overcame before he rose from his seat and turned towards Arthur. Arthur heard the movement, and, turning round, met the sad but softened look with which Adam said,

"It's true what you say, sir: I'm hard—it's in my nature. I was too hard with my father, for doing wrong. I've been a bit hard t' everybody but *her*. I felt as if nobody pitied her enough—her suffering cut into me so; and when I thought the folks at the Farm were too hard with her, I said I'd never be hard to anybody myself again. But feeling overmuch about her has perhaps made me unfair to you. I've known what it is in my life to repent and feel it's too late: I felt I'd been too harsh to my father when he was gone from me—I feel it now, when I think of him. I've no right to be hard towards them as have done wrong and repent."

Adam spoke these words with the firm distinctness of a man who is resolved to leave nothing unsaid that he is bound to say; but he went on with more hesitation.

"I wouldn't shake hands with you once, sir, when you asked me—but if you're willing to do it now, for all I refused then" . . .

Arthur's white hand was in Adam's large grasp in an instant, and with that action there was a strong rush, on both sides, of the old, boyish affection.

"Adam," Arthur said, impelled to full confession now, "it would never have happened if I'd known you loved her. That would have helped to save me from it. And I *did* struggle: I never meant to injure her. I deceived you afterwards—and that led on to worse; but I thought it was forced upon me, I thought it was the best thing I could do. And in that letter I told her to let me know if she were in any trouble: don't think I would not have done everything I could. But I was all wrong from the very first, and horrible wrong has come of it. God knows, I'd give my life if I could undo it."

They sat down again opposite each other, and Adam said, tremulously, "How did she seem when you left her, sir?"

"Don't ask me, Adam," Arthur said; "I feel sometimes as if I should go mad with thinking of her looks and what she said to me, and then, that I couldn't get a full pardon—that I couldn't save her from that wretched fate of being transported—that I can do nothing for her all those years; and she may die under it, and never know comfort any more."

"Ah, sir," said Adam, for the first time feeling his own pain merged in sympathy for Arthur, "you and me'll often be thinking o' the same thing, when we're a long way off one another. I'll pray God to help you, as I pray him to help me."

"But there's that sweet woman—that Dinah Morris," Arthur said, pursuing his own thoughts, and not knowing what had been the sense of Adam's words, "she says she shall stay with her to the very last moment—till she goes; and the poor thing clings to her as if she found some comfort in her. I could worship that woman; I don't know what I should do if she were not there. Adam, you will see her when she comes back: I could say nothing to her yesterday—nothing of what I felt towards her. Tell her," Arthur went on hurriedly, as if he wanted to hide the emotion with which he spoke, while he took off his chain and watch—"tell her I asked you to give her this in remembrance of me—of the man to whom she is the one source of comfort, when he thinks of . . . I know she doesn't care about such things—or anything else I can give her for its own sake. But she will use the watch—I shall like to think of her using it."

"I'll give it to her, sir," Adam said, "and tell her your words. She told me she should come back to the people at the Hall Farm."

"And you *will* persuade the Poysers to stay, Adam?" said Arthur, reminded of the subject which both of them had forgotten in the first interchange of revived friendship. "You *will* stay yourself, and help Mr Irwine to carry out the repairs and improvements on the estate?"

"There's one thing, sir, that perhaps you don't take account of," said Adam, with hesitating gentleness, "and that was what made me hang back longer. You see, it's the same with both me and the Poysers: if we stay, it's for our own worldly interest, and it looks as if we'd put up with anything for the sake o' that. I know that's what they'll feel, and I can't help feeling a little of it myself. When folks have got an honourable, independent spirit, they don't like to do anything that might make 'em seem base-minded."

"But no one who knows you will think that, Adam: that is not a reason strong enough against a course that is really more generous, more unselfish than the other. And it will be known—it shall be made known, that both you and the Poysers stayed at my entreaty. Adam, don't try to make things worse for me; I'm punished enough without that."

"No, sir, no," Adam said, looking at Arthur with mournful affection. "God forbid I should make things worse for you. I used to wish I could do it, in my passion;—but that was when I thought you didn't feel enough. I'll stay, sir: I'll do the best I can. It's all I've got to think of now—to do my work well, and make the world a bit better place for them as can enjoy it."

"Then we'll part now, Adam. You will see Mr. Irwine to-morrow, and consult with him about everything."

"Are you going soon, sir?" said Adam.

"As soon as possible—after I've made the necessary arrangements. Good-by, Adam. I shall think of you going about the old place."

"Good-by, sir. God bless you."

The hands were clasped once more, and Adam left the Hermitage, feeling that sorrow was more bearable now hatred was gone.

As soon as the door was closed behind him, Arthur went to the waste paper basket and took out the little pink silk handkerchief.

BOOK SIX

★

CHAPTER XLIX

AT THE HALL FARM

THE first autumnal afternoon sunshine of 1801—more than eighteen months after that parting of Adam and Arthur in the Hermitage—was on the yard at the Hall Farm, and the bulldog was in one of his most excited moments; for it was that hour of the day when the cows were being driven into the yard for their afternoon milking. No wonder the patient beasts ran confusedly into the wrong places, for the alarming din of the bulldog was mingled with more distant sounds which the timid feminine creatures, with pardonable superstition, imagined also to have some relation to their own movements—with the tremendous crack of the waggoner's whip, the roar of his voice, and the booming thunder of the waggon, as it left the rick-yard empty of its golden load.

The milking of the cows was a sight Mrs. Poyser loved, and at this hour on mild days she was usually standing at the house door, with her knitting in her hands, in quiet contemplation, only heightened to a keener interest when the vicious yellow cow, who had once kicked over a pailful of precious milk, was about to undergo the preventive punishment of having her hinder-legs strapped.

To-day, however, Mrs. Poyser gave but a divided attention to the arrival of the cows, for she was in eager discussion with Dinah, who was stitching Mr. Poyser's shirt-collars, and had borne patiently to have her thread broken three times by Totty pulling at her arm with a sudden insistence that she should look at "Baby," that is, at a large wooden doll with no legs and a long skirt, whose bald head Totty, seated in her small chair at Dinah's side, was caressing and pressing to her fat cheek with much fervour. Totty is larger by more than two years' growth than when you first saw her, and she has on a black frock under her pinafore: Mrs. Poyser too has on a black gown, which seems to heighten the family likeness between her and Dinah. In other respects there is little outward change now discernible in our old friends, or in the pleasant house-place, bright with polished oak and pewter.

"I never saw the like to you, Dinah," Mrs. Poyser was saying, "when you've once took anything into your head: there's no more moving you than the rooted tree. You may say what you like, but I don't believe *that's* religion; for what's the Sermon on the Mount about, as you're

so fond o' reading to the boys, but doing what other folks 'ud have you
do? But if it was anything unreasonable they wanted you to do, like
taking your cloak off and giving it to 'em, or letting 'em slap you i' the
face, I daresay you'd be ready enough: it's only when one 'ud have
you do what's plain common-sense and good for yourself, as you're
obstinate th' other way."

"Nay, dear aunt," said Dinah, smiling slightly as she went on with
her work, "I'm sure your wish 'ud be a reason for me to do anything
that I didn't feel it was wrong to do."

"Wrong! You drive me past bearing. What is there wrong, I should
like to know, i' staying along wi' your own friends, as are th' happier
for having you with 'em, an' are willing to provide for you, even if
your work didn't more nor pay 'em for the bit o' sparrow's victual y'
eat, and the bit o' rag you put on? An' who is it, I should like to know,
as you're bound t' help and comfort i' the world more nor your own
flesh and blood—an' me th' only aunt you've got aboveground, an' am
brought to the brink o' the grave welly every winter as comes, an' there's
the child as sits beside you 'ull break her little heart when you go, an'
the grandfather not been dead a twelvemonth, an' your uncle 'ull miss
you so as never was—a-lighting his pipe an' waiting on him, an' now I
can trust you wi' the butter, an' have had all the trouble o' teaching
you, and there's all the sewing to be done, an' I must have a strange gell
out o' Treddles'on to do it—an' all because you must go back to that
bare heap o' stones as the very crows fly over an' won't stop at."

"Dear aunt Rachel," said Dinah, looking up in Mrs. Poyser's face,
"it's your kindness makes you say I'm useful to you. You don't really
want me now; for Nancy and Molly are clever at their work, and you're
in good health now, by the blessing of God, and my uncle is of a cheerful countenance again, and you have neighbours and friends not a few—
some of them come to sit with my uncle almost daily. Indeed, you will
not miss me; and at Snowfield there are brethren and sisters in great
need, who have none of those comforts you have around you. I feel that
I am called back to those amongst whom my lot was first cast: I feel
drawn again towards the hills where I used to be blessed in carrying the
word of life to the sinful and desolate."

"You feel! yes," said Mrs. Poyser, returning from a parenthetic
glance at the cows. "That's allays the reason I'm to sit down wi', when
you've a mind to do anything contrary. What do you want to be
preaching for more than you're preaching now? Don't you go off, the
Lord knows where, every Sunday a-preaching and praying? an' haven't
you got Methodists enow at Treddles'on to go and look at, if church
folks's faces are too handsome to please you? an' isn't there them i' this
parish as you've got under hand, and they're like enough to make
friends wi' Old Harry again as soon as your back's turned? There's that
Bessy Cranage—she'll be flaunting i' new finery three weeks after
you're gone, I'll be bound: she'll no more go on in her new ways without you, than a dog 'ull stand on its hind-legs when there's nobody look-

ing. But I suppose it doesna matter so much about folks's souls i' this country, else you'd be for staying with your own aunt, for she's none so good but what you might help her to be better."

There was a certain something in Mrs. Poyser's voice just then, which she did not wish to be noticed, so she turned round hastily to look at the clock and said: "See there! It's tea-time; an' if Martin's i' the rick-yard, he'll like a cup. Here, Totty, my chicken, let mother put your bonnet on, and then you go out into the rick-yard, and see if father's there, and tell him he mustn't go away again without coming t' have a cup o' tea; and tell your brothers to come in too."

Totty trotted off in her flapping bonnet, while Mrs. Poyser set out the bright oak table, and reached down the tea-cups.

"You talk o' them gells Nancy and Molly being clever i' their work," she began again;—"it's fine talking. They're all the same, clever or stupid—one can't trust 'em out o' one's sight a minute. They want somebody's eye on 'em constant if they're to be kept to their work. An' suppose I'm ill again this winter, as I was the winter before last, who's to look after 'em then, if you're gone? An' there's that blessed child—something's sure t' happen to her—they'll let her tumble into the fire, or get at the kettle wi' the boiling lard in't, or some mischief as 'ull lame her for life; an' it'll be all your fault, Dinah."

"Aunt," said Dinah, "I promise to come back to you in the winter if you're ill. Don't think I will ever stay away from you if you're in real want of me. But indeed it is needful for my own soul that I should go away from this life of ease and luxury, in which I have all things too richly to enjoy—at least that I should go away for a short space. No one can know but myself what are my inward needs, and the besetments I am most in danger from. Your wish for me to stay is not a call of duty which I refuse to hearken to because it is against my own desires; it is a temptation that I must resist, lest the love of the creature should become like a mist in my soul shutting out the heavenly light."

"It passes my cunning to know what you mean by ease and luxury," said Mrs. Poyser, as she cut the bread and butter. "It's true there's good victual enough about you, as nobody shall ever say I don't provide enough and to spare, but if there's ever a bit o' odds and ends as nobody else 'ud eat, you're sure to pick it out . . . but look there! there's Adam Bede a-carrying the little un in. I wonder how it is he's come so early."

Mrs. Poyser hastened to the door for the pleasure of looking at her darling in a new position, with love in her eyes but reproof on her tongue. "O for shame, Totty! Little gells o' five year old should be ashamed to be carried. Why, Adam, she'll break your arm, such a big gell as that; set her down—for shame!"

"Nay, nay," said Adam, "I can lift her with my hand, I've no need to take my arm to it."

Totty, looking as serenely unconscious of remark as a fat white puppy, was set down at the door-place, and the mother enforced her reproof with a shower of kisses.

"You're surprised to see me at this hour o' the day," said Adam.

"Yes, but come in," said Mrs. Poyser, making way for him; "there's no bad news, I hope?"

"No, nothing bad," Adam answered, as he went up to Dinah and put out his hand to her. She had laid down her work and stood up, instinctively, as he approached her. A faint blush died away from her pale cheek as she put her hand in his, and looked up at him timidly.

"It's an errand to you brought me, Dinah," said Adam, apparently unconscious that he was holding her hand all the while; "mother's a bit ailing, and she's set her heart on your coming to stay the night with her, if you'll be so kind. I told her I'd call and ask you as I came from the village. She overworks herself, and I can't persuade her to have a little girl t' help her. I don't know what's to be done."

Adam released Dinah's hand as he ceased speaking, and was expecting an answer; but before she had opened her lips Mrs. Poyser said,

"Look there now! I told you there was folks enow t' help i' this parish, wi'out going further off. There's Mrs. Bede getting as old and cas'alty as can be, and she won't let anybody but you go a-nigh her hardly. The folks at Snowfield have learnt by this time to do better wi'out you nor she can."

"I'll put my bonnet on and set off directly, if you don't want anything done first, aunt," said Dinah, folding up her work.

"Yes, I do want something done. I want you t' have your tea, child; it's all ready; and you'll have a cup, Adam, if y' arena in too big a hurry."

"Yes, I'll have a cup, please; and then I'll walk with Dinah. I'm going straight home, for I've got a lot o' timber valuations to write out."

"Why, Adam lad, are you here?" said Mr. Poyser, entering warm and coatless, with the two black-eyed boys behind him, still looking as much like him as two small elephants are like a large one. "How it is we've got sight o' you so long before foddering-time?"

"I came on an errand for mother," said Adam. "She's got a touch of her old complaint, and she wants Dinah to go and stay with her a bit."

"Well, we'll spare her for your mother a little while," said Mr. Poyser. "But we wonna spare her for anybody else, on'y her husband."

"Husband!" said Marty, who was at the most prosaic and literal period of the boyish mind. "Why, Dinah hasn't got a husband."

"Spare her?" said Mrs. Poyser, placing a seed-cake on the table, and then seating herself to pour out the tea. "But we must spare her, it seems, and not for a husband neither, but for her own megrims. Tommy, what are you doing to your little sister's doll? making the child naughty when she'd be good if you'd let her. You shanna have a morsel o' cake if you behave so."

Tommy, with true brotherly sympathy, was amusing himself by turning Dolly's skirt over her bald head, and exhibiting her truncated body to the general scorn—an indignity which cut Totty to the heart.

"What do you think Dinah's been a-telling me since dinner-time?" Mrs. Poyser continued, looking at her husband.

"Eh! I'm a poor un at guessing," said Mr. Poyser.

"Why, she means to go back to Snowfield again, and work i' the mill, and starve herself, as she used to do, like a creatur as has got no friends."

Mr. Poyser did not readily find words to express his unpleasant astonishment; he only looked from his wife to Dinah, who had now seated herself beside Totty, as a bulwark against brotherly playfulness, and was busying herself with the children's tea. If he had been given to making general reflections, it would have occurred to him that there was certainly a change come over Dinah, for she never used to change colour; but, as it was, he merely observed that her face was flushed at that moment. Mr. Poyser thought she looked the prettier for it: it was a flush no deeper than the petal of a monthly rose. Perhaps it came because her uncle was looking at her so fixedly; but there is no knowing; for just then Adam was saying, with quiet surprise,

"Why, I hoped Dinah was settled among us for life. I thought she'd given up the notion o' going back to her old country."

"Thought! yes," said Mrs. Poyser; "and so would anybody else ha' thought, as had got their right end up'ards. But I suppose you must *be* a Methodist to know what a Methodist 'ull do. It's ill guessing what the bats are flying after."

"Why, what have we done to you, Dinah, as you must go away from us?" said Mr. Poyser, still pausing over his tea-cup. "It's like breaking your word, welly; for your aunt never had no thought but you'd make this your home."

"Nay, uncle," said Dinah, trying to be quite calm. "When I first came, I said it was only for a time, as long as I could be of any comfort to my aunt."

"Well, an' who said you'd ever left off being a comfort to me?" said Mrs. Poyser. "If you didna mean to stay wi' me, you'd better never ha' come. Them as ha' never had a cushion don't miss it."

"Nay, nay," said Mr. Poyser, who objected to exaggerated views. "Thee mustna say so; we should ha' been ill off wi'out her, Lady Day was a twelvemont': we mun be thankful for that, whether she stays or no. But I canna think what she mun leave a good home for, to go back int' a country where the land, most on't, isna worth ten shillings an acre, rent and profits."

"Why, that's just the reason she wants to go, as fur as she can give a reason," said Mrs. Poyser. "She says this country's too comfortable, an' here's too much t' eat, an' folks arena miserable enough. And she's going next week: I canna turn her, say what I will. It's allays the way wi' them meekfaced people; you may's well pelt a bag o' feathers as talk to 'em. But *I* say it isna religion, to be so obstinate—is it now, Adam?"

Adam saw that Dinah was more disturbed than he had ever seen her by any matter relating to herself, and, anxious to relieve her, if possible, he said, looking at her affectionately,

"Nay, I can't find fault with anything Dinah does. I believe her thoughts are better than our guesses, let 'em be what they may. I should ha' been thankful for her to stay among us; but if she thinks well to go, I wouldn't cross her, or make it hard to her by objecting. We owe her something different to that."

As it often happens, the words intended to relieve her were just too much for Dinah's susceptible feelings at this moment. The tears came into the grey eyes too fast to be hidden; and she got up hurriedly, meaning it to be understood that she was going to put on her bonnet.

"Mother, what's Dinah crying for?" said Totty. "She isn't a naughty dell."

"Thee'st gone a bit too fur," said Mr. Poyser. "We've no right t' interfere with her doing as she likes. An' thee'dst be as angry as could be wi' me, if I said a word against anything she did."

"Because you'd very like be finding fault wi'out reason," said Mrs Poyser. "But there's reason i' what I say, else I shouldna say it. It's easy talking for them as can't love her so well as her own aunt does. An' me got so used to her! I shall feel as uneasy as a new sheared sheep when she's gone from me. An' to think of her leaving a parish where she's so looked on. There's Mr. Irwine makes as much of her as if she was a lady, for all her being a Methodist, an' wi' that maggot o' preaching in her head;—God forgi'e me if I'm i' the wrong to call it so."

"Ay," said Mr. Poyser, looking jocose; "but thee dostna tell Adam what he said to thee about it one day. The missis was saying, Adam, as the preaching was th' only fault to be found wi' Dinah, and Mr. Irwine says, 'But you mustn't find fault with her for that, Mrs. Poyser; you forget she's got no husband to preach to. I'll answer for it, you give Poyser many a good sermon.' The parson had thee there," Mr. Poyser added, laughing unctuously. "I told Bartle Massey on it, an' he laughed too."

"Yes, it's a small joke sets men laughing when they sit a-staring at one another with a pipe i' their mouths," said Mrs. Poyser. "Give Bartle Massey his way, and he'd have all the sharpness to himself. If the chaff cutter had the making of us, we should all be straw, I reckon. Totty, my chicken, go up-stairs to cousin Dinah, and see what she's doing, an' give her a pretty kiss."

This errand was devised for Totty as a means of checking certain threatening symptoms about the corners of the mouth; for Tommy, no longer expectant of cake, was lifting up his eyelids with his fore-fingers and turning his eyeballs towards Totty, in a way that she felt to be disagreeably personal.

"You're rare and busy now—eh, Adam?" said Mr. Poyser. "Burge getting so bad wi' his asthmy, it's well if he'll ever do much riding about again."

"Yes, we've got a pretty bit o' building on hand now," said Adam: "what with the repairs on th' estate, and the new houses at Treddles'on."

"I'll bet a penny that new house Burge is building on his own bit o' land is for him and Mary to go to," said Mr. Poyser. "He'll be for laying by business soon, I'll warrant, and be wanting you to take to it all, and pay him so much by th' 'ear. We shall see you living on th' hill before another twelvemont's over."

"Well," said Adam, "I should like t' have the business in my own hands. It isn't as I mind much about getting any more money: we've enough and to spare now, with only our two selves and mother; but I should like t' have my own way about things: I could try plans then, as I can't do now."

"You get on pretty well wi' the new steward, I reckon?" said Mr. Poyser.

"Yes, yes; he's a sensible man enough: understands farming—he's carrying on the draining, and all that, capital. You must go some day towards the Stonyshire side, and see what alterations they're making. But he's got no notion about buildings: you can so seldom get hold of a man as can turn his brains to more nor one thing; it's just as if they wore blinkers like th' horses, and could see nothing o' one side of 'em. Now, there's Mr. Irwine has got notions o' building more nor most architects; for as for th' architects, they set up to be fine fellows, but the most of 'em don't know where to set a chimney so as it shan't be quarrelling with a door. My notion is, a practical builder, that's got a bit o' taste, makes the best architect for common things; and I've ten times the pleasure i' seeing after the work when I've made the plan myself."

Mr. Poyser listened with an admiring interest to Adam's discourse on building; but perhaps it suggested to him that the building of his corn-rick had been proceeding a little too long without the control of the master's eye; for when Adam had done speaking, he got up and said,

"Well, lad, I'll bid you good-by now, for I'm off to the rick-yard again."

Adam rose too, for he saw Dinah entering, with her bonnet on, and a little basket in her hand, preceded by Totty.

"You're ready, I see, Dinah," Adam said; "so we'll set off, for the sooner I'm at home the better."

"Mother," said Totty, with her treble pipe, "Dinah was saying her prayers and crying ever so."

"Hush, hush," said the mother: "little gells mustn't chatter."

Whereupon the father, shaking with silent laughter, set Totty on the white deal table, and desired her to kiss him. Mr. and Mrs. Poyser, you perceive, had no correct principles of education.

"Come back to-morrow if Mrs. Bede doesn't want you, Dinah," said Mrs. Poyser: "but you can stay, you know, if she's ill."

So, when the good-bys had been said, Dinah and Adam left the Hall Farm together.

CHAPTER L

IN THE COTTAGE

ADAM did not ask Dinah to take his arm when they got out into the lane. He had never yet done so, often as they had walked together; for he had observed that she never walked arm-in-arm with Seth, and he thought, perhaps, that kind of support was not agreeable to her. So they walked apart, though side by side, and the close poke of her little black bonnet hid her face from him.

"You can't be happy, then, to make the Hall Farm your home, Dinah?" Adam said, with the quiet interest of a brother, who has no anxiety for himself in the matter. "It's a pity, seeing they're so fond of you."

"You know, Adam, my heart is as their heart, so far as love for them and care for their welfare goes; but they are in no present need, their sorrows are healed, and I feel that I am called back to my old work, in which I found a blessing that I have missed of late in the midst of too abundant worldly good. I know it is a vain thought to flee from the work that God appoints us, for the sake of finding a greater blessing to our own souls, as if we could choose for ourselves where we shall find the fulness of the Divine Presence, instead of seeking it where alone it is to be found, in loving obedience. But now, I believe, I have a clear showing that my work lies elsewhere—at least for a time. In the years to come, if my aunt's health should fail, or she should otherwise need me, I shall return."

"You know best, Dinah," said Adam. "I don't believe you'd go against the wishes of them that love you, and are akin to you, without a good and sufficient reason in your own conscience. I've no right to say anything about my being sorry: you know well enough what cause I have to put you above every other friend I've got; and if it had been ordered so that you could ha' been my sister, and lived with us all our lives, I should ha' counted it the greatest blessing as could happen to us now; but Seth tells me there's no hope o' that: your feelings are different; and perhaps I'm taking too much upon me to speak about it."

Dinah made no answer, and they walked on in silence for some yards, till they came to the stone stile; where, as Adam had passed through first, and turned round to give her his hand while she mounted the unusually high step, she could not prevent him from seeing her face. It struck him with surprise; for the grey eyes, usually so mild and grave, had the bright uneasy glance which accompanies suppressed agitation, and the slight flush in her cheeks, with which she had come down-stairs, was heightened to a deep rose-colour. She looked as if she were only sister to Dinah. Adam was silent with surprise and conjecture for some moments, and then he said:

"I hope I've not hurt or displeased you, by what I've said, Dinah: perhaps I was making too free. I've no wish different from what you see to be best; and I'm satisfied for you to live thirty mile off, if you think it right. I shall think of you just as much as I do now; for you're bound up with what I can no more help remembering, than I can help my heart beating."

Poor Adam! Thus do men blunder. Dinah made no answer, but she presently said,

"Have you heard any news from that poor young man, since we last spoke of him?"

Dinah always called Arthur so; she had never lost the image of him as she had seen him in the prison.

"Yes," said Adam. "Mr. Irwine read me part of a letter from him yesterday. It's pretty certain, they say, that there'll be a peace soon, though nobody believes it'll last long; but he says he doesn't mean to come home. He's no heart for it yet; and it's better for others that he should keep away. Mr. Irwine thinks he's in the right not to come:—it's a sorrowful letter. He asks about you and the Poysers, as he always does. There's one thing in the letter cut me a good deal:—'You can't think what an old fellow I feel,' he says; 'I make no schemes now. I'm the best when I've a good day's march or fighting before me.' "

"He's of a rash, warm-hearted nature, like Esau, for whom I have always felt great pity," said Dinah. "That meeting between the brothers, where Esau is so loving and generous, and Jacob so timid and distrustful, notwithstanding his sense of the Divine favour, has always touched me greatly. Truly, I have been tempted sometimes to say that Jacob was of a mean spirit. But that is our trial:—we must learn to see the good in the midst of much that is unlovely."

"Ah," said Adam, "I like to read about Moses best, in th' Old Testament. He carried a hard business well through, and died when other folks were going to reap the fruits: a man must have courage to look at his life so, and think what'll come of it after he's dead and gone. A good solid bit o' work lasts: if it's only laying a floor down, somebody's the better for it being done well, besides the man as does it."

They were both glad to talk of subjects that were not personal, and in this way they went on till they passed the bridge across the Willow Brook, when Adam turned round and said,

"Ah, here's Seth. I thought he'd be home soon. Does he know of your going, Dinah?"

"Yes, I told him last Sabbath."

Adam remembered now that Seth had come home much depressed on Sunday evening, a circumstance which had been very unusual with him of late, for the happiness he had in seeing Dinah every week seemed long to have outweighed the pain of knowing she would never marry him. This evening he had his habitual air of dreamy benignant contentment, until he came quite close to Dinah, and saw the traces of tears on her delicate eyelids and eyelashes. He gave one rapid glance at his

brother; but Adam was evidently quite outside the current of emotion
that had shaken Dinah: he wore his everyday look of unexpectant calm.
Seth tried not to let Dinah see that he had noticed her face, and only
said,

"I'm thankful you're come, Dinah, for mother's been hungering after
the sight of you all day. She began to talk of you the first thing in the
morning."

When they entered the cottage, Lisbeth was seated in her arm-chair,
too tired with setting out the evening meal, a task she always performed
a long time beforehand, to go and meet them at the door as usual, when
she heard the approaching footsteps.

"Coom, child, thee't coom at last," she said, when Dinah went towards
her. "What dost mane by lavin' me a week, an' ne'er coomin' a-nigh
me?"

"Dear friend," said Dinah, taking her hand, "you're not well. If I'd
known it sooner, I'd have come."

"An' how's t' know if thee dostna coom? Th' lads on'y know what I
tell 'em: as long as ye can stir hand and foot the men think ye're hearty.
But I'm none so bad, on'y a bit of a cold sets me achin'. An' th' lads
tease me so t' ha' somebody wi' me t' do the work—they make me ache
worse wi' talkin'. If thee'dst come and stay wi' me, they'd let me alone.
The Poysers canna want thee so bad as I do. But take thy bonnet off,
an' let me look at thee."

Dinah was moving away, but Lisbeth held her fast, while she was
taking off her bonnet, and looked at her face, as one looks into a newly-
gathered snow-drop, to renew the old impressions of purity and gentleness.

"What's the matter wi' thee?" said Lisbeth, in astonishment; "thee'st
been a-cryin'."

"It's only a grief that'll pass away," said Dinah, who did not wish
just now to call forth Lisbeth's remonstrances by disclosing her intention to leave Hayslope. "You shall know about it shortly—we'll talk of it
to-night. I shall stay with you to-night."

Lisbeth was pacified by this prospect; and she had the whole evening
to talk with Dinah alone; for there was a new room in the cottage, you
remember, built nearly two years ago, in the expectation of a new inmate; and here Adam always sat when he had writing to do, or plans
to make. Seth sat there too this evening, for he knew his mother would
like to have Dinah all to herself.

There were two pretty pictures on the two sides of the wall in the
cottage. On one side there was the broad-shouldered, large-featured,
hardy old woman, in her blue jacket and buff kerchief, with her dim-
eyed anxious looks turned continually on the lily face and the slight
form in the black dress that were either moving lightly about in helpful
activity, or seated close by the old woman's arm-chair, holding her
withered hand, with eyes lifted up towards her to speak a language which

Lisbeth understood far better than the Bible or the hymn-book. She would scarcely listen to reading at all to-night. "Nay, nay, shut the book," she said. "We mun talk. I want t' know what thee wast cryin' about. Hast got troubles o' thy own, like other folks?"

On the other side of the wall there were the two brothers, so like each other in the midst of their unlikeness: Adam, with knit brows, shaggy hair, and dark vigorous colour, absorbed in his "figuring"; Seth, with large rugged features, the close copy of his brother's, but with thin wavy brown hair and blue dreamy eyes, as often as not looking vaguely out of the window instead of at his book, although it was a newly bought book—Wesley's abridgement of Madame Guyon's life, which was full of wonder and interest for him. Seth had said to Adam, "Can I help thee with anything in here to-night? I don't want to make a noise in the shop."

"No, lad," Adam answered, "there's nothing but what I must do myself. Thee'st got thy new book to read."

And often, when Seth was quite unconscious, Adam, as he paused after drawing a line with his ruler, looked at his brother with a kind smile dawning in his eyes. He knew "th' lad liked to sit full o' thoughts he could give no account of; they'd never come t' anything, but they made him happy"; and in the last year or so, Adam had been getting more and more indulgent to Seth. It was part of that growing tenderness which came from the sorrow at work within him.

For Adam, though you see him quite master of himself, working hard and delighting in his work after his inborn inalienable nature, had not outlived his sorrow—had not felt it slip from him as a temporary burthen, and leave him the same man again. Do any of us? God forbid. It would be a poor result of all our anguish and our wrestling, if we won nothing but our old selves at the end of it—if we could return to the same blind loves, the same self-confident blame, the same light thoughts of human suffering, the same frivolous gossip over blighted human lives, the same feeble sense of that Unknown towards which we have sent forth irrepressible cries in our loneliness. Let us rather be thankful that our sorrow lives in us as an indestructible force, only changing its form, as forces do, and passing from pain into sympathy—the one poor word which includes all our best insight and our best love. Not that this transformation of pain into sympathy had completely taken place in Adam yet: there was still a great remnant of pain, and this he felt would subsist as long as *her* pain was not a memory, but an existing thing, which he must think of as renewed with the light of every new morning. But we get accustomed to mental as well as bodily pain, without, for all that, losing our sensibility to it: it becomes a habit of our lives, and we cease to imagine a condition of perfect ease as possible for us. Desire is chastened into submission; and we are contented with our day when we have been able to bear our grief in silence, and act as if we were not suffering. For it is at such periods that the sense of our lives having visible and invisible relations beyond any of which either our present or prospective self is the centre, grows like a muscle that we are obliged to lean on and exert.

That was Adam's state of mind in this second autumn of his sorrow. His work, as you know, had always been part of his religion, and from very early days he saw clearly that good carpentry was God's will— was that form of God's will that most immediately concerned him; but now there was no margin of dreams for him beyond this daylight reality, no holiday-time in the working-day world; no moment in the distance when duty would take off her iron glove and breastplate, and clasp him gently into rest. He conceived no picture of the future but one made up of hard-working days such as he lived through, with growing content-ment and intensity of interest, every fresh week: love, he thought, could never be anything to him but a living memory—a limb lopped off, but not gone from consciousness. He did not know that the power of loving was all the while gaining new force within him; that the new sensibilities bought by a deep experience were so many new fibres by which it was possible, nay, necessary to him, that his nature should intertwine with another. Yet he was aware that common affection and friendship were more precious to him than they used to be,—that he clung more to his mother and Seth, and had an unspeakable satisfaction in the sight or imagination of any small addition to their happiness. The Poysers, too —hardly three or four days passed but he felt the need of seeing them, and interchanging words and looks of friendliness with them: he would have felt this, probably, even if Dinah had not been with them; but he had only said the simplest truth in telling Dinah that he put her above all other friends in the world. Could anything be more natural? For in the darkest moments of memory the thought of her always came as the first ray of returning comfort: the early days of gloom at the Hall Farm had been gradually turned into soft moonlight by her presence; and in the cottage, too,—for she had come at every spare moment to soothe and cheer poor Lisbeth, who had been stricken with a fear that subdued even her querulousness, at the sight of her darling Adam's grief-worn face. He had become used to watching her light quiet movements, her pretty loving ways to the children, when he went to the Hall Farm; to listen for her voice as for a recurrent music; to think everything she said and did was just right, and could not have been better. In spite of his wisdom, he could not find fault with her for her over-indulgence of the children, who had managed to convert Dinah the preacher, before whom a circle of rough men had often trembled a little, into a con-venient household slave; though Dinah herself was rather ashamed of this weakness, and had some inward conflict as to her departure from the precepts of Solomon. Yes, there was one thing that might have been better; she might have loved Seth, and consented to marry him. He felt a little vexed, for his brother's sake; and he could not help thinking regretfully how Dinah, as Seth's wife, would have made their home as

happy as it could be for them all—how she was the one being that would
have soothed their mother's last days into peacefulness and rest.

"It's wonderful she doesn't love th' lad," Adam had said sometimes
to himself; "for anybody 'ud think he was just cut out for her. But her
heart's so taken up with other things. She's one o' those women that
feel no drawing towards having a husband and children o' their own.
She thinks she should be filled up with her own life then; and she's been
used so to living in other's folks's cares, she can't bear the thought of
her heart being shut up from 'em. I see how it is, well enough. She's cut
out o' different stuff from most women: I saw that long ago. She's never
easy but when she's helping somebody, and marriage 'ud interfere with
her ways,—that's true. I've no right to be contriving and thinking it 'ud
be better if she'd have Seth, as if I was wiser than she is;—or than God
either, for He made her what she is, and that's one o' the greatest
blessings I've ever had from His hands, and others besides me."

This self-reproof had recurred strongly to Adam's mind, when he
gathered from Dinah's face that he had wounded her by referring to
his wish that she had accepted Seth, and so he had endeavoured to put
into the strongest words his confidence in her decision as right—his
resignation even to her going away from them, and ceasing to make part
of their life otherwise than by living in their thoughts, if that separation
were chosen by herself. He felt sure she knew quite well enough how
much he cared to see her continually—to talk to her with the silent
consciousness of a mutual remembrance. It was not possible she should
hear anything but self-renouncing affection and respect in his assurance
that he was contented for her to go away; and yet there remained an
uneasy feeling in his mind that he had not said quite the right thing—
that, somehow, Dinah had not understood him.

Dinah must have risen a little before the sun the next morning, for
she was down-stairs about five o'clock. So was Seth; for, through Lisbeth's obstinate refusal to have any woman-helper in the house, he had
learned to make himself, as Adam said, "very handy in the housework," that he might save his mother from too great weariness; on
which ground I hope you will not think him unmanly, any more than
you can have thought the gallant Colonel Bath unmanly when he made
the gruel for his invalid sister. Adam, who had sat up late at his writing,
was still asleep, and was not likely, Seth said, to be down till breakfast-
time. Often as Dinah had visited Lisbeth during the last eighteen
months, she had never slept in the cottage since that night after Thias's
death, when, you remember, Lisbeth praised her deft movements, and
even gave a modified approval to her porridge. But in that long interval
Dinah had made great advances in household cleverness: and this morning, since Seth was there to help, she was bent on bringing everything to
a pitch of cleanliness and order that would have satisfied her aunt
Poyser. The cottage was far from that standard at present, for Lisbeth's
rheumatism had forced her to give up her old habits of dilettante scour-

ing and polishing. When the kitchen was to her mind, Dinah went into
the new room, where Adam had been writing the night before, to see
what sweeping and dusting were needed there. She opened the window
and let in the fresh morning air, and the smell of the sweet-brier, and
the bright low-slanting rays of the early sun, which made a glory about
her pale face and pale auburn hair as she held the long brush, and swept,
singing to herself in a very low tone—like a sweet summer murmur that
you have to listen for very closely—one of Charles Wesley's hymns:

> "Eternal Beam of Light Divine,
>   Fountain of unexhausted love,
> In whom the Father's glories shine,
>   Through earth beneath and heaven above;
>
> Jesus! the weary wanderer's rest,
>   Give me thy easy yoke to bear;
> With steadfast patience arm my breast,
>   With spotless love and holy fear.
>
> Speak to my warring passions, 'Peace!'
>   Say to my trembling heart, 'Be still!'
> Thy power my strength and fortress is,
>   For all things serve thy sovereign will."

She laid by the brush and took up the duster; and if you had ever
lived in Mrs. Poyser's household, you would know how the duster behaved in Dinah's hand—how it went into every small corner, and on
every ledge in and out of sight—how it went again and again round
every bar of the chairs, and every leg, and under and over everything
that lay on the table, till it came to Adam's papers and rulers, and the
open desk near them. Dinah dusted up to the very edge of these, and
then hesitated, looking at them with a longing but timid eye. It was
painful to see how much dust there was among them. As she was looking
in this way, she heard Seth's step just outside the open door, towards
which her back was turned, and said, raising her clear treble,

"Seth, is your brother wrathful when his papers are stirred?"

"Yes, very, when they are not put back in the right places," said a
deep strong voice, not Seth's.

It was as if Dinah had put her hands unawares on a vibrating chord;
she was shaken with an intense thrill, and for the instant felt nothing
else; then she knew her cheeks were glowing, and dared not look round
but stood still, distressed because she could not say good-morning in a
friendly way. Adam, finding that she did not look round so as to see the
smile on his face, was afraid she had thought him serious about his
wrathfulness, and went up to her, so that she was obliged to look at him

"What! you think I'm a cross fellow at home, Dinah?" he said
smilingly.

"Nay," said Dinah, looking up with timid eyes, "not so. But you
might be put about by finding things meddled with; and even the man
Moses, the meekest of men, was wrathful sometimes."

"Come, then," said Adam, looking at her affectionately, "I'll help you move the things, and put 'em back again, and then they can't get wrong. You're getting to be your aunt's own niece, I see, for particularness."

They began their little task together, but Dinah had not recovered herself sufficiently to think of any remark, and Adam looked at her uneasily. Dinah, he thought, had seemed to disapprove him somehow lately; she had not been so kind and open to him as she used to be. He wanted her to look at him, and be as pleased as he was himself with doing this bit of playful work. But Dinah did not look at him—it was easy for her to avoid looking at the tall man; and when at last there was no more dusting to be done, and no further excuse for him to linger near her, he could bear it no longer, and said, in rather a pleading tone,

"Dinah, you're not displeased with me for anything, are you? I've not said or done anything to make you think ill of me?"

The question surprised her, and relieved her by giving a new course to her feeling. She looked up at him now, quite earnestly, almost with the tears coming, and said,

"Oh, no, Adam! how could you think so?"

"I couldn't bear you not to feel as much a friend to me as I do to you," said Adam. "And you don't know the value I set on the very thought of you, Dinah. That was what I meant yesterday, when I said I'd be content for you to go, if you thought right. I meant, the thought of you was worth so much to me, I should feel I ought to be thankful, and not grumble, if you see right to go away. You know I do mind parting with you, Dinah?"

"Yes, dear friend," said Dinah, trembling, but trying to speak calmly, "I know you have a brother's heart towards me, and we shall often be with one another in spirit; but at this season I am in heaviness through manifold temptation; you must not mark me. I feel called to leave my kindred for a while; but it is a trial: the flesh is weak."

Adam saw that it pained her to be obliged to answer.

"I hurt you by talking about it, Dinah," he said: "I'll say no more. Let's see if Seth's ready with breakfast now."

That is a simple scene, reader. But it is almost certain that you, too, have been in love—perhaps, even, more than once, though you may not choose to say so to all your feminine friends. If so, you will no more think the slight words, the timid looks, the tremulous touches, by which two human souls approach each other gradually, like two little quivering rain-streams, before they mingle into one—you will no more think these things trivial than you will think the first detected signs of coming spring trivial, though they be but a faint, indescribable something in the air and in the song of the birds, and the tiniest perceptible budding in the hedgerow branches. Those slight words and looks and touches are part of the soul's language; and the finest language, I believe, is chiefly made up of unimposing words, such as "light," "sound," "stars," "music,"—words really not worth looking at, or hearing, in themselves, any more than "chips" or "sawdust": it is only that they happen to be the signs of something unspeakably great and beautiful. I am of opinion that love is a great and beautiful thing too; and if you agree with me, the smallest signs of it will not be chips and sawdust to you: they will rather be like those little words, "light" and "music," stirring the long-winding fibres of your memory, and enriching your present with your most precious past.

CHAPTER LI

SUNDAY MORNING

LISBETH's touch of rheumatism could not be made to appear serious enough to detain Dinah another night from the Hall Farm, now she had made up her mind to leave her aunt so soon; and at evening the friends must part. "For a long while," Dinah had said; for she had told Lisbeth of her resolve.

"Then it'll be for all my life, an' I shall ne'er see thee again," said Lisbeth. "Long while! I'n got no long while t' live. An' I shall be took bad an' die, an' thee canst ne'er come a-nigh me, an' I shall die a-longing for thee."

That had been the key-note of her wailing talk all day; for Adam was not in the house, and so she put no restraint on her complaining. She had tried poor Dinah by returning again and again to the question, why she must go away; and refusing to accept reasons, which seemed to her nothing but whim and "contrairiness"; and still more, by regretting that she "couldna ha' one o' the lads," and be her daughter.

"Thee couldstna put up wi' Seth," she said: "he isna cliver enough for thee, happen; but he'd ha' been very good t' thee— he's as handy as can be at doin' things for me when I'm bad; an' he's as fond o' the Bible an' chappellin' as thee art thysen. But happen, thee'dst like a husband better as isna just the cut o' thysen: the runnin' brook isna athirst for th' rain. Adam 'ud ha' done for thee—I know he would; an' he might come t' like thee well enough, if thee'dst stop. But he's as stubborn as th' iron bar—there's no bending him no way but's own. But he'd be a fine husband for anybody, be they who they will, so looked-on an so cliver as he is. And he'd be rare an' lovin': it does me good on'y a look o' the lad's eye, when he means kind tow'rt me."

Dinah tried to escape from Lisbeth's closest looks and questions by finding little tasks of housework, that kept her moving about; and as soon as Seth came home in the evening she put on her bonnet to go. It touched Dinah keenly to say the last good-by, and still more to look round on her way across the fields, and see the old woman still standing at the door, gazing after her till she must have been the faintest speck in the dim aged eyes. "The God of love and peace be with them," Dinah prayed, as she looked back from the last stile. "Make them glad ac cording to the days wherein thou hast afflicted them, and the years wherein they have seen evil. It is thy will that I should part from them; let me have no will but thine."

Lisbeth turned into the house at last, and sat down in the work-shop near Seth, who was busying himself there with fitting some bits of turned wood he had brought from the village, into a small work-box which he meant to give to Dinah before she went away.

"Thee't see her again o' Sunday afore she goes," were her first words. "If thee wast good for anything, thee'dst make her come in again o' Sunday night wi' thee, an' see me once more."

"Nay, mother," said Seth, "Dinah 'ud be sure to come again if she saw right to come. I should have no need to persuade her. She only thinks it 'ud be troubling thee for nought, just to come in to say good-by over again."

"She'd ne'er go away, I know, if Adam 'ud be fond on her an' marry her; but everything's so contrairy," said Lisbeth, with a burst of vexation.

Seth paused a moment, and looked up, with a slight blush, at his mother's face. "What! has she said anything o' that sort to thee, mother?" he said, in a lower tone.

"Said? nay, she'll say nothin'. It's on'y the men as have to wait till folks say things afore they find 'em out."

"Well, but what makes thee think so, mother? What's put it into thy head?"

"It's no matter what's put it into my head: my head's none so hollow as it must get in, an' nought to put it there. I know she's fond on him, as I know th' wind's comin' in at the door, an' that's anoof. An' he might be willin' to marry her if he know'd she's fond on him, but he'll ne'er think on't if somebody doesna put it into's head."

His mother's suggestion about Dinah's feeling towards Adam was not quite a new thought to Seth, but her last words alarmed him, lest she should herself undertake to open Adam's eyes. He was not sure about Dinah's feeling, and he thought he *was* sure about Adam's.

"Nay, mother, nay," he said, earnestly, "thee mustna think o' speaking o' such things to Adam. Thee'st no right to say what Dinah's feelings are if she hasna told thee; and it 'ud do nothing but mischief to say such things to Adam: he feels very grateful and affectionate toward Dinah, but he's no thoughts towards her that 'ud incline him to make her his wife; and I don't believe Dinah 'ud marry him either. I don't think she'll marry at all."

"Eh," said Lisbeth, impatiently. "Thee think'st so 'cause she wouldna ha' thee. She'll ne'er marry thee; thee mightst as well like her t' ha' thy brother."

Seth was hurt. "Mother," he said, in a remonstrating tone, "don't think that of me. I should be as thankful t' have her for a sister as thee wouldst t' have her for a daughter. I've no more thoughts about myself in that thing, and I shall take it hard if ever thee say'st it again."

"Well, well, then thee shouldstna cross me wi' sayin' things arena as I say they are."

"But, mother," said Seth, "thee'dst be doing Dinah a wrong by telling Adam what thee think'st about her. It 'ud do nothing but mischief; for it 'ud make Adam uneasy if he doesna feel the same to her. And I'm pretty sure he feels nothing o' the sort."

"Eh, donna tell me what thee't sure on; thee know'st nought about it. What's he allays goin' to the Poysers' for, if he didna want t' see her? He goes twice where he used t' go once. Happen he knowsna as he wants t' see her; he knowsna as I put salt in's broth, but he'd miss it pretty quick if it warna there. He'll ne'er think o' marrying if it isna put into's head; an' if thee'dst any love for thy mother, thee'dst put him up to't, an' not let her go away out o' my sight, when I might ha' her to make a bit o' comfort for me afore I go to bed to my old man under the white thorn."

"Nay, mother," said Seth, "thee mustna think me unkind; but I should be going against my conscience if I took upon me to say what Dinah's feelings are. And besides that, I think I should give offence to Adam by speaking to him at all about marrying; and I counsel thee not to do't. Thee may'st be quite deceived about Dinah; nay, I'm pretty sure, by words she said to me last Sabbath, as she's no mind to marry."

"Eh, thee't as contrairy as the rest on 'em. If it war summat I didna want, it 'ud be done fast enough."

Lisbeth rose from the bench at this, and went out of the workshop, leaving Seth in much anxiety lest she should disturb Adam's mind about Dinah. He consoled himself after a time with reflecting that, since Adam's trouble, Lisbeth had been very timid about speaking to him on matters of feeling, and that she would hardly dare to approach this tenderest of all subjects. Even if she did, he hoped Adam would not take much notice of what she said.

Seth was right in believing that Lisbeth would be held in restraint by timidity; and during the next three days, the intervals in which she had an opportunity of speaking to Adam were too rare and short to cause her any strong temptation. But in her long solitary hours she brooded over her regretful thoughts about Dinah, till they had grown very near that point of unmanageable strength when thoughts are apt to take wing out of their secret nest in a startling manner. And on Sunday morning, when Seth went away to chapel at Treddleston, the dangerous opportunity came.

Sunday morning was the happiest time in all the week to Lisbeth; for as there was no service at Hayslope church till the afternoon, Adam was always at home, doing nothing but reading, an occupation in which she could venture to interrupt him. Moreover, she had always a better dinner than usual to prepare for her sons—very frequently for Adam and herself alone, Seth being often away the entire day; and the smell of the roast-meat before the clear fire in the clean kitchen, the clock ticking in a peaceful Sunday manner, her darling Adam seated near her in his best clothes, doing nothing very important, so that she could go and stroke her hand across his hair if she liked, and see him look up at her and smile, while Gyp, rather jealous, poked his muzzle up between them,—all these things made poor Lisbeth's earthly paradise.

The book Adam most often read on a Sunday morning was his large pictured Bible, and this morning it lay open before him on the round white deal table in the kitchen; for he sat there in spite of the fire, because he knew his mother liked to have him with her, and it was the only day in the week when he could indulge her in that way. You would have liked to see Adam reading his Bible: he never opened it on a week-day, and so he came to it as a holiday book, serving him for history, biography, and poetry. He held one hand thrust between his waistcoat buttons, and the other ready to turn the pages; and in the course of the morning you would have seen many changes in his face. Sometimes his lips moved in semi-articulation—it was when he came to a speech that he could fancy himself uttering, such as Samuel's dying speech to the people; then his eyebrows would be raised, and the corners of his mouth would quiver a little with sad sympathy—something, perhaps old Isaac's meeting with his son, touched him closely; at other times, over the New Testament, a very solemn look would come upon his face, and he would every now and then shake his head in serious assent, or just lift up his hand and let it fall again; and on some mornings, when he read in the Apocrypha, of which he was very fond, the son of Sirach's keen-edged words would bring a delighted smile, though he also enjoyed the freedom of occasionally differing from an Apocryphal writer. For Adam knew the Articles quite well, as became a good churchman.

Lisbeth, in the pauses of attending to her dinner, always sat opposite to him and watched him, till she could rest no longer without going up to him and giving him a caress, to call his attention to her. This morning he was reading the Gospel according to St. Matthew, and Lisbeth had been standing close by him for some minutes, stroking his hair, which was smoother than usual this morning, and looking down at the large page with silent wonderment at the mystery of letters. She was encouraged to continue this caress, because when she first went up to him, he had thrown himself back in his chair to look at her affectionately and say, "Why, mother, thee look'st rare and hearty this morning. Eh, Gyp wants me t' look at him: he can't abide to think I love thee the best." Lisbeth said nothing, because she wanted to say so many things. And now there was a new leaf to be turned over, and it was a picture—that of the angel seated on the great stone that has been rolled away from the sepulchre. This picture had one strong association in Lisbeth's memory, for she had been reminded of it when she first saw Dinah; and Adam had no sooner turned the page, and lifted the book sideways that they might look at the angel, than she said, "that's her—that's Dinah."

Adam smiled, and. looking more intently at the angel's face, said,
    "It *is* a bit like her; but Dinah's prettier, I think."
    "Well, then, if thee think'st her so pretty, why arn't fond on her?"

Adam looked up in surprise. "Why, mother, dost think I don't set store by Dinah?"

"Nay," said Lisbeth, frightened at her own courage, yet feeling that she had broken the ice, and the waters must flow, whatever mischief they might do. "What's th' use o' settin' store by things as are thirty mile off? If thee wast fond enough on her thee wouldstna let her go away."

"But I've no right t' hinder her, if she thinks well," said Adam, looking at his book as if he wanted to go on reading. He foresaw a series of complaints tending to nothing. Lisbeth sat down again in the chair opposite to him, as she said,

"But she wouldna think well if thee wastna so contrairy." Lisbeth dared not venture beyond a vague phrase yet.

"Contrairy, mother?" Adam said, looking up again in some anxiety. "What have I done? What dost mean?"

"Why, thee't never look at nothin', nor think o' nothin', but thy figurin' an' thy work," said Lisbeth, half crying. "An' dost think thee canst go on all thy life, as if thee wast a man cut out o' timber? An' what wut do when thy mother's gone, an' nobody to take care on thee as thee gett'st a bit o' victual comfortable i' the mornin'?"

"What hast got i' thy mind, mother?" said Adam, vexed at this whimpering. "I canna see what thee't driving at. Is there anything I could do for thee as I don't do?"

"Ay, an' that there is. Thee might'st do as I should ha' somebody wi' me to comfort me a bit, an' wait on me when I'm bad, an' be good to me."

"Well, mother, whose fault is it there isna some tidy body i' th' house t' help thee? It isna by my wish as thee hast a stroke o' work to do. We can afford it—I've told thee often enough. It 'ud be a deal better for us."

"Eh, what's the use o' talkin' o' tidy bodies, when thee mean'st one o' th' wenches out o' th' village, or somebody from Treddles'on as I ne'er set eyes on i' my life? I'd sooner make a shift an' get into my own coffin afore I die, nor ha' them folks to put me in."

Adam was silent, and tried to go on reading. That was the utmost severity he could show towards his mother on a Sunday morning. But Lisbeth had gone too far now to check herself, and after scarcely a minute's quietness she began again.

"Thee mightst know well enough who 'tis I'd like t' ha' wi' me. It isna many folks I send for t' come an' see me, I reckon. An' thee'st had the fetchin' on her times enow."

"Thee mean'st Dinah, mother, I know," said Adam. "But it's no use setting thy mind on what can't be. If Dinah 'ud be willing to stay at Hayslope, it isn't likely she can come away from her aunt's house, where they hold her like a daughter, and where she's more bound than she is to us. If it had been so that she could ha' married Seth, that 'ud ha' been a great blessing to us, but we can't have things just as we like in this life. Thee must try and make up thy mind to do without her."

"Nay, but I canna ma' up my mind, when she's just cut out for thee;

an' nought shall ma' me believe as God didna make her an' send her there o' purpose for thee. What's it sinnify about her being a Methody? It 'ud happen wear out on her wi' marryin'."

Adam threw himself back in his chair and looked at his mother. He understood now what she had been aiming at from the beginning of the conversation. It was as unreasonable, impracticable a wish as she had ever urged, but he could not help being moved by so entirely new an idea. The chief point, however, was to chase away the notion from his mother's mind as quickly as possible.

"Mother," he said, gravely, "thee't talking wild. Don't let me hear thee say such things again. It's no good talking o' what can never be. Dinah's not for marrying; she's fixed her heart on a different sort o' life."

"Very like," said Lisbeth, impatiently, "very like she's none for marr'ing, when them as she'd be willin' t' marry wonna ax her. I shouldna ha' been for marr'ing thy feyther if he'd ne'er axed me; an' she's as fond o' thee as e'er I war o' Thias, poor fellow."

The blood rushed to Adam's face, and for a few moments he was not quite conscious where he was: his mother and the kitchen had vanished for him, and he saw nothing but Dinah's face turned up towards his. It seemed as if there were a resurrection of his dead joy. But he woke up very speedily from that dream (the waking was chill and sad); for it would have been very foolish in him to believe his mother's words; she could have no ground for them. He was prompted to express his disbelief very strongly—perhaps that he might call forth the proofs, if there were any to be offered.

"What dost say such things for, mother, when thee'st got no foundation for 'em? Thee know'st nothing as gives thee a right to say that."

"Then I knowna nought as gi'es me a right to say as the year's turned, for all I feel it fust thing when I get up i' th' mornin'. She isna fond o' Seth, I reckon, is she? She doesna want to marry *him?* But I can see as she doesna behave tow'rt thee as she does tow'rt Seth. She makes no more o' Seth's coming a-nigh her nor if he war Gyp, but she's all of a tremble when thee't a-sittin' down by her breakfast, and a-looking at her. Thee think'st thy mother knows nought, but she war alive afore thee wast born."

"But thee canstna be sure as the trembling means love?" said Adam, anxiously.

"Eh, what else should it mane? It isna hate, I reckon. An' what should she do but love thee? Thee't made to be loved—for where's there a straighter, cliverer man? An' what's it sinnify her bein' a Methody? It's on'y the marigold i' th' parridge."

Adam had thrust his hands in his pockets, and was looking down at the book on the table, without seeing any of the letters. He was trembling like a gold-seeker, who sees the strong promise of gold, but sees in the same moment a sickening vision of disappointment. He could not trust his mother's insight; she had seen what she wished to see. And yet—

and yet, now the suggestion had been made to him, he remembered so
many things, very slight things, like the stirring of the water by an
imperceptible breeze, which seemed to him some confirmation of his
mother's words.

Lisbeth noticed that he was moved. She went on:

"An' thee't find out as thee't poorly aff when she's gone. Thee't
fonder on her nor thee know'st. Thy eyes follow her about, welly as
Gyp's follow thee."

Adam could sit still no longer. He rose, took down his hat, and went
out into the fields.

The sunshine was on them: that early autumn sunshine which we
should know was not summer's, even if there were not the touches of
yellow on the lime and chestnut: the Sunday sunshine, too, which has
more than autumnal calmness for the working man: the morning sunshine, which still leaves the dew-crystals on the fine gossamer webs in
the shadow of the bushy hedgerows.

Adam needed the calm influence; he was amazed at the way in which
this new thought of Dinah's love had taken possession of him, with an
overmastering power that made all other feelings give way before the
impetuous desire to know that the thought was true. Strange, that till
that moment the possibiliy of their ever being lovers had never crossed
his mind, and yet now, all his longing suddenly went out towards that
possibility; he had no more doubt or hesitation as to his own wishes
than the bird that flies towards the opening through which the daylight
gleams and the breath of heaven enters.

The autumnal Sunday sunshine soothed him; but not by preparing
him with resignation to the disappointment if his mother—if he himself, proved to be mistaken about Dinah: it soothed him by gentle encouragement of his hopes. Her love was so like that calm sunshine that
they seemed to make one presence to him, and he believed in them both
alike. And Dinah was so bound up with the sad memories of his first
passion, that he was not forsaking them, but rather giving them a new
sacredness by loving her. Nay, his love for her had grown out of that
past: it was the noon of that morning.

But Seth? Would the lad be hurt? Hardly; for he had seemed quite
contented of late, and there was no selfish jealousy in him; he had
never been jealous of his mother's fondness for Adam. But had *he* seen
anything of what their mother talked about? Adam longed to know
this, for he thought he could trust Seth's observation better than his
mother's. He must talk to Seth before he went to see Dinah; and, with
this intention in his mind, he walked back to the cottage and said to
his mother,

"Did Seth say anything to thee about when he was coming home?
Will he be back to dinner?"

"Ay, lad; he'll be back for a wonder. He isna gone to Treddles'on.
He's gone somewhere else a-preachin' and a-prayin'."

"Hast any notion which way he's gone?" said Adam.

"Nay, but he aften goes to th' Common. Thee know'st more o's goings nor I do."

Adam wanted to go and meet Seth, but he must content himself with walking about the near fields and getting sight of him as soon as possible. That would not be for more than an hour to come, for Seth would scarcely be at home much before their dinner-time, which was twelve o'clock. But Adam could not sit down to his reading again, and he sauntered along by the brook and stood leaning against the stiles, with eager, intense eyes, which looked as if they saw something very vividly; but it was not the brook or the willows, not the fields or the sky. Again and again his vision was interrupted by wonder at the strength of his own feeling, at the strength and sweetness of this new love—almost like the wonder a man feels at the added power he finds in himself for an art which he had laid aside for a space. How is it that the poets have said so many fine things about our first love, so few about our later love? Are their first poems their best? or are not those the best which come from their fuller thought, their larger experience, their deeper-rooted affections? The boy's flute-like voice has its own spring charm; but the man's should yield a richer, deeper music.

At last, there was Seth, visible at the farthest stile, and Adam hastened to meet him. Seth was surprised, and thought something unusual must have happened: but when Adam came up, his face said plain enough that it was nothing alarming.

"Where hast been?" said Adam, when they were side by side.

"I've been to the Common," said Seth. "Dinah's been speaking the Word to a little company of hearers at Brimstone's, as they call him. They're folks as never go to church hardly—them on the Common—but they'll go and hear Dinah a bit. She's been speaking with power this forenoon from the words, 'I came not to call the righteous, but sinners to repentance.' And there was a little thing happened as was pretty to see. The women mostly bring their children with 'em, but to-day there was one stout curly-headed fellow about three or four year old, that I never saw there before. He was as naughty as could be at the beginning while I was praying, and while we was singing, but when we all sat down and Dinah began to speak, th' young un stood stock-still all at once, and began to look at her with's mouth open, and presently he ran away from's mother and went up to Dinah, and pulled at her, like a little dog, for her to take notice of him. So Dinah lifted him up and held th' lad on her lap, while she went on speaking; and he was as good as could be till he went t' sleep—and the mother cried to see him."

"It's a pity she shouldna be a mother herself," said Adam, "so fond as the children are of her. Dost think she's quite fixed against marrying, Seth? Dost think nothing 'ud turn her?"

There was something peculiar in his brother's tone, which made Seth steal a glance at his face before he answered.

"It 'ud be wrong of me to say nothing 'ud turn her," he answered. "But if thee mean'st it about myself, I've given up all thoughts as she can ever be *my* wife. She calls me her brother, and that's enough."

"But dost think she might ever get fond enough of anybody else to be willing to marry 'em?" said Adam, rather shyly.

"Well," said Seth, after some hesitation, "it's crossed my mind sometimes o' late as she might; but Dinah 'ud let no fondness for the creature draw her out o' the path as she believed God had marked out for her. If she thought the leading was not from Him, she's not one to be brought under the power of it. And she's allays seemed clear about that—as her work was to minister t' others, and make no home for herself i' this world."

"But suppose," said Adam, earnestly, "suppose there was a man as 'ud let her do just the same and not interfere with her,—she might do a good deal o' what she does now, just as well when she was married as when she was single. Other women of her sort have married—that's to say, not just like her, but women as preached and attended on the sick and needy. There's Mrs. Fletcher as she talks of."

A new light had broken in on Seth. He turned round, and laying his hand on Adam's shoulder, said, "Why, wouldst like her to marry *thee*, brother?"

Adam looked doubtfully at Seth's inquiring eyes, and said, "Wouldst be hurt if she was to be fonder o' me than o' thee?"

"Nay," said Seth, warmly, "how canst think it? Have I felt thy trouble so little, that I shouldna feel thy joy?"

There was silence a few moments as they walked on, and then Seth said,

"I'd no notion as thee'dst ever think of her for a wife."

"But is it o' any use to think of her?" said Adam—"what dost say? Mother's made me as I hardly know where I am, with what she's been saying to me this forenoon. She says she's sure Dinah feels for me more than common, and 'ud be willing t' have me. But I'm afraid she speaks without book. I want to know if thee'st seen anything."

"It's a nice point to speak about," said Seth, "and I'm afraid o' being wrong; besides, we've no right t' intermeddle with people's feelings when they wouldn't tell 'em themselves."

Seth paused.

"But thee mightst ask her," he said, presently. "She took no offence at *me* for asking, and thee'st more right than I had, only thee't not in the Society. But Dinah doesn't hold wi' them as are for keeping the Society so strict to themselves. She doesn't mind about making folks enter the Society, so as they're fit t' enter the kingdom o' God. Some o' the brethren at Treddles'on are displeased with her for that."

"Where will she be the rest o' the day?" said Adam.

"She said she shouldn't leave the Farm again to-day," said Seth, "because it's her last Sabbath there, and she's going t' read out o' the big Bible wi' the children."

Adam thought—but did not say—"Then I'll go this afternoon; for if I go to church my thoughts 'ull be with her all the while. They must sing th' anthem without me to-day."

CHAPTER LII

ADAM AND DINAH

IT was about three o'clock when Adam entered the farmyard and roused Alick and the dogs from their Sunday dozing. Alick said everybody was gone to church "but th' young missis"—so he called Dinah; but this did not disappoint Adam, although "everybody" was so liberal as to include Nancy the dairymaid, whose works of necessity were not unfrequently incompatible with church-going.

There was perfect stillness about the house: the doors were all closed, and the very stones and tubs seemed quieter than usual. Adam heard the water gently dripping from the pump—that was the only sound; and he knocked at the house door rather softly, as was suitable in that stillness.

The door opened, and Dinah stood before him, colouring deeply with the great surprise of seeing Adam at this hour, when she knew it was his regular practice to be at church. Yesterday he would have said to her without any difficulty, "I came to see you, Dinah: I knew the rest were not at home." But to-day something prevented him from saying that, and he put out his hand to her in silence. Neither of them spoke, and yet both wished they could speak, as Adam entered, and they sat down. Dinah took the chair she had just left; it was at the corner of the table near the window, and there was a book lying on the table, but it was not open: she had been sitting perfectly still, looking at the small bit of clear fire in the bright grate. Adam sat down opposite her, in Mr. Poyser's three-cornered chair.

"Your mother is not ill again, I hope, Adam?" Dinah said, recovering herself. "Seth said she was well this morning."

"No, she's very hearty to-day," said Adam, happy in the signs of Dinah's feelings at the sight of him, but shy.

"There's nobody at home, you see," Dinah said; "but you'll wait. You've been hindered from going to church to-day, doubtless."

"Yes," Adam said, and then paused, before he added, "I was thinking about you: that was the reason."

This confession was very awkward and sudden, Adam felt; for he thought Dinah must understand all he meant. But the frankness of the words caused her immediately to interpret them into a renewal of his brotherly regrets that she was going away, and she answered calmly,

"Do not be careful and troubled for me, Adam. I have all things and abound at Snowfield. And my mind is at rest, for I am not seeking my own will in going."

"But if things were different, Dinah," said Adam, hesitatingly—"if
you knew things that perhaps you don't know now" . . .

Dinah looked at him inquiringly, but instead of going on, he reached
a chair and brought it near the corner of the table where she was sitting.
She wondered, and was afraid—and the next moment her thoughts flew
to the past: was it something about those distant unhappy ones that she
didn't know?

Adam looked at her: it was so sweet to look at her eyes, which had
now a self-forgetful questioning in them,—for a moment he forgot that
he wanted to say anything or that it was necessary to tell her what he
meant.

"Dinah," he said suddenly, taking both her hands between his, "I
love you with my whole heart and soul. I love you next to God who
made me."

Dinah's lips became pale, like her cheeks, and she trembled violently
under the shock of painful joy. Her hands were cold as death between
Adam's. She could not draw them away, because he held them fast.

"Don't tell me you can't love me, Dinah. Don't tell me we must part,
and pass our lives away from one another."

The tears were trembling in Dinah's eyes, and they fell before she
could answer. But she spoke in a quiet low voice.

"Yes, dear Adam, we must submit to another Will. We must part."

"Not if you love me, Dinah—not if you love me," Adam said, passionately. "Tell me—tell me if you can love me better than a brother?"

Dinah was too entirely reliant on the Supreme guidance to attempt to
achieve any end by a deceptive concealment. She was recovering now
from the first shock of emotion, and she looked at Adam with simple
sincere eyes as she said,

"Yes, Adam, my heart is drawn strongly towards you; and of my
own will, if I had no clear showing to the contrary, I could find my happiness in being near you, and ministering to you continually. I fear I
should forget to rejoice and weep with others; nay, I fear I should forget
the Divine presence, and seek no love but yours."

Adam did not speak immediately. They sat looking at each other in
delicious silence,—for the first sense of mutual love excludes other
feelings; it will have the soul all to itself.

"Then, Dinah," Adam said at last, "how can there be anything contrary to what's right in our belonging to one another, and spending our
lives together? Who put this great love into our hearts? Can anything
be holier than that? For we can help one another in everything as is
good. I'd never think o' putting myself between you and God, and
saying you oughtn't to do this, and you oughtn't to do that. You'd follow
your conscience as much as you do now."

"Yes, Adam," Dinah said, "I know marriage is a holy state for those
who are truly called to it, and have no other drawing; but from my
childhood upward I have been led towards another path; all my peace
and my joy have come from having no life of my own, no wants, no

wishes for myself, and living only in God and those of his creatures whose sorrows and joys he has given me to know. Those have been very blessed years to me, and I feel that if I was to listen to any voice that would draw me aside from that path, I should be turning my back on the light that has shone upon me, and darkness and doubt would take hold of me. We could not bless each other, Adam, if there were doubts in my soul, and if I yearned, when it was too late, after that better part which had once been given me and I had put away from me."

"But if a new feeling has come into your mind, Dinah, and if you love me so as to be willing to be nearer to me than to other people, isn't that a sign that it's right for you to change your life? Doesn't the love make it right when nothing else would?"

"Adam, my mind is full of questionings about that; for now, since you tell me of your strong love towards me, what was clear to me has become dark again. I felt before that my heart was too strongly drawn towards you, and that your heart was not as mine; and the thought of you had taken hold of me, so that my soul had lost its freedom, and was becoming enslaved to an earthly affection, which made me anxious and careful about what should befall myself. For in all other affection I had been content with any small return, or with none; but my heart was beginning to hunger after an equal love from you. And I had no doubt that I must wrestle against that as a great temptation; and the command was clear that I must go away."

"But now, dear, dear Dinah, now you know I love you better than you love me . . . it's all different now. You won't think o' going: you'll stay, and be my dear wife, and I shall thank God for giving me my life as I never thanked him before."

"Adam, it's hard to me to turn a deaf ear . . . you know it's hard; but a great fear is upon me. It seems to me as if you were stretching out your arms to me, and beckoning me to come and take my ease, and live for my own delight, and Jesus, the Man of Sorrows, was standing looking towards me, and pointing to the sinful, and suffering, and afflicted. I have seen that again and again when I have been sitting in stillness and darkness, and a great terror has come upon me lest I should become hard, and a lover of self, and no more bear willingly the Redeemer's cross."

Dinah had closed her eyes, and a faint shudder went through her. "Adam," she went on, "you wouldn't desire that we should seek a good through any unfaithfulness to the light that is in us; you wouldn't believe that could be a good. We are of one mind in that."

"Yes, Dinah," said Adam, sadly, "I'll never be the man t' urge you against your conscience. But I can't give up the hope that you may come to see different. I don't believe your loving me could shut up your heart; it's only adding to what you've been before, not taking away from it; for it seems to me it's the same with love and happiness as with sorrow— the more we know of it the better we can feel what other people's lives are or might be, and so we shall only be more tender to 'em, and wishful to help 'em. The more knowledge a man has, the better he'll do's work; and feeling's a sort o' knowledge."

Dinah was silent; her eyes were fixed in contemplation of something visible only to herself. Adam went on presently with his pleading:

"And you can do almost as much as you do now. I won't ask you to go to church with me of a Sunday; you shall go where you like among the people, and teach 'em; for though I like church best, I don't put my soul above yours, as if my words was better for you to follow than your own conscience. And you can help the sick just as much, and you'll have more means o' making 'em a bit comfortable; and you'll be among all your own friends as love you, and can help 'em and be a blessing to 'em till their dying day. Surely, Dinah, you'd be as near to God as if you was living lonely and away from me."

Dinah made no answer for some time. Adam was still holding her hands, and looking at her with almost trembling anxiety, when she turned her grave loving eyes on his, and said, in rather a sad voice,

"Adam, there is truth in what you say, and there's many of the brethren and sisters who have greater strength than I have, and find their hearts enlarged by the cares of husband and kindred. But I have not faith that it would be so with me, for since my affections have been set above measure on you, I have had less peace and joy in God; I have felt as it were a division in my heart. And think how it is with me, Adam:—that life I have led is like a land I have trodden in blessedness since my childhood; and if I long for a moment to follow the voice which calls me to another land that I know not, I cannot but fear that my soul might hereafter yearn for that early blessedness which I had forsaken; and where doubt enters, there is not perfect love. I must wait for clearer guidance: I must go from you, and we must submit ourselves entirely to the Divine Will. We are sometimes required to lay our natural, lawful affections on the altar."

Adam dared not plead again, for Dinah's was not the voice of caprice or insincerity. But it was very hard for him; his eyes got dim as he looked at her.

"But you may come to feel satisfied . . . to feel that you may come to me again, and we may never part, Dinah?"

"We must submit ourselves, Adam. With time, our duty will be made clear. It may be, when I have entered on my former life, I shall find all these new thoughts and wishes vanish, and become as things that were not. Then I shall know that my calling is not towards marriage. But we must wait."

"Dinah," said Adam, mournfully, "you can't love me so well as I love you, else you'd have no doubts. But it's natural you shouldn't; for I'm not so good as you. I can't doubt it's right for me to love the best thing God's ever given me to know."

"Nay, Adam; it seems to me that my love for you is not weak; for my heart waits on your words and looks, almost as a little child waits on the help and tenderness of the strong on whom it depends. If the thought of you took slight hold of me, I should not fear that it would be an idol in the temple. But you will strengthen me—you will not hinder me in seeking to obey to the uttermost."

"Let us go out into the sunshine, Dinah, and walk together. I'll speak no word to disturb you."

They went out and walked towards the fields, where they would meet the family coming from church. Adam said, "Take my arm, Dinah," and she took it. That was the only change in their manner to each other since they were last walking together. But no sadness in the prospect of her going away—in the uncertainty of the issue—could rob the sweetness from Adam's sense that Dinah loved him. He thought he would stay at the Hall Farm all that evening. He would be near her as long as he could.

"Heyday! there's Adam along wi' Dinah," said Mr. Poyser, as he opened the far gate into the Home Close. "I couldna think how he happened away from church. Why," added good Martin, after a moment's pause, "what dost think has just jumped into my head?"

"Summat as hadna far to jump, for it's just under our nose. You mean as Adam's fond o' Dinah."

"Ay! hast ever had any notion of it before?"

"To be sure I have," said Mrs. Poyser, who always declined, if possible, to be taken by surprise. "I'm not one o' those as can see the cat i' the dairy, an' wonder what she's come after."

"Thee never saidst a word to me about it."

"Well, I aren't like a bird-clapper, forced to make a rattle when the wind blows on me. I can keep my own counsel when there's no good i' speaking."

"But Dinah 'll ha' none o' him; dost think she will?"

"Nay," said Mrs. Poyser, not sufficiently on her guard against a possible surprise; "she'll never marry anybody, if he isn't a Methodist and a cripple."

"It 'ud ha' been a pretty thing for 'em t' marry," said Martin, turning his head on one side, as if in pleased contemplation of his new idea. "Thee'dst ha' liked it too, wouldstna?"

"Ah! I should. I should ha' been sure of her then, as she wouldn't go away from me to Snowfield, welly thirty mile off, and me not got a creatur to look to, only neighbours, as are no kin to me, an' most of 'em women as I'd be ashamed to show my face, if *my* dairy things war like their'n. There may well be streaky butter i' the market. An' I should be glad to see the poor thing settled like a Christian woman, with a house of her own over her head; and we'd stock her well wi' linen and feathers; for I love her next to my own children. An' she makes one feel safer when she's i' the house; for she's like the driven snow: anybody might sin for two as had her at their elbow."

"Dinah," said Tommy, running forward to meet her, "mother says you'll never marry anybody but a Methodist cripple. What a silly you must be!" a comment which Tommy followed up by seizing Dinah with both arms, and dancing along by her side with incommodious fondness.

"Why, Adam, we missed you i' the singing to-day," said Mr. Poyser. "How was it?"

"I wanted to see Dinah: she's going away so soon," said Adam.

"Ah, lad! can you persuade her to stop somehow? Find her a good husband somewhere i' the parish. If you'll do that, we'll forgive you for missing church. But, anyway, she isna going before the harvest-supper o' Wednesday, and you must come then. There's Bartle Massey comin', an' happen Craig. You'll be sure an' come, now, at seven? The missis wunna have it a bit later."

"Ay," said Adam, "I'll come if I can. But I can't often say what I'll do beforehand, for the work often holds me longer than I expect. You'll stay till the end o' the week, Dinah?"

"Yes, yes!" said Mr. Poyser; "we'll have no nay."

"She's no call to be in a hurry," observed Mrs. Poyser. "Scarceness o' victual 'ull keep: there's no need to be hasty wi' the cooking. An' scarceness is what there's the biggest stock of i' that country."

Dinah smiled, but gave no promise to stay, and they talked of other things through the rest of the walk, lingering in the sunshine to look at the great flock of geese grazing, at the new corn-ricks, and at the surprising abundance of fruit on the old pear-tree; Nancy and Molly having already hastened home, side by side, each holding, carefully wrapped in her pocket-handkerchief, a prayer-book, in which she could read little beyond the large letters and the Amens.

Surely all other leisure is hurry compared with a sunny walk through the fields from "afternoon church,"—as such walks used to be in those old leisurely times, when the boat, gliding sleepily along the canal, was the newest locomotive wonder; when Sunday books had most of them old brown-leather covers, and opened with remarkable precision always in one place. Leisure is gone—gone where the spinning-wheels are gone, and the pack-horses, and the slow waggons, and the pedlars, who brought bargains to the door on sunny afternoons. Ingenious philosophers tell you, perhaps, that the great work of the steam-engine is to create leisure for mankind. Do not believe them: it only creates a vacuum for eager thought to rush in. Even idleness is eager now—eager for amusement: prone to excursion-trains, art-museums, periodical literature, and exciting novels: prone even to scientific theorising, and cursory peeps through microscopes. Old Leisure was quite a different personage: he only read one newspaper, innocent of leaders, and was free from that periodicity of sensations which we call post-time. He was a contemplative, rather stout gentleman, of excellent digestion,—of quiet perceptions, undiseased by hypothesis: happy in his inability to know the causes of things, preferring the things themselves. He lived chiefly in the country, among pleasant seats and homesteads, and was fond of sauntering by the fruit-tree wall, and scenting the apricots when they were warmed by the morning sunshine, or of sheltering himself under the orchard boughs at noon, when the summer pears were falling. He knew nothing of week-day services, and thought none the worse of the Sunday sermon if it allowed him to sleep from the text to the blessing—liking the afternoon service best, because the prayers were the shortest, and not ashamed to say so; for he had an easy, jolly conscience, broad-backed like himself, and able to carry a great deal of beer or port-wine,—not being made squeamish by doubts and qualms and lofty aspirations. Life was not a task to him, but a sinecure: he fingered the guineas in his pocket, and ate his dinners, and slept the sleep of the irresponsible; for had he not kept up his charter by going to church on the Sunday afternoons?

Fine old Leisure! Do not be severe upon him, and judge him by our modern standard: he never went to Exeter Hall, or heard a popular preacher, or read *Tracts for the Times* or *Sartor Resartus*.

CHAPTER LIII

THE HARVEST SUPPER

As Adam was going homewards, on Wednesday evening, in the six o'clock sunlight, he saw in the distance the last load of barley winding its way towards the yard-gate of the Hall Farm, and heard the chant of "Harvest Home!" rising and sinking like a wave. Fainter and fainter, and more musical through the growing distance, the falling dying sound still reached him, as he neared the Willow Brook. The low westering sun shone right on the shoulders of the old Binton Hills, turning the unconscious sheep into bright spots of light; shone on the windows of the cottage too, and made them a-flame with a glory beyond that of amber or amethyst. It was enough to make Adam feel that he was in a great temple, and that the distant chant was a sacred song.

"It's wonderful," he thought, "how that sound goes to one's heart almost like a funeral-bell, for all it tells one o' the joyfullest time o' the year, and the time when men are mostly the thankfullest. I suppose it's a bit hard to us to think anything's over and gone in our lives; and there's a parting at the root of all our joys. It's like what I feel about Dinah: I should never ha' come to know that her love 'ud be the greatest o' blessings to me, if what I counted a blessing hadn't been wrenched and torn away from me, and left me with a greater need, so as I could crave and hunger for a greater and a better comfort."

He expected to see Dinah again this evening, and get leave to accompany her as far as Oakbourne; and then he would ask her to fix some time when he might go to Snowfield, and learn whether the last best hope that had been born to him must be resigned like the rest. The work he had to do at home, besides putting on his best clothes, made it seven before he was on his way again to the Hall Farm, and it was questionable whether, with his longest and quickest strides, he should be there in time even for the roast-beef, which came after the plum-pudding; for Mrs. Poyser's supper would be punctual.

Great was the clatter of knives and pewter plates and tin cans when Adam entered the house, but there was no hum of voices to this accompaniment: the eating of excellent roast-beef, provided free of expense, was too serious a business to those good farm-labourers to be performed with a divided attention, even if they had had anything to say to each other,—which they had not; and Mr. Poyser, at the head of the table, was too busy with his carving to listen to Bartle Massey's or Mr. Craig's ready talk.

"Here, Adam," said Mrs. Poyser, who was standing and looking on to see that Molly and Nancy did their duty as waiters, "here's a place kept for you between Mr. Massey and the boys. It's a poor tale you couldn't come to see the pudding when it was whole."

Adam looked anxiously round for a fourth woman's figure; but Dinah was not there. He was almost afraid of asking about her; besides, his attention was claimed by greetings, and there remained the hope that Dinah was in the house, though perhaps disinclined to festivities on the eve of her departure.

It was a goodly sight—that table, with Martin Poyser's round good-humoured face and large person at the head of it, helping his servants to the fragrant roast-beef, and pleased when the empty plates came again. Martin, though usually blest with a good appetite, really forgot to finish his own beef to-night—it was so pleasant to him to look on in the intervals of carving, and see how the others enjoyed their supper; for were they not men who, on all the days of the year except Christmas Day and Sundays, ate their cold dinner, in a make-shift manner, under the hedgerows, and drank their beer out of wooden bottles—with relish certainly, but with their mouths towards the zenith, after a fashion more endurable to ducks than to human bipeds. Martin Poyser had some faint conception of the flavour such men must find in hot roast-beef and fresh-drawn ale. He held his head on one side, and screwed up his mouth, as he nudged Bartle Massey, and watched half-witted Tom Tholer, otherwise known as "Tom Saft," receiving his second plateful of beef. A grin of delight broke over Tom's face as the plate was set down before him, between his knife and fork, which he held erect, as if they had been sacred tapers; but the delight was too strong to continue smouldering in a grin—it burst out the next instant in a long-drawn "haw, haw!" followed by a sudden collapse into utter gravity, as the knife and fork darted down on the prey. Martin Poyser's large person shook with his silent unctuous laugh: he turned towards Mrs. Poyser to see if she, too, had been observant of Tom, and the eyes of husband and wife met in a glance of good-natured amusement.

"Tom Saft" was a great favourite on the farm, where he played the part of the old jester, and made up for his practical deficiencies by his success in repartee. His hits, I imagine, were those of the flail, which falls quite at random, but nevertheless smashes an insect now and then. They were much quoted at sheep-shearing and haymaking times; but I refrain from recording them here, lest Tom's wit should prove to be

like that of many other bygone jesters eminent in their day—rather of
a temporary nature, not dealing with the deeper and more lasting relations of things.

Tom excepted, Martin Poyser had some pride in his servants and
labourers, thinking with satisfaction that they were the best worth their
pay of any set on the estate. There was Kester Bale, for example
(Beale, probably, if the truth were known, but he was called Bale, and
was not conscious of any claim to a fifth letter),—the old man with the
close leather cap, and the network of wrinkles on his sun-browned face.
Was there any man in Loamshire who knew better the "natur" of all
farming work? He was one of those invaluable labourers who can not
only turn their hand to everything, but excel in everything they turn
their hand to. It is true Kester's knees were much bent outward by this
time, and he walked with a perpetual curtsy, as if he were among the
most reverent of men. And so he was; but I am obliged to admit that
the object of his reverence was his own skill, towards which he performed
some rather affecting acts of worship. He always thatched the ricks; for
if anything were his forte more than another, it was thatching; and when
the last touch had been put to the last beehive rick, Kester, whose home
lay at some distance from the farm, would take a walk to the rickyard
in his best clothes on a Sunday morning, and stand in the lane, at a due
distance, to contemplate his own thatching,—walking about to get each
rick from the proper point of view. As he curtsied along, with his eyes
upturned to the straw knobs imitative of golden globes at the summits of
the beehive ricks, which indeed were gold of the best sort, you might
have imagined him to be engaged in some pagan act of adoration. Kester
was an old bachelor, and reputed to have stockings full of coin, concerning which his master cracked a joke with him every pay-night: not a
new, unseasoned joke, but a good old one, that had been tried many
times before, and had worn well. "Th' young measter's a merry mon,"
Kester frequently remarked; for having begun his career by frightening
away the crows under the last Martin Poyser but one, he could never
cease to account the reigning Martin a young master. I am not ashamed
of commemorating old Kester: you and I are indebted to the hard hands
of such men—hands that have long ago mingled with the soil they tilled
so faithfully, thriftily making the best they could of the earth's fruits,
and receiving the smallest share as their own wages.

Then, at the end of the table, opposite his master, there was Alick, the
shepherd and head man, with the ruddy face and broad shoulders, not
on the best terms with old Kester; indeed, their intercourse was confined
to an occasional snarl, for though they probably differed little concerning hedging and ditching and the treatment of ewes, there was a profound difference of opinion between them as to their own respective
merits. When Tityrus and Meliboeus happen to be on the same farm,
they are not sentimentally polite to each other. Alick, indeed, was not
by any means a honeyed man: his speech had usually something of a
snarl in it, and his broad-shouldered aspect something of the bull-dog

expression—"Don't you meddle with me, and I won't meddle with you"; but he was honest even to the splitting of an oat-grain rather than he would take beyond his acknowledged share, and as "close-fisted" with his master's property as if it had been his own,—throwing very small handfuls of damaged barley to the chickens, because a large handful affected his imagination painfully with a sense of profusion. Good-tempered Tim, the waggoner, who loved his horses, had his grudge against Alick in the matter of corn: they rarely spoke to each other, and never looked at each other, even over their dish of cold potatoes; but then, as this was their usual mode of behaviour towards all mankind, it would be an unsafe conclusion that they had more than transient fits of unfriendliness. The bucolic character at Hayslope, you perceive, was not of that entirely genial, merry, broad-grinning sort, apparently observed in most districts visited by artists. The mild radiance of a smile was a rare sight on a field-labourer's face, and there was seldom any gradation between bovine gravity and a laugh. Nor was every labourer so honest as our friend Alick. At this very table, among Mr. Poyser's men, there is that Big Ben Tholoway, a very powerful thresher, but detected more than once in carrying away his master's corn in his pockets: an action which, as Ben was not a philosopher, could hardly be ascribed to absence of mind. However, his master had forgiven him, and continued to employ him; for the Tholoways had lived on the Common, time out of mind, and had always worked for the Poysers. And on the whole, I daresay, society was not much the worse because Ben had not six months of it at the treadmill; for his views of depredation were narrow, and the House of Correction might have enlarged them. As it was, Ben ate his roast-beef to-night with a serene sense of having stolen nothing more than a few peas and beans as seed for his garden, since the last harvest supper, and felt warranted in thinking that Alick's suspicious eye, for ever upon him, was an injury to his innocence.

But *now* the roast-beef was finished and the cloth was drawn, leaving a fair large deal table for the bright drinking-cans, and the foaming brown jugs, and the bright brass candlesticks, pleasant to behold. *Now,* the great ceremony of the evening was to begin—the harvest-song, in which every man must join: he might be in tune, if he liked to be singular, but he must not sit with closed lips. The movement was obliged to be in triple time; the rest was *ad libitum.*

As to the origin of this song—whether it came in its actual state from the brain of a single rhapsodist, or was gradually perfected by a school or succession of rhapsodists, I am ignorant. There is a stamp of unity, of individual genius, upon it, which inclines me to the former hypothesis, though I am not blind to the consideration that this unity may rather have arisen from that consensus of many minds which was a condition of primitive thought, foreign to our modern consciousness. Some will perhaps think that they detect in the first quatrain an indication of a lost line, which later rhapsodists, failing in imaginative vigour, have supplied by the feeble device of iteration: others, however, may rather maintain that this very iteration is an original felicity, to which none but the most prosaic minds can be insensible.

The ceremony connected with the song was a drinking ceremony. (That is perhaps a painful fact, but then, you know, we cannot reform our forefathers.) During the first and second quatrain, sung decidedly *forte,* no can was filled.

> "Here's a health unto our master,
>   The founder of the feast;
> Here's a health unto our master
>   And to our mistress!
>
> And may his doings prosper,
>   Whate'er he takes in hand,
> For we are all his servants,
>   And are at his command."

But now, immediately before the third quatrain or chorus, sung *fortis-simo,* with emphatic raps on the table, which gave the effect of cymbals and drum together, Alick's can was filled, and he was bound to empty it before the chorus ceased.

> "Then drink, boys, drink!
>   And see ye do not spill,
> For if ye do, ye shall drink two,
>   For 'tis our master's will."

When Alick had gone successfully through this test of steady-handed manliness, it was the turn of old Kester, at his right hand,—and so on, till every man had drunk his initiatory pint under the stimulus of the chorus. Tom Saft—the rogue—took care to spill a little by accident; but Mrs. Poyser (too officiously, Tom thought) interfered to prevent the exaction of the penalty.

To any listener outside the door it would have been the reverse of obvious why the "Drink, boys, drink!" should have such an immediate and often-repeated encore; but once entered, he would have seen that all faces were at present sober, and most of them serious: it was the regular and respectable thing for those excellent farm-labourers to do, as much as for elegant ladies and gentlemen to smirk and bow over their wine-glasses. Bartle Massey, whose ears were rather sensitive, had gone out to see what sort of evening it was, at an early stage in the ceremony; and had not finished his contemplation until a silence of five minutes declared that "Drink. boys, drink!" was not likely to begin again for the next twelvemonth. Much to the regret of the boys and Totty: on them the stillness fell rather flat, after that glorious thumping of the table, towards which Totty, seated on her father's knee, contributed with her small might and small fist.

When Bartle re-entered, however, there appeared to be a general desire for solo music after the choral. Nancy declared that Tim the waggoner knew a song and was "allays singing like a lark i' the stable"; whereupon

Mr. Poyser said encouragingly, "Come, Tim, lad, let's hear it." Tim looked sheepish, tucked down his head, and said he couldn't sing; but this encouraging invitation of the master's was echoed all round the table. It was a conversational opportunity: everybody could say "Come, Tim,"—except Alick, who never relaxed into the frivolity of unnecessary speech. At last, Tim's next neighbour, Ben Tholoway, began to give emphasis to his speech by nudges, at which Tim, growing rather savage, said, "Let me alooan, will ye? else I'll ma' ye sing a toon ye wonna like." A good-tempered waggoner's patience has limits, and Tim was not to be urged further.

"Well, then, David, ye're the lad to sing," said Ben, willing to show that he was not discomfited by this check. "Sing 'My loove's a roos wi'out a thorn.' "

The amatory David was a young man of an unconscious abstracted expression, which was due probably to a squint of superior intensity rather than to any mental characteristic; for he was not indifferent to Ben's invitation, but blushed and laughed and rubbed his sleeve over his mouth in a way that was regarded as a symptom of yielding. And for some time the company appeared to be much in earnest about the desire to hear David's song. But in vain. The lyrism of the evening was in the cellar at present, and was not to be drawn from that retreat just yet.

Meanwhile the conversation at the head of the table had taken a political turn. Mr. Craig was not above talking politics occasionally, though he piqued himself rather on a wise insight than on specific information. He saw so far beyond the mere facts of a case, that really it was superfluous to know them.

"I'm no reader o' the paper myself," he observed to-night, as he filled his pipe, "though I might read it fast enough if I liked, for there's Miss Lyddy has 'em, and 's done with 'em i' no time; but there's Mills, now, sits i' the chimney-corner and reads the paper pretty nigh from morning to night, and when he's got to th' end on't he's more addle-headed than he was at the beginning. He's full o' this peace now, as they talk on; he's been reading and reading, and thinks he's got to the bottom on't. 'Why, Lor' bless you, Mills,' says I, 'you see no more into this thing nor you can see into the middle of a potato. I'll tell you what it is: you think it 'll be a fine thing for the country; and I'm not again' it—. mark my words—I'm not again' it. But it's my opinion as there's them at th' head o' this country as are worse enemies to us nor Bony and all the mounseers he's got at 's back; for the mounseers, you may skewer half-a-dozen of 'em at once as if they war frogs.' "

"Ay, ay," said Martin Poyser, listening with an air of much intelligence and edification, "they ne'er ate a bit o' beef i' their lives. Mostly sallet, I reckon."

"And says I to Mills," continued Mr. Craig, " 'Will *you* try to make me believe as furriners like them can do us half th' harm them ministers do with their bad government? If King George 'ud turn 'em all away and govern by himself he'd see everything righted. He might take on Billy Pitt again if he liked; but I don't see myself what we want wi' anybody besides King and Parliament. It's that nest o' ministers does the mischief, I tell you.' "

"Ah, it's fine talking," observed Mrs. Poyser, who was now seated near her husband, with Totty on her lap—"it's fine talking. It's hard work to tell which is Old Harry when everybody's got boots on."

"As for this peace," said Mr. Poyser, turning his head on one side in a dubitative manner, and giving a precautionary puff to his pipe between each sentence, "I don't know. Th' war's a fine thing for the country, an' how'll you keep up prices wi'out it? An' them French are a wicked sort o' folks, by what I can make out; what can you do better nor fight 'em?"

"Ye're partly right there, Poyser," said Mr. Craig, "but I'm not again' the peace—to make a holiday for a bit. We can break it when we like, an' *I'm* in no fear o' Bony, for all they talk so much o' his cliverness. That's what I says to Mills this morning. Lor' bless you, he sees no more through Bony! . . . why, I put him up to more in three minutes than he gets from 's paper all the year round. Says I, 'Am I a gardener as knows his business, or aren't I, Mills? answer me that.' 'To be sure y' are, Craig,' says he—he's not a bad fellow, Mills isn't, for a butler, but weak i' the head. 'Well,' says I, 'you talk o' Bony's cliverness; would it be any use my being a first-rate gardener if I'd got nought but a quagmire to work on?' 'No,' says he. 'Well,' I says, 'that's what it is wi' Bony. I'll not deny but he may be a bit cliver—he's no Frenchman born, as I understand; but what's he got at's back but mounseers?' "

Mr. Craig paused a moment with an emphatic stare after this triumphant specimen of Socratic argument, and then added, thumping the table rather fiercely,

"Why, it's a sure thing—and there's them 'ull bear witness to't—as i' one regiment where there was one man a-missing, they put the regimentals on a big monkey, and they fit him as the shell fits the walnut, and you couldn't tell the monkey from the mounseers! "

"Ah! think o' that, now!" said Mr. Poyser, impressed at once with the political bearings of the fact, and with its striking interest as an anecdote in natural history.

"Come, Craig," said Adam, "that's a little too strong. You don't believe that. It's all nonsense about the French being such poor sticks. Mr. Irwine's seen 'em in their own country, and he says they've plenty o' fine fellows among 'em. And as for knowledge, and contrivances, and manifactures, there's a many things as we're a fine sight behind 'em in. It's poor foolishness to run down your enemies. Why, Nelson and the rest of 'em 'ud have no merit i' beating 'em, if they were such offal as folks pretend."

Mr. Poyser looked doubtfully at Mr. Craig, puzzled by this opposition of authorities. Mr. Irwine's testimony was not to be disputed; but, on the other hand, Craig was a knowing fellow, and his view was less startling. Martin had never "heard tell" of the French being good for much. Mr. Craig had found no answer but such as was implied in taking a long draught of ale, and then looking down fixedly at the proportions of his own leg, which he turned a little outward for that purpose, when Bartle Massey returned from the fireplace, where he had been smoking his first pipe in quiet, and broke the silence by saying, as he thrust his forefinger into the canister,

"Why, Adam, how happened you not to be at church on Sunday? answer me that, you rascal. The anthem went limping without you. Are you going to disgrace your schoolmaster in his old age?"

"No, Mr. Massey," said Adam. "Mr. and Mrs. Poyser can tell you where I was. I was in no bad company."

"She's gone, Adam—gone to Snowfield," said Mr. Poyser, reminded of Dinah for the first time this evening. "I thought you'd ha' persuaded her better. Nought 'ud hold her, but she must go yesterday forenoon. The missis has hardly got over it. I thought she'd ha' no sperrit for th' harvest supper."

Mrs. Poyser had thought of Dinah several times since Adam had come in, but she had had "no heart" to mention the bad news.

"What!" said Bartle, with an air of disgust. "Was there a woman concerned? Then I give you up, Adam."

"But it's a woman you'n spoke well on, Bartle," said Mr. Poyser. "Come, now, you canna draw back; you said once as women wouldna ha' been a bad invention if they'd all been like Dinah."

"I meant her voice, man—I meant her voice, that was all," said Bartle. "I can bear to hear her speak without wanting to put wool in my ears. As for other things, I daresay she's like the rest o' the women —thinks two and two 'll come to make five, if she cries and bothers enough about it."

"Ay, ay!" said Mrs. Poyser; "one 'ud think. an' hear some folks talk, as the men war 'cute enough to count the corns in a bag o' wheat wi' only smelling at it. They can see through a barn-door, *they* can. Perhaps that's the reason they can see so little o' this side on't."

Martin Poyser shook with delighted laughter, and winked at Adam, as much as to say the schoolmaster was in for it now.

"Ah!" said Bartle, sneeringly, "the women are quick enough—they're quick enough. They know the rights of a story before they hear it, and can tell a man what his thoughts are before he knows 'em himself."

"Like enough," said Mrs. Poyser; "for the men are mostly so slow, their thoughts overrun 'em an' they can only catch 'em by the tail. I can count a stocking-top while a man's getting's tongue ready; an' when he outs wi' his speech at last, there's little broth to be made on't. It's your dead chicks take the longest hatchin'. Howiver, I'm not denyin' the women are foolish: God Almighty made 'em to match the men."

"Match!" said Bartle; "ay, as vinegar matches one's teeth. If a man says a word, his wife 'll match it with a contradiction; if he's a mind for hot meat, his wife 'll match it with cold bacon; if he laughs, she'll match with whimpering. She's such a match as the horse-fly is to th' horse: she's got the right venom to sting him with—the right venom to sting him with."

"Yes," said Mrs. Poyser, "I know what the men like—a poor soft, as 'ud simper at 'em like the pictur o' the sun, whether they did right or wrong, an' say thank you for a kick, an' pretend she didna know which end she stood uppermost, till her husband told her. That's what a man wants in a wife, mostly; he wants to make sure o' one fool as 'ull tell him he's wise. But there's some men can do wi'out that—they think so much o' themselves a'ready; an' that's how it is there's old bachelors."

"Come, Craig," said Mr. Poyser, jocosely, "you mun get married pretty quick, else you'll be set down for an old bachelor; an' you see what the women 'ull think on you."

"Well," said Mr. Craig, willing to conciliate Mrs. Poyser, and setting a high value on his own compliments, "*I* like a cleverish woman—a woman o' sperrit—a managing woman."

"You're out there, Craig," said Bartle, dryly; "you're out there. You judge o' your garden-stuff on a better plan than that: you pick the things for what they can excel in—for what they can excel in. You don't value your peas for their roots, or your carrots for their flowers. Now, that's the way you should choose women: their cleverness 'll never come to much—never come to much; but they make excellent simpletons, ripe and strong-flavoured."

"What dost say to that?" said Mr. Poyser, throwing himself back and looking merrily at his wife.

"Say!" answered Mrs. Poyser, with dangerous fire kindling in her eye; "why, I say as some folks' tongues are like the clocks as run on strikin', not to tell you the time o' the day, but because there's summat wrong i' their own inside" . . .

Mrs. Poyser would probably have brought her rejoinder to a further climax, if every one's attention had not at this moment been called to the other end of the table, where the lyrism, which had at first only manifested itself by David's *sotto voce* performance of "My love's a rose without a thorn," had gradually assumed a rather deafening and complex character. Tim, thinking slightly of David's vocalisation, was impelled to supersede that feeble buzz by a spirited commencement of "Three Merry Mowers"; but David was not to be put down so easily, and showed himself capable of a copious crescendo, which was rendering it doubtful whether the rose would not predominate over the mowers, when old Kester, with an entirely unmoved and immovable aspect, suddenly set up a quavering treble,—as if he had been an alarum, and the time was come for him to go off.

The company at Alick's end of the table took this form of vocal entertainment very much as a matter of course, being free from musical prejudices; but Bartle Massey laid down his pipe and put his fingers in his ears; and Adam, who had been longing to go, ever since he had heard Dinah was not in the house, rose and said he must bid good-night.

"I'll go with you, lad," said Bartle; "I'll go with you before my ears are split."

"I'll go round by the Common, and see you home, if you like, Mr. Massey," said Adam.

"Ay, ay!" said Bartle; "then we can have a bit o' talk together. I never get hold of you now."

"Eh! it's a pity but you'd sit it out," said Martin Poyser. "They'll all go soon; for th' missis niver lets 'em stay past ten."

But Adam was resolute, so the good-nights were said, and the two friends turned out on their starlight walk together.

"There's that poor fool, Vixen, whimpering for me at home," said Bartle. "I can never bring her here with me for fear she should be struck with Mrs. Poyser's eye, and the poor bitch might go limping for ever after."

"I've never any need to drive Gyp back," said Adam, laughing. "He always turns back on his own head when he finds out I'm coming here."

"Ay, ay," said Bartle. "A terrible woman!—made of needles—made of needles. But I stick to Martin—I shall always stick to Martin. And he likes the needles, God help him! He's a cushion made on purpose for 'em."

"But she's a downright good-natur'd woman, for all that," said Adam, "and as true as the daylight. She's a bit cross wi' the dogs when they offer to come in th' house, but if they depended on her, she'd take care and have 'em well fed. If her tongue's keen her heart's tender: I've seen that in times o' trouble. She's one o' those women as are better than their word."

"Well, well," said Bartle, "I don't say th' apple isn't sound at the core; but it sets my teeth on edge—it sets my teeth on edge."

CHAPTER LIV

THE MEETING ON THE HILL

ADAM understood Dinah's haste to go away, and drew hope rather than discouragement from it. She was fearful lest the strength of her feeling towards him should hinder her from waiting and listening faithfully for the ultimate guiding voice from within.

"I wish I'd asked her to write to me, though," he thought. "And yet even that might disturb her a bit, perhaps. She wants to be quite quiet in her old way for a while. And I've no right to be impatient and interrupting her with my wishes. She's told me what her mind is; and she's not a woman to say one thing and mean another. I'll wait patiently."

That was Adam's wise resolution, and it throve excellently for the first two or three weeks on the nourishment it got from the remembrance of Dinah's confession that Sunday afternoon. There is a wonderful amount of sustenance in the first few words of love. But towards the middle of October the resolution began to dwindle perceptibly, and showed dangerous symptoms of exhaustion. The weeks were unusually long: Dinah must surely have had more than enough time to make up her mind. Let a woman say what she will after she has once told a man that she loves him, he is a little too flushed and exalted with that first draught she offers him to care much about the taste of the second: he treads the earth with a very elastic step as he walks away from her, and makes light of all difficulties. But that sort of glow dies out: memory gets sadly diluted with time, and is not strong enough to revive us. Adam was no longer so confident as he had been: he began to fear that perhaps Dinah's old life would have too strong a grasp upon her for any new feeling to triumph. If she had not felt this, she would surely have written to him to give him some comfort; but it appeared that she held it right to discourage him. As Adam's confidence waned, his patience waned with it, and he thought he must write himself; he must ask Dinah not to leave him in painful doubt longer than was needful. He sat up late one night to write her a letter, but the next morning he burnt it, afraid of its effect. It would be worse to have a discouraging answer by letter than from her own lips, for her presence reconciled him to her will.

You perceive how it was: Adam was hungering for the sight of Dinah; and when that sort of hunger reaches a certain stage, a lover is likely to still it though he may have to put his future in pawn.

But what harm could he do by going to Snowfield? Dinah could not be displeased with him for it: she had not forbidden him to go: she must surely expect that he would go before long. By the second Sunday in October this view of the case had become so clear to Adam, that he was already on his way to Snowfield; on horseback this time, for his hours were precious now, and he had borrowed Jonathan Burge's good nag for the journey.

What keen memories went along the road with him! He had often been to Oakbourne and back since that first journey to Snowfield, but beyond Oakbourne the grey stone walls, the broken country, the meagre trees, seemed to be telling him afresh the story of that painful past which he knew so well by heart. But no story is the same to us after a lapse of time; or rather, we who read it are no longer the same interpreters: and Adam this morning brought with him new thoughts through that grey country—thoughts which gave an altered significance to its story of the past.

That is a base and selfish, even a blasphemous, spirit, which rejoices and is thankful over the past evil that has blighted or crushed another, because it has been made a source of unforeseen good to ourselves: Adam could never cease to mourn over that mystery of human sorrow which had been brought so close to him: he could never thank God for another's misery. And if I were capable of that narrow-sighted joy in Adam's behalf, I should still know he was not the man to feel it for himself: he would have shaken his head at such a sentiment, and said, "Evil's evil, and sorrow's sorrow, and you can't alter its natur by

wrapping it up in other words. Other folks were not created for my
sake, that I should think all square when things turn out well for me."

But it is not ignoble to feel that the fuller life which a sad experience
has brought us is worth our own personal share of pain: surely it is not
possible to feel otherwise, any more than it would be possible for a man
with cataract to regret the painful process by which his dim blurred
sight of men as trees walking had been exchanged for clear outline and
effulgent day. The growth of higher feeling within us is like the growth
of faculty, bringing with it a sense of added strength: we can no more
wish to return to a narrower sympathy, than a painter or a musician can
wish to return to his cruder manner, or a philosopher to his less complete
formula.

Something like this sense of enlarged being was in Adam's mind this
Sunday morning, as he rode along in vivid recollection of the past. His
feeling towards Dinah, the hope of passing his life with her, had been
the distant unseen point towards which that hard journey from Snowfield eighteen months ago had been leading him. Tender and deep as
his love for Hetty had been—so deep that the roots of it would never be
torn away—his love for Dinah was better and more precious to him;
for it was the outgrowth of that fuller life which had come to him from
his acquaintance with deep sorrow. "It's like as if it was a new strength
to me," he said to himself, "to love her, and know as she loves me. I
shall look t' her to help me to see things right. For she's better than I am
—there's less o' self in her, and pride. And it's a feeling as gives you a
sort o' liberty, as if you could walk more fearless, when you've more
trust in another than y' have in yourself. I've always been thinking I
knew better than them as belonged to me, and that's a poor sort o' life,
when you can't look to them nearest to you t' help you with a bit better
thought than what you've got inside you a'ready."

It was more than two o'clock in the afternoon when Adam came in
sight of the grey town on the hill-side, and looked searchingly towards the
green valley below, for the first glimpse of the old thatched roof near the
ugly red mill. The scene looked less harsh in the soft October sunshine
than it had done in the eager time of early spring; and the one grand
charm it possessed in common with all wide-stretching woodless regions
—that it filled you with a new consciousness of the overarching sky—had
a milder, more soothing influence than usual, on this almost cloudless
day. Adam's doubts and fears melted under this influence as the delicate
web-like clouds had gradually melted away into the clear blue above
him. He seemed to see Dinah's gentle face assuring him, with its looks
alone, of all he longed to know.

He did not expect Dinah to be at home at this hour, but he got down
from his horse and tied it at the little gate, that he might ask where she
was gone to-day. He had set his mind on following her and bringing her
home. She was gone to Sloman's End, a hamlet about three miles off,
over the hill, the old woman told him: had set off directly after the

morning chapel, to preach in a cottage there, as her habit was. Anybody at the town would tell him the way to Sloman's End. So Adam got on his horse again and rode to the town, putting up at the old inn, and taking a hasty dinner there in the company of the too chatty landlord, from whose friendly questions and reminiscences he was glad to escape as soon as possible, and set out towards Sloman's End. With all his haste, it was nearly four o'clock before he could set off, and he thought that as Dinah had gone so early, she would perhaps already be near returning. The little, grey, desolate-looking hamlet, unscreened by sheltering trees, lay in sight long before he reached it; and as he came near he could hear the sound of voices singing a hymn. "Perhaps that's the last hymn before they come away," Adam thought: "I'll walk back a bit, and turn again to meet her, further off the village." He walked back till he got nearly to the top of the hill again, and seated himself on a loose stone, against the low wall, to watch till he should see the little black figure leaving the hamlet and winding up the hill. He chose this spot, almost at the top of the hill, because it was away from all eyes—no house, no cattle, not even a nibbling sheep near—no presence but the still lights and shadows, and the great bracing sky.

She was much longer coming than he expected: he waited an hour at least watching for her and thinking of her, while the afternoon shadows lengthened, and the light grew softer. At last he saw the little black figure coming from between the grey houses, and gradually approaching the foot of the hill. Slowly, Adam thought; but Dinah was really walking at her usual pace, with a light quiet step. Now she was beginning to wind along the path up the hill, but Adam would not move yet: he would not meet her too soon; he had set his heart on meeting her in this assured loneliness. And now he began to fear lest he should startle her too much; "Yet," he thought, "she's not one to be overstartled; she's always so calm and quiet, as if she was prepared for anything."

What was she thinking of as she wound up the hill? Perhaps she had found complete repose without him, and had ceased to feel any need of his love. On the verge of a decision we all tremble: hope pauses with fluttering wings.

But now at last she was very near, and Adam rose from the stone wall. It happened that just as he walked forward, Dinah had paused and turned round to look back at the village: who does not pause and look back in mounting a hill? Adam was glad; for, with the fine instinct of a lover, he felt that it would be best for her to hear his voice before she saw him. He came within three paces of her and then said, "Dinah!" She started without looking round, as if she connected the sound with no place. "Dinah!" Adam said again. He knew quite well what was in her mind. She was so accustomed to think of impressions as purely spiritual monitions, that she looked for no material visible accompaniment of the voice.

But this second time she looked round. What a look of yearning love it was that the mild grey eyes turned on the strong dark-eyed man! She did not start again at the sight of him; she said nothing, but moved towards him so that his arm could clasp her round.

And they walked on so in silence, while the warm tears fell. Adam was content, and said nothing. It was Dinah who spoke first.

"Adam," she said, "it is the Divine Will. My soul is so knit to yours that it is but a divided life I live without you. And this moment, now you are with me, and I feel that our hearts are filled with the same love, I have a fulness of strength to bear and do our heavenly Father's Will, that I had lost before."

Adam paused and looked into her sincere eyes.

"Then we'll never part any more, Dinah, till death parts us."

And they kissed each other with a deep joy.

What greater thing is there for two human souls, than to feel that they are joined for life—to strengthen each other in all labour, to rest on each other in all sorrow, to minister to each other in all pain, to be one with each other in silent unspeakable memories at the moment of the last parting?

CHAPTER LV

MARRIAGE BELLS

In little more than a month after that meeting on the hill—on a rimy morning in departing November—Adam and Dinah were married.

It was an event much thought of in the village. All Mr. Burge's men had a holiday, and all Mr. Poyser's; and most of those who had a holiday appeared in their best clothes at the wedding. I think there was hardly an inhabitant of Hayslope specially mentioned in this history and still resident in the parish on this November morning, who was not either in church to see Adam and Dinah married, or near the church door to greet them as they came forth. Mrs. Irwine and her daughters were waiting at the churchyard gates in their carriage (for they had a carriage now) to shake hands with the bride and bridegroom, and wish them well; and in the absence of Miss Lydia Donnithorne at Bath, Mrs. Best, Mr. Mills, and Mr. Craig had felt it incumbent on them to represent "the family" at the Chase on the occasion. The churchyard walk was quite lined with familiar faces, many of them faces that had first looked at Dinah when she preached on the Green; and no wonder they showed this eager interest on her marriage morning, for nothing like Dinah and the history which had brought her and Adam Bede together had been known at Hayslope within the memory of man.

Bessy Cranage, in her neatest cap and frock, was crying, though she did not exactly know why; for, as her cousin Wiry Ben, who stood near her, judiciously suggested, Dinah was not going away, and if Bessy was in low spirits, the best thing for her to do was to follow Dinah's example, and marry an honest fellow who was ready to have her. Next to Bessy, just within the church door, there were the Poyser children, peeping round the corner of the pews to get a sight of the mysterious ceremony; Totty's face wearing an unusual air of anxiety at the idea of seeing cousin Dinah come back looking rather old, for in Totty's experience no married people were young.

I envy them all the sight they had when the marriage was fairly ended and Adam led Dinah out of the church. She was not in black this morning; for her aunt Poyser would by no means allow such a risk of incurring bad luck, and had herself made a present of the wedding dress, made all of grey, though in the usual Quaker form, for on this point Dinah could not give way. So the lily face looked out with sweet gravity from under a grey Quaker bonnet, neither smiling nor blushing, but with lips trembling a little under the weight of solemn feelings. Adam, as he pressed her arm to his side, walked with his old erectness and his head thrown rather backward as if to face all the world better; but it was not because he was particularly proud this morning, as is the wont of bridegrooms, for his happiness was of a kind that had little reference to men's opinion of it. There was a tinge of sadness in his deep joy; Dinah knew it, and did not feel aggrieved.

There were three other couples, following the bride and bridegroom: first, Martin Poyser, looking as cheery as a bright fire on this rimy morning, led quiet Mary Burge, the bridesmaid; then came Seth serenely happy, with Mrs. Poyser on his arm; and last of all Bartle Massey, with Lisbeth—Lisbeth in a new gown and bonnet, too busy with her pride in her son, and her delight in possessing the one daughter she had desired, to devise a single pretext for complaint.

Bartle Massey had consented to attend the wedding at Adam's earnest request, under protest against marriage in general, and the marriage of a sensible man in particular. Nevertheless, Mr. Poyser had a joke against him after the wedding dinner, to the effect that in the vestry he had given the bride one more kiss than was necessary.

Behind this last couple came Mr. Irwine, glad at heart over this good morning's work of joining Adam and Dinah. For he had seen Adam in the worst moments of his sorrow; and what better harvest from that painful seed-time could there be than this? The love that had brought hope and comfort in the hour of despair, the love that had found its way to the dark prison cell and to poor Hetty's darker soul—this strong, gentle love was to be Adam's companion and helper till death.

There was much shaking of hands mingled with "God bless you's," and other good wishes to the four couples, at the churchyard gate, Mr. Poyser answering for the rest with unwonted vivacity of tongue, for he had all the appropriate wedding-day jokes at his command. And the women, he observed, could never do anything but put finger in eye at a wedding. Even Mrs. Poyser could not trust herself to speak as the neighbours shook hands with her; and Lisbeth began to cry in the face of the very first person who told her she was getting young again.

Mr. Joshua Rann, having a slight touch of rheumatism, did not join in the ringing of the bells this morning, and, looking on with some contempt at these informal greetings which required no official co-operation from the clerk, began to hum in his musical bass, "O what a joyful thing it is," by way of preluding a little to the effect he intended to produce in the wedding psalm next Sunday.

"That's a bit of good news to cheer Arthur," said Mr. Irwine to his mother, as they drove off. "I shall write to him the first thing when we get home."

EPILOGUE

It is near the end of June, in 1807. The workshops have been shut up half an hour or more in Adam Bede's timber-yard, which used to be Jonathan Burge's, and the mellow evening light is falling on the pleasant house with the buff walls and the soft grey thatch, very much as it did when we saw Adam bringing in the keys on that June evening nine years ago.

There is a figure we know well, just come out of the house, and shading her eyes with her hands as she looks for something in the distance; for the rays that fall on her white borderless cap and her pale auburn hair are very dazzling. But now she turns away from the sunlight and looks towards the door. We can see the sweet pale face quite well now: it's scarcely at all altered—only a little fuller, to correspond to her more matronly figure, which still seems light and active enough in the plain black dress.

"I see him, Seth," Dinah said, as she looked into the house. "Let us go and meet him. Come, Lisbeth, come with mother."

The last call was answered immediately by a small fair creature with pale auburn hair and grey eyes, little more than four years old, who ran out silently and put her hand into her mother's.

"Come, uncle Seth," said Dinah.

"Ay, ay, we're coming," Seth answered from within, and presently appeared stooping under the doorway, being taller than usual by the black head of a sturdy two-year-old nephew, who had caused some delay by demanding to be carried on uncle's shoulder.

"Better take him on thy arm, Seth," said Dinah, looking fondly at the stout black-eyed fellow. "He's troublesome to thee so."

"Nay, nay: Addy likes a ride on my shoulder. I can carry him so for a bit." A kindness which young Addy acknowledged by drumming his heels with promising force against uncle Seth's chest. But to walk by Dinah's side, and be tyrannised over by Dinah's and Adam's children, was uncle Seth's earthly happiness.

"Where didst see him?" asked Seth, as they walked on into the adjoining field. "I can't catch sight of him anywhere."

"Between the hedges by the roadside," said Dinah. "I saw his hat and his shoulder. There he is again."

"Trust thee for catching sight of him if he's anywhere to be seen," said Seth, smiling. "Thee't like poor mother used to be. She was always on the look-out for Adam, and could see him sooner than other folks, for all her eyes got dim."

"He's been longer than he expected," said Dinah, taking Arthur's watch from a small side-pocket and looking at it; "it's nigh upon seven now."

"Ay, they'd have a deal to say to one another," said Seth, "and the meeting 'ud touch 'em both pretty closish. Why, it's getting on towards eight years since they parted."

"Yes," said Dinah, "Adam was greatly moved this morning at the thought of the change he should see in the poor young man, from the sickness he has undergone, as well as the years which have changed us all. And the death of the poor wanderer, when she was coming back to us, has been sorrow upon sorrow."

"See, Addy," said Seth, lowering the young one to his arm now, and pointing, "there's father coming—at the far stile."

Dinah hastened her steps, and little Lisbeth ran on at her utmost speed till she clasped her father's leg. Adam patted her head and lifted her up to kiss her, but Dinah could see the marks of agitation on his face as she approached him, and he put her arm within his in silence.

"Well, youngster, must I take you?" he said, trying to smile, when Addy stretched out his arms—ready, with the usual baseness of infancy, to give up his uncle Seth at once, now there was some rarer patronage at hand.

"It's cut me a good deal, Dinah," Adam said at last, when they were walking on.

"Did'st find him greatly altered?" said Dinah.

"Why, he's altered and yet not altered. I should ha' known him anywhere. But his colour's changed, and he looks sadly. However, the doctors say he'll soon be set right in his own country air. He's all sound in th' inside; it's only the fever shattered him so. But he speaks just the same, and smiles at me just as he did when he was a lad. It's wonderful how he's always had just the same sort o' look when he smiles."

"I've never seen him smile, poor young man," said Dinah.

"But thee *wilt* see him smile, to-morrow," said Adam. "He asked after thee the first thing when he began to come round, and we could talk to one another. 'I hope she isn't altered,' he said, 'I remember her face so well.' I told him, 'no,'" Adam continued, looking fondly at the eyes that were turned up towards his, "only a bit plumper, as thee'dst a right to be after seven year. 'I may come and see her to-morrow, mayn't I?' he said; 'I long to tell her how I've thought of her all these years.'"

"Did'st tell him I'd always used the watch?" said Dinah.

"Ay; and we talked a deal about thee, for he says he never saw a woman a bit like thee. 'I shall turn Methodist some day,' he said, 'when she preaches out of doors, and go to hear her.' And I said, 'Nay, sir, you can't do that, for Conference has forbid the women preaching, and she's given it up, all but talking to the people a bit in their houses.' "

"Ah," said Seth, who could not repress a comment on this point, "and a sore pity it was o' Conference; and if Dinah had seen as I did, we'd ha' left the Wesleyans and joined a body that 'ud put no bonds on Christian liberty."

"Nay, lad, nay," said Adam, "she was right and thee wast wrong. There's no rule so wise but what it's a pity for somebody or other. Most o' the women do more harm nor good with their preaching—they've not got Dinah's gift nor her sperrit; and she's seen that, and she thought it right to set th' example o' submitting, for she's not held from other sorts o' teaching. And I agree with her, and approve o' what she did."

Seth was silent. This was a standing subject of difference rarely alluded to, and Dinah, wishing to quit it at once, said,

"Didst remember, Adam, to speak to Colonel Donnithorne the words my uncle and aunt intrusted to thee?"

"Yes, and he's going to the Hall Farm with Mr. Irwine the day after to-morrow. Mr. Irwine came in while we were talking about it, and he would have it as the Colonel must see nobody but thee to-morrow: he said—and he's in the right of it—as it'll be bad for him t' have his feelings stirred with seeing many people one after another. 'We must get you strong and hearty,' he said, 'that's the first thing to be done, Arthur, and then you shall have your own way. But I shall keep you under your old tutor's thumb till then.' Mr. Irwine's fine and joyful at having him home again."

Adam was silent a little while, and then said:

"It was very cutting when we first saw one another. He'd never heard about poor Hetty till Mr. Irwine met him in London, for the letters missed him on his journey. The first thing he said to me, when we'd got hold o' one another's hands was, 'I could never do anything for her, Adam—she lived long enough for all the suffering—and I'd thought so of the time when I might do something for her. But you told me the truth when you said to me once, 'There's a sort of wrong that can never be made up for.' "

"Why, there's Mr. and Mrs. Poyser coming in at the yard gate," said Seth.

"So there is," said Dinah. "Run, Lisbeth, run to meet aunt Poyser. Come in, Adam, and rest; it has been a hard day for thee."

THE
MILL ON THE FLOSS

"In their death they were not divided."

CONTENTS

★

BOOK ONE

BOY AND GIRL

BOOK TWO

SCHOOL-TIME

BOOK THREE

THE DOWNFALL

BOOK FOUR

THE VALLEY OF HUMILIATION

BOOK FIVE

WHEAT AND TARES

BOOK SIX

THE GREAT TEMPTATION

BOOK SEVEN

THE FINAL RESCUE

BOOK ONE

Boy and Girl

★

CHAPTER I

OUTSIDE DORLCOTE MILL

A WIDE plain, where the broadening Floss hurries on between its green banks to the sea, and the loving tide, rushing to meet it, checks its passage with an impetuous embrace. On this mighty tide the black ships—laden with the fresh-scented fir-planks, with rounded sacks of oil-bearing seed, or with the dark glitter of coal—are borne along to the town of St. Ogg's, which shows its aged, fluted red roofs and the broad gables of its wharves between the low wooded hill and the river brink, tinging the water with a soft purple hue under the transient glance of this February sun. Far away on each hand stretch the rich pastures, and the patches of dark earth, made ready for the seed of broad-leaved green crops, or touched already with the tint of the tender-bladed autumn-sown corn. There is a remnant still of the last year's golden clusters of beehive ricks rising at intervals beyond the hedgerows; and everywhere the hedgerows are studded with trees: the distant ships seem to be lifting their masts and stretching their red-brown sails close among the branches of the spreading ash. Just by the red-roofed town the tributary Ripple flows with a lively current into the Floss. How lovely the little river is, with its dark, changing wavelets! It seems to me like a living companion while I wander along the bank and listen to its low placid voice, as to the voice of one who is deaf and loving. I remember those large dipping willows. I remember the stone bridge.

And this is Dorlcote Mill. I must stand a minute or two here on the bridge and look at it, though the clouds are threatening, and it is far on in the afternoon. Even in this leafless time of departing February it is pleasant to look at—perhaps the chill damp season adds a charm to the trimly-kept, comfortable dwelling-house, as old as the elms and chestnuts that shelter it from the northern blast. The stream is brimful now, and lies high in this little withy plantation, and half drowns the grassy fringe of the croft in front of the house. As I look at the full stream, the vivid grass, the delicate bright-green powder softening the outline of the great trunks and branches that gleam from under the bare purple boughs, I am in love with moistness, and envy the white ducks that are dipping their heads far into the water here among the withes, unmindful of the awkward appearance they make in the drier world above.

The rush of the water, and the booming of the mill, bring a dreamy deafness, which seems to heighten the peacefulness of the scene. They are like a great curtain of sound, shutting one out from the world beyond. And now there is the thunder of the huge covered wagon coming home with sacks of grain. That honest waggoner is thinking of his dinner, getting sadly dry in the oven at this late hour; but he will not touch it till he has fed his horses,—the strong, submissive, meek-eyed beasts, who, I fancy, are looking mild reproach at him from between their blinkers, that he should crack his whip at them in that awful manner, as if they needed that hint! See how they stretch their shoulders up the slope towards the bridge, with all the more energy because they are so near home. Look at their grand shaggy feet that seem to grasp the firm earth, at the patient strength of their necks bowed under the heavy collar, at the mighty muscles of their struggling haunches! I should like well to hear them neigh over their hardly-earned feed of corn, and see them, with their moist necks freed from the harness, dipping their eager nostrils into the muddy pond. Now they are on the bridge, and down they go again at a swifter pace, and the arch of the covered wagon disappears at the turning behind the trees.

Now I can turn my eyes towards the mill again, and watch the unresting wheel sending out its diamond jets of water. That little girl is watching it too: she has been standing on just the same spot at the edge of the water ever since I paused on the bridge. And that queer white cur with the brown ear seems to be leaping and barking in ineffectual remonstrance with the wheel; perhaps he is jealous, because his playfellow in the beaver bonnet is so rapt in its movement. It is time the little playfellow went in, I think; and there is a very bright fire to tempt her: the red light shines out under the deepening grey of the sky. It is time, too, for me to leave off resting my arms on the cold stone of this bridge. . . .

Ah, my arms are really benumbed. I have been pressing my elbows on the arms of my chair, and dreaming that I was standing on the bridge in front of Dorlcote Mill, as it looked one February afternoon many years ago. Before I dozed off, I was going to tell you what Mr. and Mrs. Tulliver were talking about, as they sat by the bright fire in the left-hand parlour on that very afternoon I have been dreaming of.

CHAPTER II

MR. TULLIVER, OF DORLCOTE MILL, DECLARES HIS RESOLUTION ABOUT TOM

"WHAT I want, you know," said Mr. Tulliver—"what I want is to give Tom a good eddication; an eddication as'll be a bread to him. That was what I was thinking of when I gave notice for him to leave th' academy at Ladyday. I mean to put him to a downright good school at Midsummer. The two years at th' academy 'ud ha' done well enough, if I'd meant to make a miller and farmer of him; for he's had a fine sight more schoolin' nor *I* ever got: all the learnin' *my* father ever paid for was a bit o' birch at one end and the alphabet at th' other. But I should like Tom to be a bit of a scholard, so as he might be up to the tricks o' these fellows as talk fine and write with a flourish. It 'ud be a help to me wi' these law-suits, and arbitrations, and things. I wouldn't make a downright lawyer o' the lad—I should be sorry for him to be a raskill—but a sort o' engineer, or a surveyor, or an auctioneer and vallyer, like Riley, or one o' them smartish businesses as are all profits and no outlay, only for a big watch-chain and a high stool. They're pretty nigh all one, and they're not far off being even wi' the law, *I* believe; for Riley looks Lawyer Wakem i' the face as hard as one cat looks another. *He's* none frightened at him."

Mr. Tulliver was speaking to his wife, a blond comely woman, in a fan-shaped cap (I am afraid to think how long it is since fan-shaped caps were worn—they must be so near coming in again. At that time, when Mrs. Tulliver was nearly forty, they were new at St. Ogg's, and considered sweet things).

"Well, Mr. Tulliver, you know best: *I've* no objections. But hadn't I better kill a couple o' fowl and have th' aunts and uncles to dinner next week, so as you may hear what sister Glegg and sister Pullet have got to say about it? There's a couple o' fowl *wants* killing!"

"You may kill every fowl i' the yard, if you like, Bessy; but I shall ask neither aunt nor uncle what I'm to do wi' my own lad," said Mr. Tulliver, defiantly.

"Dear heart," said Mrs. Tulliver, shocked at this sanguinary rhetoric, "how can you talk so, Mr. Tulliver? But it's your way to speak disrespectful o' my family; and sister Glegg throws all the blame upo' me, though I'm sure I'm as innocent as the babe unborn. For nobody's ever heard *me* say as it wasn't lucky for my children to have aunts and uncles as can live independent. Howiver, if Tom's to go to a new school, I should like him to go where I can wash him and mend him; else he might as well have calico as linen, for they'd be one as yallow as th' other before they'd been washed half-a-dozen times. And then, when the box is goin' backards and forrards, I could send the lad a cake, or a pork-pie, or an apple; for he can do with an extry bit, bless him, whether they stint him at the meals or no. My children can eat as much victuals as most, thank God."

"Well, well, we won't send him out o' reach o' the carrier's cart, if other things fit in," said Mr. Tulliver. "But you mustn't put a spoke i' the wheel about the washin', if we can't get a school near enough. That's the fault I have to find wi' you, Bessy: if you see a stick i' the road, you're allays thinkin' you can't step over it. You'd want me not to hire a good waggoner, 'cause he'd got a mole on his face."

"Dear heart!" said Mrs. Tulliver, in mild surprise, "when did I iver make objections to a man because he'd got a mole on his face? I'm sure I'm rether fond o' the moles, for my brother, as is dead an' gone, had a mole on his brow. But I can't remember your iver offering to hire a waggoner with a mole, Mr. Tulliver. There was John Gibbs hadn't a mole on his face no more nor you have, an' I was all for having you hire *him;* an' so you did hire him, an' if he hadn't died o' th' inflammation, as we paid Dr. Turnbull for attending him, he'd very like ha' been driving the waggon now. He might have a mole somewhere out o' sight, but how was I to know that, Mr. Tulliver?"

"No, no, Bessy; I didn't mean justly the mole; I meant it to stand for summat else; but niver mind—it's puzzling work, talking is. What I'm thinking on, is how to find the right sort o' school to send Tom to, for I might be ta'en in again, as I've been wi' th' academy. I'll have nothing to do wi' a 'cademy again: whatever school I send Tom to, it shan't be a 'cademy; it shall be a place where the lads spend their time i' summat else besides blacking the family's shoes, and getting up the potatoes. It's an uncommon puzzling thing to know what school to pick."

Mr. Tulliver paused a minute or two, and dived with both hands into his breeches pockets as if he hoped to find some suggestion there. Apparently he was not disappointed, for he presently said, "I know what I'll do—I'll talk it over wi' Riley: he's coming to-morrow, t' arbitrate about the dam."

"Well, Mr. Tulliver, I've put the sheets out for the best bed, and Kezia's got 'em hanging at the fire. They aren't the best sheets, but they're good enough for anybody to sleep in, be he who he will; for as for them best Holland sheets, I should repent buying 'em, only they'll do to lay us out in. An' if you was to die to-morrow, Mr. Tulliver, they're mangled beautiful, an' all ready, an' smell o' lavender as it 'ud be a pleasure to lay 'em out; an' they lie at the left-hand corner o' the big oak linen-chest, at the back: not as I should trust anybody to look 'em out but myself."

As Mrs. Tulliver uttered the last sentence, she drew a bright bunch of keys from her pocket, and singled out one, rubbing her thumb and finger up and down it with a placid smile while she looked at the clear fire. If Mr. Tulliver had been a susceptible man in his conjugal relation, he might have supposed that she drew out the key to aid her imagination in anticipating the moment when he would be in a state to justify the production of the best Holland sheets. Happily he was not so; he was only susceptible in respect of his right to water-power; moreover, he had the marital habit of not listening very closely, and, since his mention of Mr. Riley, had been apparently occupied in a tactile examination of his woollen stockings.

"I think I've hit it, Bessy," was his first remark after a short silence. "Riley's as likely a man as any to know o' some school; he's had schooling himself, an' goes about to all sorts o' places—arbitratin' and vallyin'

and that. And we shall have time to talk it over to-morrow night when
the business is done. I want Tom to be such a sort o' man as Riley, you
know—as can talk pretty nigh as well as if it was all wrote out for him,
and knows a good lot o' words as don't mean much, so as you can't lay
hold of 'em i' law; and a good solid knowledge o' business too."

"Well," said Mrs. Tulliver, "so far as talking proper, and knowing
everything, and walking with a bend in his back, and setting his hair
up, I shouldn't mind the lad being brought up to that. But them fine-
talking men from the big towns mostly wear the false shirt-fronts; they
wear a frill till it's all a mess, and then hide it with a bib; I know Riley
does. And then, if Tom's to go and live at Mudport, like Riley, he'll have
a house with a kitchen hardly big enough to turn in, an' niver get a
fresh egg for his breakfast, an' sleep up three pair o' stairs—or four, for
what I know—an' be burnt to death before he can get down."

"No, no," said Mr. Tulliver, "I've no thoughts of his going to Mudport: I mean him to set up his office at St. Ogg's, close by us, an' live
at home. But," continued Mr. Tulliver after a pause, "what I'm a bit
afraid on is, as Tom hasn't got the right sort o' brains for a smart fellow. I doubt he's a bit slowish. He takes after your family, Bessy."

"Yes, that he does," said Mrs. Tulliver, accepting the last proposition
entirely on its own merits; "he's wonderful for liking a deal o' salt in
his broth. That was my brother's way, and my father's before him."

"It seems a bit of a pity, though," said Mr. Tulliver, "as the lad
should take after the mother's side i'stead o' the little wench. That's the
worst on't wi' the crossing o' breeds: you can never justly calkilate
what'll come on't. The little un takes after my side, now: she's twice as
'cute as Tom. Too 'cute for a woman, I'm afraid," continued Mr. Tulliver, turning his head dubiously first on one side and then on the other.
"It's no mischief much while she's a little un, but an o'er-'cute woman's
no better nor a long-tailed sheep—she'll fetch none the bigger price for
that."

"Yes, it *is* a mischief while she's a little un, Mr. Tulliver, for it all
runs to naughtiness. How to keep her in a clean pinafore two hours
together passes my cunning. An' now you put me i' mind," continued
Mrs. Tulliver, rising and going to the window, "I don't know where
she is now, an' it's pretty nigh tea-time. Ah, I thought so—wanderin'
up an' down by the water, like a wild thing: she'll tumble in some day."

Mrs. Tulliver rapped the window sharply, beckoned, and shook her
head,—a process which she repeated more than once before she returned
to her chair.

"You talk o' 'cuteness, Mr. Tulliver," she observed as she sat down,
"but I'm sure the child's half an idiot i' some things; for if I send her
up-stairs to fetch anything, she forgets what she's gone for, an' perhaps
'ull sit down on the floor i' the sunshine an' plait her hair an' sing to
herself like a Bedlam creatur', all the while I'm waiting for her down-
stairs. That niver run i' my family, thank God, no more nor a brown

skin as makes her look like a mulatter. I don't like to fly i' the face o'
Providence, but it seems hard as I should have but one gell, an' her so
comical."

"Pooh, nonsense!" said Mr. Tulliver, "she's a straight black-eyed
wench as anybody need wish to see. I don't know i' what she's behind
other folks's children; and she can read almost as well as the parson."

"But her hair won't curl all I can do with it, and she's so franzy about
having it put i' paper, and I've such work as never was to make her
stand and have it pinched with th' irons."

"Cut it off—cut it off short," said the father, rashly.

"How can you talk so, Mr. Tulliver? She's too big a gell, gone nine,
and tall of her age, to have her hair cut short; an' there's her cousin
Lucy's got a row o' curls round her head, an' not a hair out o' place.
It seems hard as my sister Deane should have that pretty child; I'm
sure Lucy takes more after me nor my own child does. Maggie, Maggie,"
continued the mother, in a tone of half-coaxing fretfulness, as this small
mistake of nature entered the room, "where's the use o' my telling you
to keep away from the water? You'll tumble in and be drownded some
day, an' then you'll be sorry you didn't do as mother told you."

Maggie's hair, as she threw off her bonnet, painfully confirmed her
mother's accusation: Mrs. Tulliver, desiring her daughter to have a
curled crop, "like other folks's children," had had it cut too short in
front to be pushed behind the ears; and as it was usually straight an
hour after it had been taken out of paper, Maggie was incessantly tossing her head to keep the dark heavy locks out of her gleaming black
eyes—an action which gave her very much the air of a small Shetland
pony.

"O dear, O dear, Maggie, what are you thinkin' of, to throw your
bonnet down there? Take it up-stairs, there's a good gell, an' let your
hair be brushed, an' put your other pinafore on, an' change your shoes
—do, for shame; an' come an' go on with your patchwork, like a little
lady."

"O, mother," said Maggie, in a vehemently cross tone, "I don't *want*
to do my patchwork."

"What! not your pretty patchwork, to make a counterpane for your
aunt Glegg?"

"It's foolish work," said Maggie, with a toss of her mane,—"tearing
things to pieces to sew 'em together again. And I don't want to do anything for my aunt Glegg—I don't like her."

Exit Maggie, dragging her bonnet by the string, while Mr. Tulliver
laughs audibly.

"I wonder at you, as you'll laugh at her, Mr. Tulliver," said the
mother, with feeble fretfulness in her tone. "You encourage her i'
naughtiness. An' her aunts will have it as it's me spoils her."

Mrs. Tulliver was what is called a good-tempered person—never
cried, when she was a baby, on any slighter ground than hunger and
pins; and from the cradle upwards had been healthy, fair, plump, and

dull-witted; in short, the flower of her family for beauty and amiability. But milk and mildness are not the best things for keeping, and when they turn only a little sour, they may disagree with young stomachs seriously. I have often wondered whether those early Madonnas of Raphael, with the blond faces and somewhat stupid expression, kept their placidity undisturbed when their strong-limbed, strong-willed boys got a little too old to do without clothing. I think they must have been given to feeble remonstrance, getting more and more peevish as it became more and more ineffectual.

CHAPTER III

MR. RILEY GIVES HIS ADVICE CONCERNING A SCHOOL FOR TOM

THE gentleman in the ample white cravat and shirt-frill, taking his brandy-and-water so pleasantly with his good friend Tulliver, is Mr. Riley, a gentleman with a waxen complexion and fat hands, rather highly educated for an auctioneer and appraiser, but large-hearted enough to show a great deal of *bonhommie* towards simple country acquaintances of hospitable habits. Mr. Riley spoke of such acquaintances kindly as "people of the old school."

The conversation had come to a pause. Mr. Tulliver, not without a particular reason, had abstained from a seventh recital of the cool retort by which Riley had shown himself too many for Dix, and how Wakem had had his comb cut for once in his life, now the business of the dam had been settled by arbitration, and how there never would have been any dispute at all about the height of water if everybody was what they should be, and Old Harry hadn't made the lawyers. Mr. Tulliver was on the whole a man of safe traditional opinions; but on one or two points he had trusted to his unassisted intellect, and had arrived at several questionable conclusions; among the rest, that rats, weevils, and lawyers were created by Old Harry. Unhappily he had no one to tell him that this was rampant Manichæism, else he might have seen his error. But to-day it was clear that the good principle was triumphant: this affair of the water-power had been a tangled business somehow, for all it seemed—look at it one way—as plain as water's water; but, big a puzzle as it was, it hadn't got the better of Riley. Mr. Tulliver took his brandy-and-water a little stronger than usual, and, for a man who might be supposed to have a few hundreds lying idle at his banker's, was rather incautiously open in expressing his high estimate of his friend's business talents.

But the dam was a subject of conversation that would keep; it could always be taken up again at the same point, and exactly in the same condition; and there was another subject, as you know, on which Mr. Tulliver was in pressing want of Mr. Riley's advice. This was his particular reason for remaining silent for a short space after his last draught, and rubbing his knees in a meditative manner. He was not a man to make an abrupt transition. This was a puzzling world, as he often said, and if you drive your waggon in a hurry, you may light on an awkward corner. Mr. Riley, meanwhile, was not impatient. Why should he be? Even Hotspur, one would think, must have been patient in his slippers on a warm hearth, taking copious snuff, and sipping gratuitous brandy-and-water.

"There's a thing I've got i' my head," said Mr. Tulliver at last, in rather a lower tone than usual, as he turned his head and looked stead-fastly at his companion.

"Ah!" said Mr. Riley, in a tone of mild interest. He was a man with heavy waxen eyelids and high-arched eyebrows, looking exactly the same under all circumstances. This immovability of face, and the habit of taking a pinch of snuff before he gave an answer, made him trebly oracular to Mr. Tulliver.

"It's a very particular thing," he went on; "it's about my boy Tom."

At the sound of this name, Maggie, who was seated on a low stool close by the fire, with a large book open on her lap, shook her heavy hair back and looked up eagerly. There were few sounds that roused Maggie when she was dreaming over her book, but Tom's name served as well as the shrillest whistle: in an instant she was on the watch, with gleaming eyes, like a Skye terrier suspecting mischief, or at all events determined to fly at any one who threatened it towards Tom.

"You see, I want to put him to a new school at Midsummer," said Mr. Tulliver; "he's comin' away from the 'cademy at Ladyday, an' I shall let him run loose for a quarter; but after that I want to send him to a downright good school, where they'll make a scholard of him."

"Well," said Mr. Riley, "there's no greater advantage you can give him than a good education. Not," he added, with polite significance, "not that a man can't be an excellent miller and farmer, and a shrewd sensible fellow into the bargain, without much help from the school-master."

"I believe you," said Mr. Tulliver, winking, and turning his head on one side, "but that's where it is. I don't *mean* Tom to be a miller and farmer. I see no fun i' that: why, if I made him a miller an' farmer, he'd be expectin' to take to the mill an' the land, an' a-hinting at me as it was time for me to lay by an' think o' my latter end. Nay, nay, I've seen enough o' that wi' sons. I'll niver pull my coat off before I go to bed. I shall give Tom an eddication an' put him to a business, as he may make a nest for himself, an' not want to push me out o' mine. Pretty well if he gets it when I'm dead an' gone. I shan't be put off wi' spoon-meat afore I've lost my teeth."

This was evidently a point on which Mr. Tulliver felt strongly, and the impetus which had given unusual rapidity and emphasis to his speech, showed itself still unexhausted for some minutes afterwards in a defiant motion of the head from side to side, and an occasional "Nay, nay," like a subsiding growl.

These angry symptoms were keenly observed by Maggie, and cut her to the quick. Tom, it appeared, was supposed capable of turning his father out of doors, and of making the future in some way tragic by his wickedness. This was not to be borne; and Maggie jumped up from her stool, forgetting all about her heavy book, which fell with a bang within the fender; and going up between her father's knees, said, in a half-crying, half-indignant voice—

"Father, Tom wouldn't be naughty to you ever; I know he wouldn't."

Mrs. Tulliver was out of the room superintending a choice supper-dish, and Mr. Tulliver's heart was touched; so Maggie was not scolded about the book. Mr. Riley quietly picked it up and looked at it, while the father laughed with a certain tenderness in his hard-lined face, and patted his little girl on the back, and then held her hands and kept her between his knees.

"What! they mustn't say any harm o' Tom, eh?" said Mr. Tulliver, looking at Maggie with a twinkling eye. Then, in a lower voice, turning to Mr. Riley, as though Maggie couldn't hear, "She understands what one's talking about so as never was. And you should hear her read—straight off, as if she knowed it all beforehand. And allays at her book! But it's bad—it's bad," Mr. Tulliver added, sadly, checking this blam-able exultation; "a woman's no business wi' being so clever; it'll turn to trouble, I doubt. But, bless you!"—here the exultation was clearly recovering the mastery—"she'll read the books and understand 'em better nor half the folks as are growed up."

Maggie's cheeks began to flush with triumphant excitement: she thought Mr. Riley would have a respect for her now; it had been evident that he thought nothing of her before.

Mr. Riley was turning over the leaves of the book, and she could make nothing of his face, with its high-arched eyebrows; but he presently looked at her and said,

"Come, come and tell me something about this book; here are some pictures—I want to know what they mean."

Maggie with deepening colour went without hesitation to Mr. Riley's elbow and looked over the book, eagerly seizing one corner and tossing back her mane, while she said,

"O, I'll tell you what that means. It's a dreadful picture, isn't it? But I can't help looking at it. That old woman in the water's a witch —they've put her in to find out whether she's a witch or no, and if she swims she's a witch, and if she's drowned—and killed, you know— she's innocent, and not a witch, but only a poor silly old woman. But what good would it do her then, you know, when she was drowned? Only, I suppose, she'd go to heaven, and God would make it up to her. And this dreadful blacksmith with his arms akimbo, laughing—oh, isn't he ugly?—I'll tell you what he is. He's the devil *really*" (here Maggie's voice became louder and more emphatic), "and not a right blacksmith; for the devil takes the shape of wicked men, and walks about and sets people doing wicked things, and he's oftener in the shape of a bad man than any other, because, you know, if people saw he was the devil, and he roared at 'em, they'd run away, and he couldn't make 'em do what he pleased."

Mr. Tulliver had listened to this exposition of Maggie's with petrifying wonder.

"Why, what book is it the wench has got hold on?" he burst out, at last.

" 'The History of the Devil,' by Daniel Defoe; not quite the right book for a little girl," said Mr. Riley. "How came it among your books, Tulliver?"

Maggie looked hurt and discouraged, while her father said,

"Why, it's one o' the books I bought at Partridge's sale. They was all bound alike—it's a good binding, you see—and I thought they'd be all good books. There's Jeremy Taylor's 'Holy Living and Dying' among 'em; I read in it often of a Sunday" (Mr. Tulliver felt somehow a familiarity with that great writer because his name was Jeremy); "and there's a lot more of 'em, sermons mostly, I think; but they've all got the same covers, and I thought they were all o' one sample, as you may say. But it seems one mustn't judge by th' outside. This is a puzzlin' world."

"Well," said Mr. Riley, in an admonitory patronising tone, as he patted Maggie on the head, "I advise you to put by the 'History of the Devil,' and read some prettier book. Have you no prettier books?"

"O, yes," said Maggie, reviving a little in the desire to vindicate the variety of her reading, "I know the reading in this book isn't pretty—but I like the pictures, and I make stories to the pictures out of my own head, you know. But I've got 'Æsop's Fables,' and a book about kangaroos and things, and the 'Pilgrim's Progress' " . . .

"Ah, a beautiful book," said Mr. Riley; "you can't read a better."

"Well, but there's a great deal about the devil in that," said Maggie, triumphantly, "and I'll show you the picture of him in his true shape, as he fought with Christian."

Maggie ran in an instant to the corner of the room, jumped on a chair, and reached down from the small bookcase a shabby old copy of Bunyan, which opened at once, without the least trouble of search, at the picture she wanted.

"Here he is," she said, running back to Mr. Riley, "and Tom coloured him for me with his paints when he was at home last holidays—the body all black, you know, and the eyes red, like fire, because he's all fire inside, and it shines out at his eyes."

"Go, go!" said Mr. Tulliver, peremptorily, beginning to feel rather uncomfortable at these free remarks on the personal appearance of a being powerful enough to create lawyers; "shut up the book, and let's hear no more o' such talk. It is as I thought—the child 'ull learn more mischief nor good wi' the books. Go, go and see after your mother."

Maggie shut up the book at once, with a sense of disgrace, but not being inclined to see after her mother, she compromised the matter by going into a dark corner behind her father's chair, and nursing her doll, towards which she had an occasional fit of fondness in Tom's absence, neglecting its toilette, but lavishing so many warm kisses on it that the waxen cheeks had a wasted unhealthy appearance.

"Did you ever hear the like on 't?" said Mr. Tulliver, as Maggie retired. "It's a pity but what she'd been the lad—she'd ha' been a match for the lawyers, *she* would. It's the wonderful'st thing"—here he lowered his voice—"as I picked the mother because she wasn't o'er 'cute—bein' a good-looking woman too, an' come of a rare family for managing; but I picked her from her sisters o' purpose, 'cause she was a bit weak, like; for I wasn't a-goin' to be told the rights o' things by my own fireside. But you see, when a man's got brains himself, there's no knowing where they'll run to; an' a pleasant sort o' soft woman may go on breeding you stupid lads and 'cute wenches, till it's like as if the world was turned topsy-turvy. It's an uncommon puzzlin' thing."

Mr. Riley's gravity gave way, and he shook a little under the application of his pinch of snuff, before he said—

"But your lad's not stupid, is he? I saw him, when I was here last, busy making fishing-tackle; he seemed quite up to it."

"Well, he isn't not to say stupid—he's got a notion o' things out o' door, an' a sort o' common-sense, as he'd lay hold o' things by the right handle. But he's slow with his tongue, you see, and he reads but poorly, and can't abide the books, and spells all wrong, they tell me, an' as shy as can be wi' strangers, an' you never hear him say 'cute things like the little wench. Now, what I want is to send him to a school where they'll make him a bit nimble with his tongue and his pen, and make a smart chap of him. I want my son to be even wi' these fellows as have got the start o' me with having better schooling. Not but what, if the world had been left as God made it, I could ha' seen my way, and held my own wi' the best of 'em; but things have got so twisted round and wrapped up i' unreasonable words, as arn't a bit like 'em, as I'm clean at fault, often an' often. Everything winds about so—the more straightforrard you are, the more you're puzzled."

Mr. Tulliver took a draught, swallowed it slowly, and shook his head in a melancholy manner, conscious of exemplifying the truth that a perfectly sane intellect is hardly at home in this insane world.

"You're quite in the right of it, Tulliver," observed Mr. Riley. "Better spend an extra hundred or two on your son's education, than leave it him in your will. I know I should have tried to do so by a son of mine, if I'd had one, though, God knows, I haven't your ready-money to play with, Tulliver; and I have a houseful of daughters into the bargain."

"I daresay, now, you know of a school as 'ud be just the thing for Tom," said Mr. Tulliver, not diverted from his purpose by any sympathy with Mr. Riley's deficiency of ready cash.

Mr. Riley took a pinch of snuff, and kept Mr. Tulliver in suspense by a silence that seemed deliberative, before he said—

"I know of a very fine chance for any one that's got the necessary money, and that's what you have, Tulliver. The fact is, I wouldn't recommend any friend of mine to send a boy to a regular school, if he could afford to do better. But if any one wanted his boy to get superior instruction and training, where he would be the companion of his master, and that master a first-rate fellow—I know his man. I wouldn't mention the chance to everybody, because I don't think everybody would succeed in getting it, if he were to try; but I mention it to you, Tulliver—between ourselves."

The fixed inquiring glance with which Mr. Tulliver had been watching his friend's oracular face became quite eager.

"Ay, now, let's hear," he said, adjusting himself in his chair with the complacency of a person who is thought worthy of important communications.

"He's an Oxford man," said Mr. Riley, sententiously, shutting his mouth close, and looking at Mr. Tulliver to observe the effect of this stimulating information.

"What! a parson?" said Mr. Tulliver, rather doubtfully.

"Yes—and an M.A. The bishop, I understand, thinks very highly of him: why, it was the bishop who got him his present curacy."

"Ah?" said Mr. Tulliver, to whom one thing was as wonderful as another concerning these unfamiliar phenomena. "But what can he want wi' Tom, then?"

"Why, the fact is, he's fond of teaching, and wishes to keep up his studies, and a clergyman has but little opportunity for that in his parochial duties. He's willing to take one or two boys as pupils to fill up his time profitably. The boys would be quite of the family—the finest thing in the world for them; under Stelling's eye continually."

"But do you think they'd give the poor lad twice o' pudding?" said Mrs. Tulliver, who was now in her place again. "He's such a boy for pudding as never was; an' a growing boy like that—it's dreadful to think o' their stintin' him."

"And what money 'ud he want?" said Mr. Tulliver, whose instinct told him that the services of this admirable M.A. would bear a high price.

"Why, I know of a clergyman who asks a hundred and fifty with his youngest pupils, and he's not to be mentioned with Stelling, the man I speak of. I know, on good authority, that one of the chief people at Oxford said, 'Stelling might get the highest honours if he chose.' But he didn't care about university honours. He's a quiet man—not noisy."

"Ah, a deal better—a deal better," said Mr. Tulliver; "but a hundred and fifty's an uncommon price. I never thought o' payin' so much as that."

"A good education, let me tell you, Tulliver—a good education is cheap at the money. But Stelling is moderate in his terms—he's not a grasping man. I've no doubt he'd take your boy at a hundred, and that's what you wouldn't get many other clergymen to do. I'll write to him about it, if you like."

Mr. Tulliver rubbed his knees, and looked at the carpet in a meditative manner.

"But belike he's a bachelor," observed Mrs. Tulliver in the interval, "an' I've no opinion o' housekeepers. There was my brother, as is dead an' gone, had a housekeeper once, an' she took half the feathers out o' the best bed, an' packed 'em up an' sent 'em away. An' it's unknown the linen she made away with—Stott her name was. It 'ud break my heart to send Tom where there's a housekeeper, an' I hope you won't think of it, Mr. Tulliver."

"You may set your mind at rest on that score, Mrs. Tulliver," said Mr. Riley, "for Stelling is married to as nice a little woman as any man need wish for a wife. There isn't a kinder little soul in the world; I know her family well. She has very much your complexion—light curly hair. She comes of a good Mudport family, and it's not every offer that would have been acceptable in that quarter. But Stelling's not an everyday man. Rather a particular fellow as to the people he chooses to be connected with. But I *think* he would have no objection to take your son—I *think* he would not, on my representation."

"I don't know what he could have *against* the lad," said Mrs. Tulliver, with a slight touch of motherly indignation, "a nice fresh-skinned lad as anybody need wish to see."

"But there's one thing I'm thinking on," said Mr. Tulliver, turning his head on one side and looking at Mr. Riley, after a long perusal of the carpet. "Wouldn't a parson be almost too high-learnt to bring up a lad to be a man o' business? My notion o' the parsons was as they'd got a sort o' learning as lay mostly out o' sight. And that isn't what I want for Tom. I want him to know figures, and write like print, and see into things quick, and know what folks mean, and how to wrap things up in words as aren't actionable. It's an uncommon fine thing, that is," concluded Mr. Tulliver, shaking his head, "when you can let a man know what you think of him without paying for it."

"O, my dear Tulliver," said Mr. Riley, "you're quite under a mistake about the clergy; all the best schoolmasters are of the clergy. The schoolmasters who are not clergymen, are a very low set of men generally" . . .

"Ay, that Jacobs is, at the 'cademy," interposed Mr. Tulliver.

"To be sure—men who have failed in other trades, most likely. Now a clergyman is a gentleman by profession and education; and besides that, he has the knowledge that will ground a boy, and prepare him for entering on any career with credit. There may be some clergymen who are mere book-men; but you may depend upon it, Stelling is not one of them—a man that's wide awake, let me tell you. Drop him a hint, and that's enough. You talk of figures, now; you have only to say to Stelling, 'I want my son to be a thorough arithmetician,' and you may leave the rest to him."

Mr. Riley paused a moment, while Mr. Tulliver, somewhat reassured as to clerical tutorship, was inwardly rehearsing to an imaginary Mr. Stelling the statement, "I want my son to know 'rethmetic."

"You see, my dear Tulliver," Mr. Riley continued, "when you get a thoroughly educated man, like Stelling, he's at no loss to take up any branch of instruction. When a workman knows the use of his tools, he can make a door as well as a window."

"Ay, that's true," said Mr. Tulliver, almost convinced now that the clergy must be the best of schoolmasters.

"Well, I'll tell you what I'll do for you," said Mr. Riley, "and I wouldn't do it for everybody. I'll see Stelling's father-in-law, or drop him a line when I get back to Brassing, to say that you wish to place your boy with his son-in-law, and I daresay Stelling will write to you, and send you his terms."

"But there's no hurry, is there?" said Mrs. Tulliver; "for I hope, Mr. Tulliver, you won't let Tom begin at his new school before Midsummer. He began at the 'cademy at the Ladyday quarter, and you see what good's come of it."

"Ay, ay, Bessy, never brew wi' bad malt upo' Michaelmas day, else you'll have a poor tap," said Mr. Tulliver, winking and smiling at Mr. Riley with the natural pride of a man who has a buxom wife conspicuously his inferior in intellect. "But it's true there's no hurry—you've hit it there, Bessy."

"It might be as well not to defer the arrangement too long," said Mr. Riley, quietly, "for Stelling may have propositions from other parties, and I know he would not take more than two or three boarders, if so many. If I were you, I think I would enter on the subject with Stelling at once: there's no necessity for sending the boy before Midsummer, but I would be on the safe side, and make sure that nobody forestalls you."

"Ay, there's summat in that," said Mr. Tulliver.

"Father," broke in Maggie, who had stolen unperceived to her father's elbow again, listening with parted lips, while she held her doll topsy-turvy, and crushed its nose against the wood of the chair—"Father, is it a long way off where Tom is to go? shan't we ever go to see him?"

"I don't know, my wench," said the father, tenderly. "Ask Mr. Riley; he knows."

Maggie came round promptly in front of Mr. Riley, and said, "How far is it, please sir?"

"O, a long long way off," that gentleman answered, being of opinion that children, when they are not naughty, should always be spoken to jocosely. "You must borrow the seven-leagued boots to get to him."

"That's nonsense!" said Maggie, tossing her head haughtily, and turning away with the tears springing in her eyes. She began to dislike

Mr. Riley: it was evident he thought her silly and of no consequence.

"Hush, Maggie, for shame of you, asking questions and chattering," said her mother. "Come and sit down on your little stool and hold your tongue, do. But," added Mrs. Tulliver, who had her own alarm awakened, "is it so far off as I couldn't wash him and mend him?"

"About fifteen miles, that's all," said Mr. Riley. "You can drive there and back in a day quite comfortably. Or—Stelling is a hospitable, pleasant man—he'd be glad to have you stay."

"But it's too far off for the linen, I doubt," said Mrs. Tulliver, sadly.

The entrance of supper opportunely adjourned this difficulty, and relieved Mr. Riley from the labour of suggesting some solution or compromise—a labour which he would otherwise doubtless have undertaken; for, as you perceive, he was a man of very obliging manners. And he had really given himself the trouble of recommending Mr. Stelling to his friend Tulliver without any positive expectation of a solid, definite advantage resulting to himself, notwithstanding the subtle indications to the contrary which might have misled a too sagacious observer. For there is nothing more widely misleading than sagacity if it happens to get on a wrong scent; and sagacity persuaded that men usually act and speak from distinct motives, with a consciously proposed end in view, is certain to waste its energies on imaginary game. Plotting covetousness and deliberate contrivance, in order to compass a selfish end, are nowhere abundant but in the world of the dramatist: they demand too intense a mental action for many of our fellow-parishioners to be guilty of them. It is easy enough to spoil the lives of our neighbours without taking so much trouble: we can do it by lazy acquiescence and lazy omission, by trivial falsities for which we hardly know a reason, by small frauds neutralised by small extravagancies, by maladroit flatteries, and clumsily improvised insinuations. We live from hand to mouth, most of us, with a small family of immediate desires—we do little else than snatch a morsel to satisfy the hungry brood, rarely thinking of seed-corn or the next year's crop.

Mr. Riley was a man of business, and not cold towards his own interest, yet even he was more under the influence of small promptings than of far-sighted designs. He had no private understanding with the Rev. Walter Stelling; on the contrary, he knew very little of that M.A. and his acquirements—not quite enough perhaps to warrant so strong a recommendation of him as he had given to his friend Tulliver. But he believed Mr. Stelling to be an excellent classic, for Gadsby had said so, and Gadsby's first cousin was an Oxford tutor; which was better ground for the belief even than his own immediate observation would have been, for though Mr. Riley had received a tincture of the classics at the great Mudport Free School, and had a sense of understanding Latin generally, his comprehension of any particular Latin was not ready. Doubtless there remained a subtle aroma from his juvenile contact with the *De Senectute* and the Fourth Book of the *Æneid*, but it had ceased to be distinctly recognisable as classical, and was only perceived in the higher finish and force of his auctioneering style. Then, Stelling was an Oxford man, and the Oxford men were always—no, no, it was the Cambridge men who were always good mathematicians. But a man who had had a university education could teach anything he likes; especially a man like Stelling, who had made a speech at a Mudport dinner on a political occasion, and had acquitted himself so well that it was generally remarked, this son-in-law of Timpson's was a sharp fellow. It was to be expected of a Mudport man, from the parish of St. Ursula, that he would not omit to do a good turn to a son-in-law of Timpson's, for Timpson was one of the most useful and influential men in the parish, and had a good deal of business, which he knew how to put into the right hands. Mr. Riley liked such men, quite apart from any money which might be diverted, through their good judgment, from less worthy pockets into his own; and it would be a satisfaction to him to say to Timpson on his return home, "I've secured a good pupil for your son-in-law." Timpson had a large family of daughters; Mr. Riley felt for him: besides, Louisa Timpson's face, with its light curls, had been a familiar object to him over the pew wainscot on a Sunday for nearly fifteen years;—it was natural her husband should be a commendable tutor. Moreover, Mr. Riley knew of no other schoolmaster whom he had any ground for recommending in preference: why then should he not recommend Stelling? His friend Tulliver had asked him for an opinion: it is always chilling, in friendly intercourse, to say you have no opinion to give. And if you deliver an opinion at all, it is mere stupidity not to do it with an air of conviction and well-founded knowledge. You make it your own in uttering it, and naturally get fond of it. Thus, Mr. Riley, knowing no harm of Stelling to begin with, and wishing him well, so far as he had any wishes at all concerning him, had no sooner recommended him than he began to think with admiration of a man recommended on such high authority, and would soon have gathered so warm an interest on the subject, that if Mr. Tulliver had in the end declined to send Tom to Stelling, Mr. Riley would have thought his friend of the old school a thoroughly pig-headed fellow.

If you blame Mr. Riley very severely for giving a recommendation on such slight grounds, I must say you are rather hard upon him. Why should an auctioneer and appraiser thirty years ago, who had as good as forgotten his free-school Latin, be expected to manifest a delicate scrupulosity which is not always exhibited by gentlemen of the learned professions, even in our present advanced stage of morality?

Besides, a man with the milk of human kindness in him can scarcely abstain from doing a good-natured action, and one cannot be good-natured all round. Nature herself occasionally quarters an inconvenient parasite on an animal towards whom she has otherwise no ill-will. What then? We admire her care for the parasite. If Mr. Riley had shrunk from giving a recommendation that was not based on valid evidence, he would not have helped Mr. Stelling to a paying pupil, and that would not have been so well for the reverend gentleman. Consider, too, that all the pleasant little dim ideas and complacencies—of standing well with Timpson, of dispensing advice when he was asked for it, of impressing his friend Tulliver with additional respect, of saying something, and saying it emphatically, with other inappreciably minute ingredients that went along with the warm hearth and the brandy-and-water to make up Mr. Riley's consciousness on this occasion—would have been a mere blank.

CHAPTER IV

TOM IS EXPECTED

It was a heavy disappointment to Maggie that she was not allowed to go with her father in the gig when he went to fetch Tom home from the academy; but the morning was too wet, Mrs. Tulliver said, for a little girl to go out in her best bonnet. Maggie took the opposite view very strongly, and it was a direct consequence of this difference of opinion that when her mother was in the act of brushing out the reluctant black crop, Maggie suddenly rushed from under her hands and dipped her head in a basin of water standing near—in the vindictive determination that there should be no more chance of curls that day.

"Maggie, Maggie," exclaimed Mrs. Tulliver, sitting stout and helpless with the brushes on her lap, "what is to become of you if you're so naughty? I'll tell your aunt Glegg and your aunt Pullet when they come next week, and they'll never love you any more. O dear, O dear! look at your clean pinafore, wet from top to bottom. Folks 'ull think it's a judgment on me as I've got such a child—they'll think I've done summat wicked."

Before this remonstrance was finished, Maggie was already out of hearing, making her way towards the great attic that ran under the old high-pitched roof, shaking the water from her black locks as she ran, like a Skye terrier escaped from his bath. This attic was Maggie's favourite retreat on a wet day, when the weather was not too cold; here she fretted out all her ill-humours, and talked aloud to the worm-eaten floors and the worm-eaten shelves, and the dark rafters festooned with cobwebs; and here she kept a Fetish which she punished for all her misfortunes. This was the trunk of a large wooden doll, which once stared with the roundest of eyes above the reddest of cheeks; but was now entirely defaced by a long career of vicarious suffering. Three nails driven into the head commemorated as many crises in Maggie's nine years of earthly struggle; that luxury of vengeance having been suggested to her by the picture of Jael destroying Sisera in the old Bible. The last nail had been driven in with a fiercer stroke than usual, for the Fetish on that occasion represented aunt Glegg. But immediately afterwards Maggie had reflected that if she drove many nails in, she would not be so well able to fancy that the head was hurt when she knocked it against the wall, nor to comfort it, and make believe to poultice it, when her fury was abated; for even aunt Glegg would be pitiable when she had been hurt very much, and thoroughly humiliated, so as to beg her niece's pardon. Since then she had driven no more nails in, but had soothed herself by alternately grinding and beating the wooden head against the rough brick of the great chimneys that made two square pillars supporting the roof. That was what she did this morning on reaching the attic, sobbing all the while with a passion that expelled every other form of consciousness—even the memory of the grievance that had caused it. As at last the sobs were getting quieter, and the grinding less fierce, a sudden beam of sunshine, falling through the wire lattice across the worm-eaten shelves, made her throw away the Fetish and run to the window. The sun was really breaking out; the sound of the mill seemed cheerful again; the granary doors were open; and there was Yap, the queer white-and-brown terrier, with one ear turned back, trotting about and sniffing vaguely as if he were in search of a companion. It was irresistible. Maggie tossed her hair back and ran down-stairs, seized her bonnet without putting it on, peeped, and then dashed along the passage lest she should encounter her mother, and was quickly out in the yard, whirling round like a Pythoness, and singing as she whirled, "Yap, Yap, Tom's coming home!" while Yap danced and barked round her, as much as to say, if there was any noise wanted he was the dog for it.

"Hegh, hegh, Miss, you'll make yourself giddy, an' tumble down i' the dirt," said Luke, the head miller, a tall broad-shouldered man of forty, black-eyed and black-haired, subdued by a general mealiness, like an auricula.

Maggie paused in her whirling and said, staggering a little, "O, no, it doesn't make me giddy, Luke; may I go into the mill with you?"

Maggie loved to linger in the great spaces of the mill, and often came out with her black hair powdered to a soft whiteness that made her dark eyes flash out with new fire. The resolute din, the unresting motion of the great stones, giving her a dim delicious awe as at the presence of an uncontrollable force—the meal for ever pouring, pouring—the fine white powder softening all surfaces, and making the very spider-nets look like a fairy lacework—the sweet pure scent of the meal—all helped to make Maggie feel that the mill was a little world apart from her outside everyday life. The spiders were especially a subject of speculation with her. She wondered if they had any relations outside the mill, for in that case there must be a painful difficulty in their family intercourse—a fat and floury spider, accustomed to take his fly well dusted with meal, must suffer a little at a cousin's table where the fly was *au naturel*, and the lady-spiders must be mutually shocked at each other's appearance. But the part of the mill she liked best was the topmost story—the corn-hutch, where there were the great heaps of grain, which she could sit on and slide down continually. She was in the habit of taking this recreation as she conversed with Luke, to whom she was very communicative, wishing him to think well of her understanding, as her father did.

Perhaps she felt it necessary to recover her position with him on the present occasion, for, as she sat sliding on the heap of grain near which he was busying himself, she said, at that shrill pitch which was requisite in mill-society—

"I think you never read any book but the Bible—did you, Luke?"

"Nay, Miss—an' not much o' that," said Luke, with great frankness. "I'm no reader, I arn't."

"But if I lent you one of my books, Luke? I've not got any *very* pretty books that would be easy for you to read; but there's 'Pug's Tour of Europe'—that would tell you all about the different sorts of people in the world, and if you didn't understand the reading, the pictures would help you—they show the looks and ways of the people, and what they do. There are the Dutchmen, very fat, and smoking, you know—and one sitting on a barrel."

"Nay, Miss, I'n no opinion o' Dutchmen. There ben't much good i' knowin' about *them*."

"But they're our fellow-creatures, Luke—we ought to know about our fellow-creatures."

"Not much o' fellow-creaturs, I think, Miss; all I know—my old master, as war a knowin' man, used to say, says he, 'If e'er I sow my wheat wi'out brinin', I'm a Dutchman,' says he; an' that war as much as to say as a Dutchman war a fool, or next door. Nay, nay, I arn't goin' to bother mysen about Dutchmen. There's fools enoo—an' rogues enoo—wi'out lookin' i' books for em."

"O, well," said Maggie, rather foiled by Luke's unexpectedly decided views about Dutchmen, "perhaps you would like 'Animated Nature' better—that's not Dutchmen, you know, but elephants, and kangaroos, and the civet cat, and the sun-fish, and a bird sitting on its tail—I forget its name. There are countries full of those creatures, instead of horses and cows, you know. Shouldn't you like to know about them, Luke?"

"Nay, Miss, I'n got to keep count o' the flour an' corn—I can't do wi' knowin' so many things besides my work. That's what brings folks to the gallows—knowin' everything but what they'n got to get their bread by. An' they're mostly lies, I think, what's printed i' the books: them printed sheets are, anyhow, as the men cry i' the streets."

"Why, you're like my brother Tom, Luke," said Maggie, wishing to turn the conversation agreeably; "Tom's not fond of reading. I love Tom so dearly, Luke—better than anybody else in the world. When he grows up, I shall keep his house, and we shall always live together. I can tell him everything he doesn't know. But I think Tom's clever, for all he doesn't like books: he makes beautiful whipcord and rabbit-pens."

"Ah," said Luke, "but he'll be fine an' vexed, as the rabbits are all dead."

"Dead!" screamed Maggie, jumping up from her sliding seat on the corn. "O dear, Luke! What! the lop-eared one, and the spotted doe that Tom spent all his money to buy?"

"As dead as moles," said Luke, fetching his comparison from the un-mistakable corpses nailed to the stable-wall.

"O dear, Luke," said Maggie, in a piteous tone, while the big tears rolled down her cheek; "Tom told me to take care of 'em, and I forgot. What *shall* I do?"

"Well, you see, Miss, they were in that far tool-house, an' it was nobody's business to see to 'em. I reckon Master Tom told Harry to feed 'em, but there's no countin' on Harry—*he's* a offal creatur as iver come about the primises, he is. He remembers nothing but his own in-side—an' I wish it 'ud gripe him."

"O, Luke, Tom told me to be sure and remember the rabbits every day; but how could I, when they did not come into my head, you know? O, he will be so angry with me, I know he will, and so sorry about his rabbits—and so am I sorry. O, what *shall* I do?"

"Don't you fret, Miss," said Luke, soothingly, "they're nash things, them lop-eared rabbits—they'd happen ha' died, if they'd been fed. Things out o' natur niver thrive: God A'mighty doesn't like 'em. He made the rabbits' ears to lie back, an' it's nothin' but contrairiness to make 'em hing down like a mastiff dog's. Master Tom 'ull know better nor buy such things another time. Don't you fret, Miss. Will you come along home wi' me, and see my wife? I'm a-goin' this minute."

The invitation offered an agreeable distraction to Maggie's grief, and her tears gradually subsided as she trotted along by Luke's side to his pleasant cottage, which stood with its apple and pear trees, and with the added dignity of a lean-to pig-sty, close by the brink of the Ripple. Mrs. Moggs, Luke's wife, was a decidedly agreeable acquaintance. She exhibited her hospitality in bread and treacle, and possessed various works of art. Maggie actually forgot that she had any special cause of sadness this morning, as she stood on a chair to look at a remarkable series of pictures representing the Prodigal Son in the costume of Sir Charles Grandison, except that, as might have been expected from his defective moral character, he had not, like that accomplished hero, the taste and strength of mind to dispense with a wig. But the indefin-able weight the dead rabbits had left on her mind caused her to feel more than usual pity for the career of this weak young man, particu-larly when she looked at the picture where he leaned against a tree with a flaccid appearance, his knee-breeches unbuttoned and his wig awry, while the swine, apparently of some foreign breed, seemed to insult him by their good spirits over their feast of husks.

"I'm very glad his father took him back again—aren't you, Luke?" she said. "For he was very sorry, you know, and wouldn't do wrong again."

"Eh, Miss," said Luke, "he'd be no great shakes, I doubt, let's feyther do what he would for him."

That was a painful thought to Maggie, and she wished much that the subsequent history of the young man had not been left a blank.

CHAPTER V

TOM COMES HOME

Tom was to arrive early in the afternoon, and there was another fluttering heart besides Maggie's when it was late enough for the sound of the gig-wheels to be expected; for if Mrs. Tulliver had a strong feeling, it was fondness for her boy. At last the sound came—that quick light bowling of the gig-wheels—and in spite of the wind, which was blowing the clouds about, and was not likely to respect Mrs. Tulliver's curls and cap-strings, she came outside the door, and even held her hand on Maggie's offending head, forgetting all the griefs of the morning.

"There he is, my sweet lad! But, Lord ha' mercy! he's got never a collar on; it's been lost on the road, I'll be bound, and spoilt the set."

Mrs. Tulliver stood with her arms open; Maggie jumped first on one leg and then on the other; while Tom descended from the gig, and said, with masculine reticence as to the tender emotions, "Hallo! Yap—what! are you there?"

Nevertheless he submitted to be kissed willingly enough, though Maggie hung on his neck in rather a strangling fashion, while his blue-grey eyes wandered towards the croft and the lambs and the river, where he promised himself that he would begin to fish the first thing to-morrow morning. He was one of those lads that grow everywhere in England, and, at twelve or thirteen years of age, look as much alike as goslings:— a lad with light-brown hair, cheeks of cream and roses, full lips, indeterminate nose and eyebrows—a physiognomy in which it seems impossible to discern anything but the generic character of boyhood; as different as possible from poor Maggie's phiz, which Nature seemed to have moulded and coloured with the most decided intention. But that same Nature has the deep cunning which hides itself under the appearance of openness, so that simple people think they can see through her quite well, and all the while she is secretly preparing a refutation of their confident prophecies. Under these average boyish physiognomies that she seems to turn off by the gross, she conceals some of her most rigid, inflexible purposes, some of her most unmodifiable characters; and the dark-eyed, demonstrative, rebellious girl may after all turn out to be a passive being compared with this pink-and-white bit of masculinity with the indeterminate features.

"Maggie," said Tom, confidentially, taking her into a corner, as soon as his mother was gone out to examine his box, and the warm parlour had taken off the chill he had felt from the long drive, "you don't know what I've got in *my* pockets," nodding his head up and down as a means of rousing her sense of mystery.

"No," said Maggie. "How stodgy they look, Tom! Is it marls (marbles) or cobnuts?" Maggie's heart sank a little, because Tom always

415

said it was "no good" playing with *her* at those games—she played so badly.

"Marls! no; I've swopped all my marls with the little fellows, and cobnuts are no fun, you silly, only when the nuts are green. But see here!" He drew something half out of his right-hand pocket.

"What is it?" said Maggie, in a whisper. "I can see nothing but a bit of yellow."

"Why it's . . . a . . . new . . . guess, Maggie!"

"O, I *can't* guess, Tom," said Maggie, impatiently.

"Don't be a spitfire, else I won't tell you," said Tom, thrusting his hand back into his pocket, and looking determined.

"No, Tom," said Maggie, imploringly, laying hold of the arm that was held stiffly in the pocket. "I'm not cross, Tom; it was only because I can't bear guessing. *Please* be good to me."

Tom's arm slowly relaxed, and he said, "Well, then, it's a new fish-line—two new uns—one for you, Maggie, all to yourself. I wouldn't go halves in the toffee and gingerbread on purpose to save the money; and Gibson and Spouncer fought with me because I wouldn't. And here's hooks; see here! . . . I say, *won't* we go and fish to-morrow down by Round Pool? And you shall catch your own fish, Maggie, and put the worms on, and everything—won't it be fun?"

Maggie's answer was to throw her arms round Tom's neck and hug him, and hold her cheek against his without speaking, while he slowly unwound some of the line, saying, after a pause,

"Wasn't I a good brother, now, to buy you a line all to yourself? You know, I needn't have bought it, if I hadn't liked."

"Yes, very, very good. . . . I *do* love you, Tom."

Tom had put the line back in his pocket, and was looking at the hooks one by one, before he spoke again.

"And the fellows fought me, because I wouldn't give in about the toffee."

"O dear! I wish they wouldn't fight at your school, Tom. Didn't it hurt you?"

"Hurt me? No," said Tom, putting up the hooks again, taking out a large pocket-knife, and slowly opening the largest blade, which he looked at meditatively as he rubbed his finger along it. Then he added—

"I gave Spouncer a black eye, I know—that's what he got by wanting to leather *me;* I wasn't going to go halves because anybody leathered me."

"O, how brave you are, Tom! I think you're like Samson. If there came a lion roaring at me, I think you'd fight him—wouldn't you, Tom?"

"How can a lion come roaring at you, you silly thing? There's no lions, only in the shows."

"No; but if we were in the lion countries—I mean, in Africa, where it's very hot—the lions eat people there. I can show it you in the book where I read it."

"Well, I should get a gun and shoot him."

"But if you hadn't got a gun—we might have gone out, you know, not thinking—just as we go fishing; and then a great lion might run towards us roaring, and we couldn't get away from him. What should you do, Tom?"

Tom paused, and at last turned away contemptuously, saying, "But the lion *isn't* coming. What's the use of talking?"

"But I like to fancy how it would be," said Maggie, following him. "Just think what you would do, Tom."

"O, don't bother, Maggie! You're such a silly—I shall go and see my rabbits."

Maggie's heart began to flutter with fear. She dared not tell the sad truth at once, but she walked after Tom in trembling silence as he went out, thinking how she could tell him the news so as to soften at once his sorrow and his anger; for Maggie dreaded Tom's anger of all things —it was quite a different anger from her own.

"Tom," she said, timidly, when they were out of doors, "how much money did you give for your rabbits?"

"Two half-crowns and a sixpence," said Tom, promptly.

"I think I've got a great deal more than that in my steel purse upstairs. I'll ask mother to give it you."

"What for?" said Tom. "I don't want *your* money, you silly thing. I've got a great deal more money than you, because I'm a boy. I always have half-sovereigns and sovereigns for my Christmas boxes, because I shall be a man, and you only have five-shilling pieces, because you're only a girl."

"Well, but, Tom—if mother would let me give you two half-crowns and a sixpence out of my purse to put into your pocket and spend, you know; and buy some more rabbits with it?"

"More rabbits? I don't want any more."

"O, but Tom, they're all dead."

Tom stopped immediately in his walk and turned round towards Maggie. "You forgot to feed 'em, then, and Harry forgot?" he said, his colour heightening for a moment, but soon subsiding. "I'll pitch into Harry—I'll have him turned away. And I don't love you, Maggie. You shan't go fishing with me to-morrow. I told you to go and see the rabbits every day." He walked on again.

"Yes, but I forgot—and I couldn't help it, indeed, Tom. I'm so very sorry," said Maggie, while the tears rushed fast.

"You're a naughty girl," said Tom, severely, "and I'm sorry I bought you the fish-line. I don't love you."

"O, Tom, it's very cruel," sobbed Maggie. "I'd forgive you, if *you* forgot anything—I wouldn't mind what you did—I'd forgive you and love you."

"Yes, you're a silly—but I never *do* forget things—I don't."

"O, please forgive me, Tom; my heart will break," said Maggie, shaking with sobs, clinging to Tom's arm, and laying her wet cheek on his shoulder.

Tom shook her off, and stopped again, saying in a peremptory tone, "Now, Maggie, you just listen. Aren't I a good brother to you?"

"Ye-ye-es," sobbed Maggie, her chin rising and falling convulsedly.

"Didn't I think about your fish-line all this quarter, and mean to buy it, and saved my money o' purpose, and wouldn't go halves in the toffee, and Spouncer fought me because I wouldn't?"

"Ye-ye-es . . . and I . . . lo-lo-love you so, Tom."

"But you're a naughty girl. Last holidays you licked the paint off my lozenge-box, and the holidays before that you let the boat drag my fish-line down when I'd set you to watch it, and you pushed your head through my kite, all for nothing."

"But I didn't mean," said Maggie; "I couldn't help it."

"Yes, you could," said Tom, "if you'd minded what you were doing. And you're a naughty girl, and you shan't go fishing with me to-morrow."

With this terrible conclusion, Tom ran away from Maggie towards the mill, meaning to greet Luke there, and complain to him of Harry.

Maggie stood motionless, except from her sobs, for a minute or two; then she turned round and ran into the house, and up to her attic, where she sat on the floor, and laid her head against the worm-eaten shelf, with a crushing sense of misery. Tom was come home, and she had thought how happy she should be—and now he was cruel to her. What use was anything, if Tom didn't love her? O, he was very cruel! Hadn't she wanted to give him the money, and said how very sorry she was? She knew she was naughty to her mother, but she had never been naughty to Tom—had never *meant* to be naughty to him.

"O, he is cruel!" Maggie sobbed aloud, finding a wretched pleasure in the hollow resonance that came through the long empty space of the attic. She never thought of beating or grinding her Fetish; she was too miserable to be angry.

These bitter sorrows of childhood! when sorrow is all new and strange, when hope has not yet got wings to fly beyond the days and weeks, and the space from summer to summer seems measureless.

Maggie soon thought she had been hours in the attic, and it must be tea-time, and they were all having their tea, and not thinking of her. Well, then, she would stay up there and starve herself—hide herself behind the tub, and stay there all night; and then they would all be frightened, and Tom would be sorry. Thus Maggie thought in the pride of her heart, as she crept behind the tub; but presently she began to cry again at the idea that they didn't mind her being there. If she went down again to Tom now—would he forgive her?—perhaps her father would be there, and he would take her part. But, then, she wanted Tom to forgive her because he loved her, not because his father told him. No, she would never go down if Tom didn't come to fetch her. This resolution lasted in great intensity for five dark minutes behind the tub; but then the need of being loved, the strongest need in poor Maggie's nature, began to wrestle with her pride, and soon threw it. She crept from behind her tub into the twilight of the long attic, but just then she heard a quick footstep on the stairs.

Tom had been too much interested in his talk with Luke, in going the round of the premises, walking in and out where he pleased, and whittling sticks without any particular reason, except that he didn't whittle sticks at school, to think of Maggie and the effect his anger had produced on her. He meant to punish her, and that business having been performed, he occupied himself with other matters, like a practical person. But when he had been called in to tea, his father said, "Why, where's the little wench?" and Mrs. Tulliver, almost at the same moment, said, "Where's your little sister?"—both of them having supposed that Maggie and Tom had been together all the afternoon.

"I don't know," said Tom. He didn't want to "tell" of Maggie, though he was angry with her; for Tom Tulliver was a lad of honour.

"What! hasn't she been playing with you all this while?" said the father. "She'd been thinking o' nothing but your coming home."

"I haven't seen her this two hours," says Tom, commencing on the plumcake.

"Goodness heart! she's got drownded," exclaimed Mrs. Tulliver, rising from her seat and running to the window. "How could you let her do so?" she added, as became a fearful woman, accusing she didn't know whom of she didn't know what.

"Nay, nay, she's none drownded," said Mr. Tulliver. "You've been naughty to her, I doubt, Tom."

"I'm sure I haven't, father," said Tom, indignantly. "I think she's in the house."

"Perhaps up in that attic," said Mrs. Tulliver, "a-singing and talking to herself, and forgetting all about meal-times."

"You go and fetch her down, Tom," said Mr. Tulliver, rather sharply, his perspicacity or his fatherly fondness for Maggie making him suspect that the lad had been hard upon "the little un," else she would never have left his side. "And be good to her, do you hear? Else I'll let you know better."

Tom never disobeyed his father, for Mr. Tulliver was a peremptory man, and, as he said, would never let anybody get hold of his whip-hand; but he went out rather sullenly, carrying his piece of plumcake, and not intending to reprieve Maggie's punishment, which was no more than she deserved. Tom was only thirteen, and had no decided views in grammar and arithmetic, regarding them for the most part as open questions, but he was particularly clear and positive on one point—namely, that he would punish everybody who deserved it: why, he wouldn't have minded being punished himself, if he deserved it; but, then, he never *did* deserve it.

It was Tom's step, then, that Maggie heard on the stairs, when her need of love had triumphed over her pride, and she was going down with her swollen eyes and dishevelled hair to beg for pity. At least her father would stroke her head and say, "Never mind, my wench." It is a wonderful subduer, this need of love—this hunger of the heart—as peremptory as that other hunger by which Nature forces us to submit to the yoke, and change the face of the world.

But she knew Tom's step, and her heart began to beat violently with the sudden shock of hope. He only stood still at the top of the stairs and said, "Maggie, you're to come down." But she rushed to him and clung round his neck, sobbing, "O, Tom, please forgive me—I can't bear it—I will always be good—always remember things—do love me—please, dear Tom?"

We learn to restrain ourselves as we get older. We keep apart when we have quarrelled, express ourselves in well-bred phrases, and in this way preserve a dignified alienation, showing much firmness on one side, and swallowing much grief on the other. We no longer approximate in our behaviour to the mere impulsiveness of the lower animals, but conduct ourselves in every respect like members of a highly civilised society. Maggie and Tom were still very much like young animals, and so she could rub her cheek against his, and kiss his ear in a random, sobbing way; and there were tender fibres in the lad that had been used to answer to Maggie's fondling; so that he behaved with a weakness quite inconsistent with his resolution to punish her as much as she deserved: he actually began to kiss her in return, and say—

"Don't cry, then, Magsie—here, eat a bit o' cake."

Maggie's sobs began to subside, and she put out her mouth for the cake and bit a piece; and then Tom bit a piece, just for company, and they ate together and rubbed each other's cheeks and brows and noses together, while they ate, with a humiliating resemblance to two friendly ponies.

"Come along, Magsie, and have tea," said Tom at last, when there was no more cake except what was down-stairs.

So ended the sorrows of this day, and the next morning Maggie was trotting with her own fishing-rod in one hand and a handle of the basket in the other, stepping always, by a peculiar gift, in the muddiest places, and looking darkly radiant from under her beaver-bonnet because Tom was good to her. She had told Tom, however, that she should like him to put the worms on the hook for her, although she accepted his word when he assured her that worms couldn't feel (it was Tom's private opinion that it didn't much matter if they did). He knew all about worms, and fish, and those things; and what birds were mischievous, and how padlocks opened, and which way the handles of the gates were to be lifted. Maggie thought this sort of knowledge was very wonderful —much more difficult than remembering what was in the books; and she was rather in awe of Tom's superiority, for he was the only person who called her knowledge "stuff," and did not feel surprised at her cleverness. Tom, indeed, was of opinion that Maggie was a silly little thing; all girls were silly—they couldn't throw a stone so as to hit anything, couldn't do anything with a pocket-knife, and were frightened at frogs. Still he was very fond of his sister, and meant always to take care of her, make her his housekeeper, and punish her when she did wrong.

They were on their way to the Round Pool—that wonderful pool, which the floods had made a long while ago: no one knew how deep it was; and it was mysterious, too, that it should be almost a perfect round, framed in with willows and tall reeds, so that the water was only to be seen when you got close to the brink. The sight of the old favourite spot always heightened Tom's good-humour, and he spoke to Maggie in the most amicable whispers, as he opened the precious basket and prepared their tackle. He threw her line for her, and put the rod into her hand. Maggie thought it probable that the small fish would come to her hook, and the large ones to Tom's. But she had forgotten all about the fish, and was looking dreamily at the glassy water, when Tom said, in a loud whisper, "Look, look, Maggie!" and came running to prevent her from snatching her line away.

Maggie was frightened lest she had been doing something wrong, as usual, but presently Tom drew out her line and brought a large tench bouncing on the grass.

Tom was excited.

"O, Magsie! you little duck! Empty the basket."

Maggie was not conscious of unusual merit, but it was enough that Tom called her Magsie, and was pleased with her. There was nothing to mar her delight in the whispers and the dreamy silences, when she listened to the light dipping sounds of the rising fish, and the gentle rustling, as if the willows and the reeds and the water had their happy whisperings also. Maggie thought it would make a very nice heaven to sit by the pool in that way, and never be scolded. She never knew she had a bite till Tom told her, but she liked fishing very much.

It was one of their happy mornings. They trotted along and sat down together, with no thought that life would ever change much for them: they would only get bigger and not go to school, and it would always be like the holidays; they would always live together and be fond of each other. And the mill with its booming—the great chestnut-tree under which they played at houses—their own little river, the Ripple, where the banks seemed like home, and Tom was always seeing the water-rats, while Maggie gathered the purple plumy tops of the reeds, which she forgot and dropped afterwards—above all, the great Floss, along which they wandered with a sense of travel, to see the rushing spring-tide, the awful Eagre, come up like a hungry monster, or to see the Great Ash which had once wailed and groaned like a man—these things would always be just the same to them. Tom thought people were at a disadvantage who lived on any other spot of the globe; and Maggie, when she read about Christiana passing "the river over which there is no bridge," always saw the Floss between the green pastures by the Great Ash.

Life did change for Tom and Maggie; and yet they were not wrong in believing that the thoughts and loves of these first years would always make part of their lives. We could never have loved the earth so well if we had had no childhood in it,—if it were not the earth where the same flowers come up again every spring that we used to gather with our tiny fingers as we sat lisping to ourselves on the grass—the same hips and haws on the autumn hedgerows—the same redbreasts that we used to call "God's birds," because they did no harm to the precious crops. What novelty is worth that sweet monotony where everything is known, and *loved* because it is known?

The wood I walk in on this mild May day, with the young yellow-brown foliage of the oaks between me and the blue sky, the white star-flowers and the blue-eyed speedwell and the ground ivy at my feet—what grove of tropic palms, what strange ferns or splendid broad-petalled blossoms, could ever thrill such deep and delicate fibres within me as this home-scene? These familiar flowers, these well-remembered bird-notes, this sky with its fitful brightness, these furrowed and grassy fields, each with a sort of personality given to it by the capricious hedge-rows—such things as these are the mother tongue of our imagination, the language that is laden with all the subtle inextricable associations the fleeting hours of our childhood left behind them. Our delight in the sun-shine on the deep-bladed grass to-day, might be no more than the faint perception of wearied souls, if it were not for the sunshine and the grass in the far-off years, which still live in us, and transform our per-ception into love.

CHAPTER VI

THE AUNTS AND UNCLES ARE COMING

It was Easter week, and Mrs. Tulliver's cheese-cakes were more ex-quisitely light than usual: "a puff o' wind 'ud make 'em blow about like feathers," Kezia the house-maid said,—feeling proud to live under a mistress who could make such pastry; so that no season or circumstances could have been more propitious for a family party, even if it had not been advisable to consult sister Glegg and sister Pullet about Tom's going to school.

"I'd as lief not invite sister Deane this time," said Mrs. Tulliver, "for she's as jealous and having as can be, and 's allays trying to make the worst o' my poor children to their aunts and uncles."

"Yes, yes," said Mr. Tulliver, "ask her to come. I never hardly get a bit o' talk with Deane now: we haven't had him this six months. What's it matter what she says?—my children need be beholding to nobody."

"That's what you allays say, Mr. Tulliver; but I'm sure there's nobody o' your side, neither aunt nor uncle, to leave 'em so much as a five-pound note for a leggicy. And there's sister Glegg, and sister Pullet too, saving money unknown—for they put by all their own interest and butter-money too; their husbands buy 'em everything." Mrs. Tulliver was a mild woman, but even a sheep will face about a little when she has lambs.

"Tchuh!" said Mr. Tulliver. "It takes a big loaf when there's many to breakfast. What signifies your sisters' bits o' money when they've got half-a-dozen nevvies and nieces to divide it among? And your sister Deane won't get 'em to leave all to one, I reckon, and make the country cry shame on 'em when they are dead?"

"I don't know what she won't get 'em to do," said Mrs. Tulliver, "for my children are so awk'ard wi' their aunts and uncles. Maggie's ten times naughtier when they come than she is other days, and Tom doesn't like 'em, bless him—though it's more nat'ral in a boy than a gell. And there's Lucy Deane's such a good child—you may set her on a stool, and there she'll sit for an hour together, and never offer to get off. I can't help loving the child as if she was my own; and I'm sure she's more like *my* child than sister Deane's, for she'd allays a very poor colour for one of our family, sister Deane had."

"Well, well, if you're fond o' the child, ask her father and mother to bring her with 'em. And won't you ask their aunt and uncle Moss too? and some o' *their* children?"

"O dear, Mr. Tulliver, why, there'd be eight people besides the children, and I must put two more leaves i' the table, besides reaching down more o' the dinner-service; and you know as well as I do, as *my* sisters and *your* sisters don't suit well together."

"Well, well, do as you like, Bessy," said Mr. Tulliver, taking up his hat and walking out to the mill. Few wives were more submissive than Mrs. Tulliver on all points unconnected with her family relations; but she had been a Miss Dodson, and the Dodsons were a very respectable family indeed—as much looked up to as any in their own parish, or the next to it. The Miss Dodsons had always been thought to hold up their heads very high, and no one was surprised the two eldest had married so well—not at an early age, for that was not the practice of the Dodson family. There were particular ways of doing everything in that family: particular ways of bleaching the linen, of making the cowslip wine, curing the hams, and keeping the bottled gooseberries; so that no daughter of that house could be indifferent to the privilege of having been born a Dodson, rather than a Gibson or a Watson. Funerals were always conducted with peculiar propriety in the Dodson family: the hat-bands were never of a blue shade, the gloves never split at the thumb, everybody was a mourner who ought to be, and there were always scarfs for the bearers. When one of the family was in trouble or sickness, all the rest went to visit the unfortunate member, usually at the same time, and did not shrink from uttering the most disagreeable truths that correct family feeling dictated: if the illness or trouble was the sufferer's own fault, it was not in the practice of the Dodson family to shrink from saying so. In short, there was in this family a peculiar tradition as to what was the right thing in household management and social demeanour, and the only bitter circumstance attending this superiority was a painful inability to approve the condiments or the conduct of families ungoverned by the Dodson tradition. A female Dodson, when in "strange houses," always ate dry bread with her tea, and declined any sort of preserves, having no confidence in the butter, and thinking that the preserves had probably begun to ferment from want of due sugar and boiling. There were some Dodsons less like the family than others—that was admitted; but in so far as they were "kin," they were of necessity better than those who were "no kin." And it is remarkable that while no individual Dodson was satisfied with any other individual Dodson, each was satisfied, not only with him or her self, but with the Dodsons collectively. The feeblest member of a family—the one who has the least character—is often the merest epitome of the family habits and traditions; and Mrs. Tulliver was a thorough Dodson, though a mild one, as small-beer, so long as it is anything, is only describable as very weak ale: and though she had groaned a little in her youth under the yoke of her elder sisters, and still shed occasional tears at their sisterly reproaches, it was not in Mrs. Tulliver to be an innovator on the family ideas. She was thankful to have been a Dodson, and to have one child who took after her own family, at least in his features and complexion, in liking salt and in eating beans, which a Tulliver never did.

In other respects the true Dodson was partly latent in Tom, and he was as far from appreciating his "kin" on the mother's side as Maggie herself; generally absconding for the day with a large supply of the most portable food, when he received timely warning that his aunts and uncles were coming; a moral symptom from which his aunt Glegg deduced the gloomiest views of his future. It was rather hard on Maggie that Tom always absconded without letting her into the secret, but the weaker sex are acknowledged to be serious *impedimenta* in cases of flight.

On Wednesday, the day before the aunts and uncles were coming, there were such various and suggestive scents, as of plumcakes in the oven and jellies in the hot state, mingled with the aroma of gravy, that it was impossible to feel altogether gloomy: there was hope in the air. Tom and Maggie made several inroads into the kitchen, and, like other marauders, were induced to keep aloof for a time only by being allowed to carry away a sufficient load of booty.

"Tom," said Maggie, as they sat on the boughs of the elder-tree, eating their jam puffs, "shall you run away to-morrow?"

"No," said Tom, slowly, when he had finished his puff, and was eyeing the third, which was to be divided between them—"No, I shan't."

"Why, Tom? Because Lucy's coming?"

"No," said Tom, opening his pocket-knife and holding it over the puff, with his head on one side in a dubitative manner. (It was a difficult problem to divide that very irregular polygon into two equal parts.) "What do *I* care about Lucy? She's only a girl—*she* can't play at bandy."

"Is it the tipsy-cake, then?" said Maggie, exerting her hypothetic

powers, while she leaned forward towards Tom with her eyes fixed on the
hovering knife.

"No, you silly, that'll be good the day after. It's the pudden. I know
what the pudden's to be—apricot roll-up—O, my buttons!"

With this interjection, the knife descended on the puff and it was in
two, but the result was not satisfactory to Tom, for he still eyed the
halves doubtfully. At last he said—

"Shut your eyes, Maggie."

"What for?"

"You never mind what for. Shut 'em, when I tell you."

Maggie obeyed.

"Now, which'll you have, Maggie—right hand or left?"

"I'll have that with the jam run out," said Maggie, keeping her eyes
shut to please Tom.

"Why, you don't like that, you silly. You may have it if it comes to
you fair, but I shan't give it you without. Right or left—you choose,
now. Ha-a-a!" said Tom, in a tone of exasperation, as Maggie peeped.
"You keep your eyes shut, now, else you shan't have any."

Maggie's power of sacrifice did not extend so far; indeed, I fear she
cared less that Tom should enjoy the utmost possible amount of puff,
than that he should be pleased with her for giving him the best bit. So
she shut her eyes quite close, till Tom told her to "say which," and then
she said, "Left-hand."

"You've got it," said Tom, in rather a bitter tone.

"What! the bit with the jam run out?"

"No; here, take it," said Tom, firmly, handing decidedly the best
piece to Maggie.

"O, please, Tom, have it: I don't mind—I like the other: please
take this."

"No, I shan't," said Tom, almost crossly, beginning on his own inferior piece.

Maggie, thinking it was no use to contend further, began too, and ate
up her half puff with considerable relish as well as rapidity. But Tom
had finished first, and had to look on while Maggie ate her last morsel
or two, feeling in himself a capacity for more. Maggie didn't know Tom
was looking at her: she was seesawing on the elder bough, lost to almost
everything but a vague sense of jam and idleness.

"O, you greedy thing!" said Tom, when she had swallowed the last
morsel. He was conscious of having acted very fairly, and thought she
ought to have considered this, and made up to him for it. He would have
refused a bit of hers beforehand, but one is naturally at a different point
of view before and after one's own share of puff is swallowed.

Maggie turned quite pale. "O, Tom, why didn't you ask me?"

"*I* wasn't going to ask you for a bit, you greedy. You might have
thought of it without, when you knew I gave you the best bit."

"But I wanted you to have it—you know I did," said Maggie, in an
injured tone.

"Yes, but I wasn't going to do what wasn't fair, like Spouncer. He always takes the best bit, if you don't punch him for it; and if you choose the best with your eyes shut, he changes his hands. But if I go halves, I'll go 'em fair—only I wouldn't be a greedy."

With this cutting innuendo, Tom jumped down from his bough, and threw a stone with a "hoigh!" as a friendly attention to Yap, who had also been looking on while the eatables vanished, with an agitation of his ears and feelings which could hardly have been without bitterness. Yet the excellent dog accepted Tom's attention with as much alacrity as if he had been treated quite generously.

But Maggie, gifted with that superior power of misery which distinguishes the human being, and places him at a proud distance from the most melancholy chimpanzee, sat still on her bough, and gave herself up to the keen sense of unmerited reproach. She would have given the world not to have eaten all her puff, and to have saved some of it for Tom. Not but that the puff was very nice, for Maggie's palate was not at all obtuse, but she would have gone without it many times over, sooner than Tom should call her greedy and be cross with her. And he had said he wouldn't have it—and she ate it without thinking—how could she help it? The tears flowed so plentifully that Maggie saw nothing around her for the next ten minutes; but by that time resentment began to give way to the desire of reconciliation, and she jumped from her bough to look for Tom. He was no longer in the paddock behind the rickyard—where was he likely to be gone, and Yap with him? Maggie ran to the high bank against the great holly-tree, where she could see far away towards the Floss. There was Tom; but her heart sank again as she saw how far off he was on his way to the great river, and that he had another companion besides Yap—naughty Bob Jakin, whose official, if not natural function, of frightening the birds, was just now at a standstill. Maggie felt sure that Bob was wicked, without very distinctly knowing why; unless it was because Bob's mother was a dreadfully large fat woman, who lived at a queer round house down the river; and once, when Maggie and Tom had wandered thither, there rushed out a brindled dog that wouldn't stop barking; and when Bob's mother came out after it, and screamed above the barking to tell them not to be frightened, Maggie thought she was scolding them fiercely, and her heart beat with terror. Maggie thought it very likely that the round house had snakes on the floor, and bats in the bedroom; for she had seen Bob take off his cap to show Tom a little snake that was inside it, and another time he had a handful of young bats: altogether, he was an irregular character, perhaps even slightly diabolical, judging from his intimacy with snakes and bats; and to crown all, when Tom had Bob for a companion, he didn't mind about Maggie, and would never let her go with him.

It must be owned that Tom was fond of Bob's company. How could it be otherwise? Bob knew, directly he saw a bird's egg, whether it was a swallow's, or a tomtit's, or a yellowhammer's; he found out all the wasps' nests, and could set all sorts of traps; he could climb the trees like a squirrel, and had quite a magical power of detecting hedgehogs and stoats; and he had courage to do things that were rather naughty, such as making gaps in the hedgerows, throwing stones after the sheep, and killing a cat that was wandering *incognito*. Such qualities in an inferior, who could always be treated with authority in spite of his superior knowingness, had necessarily a fatal fascination for Tom; and every holiday-time Maggie was sure to have days of grief because he had gone off with Bob.

Well! there was no hope for it: he was gone now, and Maggie could think of no comfort but to sit down by the holly, or wander by the hedgerow, and fancy it was all different, refashioning her little world into just what she should like it to be.

Maggie's was a troublous life, and this was the form in which she took her opium.

Meanwhile Tom, forgetting all about Maggie and the sting of reproach which he had left in her heart, was hurrying along with Bob, whom he had met accidentally, to the scene of a great rat-catching in a neighbouring barn. Bob knew all about this particular affair, and spoke of the sport with an enthusiasm which no one who is not either divested of all manly feeling, or pitiably ignorant of rat-catching, can fail to imagine. For a person suspected of preternatural wickedness, Bob was really not so very villanous-looking; there was even something agreeable in his snub-nosed face, with its close-curled border of red hair. But then his trousers were always rolled up at the knee, for the convenience of wading on the slightest notice; and his virtue, supposing it to exist, was undeniably "virtue in rags," which, on the authority even of bilious philosophers, who think all well-dressed merit over-paid, is notoriously likely to remain unrecognised (perhaps because it is seen so seldom).

"I know the chap as owns the ferrets," said Bob in a hoarse treble voice, as he shuffled along, keeping his blue eyes fixed on the river, like an amphibious animal who foresaw occasion for darting in. "He lives up the Kennel Yard at Sut Ogg's—he does. He's the biggest rot-catcher anywhere—he is. I'd sooner be a rot-catcher nor anything—I would. The moles is nothing to the rots. But Lors! you mun ha' ferrets. Dogs is no good. Why, there's that dog, now!" Bob continued, pointing with an air of disgust towards Yap, "he's no more good wi' a rot nor nothin'. I see it myself—I did—at the rot-catchin' i' your feyther's barn."

Yap, feeling the withering influence of this scorn, tucked his tail in and shrank close to Tom's leg, who felt a little hurt for him, but had not the superhuman courage to seem behindhand with Bob in contempt for a dog who made so poor a figure.

"No, no," he said, "Yap's no good at sport. I'll have regular good dogs for rats and everything, when I've done school."

"Hev ferrets, Measter Tom," said Bob, eagerly,—"them white ferrets wi' pink eyes; Lors, you might catch your own rots, an' you might put a rot in a cage wi' a ferret, an' see 'em fight—you might. That's what

I'd do, I know, an' it 'ud be better fun a'most nor seein' two chaps fight —if it wasn't them chaps as sell cakes an' oranges at the Fair, as the things flew out o' their baskets, an' some o' the cakes was smashed . . . But they tasted just as good," added Bob, by way of note or addendum, after a moment's pause.

"But, I say, Bob," said Tom, in a tone of deliberation, "ferrets are nasty biting things—they'll bite a fellow without being set on."

"Lors! why that's the beauty on 'em. If a chap lays hold o' your ferret, he won't be long before he hollows out a good un—*he* won't."

At this moment a striking incident made the boys pause suddenly in their walk. It was the plunging of some small body in the water from among the neighbouring bulrushes—if it was not a water-rat, Bob intimated that he was ready to undergo the most unpleasant consequences.

"Hoigh! Yap—hoigh! there he is," said Tom, clapping his hands, as the little black snout made its arrowy course to the opposite bank. "Seize him, lad, seize him!"

Yap agitated his ears and wrinkled his brows, but declined to plunge, trying whether barking would not answer the purpose just as well.

"Ugh! you coward!" said Tom, and kicked him over, feeling humiliated as a sportsman to possess so poor-spirited an animal. Bob abstained from remark and passed on, choosing, however, to walk in the shallow edge of the overflowing river by way of change.

"He's none so full now, the Floss isn't," said Bob, as he kicked the water up before him, with an agreeable sense of being insolent to it. "Why, last 'ear, the meadows was all one sheet o' water, they was."

"Ay, but," said Tom, whose mind was prone to see an opposition between statements that were really quite accordant, "but there was a big flood once, when the Round Pool was made. *I* know there was, 'cause father says so. And the sheep and cows were all drowned, and the boats went all over the fields ever such a way."

"*I* don't care about a flood comin'," said Bob; "I don't mind the water, no more nor the land. I'd swim—*I* would."

"Ah, but if you got nothing to eat for ever so long?" said Tom, his imagination becoming quite active under the stimulus of that dread. "When I'm a man, I shall make a boat with a wooden house on the top of it, like Noah's ark, and keep plenty to eat in it—rabbits and things— all ready. And then if the flood came, you know, Bob, I shouldn't mind. . . . And I'd take you in, if I saw you swimming," he added, in the tone of a benevolent patron.

"I aren't frighted," said Bob, to whom hunger did not appear so appalling. "But I'd get in an' knock the rabbits on th' head when you wanted to eat 'em."

"Ah, and I should have halfpence, and we'd play at heads-and-tails," said Tom, not contemplating the possibility that this recreation might have fewer charms for his mature age. "I'd divide fair to begin with, and then we'd see who'd win."

"I'n got a halfpenny o' my own," said Bob, proudly, coming out of the water and tossing his halfpenny in the air. "Yeads or tails?"

"Tails," said Tom, instantly fired with the desire to win.

"It's yeads," said Bob, hastily, snatching up the halfpenny as it fell.

"It wasn't," said Tom, loudly and peremptorily. "You give me the halfpenny—I've won it fair."

"I shan't," said Bob, holding it tight in his pocket.

"Then I'll make you—see if I don't," said Tom.

"You can't make me do nothing, you can't," said Bob.

"Yes, I can."

"No, you can't."

"I'm master."

"I don't care for you."

"But I'll make you care, you cheat," said Tom, collaring Bob and shaking him.

"You get out wi' you," said Bob, giving Tom a kick.

Tom's blood was thoroughly up: he went at Bob with a lunge and threw him down, but Bob seized hold and kept it like a cat, and pulled Tom down after him. They struggled fiercely on the ground for a moment or two, till Tom, pinning Bob down by the shoulders, thought he had the mastery.

"*You* say you'll give me the halfpenny now," he said, with difficulty, while he exerted himself to keep the command of Bob's arms.

But at this moment, Yap, who had been running on before, returned barking to the scene of action, and saw a favourable opportunity for biting Bob's bare leg not only with impunity but with honour. The pain from Yap's teeth, instead of surprising Bob into a relaxation of his hold, gave it a fiercer tenacity, and, with a new exertion of his force, he pushed Tom backward and got uppermost. But now Yap, who could get no sufficient purchase before, set his teeth in a new place, so that Bob, harassed in this way, let go his hold of Tom, and, almost throttling Yap, flung him into the river. By this time Tom was up again, and before Bob had quite recovered his balance after the act of swinging Yap, Tom fell upon him, threw him down, and got his knees firmly on Bob's chest.

"You give me the halfpenny now," said Tom.

"Take it," said Bob, sulkily.

"No, I shan't take it; you give it me."

Bob took the halfpenny out of his pocket, and threw it away from him on the ground.

Tom loosed his hold, and left Bob to rise.

"There the halfpenny lies," he said. "I don't want your halfpenny; I wouldn't have kept it. But you wanted to cheat: I hate a cheat. I shan't go along with you any more," he added, turning round homeward, not without casting a regret towards the rat-catching and other pleasures which he must relinquish along with Bob's society.

"You may let it alone, then," Bob called out after him. "I shall cheat if I like; there's no fun i' playing else; and I know where there's a goldfinch's nest, but I'll take care *you* don't. . . . An' you're a nasty fightin' turkey-cock, you are. . . ."

Tom walked on without looking round, and Yap followed his example, the cold bath having moderated his passions.

"Go along wi' you, then, wi' your drownded dog; I wouldn't own such a dog—*I* wouldn't," said Bob, getting louder, in a last effort to sustain his defiance. But Tom was not to be provoked into turning round, and Bob's voice began to falter a little as he said,

"An' I'n gi'en you everything, an' showed you everything, an' niver wanted nothin' from you. . . . An' there's your horn-handed knife, then, as you gi'en me. . . ." Here Bob flung the knife as far as he could after Tom's retreating footsteps. But it produced no effect, except the sense in Bob's mind that there was a terrible void in his lot, now that knife was gone.

He stood still till Tom had passed through the gate and disappeared behind the hedge. The knife would do no good on the ground there—it wouldn't vex Tom, and pride or resentment was a feeble passion in Bob's mind compared with the love of a pocket-knife. His very fingers sent entreating thrills that he would go and clutch that familiar rough buck's-horn handle, which they had so often grasped for mere affection as it lay idle in his pocket. And there were two blades, and they had just been sharpened! What is life without a pocket-knife to him who has once tasted a higher existence? No: to throw the handle after the hatchet is a comprehensible act of desperation, but to throw one's pocket-knife after an implacable friend is clearly in every sense a hyperbole, or throwing beyond the mark. So Bob shuffled back to the spot where the beloved knife lay in the dirt, and felt quite a new pleasure in clutching it again after the temporary separation, in opening one blade after the other, and feeling their edge with his well-hardened thumb. Poor Bob! he was not sensitive on the point of honour—not a chivalrous character. That fine moral aroma would not have been thought much of by the public opinion of Kennel Yard, which was the very focus or heart of Bob's world, even if it could have made itself perceptible there; yet, for all that, he was not utterly a sneak and a thief, as our friend Tom had hastily decided.

But Tom, you perceive, was rather a Rhadamanthine personage, having more than the usual share of boy's justice in him—the justice that desires to hurt culprits as much as they deserve to be hurt, and is troubled with no doubts concerning the exact amount of their deserts. Maggie saw a cloud on his brow when he came home, which checked her joy at his coming so much sooner than she had expected, and she dared hardly speak to him as he stood silently throwing the small gravel-stones into the mill-dam. It is not pleasant to give up a rat-catching when you have set your mind on it. But if Tom had told his strongest feeling at that moment, he would have said, "I'd do just the same again." That was his usual mode of viewing his past actions; whereas Maggie was always wishing she had done something different.

CHAPTER VII

ENTER THE AUNTS AND UNCLES

The Dodsons were certainly a handsome family, and Mrs. Glegg was not the least handsome of the sisters. As she sat in Mrs. Tulliver's arm-chair, no impartial observer could have denied that for a woman of fifty she had a very comely face and figure, though Tom and Maggie considered their aunt Glegg as the type of ugliness. It is true she despised the advantages of costume, for though, as she often observed, no woman had better clothes, it was not her way to wear her new things out before her old ones. Other women, if they liked, might have their best thread-lace in every wash, but when Mrs. Glegg died, it would be found that she had better lace laid by in the right-hand drawer of her wardrobe, in the Spotted Chamber, than ever Mrs. Wooll of St. Ogg's had bought in her life, although Mrs. Wooll wore her lace before it was paid for. So of her curled fronts: Mrs. Glegg had doubtless the glossiest and crispest brown curls in her drawers, as well as curls in various degrees of fuzzy laxness; but to look out on the week-day world from under a crisp and glossy front, would be to introduce a most dream-like and unpleasant confusion between the sacred and the secular. Occasionally, indeed, Mrs. Glegg wore one of her third-best fronts on a week-day visit, but not at a sister's house; especially not at Mrs. Tulliver's, who, since her marriage, had hurt her sisters' feelings greatly by wearing her own hair, though, as Mrs. Glegg observed to Mrs. Deane, a mother of a family, like Bessy, with a husband always going to law, might have been expected to know better. But Bessy was always weak!

So if Mrs. Glegg's front to-day was more fuzzy and lax than usual, she had a design under it: she intended the most pointed and cutting allusion to Mrs. Tulliver's bunches of blond curls, separated from each other by a due wave of smoothness on each side of the parting. Mrs. Tulliver had shed tears several times at sister Glegg's unkindness on the subject of these unmatronly curls, but the consciousness of looking the handsomer for them, naturally administered support: Mrs. Glegg chose to wear her bonnet in the house to-day—untied and tilted slightly, of course —a frequent practice of hers when she was on a visit, and happened to be in a severe humour: she didn't know what draughts there might be in strange houses. For the same reason she wore a small sable tippet, which reached just to her shoulders, and was very far from meeting across her well-formed chest, while her long neck was protected by a *chevaux-de-frise* of miscellaneous frilling. One would need to be learned in the fashions of those times to know how far in the rear of them Mrs. Glegg's slate-coloured silk-gown must have been; but from certain constellations of small yellow spots upon it, and a mouldy odour about it suggestive of a damp clothes-chest, it was probable that it belonged to a stratum of garments just old enough to have come recently into wear.

Mrs. Glegg held her large gold-watch in her hand with the many-doubled chain round her fingers, and observed to Mrs. Tulliver, who had just returned from a visit to the kitchen, that whatever it might be by other people's clocks and watches, it was gone half-past twelve by hers.

"I don't know what ails sister Pullet," she continued. "It used to be the way in our family for one to be as early as another—I'm sure it was so in my poor father's time—and not for one sister to sit half an hour before the others came. But if the ways o' the family are altered, it shan't be *my* fault—*I'll* never be the one to come into a house when all the rest are going away. I wonder *at* sister Deane—she used to be more like me. But if you'll take my advice, Bessy, you'll put the dinner forrard a bit, sooner than put it back, because folks are late as ought to ha' known better."

"O dear, there's no fear but what they'll be all here in time, sister," said Mrs. Tulliver, in her mild-peevish tone. "The dinner won't be ready till half-past one. But if it's long for you to wait, let me fetch you a cheese-cake and a glass o' wine."

"Well, Bessy!" said Mrs. Glegg, with a bitter smile, and a scarcely perceptible toss of her head, "I should ha' thought you'd know your own sister better. I never *did* eat between meals, and I'm not going to begin. Not but what I hate that nonsense of having your dinner at half-past one, when you might have it at one. You was never brought up in that way, Bessy."

"Why, Jane, what can I do? Mr. Tulliver doesn't like his dinner before two o'clock, but I put it half an hour earlier because o' you."

"Yes, yes, I know how it is wi' husbands—they're for putting everything off—they'll put the dinner off till after tea, if they've got wives as are weak enough to give in to such work; but it's a pity for you, Bessy, as you haven't got more strength o' mind. It'll be well if your children don't suffer for it. And I hope you've not gone and got a great dinner for us—going to expense, for your sisters as 'ud sooner eat a crust o' dry bread nor help to ruin you with extravagance. I wonder you don't take pattern by your sister Deane—she's far more sensible. And here you've got two children to provide for, and your husband's spent your fortin i' going to law, and's like to spend his own too. A boiled joint, as you could make broth of for the kitchen," Mrs. Glegg added, in a tone of emphatic protest, "and a plain pudding, with a spoonful o' sugar and no spice, 'ud be far more becoming."

With sister Glegg in this humour, there was a cheerful prospect for the day. Mrs. Tulliver never went the length of quarrelling with her, any more than a waterfowl that puts out its leg in a deprecating manner can be said to quarrel with a boy who throws stones. But this point of the dinner was a tender one, and not at all new, so that Mrs. Tulliver could make the same answer she had often made before.

"Mr. Tulliver says he always *will* have a good dinner for his friends while he can pay for it," she said, "and he's a right to do as he likes in his own house, sister."

"Well, Bessy, *I* can't leave your children enough, out o' my savings, to keep 'em from ruin. And you mustn't look to having any o' Mr. Glegg's money, for it's well if I don't go first—he comes of a long-lived family; and if he was to die and leave me well for my life, he'd tie all the money up to go back to his own kin."

The sound of wheels while Mrs. Glegg was speaking was an interruption highly welcome to Mrs. Tulliver, who hastened out to receive sister Pullet—it must be sister Pullet, because the sound was that of a four-wheel.

Mrs. Glegg tossed her head and looked rather sour about the mouth at the thought of the "four-wheel." She had a strong opinion on that subject.

Sister Pullet was in tears when the one-horse chaise stopped before Mrs. Tulliver's door, and it was apparently requisite that she should shed a few more before getting out, for though her husband and Mrs. Tulliver stood ready to support her, she sat still and shook her head sadly, as she looked through her tears at the vague distance.

"Why, whativer is the matter, sister?" said Mrs. Tulliver. She was not an imaginative woman, but it occurred to her that the large toilet-glass in sister Pullet's best bedroom was possibly broken for the second time.

There was no reply but a further shake of the head, as Mrs. Pullet slowly rose and got down from the chaise, not without casting a glance at Mr. Pullet to see that he was guarding her handsome silk dress from injury. Mr. Pullet was a small man with a high nose, small twinkling eyes, and thin lips, in a fresh-looking suit of black and a white cravat, that seemed to have been tied very tight on some higher principle than that of mere personal ease. He bore about the same relation to his tall, good-looking wife, with her balloon sleeves, abundant mantle, and large be-feathered and be-ribboned bonnet, as a small fishing-smack bears to a brig with all its sails spread.

It is a pathetic sight and a striking example of the complexity introduced into the emotions by a high state of civilisation—the sight of a fashionably drest female in grief. From the sorrow of a Hottentot to that of a woman in large buckram sleeves, with several bracelets on each arm, an architectural bonnet, and delicate ribbon-strings—what a long series of gradations! In the enlightened child of civilisation the abandonment characteristic of grief is checked and varied in the subtlest manner, so as to present an interesting problem to the analytic mind. If, with a crushed heart and eyes half-blinded by the mist of tears, she were to walk with a too devious step through a door-place, she might crush her buckram sleeves too, and the deep consciousness of this possibility produces a composition of forces by which she takes a line that just clears the doorpost. Perceiving that the tears are hurrying fast, she unpins her strings and throws them languidly backward—a touching gesture, indicative, even in the deepest gloom, of the hope in future dry moments when cap-strings will once more have a charm. As the tears subside a little, and with her head leaning backward at the angle that will not injure her bonnet, she endures that terrible moment when grief, which has made all things else a weariness, has itself become weary; she looks down pensively at her bracelets, and adjusts their clasps with that pretty studied fortuity which would be gratifying to her mind if it were once more in a calm and healthy state.

Mrs. Pullet brushed each doorpost with great nicety, about the latitude of her shoulders (at that period a woman was truly ridiculous to an instructed eye if she did not measure a yard and a half across the shoulders), and having done that, sent the muscles of her face in quest of fresh tears as she advanced into the parlour where Mrs. Glegg was seated.

"Well, sister, you're late; what's the matter?" said Mrs. Glegg, rather sharply, as they shook hands.

Mrs. Pullet sat down—lifting up her mantle carefully behind, before she answered,——

"She's gone," unconsciously using an impressive figure of rhetoric.

"It isn't the glass this time, then," thought Mrs. Tulliver.

"Died the day before yesterday," continued Mrs. Pullet; "an' her legs was as thick as my body," she added, with deep sadness, after a pause. "They'd tapped her no end o' times, and the water—they say you might ha' swum in it, if you'd liked."

"Well, Sophy, it's a mercy she's gone, then, whoiver she may be," said Mrs. Glegg with the promptitude and emphasis of a mind naturally clear and decided; "but I can't think who you're talking of, for my part."

"But I know," said Mrs. Pullet, sighing and shaking her head; "and there isn't another such a dropsy in the parish. I know as it's old Mrs. Sutton o' the Twentylands."

"Well, she's no kin o' yours, nor much acquaintance as I've ever heard of," said Mrs. Glegg, who always cried just as much as was proper when anything happened to her own "kin," but not on other occasions.

"She's so much acquaintance as I've seen her legs when they was like bladders. . . . And an old lady as had doubled her money over and over again, and kept it all in her own management to the last, and had her pocket with her keys in under her pillow constant. There isn't many old *par*ish'ners like her, I doubt."

"And they say she'd took as much physic as 'ud fill a waggon," observed Mr. Pullet.

"Ah," sighed Mrs. Pullet, "she'd another complaint ever so many years before she had the dropsy, and the doctors couldn't make out what it was. And she said to me, when I went to see her last Christmas, she said, 'Mrs. Pullet, if iver you have the dropsy, you'll think o' me.' She *did* say so," added Mrs. Pullet, beginning to cry bitterly again; "those were her very words. And she's to be buried o' Saturday, and Pullet's bid to the funeral."

"Sophy," said Mrs. Glegg, unable any longer to contain her spirit of rational remonstrance—"Sophy, I wonder *at* you, fretting and injuring your health about people as don't belong to you. Your poor father never did so, nor your aunt Frances neither, nor any o' the family as I ever heard of. You couldn't fret no more than this, if we'd heard as our cousin Abbott had died sudden without making his will."

Mrs. Pullet was silent, having to finish her crying, and rather flattered than indignant at being upbraided for crying too much. It was not everybody who could afford to cry so much about their neighbours who had left them nothing; but Mrs. Pullet had married a gentleman farmer, and had leisure and money to carry her crying and everything else to the highest pitch of respectability.

"Mrs. Sutton didn't die without making her will, though," said Mr. Pullet, with a confused sense that he was saying something to sanction his wife's tears; "ours is a rich parish, but they say there's nobody else to leave as many thousands behind 'em as Mrs. Sutton. And she's left no leggicies, to speak on—left it all in a lump to her husband's nevvy."

"There wasn't much good i' being so rich, then," said Mrs. Glegg, "if she'd got none but husband's kin to leave it to. It's poor work when that's all you've got to pinch yourself for;—not as I'm one o' those as 'ud like to die without leaving more money out at interest than other folks had reckoned. But it's a poor tale when it must go out o' your own family."

"I'm sure, sister," said Mrs. Pullet, who had recovered sufficiently to take off her veil and fold it carefully, "it's a nice sort o' man as Mrs. Sutton has left her money to, for he's troubled with the asthmy, and goes to bed every night at eight o'clock. He told me about it himself —as free as could be—one Sunday when he came to our church. He wears a hare-skin on his chest, and has a trembling in his talk—quite a gentleman sort o' man. I told him there wasn't many months in the year as I wasn't under the doctor's hands. And he said, 'Mrs. Pullet, I can feel for you.' That was what he said—the very words. Ah!" sighed Mrs. Pullet, shaking her head at the idea that there were but few who could enter fully into her experiences in pink mixture and white mixture, strong stuff in small bottles, and weak stuff in large bottles, damp boluses at a shilling, and draughts at eighteenpence. "Sister, I may as well go and take my bonnet off now. Did you see as the cap-box was put out?" she added, turning to her husband.

Mr. Pullet, by an unaccountable lapse of memory, had forgotten it, and hastened out, with a stricken conscience, to remedy the omission.

"They'll bring it up-stairs, sister," said Mrs. Tulliver, wishing to go at once, lest Mrs. Glegg should begin to explain her feelings about Sophy's being the first Dodson who ever ruined her constitution with doctor's stuff.

Mrs. Tulliver was fond of going up-stairs with her sister Pullet, and looking thoroughly at her cap before she put it on her head, and discussing millinery in general. This was part of Bessy's weakness that stirred Mrs. Glegg's sisterly compassion: Bessy went far too well drest, considering; and she was too proud to dress her child in the good clothing her sister Glegg gave her from the primeval strata of her wardrobe; it was a sin and a shame to buy anything to dress that child, if it wasn't a pair of shoes. In this particular, however, Mrs. Glegg did her sister Bessy some injustice, for Mrs. Tulliver had really made great efforts to induce Maggie to wear a leghorn bonnet and a dyed silk frock made out of her aunt Glegg's, but the results had been such that Mrs. Tulliver was obliged to bury them in her maternal bosom; for Maggie, declaring that the frock smelt of nasty dye, had taken an opportunity of basting it together with the roast-beef the first Sunday she wore it, and, finding this scheme answer, she had subsequently pumped on the bonnet with its green ribbons, so as to give it a general resemblance to a sage cheese garnished with withered lettuces. I must urge in excuse for Maggie, that Tom had laughed at her in the bonnet, and said she looked like an old Judy. Aunt Pullet, too, made presents of clothes, but these were always pretty enough to please Maggie as well as her mother. Of all her sisters, Mrs. Tulliver certainly preferred her sister Pullet, not without a return of preference; but Mrs. Pullet was sorry Bessy had those naughty awkward children; she would do the best she could by them, but it was a pity they weren't as good and as pretty as sister Deane's child. Maggie and Tom, on their part, thought their aunt Pullet tolerable, chiefly because she was not their aunt Glegg. Tom always declined to go more than once, during his holidays, to see either of them: both his uncles tipped him that once, of course; but at his aunt Pullet's there were a great many toads to pelt in the cellar-area, so that he preferred the visit to her. Maggie shuddered at the toads, and dreamed of them horribly, but she liked her uncle Pullet's musical snuff-box. Still, it was agreed by the sisters, in Mrs. Tulliver's absence, that the Tulliver blood did not mix well with the Dodson blood; that, in fact, poor Bessy's children were Tullivers, and that Tom, notwithstanding he had the Dodson complexion, was likely to be as "contrairy" as his father. As for Maggie, she was the picture of her aunt Moss, Mr. Tulliver's sister, —a large-boned woman, who had married as poorly as could be; had no china, and had a husband who had much ado to pay his rent. But when Mrs. Pullet was alone with Mrs. Tulliver up-stairs, the remarks were naturally to the disadvantage of Mrs. Glegg, and they agreed, in confidence, that there was no knowing what sort of fright sister Jane would come out next. But their *tête-à-tête* was curtailed by the appearance of Mrs. Deane with little Lucy; and Mrs. Tulliver had to look on with a silent pang while Lucy's blond curls were adjusted. It was quite unaccountable that Mrs. Deane, the thinnest and sallowest of all the Miss Dodsons, should have had this child, who might have been taken for Mrs. Tulliver's any day. And Maggie always looked twice as dark as usual when she was by the side of Lucy.

She did to-day, when she and Tom came in from the garden with their father and their uncle Glegg. Maggie had thrown her bonnet off very carelessly, and, coming in with her hair rough as well as out of curl, rushed at once to Lucy, who was standing by her mother's knee.

Certainly the contrast between the cousins was conspicuous, and, to superficial eyes, was very much to the disadvantage of Maggie, though a connoisseur might have seen "points" in her which had a higher promise for maturity than Lucy's natty completeness. It was like the contrast between a rough, dark, overgrown puppy and a white kitten. Lucy put up the neatest little rosebud mouth to be kissed: everything about her was neat—her little round neck, with the row of coral beads; her little straight nose, not at all snubby; her little clear eyebrows, rather darker than her curls, to match her hazel eyes, which looked up with shy pleasure at Maggie, taller by the head, though scarcely a year older. Maggie always looked at Lucy with delight. She was fond of fancying a world where the people never got any larger than children of their own age, and she made the queen of it just like Lucy, with a little crown on her head and a little sceptre in her hand . . . only the queen was Maggie herself in Lucy's form.

"O, Lucy," she burst out, after kissing her, "you'll stay with Tom and me, won't you? O, kiss her, Tom."

Tom, too, had come up to Lucy, but he was not going to kiss her —no; he came up to her with Maggie because it seemed easier, on the whole, than saying, "How do you do?" to all those aunts and uncles: he stood looking at nothing in particular, with the blushing, awkward air and semi-smile which are common to shy boys when in company —very much as if they had come into the world by mistake, and found it in a degree of undress that was quite embarrassing.

"Heyday!" said aunt Glegg, with loud emphasis. "Do little boys and gells come into a room without taking notice o' their uncles and aunts? That wasn't the way when *I* was a little gell."

"Go and speak to your aunts and uncles, my dears," said Mrs. Tulliver, looking anxious and melancholy. She wanted to whisper to Maggie a command to go and have her hair brushed.

"Well, and how do you do? And I hope you're good children, are you?" said aunt Glegg, in the same loud emphatic way, as she took their hands, hurting them with her large rings, and kissing their cheeks much against their desire. "Look up, Tom, look up. Boys as go to boarding-schools should hold their heads up. Look at me now." Tom declined that pleasure apparently, for he tried to draw his hand away. "Put your hair behind your ears, Maggie, and keep your frock on your shoulder."

Aunt Glegg always spoke to them in this loud emphatic way, as if she considered them deaf, or perhaps rather idiotic: it was a means, she thought, of making them feel that they were accountable creatures, and might be a salutary check on naughty tendencies. Bessy's children were so spoiled—they'd need have somebody to make them feel their duty.

"Well, my dears," said aunt Pullet, in a compassionate voice, "you grow wonderful fast. I doubt they'll outgrow their strength," she added, looking over their heads, with a melancholy expression, at their mother. "I think the gell has too much hair. I'd have it thinned and cut shorter, sister, if I was you: it isn't good for her health. It's that as makes her skin so brown, I shouldn't wonder. Don't you think so, sister Deane?"

"I can't say, I'm sure, sister," said Mrs. Deane, shutting her lips close again, and looking at Maggie with a critical eye.

"No, no," said Mr. Tulliver, "the child's healthy enough—there's nothing ails her. There's red wheat as well as white, for that matter, and some like the dark grain best. But it 'ud be as well if Bessy 'ud have the child's hair cut, so as it 'ud lie smooth."

A dreadful resolve was gathering in Maggie's breast, but it was arrested by the desire to know from her aunt Deane whether she would leave Lucy behind: aunt Deane would hardly ever let Lucy come to see them. After various reasons for refusal, Mrs. Deane appealed to Lucy herself.

"You wouldn't like to stay behind without mother, should you, Lucy?"

"Yes, please, mother," said Lucy, timidly, blushing very pink all over her little neck.

"Well done, Lucy! Let her stay, Mrs. Deane, let her stay," said Mr. Deane, a large but alert-looking man, with a type of physique to be seen in all ranks of English society—bald crown, red whiskers, full forehead, and general solidity without heaviness. You may see noblemen like Mr. Deane, and you may see grocers or day-labourers like him; but the keenness of his brown eyes was less common than his contour. He held a silver snuff-box very tightly in his hand, and now and then exchanged a pinch with Mr. Tulliver, whose box was only silver-mounted, so that it was naturally a joke between them that Mr. Tulliver wanted to exchange snuff-boxes also. Mr. Deane's box had been given him by the superior partners in the firm to which he belonged, at the same time that they gave him a share in the business, in acknowledgment of his valuable services as manager. No man was thought more highly of in St. Ogg's than Mr. Deane, and some persons were even of opinion that Miss Susan Dodson, who was held to have made the worst match of all the Dodson sisters, might one day ride in a better carriage, and live in a better house, even than her sister Pullet. There was no knowing where a man would stop, who had got his foot into a great mill-owning, ship-owning business like that of Guest & Co., with a banking concern attached. And Mrs. Deane, as her intimate female friends observed, was proud and "having" enough: *she* wouldn't let her husband stand still in the world for want of spurring.

"Maggie," said Mrs. Tulliver, beckoning Maggie to her, and whispering in her ear, as soon as this point of Lucy's staying was settled, "go and get your hair brushed—do, for shame. I told you not to come in without going to Martha first; you know I did."

"Tom, come out with me," whispered Maggie, pulling his sleeve as she passed him; and Tom followed willingly enough.

"Come up-stairs with me, Tom," she whispered when they were outside the door. "There's something I want to do before dinner."

"There's no time to play at anything before dinner," said Tom, whose imagination was impatient of any intermediate prospect.

"O, yes, there is time for this—*do* come, Tom."

Tom followed Maggie up-stairs into her mother's room, and saw her go at once to a drawer, from which she took out a large pair of scissors.

"What are they for, Maggie?" said Tom, feeling his curiosity awakened.

Maggie answered by seizing her front locks and cutting them straight across the middle of her forehead.

"O, my buttons, Maggie, you'll catch it!" exclaimed Tom; "you'd better not cut any more off."

Snip! went the great scissors again while Tom was speaking; and he couldn't help feeling it was rather good fun: Maggie would look so queer.

"Here, Tom, cut it behind for me," said Maggie, excited by her own daring, and anxious to finish the deed.

"You'll catch it, you know," said Tom, nodding his head in an admonitory manner, and hesitating a little as he took the scissors.

"Never mind—make haste!" said Maggie, giving a little stamp with her foot. Her cheeks were quite flushed.

The black locks were so thick—nothing could be more tempting to a lad who had already tasted the forbidden pleasure of cutting the pony's mane. I speak to those who know the satisfaction of making a pair of shears meet through a duly resisting mass of hair. One delicious grinding snip, and then another and another, and the hinder-locks fell heavily on the floor, and Maggie stood cropped in a jagged uneven manner, but with a sense of clearness and freedom, as if she had emerged from a wood into the open plain.

"O, Maggie," said Tom, jumping round her, and slapping his knees as he laughed, "O, my buttons, what a queer thing you look! Look at yourself in the glass—you look like the idiot we throw our nutshells to at school."

Maggie felt an unexpected pang. She had thought beforehand chiefly of her own deliverance from her teasing hair and teasing remarks about it, and something also of the triumph she should have over her mother and her aunts by this very decided course of action: she didn't want her hair to look pretty—that was out of the question—she only wanted people to think her a clever little girl, and not to find fault with her. But now, when Tom began to laugh at her, and say she was like the idiot, the affair had quite a new aspect. She looked in the glass, and still Tom laughed and clapped his hands, and Maggie's flushed cheeks began to pale, and her lips to tremble a little.

"O, Maggie, you'll have to go down to dinner directly," said Tom. "O my!"

"Don't laugh at me, Tom," said Maggie, in a passionate tone, with an outburst of angry tears, stamping, and giving him a push.

"Now, then, spitfire!" said Tom. "What did you cut it off for, then? I shall go down: I can smell the dinner going in."

He hurried down-stairs and left poor Maggie to that bitter sense of the irrevocable which was almost an everyday experience of her small soul. She could see clearly enough, now the thing was done, that it was very foolish, and that she should have to hear and think more about her hair than ever; for Maggie rushed to her deeds with passionate impulse, and then saw not only their consequences, but what would have happened if they had not been done, with all the detail and exaggerated circumstance of an active imagination. Tom never did the same sort of foolish things as Maggie, having a wonderful, instinctive discernment of what would turn to his advantage or disadvantage; and so it happened, that though he was much more wilful and inflexible than Maggie, his mother hardly ever called him naughty. But if Tom did make a mistake of that sort, he espoused it, and stood by it: he "didn't mind." If he broke the lash of his father's gig-whip by lashing the gate, he couldn't help it—the whip shouldn't have got caught in the hinge. If Tom Tulliver whipped a gate, he was convinced, not that the whipping of gates by all boys was a justifiable act, but that he, Tom Tulliver, was justifiable in whipping that particular gate, and he wasn't going to be sorry. But Maggie, as she stood crying before the glass, felt it impossible that she should go down to dinner and endure the severe eyes and severe words of her aunts, while Tom, and Lucy, and Martha, who waited at table, and perhaps her father and her uncles, would laugh at her,— for if Tom had laughed at her, of course every one else would; and if she had only let her hair alone, she could have sat with Tom and Lucy, and had the apricot pudding and the custard! What could she do but sob? She sat as helpless and despairing among her black locks as Ajax among the slaughtered sheep. Very trivial, perhaps, this anguish seems to weather-worn mortals who have to think of Christmas bills, dead loves, and broken friendships; but it was not less bitter to Maggie —perhaps it was even more bitter—than what we are fond of calling antithetically the real troubles of mature life. "Ah, my child, you will have real troubles to fret about by-and-by," is the consolation we have almost all of us had administered to us in our childhood, and have repeated to other children since we have been grown up. We have all of us sobbed so piteously, standing with tiny bare legs above our little socks, when we lost sight of our mother or nurse in some strange place; but we can no longer recall the poignancy of that moment and weep over it, as we do over the remembered sufferings of five or ten years ago. Every one of those keen moments has left its trace, and lives in us still, but such traces have blent themselves irrecoverably with the firmer texture of our youth and manhood; and so it comes that we can look on at the troubles of our chidren with a smiling disbelief in the reality of their pain. Is there any one who can recover the experience of his childhood, not merely with a memory of what he did and what happened to him, of what he liked and disliked when he was in frock and trousers, but with an intimate penetration, a revived consciousness of what he felt then —when it was so long from one Midsummer to another? what he felt when his schoolfellows shut him out of their game because he would pitch the ball wrong out of mere wilfulness; or on a rainy day in the holidays, when he didn't know how to amuse himself, and fell from idleness into mischief, from mischief into defiance, and from defiance into sulkiness; or when his mother absolutely refused to let him have a tailed coat that "half," although every other boy of his age had gone into tails already? Surely if we could recall that early bitterness, and the dim guesses, the strangely perspectiveless conception of life that gave the bitterness its intensity, we should not pooh-pooh the griefs of our children.

"Miss Maggie, you're to come down this minute," said Kezia, entering the room hurriedly. "Lawks! what have you been a-doing? I niver *see* such a fright."

"Don't, Kezia," said Maggie, angrily. "Go away!"

"But I tell you, you're to come down, Miss, this minute: your mother says so," said Kezia, going up to Maggie and taking her by the hand to raise her from the floor.

"Get away, Kezia; I don't want any dinner," said Maggie, resisting Kezia's arm. "I shan't come."

"O, well, I can't stay. I've got to wait at dinner," said Kezia, going out again.

"Maggie, you little silly," said Tom, peeping into the room ten minutes after, "why don't you come and have your dinner? There's lots o' goodies, and mother says you're to come. What are you crying for, you little spooney?"

O, it was dreadful! Tom was so hard and unconcerned: if *he* had been crying on the floor, Maggie would have cried too. And there was the dinner, so nice; and she was *so* hungry. It was very bitter.

But Tom was not altogether hard. He was not inclined to cry, but did not feel that Maggie's grief spoiled his prospect of the sweets; but he went and put his head near her, and said in a lower, comforting tone—

"Won't you come, then, Magsie? Shall I bring you a bit o' pudding when I've had mine? . . . and a custard and things?"

"Ye-e-es," said Maggie, beginning to feel life a little more tolerable.

"Very well," said Tom, going away. But he turned again at the door and said, "But you'd better come, you know. There's the dessert—nuts, you know—and cowslip wine."

Maggie's tears had ceased, and she looked reflective as Tom left her. His good-nature had taken off the keenest edge of her suffering, and nuts with cowslip wine began to assert their legitimate influence.

Slowly she rose from amongst her scattered locks, and slowly she made her way down-stairs. Then she stood leaning with one shoulder against the frame of the dining-parlour door, peeping in when it was ajar. She saw Tom and Lucy with an empty chair between them, and there were the custards on a side-table—it was too much. She slipped in and went towards the empty chair. But she had no sooner sat down than she repented, and wished herself back again.

Mrs. Tulliver gave a little scream as she saw her, and felt such a "turn" that she dropt the large gravy-spoon into the dish with the most serious results to the table-cloth. For Kezia had not betrayed the reason of Maggie's refusal to come down, not liking to give her mistress a shock in the moment of carving, and Mrs. Tulliver thought there was nothing worse in question than a fit of perverseness, which was inflicting its own punishment by depriving Maggie of half her dinner.

Mrs. Tulliver's scream made all eyes turn towards the same point as her own, and Maggie's cheeks and ears began to burn, while uncle Glegg, a kind-looking, white-haired old gentleman, said——

"Hey-day! what little gell's this—why, I don't know her. Is it some little gell you've picked up in the road, Kezia?"

"Why, she's gone and cut her hair herself," said Mr. Tulliver in an under-tone to Mr. Deane, laughing with much enjoyment. "Did you ever know such a little hussy as it is?"

"Why, little miss, you've made yourself look very funny," said uncle Pullet, and perhaps he never in his life made an observation which was felt to be so lacerating.

"Fie, for shame!" said aunt Glegg, in her loudest, severest tone of reproof. "Little gells as cut their own hair should be whipped and fed on bread-and-water—not come and sit down with their aunts and uncles."

"Ay, ay," said uncle Glegg, meaning to give a playful turn to this denunciation, "she must be sent to jail, I think, and they'll cut the rest of her hair off there, and make it all even."

"She's more like a gypsy nor ever," said aunt Pullet, in a pitying tone; "it's very bad luck, sister, as the gell should be so brown—the boy's fair enough. I doubt it'll stand in her way i' life, to be so brown."

"She's a naughty child, as 'll break her mother's heart," said Mrs. Tulliver, with the tears in her eyes.

Maggie seemed to be listening to a chorus of reproach and derision. Her first flush came from anger, which gave her a transient power of defiance, and Tom thought she was braving it out, supported by the recent appearance of the pudding and custard. Under this impression, he whispered, "O my! Maggie, I told you you'd catch it." He meant to be friendly, but Maggie felt convinced that Tom was rejoicing in her ignominy. Her feeble power of defiance left her in an instant, her heart swelled, and, getting up from her chair, she ran to her father, hid her face on his shoulder, and burst out into loud sobbing.

"Come, come, my wench," said her father, soothingly, putting his arm round her, "never mind; you was i' the right to cut it off if it plagued you; give over crying: father 'll take your part."

Delicious words of tenderness! Maggie never forgot any of these moments when her father "took her part;" she kept them in her heart.

and thought of them long years after, when every one else said that her father had done very ill by his children.

"How your husband does spoil that child, Bessy!" said Mrs. Glegg, in a loud "aside," to Mrs. Tulliver. "It'll be the ruin of her, if you don't take care. *My* father niver brought his children up so, else we should ha' been a different sort o' family to what we are."

Mrs. Tulliver's domestic sorrows seemed at this moment to have reached the point at which insensibility begins. She took no notice of her sister's remark, but threw back her cap-strings and dispensed the pudding, in mute resignation.

With the dessert there came entire deliverance for Maggie, for the children were told they might have their nuts and wine in the summer-house, since the day was so mild, and they scampered out among the budding bushes of the garden with the alacrity of small animals getting from under a burning-glass.

Mrs. Tulliver had her special reason for this permission: now the dinner was despatched, and every one's mind disengaged, it was the right moment to communicate Mr. Tulliver's intention concerning Tom, and it would be as well for Tom himself to be absent. The children were used to hear themselves talked of as freely as if they were birds, and could understand nothing, however they might stretch their necks and listen; but on this occasion Mrs. Tulliver manifested an unusual discretion, because she had recently had evidence that the going to school to a clergyman was a sore point with Tom, who looked at it as very much on a par with going to school to a constable. Mrs. Tulliver had a sighing sense that her husband would do as he liked, whatever sister Glegg said, or sister Pullet either, but at least they would not be able to say, if the thing turned out ill, that Bessy had fallen in with her husband's folly without letting her own friends know a word about it.

"Mr. Tulliver," she said, interrupting her husband in his talk with Mr. Deane, "it's time now to tell the children's aunts and uncles what you're thinking of doing with Tom, isn't it?"

"Very well," said Mr. Tulliver, rather sharply, "I've no objections to tell anybody what I mean to do with him. I've settled," he added, looking towards Mr. Glegg and Mr. Deane—"I've settled to send him a Mr. Stelling, a parson, down at King's Lorton, there—an uncommon clever fellow, I understand—as'll put him up to most things."

There was a rustling demonstration of surprise in the company, such as you may have observed in a country congregation when they hear an allusion to their week-day affairs from the pulpit. It was equally astonishing to the aunts and uncles to find a parson introduced into Mr. Tulliver's family arrangements. As for uncle Pullet, he could hardly have been more thoroughly obfuscated if Mr. Tulliver had said that he was going to send Tom to the Lord Chancellor: for uncle Pullet belonged to that extinct class of British yeomen who, dressed in good broadcloth, paid high rates and taxes, went to church, and ate a particularly good dinner on Sunday, without dreaming that the British constitution in

Church and State had a traceable origin any more than the solar system and the fixed stars. It is melancholy, but true, that Mr. Pullet had the most confused idea of a bishop as a sort of a baronet, who might or might not be a clergyman; and as the rector of his own parish was a man of high family and fortune, the idea that a clergyman could be a school-master was too remote from Mr. Pullet's experience to be readily conceivable. I know it is difficult for people in these instructed times to believe in uncle Pullet's ignorance; but let them reflect on the remarkable results of a great natural faculty under favouring circumstances. And uncle Pullet had a great natural faculty for ignorance. He was the first to give utterance to his astonishment.

"Why, what can you be going to send him to a parson for?" he said, with an amazed twinkling in his eyes, looking at Mr. Glegg and Mr. Deane, to see if they showed any signs of comprehension.

"Why, because the parsons are the best schoolmasters, by what I can make out," said poor Mr. Tulliver, who, in the maze of this puzzling world, laid hold of any clue with great readiness and tenacity. "Jacobs at th' academy's no parson, and he's done very bad by the boy; and I made up my mind, if I sent him to school again, it should be to somebody different to Jacobs. And this Mr. Stelling, by what I can make out, is the sort o' man I want. And I mean my boy to go to him at Mid-summer," he concluded, in a tone of decision, tapping his snuff-box and taking a pinch.

"You'll have to pay a swinging half-yearly bill then, eh, Tulliver? The clergymen have highish notions, in general," said Mr. Deane, taking snuff vigorously, as he always did when wishing to maintain a neutral position.

"What! do you think the parson 'll teach him to know a good sample o' wheat when he sees it, neighbour Tulliver?" said Mr. Glegg, who was fond of his jest; and, having retired from business, felt that it was not only allowable but becoming in him to take a playful view of things.

"Why, you see, I've got a plan i' my head about Tom," said Mr. Tulliver, pausing after that statement and lifting up his glass.

"Well, if I may be allowed to speak, and it's seldom as I am," said Mrs. Glegg, with a tone of bitter meaning, "I should like to know what good is to come to the boy, by bringin' him up above his fortin."

"Why," said Mr. Tulliver, not looking at Mrs. Glegg, but at the male part of his audience, "you see, I've made up my mind not to bring Tom up to my own business. I've had my thoughts about it all along, and I made up my mind by what I saw with Garnett and *his* son. I mean to put him to some business, as he can go into without capital, and I want to give him an eddication as he'll be even wi' the lawyers and folks, and put me up to a notion now an' then."

Mrs. Glegg emitted a long sort of guttural sound with closed lips, that smiled in mingled pity and scorn.

"It 'ud be a fine deal better for some people," she said, after that introductory note, "if they'd let the lawyers alone."

"Is he at the head of a grammar school, then, this clergyman—such as that at Market Bewley?" said Mr. Deane.

"No—nothing o' that," said Mr. Tulliver. "He won't take more than two or three pupils—and so he'll have the more time to attend to 'em, you know."

"Ah, and get his eddication done the sooner: they can't learn much at a time when there's so many of 'em," said uncle Pullet, feeling that he was getting quite an insight into this difficult matter.

"But he'll want the more pay, I doubt," said Mr. Glegg.

"Ay, ay, a cool hundred a-year—that's all," said Mr. Tulliver, with some pride at his own spirited course. "But then, you know, it's an investment; Tom's eddication 'ull be so much capital to him."

"Ay, there's something in that," said Mr. Glegg. "Well, well, neighbour Tulliver, you may be right, you may be right:

'When land is gone and money's spent,
Then learning is most excellent.'

I remember seeing those two lines wrote on a window at Buxton. But us that have got no learning had better keep our money, eh, neighbour Pullet?" Mr. Glegg rubbed his knees and looked very pleasant.

"Mr. Glegg, I wonder *at* you," said his wife. "It's very unbecoming in a man o' your age and belongings."

"What's unbecoming, Mrs. G.?" said Mr. Glegg, winking pleasantly at the company. "My new blue coat as I've got on?"

"I pity your weakness, Mr. Glegg. I say it's unbecoming to be making a joke when you see your own kin going headlongs to ruin."

"If you mean me by that," said Mr. Tulliver, considerably nettled, "you needn't trouble yourself to fret about me. I can manage my own affairs without troubling other folks."

"Bless me," said Mr. Deane, judiciously introducing a new idea, "why, now I come to think of it, somebody said Wakem was going to send *his* son—the deformed lad—to a clergyman, didn't they, Susan?" (appealing to his wife).

"I can give no account of it, I'm sure," said Mrs. Deane, closing her lips very tightly again. Mrs. Deane was not a woman to take part in a scene where missiles were flying.

"Well," said Mr. Tulliver, speaking all the more cheerfully that Mrs. Glegg might see he didn't mind her, "if Wakem thinks o' sending his son to a clergyman, depend on it I shall make no mistake i' sending Tom to one. Wakem's as big a scoundrel as Old Harry ever made, but he knows the length of every man's foot he's got to deal with. Ay, ay, tell me who's Wakem's butcher, and I'll tell you where to get your meat."

"But lawyer Wakem's son's got a hump-back," said Mrs. Pullet, who felt as if the whole business had a funereal aspect; "it's more nat'ral to send *him* to a clergyman."

"Yes," said Mr. Glegg, interpreting Mrs. Pullet's observation with erroneous plausibility, "you must consider that, neighbour Tulliver;

Wakem's son isn't likely to follow any business. Wakem 'ull make a gentleman of him, poor fellow."

"Mr. Glegg," said Mrs. G., in a tone which implied that her indignation would fizz and ooze a little, though she was determined to keep it corked up, "you'd far better hold your tongue. Mr. Tulliver doesn't want to know your opinion nor mine neither. There's folks in the world as know better than everybody else."

"Why, I should think that's you, if we're to trust your own tale," said Mr. Tulliver, beginning to boil up again.

"O, *I* say nothing," said Mrs. Glegg, sarcastically. "My advice has never been asked, and I don't give it."

"It'll be the first time, then," said Mr. Tulliver. "It's the only thing you're over-ready at giving."

"I've been over-ready at lending, then, if I haven't been over-ready at giving," said Mrs. Glegg. "There's folks I've lent money to, as perhaps I shall repent o' lending money to kin."

"Come, come, come," said Mr. Glegg, soothingly. But Mr. Tulliver was not to be hindered of his retort.

"You've got a bond for it, I reckon," he said; "and you've had your five per cent, kin or no kin."

"Sister," said Mrs. Tulliver, pleadingly, "drink your wine, and let me give you some almonds and raisins."

"Bessy, I'm sorry for you," said Mrs. Glegg, very much with the feeling of a cur that seizes the opportunity of diverting his bark towards the man who carries no stick. "It's poor work, talking o' almonds and raisins."

"Lors, sister Glegg, don't be so quarrelsome," said Mrs. Pullet, beginning to cry a little. "You may be struck with a fit, getting so red in the face after dinner, and we are but just out o' mourning, all of us—and all wi' gowns craped alike and just put by—it's very bad among sisters."

"I should think it *is* bad," said Mrs. Glegg. "Things are come to a fine pass when one sister invites the other to her house o' purpose to quarrel with her and abuse her."

"Softly, softly, Jane—be reasonable—be reasonable," said Mr. Glegg. But while he was speaking, Mr. Tulliver, who had by no means said enough to satisfy his anger, burst out again.

"Who wants to quarrel with you?" he said. "It's you as can't let people alone, but must be gnawing at 'em for ever. *I* should never want to quarrel with any woman, if she kept her place."

"My place, indeed!" said Mrs. Glegg, getting rather more shrill. "There's your betters, Mr. Tulliver, as are dead and in their grave, treated me with a different sort o' respect to what you do—*though* I've got a husband as 'll sit by and see me abused by them as 'ud never ha' had the chance if there hadn't been them in our family as married worse than they might ha' done."

"If you talk o' that," said Mr. Tulliver, "my family's as good as yours—and better, for it hasn't got a damned ill-tempered woman in it."

"Well!" said Mrs. Glegg, rising from her chair, "I don't know whether you think it's a fine thing to sit by and hear me swore at, Mr. Glegg; but I'm not going to stay a minute longer in this house. You can stay behind, and come home with the gig—and I'll walk home."

"Dear heart, dear heart!" said Mr. Glegg in a melancholy tone, as he followed his wife out of the room.

"Mr. Tulliver, how could you talk so?" said Mrs. Tulliver, with the tears in her eyes.

"Let her go," said Mr. Tulliver, too hot to be damped by any amount of tears. "Let her go, and the sooner the better: she won't be trying to domineer over *me* again in a hurry."

"Sister Pullet," said Mrs. Tulliver, helplessly, "do you think it 'ud be any use for you to go after her and try to pacify her?"

"Better not, better not," said Mr. Deane. "You'll make it up another day."

"Then, sisters, shall we go and look at the children?" said Mrs. Tulliver, drying her eyes.

No proposition could have been more seasonable. Mr. Tulliver felt very much as if the air had been cleared of obtrusive flies now the women were out of the room. There were few things he liked better than a chat with Mr. Deane, whose close application to business allowed the pleasure very rarely. Mr. Deane, he considered, was the "knowing-est" man of his acquaintance, and he had besides a ready causticity of tongue that made an agreeable supplement to Mr. Tulliver's own tendency that way, which had remained in rather an inarticulate condition. And now the women were gone, they could carry on their serious talk without frivolous interruption. They would exchange their views concerning the Duke of Wellington, whose conduct in the Catholic Question had thrown such an entirely new light on his character; and speak slightingly of his conduct at the battle of Waterloo, which he would never have won if there hadn't been a great many Englishmen at his back, not to speak of Blucher and the Prussians, who, as Mr. Tulliver had heard from a person of particular knowledge in that matter, had come up in the very nick of time; though here there was a slight dissidence, Mr. Deane remarking that he was not disposed to give much credit to the Prussians,—the build of their vessels, together with the unsatisfactory character of transactions in Dantzic beer, inclining him to form rather a low view of Prussian pluck generally. Rather beaten on this ground, Mr. Tulliver proceeded to express his fears that the country could never again be what it used to be; but Mr. Deane, attached to a firm of which the returns were on the increase, naturally took a more lively view of the present; and had some details to give concerning the state of the imports, especially in hides and spelter, which soothed Mr. Tulliver's imagination by throwing into more distant perspective the period when the country would become utterly the prey of Papists and Radicals, and there would be no more chance for honest men.

Uncle Pullet sat by and listened with twinkling eyes to these high matters. He didn't understand politics himself—thought they were a natural gift—but by what he could make out, this Duke of Wellington was no better than he should be.

CHAPTER VIII

MR. TULLIVER SHOWS HIS WEAKER SIDE

"Suppose sister Glegg should call her money in—it 'ud be very awkward for you to have to raise five hundred pounds now," said Mrs. Tulliver to her husband that evening, as she took a plaintive review of the day.

Mrs. Tulliver had lived thirteen years with her husband, yet she retained in all the freshness of her early married life a facility of saying things which drove him in the opposite direction to the one she desired. Some minds are wonderful for keeping their bloom in this way, as a patriarchal gold-fish apparently retains to the last its youthful illusion that it can swim in a straight line beyond the encircling glass. Mrs. Tulliver was an amiable fish of this kind, and, after running her head against the same resisting medium for thirteen years, would go at it again to-day with undulled alacrity.

This observation of hers tended directly to convince Mr. Tulliver that it would not be at all awkward for him to raise five hundred pounds; and when Mrs. Tulliver became rather pressing to know *how* he would raise it without mortgaging the mill and the house which he had said he never *would* mortgage, since nowadays people were none so ready to lend money without security, Mr. Tulliver, getting warm, declared that Mrs. Glegg might do as she liked about calling in her money—he should pay it in, whether or not. He was not going to be beholding to his wife's sisters. When a man had married into a family where there was a whole litter of women, he might have plenty to put up with if he choose. But Mr. Tulliver did *not* choose.

Mrs. Tulliver cried a little in a trickling quiet way as she put on her nightcap; but presently sank into a comfortable sleep, lulled by the thought that she would talk everything over with her sister Pullet to-morrow, when she was to take the children to Garum Firs to tea. Not that she looked forward to any distinct issue from that talk; but it seemed impossible that past events should be so obstinate as to remain unmodified when they were complained against.

Her husband lay awake rather longer, for he too was thinking of a visit he would pay on the morrow, and his ideas on the subject were not of so vague and soothing a kind as those of his amiable partner.

Mr. Tulliver, when under the influence of a strong feeling, had a promptitude in action that may seem inconsistent with that painful sense of the complicated puzzling nature of human affairs under which his more dispassionate deliberations were conducted; but it is really not improbable that there was a direct relation between these apparently contradictory phenomena, since I have observed that for getting a strong impression that a skein is tangled, there is nothing like snatching hastily at a single thread. It was owing to this promptitude that Mr. Tulliver was on horseback soon after dinner the next day (he was not dyspeptic) on his way to Basset to see his sister Moss and her husband. For having made up his mind irrevocably that he would pay Mrs. Glegg her loan of five hundred pounds, it naturally occurred to him that he had a promissory note for three hundred pounds lent to his brother-in-law Moss, and if said brother-in-law could manage to pay in the money within a given time, it would go far to lessen the fallacious air of inconvenience which Mr. Tulliver's spirited step might have worn in the eyes of weak people who require to know precisely *how* a thing is to be done before they are strongly confident that it will be easy.

For Mr. Tulliver was in a position neither new nor striking, but, like other everyday things, sure to have a cumulative effect that will be felt in the long run: he was held to be a much more substantial man than he really was. And as we are all apt to believe what the world believes about us, it was his habit to think of failure and ruin with the same sort of remote pity with which a spare long-necked man hears that his plethoric short-necked neighbour is stricken with apoplexy. He had been always used to hear pleasant jokes about his advantages as a man who worked his own mill, and owned a pretty bit of land; and these jokes naturally kept up his sense that he was a man of considerable substance. They gave a pleasant flavour to his glass on a market-day, and if it had not been for the recurrence of half-yearly payments, Mr. Tulliver would really have forgotten that there was a mortgage of two thousand pounds on his very desirable freehold. That was not altogether his own fault, since one of the thousand pounds was his sister's fortune, which he had had to pay on her marriage; and a man who has neighbours that *will* go to law with him, is not likely to pay off his mortgages, especially if he enjoys the good opinion of acquaintances who want to borrow a hundred pounds on security too lofty to be represented by parchment. Our friend Mr. Tulliver had a good-natured fibre in him, and did not like to give harsh refusals even to a sister, who had not only come into the world in that superfluous way characteristic of sisters, creating a necessity for mortgages, but had quite thrown herself away in marriage, and had crowned her mistakes by having an eighth baby. On this point Mr. Tulliver was conscious of being a little weak; but he apologised to himself by saying that poor Gritty had been a good-looking wench before she married Moss—he would sometimes say this even with a slight tremulousness in his voice. But this morning he was in a mood more becoming a man of business, and in the course of his ride along the Basset lanes, with their deep ruts,—lying so far away from a market-town that the labour of drawing produce and manure was enough to take away the best part of the profits on such poor land as that parish was made of, —he got up a due amount of irritation against Moss as a man without

capital, who, if murrain and blight were abroad, was sure to have his
share of them, and who, the more you tried to help him out of the mud,
would sink the further in. It would do him good rather than harm,
now, if he were obliged to raise this three hundred pounds: it would
make him look about him better, and not act so foolishly about his wool
this year as he did the last: in fact, Mr. Tulliver had been too easy with
his brother-in-law, and because he had let the interest run on for two
years, Moss was likely enough to think that he should never be troubled
about the principal. But Mr. Tulliver was determined not to encourage
such shuffling people any longer; and a ride along the Basset lanes was
not likely to enervate a man's resolution by softening his temper. The
deep-trodden hoof-marks, made in the muddiest days of winter, gave
him a shake now and then which suggested a rash but stimulating snarl
at the father of lawyers, who, whether by means of his hoof or otherwise,
had doubtless something to do with this state of the roads; and the
abundance of foul land and neglected fences that met his eye, though
they made no part of his brother Moss's farm, strongly contributed to
his dissatisfaction with that unlucky agriculturist. If this wasn't Moss's
fallow, it might have been: Basset was all alike; it was a beggarly parish in Mr. Tulliver's opinion, and his opinion was certainly not ground-
less. Basset had a poor soil, poor roads, a poor non-resident landlord, a
poor non-resident vicar, and rather less than half a curate, also poor. If
any one strongly impressed with the power of the human mind to triumph over circumstances, will contend that the parishioners of Basset
might nevertheless have been a very superior class of people, I have
nothing to urge against that abstract proposition; I only know that, in
point of fact, the Basset mind was in strict keeping with its circumstances. The muddy lanes, green or clayey, that seemed to the unaccustomed eye to lead nowhere but into each other, did really lead, with
patience, to a distant high-road; but there were many feet in Basset
which they led more frequently to a centre of dissipation, spoken of
formally as the "Markis o' Granby," but among intimates as "Dickison's." A large low room with a sanded floor, a cold scent of tobacco,
modified by undetected beer-dregs, Mr. Dickinson leaning against the
doorpost with a melancholy pimpled face, looking as irrelevant to the
daylight as a last night's guttered candle—all this may not seem a very
seductive form of temptation; but the majority of men in Basset found
it fatally alluring when encountered on their road towards four o'clock
on a wintry afternoon; and if any wife in Basset wished to indicate that
her husband was not a pleasure-seeking man, she could hardly do it more
emphatically than by saying that he didn't spend a shilling at Dickison's
from one Whitsuntide to another. Mrs. Moss had said so of *her* husband
more than once, when her brother was in a mood to find fault with him,
as he certainly was to-day. And nothing could be less pacifying to Mr.
Tulliver than the behaviour of the farmyard gate, which he no sooner
attempted to push open with his riding-stick, than it acted as gates
without the upper hinge are known to do, to the peril of shins, whether

equine or human. He was about to get down and lead his horse through the damp dirt of the hollow farmyard, shadowed drearily by the large half-timbered buildings, up to the long line of tumble-down dwelling-house standing on a raised causeway, but the timely appearance of a cowboy saved him that frustration of a plan he had determined on—namely, not to get down from his horse during this visit. If a man means to be hard, let him keep in his saddle and speak from that height, above the level of pleading eyes, and with the command of a distant horizon. Mrs. Moss heard the sound of the horse's feet, and, when her brother rode up, was already outside the kitchen door, with a half-weary smile on her face, and a black-eyed baby in her arms. Mrs. Moss's face bore a faded resemblance to her brother's; baby's little fat hand, pressed against her cheek, seemed to show more strikingly that the cheek was faded.

"Brother, I'm glad to see you," she said, in an affectionate tone. "I didn't look for you to-day. How do you do?"

"Oh, . . . pretty well, Mrs. Moss . . . pretty well," answered the brother, with cool deliberation, as if it were rather too forward of her to ask that question. She knew at once that her brother was not in a good humour: he never called her Mrs. Moss except when he was angry, and when they were in company. But she thought it was in the order of nature that people who were poorly off should be snubbed. Mrs. Moss did not take her stand on the equality of the human race: she was a patient, prolific, loving-hearted woman.

"Your husband isn't in the house, I suppose?" added Mr. Tulliver, after a grave pause, during which four children had run out, like chickens whose mother has been suddenly in eclipse behind the hencoop.

"No," said Mrs. Moss, "but he's only in the potato-field yonders. Georgy, run to the Far Close in a minute, and tell father your uncle's come. You'll get down, brother, won't you, and take something?"

"No, no; I can't get down. I must be going home again directly," said Mr. Tulliver, looking at the distance.

"And how's Mrs. Tulliver and the children?" said Mrs. Moss, humbly, not daring to press her invitation.

"Oh, . . . pretty well. Tom's going to a new school at Midsummer —a deal of expense to me. It's bad work for me, lying out o' my money."

"I wish you'd be so good as let the children come and see their cousins some day. My little uns want to see their cousin Maggie, so as never was. And me her god-mother, and so fond of her—there's nobody 'ud make a bigger fuss with her, according to what they've got. And I know she likes to come, for she's a loving child, and how quick and clever she is, to be sure!"

If Mrs. Moss had been one of the most astute women in the world, instead of being one of the simplest, she could have thought of nothing more likely to propitiate her brother than this praise of Maggie. He seldom found any one volunteering praise of "the little wench:" it was usually left entirely to himself to insist on her merits. But Maggie al-

ways appeared in the most amiable light at her aunt Moss's: it was her
Alsatia, where she was out of the reach of law—if she upset anything,
dirtied her shoes, or tore her frock, these things were matters of course
at her aunt Moss's. In spite of himself, Mr. Tulliver's eyes got milder,
and he did not look away from his sister, as he said,

"Ay: she's fonder o' you than o' the other aunts, I think. She takes
after our family: not a bit of her mother's in her."

"Moss says she's just like what I used to be," said Mrs. Moss,
"though I was never so quick and fond o' the books. But I think my
Lizzy's like her—*she's* sharp. Come here, Lizzy, my dear, and let your
uncle see you: he hardly knows you; you grow so fast."

Lizzy, a black-eyed child of seven, looked very shy when her mother
drew her forward, for the small Mosses were much in awe of their
uncle from Dorlcote Mill. She was inferior enough to Maggie in fire
and strength of expression, to make the resemblance between the two
entirely flattering to Mr. Tulliver's fatherly love.

"Ay, they're a bit alike," he said, looking kindly at the little figure in
the soiled pinafore. "They both take after our mother. You've got
enough o' gells, Gritty," he added, in a tone half compassionate, half
reproachful.

"Four of 'em, bless 'em," said Mrs. Moss, with a sigh, stroking Lizzy's
hair on each side of her forehead; "as many as there's boys. They've got
a brother a-piece."

"Ah, but they must turn out and fend for themselves," said Mr.
Tulliver, feeling that his severity was relaxing, and trying to brace it by
throwing out a wholesome hint. "They mustn't look to hanging on their
brothers."

"No: but I hope their brothers 'ull love the poor things, and remember they came o' one father and mother: the lads 'ull never be the
poorer for that," said Mrs. Moss, flashing out with hurried timidity,
like a half-smothered fire.

Mr. Tulliver gave his horse a little stroke on the flank, then checked
it, and said, angrily, "Stand still with you!" much to the astonishment
of that innocent animal.

"And the more there is of 'em, the more they must love one another,"
Mrs. Moss went on, looking at her children with a didactic purpose. But
she turned towards her brother again to say, "Not but what I hope
your boy 'ull allays be good to his sister, though there's but two of 'em,
like you and me, brother."

That arrow went straight to Mr. Tulliver's heart. He had not a rapid
imagination, but the thought of Maggie was very near to him, and he
was not long in seeing his relation to his own sister side by side with
Tom's relation to Maggie. Would the little wench ever be poorly off,
and Tom rather hard upon her?

"Ay, ay, Gritty," said the miller, with a new softness in his tone,
"but I've allays done what I could for you," he added, as if vindicating
himself from a reproach.

"I'm not denying that, brother, and I'm noways ungrateful," said poor Mrs. Moss, too fagged by toil and children to have strength left for any pride. "But here's the father. What a while you've been, Moss!"

"While, do you call it?" said Mr. Moss, feeling out of breath and injured. "I've been running all the way. Won't you 'light, Mr. Tulliver?"

"Well, I'll just get down, and have a bit o' talk with you in the garden," said Mr. Tulliver, feeling that he should be more likely to show a due spirit of resolve if his sister were not present.

He got down, and passed with Mr. Moss into the garden, towards an old yew-tree arbour, while his sister stood tapping her baby on the back, and looking wistfully after them.

Their entrance into the yew-tree arbour surprised several fowls that were recreating themselves by scratching deep holes in the dusty ground, and at once took flight with much pother and cackling. Mr. Tulliver sat down on the bench, and tapping the ground curiously here and there with his stick, as if he suspected some hollowness, opened the conversation by observing, with something like a snarl in his tone——

"Why, you've got wheat again in that Corner Close, I see; and never a bit o' dressing on it. You'll do no good with it this year."

Mr. Moss, who, when he married Miss Tulliver, had been regarded as the buck of Basset, now wore a beard nearly a week old, and had the depressed, unexpectant air of a machine-horse. He answered in a patient-grumbling tone, "Why, poor farmers like me must do as they can: they must leave it to them as have got money to play with, to put half as much into the ground as they mean to get out of it."

"I don't know who should have money to play with, if it isn't them as can borrow money without paying interest," said Mr. Tulliver, who wished to get into a slight quarrel; it was the most natural and easy introduction to calling in money.

"I know I'm behind with the interest," said Mr. Moss, "but I was so unlucky wi' the wool last year; and what with the Missis being laid up so, things have gone awk'arder nor usual."

"Ay," snarled Mr. Tulliver, "there's folks as things 'ull allays go awk'ard with: empty sacks 'ull never stand upright."

"Well, I don't know what fault you've got to find wi' me, Mr. Tulliver," said Mr. Moss, deprecatingly; "I know there isn't a day-labourer works harder."

"What's the use o' that," said Mr. Tulliver, sharply, "when a man marries, an's got no capital to work his farm but his wife's bit o' fortin? I was against it from the first; but you'd neither of you listen to me. And I can't lie out o' my money any longer, for I've got to pay five hundred o' Mrs. Glegg's, and there 'ull be Tom an expense to me, as I should find myself short, even saying I'd got back all as is my own. You must look about and see how you can pay me the three hundred pound."

"Well, if that's what you mean," said Mr. Moss, looking blankly before him, "we'd better be sold up, and ha' done with it; I must part wi' every head o' stock I'n got, to pay you and the landlord too."

Poor relations are undeniably irritating—their existence is so entirely uncalled for on our part, and they are almost always very faulty people. Mr. Tulliver had succeeded in getting quite as much irritated with Mr. Moss as he had desired, and he was able to say angrily, rising from his seat——

"Well, you must do as you can. *I* can't find money for everybody else as well as myself. I must look to my own business, and my own family. I can't lie out o' my money any longer. You must raise it as quick as you can."

Mr. Tulliver walked abruptly out of the arbour as he uttered the last sentence, and, without looking round at Mr. Moss, went on to the kitchen door, where the eldest boy was holding his horse, and his sister was waiting in a state of wondering alarm, which was not without its alleviations, for baby was making pleasant gurgling sounds, and performing a great deal of finger practice on the faded face. Mrs. Moss had eight children, but could never overcome her regret that the twins had not lived. Mr. Moss thought their removal was not without its consolations. "Won't you come in, brother?" she said, looking anxiously at her husband, who was walking slowly up, while Mr. Tulliver had his foot already in the stirrup.

"No, no; good-by," said he, turning his horse's head, and riding away.

No man could feel more resolute till he got outside the yard-gate, and a little way along the deep-rutted lane; but before he reached the next turning, which would take him out of sight of the dilapidated farm-buildings, he appeared to be smitten by some sudden thought. He checked his horse, and made it stand still in the same spot for two or three minutes, during which he turned his head from side to side in a melancholy way, as if he were looking at some painful object on more sides than one. Evidently, after his fit of promptitude, Mr. Tulliver was relapsing into the sense that this is a puzzling world. He turned his horse, and rode slowly back, giving vent to the climax of feeling which had determined this movement by saying aloud, as he struck his horse, "Poor little wench! she'll have nobody but Tom, belike, when I'm gone."

Mr. Tulliver's return into the yard was descried by several young Mosses, who immediately ran in with the exciting news to their mother, so that Mrs. Moss was again on the door-step when her brother rode up. She had been crying, but was rocking baby to sleep in her arms now, and made no ostentatious show of sorrow as her brother looked at her, but merely said—

"The father's gone to the field again, if you want him, brother."

"No, Gritty, no," said Mr. Tulliver, in a gentle tone. "Don't you fret—that's all—I'll make a shift without the money a bit—only you must be as cliver and contriving as you can."

Mrs. Moss's tears came again at this unexpected kindness, and she could say nothing.

"Come, come!—the little wench shall come and see you. I'll bring

her and Tom some day before he goes to school. You mustn't fret
. . . I'll allays be a good brother to you."

"Thank you for that word, brother," said Mrs. Moss, drying hei
tears; then turning to Lizzy, she said, "Run now, and fetch the col·
oured egg for cousin Maggie." Lizzy ran in, and quickly reappeared
with a small paper parcel.

"It's boiled hard, brother, and coloured with thrums—very pretty:
it was done o' purpose for Maggie. Will you please to carry it in your
pocket?"

"Ay, ay," said Mr. Tulliver, putting it carefully in his side-pocket.
"Good-by."

And so the respectable miller returned along the Basset lanes
rather more puzzled than before as to ways and means, but still with
the sense of a danger escaped. It had come across his mind that if he
were hard upon his sister, it might somehow tend to make Tom hard
upon Maggie at some distant day, when her father was no longer
there to take her part; for simple people, like our friend Mr. Tulliver,
are apt to clothe unimpeachable feelings in erroneous ideas, and this
was his confused way of explaining to himself that his love and
anxiety for "the little wench" had given him a new sensibility towards
his sister.

CHAPTER IX

TO GARUM FIRS

While the possible troubles of Maggie's future were occupying her
father's mind, she herself was tasting only the bitterness of the present. Childhood has no forebodings; but then, it is soothed by no
memories of outlived sorrow.

The fact was, the day had begun ill with Maggie. The pleasure of having Lucy to look at, and the prospect of the afternoon visit
to Garum Firs, where she would hear uncle Pullet's musical-box, had
been marred as early as eleven o'clock by the advent of the hair-
dresser from St. Ogg's, who had spoken in the severest terms of the
condition in which he had found her hair, holding up one jagged lock
after another and saying, "See here! tut—tut—tut!" in a tone of
mingled disgust and pity, which to Maggie's imagination was equivalent to the strongest expression of public opinion. Mr. Rappit, the
hair-dresser, with his well-anointed coronal locks tending wavily upward, like the simulated pyramid of flame on a monumental urn,
seemed to her at that moment the most formidable of her contemporaries, into whose street at St. Ogg's she would carefully refrain
from entering through the rest of her life.

Moreover, the preparation for a visit being always a serious affair
in the Dodson family, Martha was enjoined to have Mrs. Tulliver's

room ready an hour earlier than usual, that the laying-out of the best clothes might not be deferred till the last moment, as was sometimes the case in families of lax views, where the ribbon-strings were never rolled up, where there was little or no wrapping in silver paper, and where the sense that the Sunday clothes could be got at quite easily produced no shock to the mind. Already, at twelve o'clock, Mrs. Tulliver had on her visiting costume, with a protective apparatus of brown holland, as if she had been a piece of satin furniture in danger of flies; Maggie was frowning and twisting her shoulders, that she might if possible shrink away from the prickliest of tuckers, while her mother was remonstrating, "Don't, Maggie, my dear—don't look so ugly!" and Tom's cheeks were looking particularly brilliant as a relief to his best blue suit, which he wore with becoming calmness; having, after a little wrangling, effected what was always the one point of interest to him in his toilette—he had transformed all the contents of his everyday pockets to those actually in wear.

As for Lucy, she was just as pretty and neat as she had been yesterday: no accidents ever happened to her clothes, and she was never uncomfortable in them, so that she looked with wondering pity at Maggie pouting and writhing under the exasperating tucker. Maggie would certainly have torn it off, if she had not been checked by the remembrance of her recent humiliation about her hair: as it was, she confined herself to fretting and twisting, and behaving peevishly about the card-houses which they were allowed to build till dinner, as a suitable amusement for boys and girls in their best clothes. Tom could build perfect pyramids of houses; but Maggie's would never bear the laying-on of the roof:—it was always so with the things that Maggie made; and Tom had deduced the conclusion that no girls could ever make anything. But it happened that Lucy proved wonderfully clever at building: she handled the cards so lightly, and moved so gently, that Tom condescended to admire her houses as well as his own, the more readily because she had asked him to teach her. Maggie, too, would have admired Lucy's houses, and would have given up her own unsuccessful building to contemplate them, without ill-temper, if her tucker had not made her peevish, and if Tom had not inconsiderately laughed when her houses fell, and told her she was "a stupid."

"Don't laugh at me, Tom!" she burst out, angrily, "I'm not a stupid. I know a great many things you don't."

"O, I daresay, Miss Spitfire! I'd never be such a cross thing as you —making faces like that. Lucy doesn't do so. I like Lucy better than you: *I* wish Lucy was *my* sister."

"Then it's very wicked and cruel of you to wish so," said Maggie, starting up hurriedly from her place on the floor, and upsetting Tom's wonderful pagoda. She really did not mean it, but the circumstantial evidence was against her, and Tom turned white with anger, but said nothing: he would have struck her, only he knew it was cowardly to strike a girl, and Tom Tulliver was quite determined he would never do anything cowardly.

Maggie stood in dismay and terror while Tom got up from the floor and walked away, pale, from the scattered ruins of his pagoda, and Lucy looked on mutely, like a kitten pausing from its lapping.

"O Tom," said Maggie, at last, going half-way towards him, "I didn't mean to knock it down—indeed, indeed I didn't."

Tom took no notice of her, but took, instead, two or three hard peas out of his pocket, and shot them with his thumb-nail against the window—vaguely at first, but presently with the distinct aim of hitting a superannuated blue-bottle which was exposing its imbecility in the spring sunshine, clearly against the views of nature, who had provided Tom and the peas for the speedy destruction of this weak individual.

Thus the morning had been made heavy to Maggie, and Tom's persistent coldness to her all through their walk spoiled the fresh air and sunshine for her. He called Lucy to look at the half-built bird's nest without caring to show it Maggie, and peeled a willow switch for Lucy and himself, without offering one to Maggie. Lucy had said, "Maggie, shouldn't *you* like one?" but Tom was deaf.

Still the sight of the peacock opportunely spreading his tail on the stackyard wall, just as they reached Garum Firs, was enough to divert the mind temporarily from personal grievances. And this was only the beginning of beautiful sights at Garum Firs. All the farmyard life was wonderful there—bantams, speckled and top-knotted; Friesland hens, with their feathers all turned the wrong way; Guinea fowls that flew and screamed and dropped their pretty-spotted feathers; pouter pigeons and a tame magpie; nay, a goat, and a wonderful brindled dog, half mastiff half bull-dog, as large as a lion. Then there were white railings and white gates all about, and glittering weathercocks of various design, and garden-walks paved with pebbles in beautiful patterns—nothing was quite common at Garum Firs: and Tom thought that the unusual size of the toads there was simply due to the general unusualness which characterised uncle Pullet's possessions as a gentleman farmer. Toads who paid rent were naturally leaner. As for the house, it was not less remarkable: it had a receding centre, and two wings with battlemented turrets, and was covered with glittering white stucco.

Uncle Pullet had seen the expected party approaching from the window, and made haste to unbar and unchain the front door, kept always in this fortified condition from fear of tramps, who might be supposed to know of the glass-case of stuffed birds in the hall, and to contemplate rushing in and carrying it away on their heads. Aunt Pullet, too, appeared at the doorway, and as soon as her sister was within hearing, said, "Stop the children, for God's sake, Bessy— don't let 'em come up the door-steps: Sally's bringing the old mat and the duster, to rub their shoes."

Mrs. Pullet's front-door mats were by no means intended to wipe shoes on: the very scraper had a deputy to do its dirty work. Tom rebelled particularly against this shoe-wiping, which he always considered in the light of an indignity to his sex. He felt it as the beginning of the disagreeables incident to a visit at aunt Pullet's, where he had once been compelled to sit with towels wrapped round his boots; a fact which may serve to correct the too hasty conclusion that a visit to Garum Firs must have been a great treat to a young gentleman fond of animals—fond, that is, of throwing stones at them.

The next disagreeable was confined to his feminine companions: it was the mounting of the polished oak stairs, which had very handsome carpets rolled up and laid by in a spare bedroom, so that the ascent of these glossy steps might have served, in barbarous times, as a trial by ordeal from which none but the most spotless virtue could have come off with unbroken limbs. Sophy's weakness about these polished stairs was always a subject of bitter remonstrance on Mrs. Glegg's part; but Mrs. Tulliver ventured on no comment, only thinking to herself it was a mercy when she and the children were safe on the landing.

"Mrs. Gray has sent home my new bonnet, Bessy," said Mrs. Pullet, in a pathetic tone, as Mrs. Tulliver adjusted her cap.

"Has she, sister?" said Mrs. Tulliver, with an air of much interest. "And how do you like it?"

"It's apt to make a mess with clothes, taking 'em out and putting 'em in again," said Mrs. Pullet, drawing a bunch of keys from her pocket and looking at them earnestly, "but it 'ud be a pity for you to go away without seeing it. There's no knowing what may happen."

Mrs. Pullet shook her head slowly at this last serious consideration, which determined her to single out a particular key.

"I'm afraid it'll be troublesome to you getting it out, sister," said Mrs. Tulliver, "but I *should* like to see what sort of a crown she's made you."

Mrs. Pullet rose with a melancholy air and unlocked one wing of a very bright wardrobe, where you may have hastily supposed she would find the new bonnet. Not at all. Such a supposition could only have arisen from a too superficial acquaintance with the habits of the Dodson family. In this wardrobe Mrs. Pullet was seeking something small enough to be hidden among layers of linen—it was a door-key.

"You must come with me into the best room," said Mrs. Pullet.

"May the children come too, sister?" inquired Mrs. Tulliver, who saw that Maggie and Lucy were looking rather eager.

"Well," said aunt Pullet, reflectively, "it'll perhaps be safer for 'em to come—they'll be touching something if we leave 'em behind."

So they went in procession along the bright and slippery corridor, dimly lighted by the semi-lunar top of the window which rose above the closed shutter: it was really quite solemn. Aunt Pullet paused and unlocked a door which opened on something still more solemn than the passage: a darkened room, in which the outer light, entering feebly, showed what looked like the corpses of furniture in white shrouds. Everything that was not shrouded stood with its legs upwards. Lucy laid hold of Maggie's frock, and Maggie's heart beat rapidly.

Aunt Pullet half-opened the shutter and then unlocked the wardrobe, with a melancholy deliberateness which was quite in keeping with the funereal solemnity of the scene. The delicious scent of rose-leaves that issued from the wardrobe, made the process of taking out sheet after sheet of silver-paper quite pleasant to assist at, though the sight of the bonnet at last was an anticlimax to Maggie, who would have preferred something more strikingly preternatural. But few things could have been more impressive to Mrs. Tulliver. She looked all round it in silence for some moments, and then said emphatically, "Well, sister, I'll never speak against the full crowns again!"

It was a great concession, and Mrs. Pullet felt it: she felt something was due to it.

"You'd like to see it on, sister?" she said, sadly. "I'll open the shutter a bit further."

"Well, if you don't mind taking off your cap, sister," said Mrs. Tulliver.

Mrs. Pullet took off her cap, displaying the brown silk scalp with a jutting promontory of curls which was common to the more mature and judicious women of those times, and, placing the bonnet on her head, turned slowly round, like a draper's lay-figure, that Mrs. Tulliver might miss no point of view.

"I've sometimes thought there's a loop too much o' ribbon on this left side, sister; what do you think?" said Mrs. Pullet.

Mrs. Tulliver looked earnestly at the point indicated, and turned her head on one side. "Well, I think it's best as it is; if you meddled with it, sister, you might repent."

"That's true," said aunt Pullet, taking off the bonnet and looking at it contemplatively.

"How much might she charge you for that bonnet, sister?" said Mrs. Tulliver, whose mind was actively engaged on the possibility of getting a humble imitation of this *chef-d'œuvre* made from a piece of silk she had at home.

Mrs. Pullet screwed up her mouth and shook her head, and then whispered, "Pullet pays for it; he said I was to have the best bonnet at Garum Church, let the next best be whose it would."

She began slowly to adjust the trimmings in preparation for returning it to its place in the wardrobe, and her thoughts seemed to have taken a melancholy turn, for she shook her head.

"Ah," she said at last, "I may never wear it twice, sister; who knows?"

"Don't talk o' that, sister," answered Mrs. Tulliver. "I hope you'll have your health this summer."

"Ah! but there may come a death in the family, as there did soon after I had my green satin bonnet. Cousin Abbott may go, and we can't think o' wearing crape less nor half a year for him."

"That *would* be unlucky," said Mrs. Tulliver, entering thoroughly into the possibility of an inopportune decease. "There's never so much pleasure i' wearing a bonnet the second year, especially when the crowns are so chancy—never two summers alike."

"Ah, it's the way i' this world," said Mrs. Pullet, returning the bonnet to the wardrobe and locking it up. She maintained a silence characterised by head-shaking, until they had all issued from the solemn chamber and were in her own room again. Then, beginning to cry, she said, "Sister, if you should never see that bonnet again till I'm dead and gone, you'll remember I showed it you this day."

Mrs. Tulliver felt that she ought to be affected, but she was a woman of sparse tears, stout and healthy—she couldn't cry so much as her sister Pullet did, and had often felt her deficiency at funerals. Her effort to bring tears into her eyes issued in an odd contraction of her face. Maggie, looking on attentively, felt that there was some painful mystery about her aunt's bonnet which she was considered too young to understand; indignantly conscious, all the while, that she could have understood that, as well as everything else, if she had been taken into confidence.

When they went down, uncle Pullet observed, with some acumen, that he reckoned the missis had been showing her bonnet—that was what had made them so long up-stairs. With Tom the interval had seemed still longer, for he had been seated in irksome constraint on the edge of a sofa directly opposite his uncle Pullet, who regarded him with twinkling grey eyes, and occasionally addressed him as "Young sir."

"Well, young sir, what do you learn at school?" was a standing question with uncle Pullet; whereupon Tom always looked sheepish, rubbed his hand across his face, and answered, "I don't know." It was altogether so embarrassing to be seated *tête-à-tête* with uncle Pullet, that Tom could not even look at the prints on the walls, or the fly-cages, or the wonderful flower-pots; he saw nothing but his uncle's gaiters. Not that Tom was in awe of his uncle's mental superiority; indeed, he had made up his mind that he didn't want to be a gentleman farmer, because he shouldn't like to be such a thin-legged silly fellow as his uncle Pullet—a mollycoddle, in fact. A boy's sheepishness is by no means a sign of overmastering reverence; and while you are making encouraging advances to him under the idea that he is overwhelmed by a sense of your age and wisdom, ten to one he is thinking you extremely queer. The only consolation I can suggest to you is, that the Greek boys probably thought the same of Aristotle. It is only when you have mastered a restive horse, or thrashed a drayman, or have got a gun in your hand, that these shy juniors feel you to be a truly admirable and enviable character. At least, I am quite sure of Tom Tulliver's sentiments on these points. In very tender years, when he still wore a lace border under his out-door cap, he was often observed peeping through the bars of a gate and making minatory gestures with his small forefinger while he scolded the sheep with an inarticulate burr, intended to strike terror into their astonished minds; indicating, thus early, that desire for mastery over the inferior animals, wild and domestic, including cockchafers, neighbours' dogs, and small sisters, which in all ages has been an attribute of so much promise for the fortunes of our race. Now Mr. Pullet never rode anything taller than a low pony, and was the least predatory of men, considering firearms dangerous, as apt to go off of themselves by nobody's particular desire. So that Tom was not without strong reasons when, in confidential talk with a chum, he had described uncle Pullet as a nincompoop, taking care at the same time to observe that he was a very "rich fellow."

The only alleviating circumstance in a *tête-à-tête* with uncle Pullet was that he kept a variety of lozenges and peppermint drops about his person, and when at a loss for conversation, he filled up the void by proposing a mutual solace of this kind.

"Do you like peppermints, young sir?" required only a tacit answer when it was accompanied by a presentation of the article in question.

The appearance of the little girls suggested to uncle Pullet the further solace of small sweet-cakes, of which he also kept a stock under lock and key for his own private eating on wet days; but the three children had no sooner got the tempting delicacy between their fingers, than aunt Pullet desired them to abstain from eating it till the tray and the plates came, since with those crisp cakes they would make the floor "all over" crumbs. Lucy didn't mind that much, for the cake was so pretty, she thought it was rather a pity to eat it; but Tom, watching his opportunity while the elders were talking, hastily stowed it in his mouth at two bites, and chewed it furtively. As for Maggie, becoming fascinated, as usual, by a print of Ulysses and Nausicaa, which uncle Pullet had bought as a "pretty Scripture thing," she presently let fall her cake, and in an unlucky movement crushed it beneath her foot—a source of so much agitation to aunt Pullet and conscious disgrace to Maggie, that she began to despair of hearing the musical snuff-box to-day, till, after some reflection, it occurred to her that Lucy was in high favour enough to venture on asking for a tune. So she whispered to Lucy, and Lucy, who always did what she was desired to do, went up quietly to her uncle's knee, and, blushing all over her neck while she fingered her necklace, said, "Will you please play us a tune, uncle?"

Lucy thought it was by reason of some exceptional talent in uncle Pullet that the snuff-box played such beautiful tunes, and indeed the thing was viewed in that light by the majority of his neighbours in

Garum. Mr. Pullet had *bought* the box, to begin with, and he under-stood winding it up, and knew which tune it was going to play before-hand; altogether, the possession of this unique "piece of music" was a proof that Mr. Pullet's character was not of that entire nullity which might otherwise have been attributed to it. But uncle Pullet, when entreated to exhibit his accomplishment, never depreciated it by a too ready consent. "We'll see about it," was the answer he always gave, carefully abstaining from any sign of compliance till a suitable number of minutes had passed. Uncle Pullet had a programme for all great social occasions, and in this way fenced himself in from much painful confusion and perplexing freedom of will.

Perhaps the suspense did heighten Maggie's enjoyment when the fairy tune began: for the first time she quite forgot that she had a load on her mind—that Tom was angry with her; and by the time "Hush, ye pretty warbling choir," had been played, her face wore that bright look of happiness, while she sat immovable with her hands clasped, which sometimes comforted her mother with the sense that Maggie could look pretty now and then, in spite of her brown skin. But when the magic music ceased, she jumped up, and, running towards Tom, put her arm round his neck and said, "O, Tom, isn't it pretty?"

Lest you should think it showed a revolting insensibility in Tom that he felt any new anger towards Maggie for this uncalled-for, and, to him, inexplicable caress, I must tell you that he had his glass of cowslip wine in his hand, and that she jerked him so as to make him spill half of it. He must have been an extreme milksop not to say angrily, "Look there, now!" especially when his resentment was sanctioned, as it was, by general disapprobation of Maggie's behaviour.

"Why don't you sit still, Maggie?" her mother said peevishly.

"Little gells mustn't come to see me if they behave in that way," said aunt Pullet.

"Why, you're too rough, little miss," said uncle Pullet.

Poor Maggie sat down again, with the music all chased out of her soul, and the seven small demons all in again.

Mrs. Tulliver, foreseeing nothing but misbehaviour while the chil-dren remained in-doors, took an early opportunity of suggesting that, now they were rested after their walk, they might go and play out of doors; and aunt Pullet gave permission, only enjoining them not to go off the paved walks in the garden, and if they wanted to see the poultry fed, to view them from a distance on the horse-block; a restriction which had been imposed ever since Tom had been found guilty of running after the peacock, with an illusory idea that fright would make one of its feathers drop off.

Mrs. Tulliver's thoughts had been temporarily diverted from the quarrel with Mrs. Glegg by millinery and maternal cares, but now the great theme of the bonnet was thrown into perspective, and the children were out of the way, yesterday's anxieties recurred.

"It weighs on my mind so as never was," she said, by way of opening the subject, "sister Glegg's leaving the house in that way. I'm sure I'd no wish t' offend a sister."

"Ah," said aunt Pullet, "there's no accounting for what Jane 'ull do. I wouldn't speak of it out o' the family—if it wasn't to Dr. Turnbull; but it's my belief Jane lives too low. I've said so to Pullet often and often, and he knows it."

"Why, you said so last Monday was a week, when we came away from drinking tea with 'em," said Mr. Pullet, beginning to nurse his knee and shelter it with his pocket-handkerchief, as was his way when the conversation took an interesting turn.

"Very like I did," said Mrs. Pullet, "for you remember when I said things, better than I can remember myself. He's got a wonderful memory, Pullet has," she continued, looking pathetically at her sister. "I should be poorly off if he was to have a stroke, for he always remembers when I've got to take my doctor's stuff—and I'm taking three sorts now."

"There's the 'pills as before' every other night, and the new drops at eleven and four, and the 'fervescing mixture 'when agreeable,' " rehearsed Mr. Pullet, with a punctuation determined by a lozenge on his tongue.

"Ah, perhaps it 'ud be better for sister Glegg, if *she*'d go to the doctor sometimes, instead o' chewing Turkey rhubarb whenever there's anything the matter with her," said Mrs. Tulliver, who naturally saw the wide subject of medicine chiefly in relation to Mrs. Glegg.

"It's dreadful to think on," said aunt Pullet, raising her hands and letting them fall again, "people playing with their own insides in that way! And it's flying i' the face o' Providence; for what are the doctors for, if we aren't to call 'em in? And when folks have got the money to pay for a doctor, it isn't respectable, as I've told Jane many a time. I'm ashamed of acquaintance knowing it."

"Well, *we*'ve no call to be ashamed," said Mr. Pullet, "for Doctor Turnbull hasn't got such another patient as you i' this parish, now old Mrs. Sutton's gone."

"Pullet keeps all my physic-bottles—did you know, Bessy?" said Mrs. Pullet. "He won't have one sold. He says it's nothing but right, folks should see 'em when I'm gone. They fill two o' the long storeroom shelves a'ready—but," she added, beginning to cry, "it's well if they ever fill three. I may go before I've made up the dozen o' these last sizes. The pill-boxes are in the closet in my room—you'll remember that, sister—but there's nothing to show for the boluses, if it isn't the bills."

"Don't talk o' your going, sister," said Mrs. Tulliver; "I should have nobody to stand between me and sister Glegg if you was gone. And there's nobody but you can get her to make it up wi' Mr. Tulliver, for sister Deane's never o' my side, and if she was, it's not to be looked for as she can speak like them as have got an independent fortin."

"Well, your husband *is* awk'ard, you know, Bessy," said Mrs. Pullet, good-naturedly ready to use her deep depression on her sister's account as well as her own. "He's never behaved quite so pretty to our family as he should do, and the children take after him—the boy's very mischievous, and runs away from his aunts and uncles, and the gell's rude and brown. It's your bad luck, and I'm sorry for you, Bessy; for you was allays my favourite sister, and we allays liked the same patterns."

"I know Tulliver's hasty, and says odd things," said Mrs. Tulliver, wiping away one small tear from the corner of her eye, "but I'm sure he's never been the man, since he married me, to object to my making the friends o' my side o' the family welcome to the house."

"*I* don't want to make the worst of you, Bessy," said Mrs. Pullet, compassionately, "for I doubt you'll have trouble enough without that; and your husband's got that poor sister and her children hanging on him, and so given to lawing, they say. I doubt he'll leave you poorly off when he dies. Not as I'd have it said out o' the family."

This view of her position was naturally far from cheering to Mrs. Tulliver. Her imagination was not easily acted on, but she could not help thinking that her case was a hard one, since it appeared that other people thought it hard.

"I'm sure, sister, I can't help myself," she said, urged by the fear lest her anticipated misfortunes might be held retributive, to take a comprehensive review of her past conduct. "There's no woman strives more for her children; and I'm sure, at scouring-time this Ladyday as I've had all the bed-hangings taken down, I did as much as the two gells put together; and there's this last elder-flower wine I've made—beautiful! I allays offer it along with the sherry, though sister Glegg will have it I'm so extravagant; and as for liking to have my clothes tidy, and not go a fright about the house, there's nobody in the parish can say anything against me in respect o' backbiting and making mischief, for I don't wish anybody any harm; and nobody loses by sending me a pork-pie, for my pies are fit to show with the best o' my neighbours'; and the linen's so in order, as if I was to die to-morrow I shouldn't be ashamed. A woman can do no more nor she can."

"But it's all o' no use, you know, Bessy," said Mrs. Pullet, holding her head on one side, and fixing her eyes pathetically on her sister, "if your husband makes away with his money. Not but what if you was sold up, and other folks bought your furniture, it's a comfort to think as you've kept it well rubbed. And there's the linen, with your maiden mark on, might go all over the country. It 'ud be a sad pity for our family." Mrs. Pullet shook her head slowly.

"But what can I do, sister?" said Mrs. Tulliver. "Mr. Tulliver's not a man to be dictated to—not if I was to go to the parson, and get by heart what I should tell my husband for the best. And I'm sure I don't pretend to know anything about putting out money and all that. I could never see into men's business as sister Glegg does."

"Well, you're like me in that, Bessy," said Mrs. Pullet; "and I think it 'ud be a deal more becoming o' Jane if she'd have that pierglass rubbed oftener—there was ever so many spots on it last week —instead o' dictating to folks as have more comings in than she ever had, and telling 'em what they've to do with their money. But Jane and me were allays contrairy: she *would* have striped things, and I like spots. You like a spot too, Bessy: we allays hung together i' that."

Mrs. Pullet, affected by this last reminiscence, looked at her sister pathetically.

"Yes, Sophy," said Mrs. Tulliver, "I remember our having a blue ground with a white spot both alike—I've got a bit in a bed-quilt now; and if you would but go and see sister Glegg, and persuade her to make it up with Tulliver, I should take it very kind of you. You was allays a good sister to me."

"But the right thing 'ud be for Tulliver to go and make it up with her himself, and say he was sorry for speaking so rash. If he's borrowed money of her, he shouldn't be above that," said Mrs. Pullet, whose partiality did not blind her to principles: she did not forget what was due to people of independent fortune.

"It's no use talking o' that," said poor Mrs. Tulliver, almost peevishly. "If I was to go down on my bare knees on the gravel to Tulliver, he'd never humble himself."

"Well, you can't expect me to persuade *Jane* to beg pardon," said Mrs. Pullet. "Her temper's beyond everything; it's well if it doesn't carry her off her mind, though there never *was* any of our family went to a madhouse."

"I'm not thinking of her begging pardon," said Mrs. Tulliver. "But if she'd just take no notice, and not call her money in; as it's not so much for one sister to ask of another; time 'ud mend things, and Tulliver 'ud forget all about it, and they'd be friends again."

Mrs. Tulliver, you perceive, was not aware of her husband's irrevocable determination to pay in the five hundred pounds; at least such a determination exceeded her powers of belief.

"Well, Bessy," said Mrs. Pullet, mournfully, "*I* don't want to help you on to ruin. I won't be behindhand i' doing you a good turn, if it is to be done. And I don't like it said among acquaintance as we've got quarrels in the family. I shall tell Jane that; and I don't mind driving to Jane's to-morrow, if Pullet doesn't mind. What do you say, Mr. Pullet?"

"I've no objections," said Mr. Pullet, who was perfectly contented with any course the quarrel might take, so that Mr. Tulliver did not apply to *him* for money. Mr. Pullet was nervous about his investments, and did not see how a man could have any security for his money unless he turned it into land.

After a little further discussion as to whether it would not be better for Mrs. Tulliver to accompany them on the visit to sister Glegg, Mrs. Pullet, observing that it was tea-time, turned to reach from a drawer a delicate damask napkin, which she pinned before her in the fashion of an apron. The door did, in fact, soon open, but instead of the tea-tray, Sally introduced an object so startling that both Mrs. Pullet and Mrs. Tulliver gave a scream, causing uncle Pullet to swallow his lozenge—for the fifth time in his life, as he afterwards noted.

CHAPTER X

MAGGIE BEHAVES WORSE THAN SHE EXPECTED

THE startling object which thus made an epoch for uncle Pullet was no other than little Lucy, with one side of her person, from her small foot to her bonnet-crown, wet and discoloured with mud, holding out two tiny blackened hands, and making a very piteous face. To account for this unprecedented apparition in aunt Pullet's parlour, we must return to the moment when the three children went to play out of doors, and the small demons who had taken possession of Maggie's soul at an early period of the day had returned in all the greater force after a temporary absence. All the disagreeable recollections of the morning were thick upon her, when Tom, whose displeasure towards her had been considerably refreshed by her foolish trick of causing him to upset his cowslip wine, said, "Here, Lucy, you come along with me," and walked off to the area where the toads were, as if there were no Maggie in existence. Seeing this, Maggie lingered at a distance, looking like a small Medusa with her snakes cropped. Lucy was naturally pleased that cousin Tom was so good to her, and it was very amusing to see him tickling a fat toad with a piece of string when the toad was safe down the area, with an iron grating over him. Still Lucy wished Maggie to enjoy the spectacle also, especially as she would doubtless find a name for the toad, and say what had been his past history; for Lucy had a delighted semi-belief in Maggie's stories about the live things they came upon by accident—how Mrs Earwig had a wash at home, and one of her children had fallen into the hot copper, for which reason she was running so fast to fetch the doctor. Tom had a profound contempt for this nonsense of Maggie's, smashing the earwig at once as a superfluous yet easy means of proving the entire unreality of such a story; but Lucy, for the life of her, could not help fancying there was something in it, and at all events thought it was very pretty make-believe. So now the desire to know the history of a very portly toad, added to her habitual affectionateness, made her run back to Maggie and say, "O, there is such a big, funny toad, Maggie! Do come and see."

Maggie said nothing, but turned away from her with a deeper frown. As long as Tom seemed to prefer Lucy to her, Lucy made part of his unkindness. Maggie would have thought a little while ago that she could never be cross with pretty little Lucy, any more than she could be cruel to a little white mouse; but then, Tom had always been quite indifferent to Lucy before, and it had been left to Maggie to pet and make much of her. As it was, she was actually beginning to think that she should like to make Lucy cry, by slapping or pinching her, especially as it might vex Tom, whom it was of no use to slap, even if she dared, because he didn't mind it. And if Lucy hadn't been there, Maggie was sure he would have got friends with her sooner.

Tickling a fat toad who is not highly sensitive, is an amusement that it is possible to exhaust, and Tom by-and-by began to look round for some other mode of passing the time. But in so prim a garden, where they were not to go off the paved walks, there was not a great choice of sport. The only great pleasure such a restriction allowed was the pleasure of breaking it, and Tom began to meditate an insurrectionary visit to the pond, about a field's length beyond the garden.

"I say, Lucy," he began, nodding his head up and down with great significance, as he coiled up his string again, "what do you think I mean to do?"

"What, Tom?" said Lucy, with curiosity.

"I mean to go to the pond, and look at the pike. You may go with me if you like," said the young sultan.

"O, Tom, *dare* you?" said Lucy. "Aunt said we mustn't go out of the garden."

"O, I shall go out at the other end of the garden," said Tom. "Nobody 'ull see us. Besides, I don't care if they do—I'll run off home."

"But *I* couldn't run," said Lucy, who had never before been exposed to such severe temptation.

"O, never mind—they won't be cross with *you*," said Tom. "You say I took you."

Tom walked along, and Lucy trotted by his side, timidly enjoying the rare treat of doing something naughty—excited also by the mention of that celebrity, the pike, about which she was quite uncertain whether it was a fish or a fowl. Maggie saw them leaving the garden, and could not resist the impulse to follow. Anger and jealousy can no more bear to lose sight of their objects than love, and that Tom and Lucy should do or see anything of which she was ignorant would have been an intolerable idea to Maggie. So she kept a few yards behind them, unobserved by Tom, who was presently absorbed in watching for the pike—a highly interesting monster; he was said to be so very old, so very large, and to have such a remarkable appetite. The pike, like other celebrities, did not show when he was watched for, but Tom caught sight of something in rapid movement in the water, which attracted him to another spot on the brink of the pond.

"Here, Lucy!" he said in a loud whisper, "come here! take care! keep on the grass—don't step where the cows have been!" he added, pointing to a peninsula of dry grass, with trodden mud on each side of it; for Tom's contemptuous conception of a girl included the attribute of being unfit to walk in dirty places.

Lucy came carefully as she was bidden, and bent down to look at what seemed a golden arrow-head darting through the water. It was a water-snake, Tom told her, and Lucy at last could see the serpentine wave of its body, very much wondering that a snake could swim. Maggie had drawn nearer and nearer—she *must* see it too, though it was bitter to her like everything else, since Tom did not care about her seeing it. At last, she was close by Lucy, and Tom, who had been aware of her approach, but would not notice it till he was obliged, turned round and said—

"Now, get away, Maggie. There's no room for you on the grass here. Nobody asked *you* to come."

There were passions at war in Maggie at that moment to have made a tragedy, if tragedies were made by passion only, but the essential τι μέγεθος which was present in the passion was wanting to the action; the utmost Maggie could do, with a fierce thrust of her small brown arm, was to push poor little pink-and-white Lucy into the cow-trodden mud.

Then Tom could not restrain himself, and gave Maggie two smart slaps on the arm as he ran to pick up Lucy, who lay crying helplessly. Maggie retreated to the roots of a tree a few yards off, and looked on impenitently. Usually her repentance came quickly after one rash deed, but now Tom and Lucy had made her so miserable she was glad to spoil their happiness—glad to make everybody uncomfortable. Why should she be sorry? Tom was very slow to forgive *her*, however sorry she might have been.

"I shall tell mother, you know, Miss Mag," said Tom, loudly and emphatically, as soon as Lucy was up and ready to walk away. It was not Tom's practice to "tell," but here justice clearly demanded that Maggie should be visited with the utmost punishment: not that Tom had learnt to put his views in that abstract form; he never mentioned "justice," and had no idea that his desire to punish might be called by that fine name. Lucy was too entirely absorbed by the evil that had befallen her—the spoiling of her pretty best clothes, and the discomfort of being wet and dirty—to think much of the cause which was entirely mysterious to her. She could never have guessed what she had done to make Maggie angry with her; but she felt that Maggie was very unkind and disagreeable, and made no magnanimous entreaties to Tom that he would not "tell," only running along by his side and crying piteously, while Maggie sat on the roots of the tree and looked after them with her small Medusa face.

"Sally," said Tom, when they reached the kitchen door, and Sally looked at them in speechless amaze, with a piece of bread-and-butter in her mouth and a toasting-fork in her hand—"Sally, tell mother it was Maggie pushed Lucy into the mud."

"But Lors ha' massy, how did you get near such mud as that?" said Sally, making a wry face, as she stooped down and examined the *corpus delicti.*

Tom's imagination had not been rapid and capacious enough to include this question among the foreseen consequences, but it was no sooner put than he foresaw whither it tended, and that Maggie would not be considered the only culprit in the case. He walked quietly away from the kitchen door, leaving Sally to that pleasure of guessing which active minds notoriously prefer to ready-made knowledge.

Sally, as you are aware, lost no time in presenting Lucy at the parlour door, for to have so dirty an object introduced into the house at Garum Firs was too great a weight to be sustained by a single mind.

"Goodness gracious!" aunt Pullet exclaimed, after preluding by an inarticulate scream; "keep her at the door, Sally! Don't bring her off the oilcloth, whatever you do."

"Why, she's tumbled into some nasty mud," said Mrs. Tulliver, going up to Lucy to examine into the amount of damage to clothes for which she felt herself responsible to her sister Deane.

"If you please, 'um, it was Miss Maggie as pushed her in," said Sally; "Master Tom's been and said so, and they must ha' been to the pond, for it's only there they could ha' got into such dirt."

"There it is, Bessy; it's what I've been telling you," said Mrs. Pullet, in a tone of prophetic sadness; "it's your children—there's no knowing what they'll come to."

Mrs. Tulliver was mute, feeling herself a truly wretched mother. As usual, the thought pressed upon her that people would think she had done something wicked to deserve her maternal troubles, while Mrs. Pullet began to give elaborate directions to Sally how to guard the premises from serious injury in the course of removing the dirt. Meantime tea was to be brought in by the cook, and the two naughty children were to have theirs in an ignominious manner in the kitchen. Mrs. Tulliver went out to speak to these naughty children, supposing them to be close at hand; but it was not until after some search that she found Tom leaning with rather a hardened careless air against the white paling of the poultry-yard, and lowering his piece of string on the other side as a means of exasperating the turkey-cock.

"Tom, you naughty boy, where's your sister?" said Mrs. Tulliver in a distressed voice.

"I don't know," said Tom; his eagerness for justice on Maggie had diminished since he had seen clearly that it could hardly be brought about without the injustice of some blame on his own conduct.

"Why, where did you leave her?" said his mother, looking round.

"Sitting under the tree against the pond," said Tom, apparently indifferent to everything but the string and the turkey-cock.

"Then go and fetch her in this minute, you naughty boy. And how could you think o' going to the pond, and taking your sister where there was dirt? You know she'll do mischief, if there's mischief to be done."

It was Mrs. Tulliver's way, if she blamed Tom, to refer his misdemeanour, somehow or other, to Maggie.

The idea of Maggie sitting alone by the pond, roused an habitual fear in Mrs. Tulliver's mind, and she mounted the horse-block to satisfy herself by a sight of that fatal child, while Tom walked—not very quickly—on his way towards her.

"They're such children for the water, mine are," she said aloud, without reflecting that there was no one to hear her; "they'll be brought in dead and drownded some day. I wish that river was far enough."

But when she not only failed to discern Maggie, but presently saw Tom returning from the pool alone, this hovering fear entered and took complete possession of her, and she hurried to meet him.

"Maggie's nowhere about the pond, mother," said Tom; "she's gone away."

You may conceive the terrified search for Maggie, and the difficulty of convincing her mother that she was not in the pond. Mrs. Pullet observed that the child might come to a worse end if she lived —there was no knowing; and Mr. Pullet, confused and overwhelmed by this revolutionary aspect of things—the tea deferred and the poultry alarmed by the unusual running to and fro—took up his spud as an instrument of search, and reached down a key to unlock the goose-pen, as a likely place for Maggie to lie concealed in.

Tom, after a while, started the idea that Maggie was gone home (without thinking it necessary to state that it was what he should have done himself under the circumstances), and the suggestion was seized as a comfort by his mother.

"Sister, for goodness' sake, let 'em put the horse in the carriage and take me home—we shall perhaps find her on the road. Lucy can't walk in her dirty clothes," she said, looking at that innocent victim, who was wrapped up in a shawl, and sitting with naked feet on the sofa.

Aunt Pullet was quite willing to take the shortest means of restoring her premises to order and quiet, and it was not long before Mrs.

Tulliver was in the chaise looking anxiously at the most distant point before her. What the father would say if Maggie was lost? was a question that predominated over every other.

CHAPTER XI

MAGGIE TRIES TO RUN AWAY FROM HER SHADOW

MAGGIE's intentions, as usual, were on a larger scale than Tom had imagined. The resolution that gathered in her mind, after Tom and Lucy had walked away, was not so simple as that of going home. No! she would run away and go to the gypsies, and Tom should never see her any more. That was by no means a new idea to Maggie; she had been so often told she was like a gypsy, and "half wild," that when she was miserable it seemed to her the only way of escaping opprobrium, and being entirely in harmony with circumstances, would be to live in a little brown tent on the commons: the gypsies, she considered, would gladly receive her, and pay her much respect on account of her superior knowledge. She had once mentioned her views on this point to Tom, and suggested that he should stain his face brown, and they should run away together; but Tom rejected the scheme with contempt, observing that gypsies were thieves, and hardly got anything to eat, and had nothing to drive but a donkey. To-day, however, Maggie thought her misery had reached a pitch at which gypsydom was her only refuge, and she rose from her seat on the roots of the tree with the sense that this was a great crisis in her life; she would run straight away till she came to Dunlow Common, where there would certainly be gypsies; and cruel Tom, and the rest of her relations who found fault with her, should never see her any more. She thought of her father as she ran along, but she reconciled herself to the idea of parting with him, by determining that she would secretly send him a letter by a small gypsy, who would run away without telling where she was, and just let him know that she was well and happy, and always loved him very much.

Maggie soon got out of breath with running, but by the time Tom got to the pond again, she was at the distance of three long fields, and was on the edge of the lane leading to the high-road. She stopped to pant a little, reflecting that running away was not a pleasant thing until one had got quite to the common where the gypsies were, but her resolution had not abated: she presently passed through the gate into the lane, not knowing where it would lead her, for it was not this way that they came from Dorlcote Mill to Garum Firs, and she felt all the safer for that, because there was no chance of her being overtaken. But she was soon aware, not without trembling, that there were two men coming along the lane in front of her: she had not thought of meeting strangers—she had been too much occupied with the idea of her friends coming after her. The formidable strangers were two shabby-looking men with flushed faces, one of them carrying a bundle on a stick over his shoulder: but to her surprise, while she was dreading their disapprobation as a runaway, the man with the bundle stopped, and in a half-whining half-coaxing tone asked her if she had a copper to give a poor man. Maggie had a sixpence in her pocket—her uncle Glegg's present—which she immediately drew out and gave this poor man with a polite smile, hoping he would feel very kindly towards her as a generous person. "That's the only money I've got," she said, apologetically. "Thank you, little miss," said the man in a less respectful and grateful tone than Maggie anticipated, and she even observed that he smiled and winked at his companion. She walked on hurriedly, but was aware that the two men were standing still, probably to look after her, and she presently heard them laughing loudly. Suddenly it occurred to her that they might think she was an idiot: Tom had said that her cropped hair made her look like an idiot, and it was too painful an idea to be readily forgotten. Besides, she had no sleeves on—only a cape and a bonnet. It was clear that she was not likely to make a favourable impression on passengers, and she thought she would turn into the fields again; but not on the same side of the lane as before, lest they should still be uncle Pullet's fields. She turned through the first gate that was not locked, and felt a delightful sense of privacy in creeping along by the hedgerows, after her recent humiliating encounter. She was used to wandering about the fields by herself, and was less timid there than on the high-road. Sometimes she had to climb over high gates, but that was a small evil; she was getting out of reach very fast, and she should probably soon come within sight of Dunlow Common, or at least of some other common, for she had heard her father say that you couldn't go very far without coming to a common. She hoped so, for she was getting rather tired and hungry, and until she reached the gypsies there was no definite prospect of bread-and-butter. It was still broad daylight, for aunt Pullet, retaining the early habits of the Dodson family, took tea at half-past four by the sun, and at five by the kitchen clock; so, though it was nearly an hour since Maggie started, there was no gathering gloom on the fields to remind her that the night would come. Still, it seemed to her that she had been walking a very great distance indeed, and it was really surprising that the common did not come within sight. Hitherto she had been in the rich parish of Garum, where there was a great deal of pasture land, and she had only seen one labourer at a distance. That was fortunate in some respects, as labourers might be too ignorant to understand the propriety of her wanting to go to Dunlow Common; yet it would have been better if she could have met some one who would tell her the way without wanting to know anything about her private business. At last, however, the green fields came to an end, and Maggie found herself looking through the bars of a gate into a lane with a wide margin of grass on each side of it. She had never seen such a wide lane before, and, without her knowing why, it gave her the impression that the common could not be far off; perhaps it was because she saw a donkey with a log to his foot feeding on the grassy margin, for she had seen a donkey with that pitiable encumbrance on Dunlow Common when she had been across it in her father's gig. She crept through the bars of the gate and walked on with new spirit, though not without haunting images of Apollyon, and a highwayman with a pistol, and a blinking dwarf in yellow, with a mouth from ear to ear, and other miscellaneous dangers. For poor little Maggie had at once the timidity of an active imagination, and the daring that comes from overmastering impulse. She had rushed into the adventure of seeking her unknown kindred, the gypsies; and now she was in this strange lane, she hardly dared look on one side of her, lest she should see the diabolical blacksmith in his leathern apron, grinning at her with arms akimbo. It was not without a leaping of the heart that she caught sight of a small pair of bare legs sticking up, feet uppermost, by the side of a hillock; they seemed something hideously preternatural—a diabolical kind of fungus; for she was too much agitated at the first glance to see the ragged clothes and the dark shaggy head attached to them. It was a boy asleep, and Maggie trotted along faster and more lightly, lest she should wake him: it did not occur to her that he was one of her friends the gypsies, who in all probability would have very genial manners. But the fact was so, for at the next bend in the lane, Maggie actually saw the little semi-circular black tent with the blue smoke rising before it, which was to be her refuge from all the blighting obloquy that had pursued her in civilised life. She even saw a tall female figure by the column of smoke —doubtless the gypsy-mother, who provided the tea and other groceries; it was astonishing to herself that she did not feel more delighted. But it was startling to find the gypsies in a lane, after all, and not on a common; indeed, it was rather disappointing; for a mysterious illimitable common, where there were sand-pits to hide in, and one was out of everybody's reach, had always made part of Maggie's picture of gypsy life. She went on, however, and thought with some comfort that gypsies most likely knew nothing about idiots, so there was no danger of their falling into the mistake of setting her down at the first glance as an idiot. It was plain she had attracted attention; for the tall figure, who proved to be a young woman with a baby on her arm, walked slowly to meet her. Maggie looked up in the new face rather tremblingly as it approached, and was reassured by the thought that her aunt Pullet and the rest were right when they called her a gypsy, for this face, with the bright dark eyes and the long hair, was really something like what she used to see in the glass before she cut her hair off.

"My little lady, where are you going to?" the gypsy said, in a tone of coaxing deference.

It was delightful, and just what Maggie expected: the gypsies saw at once that she was a little lady, and were prepared to treat her accordingly.

"Not any farther," said Maggie, feeling as if she were saying what she had rehearsed in a dream. "I'm come to stay with *you*, please."

"That's pritty; come, then. Why, what a nice little lady you are, to be sure," said the gypsy, taking her by the hand. Maggie thought her very agreeable, but wished she had not been so dirty.

There was quite a group round the fire when they reached it. An old gypsy-woman was seated on the ground nursing her knees, and occasionally poking a skewer into the round kettle that sent forth an odorous steam: two small shock-headed children were lying prone and resting on their elbows something like small sphinxes; and a placid donkey was bending his head over a tall girl, who, lying on her back, was scratching his nose and indulging him with a bite of excellent stolen hay. The slanting sunlight fell kindly upon them, and the scene was really very pretty and comfortable, Maggie thought, only she hoped they would soon set out the tea-cups. Everything would be quite charming when she had taught the gypsies to use a washing-basin, and to feel an interest in books. It was a little confusing, though, that the young woman began to speak to the old one in a language which Maggie did not understand, while the tall girl, who was feeding the donkey, sat up and stared at her without offering any salutation. At last the old woman said—

"What, my pretty lady, are you come to stay with us? Sit ye down, and tell us where you come from."

It was just like a story: Maggie liked to be called pretty lady and treated in this way. She sat down and said—

"I'm come from home because I'm unhappy, and I mean to be a gypsy. I'll live with you, if you like, and I can teach you a great many things."

"Such a clever little lady," said the woman with the baby, sitting down by Maggie, and allowing baby to crawl; "and such a pritty bonnet and frock," she added, taking off Maggie's bonnet and looking at it while she made an observation to the old woman, in the unknown language. The tall girl snatched the bonnet and put it on her own head hind-foremost with a grin; but Maggie was determined not to show any weakness on this subject, as if she were susceptible about her bonnet.

"I don't want to wear a bonnet," she said, "I'd rather wear a red handkerchief, like yours" (looking at her friend by her side); "my hair was quite long till yesterday, when I cut it off: but I daresay it will grow again very soon," she added apologetically, thinking it probable the gypsies had a strong prejudice in favour of long hair. And Maggie had forgotten even her hunger at that moment in the desire to conciliate gypsy opinion.

"O, what a nice little lady!—and rich, I'm sure," said the old woman. "Didn't you live in a beautiful house at home?"

"Yes, my home is pretty, and I'm very fond of the river, where we go fishing—but I'm often very unhappy. I should have liked to bring my books with me, but I came away in a hurry, you know. But I can tell you almost everything there is in my books, I've read them so many times—and that will amuse you. And I can tell you something about Geography too—that's about the world we live in—very useful and interesting. Did you ever hear about Columbus?"

Maggie's eyes had begun to sparkle and her cheeks to flush—she was really beginning to instruct the gypsies, and gaining great influence over them. The gypsies themselves were not without amazement at this talk, though their attention was divided by the contents of Maggie's pocket, which the friend at her right hand had by this time emptied without attracting her notice.

"Is that where you live, my little lady?" said the old woman, at the mention of Columbus.

"O, no!" said Maggie, with some pity; "Columbus was a very wonderful man, who found out half the world, and they put chains on him and treated him very badly, you know—it's in my Catechism of Geography—but perhaps it's rather too long to tell before tea . . . *I want my tea so.*"

The last words burst from Maggie, in spite of herself, with a sudden drop from patronising instruction to simple peevishness.

"Why, she's hungry, poor little lady," said the younger woman. "Give her some o' the cold victual. You've been walking a good way, I'll be bound, my dear. Where's your home?"

"It's Dorlcote Mill, a good way off," said Maggie. "My father is Mr. Tulliver, but we mustn't let him know where I am, else he'll fetch me home again. Where does the queen of the gypsies live?"

"What! do you want to go to her, my little lady?" said the younger woman. The tall girl meanwhile was constantly staring at Maggie and grinning. Her manners were certainly not agreeable.

"No," said Maggie, "I'm only thinking that if she isn't a very good queen you might be glad when she died, and you could choose another. If I was a queen, I'd be a very good queen, and kind to everybody."

"Here's a bit o' nice victual, then," said the old woman, handing to Maggie a lump of dry bread, which she had taken from a bag of scraps, and a piece of cold bacon.

"Thank you," said Maggie, looking at the food without taking it; "but will you give me some bread-and-butter and tea instead? I don't like bacon."

"We've got no tea nor butter," said the old woman with something like a scowl, as if she were getting tired of coaxing.

"O, a little bread and treacle would do," said Maggie.

"We ha'nt got no treacle," said the old woman crossly, whereupon there followed a sharp dialogue between the two women in their unknown tongue, and one of the small sphinxes snatched at the bread-and-bacon, and began to eat it. At this moment the tall girl, who had gone a few yards off, came back and said something which produced a strong effect. The old woman, seeming to forget Maggie's hunger, poked the skewer into the pot with new vigour, and the younger crept under the tent, and reached out some platters and spoons. Maggie trembled a little, and was afraid the tears would come into her eyes. Meanwhile the tall girl gave a shrill cry, and presently came running up the boy, whom Maggie had passed as he was sleeping—a rough urchin about the age of Tom. He stared at Maggie, and there ensued much incomprehensible chattering. She felt very lonely, and was quite sure she should begin to cry before long: the gypsies didn't seem to mind her at all, and she felt quite weak among them. But the springing tears were checked by a new terror, when two men came up, whose approach had been the cause of the sudden excitement. The elder of the two carried a bag, which he flung down, addressing the women in a loud and scolding tone, which they answered by a shower of treble sauciness; while a black cur ran barking up to Maggie, and threw her into a tremor that only found a new cause in the curses with which the younger man called the dog off, and gave him a rap with a great stick he held in his hand.

Maggie felt that it was impossible she should ever be queen of these people, or ever communicate to them amusing and useful knowledge.

Both the men now seemed to be inquiring about Maggie, for they looked at her, and the tone of the conversation became of that pacific kind which implies curiosity on one side and the power of satisfying it on the other. At last the younger woman said in her previous deferential coaxing tone—

"This nice little lady's come to live with us: aren't you glad?"

"Ay, very glad," said the younger man, who was looking at Maggie's silver thimble and other small matters that had been taken from her pocket. He returned them all except the thimble to the younger woman, with some observation, and she immediately restored them to Maggie's pocket, while the men seated themselves, and began to attack the contents of the kettle—a stew of meat and potatoes—which had been taken off the fire and turned out into a yellow platter.

Maggie began to think that Tom must be right about the gypsies —they must certainly be thieves, unless the man meant to return her thimble by-and-by. She would willingly have given it to him, for she was not at all attached to her thimble; but the idea that she was among thieves prevented her from feeling any comfort in the revival of deference and attention towards her—all thieves except Robin Hood were wicked people. The women saw she was frightened.

"We've got nothing nice for a lady to eat," said the old woman, in her coaxing tone. "And she's so hungry, sweet little lady."

"Here, my dear, try if you can eat a bit o' this," said the younger woman, handing some of the stew on a brown dish with an iron spoon to Maggie, who, remembering that the old woman had seemed angry with her for not liking the bread-and-bacon, dared not refuse the stew, though fear had chased away her appetite. If her father would but come by in the gig and take her up! Or even if Jack the Giantkiller, or Mr. Greatheart, or St. George who slew the dragon on the halfpennies, would happen to pass that way! But Maggie thought with a sinking heart that these heroes were never seen in the neighbourhood of St. Ogg's—nothing very wonderful ever came there.

Maggie Tulliver, you perceive, was by no means that well-trained, well-informed young person that a small female of eight or nine necessarily is in these days: she had only been to school a year at St. Ogg's, and had so few books that she sometimes read the dictionary; so that in travelling over her small mind you would have found the most unexpected ignorance as well as unexpected knowledge. She could have informed you that there was such a word as "polygamy," and being also acquainted with "polysyllable," she had deduced the conclusion that "poly" meant "many;" but she had had no idea that gypsies were not well supplied with groceries, and her thoughts generally were the oddest mixture of clear-eyed acumen and blind dreams.

Her ideas about the gypsies had undergone a rapid modification in the last five minutes. From having considered them very respectful companions, amenable to instruction, she had begun to think that they meant perhaps to kill her as soon as it was dark, and cut up her body for gradual cooking: the suspicion crossed her that the fierce-eyed old man was in fact the devil, who might drop that transparent disguise at any moment, and turn either into the grinning blacksmith or else a fiery-eyed monster with dragon's wings. It was no use trying to eat the stew, and yet the thing she most dreaded was to offend the gypsies, by betraying her extremely unfavourable opinion of them, and she wondered with a keenness of interest that no theologian could have exceeded, whether, if the devil were really present, he would know her thoughts.

"What! you don't like the smell of it, my dear," said the young woman, observing that Maggie did not even take a spoonful of the stew. "Try a bit—come."

"No, thank you," said Maggie, summoning all her force for a desperate effort, and trying to smile in a friendly way. "I haven't time, I think—it seems getting darker. I think I must go home now, and come again another day, and then I can bring you a basket with some jam-tarts and things."

Maggie rose from her seat as she threw out this illusory prospect, devoutly hoping that Apollyon was gullible; but her hope sank when the old gypsy-woman said, "Stop a bit, stop a bit, little lady—we'll take you home, all safe, when we've done supper: you shall ride home, like a lady."

Maggie sat down again, with little faith in this promise, though she presently saw the tall girl putting a bridle on the donkey, and throwing a couple of bags on his back.

"Now, then, little missis," said the younger man, rising, and leading the donkey forward, "tell us where you live—what's the name o' the place?"

"Dorlcote Mill is my home," said Maggie, eagerly. "My father is Mr. Tulliver—he lives there."

"What! a big mill a little way this side o' St. Ogg's?"

"Yes," said Maggie. "Is it far off? I think I should like to walk there, if you please."

"No, no, it'll be getting dark, we must make haste. And the donkey 'll carry you as nice as can be—you'll see."

He lifted Maggie as he spoke, and set her on the donkey. She felt relieved that it was not the old man who seemed to be going with her, but she had only a trembling hope that she was really going home.

"Here's your pretty bonnet," said the younger woman, putting that recently despised but now welcome article of costume on Maggie's head; "and you'll say we've been very good to you, won't you? and what a nice little lady we said you was."

"O, yes, thank you," said Maggie, "I'm very much obliged to you. But I wish you'd go with me too." She thought anything was better than going with one of the dreadful men alone: it would be more cheerful to be murdered by a larger party.

"Ah, you're fondest o' me, aren't you?" said the woman. "But I can't go—you'll go too fast for me."

It now appeared that the man also was to be seated on the donkey, holding Maggie before him, and she was as incapable of remonstrating against this arrangement as the donkey himself, though no nightmare had ever seemed to her more horrible. When the woman had patted her on the back, and said, "good-by," the donkey, at a strong hint from the man's stick, set off at a rapid walk along the lane towards the point Maggie had come from an hour ago, while the tall girl and the rough urchin, also furnished with sticks, obligingly escorted them for the first hundred yards, with much screaming and thwacking.

Not Leonore, in that preternatural midnight excursion with her phantom lover, was more terrified than poor Maggie in this entirely natural ride on a short-paced donkey, with a gypsy behind her, who considered that he was earning half-a-crown. The red light of the setting sun seemed to have a portentous meaning, with which the alarming bray of the second donkey with the log on its foot must surely have some connection. Two low thatched cottages—the only houses they passed in this lane—seemed to add to its dreariness: they had no windows to speak of, and the doors were closed: it was probable that they were inhabited by witches, and it was a relief to find that the donkey did not stop there.

At last—O, sight of joy!—this lane, the longest in the world, was coming to an end, was opening on a broad high-road, where there was actually a coach passing! And there was a finger-post at the corner: she had surely seen that finger-post before—"To St. Ogg's, 2 miles." The gypsy really meant to take her home, then: he was probably a good man, after all, and might have been rather hurt at the thought that she didn't like coming with him alone. This idea became stronger as she felt more and more certain that she knew the road quite well, and she was considering how she might open a conversation with the injured gypsy, and not only gratify his feelings but efface the impression of her cowardice, when, as they reached a cross-road, Maggie caught sight of some one coming on a white-faced horse.

"O, stop, stop!" she cried out. "There's my father! O, father, father!"

The sudden joy was almost painful, and before her father reached her, she was sobbing. Great was Mr. Tulliver's wonder, for he had made a round from Basset, and had not yet been home.

"Why, what's the meaning o' this?" he said, checking his horse, while Maggie slipped from the donkey and ran to her father's stirrup.

"The little miss lost herself, I reckon," said the gypsy. "She'd come to our tent at the far end o' Dunlow Lane, and I was bringing her where she said her home was. It's a good way to come arter being on the tramp all day."

"O, yes, father, he's been very good to bring me home," said Maggie. "A very kind, good man!"

"Here, then, my man," said Mr. Tulliver, taking out five shillings. "It's the best day's work *you* ever did. I couldn't afford to lose the little wench; here, lift her up before me."

"Why, Maggie, how's this, how's this?" he said, as they rode along, while she laid her head against her father, and sobbed. "How came you to be rambling about and lose yourself?"

"O, father," sobbed Maggie, "I ran away because I was so unhappy—Tom was so angry with me. I couldn't bear it."

"Pooh, pooh," said Mr. Tulliver, soothingly, "you mustn't think o' running away from father. What 'ud father do without his little wench?"

"O, no, I never will again, father—never."

Mr. Tulliver spoke his mind very strongly when he reached home that evening, and the effect was seen in the remarkable fact, that Maggie never heard one reproach from her mother, or one taunt from Tom, about this foolish business of her running away to the gypsies. Maggie was rather awe-stricken by this unusual treatment, and sometimes thought that her conduct had been too wicked to be alluded to.

CHAPTER XII

MR. AND MRS. GLEGG AT HOME

In order to see Mr. and Mrs. Glegg at home, we must enter the town of St. Ogg's—that venerable town with the red-fluted roofs and the broad warehouse gables, where the black ships unlade themselves of their burthens from the far north, and carry away, in exchange, the precious inland products, the well-crushed cheese and the soft fleeces, which my refined readers have doubtless become acquainted with through the medium of the best classic pastorals.

It is one of those old, old towns which impress one as a continuation and outgrowth of nature, as much as the nests of the bower-birds or the winding galleries of the white ants: a town which carries the traces of its long growth and history like a millenial tree, and has sprung up and developed in the same spot between the river and the low hill from the time when the Roman legions turned their backs on it from the camp on the hill-side, and the long-haired sea-kings came up the river and looked with fierce, eager eyes at the fatness of the land. It is a town "familiar with forgotten years." The shadow of the Saxon hero-king still walks there fitfully, reviewing the scenes of his youth and love-time, and is met by the gloomier shadow of the dreadful heathen Dane, who was stabbed in the midst of his warriors by the sword of an invisible avenger, and who rises on autumn evenings like a white mist from his tumulus on the hill, and hovers in the court of the old hall by the river-side—the spot where he was thus miraculously slain in the days before the old hall was built. It was the Normans who began to build that fine old hall, which is like the town, telling of the thoughts and hands of widely-sundered generations; but it is all so old that we look with loving pardon at its inconsistencies, and are well content that they who built the stone oriel, and they who built the Gothic façade and towers of finest small brickwork with the trefoil ornament, and the windows and battlements defined with stone, did not sacrilegiously pull down the ancient half-timbered body with its oak-roofed banqueting-hall.

But older even than this old hall is perhaps the bit of wall now built into the belfry of the parish church, and said to be a remnant of the original chapel dedicated to St. Ogg, the patron saint of this ancient town, of whose history I possess several manuscript versions. I incline to the briefest, since, if it should not be wholly true, it is at least likely to contain the least falsehood. "Ogg the son of Beorl," says my private hagiographer, "was a boatman who gained a scanty living by ferrying passengers across the river Floss. And it came to pass, one evening when the winds were high, that there sat moaning by the brink of the river a woman with a child in her arms; and she was clad in rags, and had a worn and withered look, and she craved to be rowed across the river. And the men thereabout questioned her, and said, 'Wherefore dost thou desire to cross the river? Tarry till the morning, and take shelter here for the night: so shalt thou be wise, and not foolish.' Still she went on to mourn and crave. But Ogg the son of Beorl came up and said, 'I will ferry thee across: it is enough that thy heart needs it.' And he ferried her across. And it came to pass, when she stepped ashore, that her rags were turned into robes of flowing white, and her face became bright with exceeding beauty, and there was a glory around it, so that she shed a light on the water like the moon in its brightness. And she said—'Ogg the son of Beorl, thou art blessed in that thou didst not question and wrangle with the heart's need, but wast smitten with pity, and didst straightway relieve the same. And from henceforth whoso steps into thy boat shall be in no peril from the storm; and whenever it puts forth to the rescue, it shall save the lives both of men and beasts.' And when the floods came, many were saved by reason of that blessing on the boat. But when Ogg the son of Beorl died, behold, in the parting of his soul, the boat loosed itself from its moorings, and was floated with the ebbing tide in great swiftness to the ocean, and was seen no more. Yet it was witnessed in the floods of after-time, that at the coming on of even, Ogg the son of Beorl was always seen with his boat upon the wide-spreading waters, and the Blessed Virgin sat in the prow, shedding a light around as of the moon in its brightness, so that the rowers in the gathering darkness took heart and pulled anew."

This legend, one sees, reflects from a far-off time the visitation of the floods, which, even when they left human life untouched, were widely fatal to the helpless cattle, and swept as sudden death over all smaller living things. But the town knew worse troubles even than the floods—troubles of the civil wars, when it was a continual fighting-place, where first Puritans thanked God for the blood of the Loyalists, and then Loyalists thanked God for the blood of the Puritans. Many honest citizens lost all their possessions for conscience' sake in those times, and went forth beggared from their native town. Doubtless there are many houses standing now on which those honest citizens turned their backs in sorrow: quaint-gabled houses looking on the river, jammed between newer warehouses, and penetrated by surprising passages, which turn and turn at sharp angles till they lead you out on a muddy strand overflowed continually by the rushing tide. Everywhere the brick houses have a mellow look, and in Mrs. Glegg's day there was no incongruous new-fashioned smartness, no plate-glass in shop windows, no fresh stucco-facing or other fallacious attempt to make fine old red St. Ogg's wear the air of a town that sprang up yesterday. The shop windows were small and unpretending; for the farmers' wives and daughters who came to do their shopping on market-days were not to be withdrawn from their regular, well-known shops; and the tradesmen had no wares intended for customers who would go on their way and be seen no more. Ah! even Mrs. Glegg's day seems far back in the past now, separated from us by changes that widen the years. War and the rumour of war had then died out from the minds of men, and if they were ever thought of by the farmers in drab greatcoats, who shook the grain out of their sample-bags and buzzed over it in the full market-place, it was as a state of things that belonged to a past golden age, when prices were high. Surely the time was gone for ever when the broad river could bring up unwelcome ships: Russia was only the place where the linseed came from—the more the better—making grist for the great vertical millstones with their scythe-like arms, roaring and grinding and carefully sweeping as if an informing soul were in them. The Catholics, bad harvests, and the mysterious fluctuations of trade, were the three evils mankind had to fear: even the floods had not been great of late years. The mind of St. Ogg's did not look extensively before or after. It inherited a long past without thinking of it, and had no eyes for the spirits that walked the streets. Since the centuries when St. Ogg with his boat and the Virgin Mother at the prow had been seen on the wide water, so many memories had been left behind, and had gradually vanished like the receding hill-tops! And the present time was like the level plain where men lose their belief in volcanoes and earthquakes, thinking to-morrow will be as yesterday, and the giant forces that used to shake the earth are for ever laid to sleep. The days were gone when people could be greatly wrought upon by their faith, still less change it: the Catholics were formidable because they would lay hold of government and property, and burn men alive; not because any sane and honest parishioner of St. Ogg's could be brought to believe in the Pope. One aged person remembered how a rude multitude had been swayed when John Wesley preached in the cattle-market; but for a long while it had not been expected of preachers that they should shake the souls of men. An occasional burst of fervour, in Dissenting pulpits, on the subject of infant baptism, was the only symptom of a zeal unsuited to sober times when men had done with change. Protestantism sat at ease, unmindful of schisms, careless of proselytism: Dissent was an inheritance along with a superior pew and a business connection; and Churchmanship only wondered contemptuously at Dissent as a foolish habit that clung greatly to families in the grocery and chandlering lines, though not incompatible with prosperous wholesale dealing. But with the Catholic Question had come a slight wind of controversy to break the calm: the elderly rector had become occasionally historical and argumentative, and Mr. Spray, the Independent minister, had begun to preach political sermons, in which he distinguished with much subtlety between his fervent belief in the right of the Catholics to the franchise and his fervent belief in their eternal perdition. But most of Mr. Spray's hearers were incapable of following his subtleties, and many old-fashioned Dissenters were much pained by his "siding with the Catholics;" while others thought he had better let politics alone. Public spirit was not held in high esteem at St. Ogg's, and men who busied themselves with political questions were re, garded with some suspicion as dangerous characters: they were usu, ally persons who had little or no business of their own to manage, or, if they had, were likely enough to become insolvent.

This was the general aspect of things at St. Ogg's in Mrs. Glegg's day, and at that particular period in her family history when she had had her quarrel with Mr. Tulliver. It was a time when ignorance was much more comfortable than at present, and was received with all the honours in very good society, without being obliged to dress itself in an elaborate costume of knowledge; a time when cheap periodicals were not, and when country surgeons never thought of asking their female patients if they were fond of reading, but simply took it for granted that they preferred gossip; a time when ladies in rich silk-gowns wore large pockets, in which they carried a mutton-bone to secure them against cramp. Mrs. Glegg carried such a bone, which she had inherited from her grandmother with a brocaded gown that would stand up empty, like a suit of armour, and a silver-headed walking-stick; for the Dodson family had been respectable for many generations.

Mrs. Glegg had both a front and a back parlour in her excellent house at St. Ogg's, so that she had two points of view from which she could observe the weaknesses of her fellow-beings, and reinforce her thankfulness for her own exceptional strength of mind. From her front windows she could look down the Tofton Road, leading out of St. Ogg's, and note the growing tendency to "gadding about" in the wives of men not retired from business, together with a practice of wearing woven cotton stockings, which opened a dreary prospect for the coming generation; and from her back windows she could look down the pleasant garden and orchard which stretched to the river, and observe the folly of Mr. Glegg in spending his time among "them flowers and vegetables." For Mr. Glegg, having retired from active business as a wool-stapler, for the purpose of enjoying himself through the rest of his life, had found this last occupation so much more severe than his business, that he had been driven into amateur hard labour as a dissipation, and habitually relaxed by doing the work of two ordinary gardeners. The economising of a gardener's wages might perhaps have induced Mrs. Glegg to wink at this folly, if it were possible for a healthy female mind even to simulate respect for a husband's hobby. But it is well known that this conjugal complacency belongs only to the weaker portion of the sex, who are scarcely alive to the responsibilities of a wife as a constituted check on her husband's pleasures, which are hardly ever of a rational or commendable kind.

Mr. Glegg on his side, too, had a double source of mental occupation, which gave every promise of being inexhaustible. On the one

hand, he surprised himself by his discoveries in natural history, finding that his piece of garden-ground contained wonderful caterpillars,
slugs, and insects, which, so far as he had heard, had never before
attracted human observation; and he noticed remarkable coincidences
between these zoological phenomena and the great events of that
time,—as, for example, that before the burning of York Minster
there had been mysterious serpentine marks on the leaves of the rose-
trees, together with an unusual prevalence of slugs, which he had
been puzzled to know the meaning of, until it flashed upon him with
this melancholy conflagration. (Mr. Glegg had an unusual amount
of mental activity, which, when disengaged from the wool business,
naturally made itself a pathway in other directions.) And his second
subject of meditation was the "contrairiness" of the female mind, as
typically exhibited in Mrs. Glegg. That a creature made—in a genea-
logical sense—out of a man's rib, and in this particular case maintained in the highest respectability without any trouble of her own,
should be normally in a state of contradiction to the blandest propositions and even to the most accommodating concessions, was a mystery in the scheme of things to which he had often in vain sought a
clue in the early chapters of Genesis. Mr. Glegg had chosen the eldest
Miss Dodson as a handsome embodiment of female prudence and
thrift, and being himself of a money-getting, money-keeping turn, had
calculated on much conjugal harmony. But in that curious compound,
the feminine character, it may easily happen that the flavour is unpleasant in spite of excellent ingredients; and a fine systematic stinginess may be accompanied with a seasoning that quite spoils its
relish. Now good Mr. Glegg himself was stingy in the most amiable
manner: his neighbours called him "near," which always means that
the person in question is a lovable skinflint. If you expressed a preference for cheese-parings, Mr. Glegg would remember to save them
for you, with a good-natured delight in gratifying your palate, and
he was given to pet all animals which required no appreciable keep.
There was no humbug or hypocrisy about Mr. Glegg: his eyes would
have watered with true feeling over the sale of a widow's furniture,
which a five-pound note from his side-pocket would have prevented;
but a donation of five pounds to a person "in a small way of life"
would have seemed to him a mad kind of lavishness rather than
"charity," which had always presented itself to him as a contribution of small aids, not a neutralising of misfortune. And Mr. Glegg
was just as fond of saving other people's money as his own: he would
have ridden as far round to avoid a turnpike when his expenses were
to be paid for him, as when they were to come out of his own pocket,
and was quite zealous in trying to induce indifferent acquaintances
to adopt a cheap substitute for blacking. This inalienable habit of
saving, as an end in itself, belonged to the industrious men of business of a former generation, who made their fortunes slowly, almost
as the tracking of the fox belongs to the harrier—it constituted them

a "race," which is nearly lost in these days of rapid money-getting, when lavishness comes close on the back of want. In old-fashioned times, an "independence" was hardly ever made without a little miserliness as a condition, and you would have found that quality in every provincial district, combined with characters as various as the fruits from which we can extract acid. The true Harpagons were always marked and exceptional characters: not so the worthy tax-payers, who, having once pinched from real necessity, retained even in the midst of their comfortable retirement, with their wall-fruit and wine-bins, the habit of regarding life as an ingenious process of nibbling out one's livelihood without leaving any perceptible deficit, and who would have been as immediately prompted to give up a newly-taxed luxury when they had their clear five hundred a-year, as when they had only five hundred pounds of capital. Mr. Glegg was one of these men, found so impracticable by chancellors of the ex-chequer; and knowing this, you will be the better able to understand why he had not swerved from the conviction that he had made an eligible marriage, in spite of the too pungent seasoning that nature had given to the eldest Miss Dodson's virtues. A man with an affec-tionate disposition, who finds a wife to concur with his fundamental idea of life, easily comes to persuade himself that no other woman would have suited him so well, and does a little daily snapping and quarrelling without any sense of alienation. Mr. Glegg, being of a reflective turn, and no longer occupied with wool, had much wonder-ing meditation on the peculiar constitution of the female mind as unfolded to him in his domestic life; and yet he thought Mrs. Glegg's household ways a model for her sex: it struck him as a pitiable irregularity in other women if they did not roll up their table-napkins with the same tightness and emphasis as Mrs. Glegg did, if their pas-try had a less leathery consistence, and their damson cheese a less venerable hardness than hers: nay, even the peculiar combination of grocery and drug-like odours in Mrs. Glegg's private cupboard impressed him as the only right thing in the way of cupboard smells. I am not sure that he would not have longed for the quarrelling again, if it had ceased for an entire week; and it is certain that an acquies-cent mild wife would have left his meditations comparatively jejune and barren of mystery.

Mr. Glegg's unmistakable kind-heartedness was shown in this, that it pained him more to see his wife at variance with others— even with Dolly, the servant—than to be in a state of cavil with her himself; and the quarrel between her and Mr. Tulliver vexed him so much that it quite nullified the pleasure he would otherwise have had in the state of his early cabbages, as he walked in his garden before breakfast the next morning. Still he went in to breakfast with some slight hope that, now Mrs. Glegg had "slept upon it," her anger might be subdued enough to give way to her usually strong sense of family decorum. She had been used to boast that there had never been any of those deadly quarrels among the Dodsons which had disgraced other families; that no Dodson had ever been "cut off with a shilling," and no cousin of the Dodsons disowned; as, indeed, why should they be? for they had no cousins who had not money out at use, or some houses of their own, at the very least.

There was one evening-cloud which had always disappeared from Mrs. Glegg's brow when she sat at the breakfast-table: it was her fuzzy front of curls; for as she occupied herself in household matters in the morning, it would have been a mere extravagance to put on anything so superfluous to the making of leathery pastry as a fuzzy curled front. By half-past ten decorum demanded the front: until then Mrs. Glegg could economise it, and society would never be any the wiser. But the absence of that cloud only left it more apparent that the cloud of severity remained; and Mr. Glegg, perceiving this, as he sat down to his milk-porridge, which it was his old frugal habit to stem his morning hunger with, prudently resolved to leave the first remark to Mrs. Glegg, lest, to so delicate an article as a lady's temper, the slightest touch should do mischief. People who seem to enjoy their ill-temper have a way of keeping it in fine condition by inflicting privations on themselves. That was Mrs. Glegg's way: she made her tea weaker than usual this morning, and declined butter. It was a hard case that a vigorous mood for quarrelling, so highly capable of using any opportunity, should not meet with a single remark from Mr. Glegg on which to exercise itself. But by-and-by it appeared that his silence would answer the purpose, for he heard himself apostrophised at last in that tone peculiar to the wife of one's bosom.

"Well, Mr. Glegg! it's a poor return I get for making you the wife I've made you all these years. If this is the way I'm to be treated, I'd better ha' known it before my poor father died, and then, when I'd wanted a home, I should ha' gone elsewhere—as the choice was offered me."

Mr. Glegg paused from his porridge and looked up—not with any new amazement, but simply with that quiet, habitual wonder with which we regard constant mysteries.

"Why, Mrs. G., what have I done now?"

"Done now, Mr. Glegg? *done now?* . . . I'm sorry for you."

Not seeing his way to any pertinent answer, Mr. Glegg reverted to his porridge.

"There's husbands in the world," continued Mrs. Glegg after a pause, "as 'ud have known how to do something different to siding with everybody else against their own wives. Perhaps I'm wrong, and you can teach me better—but I've allays heard as it's the husband's place to stand by the wife, instead o' rejoicing and triumphing when folks insult her."

"Now, what call have you to say that?" said Mr. Glegg, rather warmly, for though a kind man, he was not as meek as Moses. "When did I rejoice or triumph over you?"

"There's ways o' doing things worse than speaking out plain, Mr. Glegg. I'd sooner you'd tell me to my face as you make light of me, than try to make out as everybody's in the right but me, and come to your breakfast in the morning, as I've hardly slept an hour this night, and sulk at me as if I was the dirt under your feet."

"Sulk at you?" said Mr. Glegg, in a tone of angry facetiousness. "You're like a tipsy man as thinks everybody's had too much but himself."

"Don't lower yourself with using coarse language to *me*, Mr. Glegg! It makes you look very small, though you can't see yourself," said Mrs. Glegg, in a tone of energetic compassion. "A man in your place should set an example, and talk more sensible."

"Yes; but will you listen to sense?" retorted Mr. Glegg, sharply. "The best sense I can talk to you is what I said last night—as you're i' the wrong to think o' calling in your money, when it's safe enough if you'd let it alone, all because of a bit of a tiff, and I was in hopes you'd ha' altered your mind this morning. But if you'd like to call it in, don't do it in a hurry now, and breed more enmity in the family— but wait till there's a pretty mortgage to be had without any trouble. You'd have to set the lawyer to work now to find an investment, and make no end o' expense."

Mrs. Glegg felt there was really something in this, but she tossed her head and emitted a guttural interjection to indicate that her silence was only an armistice, not a peace. And, in fact, hostilities soon broke out again.

"I'll thank you for my cup o' tea, now, Mrs. G.," said Mr. Glegg, seeing that she did not proceed to give it to him as usual, when he had finished his porridge. She lifted the teapot with a slight toss of the head, and said,

"I'm glad to hear you'll *thank* me, Mr. Glegg. It's little thanks *I* get for what I do for folks i' this world. Though there's never a woman o' *your* side i' the family, Mr. Glegg, as is fit to stand up with me, and I'd say it if I was on my dying bed. Not but what I've allays conducted myself civil to your kin, and there isn't one of 'em can say the contrary, though my equils they aren't, and nobody shall make me say it."

"You'd better leave finding fault wi' my kin till you've left off quarrelling with your own, Mrs. G.," said Mr. Glegg, with angry sarcasm. "I'll trouble you for the milk-jug."

"That's as false a word as ever you spoke, Mr. Glegg," said the lady, pouring out the milk with unusual profuseness, as much as to say, if he wanted milk, he should have it with a vengeance. "And you know it's false. I'm not the woman to quarrel with my own kin: *you* may, for I've known you do it."

"Why, what did you call it yesterday, then, leaving your sister's house in a tantrum?"

"I'd no quarrel wi' my sister, Mr. Glegg, and it's false to say it,

Mr. Tulliver's none o' my blood, and it was him quarrelled with me, and drove me out o' the house. But perhaps you'd have had me stay and be swore at, Mr. Glegg; perhaps you was vexed not to hear more abuse and foul language poured out upo' your own wife. But, let me tell you, it's *your* disgrace."

"Did ever anybody hear the like i' this parish?" said Mr. Glegg, getting hot. "A woman, with everything provided for her, and allowed to keep her own money the same as if it was settled on her, and with a gig new stuffed and lined at no end o' expense, and provided for when I die beyond anything she could expect . . . to go on i' this way, biting and snapping like a mad dog! It's beyond everything as God A'mighty should ha' made women so." (These last words were uttered in a tone of sorrowful agitation. Mr. Glegg pushed his tea from him, and tapped the table with both his hands.)

"Well, Mr. Glegg! if those are your feelings, it's best they should be known," said Mrs. Glegg, taking off her napkin, and folding it in an excited manner. "But if you talk o' my being provided for beyond what I could expect, I beg leave to tell you as I'd a right to expect a many things as I don't find. And as to my being like a mad dog, it's well if you're not cried shame on by the county for your treatment of me, for it's what I can't bear, and I won't bear. . . ."

Here Mrs. Glegg's voice intimated that she was going to cry, and, breaking off from speech, she rang the bell violently.

"Sally," she said, rising from her chair, and speaking in rather a choked voice, "light a fire up-stairs, and put the blinds down. Mr. Glegg, you'll please to order what you'd like for dinner. I shall have gruel."

Mrs. Glegg walked across the room to the small book-case, and took down Baxter's "Saints' Everlasting Rest," which she carried with her up-stairs. It was the book she was accustomed to lay open before her on special occasions: on wet Sunday mornings, or when she heard of a death in the family, or when, as in this case, her quarrel with Mr. Glegg had been set an octave higher than usual.

But Mrs. Glegg carried something else up-stairs with her, which, together with the "Saints' Rest" and the gruel, may have had some influence in gradually calming her feelings, and making it possible for her to endure existence on the ground-floor shortly before tea-time. This was, partly, Mr. Glegg's suggestion, that she would do well to let her five hundred lie still until a good investment turned up; and, further, his parenthetic hint at his handsome provision for her in case of his death. Mr. Glegg, like all men of his stamp, was extremely reticent about his will; and Mrs. Glegg, in her gloomier moments, had forebodings that, like other husbands of whom she had heard, he might cherish the mean project of heightening her grief at his death by leaving her poorly off, in which case she was firmly resolved that she would have scarcely any weeper on her bonnet, and would cry no more than if he had been a second husband.

But if he had really shown her any testamentary tenderness, it would be affecting to think of him, poor man, when he was gone; and even his foolish fuss about the flowers and garden-stuff, and his insistence on the subject of snails, would be touching when it was once fairly at an end. To survive Mr. Glegg, and talk eulogistically of him as a man who might have his weaknesses, but who had done the right thing by her, notwithstanding his numerous poor relations—to have sums of interest coming in more frequently, and secrete it in various corners, baffling to the most ingenious of thieves (for, to Mrs. Glegg's mind, banks and strong-boxes would have nullified the pleasure of property— she might as well have taken her food in capsules)—finally, to be looked up to by her own family and the neighbourhood, so as no woman can ever hope to be who has not the præterite and present dignity comprised in being a "widow well left,"—all this made a flattering and conciliatory view of the future. So that when good Mr. Glegg, restored to good-humour by much hoeing, and moved by the sight of his wife's empty chair, with her knitting rolled up in the corner, went upstairs to her, and observed that the bell had been tolling for poor Mr. Morton, Mrs. Glegg answered magnanimously, quite as if she had been an uninjured woman, "Ah! then, there'll be a good business for somebody to take to."

Baxter had been open at least eight hours by this time, for it was nearly five o'clock; and if people are to quarrel often, it follows as a corollary that their quarrels cannot be protracted beyond certain limits.

Mr. and Mrs. Glegg talked quite amicably about the Tullivers that evening. Mr. Glegg went the length of admitting that Tulliver was a sad man for getting into hot water, and was like enough to run through his property; and Mrs. Glegg, meeting this acknowledgment half-way, declared that it was beneath her to take notice of such a man's conduct, and that, for her sister's sake, she would let him keep the five hundred a while longer, for when she put it out on a mortgage she should only get four per cent.

CHAPTER XIII

MR. TULLIVER FURTHER ENTANGLES THE SKEIN OF LIFE

Owing to this new adjustment of Mrs. Glegg's thoughts, Mrs. Pullet found her task of mediation the next day surprisingly easy. Mrs. Glegg, indeed, checked her rather sharply for thinking it would be necessary to tell her elder sister what was the right mode of behaviour in family matters. Mrs. Pullet's argument that it would look ill in the neighbourhood if people should have it in their power to say that there was a quarrel in the family, was particularly offensive. If the family name never suffered except through Mrs. Glegg, Mrs. Pullet might lay her head on her pillow in perfect confidence.

"It's not to be expected, I suppose," observed Mrs. Glegg, by way of winding up the subject, "as I shall go to the mill again before Bessy comes to see me, or as I shall go and fall down o' my knees to Mr. Tulliver and ask his pardon for showing him favours; but I shall bear no malice, and when Mr. Tulliver speaks civil to me, I'll speak civil to him. Nobody has any call to tell me what's becoming."

Finding it unnecessary to plead for the Tullivers, it was natural that aunt Pullet should relax a little in her anxiety for them, and recur to the annoyance she had suffered yesterday from the offspring of that apparently ill-fated house. Mrs. Glegg heard a curcumstantial narrative, to which Mr. Pullet's remarkable memory furnished some items; and while aunt Pullet pitied poor Bessy's bad-luck with her children, and expressed a half-formed project of paying for Maggie's being sent to a distant boarding-school, which would not prevent her being so brown, but might tend to subdue some other vices in her, aunt Glegg blamed Bessy for her weakness, and appealed to all witnesses who should be living when the Tulliver children had turned out ill, that she, Mrs. Glegg, had always said how it would be from the very first, observing that it was wonderful to herself how all her words came true.

"Then I may call and tell Bessy you'll bear no malice, and everything be as it was before?" Mrs. Pullet said, just before parting.

"Yes, you may, Sophy," said Mrs. Glegg; "you may tell Mr. Tulliver, and Bessy too, as I'm not going to behave ill because folks behave ill to me: I know it's my place, as the eldest, to set an example in every respect, and I do it. Nobody can say different of me, if they'll keep to the truth."

Mrs. Glegg being in this state of satisfaction in her own lofty magnanimity, I leave you to judge what effect was produced on her by the reception of a short letter from Mr. Tulliver, that very evening, after Mrs. Pullet's departure, informing her that she needn't trouble her mind about her five hundred pounds, for it should be paid back to her in the course of the next month at farthest, together with the interest due thereon until the time of payment. And furthermore, that Mr. Tulliver had no wish to behave uncivilly to Mrs. Glegg, and she was welcome to his house whenever she liked to come, but he desired no favours from her, either for himself or his children.

It was poor Mrs. Tulliver who had hastened this catastrophe, entirely through that irrepressible hopefulness of hers which led her to expect that similar causes may at any time produce different results. It had very often occurred in her experience that Mr. Tulliver had done something because other people had said he was not able to do it, or had pitied him for his supposed inability, or in any other way piqued his pride; still, she thought today, if she told him when he came in to tea that sister Pullet was gone to try and make everything up with sister Glegg, so that he needn't think about paying in the money, it would give a cheerful effect to the meal. Mr. Tulliver had never slackened in his resolve to raise the money, but now he at once determined to write a letter to Mrs. Glegg which should cut off all possibility of mistake. Mrs. Pullet gone to beg and pray for *him,* indeed! Mr. Tulliver did not willingly write a letter, and found the relation between spoken and written language, briefly known as spelling, one of the most puzzling things in this puzzling world. Nevertheless, like all fervid writing, the task was done in less time than usual, and if the spelling differed from Mrs. Glegg's—why, she belonged, like himself, to a generation with whom spelling was a matter of private judgment.

Mrs. Glegg did not alter her will in consequence of this letter, and cut off the Tulliver children from their sixth and seventh share in her thousand pounds; for she had her principles. No one must be able to say of her when she was dead that she had not divided her money with perfect fairness among her own kin: in the matter of wills, personal qualities were subordinate to the great fundamental fact of blood; and to be determined in the distribution of your property by caprice, and not make your legacies bear a direct ratio to degrees of kinship, was a prospective disgrace that would have embittered her life. This had always been a principle in the Dodson family; it was one form of that sense of honour and rectitude which was a proud tradition in such families—a tradition which has been the salt of our provincial society.

But though the letter could not shake Mrs. Glegg's principles, it made the family breach much more difficult to mend; and as to the effect it produced on Mrs. Glegg's opinion of Mr. Tulliver—she begged to be understood from that time forth that she had nothing whatever to say about him: his state of mind, apparently, was too corrupt for her to contemplate it for a moment. It was not until the evening before Tom went to school, at the beginning of August, that Mrs. Glegg paid a visit to her sister Tulliver, sitting in her gig all the while, and showing her displeasure by markedly abstaining from all advice and criticism, for, as she observed to her sister Deane, "Bessy must bear the consequences o' having such a husband, though I'm sorry for her," and Mrs. Deane agreed that Bessy was pitiable.

That evening Tom observed to Maggie, "O my! Maggie, aunt Glegg's beginning to come again; I'm glad I'm going to school. *You'll* catch it all now!"

Maggie was already so full of sorrow at the thought of Tom's going away from her, that this playful exultation of his seemed very unkind, and she cried herself to sleep that night.

Mr. Tulliver's prompt procedure entailed on him further promptitude in finding the convenient person who was desirous of lending five hundred pounds on bond. "It must be no client of Wakem's," he said to himself; and yet at the end of a fortnight it turned out to the contrary; not because Mr. Tulliver's will was feeble, but because external fact was stronger. Wakem's client was the only convenient person to be found. Mr. Tulliver had a destiny as well as Œdipus, and in this case he might plead, like Œdipus, that his deed was inflicted on him rather than committed by him.

BOOK TWO

School-Time

★

CHAPTER I

TOM'S "FIRST HALF"

TOM TULLIVER's sufferings during the first quarter he was at King's Lorton, under the distinguished care of the Rev. Walter Stelling, were rather severe. At Mr. Jacobs' academy, life had not presented itself to him as a difficult problem: there were plenty of fellows to play with, and Tom being good at all active games—fighting especially—had that precedence among them which appeared to him inseparable from the personality of Tom Tulliver. Mr. Jacobs himself, familiarly known as Old Goggles, from his habit of wearing spectacles, imposed no painful awe; and if it was the property of snuffy old hypocrites like him to write like copperplate and surround their signatures with arabesques, to spell without forethought, and to spout "My name is Norval" without bungling, Tom, for his part, was rather glad he was not in danger of those mean accomplishments. He was not going to be a snuffy school-master—he; but a substantial man, like his father, who used to go hunting when he was younger, and rode a capital black mare—as pretty a bit of horse-flesh as ever you saw: Tom had heard what her points were a hundred times. *He* meant to go hunting too, and to be generally respected. When people were grown up, he considered, nobody inquired about their writing and spelling: when he was a man, he should be master of everything, and do just as he liked. It had been very difficult for him to reconcile himself to the idea that his school-time was to be prolonged, and that he was not to be brought up to his father's business, which he had always thought extremely pleasant, for it was nothing but riding about, giving orders, and going to market; and he thought that a clergyman would give him a great many Scripture lessons, and probably make him learn the Gospel and Epistle on a Sunday as well as the Collect. But in the absence of specific information, it was impossible for him to imagine that school and a school-master would be something entirely different from the academy of Mr. Jacobs. So, not to be at a deficiency, in case of his finding genial companions, he had taken care to carry with him a small box of percussion-caps; not that there was anything particular to be done with them, but they would serve to impress strange boys with a sense of his familiarity with guns. Thus poor Tom, though he saw very clearly through Maggie's illusions, was not without illusions of his own, which were to be cruelly dissipated by his enlarged experience at King's Lorton.

He had not been there a fortnight before it was evident to him that life, complicated not only with the Latin grammar but with a new standard of English pronunciation, was a very difficult business, made all the more obscure by a thick mist of bashfulness. Tom, as you have observed, was never an exception among boys for ease of address; but the difficulty of enunciating a monosyllable in reply to Mr. or Mrs. Stelling was so great, that he even dreaded to be asked at table whether he would have more pudding. As to the percussion-caps, he had almost resolved, in the bitterness of his heart, that he would throw them into a neighbouring pond; for not only was he the solitary pupil, but he began even to have a certain scepticism about guns, and a general sense that his theory of life was undermined. For Mr. Stelling thought nothing of guns, or horses either, apparently; and yet it was impossible for Tom to despise Mr. Stelling as he had despised Old Goggles. If there were anything that was not thoroughly genuine about Mr. Stelling, it lay quite beyond Tom's power to detect it: it is only by a wide comparison of facts that the wisest full-grown man can distinguish well-rolled barrels from more supernal thunder.

Mr. Stelling was a well-sized, broad-chested man, not yet thirty, with flaxen hair standing erect, and large lightish-grey eyes, which were always very wide open; he had a sonorous bass voice, and an air of defiant self-confidence inclining to brazenness. He had entered on his career with great vigour, and intended to make a considerable impression on his fellow-men. The Rev. Walter Stelling was not a man who would remain among the "inferior clergy" all his life. He had a true British determination to push his way in the world. As a schoolmaster, in the first place; for there were capital masterships of grammar-schools to be had, and Mr. Stelling meant to have one of them. But as a preacher also, for he meant always to preach in a striking manner, so as to have his congregation swelled by admirers from neighbouring parishes, and to produce a great sensation whenever he took occasional duty for a brother clergyman of minor gifts. The style of preaching he had chosen was the extemporaneous, which was held little short of the miraculous in rural parishes like King's Lorton. Some passages of Massillon and Bourdaloue, which he knew by heart, were really very effective when rolled out in Mr. Stelling's deepest tones; but as comparatively feeble appeals of his own were delivered in the same loud and impressive manner, they were often thought quite as striking by his hearers. Mr. Stelling's doctrine was of no particular school; if anything, it had a tinge of evangelicalism, for that was "the telling thing" just then in the diocese to which King's Lorton belonged. In short, Mr. Stelling was a man who meant to rise in his profession, and to rise by merit, clearly, since he had no interest beyond what might be promised by a problematic relationship to a great lawyer who had not yet become Lord Chancellor. A clergyman who has such vigorous intentions naturally gets a little into debt at starting; it is not to be expected that he will live in the meagre style of a man who means to be a poor curate all his life, and if the few hundreds Mr. Timpson advanced towards his daughter's fortune did not suffice for the purchase of handsome furniture, together with a stock of wine, a grand piano, and the laying-out of a superior flower-garden, it followed in the most rigorous manner, either that these things must be procured by some other means, or else that the Rev. Mr. Stelling must go without them—· which last alternative would be an absurd procrastination of the fruits of success, where success was certain. Mr. Stelling was so broad-chested and resolute that he felt equal to anything; he would become celebrated by shaking the consciences of his hearers, and he would by-and-by edit a Greek play, and invent several new readings. He had not yet selected the play, for having been married little more than two years, his leisure time had been much occupied with attentions to Mrs. Stelling; but he had told that fine woman what he meant to do some day, and she felt great confidence in her husband, as a man who understood everything of that sort.

But the immediate step to future success was to bring on Tom Tulliver during this first half-year; for, by a singular coincidence, there had been some negotiation concerning another pupil from the same neighbourhood, and it might further a decision in Mr. Stelling's favour, if it were understood that young Tulliver, who, Mr. Stelling observed in conjugal privacy, was rather a rough cub, had made prodigious progress in a short time. It was on this ground that he was severe with Tom about his lessons: he was clearly a boy whose powers would never be developed through the medium of the Latin grammar, without the application of some sternness. Not that Mr. Stelling was a harsh-tempered or unkind man—quite the contrary: he was jocose with Tom at table, and corrected his provincialisms and his deportment in the most playful manner; but poor Tom was only the more cowed and confused by this double novelty, for he had never been used to jokes at all like Mr. Stelling's; and for the first time in his life he had a painful sense that he was all wrong somehow. When Mr. Stelling said, as the roast-beef was being uncovered, "Now, Tulliver! which would you rather decline, roast-beef or the Latin for it?"—Tom, to whom in his coolest moments a pun would have been a hard nut, was thrown into a state of embarrassed alarm that made everything dim to him except the feeling that he would rather not have anything to do with Latin: of course he answered, "Roast-beef," whereupon there followed much laughter and some practical joking with the plates, from which Tom gathered that he had in some mysterious way refused beef, and, in fact, made himself appear "a silly." If he could have seen a fellow-pupil undergo these painful operations and survive them in good spirits, he might sooner have taken them as a matter of course. But there are two expensive forms of education, either of which a parent may procure for his son by sending him as solitary pupil to a clergyman: one is, the enjoyment of the reverend gentleman's undivided neglect; the other is, the endurance of the reverend gentleman's undivided attention. It was the latter privilege for which Mr. Tulliver paid a high price in Tom's initiatory months at King's Lorton.

That respectable miller and maltster had left Tom behind, and driven homeward in a state of great mental satisfaction. He considered that it was a happy moment for him when he had thought of asking Riley's advice about a tutor for Tom. Mr. Stelling's eyes were so wide open, and he talked in such an off-hand, matter-of-fact way,—answering every difficult slow remark of Mr. Tulliver's with, "I see, my good sir, I see;" "To be sure, to be sure!" "You want your son to be a man who will make his way in the world,"—that Mr. Tulliver was delighted to find in him a clergyman whose knowledge was so applicable to the everyday affairs of this life. Except Counsellor Wylde, whom he had heard at the last sessions, Mr. Tulliver thought the Rev. Mr. Stelling was the shrewdest fellow he had ever met with—not unlike Wylde, in fact: he had the same way of sticking his thumbs in the armholes of his waistcoat. Mr. Tulliver was not by any means an exception in mistaking brazenness for shrewdness: most laymen thought Stelling shrewd, and a man of remarkable powers generally: it was chiefly by his clerical brethren that he was considered rather a dull fellow. But he told Mr. Tulliver several stories about "swing" and incendiarism, and asked his advice about feeding pigs in so thoroughly secular and judicious a manner, with so much polished glibness of tongue, that the miller thought, here was the very thing he wanted for Tom. He had no doubt this first-rate man was acquainted with every branch of information, and knew exactly what Tom must learn in order to become a match for the lawyers—which poor Mr. Tulliver himself did *not* know, and so was necessarily thrown for self-direction on this wide kind of inference. It is hardly fair to laugh at him, for I have known much more highly-instructed persons than he make inferences quite as wide, and not at all wiser.

As for Mrs. Tulliver—finding that Mrs. Stelling's views as to the airing of linen and the frequent recurrence of hunger in a growing boy, entirely coincided with her own; moreover, that Mrs. Stelling, though so young a woman, and only anticipating her second confinement, had gone through very nearly the same experience as herself with regard to the behaviour and fundamental character of the monthly nurse, she expressed great contentment to her husband, when they drove away, at leaving Tom with a woman who, in spite of her youth, seemed quite sensible and motherly, and asked advice as prettily as could be.

"They must be very well off, though," said Mrs. Tulliver, "for everything's as nice as can be all over the house, and that watered-silk she had on cost a pretty penny. Sister Pullet has got one like it."

"Ah," said Mr. Tulliver, "he's got some income besides the curacy,

I reckon. Perhaps her father allows 'em something. There's Tom 'ull be another hundred to him, and not much trouble either, by his own account: he says teaching comes natural to him. That's wonderful, now," added Mr. Tulliver, turning his head on one side, and giving his horse a meditative tickling on the flank.

Perhaps it was because teaching came naturally to Mr. Stelling, that he set about it with that uniformity of method and independence of circumstances, which distinguish the actions of animals understood to be under the immediate teaching of nature. Mr. Broderip's amiable beaver, as that charming naturalist tells us, busied himself as earnestly in constructing a dam, in a room up three pair of stairs in London, as if he had been laying his foundation in a stream or lake in Upper Canada. It was "Binny's" function to build: the absence of water or of possible progeny was an accident for which he was not accountable. With the same unerring instinct Mr. Stelling set to work at his natural method of instilling the Eton Grammar and Euclid into the mind of Tom Tulliver. This, he considered, was the only basis of solid instruction: all other means of education were mere charlatanism, and could produce nothing better than smatterers. Fixed on this firm basis, a man might observe the display of various or special knowledge made by irregularly educated people with a pitying smile: all that sort of thing was very well, but it was impossible these people could form sound opinions. In holding this conviction Mr. Stelling was not biassed, as some tutors have been, by the excessive accuracy or extent of his own scholarship; and as to his views about Euclid, no opinion could have been freer from personal partiality. Mr. Stelling was very far from being led astray by enthusiasm, either religious or intellectual: on the other hand, he had no secret belief that everything was humbug. He thought religion was a very excellent thing, and Aristotle a great authority, and deaneries and prebends useful institutions, and Great Britain the providential bulwark of Protestantism, and faith in the unseen a great support to afflicted minds: he believed in all these things, as a Swiss hotel-keeper believes in the beauty of the scenery around him, and in the pleasure it gives to artistic visitors. And in the same way Mr. Stelling believed in his method of education: he had no doubt that he was doing the very best thing for Mr. Tulliver's boy. Of course, when the miller talked of "mapping" and "summing" in a vague and diffident manner, Mr. Stelling had set his mind at rest by an assurance that he understood what was wanted; for how was it possible the good man could form any reasonable judgment about the matter? Mr. Stelling's duty was to teach the lad in the only right way—indeed, he knew no other: he had not wasted his time in the acquirement of anything abnormal.

He very soon set down poor Tom as a thoroughly stupid lad; for though by hard labour he could get particular declensions into his brain, anything so abstract as the relation between cases and terminations could by no means get such a lodgment there as to enable him to recognise a chance genitive or dative. This struck Mr. Stelling as some-thing more than natural stupidity: he suspected obstinacy, or, at any rate, indifference; and lectured Tom severely on his want of thorough application. "You feel no interest in what you're doing, sir," Mr. Stelling would say, and the reproach was painfully true. Tom had never found any difficulty in discerning a pointer from a setter, when once he had been told the distinction, and his perceptive powers were not at all deficient. I fancy they were quite as strong as those of the Rev. Mr. Stelling; for Tom could predict with accuracy what number of horses were cantering behind him, he could throw a stone right into the centre of a given ripple, he could guess to a fraction how many lengths of his stick it would take to reach across the playground, and could draw almost perfect squares on his slate without any measurement. But Mr. Stelling took no note of these things: he only observed that Tom's faculties failed him before the abstractions hideously symbolised to him in the pages of the Eton Grammar, and that he was in a state bordering on idiocy with regard to the demonstration that two given triangles must be equal—though he could discern with great promptitude and certainty the fact that they *were* equal. Whence Mr. Stelling concluded that Tom's brain, being peculiarly impervious to etymology and demon-strations, was peculiarly in need of being ploughed and harrowed by these patent implements: it was his favourite metaphor, that the classics and geometry constituted that culture of the mind which prepared it for the reception of any subsequent crop. I say nothing against Mr. Stelling's theory: if we are to have one regimen for all minds, his seems to me as good as any other. I only know it turned out as uncomfortably for Tom Tulliver as if he had been plied with cheese in order to remedy a gastric weakness which prevented him from digesting it. It is astonishing what a different result one gets by changing the metaphor! Once call the brain an intellectual stomach, and one's ingenious conception of the classics and geometry as ploughs and harrows seems to settle noth-ing. But then it is open to some one else to follow great authorities, and call the mind a sheet of white paper or a mirror, in which case one's knowledge of the digestive process becomes quite irrelevant. It was doubtless an ingenious idea to call the camel the ship of the desert, but it would hardly lead one far in training that useful beast. O Aristotle! if you had had the advantage of being "the freshest modern" instead of the greatest ancient, would you not have mingled your praise of metaphorical speech, as a sign of high intelligence, with a lamentation that intelligence so rarely shows itself in speech without metaphor,—that we can so seldom declare what a thing is, except by saying it is something else?

Tom Tulliver, being abundant in no form of speech, did not use any metaphor to declare his views as to the nature of Latin: he never called it an instrument of torture; and it was not until he had got on some way in the next half-year, and in the Delectus, that he was ad-vanced enough to call it a "bore" and "beastly stuff." At present, in relation to this demand that he should learn Latin declensions and conjugations, Tom was in a state of as blank unimaginativeness concerning the cause and tendency of his sufferings, as if he had been an innocent shrewmouse imprisoned in the split trunk of an ash tree in order to cure lameness in cattle. It is doubtless almost incredible to instructed minds of the present day that a boy of twelve, not belonging strictly to "the masses," who are now understood to have the monopoly of mental darkness, should have had no distinct idea how there came to be such a thing as Latin on this earth: yet so it was with Tom. It would have taken a long while to make conceivable to him that there ever existed a people who bought and sold sheep and oxen, and transacted the everyday affairs of life, through the medium of this language, and still longer to make him understand why he should be called upon to learn it, when its connection with those affairs had become entirely latent. So far as Tom had gained any acquaintance with the Romans at Mr. Jacobs' academy, his knowledge was strictly correct, but it went no farther than the fact that they were "in the New Testament;" and Mr. Stelling was not the man to enfeeble and emasculate his pupil's mind by simplifying and explaining, or to reduce the tonic effect of etymology by mixing it with smattering, extraneous information such as is given to girls.

Yet, strange to say, under this vigorous treatment Tom became more like a girl than he had ever been in his life before. He had a large share of pride, which had hitherto found itself very comfortable in the world, despising Old Goggles, and reposing in the sense of unquestioned rights; but now this same pride met with nothing but bruises and crushings. Tom was too clear-sighted not to be aware that Mr. Stelling's standard of things was quite different, was certainly something higher in the eyes of the world, than that of the people he had been living amongst, and that, brought in contact with it, he, Tom Tulliver, appeared uncouth and stupid: he was by no means indifferent to this, and his pride got into an uneasy condition which quite nullified his boyish self-satisfaction, and gave him something of the girl's susceptibility. He was of a very firm, not to say obstinate, disposition, but there was no brute-like rebellion and recklessness in his nature: the human sensibilities predominated, and if it had occurred to him that he could enable himself to show some quickness at his lessons, and so acquire Mr. Stelling's approbation, by standing on one leg for an inconvenient length of time, or rapping his head moderately against the wall, or any voluntary action of that sort, he would certainly have tried it. But no—Tom had never heard that these measures would brighten the understanding, or strengthen the verbal memory; and he was not given to hypothesis and experiment. It did occur to him that he could perhaps get some help by praying for it; but as the prayers he said every evening were forms learned by heart, he rather shrank from the novelty and irregularity of introducing an extempore passage on a topic of petition for which he was not aware of any precedent. But one day when he had broken down, for the fifth time, in the supines of the third conjugation, and Mr. Stelling, convinced that this must be carelessness, since it transcended the bounds of possible stupidity, had lectured him very seriously, pointing out that if he failed to seize the present golden opportunity of learning supines, he would have to regret it when he became a man,— Tom, more miserable than usual, determined to try his sole resource; and that evening, after his usual form of prayer for his parents and "little sister" (he had begun to pray for Maggie when she was a baby), and that he might be able always to keep God's commandments, he added, in the same low whisper, "and please to make me always remember my Latin." He paused a little to consider how he should pray about Euclid —whether he should ask to see what it meant, or whether there was any other mental state which would be more applicable to the case. But at last he added—"And make Mr. Stelling say I shan't do Euclid any more. Amen."

The fact that he got through his supines without mistake the next day, encouraged him to persevere in this appendix to his prayers, and neutralised any scepticism that might have arisen from Mr. Stelling's continued demand for Euclid. But his faith broke down under the apparent absence of all help when he got into the irregular verbs. It seemed clear that Tom's despair under the caprices of the present tense did not constitute a *nodus* worthy of interference, and since this was the climax of his difficulties, where was the use of praying for help any longer? He made up his mind to this conclusion in one of his dull, lonely evenings, which he spent in the study, preparing his lessons for the morrow. His eyes were apt to get dim over the page—though he hated crying, and was ashamed of it: he couldn't help thinking with some affection even of Spouncer, whom he used to fight and quarrel with; he would have felt at home with Spouncer, and in a condition of superiority. And then the mill, and the river, and Yap pricking up his ears, ready to obey the least sign when Tom said "Hoigh!" would all come before him in a sort of calenture, when his fingers played absently in his pocket with his great knife and his coil of whip-cord, and other relics of the past. Tom, as I said, had never been so much like a girl in his life before, and at that epoch of irregular verbs his spirit was further depressed by a new means of mental development, which had been thought of for him out of school hours. Mrs. Stelling had lately had her second baby, and as nothing could be more salutary for a boy than to feel himself useful, Mrs. Stelling considered she was doing Tom a service by setting him to watch the little cherub Laura while the nurse was occupied with the sickly baby. It was quite a pretty employment for Tom to take little Laura out in the sunniest hour of the autumn day—it would help to make him feel that Lorton Parsonage was a home for him, and that he was one of the family. The little cherub Laura, not being an accomplished walker at present, had a ribbon fastened round her waist, by which Tom held her as if she had been a little dog during the minutes in which she chose to walk; but as these were rare, he was for the most part carrying this fine child round and round the garden, within sight of Mrs. Stelling's window—according to orders. If any one considers this unfair and even oppressive towards Tom, I beg him to consider that there are feminine virtues which are with difficulty combined, even if they are not incompatible. When the wife of a poor curate contrives, under all her disadvantages, to dress extremely well, and to have a style of coiffure which requires that her nurse shall occasionally officiate as lady's maid,—when, moreover, her dinner-parties and her drawing-room show that effort at elegance and completeness of appointment to which ordinary women might imagine a large income necessary, it would be unreasonable to expect of her that she should employ a second nurse, or even act as a nurse herself. Mr. Stelling knew better: he saw that his wife did wonders already, and was proud of her: it was certainly not the best thing in the world for young Tulliver's gait to carry a heavy child, but he had plenty of exercise in long walks with himself, and next half-year Mr. Stelling would see about having a drilling-master. Among the many means whereby Mr. Stelling intended to be more fortunate than the bulk of his fellow-men, he had entirely given up that of having his own way in his own house. What then? he had married "as kind a little soul as ever breathed," according to Mr. Riley, who had been acquainted with Mrs. Stelling's blond ringlets and smiling demeanour throughout her maiden life, and on the strength of that knowledge would have been ready any day to pronounce that whatever domestic differences might arise in her married life must be entirely Mr. Stelling's fault.

If Tom had had a worse disposition, he would certainly have hated the little cherub Laura, but he was too kind-hearted a lad for that—there was too much in him of the fibre that turns to true manliness, and to protecting pity for the weak. I am afraid he hated Mrs. Stelling, and contracted a lasting dislike to pale blond ringlets and broad plaits, as directly associated with haughtiness of manner and a frequent reference to other people's "duty." But he couldn't help playing with little Laura, and liking to amuse her: he even sacrificed his percussion-caps for her sake, in despair of their ever serving a greater purpose—thinking the small flash and bang would delight her, and thereby drawing down on himself a rebuke from Mrs. Stelling for teaching her child to play with fire. Laura was a sort of playfellow—and O, how Tom longed for playfellows! In his secret heart he yearned to have Maggie with him, and was almost ready to doat on her exasperating acts of forgetfulness; though, when he was at home, he always represented it as a great favour on his part to let Maggie trot by his side on his pleasure excursions.

And before this dreary half-year was ended, Maggie actually came. Mrs. Stelling had given a general invitation for the little girl to come and stay with her brother; so when Mr. Tulliver drove over to King's Lorton late in October, Maggie came too, with the sense that she was taking a great journey, and beginning to see the world. It was Mr. Tulliver's first visit to see Tom, for the lad must learn not to think too much about home.

"Well, my lad," he said to Tom, when Mr. Stelling had left the room to announce the arrival to his wife, and Maggie had begun to kiss Tom freely, "you look rarely! School agrees with you."

Tom wished he had looked rather ill.

"I don't think I *am* well, father," said Tom; "I wish you'd ask Mr. Stelling not to let me do Euclid—it brings on the toothache, I think."

(The toothache was the only malady to which Tom had ever been subject.)

"Euclid, my lad—why, what's that?" said Mr. Tulliver.

"O, I don't know: it's definitions, and axioms, and triangles, and things. It's a book I've got to learn in—there's no sense in it."

"Go, go!" said Mr. Tulliver, reprovingly, "you mustn't say so. You must learn what your master tells you. He knows what it's right for you to learn."

"*I'll* help you now, Tom," said Maggie, with a little air of patronising consolation. "I'm come to stay ever so long, if Mrs. Stelling asks me. I've brought my box and my pinafores, haven't I, father?"

"*You* help me, you silly little thing!" said Tom, in such high spirits at this announcement that he quite enjoyed the idea of confounding Maggie by showing her a page of Euclid. "I should like to see you doing one of *my* lessons! Why, I learn Latin too! Girls never learn such things. They're too silly."

"I know what Latin is very well," said Maggie, confidently. "Latin's a language. There are Latin words in the Dictionary. There's bonus, a gift."

"Now, you're just wrong there, Miss Maggie!" said Tom, secretly astonished. "You think you're very wise! But 'bonus' means 'good,' as it happens—bonus, bona, bonum."

"Well, that's no reason why it shouldn't mean 'gift,'" said Maggie, stoutly. "It may mean several things—almost every word does. There's 'lawn,'— it means the grass-plot, as well as the stuff pocket-handker-chiefs are made of."

"Well done, little 'un," said Mr. Tulliver, laughing, while Tom felt rather disgusted with Maggie's knowingness, though beyond measure cheerful at the thought that she was going to stay with him. Her conceit would soon be overawed by the actual inspection of his books.

Mrs. Stelling, in her pressing invitation, did not mention a longer time than a week for Maggie's stay; but Mr. Stelling, who took her between his knees, and asked her where she stole her dark eyes from, insisted that she must stay a fortnight. Maggie thought Mr. Stelling was a charming man, and Mr. Tulliver was quite proud to leave his little wench where she would have an opportunity of showing her clever-ness to appreciating strangers. So it was agreed that she should not be fetched home till the end of the fortnight.

"Now, then, come with me into the study, Maggie," said Tom, as their father drove away. "What do you shake and toss your head now for, you silly?" he continued; for though her hair was now under a new dispensation, and was brushed smoothly behind her ears, she seemed still in imagination to be tossing it out of her eyes. "It makes you look as if you were crazy."

"O, I can't help it," said Maggie, impatiently. "Don't tease me, Tom. O, what books!" she exclaimed, as she saw the book-cases in the study. "How I should like to have as many books as that!"

"Why, you couldn't read one of 'em," said Tom, triumphantly. "They're all Latin."

"No, they aren't," said Maggie. "I can read the back of this . . . History of the Decline and Fall of the Roman Empire."

"Well, what does that mean? *You* don't know," said Tom, wagging his head.

"But I could soon find out," said Maggie, scornfully.

"Why, how?"

"I should look inside, and see what it was about."

"You'd better not, Miss Maggie," said Tom, seeing her hand on the volume. "Mr. Stelling lets nobody touch his books without leave, and *I* shall catch it, if you take it out."

"O, very well! Let me see all *your* books, then," said Maggie, turning to throw her arms round Tom's neck, and rub his cheek with her small round nose.

Tom, in the gladness of his heart at having dear old Maggie to dispute with and crow over again, seized her round the waist, and began to jump with her round the large library table. Away they jumped with more and more vigour, till Maggie's hair flew from behind her ears, and twirled about like an animated mop. But the revolutions round the table became more and more irregular in their sweep, till at last reaching Mr. Stelling's reading-stand, they sent it thundering down with its heavy lexicons to the floor. Happily it was the ground-floor, and the study was a one-storied wing to the house, so that the downfall made no alarming resonance, though Tom stood dizzy and aghast for a few minutes, dreading the appearance of Mr. or Mrs. Stelling.

"O, I say, Maggie," said Tom at last, lifting up the stand, "we must keep quiet here, you know. If we break anything, Mrs. Stelling 'll make us cry peccavi."

"What's that?" said Maggie.

"O, it's the Latin for a good scolding," said Tom, not without some pride in his knowledge.

"Is she a cross woman?" said Maggie.

"I believe you!" said Tom, with an emphatic nod.

"I think all women are crosser than men," said Maggie. "Aunt Glegg's a great deal crosser than Uncle Glegg, and mother scolds me more than father does."

"Well, *you'll* be a woman some day," said Tom, "so *you* needn't talk."

"But I shall be a *clever* woman," said Maggie, with a toss.

"O, I daresay, and a nasty conceited thing. Everybody 'll hate you."

"But you oughtn't to hate me, Tom: it'll be very wicked of you, for I shall be your sister."

"Yes, but if you're a nasty disagreeable thing, I *shall* hate you."

"O, but, Tom, you won't! I shan't be disagreeable. I shall be very good to you—and I shall be good to everybody. You won't hate me really, will you, Tom?"

"O, bother! never mind! Come, it's time for me to learn my lessons. See here! what I've got to do," said Tom, drawing Maggie towards him and showing her his theorem, while she pushed her hair behind her ears, and prepared herself to prove her capability of helping him in Euclid. She began to read with full confidence in her own powers, but presently, becoming quite bewildered, her face flushed with irritation. It was unavoidable—she must confess her incompetency, and she was not fond of humiliation.

"It's nonsense!" she said, "and very ugly stuff—nobody need want to make it out."

"Ah, there now, Miss Maggie!" said Tom, drawing the book away, and wagging his head at her, "you see you're not so clever as you thought you were."

"O," said Maggie, pouting, "I daresay I could make it out, if I'd learned what goes before, as you have."

"But that's what you just couldn't, Miss Wisdom," said Tom. "For it's all the harder when you know what goes before: for then you've got to say what definition 3. is, and what axiom V. is. But get along with you now: I must go on with this. Here's the Latin Grammar. See what you can make of that."

Maggie found the Latin Grammar quite soothing after her mathematical mortification; for she delighted in new words, and quickly found that there was an English Key at the end, which would make her very wise about Latin, at slight expense. She presently made up her mind to skip the rules in the Syntax—the examples became so absorbing. These mysterious sentences, snatched from an unknown context,—like strange horns of beasts, and leaves of unknown plants, brought from some far-off region,—gave boundless scope to her imagination, and were all the more fascinating because they were in a peculiar tongue of their own, which she could learn to interpret. It was really very interesting—the Latin Grammar that Tom had said no girls could learn: and she was proud because she found it interesting. The most fragmentary examples were her favorites. *Mors omnibus est communis* would have been jejune, only she liked to know the Latin; but the fortunate gentleman whom every one congratulated because he had a son "endowed with *such* a disposition" afforded her a great deal of pleasant conjecture, and she was quite lost in the "thick grove penetrable by no star," when Tom called out,

"Now, then, Magsie, give us the Grammar!"

"O Tom, it's such a pretty book!" she said, as she jumped out of the large arm-chair to give it him; "it's much prettier than the Dictionary. I could learn Latin very soon. I don't think it's at all hard."

"O, I know what you've been doing," said Tom; "you've been reading the English at the end. Any donkey can do that."

Tom seized the book and opened it with a determined and businesslike air, as much as to say that he had a lesson to learn which no donkeys would find themselves equal to. Maggie, rather piqued, turned to the book-cases to amuse herself with puzzling out the titles.

Presently Tom called to her: "Here, Magsie, come and hear if I can say this. Stand at that end of the table, where Mr. Stelling sits when he hears me."

Maggie obeyed and took the open book.

"Where do you begin, Tom?"

"O, I begin at '*Appellativa arborum*,' because I say all over again what I've been learning this week."

Tom sailed along pretty well for three lines; and Maggie was beginning to forget her office of prompter, in speculating as to what *mas* could mean, which came twice over, when he stuck fast at *Sunt etiam volucrum.*

"Don't tell me, Maggie; *Sunt etiam volucrum. . . . Sunt etiam volucrum . . . ut ostrea, cetus . . .*"

"No," said Maggie, opening her mouth and shaking her head.

"*Sunt etiam volucrum,*" said Tom, very slowly, as if the next words might be expected to come sooner when he gave them this strong hint that they were waited for.

"C, e, u," said Maggie, getting impatient.

"O, I know—hold your tongue," said Tom."*Ceu passer, hirundo; Ferarum . . . ferarum . . .*" Tom took his pencil and made several hard dots with it on his book-cover . . . "*ferarum . . .*"

"O dear, O dear, Tom," said Maggie, "what a time you are! *Ut . . .*"

"*Ut, ostrea . . .*"

"No, no," said Maggie, "*ut, tigris . . .*"

"O yes, now I can do," said Tom; "it was *tigris, vulpes,* I'd forgotten: *Ut tigris, vulpes; et Piscium.*"

With some further stammering and repetition, Tom got through the next few lines.

"Now, then," he said, "the next is what I've just learnt for tomorrow. Give me hold of the book a minute."

After some whispered gabbling, assisted by the beating of his fist on the table, Tom returned the book.

"*Mascula nomina in a,*" he began.

"No, Tom," said Maggie, "that doesn't come next. It's *Nomen non creskens genittivo . . .*"

"*Creskens genittivo,*" exclaimed Tom, with a derisive laugh, for Tom had learned this omitted passage for his yesterday's lesson, and a young gentleman does not require an intimate or extensive acquaintance with

Latin before he can feel the pitiable absurdity of a false quantity. *"Creskens genittivo!* What a little silly you are, Maggie!"

"Well, you needn't laugh, Tom, for you didn't remember it at all. I'm sure it's spelt so; how was I to know?"

"Phee-e-e-h! I told you girls couldn't learn Latin. It's *Nomen non crescens genitivo.*"

"Very well, then," said Maggie, pouting. "I can say that as well as you can. And you don't mind your stops. For you ought to stop twice as long at a semicolon as you do at a comma, and you make the longest stops where there ought to be no stop at all."

"O, well, don't chatter. Let me go on."

They were presently fetched to spend the rest of the evening in the drawing-room, and Maggie became so animated with Mr. Stelling, who, she felt sure, admired her cleverness, that Tom was rather amazed and alarmed at her audacity. But she was suddenly subdued by Mr. Stelling's alluding to a little girl of whom he had heard that she once ran away to the gypsies.

"What a very odd little girl that must be!" said Mrs. Stelling, meaning to be playful—but a playfulness that turned on her supposed oddity was not at all to Maggie's taste. She feared Mr. Stelling, after all, did not think much of her, and went to bed in rather low spirits. Mrs. Stelling, she felt, looked at her as if she thought her hair was very ugly because it hung down straight behind.

Nevertheless it was a very happy fortnight to Maggie, this visit to Tom. She was allowed to be in the study while he had his lessons, and in her various readings got very deep into the examples in the Latin Grammar. The astronomer who hated women generally, caused her so much puzzling speculation that she one day asked Mr. Stelling if all astronomers hated women, or whether it was only this particular astronomer. But, forestalling his answer, she said,

"I suppose it's all astronomers: because, you know, they live up in high towers, and if the women came there, they might talk and hinder them from looking at the stars."

Mr. Stelling liked her prattle immensely, and they were on the best terms. She told Tom she should like to go to school to Mr. Stelling, as he did, and learn just the same things. She knew she could do Euclid, for she had looked into it again, and she saw what A B C meant: they were the names of the lines.

"I'm sure you couldn't do it, now," said Tom; "and I'll just ask Mr. Stelling if you could."

"I don't mind," said the little conceited minx. "I'll ask him myself."

"Mr. Stelling," she said, that same evening when they were in the drawing-room, "couldn't I do Euclid, and all Tom's lessons, if you were to teach me instead of him?"

"No; you couldn't," said Tom, indignantly. "Girls can't do Euclid: can they, sir?"

"They can pick up a little of everything, I daresay," said Mr. Stelling. "They've a great deal of superficial cleverness; but they couldn't go far into anything. They're quick and shallow."

Tom, delighted with this verdict, telegraphed his triumph by wagging his head at Maggie behind Mr. Stelling's chair. As for Maggie, she had hardly ever been so mortified. She had been so proud to be called "quick" all her little life, and now it appeared that this quickness was the brand of inferiority. It would have been better to be slow, like Tom.

"Ha, ha! Miss Maggie!" said Tom, when they were alone, "you see it's not such a fine thing to be quick. You'll never go far into anything, you know."

And Maggie was so oppressed by this dreadful destiny that she had no spirit for a retort.

But when this small apparatus of shallow quickness was fetched away in the gig by Luke, and the study was once more quite lonely for Tom, he missed her grievously. He had really been brighter, and had got through his lessons better, since she had been there; and she had asked Mr. Stelling so many questions about the Roman empire, and whether there really ever was a man who said, in Latin, "I would not buy it for a farthing or a rotten nut," or whether that had only been turned into Latin, that Tom had actually come to a dim understanding of the fact that there had once been people upon the earth who were so fortunate as to know Latin without learning it through the medium of the Eton Grammar. This luminous idea was a great addition to his historical acquirements during this half-year, which were otherwise confined to an epitomised history of the Jews.

But the dreary half-year *did* come to an end. How glad Tom was to see the last yellow leaves fluttering before the cold wind! The dark afternoons, and the first December snow, seemed to him far livelier than the August sunshine; and that he might make himself the surer about the flight of the days that were carrying him homeward, he stuck twenty-one sticks deep in a corner of the garden, when he was three weeks from the holidays, and pulled one up every day with a great wrench, throwing it to a distance with a vigour of will which would have carried it to limbo, if it had been in the nature of sticks to travel so far.

But it was worth purchasing, even at the heavy price of the Latin Grammar—the happiness of seeing the bright light in the parlour at home, as the gig passed noiselessly over the snow-covered bridge: the happiness of passing from the cold air to the warmth, and the kisses and the smiles of that familiar hearth, where the pattern of the rug and the grate and the fire-irons were "first ideas" that it was no more possible to criticise than the solidity and extension of matter. There is no sense of ease like the ease we felt in those scenes where we were born, where objects became dear to us before we had known the labour of choice, and where the outer world seemed only an extension of our own personality: we accepted and loved it as we accepted our own sense of existence and our own limbs. Very commonplace, even ugly, that furniture of our early home might look if it were put up to auction; an improved taste in upholstery scorns it; and is not the striving after something better and better in our surroundings, the grand characteristic that distinguishes man from the brute—or, to satisfy a scrupulous accuracy of definition, that distinguishes the British man from the foreigr brute? But heaven knows where that striving might lead us, if our affections had not a trick of twining round those old inferior things—if the loves and sanctities of our life had no deep immovable roots in memory. One's delight in an elderberry bush overhanging the confused leafage of a hedgerow bank, as a more gladdening sight than the finest cistus or fuchsia spreading itself on the softest undulating turf, is an entirely unjustifiable preference to a landscape-gardener, or to any of those severely regulated minds who are free from the weakness of any attachment that does not rest on a demonstrable superiority of qualities. And there is no better reason for preferring this elderberry bush than that it stirs an early memory—that it is no novelty in my life, speaking to me merely through my present sensibilities to form and colour, but the long companion of my existence, that wove itself into my joys when joys were vivid.

CHAPTER II

THE CHRISTMAS HOLIDAYS

FINE old Christmas, with the snowy hair and ruddy face, had done his duty that year in the noblest fashion, and had set off his rich gifts of warmth and colour with all the heightening contrast of frost and snow.

Snow lay on the croft and river-bank in undulations softer than the limbs of infancy; it lay with the neatliest finished border on every sloping roof, making the dark-red gables stand out with a new depth of colour; it weighed heavily on the laurels and fir-trees till it fell from them with a shuddering sound; it clothed the rough turnip-field with whiteness, and made the sheep look like dark blotches; the gates were all blocked up with the sloping drifts, and here and there a disregarded four-footed beast stood as if petrified "in unrecumbent sadness;" there was no gleam, no shadow, for the heavens, too, were one still, pale cloud—no sound or motion in anything but the dark river, that flowed and moaned like an unresting sorrow. But old Christmas smiled as he laid this cruel-seeming spell on the out-door world, for he meant to light up home with new brightness, to deepen all the richness of indoor colour, and give a keener edge of delight to the warm fragrance of food: he meant to prepare a sweet imprisonment that would strengthen the primitive fellowship of kindred, and make the sunshine of familiar human faces as welcome as the hidden day-star. His kindness fell but hardly on the homeless—fell but hardly on the homes where the hearth was not very warm, and where the food had little fragrance; where the

508 THE MILL ON THE FLOSS

human faces had no sunshine in them, but rather the leaden, blank-eyed gaze of unexpectant want. But the fine old season meant well; and if he has not learnt the secret how to bless men impartially, it is because his father Time, with ever-unrelenting purpose, still hides that secret in his own mighty, slow-beating heart.

And yet this Christmas day, in spite of Tom's fresh delight in home, was not, he thought, somehow or other, quite so happy as it had always been before. The red berries were just as abundant on the holly, and he and Maggie had dressed all the windows and mantelpieces and picture-frames on Christmas eve with as much taste as ever, wedding the thick-set scarlet clusters with branches of the black-berried ivy. There had been singing under the windows after midnight—supernatural singing, Maggie always felt, in spite of Tom's contemptuous insistence that the singers were old Patch, the parish clerk, and the rest of the church choir: she trembled with awe when their caroling broke in upon her dreams, and the image of men in fustian clothes was always thrust away by the vision of angels resting on the parted cloud. But the midnight chant had helped as usual to lift the morning above the level of common days; and then there was the smell of hot toast and ale from the kitchen, at the breakfast hour; the favourite anthem, the green boughs, and the short sermon, gave the appropriate festal character to the church-going; and aunt and uncle Moss, with all their seven children, were looking like so many reflectors of the bright parlour fire, when the church-goers came back, stamping the snow from their feet. The plum-pudding was of the same handsome roundness as ever, and came in with the symbolic blue flames around it, as if it had been heroically snatched from the nether fires into which it had been thrown by dyspeptic Puritans; the dessert was as splendid as ever, with its golden oranges, brown nuts, and the crystalline light and dark of apple jelly and damson cheese: in all these things Christmas was as it had always been since Tom could remember; it was only distinguished, if by anything, by superior sliding and snowballs.

Christmas was cheery, but not so Mr. Tulliver. He was irate and defiant, and Tom, though he espoused his father's quarrels and shared his father's sense of injury, was not without some of the feeling that oppressed Maggie when Mr. Tulliver got louder and more angry in narration and assertion with the increased leisure of dessert. The attention that Tom might have concentrated on his nuts and wine was distracted by a sense that there were rascally enemies in the world, and that the business of grown-up life could hardly be conducted without a good deal of quarrelling. Now Tom was not fond of quarrelling, unless it could soon be put an end to by a fair stand-up fight with an adversary whom he had every chance of thrashing; and his father's irritable talk made him uncomfortable, though he never accounted to himself for the feeling, or conceived the notion that his father was faulty in this respect.

The particular embodiment of the evil principle now exciting Mr.

Tulliver's determined resistance was Mr. Pivart, who, having lands higher up the Ripple, was taking measures for their irrigation, which either were, or would be, or were bound to be (on the principle that water was water), an infringement on Mr. Tulliver's legitimate share of water-power. Dix, who had a mill on the stream, was a feeble auxiliary of Old Harry compared with Pivart. Dix had been brought to his senses by arbitration, and Wakem's advice had not carried *him* far; no: Dix, Mr. Tulliver considered, had been as good as nowhere in point of law; and in the intensity of his indignation against Pivart, his contempt for a baffled adversary like Dix began to wear the air of a friendly attachment. He had no male audience to-day except Mr. Moss, who knew nothing, as he said, of the "natur' o' mills," and could only assent to Mr. Tulliver's arguments on the *a priori* ground of family relationship and monetary obligation; but Mr. Tulliver did not talk with the futile intention of convincing his audience—he talked to relieve himself; while good Mr. Moss made strong efforts to keep his eyes wide open, in spite of the sleepiness which an unusually good dinner produced in his hard-worked frame. Mrs. Moss, more alive to the subject, and interested in everything that affected her brother, listened and put in a word as often as maternal preoccupations allowed.

"Why, Pivart's a new name hereabout, brother, isn't it?" she said: "he didn't own the land in father's time, nor yours either, before I was married."

"New name? Yes—I should think it *is* a new name," said Mr. Tulliver, with angry emphasis. "Dorlcote Mill's been in our family a hundred year and better, and nobody ever heard of a Pivart meddling with the river, till this fellow came and bought Bincome's farm out of hand, before anybody else could so much as say 'snap.' But I'll *Pivart* him!" added Mr. Tulliver, lifting his glass with a sense that he had defined his resolution in an unmistakable manner.

"You won't be forced to go to law with him, I hope, brother?" said Mrs. Moss, with some anxiety.

"I don't know what I shall be forced to; but I know what I shall force him to, with his dykes and erigations, if there's any law to be brought to bear o' the right side. I know well enough who's at the bottom of it; he's got Wakem to back him and egg him on. I know Wakem tells him the law can't touch him for it, but there's folks can handle the law besides Wakem. It takes a big raskil to beat him; but there's bigger to be found, as know more o' th' ins and out o' the law, else how came Wakem to lose Brumley's suit for him?"

Mr. Tulliver was a strictly honest man, and proud of being honest, but he considered that in law the ends of justice could only be achieved by employing a stronger knave to frustrate a weaker. Law was a sort of cock-fight, in which it was the business of injured honesty to get a game bird with the best pluck and the strongest spurs.

"Gore's no fool—you needn't tell me that," he observed presently, in a pugnacious tone, as if poor Gritty had been urging that lawyer's capabilities; "but, you see, he isn't up to the law as Wakem is. And water's a very particular thing—you can't pick it up with a pitchfork. That's why it's been nuts to Old Harry and the lawyers. It's plain enough what's the rights and the wrongs of water, if you look at it straightforward; for a river's a river, and if you've got a mill, you must have water to turn it; and it's no use telling me, Pivart's erigation and nonsense won't stop my wheel: I know what belongs to water better than that. Talk to me o' what th' engineers say! I say it's common sense, as Pivart's dykes must do me an injury. But if that's their engineering, I'll put Tom to it by-and-by, and he shall see if he can't find a bit more sense in th' engineering business than what *that* comes to."

Tom, looking round with some anxiety at this announcement of his prospects, unthinkingly withdrew a small rattle he was amusing Baby Moss with, whereupon she, being a baby that knew her own mind with remarkable clearness, instantaneously expressed her sentiments in a piercing yell, and was not to be appeased even by the restoration of the rattle, feeling apparently that the original wrong of having it taken from her remained in all its force. Mrs. Moss hurried away with her into another room, and expressed to Mrs. Tulliver, who accompanied her, the conviction that the dear child had good reasons for crying; implying that if it was supposed to be the rattle that baby clamoured for, she was a misunderstood baby. The thoroughly justifiable yell being quieted, Mrs. Moss looked at her sister-in-law and said—

"I'm sorry to see brother so put out about this water work."

"It's your brother's way, Mrs. Moss; I'd never anything o' that sort before I was married," said Mrs. Tulliver, with a half-implied reproach. She always spoke of her husband as "your brother" to Mrs. Moss, in any case when his line of conduct was not matter of pure admiration. Amiable Mrs. Tulliver, who was never angry in her life, had yet her mild share of that spirit without which she could hardly have been at once a Dodson and a woman. Being always on the defensive towards her own sisters, it was natural that she should be keenly conscious of her superiority, even as the weakest Dodson, over a husband's sister, who, besides being poorly off, and inclined to "hang on" her brother, had the good-natured submissiveness of a large, easy-tempered, untidy, prolific woman, with affection enough in her not only for her own husband and abundant children, but for any number of collateral relations.

"I hope and pray he won't go to law," said Mrs. Moss, "for there's never any knowing where that 'll end. And the right doesn't allays win. This Mr. Pivart's a rich man, by what I can make out, and the rich mostly get things their own way."

"As to that," said Mrs. Tulliver, stroking her dress down, "I've seen what riches are in my own family; for my sisters have got husbands as can afford to do pretty much what they like. But I think sometimes I shall be drove off my head with the talk about this law and erigation; and my sisters lay all the fault to me, for they don't know what it is to marry a man like your brother—how should they? Sister Pullet has her own way from morning till night."

"Well," said Mrs. Moss, "I don't think I should like my husband if he hadn't got any wits of his own, and I had to find head-piece for him. It's a deal easier to do what pleases one's husband, than to be puzzling what else one should do."

"If people come to talk o' doing what pleases their husbands," said Mrs. Tulliver, with a faint imitation of her sister Glegg, "I'm sure your brother might have waited a long while before he'd have found a wife that 'ud have let him have his say in everything, as I do. It's nothing but law and erigation now, from when we first get up in the morning till we go to bed at night; and I never contradict him; I only say— 'Well, Mr. Tulliver, do as you like; but whativer you do, don't go to law.' "

Mrs. Tulliver, as we have seen, was not without influence over her husband. No woman is; she can always incline him to do either what she wishes, or the reverse; and on the composite impulses that were threatening to hurry Mr. Tulliver into "law," Mrs. Tulliver's monotonous pleading had doubtless its share of force; it might even be comparable to that proverbial feather which has the credit or discredit of breaking the camel's back; though, on a strictly impartial view, the blame ought rather to lie with the previous weight of feathers which had already placed the back in such imminent peril, that an otherwise innocent feather could not settle on it without mischief. Not that Mrs. Tulliver's feeble beseeching could have had this feather's weight in virtue of her single personality; but whenever she departed from entire assent to her husband, he saw in her the representative of the Dodson family; and it was a guiding principle with Mr. Tulliver, to let the Dodsons know that they were not to domineer over *him*, or—more specifically—that a male Tulliver was far more than equal to four female Dodsons, even though one of them was Mrs. Glegg.

But not even a direct argument from that typical Dodson female herself against his going to law, could have heightened his disposition towards it so much as the mere thought of Wakem, continually freshened by the sight of the too able attorney on market-days. Wakem, to his certain knowledge, was (metaphorically speaking) at the bottom of Pivart's irrigation: Wakem had tried to make Dix stand out, and go to law about the dam: it was unquestionably Wakem who had caused Mr. Tulliver to lose the suit about the right of road and the bridge that made a thoroughfare of his land for every vagabond who preferred an opportunity of damaging private property to walking like an honest man along the high-road: all lawyers were more or less rascals, but Wakem's rascality was of that peculiarly aggravated kind which placed itself in opposition to that form of right embodied in Mr. Tulliver's interests and opinions. And as an extra touch of bitterness, the injured miller had recently, in borrowing the five hundred pounds, been obliged to carry a little business to Wakem's office on his own account. A hook-nosed glib fellow! as cool as a cucumber—always looking so sure of his game! And it was vexatious that Lawyer Gore was not more like him, but was a bald, round-featured man, with bland manners and fat hands; a game-cock that you would be rash to bet upon against Wakem. Gore was a sly fellow; his weakness did not lie on the side of scrupulosity: but the largest amount of winking, however significant, is not equivalent to seeing through a stone wall; and confident as Mr. Tulliver was in his principle that water was water, and in the direct inference that Pivart had not a leg to stand on in this affair of irrigation, he had an uncomfortable suspicion that Wakem had more law to show against this (rationally) irrefragable inference, than Gore could show for it. But then, if they went to law, there was a chance for Mr. Tulliver to employ Counsellor Wylde on his side, instead of having that admirable bully against him; and the prospect of seeing a witness of Wakem's made to perspire and become confounded, as Mr. Tulliver's witness had once been, was alluring to the love of retributive justice.

Much rumination had Mr. Tulliver on these puzzling subjects during his rides on the grey horse—much turning of the head from side to side, as the scales dipped alternately; but the probable result was still out of sight, only to be reached through much hot argument and iteration in domestic and social life. That initial stage of the dispute which consisted in the narration of the case and the enforcement of Mr. Tulliver's views concerning it throughout the entire circle of his connections would necessarily take time, and at the beginning of February, when Tom was going to school again, there were scarcely any new items to be detected in his father's statement of the case against Pivart, or any more specific indication of the measures he was bent on taking against that rash contravener of the principle that water was water. Iteration, like friction, is likely to generate heat instead of progress, and Mr. Tulliver's heat was certainly more and more palpable. If there had been no new evidence on any other point, there had been new evidence that Pivart was as "thick as mud" with Wakem.

"Father," said Tom, one evening near the end of the holidays, "uncle Glegg says Lawyer Wakem *is* going to send his son to Mr. Stelling. It isn't true—what they said about his going to be sent to France. You won't like me to go to school with Wakem's son, shall you?"

"It's no matter for that, my boy," said Mr. Tulliver; "don't you learn anything bad of him, that's all. The lad's a poor deformed creatur, and takes after his mother in the face: I think there isn't much of his father in him. It's a sign Wakem thinks high o' Mr. Stelling, as he sends his son to him, and Wakem knows meal from bran."

Mr. Tulliver in his heart was rather proud of the fact that his son was to have the same advantages as Wakem's: but Tom was not at all easy on the point; it would have been much clearer if the lawyer's son had not been deformed, for then Tom would have had the prospect of pitching into him with all that freedom which is derived from a high moral sanction.

CHAPTER III

THE NEW SCHOOLFELLOW

IT was a cold, wet January day on which Tom went back to school; a day quite in keeping with this severe phase of his destiny. If he had not carried in his pocket a parcel of sugar-candy and a small Dutch doll for little Laura, there would have been no ray of expected pleasure to enliven the general gloom. But he liked to think how Laura would put out her lips and her tiny hands for the bits of sugar-candy; and, to give the greater keenness to these pleasures of imagination, he took out the parcel, made a small hole in the paper, and bit off a crystal or two, which had so solacing an effect under the confined prospect and damp odours of the gig-umbrella, that he repeated the process more than once on his way.

"Well, Tulliver, we're glad to see you again," said Mr. Stelling, heartily. "Take off your wrappings and come into the study till dinner. You'll find a bright fire there, and a new companion."

Tom felt in an uncomfortable flutter as he took off his woollen comforter and other wrappings. He had seen Philip Wakem at St. Ogg's, but had always turned his eyes away from him as quickly as possible. He would have disliked having a deformed boy for his companion, even if Philip had not been the son of a bad man. And Tom did not see how a bad man's son could be very good. His own father was a good man, and he would readily have fought any one who said the contrary. He was in a state of mingled embarrassment and defiance as he followed Mr. Stelling to the study.

"Here is a new companion for you, to shake hands with, Tulliver," said that gentleman on entering the study—"Master Philip Wakem. I shall leave you to make acquaintance by yourselves. You already know something of each other, I imagine; for you are neighbours at home."

Tom looked confused and awkward, while Philip rose and glanced at him timidly. Tom did not like to go up and put out his hand, and he was not prepared to say, "How do you do?" on so short a notice.

Mr. Stelling wisely turned away, and closed the door behind him: boys' shyness only wears off in the absence of their elders.

Philip was at once too proud and too timid to walk towards Tom. He thought, or rather felt, that Tom had an aversion to looking at him: every one, almost, disliked looking at him; and his deformity was more conspicuous when he walked. So they remained without shaking hands or even speaking, while Tom went to the fire and warmed himself, every now and then casting furtive glances at Philip, who seemed to be drawing absently first one object and then another on a piece of paper he had before him. He had seated himself again, and as he drew, was thinking what he could say to Tom, and trying to overcome his own repugnance to making the first advances.

Tom began to look oftener and longer at Philip's face, for he could see it without noticing the hump, and it was really not a disagreeable face—very old-looking, Tom thought. He wondered how much older Philip was than himself. An anatomist—even a mere physiognomist—would have seen that the deformity of Philip's spine was not a congenital hump, but the result of an accident in infancy; but you do not expect from Tom any acquaintance with such distinctions: to him, Philip was simply a humpback. He had a vague notion that the deformity of Wakem's son had some relation to the lawyer's rascality, of which he had so often heard his father talk with hot emphasis; and he felt, too, a half-admitted fear of him as probably a spiteful fellow, who, not being able to fight you, had cunning ways of doing you a mischief by the sly. There was a humpbacked tailor in the neighbourhood of Mr. Jacobs' academy, who was considered a very unamiable character, and was much hooted after by public-spirited boys solely on the ground of his unsatisfactory moral qualities; so that Tom was not without a basis of fact to go upon. Still, no face could be more unlike that ugly tailor's than this melancholy boy's face; the brown hair round it waved and curled at the ends like a girl's: Tom thought that truly pitiable. This Wakem was a pale, puny fellow, and it was quite clear he would not be able to play at anything worth speaking of; but he handled his pencil in an enviable manner, and was apparently making one thing after another without any trouble. What was he drawing? Tom was quiet warm now, and wanted something new to be going forward. It was certainly more agreeable to have an ill-natured humpback as a companion than to stand looking out of the study window at the rain, and kicking his foot against the washboard in solitude; something would happen every day—"a quarrel or something;" and Tom thought he should rather like to show Philip that he had better not try his spiteful tricks on *him*. He suddenly walked across the hearth, and looked over Philip's paper.

"Why, that's a donkey with panniers—and a spaniel, and partridges in the corn!" he exclaimed, his tongue being completely loosed by surprise and admiration. "O, my buttons! I wish I could draw like that. I'm to learn drawing this half—I wonder if I shall learn to make dogs and donkeys!"

"O, you can do them without learning," said Philip; "I never learned drawing."

"Never learned?" said Tom, in amazement. "Why, when I make dogs and horses, and those things, the heads and the legs won't come right; though I can see how they ought to be very well. I can make houses, and all sorts of chimneys—chimneys going all down the wall, and windows in the roof, and all that. But I daresay I could do dogs and horses if I was to try more," he added, reflecting that Philip might falsely suppose that he was going to "knock under," if he were too frank about the imperfection of his accomplishments.

"O, yes," said Philip, "it's very easy. You've only to look well at things, and draw them over and over again. What you do wrong once, you can alter the next time."

"But haven't you been taught *any*thing?" said Tom, beginning to have a puzzled suspicion that Philip's crooked back might be the source of remarkable faculties. "I thought you'd been to school a long while."

"Yes," said Philip, smiling, "I've been taught Latin, and Greek, and mathematics,—and writing, and such things."

"O, but, I say, you don't like Latin, though, do you?" said Tom, lowering his voice confidentially.

"Pretty well; I don't care much about it," said Philip.

"Ah, but perhaps you haven't got into the *Propriæ quæ maribus,*" said Tom, nodding his head sideways, as much as to say, "that was the test: it was easy talking till you came to *that.*"

Philip felt some bitter complacency in the promising stupidity of this well-made active-looking boy; but made polite by his own extreme sensitiveness, as well as by his desire to conciliate, he checked his inclination to laugh, and said, quietly,

"I've done with the grammar; I don't learn that any more."

"Then you won't have the same lessons as I shall?" said Tom, with a sense of disappointment.

"No; but I daresay I can help you. I shall be very glad to help you if I can."

Tom did not say "Thank you," for he was quite absorbed in the thought that Wakem's son did not seem so spiteful a fellow as might have been expected.

"I say," he said presently, "do you love your father?"

"Yes," said Philip, colouring deeply; "don't you love yours?"

"O, yes. . . . I only wanted to know," said Tom, rather ashamed of himself, now he saw Philip colouring and looking uncomfortable. He found much difficulty in adjusting his attitude of mind towards the son of Lawyer Wakem, and it had occurred to him that if Philip disliked his father, that fact might go some way towards clearing up his perplexity.

"Shall you learn drawing now?" he said, by way of changing the subject.

"No," said Philip. "My father wishes me to give all my time to other things now."

"What! Latin, and Euclid, and those things?" said Tom.

"Yes," said Philip, who had left off using his pencil, and was resting his head on one hand, while Tom was leaning forward on both elbows, and looking with increasing admiration at the dog and the donkey.

"And you don't mind that?" said Tom, with strong curiosity.

"No: I like to know what everybody else knows. I can study what I like by-and-by."

"I can't think why anybody should learn Latin," said Tom. "It's no good."

"It's part of the education of a gentleman," said Philip. "All gentlemen learn the same things."

"What! do you think Sir John Crake, the master of the harriers, knows Latin?" said Tom, who had often thought he should like to resemble Sir John Crake.

"He learnt it when he was a boy, of course," said Philip. "But I daresay he's forgotten it."

"O, well, I can do that, then," said Tom, not with any epigrammatic intention, but with serious satisfaction at the idea that, as far as Latin was concerned, there was no hindrance to his resembling Sir John Crake. "Only you're obliged to remember it while you're at school, else you've got to learn ever so many lines of 'Speaker.' Mr. Stelling's very particular—did you know? He'll have you up ten times if you say 'nam' for 'jam' . . . he won't let you go a letter wrong, *I* can tell you."

"O, I don't mind," said Philip, unable to choke a laugh; "I can remember things easily. And there are some lessons I'm very fond of. I'm very fond of Greek history, and everything about the Greeks. I should like to have been a Greek and fought the Persians, and then have come home and have written tragedies, or else have been listened to by everybody for my wisdom, like Socrates, and have died a grand death." (Philip, you perceive, was not without a wish to impress the well-made barbarian with a sense of his mental superiority.)

"Why, were the Greeks great fighters?" said Tom, who saw a vista in this direction. "Is there anything like David, and Goliath, and Samson, in the Greek history? Those are the only bits I like in the history of the Jews."

"O, there are very fine stories of that sort about the Greeks—about the heroes of early times who killed the wild beasts, as Samson did. And in the *Odyssey*—that's a beautiful poem—there's a more wonderful giant than Goliath—Polypheme, who had only one eye in the middle of his forehead; and Ulysses, a little fellow, but very wise and cunning, got a red-hot pine-tree and stuck it into this one eye, and made him roar like a thousand bulls."

"O, what fun!" said Tom, jumping away from the table, and stamping first with one leg and then the other. "I say, can you tell me all about those stories? Because I shan't learn Greek, you know. . . . Shall I?" he added, pausing in his stamping with a sudden alarm, lest the contrary might be possible. "Does every gentleman learn Greek? . . . Will Mr. Stelling make me begin with it, do you think?"

"No, I should think not—very likely not," said Philip. "But you may read those stories without knowing Greek. I've got them in English."

"O, but I don't like reading; I'd sooner have you tell them me. But only the fighting ones, you know. My sister Maggie is always wanting to tell me stories—but they're stupid things. Girls' stories always are. Can you tell a good many fighting stories?"

"O, yes," said Philip; "lots of them, besides the Greek stories. I can tell you about Richard Cœur-de-Lion and Saladin, and about William Wallace, and Robert Bruce, and James Douglas—I know no end."

"You're older than I am, aren't you?" said Tom.

"Why, how old are *you?* I'm fifteen."

"I'm only going in fourteen," said Tom. "But I thrashed all the fellows at Jacobs'—that's where I was before I came here. And I beat 'em all at bandy and climbing. And I wish Mr. Stelling would let us go fishing. *I* could show you how to fish. You *could* fish, couldn't you? It's only standing, and sitting still, you know."

Tom, in his turn, wished to make the balance dip in his favour. This hunchback must not suppose that his acquaintance with fighting stories put him on a par with an actual fighting hero like Tom Tulliver. Philip winced under this allusion to his unfitness for active sports, and he answered almost peevishly—

"I can't bear fishing. I think people look like fools sitting watching a line hour after hour—or else throwing and throwing, and catching nothing."

"Ah, but you wouldn't say they looked like fools when they landed a big pike, I can tell you," said Tom, who had never caught anything that was "big" in his life, but whose imagination was on the stretch with indignant zeal for the honour of sport. Wakem's son, it was plain, had his disagreeable points, and must be kept in due check. Happily for the harmony of this first interview, they were now called to dinner, and Philip was not allowed to develop farther his unsound views on the subject of fishing. But Tom said to himself, that was just what he should have expected from a hunchback.

CHAPTER IV

"THE YOUNG IDEA"

THE alternations of feeling in that first dialogue between Tom and Philip continued to mark their intercourse even after many weeks of schoolboy intimacy. Tom never quite lost the feeling that Philip, being the son of a "rascal," was his natural enemy, never thoroughly overcame his repulsion to Philip's deformity: he was a boy who adhered tenaciously to impressions once received: as with all minds in which mere perception predominates over thought and emotion, the external remained to him rigidly what it was in the first instance. But then, it was impossible not to like Philip's company when he was in a good humour; he could help one so well in one's Latin exercises, which Tom regarded as a kind of puzzle that could only be found out by a lucky chance; and he could tell such wonderful fighting stories about Hal of the Wynd, for example, and other heroes who were especial favourites with Tom, because they laid about them with heavy strokes. He had small opinion of Saladin, whose scimitar could cut a cushion in two in an instant, who wanted to cut cushions? That was a stupid story, and he didn't care to hear it again. But when Robert Bruce, on the black pony, rose in his stirrups, and, lifting his good battle-axe, cracked at once the helmet and the skull of the too-hasty knight at Bannockburn, then Tom felt all the exaltation of sympathy, and if he had had a cocoanut at hand, he would have cracked it at once with the poker. Philip, in his happier moods, indulged Tom to the top of his bent, heightening the crash and bang and fury of every fight with all the artillery of epithets and similies at his command. But he was not always in a good humour or happy mood. The slight spurt of peevish susceptibility which had escaped him in their first interview, was a symptom of a perpetually-recurring mental ailment—half of it nervous irritability, half of it the heart-bitterness produced by the sense of his deformity. In these fits of susceptibility every glance seemed to him to be charged either with offensive pity or with ill-repressed disgust—at the very least it was an indifferent glance, and Philip felt indifference as a child of the south feels the chill air of a northern spring. Poor Tom's blundering patronage when they were out of doors together would sometimes make him turn upon the well-meaning lad quite savagely; and his eyes, usually sad and quiet, would flash with anything but playful lightning. No wonder Tom retained his suspicions of the humpback.

But Philip's self-taught skill in drawing was another link between them; for Tom found, to his disgust, that his new drawing-master gave him no dogs and donkeys to draw, but brooks and rustic bridges and ruins, all with a general softness of black-lead surface, indicating that nature, if anything, was rather satiny; and as Tom's feeling for the picturesque in landscape was at present quite latent, it is not surprising that Mr. Goodrich's productions seemed to him an uninteresting form of art. Mr. Tulliver, having a vague intention that Tom should be put to some business which included the drawing out of plans and maps, had complained to Mr. Riley, when he saw him at Mudport, that Tom seemed to be learning nothing of that sort; whereupon that obliging adviser had suggested that Tom should have drawing-lessons. Mr. Tulliver must not mind paying extra for drawing: let Tom be made a good draughtsman, and he would be able to turn his pencil to any purpose. So it was ordered that Tom should have drawing-lessons; and whom should Mr. Stelling have selected as a master if not Mr. Goodrich, who was considered quite at the head of his profession within a circuit of twelve miles round King's Lorton? By which means Tom learned to make an extremely fine point to his pencil, and to represent landscape with a "broad generality," which, doubtless from a narrow tendency in his mind to details, he thought extremely dull.

All this, you remember, happened in those dark ages when there were no schools of design—before schoolmasters were invariably men of scrupulous integrity, and before the clergy were all men of enlarged minds and varied culture. In those less-favoured days, it is no fable that there were other clergymen besides Mr. Stelling who had narrow intellects and large wants, and whose income, by a logical confusion to which Fortune, being a female as well as blindfold, is peculiarly liable, was proportioned not to their wants but to their intellect—with which income has clearly no inherent relation. The problem these gentlemen had to solve was to readjust the proportion between their wants and their income; and since wants are not easily starved to death, the simpler method appeared to be—to raise their income. There was but one way of doing this: any of those low callings in which men are obliged to do good work at a low price were forbidden to clergymen: was it their fault if their only resource was to turn out very poor work at a high price? Besides, how should Mr. Stelling be expected to know that education was a delicate and difficult business? any more than an animal endowed with a power of boring a hole through a rock should be expected to have wide views of excavation. Mr. Stelling's faculties had been early trained to boring in a straight line, and he had no faculty to spare. But among Tom's contemporaries, whose fathers cast their sons on clerical instruction to find them ignorant after many days, there were many far less lucky than Tom Tulliver. Education was almost entirely a matter of luck—usually of ill-luck—in those distant days. The state of mind in which you take a billiard-cue or a dice-box in your hand is one of sober certainty compared with that of old-fashioned fathers, like Mr. Tulliver, when they selected a school or a tutor for their sons. Excellent men, who had been forced all their lives to spell on an impromptu-phonetic system, and having carried on a successful business in spite of this disadvantage, had acquired money enough to give their sons a better start in life than they had had themselves, must necessarily take their chances as to the conscience and the competence of the schoolmaster whose circular fell in their way, and appeared to promise so much more than they would ever have thought of asking for, including the return of linen, fork, and spoon. It was happy for them if some ambitious draper of their acquaintance had not brought up his son to the Church, and if that young gentleman, at the age of four-and-twenty, had not closed his college dissipations by an imprudent marriage: otherwise, these innocent fathers, desirous of doing the best for their offspring, could only escape the draper's son by happening to be on the foundation of a grammar-school as yet unvisited by commissioners, where two or three boys could have, all to themselves, the advantages of a large and lofty building, together with a head-master, toothless, dim-eyed, and deaf, whose erudite indistinctness and inattention were engrossed by them at the rate of three hundred pounds a-head—a ripe scholar, doubtless, when first appointed; but all ripeness beneath the sun has a further stage less esteemed in the market.

Tom Tulliver, then, compared with many other British youths of his time who have since had to scramble through life wth some fragments of more or less relevant knowledge, and a great deal of strictly relevant ignorance, was not so very unlucky. Mr. Stelling was a broad-chested

healthy man, with the bearing of a gentleman, a conviction that a growing boy required a sufficiency of beef, and a certain hearty kindness in
him that made him like to see Tom looking well and enjoying his dinner;
not a man of refined conscience, or with any deep sense of the infinite
issues belonging to everyday duties; not quite competent to his high
offices; but incompetent gentlemen must live, and without private fortune it is difficult to see how they could all live genteely if they had
nothing to do with education or government. Besides, it was the fault of
Tom's mental constitution that his faculties could not be nourished on
the sort of knowledge Mr. Stelling had to communicate. A boy born
with a deficient power of apprehending signs and abstractions must
suffer the penalty of his congenital deficiency, just as if he had been
born with one leg shorter than the other. A method of education sanctioned by the long practice of our venerable ancestors was not to give
way before the exceptional dulness of a boy who was merely living at
the time then present. And Mr. Stelling was convinced that a boy so
stupid at signs and abstractions must be stupid at everything else, even
if that reverend gentleman could have taught him everything else. It
was the practice of our venerable ancestors to apply that ingenious instrument the thumb-screw, and to tighten and tighten it in order to elicit
non-existent facts: they had a fixed opinion to begin with, that the facts
were existent, and what had they to do but to tighten the thumb-screw?
In like manner, Mr. Stelling had a fixed opinion that all boys with any
capacity could learn what it was the only regular thing to teach: if
they were slow, the thumb-screw must be tightened—the exercises must
be insisted on with increased severity, and a page of Virgil be awarded
as a penalty, to encourage and stimulate a too languid inclination to
Latin verse.

   Nevertheless the thumb-screw was relaxed a little during this second
half-year. Philip was so advanced in his studies, and so apt, that Mr.
Stelling could obtain credit by his facility, which required little help,
much more easily than by the troublesome process of overcoming Tom's
dulness. Gentlemen with broad chests and ambitious intentions do
sometimes disappoint their friends by failing to carry the world before
them. Perhaps it is, that high achievements demand some other unusual
qualification besides an unusual desire for high prizes; perhaps it is
that these stalwart gentlemen are rather indolent, their *divinæ particu-
lum auræ* being obstructed from soaring by a too hearty appetite. Some
reason or other there was why Mr. Stelling deferred the execution of
many spirited projects—why he did not begin the editing of his Greek
play, or any other work of scholarship, in his leisure hours, but, after
turning the key of his private study with much resolution, sat down
to one of Theodore Hook's novels. Tom was gradually allowed to
shuffle through his lessons with less rigour, and having Philip to help
him, he was able to make some show of having applied his mind in a
confused and blundering way, without being cross-examined into a
betrayal that his mind had been entirely neutral in the matter. He

thought school much more bearable under this modification of circumstances; and he went on contentedly enough, picking up a promiscuous education chiefly from things that were not intended as education at all. What was understood to be his education, was simply the practice of reading, writing, and spelling, carried on by an elaborate appliance of unintelligible ideas, and by much failure in the effort to learn by rote.

Nevertheless, there was a visible improvement in Tom under this training; perhaps because he was not a boy in the abstract, existing solely to illustrate the evils of a mistaken education, but a boy made of flesh and blood, with dispositions not entirely at the mercy of circumstances.

There was a great improvement in his bearing, for example, and some credit on this score was due to Mr. Poulter, the village schoolmaster, who, being an old Peninsular soldier, was employed to drill Tom—a source of high mutual pleasure. Mr. Poulter, who was understood by the company at the Black Swan to have once struck terror into the hearts of the French, was no longer personally formidable. He had rather a shrunken appearance, and was tremulous in the mornings, not from age, but from the extreme perversity of the King's Lorton boys, which nothing but gin could enable him to sustain with any firmness. Still, he carried himself with martial erectness, had his clothes scrupulously brushed, and his trousers tightly strapped; and on the Wednesday and Saturday afternoons, when he come to Tom, he was always inspired with gin and old memories, which gave him an exceptionally spirited air, as of a superannuated charger who hears the drum. The drilling-lessons were always protracted by episodes of warlike narrative, much more interesting to Tom than Philip's stories out of the *Iliad;* for there were no cannon in the *Iliad,* and, besides, Tom had felt some disgust on learning that Hector and Achilles might possibly never have existed. But the Duke of Wellington was really alive, and Bony had not been long dead—therefore Mr. Poulter's reminiscences of the Peninsular War were removed from all suspicion of being mythical. Mr. Poulter, it appeared, had been a conspicuous figure at Talavera, and had contributed not a little to the peculiar terror with which his regiment of infantry was regarded by the enemy. On afternoons, when his memory was more stimulated than usual, he remembered that the Duke of Wellington had (in strict privacy, lest jealousies should be awakened) expressed his esteem for that fine fellow Poulter. The very surgeon who attended him in the hospital after he had received his gun-shot wound, had been profoundly impressed with the superiority of Mr. Poulter's flesh: no other flesh would have healed in anything like the same time. On less personal matters connected with the important warfare in which he had been engaged, Mr. Poulter was more reticent, only taking care not to give the weight of his authority to any loose notions concerning military history. Any one who pretended to a knowledge of what occurred at the siege of Badajos, was especially an object of silent pity to Mr. Poulter; he wished that prating person had been run down, and had the breath trampled out of him at the first go-off, as he himself had —he might talk about the siege of Badajos then! Tom did not escape irritating his drilling-master occasionally, by his curiosity concerning other military matters than Mr. Poulter's personal experience.

"And General Wolfe, Mr. Poulter? wasn't he a wonderful fighter?" said Tom, who held the notion that all the martial heroes commemorated on the public-house signs were engaged in the war with Bony.

"Not at all!" said Mr. Poulter, contemptuously. "Nothing o' the sort! . . . Heads up!" he added, in a tone of stern command, which delighted Tom, and made him feel as if he were a regiment in his own person.

"No, no!" Mr. Poulter would continue, on coming to a pause in his discipline. "They'd better not talk to me about General Wolfe. He did nothing but die of his wound; that's a poor haction, I consider. Any other man 'ud have died o' the wounds I've had. . . . One of my sword-cuts 'ud ha' killed a fellow like General Wolfe."

"Mr. Poulter," Tom would say, at any allusion to the sword, "I wish you'd bring your sword and do the sword-exercise!"

For a long while Mr. Poulter only shook his head in a significant manner at this request, and smiled patronisingly, as Jupiter may have done when Semele urged her too ambitious request. But one afternoon, when a sudden shower of heavy rain had detained Mr. Poulter twenty minutes longer than usual at the Black Swan, the sword was brought —just for Tom to look at.

"And this is the real sword you fought with in all the battles, Mr. Poulter?" said Tom, handling the hilt. "Has it ever cut a Frenchman's head off?"

"Head off? Ah! and would, if he'd had three heads."

"But you had a gun and bayonet besides?" said Tom. "*I* should like the gun and bayonet best, because you could shoot 'em first and spear 'em after. Bang! Ps-s-s-s!" Tom gave the requisite pantomime to indicate the double enjoyment of pulling the trigger and thrusting the spear.

"Ah, but the sword's the thing when you come to close fighting," said Mr. Poulter, involuntarily falling in with Tom's enthusiasm, and drawing the sword so suddenly that Tom leaped back with much agility.

"O, but, Mr. Poulter, if you're going to do the exercise," said Tom, a little conscious that he had not stood his ground as became an Englishman, "let me go and call Philip. He'll like to see you, you know."

"What! the humpbacked lad?" said Mr. Poulter, contemptuously "What's the use of *his* looking on?"

"O, but he knows a great deal about fighting," said Tom; "and how they used to fight with bows and arrows, and battle-axes."

"Let him come then. I'll show him something different from his bows and arrows," said Mr. Poulter, coughing, and drawing himself up, while he gave a little preliminary play to his wrist.

Tom ran in to Philip, who was enjoying his afternoon's holiday at the piano, in the drawing-room, picking out tunes for himself and singing them. He was supremely happy, perched like an amorphous bundl

on the high stool, with his head thrown back, his eyes fixed on the opposite cornice, and his lips wide open, sending forth, with all his might,
impromptu syllables to a tune of Arne's, which had hit his fancy.

"Come, Philip," said Tom, bursting in; "don't stay roaring 'la la'
there—come and see old Poulter do his sword-exercise in the carriage-
house!"

The jar of this interruption—the discord of Tom's tones coming across
the notes to which Philip was vibrating in soul and body, would have
been enough to unhinge his temper, even if there had been no question
of Poulter the drilling-master; and Tom, in the hurry of seizing something to say to prevent Mr. Poulter from thinking he was afraid of the
sword when he sprang away from it, had alighted on this proposition to
fetch Philip—though he knew well enough that Philip hated to hear him
mention his drilling-lessons. Tom would never have done so inconsider-
ate a thing except under the severe stress of his personal pride.

Philip shuddered visibly as he paused from his music. Then turning
red, he said, with violent passion,——

"Get away, you lumbering idiot! Don't come bellowing at me—you're
not fit to speak to anything but a cart-horse!"

It was not the first time Philip had been made angry by him, but
Tom had never before been assailed with verbal missiles that he understood so well.

"I'm fit to speak to something better than you—you poor-spirited
imp!" said Tom, lighting up immediately at Philip's fire. "You know I
won't hit you, because you're no better than a girl. But I'm an honest
man's son, and *your* father's a rogue—everybody says so!"

Tom flung out of the room, and slammed the door after him, made
strangely heedless by his anger; for to slam doors within the hearing
of Mrs. Stelling, who was probably not far off, was an offence only to
be wiped out by twenty lines of Virgil. In fact, that lady did presently
descend from her room, in double wonder at the noise and the subsequent cessation of Philip's music. She found him sitting in a heap on
the hassock, and crying bitterly.

"What's the matter, Wakem? What was that noise about? Who
slammed the door?"

Philip looked up, and hastily dried his eyes. "It was Tulliver who
came in . . . to ask me to go out with him."

"And what are you in trouble about?" said Mrs. Stelling.

Philip was not her favourite of the two pupils; he was less obliging
than Tom, who was made useful in many ways. Still his father paid
more than Mr. Tulliver did, and she meant him to feel that she behaved
exceedingly well to him. Philip, however, met her advances towards a
good understanding very much as a caressed mollusc meets an invitation to show himself out of his shell. Mrs. Stelling was not a loving,
tender-hearted woman: she was a woman whose skirt sat well, who
adjusted her waist and patted her curls with a preoccupied air when she
inquired after your welfare. These things, doubtless, represent a great

social power, but it is not the power of love—and no other power could win Philip from his personal reserve.

He said, in answer to her question, "My toothache came on, and made me hysterical again."

This had been the fact once, and Philip was glad of the recollection—it was like an inspiration to enable him to excuse his crying. He had to accept eau-de-cologne, and to refuse creosote in consequence; but that was easy.

Meanwhile Tom, who had for the first time sent a poisoned arrow into Phillip's heart, had returned to the carriage-house, where he found Mr. Poulter, with a fixed and earnest eye, wasting the perfections of his sword-exercise on probably observant but inappreciative rats. But Mr. Poulter was a host in himself; that is to say, he admired himself more than a whole army of spectators could have admired him. He took no notice of Tom's return, being too entirely absorbed in the cut and thrust—the solemn one, two, three, four; and Tom, not without a slight feeling of alarm at Mr. Poulter's fixed eye and hungry-looking sword, which seemed impatient for something else to cut besides the air, admired the performance from as great a distance as possible. It was not until Mr. Poulter paused and wiped the perspiration from his forehead, that Tom felt the full charm of the sword-exercise, and wished it to be repeated.

"Mr. Poulter," said Tom, when the sword was being finally sheathed, "I wish you'd lend me your sword a little while to keep."

"No, no, young gentleman," said Mr. Poulter, shaking his head decidedly, "you might do yourself some mischief with it."

"No, I'm sure I wouldn't—I'm sure I'd take care and not hurt myself. I shouldn't take it out of the sheath much, but I could ground arms with it, and all that."

"No, no, it won't do, I tell you; it won't do," said Mr. Poulter, preparing to depart. "What 'ud Mr. Stelling say to me?"

"O, I say, do, Mr. Poulter! I'd give you my five-shilling piece if you'd let me keep the sword a week. Look here!" said Tom, reaching out the attractively large round of silver. The young dog calculated the effect as well as if he had been a philosopher.

"Well," said Mr. Poulter, with still deeper gravity, "you must keep it out of sight, you know."

"O, yes, I'll keep it under the bed," said Tom, eagerly, "or else at the bottom of my large box."

"And let me see, now, whether you can draw it out of the sheath without hurting yourself."

That process having been gone through more than once, Mr. Poulter felt that he had acted with scrupulous conscientiousness, and said, "Well, now, Master Tulliver, if I take the crown-piece, it is to make sure as you'll do no mischief with the sword."

"O, no, indeed, Mr. Poulter," said Tom, delightedly handing him the crown-piece, and grasping the sword, which, he thought, might have been lighter with advantage.

"But if Mr. Stelling catches you carrying it in," said Mr. Poulter, pocketing the crown-piece provisionally while he raised this new doubt.

"O, he always keeps in his up-stairs study on Saturday afternoons," said Tom, who disliked anything sneaking, but was not disinclined to a little stratagem in a worthy cause. So he carried off the sword in triumph, mixed with dread—dread that he might encounter Mr. or Mrs. Stelling —to his bedroom, where, after some consideration, he hid it in the closet behind some hanging clothes. That night he fell asleep in the thought that he would astonish Maggie with it when she came—tie it round his waist with his red comforter, and make her believe that the sword was his own, and that he was going to be a soldier. There was nobody but Maggie who would be silly enough to believe him, or whom he dared allow to know that he had a sword; and Maggie was really coming next week to see Tom, before she went to a boarding-school with Lucy.

If you think a lad of thirteen would not have been so childish, you must be an exceptionally wise man, who, although you are devoted to a civil calling, requiring you to look bland rather than formidable, yet never, since you had a beard, threw yourself into a martial attitude, and frowned before the looking-glass. It is doubtful whether our soldiers would be maintained if there were not pacific people at home who like to fancy themselves soldiers. War, like other dramatic spectacles, might possibly cease for want of a "public."

CHAPTER V

MAGGIE'S SECOND VISIT

THIS last breach between the two lads was not readily mended, and for some time they spoke to each other no more than was necessary. Their natural antipathy of temperament made resentment an easy passage to hatred, and in Philip the transition seemed to have begun: there was no malignity in his disposition, but there was a susceptibility that made him peculiarly liable to a strong sense of repulsion. The ox—we may venture to assert it on the authority of a great classic—is not given to use his teeth as an instrument of attack; and Tom was an excellent bovine lad, who ran at questionable objects in a truly ingenuous bovine manner; but he had blundered on Philip's tenderest point, and had caused him as much acute pain as if he had studied the means with the nicest precision and the most envenomed spite. Tom saw no reason why they should not make up this quarrel as they had done many others, by behaving as if nothing had happened; for though he had never before said to Philip that his father was a rogue, this idea had so habitually made part of his feeling as to the relation between himself and his dubious schoolfellow, whom he could neither like nor dislike, that the mere utterance did not make such an epoch to him as it did to Philip. And he had a right to say so, when Philip hectored over *him*, and called him names. But perceiving that his first advances towards amity were not met, he relapsed into his least favourable disposition towards Philip, and resolved never to appeal to him either about drawing or exercises again. They were only so far civil to each other as was necessary to prevent their state of feud from being observed by Mr. Stelling, who would have "put down" such nonsense with great vigour.

When Maggie came, however, she could not help looking with growing interest at the new schoolfellow, although he was the son of that wicked Lawyer Wakem, who made her father so angry. She had arrived in the middle of school-hours, and had sat by while Philip went through his lessons with Mr. Stelling. Tom, some weeks ago, had sent her word that Philip knew no end of stories—not stupid stories like hers; and she was convinced now from her own observation that he must be very clever: she hoped he would think *her* rather clever too, when she came to talk to him. Maggie, moreover, had rather a tenderness for deformed things; she preferred the wry-necked lambs, because it seemed to her that the lambs which were quite strong and well made wouldn't mind so much about being petted; and she was especially fond of petting objects that would think it very delightful to be petted by her. She loved Tom very dearly, but she often wished that he *cared* more about her loving him.

"I think Philip Wakem seems a nice boy, Tom," she said, when they went out of the study together into the garden, to pass the interval before dinner. "He couldn't choose his father, you know; and I've read of very bad men who had good sons, as well as good parents who had bad children. And if Philip is good, I think we ought to be the more sorry for him because his father is not a good man. *You* like him, don't you?"

"O, he's a queer fellow," said Tom, curtly, "and he's as sulky as can be with me, because I told him his father was a rogue. And I'd a right to tell him so, for it was true—and *he* began it, with calling me names. But you stop here by yourself a bit, Magsie, will you? I've got something I want to do up-stairs."

"Can't I go too?" said Maggie, who, in this first day of meeting again, loved Tom's shadow.

"No, it's something I'll tell you about by-and-by, not yet," said Tom, skipping away.

In the afternoon the boys were at their books in the study, preparing the morrow's lessons, that they might have a holiday in the evening in honour of Maggie's arrival. Tom was hanging over his Latin grammar, moving his lips inaudibly like a strict but impatient Catholic repeating his tale of paternosters; and Philip, at the other end of the room, was busy with two volumes, with a look of contented diligence that excited Maggie's curiosity; he did not look at all as if he were learning a lesson. She sat on a low stool at nearly a right angle with the two boys, watching first one and then the other; and Philip, looking off his book once towards the fireplace, caught the pair of questioning dark eyes fixed upon him. He thought this sister of Tulliver's seemed a nice little thing, quite unlike her brother; he wished *he* had a little sister. What was it, he wondered, that made Maggie's dark eyes remind him of the stories about princesses being turned into animals? . . . I think it was that her eyes were full of unsatisfied intelligence, and unsatisfied, beseeching affection.

"I say, Magsie," said Tom at last, shutting his books and putting them away with the energy and decision of a perfect master in the art of leaving off, "I've done my lessons now. Come up-stairs with me."

"What is it?" said Maggie, when they were outside the door, a slight suspicion crossing her mind as she remembered Tom's preliminary visit up-stairs. "It isn't a trick you're going to play me, now?"

"No, no, Maggie," said Tom, in his most coaxing tone; "it's something you'll like *ever so.*"

He put his arm round her neck, and she put hers round his waist, and, twined together in this way, they went up-stairs.

"I say, Magsie, you must not tell anybody, you know," said Tom, "else I shall get fifty lines."

"Is it alive?" said Maggie, whose imagination had settled for the moment on the idea that Tom kept a ferret clandestinely.

"O, I shan't tell you," said he. "Now you go into that corner and hide your face, while I reach it out," he added, as he locked the bed-room door behind them. "I'll tell you when to turn round. You mustn't squeal out, you know."

"O, but if you frighten me, I shall," said Maggie, beginning to look rather serious.

"You won't be frightened, you silly thing," said Tom. "Go and hide your face, and mind you don't peep."

"Of course I shan't peep," said Maggie, disdainfully; and she buried her face in the pillow like a person of strict honour.

But Tom looked round warily as he walked to the closet; then he stepped into the narrow space, and almost closed the door. Maggie kept her face buried without the aid of principle, for in that dream-suggestive attitude she had soon forgotten where she was, and her thoughts were busy with the poor deformed boy, who was so clever, when Tom called out, "Now then, Magsie!"

Nothing but long meditation and preconcerted arrangement of effects could have enabled Tom to present so striking a figure as he did to Maggie when she looked up. Dissatisfied with the pacific aspect of a face which had no more than the faintest hint of flaxen eyebrow, together with a pair of amiable blue-grey eyes and round pink cheeks that refused to look formidable, let him frown as he would before the looking-glass—(Philip had once told him of a man who had a horse-shoe brown, and Tom had tried with all his frowning-might to make a horse-shoe on his forehead)—he had had recourse to that unfailing source of the terrible, burnt cork, and had made himself a pair of black eyebrows that met in a satisfactory manner over his nose, and were matched by a less carefully adjusted blackness about the chin. He had wound a red handkerchief round his cloth cap to give it the air of a turban, and his red comforter across his breast as a scarf—an amount of red which, with the tremendous frown on his brow, and the decision with which he grasped the sword, as he held it with its point resting on the ground, would suffice to convey an approximative idea of his fierce and bloodthirsty disposition.

Maggie looked bewildered for a moment, and Tom enjoyed that moment keenly; but in the next, she laughed, clapped her hands together, and said, "O, Tom, you've made yourself like Bluebeard at the show."

It was clear she had not been struck with the presence of the sword —it was not unsheathed. Her frivolous mind required a more direct appeal to its sense of the terrible, and Tom prepared for his master-stroke. Frowning with a double amount of intention, if not of corrugation, he (carefully) drew the sword from its sheath and pointed it at Maggie.

"O, Tom, please don't," exclaimed Maggie, in a tone of suppressed dread, shrinking away from him into the opposite corner, "I *shall* scream—I'm sure I shall! O, don't! I wish I'd never come up-stairs!"

The corners of Tom's mouth showed an inclination to a smile of complacency that was immediately checked as inconsistent with the severity of a great warrior. Slowly he let down the scabbard on the floor, lest it should make too much noise, and then said, sternly,——

"I'm the Duke of Wellington! March!" stamping forward with the right leg a little bent, and the sword still pointing towards Maggie, who, trembling, and with tear-filled eyes, got upon the bed, as the only means of widening the space between them.

Tom, happy in this spectator of his military performances, even though the spectator was only Maggie, proceeded, with the utmost exertion of his force, to such an exhibition of the cut and thrust as would necessarily be expected of the Duke of Wellington.

"Tom, I *will not* bear it—I *will* scream," said Maggie, at the first movement of the sword. "You'll hurt yourself; you'll cut your head off!"

"One—two," said Tom, resolutely, though at "two" his wrist trembled a little. "Three," came more slowly, and with it the sword swung downwards, and Maggie gave a loud shriek. The sword had fallen, with its edge on Tom's foot, and in a moment after, he had fallen too. Maggie leaped from the bed, still shrieking, and immediately there was a rush of footsteps towards the room. Mr. Stelling, from his up-stairs study, was the first to enter. He found both the children on the floor. Tom had fainted, and Maggie was shaking him by the collar of his jacket, screaming, with wild eyes. She thought he was dead, poor child! and yet she shook him, as if that would bring him back to life. In another minute she was sobbing with joy because Tom had opened his eyes: she couldn't sorrow yet that he had hurt his foot—it seemed as if all happiness lay in his being alive.

CHAPTER VI

A LOVE SCENE

POOR Tom bore his severe pain heroically, and was resolute in not "telling" of Mr. Poulter more than was unavoidable: the five-shilling piece remained a secret even to Maggie. But there was a terrible dread weighing on his mind—so terrible that he dared not even ask the question which might bring the fatal "yes"—he dared not ask the surgeon or Mr. Stelling, "Shall I be lame, sir?" He mastered himself so as not to cry out at the pain, but when his foot had been dressed, and he was left alone with Maggie seated by his bedside, the children sobbed together with their heads laid on the same pillow. Tom was thinking of himself walking about on crutches, like the wheelwright's son; and Maggie, who did not guess what was in his mind, sobbed for company. It had not occurred to the surgeon or to Mr. Stelling to anticipate this dread in Tom's mind, and to reassure him by hopeful words. But Philip watched the surgeon out of the house, and waylaid Mr. Stelling to ask the very question that Tom had not dared to ask for himself.

"I beg your pardon, sir,—but does Mr. Askern say Tulliver will be lame?"

"O, no, O, no," said Mr. Stelling, "not permanently, only for a little while."

"Did he tell Tulliver so, sir, do you think?"

"No: nothing was said to him on the subject."

"Then may I go and tell him, sir?"

"Yes, to be sure: now you mention it, I daresay he may be troubling about that. Go to his bedroom, but be very quiet at present."

It had been Philip's first thought when he heard of the accident—"Will Tulliver be lame? It will be very hard for him if he is"—and Tom's hitherto unforgiven offences were washed out by that pity. Philip felt that they were no longer in a state of repulsion, but were being drawn into a common current of suffering and sad privation. His imagination did not dwell on the outward calamity and its future effect on Tom's life, but it made vividly present to him the probable state of Tom's feeling: he had only lived fourteen years, but those years had, most of them, been steeped in the sense of a lot irremediably hard.

"Mr. Askern says you'll soon be all right again, Tulliver, did you know?" he said, rather timidly, as he stepped gently up to Tom's bed. "I've just been to ask Mr. Stelling, and he says you'll walk as well as ever again, by-and-by."

Tom looked up with that momentary stopping of the breath which comes with a sudden joy; then he gave a long sigh, and turned his blue-grey eyes straight on Philip's face, as he had not done for a fortnight or more. As for Maggie, this intimation of a possibility she had not thought of before, affected her as a new trouble; the bare idea of Tom's being always lame overpowered the assurance that such a misfortune was not likely to befall him, and she clung to him and cried afresh.

"Don't be a little silly, Magsie," said Tom, tenderly, feeling very brave now. "I shall soon get well."

"Good-by, Tulliver," said Philip, putting out his small, delicate hand, which Tom clasped immediately with his more substantial fingers.

"I say," said Tom, "ask Mr. Stelling to let you come and sit with me sometimes, till I get up again, Wakem—and tell me about Robert Bruce, you know."

After that, Philip spent all his time out of school-hours with Tom and Maggie. Tom liked to hear fighting stories as much as ever, but he insisted strongly on the fact that those great fighters, who did so many wonderful things and came off unhurt, wore excellent armour from head to foot, which made fighting easy work, he considered. He should not have hurt his foot if he had had an iron shoe on. He listened with great interest to a new story of Philip's about a man who had a very bad wound in his foot, and cried out so dreadfully with the pain that his friends could bear with him no longer, but put him ashore on a desert island, with nothing but some wonderful poisoned arrows to kill animals with for food.

"I didn't roar out a bit, you know," Tom said, "and I daresay my foot was as bad as his. It's cowardly to roar."

But Maggie would have it that when anything hurt you very much, it was quite permissible to cry out, and it was cruel of people not to bear it. She wanted to know if Philoctetes had a sister, and why *she* didn't go with him on the desert island and take care of him.

One day, soon after Philip had told this story, he and Maggie were in the study alone together while Tom's foot was being dressed. Philip was at his books, and Maggie, after sauntering idly round the room, not caring to do anything in particular, because she would soon go to Tom again, went and leaned on the table near Philip to see what he was doing, for they were quite old friends now, and perfectly at home with each other.

"What are you reading about in Greek?" she said. "It's poetry—can see that, because the lines are so short."

"It's about Philoctetes—the lame man I was telling you of yesterday," he answered, resting his head on his hand and looking at her, as if he were not at all sorry to be interrupted. Maggie, in her absent way, continued to lean forward, resting on her arms and moving her feet about, while her dark eyes got more and more fixed and vacant, as if she had quite forgotten Philip and his book.

"Maggie," said Philip, after a minute or two, still leaning on his elbow and looking at her, "if you had had a brother like me, do you think you should have loved him as well as Tom?"

Maggie started a little on being roused from her reverie, and said "What?" Philip repeated his question.

"O, yes, better," she answered, immediately. "No, not better; because I don't think I *could* love you better than Tom. But I should be so sorry —*so sorry* for you."

Philip coloured: he had meant to imply, would she love him as well in spite of his deformity, and yet when she alluded to it so plainly, he winced under her pity. Maggie, young as she was, felt her mistake. Hitherto she had instinctively behaved as if she were quite unconscious of Philip's deformity: her own keen sensitiveness and experience under family criticism sufficed to teach her this, as well as if she had been directed by the most finished breeding.

"But you are so very clever, Philip, and you can play and sing," she added, quickly. "I wish you *were* my brother. I'm very fond of you. And you would stay at home with me when Tom went out, and you would teach me everything—wouldn't you? Greek and everything?"

"But you'll go away soon, and go to school, Maggie," said Philip, "and then you'll forget all about me, and not care for me any more. And then I shall see you when you're grown up, and you'll hardly take any notice of me."

"O, no, I shan't forget you, I'm sure," said Maggie, shaking her head very seriously. "I never forget anything, and I think about everybody when I'm away from them. I think about poor Yap—he's got a lump in his throat, and Luke says he'll die. Only don't you tell Tom, because it will vex him so. You never saw Yap: he's a queer little dog—nobody cares about him but Tom and me."

"Do you care as much about me as you do about Yap, Maggie?" said Philip, smiling rather sadly.

"O, yes, I should think so," said Maggie, laughing.

"I'm very fond of *you,* Maggie; I shall never forget *you,*" said Philip, "and when I'm very unhappy, I shall always think of you, and wish I had a sister with dark eyes, just like yours."

"Why do you like my eyes?" said Maggie, well pleased. She had never heard any one but her father speak of her eyes as if they had merit.

"I don't know," said Philip. "They're not like any other eyes. They seem trying to speak—trying to speak kindly. I don't like other people to look at me much, but I like you to look at me, Maggie."

"Why, I think you're fonder of me than Tom is," said Maggie, rather sorrowfully. Then, wondering how she could convince Philip that he could like him just as well, although he was crooked, she said, "Should you like me to kiss you, as I do Tom? I will, if you like."

"Yes, very much: nobody kisses me."

Maggie put her arm round his neck and kissed him quite earnestly.

"There now," she said, "I shall always remember you, and kiss you when I see you again, if it's ever so long. But I'll go now, because I think Mr. Askern's done with Tom's foot."

When their father came the second time, Maggie said to him, "O, father, Philip Wakem is so very good to Tom—he is such a clever boy, and I *do* love him. And you love him too, Tom, don't you? *Say* you love him," she added, entreatingly.

Tom coloured a little as he looked at his father and said, "I shan't be friends with him when I leave school, father, but we've made it up now, since my foot has been bad, and he's taught me to play at draughts, and I can beat him."

"Well, well," said Mr. Tulliver, "if he's good to you, try and make him amends, and be good to *him*. He's a poor crooked creatur, and takes after his dead mother. But don't you be getting too thick with him—he's got his father's blood in him too. Ay, ay, the grey colt may chance to kick like his black sire."

The jarring natures of the two boys effected what Mr. Tulliver's admonition alone might have failed to effect: in spite of Philip's new kindness, and Tom's answering regard in this time of his trouble, they never became close friends. When Maggie was gone, and when Tom by-and-by began to walk about as usual, the friendly warmth that had been kindled by pity and gratitude died out by degrees, and left them in their old relation to each other. Philip was often peevish and contemptuous; and Tom's more specific and kindly impressions gradually melted into the old background of suspicion and dislike towards him as a queer fellow, a humpback, and the son of a rogue. If boys and men are to be welded together in the glow of transient feeling, they must be made of metal that will mix, else they inevitably fall asunder when the heat dies out.

CHAPTER VII

THE GOLDEN GATES ARE PASSED

So Tom went on even to the fifth half-year—till he was turned sixteen—at King's Lorton, while Maggie was growing, with a rapidity which her aunts considered highly reprehensible, at Miss Firniss's boarding-school in the ancient town of Laceham on the Floss, with cousin Lucy for her companion. In her early letters to Tom she had always sent her love to Philip, and asked many questions about him, which were answered by brief sentences about Tom's toothache, and a turf-house which he was helping to build in the garden, with other items of that kind. She was pained to hear Tom say in the holidays that Philip was as queer as ever again, and often cross: they were no longer very good friends, she perceived; and when she reminded Tom that he ought always to love Philip for being so good to him when his foot was bad, he answered, "Well, it isn't my fault: *I* don't do anything to him." She hardly ever saw Philip during the remainder of their school-life; in the Midsummer holidays he was always away at the seaside, and at Christmas she could only meet him at long intervals in the streets of St Ogg's. When they did meet, she remembered her promise to kiss him out, as a young lady who had been at a boarding-school, she knew now that such a greeting was out of the question, and Philip would not expect it. The promise was void, like so many other sweet, illusory promises of our childhood; void as promises made in Eden before the seasons were divided, and when the starry blossoms grew side by side with the ripening peach—impossible to be fulfilled when the golden gates had been passed.

But when their father was actually engaged in the long-threatened lawsuit, and Wakem, as the agent at once of Pivart and Old Harry, was acting against him, even Maggie felt, with some sadness, that they were not likely ever to have any intimacy with Philip again: the very name of Wakem made her father angry, and she had once heard him say, that if that crookbacked son lived to inherit his father's ill-gotten gains, there would be a curse upon him. "Have as little to do with him at school as you can, my lad," he said to Tom; and the command was obeyed the more easily because Mr. Stelling by this time had two additional pupils; for though this gentleman's rise in the world was not of that meteor-like rapidity which the admirers of his extemporaneous eloquence had expected for a preacher whose voice demanded so wide a sphere, he had yet enough of growing prosperity to enable him to increase his expenditure in continued disproportion to his income.

As for Tom's school course, it went on with mill-like monotony, his mind continuing to move with a slow, half-stifled pulse in a medium of uninteresting or unintelligible ideas. But each vacation he brought home larger and larger drawings with the satiny rendering of landscape, and water-colours in vivid greens, together with manuscript books full of exercises and problems, in which the handwriting was all the finer because he gave his whole mind to it. Each vacation he brought home a new book or two, indicating his progress through different stages of history, Christian doctrine, and Latin literature; and that passage was not entirely without result, besides the possession of the books. Tom's ear and tongue had become accustomed to a great many words and phrases which are understood to be signs of an educated condition; and though he had never really applied his mind to any one of his lessons, the lessons had left a deposit of vague, fragmentary, ineffectual notions. Mr. Tulliver, seeing signs of acquirement beyond the reach of his own criticism, thought it was probably all right with Tom's education: he observed, indeed, that there were no maps, and not enough "summing;" but he made no formal complaint to Mr. Stelling. It was a puzzling business, this schooling; and if he took Tom away, where could he send him with better effect?

By the time Tom had reached his last quarter at King's Lorton, the years had made striking changes in him since the day we saw him returning from Mr. Jacobs' academy. He was a tall youth now, carrying himself without the least awkwardness, and speaking without more shyness than was a becoming symptom of blended diffidence and pride: he wore his tail-coat and his stand-up collars, and watched the down on his lip with eager impatience, looking every day at his virgin razor, with which he had provided himself in the last holidays. Philip had already left—at the autumn quarter—that he might go to the south for the winter, for the sake of his health; and this change helped to give Tom the unsettled, exultant feeling that usually belongs to the last months before leaving school. This quarter, too, there was some hope of his father's lawsuit being decided: *that* made the prospect of home more entirely pleasurable. For Tom, who had gathered his view of the case from his father's conversation, had no doubt that Pivart would be beaten.

Tom had not heard anything from home for some weeks—a fact which did not surprise him, for his father and mother were not apt to manifest their affection in unnecessary letters—when, to his great surprise, on the morning of a dark cold day near the end of November, he was told, soon after entering the study at nine o'clock, that his sister was in the drawing-room. It was Mrs. Stelling who had come into the study to tell him, and she left him to enter the drawing-room alone.

Maggie, too, was tall now, with braided and coiled hair: she was almost as tall as Tom, though she was only thirteen; and she really looked older than he did at that moment. She had thrown off her bonnet, her heavy braids were pushed back from her forehead, as if it would not bear that extra load, and her young face had a strangely worn look, as her eyes turned anxiously towards the door. When Tom entered she did not speak, but only went up to him, put her arms round his neck, and kissed him earnestly. He was used to various moods of hers, and felt no alarm at the unusual seriousness of her greeting.

"Why, how is it you're come so early this cold morning, Maggie? Did you come in the gig?" said Tom, as she backed towards the sofa, and drew him to her side.

"No, I came by the coach. I've walked from the turnpike."

"But how is it you're not at school? The holidays have not begun yet?"

"Father wanted me at home," said Maggie, with a slight trembling of the lip. "I came home three or four days ago."

"Isn't my father well?" said Tom, rather anxiously.

"Not quite," said Maggie. "He's very unhappy, Tom. The lawsuit is ended, and I came to tell you, because I thought it would be better for you to know it before you came home, and I didn't like only to send you a letter."

"My father hasn't lost?" said Tom, hastily, springing from the sofa and standing before Maggie with his hands suddenly thrust in his pockets.

"Yes, dear Tom," said Maggie, looking up at him with trembling.

Tom was silent a minute or two, with his eyes fixed on the floor. Then he said——

"My father will have to pay a good deal of money, then?"

"Yes," said Maggie, rather faintly.

"Well, it can't be helped," said Tom, bravely, not translating the loss of a large sum of money into any tangible results. "But my father's very much vexed, I daresay?" he added, looking at Maggie, and thinking that her agitated face was only part of her girlish way of taking things.

"Yes," said Maggie, again faintly. Then, urged to fuller speech by Tom's freedom from apprehension, she said loudly and rapidly, as if the words *would* burst from her, "O, Tom, he will lose the mill and the land, and everything; he will have nothing left."

Tom's eyes flashed out one look of surprise at her, before he turned pale and trembled visibly. He said nothing, but sat down on the sofa again, looking vaguely out of the opposite window.

Anxiety about the future had never entered Tom's mind. His father had always ridden a good horse, kept a good house, and had the cheerful, confident air of a man who has plenty of property to fall back upon. Tom had never dreamed that his father would "fail;" *that* was a form of misfortune which he had always heard spoken of as a deep disgrace, and disgrace was an idea that he could not associate with any of his relations, least of all with his father. A proud sense of family respectability was part of the very air Tom had been born and brought up in. He knew there were people in St. Ogg's who made a show without money to support it, and he had always heard such people spoken of by his own friends with contempt and reprobation. He had a strong belief, which was a life-long habit, and required no definite evidence to rest on, that his father could spend a great deal of money if he chose; and since his education at Mr. Stelling's had given him a more expensive view of life, he had often thought that when he got older he would make a figure in the world, with his horse and dogs and saddle, and other accoutrements of a fine young man, and show himself equal to any of his contemporaries at St. Ogg's, who might consider themselves a grade above him in society, because their fathers were professional men, or had large oil-mills. As to the prognostics and head-shaking of his aunts and uncles, they had never produced the least effect on him, except to make him think that aunts and uncles were disagreeable society: he had heard them find fault in much the same way as long as he could remember. His father knew better than they did.

The down had come on Tom's lip, yet his thoughts and expectations had been hitherto only the reproduction, in changed forms, of the boyish dreams in which he had lived three years ago. He was awakened now with a violent shock.

Maggie was frightened at Tom's pale, trembling silence. There was something else to tell him—something worse. She threw her arms round him at last, and said, with a half sob——

"O, Tom—dear, dear Tom, don't fret too much—try and bear it well."

Tom turned his cheek passively to meet her entreating kisses, and there gathered a moisture in his eyes, which he just rubbed away with his hand. The action seemed to rouse him, for he shook himself and said, "I shall go home with you, Maggie. Didn't my father say I was to go?"

"No, Tom, father didn't wish it," said Maggie, her anxiety about *his* feeling helping her to master her agitation. What *would* he do when she told him all? "But mother wants you to come—poor mother!—she cries so. O, Tom, it's very dreadful at home."

Maggie's lips grew whiter, and she began to tremble almost as Tom had done. The two poor things clung closer to each other—both trembling—the one at an unshapen fear, the other at the image of a terrible certainty. When Maggie spoke, it was hardly above a whisper.

"And . . . and . . . poor father . . ."

Maggie could not utter it. But the suspense was intolerable to Tom. A vague idea of going to prison, as a consequence of debt, was the shape his fears had begun to take.

"Where's my father?" he said, impatiently. "*Tell* me, Maggie."

"He's at home," said Maggie, finding it easier to reply to that question. "But," she added, after a pause, "not himself. . . . He fell off his horse. . . . He has known nobody but me ever since. . . . He seems to have lost his senses. . . . O, father, father . . ."

With these last words, Maggie's sobs burst forth with the more violence for the previous struggle against them. Tom felt that pressure of the heart which forbids tears: he had no distinct vision of their troubles as Maggie had, who had been at home: he only felt the crushing weight of what seemed unmitigated misfortune. He tightened his arm almost convulsively round Maggie as she sobbed, but his face looked rigid and tearless—his eyes blank—as if a black curtain of cloud had suddenly fallen on his path.

But Maggie soon checked herself abruptly: a single thought had acted on her like a startling sound.

"We must set out, Tom—we must not stay—father will miss me—we must be at the turnpike at ten to meet the coach." She said this with hasty decision, rubbing her eyes, and rising to seize her bonnet.

Tom at once felt the same impulse, and rose too. "Wait a minute, Maggie," he said. "I must speak to Mr. Stelling, and then we'll go."

He thought he must go to the study where the pupils were, but on his way he met Mr. Stelling, who had heard from his wife that Maggie appeared to be in trouble when she asked for her brother; and, now that he thought the brother and sister had been alone long enough, was coming to inquire and offer his sympathy.

"Please, sir, I must go home," Tom said, abruptly, as he met Mr. Stelling in the passage. "I must go back with my sister directly. My father's lost his lawsuit—he's lost all his property—and he's very ill."

Mr. Stelling felt like a kind-hearted man; he foresaw a probable money loss for himself, but this had no appreciable share in his feeling while he looked with grave pity at the brother and sister for whom youth and sorrow had begun together. When he knew how Maggie had come, and how eager she was to get home again, he hurried their departure, only whispering something to Mrs. Stelling, who had followed him, and who immediately left the room.

Tom and Maggie were standing on the door-step, ready to set out, when Mrs. Stelling came with a little basket, which she hung on Mag

gie's arms, saying, "Do remember to eat something on the way, dear."
Maggie's heart went out towards this woman whom she had never liked,
and she kissed her silently. It was the first sign within the poor child of
that new sense which is the gift of sorrow—that susceptibility to the
bare offices of humanity which raises them into a bond of loving fellowship, as to haggard men among the icebergs the mere presence of an
ordinary comrade stirs the deep fountains of affection.

Mr. Stelling put his hand on Tom's shoulder and said, "God bless you,
my boy: let me know how you get on." Then he pressed Maggie's hand;
but there were no audible good-bys. Tom had so often thought how
joyful he should be the day he left school "for good!" And now his
school-years seemed like a holiday that had come to an end.

The two slight youthful figures soon grew indistinct on the distant
road—were soon lost behind the projecting hedgerow.

They had gone forth together into their new life of sorrow, and they
would never more see the sunshine undimmed by remembered cares.
They had entered the thorny wilderness, and the golden gates of their
childhood had for ever closed behind them.

BOOK THREE

The Downfall

★

CHAPTER I

WHAT HAD HAPPENED AT HOME

WHEN Mr. Tulliver first knew the fact that the lawsuit was decided against him, and that Pivart and Wakem were triumphant, every one who happened to observe him at the time thought that, for so confident and hot-tempered a man, he bore the blow remarkably well. He thought so himself: he thought he was going to show that if Wakem or anybody else considered him crushed, they would find themselves mistaken. He could not refuse to see that the costs of this protracted suit would take more than he possessed to pay them; but he appeared to himself to be full of expedients by which he could ward off any results but such as were tolerable, and could avoid the appearance of breaking down in the world. All the obstinacy and defiance of his nature, driven out of their old channel, found a vent for themselves in the immediate formation of plans by which he would meet his difficulties, and remain Mr. Tulliver of Dorlcote Mill in spite of them. There was such a rush of projects in his brain, that it was no wonder his face was flushed when he came away from his talk with his attorney, Mr. Gore, and mounted his horse to ride home from Lindum. There was Furley, who held the mortgage on the land—a reasonable fellow, who would see his own interest, Mr Tulliver was convinced, and who would be glad not only to purchase the whole estate, including the mill and homestead, but would accept Mr Tulliver as tenant, and he willing to advance money to be repaid with high interest out of the profits of the business, which would be made over to him, Mr. Tulliver only taking enough barely to maintain himsel and his family. Who would neglect such a profitable investment? Certainly not Furley, for Mr. Tulliver had determined that Furley shoulc meet his plans with the utmost alacrity; and there are men whose brain have not yet been dangerously heated by the loss of a lawsuit, who ar apt to see in their own interest or desires a motive for other men' actions. There was no doubt (in the miller's mind) that Furley would d just what was desirable; and if he did—why, things would not be so ver; much worse. Mr. Tulliver and his family must live more meagrely an humbly, but it would only be till the profits of the business had paid off Furley's advances, and that might be while Mr. Tulliver had still a good many years of life before him. It was clear that the costs of the suit could be paid without his being obliged to turn out of his old place, and look like a ruined man. It was certainly an awkward moment in his affairs. There was that suretyship for poor Riley, who had died suddenly last April, and left his friend saddled with a debt of two hundred and fifty pounds—a fact which had helped to make Mr. Tulliver's banking book less pleasant reading than a man might desire towards Christmas. Well! he had never been one of those poor-spirited sneaks who would refuse to give a helping hand to a fellow-traveller in this puzzling world. The really vexatious business was the fact that some months ago the creditor who had lent him the five hundred pounds to repay Mrs. Glegg, had become uneasy about his money (set on by Wakem, of course), and Mr. Tulliver, still confident that he should gain his suit, and finding it eminently inconvenient to raise the said sum until that desirable issue had taken place, had rashly acceded to the demand that he should give a bill of sale on his household furniture, and some other effects, as security in lieu of the bond. It was all one, he had said to himself: he should soon pay off the money, and there was no harm in giving that security any more than another. But now the consequences of this bill of sale occurred to him in a new light, and he remembered that the time was close at hand, when it would be enforced unless the money were repaid. Two months ago he would have declared stoutly that he would never be beholden to his wife's friends; but now he told himself as stoutly that it was nothing but right and natural that Bessy should go to the Pullets and explain the thing to them: they would hardly let Bessy's furniture be sold, and it might be security to Pullet if he advanced the money—there would, after all, be no gift or favour in the matter. Mr. Tulliver would never have asked for anything from so poor-spirited a fellow for himself, but Bessy might do so if she liked.

It is precisely the proudest and most obstinate men who are the most liable to shift their position and contradict themselves in this sudden manner: everything is easier to them than to face the simple fact that they have been thoroughly defeated, and must begin life anew. And Mr. Tulliver, you perceive, though nothing more than a superior miller and maltster, was as proud and obstinate as if he had been a very lofty personage, in whom such dispositions might be a source of that conspicuous, far-echoing tragedy, which sweeps the stage in regal robes, and makes the dullest chronicler sublime. The pride and obstinacy of millers, and other insignificant people, whom you pass unnoticingly on the road every day, have their tragedy too; but it is of that unwept, hidden sort, that goes on from generation to generation, and leaves no record—such tragedy, perhaps, as lies in the conflicts of young souls, hungry for joy, under a lot made suddenly hard to them, under the dreariness of a home where the morning brings no promise with it, and where the unexpectant discontent of worn and disappointed parents weighs on the children like a damp, thick air, in which all the functions of life are depressed; or such tragedy as lies in the slow or sudden death that follows on a bruised passion, though it may be a death that finds only a parish funeral. There are certain animals to which tenacity of position is a law of life—they can never flourish again, after a single wrench: and there are certain human beings to whom predominance is a law of life—they can only sustain humiliation so long as they can refuse to believe in it, and, in their own conception, predominate still.

Mr. Tulliver was still predominating in his own imagination as he approached St. Ogg's, through which he had to pass on his way homeward. But what was it that suggested to him, as he saw the Laceham coach entering the town, to follow it to the coach-office, and get the clerk there to write a letter, requiring Maggie to come home the very next day? Mr. Tulliver's own hand shook too much under his excitement for him to write himself, and he wanted the letter to be given to the coachman to deliver at Miss Firniss's school in the morning. There was a craving which he would not account for to himself, to have Maggie near him—without delay—she must come back by the coach to-morrow.

To Mrs. Tulliver, when he got home, he would admit no difficulties, and scolded down her burst of grief on hearing that the lawsuit was lost, by angry assertions that there was nothing to grieve about. He said nothing to her that night about the bill of sale, and the application to Mrs. Pullet, for he had kept her in ignorance of the nature of that transaction, and had explained the necessity for taking an inventory of the goods as a matter connected with his will. The possession of a wife conspicuously one's inferior in intellect, is, like other high privileges, attended with a few inconveniences, and among the rest, with the occasional necessity for using a little deception.

The next day Mr. Tulliver was again on horseback in the afternoon, on his way to Mr. Gore's office at St. Ogg's. Gore was to have seen Furley in the morning, and to have sounded him in relation to Mr. Tulliver's affairs. But he had not gone half-way when he met a clerk from Mr. Gore's office, who was bringing a letter to Mr. Tulliver. Mr. Gore had been prevented by a sudden call of business from waiting at his office to see Mr. Tulliver, according to appointment, but would be at his office at eleven to-morrow morning, and meanwhile had sent some important information by letter.

"O!" said Mr. Tulliver, taking the letter, but not opening it. "Then tell Gore I'll see him to-morrow at eleven;" and he turned his horse.

The clerk, struck with Mr. Tulliver's glistening excited glance, looked after him for a few moments, and then rode away. The reading of a letter was not the affair of an instant to Mr. Tulliver; he took in the sense of a statement very slowly through the medium of written or even printed characters; so he had put the letter in his pocket, thinking he would open it in his armchair at home. But by-and-by it occurred to him that there might be something in the letter Mrs. Tulliver must not know about, and if so, it would be better to keep it out of her sight altogether. He stopped his horse, took out the letter and read it. It was only a short letter; the substance was, that Mr. Gore had ascertained, on secret but sure authority, that Furley had been lately much straitened for money, and had parted with his securities—among the rest, the mortgage on Mr. Tulliver's property, which he had transferred to—Wakem.

In half an hour after this, Mr. Tulliver's own waggoner found him lying by the roadside insensible, with an open letter near him, and his grey horse snuffing uneasily about him.

When Maggie reached home that evening, in obedience to her father's call, he was no longer insensible. About an hour before, he had become conscious, and after vague, vacant looks around him, had muttered something about "a letter," which he presently repeated impatiently. At the instance of Mr. Turnbull, the medical man, Gore's letter was brought and laid on the bed, and the previous impatience seemed to be allayed. The stricken man lay for some time with his eyes fixed on the letter, as if he were trying to knit up his thoughts by its help. But presently a new wave of memory seemed to have come and swept the other away; he turned his eyes from the letter to the door, and after looking uneasily, as if striving to see something his eyes were too dim for, he said, "The little wench."

He repeated the words impatiently from time to time, appearing entirely unconscious of everything except this one importunate want, and giving no sign of knowing his wife or any one else; and poor Mrs. Tulliver, her feeble faculties almost paralysed by this sudden accumulation of troubles, went backwards and forwards to the gate to see if the Laceham coach were coming, though it was not yet time.

But it came at last, and set down the poor anxious girl, no longer the "little wench," except to her father's fond memory.

"O, mother, what is the matter?" Maggie said, with pale lips, as her mother came towards her crying. She didn't think her father was ill, because the letter had come at his dictation from the office at St. Ogg's.

But Mr. Turnbull came now to meet her: a medical man is the good angel of the troubled house, and Maggie ran towards the kind old friend, whom she remembered as long as she could remember anything, with a trembling, questioning look.

"Don't alarm yourself too much, my dear," he said, taking her hand. "Your father has had a sudden attack, and has not quite recovered his memory. But he has been asking for you, and it will do him good to see you. Keep as quiet as you can; take off your things and come up-stairs with me."

Maggie obeyed, with that terrible beating of the heart which makes existence seem simply a painful pulsation. The very quietness with which Mr. Turnbull spoke had frightened her susceptible imagination. Her father's eyes were still turned uneasily towards the door when she entered and met the strange, yearning, helpless look that had been seeking her in vain. With a sudden flash and movement, he raised himself in the bed—she rushed towards him, and clasped him with agonised kisses.

Poor child! it was very early for her to know one of those supreme moments in life when all we have hoped or delighted in, all we can dread or endure, falls away from our regard as insignificant—is lost, like a trivial memory, in that simple, primitive love which knits us to the beings who have been nearest to us, in their times of helplessness or of anguish.

But that flash of recognition had been too great a strain on the father's bruised, enfeebled powers. He sank back again in renewed insensibility and rigidity, which lasted for many hours, and was only broken by a flickering return of consciousness, in which he took passively everything that was given to him, and seemed to have a sort of infantine satisfaction in Maggie's near presence—such satisfaction as a baby has when it is returned to the nurse's lap.

Mrs. Tulliver sent for her sisters, and there was much wailing and lifting up of hands below stairs: both uncles and aunts saw that the ruin of Bessy and her family was as complete as they had ever foreboded it, and there was a general family sense that a judgment had fallen on Mr. Tulliver, which it would be an impiety to counteract by too much kindness. But Maggie heard little of this, scarcely ever leaving her father's bedside, where she sat opposite him with her hand on his. Mrs. Tulliver wanted to have Tom fetched home, and seemed to be thinking more of her boy even than of her husband; but the aunts and uncles opposed this. Tom was better at school, since Mr. Turnbull said there was no immediate danger, he believed. But at the end of the second day, when Maggie had become more accustomed to her father's fits of insensibility, and to the expectation that he would revive from them, the thought of Tom had become urgent with *her* too; and when her mother sate crying at night and saying, "My poor lad . . . it's nothing but right he should come home;" Maggie said, "Let me go for him, and tell him, mother: I'll go to-morrow morning if father doesn't know me and want me. It would be so hard for Tom to come home and not know anything about it beforehand."

And the next morning Maggie went, as we have seen. Sitting on the coach on their way home, the brother and sister talked to each other in sad, interrupted whispers.

"They say Mr. Wakem has got a mortgage or something on the land, Tom," said Maggie. "It was the letter with that news in it that made father ill, they think."

"I believe that scoundrel's been planning all along to ruin my father," said Tom, leaping from the vaguest impressions to a definite conclusion. "I'll make him feel for it when I'm a man. Mind you never speak to Philip again."

"O, Tom!" said Maggie, in a tone of sad remonstrance; but she had no spirit to dispute anything then, still less to vex Tom by opposing him.

CHAPTER II

WHEN the coach set down Tom and Maggie, it was five hours since she had started from home, and she was thinking with some trembling that her father had perhaps missed her, and asked for "the little wench" in vain. She thought of no other change that might have happened.

She hurried along the gravel-walk and entered the house before Tom; but in the entrance she was startled by a strong smell of tobacco. The parlour door was ajar—that was where the smell came from. It was very strange: could any visitor be smoking at a time like this? Was her mother there? If so, she must be told that Tom was come. Maggie, after this pause of surprise, was only in the act of opening the door when Tom came up, and they both looked in the parlour together. There was a coarse, dingy man, of whose face Tom had some vague recollection, sitting in his father's chair, smoking, with a jug and glass beside him.

The truth flashed on Tom's mind in an instant. To "have the bailiff in the house," and "to be sold up," were phrases which he had been used to, even as a little boy: they were part of the disgrace and misery of "failing," of losing all one's money, and being ruined—sinking into the condition of poor working people. It seemed only natural this should happen since his father had lost all his property, and he thought of no more special cause for this particular form of misfortune than the loss of the lawsuit. But the immediate presence of this disgrace was so much keener an experience to Tom than the worst form of apprehension, that he felt at this moment as if his real trouble had only just begun: it was a touch on the irritated nerve compared with its spontaneous dull aching.

"How do you do, sir?" said the man, taking the pipe out of his mouth, with rough, embarrassed civility. The two young startled faces made him a little uncomfortable.

But Tom turned away hastily without speaking: the sight was too hateful. Maggie had not understood the appearance of this stranger, as Tom had. She followed him, whispering "Who can it be, Tom?— what is the matter?" Then, with a sudden undefined dread lest this stranger might have something to do with a change in her father, she rushed up-stairs, checking herself at the bedroom door to throw off her bonnet, and enter on tiptoe. All was silent there: her father was lying, heedless of everything around him, with his eyes closed as when she had left him. A servant was there, but not her mother.

"Where's my mother?" she whispered. The servant did not know.

Maggie hastened out, and said to Tom, "Father is lying quiet: let us go and look for my mother. I wonder where she is."

Mrs. Tulliver was not down-stairs—not in any of the bedrooms. There was but one room below the attic which Maggie had left unsearched: it was the store-room, where her mother kept all her linen and all the precious "best things" that were only unwrapped and brought out on special occasions. Tom, preceding Maggie as they returned along the passage, opened the door of this room, and immediately said, "Mother!"

Mrs. Tulliver was seated there with all her laid-up treasures. One of the linen-chests was open: the silver teapot was unwrapped from its many folds of paper, and the best china was laid out on the top of the closed linen-chest; spoons and skewers and ladles were spread in rows on the shelves; and the poor woman was shaking her head and weeping, with a bitter tension of the mouth, over the mark, "Elizabeth Dodson," on the corner of some table-cloths she held in her lap.

She dropped them, and started up as Tom spoke.

"O, my boy, my boy!" she said, clasping him round the neck. "To think as I should live to see this day! We're ruined . . . everything's going to be sold up . . . to think as your father should ha' married me to bring me to this! We've got nothing . . . we shall be beggars . . . we must go to the workhouse . . ."

She kissed him, then seated herself again, and took another table-cloth on her lap, unfolding it a little way to look at the pattern, while the children stood by in mute wretchedness—their minds quite filled for the moment with the words "beggars" and "workhouse."

"To think o' these cloths as I spun myself," she went on, lifting things out and turning them over with an excitement all the more strange and piteous because the stout blond woman was usually so passive: if she had been ruffled before, it was at the surface merely: "and Job Haxey wove 'em, and brought the piece home on his back, as I remember standing at the door and seeing him come, before I ever thought o' marrying your father! And the pattern as I chose myself—and bleached so beautiful, and I marked 'em so as nobody ever saw such marking—they must cut the cloth to get it out, for it's a particular stitch. And they're all to be sold—and go into strange people's houses, and perhaps be cut with the knives, and wore out before I'm dead. You'll never have one of 'em, my boy," she said, looking up at Tom with her eyes full of tears, "and I meant 'em for you. I wanted you to have all o' this pattern. Maggie could have had the large check—it never shows so well when the dishes are on it."

Tom was touched to the quick, but there was an angry reaction immediately. His face flushed as he said—

"But will my aunts let them be sold, mother? Do they know about it? They'll never let your linen go, will they? Haven't you sent to them?"

"Yes, I sent Luke directly they'd put the bailies in, and your aunt Pullet's been—and, O dear, O dear, she cries so, and says your father's disgraced my family and made it the talk o' the country; and she'll buy the spotted cloths for herself, because she's never had so many as she wanted o' that pattern, and they shan't go to strangers, but she's got more checks a'ready nor she can do with." (Here Mrs. Tulliver began to lay back the table-cloths in the chest, folding and stroking them auto-matically.) "And your uncle Glegg's been too, and he says things must be bought in for us to lie down on, but he must talk to your aunt; and they're all coming to consult. . . . But I know they'll none of 'em take my chany," she added, turning towards the cups and saucers—"for they all found fault with 'em when I bought 'em, 'cause o' the small gold sprig all over 'em, between the flowers. But there's none of 'em got bet-ter chany, not even your aunt Pullet herself,—and I bought it wi' my own money as I'd saved ever since I was turned fifteen; and the silver teapot, too—your father never paid for 'em. And to think as he should ha' married me, and brought me to this."

Mrs. Tulliver burst out crying afresh, and she sobbed with her hand-kerchief at her eyes a few moments, but then removing it, she said in a deprecating way, still half-sobbing, as if she were called upon to speak before she could command her voice—

"And I *did* say to him times and times, 'Whatever you do, don't go to law'—and what more could I do? I've had to sit by while my own fortin's been spent, and what should ha' been my children's, too. You'll have niver a penny, my boy . . . but it isn't your poor mother's fault."

She put out one arm towards Tom, looking up at him piteously with her helpless, childish blue eyes. The poor lad went to her and kissed her, and she clung to him. For the first time Tom thought of his father with some reproach. His natural inclination to blame, hitherto kept en-tirely in abeyance towards his father by the predisposition to think him always right, simply on the ground that he was Tom Tulliver's father —was turned into this new channel by his mother's plaints, and with his indignation against Wakem there began to mingle some indignation of another sort. Perhaps his father might have helped bringing them all down in the world, and making people talk of them with contempt; but no one should talk long of Tom Tulliver with contempt. The natural strength and firmness of his nature was beginning to assert itself, urged by the double stimulus of resentment against his aunts, and the sense that he must behave like a man and take care of his mother.

"Don't fret, mother," he said, tenderly. "I shall soon be able to get money: I'll get a situation of some sort."

"Bless you, my boy!" said Mrs. Tulliver, a little soothed. Then, look-ing round sadly, "But I shouldn't ha' minded so much if we could ha' kept the things wi' my name on 'em."

Maggie had witnessed this scene with gathering anger. The implied reproaches against her father—her father, who was lying there in a sort of living death—neutralised all her pity for griefs about table-cloths and china; and her anger on her father's account was heightened by some egoistic resentment at Tom's silent concurrence with her mother in shutting her out from the common calamity. She had become almost indifferent to her mother's habitual depreciation of her, but she was keenly alive to any sanction of it, however passive, that she might sus-pect in Tom. Poor Maggie was by no means made up of unalloyed devotedness, but put forth large claims for herself where she loved strongly. She burst out at last in an agitated, almost violent tone, "Mother, how can you talk so? as if you cared only for things with *your* name on, and not for what has my father's name too—and to care about anything but dear father himself!—when he's lying there, and may never speak to us again. Tom, you ought to say so too—you ought not to let any one find fault with my father."

Maggie, almost choked with mingled grief and anger, left the room, and took her old place on her father's bed. Her heart went out to him with a stronger movement than ever, at the thought that people would blame him. Maggie hated blame: she had been blamed all her life, and nothing had come of it but evil tempers. Her father had always defended and excused her, and her loving remembrance of his tenderness was a force within her that would enable her to do or bear anything for his sake.

Tom was a little shocked at Maggie's outburst—telling *him* as well as his mother what it was right to do! She ought to have learned better than have those hectoring, assuming manners by this time. But he presently went into his father's room, and the sight there touched him in a way that effaced the slighter impressions of the previous hour. When Maggie saw how he was moved, she went to him and put her arm round his neck as he sat by the bed, and the two children forgot everything else in the sense that they had one father and one sorrow.

CHAPTER III

THE FAMILY COUNCIL

IT was at eleven o'clock the next morning that the aunts and uncles came to hold their consultation. The fire was lighted in the large parlour, and poor Mrs. Tulliver, with a confused impression that it was a great occasion, like a funeral, unbagged the bell-rope tassels, and unpinned the curtains, adjusting them in proper folds—looking round and shaking her head sadly at the polished tops and legs of the tables, which sister Pullet herself could not accuse of insufficient brightness.

Mr. Deane was not coming—he was away on business; but Mrs. Deane appeared punctually in that handsome new gig with the head to it, and the livery-servant driving it, which had thrown so clear a light on several traits in her character to some of her female friends in St. Ogg's. Mr. Deane had been advancing in the world as rapidly as Mr. Tulliver had been going down in it; and in Mrs. Deane's house, the Dodson linen and plate were beginning to hold quite a subordinate position, as a mere supplement to the handsomer articles of the same kind, purchased in recent years: a change which had caused an occasional coolness in the sisterly intercourse between her and Mrs. Glegg, who felt that Susan was getting "like the rest," and there would soon be little of the true Dodson spirit surviving except in herself, and, it might be hoped, in those nephews who supported the Dodson name on the family land, far away in the Wolds. People who live at a distance are naturally less faulty than those immediately under our own eyes; and it seems superfluous, when we consider the remote geographical position of the Ethiopians, and how very little the Greeks had to do with them, to inquire further why Homer calls them "blameless."

Mrs. Deane was the first to arrive; and when she had taken her seat in the large parlour, Mrs. Tulliver came down to her with her comely face a little distorted, nearly as it would have been if she had been crying: she was not a woman who could shed abundant tears, except in moments when the prospect of losing her furniture became unusually vivid, but she felt how unfitting it was to be quite calm under present circumstances.

"O, sister, what a world this is!" she exclaimed as she entered; "what trouble, O dear!"

Mrs. Deane was a thin-lipped woman, who made small well-considered speeches on peculiar occasions, repeating them afterwards to her husband, and asking him if she had not spoken very properly.

"Yes, sister," she said, deliberately, "this is a changing world, and we don't know to-day what may happen to-morrow. But it's right to be prepared for all things, and if trouble's sent, to remember, as it isn't sent without a cause. I'm very sorry for you as a sister, and if the doctor orders jelly for Mr. Tulliver, I hope you'll let me know: I'll send it willingly. For it is but right he should have proper attendance while he's ill."

"Thank you, Susan," said Mrs. Tulliver, rather faintly, withdrawing her fat hand from her sister's thin one. "But there's been no talk o' jelly yet." Then after a moment's pause she added, "There's a dozen o' cut jelly-glasses up-stairs. . . . I shall niver put jelly into 'em no more."

Her voice was rather agitated as she uttered the last words, but the sound of wheels diverted her thoughts. Mr. and Mrs. Glegg were come, and were almost immediately followed by Mr. and Mrs. Pullet.

Mrs. Pullet entered crying, as a compendious mode, at all times, of expressing what were her views of life in general, and what, in brief, were the opinions she held concerning the particular case before her.

Mrs. Glegg had on her fuzziest front, and garments which appeared to have had a recent resurrection from rather a creasy form of burial; a costume selected with the high moral purpose of instilling perfect humility into Bessy and her children.

"Mrs. G., won't you come nearer the fire?" said her husband, unwilling to take the more comfortable seat without offering it to her.

"You see I've seated myself here, Mr. Glegg," returned this superior woman; "*you* can roast yourself, if you like."

"Well," said Mr. Glegg, seating himself good-humouredly, "and how's the poor man up-stairs?"

"Dr. Turnbull thought him a deal better this morning," said Mrs.

Tulliver; "he took more notice, and spoke to me; but he's never known Tom yet—looks at the poor lad as if he was a stranger, though he said something once about Tom and the pony. The doctor says his memory's gone a long way back, and he doesn't know Tom because he's thinking of him when he was little. Eh dear, eh dear!"

"I doubt it's the water got on his brain," said aunt Pullet, turning round from adjusting her cap in a melancholy way at the pier-glass. "It's much if he ever gets up again; and if he does, he'll most like be childish, as Mr. Carr was, poor man! They fed him with a spoon as if he'd been a babby for three year. He'd quite lost the use of his limbs; but then he'd got a Bath chair, and somebody to draw him; and that's what you won't have, I doubt, Bessy."

"Sister Pullet," said Mrs. Glegg, severely, "if I understand right, we've come together this morning to advise and consult about what's to be done in this disgrace as has fallen upon the family, and not to talk o' people as don't belong to us. Mr. Carr was none of our blood, nor noways connected with us, as I've ever heared."

"Sister Glegg," said Mrs. Pullet, in a pleading tone, drawing on her gloves again, and stroking the fingers in an agitated manner, "if you've got anything disrespectful to say o' Mr. Carr, I do beg of you as you won't say it to me. *I* know what he was," she added, with a sigh; "his breath was short to that degree as you could hear him two rooms off."

"Sophy!" said Mrs. Glegg, with indignant disgust, "you *do* talk o' people's complaints till it's quite undecent. But I say again, as I said before, I didn't come away from home to talk about acquaintance, whether they'd short breath or long. If we aren't come together for one to hear what the other 'ull do to save a sister and her children from the parish, *I* shall go back. *One* can't act without the other, I suppose; it isn't to be expected as *I* should do everything."

"Well, Jane," said Mrs. Pullet, "I don't see as you've been so very forrard at doing. So far as I know, this is the first time as here you've been, since it's been known as the bailiff's in the house; and I was here yesterday, and looked at all Bessy's linen and things, and I told her I'd buy in the spotted table-cloths. I couldn't speak fairer; for as for the teapot as she doesn't want to go out o' the family, it stands to sense I can't do with two silver teapots, not if it *hadn't* a strait spout—but the spotted damask I was allays fond on."

"I wish it could be managed so as my teapot and chany and the best castors needn't be put up for sale," said poor Mrs. Tulliver, beseechingly, "and the sugar-tongs, the first things ever I bought."

"But that can't be helped, you know," said Mr. Glegg. "If one o' the family chooses to buy 'em in, they can, but one thing must be bid for as well as another."

"And it isn't to be looked for," said uncle Pullet, with unwonted independence of idea, "as your own family should pay more for things nor they'll fetch. They may go for an old song by auction."

"O dear, O dear," said Mrs. Tulliver, "to think o' my chany being sold i' that way—and I bought it when I was married, just as you did yours, Jane and Sophy: and I know you didn't like mine, because o' the sprig, but I was fond of it; and there's never been a bit broke, for I've washed it myself—and there's the tulips on the cups, and the roses, as anybody might go and look at 'em for pleasure. You wouldn't like *your* chany to go for an old song and be broke to pieces, though yours has got no colour in it, Jane—it's all white and fluted, and didn't cost so much as mine. And there's the castors—sister Deane, I can't think but you'd like to have the castors, for I've heard you say they're pretty."

"Well, I've no objection to buy some of the best things," said Mrs. Deane, rather loftily; "we can do with extra things in our house."

"Best things!" exclaimed Mrs. Glegg with severity, which had gathered intensity from her long silence. "It drives me past patience to hear you all talking o' best things, and buying in this, that, and the other, such as silver and chany. You must bring your mind to your circumstances, Bessy, and not be thinking o' silver and chany; but whether you shall get so much as a flock bed to lie on, and a blanket to cover you, and a stool to sit on. You must remember, if you get 'em, it'll be because your friends have bought 'em for you, for you're dependent upon *them* for everything; for your husband lies there helpless, and hasn't got a penny i' the world to call his own. And it's for your own good I say this, for it's right you should feel what your state is, and what disgrace your husband's brought on your own family, as you've got to look to for everything—and be humble in your mind."

Mrs. Glegg paused, for speaking with much energy for the good of others is naturally exhausting. Mrs. Tulliver, always borne down by the family predominance of sister Jane, who had made her wear the yoke of a younger sister in very tender years, said pleadingly—

"I'm sure, sister, I've never asked anybody to do anything, only buy things as it 'ud be a pleasure to 'em to have, so as they mightn't go and be spoiled i' strange houses. I never asked anybody to buy the things in for me and my children; though there's the linen I spun, and I thought when Tom was born—I thought one o' the first things when he was lying i' the cradle, as all the things I'd bought wi' my own money, and been so careful of, 'ud go to him. But I've said nothing as I wanted my sisters to pay their money for me. What my husband has done for *his* sister's unknown, and we should ha' been better off this day if it hadn't been as he's lent money and never asked for it again."

"Come, come," said Mr. Glegg, kindly, "don't let us make things too dark. What's done can't be undone. We shall make a shift among us to buy what's sufficient for you; though, as Mrs. G. says, they must be useful, plain things. We mustn't be thinking o' what's unnecessary. A table, and a chair or two, and kitchen things, and a good bed, and suchlike. Why, I've seen the day when I shouldn't ha' known myself if I'd lain on sacking i'stead o' the floor. We get a deal o' useless things about us, only because we've got the money to spend."

"Mr. Glegg," said Mrs. G., "if you'll be kind enough to let me speak, i'stead o' taking the words out o' my mouth—I was going to say, Bessy, as it's fine talking for you to say as you've never asked us to buy anything for you; let me tell you, you *ought* to have asked us. Pray, how are you to be purvided for, if your own family don't help you? You must go to the parish, if they didn't. And you ought to know that, and keep it in mind, and ask us humble to do what we can for you, i'stead o' saying, and making a boast, as you've never asked us for anything."

"You talked o' the Mosses, and what Mr. Tulliver's done for 'em," said uncle Pullet, who became unusually suggestive where advances of money were concerned. "Haven't *they* been anear you? They ought to do something, as well as other folks; and if he's lent 'em money, they ought to be made to pay it back."

"Yes, to be sure," said Mrs. Deane; "I've been thinking so. How is it Mr. and Mrs. Moss aren't here to meet us? It is but right they should do their share."

"O dear!" said Mrs. Tulliver, "I never sent 'em word about Mr. Tulliver, and they live so back'ard among the lanes at Basset, they niver hear anything only when Mr. Moss comes to market. But I niver gave 'em a thought. I wonder Maggie didn't, though, for she was allays so fond of her aunt Moss."

"Why don't your children come in, Bessy?" said Mrs. Pullet, at the mention of Maggie. "They should hear what their aunts and uncles have got to say: and Maggie—when it's me as have paid for half her schooling, she ought to think more of her aunt Pullet nor of aunt Mosses. I may go off sudden when I get home to-day—there's no telling."

"If I'd had *my* way," said Mrs. Glegg, "the children 'ud ha' been in the room from the first. It's time they knew who they've to look to, and it's right as *somebody* should talk to 'em, and let 'em know their condition i' life, and what they're come down to, and make 'em feel as they've got to suffer for their father's faults."

"Well, I'll go and fetch 'em, sister," said Mrs. Tulliver, resignedly. She was quite crushed now, and thought of the treasures in the storeroom with no other feeling than blank despair.

She went up-stairs to fetch Tom and Maggie, who were both in their father's room, and was on her way down again, when the sight of the store-room door suggested a new thought to her. She went towards it, and left the children to go down by themselves.

The aunts and uncles appeared to have been in warm discussion when the brother and sister entered—both with shrinking reluctance; for though Tom, with a practical sagacity which had been roused into activity by the strong stimulus of the new emotions he had undergone since yesterday, had been turning over in his mind a plan which he meant to propose to one of his aunts or uncles, he felt by no means amicably towards them, and dreaded meeting them all at once as he would have dreaded a large dose of concentrated physic, which was but just endurable in small draughts. As for Maggie, she was peculiarly depressed this morning: she had been called up, after brief rest, at three o'clock, and had that strange dreamy weariness which comes from watching in a sick-room through the chill hours of early twilight and breaking day—in which the outside daylight life seems to have no importance, and to be a mere margin to the hours in the darkened chamber. Their entrance interrupted the conversation. The shaking of hands was a melancholy and silent ceremony, till uncle Pullet observed, as Tom approached him—

"Well, young sir, we've been talking as we should want your pen and ink; you can write rarely now, after all your schooling, I should think."

"Ay, ay," said uncle Glegg, with admonition which he meant to be kind, "we must look to see the good of all this schooling, as your father's sunk so much money in, now——

'When land is gone and money spent,
Then learning is most excellent.'

Now's the time, Tom, to let us see the good o' your learning. Let us see whether you can do better than I can, as have made my fortin' without it. But I began wi' doing with little, you see: I could live on a basin o' porridge and a crust o' bread-and-cheese. But I doubt high living and high learning 'ull make it harder for you, young man, nor it was for me."

"But he must do it," interposed aunt Glegg, energetically, "whether it's hard or no. He hasn't got to consider what's hard; he must consider as he isn't to trusten to his friends to keep him in idleness and luxury: he's got to bear the fruits of his father's misconduct, and bring his mind to fare hard and to work hard. And he must be humble and grateful to his aunts and uncles for what they're doing for his mother and father, as must be turned out into the streets and go to the workhouse if they didn't help 'em. And his sister, too," continued Mrs. Glegg, looking severely at Maggie, who had sat down on the sofa by her aunt Deane, drawn to her by the sense that she was Lucy's mother, "she must make up her mind to be humble and work; for there'll be no servants to wait on her any more—she must remember that. She must do the work o' the house, and she must respect and love her aunts as have done so much for her, and saved their money to leave to their nepheys and nieces."

Tom was still standing before the table in the centre of the group. There was a heightened colour in his face, and he was very far from looking humbled, but he was preparing to say, in a respectful tone, something he had previously meditated, when the door opened and his mother re-entered.

Poor Mrs. Tulliver had in her hands a small tray, on which she had placed her silver teapot, a specimen teacup and saucer, the castors, and sugar-tongs.

"See here, sister," she said, looking at Mrs. Deane, as she set the tray on the table, "I thought, perhaps, if you looked at the teapot again—it's a good while since you saw it—you might like the pattern better: it makes beautiful tea, and there's a stand and everything: you might use it for every day, or else lay it by for Lucy when she goes to house-keeping. I should be so loth for 'em to buy it at the Golden Lion," said the poor woman, her heart swelling, and the tears coming, "my teapot as I bought when I was married, and to think o' its being scratched, and set before the travellers and folks, and my letters on it—see here, E. D.—and everybody to see 'em."

"Ah, dear, dear!" said aunt Pullet, shaking her head with deep sad-ness, "it's very bad—to think o' the family initials going about every-where—it niver was so before: you're a very unlucky sister, Bessy. But what's the use o' buying the teapot, when there's the linen and spoons and everything to go, and some of 'em with your full name—and when it's got that straight spout too."

"As to disgrace o' the family," said Mrs. Glegg, "that can't be helped wi' buying teapots. The disgrace is, for one o' the family to ha' married a man as has brought her to beggary. The disgrace is, as they're to be sold up. We can't hinder the country from knowing that."

Maggie had started up from the sofa at the allusion to her father, but Tom saw her action and flushed face in time to prevent her from speaking. "Be quiet, Maggie," he said, authoritatively, pushing her aside. It was a remarkable manifestation of self-command and prac-tical judgment in a lad of fifteen, that when his aunt Glegg ceased, he began to speak in a quiet and respectful manner, though with a good deal of trembling in his voice; for his mother's words had cut him to the quick.

"Then, aunt," he said, looking straight at Mrs. Glegg, "if you think it's a disgrace to the family that we should be sold up, wouldn't it be better to prevent it altogether? And if you and my aunt Pullet," he continued, looking at the latter, "think of leaving any money to me and Maggie, wouldn't it be better to give it now, and pay the debt we're going to be sold up for, and save my mother from parting with her furniture?"

There was silence for a few moments, for every one, including Maggie, was astonished at Tom's sudden manliness of tone. Uncle Glegg was the first to speak.

"Ay, ay, young man—come now! You show some notion o' things. But there's the interest, you must remember; your aunts get five per cent on their money, and they'd lose that if they advanced it—you haven't thought o' that."

"I could work and pay that every year," said Tom, promptly. "I'd do anything to save my mother from parting with her things."

"Well done!" said uncle Glegg, admiringly. He had been drawing Tom out, rather than reflecting on the practicability of his proposal. But he had produced the unfortunate result of irritating his wife.

"Yes, Mr. Glegg!" said that lady, with angry sarcasm. "It's pleasant work for you to be giving my money away, as you've pretended to leave at my own disposial. And my money, as was my own father's gift, and not yours, Mr. Glegg; and I've saved it, and added to it myself, and had more to put out almost every year, and it's to go and be sunk in other folks's furniture, and encourage 'em in luxury and extravagance as they've no means of supporting; and I'm to alter my will, or have a codicil made, and leave two or three hundred less behind me when I die—me as have allays done right and been careful, and the eldest o' the family; and my money's to go and be squandered on them as have had the same chance as me, only they've been wicked and wasteful. Sister Pullet, *you* may do as you like, and you may let your husband rob you back again o' the money he's given you, but that isn't *my* sperrit."

"La, Jane, how fiery you are!" said Mrs. Pullet. "I'm sure you'll have the blood in your head, and have to be cupped. I'm sorry for Bessy and her children—I'm sure I think of 'em o' nights dreadful, for I sleep very bad wi' this new medicine: but it's no use for me to think o' doing anything, if you won't meet me half-way."

"Why, there's this to be considered," said Mr. Glegg. "It's no use to pay off this debt and save the furniture, when there's all the law debts behind, as 'ud take every shilling, and more than could be made out o' land and stock, for I've made that out from Lawyer Gore. We'd need save our money to keep the poor man with, instead o' spending it on furniture as he can neither eat nor drink. You *will* be so hasty, Jane, as if I didn't know what was reasonable."

"Then speak accordingly, Mr. Glegg!" said his wife, with slow, loud emphasis, bending her head towards him significantly.

Tom's countenance had fallen during this conversation, and his lip quivered; but he was determined not to give way. He would behave like a man. Maggie, on the contrary, after her momentary delight in Tom's speech, had relapsed into her state of trembling indignation. Her mother had been standing close by Tom's side, and had been clinging to his arm ever since he had last spoken: Maggie suddenly started up and stood in front of them, her eyes flashing like the eyes of a young lioness.

"Why do you come, then," she burst out, "talking, and interfering with us and scolding us, if you don't mean to do anything to help my poor mother—your own sister—if you've no feeling for her when she's in trouble, and won't part with anything, though you would never miss it, to save her from pain? Keep away from us then, and don't come to find fault with my father—he was better than any of you—he was kind —he would have helped *you,* if you had been in trouble. Tom and I don't ever want to have any of your money, if you won't help my mother. We'd rather not have it! we'll do without you."

Maggie, having hurled her defiance at aunts and uncles in this way, stood still, with her large dark eyes glaring at them, as if she were ready to await all consequences.

Mrs. Tulliver was frightened; there was something portentous in this mad outbreak; she did not see how life could go on after it. Tom was vexed; it was no *use* to talk so. The aunts were silent with surprise for some moments. At length, in a case of aberration such as this, comment presented itself as more expedient than any answer.

"You haven't seen the end o' your trouble wi' that child, Bessy," said Mrs. Pullet; "she's beyond everything for boldness and unthankfulness. It's dreadful. I might ha' let alone paying for her schooling, for she's worse nor ever."

"It's no more than what I've allays said," followed Mrs. Glegg. "Other folks may be surprised, but I'm not. I've said over and over again— years ago I've said—'Mark my words; that child 'ull come to no good: there isn't a bit of our family in her.' And as for her having so much schooling, I never thought well o' that. I'd my reasons when I said *I* wouldn't pay anything towards it."

"Come, come," said Mr. Glegg, "let's waste no more time in talking —let's go to business. Tom now, get the pen and ink——"

While Mr. Glegg was speaking, a tall dark figure was seen hurrying past the window.

"Why, there's Mrs. Moss," said Mrs. Tulliver. "The bad news must ha' reached her, then;" and she went out to open the door, Maggie eagerly following her.

"That's fortunate," said Mrs. Glegg. "She can agree to the list o' things to be bought in. It's but right she should do her share when it's her own brother."

Mrs. Moss was in too much agitation to resist Mrs. Tulliver's movement, as she drew her into the parlour, automatically, without reflecting that it was hardly kind to take her among so many persons in the first painful moment of arrival. The tall, worn, dark-haired woman was a strong contrast to the Dodson sisters as she entered in her shabby dress, with her shawl and bonnet looking as if they had been hastily huddled on, and with that entire absence of self-consciousness which belongs to keenly-felt trouble. Maggie was clinging to her arm; and Mrs. Moss seemed to notice no one else except Tom, whom she went straight up to and took by the hand.

"O, my dear children," she burst out, "you've no call to think well o' me; I'm a poor aunt to you, for I'm one o' them as take all and give nothing. How's my poor brother?"

"Mr. Turnbull thinks he'll get better," said Maggie. "Sit down, aunt Gritty. Don't fret."

"O, my sweet child, I feel torn i' two," said Mrs. Moss, allowing Maggie to lead her to the sofa, but still not seeming to notice the presence of the rest. "We've three hundred pounds o' my brother's money, and now he wants it, and you all want it, poor things!—and yet we must be sold up to pay it, and there's my poor children—eight of 'em, and the little un of all can't speak plain. And I feel as if I was a robber. But I'm sure I'd no thought as my brother . . ."

The poor woman was interrupted by a rising sob.

"Three hundred pounds! O dear, dear," said Mrs. Tulliver, who, when she had said that her husband had done "unknown" things for his sister, had not had any particular sum in her mind, and felt a wife's irritation at having been kept in the dark.

"What madness, to be sure!" said Mrs. Glegg. "A man with a family! He'd no right to lend his money i' that way; and without security, I'll be bound, if the truth was known."

Mrs. Glegg's voice had arrested Mrs. Moss's attention, and, looking up, she said—

"Yes, there *was* security: my husband gave a note for it. We're not that sort o' people, neither of us, as 'ud rob my brother's children; and we looked to paying back the money, when the times got a bit better."

"Well, but now," said Mr. Glegg, gently, "hasn't your husband no way o' raising this money? Because it 'ud be a little fortin', like, for these folks, if we can do without Tulliver's being made a bankrupt. Your husband's got stock: it is but right he should raise the money, as it seems to me—not but what I'm sorry for you, Mrs. Moss."

"O, sir, you don't know what bad luck my husband's had with his stock. The farm's suffering so as never was for want o' stock; and we've sold all the wheat, and we're behind with our rent . . . not but what we'd like to do what's right, and I'd sit up and work half the night, if it 'ud be any good . . . but there's them poor children . . . four of 'em such little uns . . ."

"Don't cry so, aunt—don't fret," whispered Maggie, who had kept hold of Mrs. Moss's hand.

"Did Mr. Tulliver let you have the money all at once?" said Mrs. Tulliver, still lost in the conception of things which had been "going on" without her knowledge.

"No; at twice," said Mrs. Moss, rubbing her eyes, and making an effort to restrain her tears. "The last was after my bad illness, four years ago, as everything went wrong, and there was a new note made then. What with illness and bad luck, I've been nothing but cumber all my life."

"Yes, Mrs. Moss," said Mrs. Glegg, with decision. "Yours is a very unlucky family; the more's the pity for *my* sister."

"I set off in the cart as soon as ever I heard o' what had happened," said Mrs. Moss, looking at Mrs. Tulliver. "I should never ha' staid away all this while, if you'd thought well to let me know. And it isn't as I'm thinking all about ourselves, and nothing about my brother— only the money was so on my mind, I couldn't help speaking about it. And my husband and me desire to do the right thing, sir," she added, looking at Mr. Glegg, "and we'll make shift and pay the money, come what will, if that's all my brother's got to trust to. We've been used to trouble, and don't look for much else. It's only the thought o' my poor children pulls me i' two."

"Why, there's this to be thought on, Mrs. Moss," said Mr. Glegg, "and it's right to warn you;—if Tulliver's made a bankrupt, and he's got a note-of-hand of your husband's for three hundred pounds, you'll be obliged to pay it: th' assignees 'ull come on you for it."

"O dear, O dear!" said Mrs. Tulliver, thinking of the bankruptcy, and not of Mrs. Moss's concern in it. Poor Mrs. Moss herself listened in trembling submission, while Maggie looked with bewildered distress at Tom to see if *he* showed any signs of understanding this trouble, and caring about poor aunt Moss. Tom was only looking thoughtful, with his eyes on the table-cloth.

"And if he isn't made bankrupt," continued Mr. Glegg, "as I said before, three hundred pounds 'ud be a little fortin' for him, poor man. We don't know but what he may be partly helpless, if he ever gets up again. I'm very sorry if it goes hard with you, Mrs. Moss—but my opinion is, looking at it one way, it'll be right for you to raise the money; and looking at it th' other way, you'll be obliged to pay it. You won't think ill o' me for speaking the truth."

"Uncle," said Tom, looking up suddenly from his meditative view of the table-cloth, "I don't think it would be right for my aunt Moss to pay the money, if it would be against my father's will for her to pay it; would it?"

Mr. Glegg looked surprised for a moment or two before he said, "Why, no, perhaps not, Tom; but then he'd ha' destroyed the note, you know. We must look for the note. What makes you think it 'ud be against his will?"

"Why," said Tom, colouring, but trying to speak firmly, in spite of a boyish tremor, "I remember quite well, before I went to school to Mr. Stelling, my father said to me one night, when we were sitting by the fire together, and no one else was in the room . . ."

Tom hesitated a little, and then went on.

"He said something to me about Maggie, and then he said, 'I've always been good to my sister, though she married against my will—and I've lent Moss money; but I shall never think of distressing him to pay it: I'd rather lose it. My children must not mind being the poorer for that.' And now my father's ill, and not able to speak for himself, I shouldn't like anything to be done contrary to what he said to me."

"Well, but then, my boy," said uncle Glegg, whose good feeling led him to enter into Tom's wish, but who could not at once shake off his habitual abhorrence of such recklessness as destroying securities, or alienating anything important enough to make an appreciable difference in a man's property, "we should have to make away wi' the note, you know, if we're to guard against what may happen, supposing your father's made bankrupt . . ."

"Mr. Glegg," interrupted his wife, severely, "mind what you're saying. You're putting yourself very forrard in other folks's business. If you speak rash, don't say it was my fault."

"That's such a thing as I never heared of before," said uncle Pullet, who had been making haste with his lozenge in order to express his amazement; "making away with a note! I should think anybody could set the constable on you for it."

"Well, but," said Mrs. Tulliver, "if the note's worth all that money, why can't we pay it away, and save my things from going away? We've no call to meddle with your uncle and aunt Moss, Tom, if you think your father 'ud be angry when he gets well."

Mrs. Tulliver had not studied the question of exchange, and was straining her mind after original ideas on the subject.

"Pooh, pooh, pooh! you women don't understand these things," said uncle Glegg. "There's no way o' making it safe for Mr. and Mrs. Moss but destroying the note."

"Then I hope you'll help me to do it, uncle," said Tom, earnestly. "If my father shouldn't get well, I should be very unhappy to think anything had been done against his will, that I could hinder. And I'm sure he meant me to remember what he said that evening. I ought to obey my father's wish about his property."

Even Mrs. Glegg could not withhold her approval from Tom's words: she felt that the Dodson blood was certainly speaking in him, though, if his father had been a Dodson, there would never have been this wicked alienation of money. Maggie would hardly have restrained herself from leaping on Tom's neck, if her aunt Moss had not prevented her by herself rising and taking Tom's hand, while she said, with rather a choked voice—

"You'll never be the poorer for this, my dear boy, if there's a God above; and if the money's wanted for your father, Moss and me 'ull pay it, the same as if there was ever such security. We'll do as we'd be done by; for if my children have got no other luck, they've got an honest father and mother."

"Well," said Mr. Glegg, who had been meditating after Tom's words, "we shouldn't be doing any wrong by the creditors, supposing your father *was* bankrupt. I've been thinking o' that, for I've been a creditor myself, and seen no end o' cheating. If he meant to give your aunt the money before ever he got into this sad work o' lawing, it's the same as if he'd made away with the note himself; for he'd made up his mind to be that much poorer. But there's a deal o' things to be considered, young man," Mr. Glegg added, looking admonishingly at Tom, "when you come to money business, and you may be taking one man's dinner away to make another man's breakfast. You don't understand that, I doubt?"

"Yes, I do," said Tom, decidedly. "I know if I owe money to one man, I've no right to give it to another. But if my father had made up his mind to give my aunt the money before he was in debt, he had a right to do it."

"Well done, young man! I didn't think you'd been so sharp," said uncle Glegg, with much candour. "But perhaps your father *did* make away with the note. Let us go and see if we can find it in the chest."

"It's in my father's room. Let us go too. aunt Gritty," whispered Maggie.

CHAPTER IV

A VANISHING GLEAM

Mr. Tulliver, even between the fits of spasmodic rigidity which had recurred at intervals ever since he had been found fallen from his horse, was usually in so apathetic a condition that the exits and entrances into his room were not felt to be of great importance. He had lain so still, with his eyes closed, all this morning, that Maggie told her aunt Moss she must not expect her father to take any notice of them.

They entered very quietly, and Mrs. Moss took her seat near the head of the bed, while Maggie sat in her old place on the bed, and put her hand on her father's, without causing any change in his face.

Mr. Glegg and Tom had also entered, treading softly, and were busy selecting the key of the old oak chest from the bunch which Tom had brought from his father's bureau. They succeeded in opening the chest —which stood opposite the foot of Mr. Tulliver's bed—and propping the lid with the iron holder, without much noise.

"There's a tin box," whispered Mr. Glegg; "he'd most like put a small thing like a note in there. Lift it out, Tom; but I'll just lift up these deeds—they're the deeds o' the house and mill, I suppose—and see what there is under 'em."

Mr. Glegg had lifted out the parchments, and had fortunately drawn back a little, when the iron holder gave way, and the heavy lid fell with a loud bang, that resounded over the house.

Perhaps there was something in that sound more than the mere fact of the strong vibration that produced the instantaneous effect on the frame of the prostrate man, and for the time completely shook off the obstruction of paralysis. The chest had belonged to his father and his father's father, and it had always been rather a solemn business to visit it. All long-known objects, even a mere window-fastening or a particular door-latch, have sounds which are a sort of recognised voice to us —a voice that will thrill and awaken, when it has been used to touch deep-lying fibres. In the same moment when all the eyes in the room were turned upon him, he started up and looked at the chest, the parchments in Mr. Glegg's hand, and Tom holding the tin box, with a glance of perfect consciousness and recognition.

"What are you going to do with those deeds?" he said, in his ordinary tone of sharp questioning whenever he was irritated. "Come here, Tom. What do you do, going to my chest?"

Tom obeyed, with some trembling: it was the first time his father had recognised him. But instead of saying anything more to him, his father continued to look with a growing distinctness of suspicion at Mr. Glegg and the deeds.

"What's been happening, then?" he said, sharply. "What are you meddling with my deeds for? Is Wakem laying hold of everything? . . . Why don't you tell me what you've been a-doing?" he added, impatiently, as Mr. Glegg advanced to the foot of the bed before speaking.

"No, no, friend Tulliver," said Mr. Glegg, in a soothing tone. "Nobody's getting hold of anything as yet. We only came to look and see what was in the chest. You've been ill, you know, and we've had to look after things a bit. But let's hope you'll soon be well enough to attend to everything yourself."

Mr. Tulliver looked round him meditatively—at Tom, at Mr. Glegg, and at Maggie; then suddenly appearing aware that some one was seated by his side at the head of the bed, he turned sharply round and saw his sister.

"Eh, Gritty!" he said, in the half-sad, affectionate tone in which he had been wont to speak to her. "What! you're there, are you? How could you manage to leave the children?"

"O, brother!" said good Mrs. Moss, too impulsive to be prudent, "I'm thankful I'm come now to see you yourself again—I thought you'd never know us any more."

"What! have I had a stroke?" said Mr. Tulliver, anxiously, looking at Mr. Glegg.

"A fall from your horse—shook you a bit—that's all, I think," said Mr. Glegg. "But you'll soon get over it, let's hope."

Mr. Tulliver fixed his eyes on the bed-clothes, and remained silent for two or three minutes. A new shadow came over his face. He looked up at Maggie first, and said in a lower tone, "You got the letter, then, my wench?"

"Yes, father," she said, kissing him with a full heart. She felt as if her father were come back to her from the dead, and her yearning to show him how she had always loved him could be fulfilled.

"Where's your mother?" he said, so preoccupied that he received the kiss as passively as some quiet animal might have received it.

"She's down-stairs with my aunts, father: shall I fetch her?"

"Ay, ay: poor Bessy!" and his eyes turned towards Tom as Maggie left the room.

"You'll have to take care of 'em both if I die, you know, Tom. You'll be badly off, I doubt. But you must see and pay everybody. And mind—there's fifty pound o' Luke's as I put into the business—he gave it me a bit at a time, and he's got nothing to show for it. You must pay him first thing."

Uncle Glegg involuntarily shook his head, and looked more concerned than ever, but Tom said firmly—

"Yes, father. And haven't you a note from my uncle Moss for three hundred pounds? We came to look for that. What do you wish to be done about it, father?"

"Ah! I'm glad you thought o' that, my lad," said Mr. Tulliver. "I allays meant to be easy about that money, because o' your aunt. You mustn't mind losing the money, if they can't pay it—and it's like enough they can't. The note's in that box, mind! I allays meant to be good to you, Gritty," said Mr. Tulliver, turning to his sister; "but, you know, you aggravated me when you would have Moss."

At this moment Maggie re-entered with her mother, who came in much agitated by the news that her husband was quite himself again.

"Well, Bessy," he said, as she kissed him, "you must forgive me if you're worse off than you ever expected to be. But it's the fault o' the law—it's none o' mine," he added, angrily. "It's the fault o' raskills! Tom—you mind this: if ever you've got the chance, you make Wakem smart. If you don't, you're a good-for-nothing son. You might horse-whip him—but he'd set the law on you—the law's made to take care o' raskills."

Mr. Tulliver was getting excited, and an alarming flush was on his face. Mr. Glegg wanted to say something soothing, but he was prevented by Mr. Tulliver's speaking again to his wife. "They'll make a shift to pay everything, Bessy," he said, "and yet leave you your furniture; and your sisters'll do something for you . . . and Tom 'll grow up . . . though what he's to be I don't know . . . I've done what I could . . . I've given him a eddication . . . and there's the little wench, she'll get married . . . but it's a poor tale . . ."

The sanative effect of the strong vibration was exhausted, and with the last words the poor man fell again, rigid and insensible. Though this was only a recurrence of what had happened before, it struck all present as if it had been death, not only from its contrast with the completeness of the revival, but because his words had all had reference to the possibility that his death was near. But with poor Tulliver death was not to be a leap: it was to be a long descent under thickening shadows.

Mr. Turnbull was sent for; but when he heard what had passed, he said this complete restoration, though only temporary, was a hopeful sign, proving that there was no permanent lesion to prevent ultimate recovery.

Among the threads of the past which the stricken man had gathered up, he had omitted the bill of sale; the flash of memory had only lit up prominent ideas, and he sank into forgetfulness again with half his humiliation unlearned.

But Tom was clear upon two points—that his uncle Moss's note must be destroyed, and that Luke's money must be paid, if in no other way, out of his own and Maggie's money now in the savings' bank. There were subjects, you perceive, on which Tom was much quicker than on the niceties of classical construction, or the relations of a mathematical demonstration.

CHAPTER V

TOM APPLIES HIS KNIFE TO THE OYSTER

THE next day, at ten o'clock, Tom was on his way to St. Ogg's, to see his uncle Deane, who was to come home last night, his aunt had said; and Tom had made up his mind that his uncle Deane was the right person to ask for advice about getting some employment. He was in a great way of business; he had not the narrow notions of uncle Glegg; and he had risen in the world on a scale of advancement which accorded with Tom's ambition.

It was a dark, chill, misty morning, likely to end in rain—one of those mornings when even happy people take refuge in their hopes. And Tom was very unhappy: he felt the humiliation as well as the prospective hardships of his lot with all the keenness of a proud nature; and with all his resolute dutifulness towards his father there mingled an irrepressible indignation against him which gave misfortune the less endurable aspect of a wrong. Since these were the consequences of going to law, his father was really blamable, as his aunts and uncles had always said he was; and it was a significant indication of Tom's character, that though he thought his aunts ought to do something more for his mother, he felt nothing like Maggie's violent resentment against them for showing no eager tenderness and generosity. There were no impulses in Tom that led him to expect what did not present itself to him as a right to be demanded. Why should people give away their money plentifully to those who had not taken care of their own money? Tom saw some justice in severity; and all the more, because he had confidence in himself that he should never deserve that just severity. It was very hard upon him that he should be put at this disadvantage in life by his father's want of prudence; but he was not going to complain and to find fault with people because they did not make everything easy for him. He would ask no one to help him, more than to give him work and pay him for it. Poor Tom was not without his hopes to take refuge in under the chill damp imprisonment of the December fog which seemed only like a part of his home troubles. At sixteen, the mind that has the strongest affinity for fact cannot escape illusion and self-flattery; and Tom, in sketching his future, had no other guide in arranging his facts than the suggestions of his own brave self-reliance. Both Mr. Glegg and Mr. Deane, he knew, had been very poor once: he did not want to save money slowly and retire on a moderate fortune like his uncle Glegg, but he would be like his uncle Deane—get a situation in some great house of business and rise fast. He had scarcely seen anything of his uncle Deane for the last three years—the two families had been getting wider apart; but for this very reason Tom was the more hopeful about applying to him. His uncle Glegg, he felt sure, would never encourage any spirited project, but he had a vague imposing idea of the resources at his uncle Deane's command. He had heard his father say, long ago, how Deane had made himself so valuable to Guest & Co. that they were glad enough to offer him a share in the business: that was what Tom resolved *he* would do. It was intolerable to think of being poor and looked down upon all one's life. He would provide for his mother and sister, and make every one say that he was a man of high character. He leaped over the years in this way, and in the haste of strong purpose and strong desire, did not see how they would be made up of slow days, hours, and minutes.

By the time he had crossed the stone bridge over the Floss, and was entering St. Ogg's, he was thinking that he would buy his father's mill and land again when he was rich enough, and improve the house and live there: he should prefer it to any smarter, newer place, and he could keep as many horses and dogs as he liked.

Walking along the street with a firm, rapid step, at this point in his reverie he was startled by some one who had crossed without his notice, and who said to him in a rough, familiar voice—

"Why, Master Tom, how's your father this morning?" It was a publican of St. Ogg's—one of his father's customers.

Tom disliked being spoken to just then; but he said civilly, "He's still very ill, thank you."

"Ay, it's been a sore chance for you, young man, hasn't it?—this lawsuit turning out against him," said the publican, with a confused beery idea of being good-natured.

Tom reddened and passed on: he would have felt it like the handling of a bruise, even if there had been the most polite and delicate reference to his position.

"That's Tulliver's son," said the publican to a grocer standing on the adjacent door-step.

"Ah!" said the grocer, "I thought I knew his features, like. He takes after his mother's family: she was a Dodson. He's a fine, straight youth: what's he been brought up to?"

"O! to turn up his nose at his father's customers, and be a fine gentleman—not much else, I think."

Tom, roused from his dream of the future to a thorough consciousness of the present, made all the greater haste to reach the warehouse offices of Guest & Co., where he expected to find his uncle Deane. But this was Mr. Deane's morning at the bank, a clerk told him, with some contempt for his ignorance: Mr. Deane was not to be found in River Street on a Thursday morning.

At the bank Tom was admitted into the private room where his uncle was, immediately after sending in his name. Mr. Deane was auditing accounts; but he looked up as Tom entered, and, putting out his hand, said, "Well, Tom, nothing fresh the matter at home, I hope? How's your father?"

"Much the same, thank you, uncle," said Tom, feeling nervous. "But I want to speak to you, please, when you're at liberty."

"Sit down, sit down," said Mr. Deane, relapsing into his accounts, in which he and the managing-clerk remained so absorbed for the next half-hour that Tom began to wonder whether he should have to sit in this way till the bank closed—there seemed so little tendency towards a conclusion in the quiet monotonous procedure of these sleek, prosperous men of business. Would his uncle give him a place in the bank? it would be very dull, prosy work, he thought, writing there for ever to the loud ticking of a time-piece. He preferred some other way of getting rich. But at last there was a change: his uncle took a pen and wrote something with a flourish at the end.

"You'll just step up to Torry's now, Mr. Spence, will you?" said Mr. Deane, and the clock suddenly became less loud and deliberate in Tom's ears.

"Well, Tom," said Mr. Deane, when they were alone, turning his substantial person a little in his chair, and taking out his snuff-box, "what's the business, my boy—what's the business?" Mr. Deane, who had heard from his wife what had passed the day before, thought Tom was come to appeal to him for some means of averting the sale.

"I hope you'll excuse me for troubling you, uncle," said Tom, colouring, but speaking in a tone which, though tremulous, had a certain proud independence in it; "but I thought you were the best person to advise me what to do."

"Ah?" said Mr. Deane, reserving his pinch of snuff, and looking at Tom with new attention, "let us hear."

"I want to get a situation, uncle, so that I may earn some money," said Tom, who never fell into circumlocution.

"A situation?" said Mr. Deane, and then took his pinch of snuff with elaborate justice to each nostril. Tom thought snuff-taking a most provoking habit.

"Why, let me see, how old are you?" said Mr. Deane, as he threw himself backward again.

"Sixteen—I mean, I am going in seventeen," said Tom, hoping his uncle noticed how much beard he had.

"Let me see—your father had some notion of making you an engineer, I think?"

"But I don't think I could get any money at that for a long while, could I?"

"That's true; but people don't get much money at anything, my boy, when they're only sixteen. You've had a good deal of schooling, however: I suppose you're pretty well up in accounts, eh? You understand book-keeping?"

"No," said Tom, rather falteringly. "I was in Practice. But Mr. Stelling says I write a good hand, uncle. That's my writing," added Tom, laying on the table a copy of the list he had made yesterday.

"Ah! that's good, that's good. But, you see, the best hand in the world 'll not get you a better place than a copying-clerk's, if you know nothing of book-keeping—nothing of accounts. And a copying-clerk's a cheap article. But what have you been learning at school, then?"

Mr. Deane had not occupied himself with methods of education, and had no precise conception of what went forward in expensive schools.

"We learned Latin," said Tom, pausing a little between each item, as if he were turning over the books in his school-desk to assist his memory—"a good deal of Latin; and the last year I did Themes, one week in Latin and one in English; and Greek and Roman History; and Euclid; and I began Algebra, but I left it off again; and we had one day every week for Arithmetic. Then I used to have drawing-lessons; and there were several other books we either read or learned out of, English Poetry, and Horæ Paulinæ, and Blair's Rhetoric, the last Half."

Mr. Deane tapped his snuff-box again, and screwed up his mouth: he felt in the position of many estimable persons when they had read the New Tariff, and found how many commodities were imported of which they knew nothing: like a cautious man of business, he was not going to speak rashly of a raw material in which he had had no experience. But the presumption was, that if it had been good for anything, so successful a man as himself would hardly have been ignorant of it. About Latin he had an opinion, and thought that in case of another war, since people would no longer wear hair-powder, it would be well to put a tax upon Latin, as a luxury much run upon by the higher classes, and not telling at all on the ship-owning department. But, for what he knew, the Horæ Paulinæ might be something less neutral. On the whole, this list of acquirements gave him a sort of repulsion towards poor Tom.

"Well," he said, at last, in rather a cold, sardonic tone, "you've had three years at these things—you must be pretty strong in 'em. Hadn't you better take up some line where they'll come in handy?"

Tom coloured, and burst out, with new energy—

"I'd rather not have any employment of that sort, uncle. I don't like Latin and those things. I don't know what I could do with them unless I went as usher in a school; and I don't know them well enough for that: besides, I would as soon carry a pair of panniers. I don't want to be that sort of person. I should like to enter into some business where I can get on—a manly business, where I should have to look after things, and get credit for what I did. And I shall want to keep my mother and sister."

"Ah, young gentleman," said Mr. Deane, with that tendency to repress youthful hopes which stout and successful men of fifty find one of their easiest duties, "that's sooner said than done—sooner said than done."

"But didn't *you* get on in that way, uncle?" said Tom, a little irritated that Mr. Deane did not enter more rapidly into his views. "I mean, didn't you rise from one place to another through your abilities and good conduct?"

"Ay, ay, sir," said Mr. Deane, spreading himself in his chair a little, and entering with great readiness into a retrospect of his own career. "But I'll tell you how I got on. It wasn't by getting astride a stick, and thinking it would turn into a horse if I sat on it long enough. I kept my eyes and ears open, sir, and I wasn't too fond of my own back, and I made my master's interest my own. Why, with only looking into what went on in the mill, I found out how there was a waste of five hundred a-year that might be hindered. Why, sir, I hadn't more schooling to begin with than a charity boy; but I saw pretty soon that I couldn't get on far without mastering accounts, and I learned 'em between working hours, after I'd been unlading. Look here." Mr. Deane opened a book, and pointed to the page. "I write a good hand enough, and I'll match anybody at all sorts of reckoning by the head, and I got it all by hard work, and paid for it out of my own earnings—often out of my own dinner and supper. And I looked into the nature of all the things we had to do with in the business, and picked up knowledge as I went about my work, and turned it over in my head. Why, I'm no mechanic—I never pretended to be—but I've thought of a thing or two that the mechanics never thought of, and it's made a fine difference in our returns. And there isn't an article shipped or unshipped at our wharf but I know the quality of it. If I got places, sir, it was because I made myself fit for 'em. If you want to slip into a round hole, you must make a ball of yourself—that's where it is."

Mr. Deane tapped his box again. He had been led on by pure enthusiasm in his subject, and had really forgotten what bearing this retrospective survey had on his listener. He had found occasion for saying the same thing more than once before, and was not distinctly aware that he had not his port-wine before him.

"Well, uncle," said Tom, with a slight complaint in his tone, "that's what I should like to do. Can't *I* get on in the same way?"

"In the same way?" said Mr. Deane, eyeing Tom with quiet deliberation. "There go two or three questions to that, Master Tom. That depends on what sort of material you are, to begin with, and whether you've been put into the right mill. But I'll tell you what it is. Your poor father went the wrong way to work in giving you an education. It wasn't my business, and I didn't interfere: but it is as I thought it would be. You've had a sort of learning that's all very well for a young fellow like our Mr. Stephen Guest, who'll have nothing to do but sign cheques all his life, and may as well have Latin inside his head as any other sort of stuffing."

"But, uncle," said Tom, earnestly, "I don't see why the Latin need hinder me from getting on in business. I shall soon forget it all: it makes no difference to me. I had to do my lessons at school; but I always thought they'd never be of any use to me afterwards—I didn't care about them."

"Ay, ay, that's all very well," said Mr. Deane; "but it doesn't alter what I was going to say. Your Latin and rigmarole may soon dry off you, but you'll be but a bare stick after that. Besides, it's whitened your hands and taken the rough work out of you. And what do you know? Why, you know nothing about book-keeping, to begin with, and not so much of reckoning as a common shopman. You'll have to begin at a low round of the ladder, let me tell you, if you mean to get on in life. It's no use forgetting the education your father's been paying for, if you don't give yourself a new un."

Tom bit his lips hard; he felt as if the tears were rising, and he would rather die than let them.

"You want me to help you to a situation," Mr. Deane went on; "well, I've no fault to find with that. I'm willing to do something for you. But you youngsters nowadays think you're to begin with living well and working easy: you've no notion of running afoot before you get on horseback. Now, you must remember what you are—you're a lad of sixteen, trained to nothing particular. There's heaps of your sort, like so many pebbles, made to fit in nowhere. Well, you might be apprenticed to some business—a chemist's and druggist's perhaps: your Latin might come in a bit there . . ."

Tom was going to speak, but Mr. Deane put up his hand, and said—

"Stop! hear what I've got to say. You don't want to be a 'prentice—I know, I know—you want to make more haste—and you don't want to stand behind a counter. But if you're a copying-clerk, you'll have to stand behind a desk, and stare at your ink and paper all day: there isn't much outlook there, and you won't be much wiser at the end of the year than at the beginning. The world isn't made of pen, ink, and paper, and if you're to get on in the world, young man, you must know what the world's made of. Now the best chance for you 'ud be to have a place on a wharf, or in a warehouse, where you'd learn the smell of things—but you wouldn't like that, I'll be bound; you'd have to stand cold and wet, and be shouldered about by rough fellows. You're too fine a gentleman for that."

Mr. Deane paused and looked hard at Tom, who certainly felt some inward struggle before he could reply.

"I would rather do what will be best for me in the end, sir: I would put up with what was disagreeable."

"That's well, if you can carry it out. But you must remember it isn't only laying hold of a rope—you must go on pulling. It's the mistake you lads make that have got nothing either in your brains or your pocket, to think you've got a better start in the world if you stick yourselves in a place where you can keep your coats clean, and have the shop-wenches take you for fine gentlemen. That wasn't the way *I* started, young man: when I was sixteen, my jacket smelt of tar, and I wasn't afraid of handling cheeses. That's the reason I can wear good broadcloth now, and have my legs under the same table with the heads of the best firms in St. Ogg's."

Uncle Deane tapped his box, and seemed to expand a little under his waistcoat and gold chain, as he squared his shoulders in the chair.

"Is there any place at liberty that you know of now, uncle, that I should do for? I should like to set to work at once," said Tom, with a slight tremor in his voice.

"Stop a bit, stop a bit; we mustn't be in too great a hurry. You must bear in mind, if I put you in a place you're a bit young for, because you happen to be my nephew, I shall be responsible for you. And there's no better reason, you know, than your being my nephew; because it remains to be seen whether you're good for anything."

"I hope I should never do you any discredit, uncle," said Tom, hurt, as all boys are at the statement of the unpleasant truth that people feel no ground for trusting them. "I care about my own credit too much for that."

"Well done, Tom, well done! That's the right spirit, and I never refuse to help anybody, if they've a mind to do themselves justice. There's a young man of two-and-twenty I've got my eye on now. I shall do what I can for that young man—he's got some pith in him. But then, you see, he's made good use of his time—a first-rate calculator—can tell you the cubic contents of anything in no time, and put me up the other day to a new market for Swedish bark; he's uncommonly knowing in manufactures, that young fellow."

"I'd better set about learning book-keeping, hadn't I, uncle?" said Tom, anxious to prove his readiness to exert himself.

"Yes, yes, you can't do amiss there. But . . . ah, Spence, you're back again. Well, Tom, there's nothing more to be said just now, I think, and I must go to business again. Good-by. Remember me to your mother."

Mr. Deane put out his hand, with an air of friendly dismissal, and Tom had not courage to ask another question, especially in the presence of Mr. Spence. So he went out again into the cold damp air. He had to call at his uncle Glegg's about the money in the Savings' Bank, and by the time he set out again, the mist had thickened, and he could not see very far before him; but going along River Street again, he was startled, when he was within two yards of the projecting side of a shop window, by the words "Doricote Mill" in large letters on a hand-bill, placed as if on purpose to stare at him. It was the catalogue of the sale to take place the next week—it was a reason for hurrying faster out of the town.

Poor Tom formed no visions of the distant future as he made his way homeward; he only felt that the present was very hard. It seemed a wrong towards him that his uncle Deane had no confidence in him—did not see at once that he should acquit himself well, which Tom himself was as certain of as of the daylight. Apparently he, Tom Tulliver, was likely to be held of small account in the world, and for the first time he felt a sinking of heart under the sense that he really was very ignorant, and could do very little. Who was that enviable young man, that could tell the cubic contents of things in no time, and make suggestions about Swedish bark? Swedish bark! Tom had been used to be so entirely satisfied with himself in spite of his breaking down in a demonstration, and construing *nunc illas promite vires,* as "now promise those men;" but now he suddenly felt at a disadvantage, because he knew less than some one else knew. There must be a world of things connected with that Swedish bark, which, if he only knew them, might have helped him to get on. It would have been much easier to make a figure with a spirited horse and a new saddle.

Two hours ago, as Tom was walking to St. Ogg's, he saw the distant future before him, as he might have seen a tempting stretch of smooth sandy beach beyond a belt of flinty shingles; he was on the grassy bank then, and thought the shingles might soon be passed. But now his feet were on the sharp stones; the belt of shingles had widened, and the stretch of sand had dwindled into narrowness.

"What did my uncle Deane say, Tom?" said Maggie, putting her arm through Tom's as he was warming himself rather drearily by the kitchen fire. "Did he say he would give you a situation?"

"No, he didn't say that. He didn't quite promise me anything; he seemed to think I couldn't have a very good situation. I'm too young."

"But didn't he speak kindly, Tom?"

"Kindly? Pooh! what's the use of talking about that? I wouldn't care about his speaking kindly, if I could get a situation. But it's such a nuisance and bother—I've been at school all this while learning Latin and things—not a bit of good to me—and now my uncle says, I must set about learning book-keeping and calculation, and those things. He seems to make out I'm good for nothing."

Tom's mouth twitched with a bitter expression as he looked at the fire.

"O, what a pity we haven't got Dominie Sampson," said Maggie, who couldn't help mingling some gaiety with their sadness. "If he had taught me book-keeping by double entry and after the Italian method, as he did Lucy Bertram, I could teach you, Tom."

"*You* teach! Yes, I daresay. That's always the tone you take," said Tom.

"Dear Tom! I was only joking," said Maggie, putting her cheek against his coat sleeve.

"But it's always the same, Maggie," said Tom, with the little frown he put on when he was about to be justifiably severe. "You're always setting yourself up above me and every one else, and I've wanted to tell you about it several times. You ought not to have spoken as you did to my uncles and aunts—you should leave it to me to take care of my mother and you, and not put yourself forward. You think you know better than any one, but you're almost always wrong. I can judge much better than you can."

Poor Tom! he had just come from being lectured and made to feel his inferiority: the reaction of his strong, self-asserting nature must take place somehow; and here was a case in which he could justly show himself dominant. Maggie's cheek flushed and her lip quivered with conflicting resentment and affection, and a certain awe as well as admiration of Tom's firmer and more effective character. She did not answer immediately; very angry words rose to her lips, but they were driven back again, and she said at last—

"You often think I'm conceited, Tom, when I don't mean what I say at all in that way. I don't mean to put myself above you—I know you behaved better than I did yesterday. But you are always so harsh to me, Tom."

With the last words the resentment was rising again.

"No, I'm not harsh," said Tom, with severe decision. "I'm always kind to you; and so I shall be: I shall always take care of you. But you must mind what I say."

Their mother came in now, and Maggie rushed away, that her burst of tears, which she felt must come, might not happen till she was safe up-stairs. They were very bitter tears: everybody in the world seemed so hard and unkind to Maggie: there was no indulgence, no fondness, such as she imagined when she fashioned the world afresh in her own thoughts. In books there were people who were always agreeable or tender, and delighted to do things that made one happy, and who did not show their kindness by finding fault. The world outside the books was not a happy one, Maggie felt: it seemed to be a world where people behaved the best to those they did not pretend to love, and that did not belong to them. And if life had no love in it, what else was there for Maggie? Nothing but poverty and the companionship of her mother's narrow griefs—perhaps of her father's heart-cutting childish dependence. There is no hopelessness so sad as that of early youth, when the soul is made up of wants, and has no long memories, no superadded life in the life of others; though we who look on think lightly of such premature despair, as if our vision of the future lightened the blind sufferer's present.

Maggie in her brown frock, with her eyes reddened and her heavy hair pushed back, looking from the bed where her father lay, to the dull walls of this sad chamber which was the centre of her world, was a creature full of eager, passionate longings for all that was beautiful and glad; thirsty for all knowledge; with an ear straining after dreamy music that died away and would not come near to her; with a blind, unconscious yearning for something that would link together the wonderful impressions of this mysterious life, and give her soul a sense of home in it.

No wonder, when there is this contrast between the outward and the inward, that painful collisions come of it.

CHAPTER VI

TENDING TO REFUTE THE POPULAR PREJUDICE AGAINST THE PRESENT
OF A POCKET-KNIFE

In that dark time of December, the sale of the household furniture lasted
beyond the middle of the second day. Mr. Tulliver, who had begun, in
his intervals of consciousness, to manifest an irritability which often
appeared to have as a direct effect the recurrence of spasmodic rigidity
and insensibility, had lain in this living death throughout the critical
hours when the noise of the sale came nearest to his chamber. Mr. Turnbull had decided that it would be a less risk to let him remain where he
was, than to move him to Luke's cottage—a plan which the good Luke
had proposed to Mrs. Tulliver, thinking it would be very bad if the
master were "to waken up" at the noise of the sale; and the wife and
children had sat imprisoned in the silent chamber, watching the large
prostrate figure on the bed, and trembling lest the blank face should
suddenly show some response to the sounds which fell on their own ears
with such obstinate, painful repetition.

But it was over at last—that time of importunate certainty and eye-
straining suspense. The sharp sound of a voice, almost as metallic as
the rap that followed it, had ceased; the tramping of footsteps on the
gravel had died out. Mrs. Tulliver's blond face seemed aged ten years
by the last thirty hours: the poor woman's mind had been busy divining when her favourite things were being knocked down by the terrible
hammer; her heart had been fluttering at the thought that first one
thing and then another had gone to be identified as hers in the hateful
publicity of the Golden Lion; and all the while she had to sit and make
no sign of this inward agitation. Such things bring lines in well-rounded
faces, and broaden the streaks of white among the hairs that once looked
as if they had been dipped in pure sunshine. Already, at three o'clock,
Kezia, the good-hearted, bad-tempered housemaid, who regarded all
people that came to the sale as her personal enemies, the dirt on whose
feet was of a peculiarly vile quality, had begun to scrub and swill with
an energy much assisted by a continual low muttering against "folks
as came to buy up other folks's things," and made light of "scrazing"
the tops of mahogany tables over which better folks than themselves
had had to—suffer a waste of tissue through evaporation. She was not
scrubbing indiscriminately, for there would be further dirt of the same
atrocious kind made by people who had still to fetch away their purchases: but she was bent on bringing the parlour, where that "pipe-
smoking pig" the bailiff had sat, to such an appearance of scant comfort as could be given to it by cleanliness, and the few articles of furniture bought in for the family. Her mistress and the young folks should
have their tea in it that night, Kezia was determined.

It was between five and six o'clock, near the usual tea-time, when she came up-stairs and said that Master Tom was wanted. The person who wanted him was in the kitchen, and in the first moments, by the imperfect fire and candle-light, Tom had not even an indefinite sense of any acquaintance with the rather broad-set but active figure, perhaps two years older than himself, that looked at him with a pair of blue eyes set in a disc of freckles, and pulled some curly red locks with a strong intention of respect. A low-crowned oilskin-covered hat, and a certain shiny deposit of dirt on the rest of the costume, as of tablets prepared for writing upon, suggested a calling that had to do with boats; but this did not help Tom's memory.

"Sarvant, Mister Tom," said he of the red locks, with a smile which seemed to break through a self-imposed air of melancholy. "You don' know me again, I doubt," he went on, as Tom continued to look at him inquiringly; "but I'd like to talk to you by yourself a bit, please."

"There's a fire i' the parlour, Master Tom," said Kezia, who objected to leaving the kitchen in the crisis of toasting.

"Come this way, then," said Tom, wondering if this young fellow belonged to Guest & Co.'s Wharf; for his imagination ran continually towards that particular spot, and uncle Deane might any time be sending for him to say that there was a situation at liberty.

The bright fire in the parlour was the only light that showed the few chairs, the bureau, the carpetless floor, and the one table—no, not the *one* table: there was a second table in a corner, with a large Bible and a few other books upon it. It was this new strange bareness that Tom felt first, before he thought of looking again at the face which was also lit up by the fire, and which stole a half-shy, questioning glance at him as the entirely strange voice said—

"Why! you don't remember Bob, then, as you gen the pocket-knife, Mr. Tom?"

The rough-handled pocket-knife was taken out in the same moment, and the largest blade opened by way of irresistible demonstration.

"What! Bob Jakin?" said Tom—not with any cordial delight, for he felt a little ashamed of that early intimacy symbolised by the pocket-knife, and was not at all sure that Bob's motives for recalling it were entirely admirable.

"Ay, ay, Bob Jakin—if Jakin it must be, 'cause there's so many Bobs, as you went arter the squerrils with, that day as I plumped right down from the bough, and bruised my shins a good un—but I got the squerril tight for all that, an' a scratter it was. An' this littlish blade's broke, you see, but I wouldn't hev a new un put in, 'cause they might be cheatin' me an' givin' me another knife istid, for there isn't such a blade i' the country—it's got used to my hand, like. An' there was niver nobody else gen me nothin' but what I got by my own sharpness, only you, Mr. Tom; if it wasn't Bill Fawks as gen me the terrier pup istid o' drowndin' it, an' I had to jaw him a good un afore he'd give it me."

Bob spoke with a sharp and rather treble volubility, and got through his long speech with surprising despatch, giving the blade of his knife an affectionate rub on his sleeve when he had finished.

"Well, Bob," said Tom, with a slight air of patronage, the foregoing reminiscences having disposed him to be as friendly as was becoming, though there was no part of his acquaintance with Bob that he remembered better than the cause of their parting quarrel; "is there anything I can do for you?"

"Why, no, Mr. Tom," answered Bob, shutting up his knife with a click and returning it to his pocket, where he seemed to be feeling for something else. "I shouldn't ha' come back upon you now ye're i' trouble, an' folks say as the master, as I used to frighten the birds for, an' he flogged me a bit for fun when he catched me eatin' the turnip, as they say he'll niver lift up his yead no more—I shouldn't ha' come now to ax you to gi' me another knife, 'cause you gen me one afore. If a chap gives me one black eye, that's enough for me: I shan't ax him for another afore I sarve him out; an' a good turn's worth as much as a bad un, anyhow. I shall niver grow down'ards again, Mr. Tom, an' you war the little chap as I liked the best when *I* war a little chap, for all you leathered me, and wouldn't look at me again. There's Dick Brumby, there, I could leather him as much as I'd a mind; but lors! you get tired o' leatherin' a chap when you can niver make him see what you want him to shy at. I'n seen chaps as 'ud stand starin' at a bough till their eyes shot out, afore they'd see as a bird's tail warn't a leaf. It's poor work goin' wi' such raff—but you war allays a rare un at shying, Mr. Tom, an' I could trusten to you for droppin' down wi' your stick in the nick o' time at a runnin' rat, or a stoat, or that, when I war a-beatin' the bushes."

Bob had drawn out a dirty canvass bag, and would perhaps not have paused just then if Maggie had not entered the room and darted a look of surprise and curiosity at him, whereupon he pulled his red locks again with due respect. But the next moment the sense of the altered room came upon Maggie with a force that overpowered the thought of Bob's presence. Her eyes had immediately glanced from him to the place where the book-case had hung; there was nothing now but the oblong unfaded space on the wall, and below it the small table with the Bible and the few other books.

"O, Tom," she burst out, clasping her hands, "where are the books? I thought my uncle Glegg said he would buy them—didn't he?—are those all they've left us?"

"I suppose so," said Tom, with a sort of desperate indifference. "Why should they buy many books when they bought so little furniture?"

"O, but, Tom," said Maggie, her eyes filling with tears, as she rushed up to the table to see what books had been rescued, "our dear old Pilgrim's Progress that you coloured with your little paints; and that picture of Pilgrim with a mantle on, looking just like a turtle—O dear!" Maggie went on, half sobbing as she turned over the few books. "I thought we should never part with that while we lived—everything is going away from us—the end of our lives will have nothing in it like the beginning!"

Maggie turned away from the table and threw herself into a chair, with the big tears ready to roll down her cheeks—quite blinded to the presence of Bob, who was looking at her with the pursuant gaze of an intelligent dumb animal, with perceptions more perfect than his comprehension.

"Well, Bob," said Tom, feeling that the subject of the books was unseasonable, "I suppose you just came to see me because we're in trouble? That was very good-natured of you."

"I'll tell you how it is, Master Tom," said Bob, beginning to untwist his canvass bag. "You see, I'n been with a barge this two 'ear—that's how I'n been gettin' my livin'—if it wasn't when I was tentin' the furnace, between whiles, at Torry's mill. But a fortni't ago I'd a rare bit o' luck—I allays thought I was a lucky chap, for I niver set a trap but what I catched so'thing; but this wasn't a trap, it was a fire i' Torry's mill, an' I doused it, else it 'ud ha' set th' oil alight, an' the genelman gen me ten suvreigns—he gen me 'em himself last week. An' he said first, I was a sperrited chap—but I knowed that afore—but then he outs wi' the ten suvreigns, an' that war summat new. Here they are—all but one!" Here Bob emptied the canvass bag on the table. "An' when I'd got 'em, my head was all of a boil like a kettle o' broth, thinkin' what sort o' life I should take to—for there war a many trades I'd thought on; for as for the barge, I'm clean tired out wi't, for it pulls the days out till they're as long as pigs' chitterlings. An' I thought first I'd ha' ferrets an' dogs, an' be a rat-ketcher; an' then I thought as I should like a bigger way o' life, as I didn't know so well; for I'n seen to the bottom o' rat-ketching; an' I thought an' thought till at last I settled I'd be a packman, for they're knowin' fellers, the packmen are—an' I'd carry the lightest things I could i' my pack—an' there'd be a use for a feller's tongue, as is no use, neither wi' rats nor barges. An' I should go about the country far an' wide, an' come round the women wi' my tongue, an' get my dinner hot at the public—lors! it 'ud be a lovely life!"

Bob paused, and then said, with defiant decision, as if resolutely turning his back on that paradisaic picture—

"But I don't mind about it, not a chip! An' I'n changed one o' the suvreigns to buy my mother a goose for dinner, an' I'n bought a blue plush wescoat an' a sealskin cap—for if I meant to be a packman, I'd do it respectable. But I don't mind about it—not a chip! My yead isn't a turnup, an' I shall p'r'aps have a chance o' dousing another fire afore long. I'm a lucky chap. So I'll thank you to take the nine suvreigns, Mr. Tom, and set yoursen up with 'em somehow—if it's true as the master's broke. They mayn't go fur enough—but they'll help."

Tom was touched keenly enough to forget his pride and suspicion.

"You're a very kind fellow, Bob," he said, colouring, with that little diffident tremor in his voice, which gave a certain charm even to Tom's pride and severity, "and I sha'n't forget you again, though I didn't know you this evening. But I can't take the nine sovereigns: I should be taking your little fortune from you, and they wouldn't do me much good either."

"Wouldn't they, Mr. Tom?" said Bob, regretfully. "Now don't say so 'cause you think I want 'em. I aren't a poor chap. My mother gets a good penn'orth wi' picking feathers an' things; an' if she eats nothin' but bread-an'-water, it runs to fat. An' I'm such a lucky chap: an' I doubt you aren't quite so lucky, Mr. Tom—th' old master isn't, any-now—an' so you might take a slice o' my luck, an' no harm done. Lors! I found a leg o' pork i' the river one day: it had tumbled out o' one o' them round-sterned Dutchmen, I'll be bound. Come, think better on it, Mr. Tom, for old 'quintance sake—else I shall think you bear me a grudge."

Bob pushed the sovereigns forward, but before Tom could speak, Maggie, clasping her hands, and looking penitently at Bob, said—

"O, I'm so sorry, Bob—I never thought you were so good. Why, I think you're the kindest person in the world!"

Bob had not been aware of the injurious opinion for which Maggie was performing an inward act of penitence, but he smiled with pleasure at this handsome eulogy—especially from a young lass who, as he informed his mother that evening, had "such uncommon eyes, they looked somehow as they made him feel nohow."

"No, indeed, Bob, I can't take them," said Tom; "but don't think I feel your kindness less because I say no. I don't want to take anything from anybody, but to work my own way. And those sovereigns wouldn't help me much—they wouldn't, really—if I were to take them. Let me shake hands with you instead."

Tom put out his pink palm, and Bob was not slow to place his hard, grimy hand within it.

"Let me put the sovereigns in the bag again," said Maggie; "and you'll come and see us when you've bought your pack, Bob."

"It's like as if I'd come out o' make-believe, o' purpose to show 'em you," said Bob, with an air of discontent, as Maggie gave him the bag again, "a-taking 'em back i' this way. I *am* a bit of a Do, you know; but it isn't that sort o' Do: it's on'y when a feller's a big rogue, or a big flat, I like to let him in a bit, that's all."

"Now, don't you be up to any tricks, Bob," said Tom, "else you'll get transported some day."

"No, no; not me, Mr. Tom," said Bob, with an air of cheerful confidence. "There's no law again' fleabites. If I wasn't to take a fool in now and then, he'd niver get any wiser. But, lors! hev a suvreign to buy you and Miss summat, on'y for a token—just to match my pocket-knife."

While Bob was speaking he laid down the sovereign, and resolutely twisted up his bag again. Tom pushed back the gold, and said, "No, indeed, Bob; thank you heartily; but I can't take it." And Maggie, taking it between her fingers, held it up to Bob, and said, more persuasively—

"Not now—but perhaps another time. If ever Tom or my father wants help that you can give, we'll let you know—won't we, Tom? That's what you would like—to have us always depend on you as a friend that we can go to—isn't it, Bob?"

"Yes, Miss, and thank you," said Bob, reluctantly taking the money; "that's what I'd like—anything as you like. An' I wish you good-by, Miss, and good-luck, Mr. Tom, and thank you for shaking hands wi' me, *though* you wouldn't take the money."

Kezia's entrance, with very black looks, to inquire if she shouldn't bring in the tea now, or whether the toast was to get hardened to a brick, was a seasonable check on Bob's flux of words, and hastened his parting bow.

CHAPTER VII

HOW A HEN TAKES TO STRATAGEM

THE days passed, and Mr. Tulliver showed, at least to the eyes of the medical man, stronger and stronger symptoms of a gradual return to his normal condition: the paralytic obstruction was, little by little, losing its tenacity, and the mind was rising from under it with fitful struggles, like a living creature making its way from under a great snow-drift, that slides and slides again, and shuts up the newly-made opening.

Time would have seemed to creep to the watchers by the bed, if it had only been measured by the doubtful distant hope which kept count of the moments within the chamber; but it was measured for them by a fast-approaching dread which made the nights come too quickly. While Mr. Tulliver was slowly becoming himself again, his lot was hastening towards its moment of most palpable change. The taxing-masters had done their work like any respectable gunsmith conscientiously preparing the musket, that, duly pointed by a brave arm, will spoil a life or two. Allocaturs, filing of bills in Chancery, decrees of sale, are legal chain-shot or bomb-shells that can never hit a solitary mark, but must fall with widespread shattering. So deeply inherent is it in this life of ours that men have to suffer for each other's sins, so inevitably diffusive is human suffering, that even justice makes its victims, and we can conceive no retribution that does not spread beyond its mark in pulsations of unmerited pain.

By the beginning of the second week in January the bills were out advertising the sale, under a decree of Chancery, of Mr. Tulliver's farming and other stock, to be followed by a sale of the mill and land, held in the proper after-dinner hour at the Golden Lion. The miller himself, unaware of the lapse of time, fancied himself still in that first stage of his misfortunes when expedients might be thought of; and often in his conscious hours talked in a feeble, disjointed manner, of plans he would carry out when he "got well." The wife and children were not without hope of an issue that would at least save Mr. Tulliver from leaving the old spot, and seeking an entirely strange life. For uncle Deane had been induced to interest himself in this stage of the business. It would not, he acknowledged, be a bad speculation for Guest & Co. to buy Dorlcote Mill, and carry on the business, which was a good one, and might be increased by the addition of steam-power; in which case Tulliver might be retained as manager. Still Mr. Deane would say nothing decided about the matter: the fact that Wakem held the mortgage on the land might put it into his head to bid for the whole estate, and further, to outbid the cautious firm of Guest & Co., who did not carry on business on sentimental grounds. Mr. Deane was obliged to tell Mrs. Tulliver something to that effect, when he rode over to the mill to inspect the books in company with Mrs. Glegg: for she had observed that "if Guest & Co. would only think about it, Mr. Tulliver's father and grandfather had been carrying on Dorlcote Mill long before the oil-mill of that firm had been so much as thought of." Mr. Deane, in reply, doubted whether that was precisely the relation between the two mills which would determine their value as invest-ments. As for uncle Glegg, the thing lay quite beyond his imagination; the good-natured man felt sincere pity for the Tulliver family, but his money was all locked up in excellent mortgages, and he could run no risk; that would be unfair to his own relatives; but he had made up his mind that Tulliver should have some new flannel waistcoats which he had himself renounced in favour of a more elastic commodity, and that he would buy Mrs. Tulliver a pound of tea now and then; it would be a journey which his benevolence delighted in beforehand, to carry the tea, and see her pleasure on being assured it was the best black.

Still, it was clear that Mr. Deane was kindly disposed towards the Tullivers. One day he had brought Lucy, who was come home for the Christmas holidays, and the little blond angel-head had pressed itself against Maggie's darker cheek with many kisses and some tears. These fair slim daughters keep up a tender spot in the heart of many a respec-table partner in a respectable firm, and perhaps Lucy's anxious pitying questions about her poor cousins helped to make uncle Deane more prompt in finding Tom a temporary place in the warehouse, and in putting him in the way of getting evening lessons in book-keeping and calculation.

That might have cheered the lad and fed his hopes a little, if there had not come at the same time the much-dreaded blow of finding that his father must be a bankrupt, after all; at least, the creditors must be asked to take less than their due, which to Tom's untechnical mind was the same thing as bankruptcy. His father must not only be said to have "lost his property," but to have "failed"—the word that carried the worst obloquy to Tom's mind. For when the defendant's claim for costs had been satisfied, there would remain the friendly bill of Mr.

Gore, and the deficiency at the bank, as well as the other debts, which would make the assets shrink into unequivocal disproportion: "not more than ten or twelve shillings in the pound," predicted Mr. Deane, in a decided tone, tightening his lips; and the words fell on Tom like a scalding liquid, leaving a continual smart.

He was sadly in want of something to keep up his spirits a little in the unpleasant newness of his position—suddenly transported from the easy carpeted ennui of study-hours at Mr. Stelling's, and the busy idleness of castle-building in a "last half" at school, to the companionship of sacks and hides, and bawling men thundering down heavy weights at his elbow. The first step towards getting on in the world was a chill, dusty, noisy affair, and implied going without one's tea in order to stay in St. Ogg's and have an evening lesson from a one-armed elderly clerk, in a room smelling strongly of bad tobacco. Tom's young pink-and-white face had its colours very much deadened by the time he took off his hat at home, and sat down with keen hunger to his supper. No wonder he was a little cross if his mother or Maggie spoke to him.

But all this while Mrs. Tulliver was brooding over a scheme by which she, and no one else, would avert the result most to be dreaded, and prevent Wakem from entertaining the purpose of bidding for the mill. Imagine a truly respectable and amiable hen, by some portentous anomaly, taking to reflection and inventing combinations by which she might prevail on Hodge not to wring her neck, or send her and her chicks to market: the result could hardly be other than much cackling and fluttering. Mrs. Tulliver, seeing that everything had gone wrong, had begun to think that she had been too passive in life; and that, if she had applied her mind to business, and taken a strong resolution now and then, it would have been all the better for her and her family. Nobody, it appeared, had thought of going to speak to Wakem on this business of the mill; and yet, Mrs. Tulliver reflected, it would have been quite the shortest method of securing the right end. It would have been of no use, to be sure, for Mr. Tulliver to go—even if he had been able and willing—for he had been "going to law against Wakem" and abusing him for the last ten years; Wakem was always likely to have a spite against him. And now that Mrs. Tulliver had come to the conclusion that her husband was very much in the wrong to bring her into this trouble, she was inclined to think that his opinion of Wakem was wrong too. To be sure, Wakem had "put the bailies in the house, and sold them up;" but she supposed he did that to please the man that lent Mr. Tulliver the money, for a lawyer had more folks to please than one, and he wasn't likely to put Mr. Tulliver, who had gone to law with him, above everybody else in the world. The attorney might be a very reasonable man—why not? He had married a Miss Clint, and at the time Mrs. Tulliver had heard of that marriage, the summer when she wore her blue satin spencer, and had not yet any thoughts of Mr. Tulliver, she knew no harm of Wakem. And certainly towards herself —whom he knew to have been a Miss Dodson—it was out of all possibility that he could entertain anything but good-will, when it was once brought home to his observation that she, for her part, had never wanted to go to law, and indeed was at present disposed to take Mr. Wakem's view of all subjects rather than her husband's. In fact, if that attorney saw a respectable matron like herself disposed "to give him good words," why shouldn't he listen to her representations? For she would put the matter clearly before him, which had never been done yet. And he would never go and bid for the mill on purpose to spite her, an innocent woman, who thought it likely enough that she had danced with him in their youth at Squire Darleigh's, for at those big dances she had often and often danced with young men whose names she had forgotten.

Mrs. Tulliver hid these reasonings in her own bosom; for when she had thrown out a hint to Mr. Deane and Mr. Glegg, that she wouldn't mind going to speak to Wakem herself, they had said, "No, no, no," and "Pooh, pooh," and "Let Wakem alone," in the tone of men who were not likely to give a candid attention to a more definite exposition of her project; still less dared she mention the plan to Tom and Maggie, for "the children were always so against everything their mother said;" and Tom, she observed, was almost as much set against Wakem as his father was. But this unusual concentration of thought naturally gave Mrs. Tulliver an unusual power of device and determination; and a day or two before the sale, to be held at the Golden Lion, when there was no longer any time to be lost, she carried out her plan by a stratagem. There were pickles in question—a large stock of pickles and ketchup which Mrs. Tulliver possessed, and which Mr. Hyndmarsh the grocer would certainly purchase if she could transact the business in a personal interview, so she would walk with Tom to St. Ogg's that morning: and when Tom urged that she might let the pickles be, at present —he didn't like her to go about just yet—she appeared so hurt at this conduct in her son, contradicting her about pickles which she had made after the family receipts inherited from his own grandmother, who had died when his mother was a little girl, that he gave way, and they walked together until she turned towards Danish Street, where Mr. Hyndmarsh retailed his grocery, not far from the offices of Mr. Wakem.

That gentleman was not yet come to his office: would Mrs. Tulliver sit down by the fire in his private room and wait for him? She had not long to wait before the punctual attorney entered, knitting his brow with an examining glance at the stout blond woman who rose, curtsying deferentially:—a tallish man, with an aquiline nose and abundant iron-grey hair. You have never seen Mr. Wakem before, and are possibly wondering whether he was really as eminent a rascal, and as crafty, bitter an enemy of honest humanity in general, and of Mr. Tulliver in particular, as he is represented to be in that eidolon or portrait of him which we have seen to exist in the miller's mind.

It is clear that the irascible miller was a man to interpret any chance-shot that grazed him as an attempt on his own life, and was liable to entanglements in this puzzling world, which, due consideration had to his own infallibility, required the hypothesis of a very active diabolical agency to explain them. It is still possible to believe that the attorney was not more guilty towards him, than an ingenious machine, which performs its work with much regularity, is guilty towards the rash man who, venturing too near it, is caught up by some fly-wheel or other, and suddenly converted into unexpected sausages.

But it is really impossible to decide this question by a glance at his person: the lines and lights of the human countenance are like other symbols—not always easy to read without a key. On an *a priori* view of Wakem's aquiline nose, which offended Mr. Tulliver, there was not more rascality than in the shape of his stiff shirt-collar, though this too, along with his nose, might have become fraught with damnatory meaning when once the rascality was ascertained.

"Mrs. Tulliver, I think?" said Mr. Wakem.

"Yes, sir. Miss Elizabeth Dodson as was."

"Pray be seated. You have some business with me?"

"Well, sir, yes," said Mrs. Tulliver, beginning to feel alarmed at her own courage, now she was really in presence of the formidable man, and reflecting that she had not settled with herself how she should begin. Mr. Wakem felt in his waistcoat pockets, and looked at her in silence.

"I hope, sir," she began at last—"I hope, sir, you're not a-thinking as *I* bear you any ill-will because o' my husband's losing his lawsuit, and the bailies being put in, and the linen being sold—O dear! . . . for I wasn't brought up in that way. I'm sure you remember my father, sir, for he was close friends with Squire Darleigh, and we allays went to the dances there—the Miss Dodsons—nobody could be more looked on—and justly, for there was four of us, and you're quite aware as Mrs. Glegg and Mrs. Deane are my sisters. And as for going to law, and losing money, and having sales before you're dead, I never saw anything o' that before I was married, nor for a long while after. And I'm not to be answerable for my bad luck i' marrying out o' my own family into one where the goings-on was different. And as for being drawn in t' abuse you as other folks abuse you, sir, *that* I niver was, and nobody can say it of me."

Mrs. Tulliver shook her head a little, and looked at the hem of her pocket-handkerchief.

"I've no doubt of what you say, Mrs. Tulliver," said Mr. Wakem, with cold politeness. "But you have some question to ask me?"

"Well, sir, yes. But that's what I've said to myself—I've said you'd have some nat'ral feeling; and as for my husband, as hasn't been himself for this two months, I'm not a-defending him, in no way, for being so hot about th' erigation—not but what there's worse men, for he never wronged nobody of a shilling nor a penny, not willingly—and as for his fieriness and lawing, what could I do? And him struck as if it was with death when he got the letter as said you'd the hold upo' the land. But I can't believe but what you'll behave as a gentleman."

"What does all this mean, Mrs. Tulliver?" said Mr. Wakem, rather sharply. "What do you want to ask me?"

"Why, sir, if you'll be so good," said Mrs. Tulliver, starting a little, and speaking more hurriedly, "if you'll be so good not to buy the mill an' the land—the land wouldn't so much matter, only my husband 'ull be like mad at your having it."

Something like a new thought flashed across Mr. Wakem's face as he said, "Who told you I meant to buy it?"

"Why, sir, it's none o' my inventing; and I should never ha' thought of it, for my husband, as ought to know about the law, he allays used to say as lawyers had never no call to buy anything—either lands or houses—for they allays got 'em into their hands other ways. An' I should think that 'ud be the way with you, sir; and I niver said as you'd be the man to do contrairy to that."

"Ah, well, who was it that *did* say so?" said Wakem, opening his desk, and moving things about, with the accompaniment of an almost inaudible whistle.

"Why, sir, it was Mr. Glegg and Mr. Deane, as have all the management: and Mr. Deane thinks as Guest & Co. 'ud buy the mill and let Mr. Tulliver work it for 'em, if you didn't bid for it and raise the price. And it 'ud be such a thing for my husband to stay where he is, if he could get his living: for it was his father's before him, the mill was, and his grandfather built it, though I wasn't fond o' the noise of it, when first I was married, for there was no mills in our family—not the Dodsons—and if I'd known as the mills had so much to do with the law, it wouldn't have been me as 'ud have been the first Dodson to marry one; but I went into it blindfold, that I did, erigation and everything."

"What! Guest & Co. would keep the mill in their own hands, I suppose, and pay your husband wages?"

"O dear, sir, it's hard to think of," said poor Mrs. Tulliver, a little tear making its way, "as my husband should take wage. But it 'ud look more like what used to be, to stay at the mill than to go anywhere else; and if you'll only think—if you was to bid for the mill and buy it, my husband might be struck worse than he was before, and niver get better again as he's getting now."

"Well, but if I bought the mill, and allowed your husband to act as my manager in the same way, how then?" said Mr. Wakem.

"O, sir, I doubt he could niver be got to do it, not if the very mill stood still to beg and pray of him. For your name's like poison to him, it's so as never was; and he looks upon it as you've been the ruin of him all along, ever since you set the law on him about the road through the meadow—that's eight year ago, and he's been going on ever since—as I've allays told him he was wrong . . ."

"He's a pig-headed, foul-mouthed fool!" burst out Mr. Wakem, forgetting himself.

"O dear, sir!" said Mrs. Tulliver, frightened at a result so different from the one she had fixed her mind on; "I wouldn't wish to contradict you, but it's like enough he's changed his mind with this illness—he's forgot a many things he used to talk about. And you wouldn't like to have a corpse on your mind, if he was to die; and they *do* say as it's allays unlucky when Dorlcote Mill changes hands, and the water might all run away, and *then* . . . not as I'm wishing you any ill-luck, sir, for I forgot to tell you as I remember your wedding as if it was yesterday—Mrs. Wakem was a Miss Clint, I know *that*—and my boy, as there isn't a nicer, handsomer, straighter boy nowhere, went to school with your son . . ."

Mr. Wakem rose, opened the door, and called to one of his clerks.

"You must excuse me for interrupting you, Mrs. Tulliver; I have business that must be attended to; and I think there is nothing more, necessary to be said."

"But if you *would* bear it in mind, sir," said Mrs. Tulliver, rising, "and not run against me and my children; and I'm not denying Mr. Tulliver's been in the wrong, but he's been punished enough, and there's worse men, for it's been giving to other folks has been his fault. He's done nobody any harm but himself and his family—the more's the pity —and I go and look at the bare shelves every day, and think where all my things used to stand."

"Yes, yes, I'll bear it in mind," said Mr. Wakem, hastily, looking towards the open door.

"And if you'd please not to say as I've been to speak to you, for my son 'ud be very angry with me for demeaning myself, I know he would, and I've trouble enough without being scolded by my children."

Poor Mrs. Tulliver's voice trembled a little, and she could make no answer to the attorney's "good morning," but curtsied and walked out in silence.

"Which day is it that Dorlcote Mill is to be sold? Where's the bill?" said Mr. Wakem to his clerk when they were alone.

"Next Friday is the day: Friday, at six o'clock."

"Oh! just run to Winship's, the auctioneer, and see if he's at home. I have some business for him: ask him to come up."

Although, when Mr. Wakem entered his office that morning, he had had no intention of purchasing Dorlcote Mill, his mind was already made up: Mrs. Tulliver had suggested to him several determining motives, and his mental glance was very rapid: he was one of those men who can be prompt without being rash, because their motives run in fixed tracks, and they have no need to reconcile conflicting aims.

To suppose that Wakem had the same sort of inveterate hatred towards Tulliver, that Tulliver had towards him, would be like supposing that a pike and a roach can look at each other from a similar point of view. The roach necessarily abhors the mode in which the pike gets his living, and the pike is likely to think nothing further even of the most indignant roach than that he is excellent good eating; it could only be when the roach choked him that the pike could entertain a strong personal animosity. If Mr. Tulliver had ever seriously injured or thwarted

the attorney, Wakem would not have refused him the distinction of
being a special object of his vindictiveness. But when Mr. Tulliver
called Wakem a rascal at the market dinner-table, the attorney's clients
were not a whit inclined to withdraw their business from him; and if,
when Wakem himself happened to be present, some jocose cattle-
feeder, stimulated by opportunity and brandy, made a thrust at him by
alluding to old ladies' wills, he maintained perfect *sang froid,* and knew
quite well that the majority of substantial men then present were perfectly contented with the fact that "Wakem was Wakem;" that is to
say, a man who always knew the stepping-stones that would carry him
through very muddy bits of practice. A man who had made a large
fortune, had a handsome house among the trees at Tofton, and decidedly the finest stock of port-wine in the neighbourhood of St. Ogg's,
was likely to feel himself on a level with public opinion. And I am not
sure that even honest Mr. Tulliver himself, with his general view of law
as a cockpit, might not, under opposite circumstances, have seen a fine
appropriateness in the truth that "Wakem was Wakem;" since I have
understood from persons versed in history, that mankind is not disposed
to look narrowly into the conduct of great victors when their victory is
on the right side. Tulliver, then, could be no obstruction to Wakem;
on the contrary, he was a poor devil whom the lawyer had defeated
several times—a hot-tempered fellow, who would always give you a
handle against him. Wakem's conscience was not uneasy because he had
used a few tricks against the miller: why should he hate that unsuccessful plaintiff—that pitiable, furious bull entangled in the meshes of
a net?

Still, among the various excesses to which human nature is subject,
moralists have never numbered that of being too fond of the people who
openly revile us. The successful Yellow candidate for the borough of
Old Topping, perhaps, feels no pursuant meditative hatred toward the
Blue editor who consoles his subscribers with vituperative rhetoric
against Yellow men who sell their country, and are the demons of
private life; but he might not be sorry, if law and opportunity favoured,
to kick that Blue editor to a deeper shade of his favourite colour.
Prosperous men take a little vengeance now and then, as they take a
diversion, when it comes easily in their way, and is no hindrance to
business; and such small unimpassioned revenges have an enormous
effect in life, running through all degrees of pleasant infliction, blocking
the fit men out of places, and blackening characters in unpremeditated
talk. Still more, to see people who have been only insignificantly offensive to us, reduced in life and humiliated without any special efforts
of ours, is apt to have a soothing, flattering influence: Providence, or
some other prince of this world, it appears, has undertaken the task of
retribution for us; and really, by an agreeable constitution of things,
our enemies, somehow, *don't* prosper.

Wakem was not without this parenthetic vindictiveness towards the
uncomplimentary miller; and now Mrs. Tulliver had put the notion into

his head, it presented itself to him as a pleasure to do the very thing that would cause Mr. Tulliver the most deadly mortification,—and a pleasure of a complex kind, not made up of crude malice, but mingling with it the relish of self-approbation. To see an enemy humiliated gives a certain contentment, but this is jejune compared with the highly blent satisfaction of seeing him humiliated by your benevolent action or concession on his behalf. That is a sort of revenge which falls into the scale of virtue, and Wakem was not without an intention of keeping that scale respectably filled. He had once had the pleasure of putting an old enemy of his into one of the St. Ogg's alms-houses, to the rebuilding of which he had given a large subscription; and here was an opportunity of providing for another by making him his own servant. Such things give a completeness to prosperity, and contribute elements of agreeable consciousness that are not dreamed of by that short-sighted, over-heated vindictiveness, which goes out of its way to wreak itself in direct injury. And Tulliver, with his rough tongue filed by a sense of obligation, would make a better servant than any chance-fellow who was cap-in-hand for a situation. Tulliver was known to be a man of proud honesty, and Wakem was too acute not to believe in the existence of honesty. He was given to observing individuals, not to judging of them according to maxims, and no one knew better than he that all men were not like himself. Besides, he intended to overlook the whole business of land and mill pretty closely: he was fond of these practical rural matters. But there were good reasons for purchasing Dorlcote Mill, quite apart from any benevolent vengeance on the miller. It was really a capital investment; besides, Guest & Co. were going to bid for it. Mr. Guest and Mr. Wakem were on friendly dining terms, and the attorney liked to predominate over a ship-owner and mill-owner who was a little too loud in the town affairs as well as in his table-talk. For Wakem was not a mere man of business: he was considered a pleasant fellow in the upper circles of St. Ogg's—chatted amusingly over his port-wine, did a little amateur farming, and had certainly been an excellent husband and father: at church, when he went there, he sat under the handsomest of mural monuments erected to the memory of his wife. Most men would have married again under his circumstances, but he was said to be more tender to his deformed son than most men were to their best-shapen offspring. Not that Mr. Wakem had not other sons besides Philip; but towards them he held only a chiaroscuro parentage, and provided for them in a grade of life duly beneath his own. In this fact, indeed, there lay the clenching motive to the purchase of Dorlcote Mill. While Mrs. Tulliver was talking, it had occurred to the rapid-minded lawyer, among all the other circumstances of the case, that this purchase would, in a few years to come, furnish a highly suitable position for a certain favourite lad whom he meant to bring on in the world.

These were the mental conditions on which Mrs. Tulliver had undertaken to act persuasively, and had failed: a fact which may receive some illustration from the remark of a great philosopher, that fly-fishers fail in preparing their bait so as to make it alluring in the right quarter, for want of a due acquaintance with the subjectivity of fishes.

CHAPTER VIII

DAYLIGHT ON THE WRECK

It was a clear frosty January day on which Mr. Tulliver first came down-stairs: the bright sun on the chestnut boughs and the roofs opposite his window had made him impatiently declare that he would be caged up no longer: he thought everywhere would be more cheery under this sunshine than his bedroom; for he knew nothing of the bareness below, which made the flood of sunshine importunate, as if it had an unfeeling pleasure in showing the empty places, and the marks where well-known objects once had been. The impression on his mind that it was but yesterday when he received the letter from Mr. Gore was so continually implied in his talk, and the attempts to convey to him the idea that many weeks had passed and much had happened since then, had been so soon swept away by recurrent forgetfulness, that even Mr. Turnbull had begun to despair of preparing him to meet the facts by previous knowledge. The full sense of the present could only be imparted gradually by new experience—not by mere words, which must remain weaker than the impressions left by the *old* experience. This resolution to come down-stairs was heard with trembling by the wife and children. Mrs. Tulliver said Tom must not go to St. Ogg's at the usual hour—he must wait and see his father down-stairs: and Tom complied, though with an intense inward shrinking from the painful scene. The hearts of all three had been more deeply dejected than ever during the last few days. For Guest & Co. had not bought the mill: both mill and land had been knocked down to Wakem, who had been over the premises, and had laid before Mr. Deane and Mr. Glegg, in Mrs. Tulliver's presence, his willingness to employ Mr. Tulliver, in case of his recovery, as a manager of the business. This proposition had occasioned much family debating. Uncles and aunts were almost unanimously of opinion that such an offer ought not to be rejected when there was nothing in the way but a feeling in Mr. Tulliver's mind, which, as neither aunts nor uncles shared it, was regarded as entirely unreasonable and childish—indeed, as a transferring towards Wakem of that indignation and hatred which Mr. Tulliver ought properly to have directed against himself for his general quarrelsomeness, and his special exhibition of it in going to law. Here was an opportunity for Mr. Tulliver to provide for his wife and daughter without any assistance from his wife's relations, and without that too evident descent into pauperism which makes it annoying to respectable people to meet the degraded member of the family by the wayside. Mr. Tulliver, Mrs. Glegg considered, must be made to feel, when he came to his right mind, that he could never humble himself enough; for *that* had come which she had always foreseen would come of his insolence in time past "to them as were the best friends he'd got to look to." Mr. Glegg and Mr. Deane were less stern in their views, but they both of them thought Tulliver had done enough harm by his hot-tempered crotchets, and ought to put them out of the question when a livelihood was offered him: Wakem showed a right feeling about the matter—*he* had no grudge against Tulliver. Tom had protested against entertaining the proposition: he shouldn't like his father to be under Wakem; he thought it would look mean-spirited; but his mother's main distress was the utter impossibility of ever "turning Mr. Tulliver round about Wakem," or getting him to hear reason—no, they would all have to go and live in a pigsty on purpose to spite Wakem, who spoke "so as nobody could be fairer." Indeed, Mrs. Tulliver's mind was reduced to such confusion by living in this strange medium of unaccountable sorrow, against which she continually appealed by asking, "O dear, what *have* I done to deserve worse than other women?" that Maggie began to suspect her poor mother's wits were quite going.

"Tom," she said, when they were out of their father's room together, "we *must* try to make father understand a little of what has happened before he goes down-stairs. But we must get my mother away. She will say something that will do harm. Ask Kezia to fetch her down, and keep her engaged with something in the kitchen."

Kezia was equal to the task. Having declared her intention of staying till the master could get about again, "wage or no wage," she had found a certain recompense in keeping a strong hand over her mistress, scolding her for "moithering" herself, and going about all day without changing her cap, and looking as if she was "mushed." Altogether, this time of trouble was rather a Saturnalian time to Kezia: she could scold her betters with unreproved freedom. On this particular occasion there were drying clothes to be fetched in: she wished to know if one pair of hands could do everything indoors and out, and observed that *she* should have thought it would be good for Mrs. Tulliver to put on her bonnet, and get a breath of fresh air by doing that needful piece of work. Poor Mrs. Tulliver went submissively down-stairs: to be ordered about by a servant was the last remnant of her household dignities— she would soon have no servant to scold her.

Mr. Tulliver was resting in his chair a little after the fatigue of dressing, and Maggie and Tom were seated near him, when Luke entered to ask if he should help master down-stairs.

"Ay, ay, Luke, stop a bit, sit down," said Mr. Tulliver, pointing his stick towards a chair, and looking at him with that pursuant gaze which convalescent persons often have for those who have tended them, reminding one of an infant gazing about after its nurse. For Luke had been a constant night-watcher by his master's bed.

"How's the water now, eh, Luke?" said Mr. Tulliver. "Dix hasn't been choking you up again, eh?"

"No, sir, it's all right."

"Ay, I thought not: he won't be in a hurry at that again, now Riley's been to settle him. That was what I said to Riley yesterday . . . I said . . ."

Mr. Tulliver leaned forward, resting his elbows on the arm-chair, and looking on the ground as if in search of something—striving after vanishing images like a man struggling against a doze. Maggie looked at Tom in mute distress—their father's mind was so far off the present, which would by-and-by thrust itself on his wandering consciousness! Tom was almost ready to rush away, with that impatience of painful emotion which makes one of the differences between youth and maiden, man and woman.

"Father," said Maggie, laying her hand on his, "don't you remember that Mr. Riley is dead?"

"Dead?" said Mr. Tulliver, sharply, looking in her face with a strange, examining glance.

"Yes, he died of apoplexy nearly a year ago; I remember hearing you say you had to pay money for him; and he left his daughters badly off —one of them is under-teacher at Miss Firniss's, where I've been to school, you know . . ."

"Ah?" said her father, doubtfully, still looking in her face. But as soon as Tom began to speak he turned to look at *him* with the same inquiring glances, as if he were rather surprised at the presence of these two young people. Whenever his mind was wandering in the far past, he fell into this oblivion of their actual faces: they were not those of the lad and the little wench who belonged to that past.

"It's a long while since you had the dispute with Dix, father," said Tom. "I remember your talking about it three years ago, before I went to school at Mr. Stelling's. I've been at school there three years; don't you remember?"

Mr. Tulliver threw himself backward again, losing the childlike outward glance under a rush of new ideas, which diverted him from external impressions.

"Ay, ay," he said, after a minute or two, "I've paid a deal o' money . . . I was determined my son should have a good eddication: I'd none myself, and I've felt the miss of it. And he'll want no other fortin': that's what I say . . . if Wakem was to get the better of me again . . ."

The thought of Wakem roused new vibrations, and after a moment's pause he began to look at the coat he had on, and to feel in his side-pocket. Then he turned to Tom, and said in his old sharp way, "Where have they put Gore's letter?"

It was close at hand in a drawer, for he had often asked for it before.

"You know what there is in the letter, father?" said Tom, as he gave it to him.

"To be sure I do," said Mr. Tulliver, rather angrily. "What o' that? If Furley can't take to the property, somebody else can: there's plenty o' people in the world besides Furley. But it's hindering—my not being well—go and tell 'em to get the horse in the gig, Luke: I can get down to St. Ogg's well enough—Gore's expecting me."

"No, dear father!" Maggie burst out entreatingly, "it's a very long while since all that: you've been ill a great many weeks—more than two months—everything is changed."

Mr. Tulliver looked at them all three alternately with a startled gaze: the idea that much had happened of which he knew nothing had often transiently arrested him before, but it came upon him now with entire novelty.

"Yes, father," said Tom, in answer to the gaze. "You needn't trouble your mind about business until you are quite well: everything is settled about that for the present—about the mill and the land and the debts."

"What's settled, then?" said his father, angrily.

"Don't you take on too much about it, sir," said Luke. "You'd ha' paid iverybody if you could—that's what I said to Master Tom—I said you'd ha' paid iverybody if you could."

Good Luke felt, after the manner of contented hard-working men whose lives have been spent in servitude, that sense of natural fitness in rank which made his master's downfall a tragedy to him. He was urged, in his slow way, to say something that would express his share in the family sorrow, and these words, which he had used over and over again to Tom when he wanted to decline the full payment of his fifty pounds out of the children's money, were the most ready to his tongue. They were just the words to lay the most painful hold on his master's bewildered mind.

"Paid everybody?" he said, with vehement agitation, his face flushing, and his eye lighting up. "Why . . . what . . . have they made me a *bankrupt?*"

"O, father, dear father!" said Maggie, who thought that terrible word really represented the fact; "bear it well—because we love you—your children will always love you. Tom will pay them all; he says he will, when he's a man."

She felt her father beginning to tremble—his voice trembled too, as he said, after a few moments—

"Ay, my little wench, but I shall never live twice o'er."

"But perhaps you will live to see me pay everybody, father," said Tom, speaking with a great effort.

"Ah, my lad," said Mr. Tulliver, shaking his head slowly, "but what's broke can never be whole again: it 'ud be your doing, not mine." Then, looking up at him, "You're only sixteen—it's an up-hill fight for you— but you mustn't throw it at your father; the raskills have been too many for him. I've given you a good eddication—that'll start you."

Something in his throat half-choked the last words; the flush which had alarmed his children because it had so often preceded a recurrence of paralysis, had subsided, and his face looked pale and tremulous.

Tom said nothing: he was still struggling against his inclination to rush away. His father remained quiet a minute or two, but his mind did not seem to be wandering again.

"Have they sold me up, then?" he said, more calmly, as if he were possessed simply by the desire to know what had happened.

"Everything is sold, father; but we don't know all about the mill and the land yet," said Tom, anxious to ward off any question leading to the fact that Wakem was the purchaser.

"You must not be surprised to see the room look very bare downstairs, father," said Maggie; "but there's your chair and the bureau—*they're* not gone."

"Let us go—help me down, Luke—I'll go and see everything," said Mr. Tulliver, leaning on his stick, and stretching out his other hand towards Luke.

"Ay, sir," said Luke, as he gave his arm to his master, "you'll make up your mind to't a bit better when you've seen iverything: you'll get used to't. That's what my mother says about her shortness o' breath—she says she's made friends wi't now, though she fought again' it sore when it fust come on."

Maggie ran on before to see that all was right in the dreary parlour, where the fire, dulled by the frosty sunshine, seemed part of the general shabbiness. She turned her father's chair, and pushed aside the table to make an easy way for him, and then stood with a beating heart to see him enter and look round for the first time. Tom advanced before him, carrying the leg-rest, and stood beside Maggie on the hearth. Of those two young hearts Tom's suffered the most unmixed pain, for Maggie, with all her keen susceptibility, yet felt as if the sorrow made larger room for her love to flow in, and gave breathing-space to her passionate nature. No true boy feels that: he would rather go and slay the Nemean lion, or perform any round of heroic labours, than endure perpetual appeals to his pity, for evils over which he can make no conquest.

Mr. Tulliver paused just inside the door, resting on Luke, and looking round him at all the bare places, which for him were filled with the shadows of departed objects—the daily companions of his life. His faculties seemed to be renewing their strength from getting a footing on this demonstration of the senses.

"Ah!" he said, slowly, moving towards his chair, "they've sold me up . . . they've sold me up."

Then seating himself, and laying down his stick, while Luke left the room, he looked round again.

"They'n left the big Bible," he said. "It's got everything in—when I was born and married—bring it me, Tom."

The quarto Bible was laid open before him at the fly-leaf, and while he was reading with slowly-travelling eyes, Mrs. Tulliver entered the room, but stood in mute surprise to find her husband down already, and with the great Bible before him.

"Ah," he said, looking at a spot where his finger rested, "my mother was Margaret Beaton—she died when she was forty-seven: hers wasn't a long-lived family—we're our mother's children—Gritty and me are—we shall go to our last bed before long."

He seemed to be pausing over the record of his sister's birth and marriage, as if it were suggesting new thoughts to them: then he suddenly looked up at Tom, and said, in a sharp tone of alarm—

"They haven't come upo' Moss for the money as I lent him, have they?"

"No, father," said Tom, "the note was burnt."

Mr. Tulliver turned his eyes on the page again, and presently said—

"Ah . . . Elizabeth Dodson . . . it's eighteen year since I married her . . ."

"Come next Ladyday," said Mrs. Tulliver, going up to his side and looking at the page.

Her husband fixed his eyes earnestly on her face.

"Poor Bessy," he said, "you was a pretty lass then—everybody said so—and I used to think you kept your good looks rarely. But you're sorely aged . . . don't you bear me ill-will . . . I meant to do well by you. . . . We promised one another for better or for worse. . . ."

"But I never thought it 'ud be so for worse as this," said poor Mrs. Tulliver, with the strange, scared look that had come over her of late, "and my poor father gave me away . . . and to come on so all at once . . ."

"O, mother," said Maggie, "don't talk in that way."

'No, I know you won't let your poor mother speak . . . that's been the way all my life . . . your father never minded what I said . . . it 'ud have been o' no use for me to beg and pray . . . and it 'ud be no use now, not if I was to go down o' my hands and knees . . ."

"Don't say so, Bessy," said Mr. Tulliver, whose pride, in these first moments of humiliation, was in abeyance to the sense of some justice in his wife's reproach. "If there's anything left as I could do to make you amends, I wouldn't say you nay."

"Then we might stay here and get a living, and I might keep among my own sisters . . . and me been such a good wife to you, and never crossed you from week's end to week's end . . . and they all say so . . . they say it 'ud be nothing but right . . . only you're so turned against Wakem."

"Mother," said Tom, severely, "this is not the time to talk about that."

"Let her be," said Mr. Tulliver. "Say what you mean, Bessy."

"Why, now the mill and the land's all Wakem's, and he's got everything in his hands, what's the use o' setting your face against him?—when he says you may stay here, and speaks as fair as can be, and says you may manage the business, and have thirty shilling a-week, and a horse to ride about to market? And where have we got to put our heads? We must go into one o' the cottages in the village . . . and me and my children brought down to that . . . and all because you must set your mind against folks till there's no turning you."

Mr. Tulliver had sunk back in his chair, trembling.

"You may do as you like wi' me, Bessy," he said in a low voice; "I'n been the bringing of you to poverty . . . this world's too many for me . . . I'm nought but a bankrupt—it's no use standing up for anything now."

"Father," said Tom, "I don't agree with my mother or my uncles, and I don't think you ought to submit to be under Wakem. I get a pound a-week now, and you can find something else to do when you get well."

"Say no more, Tom, say no more: I've had enough for this day. Give me a kiss, Bessy, and let us bear one another no ill-will: we shall never be young again. . . . This world's been too many for me."

CHAPTER IX

AN ITEM ADDED TO THE FAMILY REGISTER

THAT first moment of renunciation and submission was followed by days of violent struggle in the miller's mind, as the gradual access of bodily strength brought with it increasing ability to embrace in one view all the conflicting conditions under which he found himself. Feeble limbs easily resign themselves to be tethered, and when we are subdued by sickness it seems possible to us to fulfil pledges which the old vigour comes back and breaks. There were times when poor Tulliver thought the fulfilment of his promise to Bessy was something quite too hard for human nature: he had promised her without knowing what she was going to say—she might as well have asked him to carry a ton weight on his back. But again, there were many feelings arguing on her side, besides the sense that life had been made hard to her by having married him. He saw a possibility, by much pinching, of saving money out of his salary towards paying a second dividend to his creditors, and it would not be easy elsewhere to get a situation such as he could fill. He had led an easy life, ordering much and working little, and had no aptitude for any new business. He must perhaps take to day-labour, and his wife must have help from her sisters—a prospect doubly bitter to him, now they had let all Bessy's precious things be sold, probably because they liked to set her against him, by making her feel that he had brought her to that pass. He listened to their admonitory talk, when they came to urge on him what he was bound to do for poor Bessy's sake, with averted eyes, that every now and then flashed on them furtively when their backs were turned. Nothing but the dread of needing their help could have made it an easier alternative to take their advice.

But the strongest influence of all was the love of the old premises where he had run about when he was a boy, just as Tom had done after him. The Tullivers had lived on this spot for generations, and he had sat listening on a low stool on winter evenings while his father talked of the old half-timbered mill that had been there before the last great floods which damaged it so that his grandfather pulled it down and built the new one. It was when he got able to walk about and look at all the old objects, that he felt the strain of this clinging affection for the old home as part of his life, part of himself. He couldn't bear to think of himself living on any other spot than this, where he knew the sound of every gate and door, and felt that the shape and colour of every roof and weather-stain and broken hillock was good, because his growing senses had been fed on them. Our instructed vagrancy, which has hardly time to linger by the hedgerows, but runs away early to the tropics, and is at home with palms and banyans,—which is nourished on books of travel, and stretches the theatre of its imagination to the Zambesi, can hardly get a dim notion of what an old-fashioned man like Tulliver felt for this spot, where all his memories centred, and where life seemed like a familiar smooth-handled tool that the fingers clutch with loving ease. And just now he was living in that freshened memory of the far-off time which comes to us in the passive hours of recovery from sickness.

"Ay, Luke," he said, one afternoon, as he stood looking over the orchard gate, "I remember the day they planted those apple-trees. My father was a huge man for planting—it was like a merry-making to him to get a cart full o' young trees—and I used to stand i' the cold with him, and follow him about like a dog."

Then he turned round, and, leaning against the gate-post, looked at the opposite buildings.

"The old mill 'ud miss me, I think, Luke. There's a story as when the mill changes hands, the river's angry—I've heard my father say it many a time. There's no telling whether there mayn't be summat *in* the story, for this is a puzzling world, and Old Harry's got a finger in it—it's been too many for me, I know."

"Ay, sir," said Luke, with soothing sympathy, "what wi' the rust on the wheat, an' the firin' o' the ricks an' that, as I've seen i' my time—things often looks comical: there's the bacon fat wi' our last pig runs away like butter—it leaves nought but a scratchin'."

"It's just as if it was yesterday, now," Mr. Tulliver went on, "when my father began the malting. I remember, the day they finished the malt-house, I thought summat great was to come of it; for we'd a plum-pudding that day and a bit of a feast, and I said to my mother—she was a fine dark-eyed woman, my mother was—the little wench 'ull be as like her as two peas."—Here Mr. Tulliver put his stick between his legs, and took out his snuff-box, for the greater enjoyment of this anec-dote, which dropped from him in fragments, as if he every other mo-ment lost narration in vision. "I was a little chap no higher much than my mother's knee—she was sore fond of us children, Gritty and me—

and so I said to her, 'Mother,' I said, 'shall we have plum-pudding *every* day because o' the malt-house?' She used to tell me o' that till her dying day. She was but a young woman when she died, my mother was. But it's forty good year since they finished the malt-house, and it isn't many days out of 'em all, as I haven't looked out in the yard there, the first thing in the morning—all weathers, from year's end to year's end. I should go off my head in a new place. I should be like as if I'd lost my way. It's all hard, whichever way I look at it—the harness 'ull gall me—but it 'ud be summat to draw along the old road, istead of a new un."

"Ay, sir," said Luke, "you'd be a deal better here nor in some new place. I can't abide new places mysen: things is allays awk'ard—narrow-wheeled waggins, belike, and the stiles all another sort, an' oatcake i' some places, tow'rt th' head o' the Floss, there. It's poor work, changing your country-side."

"But I doubt, Luke, they'll be for getting rid o' Ben, and making you do with a lad—and I must help a bit wi' the mill. You'll have a worse place."

"Ne'er mind, sir," said Luke, "I shan't plague mysen. I'n been wi' you twenty year, an' you can't get twenty year wi' whistlin' for 'em, no more nor you can make the trees grow: you mun wait till God A'mighty sends 'em. I can't abide new victual nor new faces, *I* can't—you niver know but what they'll gripe you."

The walk was finished in silence after this, for Luke had disburthened himself of thoughts to an extent that left his conversational resources quite barren, and Mr. Tulliver had relapsed from his recollections into a painful meditation on the choice of hardships before him. Maggie noticed that he was unusually absent that evening at tea; and afterwards he sat leaning forward in his chair, looking at the ground, moving his lips, and shaking his head from time to time. Then he looked hard at Mrs. Tulliver, who was knitting opposite him, then at Maggie, who, as she bent over her sewing, was intensely conscious of some drama going forward in her father's mind. Suddenly he took up the poker and broke the large coal fiercely.

"Dear heart, Mr. Tulliver, what can you be thinking of?" said his wife, looking up in alarm: "it's very wasteful, breaking the coal, and we've got hardly any large coal left, and I don't know where the rest is to come from."

"I don't think you're quite so well to-night, are you, father?" said Maggie; "you seem uneasy."

"Why, how is it Tom doesn't come?" said Mr. Tulliver, impatiently.

"Dear heart! is it time? I must go and get his supper," said Mrs. Tulliver, laying down her knitting, and leaving the room.

"It's nigh upon half-past eight," said Mr. Tulliver. "He'll be here soon. Go, go and get the big Bible, and open it at the beginning, where everything's set down. And get the pen and ink."

Maggie obeyed, wondering: but her father gave no further orders, and only sat listening for Tom's footfall on the gravel, apparently irritated by the wind, which had risen and was roaring so as to drown all other sounds. There was a strange light in his eyes that rather frightened Maggie: *she* began to wish that Tom would come, too.

"There he is, then," said Mr. Tulliver, in an excited way, when the knock came at last. Maggie went to open the door, but her mother came out of the kitchen hurriedly, saying, "Stop a bit, Maggie; I'll open it."

Mrs. Tulliver had begun to be a little frightened at her boy, but she was jealous of every office others did for him.

"Your supper's ready by the kitchen fire, my boy," she said, as he took off his hat and coat. "You shall have it by yourself, just as you like, and I won't speak to you."

"I think my father wants Tom, mother," said Maggie; "he must come into the parlour first."

Tom entered with his usual saddened evening face, but his eyes fell immediately on the open Bible and the inkstand, and he glanced with a look of anxious surprise at his father, who was saying—

"Come, come, you're late—I want you."

"Is there anything the matter, father?" said Tom.

"You sit down—all of you," said Mr. Tulliver, peremptorily. "And, Tom, sit down here; I've got something for you to write i' the Bible."

They all three sat down, looking at him. He began to speak, slowly, looking first at his wife.

"I've made up my mind, Bessy, and I'll be as good as my word to you. There's the same grave made for us to lie down in, and we mustn't be bearing one another ill-will. I'll stop in the old place, and I'll serve under Wakem—and I'll serve him like an honest man: there's no Tulliver but what's honest, mind that, Tom"—here his voice rose: "they'll have it to throw up against me as I paid a dividend—but it wasn't my fault—it was because there's raskills in the world. They've been too many for me, and I must give in. I'll put my neck in harness—for you've a right to say as I've brought you into trouble, Bessy—and I'll serve him as honest as if he was no raskill: I'm an honest man, though I shall never hold my head up no more—I'm a tree as is broke—a tree as is broke."

He paused, and looked on the ground. Then suddenly raising his head, he said in a louder yet deeper tone—

"But I won't forgive him! I know what they say—he never meant me any harm—that's the way Old Harry props up the raskills—he's been at the bottom of everything—but he's a fine gentleman—I know, I know. I shouldn't ha' gone to law, they say. But who made it so as there was no arbitratin', and no justice to be got? It signifies nothing to him—I know that: he's one o' them fine gentlemen as get money by doing business for poorer folks, and when he's made beggars of 'em, he'll give 'em charity. I won't forgive him! I wish he might be punished with shame till his own son 'ud like to forget him. I wish he may do summat as they'd make him work at the treadmill! But he won't—he's too big a raskill to let the law lay hold on him. And you mind this, Tom—you never forgive him, neither, if you mean to be my son. There'll maybe come a time when you may make him feel—it'll never come to me—I'n got my head under the yoke. Now write—write it i' the Bible."

"O, father, what?" said Maggie, sinking down by his knee, pale and trembling. "It's wicked to curse and bear malice."

"It isn't wicked, I tell you," said her father, fiercely. "It's wicked as the raskills should prosper—it's the devil's doing. Do as I tell you, Tom. Write."

"What am I to write, father?" said Tom, with gloomy submission.

"Write as your father, Edward Tulliver, took service under John Wakem, the man as had helped to ruin him, because I'd promised my wife to make her what amends I could for her trouble, and because I wanted to die in th' old place, where I was born and my father was born. Put that i' the right words—you know how—and then write, as I don't forgive Wakem, for all that; and for all I'll serve him honest, I wish evil may befall him. Write that."

There was a dead silence as Tom's pen moved along the paper: Mrs. Tulliver looked scared, and Maggie trembled like a leaf.

"Now let me hear what you've wrote," said Mr. Tulliver. Tom read aloud, slowly.

"Now write—write as you'll remember what Wakem's done to your father, and you'll make him and his feel it, if ever the day comes. And sign your name Thomas Tulliver."

"O, no, father, dear father!" said Maggie, almost choked with fear. "You shouldn't make Tom write that."

"Be quiet, Maggie!" said Tom. "I *shall* write it."

BOOK FOUR

The Valley of Humiliation

★

CHAPTER I

A VARIATION OF PROTESTANTISM UNKNOWN TO BOSSUET

JOURNEYING down the Rhone on a summer's day, you have perhaps
felt the sunshine made dreary by those ruined villages which stud the
banks in certain parts of its course, telling how the swift river once
rose, like an angry, destroying god, sweeping down the feeble generations whose breath is in their nostrils, and making their dwellings a
desolation. Strange contrast, you may have thought, between the effect
produced on us by these dismal remnants of commonplace houses, which
in their best days were but the sign of a sordid life, belonging in all
its details to our own vulgar era; and the effect produced by those
ruins on the castled Rhine, which have crumbled and mellowed into
such harmony with the green and rocky steeps, that they seem to have
a natural fitness, like the mountain pine: nay, even in the day when
they were built they must have had this fitness, as if they had been
raised by an earth-born race, who had inherited from their mighty
parent a sublime instinct of form. And that was a day of romance! If
those robber barons were somewhat grim and drunken ogres, they had
a certain grandeur of the wild beast in them—they were forest boars
with tusks, tearing and rending, not the ordinary domestic grunter;
they represented the demon forces for ever in collision with beauty,
virtue, and the gentle uses of life; they made a fine contrast in the
picture with the wandering minstrel, the soft-lipped princess, the pious
recluse, and the timid Israelite. That was a time of colour, when the
sunlight fell on glancing steel and floating banners; a time of adventure
and fierce struggle—nay, of living, religious art and religious enthusiasm; for were not cathedrals built in those days, and did not great
emperors leave their Western palaces to die before the infidel strongholds in the sacred East? Therefore it is that these Rhine castles thrill
me with a sense of poetry: they belong to the grand historic life of
humanity, and raise up for me the vision of an epoch. But these dead-
tinted, hollow-eyed, angular skeletons of villages on the Rhone oppress
me with the feeling that human life—very much of it—is a narrow,
ugly, grovelling existence, which even calamity does not elevate, but

rather tends to exhibit in all its bare vulgarity of conception; and I have a cruel conviction that the lives these ruins are the traces of, were part of a gross sum of obscure vitality, that will be swept into the same oblivion with the generations of ants and beavers.

Perhaps something akin to this oppressive feeling may have weighed upon you in watching this old-fashioned family life on the banks of the Floss, which even sorrow hardly suffices to lift above the level of the tragi-comic. It is a sordid life, you say, this of the Tullivers and Dodsons—irradiated by no sublime principles, no romantic visions, no active, self-renouncing faith—moved by none of those wild, uncontrollable passions which create the dark shadows of misery and crime—without that primitive rough simplicity of wants, that hard submissive ill-paid toil, that child-like spelling-out of what nature has written, which gives its poetry to peasant life. Here, one has conventional worldly notions and habits without instruction and without polish—surely the most prosaic form of human life: proud respectability in a gig of unfashionable build: worldliness without side-dishes. Observing these people narrowly, even when the iron hand of misfortune has shaken them from their unquestioning hold on the world, one sees little trace of religion, still less of a distinctively Christian creed. Their belief in the Unseen, so far as it manifests itself at all, seems to be rather of a pagan kind; their moral notions, though held with strong tenacity, seem to have no standard beyond hereditary custom. You could not live among such people; you are stifled for want of an outlet towards something beautiful, great, or noble; you are irritated with these dull men and women, as a kind of population out of keeping with the earth on which they live—with this rich plain where the great river flows for ever onward, and links the small pulse of the old English town with the beatings of the world's mighty heart. A vigorous superstition, that lashes its gods or lashes its own back, seems to be more congruous with the mystery of the human lot, than the mental condition of these emmet-like Dodsons and Tullivers.

I share with you this sense of oppressive narrowness; but it is necessary that we should feel it, if we care to understand how it acted on the lives of Tom and Maggie—how it has acted on young natures in many generations, that in the onward tendency of human things have risen above the mental level of the generation before them, to which they have been nevertheless tied by the strongest fibres of their hearts. The suffering, whether of martyr or victim, which belongs to every historical advance of mankind, is represented in this way in every town, and by hundreds of obscure hearths; and we need not shrink from this comparison of small things with great; for does not science tell us that its highest striving is after the ascertainment of a unity which shall bind the smallest things with the greatest? In natural science, I have understood, there is nothing petty to the mind that has a large vision of relations, and to which every single object suggests a vast sum of conditions. It is surely the same with the observation of human life.

Certainly the religious and moral ideas of the Dodsons and Tullivers were of too specific a kind to be arrived at deductively, from the statement that they were part of the Protestant population of Great Britain. Their theory of life had its core of soundness, as all theories must have on which decent and prosperous families have been reared and have flourished; but it had the very slightest tincture of theology. If, in the maiden days of the Dodson sisters, their Bibles opened more easily at some parts than others, it was because of dried tulip-petals, which had been distributed quite impartially, without preference for the historical, devotional, or doctrinal. Their religion was of a simple, semi-pagan kind, but there was no heresy in it—if heresy properly means choice—for they didn't know there was any other religion, except that of chapel-goers, which appeared to run in families, like asthma. How *should* they know? The vicar of their pleasant rural parish was not a controversialist, but a good hand at whist, and one who had a joke always ready for a blooming female parishioner. The religion of the Dodsons consisted in revering whatever was customary and respectable: it was necessary to be baptised, else one could not be buried in the churchyard, and to take the sacrament before death as a security against more dimly understood perils; but it was of equal necessity to have the proper pall bearers and well-cured hams at one's funeral, and to leave an unimpeachable will. A Dodson would not be taxed with the omission of anything that was becoming, or that belonged to that eternal fitness of things which was plainly indicated in the practice of the most substantial parishioners, and in the family traditions—such as, obedience to parents, faithfulness to kindred, industry, rigid honesty, thrift, the thorough scouring of wooden and copper utensils, the hoarding of coins likely to disappear from the currency, the production of first-rate commodities for the market, and the general preference for whatever was home-made. The Dodsons were a very proud race, and their pride lay in the utter frustration of all desire to tax them with a breach of traditional duty or propriety. A wholesome pride in many respects, since it identified honour with perfect integrity, thoroughness of work, and faithfulness to admitted rules: and society owes some worthy qualities in many of her members to mothers of the Dodson class, who made their butter and their fromenty well, and would have felt disgraced to make it otherwise. To be honest and poor was never a Dodson motto, still less to seem rich though being poor; rather, the family badge was to be honest and rich; and not only rich, but richer than was supposed. To live respected, and have the proper bearers at your funeral, was an achievement of the ends of existence that would be entirely nullified if, on the reading of your Will, you sank in the opinion of your fellow-men, either by turning out to be poorer than they expected, or by leaving your money in a capricious manner, without strict regard to degrees of kin. The right thing must always be done towards kindred. The right thing was to correct them severely, if they were other than a credit to the family, but still not to alienate from them the smallest rightful share in the family shoe-buckles and other property. A conspicuous quality in the Dodson character was its genuineness: its vices and virtues alike were phases of a proud, honest egoism, which had a hearty dislike to whatever made against its own credit and interest, and would be frankly hard of speech to inconvenient "kin," but would never forsake or ignore them—would not let them want bread, but only require them to eat it with bitter herbs.

The same sort of traditional belief ran in the Tulliver veins, but it was carried in richer blood, having elements of generous imprudence, warm affection, and hot-tempered rashness. Mr. Tulliver's grandfather had been heard to say that he was descended from one Ralph Tulliver, a wonderfully clever fellow, who had ruined himself. It is likely enough that the clever Ralph was a high liver, rode spirited horses, and was very decidedly of his own opinion. On the other hand, nobody had ever heard of a Dodson who had ruined himself: it was not the way of that family.

If such were the views of life on which the Dodsons and Tullivers had been reared in the praiseworthy past of Pitt and high prices, you will infer from what you already know concerning the state of society in St. Ogg's, that there had been no highly modifying influence to act on them in their maturer life. It was still possible, even in that later time of anti-Catholic preaching, for people to hold many pagan ideas, and believe themselves good church-people notwithstanding; so we need hardly feel any surprise at the fact that Mr. Tulliver, though a regular church-goer, recorded his vindictiveness on the fly-leaf of his Bible. It was not that any harm could be said concerning the vicar of that charming rural parish to which Dorlcote Mill belonged: he was a man of excellent family, an irreproachable bachelor, of elegant pursuits, had taken honours, and held a fellowship. Mr. Tulliver regarded him with dutiful respect, as he did everything else belonging to the church-service; but he considered that church was one thing and common-sense another, and he wanted nobody to tell *him* what common-sense was. Certain seeds which are required to find a nidus for themselves under unfavourable circumstances, have been supplied by nature with an apparatus of hooks, so that they will get a hold on very unreceptive surfaces. The spiritual seed which had been scattered over Mr. Tulliver had apparently been destitute of any corresponding provision, and had slipped off to the winds again, from a total absence of hooks.

CHAPTER II

THE TORN NEST IS PIERCED BY THE THORNS

THERE is something sustaining in the very agitation that accompanies the first shocks of trouble, just as an acute pain is often a stimulus, and produces an excitement which is transient strength. It is in the slow, changed life that follows—in the time when sorrow has become stale, and has no longer an emotive intensity that counteracts its pain—in the time when day follows day in dull unexpectant sameness, and trial is a dreary routine;—it is then that despair threatens; it is then that the peremptory hunger of the soul is felt, and eye and ear are strained after some unlearned secret of our existence, which shall give to endurance the nature of satisfaction.

This time of utmost need was come to Maggie, with her short span of thirteen years. To the usual precocity of the girl, she added that early experience of struggle, of conflict between the inward impulse and outward fact, which is the lot of every imaginative and passionate nature; and the years since she hammered the nails into her wooden Fetish among the worm-eaten shelves of the attic, had been filled with so eager a life in the triple world of Reality, Books, and Waking Dreams, that Maggie was strangely old for her years in everything except in her entire want of that prudence and self-command which were the qualities that made Tom manly in the midst of his intellectual boyishness. And now her lot was beginning to have a still, sad monotony, which threw her more than ever on her inward self. Her father was able to attend to business again, his affairs were settled, and he was acting as Wakem's manager on the old spot. Tom went to and fro every morning and evening, and became more and more silent in the short intervals at home: what was there to say? One day was like another, and Tom's interest in life, driven back and crushed on every other side, was concentrating itself into the one channel of ambitious resistance to misfortune. The peculiarities of his father and mother were very irksome to him, now they were laid bare of all the softening accompaniments of an easy prosperous home; for Tom had very clear prosaic eyes, not apt to be dimmed by mists of feeling or imagination. Poor Mrs. Tulliver, it seemed, would never recover her old self—her placid household activity: how could she? The objects among which her mind had moved complacently were all gone—all the little hopes, and schemes, and speculations, all the pleasant little cares about her treasures which had made this world quite comprehensible to her for a quarter of a century, since she had made her first purchase of the sugar-tongs, had been suddenly snatched away from her, and she remained bewildered in this empty life. Why that should have happened to her which had not happened to other women, remained an insoluble question by which she expressed her perpetual ruminating comparison of the past with the present. It was piteous to see the comely blond stout woman getting thinner and more worn under a bodily as well as mental restlessness, which made her often wander about the empty house after her work was done, until Maggie becoming alarmed about her, would seek her, and bring her down by telling her how it vexed Tom that she was injuring her health by never sitting down and resting herself. Yet amidst this helpless imbecility there was a touching trait of humble self-devoting maternity, which made Maggie feel tenderly towards her poor mother amidst all the little wearing griefs caused by her mental feebleness. She would let Maggie do none of the work that was heaviest and most soiling to the hands, and was quite peevish when Maggie attempted to relieve her from her grate-brushing and scouring: "Let it alone, my dear; your hands 'ull get as hard as hard," she would say: "it's your mother's place to do that. I can't do the sewing—my eyes fail me." And she would still brush and carefully tend Maggie's hair, which she had become reconciled to, in spite of its refusal to curl, now it was so long and massy. Maggie was not her pet child, and, in general, would have been much better if she had been quite different; yet the womanly heart, so bruised in its small personal desires, found a future to rest on in the life of this young thing, and the mother pleased herself with wearing out her own hands to save the hands that had so much more life in them.

But the constant presence of her mother's regretful bewilderment was less painful to Maggie than that of her father's sullen incommunicative depression. As long as the paralysis was upon him, and it seemed as if he might always be in a child-like condition of dependence—as long as he was still only half-awakened to his trouble, Maggie had felt the strong tide of pitying love almost as an inspiration, a new power, that would make the most difficult life easy for his sake; but now, instead of child-like dependence there had come a taciturn hard concentration of purpose, in strange contrast with his old vehement communicativeness and high spirit; and this lasted from day to day, and from week to week, the dull eye never brightening with any eagerness or any joy. It is something cruelly incomprehensible to youthful natures, this sombre sameness in middle-aged and elderly people, whose life has resulted in disappointment and discontent, to whose faces a smile becomes so strange that the sad lines all about the lips and brow seem to take no notice of it, and it hurries away again for want of a welcome. "Why will they not kindle up and be glad sometimes?" thinks young elasticity. "It would be so easy, if they only liked to do it." And these leaden clouds that never part are apt to create impatience even in the filial affection that streams forth in nothing but tenderness and pity in the time of more obvious affliction.

Mr. Tulliver lingered nowhere away from home: he hurried away from market, he refused all invitations to stay and chat, as in old times, in the houses where he called on business. He could not be reconciled with his lot: there was no attitude in which his pride did not feel its bruises; and in all behaviour towards him, whether kind or cold, he detected an allusion to the change in his circumstances. Even the days on which Wakem came to ride round the land and inquire into the business, were not so black to him as those market-days on which he had met several creditors who had accepted a composition from him. To save something towards the repayment of those creditors, was the object towards which he was now bending all his thoughts and efforts; and under the influence of this all-compelling demand of his nature, the somewhat profuse man, who hated to be stinted or to stint any one else in his own house, was gradually metamorphosed into the keen-eyed grudger of morsels. Mrs. Tulliver could not economise enough to satisfy him, in their food and firing; and he would eat nothing himself but what was of the coarsest quality. Tom, though depressed and strongly repelled by his father's sullenness, and the dreariness of home, entered thoroughly into his father's feelings about paying the creditors; and the poor lad brought his first quarter's money, with a declicious sense of achievement, and gave it to his father to put into the tin box which held the savings. The little store of sovereigns in the tin box seemed to be the only sight that brought a faint beam of pleasure into the miller's eyes—faint and transient, for it was soon dispelled by the thought that the time would be long—perhaps longer than his life— before the narrow savings could remove the hateful incubus of debt. A deficit of more than five hundred pounds, with the accumulating interest, seemed a deep pit to fill with the savings from thirty shillings a-week, even when Tom's probable savings were to be added. On this one point there was entire community of feeling in the four widely differing beings who sat round the dying fire of sticks, which made a cheap warmth for them on the verge of bed-time. Mrs. Tulliver carried the proud integrity of the Dodsons in her blood, and had been brought up to think that to wrong people of their money, which was another phrase for debt, was a sort of moral pillory: it would have been wickedness, to her mind, to have run counter to her husband's desire to "do the right thing," and retrieve his name. She had a confused dreamy notion that, if the creditors were all paid, her plate and linen ought to come back to her; but she had an inbred perception that while people owed money they were unable to pay, they couldn't rightly call anything their own. She murmured a little that Mr. Tulliver so peremptorily refused to receive anything in repayment from Mr. and Mrs. Moss; but to all his requirements of household economy she was submissive to the point of denying herself the cheapest indulgences of mere flavour: her only rebellion was to smuggle into the kitchen something that would make rather a better supper than usual for Tom.

These narrow notions about debt, held by the old-fashioned Tullivers, may perhaps excite a smile on the faces of many readers in these days of wide commercial views and wide philosophy, according to which everything rights itself without any trouble of ours: the fact that my tradesman is out of pocket by me, is to be looked at through the serene certainty that somebody else's tradesman is in pocket by somebody else; and since there must be bad debts in the world, why, it is mere egoism not to like that we in particular should make them instead of our fellow-citizens. I am telling the history of very simple people, who had never had any illuminating doubts as to personal integrity and honour.

Under all this grim melancholy and narrowing concentration of desire, Mr. Tulliver retained the feeling towards his "little wench" which made her presence a need to him, though it would not suffice to cheer him. She was still the desire of his eyes; but the sweet spring of fatherly love was now mingled with bitterness, like everything else. When Maggie laid down her work at night, it was her habit to get a low stool and sit by her father's knee, leaning her cheek against it. How she wished he would stroke her head, or give some sign that he was soothed by the sense that he had a daughter who loved him! But now she got no answer to her little caresses, either from her father or from Tom—the two idols of her life. Tom was weary and abstracted in the short intervals when he was at home, and her father was bitterly preoccupied with the thought that the girl was growing up—was shooting up into a woman; and how was she to do well in life? She had a poor chance for marrying, down in the world as they were. And he hated the thought of her marrying poorly, as her aunt Gritty had done: *that* would be a thing to make him turn in his grave—the little wench so pulled down by children and toil, as her aunt Moss was. When uncultured minds, confined to a narrow range of personal experience, are under the pressure of continued misfortune, their inward life is apt to become a perpetually repeated round of sad and bitter thoughts: the same words, the same scenes are revolved over and over again, the same mood accompanies them—the end of the year finds them as much what they were at the beginning as if they were machines set to a recurrent series of movements.

The sameness of the days was broken by few visitors. Uncles and aunts paid only short visits now: of course, they could not stay to meals, and the constraint caused by Mr. Tulliver's savage silence, which seemed to add to the hollow resonance of the bare uncarpeted room when the aunts were talking, heightened the unpleasantness of these family visits on all sides, and tended to make them rare. As for other acquaintances —there is a chill air surrounding those who are down in the world, and people are glad to get away from them, as from a cold room: human beings, mere men and women, without furniture, without anything to offer you, who have ceased to count as anybody, present an embarrassing negation of reasons for wishing to see them, or of subjects on which to converse with them. At that distant day, there was a dreary isolation in the civilised Christian society of these realms for families that had dropped below their original level, unless they belonged to a sectarian church, which gets some warmth of brotherhood by walling in the sacred fire.

CHAPTER III

A VOICE FROM THE PAST

ONE afternoon, when the chestnuts were coming into flower, Maggie had brought her chair outside the front door, and was seated there with a book on her knees. Her dark eyes had wandered from the book, but they did not seem to be enjoying the sunshine which pierced the screen of jasmine on the projecting porch at her right, and threw leafy shadows on her pale round cheek; they seemed rather to be searching for something that was not disclosed by the sunshine. It had been a more miserable day than usual: her father, after a visit of Wakem's, had had a paroxysm of rage, in which for some trifling fault he had beaten the boy who served in the mill. Once before, since his illness, he had had a similar paroxysm, in which he had beaten his horse, and the scene had left a lasting terror in Maggie's mind. The thought had risen, that some time or other he might beat her mother if she happened to speak in her feeble way at the wrong moment. The keenest of all dread with her was, lest her father should add to his present misfortune the wretchedness of doing something irretrievably disgraceful. The battered school-book of Tom's which she held on her knees could give her no fortitude under the pressure of that dread, and again and again her eyes had filled with tears, as they wandered vaguely, seeing neither the chestnut trees nor the distant horizon, but only future scenes of home-sorrow.

Suddenly she was roused by the sound of the opening gate and of footsteps on the gravel. It was not Tom who was entering, but a man in a sealskin cap and a blue plush waistcoat, carrying a pack on his back, and followed closely by a bull-terrier of brindled coat and defiant aspect.

"O, Bob, it's you!" said Maggie, starting up with a smile of pleased recognition, for there had been no abundance of kind acts to efface the recollection of Bob's generosity; "I'm so glad to see you."

"Thank you, Miss," said Bob, lifting his cap and showing a delighted face, but immediately relieving himself of some accompanying embarrassment by looking down at his dog, and saying in a tone of disgust, "Get out wi' you, you thunderin' sawney!"

"My brother is not at home yet, Bob," said Maggie; "he is always at St. Ogg's in the daytime."

"Well, Miss," said Bob, "I should be glad to see Mr. Tom—but that isn't just what I'm come for—look here!"

Bob was in the act of depositing his pack on the door-step, and with it a row of small books fastened together with string. Apparently, however, they were not the object to which he wished to call Maggie's attention, but rather something which he had carried under his arm, wrapped in a red handkerchief.

"See here!" he said again, laying the red parcel on the others and unfolding it; "you won't think I'm a-makin' too free, Miss, I hope, but I lighted on these books, and I thought they might make up to you a bit for them as you've lost; for I heared you speak o' picturs—an' as foi picturs, *look* here!"

The opening of the red handkerchief had disclosed a superannuated "Keepsake" and six or seven numbers of a "Portrait Gallery," in royal octavo; and the emphatic request to look referred to a portrait of George the Fourth in all the majesty of his depressed cranium and voluminous neckcloth.

"There's all sorts o' genelmen here," Bob went on, turning over the leaves with some excitement, "wi' all sorts o' noses—an' some bald an' some wi' wigs—Parlament genelmen, I reckon. An' here," he added, opening the "Keepsake," "*here's* ladies for you, some wi' curly hair and some wi' smooth, an' some a-smiling wi' their heads o' one side, an' some as if they was goin' to cry—look here—a-sittin' on the ground out o' door, dressed like the ladies I'n seen get out o' the carriages at the balls in th' Old Hall there. My eyes, I wonder what the chaps wear as go a-courtin' 'em! I sot up till the clock was gone twelve last night a-lookin' at 'em—I did—till they stared at me out o' the pictures as if they'd know when I spoke to 'em. But, lors! I shouldn't know what to say to 'em. They'll be more fittin' company for you, Miss, and the man at the book-stall, he said they banged iverything for picturs—he said they was a fust-rate article."

"And you've bought them for me, Bob?" said Maggie, deeply touched by this simple kindness. "How very, very good of you! But I'm afraid you gave a great deal of money for them."

"Not me!" said Bob. "I'd ha' gev three times the money, if they'll make up to you a bit for them as was sold away from you, Miss. For I'n niver forgot how you looked when you fretted about the books bein' gone—it's stuck by me as if it was a pictur hingin' before me. An' when I see'd the book open upo' the stall, wi' the lady lookin' out of it wi' eyes a bit like your'n when you was frettin'—you'll excuse my takin' the liberty, Miss—I thought I'd make free to buy it for you, an' then I bought the books full o' genelmen to match—an then"—here Bob took up the small stringed packet of books—"I thought you might like a bit more print as well as the picturs, an' I got these for a say-so—they're cram-full o' print, an' I thought they'd do no harm comin' along wi' these better-most books. An' I hope you won't say me nay, an' tell me as you won't have 'em, like Mr. Tom did wi' the suvreigns."

"No, indeed, Bob," said Maggie, "I'm very thankful to you for thinking of me, and being so good to me and Tom. I don't think any one ever did such a kind thing for me before. I haven't many friends who care for me."

"Hev a dog, Miss!—they're better friends nor any Christian," said Bob, laying down his pack again, which he had taken up with the intention of hurrying away; for he felt considerable shyness in talking to a young lass like Maggie, though, as he usually said of himself, "his tongue overrun him" when he began to speak. "I can't give you Mumps, 'cause he'd break his heart to go away from me—eh, Mumps, what do you say, you riff-raff?"—(Mumps declined to express himself more diffusely than by a single affirmative movement of his tail.) "But I'd get you a pup, Miss, an' welcome."

"No, thank you, Bob. We have a yard dog, and I mayn't keep a dog of my own."

"Eh, that's a pity: else there's a pup—if you didn't mind about it not bein' thoroughbred: it's mother acts in the Punch show—an uncommon sensable bitch—she means more sense wi' her bark nor half the chaps can put into their talk from breakfast to sundown. There's one chap carries pots,—a poor low trade as any on the road—he says, 'Why, Toby's nought but a mongrel—there's nought to look at in her.' But I says to him, 'Why, what are you yoursen but a mongrel? There wasn't much pickin' o' *your* feyther an' mother, to look at you.' Not but what I like a bit o' breed myself, but I can't abide to see one cur grinnin' at another. I wish you good evenin', Miss," added Bob, abruptly taking up his pack again, under the consciousness that his tongue was acting in an undisciplined manner.

"Won't you come in the evening some time, and see my brother, Bob?" said Maggie.

"Yes, Miss, thank you—another time. You'll give my duty to him, if you please. Eh, he's a fine growed chap, Mr. Tom is; he took to growin' i' the legs, an *I* didn't."

The pack was down again, now—the hook of the stick having somehow gone wrong.

"You don't call Mumps a cur, I suppose?" said Maggie, divining that any interest she showed in Mumps would be gratifying to his master.

"No, Miss, a fine way off that," said Bob, with a pitying smile; "Mumps is as fine a cross as you'll see anywhere along the Floss, an' I'n been up it wi' the barge times enoo. Why, the gentry stops to look at him; but you won't catch Mumps a-lookin' at the gentry much—he minds his own business, he does."

The expression of Mumps's face, which seemed to be tolerating the superfluous existence of objects in general, was strongly confirmatory of this high praise.

"He looks dreadfully surly," said Maggie. "Would he let me pat him?"

"Ay, that would he, and thank you. He knows his company, Mumps does. He isn't a dog as 'ull be caught wi' gingerbread: he'd smell a thief a good deal stronger nor the gingerbread—he would. Lors, I talk to him by th' hour together, when I'm walking i' lone places, and if I'n done a bit o' mischief, I allays tell him. I'n got no secrets but what Mumps knows 'em. He knows about my big thumb, he does."

"Your big thumb—what's that Bob?" said Maggie.

"That's what it is, Miss," said Bob, quickly, exhibiting a singularly broad specimen of that difference between the man and the monkey. "It tells i' measuring out the flannel, you see. I carry flannel, 'cause it's light for my pack, an' it's dear stuff, you see, so a big thumb tells. I clap my thumb at the end o' the yard and cut o' the hither side of it, and the old women aren't up to't."

"But, Bob," said Maggie, looking serious, "that's cheating: I don't like to hear you say that."

"Don't you, Miss?" said Bob, regretfully. "Then I'm sorry I said it. But I'm so used to talking to Mumps, an' he doesn't mind a bit o' cheating, when it's them skinflint women, as haggle and haggle, an' 'ud like to get their flannel for nothing, an' 'ud niver ask theirselves how I got my dinner out on't. I niver cheat anybody as doesn't want to cheat me, Miss—lors, I'm a honest chap, I am; only I must hev a bit o' sport, an' now I don't go wi' the ferrets, I'n got no varmint to come over but them haggling women. I wish you good evening, Miss."

"Good-by, Bob. Thank you very much for bringing me the books. And come again to see Tom."

"Yes, Miss," said Bob, moving on a few steps; then turning half round, he said, "I'll leave off that trick wi' my big thumb, if you don't think well on me for it, Miss—but it 'ud be a pity, it would. I couldn't find another trick so good—an' what 'ud be the use o' havin' a big thumb? It might as well ha' been narrer."

Maggie, thus exalted into Bob's directing Madonna, laughed in spite of herself; at which her worshipper's blue eyes twinkled too, and under these favouring auspices he touched his cap and walked away.

The days of chivalry are not gone, notwithstanding Burke's grand dirge over them: they live still in that far-off worship paid by many a youth and man to the woman of whom he never dreams that he shall touch so much as her little finger or the hem of her robe. Bob, with the pack on his back, had as respectful an adoration for this dark-eyed maiden as if he had been a knight in armour calling aloud on her name as he pricked on to the fight.

That gleam of merriment soon died away from Maggie's face, and perhaps only made the returning gloom deeper by contrast. She was too dispirited even to like answering questions about Bob's present of books, and she carried them away to her bedroom, laying them down there and seating herself on her one stool, without caring to look at them just yet. She leaned her cheek against the window-frame, and thought that the light-hearted Bob had a lot much happier than hers.

Maggie's sense of loneliness, and utter privation of joy, had deepened with the brightness of advancing spring. All the favourite out-door nooks about home, which seemed to have done their part with her parents in nurturing and cherishing her, were now mixed up with the home-sadness, and gathered no smile from the sunshine. Every affection, every delight the poor child had had, was like an aching nerve to her. There was no music for her any more—no piano, no harmonised voices, no delicious stringed instruments, with their passionate cries of imprisoned spirits sending a strange vibration through her frame. And of all her school-life there was nothing left her now but her little collection of school-books, which she turned over with a sickening sense that she knew them all, and they were all barren of comfort. Even at school she had often wished for books with *more* in them: everything she learned there seemed like the ends of long threads that snapped immediately. And now—without the indirect charm of school-emulation—Télémaque was mere bran; so were the hard dry questions on Christian doctrine: there was no flavour in them—no strength. Sometimes Maggie thought she could have been contented with absorbing fancies: if she could have had all Scott's novels and all Byron's poems!—then, perhaps, she might have found happiness enough to dull her sensibility to her actual daily life. And yet . . . they were hardly what she wanted. She could make dream-worlds of her own—but no dream-world would satisfy her now. She wanted some explanation of this hard, real life: the unhappy-looking father, seated at the dull breakfast-table; the childish, bewildered mother; the little sordid tasks that filled the hours, or the more oppressive emptiness of weary, joyless leisure; the need of some tender, demonstrative love; the cruel sense that Tom didn't mind what she thought or felt, and that they were no longer playfellows together; the privation of all pleasant things that had come to *her* more than to others: she wanted some key that would enable her to understand, and, in understanding, endure, the heavy weight that had fallen on her young heart. If she had been taught "real learning and wisdom, such as great men knew," she thought she should have held the secrets of life; if she had only books, that she might learn for herself what wise men knew! Saints and martyrs had never interested Maggie so much as sages and poets. She knew little of saints and martyrs, and had gathered, as a general result of her teaching, that they were a temporary provision against the spread of Catholicism, and had all died at Smithfield.

In one of these meditations, it occurred to her that she had forgotten Tom's school-books, which had been sent home in his trunk. But she found the stock unaccountably shrunk down to the few old ones which had been well thumbed—the Latin Dictionary and Grammar, a Delectus, a torn Eutropius, the well-worn Virgil, Aldrich's Logic, and the exasperating Euclid. Still, Latin, Euclid, and Logic would surely be a considerable step in masculine wisdom—in that knowledge which made men contented, and even glad to live. Not that the yearning for effectual wisdom was quite unmixed: a certain mirage would now and then rise on the desert of the future, in which she seemed to see herself honoured for her surprising attainments. And so the poor child, with her soul's hunger and her illusions of self-flattery, began to nibble at this thick-rinded fruit of the tree of knowledge, filling her vacant hours with Latin, geometry, and the forms of the syllogism, and feeling a gleam of triumph now and then that her understanding was quite equal to these peculiarly masculine studies. For a week or two she went on resolutely enough, though with an occasional sinking of heart, as if she had set out toward the Promised Land alone, and found it a thirsty, trackless, uncertain journey. In the severity of her early resolution, she would take Aldrich out into the fields, and then look off her book towards the sky, where the lark was twinkling, or to the reeds and bushes by the river, from which the water-fowl rustled forth on its anxious, awkward flight —with a startled sense that the relation between Aldrich and this living world was extremely remote for her. The discouragement deepened as the days went on, and the eager heart gained faster and faster on the patient mind. Somehow, when she sat at the window with her book, her eyes *would* fix themselves blankly on the out-door sunshine; then they would fill with tears, and sometimes, if her mother was not in the room, the studies would all end in sobbing. She rebelled against her lot, she fainted under its loneliness, and fits even of anger and hatred towards her father and mother, who were so unlike what she would have them to be—towards Tom, who checked her, and met her thought or feeling always by some thwarting difference—would flow out over her affections and conscience like a lava stream, and frighten her with the sense that it was not difficult for her to become a demon. Then her brain would be busy with wild romances of a flight from home in search of something less sordid and dreary: she would go to some great man— Walter Scott, perhaps—and tell him how wretched and how clever she was, and he would surely do something for her. But, in the middle of her vision, her father would perhaps enter the room for the evening, and, surprised that she sat still without noticing him, would say, complainingly, "Come, am I to fetch my slippers myself?" The voice pierced through Maggie like a sword: there was another sadness besides her own, and she had been thinking of turning her back on it and forsaking it.

This afternoon, the sight of Bob's cheerful freckled face had given her discontent a new direction. She thought it was part of the hardship of her life that there was laid upon her the burthen of larger wants than others seemed to feel—that she had to endure this wide hopeless yearning for that something, whatever it was, that was greatest and best on this earth. She wished she could have been like Bob, with his easily satisfied ignorance, or like Tom, who had something to do on which he could fix his mind with a steady purpose, and disregard everything else. Poor child! as she leaned her head against the window-frame, with her hands clasped tighter and tighter, and her foot beating the ground, she was as lonely in her trouble as if she had been the only girl in the civilised world of that day who had come out of her school-life with a soul untrained for inevitable struggles—with no other part of her inherited share in the hard-won treasures of thought, which generations of painful toil had laid up for the race of men, than shreds and patches of feeble literature and false history—with much futile information about Saxon and other kings of doubtful example, but unhappily quite without that knowledge of the irreversible laws within and without her, which, governing the habits, becomes morality, and, developing the feelings of submission and dependence, becomes religion:—as lonely in her trouble as if every other girl besides herself had been cherished and watched over by elder minds, not forgetful of their own early time, when need was keen and impulse strong.

At last Maggie's eyes glanced down on the books that lay on the window-shelf, and she half forsook her reverie to turn over listlessly the leaves of the "Portrait Gallery," but she soon pushed this aside to ex-

amine the little row of books tied together with string. "Beauties of the
Spectator," "Rasselas," "Economy of Human Life," "Gregory's Letters"
—she knew the sort of matter that was inside all these: the "Christian
Year"—that seemed to be a hymn-book, and she laid it down again; but
Thomas à Kempis?—the name had come across her in her reading, and
she felt the satisfaction, which every one knows, of getting some ideas
to attach to a name that strays solitary in the memory. She took up the
little, old, clumsy book with some curiosity: it had the corners turned
down in many places, and some hand, now for ever quiet, had made at
certain passages strong pen-and-ink marks, long since browned by time.
Maggie turned from leaf to leaf, and read where the quiet hand pointed
. . . "Know that the love of thyself doth hurt thee more than anything
in the world. . . . . If thou seekest this or that, and wouldst be here
or there to enjoy thy own will and pleasure, thou shalt never be quiet
nor free from care: for in everything somewhat will be wanting, and in
every place there will be some that will cross thee. . . . . Both above
and below, which way soever thou dost turn thee, everywhere thou shalt
find the Cross: and everywhere of necessity thou must have patience, if
thou wilt have inward peace, and enjoy an everlasting crown. . . . . If
thou desire to mount unto this height, thou must set out courageously,
and lay the axe to the root, that thou mayst pluck up and destroy
that hidden inordinate inclination to thyself, and unto all private and
earthly good. On this sin, that a man inordinately loveth himself, almost
all dependeth, whatsoever is thoroughly to be overcome; which evil
being once overcome and subdued, there will presently ensue great
peace and tranquillity. . . . . It is but little thou sufferest in comparison of them that have suffered so much, were so strongly tempted, so
grievously afflicted, so many ways tried and exercised. Thou oughtest
therefore to call to mind the more heavy sufferings of others, that thou
mayst the easier bear thy little adversities. And if they seem not little
unto thee, beware lest thy impatience be the cause thereof. . . . .
Blessed are those ears that receive the whispers of the divine voice, and
listen not to the whisperings of the world. Blessed are those ears which
hearken not unto the voice which soundeth outwardly, but unto the
Truth which teacheth inwardly. . . . ."

A strange thrill of awe passed through Maggie while she read, as if
she had been wakened in the night by a strain of solemn music, telling
of beings whose souls had been astir while hers was in stupor. She went
on from one brown mark to another, where the quiet hand seemed to
point, hardly conscious that she was reading—seeming rather to listen
while a low voice said——

"Why dost thou here gaze about, since this is not the place of thy
rest? In heaven ought to be thy dwelling, and all earthly things are to
be looked on as they forward thy journey thither. All things pass away,
and thou together with them. Beware thou cleave not unto them, lest
thou be entangled and perish. . . . . If a man should give all his substance, yet it is as nothing. And if he should do great penances, yet

are they but little. And if he should attain to all knowledge, he is yet far off. And if he should be of great virtue, and very fervent devotion, yet is there much wanting; to wit, one thing, which is most necessary for him. What is that? That having left all, he leave himself, and go wholly out of himself, and retain nothing of self-love. . . . . I have often said unto thee, and now again I say the same, Forsake thyself, resign thyself, and thou shalt enjoy much inward peace. . . . . Then shall all vain imaginations, evil perturbations, and superfluous cares fly away; then shall immoderate fear leave thee, and inordinate love shall die."

Maggie drew a long breath and pushed her heavy hair back, as if to see a sudden vision more clearly. Here, then, was a secret of life that would enable her to renounce all other secrets—here was a sublime height to be reached without the help of outward things—here was insight, and strength, and conquest, to be won by means entirely within her own soul, where a supreme Teacher was waiting to be heard. It flashed through her like the suddenly apprehended solution of a problem, that all the miseries of her young life had come from fixing her heart on her own pleasure, as if that were the central necessity of the universe; and for the first time she saw the possibility of shifting the position from which she looked at the gratification of her own desires, of taking her stand out of herself, and looking at her own life as an insignificant part of a divinely-guided whole. She read on and on in the old book, devouring eagerly the dialogues with the invisible Teacher, the pattern of sorrow, the source of all strength; returning to it after she had been called away, and reading till the sun went down behind the willows. With all the hurry of an imagination that could never rest in the present, she sat in the deepening twilight forming plans of self-humiliation and entire devotedness; and, in the ardour of first discovery, renunciation seemed to her the entrance into that satisfaction which she had so long been craving in vain. She had not perceived—how could she until she had lived longer?—the inmost truth of the old monk's outpourings, that renunciation remains sorrow, though a sorrow borne willingly. Maggie was still panting for happiness, and was in ecstasy because she had found the key to it. She knew nothing of doctrines and systems—of mysticism or quietism; but this voice out of the far-off middle ages was the direct communication of a human soul's belief and experience, and came to Maggie as an unquestioned message.

I suppose that is the reason why the small old-fashioned book, for which you need only pay six-pence at a book-stall, works miracles to this day, turning bitter waters into sweetness: while expensive sermons and treatises, newly issued, leave all things as they were before. It was written down by a hand that waited for the heart's prompting; it is the chronicle of a solitary, hidden anguish, struggle, trust and triumph—not written on velvet cushions to teach endurance to those who are treading with bleeding feet on the stones. And so it remains to all time a lasting record of human needs and human consolations: the voice of a brother who, ages ago, felt and suffered and renounced—in the cloister, perhaps, with serge gown and tonsured head, with much chanting and long fasts, and with a fashion of speech different from ours—but under the same silent far-off heavens, and with the same passionate desires, the same strivings, the same failures, the same weariness.

In writing the history of unfashionable families, one is apt to fall into a tone of emphasis which is very far from being the tone of good society, where principles and beliefs are not only of an extremely moderate kind, but are always presupposed, no subjects being eligible but such as can be touched with a light and graceful irony. But then, good society has its claret and its velvet carpets, its dinner-engagements six weeks deep, its opera and its faëry ball-rooms; rides off its ennui on thoroughbred horses, lounges at the club, has to keep clear of crinoline vortices, gets its science done by Faraday, and its religion by the superior clergy who are to be met in the best houses: how should it have time or need for belief and emphasis? But good society, floated on gossamer wings of light irony, is of very expensive production; requiring nothing less than a wide and arduous national life condensed in unfragrant deafening factories, cramping itself in mines, sweating at furnaces, grinding, hammering, weaving under more or less oppression of carbonic acid—or else, spread over sheepwalks, and scattered in lonely houses and huts on the clayey or chalky corn-lands, where the rainy days look dreary. This wide national life is based entirely on emphasis—the emphasis of want, which urges it into all the activities necessary for the maintenance of good society and light irony: it spends its heavy years often in a chill, uncarpeted fashion, amidst family discord unsoftened by long corridors. Under such circumstances, there are many among its myriads of souls who have absolutely needed an emphatic belief: life in this unpleasurable shape demanding some solution even to unspeculative minds; just as you inquire into the stuffing of your couch when anything galls you there, whereas eider-down and perfect French springs excite no question. Some have an emphatic belief in alcohol, and seek their *ekstasis* or outside standing-ground in gin; but the rest require something that good society calls "enthusiasm," something that will present motives in an entire absence of high prizes, something that will give patience and feed human love when the limbs ache with weariness, and human looks are hard upon us—something, clearly, that lies outside personal desires, that includes resignation for ourselves and active love for what is not ourselves. Now and then, that sort of enthusiasm finds a far-echoing voice that comes from an experience springing out of the deepest need. And it was by being brought within the long lingering vibrations of such a voice that Maggie, with her girl's face and unnoted sorrows, found an effort and a hope that helped her through years of loneliness, making out a faith for herself without the aid of established authorities and appointed guides—for they were not at hand, and her need was pressing. From what you know of her, you will not be surprised that she threw some exaggeration and wilfulness, some pride and impetuosity, even into her self-renunciation: her own life was still a drama for her, in which she demanded of herself that her part should be played with intensity. And so it came to pass that she often lost the spirit of humility by being excessive in the outward act; she often strove after too high a flight, and came down with her poor little half-fledged wings dabbled in the mud. For example, she not only determined to work at plain sewing, that she might contribute something towards the fund in the tin box, but she went, in the first instance, in her zeal of self-mortification, to ask for it at a linen-shop in St. Ogg's, instead of getting it in a more quiet and indirect way; and could see nothing but what was entirely wrong and unkind, nay, persecuting, in Tom's reproof of her for this unnecessary act. "I don't like *my* sister to do such things," said Tom; "*I'll* take care that the debts are paid, without your lowering yourself in that way." Surely there was some tenderness and bravery mingled with the worldliness and self-assertion of that little speech; but Maggie held it as dross, overlooking the grains of gold, and took Tom's rebuke as one of her outward crosses. Tom was very hard to her, she used to think, in her long night-watchings—to her who had always loved him so; and then she strove to be contented with that hardness, and to require nothing. That is the path we all like when we set out on our abandonment of egoism—the path of martyrdom and endurance, where the palm-branches grow, rather than the steep highway of tolerance, just allowance, and self-blame, where there are no leafy honours to be gathered and worn.

The old books, Virgil, Euclid, and Aldrich—that wrinkled fruit of the tree of knowledge—had been all laid by; for Maggie had turned her back on the vain ambition to share the thoughts of the wise. In her first ardour she flung away the books with a sort of triumph that she had risen above the need of them; and if they had been her own, she would have burned them, believing that she would never repent. She read so eagerly and constantly in her three books, the Bible, Thomas-à-Kempis, and the "Christian Year" (no longer rejected as a "hymn-book"), that they filled her mind with a continual stream of rhythmic memories; and she was too ardently learning to see all nature and life in the light of her new faith, to need any other material for her mind to work on, as she sat with her well-plied needle, making shirts and other complicated stitchings, falsely called "plain"—by no means plain to Maggie, since wristband and sleeve and the like had a capability of being sewed in wrong side outwards in moments of mental wandering.

Hanging diligently over her sewing, Maggie was a sight any one might have been pleased to look at. That new inward life of hers, notwithstanding some volcanic upheavings of imprisoned passions, yet shone out in her face with a tender soft light that mingled itself as added loveliness with the gradually enriched colour and outline of her blossoming youth. Her mother felt the change in her with a sort of puzzled wonder that Maggie should be "growing up so good;" it was amazing that this once "contrairy" child was become so submissive, so backward to assert her own will. Maggie used to look up from her work and find her mother's eyes fixed upon her: they were watching and waiting for the large young glance, as if her elder frame got some needful warmth from it. The mother was getting fond of her tall, brown girl, the only bit of furniture now on which she could bestow her anxiety and pride; and Maggie, in spite of her own ascetic wish to have no personal adornment, was obliged to give way to her mother about her hair, and submit to have the abundant black locks plaited into a coronet on the summit of her head, after the pitiable fashion of those antiquated times.

"Let your mother have that bit o' pleasure, my dear," said Mrs. Tulliver; "I'd trouble enough with your hair once."

So Maggie, glad of anything that would soothe her mother, and cheer their long day together, consented to the vain decoration, and showed a queenly head above her old frocks—steadily refusing, however, to look at herself in the glass. Mrs. Tulliver liked to call the father's attention to Maggie's hair and other unexpected virtues, but he had a brusque reply to give.

"I knew well enough what she'd be, before now—it's nothing new to me. But it's a pity she isn't made o' commoner stuff—she'll be thrown away, I doubt: there'll be nobody to marry her as is fit for her."

And Maggie's graces of mind and body fed his gloom. He sat patiently enough while she read him a chapter, or said something timidly when they were alone together about trouble being turned into a blessing. He took it all as part of his daughter's goodness, which made his misfortunes the sadder to him because they damaged her chance in life. In a mind charged with an eager purpose and an unsatisfied vindictiveness, there is no room for new feelings: Mr. Tulliver did not want spiritual consolation—he wanted to shake off the degradation of debt, and to have his revenge.

BOOK FIVE

Wheat and Tares

★

CHAPTER I

IN THE RED DEEPS

THE family sitting-room was a long room with a window at each end; one looking towards the croft and along the Ripple to the banks of the Floss, the other into the mill-yard. Maggie was sitting with her work against the latter window when she saw Mr. Wakem entering the yard, as usual, on his fine black horse; but not alone, as usual. Some one was with him—a figure in a cloak, on a handsome pony. Maggie had hardly time to feel that it was Philip come back, before they were in front of the window, and he was raising his hat to her; while his father, catching the movement by a side-glance, looked sharply round at them both.

Maggie hurried away from the window and carried her work up-stairs; for Mr. Wakem cometimes came in and inspected the books, and Maggie felt that the meeting with Philip would be robbed of all pleasure in the presence of the two fathers. Some day, perhaps, she should see him when they could just shake hands, and she could tell him that she remembered his goodness to Tom, and the things he had said to her in the old days, though they could never be friends any more. It was not at all agitating to Maggie to see Philip again: she retained her childish gratitude and pity towards him, and remembered his cleverness; and in the early weeks of her loneliness she had continually recalled the image of him among the people who had been kind to her in life; often wishing she had him for a brother and a teacher, as they had fancied it might have been, in their talk together. But that sort of wishing had been banished along with other dreams that savoured of seeking her own will; and she thought, besides, that Philip might be altered by his life abroad —he might have become worldly, and really not care about her saying anything to him now. And yet, his face was wonderfully little altered —it was only a larger, more manly copy of the pale small-featured boy's face, with the grey eyes and the boyish waving brown hair: there was the old deformity to awaken the old pity; and after all her meditations, Maggie felt that she really *should* like to say a few words to him. He might still be melancholy, as he always used to be, and like her to look

at him kindly. She wondered if he remembered how he used to like her
eyes; with that thought Maggie glanced towards the square looking-
glass which was condemned to hang with its face towards the wall, and
she half-started from her seat to reach it down; but she checked herself
and snatched up her work, trying to repress the rising wishes by forcing
her memory to recall snatches of hymns, until she saw Philip and his
father returning along the road, and she could go down again.

It was far on in June now, and Maggie was inclined to lengthen the
daily walk which was her one indulgence; but this day and the following
she was so busy with work which must be finished that she never went
beyond the gate, and satisfied her need of the open air by sitting out of
doors. One of her frequent walks, when she was not obliged to go to
St. Ogg's, was to a spot that lay beyond what was called the "Hill"—an
insignificant rise of ground crowned by trees, lying along the side of the
road which ran by the gates of Dorlcote Mill. Insignificant I call it,
because in height it was hardly more than a bank; but there may come
moments when Nature makes a mere bank a means towards a fateful
result, and that is why I ask you to imagine this high bank crowned
with trees, making an uneven wall for some quarter of a mile along the
left side of Dorlcote Mill and the pleasant fields behind it, bounded by
the murmuring Ripple. Just where this line of bank sloped down again
to the level, a by-road turned off and led to the other side of the rise,
where it was broken into very capricious hollows and mounds by the
working of an exhausted stone-quarry—so long exhausted that both
mounds and hollows were now clothed with brambles and trees, and
here and there by a stretch of grass which a few sheep kept close-nibbled.
In her childish days Maggie held this place, called the Red Deeps, in
very great awe, and needed all her confidence in Tom's bravery to reconcile her to an excursion thither—visions of robbers and fierce animals haunting every hollow. But now it had the charm for her which
any broken ground, any mimic rock and ravine, have for the eyes that
rest habitually on the level; especially in summer, when she could sit
on a grassy hollow under the shadow of a branching ash, stooping aslant
from the steep above her, and listen to the hum of insects, like tiniest
bells on the garment of Silence, or see the sunlight piercing the distant
boughs, as if to chase and drive home the truant heavenly blue of the
wild hyacinths. In this June time too, the dog-roses were in their glory,
and that was an additional reason why Maggie should direct her walk
to the Red Deeps, rather than to any other spot, on the first day she
was free to wander at her will—a pleasure she loved so well, that sometimes, in her ardours of renunciation, she thought she ought to deny
herself the frequent indulgence in it.

You may see her now, as she walks down the favourite turning, and
enters the Deeps by a narrow path through a group of Scotch firs—her
tall figure and old lavender-gown visible through an hereditary black-
silk shawl of some wide-meshed net-like material; and now she is sure
of being unseen, she takes off her bonnet and ties it over her arm. One

would certainly suppose her to be farther on in life than her seventeenth year—perhaps because of the slow resigned sadness of the glance, from which all search and unrest seem to have departed, perhaps because her broad-chested figure has the mould of early womanhood. Youth and health have withstood well the involuntary and voluntary hardships of her lot, and the nights in which she has lain on the hard floor for a penance have left no obvious trace; the eyes are liquid, the brown cheek is firm and rounded, the full lips are red. With her dark colouring and jet crown surmounting her tall figure, she seems to have a sort of kinship with the grand Scotch firs, at which she is looking up as if she loved them well. Yet one has a sense of uneasiness in looking at her—a sense of opposing elements, of which a fierce collision is imminent: surely there is a hushed expression, such as one often sees in older faces under borderless caps, out of keeping with the resistant youth, which one expects to flash out in a sudden, passionate glance, that will dissipate all the quietude, like a damped fire leaping out again when all seemed safe.

But Maggie herself was not uneasy at this moment. She was calmly enjoying the free air, while she looked up at the old fir-trees, and thought that those broken ends of branches were the records of past storms, which had only made the red stems soar higher. But while her eyes were still turned upward, she became conscious of a moving shadow cast by the evening sun on the grassy path before her, and looked down with a startled gesture to see Philip Wakem, who first raised his hat, and then, blushing deeply, came forward to her and put out his hand. Maggie, too, coloured with surprise, which soon gave way to pleasure. She put out her hand and looked down at the deformed figure before her with frank eyes, filled for the moment with nothing but the memory of her child's feelings—a memory that was always strong in her. She was the first to speak.

"You startled me," she said, smiling faintly; "I never meet any one here. How came you to be walking here? Did you come to meet *me?*"

It was impossible not to perceive that Maggie felt herself a child again.

"Yes, I did," said Philip, still embarrassed: "I wished to see you very much. I watched a long while yesterday on the bank near your house to see if you would come out, but you never came. Then I watched again to-day, and when I saw the way you took, I kept you in sight and came down the bank, behind there. I hope you will not be displeased with me."

"No," said Maggie, with simple seriousness, walking on, as if she meant Philip to accompany her, "I'm very glad you came, for I wished very much to have an opportunity of speaking to you. I've never forgotten how good you were long ago to Tom, and me too; but I was not sure that you would remember us so well. Tom and I have had a great deal of trouble since then, and I think *that* makes one think more of what happened before the trouble came."

"I can't believe that you have thought of me so much as I have thought of you," said Philip, timidly. "Do you know, when I was away, I made a picture of you as you looked that morning in the study when you said you would not forget me."

Philip drew a large miniature-case from his pocket, and opened it. Maggie saw her old self leaning on a table, with her black locks hanging down behind her ears, looking into space with strange, dreamy eyes. It was a water-colour sketch, of real merit as a portrait.

"O dear," said Maggie, smiling, and flushed with pleasure, "what a queer little girl I was! I remember myself with my hair in that way, in that pink frock. I really *was* like a gypsy. I daresay I am now," she added, after a little pause; "am I like what you expected me to be?"

The words might have been those of a coquette, but the full bright glance Maggie turned on Philip was not that of a coquette. She really did hope he liked her face as it was now, but it was simply the rising again of her innate delight in admiration and love. Philip met her eyes and looked at her in silence for a long moment, before he said, quietly, "No, Maggie."

The light died out a little from Maggie's face, and there was a slight trembling of the lip. Her eyelids fell lower, but she did not turn away her head, and Philip continued to look at her. Then he said, slowly—

"You are very much more beautiful than I thought you would be."

"Am I?" said Maggie, the pleasure returning in a deeper flush. She turned her face away from him and took some steps, looking straight before her in silence, as if she were adjusting her consciousness to this new idea. Girls are so accustomed to think of dress as the main ground of vanity, that, in abstaining from the looking-glass, Maggie had thought more of abandoning all care for adornment than of renouncing the contemplation of her face. Comparing herself with elegant, wealthy young ladies, it had not occurred to her that she could produce any effect with her person. Philip seemed to like the silence well. He walked by her side, watching her face, as if that sight left no room for any other wish. They had passed from among the fir-trees, and had now come to a green hollow almost surrounded by an amphitheatre of the pale pink dog-roses. But as the light about them had brightened, Maggie's face had lost its glow. She stood still when they were in the hollows, and, looking at Philip again, she said in a serious, sad voice—

"I wish we could have been friends—I mean, if it would have been good and right for us. But that is the trial I have to bear in everything: I may not keep anything I used to love when I was little. The old books went; and Tom is different—and my father. It is like death. I must part with everything I cared for when I was a child. And I must part with you: we must never take any notice of each other again. That was what I wanted to speak to you for. I wanted to let you know that Tom and I can't do as we like about such things, and that if I behave as if I had forgotten all about you, it is not out of envy or pride—or—or any bad feeling."

Maggie spoke with more and more sorrowful gentleness as she went on, and her eyes began to fill with tears. The deepening expression of pain on Philip's face gave him a stronger resemblance to his boyish self, and made the deformity appeal more strongly to her pity.

"I know—I see all that you mean," he said in a voice that had become feebler from discouragement: "I know what there is to keep us apart on both sides. But it is not right, Maggie—don't you be angry with me, I am so used to call you Maggie in my thoughts—it is not right to sacrifice everything to other people's unreasonable feelings. I would give up a great deal for *my* father; but I would not give up a friendship or—or an attachment of any sort, in obedience to any wish of his that I didn't recognise as right."

"I don't know," said Maggie, musingly. "Often, when I have been angry and discontented, it has seemed to me that I was not bound to give up anything; and I have gone on thinking till it has seemed to me that I could think away all my duty. But no good has ever come of that —it was an evil state of mind. I'm quite sure that whatever I might do, I should wish in the end that I had gone without anything for myself, rather than have made my father's life harder to him."

"But would it make his life harder, if we were to see each other sometimes?" said Philip. He was going to say something else, but checked himself.

"O, I'm sure he wouldn't like it. Don't ask me why, or anything about it," said Maggie, in a distressed tone. "My father feels so strongly about some things. He is not at all happy."

"No more am I," said Philip, impetuously: "*I* am not happy."

"Why?" said Maggie, gently. "At least—I ought not to ask—but I'm very, very sorry."

Philip turned to walk on, as if he had not patience to stand still any longer, and they went out of the hollow, winding amongst the trees and bushes in silence. After that last word of Philip's, Maggie could not bear to insist immediately on their parting.

"I've been a great deal happier," she said at last, timidly, "since I have given up thinking about what is easy and pleasant, and being discontented because I couldn't have my own will. Our life is determined for us—and it makes the mind very free when we give up wishing, and only think of bearing what is laid upon us, and doing what is given us to do."

"But I can't give up wishing," said Philip, impatiently. "It seems to me we can never give up longing and wishing while we are thoroughly alive. There are certain things we feel to be beautiful and good, and we *must* hunger after them. How can we ever be satisfied without them until our feelings are deadened? I delight in fine pictures—I long to be able to paint such. I strive and strive, and can't produce what I want. That is pain to me, and always *will* be pain, until my faculties lose their keenness, like aged eyes. Then there are many other things I long for"—here Philip hesitated a little, and then said—"things that other men have, and that will always be denied me. My life will have nothing great or beautiful in it; I would rather not have lived."

"O, Philip," said Maggie, "I wish you didn't feel so." But her heart began to beat with something of Philip's discontent.

"Well, then," said he, turning quickly round and fixing his grey eyes entreatingly in her face, "I should be contented to live, if you would let me see you sometimes." Then, checked by a fear which her face suggested, he looked away again, and said more calmly, "I have no friend to whom I can tell everything—no one who cares enough about me; and if I could only see you now and then, and you would let me talk to you a little, and show me that you cared for me—and that we may always be friends in heart, and help each other—then I might come to be glad of life."

"But how can I see you, Philip?" said Maggie, falteringly. (Could she really do him good? It would be very hard to say "good-by" this day, and not speak to him again. Here was a new interest to vary the days—it was so much easier to renounce the interest before it came.)

"If you would let me see you here sometimes—walk with you here—I would be contented if it were only once or twice in a month. *That* could injure no one's happiness, and it would sweeten my life. Besides," Philip went on, with all the inventive astuteness of love at one-and-twenty, "if there is any enmity between those who belong to us, we ought all the more to try and quench it by our friendship—I mean, that by our influence on both sides we might bring about a healing of the wounds that have been made in the past, if I could know everything about them. And I don't believe there is any enmity in my own father's mind: I think he has proved the contrary."

Maggie shook her head slowly, and was silent, under conflicting thoughts. It seemed to her inclination, that to see Philip now and then, and keep up the bond of friendship with him, was something not only innocent, but good: perhaps she might really help him to find contentment, as she had found it. The voice that said this made sweet music to Maggie; but athwart it there came an urgent monotonous warning from another voice which she had been learning to obey: the warning that such interviews implied secrecy,—implied doing something she would dread to be discovered in—something that, if discovered, must cause anger and pain; and that the admission of anything so near doubleness would act as a spiritual blight. Yet the music would swell out again, like chimes borne onward by a recurrent breeze, persuading her that the wrong lay all in the faults and weaknesses of others, and that there was such a thing as futile sacrifice for one to the injury of another. It was very cruel for Philip that he should be shrunk from, because of an unjustifiable vindictiveness towards his father—poor Philip, whom some people would shrink from only because he was deformed. The idea that he might become her lover, or that her meeting him could cause disapproval in that light, had not occurred to her; and Philip saw the absence of this idea clearly enough—saw it with a certain pang, although it made her consent to his request the less unlikely. There was bitterness to him in the perception that Maggie was almost as frank and unconstrained towards him as when she was a child.

"I can't say either yes or no," she said at last, turning round and walking towards the way she had come; "I must wait, lest I should decide wrongly. I must seek for guidance."

"May I come again, then—to-morrow—or the next day—or next week?"

"I think I had better write," said Maggie, faltering again. "I have to go to St. Ogg's sometimes, and I can put the letter in the post."

"O, no," said Philip, eagerly; "that would not be so well. My father might see the letter—and—he has not any enmity, I believe, but he views things differently from me: he thinks a great deal about wealth and position. Pray let me come here once more. *Tell* me when it shall be; or if you can't tell me, I will come as often as I can till I do see you."

"I think it must be so, then," said Maggie, "for I can't be quite certain of coming here any particular evening."

Maggie felt a great relief in adjourning the decision. She was free now to enjoy the minutes of companionship: she almost thought she might linger a little; the next time they met she should have to pain Philip by telling him her determination.

"I can't help thinking," she said, looking smiling at him after a few moments of silence, "how strange it is that we should have met and talked to each other, just as if it had been only yesterday when we parted at Lorton. And yet we must both be very much altered in those five years—I think it is five years. How was it you seemed to have a sort of feeling that I was the same Maggie?—I was not quite so sure that you would be the same: I know you are so clever, and you must have seen and learnt so much to fill your mind: I was not quite sure you would care about me now."

"I have never had any doubt that you would be the same, whenever I might see you," said Philip. "I mean, the same in everything that made me like you better than any one else. I don't want to explain that: I don't think any of the strongest effects our natures are susceptible of can ever be explained. We can neither detect the process by which they are arrived at, nor the mode in which they act on us. The greatest of painters only once painted a mysteriously divine child; he couldn't have told how he did it, and we can't tell why we feel it to be divine. I think there are stores laid up in our human nature that our understanding can make no complete inventory of. Certain strains of music affect me so strangely—I can never hear them without their changing my whole attitude of mind for a time, and if the effect would last, I might be capable of heroisms."

"Ah! I know what you mean about music—*I* feel so," said Maggie, clasping her hands with her old impetuosity. "At least," she added, in a saddened tone, "I used to feel so when I had any music: I never have any now, except the organ at church."

"And you long for it, Maggie?" said Philip, looking at her with affectionate pity. "Ah, you can have very little that is beautiful in your life. Have you many books? You were so fond of them when you were a little girl."

They were come back to the hollow, round which the dog-roses grew, and they both paused under the charm of the faëry evening light, reflected from the pale-pink clusters.

"No, I have given up books," said Maggie, quietly, "except a very, very few."

Philip had already taken from his pocket a small volume, and was looking at the back, as he said—

"Ah, this is the second volume, I see, else you might have liked to take it home with you. I put it in my pocket because I am studying a scene for a picture."

Maggie had looked at the back too, and saw the title: it revived an old impression with overmastering force.

" 'The Pirate,' " she said, taking the book from Philip's hands. "O, I began that once; I read to where Minna is walking with Cleveland, and I could never get to read the rest. I went on with it in my own head, and I made several endings; but they were all unhappy. I could never make a happy ending out of that beginning. Poor Minna! I wonder what is the real end. For a long while I couldn't get my mind away from the Shetland Isles—I used to feel the wind blowing on me from the rough sea."

Maggie spoke rapidly, with glistening eyes.

"Take that volume home with you, Maggie," said Philip, watching her with delight. "I don't want it now. I shall make a picture of you, instead—you, among the Scotch firs and the slanting shadows."

Maggie had not heard a word he had said: she was absorbed in a page at which she had opened. But suddenly she closed the book, and gave it back to Philip, shaking her head with a backward movement as if to say "avaunt" to floating visions.

"Do keep it, Maggie," said Philip, entreatingly; "it will give you pleasure."

"No, thank you," said Maggie, putting it aside with her hand, and walking on. "It would make me in love with this world again, as I used to be—it would make me long to see and know many things—it would make me long for a full life."

"But you will not always be shut up in your present lot: why should you starve your mind in that way? It is narrow asceticism—I don't like to see you persisting in it, Maggie. Poetry and art and knowledge are sacred and pure."

"But not for me—not for me," said Maggie, walking more hurriedly. "Because I should want too much. I must wait—this life will not last long."

"Don't hurry away from me without saying good-by, Maggie," said Philip, as they reached the group of Scotch firs, and she continued still to walk along without speaking. "I must not go any farther, I think, must I?"

"O, no, I forgot; good-by," said Maggie, pausing, and putting out her hand to him. The action brought her feeling back in a strong current to Philip; and after they had stood looking at each other in silence for a few moments, with their hands clasped, she said, withdrawing her hand,

"I'm very grateful to you for thinking of me all those years. It is very sweet to have people love us. What a wonderful, beautiful thing it seems that God should have made your heart so that you could care about a queer little girl whom you only knew for a few weeks. I remember saying to you, that I thought you cared for me more than Tom did."

"Ah, Maggie," said Philip, almost fretfully, "you would never love me so well as you love your brother."

"Perhaps not," said Maggie, simply; "but then, you know, the first thing I ever remember in my life is standing with Tom by the side of the Floss, while he held my hand: everything before that is dark to me. But I shall never forget you—though we must keep apart."

"Don't say so, Maggie," said Philip. "If I kept that little girl in my mind for five years, didn't I earn some part in her? She ought not to take herself quite away from me."

"Not if I were free," said Maggie; "but I am not—I must submit." She hesitated a moment and then added, "And I wanted to say to you, that you had better not take more notice of my brother than just bowing to him. He once told me not to speak to you again, and he doesn't change his mind. . . . O dear, the sun is set. I am too long away. Good-by." She gave him her hand once more.

"I shall come here as often as I can, till I see you again, Maggie. Have some feeling for *me* as well as for others."

"Yes, yes, I have," said Maggie, hurrying away, and quickly disappearing behind the last fir-tree; though Philip's gaze after her remained immovable for minutes, as if he saw her still.

Maggie went home, with an inward conflict already begun; Philip went home to do nothing but remember and hope. You can hardly help blaming him severely. He was four or five years older than Maggie, and had a full consciousness of his feeling towards her to aid him in foreseeing the character his contemplated interviews with her would bear in the opinion of a third person. But you must not suppose that he was capable of a gross selfishness, or that he could have been satisfied without persuading himself that he was seeking to infuse some happiness into Maggie's life—seeking this even more than any direct ends for himself. He could give her sympathy—he could give her help. There was not the slightest promise of love towards him in her manner; it was nothing more than the sweet girlish tenderness she had shown him when she was twelve: perhaps she would never love him—perhaps no woman ever *could* love him: well, then, he would endure that; he should at least have the happiness of seeing her—of feeling some nearness to her. And he clutched passionately the possibility that she *might* love him: perhaps the feeling would grow, if she could come to associate him with that watchful tenderness which her nature would be so keenly alive to. If any woman could love him, surely Maggie was that woman: there was such wealth of love in her, and there was no one to claim it all. Then—the pity of it, that a mind like hers should be withering in its very youth, like a young forest-tree, for want of the light and space it was formed to flourish in! Could he not hinder that, by persuading her out of her system of privation? He would be her guardian angel; he would do anything, bear anything for her sake—except not seeing her.

CHAPTER II

AUNT GLEGG LEARNS THE BREADTH OF BOB'S THUMB

WHILE Maggie's life-struggles had lain almost entirely within her own soul, one shadowy army fighting another, and the slain shadows for ever rising again, Tom was engaged in a dustier, noisier warfare, grappling with more substantial obstacles, and gaining more definite conquests. So it has been since the days of Hecuba, and of Hector, tamer of horses: inside the gates, the women with streaming hair and uplifted hands offering prayers, watching the world's combat from afar, filling their long, empty days with memories and fears: outside, the men in fierce struggle with things divine and human, quenching memory in the stronger light of purpose, losing the sense of dread and even of wounds in the hurrying ardour of action.

From what you have seen of Tom, I think he is not a youth of whom you would prophesy failure in anything he had thoroughly wished: the wagers are likely to be on his side, notwithstanding his small success in the classics. For Tom had never desired success in this field of enterprise; and for getting a fine flourishing growth of stupidity there is nothing like pouring out on a mind a good amount of subjects in which it feels no interest. But now Tom's strong will bound together his integrity, his pride, his family regrets, and his personal ambition, and made them one force, concentrating his efforts and surmounting discouragements. His uncle Deane, who watched him closely, soon began to conceive hopes of him, and to be rather proud that he had brought into the employment of the firm a nephew who appeared to be made of such good commercial stuff. The real kindness of placing him in the warehouse first was soon evident to Tom, in the hints his uncle began to throw out, that after a time he might perhaps be trusted to travel at certain seasons, and buy in for the firm various vulgar commodities with which I need not shock refined ears in this place; and it was doubtless with a view to this result that Mr. Deane, when he expected to take his wine alone, would tell Tom to step in and sit with him an hour, and would pass that hour in much lecturing and catechising concerning articles of export and import, with an occasional excursus of more indirect utility on the relative advantages to the merchants of St. Ogg's of having goods brought in their own and in foreign bottoms—a subject on which Mr. Deane, as a shipowner, naturally threw off a few sparks when he got warmed with talk and wine. Already, in the second year, Tom's salary was raised; but all, except the price of his dinner and clothes, went home into the tin box; and he shunned comradeship, lest it should lead him into expenses in spite of himself. Not that Tom was moulded on the spooney type of the Industrious Apprentice; he had a very strong appetite for pleasure—would have liked to be a tamer of horses, and to make a distinguished figure in all neighbouring eyes, dispensing treats and benefits to others with well-judged liberality, and being pronounced one of the finest young fellows of those parts; nay, he determined to achieve these things sooner or later; but his practical shrewdness told him that the means to such achievements could only lie for him in present abstinence and self-denial: there were certain milestones to be passed, and one of the first was the payment of his father's debts. Having made up his mind on that point, he strode along without swerving, contracting some rather saturnine sternness, as a young man is likely to do who has a premature call upon him for self-reliance. Tom felt intensely that common cause with his father which springs from family pride, and was bent on being irreproachable as a son; but his growing experience caused him to pass much silent criticism on the rashness and imprudence of his father's past conduct: their dispositions were not in sympathy, and Tom's face showed little radiance during his few home hours. Maggie had an awe of him, against which she struggled as something unfair to her consciousness of wider thoughts and deeper motives; but it was of no use to struggle. A character at unity with itself —that performs what it intends, subdues every counteracting impulse, and has no visions beyond the dictinctly possible—is strong by its very negations.

You may imagine that Tom's more and more obvious unlikeness to his father was well fitted to conciliate the maternal aunts and uncles; and Mr. Deane's favourable reports and predictions to Mr. Glegg concerning Tom's qualifications for business, began to be discussed amongst them with various acceptance. He was likely, it appeared, to do the family credit, without causing it any expense and trouble. Mrs. Pullet had always thought it strange if Tom's excellent complexion, so entirely that of the Dodsons, did not argue a certainty that he would turn out well, his juvenile errors of running down the peacock, and general disrespect to his aunts, only indicating a tinge of Tulliver blood which he had doubtless outgrown. Mr. Glegg, who had contracted a cautious liking for Tom ever since his spirited and sensible behaviour when the execution was in the house, was now warming into a resolution to further his prospects actively—some time, when an opportunity offered of doing so in a prudent manner, without ultimate loss; but Mrs. Glegg observed that she was not given to speak without book, as some people were; that those who said least were most likely to find their words made good; and that when the right moment came, it would be seen who could do something better than talk. Uncle Pullet, after silent meditation for a period of several lozenges, came distinctly to the conclusion, that when a young man was likely to do well, it was better not to meddle with him.

Tom, meanwhile, had shown no disposition to rely on any one but himself, though, with a natural sensitiveness towards all indications of favourable opinion, he was glad to see his uncle Glegg look in on him sometimes in a friendly way during business hours, and glad to be invited to dine at his house, though he usually preferred declining on the ground that he was not sure of being punctual. But about a year ago, something had occurred which induced Tom to test his uncle Glegg's friendly disposition.

Bob Jakin, who rarely returned from one of his rounds without seeing Tom and Maggie, awaited him on the bridge as he was coming home from St. Ogg's one evening, that they might have a little private talk. He took the liberty of asking if Mr. Tom had ever thought of making money by trading a bit on his own account. Trading, how? Tom wished to know. Why, by sending out a bit of a cargo to foreign ports; because Bob had a particular friend who had offered to do a little business for him in that way in Laceham goods, and would be glad to serve Mr. Tom on the same footing. Tom was interested at once, and begged for full explanation; wondering he had not thought of this plan before. He was so well pleased with the prospect of a speculation that might change the slow process of addition into multiplication, that he at once determined to mention the matter to his father, and get his consent to appropriate some of the savings in the tin box to the purchase of a small cargo. He would rather not have consulted his father, but he had just paid his last quarter's money into the tin box, and there was no other resource. All the savings were there; for Mr. Tulliver would not consent to put the money out at interest lest he should lose it. Since he had speculated in the purchase of some corn and had lost by it, he could not be easy without keeping the money under his eye.

Tom approached the subject carefully, as he was seated on the hearth with his father that evening, and Mr. Tulliver listened, leaning forward in his armchair and looking up in Tom's face with a sceptical glance. His first impulse was to give a positive refusal, but he was in some awe of Tom's wishes, and since he had had the sense of being an "unlucky" father, he had lost some of his old peremptoriness, and determination to be master. He took the key of the bureau from his pocket, got out the key of the large chest, and fetched down the tin box—slowly, as if he were trying to defer the moment of a painful parting. Then he seated himself against the table, and opened the box with that little padlock-key which he fingered in his waistcoat pocket in all vacant moments. There they were, the dingy bank-notes and the bright sovereigns, and he counted them out on the table—only a hundred and sixteen pounds in two years, after all the pinching.

"How much do you want, then?" he said, speaking as if the words burnt his lips.

"Suppose I begin with the thirty-six pounds, father?" said Tom.

Mr. Tulliver separated this sum from the rest, and keeping his hand over it, said,——

"It's as much as I can save out o' my pay in a year."

"Yes, father: it is such slow work—saving out of the little money we get. And in this way we might double our savings."

"Ay, my lad," said the father, keeping his hand on the money, "but you might lose it—you might lose a year o' my life—and I haven't got many."

Tom was silent.

"And you know I wouldn't pay a dividend with the first hundred, because I wanted to see it all in a lump—and when I see it, I'm sure on't. If you trust to luck, it's sure to be against me. It's Old Harry's got the luck in his hands; and if I lose one year, I shall never pick it up again—death 'ull o'ertake me."

Mr. Tulliver's voice trembled, and Tom was silent for a few minutes before he said——

"I'll give it up, father, since you object to it so strongly."

But, unwilling to abandon the scheme altogether, he determined to ask his uncle Glegg to venture twenty pounds, on condition of receiving five per cent of the profits. That was really a very small thing to ask. So when Bob called the next day at the wharf to know the decision, Tom proposed that they should go together to his uncle Glegg's to open the business; for his diffident pride clung to him, and made him feel that Bob's tongue would relieve him from some embarrassment.

Mr. Glegg, at the pleasant hour of four in the afternoon of a hot August day, was naturally counting his wall-fruit to assure himself that the sum total had not varied since yesterday. To him entered Tom, in what appeared to Mr. Glegg very questionable companionship: that of a man with a pack on his back—for Bob was equipped for a new journey—and of a huge brindled bull-terrier, who walked with a slow swaying movement from side to side, and glanced from under his eyelids with a surly indifference which might after all be a cover to the most offensive designs. Mr. Glegg's spectacles, which had been assisting him in counting the fruit, made these suspicious details alarmingly evident to him.

"Heigh! heigh! keep that dog back, will you?" he shouted, snatching up a stake and holding it before him as a shield when the visitors were within three yards of him.

"Get out wi' you, Mumps," said Bob, with a kick. "He's as quiet as a lamb, sir,"—an observation which Mumps corroborated by a low growl as he retreated behind his master's legs.

"Why, whatever does this mean, Tom?" said Mr. Glegg. "Have you brought information about the scoundrels as cut my trees?" If Bob came in the character of "information," Mr. Glegg saw reasons for tolerating some irregularity.

"No, sir," said Tom: "I came to speak to you about a little matter of business of my own."

"Ay—well—but what has this dog got to do with it?" said the old gentleman, getting mild again.

"It's my dog, sir," said the ready Bob. "An' it's me as put Mr. Tom up to the bit o' business; for Mr. Tom's been a friend o' mine iver since I was a little chap: fust thing iver I did was frightenin' the birds for th' old master. An' if a bit o' luck turns up, I'm allays thinkin' if I can let Mr. Tom have a pull at it. An' it's a downright roarin' shame, as when he's got the chance o' making a bit o' money wi' sending goods out— ten or twelve per zent clear, when freight an' commission's paid—as he shouldn't lay hold o' the chance for want o' money. An' when there's the Laceham goods—lors! they're made o' purpose for folks as want to send out a little carguy; light, an' take up no room—you may pack twenty pound so as you can't see the passill: an' they're manifacturs as please fools, so I reckon they aren't like to want a market. An' I'd go to Laceham an' buy in the goods for Mr. Tom along wi' my own. An' there's the shupercargo o' the bit of a vessel as is goin' to take 'em out —I know him partic'lar; he's a solid man, an' got a family i' the town here. Salt, his name is—an' a briny chap he is, too—an' if you don't believe me, I can take you to him."

Uncle Glegg stood open-mouthed with astonishment at this unembarrassed loquacity, with which his understanding could hardly keep pace. He looked at Bob, first over his spectacles, then through them, then over them again; while Tom, doubtful of his uncle's impression, began to wish he had not brought this singular Aaron or mouthpiece: Bob's talk appeared less seemly, now some one besides himself was listening to it.

"You seem to be a knowing fellow," said Mr. Glegg, at last.

"Ay, sir, you say true," returned Bob, nodding his head aside; "I think my head's all alive inside like an old cheese, for I'm so full o' plans, one knocks another over. If I hadn't Mumps to talk to, I should get top-heavy an' tumble in a fit. I suppose it's because I niver went to school much. That's what I jaw my old mother for. I says, 'You should ha' sent me to school a bit more,' I says—'an' then I could ha' read i' the books like fun, an' kep' my head cool an' empty.' Lors, she's fine an' comfor'ble now, my old mother is: she ates her baked meat an' taters as often as she likes. For I'm gettin' so full o' money, I must hev a wife to spend it for me. But it's botherin', a wife is—and Mumps mightn't like her."

Uncle Glegg, who regarded himself as a jocose man since he had retired from business, was beginning to find Bob amusing, but he had still a disapproving observation to make, which kept his face serious.

"Ah," he said, "I should think you're at a loss for ways o' spending your money, else you wouldn't keep that big dog, to eat as much as two Christians. It's shameful—shameful!" But he spoke more in sorrow than in anger, and quickly added——

"But, come now, let's hear more about this business, Tom. I suppose you want a little sum to make a venture with. But where's all your own money? You don't spend it all—eh?"

"No, sir," said Tom, colouring; "but my father is unwilling to risk it, and I don't like to press him. If I could get twenty or thirty pounds to begin with, I could pay five per cent for it, and then I could gradually make a little capital of my own, and do without a loan."

"Ay . . . ay," said Mr. Glegg, in an approving tone; "that's not a bad notion, and I won't say as I wouldn't be your man. But it'll be as well for me to see this Salt, as you talk on. And then . . . here's this friend o' yours offers to buy the goods for you. Perhaps you've got somebody to stand surety for you if the money's put into your hands?" added the cautious old gentleman, looking over his spectacles at Bob.

"I don't think that's necessary, uncle," said Tom. "At least, I mean it would not be necessary for me, because I know Bob well; but perhaps it would be right for you to have some security."

"You get your per-centage out o' the purchase, I suppose?" said Mr. Glegg, looking at Bob.

"No, sir," said Bob, rather indignantly; "I didn't offer to get a apple for Mr. Tom, o' purpose to hev a bite out of it myself. When I play folks tricks they'll be more fun in 'em nor that."

"Well, but it's nothing but right you should have a small per-centage," said Mr. Glegg. "I've no opinion o' transactions where folks do things for nothing. It allays looks bad."

"Well, then," said Bob, whose keenness saw at once what was implied, "I'll tell you what I get by't, an' it's money in my pocket in the end:—I make myself look big, wi' makin' a bigger purchase. That's what I'm thinking on. Lors! I'm a 'cute chap—I am."

"Mr. Glegg, Mr. Glegg," said a severe voice from the open parlor window, "pray are you coming in to tea?—or are you going to stand talking with packmen till you get murdered in the open daylight?"

"Murdered?" said Mr. Glegg; "what's the woman talking of? Here's your nephey Tom come about a bit o' business."

"Murdered—yes—it isn't many 'sizes ago, since a packman murdered a young woman in a lone place, and stole her thimble, and threw her body into a ditch."

"Nay, nay," said Mr. Glegg, soothingly, "you're thinking o' the man wi' no legs, as drove a dog-cart."

"Well, it's the same thing, Mr. Glegg—only you're fond o' contradicting what I say; and if my nephey's come about business, it 'ud be more fitting if you'd bring him into the house, and let his aunt know about it, instead o' whispering in corners, in that plotting, underminding way."

"Well, well," said Mr. Glegg, "we'll come in now."

"You needn't stay here," said the lady to Bob, in a loud voice, adapted to the moral not the physical distance between them. "We don't want anything. I don't deal wi' packmen. Mind you shut the gate after you."

"Stop a bit; not so fast," said Mr. Glegg: "I haven't done with this young man yet. Come in, Tom; come in," he added, stepping in at the French window.

"Mr. Glegg," said Mrs. G., in a fatal tone, "if you're going to let that man and his dog in on my carpet, before my very face, be so good as to let me know. A wife's got a right to ask that, I hope."

"Don't you be uneasy, mum," said Bob, touching his cap. He saw at once that Mrs. Glegg was a bit of game worth running down, and longed to be at the sport; "we'll stay out upo' the gravel here—Mumps and me will. Mumps knows his company—he does. I might hish at him by th' hour together, before he'd fly at a real gentlewoman like you. It's won-derful how he knows which is the good-looking ladies—and's partic'lar fond of 'em when they've good shapes. Lors!" added Bob, laying down his pack on the gravel, "it's a thousand pities such a lady as you shouldn't deal with a packman, i'stead o' goin' into these newfangled shops, where there's half-a-dozen fine gents wi' their chins propped up wi' a stiff stock, a-looking like bottles wi' ornamental stoppers, an' all got to get their dinner out of a bit o' calico: it stan's to reason you must pay three times the price you pay a packman, as is the nat'ral way o' gettin' goods—an' pays no rent, an' isn't forced to throttle him-self till the lies are squeezed out on him, whether he will or no. But lors! mum, you know what it is better nor I do—*you* can see through them shopmen, I'll be bound."

"Yes, I reckon I can, and through the packmen too," observed Mrs. Glegg, intending to imply that Bob's flattery had produced no effect on *her;* while her husband, standing behind her with his hands in his pock-ets and legs apart, winked and smiled with conjugal delight at the prob-ability of his wife's being circumvented.

"Ay, to be sure, mum," said Bob. "Why, you must ha' dealt wi' no end o' packmen when you war a young lass—before the master here had the luck to set eyes on you. I know where you lived, I do—seen th' house many a time—close upon Squire Darleigh's—a stone house wi' steps . . ."

"Ah, that it had," said Mrs. Glegg, pouring out the tea. "You know something o' my family then . . . are you akin to that packman with a squint in his eye, as used to bring th' Irish linen?"

"Look you there now!" said Bob, evasively. "Didn't I know as you'd remember the best bargains you've made in your life was made wi' packmen? Why, you see, even a squintin' packman's better nor a shop-man as can see straight. Lors! if I'd had the luck to call at the stone house wi' my pack, as lies here,"—stooping and thumping the bundle emphatically with his fist,—"an' th' handsome young lasses all stannin' out on the stone steps, it 'ud ha' been summat like openin' a pack—that would. It's on'y the poor houses now as a packman calls on, if it isn't for the sake o' the sarvant-maids. They're paltry times—these are. Why, mum, look at the printed cottons now, an' what they was when you wore 'em—why, you wouldn't put such a thing on now, I can see. It must be first-rate quality—the manifactur as you'd buy—summat as 'ud wear as well as your own faitures."

"Yes, better quality nor any you're like to carry: you've got nothing first-rate but brazenness, I'll be bound," said Mrs. Glegg, with a triumphant sense of her insurmountable sagacity. "Mr. Glegg, are you going ever to sit down to your tea? Tom, there's a cup for you."

"You speak true there, mum," said Bob. "My pack isn't for ladies like you. The time's gone by for that. Bargains picked up dirt cheap! A bit o' damage here an' there, as can be cut out, or else niver seen i' the wearin'; but not fit to offer to rich folks as can pay for the look o' things as nobody sees. I'm not the man as 'ud offer t' open my pack to *you,* mum: no, no; I'm a imperent chap, as you say—these times makes folks imperent—but I'm not up to the mark o' that."

"Why, what goods do you carry in your pack?" said Mrs. Glegg. "Fine-coloured things, I suppose—shawls an' that?"

"All sorts, mum, all sorts," said Bob, thumping his bundle; "but let us say no more about that, if *you* please. I'm here upo' Mr. Tom's business, an' I'm not the man to take up the time wi' my own."

"And pray, what *is* this business as is to be kept from me?" said Mrs. Glegg, who, solicited by a double curiosity, was obliged to let the one-half wait.

"A little plan o' nephey Tom's here," said good-natured Mr. Glegg; "and not altogether a bad un, I think. A little plan for making money: that's the right sort o' plan for young folks as have got their fortin' to make, eh, Jane?"

"But I hope it isn't a plan where he expects iverything to be done for him by his friends: that's what the young folks think of mostly nowadays. And pray, what has this packman got to do wi' what goes on in our family? Can't you speak for yourself, Tom, and let your aunt know things, as a nephey should?"

"This is Bob Jakin, aunt," said Tom, bridling the irritation that aunt Glegg's voice always produced. "I've known him ever since we were little boys. He's a very good fellow, and always ready to do me a kindness. And he has had some experience in sending goods out—a small part of a cargo as a private speculation; and he thinks if I could begin to do a little in the same way, I might make some money. A large interest is got in that way."

"Large int'rest?" said aunt Glegg, with eagerness; "and what do you call large int'rest?"

"Ten or twelve per cent," Bob says, "after expenses are paid."

"Then why wasn't I let to know o' such things before, Mr. Glegg?" said Mrs. Glegg, turning to her husband, with a deep grating tone of reproach. "Haven't you allays told me as there was no getting more nor five per cent?"

"Pooh, pooh, nonsense, my good woman," said Mr. Glegg. "You couldn't go into trade, could you? You can't get more than five per cent with security."

"But I can turn a bit o' money for you, an' welcome, mum," said Bob, "if you'd like to risk it—not as there's any risk to speak on. But if you'd a mind to lend a bit o' money to Mr. Tom, he'd pay you six or seven per zent, an' get a trifle for himself as well; an' a good-natur'd lady like you 'ud like the feel o' the money better if your nephey took part on it."

"What do you say, Mrs. G.?" said Mr. Glegg. "I've a notion, when I've made a bit more inquiry, as I shall perhaps start Tom here with a bit of a nest-egg—he'll pay me int'rest, you know—an' if you've got some little sums lyin' idle twisted up in a stockin' toe, or that . . ."

"Mr. Glegg, it's beyond iverything! You'll go and give information to the tramps next, as they may come and rob me."

"Well, well, as I was sayin', if you like to join me wi' twenty pounds, you can—I'll make it fifty. That'll be a pretty good nest-egg—eh, Tom?"

"You're not counting on me, Mr. Glegg, I hope," said his wife. "You could do fine things wi' my money, I don't doubt."

"Very well," said Mr. Glegg, rather snappishly, "then we'll do without you. I shall go with you to see this Salt," he added, turning to Bob.

"And now, I suppose, you'll go all the other way, Mr. Glegg," said Mrs. G., "and want to shut me out o' my own nephey's business. I never said I wouldn't put money into it—I don't say as it shall be twenty pounds, though you're so ready to say it for me—but he'll see some day as his aunt's in the right not to risk the money she's saved for him till it's proved as it won't be lost."

"Ay, that's a pleasant sort o' risk, that is," said Mr. Glegg, indiscreetly winking at Tom, who couldn't avoid smiling. But Bob stemmed the injured lady's outburst.

"Ay, mum," he said, admiringly, "you know what's what—you do. An' it's nothing but fair. *You* see how the first bit of a job answers, an' then you'll come down handsome. Lors, it's a fine thing to hev good kin. I got my bit of a nest-egg, as the master calls it, all by my own sharpness—ten suvreigns it was—wi' dousing the fire at Torry's mill, an' it's growed an' growed by a bit an' a bit, till I'n got a matter o' thirty pound to lay out, besides makin' my mother comfor'ble. I should get more, on'y I'm such a soft wi' the women—I can't help lettin' 'em hev such good bargains. There's this bundle, now" (thumping it lustily), "any other chap 'ud make a pretty penny out on it. But me! . . . lors, I shall sell 'em for pretty near what I paid for 'em."

"Have you got a bit of good net, now?" said Mrs. Glegg, in a patronising tone, moving from the tea-table, and folding her napkin.

"Eh, mum, not what you'd think it worth your while to look at. I'd scorn to show it you. It 'ud be an insult to you."

"But let me see," said Mrs. Glegg, still patronising. "If they're damaged goods, they're like enough to be a bit the better quality."

"No, mum. I know my place," said Bob, lifting up his pack and shouldering it. "I'm not going t' expose the lowness o' my trade to a lady like you. Packs is come down i' the world: it 'ud cut you to th' heart to see the difference. I'm at your sarvice, sir, when you've a mind to go an' see Salt."

"All in good time," said Mr. Glegg, really unwilling to cut short the dialogue. "Are you wanted at the wharf, Tom?"

"No, sir; I left Stowe in my place."

"Come, put down your pack, and let me see," said Mrs. Glegg, drawing a chair to the window, and seating herself with much dignity.

"Don't you ask it, mum," said Bob, entreatingly.

"Make no more words," said Mrs. Glegg, severely, "but do as I tell you."

"Eh, mum, I'm loth—that I am," said Bob, slowly depositing his pack on the step, and beginning to untie it with unwilling fingers. "But what you order shall be done" (much fumbling in pauses between the sentences). "It's not as you'll buy a single thing on me. . . . I'd be sorry for you to do it . . . for think o' them poor women up i' the villages there, as niver stir a hundred yards from home . . . it 'ud be a pity for anybody to buy up their bargains. Lors, it's as good as a junketing to 'em when they see me wi' my pack . . . an' I shall niver pick up such bargains for 'em again. Least ways, I've no time now, for I'm off to Laceham. See here, now," Bob went on, becoming rapid again, and holding up a scarlet woollen kerchief with an embroidered wreath in the corner; "here's a thing to make a lass's mouth water, an' on'y two shillin'—an' why? Why, 'cause there's a bit of a moth-hole i' this plain end. Lors, I think the moths an' the mildew was sent by Providence o' purpose to cheapen the goods a bit for the good-lookin' women as han't got much money. If it hadn't been for the moths, now, every hankicher on 'em 'ud ha' gone to the rich handsome ladies, like you, mum, at five shillin' a-piece—not a farthin' less; but what does the moth do? Why, it nibbles off three shillin' o' the price i' no time, an' then a packman like me can carry't to the poor lasses as live under the dark thack, to make a bit of a blaze for 'em. Lors, it's as good as a fire, to look at such a hankicher!"

Bob held it at a distance for admiration, but Mrs. Glegg said sharply—

"Yes, but nobody wants a fire this time o' year. Put these coloured things by—let me look at your nets, if you've got 'em."

"Eh, mum, I told you how it 'ud be," said Bob, flinging aside the coloured things with an air of desperation. "I knowed it 'ud turn again' you to look at such paltry articles as I carry. Here's a piece o' figured muslin now—what's the use o' your lookin' at it? You might as well look at poor folks's victual, mum—it 'ud on'y take away your appetite. There's a yard i' the middle on't as the pattern's all missed—lors, why it's a muslin as the Princess Victoree might ha' wore—but," added

Bob, flinging it behind him onto the turf, as if to save Mrs. Glegg's eyes, "it'll be bought up by th' huckster's wife at Fibb's End—that's where *it*'ll go—ten shillin' for the whole lot—ten yards, countin' the damaged 'un—five-an'-twenty shillin' 'ud ha' been the price—not a penny less. But I'll say no more, mum; it's nothing to you—a piece o' muslin like that; you can afford to pay three times the money for a thing as isn't half so good. It's nets *you* talked on; well, I've got a piece all 'ull serve you to make fun on. . . ."

"Bring me that muslin," said Mrs. Glegg: "it's a buff—I'm partial to buff."

"Eh, but a *damaged* thing," said Bob, in a tone of deprecating disgust. "You'd do nothing with it, mum—you'd give it to the cook, I know you would—an' it 'ud be a pity—she'd look too much like a lady in it—it's unbecoming for servants."

"Fetch it and let me see you measure it," said Mrs. Glegg, authoritatively.

Bob obeyed with ostentatious reluctance.

"See what there is over measure!" he said, holding forth the extra half-yard, while Mrs. Glegg was busy examining the damaged yard, and throwing her head back to see how far the fault would be lost on a distant view.

"I'll give you six shilling for it," she said, throwing it down with the air of a person who mentions an ultimatum.

"Didn't I tell you now, mum, as it 'ud hurt your feelings to look at my pack? That damaged bit's turned your stomach now—I see it has," said Bob, wrapping the muslin up with the utmost quickness, and apparently about to fasten up his pack. "You're used to seein' a different sort o' article carried by packmen, when you lived at the Stone House. Packs is come down i' the world; I told you that: *my* goods are for common folks. Mrs. Pepper 'ull give me ten shillin' for that muslin, an' be sorry as I didn't ask her more. Such articles answer i' the wearin' —they keep their colour till the threads melt away i' the wash-tub, an' that won't be while *I*'m a young un."

"Well, seven shilling," said Mrs. Glegg.

"Put it out o' your mind, mum, now do," said Bob. "Here's a bit o' net, then, for you to look at before I tie up my pack: just for you to see what my trade's come to: spotted and sprigged, you see, beautiful, but yellow—'s been lyin' by an' got the wrong colour. I could niver ha' bought such net, if it hadn't been yellow. Lors, it's took me a deal o' study to know the vally o' such articles; when I begun to carry a pack, I was as ignirant as a pig—net or calico was all the same to me. I thought them things the most vally as was the thickest. I was took in dreadful—for I'm a straitforrard chap—up to no tricks, mum. I can on'y say my nose is my own, for if I went beyond, I should lose myself pretty quick. An' I gev five-an'-eightpence for that piece o' net—if I was to tell y' anything else I should be tellin' you fibs: an' five-an'-eightpence

I shall ask for it—not a penny more—for it's a woman's article, an' I like to 'commodate the women. Five-an'-eightpence for six yards—as cheap as if it was only the dirt on it as was paid for."

"I don't mind having three yards of it," said Mrs. Glegg.

"Why, there's but six altogether," said Bob. "No, mum, it isn't worth your while; you can go to the shop to-morrow an' get the same pattern ready whitened. It's on'y three times the money—what's that to a lady like you?" He gave an emphatic tie to his bundle.

"Come, lay me out that muslin," said Mrs. Glegg. "Here's eight shilling for it."

"You *will* be jokin', mum," said Bob, looking up with a laughing face; "I see'd you was a pleasant lady when I fust come to the winder."

"Well, put it me out," said Mrs. Glegg, peremptorily.

"But if I let you have it for ten shillin', mum, you'll be so good as not tell nobody. I should be a laughin'-stock—the trade 'ud hoot me, if they knowed it. I'm obliged to make believe as I ask more nor I do for my goods, else they'd find out I was a flat. I'm glad you don't insist upo' buyin' the net, for then I should ha' lost my two best bargains for Mrs. Pepper o' Fibb's End—an' she's a rare customer."

"Let me look at the net again," said Mrs. Glegg, yearning after the cheap spots and sprigs, now they were vanishing.

"Well, I can't deny *you,* mum," said Bob, handing it out. "Eh! see what a pattern now! Real Laceham goods. Now, this is the sort o' article I'm recommendin' Mr. Tom to send out. Lors, it's a fine thing for anybody as has got a bit o' money—these Laceham goods 'ud make it breed like maggits. If I was a lady wi' a bit o' money!—why, I know one as put thirty pound into them goods—a lady wi' a cork leg; but as sharp—you wouldn't catch *her* runnin' her head into a sack: *she'd* see her way clear out o' anything afore she'd be in a hurry to start. Well, she let out thirty pound to a young man in the drapering line, and he laid it out i' Laceham goods, an' a shupercargo o' my acquinetance (not Salt) took 'em out, an' she got her eight per zent fust go off—an' now you can't hold her but she must be sendin' out carguies wi' every ship, till she's gettin' as rich as a Jew. Bucks her name is—she doesn't live i' this town. Now then, mum, if you'll please to give me the net . . ."

"Here's fifteen shilling, then, for the two," said Mrs. Glegg. "But it's a shameful price."

"Nay, mum, you'll niver say that when you're upo' your knees i' church i' five years' time. I'm makin' you a present o' th' articles—I am, indeed. That eightpence shaves off my profit as clean as a razor. Now then, sir," continued Bob, shouldering his pack, "if you please, I'll be glad to go and see about makin' Mr. Tom's fortin'. Eh, I wish I'd got another twenty pound to lay out for *my*sen: I shouldn't stay to say my Catechism afore I know'd what to do wi't."

"Stop a bit, Mr. Glegg," said the lady, as her husband took his hat, "you never *will* give me the chance o' speaking. You'll go away now, and finish everything about this business, and come back and tell me it's too late for me to speak. As if I wasn't my nephey's own aunt, and th' head o' the family on his mother's side! and laid by guineas, all full weight, for him—as he'll know who to respect when I'm laid in my coffin."

"Well, Mrs. G., say what you mean," said Mr. G., hastily.

"Well, then, I desire as nothing may be done without my knowing. I don't say as I shan't venture twenty pounds, if you make out as everything's right and safe. And if I do, Tom," concluded Mrs. Glegg, turning impressively to her nephew, "I hope you'll allays bear it in mind and be grateful for such an aunt. I mean you to pay me interest, you know—I don't approve o' giving; we niver looked for that in *my* family."

"Thank you, aunt," said Tom, rather proudly. "I prefer having the money only lent to me."

"Very well: that's the Dodson sperrit," said Mrs. Glegg, rising to get her knitting with the sense that any further remark after this would be bathos.

Salt—that eminently "briny chap"—having been discovered in a cloud of tobacco smoke at the Anchor Tavern, Mr. Glegg commenced inquiries which turned out satisfactorily enough to warrant the advance of the "nest-egg," to which aunt Glegg contributed twenty pounds; and in this modest beginning you see the ground of a fact which might otherwise surprise you, namely, Tom's accumulation of a fund, unknown to his father, that promised in no very long time to meet the more tardy process of saving, and quite cover the deficit. When once his attention had been turned to this source of gain, Tom determined to make the most of it, and lost no opportunity of obtaining information and extending his small enterprises. In not telling his father, he was influenced by that strange mixture of opposite feelings which often gives equal truth to those who blame an action and those who admire it: partly, it was that disinclination to confidence which is seen between near kindred—that family repulsion which spoils the most sacred relations of our lives; partly, it was the desire to surprise his father with a great joy. He did not see that it would have been better to soothe the interval with a new hope, and prevent the delirium of a too sudden elation.

At the time of Maggie's first meeting with Philip, Tom had already nearly a hundred and fifty pounds of his own capital, and while they were walking by the evening light in the Red Deeps, he, by the same evening light, was riding into Laceham, proud of being on his first journey on behalf of Guest & Co., and revolving in his mind all the chances that by the end of another year he should have doubled his gains, lifted off the obloquy of debt from his father's name, and perhaps —for he should be twenty-one—have got a new start for himself, on a higher platform of employment. Did he not deserve it? He was quite sure that he did.

CHAPTER III

THE WAVERING BALANCE

I SAID that Maggie went home that evening from the Red Deeps with a mental conflict already begun. You have seen clearly enough, in her interview with Philip, what that conflict was. Here suddenly was an opening in the rocky wall which shut in the narrow valley of humiliation, where all her prospect was the remote unfathomed sky; and some of the memory-haunting earthly delights were no longer out of her reach. She might have books, converse, affection—she might hear tidings of the world from which her mind had not yet lost its sense of exile; and it would be a kindness to Philip too, who was pitiable—clearly not happy; and perhaps here was an opportunity indicated for making her mind more worthy of its highest service—perhaps the noblest, completest devoutness could hardly exist without some width of knowledge: *must* she always live in this resigned imprisonment? It was so blameless, so good a thing that there should be friendship between her and Philip; the motives that forbade it were so unreasonable—so unchristian! But the severe monotonous warning came again and again—that she was losing the simplicity and clearness of her life by admitting a ground of concealment, and that, by forsaking the simple rule of renunciation, she was throwing herself under the seductive guidance of illimitable wants. She thought she had won strength to obey the warning before she allowed herself the next week to turn her steps in the evening to the Red Deeps. But while she was resolved to say an affectionate farewell to Philip, how she looked forward to that evening walk in the still, fleckered shade of the hollows, away from all that was harsh and unlovely; to the affectionate admiring looks that would meet her; to the sense of comradeship that childish memories would give to wiser, older talk; to the certainty that Philip would care to hear everything she said, which no one else cared for! It was a half-hour that it would be very hard to turn her back upon, with the sense that there would be no other like it. Yet she said what she meant to say; she looked firm as well as sad.

"Philip, I have made up my mind—it is right that we should give each other up, in everything but memory. I could not see you without concealment—stay, I know what you are going to say—it is other people's wrong feelings that make concealment necessary; but concealment is bad, however it may be caused. I feel that it would be bad for me, for us both. And then, if our secret were discovered, there would be nothing but misery—dreadful anger; and then we must part after all, and it would be harder, when we were used to seeing each other."

Philip's face had flushed, and there was a momentary eagerness of expression, as if he had been about to resist this decision with all his might. But he controlled himself, and said with assumed calmness, "Well, Maggie, if we must part, let us try and forget it for one half-hour: let us talk together a little while—for the last time."

He took her hand, and Maggie felt no reason to withdraw it: his quietness made her all the more sure she had given him great pain, and she wanted to show him how unwillingly she had given it. They walked together hand in hand in silence.

"Let us sit down in the hollow," said Philip, "where we stood the last time. See how the dog-roses have strewed the ground, and spread their opal petals over it!"

They sat down at the roots of the slanting ash.

"I've begun my picture of you among the Scotch firs, Maggie," said Philip, "so you must let me study your face a little, while you stay—since I am not to see it again. Please, turn your head this way."

This was said in an entreating voice, and it would have been very hard of Maggie to refuse. The full lustrous face, with the bright black coronet, looked down, like that of a divinity well pleased to be worshipped, on the pale-hued, small-featured face that was turned up to it.

"I shall be sitting for my second portrait, then," she said, smiling. "Will it be larger than the other?"

"O yes, much larger. It is an oil-painting. You will look like a tall Hamadryad, dark and strong and noble, just issued from one of the fir-trees, when the stems are casting their afternoon shadows on the grass."

"You seem to think more of painting than of anything now, Philip?"

"Perhaps I do," said Philip, rather sadly; "but I think of too many things—sow all sorts of seeds, and get no great harvest from any one of them. I'm cursed with susceptibility in every direction, and effective faculty in none. I care for painting and music; I care for classic literature, and mediæval literature, and modern literature: I flutter all ways, and fly in none."

"But surely that is a happiness to have so many tastes—to enjoy so many beautiful things—when they are within your reach," said Maggie, musingly. "It always seemed to me a sort of clever stupidity only to have one sort of talent—almost like a carrier-pigeon."

"It might be a happiness to have many tastes if I were like other men," said Philip, bitterly. "I might get some power and distinction by mere mediocrity, as they do; at least I should get those middling satisfactions which make men contented to do without great ones. I might think society at St. Ogg's agreeable then. But nothing could make life worth the purchase-money of pain to me, but some faculty that would lift me above the dead level of provincial existence. Yes—there is one thing: a passion answers as well as a faculty."

Maggie did not hear the last words: she was struggling against the consciousness that Philip's words had set her own discontent vibrating again as it used to do.

"I understand what you mean," she said, "though I know so much less than you do. I used to think I could never bear life if it kept on being the same every day; and I must always be doing things of no consequence, and never know anything greater. But, dear Philip, I think we are only like children, that some one who is wiser is taking care of. Is it not right to resign ourselves entirely, whatever may be denied us? I have found great peace in that for the last two or three years—even joy in subduing my own will."

"Yes, Maggie," said Philip, vehemently; "and you are shutting yourself up in a narrow self-delusive fanaticism, which is only a way of escaping pain by starving into dulness all the highest powers of your nature. Joy and peace are not resignation: resignation is the willing endurance of a pain that is not allayed—that you don't expect to be allayed. Stupefaction is not resignation: and it is stupefaction to remain in ignorance—to shut up all the avenues by which the life of your fellow-men might become known to you. I am not resigned: I am not sure that life is long enough to learn that lesson. *You* are not resigned: you are only trying to stupefy yourself."

Maggie's lips trembled; she felt there was some truth in what Philip said, and yet there was a deeper consciousness that, for any immediate application it had to her conduct, it was no better than falsity. Her double impression corresponded to the double impulse of the speaker. Philip seriously believed what he said, but he said it with vehemence because it made an argument against the resolution that opposed his wishes. But Maggie's face, made more child-like by the gathering tears, touched him with a tenderer, less egoistic feeling. He took her hand and said gently—

"Don't let us think of such things in this short half-hour, Maggie. Let us only care about being together. . . . We shall be friends in spite of separation. . . . We shall always think of each other. I shall be glad to live as long as you are alive, because I shall think there may always come a time when I can—when you will let me help you in some way."

"What a dear, good brother you would have been, Philip," said Maggie, smiling through the haze of tears. "I think you would have made as much fuss about me, and been as pleased for me to love you, as would have satisfied even me. You would have loved me well enough to bear with me, and forgive me everything. That was what I always longed that Tom should do. I was never satisfied with a *little* of anything. That is why it is better for me to do without earthly happiness altogether. . . . I never felt that I had enough music—I wanted more instruments playing together—I wanted voices to be fuller and deeper. Do you ever sing now, Philip?" she added abruptly, as if she had forgotten what went before.

"Yes," he said, "every day, almost. But my voice is only middling—like everything else in me."

"O, sing me something—just one song. I *may* listen to that, before I go—something you used to sing at Lorton on a Saturday afternoon, when we had the drawing-room all to ourselves, and I put my apron over my head to listen."

"*I* know," said Philip, and Maggie buried her face in her hands, while he sang, *sotto voce,* "Love in her eyes sits playing;" and then said, "That's it, isn't it?"

"O, no, I won't stay," said Maggie, starting up. "It will only haunt me. Let us walk, Philip. I must go home."

She moved away, so that he was obliged to rise and follow her.

"Maggie," he said, in a tone of remonstrance, "don't persist in this wilful, senseless privation. It makes me wretched to see you benumbing and cramping your nature in this way. You were so full of life when you were a child: I thought you would be a brilliant woman—all wit and bright imagination. And it flashes out in your face still, until you draw that veil of dull quiescence over it."

"Why do you speak so bitterly to me, Philip?" said Maggie.

"Because I foresee it will not end well: you can never carry on this self-torture."

"I shall have strength given me," said Maggie, tremulously.

"No, you will not, Maggie: no one has strength given to do what is unnatural. It is mere cowardice to seek safety in negations. No character becomes strong in that way. You will be thrown into the world some day, and then every rational satisfaction of your nature that you deny now, will assault you like a savage appetite."

Maggie started and paused, looking at Philip with alarm in her face.

"Philip, how dare you shake me in this way? You are a tempter."

"No, I am not; but love gives insight, Maggie, and insight often gives foreboding. *Listen* to me—*let* me supply you with books; do let me see you sometimes—be your brother and teacher, as you said at Lorton. It is less wrong that you should see me than that you should be committing this long suicide."

Maggie felt unable to speak. She shook her head and walked on in silence, till they came to the end of the Scotch firs, and she put out her hand in sign of parting.

"Do you banish me from this place for ever, then, Maggie? Surely I may come and walk in it sometimes? If I meet you by chance, there is no concealment in that?"

It is the moment when our resolution seems about to become irrevocable—when the fatal iron gates are about to close upon us—that tests our strength. Then, after hours of clear reasoning and firm conviction, we snatch at any sophistry that will nullify our long struggles, and bring us the defeat that we love better than victory.

Maggie felt her heart leap at this subterfuge of Philip's, and there passed over her face that almost imperceptible shock which accompanies any relief. He saw it, and they parted in silence.

Philip's sense of the situation was too complete for him not to be visited with glancing fears lest he had been intervening too presumptuously in the action of Maggie's conscience—perhaps for a selfish end. But no!—he persuaded himself his end was not selfish. He had little hope that Maggie would ever return the strong feeling he had for her;

and it must be better for Maggie's future life, when these petty family obstacles to her freedom had disappeared, that the present should not be entirely sacrificed, and that she should have some opportunity of culture—some interchange with a mind above the vulgar level of those she was now condemned to live with. If we only look far enough off for the consequences of our actions, we can always find some point in the combination of results, by which those actions can be justified: by adopting the point of view of a Providence who arranges results, or of a philosopher who traces them, we shall find it possible to obtain perfect complacency in choosing to do what is most agreeable to us in the present moment. And it was in this way that Philip justified his subtle efforts to overcome Maggie's true prompting against a concealment that would introduce doubleness into her own mind, and might cause new misery to those who had the primary natural claim on her. But there was a surplus of passion in him that made him half independent of justifying motives. His longing to see Maggie, and make an element in her life, had in it some of that savage impulse to snatch an offered joy, which springs from a life in which the mental and bodily constitution have made pain predominate. He had not his full share in the common good of men: he could not even pass muster with the insignificant, but must be singled out for pity, and excepted from what was a matter of course with others. Even to Maggie he was an exception: it was clear that the thought of his being her lover had never entered her mind.

Do not think too hardly of Philip. Ugly and deformed people have great need of unusual virtues, because they are likely to be extremely uncomfortable without them: but the theory that unusual virtues spring by a direct consequence out of personal disadvantages, as animals get thicker wool in severe climates, is perhaps a little overstrained. The temptations of beauty are much dwelt upon, but I fancy they only bear the same relation to those of ugliness, as the temptation to excess at a feast, where the delights are varied for eye and ear as well as palate, bears to the temptations that assail the desperation of hunger. Does not the Hunger Tower stand as the type of the utmost trial to what is human in us?

Philip had never been soothed by that mother's love which flows out to us in the greater abundance because our need is greater, which clings to us the more tenderly because we are the less likely to be winners in the game of life; and the sense of his father's affection and indulgence towards him was marred by the keener perception of his father's faults. Kept aloof from all practical life as Philip had been, and by nature half-feminine in sensitiveness, he had some of the woman's intolerant repulsion towards worldliness and the deliberate pursuit of sensual enjoyment; and this one strong natural tie in his life—his relation as a son—was like an aching limb to him. Perhaps there is inevitably something morbid in a human being who is in any way unfavourably excepted from ordinary conditions, until the good force has had time to triumph; and it has rarely had time for that at two-and-twenty. That force was present in Philip in much strength, but the sun himself looks feeble through the morning mists.

CHAPTER IV

ANOTHER LOVE SCENE

EARLY in the following April, nearly a year after that dubious parting you have just witnessed, you may, if you like, again see Maggie entering the Red Deeps through the group of Scotch firs. But it is early afternoon and not evening, and the edge of sharpness in the spring air makes her draw her large shawl close about her and trip along rather quickly; though she looks round, as usual, that she may take in the sight of her beloved trees. There is a more eager, inquiring look in her eyes than there was last June, and a smile is hovering about her lips, as if some playful speech were awaiting the right hearer. The hearer was not long in appearing.

"Take back your *Corinne*," said Maggie, drawing a book from under her shawl. "You were right in telling me she would do me no good; but you were wrong in thinking I should wish to be like her."

"Wouldn't you really like to be a tenth Muse, then, Maggie?" said Philip, looking up in her face as we look at a first parting in the clouds that promises us a bright heaven once more.

"Not at all," said Maggie, laughing. "The Muses were uncomfortable goddesses, I think—obliged always to carry rolls and musical instruments about with them. If I carried a harp in this climate, you know, I must have a green baize cover for it—and I should be sure to leave it behind me by mistake."

"You agree with me in not liking Corinne, then?"

"I didn't finish the book," said Maggie. "As soon as I came to the blond-haired young lady reading in the park, I shut it up, and determined to read no further. I foresaw that that light-complexioned girl would win away all the love from Corinne and make her miserable. I'm determined to read no more books where the blond-haired women carry away all the happiness. I should begin to have a prejudice against them. If you could give me some story, now, where the dark woman triumphs, it would restore the balance. I want to avenge Rebecca and Flora Mac-Ivor, and Minna and all the rest of the dark unhappy ones. Since you are my tutor, you ought to preserve my mind from prejudices—you are always arguing against prejudices."

"Well, perhaps you will avenge the dark women in your own person, and carry away all the love from your cousin Lucy. She is sure to have some handsome young man of St. Ogg's at her feet now: and you have only to shine upon him—your fair little cousin will be quite quenched in your beams."

"Philip, that is not pretty of you, to apply my nonsense to anything

real," said Maggie, looking hurt. "As if I, with my old gowns and want
of all accomplishments, could be a rival of dear little Lucy, who knows
and does all sorts of charming things, and is ten times prettier than
I am—even if I were odious and base enough to wish to be her rival.
Besides, I never go to aunt Deane's when any one is there: it is only
because dear Lucy is good, and loves me, that she comes to see me, and
will have me go to see her sometimes."

"Maggie," said Philip, with surprise, "it is not like you to take playfulness literally. You must have been in St. Ogg's this morning, and
brought away a slight infection of dulness."

"Well," said Maggie, smiling, "if you meant that for a joke, it was a
poor one; but I thought it was a very good reproof. I thought you
wanted to remind me that I am vain, and wish every one to admire
me most. But it isn't for that, that I'm jealous for the dark women—
not because I'm dark myself. It's because I always care the most about
the unhappy people: if the blonde girl were forsaken, I should like *her*
best. I always take the side of the rejected lover in the stories."

"Then you would never have the heart to reject one yourself—should
you, Maggie?" said Philip, flushing a little.

"I don't know," said Maggie, hesitatingly. Then with a bright smile—
"I think perhaps I could if he were conceited; and yet, if he got
extremely humiliated afterwards, I should relent."

"I've often wondered, Maggie," Philip said, with some effort, "whether
you wouldn't really be more likely to love a man that other women were
not likely to love."

"That would depend on what they didn't like him for," said Maggie,
laughing. "He might be very disagreeable. He might look at me through
an eye-glass stuck in his eye, making a hideous face, as young Torry
does. I should think other women are not fond of that; but I never felt
any pity for young Torry. I've never any pity for conceited people, because I think they carry their comfort about with them."

"But suppose, Maggie—suppose it was a man who was not conceited
—who felt he had nothing to be conceited about—who had been marked
from childhood for a peculiar kind of suffering—and to whom you were
the day-star of his life—who loved you, worshipped you, so entirely
that he felt it happiness enough for him if you would let him see you
at rare moments . . ."

Philip paused with a pang of dread lest his confession should cut short
this very happiness—a pang of the same dread that had kept his love
mute through long months. A rush of self-consciousness told him that
he was besotted to have said all this. Maggie's manner this morning had
been as unconstrained and indifferent as ever.

But she was not looking indifferent now. Struck with the unusual
emotion in Philip's tone, she had turned quickly to look at him, and as
he went on speaking, a great change came over her face—a flush and
slight spasm of the features such as we see in people who hear some

news that will require them to readjust their conceptions of the past. She was quite silent, and, walking on towards the trunk of a fallen tree, she sat down, as if she had no strength to spare for her muscles. She was trembling.

"Maggie," said Philip, getting more and more alarmed in every fresh moment of silence, "I was a fool to say it—forget that I've said it. I shall be contented if things can be as they were."

The distress with which he spoke, urged Maggie to say something. "I am so surprised, Philip—I had not thought of it." And the effort to say this brought the tears down too.

"Has it made you hate me, Maggie?" said Philip, impetuously. "Do you think I'm a presumptuous fool?"

"O, Philip!" said Maggie, "how can you think I have such feelings? —as if I were not grateful for *any* love. But . . . but I had never thought of your being my lover. It seemed so far off—like a dream— only like one of the stories one imagines—that I should ever have a lover."

"Then can you bear to think of me as your lover, Maggie?" said Philip, seating himself by her and taking her hand, in the elation of a sudden hope. "*Do* you love me?"

Maggie turned rather pale: this direct question seemed not easy to answer. But her eyes met Philip's, which were in this moment liquid and beautiful with beseeching love. She spoke with hesitation, yet with sweet, simple, girlish tenderness.

"I think I could hardly love any one better: there is nothing but what I love you for." She paused a little while, and then added, "But it will be better for us not to say any more about it—won't it, dear Philip? You know we couldn't even be friends, if our friendship were discovered. I have never felt that I was right in giving way about seeing you— though it has been so precious to me in some ways; and now the fear comes upon me strongly again, that it will lead to evil."

"But no evil has come, Maggie; and if you had been guided by that fear before, you would only have lived through another dreary be-numbing year, instead of reviving into your real self."

Maggie shook her head. "It has been very sweet, I know—all the talking together, and the books, and the feeling that I had the walk to look forward to, when I could tell you the thoughts that had come into my head while I was away from you. But it has made me restless: it has made me think a great deal about the world; and I have impatient thoughts again—I get weary of my home—and then it cuts me to the heart afterwards, that I should ever have felt weary of my father and mother. I think what you call being benumbed was better—better for me—for then my selfish desires were benumbed."

Philip had risen again and was walking backwards and forwards im-patiently.

"No, Maggie, you have wrong ideas of self-conquest, as I've often told you. What you call self-conquest—blinding and deafening your-self to all but one train of impressions—is only the culture of mono-mania in a nature like yours."

He had spoken with some irritation, but now he sat down by her again, and took her hand.

"Don't think of the past now, Maggie; think only of our love. If you can really cling to me with all your heart, every obstacle will be over-come in time: we need only wait. I can live on hope. Look at me, Mag-gie; tell me again, it is possible for you to love me. Don't look away from me to that cloven tree; it is a bad omen."

She turned her large dark glance upon him with a sad smile.

"Come, Maggie, say one kind word, or else you were better to me at Lorton. You asked me if I should like you to kiss me—don't you re-member?—and you promised to kiss me when you met me again. You never kept the promise."

The recollection of that childish time came as a sweet relief to Mag-gie. It made the present moment less strange to her. She kissed him al-most as simply and quietly as she had done when she was twelve years old. Philip's eyes flashed with delight, but his next words were words of discontent.

"You don't seem happy enough, Maggie: you are forcing yourself to say you love me, out of pity."

"No, Philip," said Maggie, shaking her head, in her old childish way; "I'm telling you the truth. It is all new and strange to me; but I don't think I could love any one better than I love you. I should like always to live with you—to make you happy. I have always been happy when I have been with you. There is only one thing I will not do for your sake: I will never do anything to wound my father. You must never ask that from me."

"No, Maggie: I will ask nothing—I will bear everything—I'll wait another year only for a kiss, if you will only give me the first place in your heart."

"No," said Maggie, smiling, "I won't make you wait so long as that." But then, looking serious again, she added, as she rose from her seat—

"But what would your own father say, Philip? O, it is quite impos-sible we can ever be more than friends—brother and sister in secret, as we have been. Let us give up thinking of everything else."

"No, Maggie, I can't give you up—unless you are deceiving me—unless you really only care for me as if I were your brother. Tell me the truth."

"Indeed I do, Philip. What happiness have I ever had so great as being with you?—since I was a little girl—the days Tom was good to me. And your mind is a sort of world to me: you can tell me all I want to know. I think I should never be tired of being with you."

They were walking hand in hand, looking at each other; Maggie, in-deed, was hurrying along, for she felt it time to be gone. But the sense that their parting was near, made her more anxious lest she should have unintentionally left some painful impression on Philip's mind. It was one of those dangerous moments when speech is at once sincere and deceptive—when feeling, rising high above its average depth, leaves flood-marks which are never reached again.

They stopped to part among the Scotch firs.

"Then my life will be filled with hope, Maggie—and I shall be happier than other men, in spite of all? We *do* belong to each other—for always—whether we are apart or together?"

"Yes, Philip: I should like never to part: I should like to make your life very happy."

"I am waiting for something else—I wonder whether it will come."

Maggie smiled, with glistening tears, and then stooped her tall head to kiss the pale face that was full of pleading, timid love—like a woman's.

She had a moment of real happiness then—a moment of belief that, if there were sacrifice in this love, it was all the richer and more satisfying.

She turned away and hurried home, feeling that in the hour since she had trodden this road before, a new era had begun for her. The tissue of vague dreams must now get narrower and narrower, and all the threads of thought and emotion be gradually absorbed in the woof of her actual daily life.

CHAPTER V

THE CLOVEN TREE

SECRETS are rarely betrayed or discovered according to any programme our fear has sketched out. Fear is almost always haunted by terrible dramatic scenes, which recur in spite of the best-argued probabilities against them; and during a year that Maggie had had the burthen of concealment on her mind, the possibility of discovery had continually presented itself under the form of a sudden meeting with her father or Tom when she was walking with Philip in the Red Deeps. She was aware that this was not one of the most likely events; but it was the scene that most completely symbolised her inward dread. Those slight indirect suggestions which are dependent on apparently trivial coincidences and incalculable states of mind, are the favourite machinery of Fact, but are not the stuff in which imagination is apt to work.

Certainly one of the persons about whom Maggie's fears were farthest from troubling themselves was her aunt Pullet, on whom, seeing that she did not live in St. Ogg's, and was neither sharp-eyed nor sharp-tempered, it would surely have been quite whimsical of them to fix rather than on aunt Glegg. And yet the channel of fatality—the path, way of the lightning—was no other than aunt Pullet. She did not live at St. Ogg's, but the road from Garum Firs lay by the Red Deeps, at the end opposite that by which Maggie entered.

The day after Maggie's last meeting with Philip, being a Sunday on which Mr. Pullet was bound to appear in funeral hat-band and scarf at St. Ogg's church, Mrs. Pullet made this the occasion of dining with sister Glegg, and taking tea with poor sister Tulliver. Sunday was the one day in the week on which Tom was at home in the afternoon; and to-day the brighter spirits he had been in of late had flowed over in unusually cheerful open chat with his father, and in the invitation, "Come, Magsie, you come too!" when he strolled out with his mother in the garden to see the advancing cherry-blossoms. He had been better pleased with Maggie since she had been less odd and ascetic; he was even getting rather proud of her: several persons had remarked in his hearing that his sister was a very fine girl. To-day there was a peculiar brightness in her face, due in reality to an under-current of excitement, which had as much doubt and pain as pleasure in it; but it might pass for a sign of happiness.

"You look very well, my dear," said aunt Pullet, shaking her head sadly, as they sat round the tea-table. "I niver thought your girl 'ud be so good-looking, Bessy. But you must wear pink, my dear: that blue thing as your aunt Glegg gave you turns you into a crowflower. Jane never *was* tasty. Why don't you wear that gown o' mine?"

"It is so pretty and so smart, aunt. I think it's too showy for me— at least for my other clothes, that I must wear with it."

"To be sure, it 'ud be unbecoming if it wasn't well known you've got them belonging to you as can afford to give you such things when they've done with 'em themselves. It stands to reason I must give my own niece clothes now and then—such things as *I* buy every year, and never wear anything out. And as for Lucy, there's no giving to her, for she's got everything o' the choicest: sister Deane may well hold her head up, though she looks dreadful yellow, poor thing—I doubt this liver-complaint 'ull carry her off. That's what this new vicar, this Dr. Kenn, said in the funeral sermon to-day."

"Ah, he's a wonderful preacher, by all account—isn't he, Sophy?" said Mrs. Tulliver.

"Why, Lucy had got a collar on this blessed day," continued Mrs. Pullet, with her eyes fixed in a ruminating manner, "as I don't say I haven't got as good, but I must look out my best to match it."

"Miss Lucy's called the bell o' St. Ogg's, they say: that's a cur'ous word," observed Mr. Pullet, on whom the mysteries of etymology sometimes fell with an oppressive weight.

"Pooh!" said Mr. Tulliver, jealous for Maggie, "she's a small thing, not much of a figure. But fine feathers make fine birds. I see nothing to admire so much in those diminitive women; they look silly by the side o' the men—out o' proportion. When I chose my wife, I chose her the right size—neither too little nor too big."

The poor wife, with her withered beauty, smiled complacently.

"But the men aren't *all* big," said uncle Pullet, not without some self-reference; "a young fellow may be good-looking and yet not be a six-foot, like Master Tom here."

"Ah, it's poor talking about littleness and bigness,—anybody may think it's a mercy they're straight," said aunt Pullet. "There's that mis-made son o' Lawyer Wakem's—I saw him at church to-day. Dear, dear! to think o' the property he's like to have; and they say he's very queer and lonely—doesn't like much company. I shouldn't wonder if he goes out of his mind; for we never come along the road but he's a-scrambling out o' the trees and brambles at the Red Deeps."

This wide statement, by which Mrs. Pullet represented the fact that she had twice seen Philip at the spot indicated, produced an effect on Maggie which was all the stronger because Tom sate opposite her, and she was intensely anxious to look indifferent. At Philip's name she had blushed, and the blush deepened every instant from consciousness, until the mention of the Red Deeps made her feel as if the whole secret were betrayed, and she dared not even hold her tea-spoon lest she should show how she trembled. She sat with her hands clasped under the table, not daring to look round. Happily, her father was seated on the same side with herself beyond her uncle Pullet, and could not see her face without stooping forward. Her mother's voice brought the first relief—turning the conversation; for Mrs. Tulliver was always alarmed when the name of Wakem was mentioned in her husband's presence. Gradually Maggie recovered composure enough to look up; her eyes met Tom's, but he turned away his head immediately; and she went to bed that night wondering if he had gathered any suspicion from her confusion. Perhaps not: perhaps he would think it was only her alarm at her aunt's mention of Wakem before her father: that was the interpretation her mother had put on it. To her father, Wakem was like a disfiguring disease, of which he was obliged to endure the consciousness, but was exasperated to have the existence recognised by others; and no amount of sensitiveness in her about her father could be surprising, Maggie thought.

But Tom was too keen-sighted to rest satisfied with such an interpretation: he had seen clearly enough that there was something distinct from anxiety about her father in Maggie's excessive confusion. In trying to recall all the details that could give shape to his suspicions, he remembered only lately hearing his mother scold Maggie for walking in the Red Deeps when the ground was wet, and bringing home shoes clogged with red soil: still Tom, retaining all his old repulsion for Philip's deformity, shrank from attributing to his sister the probability of feeling more than a friendly interest in such an unfortunate exception to the common run of men. Tom's was a nature which had a sort of superstitious repugnance to everything exceptional. A love for a deformed man would be odious in any woman—in a sister intolerable. But if she had been carrying on any kind of intercourse whatever with Philip, a stop must be put to it at once: she was disobeying her father's strongest feelings and her brother's express commands, besides compromising herself by secret meetings. He left home the next morning in that watchful state of mind which turns the most ordinary course of things into pregnant coincidences.

That afternoon, about half-past three o'clock, Tom was standing on the wharf, talking with Bob Jakin about the probability of the good ship Adelaide coming in, in a day or two, with results highly important to both of them.

"Eh," said Bob, parenthetically, as he looked over the fields on the other side of the river, "there goes that crooked young Wakem. I know him or his shadder as far off as I can see 'em; I'm allays lighting on him o' that side the river."

A sudden thought seemed to have darted through Tom's mind. "I must go, Bob," he said, "I've something to attend to," hurrying off to the warehouse, where he left notice for some one to take his place—he was called away home on peremptory business.

The swiftest pace and the shortest road took him to the gate, and he was pausing to open it deliberately, that he might walk into the house with an appearance of perfect composure, when Maggie came out at the front door in bonnet and shawl. His conjecture was fulfilled, and he waited for her at the gate. She started violently when she saw him.

"Tom, how is it you are come home? Is there anything the matter?" Maggie spoke in a low tremulous voice.

"I'm come to walk with you to the Red Deeps and meet Philip Wakem," said Tom, the central fold in his brow, which had become habitual with him, deepening as he spoke.

Maggie stood helpless—pale and cold. By some means, then, Tom knew everything. At last she said, "I'm not going," and turned round.

"Yes, you are; but I want to speak to you first. Where is my father?"

"Out on horseback."

"And my mother?"

"In the yard, I think, with the poultry."

"I can go in, then, without her seeing me?"

They walked in together, and Tom, entering the parlour, said to Maggie, "Come in here."

She obeyed, and he closed the door behind her.

"Now, Maggie, tell me this instant everything that has passed between you and Philip Wakem."

"Does my father know anything?" said Maggie, still trembling.

"No," said Tom, indignantly. "But he *shall* know, if you attempt to use deceit towards me any further."

"I don't wish to use deceit," said Maggie, flushing into resentment at hearing this word applied to her conduct.

"Tell me the whole truth then."

"Perhaps you know it."

"Never mind whether I know it or not. Tell me exactly what has happened, or my father shall know everything," Tom threatened.

"I tell it for my father's sake, then."

"Yes, it becomes you to profess affection for your father, when you have despised his strongest feelings."

"You never do wrong, Tom," said Maggie, tauntingly.

"Not if I know it," answered Tom, with proud sincerity. "But I have nothing to say to you, beyond this: tell me what has passed between you and Philip Wakem. When did you first meet him in the Red Deeps?"

"A year ago," said Maggie, quietly. Tom's severity gave her a certain fund of defiance, and kept her sense of error in abeyance. "You need ask me no more questions. We have been friendly a year. We have met and walked together often. He has lent me books."

"Is that all?" said Tom, looking straight at her with his frown.

Maggie paused a moment; then, determined to make an end of Tom's right to accuse her of deceit, she said, haughtily—

"No, not quite all. On Saturday he told me that he loved me. I didn't think of it before then—I had only thought of him as an old friend."

"And you *encouraged* him?" said Tom, with an expression of disgust.

"I told him that I loved him too."

Tom was silent a few moments, looking on the ground and frowning, with his hands in his pockets. At last, he looked up, and said, coldly—

"Now, then, Maggie, there are but two courses for you to take; either you vow solemnly to me, with your hand on my father's Bible, that you will never have another meeting or speak another word in private with Philip Wakem, or you refuse, and I tell my father everything; and this month, when by my exertions he might be made happy once more, you will cause him the blow of knowing that you are a disobedient, deceitful daughter, who throws away her own respectability by clandestine meetings with the son of a man that has helped to ruin her father. Choose!" Tom ended with cold decision, going up to the large Bible, drawing it forward, and opening it at the fly-leaf, where the writing was.

It was a crushing alternative to Maggie.

"Tom," she said, urged out of pride into pleading, "don't ask me that. I will promise you to give up all intercourse with Philip, if you will let me see him once, or even only write to him and explain everything—to give it up as long as it would ever cause any pain to my father. . . . I feel something for Philip too. *He* is not happy."

"I don't wish to hear anything of your feelings; I have said exactly what I mean: choose—and quickly, lest my mother should come in."

"If I give you my word, that will be as strong a bond to me as if I laid my hand on the Bible. I don't require that to bind me."

"Do what *I* require," said Tom. "I can't trust you, Maggie. There is no consistency in you. Put your hand on this Bible, and say, 'I renounce all private speech and intercourse with Philip Wakem from this time forth.' Else you will bring shame on us all, and grief on my father; and what is the use of my exerting myself and giving up everything else for the sake of paying my father's debts, if you are to bring madness and vexation on him, just when he might be easy and hold up his head once more?"

"O, Tom—*will* the debts be paid soon?" said Maggie, clasping her hands, with a sudden flash of joy across her wretchedness.

"If things turn out as I expect," said Tom. "But," he added, his voice trembling with indignation, "while I have been contriving and working that my father may have some peace of mind before he dies— working for the respectability of our family—you have done all you can to destroy both."

Maggie felt a deep movement of compunction: for the moment, her mind ceased to contend against what she felt to be cruel and unreasonable, and in her self-blame she justified her brother.

"Tom," she said, in a low voice, "it was wrong of me—but I was so lonely—and I was sorry for Philip. And I think enmity and hatred are wicked."

"Nonsense!" said Tom. "Your duty was clear enough. Say no more; but promise, in the words I told you."

"I *must* speak to Philip once more."

"You will go with me now and speak to him."

"I give you my word not to meet him or write to him again without your knowledge. That is the only thing I will say. I will put my hand on the Bible if you like."

"Say it, then."

Maggie laid her hand on the page of manuscript and repeated the promise. Tom closed the book, and said, "Now, let us go."

Not a word was spoken as they walked along. Maggie was suffering in anticipation of what Philip was about to suffer, and dreading the galling words that would fall on him from Tom's lips; but she felt it was in vain to attempt anything but submission. Tom had his terrible clutch on her conscience and her deepest dread: she writhed under the demonstrable truth of the character he had given to her conduct, and yet her whole soul rebelled against it as unfair from its incompleteness. He, meanwhile, felt the impetus of his indignation diverted towards Philip. He did not know how much of an old boyish repulsion and of mere personal pride and animosity was concerned in the bitter severity of the words by which he meant to do the duty of a son and a brother. Tom was not given to inquire subtly into his own motives, any more than into other matters of an intangible kind; he was quite sure that his own motives as well as actions were good, else he would have had nothing to do with them.

Maggie's only hope was that something might, for the first time, have prevented Philip from coming. Then there would be delay—then she might get Tom's permission to write to him. Her heart beat with double violence when they got under the Scotch firs. It was the last moment of suspense, she thought; Philip always met her soon after she got beyond them. But they passed across the more open green space, and entered the narrow bushy path by the mound. Another turning, and they came so close upon him that both Tom and Philip stopped suddenly within a yard of each other. There was a moment's silence, in which Philip darted a look of inquiry at Maggie's face. He saw an answer there, in the pale parted lips, and the terrified tension of the large eyes. Her imagination, always rushing extravagantly beyond an immediate impression, saw her tall strong brother grasping the feeble Philip bodily, crushing him and trampling on him.

"Do you call this acting the part of a man and a gentleman, sir?" Tom said, in a voice of harsh scorn, as soon as Philip's eyes were turned on him again.

"What do you mean?" answered Philip, haughtily.

"Mean? Stand farther from me, lest I should lay hands on you, and I'll tell you what I mean. I mean, taking advantage of a young girl's foolishness and ignorance to get her to have secret meetings with you. I mean, daring to trifle with the respectability of a family that has a good and honest name to support."

"I deny that," interrupted Philip, impetuously. "I could never trifle with anything that affected your sister's happiness. She is dearer to me than she is to you; I honour her more than you can ever honour her; I would give up my life to her."

"Don't talk high-flown nonsense to me, sir! Do you mean to pretend that you didn't know it would be injurious to her to meet you here week after week? Do you pretend you had any right to make professions of love to her, even if you had been a fit husband for her, when neither her father nor your father would ever consent to a marriage between you? And you—you to try and worm yourself into the affections of a handsome girl who is not eighteen, and has been shut out from the world by her father's misfortunes! That's your crooked notion of honour, is it? I call it base treachery—I call it taking advantage of circumstances to win what's too good for you—what you'd never get by fair means."

"It is manly of you to talk in this way to me," said Philip, bitterly, his whole frame shaken by violent emotions. "Giants have an immemorial right to stupidity and insolent abuse. You are incapable even of understanding what I feel for your sister. I feel so much for her that I could even desire to be at friendship with you."

"I should be very sorry to understand your feelings," said Tom, with scorching contempt. "What I wish is that you should understand me— that I shall take care of my sister, and that if you dare to make the least attempt to come near her, or to write to her, or to keep the slightest hold on her mind, your puny, miserable body, that ought to have put some modesty into your mind, shall not protect you. I'll thrash you—I'll hold you up to public scorn. Who wouldn't laugh at the idea of your turning lover to a fine girl?"

"Tom, I will not bear it—I will listen no longer," Maggie burst out in a convulsed voice.

"Stay, Maggie!" said Philip, making a strong effort to speak. Then, looking at Tom, "You have dragged your sister here, I suppose, that she may stand by while you threaten and insult me. These naturally seemed to you the right means to influence me. But you are mistaken. Let your sister speak. If she says she is bound to give me up, I shall abide by her wishes to the slightest word."

"It was for my father's sake, Philip," said Maggie, imploringly. "Tom threatens to tell my father—and he couldn't bear it: I have promised, I have vowed solemnly, that we will not have any intercourse without my brother's knowledge."

"It is enough, Maggie. *I* shall not change; but I wish you to hold yourself entirely free. But trust me—remember that I can never seek for anything but good to what belongs to you."

"Yes," said Tom, exasperated by this attitude of Philip's, "you can talk of seeking good for her and what belongs to her now: did you seek her good before?"

"I did—at some risk, perhaps. But I wished her to have a friend for life—who would cherish her, who would do her more justice than a coarse and narrow-minded brother, that she has always lavished her affections on."

"Yes, my way of befriending her is different from yours; and I'll tell you what is my way. I'll save her from disobeying and disgracing her father: I'll save her from throwing herself away on you—from making herself a laughing-stock—from being flouted by a man like *your* father, because she's not good enough for his son. You know well enough what sort of justice and cherishing you were preparing for her. I'm not to be imposed upon by fine words: I can see what actions mean. Come away, Maggie."

He seized Maggie's right wrist as he spoke, and she put out her left hand. Philip clasped it an instant, with one eager look, and then hurried away.

Tom and Maggie walked on in silence for some yards. He was still holding her wrist tightly, as if he were compelling a culprit from the scene of action. At last Maggie, with a violent snatch, drew her hand away, and her pent-up, long-gathered irritation burst into utterance.

"Don't suppose that I think you are right, Tom, or that I bow to your will. I despise the feelings you have shown in speaking to Philip: I detest your insulting unmanly allusions to his deformity. You have been reproaching other people all your life—you have been always sure you yourself are right: it is because you have not a mind large enough to see that there is anything better than your own conduct and your own petty aims."

"Certainly," said Tom, coolly. "I don't see that your conduct is better, or your aims either. If your conduct, and Philip Wakem's conduct, has been right, why are you ashamed of its being known? Answer me that. I know what I have aimed at in my conduct, and I've succeeded: pray, what good has your conduct brought to you or any one else?"

"I don't want to defend myself," said Maggie, still with vehemence: "I know I've been wrong—often, continually. But yet, sometimes when I have done wrong, it has been because I have feelings that you would be the better for, if you had them. If *you* were in fault ever—if you had done anything very wrong, I should be sorry for the pain it brought you; I should not want punishment to be heaped on you. But you have always enjoyed punishing me—you have always been hard and cruel to me: even when I was a little girl, and always loved you better than any one else in the world, you would let me go crying to bed without forgiving me. You have no pity: you have no sense of your own imperfection and your own sins. It is a sin to be hard; it is not fitting for a mortal—for a Christian. You are nothing but a Pharisee. You thank God for nothing but your own virtues—you think they are great enough to win you everything else. You have not even a vision of feelings by the side of which your shining virtues are mere darkness!"

"Well," said Tom, with cold scorn, "if your feelings are so much better than mine, let me see you show them in some other way than by conduct that's likely to disgrace us all—than by ridiculous flights first into one extreme and then into another. Pray, how have you shown your love, that you talk of, either to me or my father? By disobeying and deceiving us. I have a different way of showing my affection."

"Because you are a man, Tom, and have power, and can do something in the world."

"Then, if you can do nothing, submit to those that can."

"So I *will* submit to what I acknowledge and feel to be right. I will submit even to what is unreasonable from my father, but I will not submit to it from you. You boast of your virtues as if they purchased you a right to be cruel and unmanly as you've been to-day. Don't suppose I would give up Philip Wakem in obedience to you. The deformity you insult would make me cling to him and care for him the more."

"Very well—that is your view of things," said Tom, more coldly than ever; "you need say no more to show me what a wide distance there is between us. Let us remember that in future, and be silent."

Tom went back to St. Ogg's, to fulfil an appointment with his uncle Deane, and receive directions about a journey on which he was to set out the next morning.

Maggie went up to her own room to pour out all that indignant remonstrance, against which Tom's mind was close barred, in bitter tears. Then, when the first burst of unsatisfied anger was gone by, came the recollection of that quiet time before the pleasure which had ended in to-day's misery had perturbed the clearness and simplicity of her life. She used to think in that time that she had made great conquests, and won a lasting stand on serene heights above worldly temptations and conflict. And here she was down again in the thick of a hot strife with her own and others' passions. Life was not so short, then, and perfect rest was not so near as she had dreamed when she was two years younger.

There was more struggle for her—perhaps more falling. If she had felt that she was entirely wrong, and that Tom had been entirely right, she could sooner have recovered more inward harmony; but now her penitence and submission were constantly obstructed by resentment that would present itself to her no otherwise than as a just indignation. Her heart bled for Philip: she went on recalling the insults that had been flung at him with so vivid a conception of what he had felt under them, that it was almost like a sharp bodily pain to her, making her beat the floor with her foot, and tighten her fingers on her palm.

And yet, how was it that she was now and then conscious of a certain dim background of relief in the forced separation from Philip? Surely it was only because the sense of a deliverance from concealment was welcome at any cost.

CHAPTER VI

THE HARD-WON TRIUMPH

THREE weeks later, when Dorlcote Mill was at its prettiest moment in all the year—the great chestnuts in blossom, and the grass all deep and daisied—Tom Tulliver came home to it earlier than usual in the evening, and as he passed over the bridge, he looked with the old deep-rooted affection at the respectable red brick-house, which always seemed cheerful and inviting outside, let the rooms be as bare and the hearts as sad as they might, inside. There is a very pleasant light in Tom's blue-grey eyes as he glances at the house-windows: that fold in his brow never disappears, but it is not unbecoming; it seems to imply a strength of will that may possibly be without harshness, when the eyes and mouth have their gentlest expression. His firm step becomes quicker, and the corners of his mouth rebel against the compression which is meant to forbid a smile.

The eyes in the parlour were not turned towards the bridge just then, and the group there was sitting in unexpectant silence—Mr. Tulliver in his arm-chair, tired with a long ride, and ruminating with a worn look, fixed chiefly on Maggie, who was bending over her sewing while her mother was making the tea.

They all looked up with surprise when they heard the well-known foot.

"Why, what's up now, Tom?" said his father. "You're a bit earlier than usual."

"O, there was nothing more for me to do, so I came away. Well, mother!"

Tom went up to his mother and kissed her, a sign of unusual good-humour with him. Hardly a word or look had passed between him and

Maggie in all the three weeks; but his usual incommunicativeness at home prevented this from being noticeable to their parents.

"Father," said Tom, when they had finished tea, "do you know exactly how much money there is in the tin box?"

"Only a hundred and ninety-three pound," said Mr. Tulliver. "You've brought less o' late—but young fellows like to have their own way with their money. Though I didn't do as I liked before *I* was of age." He spoke with rather timid discontent.

"Are you quite sure that's the sum, father?" said Tom: "I wish you would take the trouble to fetch the tin box down. I think you have perhaps made a mistake."

"How should I make a mistake?" said his father, sharply. "I've counted it often enough; but I can fetch it, if you won't believe me."

It was always an incident Mr. Tulliver liked, in his gloomy life, to fetch the tin box and count the money.

"Don't go out of the room, mother," said Tom, as he saw her moving when his father was gone up-stairs.

"And isn't Maggie to go?" said Mrs. Tulliver, "because somebody must take away the things."

"Just as she likes," said Tom, indifferently.

That was a cutting word to Maggie. Her heart had leaped with the sudden conviction that Tom was going to tell their father the debts could be paid—and Tom would have let her be absent when that news was told! But she carried away the tray, and came back immediately. The feeling of injury on her own behalf could not predominate at that moment.

Tom drew to the corner of the table near his father when the tin box was set down and opened, and the red evening light falling on them made conspicuous the worn, sour gloom of the dark-eyed father and the suppressed joy in the face of the fair-complexioned son. The mother and Maggie sat at the other end of the table, the one in blank patience, the other in palpitating expectation.

Mr. Tulliver counted out the money, setting it in order on the table, and then said, glancing sharply at Tom—

"There, now! you see I was right enough."

He paused, looking at the money with bitter despondency.

"There's more nor three hundred wanting—it'll be a fine while before *I* can save that. Losing that forty-two pound wi' the corn was a sore job. This world's been too many for me. It's took four year to lay *this* by—it's much if I'm above ground for another four year. . . . I must trusten to you to pay 'em," he went on with a trembling voice, "if you keep i' the same mind now you're coming o' age. . . . But you're like enough to bury me first."

He looked up in Tom's face with a querulous desire for some assurance.

"No, father," said Tom, speaking with energetic decision, though there was tremor discernible in his voice too, "you will live to see the debts all paid. You shall pay them with your own hand."

His tone implied something more than mere hopefulness or resolution. A slight electric shock seemed to pass through Mr. Tulliver, and he kept his eyes fixed on Tom with a look of eager inquiry, while Maggie, unable to restrain herself, rushed to her father's side and knelt down by him. Tom was silent a little while before he went on.

"A good while ago, my uncle Glegg lent me a little money to trade with, and that has answered. I have three hundred and twenty pounds in the bank."

His mother's arms were round his neck as soon as the last words were uttered, and she said, half-crying—

"O, my boy, I knew you'd make iverything right again, when you got a man."

But his father was silent: the flood of emotion hemmed in all power of speech. Both Tom and Maggie were struck with fear lest the shock of joy might even be fatal. But the blessed relief of tears came. The broad chest heaved, the muscles of the face gave way, and the grey-haired man burst into loud sobs. The fit of weeping gradually subsided, and he sat quiet, recovering the regularity of his breathing. At last he looked up at his wife and said, in a gentle tone—

"Bessy, you must come and kiss me now—the lad has made you amends. You'll see a bit o' comfort again belike."

When she had kissed him, and he had held her hand a minute, his thoughts went back to the money.

"I wish you'd brought me the money to look at, Tom," he said, fingering the sovereigns on the table; "I should ha' felt surer."

"You shall see it to-morrow, father," said Tom. "My uncle Deane has appointed the creditors to meet to-morrow at the Golden Lion, and he has ordered a dinner for them at two o'clock. My uncle Glegg and he will both be there. It was advertised in the *Messenger* on Saturday."

"Then Wakem knows on't!" said Mr. Tulliver, his eye kindling with triumphant fire. "Ah!" he went on, with a long-drawn guttural enunciation, taking out his snuff-box, the only luxury he had left himself, and tapping it with something of his old air of defiance—"I'll get from under *his* thumb now—though I *must* leave th' old mill. I thought I could ha' held out to die here—but I can't. . . . We've got a glass o' nothing in the house, have we, Bessy?"

"Yes," said Mrs. Tulliver, drawing out her much-reduced bunch of keys, "there's some brandy sister Deane brought me when I was ill."

"Get it me, then, get it me. I feel a bit weak."

"Tom, my lad," he said, in a stronger voice, when he had taken some brandy-and-water, "you shall make a speech to 'em. I'll tell 'em it's you as got the best part o' the money. They'll see I'm honest at last, and ha' got an honest son. Ah! Wakem 'ud be fine and glad to have a son like mine—a fine straight fellow—i'stead o' that poor crooked creatur! You'll prosper i' the world, my lad; you'll maybe see the day when

Wakem and his son 'ull be a round or two below you. You'll like enough be ta'en into partnership, as your uncle Deane was before you—you're in the right way for't; and then there's nothing to hinder your getting rich. . . . And if ever you're rich enough—mind this—try and get th' old mill again."

Mr. Tulliver threw himself back in his chair: his mind, which had so long been the home of nothing but bitter discontent and foreboding, suddenly filled, by the magic of joy, with visions of good fortune. But some subtle influence prevented him from foreseeing the good fortune as happening to himself.

"Shake hands wi' me, my lad," he said, suddenly putting out his hand. "It's a great thing when a man can be proud as he's got a good son. I've had *that* luck."

Tom never lived to taste another moment so delicious as that; and Maggie couldn't help forgetting her own grievances. Tom *was* good; and in the sweet humility that springs in us all in moments of true admiration and gratitude, she felt that the faults he had to pardon in her had never been redeemed, as his faults were. She felt no jealousy this evening that, for the first time, she seemed to be thrown into the background in her father's mind.

There was much more talk before bed-time. Mr. Tulliver naturally wanted to hear all the particulars of Tom's trading adventures, and he listened with growing excitement and delight. He was curious to know what had been said on every occasion—if possible, what had been thought; and Bob Jakin's part in the business threw him into peculiar outbursts of sympathy with the triumphant knowingness of that remarkable packman. Bob's juvenile history, so far as it had come under Mr. Tulliver's knowledge, was recalled with that sense of astonishing promise it displayed, which is observable in all reminiscences of the childhood of great men.

It was well that there was this interest of narrative to keep under the vague but fierce sense of triumph over Wakem, which would otherwise have been the channel his joy would have rushed into with dangerous force. Even as it was, that feeling from time to time gave threats of its ultimate mastery, in sudden bursts of irrelevant exclamation.

It was long before Mr. Tulliver got to sleep that night, and the sleep, when it came, was filled with vivid dreams. At half-past five o'clock in the morning, when Mrs. Tulliver was already rising, he alarmed her by starting up with a sort of smothered shout, and looking round in a bewildered way at the walls of the bedroom.

"What's the matter, Mr. Tulliver?" said his wife. He looked at her, till with a puzzled expression and said at last——

"Ah!—I was dreaming . . . . Did I make a noise? . . . . I thought I'd got hold of him."

CHAPTER VII

A DAY OF RECKONING

Mr. Tulliver was an essentially sober man—able to take his glass and not averse to it, but never exceeding the bounds of moderation. He had naturally an active Hotspur temperament, which did not crave liquid fire to set it a-glow; his impetuosity was usually equal to an exciting occasion without any such reinforcements; and his desire for the brandy-and-water implied that the too sudden joy had fallen with a dangerous shock on a frame depressed by four years of gloom and unaccustomed hard fare. But that first doubtful tottering moment passed, he seemed to gather strength with his gathering excitement; and the next day, when he was seated at table with his creditors, his eye kindling and his cheek flushed with the consciousness that he was about to make an honourable figure once more, he looked more like the proud, confident, warm-hearted and warm-tempered Tulliver of old times, than might have seemed possible to any one who had met him a week before, riding along as had been his wont for the last four years since the sense of failure and debt had been upon him—with his head hanging down, casting brief, unwilling looks on those who forced themselves on his notice. He made his speech, asserting his honest principles with his old confident eagerness, alluding to the rascals and the luck that had been against him, but that he had triumphed over, to some extent, by hard efforts and the aid of a good son; and winding up with the story of how Tom had got the best part of the needful money. But the streak of irritation and hostile triumph seemed to melt for a little while into purer fatherly pride and pleasure, when, Tom's health having been proposed, and uncle Deane having taken occasion to say a few words of eulogy on his general character and conduct, Tom himself got up and made the single speech of his life. It could hardly have been briefer: he thanked the gentlemen for the honour they had done him. He was glad that he had been able to help his father in proving his integrity and regaining his honest name, and, for his own part, he hoped he should never undo that work and disgrace that name. But the applause that followed was so great, and Tom looked so gentlemanly as well as tall and straight, that Mr. Tulliver remarked, in an explanatory manner, to his friends on his right and left, that he had spent a deal of money on his son's education.

The party broke up in very sober fashion at five o'clock. Tom remained in St. Ogg's to attend to some business, and Mr. Tulliver mounted his horse to go home, and describe the memorable things that had been said and done, to "poor Bessy and the little wench." The air of excitement that hung about him was but faintly due to good cheer or any stimulus but the potent wine of triumphant joy. He did not choose any back street to-day, but rode slowly, with uplifted head and free glance, along the principal street all the way to the bridge. Why did he not happen to meet Wakem? The want of that coincidence vexed him, and set his mind at work in an irritating way. Perhaps Wakem was gone out of town to-day on purpose to avoid seeing or hearing anything of an honorable action, which might well cause him some unpleasant twinges. If Wakem were to meet him then, Mr. Tulliver would look straight at him, and the rascal would perhaps be forsaken a little by his cool domineering impudence. He would know by-and-by that an honest man was not going to serve *him* any longer, and lend his honesty to fill a pocket already over-full of dishonest gains. Perhaps the luck was beginning to turn; perhaps the devil didn't always hold the best cards in this world.

Simmering in this way, Mr. Tulliver approached the yard-gates of Dorlcote Mill, near enough to see a well-known figure coming out of them on a fine black horse. They met about fifty yards from the gates, between the great chestnuts and elms and the high bank.

"Tulliver," said Wakem, abruptly, in a haughtier tone than usual, "what a fool's trick you did—spreading those hard lumps on that Far Close. I told you how it would be; but you men never learn to farm with any method."

"Oh!" said Tulliver, suddenly boiling up. "Get somebody else to farm for you, then, as 'll ask *you* to teach him."

"You have been drinking, I suppose," said Wakem, really believing that this was the meaning of Tulliver's flushed face and sparkling eyes.

"No, I've not been drinking," said Tulliver; "I want no drinking to help me make up my mind as I'll serve no longer under a scoundrel."

"Very well! you may leave my premises to-morrow, then: hold your insolent tongue and let me pass." (Tulliver was backing his horse across the road to hem Wakem in.)

"No, I *shan't* let you pass," said Tulliver, getting fiercer. "I shall tell you what I think of you first. You're too big a raskill to get hanged—you're . . ."

"Let me pass, you ignorant brute, or I'll ride over you."

Mr. Tulliver, spurring his horse and raising his whip, made a rush forward, and Wakem's horse, rearing and staggering backward, threw his rider from the saddle and sent him sideways on the ground. Wakem had had the presence of mind to loose the bridle at once, and as the horse only staggered a few paces and then stood still, he might have risen and remounted without more inconvenience than a bruise and a shake. But before he could rise, Tulliver was off his horse too. The sight of the long-hated predominant man down and in his power, threw him into a frenzy of triumphant vengeance, which seemed to give him preternatural agility and strength. He rushed on Wakem, who was in the act of trying to recover his feet, grasped him by the left arm so as to press Wakem's whole weight on the right arm, which rested on the ground, and flogged him fiercely across the back with his riding-whip. Wakem shouted for help, but no help came, until a woman's scream was heard, and the cry of "Father, father!"

Suddenly, Wakem felt, something had arrested Mr. Tulliver's arm; for the flogging ceased, and the grasp on his own arm was relaxed.

"Get away with you—go!" said Tulliver, angrily. But it was not to Wakem that he spoke. Slowly the lawyer rose, and, as he turned his head, saw that Tulliver's arms were being held by a girl—rather by the fear of hurting the girl that clung to him with all her young might.

"O, Luke—mother—come and help Mr. Wakem!" Maggie cried, as she heard the longed-for footsteps.

"Help me on to that low horse," said Wakem to Luke, "then I shall perhaps manage: though—confound it—I think this arm is sprained."

With some difficulty, Wakem was heaved on to Tulliver's horse. Then he turned towards the miller and said, with white rage, "You'll suffer for this, sir. Your daughter is a witness that you've assaulted me."

"I don't care," said Mr. Tulliver, in a thick, fierce voice; "go and show your back, and tell 'em I thrashed you. Tell 'em I've made things a bit more even i' the world."

"Ride my horse home with me," said Wakem to Luke. "By the Toften Ferry—not through the town."

"Father, come in!" said Maggie, imploringly. Then, seeing that Wakem had ridden off, and that no further violence was possible, she slackened her hold and burst into hysteric sobs, while poor Mrs. Tulliver stood by in silence, quivering with fear. But Maggie became conscious that as she was slackening her hold, her father was beginning to grasp her and lean on her. The surprise checked her sobs.

"I feel ill—faintish," he said. "Help me in, Bessy—I'm giddy—I've a pain i' the head."

He walked in slowly, propped by his wife and daughter, and tottered into his arm-chair. The almost purple flush had given way to paleness, and his hand was cold.

"Hadn't we better send for the doctor?" said Mrs. Tulliver.

He seemed to be too faint and suffering to hear her; but presently when she said to Maggie, "Go and see for somebody to fetch the doctor," he looked up at her with full comprehension, and said, "Doctor? No—no doctor. It's my head—that's all. Help me to bed."

Sad ending to the day that had risen on them all like a beginning of better times! But mingled seed must bear a mingled crop.

In half an hour after his father had lain down Tom came home. Bob Jakin was with him—come to congratulate "the old master," not without some excusable pride that he had had his share in bringing about Mr. Tom's good-luck; and Tom had thought his father would like nothing better, as a finish to the day, than a talk with Bob. But now Tom could only spend the evening in gloomy expectation of the unpleasant consequences that must follow on this mad outbreak of his father's long smothered hate. After the painful news had been told, he sat in silence; he had not spirit or inclination to tell his mother and sister anything about the dinner—they hardly cared to ask it. Apparently the mingled thread in the web of their life was so curiously twisted together, that there could be no joy without a sorrow coming close upon it. Tom was dejected by the thought that his exemplary effort must always be baffled by the wrong-doing of others: Maggie was living through, over and over again, the agony of the moment in which she had rushed to throw herself on her father's arm—with a vague, shuddering foreboding of wretched scenes to come. Not one of the three felt any particular alarm about Mr. Tulliver's health: the symptoms did not recall his former dangerous attack, and it seemed only a necessary consequence that his violent passion and effort of strength, after many hours of unusual excitement, should have made him feel ill. Rest would probably cure him.

Tom, tired out by his active day, fell asleep soon, and slept soundly: it seemed to him as if he had only just come to bed, when he waked to see his mother standing by him in the grey light of early morning.

"My boy, you must get up this minute: I've sent for the doctor, and your father wants you and Maggie to come to him."

"Is he worse, mother?"

"He's been very ill all night with his head, but he doesn't say it's worse—he only said sudden, 'Bessy, fetch the boy and girl. Tell 'em to make haste.' "

Maggie and Tom threw on their clothes hastily in the chill grey light, and reached their father's room almost at the same moment. He was watching for them with an expression of pain on his brow, but with sharpened anxious consciousness in his eyes. Mrs. Tulliver stood at the foot of the bed, frightened and trembling, looking worn and aged from disturbed rest. Maggie was at the bedside first, but her father's glance was towards Tom, who came and stood next to her.

"Tom, my lad, it's come upon me as I shan't get up again . . . . This world's been too many for me, my lad, but you've done what you could to make things a bit even. Shake hands wi' me again, my lad, before I go away from you."

The father and son clasped hands and looked at each other an instant. Then Tom said, trying to speak firmly——

"Have you any wish, father—that I can fulfil, when . . . ."

"Ay, my lad . . . you'll try and get the old mill back."

"Yes, father."

"And there's your mother—you'll try and make her amends, all you can, for my bad luck . . . and there's the little wench . . ."

The father turned his eyes on Maggie with a still more eager look, while she, with a bursting heart, sank on her knees, to be closer to the dear, time-worn face which had been present with her through long years, as the sign of her deepest love and hardest trial.

"You must take care of her, Tom . . . don't you fret, my wench . . . there'll come somebody as'll love you and take your part . . . and you must be good to her, my lad. I was good to *my* sister. Kiss me, Maggie. . . . Come, Bessy. . . . You'll manage to pay for a brick grave, Tom, so as your mother and me can lie together."

He looked away from them all when he had said this, and lay silent for some minutes, while they stood watching him, not daring to move. The morning light was growing clearer for them, and they could see the heaviness gathering in his face, and the dulness in his eyes. But at last he looked towards Tom and said——

"I had my turn—I beat him. That was nothing but fair. I never wanted anything but what was fair."

"But, father, dear father," said Maggie, an unspeakable anxiety predominating over her grief, "You forgive him—you forgive every one now?"

He did not move his eyes to look at her, but he said——

"No, my wench. I don't forgive him. . . . What's forgiving to do? I can't love a raskill . . ."

His voice had become thicker; but he wanted to say more, and moved his lips again and again, struggling in vain to speak. At length the words forced their way.

"Does God forgive raskills? . . . But if He does, He won't be hard wi' me."

His hands moved uneasily, as if he wanted them to remove some obstruction that weighed upon him. Two or three times there fell from him some broken words——

"This world's . . . too many . . . honest man . . . puzzling . . ."

Soon they merged into mere mutterings; the eyes had ceased to discern; and then came the final silence.

But not of death. For an hour or more the chest heaved, the loud hard breathing continued, getting gradually slower, as the cold dews gathered on the brow.

At last there was total stillness, and poor Tulliver's dimly-lighted soul had for ever ceased to be vexed with the painful riddle of this world.

Help was come now: Luke and his wife were there, and Mr. Turnbull had arrived, too late for everything but to say, "This is death."

Tom and Maggie went down-stairs together into the room where their father's place was empty. Their eyes turned to the same spot, and Maggie spoke:

"Tom, forgive me—let us always love each other," and they clung and wept together.

BOOK SIX

The Great Temptation

★

CHAPTER I

A DUET IN PARADISE

THE well-furnished drawing-room, with the open grand piano, and the pleasant outlook down a sloping garden to a boat-house by the side of the Floss, is Mr. Deane's. The neat little lady in mourning, whose light-brown ringlets are falling over the coloured embroidery with which her fingers are busy, is of course Lucy Deane; and the fine young man who is leaning down from his chair to snap the scissors in the extremely abbreviated face of the "King Charles" lying on the young lady's feet, is no other than Mr. Stephen Guest, whose diamond ring, attar of roses, and air of nonchalant leisure, at twelve o'clock in the day, are the graceful and odoriferous result of the largest oil-mill and the most extensive wharf in St. Ogg's. There is an apparent triviality in the action with the scissors, but your discernment perceives at once that there is a design in it which makes it eminently worthy of a large-headed, long-limbed young man; for you see that Lucy wants the scissors, and is compelled, reluctant as she may be, to shake her ringlets back, raise her soft hazel eyes, smile playfully down on the face that is so very nearly on a level with her knee, and holding out her little shell-pink palm, to say—

"My scissors, please, if you can renounce the great pleasure of persecuting my poor Minny."

The foolish scissors have slipped too far over the knuckles, it seems, and Hercules holds out his entrapped fingers hopelessly.

"Confound the scissors! The oval lies the wrong way. Please, draw them off for me."

"Draw them off with your other hand," says Miss Lucy, roguishly.

"O, but that's my left hand: I'm not left-handed." Lucy laughs, and the scissors are drawn off with gentle touches from tiny tips, which naturally dispose Mr. Stephen for a repetition *da capo*. Accordingly, he watches for the release of the scissors, that he may get them into his possession again.

"No, no," said Lucy, sticking them in her band, "you shall not have my scissors again—you have strained them already. Now don't set

663

Minny growling again. Sit up and behave properly, and then I will tell you some news."

"What is that?" said Stephen, throwing himself back and hanging his right arm over the corner of his chair. He might have been sitting for his portrait, which would have represented a rather striking young man of five-and-twenty, with a square forehead, short dark-brown hair standing erect, with a slight wave at the end, like a thick crop of corn, and a half-ardent, half-sarcastic glance from under his well-marked horizontal eyebrows. "Is it very important news?"

"Yes—very. Guess."

"You are going to change Minny's diet, and give him three ratafias soaked in a dessert-spoonful of cream daily."

"Quite wrong."

"Well, then, Dr. Kenn has been preaching against buckram, and you ladies have all been sending him a round-robin, saying—'This is a hard doctrine; who can bear it?'"

"For shame!" said Lucy, adjusting her little mouth gravely. "It is rather dull of you not to guess my news, because it is about something I mentioned to you not very long ago."

"But you have mentioned many things to me not long ago. Does your feminine tyranny require that when you say the thing you mean is one of several things, I should know it immediately by that mark?"

"Yes, I know you think I am silly."

"I think you are perfectly charming."

"And my silliness is part of my charm?"

"I didn't say *that*."

"But I know you like women to be rather insipid. Philip Wakem betrayed you: he said so one day when you were not here."

"O, I know Phil is fierce on that point; he makes it quite a personal matter. I think he must be love-sick for some unknown lady—some exalted Beatrice whom he met abroad."

"By the by!" said Lucy, pausing in her work, "it has just occurred to me that I have never found out whether my cousin Maggie will object to see Philip, as her brother does. Tom will not enter a room where Philip is, if he knows it: perhaps Maggie may be the same, and then we shan't be able to sing our glees—shall we?"

"What! is your cousin coming to stay with you?" said Stephen, with a look of slight annoyance.

"Yes; that was my news, which you have forgotten. She's going to leave her situation, where she has been nearly two years, poor thing—ever since her father's death; and she will stay with me a month or two—many months, I hope."

"And am I bound to be pleased at that news?"

"O, no, not at all," said Lucy, with a little air of pique. "*I* am pleased; but that, of course, is no reason why *you* should be pleased. There is no girl in the world I love so well as my cousin Maggie."

"And you will be inseparable, I suppose, when she comes. There will

e no possibility of a *tête-à-tête* with you any more, unless you can find
n admirer for her, who will pair off with her occasionally. What is the
ground of dislike to Philip? He might have been a resource."

"It is a family quarrel with Philip's father. There were very painful
ircumstances, I believe. I never quite understood them, or knew them
ll. My uncle Tulliver was unfortunate and lost all his property, and I
hink he considered Mr. Wakem was somehow the cause of it. Mr.
Wakem bought Dorlcote Mill, my uncle's old place, where he always
ved. You must remember my uncle Tulliver, don't you?"

"No," said Stephen, with rather supercilious indifference. "I've al-
ays known the name, and I daresay I knew the man by sight, apart
om his name. I know half the names and faces in the neighbourhood
n that detached, disjointed way."

"He was a very hot-tempered man. I remember, when I was a little
irl, and used to go to see my cousins, he often frightened me by talking
s if he were angry. Papa told me there was a dreadful quarrel, the very
ay before my uncle's death, between him and Mr. Wakem, but it was
ished up. That was when you were in London. Papa says my uncle was
uite mistaken in many ways: his mind had become embittered. But
om and Maggie must naturally feel it very painful to be reminded of
ese things. They have had so much—so very much trouble. Maggie
as at school with me six years ago, when she was fetched away because
her father's misfortunes, and she has hardly had any pleasure since,
think. She has been in a dreary situation in a school since uncle's
ath, because she is determined to be independent, and not live with
nt Pullet; and I could hardly wish her to come to me then, because
ar mamma was ill, and everything was so sad. That is why I want her
come to me now, and have a long, long holiday."

"Very sweet and angelic of you," said Stephen, looking at her with
admiring smile; "and all the more so if she has the conversational
alities of her mother."

"Poor aunty! You are cruel to ridicule her. She is very valuable to *me*,
know. She manages the house beautifully—much better than any
anger would—and she was a great comfort to me in mamma's illness."

"Yes, but in point of companionship, one would prefer that she should
represented by her brandy-cherries and cream-cakes. I think with a
udder that her daughter will always be present in person, and have no
reeable proxies of that kind—a fat, blonde girl, with round blue eyes,
o will stare at us silently."

"O, yes!" exclaimed Lucy, laughing wickedly and clapping her hands,
at is just my cousin Maggie. You must have seen her!"

"No, indeed: I'm only guessing what Mrs. Tulliver's daughter must
and then, if she is to banish Philip, our only apology for a tenor,
t will be an additional bore."

"But I hope that may not be. I think I will ask you to call on Philip
l tell him Maggie is coming to-morrow. He is quite aware of Tom's
ling, and always keeps out of his way; so he will understand, if you

tell him, that I asked you to warn him not to come until I write to ask him."

"I think you had better write a pretty note for me to take: Phil is so sensitive, you know, the least thing might frighten him off coming at all, and we had hard work to get him. I can never induce him to come to the Park: he doesn't like my sisters, I think. It is only your fairy touch that can lay his ruffled feathers."

Stephen mastered the little hand that was straying towards the table and touched it lightly with his lips. Little Lucy felt very proud and happy. She and Stephen were in that stage of courtship which makes the most exquisite moment of youth, the freshest blossom-time of passion —when each is sure of the other's love, but no formal declaration has been made, and all is mutual divination, exalting the most trivial word, the lightest gesture, into thrills delicate and delicious as wafted jasmine scent. The explicitness of an engagement wears off this finest edge of susceptibility: it is jasmine gathered and presented in a large bouquet.

"But it is really odd that you should have hit so exactly on Maggie's appearance and manners," said the cunning Lucy, moving to reach her desk, "because she might have been like her brother, you know; and Tom has not round eyes; and he is as far as possible from staring at people."

"O, I suppose he is like the father: he seems to be as proud as Lucifer. Not a brilliant companion, though, I should think."

"I like Tom. He gave me my Minny when I lost Lolo; and papa is very fond of him: he says Tom has excellent principles. It was through him that his father was able to pay all his debts before he died."

"Oh, ah, I've heard about that. I heard your father and mine talking about it a little while ago, after dinner, in one of their interminable discussions about business. They think of doing something for young Tulliver: he saved them from a considerable loss by riding home in some marvellous way, like Turpin, to bring them news about the stoppage of a bank, or something of that sort. But I was rather drowsy at the time."

Stephen rose from his seat, and sauntered to the piano, humming in falsetto, "Graceful Consort," as he turned over the volume of "The Creation," which stood open on the desk.

"Come and sing this," he said, when he saw Lucy rising.

"What! 'Graceful Consort?' I don't think it suits your voice."

"Never mind; it exactly suits my feeling, which, Philip will have it, is the grand element of good singing. I notice men with indifferent voices are usually of that opinion."

"Philip burst into one of his invectives against 'The Creation' the other day," said Lucy, seating herself at the piano. "He says it has a sort of sugared complacency and flattering make-believe in it, as if it were written for the birthday fête of a German Grand-Duke."

"O, pooh! He is the fallen Adam with a soured temper. We are Adam and Eve unfallen, in paradise. Now, then—the recitative, for the sake

of the moral. You will sing the whole duty of woman—'And from obedience grows my pride and happiness.' "

"O, no, I shall not respect an Adam who drags the *tempo,* as you
will,'" said Lucy, beginning to play the duet.

Surely the only courtship unshaken by doubts and fears, must be that
in which the lovers can sing together. The sense of mutual fitness that
springs from the two deep notes fulfilling expectation just at the right
moment between the notes of the silvery soprano, from the perfect accord of descending thirds and fifths, from the preconcerted loving chase
of a fugue, is likely enough to supersede any immediate demand for less
impassioned forms of agreement. The contralto will not care to catechise
the bass; the tenor will foresee no embarrassing dearth of remark in
evenings spent with the lovely soprano. In the provinces, too, where
music was so scarce in that remote time, how could the musical people
avoid falling in love with each other? Even political principle must have
been in danger of relaxation under such circumstances; and a violin,
faithful to rotten boroughs, must have been tempted to fraternise in a
demoralising way with a reforming violoncello. In this case, the linnet-
throated soprano, and the full-toned bass, singing,

> "With thee delight is ever new,
> With thee is life incessant bliss,"

believed what they sang all the more *because* they sang it.

"Now for Raphael's great song," said Lucy, when they had finished
the duet. "You do the 'heavy beasts' to perfection."

"That sounds complimentary," said Stephen, looking at his watch.
"By jove, it's nearly half-past one. Well, I can just sing this."

Stephen delivered with admirable ease the deep notes representing the
tread of the heavy beasts: but when a singer has an audience of two,
there is room for divided sentiments. Minny's mistress was charmed;
but Minny, who had intrenched himself, trembling, in his basket as soon
as the music began, found this thunder so little to his taste that he leaped
out and scampered under the remotest *chiffonière,* as the most eligible
place in which a small dog could await the crack of doom.

"Adieu, 'graceful consort,' " said Stephen, buttoning his coat across
when he had done singing, and smiling down from his tall height, with
the air of rather a patronising lover, at the little lady on the music-
stool. "My bliss is not incessant, for I must gallop home. I promised to
be there at lunch."

"You will not be able to call on Philip, then? It is of no consequence:
I have said everything in my note."

"You will be engaged with your cousin to-morrow, I suppose?"

"Yes, we are going to have a little family-party. My cousin Tom will
dine with us; and poor aunty will have her two children together for the
first time. It will be very pretty; I think a great deal about it."

"But I may come the next day?"

"O, yes! Come and be introduced to my cousin Maggie—though you can hardly be said not to have seen her, you have described her so well."

"Good-by, then." And there was that slight pressure of the hands, and a momentary meeting of the eyes, which will often leave a little lady with a slight flush and smile on her face that do not subside immediately when the door is closed, and with an inclination to walk up and down the room rather than to seat herself quietly at her embroidery, or other rational and improving occupation. At least this was the effect on Lucy; and you will not, I hope, consider it an indication of vanity predominating over more tender impulses, that she just glanced in the chimney-glass as her walk brought her near it. The desire to know that one has not looked an absolute fright during a few hours of conversation, may be construed as lying within the bounds of a laudable benevolent consideration for others. And Lucy had so much of this benevolence in her nature that I am inclined to think her small egoisms were impregnated with it, just as there are people not altogether unknown to you, whose small benevolences have a predominant and somewhat rank odour of egoism. Even now, that she is walking up and down with a little triumphant flutter of her girlish heart at the sense that she is loved by the person of chief consequence in her small world, you may see in her hazel eyes an ever-present sunny benignity, in which the momentary harmless flashes of personal vanity are quite lost; and if she is happy in thinking of her lover, it is because the thought of him mingles readily with all the gentle affections and good-natured offices with which she fills her peaceful days. Even now, her mind, with that instantaneous alternation which makes two currents of feeling or imagination seem simultaneous, is glancing continually from Stephen to the preparation she has only half finished in Maggie's room. Cousin Maggie should be treated as well as the grandest lady visitor—nay, better, for she should have Lucy's best prints and drawings in her bedroom, and the very finest bouquet of spring flowers on her table. Maggie would enjoy all that—she was so fond of pretty things! And there was poor aunt Tulliver, that no one made any account of—she was to be surprised with the present of a cap of superlative quality, and to have her health drunk in a gratifying manner, for which Lucy was going to lay a plot with her father this evening. Clearly, she had not time to indulge in long reveries about her own happy love-affairs. With this thought she walked towards the door, but paused there.

"What's the matter, then, Minny?" she said, stooping in answer to some whimpering of that small quadruped, and lifting his glossy head against her pink cheek. "Did you think I was going without you? Come, then, let us go and see Sindbad."

Sindbad was Lucy's chestnut horse, that she always fed with her own hand when he was turned out in the paddock. She was fond of feeding dependent creatures, and knew the private tastes of all the animals about the house, delighting in the little rippling sounds of her canaries when their beaks were busy with fresh seed, and in the small nibbling pleasure of certain animals which, lest she should appear too trivial, I will here call "the more familiar rodents."

Was not Stephen Guest right in his decided opinion that this slim maiden of eighteen was quite the sort of wife a man would not be likely to repent of marrying?—a woman who was loving and thoughtful for other women, not giving them Judas-kisses with eyes askance on their welcome defects, but with real care and vision for their half-hidden pains and mortifications, with long ruminating enjoyment of little pleasures prepared for them? Perhaps the emphasis of his admiration did not fall precisely on this rarest quality in her—perhaps he approved his own choice of her chiefly because she did not strike him as a remarkable rarity. A man likes his wife to be pretty: well, Lucy was pretty, but not to a maddening extent. A man likes his wife to be accomplished, gentle, affectionate, and not stupid; and Lucy had all these qualifications. Stephen was not surprised to find himself in love with her, and was conscious of excellent judgment in preferring her to Miss Leyburn, the daughter of the county member, although Lucy was only the daughter of his father's subordinate partner; besides, he had had to defy and overcome a slight unwillingness and disappointment in his father and sisters—a circumstance which gives a young man an agreeable consciousness of his own dignity. Stephen was aware that he had sense and independence enough to choose the wife who was likely to make him happy, unbiassed by any indirect considerations. He meant to choose Lucy: she was a little darling, and exactly the sort of woman he had always most admired.

CHAPTER II

FIRST IMPRESSIONS

"He is very clever, Maggie," said Lucy. She was kneeling on a footstool at Maggie's feet, after placing that dark lady in the large crimson-velvet chair. "I feel sure you will like him. I hope you will."

"I shall be very difficult to please," said Maggie, smiling, and holding up one of Lucy's long curls, that the sunlight might shine through it. "A gentleman who thinks he is good enough for Lucy must expect to be sharply criticised."

"Indeed, he's a great deal too good for me. And sometimes, when he is away, I almost think it can't really be that he loves me. But I can never doubt it when he is with me—though I couldn't bear any one but you to know that I feel in that way, Maggie."

"O, then, if I disapprove of him, you can give him up, since you are not engaged," said Maggie, with playful gravity.

"I would rather not be engaged. When people are engaged, they begin to think of being married soon," said Lucy, too thoroughly preoccupied to notice Maggie's joke; "and I should like everything to go on for a long while just as it is. Sometimes I am quite frightened lest Stephen should say that he has spoken to papa; and from something that fell from papa the other day, I feel sure he and Mr. Guest are expecting that. And Stephen's sisters are very civil to me now. At first, I think they didn't like his paying me attention; and that was natural. It *does* seem out of keeping that I should ever live in a great place like the Park House—such a little, insignificant thing as I am."

"But people are not expected to be large in proportion to the houses they live in, like snails," said Maggie, laughing. "Pray, are Mr. Guest's sisters giantesses?"

"O, no; and not handsome—that is, not very," said Lucy, half-penitent at this uncharitable remark. "But *he* is—at least he is generally considered very handsome."

"Though you are unable to share that opinion?"

"O, I don't know," said Lucy, blushing pink over brow and neck. "It is a bad plan to raise expectation; you will perhaps be disappointed. But I have prepared a charming surprise for *him;* I shall have a glorious laugh against him. I shall not tell you what it is, though."

Lucy rose from her knees and went to a little distance, holding her pretty head on one side, as if she had been arranging Maggie for a portrait, and wished to judge of the general effect.

"Stand up a moment, Maggie."

"What is your pleasure now?" said Maggie, smiling languidly as she rose from her chair and looked down on her slight, aërial cousin, whose figure was quite subordinate to her faultless drapery of silk and crape.

Lucy kept her contemplative attitude a moment or two in silence, and then said—

"I can't think what witchery it is in you, Maggie, that makes you look best in shabby clothes; though you really must have a new dress now. But do you know, last night I was trying to fancy you in a handsome fashionable dress, and do what I would, that old limp merino would come back as the only right thing for you. I wonder if Marie Antoinette looked all the grander when her gown was darned at the elbows. Now, if *I* were to put anything shabby on, I should be quite unnoticeable—I should be a mere rag."

"O, quite," said Maggie, with mock gravity. "You would be liable to be swept out of the room with the cobwebs and carpet-dust, and to find yourself under the grate, like Cinderella. Mayn't I sit down now?"

"Yes, now you may," said Lucy, laughing. Then, with an air of serious reflection, unfastening her large jet brooch, "But you must change brooches, Maggie; that little butterfly looks silly on you."

"But won't that mar the charming effect of my consistent shabbiness?" said Maggie, seating herself submissively, while Lucy knelt again and unfastened the contemptible butterfly. "I wish my mother were of your opinion, for she was fretting last night because this is my best frock. I've been saving my money to pay for some lessons: I shall never get a better situation without more accomplishments."

Maggie gave a little sigh.

"Now, don't put on that sad look again," said Lucy, pinning the large brooch below Maggie's fine throat. "You're forgetting that you've left that dreary schoolroom behind you, and have no little girls' clothes to mend."

"Yes," said Maggie. "It is with me as I used to think it would be with the poor uneasy white bear I saw at the show. I thought he must have got so stupid with the habit of turning backwards and forwards in that narrow space, that he would keep doing it if they set him free. One gets a bad habit of being unhappy."

"But I shall put you under a discipline of pleasure that will make you lose that bad habit," said Lucy, sticking the black butterfly absently in her own collar, while her eyes met Maggie's affectionately.

"You dear, tiny thing," said Maggie, in one of her bursts of loving admiration, "you enjoy other people's happiness so much, I believe you would do without any of your own. I wish I were like you."

"I've never been tried in that way," said Lucy. "I've always been so happy. I don't know whether I could bear much trouble; I never had any but poor mamma's death. You *have* been tried, Maggie; and I'm sure you feel for other people quite as much as I do."

"No, Lucy," said Maggie, shaking her head slowly, "I don't enjoy their happiness as you do—else I should be more contented. I do feel for them when they are in trouble; I don't think I could ever bear to make any one *un*happy; and yet I often hate myself, because I get angry sometimes at the sight of happy people. I think I get worse as I get older—more selfish. That seems very dreadful."

"Now, Maggie!" said Lucy, in a tone of remonstrance, "I don't believe a word of that. It is all a gloomy fancy—just because you are depressed by a dull, wearisome life."

"Well, perhaps it is," said Maggie, resolutely clearing away the clouds from her face with a bright smile, and throwing herself backward in her chair. "Perhaps it comes from the school diet—watery rice-pudding spiced with Pinnock. Let us hope it will give way before my mother's custards and this charming Geoffrey Crayon."

Maggie took up the "Sketch Book," which lay by her on the table.

"Do I look fit to be seen with this little brooch?" said Lucy, going to survey the effect in the chimney-glass.

"O, no, Mr. Guest will be obliged to go out of the room again if he sees you in it. Pray make haste and put another on."

Lucy hurried out of the room, but Maggie did not take the opportunity of opening her book: she let it fall on her knees, while her eyes wandered to the window: where she could see the sunshine falling on the rich clumps of spring flowers and on the long hedge of laurels—and beyond, the silvery breadth of the dear old Floss, that at this distance seemed to be sleeping in a morning holiday. The sweet fresh garden scent came through the open window, and the birds were busy flitting and alighting, gurgling and singing. Yet Maggie's eyes began to fill with tears. The sight of the old scenes had made the rush of memories so painful, that even yesterday she had only been able to rejoice in her mother's restored comfort and Tom's brotherly friendliness as we rejoice in good news of friends at a distance, rather than in the presence of a happiness which we share. Memory and imagination urged upon her a sense of privation too keen to let her taste what was offered in the transient present: her future, she thought, was likely to be worse than her past, for after her years of contented renunciation, she had slipped back into desire and longing: she found joyless days of distasteful occu- pation harder and harder—she found the image of the intense and varied life she yearned for, and despaired of, becoming more and more im- portunate. The sound of the opening door roused her, and, hastily wip- ing away her tears, she began to turn over the leaves of her book.

"There is one pleasure, I know, Maggie, that your deepest dismalness will never resist," said Lucy, beginning to speak as soon as she entered the room. "That is music, and I mean you to have quite a riotous feast of it. I mean you to get up your playing again, which used to be so much better than mine, when we were at Laceham."

"You would have laughed to see me playing the little girls' tunes over and over to them, when I took them to practice," said Maggie, "just for the sake of fingering the dear keys again. But I don't know whether I could play anything more difficult now than 'Begone, dull care!'"

"I know what a wild state of joy you used to be in when the glee-men came round," said Lucy, taking up her embroidery, "and we might have all those old glees that you used to love so, if I were certain that you don't feel exactly as Tom does about some things."

"I should have thought there was nothing you might be more certain of," said Maggie, smiling.

"I ought rather to have said, one particular thing. Because if you feel just as he does about that, we shall want our third voice. St. Ogg's is so miserably provided with musical gentlemen. There are really only Stephen and Philip Wakem who have any knowledge of music, so as to be able to sing a part."

Lucy had looked up from her work as she uttered the last sentence and saw that there was a change in Maggie's face.

"Does it hurt you to hear the name mentioned, Maggie? If it does, I will not speak of him again. I know Tom will not see him if he can avoid it."

"I don't feel at all as Tom does on that subject," said Maggie, rising and going to the window as if she wanted to see more of the landscape. "I've always liked Philip Wakem ever since I was a little girl, and saw him at Lorton. He was so good when Tom hurt his foot."

"O, I'm so glad!" said Lucy. "Then you won't mind his coming some- times, and we can have much more music than we could without him. I'm very fond of poor Philip, only I wish he were not so morbid about his deformity. I suppose it *is* his deformity that makes him so sad—and sometimes bitter. It is certainly very piteous to see his poor little crooked body and pale face among great strong people."

"But, Lucy," said Maggie, trying to arrest the prattling stream . . .

"Ah, there is the door bell. That must be Stephen," Lucy went on, not noticing Maggie's faint effort to speak. "One of the things I most admire in Stephen is, that he makes a greater friend of Philip than any one."

It was too late for Maggie to speak now: the drawing-room door was opening, and Minny was already growling in a small way at the entrance of a tall gentleman, who went up to Lucy and took her hand with a half-polite, half-tender glance and tone of inquiry, which seemed to indicate that he was unconscious of any other presence.

"Let me introduce you to my cousin, Miss Tulliver," said Lucy, turning with wicked enjoyment towards Maggie, who now approached from the farther window. "This is Mr. Stephen Guest."

For one instant Stephen could not conceal his astonishment at the sight of this tall dark-eyed nymph with her jet-black coronet of hair; the next, Maggie felt herself, for the first time in her life, receiving the tribute of a very deep blush and a very deep bow from a person towards whom she herself was conscious of timidity. This new experience was very agreeable to her—so agreeable, that it almost effaced her previous emotion about Philip. There was a new brightness in her eyes, and a very becoming blush on her cheek, as she seated herself.

"I hope you perceive what a striking likeness you drew the day before yesterday," said Lucy, with a pretty laugh of triumph. She enjoyed her lover's confusion—the advantage was usually on his side.

"This designing cousin of yours quite deceived me, Miss Tulliver," said Stephen, seating himself by Lucy, and stooping to play with Minny —only looking at Maggie furtively. "She said you had light hair and blue eyes."

"Nay, it was you who said so," remonstrated Lucy. "I only refrained from destroying your confidence in your own second-sight."

"I wish I could always err in the same way," said Stephen, "and find reality so much more beautiful than my preconceptions."

"Now you have proved yourself equal to the occasion," said Maggie, "and said what it was incumbent on you to say under the circumstances."

She flashed a slightly defiant look at him: it was clear to her that he had been drawing a satirical portrait of her beforehand. Lucy had said he was inclined to be satirical, and Maggie had mentally supplied the addition—"and rather conceited."

"An alarming amount of devil there," was Stephen's first thought. The second, when she had bent over her work, was, "I wish she would look at me again." The next was, to answer:

"I suppose all phrases of mere compliment have their turn to be true. A man is occasionally grateful when he says 'thank you.' It's rather hard upon him that he must use the same words with which all the world declines a disagreeable invitation—don't you think so, Miss Tulliver?"

"No," said Maggie, looking at him with her direct glance; "if we use common words on a great occasion, they are the more striking, because they are felt at once to have a particular meaning, like old banners, or everyday clothes, hung up in a sacred place."

"Then my compliment ought to be eloquent," said Stephen, really not quite knowing what he said while Maggie looked at him, "seeing that the words were so far beneath the occasion."

"No compliment can be eloquent, except as an expression of indifference," said Maggie, flushing a little.

Lucy was rather alarmed: she thought Stephen and Maggie were not going to like each other. She had always feared lest Maggie should appear too odd and clever to please that critical gentleman. "Why, dear Maggie," she interposed, "you have always pretended that you are too fond of being admired, and now, I think, you are angry because some one ventures to admire you."

"Not at all," said Maggie; "I like too well to feel that I am admired, but compliments never make me feel that."

"I will never pay you a compliment again, Miss Tulliver," said Stephen.

"Thank you; that will be a proof of respect."

Poor Maggie! She was so unused to society that she could take nothing as a matter of course, and had never in her life spoken from the lips merely, so that she must necessarily appear absurd to more experienced ladies, from the excessive feeling she was apt to throw into very trivial incidents. But she was even conscious herself of a little absurdity in this instance. It was true, she had a theoretic objection to compliments, and had once said impatiently to Philip, that she didn't see why women were to be told with a simper that they were beautiful, any more than old men were to be told that they were venerable: still, to be so irritated by a common practice in the case of a stranger like Mr. Stephen Guest, and to care about his having spoken slightingly of her before he had seen her, was certainly unreasonable, and as soon as she was silent she began to be ashamed of herself. It did not occur to her that her irritation was due to the pleasanter emotion which preceded it, just as when we are satisfied with a sense of glowing warmth, an innocent drop of cold water may fall upon us as a sudden smart.

Stephen was too well-bred not to seem unaware that the previous conversation could have been felt embarrassing, and at once began to talk of impersonal matters, asking Lucy if she knew when the bazaar was at length to take place, so that there might be some hope of seeing her rain the influence of her eyes on objects more grateful than those worsted flowers that were growing under her fingers.

"Some day next month, I believe," said Lucy. "But your sisters are doing more for it than I am: they are to have the largest stall."

"Ah, yes; but they carry on their manufactures in their own sitting-room, where I don't intrude on them. I see you are not addicted to the fashionable vice of fancy-work, Miss Tulliver," said Stephen, looking at Maggie's plain hemming.

"No," said Maggie, "I can do nothing more difficult or more elegant than shirt-making."

"And your plain sewing is so beautiful, Maggie," said Lucy, "that I think I shall beg a few specimens of you to show as fancy-work. Your exquisite sewing is quite a mystery to me—you used to dislike that sort of work so much in old days."

"It is a mystery easily explained, dear," said Maggie, looking up quietly. "Plain sewing was the only thing I could get money by; so I was obliged to try and do it well."

Lucy, good and simple as she was, could not help blushing a little: she did not quite like that Stephen should know that—Maggie need not have mentioned it. Perhaps there was some pride in the confession: the pride of poverty that will not be ashamed of itself. But if Maggie had been the queen of coquettes she could hardly have invented a means of giving greater piquancy to her beauty in Stephen's eyes: I am not sure that the quiet admission of plain sewing and poverty would have done alone, but assisted by the beauty, they made Maggie more unlike other women even than she had seemed at first.

"But I can knit, Lucy," Maggie went on, "if that will be of any use for your bazaar."

"O, yes, of infinite use. I shall set you to work with scarlet wool to-morrow. But your sister is the most enviable person," continued Lucy, turning to Stephen, "to have the talent of modelling. She is doing a wondering bust of Dr. Kenn entirely from memory."

"Why, if she can remember to put the eyes very near together, and the corners of the mouth very far apart, the likeness can hardly fail to be striking in St. Ogg's."

"Now, that is very wicked of you," said Lucy, looking rather hurt. "I didn't think you would speak disrespectfully of Dr. Kenn."

"I say anything disrespectful of Dr. Kenn? Heaven forbid! But I am not bound to respect a libellous bust of him. I think Kenn one of the finest fellows in the world. I don't care much about the tall candlesticks he has put on the communion-table, and I shouldn't like to spoil my temper by getting up to early prayers every morning. But he's the only man I ever knew personally who seems to me to have anything of the real apostle in him—a man who has eight hundred a-year, and is contented with deal furniture and boiled beef because he gives away two-thirds of his income. That was a very fine thing of him—taking into his house that poor lad Grattan who shot his mother by accident. He sacrifices more time than a less busy man could spare, to save the poor fellow from getting into a morbid state of mind about it. He takes the lad out with him constantly, I see."

"That is beautiful," said Maggie, who had let her work fall, and was listening with keen interest. "I never knew any one who did such things."

"And one admires that sort of action in Kenn all the more," said Stephen, "because his manners in general are rather cold and severe. There's nothing sugary and maudlin about him."

"O, I think he's a perfect character!" said Lucy, with pretty enthusiasm.

"No, there I can't agree with you," said Stephen shaking his head with sarcastic gravity.

"Now, what fault can you point out in him?"

"He's an Anglican."

"Well, those are the right views, I think," said Lucy, gravely.

"That settles the question in the abstract," said Stephen, "but not from a parliamentary point of view. He has set the Dissenters and the Church people by the ears; and a rising senator like myself, of whose services the country is very much in need, will find it inconvenient when he puts up for the honour of representing St Ogg's in parliament."

"Do you really think of that?" said Lucy, her eyes brightening with a proud pleasure that made her neglect the argumentative interests of Anglicanism.

"Decidedly—whenever old Mr. Leyburn's public spirit and gout induce him to give way. My father's heart is set on it; and gifts like mine, you know"—here Stephen drew himself up, and rubbed his large white hands over his hair with playful self-admiration—"gifts like mine involve great responsibilities. Don't you think so, Miss Tulliver?"

"Yes," said Maggie, smiling, but not looking up; "so much fluency and self-possession should not be wasted entirely on private occasions."

"Ah, I see how much penetration you have," said Stephen. "You have discovered already that I am talkative and impudent. Now superficial people never discern that—owing to my manner, I suppose."

"She doesn't look at me when I talk of myself," he thought, while his listeners were laughing. "I must try other subjects."

Did Lucy intend to be present at the meeting of the Book Club next week? was the next question. Then followed the recommendation to choose Southey's "Life of Cowper," unless she were inclined to be philosophical, and startle the ladies of St Ogg's by voting for one of the Bridgewater Treatises. Of course Lucy wished to know what these alarmingly learned books were; and as it is always pleasant to improve the minds of ladies by talking to them at ease on subjects of which they know nothing, Stephen became quite brilliant in an account of Buckland's Treatise, which he had just been reading. He was rewarded by seeing Maggie let her work fall, and gradually get so absorbed in his wonderful geological story that she sat looking at him, leaning forward with crossed arms, and with an entire absence of self-consciousness, as if he had been the snuffiest of old professors, and she a downy-lipped alumnus. He was so fascinated by this clear, large gaze, that at last he forgot to look away from it occasionally towards Lucy; but she, sweet child, was only rejoicing that Stephen was proving to Maggie how clever he was, and that they would certainly be good friends after all.

"I will bring you the book, shall I, Miss Tulliver?" said Stephen, when he found the stream of his recollections running rather shallow. "There are many illustrations in it that you will like to see."

"O, thank you," said Maggie, blushing with returning self-consciousness at this direct address, and taking up her work again.

"No, no," Lucy interposed. "I must forbid your plunging Maggie in books. I shall never get her away from them; and I want her to have delicious do-nothing days, filled with boating, and chatting, and riding, and driving: that is the holiday she needs."

"Apropos!" said Stephen, looking at his watch. "Shall we go out for a row on the river now? The tide will suit for us to go the Tofton way, and we can walk back."

That was a delightful proposition to Maggie, for it was years since she had been on the river. When she was gone to put on her bonnet, Lucy lingered to give an order to the servant, and took the opportunity of telling Stephen that Maggie had no objection to seeing Philip, so that it was a pity she had sent that note the day before yesterday. But she would write another to-morrow and invite him.

"I'll call and beat him up to-morrow," said Stephen, "and bring him with me in the evening, shall I? My sisters will want to call on you when I tell them your cousin is with you. I must leave the field clear for them in the morning."

"O, yes, pray bring him," said Lucy. "And you *will* like Maggie, shan't you?" she added, in a beseeching tone. "Isn't she a dear, noble-looking creature?"

"Too tall," said Stephen, smiling down upon her, "and a little too fiery. She is not my type of woman, you know."

Gentlemen, you are aware, are apt to impart these imprudent confidences to ladies concerning their unfavourable opinion of sister fair ones. That is why so many women have the advantage of knowing that they are secretly repulsive to men who have self-denyingly made ardent love to them. And hardly anything could be more distinctly characteristic of Lucy, than that she both implicitly believed what Stephen said, and was determined that Maggie should not know it. But you, who have a higher logic than the verbal to guide you, have already foreseen, as the direct sequence to that unfavourable opinion of Stephen's, that he walked down to the boat-house calculating, by the aid of a vivid imagination, that Maggie must give him her hand at least twice in consequence of this pleasant boating plan, and that a gentleman who wishes ladies to look at him is advantageously situated when he is rowing them in a boat. What then? Had he fallen in love with this surprising daughter of Mrs. Tulliver at first sight? Certainly not. Such passions are never heard of in real life. Besides, he was in love already, and half-engaged to the dearest little creature in the world; and he was not a man to make a fool of himself in any way. But when one is five-and-twenty, one has not chalk-stones at one's finger-ends that the touch of a handsome girl should be entirely indifferent. It was perfectly natural and safe to admire beauty and enjoy looking at it—at least under such circumstances as the present. And there was really something very interesting about this girl, with her poverty and troubles: it was gratifying to see the friendship between the two cousins. Generally, Stephen admitted, he was not fond of women who had any peculiarity of character—but here the peculiarity seemed really of a superior kind; and provided one is not obliged to marry such women, why, they certainly make a variety in social intercourse.

Maggie did not fulfil Stephen's hope by looking at him during the first quarter of an hour: her eyes were too full of the old banks that she knew so well. She felt lonely, cut off from Philip—the only person who had ever seemed to love her devotedly, as she had always longed to be loved. But presently the rhythmic movement of the oars attracted her, and she thought she should like to learn how to row. This roused her from her reverie, and she asked if she might take an oar. It appeared that she required much teaching, and she became ambitious. The exercise brought the warm blood into her cheeks, and made her inclined to take her lesson merrily.

"I shall not be satisfied until I can manage both oars, and row you and Lucy," she said, looking very bright as she stepped out of the boat. Maggie, we know, was apt to forget the thing she was doing, and she had chosen an inopportune moment for her remark: her foot slipped, but happily Mr. Stephen Guest held her hand, and kept her up with a firm grasp.

"You have not hurt yourself at all, I hope?" he said, bending to look in her face with anxiety. It was very charming to be taken care of in that kind graceful manner by some one taller and stronger than one's-self. Maggie had never felt just in the same way before.

When they reached home again, they found uncle and aunt Pullet seated with Mrs. Tulliver in the drawing-room, and Stephen hurried away, asking leave to come again in the evening.

"And pray bring with you the volume of Purcell that you took away," said Lucy. "I want Maggie to hear your best songs."

Aunt Pullet, under the certainty that Maggie would be invited to go out with Lucy, probably to Park House, was much shocked at the shabbiness of her clothes, which, when witnessed by the higher society of St Ogg's, would be a discredit to the family, that demanded a strong and prompt remedy; and the consultation as to what would be most suitable to this end from among the superfluities of Mrs. Pullet's wardrobe, was one that Lucy as well as Mrs. Tulliver entered into with some zeal. Maggie must really have an evening dress as soon as possible, and she was about the same height as aunt Pullet.

"But she's so much broader across the shoulders than I am—it's very ill-convenient," said Mrs. Pullet, "else she might wear that beautiful black brocade o' mine without any alteration; and her arms are beyond everything," added Mrs. Pullet, sorrowfully, as she lifted Maggie's large round arm. "She'd never get my sleeves on."

"O, never mind that, aunt: pray send us the dress," said Lucy. "I don't mean Maggie to have long sleeves, and I have abundance of black lace for trimming. Her arms will look beautiful."

"Maggie's arms *are* a pretty shape," said Mrs. Tulliver. "They're like mine used to be—only mine was never brown: I wish she'd had *our* family skin."

"Nonsense, aunty!" said Lucy, patting her aunt Tulliver's shoulder, "you don't understand those things. A painter would think Maggie's complexion beautiful."

"May be, my dear," said Mrs. Tulliver, submissively. "You know better than I do. Only when I was young a brown skin wasn't thought well on among respectable folks."

"No," said uncle Pullet, who took intense interest in the ladies' conversation, as he sucked his lozenges. "Though there was a song about the 'Nut-brown Maid,' too; I think she was crazy—crazy Kate—but I can't justly remember."

"O dear, dear!" said Maggie, laughing, but impatient; "I think that will be the end of *my* brown skin, if it is always to be talked about so much."

CHAPTER III

CONFIDENTIAL MOMENTS

WHEN Maggie went up to her bedroom that night, it appeared that she was not all inclined to undress. She set down her candle on the first table that presented itself, and began to walk up and down her room, which was a large one, with a firm, regular, and rather rapid step, which showed that the exercise was the instinctive vent of strong excitement. Her eyes and cheeks had an almost feverish brilliancy; her head was thrown backward, and her hands were clasped with the palms outward, and with that tension of the arms which is apt to accompany mental absorption.

Had anything remarkable happened?

Nothing that you are not likely to consider in the highest degree unimportant. She had been hearing some fine music sung by a fine bass voice—but then it was sung in a provincial, amateur fashion, such as would have left your critical ear much to desire. And she was conscious of having been looked at a great deal, in rather a furtive manner, from beneath a pair of well-marked horizontal eyebrows, with a glance that seemed somehow to have caught the vibratory influence of the voice. Such things could have had no perceptible effect on a thoroughly well-educated young lady, with a perfectly balanced mind, who had had all the advantages of fortune, training, and refined society. But if Maggie had been that young lady, you would probably have known nothing about her: her life would have had so few vicissitudes that it could hardly have been written; for the happiest women, like the happiest nations, have no history.

In poor Maggie's highly-strung, hungry nature—just come away from a third-rate schoolroom, with all its jarring sounds and petty round of tasks—these apparently trivial causes had the effect of rousing and exalting her imagination in a way that was mysterious to herself. It was not that she thought distinctly of Mr. Stephen Guest, or dwelt on the indications that he looked at her with admiration; it was rather that she felt the half-remote presence of a world of love and beauty and delight, made up of vague, mingled images from all the poetry and romance she had ever read, or had ever woven in her dreamy reveries. Her mind glanced back once or twice to the time when she had courted privation, when she had thought all longing, all impatience, was subdued; but that condition seemed irrecoverably gone, and she recoiled from the remembrance of it. No prayer, no striving now, would bring back that negative peace: the battle of her life, it seemed, was not to be decided in that short and easy way—by perfect renunciation at the very threshold of her youth. The music was vibrating in her still—Purcell's music, with its wild passion and fancy—and she could not stay in the recollection of that bare, lonely past. She was in her brighter aërial world again, when a little tap came at the door: of course it was her cousin, who entered in ample white dressing-gown.

"Why, Maggie, you naughty child, haven't you begun to undress?" said Lucy, in astonishment. "I promised not to come and talk to you, because I thought you must be tired. But here you are, looking as if you were ready to dress for a ball. Come, come, get on your dressing-gown, and unplait your hair."

"Well, you are not very forward," retorted Maggie, hastily reaching her own pink cotton gown, and looking at Lucy's light-brown hair brushed back in curly disorder.

"O, I have not much to do. I shall sit down and talk to you, till I see you are really on the way to bed."

While Maggie stood and unplaited her long black hair over her pink drapery, Lucy sat down near the toilette-table, watching her with affectionate eyes, and head a little aside, like a pretty spaniel. If it appears to you at all incredible that young ladies should be led on to talk confidentially in a situation of this kind, I will beg you to remember that human life furnishes many exceptional cases.

"You really have enjoyed the music to-night, haven't you, Maggie?"

"O, yes, that is what prevents me from feeling sleepy. I think I should have no other mortal wants, if I could always have plenty of music. It seems to infuse strength into my limbs and ideas into my brain. Life seems to go on without effort, when I am filled with music. At other times one is conscious of carrying a weight."

"And Stephen has a splendid voice, hasn't he?"

"Well, perhaps we are neither of us judges of that," said Maggie, laughing, as she seated herself and tossed her long hair back. "You are not impartial, and *I* think any barrel-organ splendid."

"But tell me what you think of him, now. Tell me exactly—good and bad too."

"O, I think you should humiliate him a little. A lover should not be so much at ease, and so self-confident. He ought to tremble more."

"Nonsense, Maggie! As if any one could tremble at me! You think he is conceited—I see that. But you don't dislike him, do you?"

"Dislike him! No. Am I in the habit of seeing such charming people, that I should be very difficult to please? Besides, how could I dislike any one that promised to make you happy, you dear thing!" Maggie pinched Lucy's dimpled chin.

"We shall have more music to-morrow evening," said Lucy looking happy already, "for Stephen will bring Philip Wakem with him."

"O, Lucy, I can't see him," said Maggie, turning pale. "At least, I could not see him without Tom's leave."

"Is Tom such a tyrant as that?" said Lucy, surprised. "I'll take the responsibility, then—tell him it was my fault."

"But, dear," said Maggie, falteringly, "I promised Tom very solemnly—before my father's death—I promised him I would not speak to Philip without his knowledge and consent. And I have a great dread of opening the subject with Tom—of getting into a quarrel with him again."

"But I never heard of anything so strange and unreasonable. What harm can poor Philip have done? May I speak to Tom about it?"

"O, no, pray don't, dear," said Maggie. "I'll go to him myself to-morrow, and tell him that you wish Philip to come. I've thought before of asking him to absolve me from my promise, but I've not had the courage to determine on it."

They were both silent for some moments, and then Lucy said—

"Maggie, you have secrets from me, and I have none from you."

Maggie looked meditatively away from Lucy. Then she turned to her and said, "I *should* like to tell you about Philip. But, Lucy, you must not betray that you know it to any one—least of all to Philip himself, or to Mr Stephen Guest."

The narrative lasted long, for Maggie had never before known the relief of such an outpouring: she had never before told Lucy anything of her inmost life; and the sweet face bent towards her with sympathetic interest, and the little hand pressing hers, encouraged her to speak on. On two points only she was not expansive. She did not betray fully what still rankled in her mind as Tom's great offence—the insults he had heaped on Philip. Angry as the remembrance still made her, she could not bear that any one else should know it all—both for Tom's sake and Philip's. And she could not bear to tell Lucy of the last scene between her father and Wakem, though it was this scene which she had ever since felt to be a new barrier between herself and Philip. She merely said, she saw now that Tom was, on the whole, right in regarding any prospect of love and marriage between her and Philip as put out of the question by the relation of the two families. Of course Philip's father would never consent.

"There, Lucy, you have had my story," said Maggie, smiling, with the tears in her eyes. "You see I am like Sir Andrew Ague-cheek—*I* was adored once."

"Ah, now I see how it is you know Shakespeare and everything, and have learned so much since you left school; which always seemed to me witchcraft before—part of your general uncanniness," said Lucy.

She mused a little with her eyes downward, and then added, looking at Maggie, "It is very beautiful that you should love Philip: I never thought such a happiness would befall him. And in my opinion, you ought not to give him up. There are obstacles now; but they may be done away with in time."

Maggie shook her head.

"Yes, yes," persisted Lucy; "I can't help being hopeful about it. There is something romantic in it—out of the common way—just what everything that happens to you ought to be. And Philip will adore you like a husband in a fairy tale. O, I shall puzzle my small brain to contrive some plot that will bring everybody into the right mind, so that you may marry Philip, when I marry—somebody else. Wouldn't that be a pretty ending to all my poor, poor Maggie's troubles?"

Maggie tried to smile, but shivered, as if she felt a sudden chill.

"Ah, dear, you are cold," said Lucy. "You must go to bed; and so must I. I dare not think what time it is."

They kissed each other, and Lucy went away—possessed of a confidence which had a strong influence over her subsequent impressions. Maggie had been thoroughly sincere: her nature had never found it easy to be otherwise. But confidences are sometimes blinding, even when they are sincere.

CHAPTER IV

BROTHER AND SISTER

MAGGIE was obliged to go to Tom's lodgings in the middle of the day, when he would be coming in to dinner, else she would not have found him at home. He was not lodging with entire strangers. Our friend Bob Jakin had, with Mumps's tacit consent, taken not only a wife about eight months ago, but also one of those queer old houses pierced with surprising passages, by the water-side, where, as he observed, his wife and mother could keep themselves out of mischief by letting out two "pleasure-boats," in which he had invested some of his savings, and by taking in a lodger for the parlour and spare bedroom. Under these circumstances, what could be better for the interests of all parties, sanitary considerations apart, than that the lodger should be Mr. Tom?

It was Bob's wife who opened the door to Maggie. She was a tiny woman, with the general physiognomy of a Dutch doll, looking, in comparison with Bob's mother, who filled up the passage in the rear, very much like one of those human figures which the artist finds conveniently standing near a colossal statue to show the proportions. The tiny woman curtsied and looked up at Maggie with some awe as soon as she had opened the door; but the words, "Is my brother at home?" which Maggie uttered smilingly, made her turn round with sudden excitement, and say—

"Eh, mother, mother—tell Bob!—it's Miss Maggie! Come in, Miss, for goodness do," she went on, opening a side-door, and endeavouring to flatten her person against the wall to make the utmost space for the visitor.

Sad recollections crowded on Maggie as she entered the small parlour, which was now all that poor Tom had to call by the name of "home"—that name which had once, so many years ago, meant for both of them the same sum of dear familiar objects. But everything was not strange to her in this new room: the first thing her eyes dwelt on was the large old Bible, and the sight was not likely to disperse the old memories. She stood without speaking.

"If you please to take the privilege o' sitting down, Miss," said Mrs. Jakin, rubbing her apron over a perfectly clean chair, and then lifting up the corner of that garment and holding it to her face with an air of embarrassment, as she looked wonderingly at Maggie.

"Bob is at home, then?" said Maggie, recovering herself, and smiling at the bashful Dutch doll.

"Yes, Miss; but I think he must be washing and dressing himself—I'll go and see," said Mrs. Jakin, disappearing.

But she presently came back walking with new courage a little way behind her husband, who showed the brilliancy of his blue eyes and regular white teeth in the doorway, bowing respectfully.

"How do you do, Bob?" said Maggie, coming forward and putting out her hand to him; "I always meant to pay your wife a visit, and I shall come another day on purpose for that, if she will let me. But I was obliged to come to-day, to speak to my brother."

"He'll be in before long, Miss. He's doin' finely, Mr. Tom is: he'll be one o' the first men hereabouts— you'll see that."

"Well, Bob, I'm sure he'll be indebted to you, whatever he becomes: he said so himself only the other night, when he was talking of you."

"Eh, Miss, that's his way o' takin' it. But I think the more on't when he says a thing, because his tongue doesn't overshoot him as mine does. Lors! I'm no better nor a tilted bottle, I arn't—I can't stop mysen when once I begin. But you look rarely, Miss—it does me good to see you.

What do you say now, Prissy?"—here Bob turned to his wife. "Isn't it all come true as I said? Though there isn't many sorts o' goods as I can't over-praise when I set my tongue to't."

Mrs. Bob's small nose seemed to be following the example of her eyes in turning up reverentially towards Maggie, but she was able now to smile and curtsy, and say, "I'd looked forrard like aenything to seein' you, Miss, for my husband's tongue's been runnin' on you, like as if he was light-headed, iver since first he come a-courtin' on me."

"Well, well," said Bob, looking rather silly. "Go an' see after the taters, else Mr Tom 'ull have to wait for 'em."

"I hope Mumps is friendly with Mrs. Jakin, Bob," said Maggie, smiling. "I remember you used to say, he wouldn't like your marrying."

"Eh, Miss," said Bob, grinning, "he made up his mind to't when he see'd what a little un she was. He pretends not to see her mostly, or else to think as she isn't full-growed. But about Mr. Tom, Miss," said Bob, speaking lower and looking serious, "he's as close as a iron biler, he is; but I'm a 'cutish chap, an' when I've left off carrying my pack, an' am at a loose end, I've got more brains nor I know what to do wi', an' I'm forced to busy myself wi' other folks's insides. An' it worrets me as Mr Tom 'ull sit by himself so glumpish, a-knittin' his brow, an' a-lookin' at the fire of a night. He should be a bit livelier now—a fine young fellow like him. My wife says, when she goes in sometimes, an' he takes no notice of her, he sits lookin' into the fire, and frownin' as if he was watchin' folks at work in it."

"He thinks so much about business," said Maggie.

"Ay," said Bob, speaking lower; "but do you think it's nothin' else, Miss? He's close, Mr. Tom is; but I'm a 'cute chap, I am, an' I thought tow'rt last Christmas as I'd found out a soft place in him. It was about a little black spaniel—a rare bit o'breed—as he made a fuss to get. But since then summat's come over him, as he's set his teeth again' things more nor iver, for all he's had such good-luck. An' I wanted to tell *you*, Miss, 'cause I thought you might work it out of him a bit, now you're come. He's a deal too lonely, an' doesn't go into company enough."

"I'm afraid I have very little power over him, Bob," said Maggie, a good deal moved by Bob's suggestion. It was a totally new idea to her mind, that Tom could have his love troubles. Poor fellow!—and in love with Lucy too! But it was perhaps a mere fancy of Bob's too officious brain. The present of the dog meant nothing more than cousinship and gratitude. But Bob had already said, "Here's Mr. Tom," and the outer door was opening.

"There's no time to spare, Tom," said Maggie, as soon as Bob had left the room. "I must tell you at once what I came about, else I shall be hindering you from taking your dinner."

Tom stood with his back against the chimney-piece, and Maggie was seated opposite the light. He noticed that she was tremulous, and he had a presentiment of the subject she was going to speak about. The presentiment made his voice colder and harder as he said, "What is it?"

This tone roused a spirit of resistance in Maggie, and she put her request in quite a different form from the one she had predetermined on. She rose from her seat, and, looking straight at Tom, said—

"I want you to absolve me from my promise about Philip Wakem. Or rather, I promised you not to see him without telling you. I am come to tell you that I wish to see him."

"Very well," said Tom, still more coldly.

But Maggie had hardly finished speaking in that chill, defiant manner, before she repented, and felt the dread of alienation from her brother.

"Not for myself, dear Tom. Don't be angry. I shouldn't have asked it, only that Philip, you know, is a friend of Lucy's and she wishes him to come—has invited him to come this evening; and I told her I couldn't see him without telling you. I shall only see him in the presence of other people. There will never be anything secret between us again."

Tom looked away from Maggie, knitting his brow more strongly for a little while. Then he turned to her and said, slowly and emphatically—

"You know what is my feeling on that subject, Maggie. There is no need for my repeating anything I said a year ago. While my father was living, I felt bound to use the utmost power over you, to prevent you from disgracing him as well as yourself, and all of us. But now I must leave you to your own choice. You wish to be independent—you told me so after my father's death. My opinion is not changed. If you think of Philip Wakem as a lover again, you must give up me."

"I don't wish it, dear Tom—at least as things are: I see that it would lead to misery. But I shall soon go away to another situation, and I should like to be friends with him again while I am here. Lucy wishes it."

The severity of Tom's face relaxed a little.

"I shouldn't mind your seeing him occasionally at my uncle's—I don't want you to make a fuss on the subject. But I have no confidence in you, Maggie. You would be led away to do anything."

That was a cruel word. Maggie's lip began to tremble.

"Why will you say that, Tom? It is very hard of you. Have I not done and borne everything as well as I could? And I have kept my word to you—when—when . . . My life has not been a happy one, any more than yours."

She was obliged to be childish—the tears would come. When Maggie was not angry, she was as dependent on kind or cold words as a daisy on the sunshine or the cloud: the need of being loved would always subdue her, as in old days it subdued her in the worm-eaten attic. The brother's goodness came uppermost at this appeal, but it could only show itself in Tom's fashion. He put his hand gently on her arm, and said in the tone of a kind pedagogue—

"Now listen to me, Maggie. I'll tell you what I mean. You're always in extremes—you have no judgment and self-command; and yet you think you know best, and will not submit to be guided. You know I didn't wish you to take a situation. My aunt Pullet was willing to give you a good home, and you might have lived respectably amongst your

relations, until I could have provided a home for you with my mother.
And that is what I should like to do. I wished my sister to be a lady, and
I would always have taken care of you, as my father desired, until you
were well married. But your ideas and mine never accord, and you will
not give way. Yet you might have sense enough to see that a brother,
who goes out into the world and mixes with men, necessarily knows better what is right and respectable for his sister than she can know herself.
You think I am not kind; but my kindness can only be directed by what
I believe to be good for you."

"Yes—I know—dear Tom," said Maggie, still half-sobbing, but trying
to control her tears. "I know you would do a great deal for me: I know
how you work, and don't spare yourself. I am grateful to you. But, indeed, you can't quite judge for me—our natures are very different. You
don't know how differently things affect me from what they do you."

"Yes, I *do* know: I know it too well. I know how differently you must
feel about all that affects our family, and your own dignity as a young
woman, before you could think of receiving secret addresses from Philip
Wakem. If it was not disgusting to me in every other way, I should
object to my sister's name being associated for a moment with that of
a young man whose father must hate the very thought of us all, and
would spurn you. With any one but you, I should think it quite certain
that what you witnessed just before my father's death, would secure you
from ever thinking again of Philip Wakem as a lover. But I don't feel
certain of it with you—I never feel certain about anything with *you*. At
one time you take pleasure in a sort of perverse self-denial, and at another you have no resolution to resist a thing that you know to be
wrong."

There was a terrible cutting truth in Tom's words—that hard rind of
truth which is discerned by unimaginative, unsympathetic minds. Maggie always writhed under this judgment of Tom's: she rebelled and was
humiliated in the same moment: it seemed as if he held a glass before
her to show her her own folly and weakness—as if he were a prophetic
voice predicting her future fallings—and yet, all the while, she judged
him in return: she said inwardly that he was narrow and unjust, that he
was below feeling those mental needs which were often the source of the
wrong-doing or absurdity that made her life a planless riddle to him.

She did not answer directly: her heart was too full, and she sat down,
leaning her arm on the table. It was no use trying to make Tom feel
that she was near to him. He always repelled her. Her feeling under his
words was complicated by the allusion to the last scene between her
father and Wakem; and at length that painful, solemn memory surmounted the immediate grievance. No! She did not think of such things
with frivolous indifference, and Tom must not accuse her of that. She
looked up at him with a grave, earnest gaze, and said—

"I can't make you think better of me, Tom, by anything I can say.
But I am not so shut out from all your feelings as you believe me to be.
I see as well as you do, that from our position with regard to Philip's

father—not on other grounds—it would be unreasonable—it would be wrong for us to entertain the idea of marriage; and I have given up thinking of him as a lover. . . . I am telling you the truth, and you have no right to disbelieve me: I have kept my word to you, and you have never detected me in a falsehood. I should not only not encourage, I should carefully avoid any intercourse with Philip on any other footing than that of quiet friendship. You may think that I am unable to keep my resolutions; but at least you ought not to treat me with hard contempt on the ground of faults that I have not committed yet."

"Well, Maggie," said Tom, softening under this appeal, "I don't want to overstrain matters. I think, all things considered, it will be best for you to see Philip Wakem, if Lucy wishes him to come to the house. I believe what you say—at least you believe it yourself, I know: I can only warn you. I wish to be as good a brother to you as you will let me."

There was a little tremor in Tom's voice as he uttered the last words, and Maggie's ready affection came back with as sudden a glow as when they were children, and bit their cake together as a sacrament of conciliation. She rose and laid her hand on Tom's shoulder.

"Dear Tom, I know you mean to be good. I know you have had a great deal to bear, and have done a great deal. I should like to be a comfort to you—not to vex you. You don't think I'm altogether naughty, now, do you?"

Tom smiled at the eager face: his smiles were very pleasant to see when they did come, for the grey eyes could be tender underneath the frown.

"No, Maggie."

"I may turn out better than you expect."

"I hope you will."

"And may I come some day and make tea for you, and see this extremely small wife of Bob's again?"

"Yes; but trot away now, for I've no more time to spare," said Tom, looking at his watch.

"Not to give me a kiss?"

Tom bent to kiss her cheek, and then said—

"There! Be a good girl. I've got a great deal to think of to-day. I'm going to have a long consultation with my uncle Deane this afternoon."

"You'll come to aunt Glegg's to-morrow? We're going all to dine early, that we may go there to tea. You *must* come: Lucy told me to say so."

"O, pooh! I've plenty else to do," said Tom, pulling his bell violently, and bringing down the small bell-rope.

"I'm frightened—I shall run away," said Maggie, making a laughing retreat; while Tom, with masculine philosophy, flung the bell-rope to the farther end of the room—not very far either: a touch of human experience which I flatter myself will come home to the bosoms of not a few substantial or distinguished men who were once at an early stage of their rise in the world, and were cherishing very large hopes in very small lodgings.

CHAPTER V

SHOWING THAT TOM HAD OPENED THE OYSTER

"AND now we've settled this Newcastle business, Tom," said Mr. Deane, that same afternoon, as they were seated in the private room at the Bank together, "there's another matter I want to talk to you about. Since you're likely to have rather a smoky, unpleasant time of it at Newcastle for the next few weeks, you'll want a good prospect of some sort to keep up your spirits."

Tom waited less nervously than he had done on a former occasion in this apartment, while his uncle took out his snuff-box and gratified each nostril with deliberate impartiality.

"You see, Tom," said Mr. Deane, at last, throwing himself backward, "the world goes on at a smarter pace now than it did when I was a young fellow. Why, sir, forty years ago, when I was much such a strapping youngster as you, a man expected to pull between the shafts the best part of his life, before he got the whip in his hand. The looms went slowish, and fashions didn't alter quite so fast: I'd a best suit that lasted me six years. Everything was on a lower scale, sir—in point of expenditure, I mean. It's this steam, you see, that has made the difference: it drives on every wheel double pace, and the wheel of fortune along with 'em, as our Mr. Stephen Guest said at the anniversary dinner (he hits these things off wonderfully, considering he's seen nothing of business). I don't find fault with the change, as some people do. Trade, sir, opens a man's eyes; and if the population is to get thicker upon the ground, as it's doing, the world must use its wits at inventions of one sort or other. I know I've done my share as an ordinary man of business. Somebody has said it's a fine thing to make two ears of corn grow where only one grew before; but, sir, it's a fine thing, too, to further the exchange of commodities, and bring the grains of corn to the mouths that are hungry. And that's our line of business; and I consider it as honourable a position as a man can hold, to be connected with it."

Tom knew that the affair his uncle had to speak of was not urgent; Mr. Deane was too shrewd and practical a man to allow either his reminiscences or his snuff to impede the progress of trade. Indeed, for the last month or two, there had been hints thrown out to Tom which enabled him to guess that he was going to hear some proposition for his own benefit. With the beginning of the last speech he had stretched out his legs, thrust his hands in his pockets, and prepared himself for some introductory diffuseness, tending to show that Mr. Deane had succeeded by his own merit, and that what he had to say to young men in general was, that if they didn't succeed too, it was because of their own demerit. He was rather surprised, then, when his uncle put a direct question to him.

"Let me see—it's going on for seven years now since you applied to me for a situation—eh, Tom?"

"Yes, sir; I'm three-and-twenty now," said Tom.

"Ah—it's as well not to say that, though; for you'd pass for a good deal older, and age tells well in business. I remember your coming very well: I remember I saw there was some pluck in you, and that was what made me give you encouragement. And I'm happy to say, I was right —I'm not often deceived. I was naturally a little shy at pushing my nephew, but I'm happy to say you've done me credit, sir; and if I'd had a son o' my own, I shouldn't have been sorry to see him like you."

Mr. Deane tapped his box and opened it again, repeating in a tone of some feeling—"No, I shouldn't have been sorry to see him like you."

"I'm very glad I've given you satisfaction, sir; I've done my best," said Tom, in his proud, independent way.

"Yes, Tom, you've given me satisfaction. I don't speak of your conduct as a son; though that weighs with me in my opinion of you. But what I have to do with, as a partner in our firm, is the qualities you've shown as a man o' business. Ours is a fine business—a splendid concern, sir—and there's no reason why it shouldn't go on growing: there's a growing capital, and growing outlets for it; but there's another thing that's wanted for the prosperity of every concern, large or small, and that's men to conduct it—men of the right habits; none o' your flashy fellows, but such as are to be depended on. Now this is what Mr. Guest and I see clear enough. Three years ago, we took Gell into the concern: we gave him a share in the oil-mill. And why? Why, because Gell was a fellow whose services were worth a premium. So it will always be, sir. So it was with me. And though Gell is pretty near ten years older than you, there are other points in your favour."

Tom was getting a little nervous as Mr. Deane went on speaking: he was conscious of something he had in his mind to say, which might not be agreeable to his uncle, simply because it was a new suggestion rather than an acceptance of the proposition he foresaw.

"It stands to reason," Mr. Deane went on, when he had finished his new pinch, "that your being my nephew weighs in your favour; but I don't deny that if you'd been no relation of mine at all, your conduct in that affair of Pelley's bank would have led Mr. Guest and myself to make some acknowledgment of the service you've been to us; and, backed by your general conduct and business ability, it has made us determine on giving you a share in the business—a share which we shall be glad to increase as years go on. We think that'll be better, on all grounds, than raising your salary. It'll give you more importance, and prepare you better for taking some of the anxiety off my shoulders by-and-by. I'm equal to a good deal o' work at present, thank God; but I'm getting older—there's no denying that. I told Mr. Guest I would open the subject to you; and when you come back from this northern business, we can go into particulars. This is a great stride for a young fellow of three-and-twenty, but I'm bound to say, you've deserved it."

"I'm very grateful to Mr. Guest and you, sir; of course, I feel the most indebted to *you,* who first took me into the business, and have taken a good deal of pains with me since."

Tom spoke with a slight tremor, and paused after he had said this.

"Yes, yes," said Mr. Deane. "I don't spare pains when I see they'll be of any use. I gave myself some trouble with Gell—else he wouldn't have been what he is."

"But there's one thing I should like to mention to you, uncle. I've never spoken to you of it before. If you remember, at the time my father's property was sold, there was some thought of your firm buying the Mill: I know you thought it would be a very good investment, especially if steam were applied."

"To be sure, to be sure. But Wakem outbid us—he'd made up his mind to that. He's rather fond of carrying everything over other people's heads."

"Perhaps it's of no use my mentioning it at present," Tom went on, "but I wish you to know what I have in my mind about the Mill. I've a strong feeling about it. It was my father's dying wish that I should try and get it back again whenever I could: it was in his family for five generations. I promised my father; and besides that, I'm attached to the place. I shall never like any other so well. And if it should ever suit your views to buy it for the firm, I should have a better chance of fulfilling my father's wish. I shouldn't have liked to mention the thing to you, only you've been kind enough to say my services have been of some value. And I'd give up a much greater chance in life for the sake of having the Mill again—I mean, having it in my own hands, and gradually working off the price."

Mr. Deane had listened attentively, and now looked thoughtful.

"I see, I see," he said, after a while; "the thing would be possible, if there were any chance of Wakem's parting with the property. But that I *don't* see. He's put that young Jetsome in the place; and he had his reasons when he bought it, I'll be bound."

"He's a loose fish, that young Jetsome," said Tom. "He's taking to drinking, and they say he's letting the business go down. Luke told me about it—our old miller. He says, he shan't stay unless there's an alteration. I was thinking, if things went on in that way, Wakem might be more willing to part with the Mill. Luke says he's getting very sour about the way things are going on."

"Well, I'll turn it over, Tom. I must inquire into the matter, and go into it with Mr. Guest. But, you see, it's rather striking out a new branch, and putting you to that, instead of keeping you where you are, which was what we'd wanted."

"I should be able to manage more than the mill when things were once set properly going, sir. I want to have plenty of work. There's nothing else I care about much."

There was something rather sad in that speech from a young man of three-and-twenty, even in uncle Deane's business-loving ears.

"Pooh, pooh! you'll be having a wife to care about one of these days, if you get on at this pace in the world. But as to this Mill, we mustn't reckon on our chickens too early. However, I promise you to bear it in mind, and when you come back, we'll talk of it again. I am going to dinner now. Come and breakfast with us to-morrow morning, and say good-by to your mother and sister before you start."

CHAPTER VI

ILLUSTRATING THE LAWS OF ATTRACTION

IT is evident to you now, that Maggie had arrived at a moment in her life which must be considered by all prudent persons as a great opportunity for a young woman. Launched into the higher society of St. Ogg's, with a striking person which had the advantage of being quite unfamiliar to the majority of beholders, and with such moderate assistance of costume as you have seen foreshadowed in Lucy's anxious colloquy with aunt Pullet, Maggie was certainly at a new starting-point in life. At Lucy's first evening-party, young Torry fatigued his facial muscles more than usual in order that "the dark-eyed girl there, in the corner," might see him in all the additional style conferred by his eyeglass; and several young ladies went home intending to have short sleeves with black lace, and to plait their hair in a broad coronet at the back of their head—"That cousin of Miss Deane's looked so very well." In fact, poor Maggie, with all her inward consciousness of a painful past and her presentiment of a troublous future, was on the way to become an object of some envy—a topic of discussion in the newly-established billiard-room, and between fair friends who had no secrets from each other on the subject of trimmings. The Miss Guests, who associated chiefly on terms of condescension with the families of St. Ogg's, and were the glass of fashion there, took some exception to Maggie's manners. She had a way of not assenting at once to the observations current in good society, and of saying that she didn't know whether those observations were true or not, which gave her an air of *gaucherie*, and impeded the even flow of conversation; but it is a fact capable of an amiable interpretation, that ladies are not the worse disposed towards a new acquaintance of their own sex because she has points of inferiority. And Maggie was so entirely without those pretty airs of coquetry which have the traditional reputation of driving gentlemen to despair, that she won some feminine pity for being so ineffective in spite of her beauty. She had not had many advantages, poor thing! and it must be admitted there was no pretension about her: her abruptness and unevenness of manner were plainly the result of her secluded and lowly circumstances. It was only a wonder that there was no tinge of vulgarity about her, considering what the rest of poor Lucy's relations were: an allusion which always made the Miss Guests shudder a little. It was not agreeable to think of any connection by marriage with such people as the Gleggs and the Pullets; but it was of no use to contradict Stephen, when once he had set his mind on anything, and certainly there was no possible objection to Lucy in herself—no one could help liking her. She would naturally desire that the Miss Guests should behave kindly to this cousin of whom she was so fond, and Stephen would make a great fuss if they were deficient in civility. Under these circumstances the invitations to Park House were not wanting; and elsewhere, also, Miss Deane was too popular and too distinguished a member of society in St. Ogg's for any attention towards her to be neglected.

Thus Maggie was introduced for the first time to the young lady's life, and knew what it was to get up in the morning without any imperative reason for doing one thing more than another. This new sense of leisure and unchecked enjoyment amidst the soft-breathing airs and garden-scents of advancing spring,—amidst the new abundance of music, and lingering strolls in the sunshine, and delicious dreaminess of gliding on the river,—could hardly be without some intoxicating effect on her, after her years of privation; and even in the first week Maggie began to be less haunted by her sad memories and anticipations. Life was certainly very pleasant just now: it was becoming very pleasant to dress in the evening, and to feel that she was one of the beautiful things of this spring-time. And there were admiring eyes always awaiting her now; she was no longer an unheeded person, liable to be chid, from whom attention was continually claimed, and on whom no one felt bound to confer any. It was pleasant, too, when Stephen and Lucy were gone out riding, to sit down at the piano alone, and find that the old fitness between her fingers and the keys remained, and revived, like a sympathetic kinship not to be worn out by separation—to get the tunes she had heard the evening before, and repeat them again and again until she had found out a way of producing them so as to make them a more pregnant, passionate language to her. The mere concord of octaves was a delight to Maggie, and she would often take up a book of studies rather than any melody, that she might taste more keenly by abstraction the more primitive sensation of intervals. Not that her enjoyment of music was of the kind that indicates a great specific talent; it was rather that her sensibility to the supreme excitement of music was only one form of that passionate sensibility which belonged to her whole nature, and made her faults and virtues all merge in each other—made her affections sometimes an impatient demand, but also prevented her vanity from taking the form of mere feminine coquetry and device, and gave it the poetry of ambition. But you have known Maggie a long while, and need to be told, not her characteristics, but her history, which is a thing hardly to be predicted even from the completest knowledge of characteristics. For the tragedy of our lives is not created entirely from within. "Character," says Novalis, in one of his questionable aphorisms—"character is destiny." But not the whole of our destiny. Hamlet, Prince of Denmark, was speculative and irresolute, and we have a great tragedy in consequence. But if his father had lived to a good old age, and his uncle had died an early death, we can conceive Hamlet's having married Ophelia, and got through life with a reputation of sanity notwithstanding many soliloquies, and some moody sarcasms towards the fair daughter of Polonius, to say nothing of the frankest incivility to his father-in-law.

Maggie's destiny, then, is at present hidden, and we must wait for it to reveal itself like the course of an unmapped river: we only know that the river is full and rapid, and that for all rivers there is the same final home. Under the charm of her new pleasures, Maggie herself was ceasing to think, with her eager prefiguring imagination, of her future lot; and her anxiety about her first interview with Philip was losing its predominance: perhaps, unconsciously to herself, she was not sorry that the interview had been deferred.

For Philip had not come the evening he was expected, and Mr. Stephen Guest brought word that he was gone to the coast—probably, he thought, on a sketching expedition; but it was not certain when he would return. It was just like Philip—to go off in that way without telling any one. It was not until the twelfth day that he returned, to find both Lucy's notes awaiting him: he had left before he knew of Maggie's arrival.

Perhaps one had need to be nineteen again to be quite convinced of the feelings that were crowded for Maggie into those twelve days—of the length to which they were stretched for her by the novelty of her experience in them, and the varying attitudes of her mind. The early days of an acquaintance almost always have this importance for us, and fill up a larger space in our memory than longer subsequent periods, which have been less filled with discovery and new impressions. There were not many hours in those ten days in which Mr. Stephen Guest was not seated by Lucy's side, or standing near her at the piano, or accompanying her on some out-door excursion: his attentions were clearly becoming more assiduous; and that was what every one had expected. Lucy was very happy: all the happier because Stephen's society seemed to have become much more interesting and amusing since Maggie had been there. Playful discussions—sometimes serious ones—were going forward, in which both Stephen and Maggie revealed themselves, to the admiration of the gentle unobtrusive Lucy; and it more than once crossed her mind what a charming quartet they should have through life when Maggie married Philip. Is it an inexplicable thing that a girl should enjoy her lover's society the more for the presence of a third person, and be without the slightest spasm of jealousy that the third person had the conversation habitually directed to her? Not when that girl is as tranquil-hearted as Lucy, thoroughly possessed with a belief that she knows the state of her companions' affections, and not prone to the feelings which shake such a belief in the absence of positive evidence against it. Besides, it was Lucy by whom Stephen sate, to whom he gave his arm, to whom he appealed as the person sure to agree with him; and every day there was the same tender politeness towards her, the same consciousness of her wants and care to supply them. Was there really the same?—it seemed to Lucy that there was more; and it was no wonder that the real significance of the change escaped her. It was a subtle act of conscience in Stephen that even he himself was not aware of. His personal attentions to Maggie were comparatively slight, and there had even sprung up an apparent distance between them, that prevented the renewal of that faint resemblance to gallantry into which he had fallen the first day in the boat. If Stephen came in when Lucy was out of the room—if Lucy left them together, they never spoke to each other: Stephen, perhaps, seemed to be examining books or music, and Maggie bent her head assiduously over her work. Each was oppressively conscious of the other's presence, even to the finger-ends. Yet each looked and longed for the same thing to happen the next day. Neither of them had begun to reflect on the matter, or silently to ask, "To what does all this tend?" Maggie only felt that life was revealing something quite new to her; and she was absorbed in the direct, immediate experience, without any energy left for taking account of it, and reasoning about it. Stephen wilfully abstained from self-questioning, and would not admit to himself that he felt an influence which was to have any determining effect on his conduct. And when Lucy came into the room again, they were once more unconstrained: Maggie could contradict Stephen and laugh at him, and he could recommend to her consideration the example of that most charming heroine, Miss Sophia Western, who had a great "respect for the understandings of men." Maggie could look at Stephen—which, for some reason or other, she always avoided when they were alone; and he could even ask her to play his accompaniment for him, since Lucy's fingers were so busy with that bazaar-work; and lecture her on hurrying the *tempo,* which was certainly Maggie's weak point.

One day—it was the day of Philip's return—Lucy had formed a sudden engagement to spend the evening with Mrs. Kenn, whose delicate state of health, threatening to become confirmed illness through an attack of bronchitis, obliged her to resign her functions at the coming bazaar into the hands of other ladies, of whom she wished Lucy to be one. The engagement had been formed in Stephen's presence, and he had heard Lucy promise to rise early and call at six o'clock for Miss Torry, who brought Mrs. Kenn's request.

"Here is another of the moral results of this idiotic bazaar," Stephen burst forth, as soon as Miss Torry had left the room—"taking young ladies from the duties of the domestic hearth into scenes of dissipation among urn-rugs and embroidered reticules! I should like to know what is the proper function of women, if it is not to make reasons for husbands to stay at home, and still stronger reasons for bachelors to go out. If this goes on much longer, the bonds of society will be dissolved."

"Well, it will not go on much longer," said Lucy, laughing, "for the bazaar is to take place on Monday week."

"Thank heaven!" said Stephen. "Kenn himself said the other day, that he didn't like this plan of making vanity do the work of charity; but just as the British public is not reasonable enough to bear direct taxation, so St. Ogg's has not got force of motive enough to build and endow schools without calling in the force of folly."

"Did he say so?" said little Lucy, her hazel eyes opening wide with anxiety. "I never heard him say anything of that kind: I thought he approved of what we were doing."

"I'm sure he approves *you*," said Stephen, smiling at her affectionately; "your conduct in going out to-night looks vicious, I own, but I know there is benevolence at the bottom of it."

"O, you think too well of me," said Lucy, shaking her head, with a pretty blush, and there the subject ended. But it was tacitly understood that Stephen would not come in the evening, and on the strength of that tacit understanding he made his morning visit the longer, not saying good-by until after four.

Maggie was seated in the drawing-room alone, shortly after dinner, with Minny on her lap, having left her uncle to his wine and his nap, and her mother to the compromise between knitting and nodding, which, when there was no company, she always carried on in the dining-room till tea-time. Maggie was stooping to caress the tiny silken pet, and comforting him for his mistress's absence, when the sound of a footstep on the gravel made her look up, and she saw Mr. Stephen Guest walking up the garden, as if he had come straight from the river. It was very unusual to see him so soon after dinner! He often complained that their dinner-hour was late at Park House. Nevertheless, there he was, in his black dress: he had evidently been home, and must have come again by the river. Maggie felt her cheeks glowing and her heart beating: it was natural she should be nervous, for she was not accustomed to receive visitors alone. He had seen her look up through the open window, and raised his hat as he walked towards it, to enter that way instead of by the door. He blushed too, and certainly looked as foolish as a young man of some wit and self-possession can be expected to look, as he walked in with a roll of music in his hand, and said with an air of hesitating improvisation—

"You are surprised to see me again, Miss Tulliver—I ought to apologise for coming upon you by surprise, but I wanted to come into the town, and I got our man to row me; so I thought I would bring these things from the 'Maid of Artois' for your cousin: I forgot them this morning. Will you give them to her?"

"Yes," said Maggie, who had risen confusedly with Minny in her arms, and now, not quite knowing what else to do, sat down again.

Stephen laid down his hat, with the music, which rolled on the floor, and sat down in the chair close by her. He had never done so before, and both he and Maggie were quite aware that it was an entirely new position.

"Well, you pampered minion!" said Stephen, leaning to pull the long curly ears that drooped over Maggie's arm. It was not a suggestive remark, and as the speaker did not follow it up by further development, it naturally left the conversation at a stand-still. It seemed to Stephen like some action in a dream, that he was obliged to do, and wonder at himself all the while—to go on stroking Minny's head. Yet it was very pleasant: he only wished he dared look at Maggie, and that she would look at him,—let him have one long look into those deep strange eyes of hers, and then he would be satisfied, and quite reasonable after that. He thought it was becoming a sort of monomania with him, to want that long look from Maggie; and he was racking his invention continually to find out some means by which he could have it without its appearing singular and entailing subsequent embarrassment. As for Maggie, she had no distinct thought—only the sense of a presence like that of a closely-hovering broad-winged bird in the darkness, for she was unable to look up, and saw nothing but Minny's black wavy coat.

But this must end some time—perhaps it ended very soon, and only *seemed* long, as a minute's dream does. Stephen at last sat upright sideways in his chair, leaning one hand and arm over the back and looking at Maggie. What should he say?

"We shall have a splendid sunset, I think; shan't you go out and see it?"

"I don't know," said Maggie. Then, courageously raising her eyes and looking out of the window, "If I'm not playing cribbage with my uncle."

A pause: during which Minny is stroked again, but has sufficient insight not to be grateful for it—to growl rather.

"Do you like sitting alone?"

A rather arch look came over Maggie's face, and, just glancing at Stephen, she said, "Would it be quite civil to say 'yes'?"

"It *was* rather a dangerous question for an intruder to ask," said Stephen, delighted with that glance, and getting determined to stay for another. "But you will have more than half an hour to yourself after I am gone," he added, taking out his watch. "I know Mr. Deane never comes in till half-past seven."

Another pause, during which Maggie looked steadily out of the window, till by a great effort she moved her head to look down at Minny's back again, and said—

"I wish Lucy had not been obliged to go out. We lose our music."

"We shall have a new voice to-morrow night," said Stephen. "Will you tell your cousin that our friend Philip Wakem is come back? I saw him as I went home."

Maggie gave a little start—it seemed hardly more than a vibration that passed from head to foot in an instant. But the new images summoned by Philip's name, dispersed half the oppressive spell she had been under. She rose from her chair with a sudden resolution, and, laying Minny on his cushion, went to reach Lucy's large work-basket from its corner. Stephen was vexed and disappointed: he thought, perhaps Maggie didn't like the name of Wakem to be mentioned to her in that abrupt way—for he now recalled what Lucy had told him of the family quarrel. It was of no use to stay any longer. Maggie was seating herself at the table with her work, and looking chill and proud; and he—he looked like a simpleton for having come. A gratuitous, entirely superfluous visit of that sort was sure to make a man disagreeable and ridiculous. Of course it was palpable to Maggie's thinking, that he had dined hastily in his own room for the sake of setting off again and finding her alone.

A boyish state of mind for an accomplished young gentleman of five-and-twenty, not without legal knowledge! But a reference to history, perhaps, may make it not incredible.

At this moment Maggie's ball of knitting-wool rolled along the ground, and she started up to reach it. Stephen rose too, and, picking up the ball, met her with a vexed complaining look that gave his eyes quite a new expression to Maggie, whose own eyes met them as he presented the ball to her.

"Good-by," said Stephen, in a tone that had the same beseeching discontent as his eyes. He dared not put out his hand—he thrust both hands into his tail-pockets as he spoke. Maggie thought she had perhaps been rude.

"Won't you stay?" she said timidly, not looking away, for that would have seemed rude again.

"No, thank you," said Stephen, looking still into the half-unwilling, half-fascinated eyes, as a thirsty man looks towards the track of the distant brook. "The boat is waiting for me. . . . You'll tell your cousin?"

"Yes."

"That I brought the music, I mean."

"Yes."

"And that Philip is come back."

"Yes." (Maggie did not notice Philip's name this time.)

"Won't you come out a little way into the garden?" said Stephen, in a still gentler tone, but the next moment he was vexed that she did not say, "No," for she moved away now towards the open window, and he was obliged to take his hat and walk by her side. But he thought of something to make him amends.

"Do take my arm," he said, in a low tone, as if it were a secret.

There is something strangely winning to most women in that offer of the firm arm: the help is not wanted physically at that moment, but the sense of help—the presence of strength that is outside them and yet theirs, meets a continual want of the imagination. Either on that ground or some other, Maggie took the arm. And they walked together round the grass-plot and under the drooping green of the laburnums, in the same dim dreamy state as they had been in a quarter of an hour before; only that Stephen had had the look he longed for, without yet perceiving in himself the symptoms of returning reasonableness, and Maggie had darting thoughts across the dimness:—how came she to be there? —why had she come out? Not a word was spoken. If it had been, each would have been less intensely conscious of the other.

"Take care of this step," said Stephen, at last.

"O, I will go in now," said Maggie, feeling that the step had come like a rescue. "Good evening."

In an instant she had withdrawn her arm, and was running back to the house. She did not reflect that this sudden action would only add to the embarrassing recollections of the last half-hour. She had no thought left for that. She only threw herself into the low armchair, and burst into tears.

"O, Philip, Philip, I wish we were together again—so quietly—in the Red Deeps."

Stephen looked after her a moment, then went on to the boat, and was soon landed at the wharf. He spent the evening in the billiard-room, smoking one cigar after another, and losing "lives" at pool. But he would not leave off. He was determined not to think—not to admit any more distinct remembrance than was urged upon him by the perpetual presence of Maggie. He was looking at her, and she was on his arm.

But there came the necessity of walking home in the cool starlight, and with it the necessity of cursing his own folly, and bitterly determining that he would never trust himself alone with Maggie again. It was all madness: he was in love, thoroughly attached to Lucy, and engaged —engaged as strongly as an honourable man need be. He wished he had never seen this Maggie Tulliver, to be thrown into a fever by her in this way: she would make a sweet, strange, troublesome, adorable wife to some man or other, but he would never have chosen her himself. Did she feel as he did? He hoped she did—not. He ought not to have gone. He would master himself in future. He would make himself disagreeable to her—quarrel with her perhaps. Quarrel with her? Was it possible to quarrel with a creature who had such eyes—defying and deprecating, contradicting and clinging, imperious and beseeching—full of delicious opposites. To see such a creature subdued by love for one would be a lot worth having—to another man.

There was a muttered exclamation which ended this inward soliloquy, as Stephen threw away the end of his last cigar, and, thrusting his hands into his pockets, stalked along at a quieter pace through the shrubbery. It was not of a benedictory kind.

CHAPTER VII

PHILIP RE-ENTERS

THE next morning was very wet: the sort of morning on which male neighbours who have no imperative occupation at home are likely to pay their fair friends an illimitable visit. The rain, which has been endurable enough for the walk or ride one way, is sure to become so heavy, and at the same time so certain to clear up by-and-by, that nothing but an open quarrel can abbreviate the visit: latent detestation will not do at all.

And if people happen to be lovers, what can be so delightful, in England, as a rainy morning? English sunshine is dubious; bonnets are never quite secure; and if you sit down on the grass, it may lead to catarrhs. But the rain is to be depended on. You gallop through it in a mackintosh, and presently find yourself in the seat you like best—a little above or a little below the one on which your goddess sits (it is the same thing to the metaphysical mind, and that is the reason why women are at once worshipped and looked down upon), with a satisfactory confidence that there will be no lady-callers.

"Stephen will come earlier this morning, I know," said Lucy: "he always does when it's rainy."

Maggie made no answer. She was angry with Stephen: she began to think she should dislike him; and if it had not been for the rain, she would have gone to her aunt Glegg's this morning, and so have avoided him altogether. As it was, she must find some reason for remaining out of the room with her mother.

But Stephen did not come earlier, and there was another visitor—a nearer neighbour—who preceded him. When Philip entered the room, he was going merely to bow to Maggie, feeling that their acquaintance was a secret which he was bound not to betray; but when she advanced towards him and put out her hand, he guessed at once that Lucy had been taken into her confidence. It was a moment of some agitation to both, though Philip had spent many hours in preparing for it; but like all persons who have passed through life with little expectation of sympathy, he seldom lost his self-control, and shrank with the most sensitive pride from any noticeable betrayal of emotion. A little extra paleness, a little tension of the nostril when he spoke, and the voice pitched in rather a higher key, that to strangers would seem expressive of cold indifference, were all the signs Philip usually gave of an inward drama that was not without its fierceness. But Maggie, who had little more power of concealing the impressions made upon her than if she had been constructed of musical strings, felt her eyes getting larger with tears as they took each other's hands in silence. They were not painful tears: they had rather something of the same origin as the tears women and children shed when they have found some protection to cling to, and look back on the threatened danger. For Philip, who a little while ago was associated continually in Maggie's mind with the sense that Tom might reproach her with some justice, had now, in this short space, become a sort of outward conscience to her, that she might fly to for rescue and strength. Her tranquil, tender affection for Philip, with its root deep down in her childhood, and its memories of long quiet talk confirming by distinct successive impressions the first instinctive bias— the fact that in him the appeal was more strongly to her pity and womanly devotedness than to her vanity or other egoistic excitability of her nature, seemed now to make a sort of sacred place, a sanctuary where she could find refuge from an alluring influence which the best part of herself must resist, which must bring horrible tumult within, wretchedness without. This new sense of her relation to Philip multiplied the anxious scruples she would otherwise have felt, lest she should overstep the limit of intercourse with him that Tom would sanction; and she put out her hand to him, and felt the tears in her eyes without any consciousness of an inward check. The scene was just what Lucy expected, and her kind heart delighted in bringing Philip and Maggie together again; though, even with all *her* regard for Philip, she could not resist the impression that her cousin Tom had some excuse for feeling shocked at the physical incongruity between the two—a prosaic person like cousin Tom, who didn't like poetry and fairy tales. But she began to speak as soon as possible, to set them at ease.

"This was very good and virtuous of you," she said, in her pretty treble, like the low conversational notes of little birds, "to come so soon after your arrival. And as it is, I think I will pardon you for running away in an inopportune manner, and giving your friends no notice. Come and sit down here," she went on, placing the chair that would suit him best, "and you shall find yourself treated mercifully."

"You will never govern well, Miss Deane," said Philip, as he seated himself, "because no one will ever believe in your severity. People will always encourage themselves in misdemeanors by the certainty that you will be indulgent."

Lucy gave some playful contradiction, but Philip did not hear what it was, for he had naturally turned towards Maggie, and she was looking at him with that open, affectionate scrutiny, which we give to a friend from whom we have been long separated. What a moment their parting had been! And Philip felt as if he were only in the morrow of it. He felt this so keenly—with such intense, detailed remembrance—with such passionate revival of all that had been said and looked in their last conversation—that with that jealousy and distrust which in diffident natures is almost inevitably linked with a strong feeling, he thought he read in Maggie's glance and manner the evidence of a change. The very fact that he feared and half expected it, would be sure to make this thought rush in, in the absence of positive proof to the contrary.

"I am having a great holiday, am I not?" said Maggie. "Lucy is like a fairy godmother: she has turned me from a drudge into a princess in no time. I do nothing but indulge myself all day long, and she always finds out what I want before I know it myself."

"I'm sure she is the happier for having you, then," said Philip. "You must be better than a whole menagerie of pets to her. And you look well—you are benefiting by the change."

Artificial conversation of this sort went on a little while, till Lucy, determined to put an end to it, exclaimed, with a good imitation of annoyance, that she had forgotten something, and was quickly out of the room.

In a moment Maggie and Philip leaned forward, and the hands were clasped again, with a look of sad contentment like that of friends who meet in the memory of recent sorrow.

"I told my brother I wished to see you, Philip—I asked him to release me from my promise, and he consented."

Maggie, in her impulsiveness, wanted Philip to know at once the position they must hold towards each other; but she checked herself. The things that had happened since he had spoken of his love for her were so painful that she shrank from being the first to allude to them. It seemed almost like an injury towards Philip even to mention her brother —her brother who had insulted him. But he was thinking too entirely of her to be sensitive on any other point at that moment.

"Then we can at least be friends, Maggie? There is nothing to hinder that now?"

"Will not your father object?" said Maggie, withdrawing her hand.

"I should not give you up on any ground but your own wish, Maggie," said Philip, colouring. "There are points on which I should always resist my father, as I used to tell you. *That* is one."

"Then there is nothing to hinder our being friends, Philip—seeing each other and talking to each other while I am here: I shall soon go away again. I mean to go very soon—to a new situation."

"Is that inevitable, Maggie?"

"Yes: I must not stay here long. It would unfit me for the life I must begin again at last. I can't live in dependence—I can't live with my brother—though he is very good to me. He would like to provide for me; but that would be intolerable to me."

Philip was silent a few moments, and then said in that high, feeble voice which with him indicated the resolute suppression of emotion:—

"Is there no other alternative, Maggie? Is that life, away from those who love you, the only one you will allow yourself to look forward to?"

"Yes, Philip," she said, looking at him pleadingly, as if she entreated him to believe that she was compelled to this course. "At least, as things are; I don't know what may be in years to come. But I begin to think there can never come much happiness to me from loving: I have always had so much pain mingled with it. I wish I could make myself a world outside it, as men do."

"Now, you are returning to your old thought in a new form, Maggie —the thought I used to combat," said Philip, with a slight tinge of bitterness. "You want to find out a mode of renunciation that will be an escape from pain. I tell you again, there is no such escape possible except by perverting or mutilating one's nature. What would become of me, if I tried to escape from pain? Scorn and cynicism would be my only opium; unless I could fall into some kind of conceited madness, and fancy myself a favourite of Heaven, because I am not a favourite with men."

The bitterness had taken on some impetuosity as Philip went on speaking: the words were evidently an outlet for some immediate feeling of his own, as well as an answer to Maggie. There was a pain pressing on him at that moment. He shrank with proud delicacy from the faintest allusion to the words of love—of plighted love that had passed between them. It would have seemed to him like reminding Maggie of a promise; it would have had for him something of the baseness of compulsion. He could not dwell on the fact that he himself had not changed; for that too would have had the air of an appeal. His love for Maggie was stamped, even more than the rest of his experience, with the exaggerated sense that he was an exception—that she, that every one, saw him in the light of an exception.

But Maggie was conscience-stricken.

"Yes, Philip," she said with her childish contrition when he used to chide her, "you are right, I know. I do always think too much of my own feelings, and not enough of others'—not enough of yours. I had need have you always to find fault with me and teach me: so many things have come true that you used to tell me."

Maggie was resting her elbow on the table, leaning her head on her hand and looking at Philip with half-penitent dependent affection, as she said this; while he was returning her gaze with an expression that, to her consciousness, gradually became less vague—became charged with a specific recollection. Had his mind flown back to something that *she* now remembered?—something about a lover of Lucy's? It was a thought that made her shudder: it gave new definiteness to her present position, and to the tendency of what had happened the evening before. She moved her arm from the table, urged to change her position by that positive physical oppression at the heart that sometimes accompanies a sudden mental pang.

"What is the matter, Maggie? Has something happened?" Philip said, in inexpressible anxiety—his imagination being only too ready to weave everything that was fatal to them both.

"No—nothing," said Maggie, rousing her latent will. Philip must not have that odious thought in his mind: she would banish it from her own. "Nothing," she repeated, "except in my own mind. You used to say I should feel the effect of my starved life, as you called it, and I do. I am too eager in my enjoyment of music and all luxuries, now they are come to me."

She took up her work and occupied herself resolutely, while Philip watched her, really in doubt whether she had anything more than this general allusion in her mind. It was quite in Maggie's character to be agitated by vague self-reproach. But soon there came a violent well-known ring at the door-bell resounding through the house.

"O, what a startling announcement!" said Maggie, quite mistress of herself, though not without some inward flutter. "I wonder where Lucy is."

Lucy had not been deaf to the signal, and after an interval long enough for a few solicitous but not hurried inquiries, she herself ushered Stephen in.

"Well, old fellow," he said, going straight up to Philip and shaking him heartily by the hand, bowing to Maggie in ⌐assing, "it's glorious to have you back again; only I wish you'd conduct yourself a little less like a sparrow with a residence on the house-top, and not go in and out constantly without letting the servants know. This is about the twentieth time I've had to scamper up those countless stairs to that painting-room of yours, all to no purpose, because your people thought you were at home. Such incidents embitter friendship."

"I've so few visitors—it seems hardly worth while to leave notice of my exit and entrances," said Philip, feeling rather oppressed just then by Stephen's bright strong presence and strong voice.

"Are you quite well this morning, Miss Tulliver?" said Stephen, turning to Maggie with stiff politeness, and putting out his hand with the air of fulfilling a social duty.

Maggie gave the tips of her fingers, and said, "Quite well, thank you," in a tone of proud indifference. Philip's eyes were watching them keenly; but Lucy was used to seeing variations in their manner to each other, and only thought with regret that there was some natural antipathy which every now and then surmounted their mutual good-will. "Maggie is not the sort of woman Stephen admires, and she is irritated by something in him which she interprets as conceit," was the silent observation that accounted for everything to guileless Lucy. Stephen and Maggie had no sooner completed this studied greeting than each felt hurt by the other's coldness. And Stephen, while rattling on in questions to Philip about his recent sketching expedition, was thinking all the more about Maggie because he was not drawing her into the conversation, as he had invariably done before. "Maggie and Philip are not looking happy," thought Lucy: "this first interview has been saddening to them."

"I think we people who have not been galloping," she said to Stephen, "are all a little damped by the rain. Let us have some music. We ought to take advantage of having Philip and you together. Give us the duet in 'Masaniello:' Maggie has not heard that, and I know it will suit her."

"Come, then," said Stephen, going towards the piano, and giving a foretaste of the tune in his deep "brum-brum," very pleasant to hear.

"You, please, Philip—you play the accompaniment," said Lucy, "and then I can go on with my work. You *will* like to play, shan't you?" she added, with a pretty inquiring look, anxious, as usual, lest she should have proposed what was not pleasant to another; but with yearnings towards her unfinished embroidery.

Philip had brightened at the proposition, for there is no feeling, perhaps, except the extremes of fear and grief, that does not find relief in music—that does not make a man sing or play the better; and Philip had an abundance of pent-up feeling at this moment, as complex as any trio or quartet that was ever meant to express love and jealousy, and resignation and fierce suspicion, all at the same time.

"O, yes," he said, seating himself at the piano, "it is a way of eking out one's imperfect life and being three people at once—to sing and make the piano sing, and hear them both all the while—or else to sing and paint."

"Ah, there you are an enviable fellow. I can do nothing with my hands," said Stephen. "That has generally been observed in men of great administrative capacity, I believe. A tendency to predominance of the reflective powers in me!—haven't you observed that, Miss Tulliver?"

Stephen had fallen by mistake into his habit of playful appeal to Maggie, and she could not repress the answering flush and epigram.

"I *have* observed a tendency to predominance," she said, smiling; and Philip at that moment devoutly hoped that she found the tendency disagreeable.

"Come, come," said Lucy; "music, music! We will discuss each other's qualities another time."

Maggie always tried in vain to go on with her work when music began. She tried harder than ever to-day; for the thought that Stephen knew how much she cared for his singing was one that no longer roused a merely playful resistance; and she knew, too, that it was his habit always to stand so that he could look at her. But it was of no use: she soon threw her work down, and all her intentions were lost in the vague state of emotion produced by the inspiring duet—emotion that seemed to make her at once strong and weak: strong for all enjoyment, weak for all resistance. When the strain passed into the minor, she half-started from her seat with the sudden thrill of that change. Poor Maggie! She looked very beautiful when her soul was being played on in this way by the inexorable power of sound. You might have seen the slightest perceptible quivering through her whole frame, as she leaned a little forward, clasping her hands as if to steady herself; while her eyes dilated and brightened into that wide-open, childish expression of wondering delight, which always came back in her happiest moments. Lucy, who at other times had always been at the piano when Maggie was looking in this way, could not resist the impulse to steal up to her and kiss her. Philip, too, caught a glimpse of her now and then round the open book on the desk, and felt that he had never before seen her under so strong an influence.

"More, more!" said Lucy, when the duet had been encored. "Something spirited again. Maggie always says she likes a great rush of sound."

"It must be 'Let us take the road,' then," said Stephen—"so suitable for a wet morning. But are you prepared to abandon the most sacred duties of life, and come and sing with us?"

"O, yes," said Lucy, laughing. "If you will look out the 'Beggar's Opera' from the large canterbury. It has a dingy cover."

"That is a great clue, considering there are about a score covers here of rival dinginess," said Stephen, drawing out the canterbury.

"O, play something the while, Philip," said Lucy, noticing that his fingers were wandering over the keys. "What is that you are falling into? —something delicious that I don't know."

"Don't you know that?" said Philip, bringing out the tune more definitely. "It's from the *Somnambula*—'Ah! perchè non posso odiarti.' I don't know the opera, but it appears the tenor is telling the heroine that he shall always love her though she may forsake him. You've heard me sing it to the English words, 'I love thee still.' "

It was not quite unintentionally that Philip had wandered into this song, which might be an indirect expression to Maggie of what he could not prevail on himself to say to her directly. Her ears had been open to what he was saying, and when he began to sing, she understood the plaintive passion of the music. That pleading tenor had no very fine qualities as a voice, but it was not quite new to her: it had sung to her by snatches, in a subdued way, among the grassy walks and hollows, and underneath the leaning ash-tree in the Red Deeps. There seemed to be some reproach in the words—did Philip mean that? She wished she had assured him more distinctly in their conversation that she desired not to renew the hope of love between them, *only* because it clashed with her inevitable circumstances. She was touched, not thrilled, by the song: it suggested distinct memories and thoughts, and brought quiet regret in the place of excitement.

"That's the way with you tenors," said Stephen, who was waiting with music in his hand while Philip finished the song. "You demoralise the fair sex by warbling your sentimental love and constancy under all sorts of vile treatment. Nothing short of having your heads served up in a dish like that mediæval tenor or troubadour, would prevent you from expressing your entire resignation. I must administer an antidote, while Miss Deane prepares to tear herself away from her bobbins."

Stephen rolled out, with saucy energy—

> "Shall I, wasting in despair,
> Die because a woman's fair?"

and seemed to make all the air in the room alive with a new influence. Lucy, always proud of what Stephen did, went towards the piano with laughing, admiring looks at him; and Maggie, in spite of her resistance to the spirit of the song and to the singer, was taken hold of and shaken by the invisible influence—was borne along by a wave too strong for her.

But angrily resolved not to betray herself, she seized her work, and went on making false stitches and pricking her fingers with much perseverance, not looking up or taking notice of what was going forward, until all the three voices united in "Let us take the road."

I am afraid there would have been a subtle, stealing gratification in her mind if she had known how entirely this saucy, defiant Stephen was occupied with her: how he was passing rapidly from a determination to treat her with ostentatious indifference to an irritating desire for some sign of inclination from her—some interchange of subdued word or look with her. It was not long before he found an opportunity, when they had passed to the music of "The Tempest." Maggie, feeling the need of a footstool, was walking across the room to get one, when Stephen, who was not singing just then, and was conscious of all her movements, guessed her want, and flew to anticipate her, lifting the footstool with an entreating look at her, which made it impossible not to return a glance of gratitude. And then, to have the footstool placed carefully by a too self-confident personage—not *any* self-confident personage, but one in particular, who suddenly looks humble and anxious, and lingers, bending still, to ask if there is not some draught in that position between the window and the fireplace, and if he may not be allowed to move the work-table for her—these things will summon a little of the too-ready, traitorous tenderness into a woman's eyes, compelled as she is in her girlish time to learn her life-lessons in very trivial language. And to Maggie such things had not been everyday incidents, but were a new element in her life, and found her keen appetite for homage quite fresh. That tone of gentle solicitude obliged her to look at the face that was bent towards her, and to say, "No, thank you;" and nothing could prevent that mutual glance from being delicious to both, as it had been the evening before.

It was but an ordinary act of politeness in Stephen; it had hardly taken two minutes; and Lucy, who was singing, scarcely noticed it. But to Philip's mind, filled already with a vague anxiety that was likely to find a definite ground for itself in any trivial incident, this sudden eagerness in Stephen, and the change in Maggie's face, which was plainly reflecting a beam from his, seemed so strong a contrast with the previous overwrought signs of indifference, as to be charged with painful meaning. Stephen's voice, pouring in again, jarred upon his nervous susceptibility as if it had been the clang of sheet-iron, and he felt inclined to make the piano shriek in utter discord. He had really seen no communicable ground for suspecting any unusual feeling between Stephen and Maggie: his own reason told him so, and he wanted to go home at once that he might reflect coolly on these false images, till he had convinced himself of their nullity. But then, again, he wanted to stay as long as Stephen stayed—always to be present when Stephen was present with Maggie. It seemed to poor Philip so natural, nay, inevitable, that any man who was near Maggie should fall in love with her! There was no promise of happiness for her if she were beguiled into loving Stephen Guest; and this thought emboldened Philip to view his own love for her in the light of a less unequal offering. He was beginning to play very falsely under this deafening inward tumult, and Lucy was looking at him in astonishment, when Mrs. Tulliver's entrance to summon them to lunch came as an excuse for abruptly breaking off the music.

"Ah, Mr. Philip," said Mr. Deane, when they entered the dining-room, "I've not seen you for a long while. Your father's not at home, I think, is he? I went after him to the office the other day, and they said he was out of town."

"He's been to Mudport on business for several days," said Philip; "but he's come back now."

"As fond of his farming hobby as ever, eh?"

"I believe so," said Philip, rather wondering at this sudden interest in his father's pursuits.

"Ah!" said Mr. Deane, "he's got some land in his own hands on this side the river as well as the other, I think?"

"Yes, he has."

"Ah!" continued Mr. Deane, as he dispensed the pigeon-pie; "he must find farming a heavy item—an expensive hobby. I never had a hobby myself—never would give in to that. And the worst of all hobbies are those that people think they can get money at. They shoot their money down like corn out of a sack then."

Lucy felt a little nervous under her father's apparently gratuitous criticism of Mr. Wakem's expenditure. But it ceased there, and Mr. Deane became unusually silent and meditative during his lunchon. Lucy, accustomed to watch all indications in her father, and having reasons, which had recently become strong, for an extra interest in what referred to the Wakems, felt an unusual curiosity to know what had prompted her father's questions. His subsequent silence made her suspect there had been some special reason for them in his mind.

With this idea in her head, she resorted to her usual plan when she wanted to tell or ask her father anything particular: she found a reason for her aunt Tulliver to leave the dining-room after dinner, and seated herself on a small stool at her father's knee. Mr. Deane, under those circumstances, considered that he tasted some of the most agreeable moments his merits had purchased him in life, notwithstanding that Lucy, disliking to have her hair powdered with snuff, usually began by mastering his snuff-box on such occasions.

"You don't want to go to sleep yet, papa, *do* you?" she said, as she brought up her stool and opened the large fingers that clutched the snuff-box.

"Not yet," said Mr. Deane, glancing at the reward of merit in the decanter. "But what do *you* want?" he added, pinching the dimpled chin fondly. "To coax some more sovereigns out of my pocket for your bazaar? Eh?"

"No, I have no base motives at all to-day. I only want to talk, not to beg. I want to know what made you ask Philip Wakem about his father's farming to-day, papa? It seemed rather odd, because you never hardly say anything to him about his father; and why should you care about Mr. Wakem's losing money by his hobby?"

"Something to do with business," said Mr. Deane, waving his hands, as if to repel intrusion into that mystery.

"But, papa, you always say Mr. Wakem has brought Philip up like a girl: how came you to think you should get any business knowledge out of him? Those abrupt questions sounded rather oddly. Philip thought them queer."

"Nonsense, child!" said Mr. Deane, willing to justify his social demeanor, with which he had taken some pains in his upward progress.

"There's a report that Wakem's mill and farm on the other side of the river—Dorlcote Mill, your uncle Tulliver's, you know—isn't answering so well as it did. I wanted to see if your friend Philip would let anything out about his father's being tired of farming."

"Why? Would you buy the mill, papa, if he would part with it?" said Lucy, eagerly. "O, tell me everything—here, you shall have your snuff-box if you'll tell me. Because Maggie says all their hearts are set on Tom's getting back the mill some time. It was one of the last things her father said to Tom, that he must get back the mill."

"Hush, you little puss," said Mr. Deane, availing himself of the restored snuff-box. "You must not say a word about this thing—do you hear? There's very little chance of their getting the mill, or of anybody's getting it out of Wakem's hands. And if he knew that we wanted it with a view to the Tulliver's getting it again, he'd be the less likely to part with it. It's natural, after what happened. He behaved well enough to Tulliver before; but a horse-whipping is not likely to be paid for with sugar-plums."

"Now, papa," said Lucy, with a little air of solemnity, "will you trust me? You must not ask me all my reasons for what I'm going to say—but I have very strong reasons. And I'm very cautious—I am, indeed."

"Well, let us hear."

"Why, I believe, if you will let me take Philip Wakem into our confidence—let me tell him all about your wish to buy, and what it's for—that my cousins wish to have it, and why they wish to have it—I believe Philip would help to bring it about. I know he would desire to do it."

"I don't see how that can be, child," said Mr. Deane, looking puzzled. "Why should *he* care?"—then, with a sudden penetrating looking at his daughter, "you don't think the poor lad's fond of you, and so you can make him do what you like?" (Mr. Deane felt quite safe about his daughter's affections.)

"No, papa; he cares very little about me—not so much as I care about him. But I have a reason for being quite sure of what I say. Don't you ask me. And if you ever guess, don't tell me. Only give me leave to do as I think fit about it."

Lucy rose from her stool to seat herself on her father's knee, and kissed him with that last request.

"Are you sure you won't do mischief, now?" he said, looking at her with delight.

"Yes, papa, quite sure. I'm very wise: I've got all your business talents. Didn't you admire my accompt-book, now, when I showed it you?"

"Well, well, if this youngster will keep his counsel, there won't be much harm done. And to tell the truth, I think there's not much chance for us any other way. Now, let me go off to sleep."

CHAPTER VIII

WAKEM IN A NEW LIGHT

BEFORE three days had passed after the conversation you have just overheard between Lucy and her father, she had contrived to have a private interview with Philip during a visit of Maggie's to her aunt Glegg. For a day and a night Philip turned over in his mind with restless agitation all that Lucy had told him in that interview, till he had thoroughly resolved on a course of action. He thought he saw before him now a possibility of altering his position with respect to Maggie, and removing at least one obstacle between them. He laid his plan and calculated all his moves with the fervid deliberation of a chess-player in the days of his first ardour, and was amazed himself at his sudden genius as a tactician. His plan was as bold as it was thoroughly calculated. Having watched for a moment when his father had nothing more urgent on his hands than the newspaper, he went behind him, laid a hand on his shoulder, and said—

"Father, will you come up into my sanctum, and look at my new sketches? I've arranged them now."

"I'm getting terribly stiff in the joints, Phil, for climbing those stairs of yours," said Wakem, looking kindly at his son as he laid down his paper. "But come along, then."

"This is a nice place for you, isn't it, Phil?—a capital light that from the roof, eh?" was, as usual, the first thing he said on entering the painting-room. He liked to remind himself and his son too that his fatherly indulgence had provided the accommodation. He had been a good father. Emily would have nothing to reproach him with there, if she came back again from her grave.

"Come, come," he said, putting his double eye-glass over his nose, and seating himself to take a general view while he rested, "you've got a famous show here. Upon my word, I don't see that your things aren't as good as that London artist's—what's his name—that Leyburn gave so much money for."

Philip shook his head and smiled. He had seated himself on his painting-stool, and had taken a lead pencil in his hand, with which he was making strong marks to counteract the sense of tremulousness. He watched his father get up, and walk slowly round, good-naturedly dwelling on the pictures much longer than his amount of genuine taste for landscape would have prompted, till he stopped before a stand on which two pictures were placed—one much larger than the other—the smaller one in a leather case.

"Bless me! what have you here?" said Wakem, startled by a sudden transition from landscape to portrait. "I thought you'd left off figures. Who are these?"

"They are the same person," said Philip, with calm promptness, "at different ages."

"And what person?" said Wakem, sharply, fixing his eyes with a growing look of suspicion on the larger picture.

"Miss Tulliver. The small one is something like what she was when I was at school with her brother at King's Lorton: the larger one is not quite so good a likeness of what she was when I came from abroad."

Wakem turned round fiercely, with a flushed face, letting his eyeglass fall, and looking at his son with a savage expression for a moment, as if he was ready to strike that daring feebleness from the stool. But he threw himself into the armchair again, and thrust his hands into his trouser-pockets, still looking angrily at his son, however. Philip did not return the look, but sat quietly watching the point of his pencil.

"And do you mean to say, then, that you have had any acquaintance with her since you came from abroad?" said Wakem, at last, with that vain effort which rage always makes to throw as much punishment as it desires to inflict into words and tones, since blows are forbidden.

"Yes: I saw a great deal of her for a whole year before her father's death. We met often, in that thicket—the Red Deeps—near Dorlcote Mill. I love her dearly: I shall never love any other woman. I have thought of her ever since she was a little girl."

"Go on, sir!—and you have corresponded with her all this while?"

"No. I never told her I loved her till just before we parted, and she promised her brother not to see me again or to correspond with me. I am not sure that she loves me, or would consent to marry me. But if she would consent—if she *did* love me well enough—I should marry her."

"And this is the return you make me for all the indulgences I've heaped on you?" said Wakem, getting white, and beginning to tremble under an enraged sense of impotence before Philip's calm defiance and concentration of purpose.

"No, father," said Philip, looking up at him for the first time. "I don't regard it as a return. You have been an indulgent father to me; but I have always felt that it was because you had an affectionate wish to give me as much happiness as my unfortunate lot would admit of— not that it was a debt you expected me to pay by sacrificing all my chances of happiness to satisfy feelings of yours, which I can never share."

"I think most sons would share their father's feelings in this case," said Wakem, bitterly. "The girl's father was an ignorant mad brute, who was within an inch of murdering me. The whole town knows it. And the brother is just as insolent, only in a cooler way. He forbade her seeing you, you say; he'll break every bone in your body, for your greater happiness, if you don't take care. But you seem to have made up your mind: you have counted the consequences, I suppose. Of course you are independent of me: you can marry this girl to-morrow, if you like: you are a man of five-and-twenty—you can go your way, and I can go mine. We need have no more to do with each other."

Wakem rose and walked towards the door, but something held him back, and instead of leaving the room, he walked up and down it. Philip was slow to reply, and when he spoke, his tone had a more incisive quietness and clearness than ever.

"No: I can't marry Miss Tulliver, even if she would have me—if I have only my own resources to maintain her with. I have been brought up to no profession. I can't offer her poverty as well as deformity."

"Ah, *there* is a reason for your clinging to me, doubtless," said Wakem, still bitterly, though Philip's last words had given him a pang: they had stirred a feeling which had been a habit for a quarter of a century. He threw himself into the chair again.

"I expected all this," said Philip. "I know these scenes are often happening between father and son. If I were like other men of my age, I might answer your angry words by still angrier—we might part—I should marry the woman I love, and have a chance of being as happy as the rest. But if it will be a satisfaction to you to annihilate the very object of everything you've done for me, you have an advantage over most fathers: you can completely deprive me of the only thing that would make my life worth having."

Philip paused, but his father was silent.

"You know best what satisfaction you would have, beyond that of gratifying a ridiculous rancour worthy only of wandering savages."

"Ridiculous rancour!" Wakem burst out. "What do you mean? Damn it! is a man to be horse-whipped by a boor and love him for it? Besides, there's that cold, proud devil of a son, who said a word to me I shall not forget when we had the settling. He would be as pleasant a mark for a bullet as I know—if he were worth the expense."

"I don't mean your resentment towards them," said Philip, who had his reasons for some sympathy with this view of Tom, "though a feeling of revenge is not worth much, that you should care to keep it. I mean your extending the enmity to a helpless girl, who has too much sense and goodness to share their narrow prejudices. *She* has never entered into the family quarrels."

"What does that signify? We don't ask what a woman does—we ask whom she belongs to. It's altogether a degrading thing to you—to think of marrying old Tulliver's daughter."

For the first time in the dialogue, Philip lost some of his self-control, and coloured with anger.

"Miss Tulliver," he said, with bitter incisiveness, "has the only grounds of rank that anything but vulgar folly can suppose to belong to the middle class: she is thoroughly refined, and her friends, whatever else they may be, are respected for irreproachable honour and integrity. All St. Ogg's, I fancy, would pronounce her to be more than my equal."

Wakem darted a glance of fierce question at his son; but Philip was not looking at him, and with a certain penitent consciousness went on, in a few moments, as if in amplification of his last words—

"Find a single person in St. Ogg's who will not tell you that a beautiful creature like her would be throwing herself away on a pitiable object like me."

"Not she!" said Wakem, rising again, and forgetting everything else in a burst of resentful pride, half fatherly, half personal. "It would be a deuced fine match for her. It's all stuff about an accidental deformity, when a girl's really attached to a man."

"But girls are not apt to get attached under those circumstances," said Philip.

"Well, then," said Wakem, rather brutally, trying to recover his previous position, "if she doesn't care for you, you might have spared yourself the trouble of talking to me about her—and you might have spared me the trouble of refusing my consent to what was never likely to happen."

Wakem strode to the door, and, without looking round again, banged it after him.

Philip was not without confidence that his father would be ultimately wrought upon as he had expected, by what had passed; but the scene had jarred upon his nerves, which were as sensitive as a woman's. He determined not to go down to dinner: he couldn't meet his father again that day. It was Wakem's habit, when he had no company at home, to go out in the evening—often as early as half-past seven; and as it was far on in the afternoon now, Philip locked up his room and went out for a long ramble, thinking he would not return until his father was out of the house again. He got into a boat, and went down the river to a favourite village, where he dined, and lingered till it was late enough for him to return. He had never had any sort of quarrel with his father before, and had a sickening fear that this contest, just begun, might go on for weeks—and what might not happen in that time? He would not allow himself to define what that involuntary question meant. But if he could once be in the position of Maggie's accepted, acknowledged lover, there would be less room for vague dread. He went up to his painting-room again, and threw himself, with a sense of fatigue, into the armchair, looking round absently at the views of water and rock that were ranged around, till he fell into a doze, in which he fancied Maggie was slipping down a glistening, green, slimy channel of a waterfall, and he was looking on helpless, till he was awakened by what seemed a sudden, awful crash.

It was the opening of the door, and he could hardly have dozed more than a few moments, for there was no perceptible change in the evening light. It was his father who entered; and when Philip moved to vacate the chair for him, he said—

"Sit still. I'd rather walk about."

He stalked up and down the room once or twice, and then standing opposite Philip, with his hands thrust in his side-pockets, he said, as if continuing a conversation that had not been broken off—

"But this girl seems to have been fond of you, Phil, else she wouldn't have met you in that way."

Philip's heart was beating rapidly, and a transient flush passed over his face like a gleam. It was not quite easy to speak at once.

"She liked me at King's Lorton, when she was a little girl, because I used to sit with her brother a great deal when he had hurt his foot. She had kept that in her memory, and thought of me as a friend of a long while ago. She didn't think of me as a lover, when she met me."

"Well, but you made love to her at last. What did she say then?" said Wakem, walking about again.

"She said she *did* love me then."

"Confound it, then, what else do you want? Is she a jilt?"

"She was very young then," said Philip, hesitatingly. "I'm afraid she hardly knew what she felt. I'm afraid our long separation, and the idea that events must always divide us, may have made a difference."

"But she's in the town. I've seen her at church. Haven't you spoken to her since you came back?"

"Yes, at Mr. Deane's. But I couldn't renew my proposals to her on several grounds. One obstacle would be removed if you would give your consent—if you would be willing to think of her as a daughter-in-law."

Wakem was silent a little while, pausing before Maggie's picture.

"She's not the sort of woman your mother was, though, Phil," he said, at last. "I saw her at church—she's handsomer than this—deuced fine eyes and fine figure, I saw; but rather dangerous and unmanageable, eh?"

"She's very tender and affectionate; and so simple—without the airs and petty contrivances other women have."

"Ah?" said Wakem. Then looking round at his son, "But your mother looked gentler: she had that brown wavy hair and grey eyes, like yours. You can't remember her very well. It was a thousand pities I'd no likeness of her."

"Then, shouldn't you be glad for me to have the same sort of happiness, father—to sweeten my life for me? There can never be another tie so strong to you as that which began eight-and-twenty years ago, when you married my mother, and you have been tightening it ever since."

"Ay, Phil—you're the only fellow that knows the best of me," said Wakem, giving his hand to his son. "We must keep together, if we can. And now, what am I to do? You must come down-stairs and tell me. Am I to go and call on this dark-eyed damsel?"

The barrier once thrown down in this way, Philip could talk freely to his father of their entire relation with the Tullivers—of the desire to get the mill and land back into the family—and of its transfer to Guest & Co. as an intermediate step. He could venture now to be persuasive

and urgent, and his father yielded with more readiness than he had calculated on.

"*I* don't care about the mill," he said at last, with a sort of angry compliance. "I've had an infernal deal of bother lately about the mill. Let
them pay me for my improvements, that's all. But there's one thing
you needn't ask me. I shall have no direct transactions with young Tulliver. If you like to swallow him, for his sister's sake, you may; but I've
no sauce that will make him go down."

I leave you to imagine the agreeable feelings with which Philip went
to Mr. Deane the next day, to say that Mr. Wakem was ready to open
the negotiations, and Lucy's pretty triumph as she appealed to her father
whether she had not proved her great business abilities. Mr. Deane was
rather puzzled, and suspected that there had been something "going
on" among the young people to which he wanted a clue. But to men of
Mr. Deane's stamp, what goes on among the young people is as extraneous to the real business of life as what goes on among the birds
and butterflies—until it can be shown to have a malign bearing on
monetary affairs. And in this case the bearing appeared to be entirely
propitious.

CHAPTER IX

CHARITY IN FULL-DRESS

THE culmination of Maggie's career as an admired member of society
in St. Ogg's was certainly the day of the bazaar, when her simple noble
beauty, clad in a white muslin of some soft-floating kind, which I
suspect must have come from the stores of aunt Pullet's wardrobe, appeared with marked distinction among the more adorned and conventional women around her. We perhaps never detect how much of our
social demeanour is made up of artificial airs, until we see a person who
is at once beautiful and simple: without the beauty, we are apt to call
simplicity awkwardness. The Miss Guests were much too well-bred to
have any of the grimaces and affected tones that belong to pretentious
vulgarity; but their stall being next to the one where Maggie sat, it
seemed newly obvious today that Miss Guest held her chin too high,
and that Miss Laura spoke and moved continually with a view to effect.

All well-drest St. Ogg's and its neighbourhood were there; and it
would have been worth while to come, even from a distance, to see the
fine old hall, with its open roof and carved oaken rafters, and great oaken
folding-doors, and light shed down from a height on the many-colored
show beneath: a very quaint place, with broad faded stripes painted on
the walls, and here and there a show of heraldic animals of a bristly,
long-snouted character, the cherished emblems of a noble family once
the seigniors of this now civic hall. A grand arch, cut in the upper wall

at one end, surmounted an oaken orchestra, with an open room behind it, where hothouse plants and stalls for refreshments were disposed: an agreeable resort for gentlemen disposed to loiter, and yet to exchange the occasional crush down below for a more commodious point of view. In fact, the perfect fitness of this ancient building for an admirable modern purpose, that made charity truly elegant, and led through vanity up to the supply of a deficit, was so striking that hardly a person entered the room without exchanging the remark more than once. Near the great arch over the orchestra was the stone oriel with painted glass, which was one of the venerable inconsistencies of the old hall; and it was close by this that Lucy had her stall, for the convenience of certain large plain articles which she had taken charge of for Mrs. Kenn. Maggie had begged to sit at the open end of the stall, and to have the sale of these articles rather than of bead-mats and other elaborate products, of which she had but a dim understanding. But it soon appeared that the gentlemen's dressing-gowns, which were among her commodities, were objects of such general attention and inquiry, and excited so troublesome a curiosity as to their lining and comparative merits, together with a determination to test them by trying on, as to make her post a very conspicuous one. The ladies who had commodities of their own to sell, and did not want dressing-gowns, saw at once the frivolity and bad taste of this masculine preference for goods which any tailor could furnish; and it is possible that the emphatic notice of various kinds which was drawn towards Miss Tulliver on this public occasion, threw a very strong and unmistakable light on her subsequent conduct in many minds then present. Not that anger, on account of spurned beauty, can dwell in the celestial breasts of charitable ladies, but rather, that the errors of persons who have once been much admired necessarily take a deeper tinge from the mere force of contrast; and also, that today Maggie's conspicuous position, for the first time, made evident certain characteristics which were subsequently felt to have an explanatory bearing. There was something rather bold in Miss Tulliver's direct gaze, and something undefinably coarse in the style of her beauty, which placed her, in the opinion of all feminine judges, far below her cousin Miss Deane; for the ladies of St. Ogg's had now completely ceded to Lucy their hypothetic claims on the admiration of Mr. Stephen Guest.

As for dear little Lucy herself, her late benevolent triumph about the Mill, and all the affectionate projects she was cherishing for Maggie and Philip, helped to give her the highest spirits to-day, and she felt nothing but pleasure in the evidence of Maggie's attractiveness. It is true, she was looking very charming herself, and Stephen was paying her the utmost attention on this public occasion; jealously buying up the articles he had seen under her fingers in the process of making, and gaily helping her to cajole the male customers into the purchase of the most effeminate futilities. He chose to lay aside his hat and wear a scarlet fez of her embroidering; but by superficial observers this was necessarily liable to be interpreted less as a compliment to Lucy than as a mark of coxcombry. "Guest is a great coxcomb," young Torry observed; "but then he is a privileged person in St. Ogg's—he carries all before him: if another fellow did such things, everybody would say be made a fool of himself."

And Stephen purchased absolutely nothing from Maggie, until Lucy said, in rather a vexed undertone—

"See, now; all the things of Maggie's knitting will be gone, and you will not have bought one. There are those deliciously soft warm things for the wrists—do buy them."

"O, no," said Stephen, "they must be intended for imaginative persons, who can chill themselves on this warm day by thinking of the frosty Caucasus. Stern reason is my forte, you know. You must get Philip to buy those. By the way, why doesn't he come?"

"He never likes going where there are many people, though I enjoined him to come. He said he would buy up any of my goods that the rest of the world rejected. But now, do go and buy something of Maggie."

"No, no—see—she has got a customer: there is old Wakem himself just coming up."

Lucy's eyes turned with anxious interest towards Maggie, to see how she went through this first interview, since a sadly memorable time, with a man towards whom she must have so strange a mixture of feelings; but she was pleased to notice that Wakem had tact enough to enter at once into talk about the bazaar wares, and appear interested in purchasing, smiling now and then kindly at Maggie, and not calling on her to speak much, as if he observed that she was rather pale and tremulous.

"Why, Wakem is making himself particularly amiable to your cousin," said Stephen, in an undertone to Lucy; "is it pure magnanimity? you talked of a family quarrel."

"O, that will soon be quite healed, I hope," said Lucy, becoming a little indiscreet in her satisfaction, and speaking with an air of significance. But Stephen did not appear to notice this, and as some lady-purchasers came up, he lounged on towards Maggie's end, handling trifles and standing aloof until Wakem, who had taken out his purse, had finished his transactions.

"My son came with me," he overheard Wakem saying, "but he has vanished into some other part of the building, and has left all these charitable gallantries to me. I hope you'll reproach him for his shabby conduct."

She returned his smile and bow without speaking, and he turned away, only then observing Stephen and nodding to him. Maggie, conscious that Stephen was still there, busied herself with counting money, and avoided looking up. She had been well pleased that he had devoted himself to Lucy to-day, and had not come near her. They had begun the morning with an indifferent salutation, and both had rejoiced in being aloof from each other, like a patient who has actually done without his opium, in spite of former failures in resolution. And during the last few days they had even been making up their minds to failures, looking to the outward events that must soon come to separate them, as a reason for dispensing with self-conquest in detail.

Stephen moved step by step as if he were being unwillingly dragged, until he had got round the open end of the stall, and was half hidden by a screen of draperies. Maggie went on counting her money till she suddenly heard a deep gentle voice saying, "Aren't you very tired? Do let me bring you something—some fruit or jelly—mayn't I?"

The unexpected tones shook her like a sudden accidental vibration of a harp close by her.

"O, no, thank you," she said, faintly, and only half looking up for an instant.

"You look so pale," Stephen insisted, in a more entreating tone. "I'm sure you're exhausted. I must disobey you, and bring something."

"No, indeed, I couldn't take it."

"Are you angry with me? What have I done? *Do* look at me."

"Pray, go away," said Maggie, looking at him helplessly, her eyes glancing immediately from him to the opposite corner of the orchestra, which was half hidden by the folds of the old faded green curtain. Maggie had no sooner uttered this entreaty than she was wretched at the admission it implied; but Stephen turned away at once, and, following her upward glance, he saw Philip Wakem seated in the half-hidden corner, so that he could command little more than that angle of the hall in which Maggie sat. An entirely new thought occurred to Stephen, and, linking itself with what he had observed of Wakem's manner, and with Lucy's reply to his observation, it convinced him that there had been some former relation between Philip and Maggie beyond that childish one of which he had heard. More than one impulse made him immediately leave the hall, and go up-stairs to the refreshment-room, where, walking up to Philip, he sat down behind him, and put his hand on his shoulder.

"Are you studying for a portrait, Phil," he said, "or for a sketch of that oriel window? By George, it makes a capital bit from this dark corner, with the curtain just marking it off."

"I have been studying expression," said Philip, curtly.

"What, Miss Tulliver's? It's rather of the savage-moody order to-day, I think—something of the fallen princess serving behind a counter. Her cousin sent me to her with a civil offer to get her some refreshment, but I have been snubbed, as usual. There's a natural antipathy between us, I suppose: I have seldom the honour to please her."

"What a hypocrite you are!" said Philip, flushing angrily.

"What, because experience must have told me that I'm universally pleasing? I admit the law, but there's some disturbing force here."

"I am going," said Philip, rising abruptly.

"So am I—to get a breath of fresh air; this place gets oppressive. I think I have done suit and service long enough."

The two friends walked down-stairs together without speaking. Philip turned through the outer door into the courtyard, but Stephen, saying,

"O, by the by, I must call in here," went on along the passage to one of the rooms at the other end of the building, which were appropriated 'o the town library. He had the room all to himself, and a man requires nothing less than this, when he wants to dash his cap on the table, throw himself astride a chair, and stare at a high brick wall with a frown which would not have been beneath the occasion if he had been slaying "the giant Python." The conduct that issues from a moral conflict has often so close a resemblance to vice, that the distinction escapes all outward judgments, founded on a mere comparison of actions. It is clear to you, I hope, that Stephen was not a hypocrite—capable of deliberate doubleness for a selfish end; and yet his fluctuations between the indulgence of a feeling and the systematic concealment of it, might have made a good case in support of Philip's accusation.

Meanwhile, Maggie sate at her stall cold and trembling, with that painful sensation in the eyes which comes from resolutely repressed tears. Was her life to be always like this?—always bringing some new source of inward strife? She heard confusedly the busy indifferent voices around her, and wished her mind could flow into that easy, babbling current. It was at this moment that Dr. Kenn, who had quite lately come into the hall, and was now walking down the middle with his hands behind him, taking a general view, fixed his eyes on Maggie for the first time, and was struck with the expression of pain on her beautiful face. She was sitting quite still, for the stream of customers had lessened at this late hour in the afternoon: the gentlemen had chiefly chosen the middle of the day, and Maggie's stall was looking rather bare. This, with her absent, pained expression, finished the contrast between her and her companions, who were all bright, eager, and busy. He was strongly arrested. Her face had naturally drawn his attention as a new and striking one at church, and he had been introduced to her during a short call on business at Mr. Deane's, but he had never spoken more than three words to her. He walked towards her now, and Maggie, perceiving some one approaching, roused herself to look up and be prepared to speak. She felt a child-like, instinctive relief from the sense of uneasiness in this exertion, when she saw it was Dr. Kenn's face that was looking at her: that plain, middle-aged face, with a grave, penetrating kindness in it, seeming to tell of a human being who had reached a firm, safe stand, but was looking with helpful pity towards the strugglers still tossed by the waves, had an effect on Maggie at this moment which was afterwards remembered by her as if it had been a promise. The middle-aged, who have lived through their strongest emotions, but are yet in the time when memory is still half passionate and not merely contemplative, should surely be a sort of natural priesthood, whom life has disciplined and consecrated to be the refuge and rescue of early stumblers and victims of self-despair. Most of us, at some moment in our young lives, would have welcomed a priest of that natural order in any sort of canonicals or uncanonicals, but had to scramble upwards into all the difficulties of nineteen entirely without such aid, as Maggie did.

"You find your office rather a fatiguing one, I fear, Miss Tulliver?" said Dr. Kenn.

"It is, rather," said Maggie, simply, not being accustomed to simper amiable denials of obvious facts.

"But I can tell Mrs. Kenn that you have disposed of her goods very quickly," he added; "she will be very much obliged to you."

"O, I have done nothing: the gentlemen came very fast to buy the dressing-gowns and embroidered waistcoats, but I think any of the other ladies would have sold more: I didn't know what to say about them."

Dr. Kenn smiled. "I hope I'm going to have you as a permanent parishioner now, Miss Tulliver—am I? You have been at a distance from us hitherto."

"I have been a teacher in a school, and I'm going into another situation of the same kind very soon."

"Ah? I was hoping you would remain among your friends, who are all in this neighbourhood, I believe."

"O, _I must go_," said Maggie, earnestly, looking at Dr. Kenn with an expression of reliance, as if she had told him her history in those three words. It was one of those moments of implicit revelation which will sometimes happen even between people who meet quite transiently —on a mile's journey, perhaps, or when resting by the wayside. There is always this possibility of a word or look from a stranger to keep alive the sense of human brotherhood.

Dr. Kenn's ear and eye took in all the signs that this brief confidence of Maggie's was charged with meaning.

"I understand," he said; "you feel it right to go. But that will not prevent our meeting again, I hope: it will not prevent my knowing you better, if I can be of any service to you."

He put out his hand and pressed hers kindly before he turned away.

"She has some trouble or other at heart," he thought. "Poor child! she looks as if she might turn out to be one of

'The souls by nature pitch'd too high,
By suffering plung'd too low.'

There's something wonderfully honest in those beautiful eyes."

It may be surprising that Maggie, among whose many imperfections an excessive delight in admiration and acknowledged supremacy were not absent now, any more than when she was instructing the gypsies with a view towards achieving a royal position among them, was not more elated on a day when she had had the tribute of so many looks and smiles, together with that satisfactory consciousness which had necessarily come from being taken before Lucy's cheval-glass, and made to look at the full length of her tall beauty, crowned by the night of her massy hair. Maggie had smiled at herself then, and for the moment had forgotten everything in the sense of her own beauty. If that state of mind could have lasted, her choice would have been to have Stephen Guest at her feet, offering her a life filled with all luxuries, with daily incense of adoration near and distant, and with all possibilities of culture at her command. But there were things in her stronger than vanity—passion, and affection, and long deep memories of early discipline and effort, of early claims on her love and pity; and the stream of vanity was soon swept along and mingled imperceptibly with that wider current which was at its highest force to-day, under the double urgency of the events and inward impulses brought by the last week.

Philip had not spoken to her himself about the removal of obstacles between them on his father's side—he shrank from that; but he had told everything to Lucy, with the hope that Maggie, being informed through her, might give him some encouraging sign that their being brought thus much nearer to each other was a happiness to her. The rush of conflicting feelings was too great for Maggie to say much when Lucy, with a face breathing playful joy, like one of Correggio's cherubs, poured forth her triumphant revelation; and Lucy could hardly be surprised that she could do little more than cry with gladness at the thought of her father's wish being fulfilled, and of Tom's getting the Mill again in reward for all his hard striving. The details of preparation for the bazaar had then come to usurp Lucy's attention for the next few days, and nothing had been said by the cousins on subjects that were likely to rouse deeper feelings. Philip had been to the house more than once, but Maggie had had no private conversation with him, and thus she had been left to fight her inward battle without interference.

But when the bazaar was fairly ended, and the cousins were alone again, resting together at home, Lucy said—

"You must give up going to stay with your aunt Moss the day after to-morrow, Maggie: write a note to her, and tell her you have put it off at my request, and I'll send the man with it. She won't be displeased; you'll have plenty of time to go by-and-by; and I don't want you to go out of the way just now."

"Yes, indeed I must go, dear; I can't put it off. I wouldn't leave aunt Gritty out for the world. And I shall have very little time, for I'm going away to a new situation on the 25th of June."

"Maggie!" said Lucy, almost white with astonishment.

"I didn't tell you, dear," said Maggie, making a great effort to command herself, "because you've been so busy. But some time ago I wrote to our old governess, Miss Firniss, to ask her to let me know if she met with any situation that I could fill, and the other day I had a letter from her telling me that I could take three orphan pupils of hers to the coast during the holidays, and then make trial of a situation with her as teacher. I wrote yesterday to accept the offer."

Lucy felt so hurt that for some moments she was unable to speak.

"Maggie," she said at last, "how could you be so unkind to me—not to tell me—to take *such* a step—and now!" She hesitated a little, and then added—"And Philip? I thought everything was going to be so happy. O, Maggie—what is the reason? Give it up; let me write. There is nothing now to keep you and Philip apart."

"Yes," said Maggie, faintly. "There is Tom's feeling. He said I must give him up if I married Philip. And I know he will not change—at least not for a long while—unless something happened to soften him."

"But I will talk to him: he's coming back this week. And this good news about the Mill will soften him. And I'll talk to him about Philip. Tom's always very compliant to me: I don't think he's so obstinate."

"But I must go," said Maggie, in a distressed voice. "I must leave some time to pass. Don't press me to stay, dear Lucy."

Lucy was silent for two or three minutes, looking away and ruminating. At length she knelt down by her cousin, and, looking up in her face with anxious seriousness, said—

"Maggie, is it that you don't love Philip well enough to marry him? —tell me—trust me."

Maggie held Lucy's hands tightly in silence a little while. Her own hands were quite cold. But when she spoke, her voice was quite clear and distinct.

"Yes, Lucy, I would choose to marry him. I think it would be the best and highest lot for me—to make his life happy. He loved me first. No one else could be quite what he is to me. But I can't divide myself from my brother for life. I must go away, and wait. Pray, don't speak to me again about it."

Lucy obeyed in pain and wonder. The next word she said was—

"Well, dear Maggie, at least you will go to the dance at Park House to-morrow, and have some music and brightness, before you go to pay these dull, dutiful visits. Ah! here come aunty and the tea."

CHAPTER X

THE SPELL SEEMS BROKEN

THE suite of rooms opening into each other at Park House looked duly brilliant with lights and flowers and the personal splendours of sixteen couples, with attendant parents and guardians. The focus of brilliancy was the long drawing-room, where the dancing went forward, under the inspiration of the grand piano; the library, into which it opened at one end, had the more sober illumination of maturity, with caps and cards; and at the other end, the pretty sitting-room, with a conservatory attached, was left as an occasional cool retreat. Lucy, who had laid aside her black for the first time, and had her pretty slimness set off by an abundant dress of white crape, was the acknowledged queen of the occasion; for this was one of the Miss Guests' thoroughly condescending parties, including no member of any aristocracy higher than that of St. Ogg's, and stretching to the extreme limits of commercial and professional gentility.

Maggie at first refused to dance, saying that she had forgotten all the figures—it was so many years since she had danced at school; and she was glad to have that excuse, for it is ill dancing with a heavy heart. But at length the music wrought in her young limbs, and the longing came; even though it was the horrible young Torry, who walked up a second time to try and persuade her. She warned him that she could not dance anything but a country dance; but he, of course, was willing to wait for that high felicity, meaning only to be complimentary when he assured her at several intervals that it was a "great bore" that she couldn't waltz—he would have liked so much to waltz with her. But at last it was the turn of the good old-fashioned dance, which has the least of vanity and the most of merriment in it, and Maggie quite forgot her troublous life in a childlike enjoyment of that half-rustic rhythm which seems to banish pretentious etiquette. She felt quite charitably towards young Torry, as his hand bore her along and held her up in the dance; her eyes and cheeks had that fire of young joy in them which will flame out if it can find the least breath to fan it; and her simple black dress, with its bit of black lace, seemed like the dim setting of a jewel.

Stephen had not yet asked her to dance—had not yet paid her more than a passing civility. Since yesterday, that inward vision of her which perpetually made part of his consciousness, had been half-screened by the image of Philip Wakem, which came across it like a blot: there was some attachment between her and Philip; at least there was an attachment on his side, which made her feel in some bondage. Here then, Stephen told himself, was another claim of honour which called on him to resist the attraction that was continually threatening to overpower him. He told himself so; and yet he had once or twice felt a certain savage resistance, and at another moment a shuddering repugnance, to this intrusion of Philip's image, which almost made it a new incitement to rush towards Maggie and claim her for himself. Nevertheless he had done what he meant to do this evening: he had kept aloof from her; he had hardly looked at her; and he had been gaily assiduous to Lucy. But now his eyes were devouring Maggie: he felt inclined to kick young Torry out of the dance, and take his place. Then he wanted the dance to end that he might get rid of his partner. The possibility that he too should dance with Maggie, and have her hand in his so long, was beginning to possess him like a thirst. But even now their hands were meeting in the dance—were meeting still to the very end of it, though they were far off each other.

Stephen hardly knew what happened, or in what automatic way he got through the duties of politeness in the interval, until he was free and saw Maggie seated alone again, at the farther end of the room. He made his way towards her round the couples that were forming for the waltz, and when Maggie became conscious that she was the person he sought, she felt, in spite of all the thoughts that had gone before, a glowing gladness at heart. Her eyes and cheeks were still brightened with her child-like enthusiasm in the dance; her whole frame was set to joy and tenderness; even the coming pain could not seem bitter—she was ready to welcome it as a part of life, for life at this moment seemed a keen vibrating consciousness poised above pleasure or pain. This one, this last night, she might expand unrestrainedly in the warmth of the present, without those chill eating thoughts of the past and the future.

"They're going to waltz again," said Stephen, bending to speak to her, with that glance and tone of subdued tenderness which young dreams create to themselves in the summer woods when low cooing voices fill the air. Such glances and tones bring the breath of poetry with them into a room that is half-stifling with glaring gas and hard flirtation.

"They are going to waltz again: it is rather dizzy work to look on, and the room is very warm. Shall we walk about a little?"

He took her hand and placed it within his arm, and they walked on into the sitting-room, where the tables were strewn with engravings for the accommodation of visitors who would not want to look at them. But no visitors were here at this moment. They passed on into the conservatory.

"How strange and unreal the trees and flowers look with the lights among them," said Maggie, in a low voice. "They look as if they belonged to an enchanted land, and would never fade away:—I could fancy they were all made of jewels."

She was looking at the tier of geraniums as she spoke, and Stephen made no answer; but he was looking at her—and does not a supreme poet blend light and sound into one, calling darkness mute, and light eloquent? Something strangely powerful there was in the light of Stephen's long gaze, for it made Maggie's face turn towards it and look upward at it—slowly, like a flower at the ascending brightness. And they walked unsteadily on, without feeling that they were walking—without feeling anything but that long grave mutual gaze which has the solemnity belonging to all deep human passion. The hovering thought that they must and would renounce each other made this moment of mute confession more intense in its rapture.

But they had reached the end of the conservatory, and were obliged to pause and turn. The change of movement brought a new consciousness to Maggie: she blushed deeply, turned away her head, and drew her arm from Stephen's, going up to some flowers to smell them. Stephen stood motionless, and still pale.

"O, may I get this rose?" said Maggie, making a great effort to say something, and dissipate the burning sense of irretrievable confession. "I think I am quite wicked with roses—I like to gather them and smell them till they have no scent left."

Stephen was mute: he was incapable of putting a sentence together, and Maggie bent her arm a little upward towards the large half-opened rose that had attracted her. Who has not felt the beauty of a woman's arm?—the unspeakable suggestions of tenderness that lie in the dimpled elbow, and all the varied gently-lessening curves down to the delicate wrist, with its tiniest, almost imperceptible nicks in the firm softness. A woman's arm touched the soul of a great sculptor two thousand years ago, so that he wrought an image of it for the Parthenon which moves us still as it clasps lovingly the time-worn marble of a headless trunk. Maggie's was such an arm as that—and it had the warm tints of life.

A mad impulse seized on Stephen; he darted towards the arm, and showered kisses on it, clasping the wrist.

But the next moment Maggie snatched it from him, and glared at him like a wounded war-goddess, quivering with rage and humiliation.

"How dare you?"—she spoke in a deeply shaken, half-smothered voice. "What right have I given you to insult me?"

She darted from him into the adjoining room, and threw herself on the sofa, panting and trembling.

A horrible punishment was come upon her for the sin of allowing a moment's happiness that was treachery to Lucy, to Philip—to her own better soul. That momentary happiness had been smitten with a blight —a leprosy: Stephen thought more lightly of *her* than he did of Lucy.

As for Stephen, he leaned back against the framework of the conservatory, dizzy with the conflict of passions—love, rage, and confused despair: despair at his want of self-mastery, and despair that he had offended Maggie.

The last feeling surmounted every other: to be by her side again and entreat forgiveness was the only thing that had the force of a motive for him, and she had not been seated more than a few minutes when he came and stood humbly before her. But Maggie's bitter rage was unspent.

"Leave me to myself, if you please," she said, with impetuous haughtiness, "and for the future avoid me."

Stephen turned away, and walked backwards and forwards at the other end of the room. There was the dire necessity of going back into the dancing-room again, and he was beginning to be conscious of that. They had been absent so short a time, that when he went in again the waltz was not ended.

Maggie, too, was not long before she re-entered. All the pride of her nature was stung into activity: the hateful weakness which had dragged her within reach of this wound to her self-respect, had at least wrought its own cure. The thoughts and temptations of the last month should all be flung away into an unvisited chamber of memory: there was nothing to allure her now; duty would be easy, and all the old calm purposes would reign peacefully once more. She re-entered the drawing-room still with some excited brightness in her face, but with a sense of proud self-command that defied anything to agitate her. She refused to dance again, but she talked quite readily and calmly with every one who addressed her. And when they got home that night, she kissed Lucy with a free heart, almost exulting in this scorching moment, which had delivered her from the possibility of another word or look that would have the stamp of treachery towards that gentle, unsuspicious sister.

The next morning Maggie did not set off to Basset quite so soon as she had expected. Her mother was to accompany her in the carriage, and household business could not be dispatched hastily by Mrs. Tulliver. So Maggie, who had been in a hurry to prepare herself, had to sit waiting, equipped for the drive, in the garden. Lucy was busy in the house wrapping up some bazaar presents for the younger ones at Basset, and when there was a loud ring at the door-bell, Maggie felt some alarm lest Lucy should bring out Stephen to her: it was sure to be Stephen.

But presently the visitor came out into the garden alone, and seated himself by her on the garden-chair. It was not Stephen.

"We can just catch the tips of the Scotch firs, Maggie, from this seat," said Philip.

They had taken each other's hands in silence, but Maggie had looked at him with a more complete revival of the old childlike affectionate smile than he had seen before, and he felt encouraged.

"Yes," she said, "I often look at them, and wish I could see the low sunlight on the stems again. But I have never been that way but once —to the churchyard, with my mother."

"I have been there—I go there—continually," said Philip. "I have nothing but the past to live upon."

A keen remembrance and keen pity impelled Maggie to put her hand in Philip's. They had so often walked hand-in-hand!

"I remember all the spots," she said—"just where you told me of particular things—beautiful stories that I had never heard of before."

"You will go there again soon—won't you, Maggie?" said Philip, getting timid. "The Mill will soon be your brother's home again."

"Yes; but I shall not be there," said Maggie. "I shall only hear of that happiness. I am going away again—Lucy has not told you, perhaps?"

"Then the future will never join on to the past again, Maggie? That book is quite closed?"

The grey eyes that had so often looked up at her with entreating worship, looked up at her now, with a last struggling ray of hope in them, and Maggie met them with her large sincere gaze.

"That book never will be closed, Philip," she said, with grave sadness; "I desire no future that will break the ties of the past. But the tie to my brother is one of the strongest. I can do nothing willingly that will divide me always from him."

"Is that the only reason that would keep us apart for ever, Maggie?" said Philip, with a desperate determination to have a definite answer.

"The only reason," said Maggie, with calm decision. And she believed it. At that moment she felt as if the enchanted cup had been dashed to the ground. The reactionary excitement that gave her a proud self-mastery had not subsided, and she looked at the future with a sense of calm choice.

They sat hand-in-hand without looking at each other or speaking for a few minutes: in Maggie's mind the first scenes of love and parting were more present than the actual moment, and she was looking at Philip in the Red Deeps.

Philip felt that he ought to have been thoroughly happy in that answer of hers: she was as open and transparent as a rock-pool. Why was he not thoroughly happy? Jealousy is never satisfied with anything short of an omniscience that would detect the subtlest fold of the heart.

CHAPTER XI

IN THE LANE

MAGGIE had been four days at her aunt Moss's, giving the early June sunshine quite a new brightness in the care-dimmed eyes of that affectionate woman, and making an epoch for her cousins great and small, who were learning her words and actions by heart, as if she had been a transient avatar of perfect wisdom and beauty.

She was standing on the causeway with her aunt and a group of cousins feeding the chickens, at that quiet moment in the life of the farmyard before the afternoon milking-time. The great buildings round the hollow yard were as dreary and tumbledown as ever, but over the old garden-wall the straggling rose-bushes were beginning to toss their summer weight, and the grey wood and old bricks of the house, on its higher level, had a look of sleepy age in the broad afternoon sunlight, that suited the quiescent time. Maggie, with her bonnet over her arm, was smiling down at the hatch of small fluffy chickens, when her aunt exclaimed—

"Goodness me! who is that gentleman coming in at the gate?"

It was a gentleman on a tall bay horse; and the flanks and neck of the horse were streaked black with fast riding. Maggie felt a beating at head and heart—horrible as the sudden leaping to life of a savage enemy who had feigned death.

"Who is it, my dear?" said Mrs. Moss, seeing in Maggie's face the evidence that she knew.

"It is Mr. Stephen Guest," said Maggie, rather faintly. "My cousin Lucy's——a gentleman who is very intimate at my cousin's."

Stephen was already close to them, had jumped off his horse, and now raised his hat as he advanced.

"Hold the horse, Willy," said Mrs. Moss to the twelve-year-old boy.

"No, thank you," said Stephen, pulling at the horse's impatiently tossing head. "I must be going again immediately. I have a message to deliver to you, Miss Tulliver—on private business. May I take the liberty of asking you to walk a few yards with me?"

He had a half-jaded, half-irritated look, such as a man gets when he has been dogged by some care or annoyance that makes his bed and his dinner of little use to him. He spoke almost abruptly, as if his errand were too pressing for him to trouble himself about what would be thought by Mrs. Moss of his visit and request. Good Mrs. Moss, rather nervous in the presence of this apparently haughty gentleman, was inwardly wondering whether she would be doing right or wrong to invite him again to leave his horse and walk in, when Maggie, feeling all the embarrassment of the situation, and unable to say anything, put on her bonnet, and turned to walk towards the gate.

Stephen turned too, and walked by her side, leading his horse.

Not a word was spoken till they were out in the lane, and had walked four or five yards, when Maggie, who had been looking straight before her all the while, turned again to walk back, saying, with haughty resentment—

"There is no need for me to go any farther. I don't know whether you consider it gentlemanly and delicate conduct to place me in a position that forced me to come out with you—or whether you wished to insult me still further by thrusting an interview upon me in this way."

"Of course you are angry with me for coming," said Stephen, bitterly. "Of course it is of no consequence what a man has to suffer—it is only your woman's dignity that you care about."

Maggie gave a slight start, such as might have come from the slightest possible electric shock.

"As if it were not enough that I'm entangled in this way—that I'm mad with love for you—that I resist the strongest passion a man can feel, because I try to be true to other claims—but you must treat me as if I were a coarse brute, who would willingly offend you. And when, if I had my own choice, I should ask you to take my hand, and my fortune, and my whole life, and do what you liked with them! I know I forgot myself. I took an unwarrantable liberty. I hate myself for having done it. But I repented immediately—I've been repenting ever since. You ought not to think it unpardonable: a man who loves with his whole soul, as I do you, is liable to be mastered by his feelings for a moment; but you know—you must believe—that the worst pain I could have is to have pained you—that I would give the world to recall the error."

Maggie dared not speak—dared not turn her head. The strength that had come from resentment was all gone, and her lips were quivering visibly. She could not trust herself to utter the full forgiveness that rose in answer to that confession.

They were come nearly in front of the gate again, and she paused, trembling.

"You must not say these things—I must not hear them," she said, looking down in misery, as Stephen came in front of her, to prevent her from going farther towards the gate. "I'm very sorry for any pain you have to go through; but it is of no use to speak."

"Yes, it *is* of use," said Stephen, impetuously. "It would be of use if you would treat me with some sort of pity and consideration, instead of doing me vile injustice in your mind. I could bear everything more quietly if I knew you didn't hate me for an insolent coxcomb. Look at me—see what a hunted devil I am: I've been riding thirty miles every day to get away from the thought of you."

Maggie did not—dared not look. She had already seen the harassed face. But she said gently—

"I don't think any evil of you."

"Then, dearest, look at me," said Stephen, in deepest, tenderest tones of entreaty. "Don't go away from me yet. Give me a moment's happiness—make me feel you've forgiven me."

"Yes, I do forgive you," said Maggie, shaken by those tones, and all the more frightened at herself. "But pray let me go in again. Pray go away."

A great tear fell from under her lowered eyelids.

"I can't go away from you—I can't leave you," said Stephen, with still more passionate pleading. "I shall come back again if you send me away with this coldness—I can't answer for myself. But if you will go with me only a little way, I can live on that. You see plainly enough that your anger has only made me ten times more unreasonable."

Maggie turned. But Tancred, the bay horse, began to make such spirited remonstrances against this frequent change of direction, that Stephen, catching sight of Willy Moss peeping through the gate, called out, "Here! just come and hold my horse for five minutes."

"O, no," said Maggie, hurriedly, "my aunt will think it so strange."

"Never mind," Stephen answered impatiently; "they don't know the people at St. Ogg's. Lead him up and down just here, for five minutes," he added to Willy, who was now close to them; and then he turned to Maggie's side, and they walked on. It was clear that she *must* go on now.

"Take my arm," said Stephen, entreatingly; and she took it, feeling all the while as if she were sliding downwards in a nightmare.

"There is no end to this misery," she began, struggling to repel the influence by speech. "It is wicked—base—ever allowing a word or look that Lucy—that others might not have seen. Think of Lucy."

"I do think of her—bless her. If I didn't——" Stephen had laid his hand on Maggie's that rested on his arm, and they both felt it difficult to speak.

"And I have other ties," Maggie went on, at last, with a desperate effort,—"even if Lucy did not exist."

"You are engaged to Philip Wakem," said Stephen, hastily. "Is it so?"

"I consider myself engaged to him—I don't mean to marry any one else."

Stephen was silent again until they had turned out of the sun into a side lane, all grassy and sheltered. Then he burst out impetuously—

"It is unnatural—it is horrible. Maggie, if you loved me as I love you, we should throw everything else to the winds for the sake of belonging to each other. We should break all these mistaken ties that were made in blindness, and determine to marry each other."

"I would rather die than fall into that temptation," said Maggie, with deep, slow distinctness,—all the gathered spiritual force of pain-

ful years coming to her aid in this extremity. She drew her arm from
his as she spoke.

"Tell me, then, that you don't care for me," he said, almost violently.
"Tell me that you love some one else better."

It darted through Maggie's mind that here was a mode of releasing
herself from outward struggle—to tell Stephen that her whole heart was
Philip's. But her lips would not utter that, and she was silent.

"If you do love me, dearest," said Stephen, gently, taking up her
hand again and laying it within his arm, "it is better—it is right that
we should marry each other. We can't help the pain it will give. It is
come upon us without our seeking: it is natural—it has taken hold of
me in spite of every effort I have made to resist it. God knows, I've been
trying to be faithful to tacit engagements, and I've only made things
worse—I'd better have given way at first."

Maggie was silent. If it were *not* wrong—if she were once convinced
of that, and need no longer beat and struggle against this current, soft
and yet strong as the summer stream!

"Say 'yes,' dearest," said Stephen, leaning to look entreatingly in
her face. "What could we care about in the whole world beside, if we
belonged to each other?"

Her breath was on his face—his lips were very near hers—but there
was a great dread dwelling in his love for her.

Her lips and eyelids quivered; she opened her eyes full on his for
an instant, like a lovely wild animal timid and struggling under caresses,
and then turned sharp round towards home again.

"And after all," he went on, in an impatient tone, trying to defeat his
own scruples as well as hers, "I am breaking no positive engagement:—
if Lucy's affections had been withdrawn from me and given to some
one else, I should have felt no right to assert a claim on her. If you
are not absolutely pledged to Philip, we are neither of us bound."

"You don't believe that—it is not your real feeling," said Maggie,
earnestly. "You feel, as I do, that the real tie lies in the feelings and
expectations we have raised in other minds. Else all pledges might be
broken, when there was no outward penalty. There would be no such
thing as faithfulness."

Stephen was silent: he could not pursue that argument; the opposite conviction had wrought in him too strongly through his previous
time of struggle. But it soon presented itself in a new form.

"The pledge *can't* be fulfilled," he said, with impetuous insistence,
"It is unnatural: we can only pretend to give ourselves to any one else.
There is wrong in that too—there may be misery in it for *them* as well
as for us. Maggie, you must see that—you do see that."

He was looking eagerly at her face for the least sign of compliance;
his large, firm, gentle grasp was on her hand. She was silent for a few
moments, with her eyes fixed on the ground; then she drew a deep
breath, and said, looking up at him with solemn sadness—

"O, it is difficult—life is very difficult. It seems right to me sometimes that we should follow our strongest feeling;—but then, such feelings continually come across the ties that all our former life has made for us—the ties that have made others dependent on us—and would cut them in two. If life were quite easy and simple, as it might have been in paradise, and we could always see that one being first towards whom . . . I mean, if life did not make duties for us before love comes—love would be a sign that two people ought to belong to each other. But I see—I feel it is not so now: there are things we must renounce in life: some of us must resign love. Many things are difficult and dark to me; but I see one thing quite clearly—that I must not, cannot seek my own happiness by sacrificing others. Love is natural; but surely pity and faithfulness and memory are natural too. And they would live in me still, and punish me if I did not obey them. I should be haunted by the suffering I had caused. Our love would be poisoned. Don't urge me; help me—help me, *because* I love you."

Maggie had become more and more earnest as she went on; her face had become flushed, and her eyes fuller and fuller of appealing love. Stephen had the fibre of nobleness in him that vibrated to her appeal; but in the same moment—how could it be otherwise?—that pleading beauty gained new power over him.

"Dearest," he said, in scarcely more than a whisper, while his arm stole round her, "I'll do, I'll bear anything you wish. But—one kiss—one—the last—before we part."

One kiss—and then a long look—until Maggie said, tremulously, "Let me go—let us make haste back."

She hurried along, and not another word was spoken. Stephen stood still and beckoned when they came within sight of Willy and the horse, and Maggie went on through the gate. Mrs. Moss was standing alone at the door of the old porch: she had sent all the cousins in, with kind thoughtfulness. It might be a joyful thing that Maggie had a rich and handsome lover, but she would naturally feel embarrassed at coming in again:—and it might *not* be joyful. In either case, Mrs. Moss waited anxiously to receive Maggie by herself. The speaking face told plainly enough that, if there was joy, it was of a very agitating dubious sort.

"Sit down here a bit, my dear." She drew Maggie into the porch, and sat down on the bench by her:—there was no privacy in the house.

"O, aunt Gritty, I'm very wretched. I wish I could have died when I was fifteen. It seemed so easy to give things up then—it is so hard now."

The poor child threw her arms round her aunt's neck, and fell into long, deep sobs.

CHAPTER VII

A FAMILY PARTY

MAGGIE left her good aunt Gritty at the end of the week, and went to Garum Firs to pay her visit to aunt Pullet according to agreement. In

the mean time, very unexpected things had happened, and there was to
be a family party at Garum to discuss and celebrate a change in the
fortunes of the Tullivers, which was likely finally to carry away the
shadow of their demerits like the last limb of an eclipse, and cause
their hitherto obscured virtues to shine forth in full-rounded splendour.
It is pleasant to know that a new ministry just come into office are
not the only fellow-men who enjoy a period of high appreciation and
full-blown eulogy: in many respectable families throughout this realm,
relatives becoming creditable meet with a similar cordiality of recognition, which, in its fine freedom from the coercion of any antecedents,
suggests the hopeful possibility that we may some day without any notice find ourselves in full millennium, with cockatrices who have ceased
to bite, and wolves that no longer show their teeth with any but the
blandest intentions.

Lucy came so early as to have the start even of aunt Glegg; for she
longed to have some undisturbed talk with Maggie about the wonderful news. It seemed—did it not? said Lucy, with her prettiest air of
wisdom—as if everything, even other people's misfortunes (poor creatures!) were conspiring now to make poor dear aunt Tulliver, and
cousin Tom, and haughty Maggie too, if she were not obstinately bent
on the contrary, as happy as they deserved to be after all their troubles.
To think that the very day—the *very day*—after Tom had come back
from Newcastle, that unfortunate young Jetsome, whom Mr. Wakem
had placed at the mill, had been pitched off his horse in a drunken fit,
and was lying at St. Ogg's in a dangerous state, so that Wakem had signified his wish that the new purchasers should enter on the premises
at once! It was very dreadful for that unhappy young man, but it did
seem as if the misfortune had happened then, rather than at any other
time, in order that cousin Tom might all the sooner have the fit reward
of his exemplary conduct—papa thought so very highly of him. Aunt
Tulliver must certainly go to the Mill now, and keep house for Tom:
that was rather a loss to Lucy in the matter of household comfort; but
then, to think of poor aunty being in her old place again, and gradually
getting comforts about her there!

On this last point Lucy had her cunning projects, and when she and
Maggie had made their dangerous way down the bright stairs into the
handsome parlour, where the very sunbeams seemed cleaner than elsewhere, she directed her manœuvres, as any other great tactician would
have done, against the weaker side of the enemy.

"Aunt Pullet," she said, seating herself on the sofa, and caressingly
adjusting that lady's floating cap-string, "I want you to make up your
mind what linen and things you will give Tom towards housekeeping;
because you're always so generous—you give such nice things, you
know; and if you set the example, aunt Glegg will follow."

"That she never can, my dear," said Mrs. Pullet, with unusual vigour,
"for she hasn't got the linen to follow suit wi' mine, I can tell you. She'd
niver the taste, not if she'd spend the money. Big checks and live things,

like stags and foxes, all her table-linen is—not a spot nor a diamont among 'em. But it's poor work, dividing one's linen before one dies— I niver thought to ha' done that, Bessy," Mrs. Pullet continued, shaking her head and looking at her sister Tulliver, "when you and me chose the double diamont, the first flax iver we'd spun—and the Lord knows where yours is gone."

"I'd no choice, I'm sure, sister," said poor Mrs. Tulliver, accustomed to consider herself in the light of an accused person. "I'm sure it was no wish o' mine, iver, as I should lie awake o' nights thinking o' my best bleached linen all over the country."

"Take a peppermint, Mrs. Tulliver," said uncle Pullet, feeling that he was offering a cheap and wholesome form of comfort, which he was recommending by example.

"O, but, aunt Pullet," said Lucy, "you've so much beautiful linen. And suppose you had had daughters! Then you must have divided it, when they were married."

"Well, I don't say as I won't do it," said Mrs. Pullet, "for now Tom's so lucky, it's nothing but right his friends should look on him and help him. There's the table-cloths I bought at your sale, Bessy; it was nothing but good-natur o' me to buy 'em, for they've been lying in the chest ever since. But I'm not going to give Maggie any more o' my Indy muslin and things, if she's to go into service again, when she might stay and keep me company, and do my sewing for me, if she wasn't wanted at her brother's."

"Going into service" was the expression by which the Dodson mind represented to itself the position of teacher or governess, and Maggie's return to that menial condition, now circumstances offered her more eligible prospects, was likely to be a sore point with all her relatives, besides Lucy. Maggie in her crude form, with her hair down her back, and altogether in a state of dubious promise, was a most undesirable niece; but now, she was capable of being at once ornamental and useful. The subject was revived in aunt and uncle Glegg's presence, over the tea and muffins.

"Hegh, hegh!" said Mr. Glegg, good-naturedly patting Maggie on the back, "nonsense, nonsense! Don't let us hear of you taking a place again, Maggie. Why, you must ha' picked up half-a-dozen sweethearts at the bazaar: isn't there one of 'em the right sort of article? Come now?"

"Mr. Glegg," said his wife, with that shade of increased politeness in her severity which she always put on with her crisper fronts, "you'l excuse me, but you're far too light for a man of your years. It's respect and duty to her aunts, and the rest of her kin as are so good to her, should have kept my niece from fixing about going away again without consulting us—not sweethearts, if I'm to use such a word though it was never heared in *my* family."

"Why, what did they call us, when we went to see 'em, then, eh neighbour Pullet? They thought us sweet enough then," said Mr. Glegg winking pleasantly, while Mr. Pullet, at the suggestion of sweetness, took a little more sugar.

"Mr. Glegg," said Mrs. G., "if you're going to be undelicate, let me know."

"La, Jane, your husband's only joking," said Mrs. Pullet; "let him joke while he's got health and strength. There's poor Mr. Tilt got his mouth drawn all o' one side, and couldn't laugh if he was to try."

"I'll trouble you for the muffineer, then, Mr. Glegg," said Mrs. G., "if I may be so bold to interrupt your joking. Though it's other people must see the joke in a niece's putting a slight on her mother's eldest sister, as is the head o' the family; and only coming in and out on short visits, all the time she's been in the town, and then settling to go away without my knowledge—as I'd laid caps out on purpose for her to make 'em up for me,—and me as have divided my money so equal——"

"Sister," Mrs. Tulliver broke in, anxiously, "I'm sure Maggie never thought o' going away without staying at your house as well as the others. Not as it's my wish she should go away at all—but quite contrairy. I'm sure I'm innocent. I've said over and over again, 'My dear, you've no call to go away.' But there's ten days or a fortnight Maggie'll have before she's fixed to go: she can stay at your house just as well, and I'll step in when I can, and so will Lucy."

"Bessy," said Mrs. Glegg, "if you'd exercise a little more thought, you might know I should hardly think it was worth while to unpin a bed, and go to all that trouble now, just at the end o' the time, when our house isn't above a quarter of an hour's walk from Mr. Deane's. She can come the first thing in the morning, and go back the last at night, and be thankful she's got a good aunt so close to her to come and sit with. I know *I* should, when I was her age."

"La, Jane," said Mrs. Pullet, "it 'ud do your beds good to have somebody to sleep in 'em. There's that striped room smells dreadful mouldy, and the glass mildewed like anything. I'm sure I thought I should be struck with death when you took me in."

"O, there is Tom!" exclaimed Lucy, clapping her hands. "He's come on Sindbad, as I told him. I was afraid he was not going to keep his promise."

Maggie jumped up to kiss Tom as he entered, with strong feeling, at this first meeting since the prospect of returning to the Mill had been opened to him; and she kept his hand, leading him to the chair by her side. To have no cloud between herself and Tom was still a perpetual yearning in her, that had its root deeper than all change. He smiled at her very kindly this evening, and said, "Well, Magsie, how's aunt Moss?"

"Come, come, sir," said Mr. Glegg, putting out his hand. "Why, you're such a big man, you carry all before you, it seems. You're come into your luck a good deal earlier than us old folks did—but I wish you joy, I wish you joy. You'll get the Mill all for your own again, some day, I'll be bound. You won't stop half-way up the hill."

"But I hope he'll bear in mind as it's his mother's family as he owes it to," said Mrs. Glegg. "If he hadn't had them to take after, he'd ha' been poorly off. There was never any failures, nor lawing, nor wastefulness in our family—nor dying without wills——"

"No, nor sudden deaths," said aunt Pullet; "allays the doctor called in. But Tom had the Dodson skin: I said that from the first. And I don't know what *you* mean to do, sister Glegg, but I mean to give him a table-cloth of all my three biggest sizes but one, besides sheets. I don't say what more I shall do; but *that* I shall do, and if I should die to-morrow, Mr. Pullet, you'll bear it in mind—though you'll be blundering with the keys, and never remember as that on the third shelf o' the left-hand wardrobe, behind the night-caps with the broad ties—not the narrow-frilled uns—is the key o' the drawer in the Blue Room, where the key o' the Blue Closet is. You'll make a mistake, and I shall niver be worthy to know it. You've a memory for my pills and draughts, wonderful—I'll allays say that of you—but you're lost among the keys." This gloomy prospect of the confusion that would ensue on her decease was very affecting to Mrs. Pullet.

"You carry it too far, Sophy—that locking in and out," said Mrs. Glegg, in a tone of some disgust at this folly. "You go beyond your own family. There's nobody can say I don't lock up; but I do what's reasonable, and no more. And as for the linen, I shall look out what's serviceable, to make a present of to my nephey: I've got cloth as has never been whittened, better worth having than other people's fine holland; and I hope he'll lie down in it and think of his aunt."

Tom thanked Mrs. Glegg, but evaded any promise to meditate nightly on her virtues; and Mr. Glegg effected a diversion for him by asking about Mr. Deane's intentions concerning steam.

Lucy had had her far-sighted views in begging Tom to come on Sindbad. It appeared, when it was time to go home, that the man-servant was to ride the horse, and cousin Tom was to drive home his mother and Lucy. "You must sit by yourself, aunty," said that contriving young lady, "because I must sit by Tom; I've a great deal to say to him."

In the eagerness of her affectionate anxiety for Maggie, Lucy could not persuade herself to defer a conversation about her with Tom, who, she thought, with such a cup of joy before him as this rapid fulfilment of his wish about the Mill, must become pliant and flexible. Her nature supplied her with no key to Tom's; and she was puzzled as well as pained to notice the unpleasant change on his countenance when she gave him the history of the way in which Philip had used his influence with his father. She had counted on this revelation as a great stroke of policy, which was to turn Tom's heart towards Philip at once, and, besides that, prove that the elder Wakem was ready to receive Maggie with all the honours of a daughter-in-law. Nothing was wanted, then, but for dear Tom, who always had that pleasant smile when he looked at cousin Lucy, to turn completely round, say the opposite of what he had always said before, and declare that he, for his part, was delighted that all the old grievances should be healed, and that Maggie should have Philip with all suitable despatch: in cousin Lucy's opinion nothing could be easier.

But to minds strongly marked by the positive and negative qualities that create severity—strength of will, conscious rectitude of purpose, narrowness of imagination and intellect, great power of self-control, and a disposition to exert control over others—prejudices come as the natural food of tendencies which can get no sustenance out of that complex, fragmentary, doubt-provoking knowledge which we call truth. Let a prejudice be bequeathed, carried in the air, adopted by hearsay, caught in through the eye—however it may come, these minds will give it a habitation: it is something to assert strongly and bravely, something to fill up the void of spontaneous ideas, something to impose on others with the authority of conscious right: it is at once a staff and a baton. Every prejudice that will answer these purposes is self-evident. Our good up-right Tom Tulliver's mind was of this class: his inward criticism of his father's faults did not prevent him from adopting his father's prejudice; it was a prejudice against a man of lax principle and lax life, and it was a meeting-point for all the disappointed feelings of family and personal pride. Other feelings added their force to produce Tom's bitter repugnance to Philip, and to Maggie's union with him; and notwithstanding Lucy's power over her strong-willed cousin, she got nothing but a cold refusal ever to sanction such a marriage: "but of course Maggie could do as she liked—she had declared her determination to be independent. For Tom's part, he held himself bound by his duty to his father's memory, and by every manly feeling, never to consent to any relation with the Wakems."

Thus, all that Lucy had effected by her zealous mediation was to fill Tom's mind with the expectation that Maggie's perverse resolve to go into a situation again, would presently metamorphose itself, as her resolves were apt to do, into something equally perverse, but entirely different—a marriage with Philip Wakem.

CHAPTER XIII

BORNE ALONG BY THE TIDE

IN less than a week Maggie was at St. Ogg's again,—outwardly in much the same position as when her visit there had just begun. It was easy for her to fill her mornings apart from Lucy without any obvious effort; for she had her promised visits to pay to her aunt Glegg, and it was nat-ural that she should give her mother more than usual of her companion-ship in these last weeks, especially as there were preparations to be thought of for Tom's housekeeping. But Lucy would hear of no pretext for her remaining away in the evenings: she must always come from aunt Glegg's before dinner—"else what shall I have of you?" said Lucy, with a tearful pout that could not be resisted. And Mr. Stephen Guest had unaccountably taken to dining at Mr. Deane's as often as possible, instead of avoiding that, as he used to do. At first he began his mornings with a resolution that he would not dine there—not even go in the evening, till Maggie was away. He had even devised a plan of starting off on a journey in this agreeable June weather: the headaches which he had constantly been alleging as a ground for stupidity and silence were a sufficient ostensible motive. But the journey was not taken, and by the fourth morning no distinct resolution was formed about the evenings: they were only foreseen as times when Maggie would still be present for a little while—when one more touch, one more glance, might be snatched. For, why not? There was nothing to conceal between them: they knew—they had confessed their love, and they had renounced each other: they were going to part. Honour and conscience were going to divide them: Maggie, with that appeal from her inmost soul, had decided it; but surely they might cast a lingering look at each other across the gulf, before they turned away never to look again till that strange light had for ever faded out of their eyes.

Maggie, all this time, moved about with a quiescence and even torpor of manner, so contrasted with her usual fitful brightness and ardour, that Lucy would have had to seek some other cause for such a change, if she had not been convinced that the position in which Maggie stood between Philip and her brother, and the prospect of her self-imposed wearisome banishment, were quite enough to account for a large amount of depression. But under this torpor there was a fierce battle of emotions, such as Maggie in all her life of struggle had never known or foreboded: it seemed to her as if all the worst evil in her had lain in ambush till now, and had suddenly started up full-armed with hideous, overpowering strength! There were moments in which a cruel selfishness seemed to be getting possession of her: why should not Lucy—why should not Philip suffer? *She* had had to suffer through many years of her life; and who had renounced anything for her? And when something like that fulness of existence—love, wealth, ease, refinement—all that her nature craved, was brought within her reach, why was she to forego it, that another might have it—another, who perhaps needed it less? But amidst all this new passionate tumult there were the old voices making themselves heard with rising power, till, from time to time, the tumult seemed quelled. *Was* that existence which tempted her the full existence she dreamed? Where, then, would be all the memories of early striving, all the deep pity for another's pain, which had been nurtured in her through years of affection and hardship, all the divine presentiment of something higher than mere personal enjoyment which had made the sacredness of life? She might as well hope to enjoy walking by maiming her feet, as hope to enjoy an existence in which she set out by maiming the faith and sympathy that were the best organs of her soul. And then, if pain were so hard to *her*, what was it to others?—"Ah, God! preserve me from inflicting—give me strength to bear it."—How had she sunk into this struggle with a temptation that she would once have thought herself as secure from, as from deliberate crime? When was that first hateful moment in which she had been conscious of a feeling that clashed with her truth, affection, and gratitude, and had not shaken it from her with horror, as if it had been a loathsome thing?—And yet, since this strange, sweet, subduing influence did not, should not conquer her— since it was to remain simply her own suffering . . . her mind was meeting Stephen's in that thought of his, that they might still snatch moments of mute confession before the parting came. For was not he suffering too? She saw it daily—saw it in the sickened look of fatigue with which, as soon as he was not compelled to exert himself, he relapsed into indifference towards everything but the possibility of watching her. Could she refuse sometimes to answer that beseeching look which she felt to be following her like a low murmur of love and pain? She refused it less and less, till at last the evening for them both was sometimes made of a moment's mutual gaze:—they thought of it till it came, and when it had come, they thought of nothing else. One other thing Stephen seemed now and then to care for, and that was, to sing: it was a way of speaking to Maggie. Perhaps he was not distinctly conscious that he was impelled to it by a secret longing—running counter to all his self-confessed resolves—to deepen the hold he had on her. Watch your own speech, and notice how it is guided by your less conscious purposes, and you will understand that contradiction in Stephen.

Philip Wakem was a less frequent visitor, but he came occasionally in the evening, and it happened that he was there when Lucy said, as they sat out on the lawn, near sunset—

"Now Maggie's tale of visits to aunt Glegg is completed, I mean that we shall go out boating every day until she goes. She has not had half enough boating, because of these tiresome visits, and she likes it better than anything. Don't you, Maggie?"

"Better than any sort of locomotion, I hope you mean," said Philip, smiling at Maggie, who was lolling backward in a low garden-chair, "else she will be selling her soul to that ghostly boatman who haunts the Floss—only for the sake of being drifted in a boat for ever."

"Should you like to be her boatman?" said Lucy. "Because, if you would, you can come with us and take an oar. If the Floss were but a quiet lake instead of a river, we should be independent of any gentleman, for Maggie can row splendidly. As it is, we are reduced to ask services of knights and squires, who do not seem to offer them with great alacrity."

She looked playful reproach at Stephen, who was sauntering up and down, and was just singing in pianissimo falsetto—

> "The thirst that from the soul doth rise,
> Doth ask a drink divine."

He took no notice, but still kept aloof: he had done so frequently during Philip's recent visits.

"You don't seem inclined for boating," said Lucy, when he came to sit down by her on the bench. "Doesn't rowing suit you now?"

"O, I hate a large party in a boat," he said, almost irritably. "I'll come when you have no one else."

Lucy coloured, fearing that Philip would be hurt: it was quite a new thing for Stephen to speak in that way; but he had certainly not been well of late. Philip coloured too, but less from a feeling of personal offence than from a vague suspicion that Stephen's moodiness had some relation to Maggie, who had started up from her chair as he spoke, and had walked towards the hedge of laurels to look at the descending sunlight on the river.

"As Miss Deane didn't know she was excluding others by inviting me," said Philip, "I am bound to resign."

"No, indeed, you shall not," said Lucy, much vexed. "I particularly wish for your company to-morrow. The tide will suit at half-past ten: it will be a delicious time for a couple of hours to row to Luckreth and walk back, before the sun gets too hot. And how can you object to four people in a boat?" she added, looking at Stephen.

"I don't object to the people, but the number," said Stephen, who had recovered himself, and was rather ashamed of his rudeness. "If I voted for a fourth at all, of course it would be you, Phil. But we won't divide the pleasure of escorting the ladies; we'll take it alternately. I'll go the next day."

This incident had the effect of drawing Philip's attention with freshened solicitude towards Stephen and Maggie; but when they re-entered the house, music was proposed, and Mrs. Tulliver and Mr. Deane being occupied with cribbage, Maggie sat apart near the table where the books and work were placed—doing nothing, however, but listening abstractedly to the music. Stephen presently turned to a duet which he insisted that Lucy and Philip should sing: he had often done the same thing before; but this evening Philip thought he divined some double intention in every word and look of Stephen's, and watched him keenly —angry with himself all the while for this clinging suspicion. For had not Maggie virtually denied any ground for his doubts on her side? and she was truth itself: it was impossible not to believe her word and glance when they had last spoken together in the garden. Stephen might be strongly fascinated by her (what was more natural?), but Philip felt himself rather base for intruding on what must be his friend's painful secret. Still, he watched. Stephen, moving away from the piano, sauntered slowly towards the table near which Maggie sat, and turned over the newspapers, apparently in mere idleness. Then he seated himself with his back to the piano, dragging a newspaper under his elbow, and thrusting his hand through his hair, as if he had been attracted by some bit of local news in the *Laceham Courier*. He was in reality looking at Maggie, who had not taken the slightest notice of his approach. She had always additional strength of resistance when Philip was present, just as we can restrain our speech better in a spot that we feel to be hallowed.

But at last she heard the word "dearest," uttered in the softest tone of pained entreaty, like that of a patient who asks for something that ought to have been given without asking. She had never heard that word since the moments in the lane at Basset, when it had come from Stephen again and again, almost as involuntarily as if it had been an inarticulate cry. Philip could hear no word, but he had moved to the opposite side of the piano, and could see Maggie start and blush, raise her eyes an instant towards Stephen's face, but immediately look apprehensively towards himself. It was not evident to her that Philip had observed her; but a pang of shame, under the sense of this concealment, made her move from her chair and walk to her mother's side to watch the game at cribbage.

Philip went home soon after in a state of hideous doubt mingled with wretched certainty. It was impossible for him now to resist the conviction that there was some mutual consciousness between Stephen and Maggie; and for half the night his irritable, susceptible nerves were pressed upon almost to frenzy by that one wretched fact: he could attempt no explanation that would reconcile it with her words and actions. When, at last, the need for belief in Maggie rose to its habitual predominance, he was not long in imagining the truth:—she was struggling, she was banishing herself—this was the clue to all he had seen since his return. But athwart that belief there came other possibilities that would not be driven out of sight. His imagination wrought out the whole story: Stephen was madly in love with her; he must have told her so; she had rejected him, and was hurrying away. But would he give her up, knowing—Philip felt the fact with heart-crushing despair—that she was made half helpless by her feeling towards him?

When the morning came, Philip was too ill to think of keeping his engagement to go in the boat. In his present agitation he could decide on nothing: he could only alternate between contradictory intentions. First, he thought he must have an interview with Maggie and entreat her to confide in him; then again, he distrusted his own interference. Had he not been thrusting himself on Maggie all along? She had uttered words long ago in her young ignorance; it was enough to make her hate him that these should be continually present with her as a bond. And had he any right to ask her for a revelation of feelings which she had evidently intended to withhold from him? He would not trust himself to see her, till he had assured himself that he could act from pure anxiety for her, and not from egoistic irritation. He wrote a brief note to Stephen, and sent it early by the servant, saying that he was not well enough to fulfil his engagement to Miss Deane. Would Stephen take his excuse, and fill his place?

Lucy had arranged a charming plan, which had made her quite content with Stephen's refusal to go in the boat. She discovered that her father was to drive to Lindum this morning at ten: Lindum was the very place she wanted to go to, to make purchases—important purchases, which must by no means be put off to another opportunity; and aunt

Tulliver must go too, because she was concerned in some of the purchases.

"You will have your row in the boat just the same, you know," she said to Maggie when they went out of the breakfast-room and up-stairs together; "Philip will be here at half-past ten, and it is a delicious morning. Now, don't say a word against it, you dear dolorous thing. What is the use of my being a fairy godmother, if you set your face against all the wonders I work for you? Don't think of awful cousin Tom: you may disobey him a little."

Maggie did not persist in objecting. She was almost glad of the plan; for perhaps it would bring her some strength and calmness to be alone with Philip again: it was like revisiting the scene of a quieter life, in which the very struggles were repose, compared with the daily tumult of the present. She prepared herself for the boat, and at half-past ten sat waiting in the drawing-room.

The ring of the door-bell was punctual, and she was thinking with half-sad, affectionate pleasure of the surprise Philip would have in finding that he was to be with her alone, when she distinguished a firm rapid step across the hall, that was certainly not Philip's: the door opened, and Stephen Guest entered.

In the first moment they were both too much agitated to speak; for Stephen had learned from the servant that the others were gone out. Maggie had started up and sat down again, with her heart beating violently; and Stephen, throwing down his cap and gloves, came and sat by her in silence. She thought Philip would be coming soon; and with great effort—for she trembled visibly—she rose to go to a distant chair.

"He is not coming," said Stephen, in a low tone. "*I* am going in the boat."

"O, we can't go," said Maggie, sinking into her chair again. "Lucy did not expect—she would be hurt. Why is not Philip come?"

"He is not well; he asked me to come instead."

"Lucy is gone to Lindum," said Maggie, taking off her bonnet, with hurried, trembling fingers. "We must not go."

"Very well," said Stephen, dreamily, looking at her, as he rested his arm on the back of his chair. "Then we'll stay here."

He was looking into her deep, deep eyes—far-off and mysterious as the starlit blackness, and yet very near, and timidly loving. Maggie sat perfectly still—perhaps for moments, perhaps for minutes—until the helpless trembling had ceased, and there was a warm glow on her check.

"The man is waiting—he has taken the cushions," she said. "Will you go and tell him?"

"What shall I tell him?" said Stephen, almost in a whisper. He was looking at the lips now.

Maggie made no answer.

"Let us go," Stephen murmured, entreatingly, rising, and taking her hand to raise her too. "We shall not be long together."

And they went. Maggie felt that she was being led down the garden

among the roses, being helped with firm tender care into the boat, having
the cushion and cloak arranged for her feet, and her parasol opened for
her (which she had forgotten)—all by this stronger presence that seemed
to bear her along without any act of her own will, like the added self
which comes with the sudden exalting influence of a strong tonic—and
she felt nothing else. Memory was excluded.

They glided rapidly along, Stephen rowing, helped by the backward-
flowing tide, past the Tofton trees and houses—on between the silent
sunny fields and pastures, which seemed filled with a natural joy that
had no reproach for theirs. The breath of the young, unwearied day, the
delicious rhythmic dip of the oars, the fragmentary song of a passing
bird heard now and then, as if it were only the overflowing of brim-full
gladness, the sweet solitude of a twofold consciousness that was mingled
into one by that grave untiring gaze which need not be averted—what
else could there be in their minds for the first hour? Some low, subdued,
languid exclamation of love came from Stephen from time to time, as
he went on rowing idly, half automatically: otherwise, they spoke no
word; for what could words have been but an inlet to thought? and
thought did not belong to that enchanted haze in which they were en-
veloped—it belonged to the past and the future that lay outside the haze.
Maggie was only dimly conscious of the banks, as they passed them, and
dwelt with no recognition on the villages: she knew there were several
to be passed before they reached Luckreth, where they always stopped
and left the boat. At all times she was so liable to fits of absence, that
she was likely enough to let her way-marks pass unnoticed.

But at last Stephen, who had been rowing more and more idly, ceased
to row, laid down the oars, folded his arms, and looked down on the
water as if watching the pace at which the boat glided without his help.
This sudden change roused Maggie. She looked at the far-stretching
fields—at the banks close by—and felt that they were entirely strange
to her. A terrible alarm took possession of her.

"O, have we passed Luckreth—where we were to stop?" she exclaimed,
looking back to see if the place were out of sight. No village was to be
seen. She turned round again, with a look of distressed questioning at
Stephen.

He went on watching the water, and said, in a strange, dreamy, absent
tone, "Yes—a long way."

"O, what shall I do?" cried Maggie, in an agony. "We shall not get
home for hours—and Lucy—O, God, help me!"

She clasped her hands and broke into a sob, like a frightened child:
she thought of nothing but of meeting Lucy, and seeing her look of
pained surprise and doubt—perhaps of just upbraiding.

Stephen moved and sat beside her, and gently drew down the clasped
hands.

"Maggie," he said, in a deep tone of slow decision, "let us never go
home again—till no one can part us—till we are married."

The unusual tone, the startling words, arrested Maggie's sob, and she sat quite still—wondering: as if Stephen might have seen some possibilities that would alter everything, and annul the wretched facts.

"See, Maggie, how everything has come without our seeking—in spite of all our efforts. We never thought of being alone together again: it has all been done by others. See how the tide is carrying us out—away from all those unnatural bonds that we have been trying to make faster round us—and trying in vain. It will carry us on to Torby, and we can land there, and get some carriage, and hurry on to York, and then to Scotland—and never pause a moment till we are bound to each other, so that only death can part us. It is the only right thing, dearest: it is the only way of escaping from this wretched entanglement. Everything has concurred to point it out to us. We have contrived nothing, we have thought of nothing ourselves."

Stephen spoke with deep, earnest pleading. Maggie listened—passing from her startled wonderment to the yearning after that belief, that the tide was doing it all—that she might glide along with the swift, silent stream, and not struggle any more. But across that stealing influence came the terrible shadow of past thoughts; and the sudden horror lest now, at last, the moment of fatal intoxication was close upon her, called up feelings of angry resistance towards Stephen.

"Let me go!" she said, in an agitated tone, flashing an indignant look at him, and trying to get her hands free. "You have wanted to deprive me of any choice. You knew we were come too far—you have dared to take advantage of my thoughtlessness. It is unmanly to bring me into such a position."

Stung at this reproach, he released her hands, moved back to his former place, and folded his arms, in a sort of desperation at the difficulty Maggie's words had made present to him. If she would not consent to go on, he must curse himself for the embarrassment he had led her into. But the reproach was the unendurable thing: the one thing worse than parting with her was, that she should feel he had acted unworthily towards her. At last he said, in a tone of suppressed rage—

"I didn't notice that we had passed Luckreth till we had got to the next village; and then it came into my mind that we would go on. I can't justify it: I ought to have told you. It is enough to make you hate me—since you don't love me well enough to make everything else indifferent to you—as I do you. Shall I stop the boat, and try to get you out here? I'll tell Lucy that I was mad—and that you hate me—and you shall be clear of me for ever. No one can blame you, because I have behaved unpardonably to you."

Maggie was paralysed: it was easier to resist Stephen's pleading, than this picture he had called up of himself suffering, while she was vindicated—easier even to turn away from his look of tenderness than from this look of angry misery, that seemed to place her in selfish isolation from him. He had called up a state of feeling in which the reasons which had acted on her conscience seemed to be transmuted into mere self-regard. The indignant fire in her eyes was quenched, and she began to look at him with timid distress. She had reproached him for being hurried into irrevocable trespass—she, who had been so weak herself.

"As if I shouldn't feel what happened to you—just the same," she said, with reproach of another kind—the reproach of love, asking for more trust. This yielding to the idea of Stephen's suffering was more fatal than the other yielding, because it was less distinguishable from that sense of others' claims which was the moral basis of her resistance.

He felt all the relenting in her look and tone—it was heaven opening again. He moved to her side, and took her hand, leaning his elbow on the back of the boat, and saying nothing. He dreaded to utter another word; he dreaded to make another movement, that might provoke another reproach or denial from her. Life hung on her consent: everything else was hopeless, confused, sickening misery. They glided along in this way, both resting in that silence as in a haven, both dreading lest their feelings should be divided again—till they became aware that the clouds had gathered, and that the slightest perceptible freshening of the breeze was growing and growing, till the whole character of the day was altered.

"You will be chill, Maggie, in this thin dress. Let me raise the cloak over your shoulders. Get up an instant, dearest."

Maggie obeyed: there was an unspeakable charm in being told what to do, and having everything decided for her. She sat down again, covered with the cloak, and Stephen took to his oars again, making haste; for they must try to get to Torby as fast as they could. Maggie was hardly conscious of having said or done anything decisive. All yielding is attended with a less vivid consciousness than resistance; it is the partial sleep of thought; it is the submergence of our own personality by another. Every influence tended to lull her into acquiescence: that dreamy gliding in the boat, which had lasted for four hours, and had brought some weariness and exhaustion—the recoil of her fatigued sensations from the impracticable difficulty of getting out of the boat at this unknown distance from home, and walking for long miles—all helped to bring her into more complete subjection to that strong mysterious charm which made a last parting from Stephen seem the death of all joy—which made the thought of wounding him like the first touch of the torturing iron before which resolution shrank. And then there was the present happiness of being with him, which was enough to absorb all her languid energy.

Presently Stephen observed a vessel coming after them. Several vessels, among them the steamer to Mudport, had passed them with the early tide, but for the last hour they had seen none. He looked more and more eagerly at this vessel, as if a new thought had come into his mind along with it, and then he looked at Maggie, hesitatingly.

"Maggie, dearest," he said, at last, "if this vessel should be going to Mudport, or to any convenient place on the coast northward, it would be our best plan to get them to take us on board. You are fatigued—and it may soon rain—it may be a wretched business, getting to Torby in this boat. It's only a trading-vessel, but I daresay you can be made tolerably comfortable. We'll take the cushions out of the boat. It is really our best plan. They'll be glad enough to take us: I've got plenty of money about me; I can pay them well."

Maggie's heart began to beat with reawakened alarm at this new proposition; but she was silent—one course seemed as difficult as another.

Stephen hailed the vessel. It was a Dutch vessel going to Mudport, the English mate informed him, and, if this wind held, would be there in less than two days.

"We had got out too far with our boat," said Stephen. "I was trying to make for Torby. But I'm afraid of the weather; and this lady—my wife—will be exhausted with fatigue and hunger. Take us on board—will you?—and haul up the boat. I'll pay you well."

Maggie, now really faint and trembling with fear, was taken on board, making an interesting object of contemplation to admiring Dutchmen. The mate feared the lady would have a poor time of it on board, for they had no accommodation for such entirely unlooked-for passengers—no private cabin larger than an old-fashioned church-pew. But at least they had Dutch cleanliness, which makes all other inconveniences tolerable; and the boat-cushions were spread into a couch for Maggie on the poop with all alacrity. But to pace up and down the deck leaning on Stephen—being upheld by his strength—was the first change that she needed: then came food, and then quiet reclining on the cushions, with the sense that no new resolution *could* be taken that day. Everything must wait till to-morrow. Stephen sat beside her, with her hand in his; they could only speak to each other in low tones, only look at each other now and then, for it would take a long while to dull the curiosity of the five men on board, and reduce these handsome young strangers to that minor degree of interest which belongs, in a sailor's regard, to all objects nearer than the horizon. But Stephen was triumphantly happy. Every other thought or care was thrown into unmarked perspective by the certainty that Maggie must be his. The leap had been taken now: he had been tortured by scruples, he had fought fiercely with overmastering inclination, he had hesitated; but repentance was impossible. He murmured forth in fragmentary sentences his happiness—his adoration—his tenderness—his belief that their life together must be heaven—that her presence with him would give rapture to every common day—that to satisfy her lightest wish was dearer to him than all other bliss—that everything was easy for her sake, except to part with her: and now they never *would* part; he would belong to her for ever—and all that was his was hers—had no value for him except as it was hers. Such things, uttered in low broken tones by the one voice that has first stirred the fibre of young passion, have only a feeble effect—on experienced minds at a distance from them. To poor Maggie they were very near: they were like nectar held close to thirsty lips: there was, there *must* be, then, a life for mortals here below which was not hard and chill—in which affection would no longer be self-sacrifice. Stephen's passionate words made the vision of such a life more fully present to her than it had ever been before; and the vision for the time excluded all realities—all except the returning sun-gleams which broke out on the waters as the evening approached, and mingled with the visionary sunlight of promised happiness—all except the hand that pressed hers, and the voice that spoke to her, and the eyes that looked at her with grave, unspeakable love.

There was to be no rain, after all; the clouds rolled off to the horizon again, making the great purple rampart and long purple isles of that wondrous land which reveals itself to us when the sun goes down—the land that the evening star watches over. Maggie was to sleep all night on the poop; it was better than going below; and she was covered with the warmest wrappings the ship could furnish. It was still early, when the fatigues of the day brought on a drowsy longing for perfect rest, and she laid down her head, looking at the faint dying flush in the west, where the one golden lamp was getting brighter and brighter. Then she looked up at Stephen, who was still seated by her, hanging over her as he leaned his arm against the vessel's side. Behind all the delicious visions of these last hours, which had flowed over her like a soft stream and made her entirely passive, there was the dim consciousness that the condition was a transient one, and that the morrow must bring back the old life of struggle—that there were thoughts which would presently avenge themselves for this oblivion. But now nothing was distinct to her: she was being lulled to sleep with that soft stream still flowing over her, with those delicious visions melting and fading like the wondrous aërial land of the west.

CHAPTER XIV

WAKING

WHEN Maggie was gone to sleep, Stephen, weary too with his unaccustomed amount of rowing, and with the intense inward life of the last twelve hours, but too restless to sleep, walked and lounged about the deck, with his cigar, far on into midnight, not seeing the dark water— hardly conscious there were stars—living only in the near and distant future. At last fatigue conquered restlessness, and he rolled himself up in a piece of tarpauling on the deck near Maggie's feet.

She had fallen asleep before nine, and had been sleeping for six hours before the faintest hint of a midsummer daybreak was discernible. She awoke from that vivid dreaming which makes the margin of our deeper rest: She was in a boat on the wide water with Stephen, and in the gathering darkness something like a star appeared, that grew and grew till they saw it was the Virgin seated in St. Ogg's boat, and it came nearer and nearer, till they saw the Virgin was Lucy and the boatman was Philip—no, not Philip, but her brother, who rowed past without looking at her; and she rose to stretch out her arms and call to him, and their own boat turned over with the movement, and they began to sink, till with one spasm of dread she seemed to awake, and find she was a child again in the parlour at evening twilight, and Tom was not really angry. From the soothed sense of that false waking she passed to the real waking—to the plash of water against the vessel, and the sound of a footstep on the deck, and the awful starlit sky. There was a moment of utter bewilderment before her mind could get disentangled from the confused web of dreams, but soon the whole terrible truth urged itself upon her. Stephen was not by her now: she was alone with her own memory and her own dread. The irrevocable wrong that must blot her life had been committed: she had brought sorrow into the lives of others—into the lives that were knit up with hers by trust and love. The feeling of a few short weeks had hurried her into the sins her nature had most recoiled from—breach of faith and cruel selfishness; she had rent the ties that had given meaning to duty, and had made herself an outlawed soul, with no guide but the wayward choice of her own passion. And where would that lead her?—where had it led her now? She had said she would rather die than fall into that temptation. She felt it now—now that the consequences of such a fall had come before the outward act was completed. There was at least this fruit from all her years of striving after the highest and best—that her soul, though betrayed, beguiled, ensnared, could never deliberately consent to a choice of the lower. And a choice of what? O, God—not a choice of joy, but of conscious cruelty and hardness; for could she ever cease to see before her Lucy and Philip, with their murdered trust and hopes? Her life with Stephen could have no sacredness: she must for ever sink and wander vaguely, driven by uncertain impulse; for she had let go the clue of life—that clue which once in the far-off years her young need had clutched so strongly. She had renounced all delights then, before she knew them, before they had come within her reach. Philip had been right when he told her that she knew nothing of renunciation: she had thought it was quiet ecstasy; she saw it face to face now—that sad patient living strength which holds the clue of life, and saw that the thorns were for ever pressing on its brow. The yesterday, which could never be revoked—if she could change it now for any length of inward silent endurance, she would have bowed beneath that cross with a sense of rest.

Daybreak came and the reddening eastern light, while her past life was grasping her in this way, with that tightening clutch which comes in the last moments of possible rescue. She could see Stephen now lying on the deck still fast asleep, and with the sight of him there came a wave of anguish that found its way in a long-suppressed sob. The worst bitterness of parting—the thought that urged the sharpest inward cry for help, was the pain it must give to *him*. But surmounting everything was the horror at her own possible failure, the dread lest her conscience should be benumbed again, and not rise to energy till it was too late.— Too late! It was too late already not to have caused misery—too late

for everything, perhaps, but to rush away from the last act of baseness—
the tasting of joys that were wrung from crushed hearts.

The sun was rising now, and Maggie started up with the sense that
a day of resistance was beginning for her. Her eyelashes were still wet
with tears, as, with her shawl over her head, she sat looking at the
slowly-rounding sun. Something roused Stephen too, and, getting up
from his hard bed, he came to sit beside her. The sharp instinct of
anxious love saw something to give him alarm in the very first glance.
He had a hovering dread of some resistance in Maggie's nature that he
would be unable to overcome. He had the uneasy consciousness that he
had robbed her of perfect freedom yesterday: there was too much native
honour in him, for him not to feel that if her will should recoil, his conduct would have been odious, and she would have a right to reproach
him.

But Maggie did not feel that right: she was too conscious of fatal
weakness in herself—too full of the tenderness that comes with the foreseen need for inflicting a wound. She let him take her hand when he
came to sit down beside her, and smiled at him—only with rather a sad
glance; she could say nothing to pain him till the moment of possible
parting was nearer. And so they drank their cup of coffee together, and
walked about the deck, and heard the captain's assurance that they
should be in at Mudport by five o'clock, each with an inward burthen;
but in him it was an undefined fear, which he trusted to the coming
hours to dissipate; in her it was a definite resolve on which she was trying silently to tighten her hold. Stephen was continually, through the
morning, expressing his anxiety at the fatigue and discomfort she was
suffering, and alluded to landing and to the change of motion and repose she would have in a carriage, wanting to assure himself more completely by pre-supposing that everything would be as he had arranged it.
For a long while Maggie contented herself with assuring him that she
had had a good night's rest, and that she didn't mind about being on the
vessel—it was not like being on the open sea—it was only a little less
pleasant than being in a boat on the Floss. But a suppressed resolve will
betray itself in the eyes, and Stephen became more and more uneasy as
the day advanced, under the sense that Maggie had entirely lost her
passiveness. He longed, but did not dare, to speak of their marriage—
of where they would go after it, and the steps he would take to inform
his father and the rest of what had happened. He longed to assure himself of a tacit assent from her. But each time he looked at her, he
gathered a stronger dread of the new, quiet sadness with which she met
his eyes. And they were more and more silent.

"Here we are in sight of Mudport," he said, at last. "Now, dearest,"
he added, turning towards her with a look that was half-beseeching, "the
worst part of your fatigue is over. On the land we can command swiftness. In another hour and a half we shall be in a chaise together—and
that will seem rest to you after this."

Maggie felt it was time to speak: it would only be unkind now to assent by silence. She spoke in the lowest tone, as he had done, but with distinct decision.

"We shall not be together—we shall have parted."

The blood rushed to Stephen's face.

"We shall not," he said. "I'll die first."

It was as he had dreaded—there was a struggle coming. But neither of them dared to say another word, till the boat was let down, and they were taken to the landing-place. Here there was a cluster of gazers and passengers awaiting the departure of the steamboat to St. Ogg's. Maggie had a dim sense, when she had landed, and Stephen was hurrying her along on his arm, that some one had advanced towards her from that cluster as if he were coming to speak to her. But she was hurried along, and was indifferent to everything but the coming trial.

A porter guided them to the nearest inn and posting-house, and Stephen gave the order for the chaise as they passed through the yard. Maggie took no notice of this, and only said, "Ask them to show us into a room where we can sit down."

When they entered, Maggie did not sit down, and Stephen, whose face had a desperate determination in it, was about to ring the bell, when she said, in a firm voice:—

"I'm not going: we must part here."

"Maggie," he said, turning round towards her, and speaking in the tones of a man who feels a process of torture beginning, "do you mean to kill me? What is the use of it now? The whole thing is done."

"No, it is not done," said Maggie. "Too much is done: more than we can ever remove the trace of. But I will go no farther. Don't try to prevail with me again. I couldn't choose yesterday."

What was he to do? He dared not go near her—her anger might leap out, and make a new barrier. He walked backwards and forwards in maddening perplexity.

"Maggie," he said, at last, pausing before her, and speaking in a tone of imploring wretchedness, "have some pity—hear me—forgive me for what I did yesterday. I will obey you now—I will do nothing without your full consent. But don't blight our lives for ever by a rash perversity that can answer no good purpose to any one—that can only create new evils. Sit down, dearest; wait—think what you are going to do. Don't treat me as if you couldn't trust me."

He had chosen the most effective appeal; but Maggie's will was fixed unswervingly on the coming wrench. She had made up her mind to suffer.

"We must not wait," she said, in a low but distinct voice; "we must part at once."

"We *can't* part, Maggie," said Stephen, more impetuously. "I can't bear it. What is the use of inflicting that misery on me? The blow—whatever it may have been—has been struck now. Will it help any one else that you should drive me mad?"

"I will not begin any future, even for you," said Maggie, tremulously, "with a deliberate consent to what ought not to have been. What I told you at Basset I feel now: I would rather have died than fall into this temptation. It would have been better if we had parted for ever then. But we must part now."

"We will *not* part," Stephen burst out, instinctively placing his back against the door—forgetting everything he had said a few moments before; "I will not endure it. You'll make me desperate—I shan't know what I do."

Maggie trembled. She felt that the parting could not be effected suddenly. She must rely on a slower appeal to Stephen's better self—she must be prepared for a harder task than that of rushing away while resolution was fresh. She sat down. Stephen, watching her with that look of desperation which had come over him like a lurid light, approached slowly from the door, seated himself close beside her, and grasped her hand. Her heart beat like the heart of a frightened bird; but this direct opposition helped her. She felt her determination growing stronger.

"Remember what you felt weeks ago," she began, with beseeching earnestness—"remember what we both felt—that we owed ourselves to others, and must conquer every inclination which could make us false to that debt. We have failed to keep our resolutions; but the wrong remains the same."

"No, it does *not* remain the same," said Stephen. "We have proved that it was impossible to keep our resolutions. We have proved that the feeling which draws us towards each other is too strong to be overcome: that natural law surmounts every other; we can't help what it clashes with."

"It is not so, Stephen—I'm quite sure that is wrong. I have tried to think it again and again; but I see, if we judged in that way, there would be a warrant for all treachery and cruelty—we should justify breaking the most sacred ties that can ever be formed on earth. If the past is not to bind us, where can duty lie? We should have no law but the inclination of the moment."

"But there are ties that can't be kept by mere resolution," said Stephen, starting up and walking about again. "What is outward faithfulness? Would they have thanked us for anything so hollow as constancy without love?"

Maggie did not answer immediately. She was undergoing an inward as well as an outward contest. At last she said, with a passionate assertion of her conviction, as much against herself as against him—

"That seems right—at first; but when I look further, I'm sure it is *not* right. Faithfulness and constancy mean something else besides doing what is easiest and pleasantest to ourselves. They mean renouncing whatever is opposed to the reliance others have in us—whatever would cause misery to those whom the course of our lives has made dependent on us. If we—if I had been better, nobler, those claims would have been so strongly present with me—I should have felt them pressing on my heart so continually, just as they do now in the moments when my conscience is awake—that the opposite feeling would never have grown in me, as it has done: it would have been quenched at once—I should have prayed for help so earnestly—I should have rushed away, as we rush from hideous danger. I feel no excuse for myself—none. I should never have failed towards Lucy and Philip as I have done, if I had not been weak, selfish, and hard—able to think of their pain without a pain to myself that would have destroyed all temptation. O, what is Lucy feeling now? She believed in me—she loved me—she was so good to me. Think of her. . ."

Maggie's voice was getting choked as she uttered these last words.

"I *can't* think of her," said Stephen, stamping as if with pain. "I can think of nothing but you, Maggie. You demand of a man what is impossible. I felt that once; but I can't go back to it now. And where is the use of *your* thinking of it, except to torture me? You can't save them from pain now; you can only tear yourself from me, and make my life worthless to me. And even if we could go back, and both fulfil our engagements—if that were possible now—it would be hateful—horrible, to think of your ever being Philip's wife—of your ever being the wife of a man you didn't love. We have both been rescued from a mistake."

A deep flush came over Maggie's face, and she couldn't speak. Stephen saw this. He sat down again, taking her hand in his, and looking at her with passionate entreaty.

"Maggie! Dearest! If you love me, you are mine. Who can have so great a claim on you as I have? My life is bound up in your love. There is nothing in the past that can annul our right to each other: it is the first time we have either of us loved with our whole heart and soul."

Maggie was still silent for a little while—looking down. Stephen was in a flutter of new hope: he was going to triumph. But she raised her eyes and met his with a glance that was filled with the anguish of regret —not with yielding.

"No—not with my whole heart and soul, Stephen," she said, with timid resolution. "I have never consented to it with my whole mind. There are memories, and affections, and longing after perfect goodness, that have such a strong hold on me; they would never quit me for long; they would come back and be pain to me—repentance. I couldn't live in peace if I put the shadow of a wilful sin between myself and God. I have caused sorrow already—I know—I feel it; but I have never deliberately consented to it: I have never said, 'They shall suffer, that I may have joy.' It has never been my will to marry you: if you were to win consent from the momentary triumph of my feeling for you, you would not have my whole soul. If I could wake back again into the time before yesterday, I would choose to be true to my calmer affections, and live without the joy of love."

Stephen loosed her hand, and, rising impatiently, walked up and down the room in suppressed rage.

"Good God!" he burst out, at last, "what a miserable thing a woman's love is to a man's. I could commit crimes for you—and you can balance and choose in that way. But you *don't* love me: if you had a tithe of the feeling for me that I have for you, it would be impossible to you to think for a moment of sacrificing me. But it weighs nothing with you that you are robbing me of *my* life's happiness."

Maggie pressed her fingers together almost convulsively as she held them clasped on her lap. A great terror was upon her, as if she were ever and anon seeing where she stood by great flashes of lightning, and then again stretched forth her hands in the darkness.

"No—I don't sacrifice you—I couldn't sacrifice you," she said, as soon as she could speak again; "but I can't believe in a good for you, that I feel—that we both feel is a wrong towards others. We can't choose happiness either for ourselves or for another: we can't tell where that will lie. We can only choose whether we will indulge ourselves in the present moment, or whether we will renounce that, for the sake of obeying the divine voice within us—for the sake of being true to all the motives that sanctify our lives. I know this belief is hard: it has slipped away from me again and again; but I have felt that if I let it go for ever, I should have no light through the darkness of this life."

"But Maggie," said Stephen, seating himself by her again, "is it possible you don't see that what happened yesterday has altered the whole position of things? What infatuation is it—what obstinate pre-possession that blinds you to that? It is too late to say what we might have done or what we ought to have done. Admitting the very worst view of what has been done, it is a fact we must act on now; our position is altered; the right course is no longer what it was before. We must accept our own actions, and start afresh from them. Suppose we had been married yesterday? It is nearly the same thing. The effect on others would not have been different. It would only have made this difference to ourselves," Stephen added, bitterly, "that you might have acknowledged then that your tie to me was stronger than to others."

Again a deep flush came over Maggie's face, and she was silent. Stephen thought again that he was beginning to prevail—he had never yet believed that he should *not* prevail: there are possibilities which our minds shrink from too completely for us to fear them.

"Dearest," he said, in his deepest, tenderest tone, leaning towards her and putting his arm round her, "you *are* mine now—the world believes it—duty must spring out of that now: in a few hours you will be legally mine, and those who had claims on us will submit—they will see that there was a force which declared against their claims.

Maggie's eyed opened wide in one terrified look at the face that was close to hers, and she started up—pale again.

"O, I can't do it," she said, in a voice almost of agony—"Stephen—don't ask me—don't urge me. I can't argue any longer—I don't know what is wise; but my heart will not let me do it. I see—I feel their trouble now: it is as if it were branded on my mind. *I* have suffered, and had no one to pity me; and now I have made others suffer. It would never leave me; it would embitter your love to me. I *do* care for Philip —in a different way: I remember all we said to each other; I know how he thought of me as the one promise of his life. He was given to me that I might make his lot less hard; and I have forsaken him. And Lucy—she has been deceived—she who trusted me more than any one. I cannot marry you: I cannot take a good for myself that has been wrung out of their misery. It is not the force that ought to rule us—this that we feel for each other; it would rend me away from all that my past life has made dear and holy to me. I can't set out on a fresh life, and forget that: I must go back to it, and cling to it, else I shall feel as if there were nothing firm beneath my feet."

"Good God, Maggie!" said Stephen, rising too and grasping her arm, "you rave. How can you go back without marrying me? You don't know what will be said, dearest. You see nothing as it really is."

"Yes, I do. But they will believe me. I will confess everything. Lucy will believe me—she will forgive you, and—and—O, *some* good will come by clinging to the right. Dear, dear Stephen, let me go!—don't drag me into deeper remorse. My whole soul has never consented—it does not consent now."

Stephen let go her arm, and sank back on his chair, half stunned by despairing rage. He was silent a few moments, not looking at her; while her eyes were turned towards him yearningly, in alarm at this sudden change. At last he said, still without looking at her—

"Go, then—leave me—don't torture me any longer—I can't bear it."

Involuntarily she leaned towards him and put out her hand to touch his. But he shrank from it as if it had been burning iron, and said again—

"Leave me."

Maggie was not conscious of a decision as she turned away from that gloomy averted face, and walked out of the room: it was like an automatic action that fulfils a forgotten intention. What came after? A sense of stairs descended as if in a dream—of flagstones—of a chaise and horses standing—then a street, and a turning into another street where a stage-coach was standing, taking in passengers—and the darting thought that that coach would take her away, perhaps towards home. But she could ask nothing yet; she only got into the coach.

Home—where her mother and brother were—Philip—Lucy—the scene of her very cares and trials—was the haven towards which her mind tended—the sanctuary where sacred relics lay—where she would be rescued from more falling. The thought of Stephen was like a horrible throbbing pain, which yet, as such pains do, seemed to urge all other thoughts into activity. But among her thoughts, what others would say and think of her conduct was hardly present. Love and deep pity and remorseful anguish left no room for that.

The coach was taking her to York—farther away from home; but she did not learn that until she was set down in the old city at midnight. It was no matter: she could sleep there, and start home the next day.

She had her purse in her pocket, with all her money in it—a bank-note and a sovereign: she had kept it in her pocket from forgetfulness, after going out to make purchases the day before yesterday.

Did she lie down in the gloomy bedroom of the old inn that night with her will bent unwaveringly on the path of penitent sacrifice? The great struggles of life are not so easy as that; the great problems of life are not so clear. In the darkness of that night she saw Stephen's face turned towards her in passionate, reproachful misery; she lived through again all the tremulous delights of his presence with her that made existence an easy floating in a stream of joy, instead of a quiet resolved endurance and effort. The love she had renounced came back upon her with a cruel charm; she felt herself opening her arms to receive it once more; and then it seemed to slip away and fade and vanish, leaving only the dying sound of a deep, thrilling voice that said, "Gone— for ever gone."

BOOK SEVEN

The Final Rescue

★

CHAPTER I

THE RETURN TO THE MILL

BETWEEN four and five o'clock on the afternoon of the fifth day from that on which Stephen and Maggie had left St. Ogg's, Tom Tulliver was standing on the gravel-walk outside the old house at Dorlcote Mill. He was master there now: he had half fulfilled his father's dying wish, and by years of steady self-government and energetic work he had brought himself near to the attainment of more than the old respectability which had been the proud inheritance of the Dodsons and Tullivers.

But Tom's face, as he stood in the hot still sunshine of that summer afternoon, had no gladness, no triumph in it. His mouth wore its bitterest expression, his severe brow its hardest and deepest fold, as he drew down his hat farther over his eyes to shelter them from the sun, and thrusting his hands deep into his pockets, began to walk up and down the gravel. No news of his sister had been heard since Bob Jakin had come back in the steamer from Mudport, and put an end to all improbable suppositions of an accident on the water by stating that he had seen her land from a vessel with Mr. Stephen Guest. Would the next news be that she was married—or what? Probably that she was not married: Tom's mind was set to the expectation of the worst that could happen—not death, but disgrace.

As he was walking with his back towards the entrance gate, and his face towards the rushing mill-stream, a tall dark-eyed figure, that we know well, approached the gate, and paused to look at him, with a fast-beating heart. Her brother was the human being of whom she had been most afraid, from her childhood upwards; afraid with that fear which springs in us when we love one who is inexorable, unbending, unmodifiable—with a mind that we can never mould ourselves upon, and yet that we cannot endure to alienate from us. That deep-rooted fear was shaking Maggie now; but her mind was unswervingly bent on returning to her brother, as the natural refuge that had been given her. In her deep humiliation under the retrospect of her own weakness—in her anguish at the injury she had inflicted—she almost desired to endure the severity of Tom's reproof, to submit in patient silence to that harsh disapproving judgment against which she had so often rebelled: it seemed no more than just to her now—who was weaker than she was? She craved that outward help to her better purpose which would come from complete, submissive confession—from being in the presence of those whose looks and words would be a reflection of her own conscience.

Maggie had been kept on her bed at York for a day with that prostrating headache which was likely to follow on the terrible strain of the previous day and night. There was an expression of physical pain still about her brow and eyes, and her whole appearance, with her dress so long unchanged, was worn and distressed. She lifted the latch of the gate and walked in—slowly. Tom did not hear the gate, he was just then close upon the roaring dam; but he presently turned, and, lifting up his eyes, saw the figure whose worn look and loneliness seemed to him a confirmation of his worst conjectures. He paused, trembling and white with disgust and indignation.

Maggie paused too—three yards before him. She felt the hatred in his face: felt it rushing through her fibres; but she must speak.

"Tom," she began, faintly, "I am come back to you—I am come back home—for refuge—to tell you everything."

"You will find no home with me," he answered with tremulous rage. "You have disgraced us all. You have disgraced my father's name. You have been a curse to your best friends. You have been base—deceitful —no motives are strong enough to restrain you. I wash my hands of you for ever. You don't belong to me."

Their mother had come to the door now. She stood paralysed by the double shock of seeing Maggie and hearing Tom's words.

"Tom," said Maggie, with more courage, "I am perhaps not so guilty as you believe me to be. I never meant to give way to my feelings. I struggled against them. I was carried too far in the boat to come back on Tuesday. I came back as soon as I could."

"I can't believe in you any more," said Tom, gradually passing from the tremulous excitement of the first moment to cold inflexibility. "You have been carrying on a clandestine relation with Stephen Guest—as you did before with another. He went to see you at my aunt Moss's; you walked alone with him in the lanes; you must have behaved as no modest girl would have done to her cousin's lover, else that could never have happened. The people at Luckreth saw you pass—you passed all the other places; you knew what you were doing. You have been using Philip Wakem as a screen to deceive Lucy—the kindest friend you ever had. Go and see the return you have made her: she's ill—unable to speak—my mother can't go near her, lest she should remind her of *you*."

Maggie was half stunned—too heavily pressed upon by her anguish even to discern any difference between her actual guilt and her brother's accusations, still less to vindicate herself.

"Tom," she said, crushing her hands together under her cloak, in the effort to speak again. "Whatever I have done, I repent it bitterly. I want to make amends. I will endure anything. I want to be kept from doing wrong again."

"What *will* keep you?" said Tom, with cruel bitterness. "Not religion; not your natural feelings of gratitude and honour. And he—he would deserve to be shot, if it were not—But you are ten times worse than he is. I loathe your character and your conduct. You struggled with your feelings, you say. Yes! *I* have had feelings to struggle with; but I conquered them. I have had a harder life than you have had; but I have found *my* comfort in doing my duty. But I will sanction no such character as yours: the world shall know that *I* feel the difference between right and wrong. If you are in want, I will provide for you—let my mother know. But you shall not come under my roof. It is enough that I have to bear the thought of your disgrace: the sight of you is hateful to me."

Slowly Maggie was turning away, with despair in her heart. But the poor frightened mother's love leaped out now, stronger than all dread.

"My child! I'll go with you. You've got a mother."

O, the sweet rest of that embrace to the heart-stricken Maggie! More helpful than all wisdom is one draught of simple human pity that will not forsake us.

Tom turned and walked into the house.

"Come in, my child," Mrs. Tulliver whispered. "He'll let you stay and sleep in my bed. He won't deny that, if I ask him."

"No, mother," said Maggie, in a low tone, like a moan. "I will never go in."

"Then wait for me outside. I'll get ready and come with you."

When his mother appeared with her bonnet on, Tom came out to her in the passage, and put money into her hands.

"My house is yours, mother, always," he said. "You will come and let me know everything you want—you will come back to me."

Poor Mrs. Tulliver took the money, too frightened to say anything. The only thing clear to her was the mother's instinct, that she would go with her unhappy child.

Maggie was waiting outside the gate; she took her mother's hand, and they walked a little way in silence.

"Mother," said Maggie, at last, "we will go to Luke's cottage. Luke will take me in. He was very good to me when I was a little girl."

"He's got no room for us, my dear, now; his wife's got so many children. I don't know where to go, if it isn't to one o' your aunts; and I hardly durst," said poor Mrs. Tulliver, quite destitute of mental resources in this extremity.

Maggie was silent a little while, and then said—

"Let us go to Bob Jakin's, mother: his wife will have room for us, if they have no other lodger."

So they went on their way to St. Ogg's—to the old house by the riverside.

Bob himself was at home, with a heaviness at heart which resisted even the new joy and pride of possessing a two months' old baby—quite the liveliest of its age that had ever been born to prince or packman. He would perhaps not so thoroughly have understood all the dubiousness of Maggie's appearance with Mr. Stephen Guest on the quay at Mudport, if he had not witnessed the effect it produced on Tom when he went to report it; and since then, the circumstances which in any case gave a disastrous character to her elopement, had passed beyond the more polite circles of St. Ogg's, and had become matter of common talk, accessible to the grooms and errand-boys. So that when he opened the door and saw Maggie standing before him in her sorrow and weariness, he had no questions to ask, except one, which he dared only ask himself—where was Mr. Stephen Guest? Bob, for his part, hoped he might be in the warmest department of an asylum understood to exist in the other world for gentlemen who are likely to be in fallen circumstances there.

The lodgings were vacant, and both Mrs. Jakin the larger and Mrs. Jakin the less were commanded to make all things comfortable for "the old Missis and the young Miss"—alas! that she was still "Miss." The ingenious Bob was sorely perplexed as to how this result could have come about—how Mr. Stephen Guest could have gone away from her, or could have let her go away from him, when he had the chance of keeping her with him. But he was silent, and would not allow his wife to ask him a question; would not present himself in the room, lest it should appear like intrusion and a wish to pry; having the same chivalry towards dark-eyed Maggie, as in the days when he had bought her the memorable present of books.

But after a day or two Mrs. Tulliver was gone to the Mill again for a few hours to see to Tom's household matters. Maggie had wished this: after the first violent outburst of feeling, which came as soon as she had no longer any active purpose to fulfil, she was less in need of her mother's presence; she even desired to be alone with her grief. But she had been solitary only a little while in the old sitting-room that looked on the river, when there came a tap at the door, and turning round her sad face as she said, "Come in," she saw Bob enter with the baby in his arms, and Mumps at his heels.

"We'll go back, if it disturbs you, Miss," said Bob.

"No," said Maggie, in a low voice, wishing she could smile.

Bob, closing the door behind him, came and stood before her.

"You see, we've got a little un, Miss, and I wanted you to look at it, and take it in your arms, if you'd be so good. For we made free to name it after you, and it 'ud be better for your takin' a bit o' notice on it."

Maggie could not speak, but she put out her arms to receive the tiny baby, while Mumps snuffed at it anxiously, to ascertain that this transference was all right. Maggie's heart had swelled at this action and speech of Bob's: she knew well enough that it was a way he had chosen to show his sympathy and respect.

"Sit down, Bob," she said presently, and he sat down in silence, finding his tongue unmanageable in quite a new fashion, refusing to say what he wanted it to say.

"Bob," she said, after a few moments, looking down at the baby, and holding it anxiously, as if she feared it might slip from her mind and her fingers, "I have a favour to ask of you."

"Don't you speak so, Miss," said Bob, grasping the skin of Mumps's neck; "if there's anything I can do for you, I should look upon it as a day's earnings."

"I want you to go to Dr. Kenn's, and ask to speak to him, and tell him that I am here, and should be very grateful if he would come to me while my mother is away. She will not come back till evening."

"Eh, Miss—I'd do it in a minute—it is but a step; but Dr. Kenn's wife lies dead—she's to be buried to-morrow—died the day I come from Mudport. It's all the more pity she should ha' died just now, if you want him. I hardly like to go a-nigh him yet."

"O, no, Bob," said Maggie, "we must let it be—till after a few days, perhaps—when you hear that he is going about again. But perhaps he may be going out of town—to a distance," she added, with a new sense of despondency at this idea.

"Not he, Miss," said Bob. "*He'll* none go away. He isn't one o' them gentlefolks as go to cry at waterin'-places when their wives die; he's got summat else to do. He looks fine an' sharp after the parish—he does. He christened the little un; an' he was *at* me to know what I did of a Sunday, as I didn't come to church. But I told him I was upo' the travel three parts o' the Sundays—an' then I'm so used to bein' on my legs, I can't sit so long on end—'an' lors, sir,' says I, 'a packman can do wi' a small 'lowance o' church: it tastes strong,' says I; 'there's no call to lay it on thick.' Eh, Miss, how good the little un is wi' you! It's like as if it knowed you: it partly does, I'll be bound—like the birds know the mornin'."

Bob's tongue was now evidently loosed from its unwonted bondage, and might even be in danger of doing more work than was required of it. But the subjects on which he longed to be informed were so steep and difficult of approach, that his tongue was likely to run on along the level rather than to carry him on that unbeaten road. He felt this, and was silent again for a little while, ruminating much on the possible forms in which he might put a question. At last he said, in a more timid voice than usual,—

"Will you give me leave to ask you only one thing, Miss?"

Maggie was rather startled, but she answered, "Yes, Bob, if it is about myself—not about any one else."

"Well, Miss, it's this: *Do* you owe anybody a grudge?"

"No, not any one," said Maggie, looking up at him inquiringly. "Why?"

"O, lors, Miss," said Bob, pinching Mumps's neck harder than ever,

"I wish you did—an' 'ud tell me—I'd leather him till I couldn't see—I would—an' the Justice might do what he liked to me arter."

"O, Bob," said Maggie, smiling faintly, "you're a very good friend to me. But I shouldn't like to punish any one, even if they'd done me wrong; I've done wrong myself too often."

This view of things was puzzling to Bob, and threw more obscurity than ever over what could possibly have happened between Stephen and Maggie. But further questions would have been too intrusive, even if he could have framed them suitably, and he was obliged to carry baby away again to an expectant mother.

"Happen you'd like Mumps for company, Miss," he said, when he had taken the baby again. "He's rare company—Mumps is—he knows iverything, an' makes no bother about it. If I tell him, he'll lie before you an' watch you—as still—just as he watches my pack. You'd better let me leave him a bit—he'll get fond on you. Lors, it's a fine thing to hev a dumb brute fond on you; it'll stick to you, an' make no jaw."

"Yes, do leave him, please," said Maggie. "I think I should like to have Mumps for a friend."

"Mumps, lie down there," said Bob, pointing to a place in front of Maggie, "an' niver do you stir till you're spoke to."

Mumps lay down at once, and made no sign of restlessness when his master left the room.

CHAPTER II

ST. OGG'S PASSES JUDGMENT

IT was soon known throughout St. Ogg's that Miss Tulliver was come back: she had not, then, eloped in order to be married to Mr. Stephen Guest—at all events, Mr. Stephen Guest had not married her—which came to the same thing, so far as her culpability was concerned. We judge others according to results; how else?—not knowing the process by which results are arrived at. If Miss Tulliver, after a few months of well-chosen travel, had returned as Mrs. Stephen Guest—with a post-marital *trousseau*, and all the advantages possessed even by the most unwelcome wife of an only son, public opinion, which at St. Ogg's, as elsewhere, always knew what to think, would have judged in strict consistency with those results. Public opinion, in these cases, is always of the feminine gender—not the world, but the world's wife: and she would have seen, that two handsome young people—the gentleman of quite the first family in St. Ogg's—having found themselves in a false position, had been led into a course which, to say the least of it, was highly injudicious, and productive of sad pain and disappointment, especially to that sweet young thing, Miss Deane. Mr. Stephen Guest had certainly not behaved well; but then, young men were liable to those sudden infatuated attachments; and bad as it might seem in Mrs. Stephen Guest to admit the faintest advances from her cousin's lover (indeed it *had* been said that she was actually engaged to young Wakem—old Wakem himself had mentioned it), still she was very young—"and a deformed young man, you know!—and young Guest so very fascinating; and, they say, he positively worships her (to be sure, that can't last!) and he ran away with her in the boat quite against her will—and what could she do? She couldn't come back then: no one would have spoken to her. And how very well that maize-colored satinette becomes her complexion! It seems as if the folds in front were quite come in; several of her dresses are made so;—they say, he thinks nothing too handsome to buy for her. Poor Miss Deane! She is very pitiable; but then, there was no positive engagement; and the air at the coast will do her good. After all, if young Guest felt no more for her than *that,* it was better for her not to marry him. What a wonderful marriage for a girl like Miss Tulliver—quite romantic! Why, young Guest will put up for the borough at the next election. Nothing like commerce nowadays! That young Wakem nearly went out of his mind—he always *was* rather queer; but he's gone abroad again to be out of the way—quite the best thing for a deformed young man. Miss Unit declares she will never visit Mr. and Mrs. Stephen Guest—such nonsense! pretending to be better than other people. Society couldn't be carried on if we inquired into private conduct in that way—and Christianity tells us to think no evil—and my belief is, that Miss Unit had no cards sent her."

But the results, we know, were not of a kind to warrant this extenuation of the past. Maggie had returned without a *trousseau,* without a husband—in that degraded and outcast condition to which error is well known to lead; and the world's wife, with that fine instinct which is given her for the preservation of Society, saw at once that Miss Tulliver's conduct had been of the most aggravated kind. Could anything be more detestable? A girl so much indebted to her friends—whose mother as well as herself had received so much kindness from the Deanes—to lay the design of winning a young man's affections away from her own cousin, who had behaved like a sister to her! Winning his affections? That was not the phrase for such a girl as Miss Tulliver: it would have been more correct to say that she had been actuated by mere unwomanly boldness and unbridled passion. There was always something questionable about her. That connection with young Wakem, which, they said, had been carried on for years, looked very ill—disgusting, in fact! But with a girl of that disposition!—To the world's wife there had always been something in Miss Tulliver's very physique that a refined instinct felt to be prophetic of harm. As for poor Mr. Stephen Guest, he was rather pitiable than otherwise: a young man of five-and-twenty is not to be too severely judged in these cases—he is really very much at the mercy of a designing bold girl. And it was clear that he had given way in spite of himself: he had shaken her off as soon as he could; indeed, their having parted so soon looked very black indeed—*for her.* To be sure, he had written a letter, laying all the blame on himself, and telling the story in a romantic fashion so as to try and make her appear quite innocent: of course he could do that! But the refined instinct of the world's wife was not to be deceived: providentially!—else what would become of Society? Why—her own brother had turned her from his door:—he had seen enough, you might be sure, before he would do that. A truly respectable young man—Mr. Tom Tulliver: quite likely to rise in the world! His sister's disgrace was naturally a heavy blow to him. It was to be hoped that she would go out of the neighbourhood—to America, or anywhere—so as to purify the air of St. Ogg's from the taint of her presence—extremely dangerous to daughters there! No good could happen to her: it was only to be hoped she would repent, and that God would have mercy on her: He had not the care of Society on His hands—as the world's wife had.

It required nearly a fortnight for fine instinct to assure itself of these inspirations; indeed, it was a whole week before Stephen's letter came, telling his father the facts, and adding that he was gone across to Holland—had drawn upon the agent at Mudport for money—was incapable of any resolution at present.

Maggie, all this while, was too entirely filled with a more agonising anxiety, to spend any thought on the view that was being taken of her conduct by the world of St. Ogg's: anxiety about Stephen—Lucy—Philip—beat on her poor heart in a hard, driving, ceaseless storm of mingled love, remorse, and pity. If she had thought of rejection and injustice at all, it would have seemed to her that they had done their worst —that she could hardly feel any stroke from them intolerable since the words she had heard from her brother's lips. Across all her anxiety for the loved and the injured, those words shot again and again, like a horrible pang that would have brought misery and dread even into a heaven of delights. The idea of ever recovering happiness never glimmered in her mind for a moment; it seemed as if every sensitive fibre in her were too entirely preoccupied by pain ever to vibrate again to another influence. Life stretched before her as one act of penitence, and all she craved, as she dwelt on her future lot, was something to guarantee her from more falling: her own weakness haunted her like a vision of hideous possibilities, that made no peace conceivable except such as lay in the sense of a sure refuge.

But she was not without practical intentions: the love of independence was too strong an inheritance and a habit for her not to remember that she must get her bread; and when other projects looked vague, she fell back on that of returning to her plain sewing, and so getting enough to pay for her lodging at Bob's. She meant to persuade her mother to return to the Mill by-and-by, and live with Tom again; and somehow or other she would maintain herself at St. Ogg's. Dr. Kenn would perhaps help her and advise her. She remembered his parting words at the bazaar. She remembered the momentary feeling of reliance that had sprung in her when he was talking with her, and she waited with yearning expectation for the opportunity of confiding everything to him. Her mother called every day at Mr. Deane's to learn how Lucy was: the report was always sad—nothing had yet roused her from the feeble passivity which had come on with the first shock. But of Philip, Mrs. Tulliver had learned nothing: naturally, no one whom she met would speak to her about what related to her daughter. But at last she summoned courage to go and see sister Glegg, who of course would know everything, and had even been to see Tom at the Mill in Mrs. Tulliver's absence, though he had said nothing of what had passed on the occasion.

As soon as her mother was gone, Maggie put on her bonnet. She had resolved on walking to the Rectory and asking to see Dr. Kenn: he was in deep grief—but the grief of another does not jar upon us in such circumstances. It was the first time she had been beyond the door since her return; nevertheless her mind was so bent on the purpose of her walk, that the unpleasantness of meeting people on the way, and being stared at, did not occur to her. But she had no sooner passed beyond the narrower streets which she had to thread from Bob's dwelling, than she became aware of unusual glances cast at her; and this consciousness made her hurry along nervously, afraid to look to right or left. Presently, however, she came full on Mrs. and Miss Turnbull, old acquaintances of her family; they both looked at her strangely, and turned a little aside without speaking. All hard looks were pain to Maggie, but her self-reproach was too strong for resentment: no wonder they will not speak to me, she thought—they are very fond of Lucy. But now she knew that she was about to pass a group of gentlemen, who were standing at the door of the billiard-rooms, and she could not help seeing young Torry step out a little with his glass at his eye, and bow to her with that air of nonchalance which he might have bestowed on a friendly bar-maid. Maggie's pride was too intense for her not to feel that sting, even in the midst of her sorrow; and for the first time the thought took strong hold of her that she would have other obloquy cast on her besides that which was felt to be due to her breach of faith towards Lucy. But she was at the Rectory now; there, perhaps, she would find something else than retribution. Retribution may come from any voice: the hardest, cruelest, most imbruted urchin at the street-corner can inflict it: surely help and pity are rarer things—more needful for the righteous to bestow.

She was shown up at once, after being announced, into Dr. Kenn's study, where he sat amongst piled-up books, for which he had little appetite, leaning his cheek against the head of his youngest child, a girl of three. The child was sent away with the servant, and when the door was closed, Dr. Kenn said, placing a chair for Maggie,—

"I was coming to see you, Miss Tulliver; you have anticipated me; I am glad you did."

Maggie looked at him with her childlike directness as she had done at the bazaar, and said, "I want to tell you everything." But her eyes filled fast with tears as she said it, and all the pent-up excitement of her humiliating walk would have its vent before she could say more.

"Do tell me everything," Dr. Kenn said, with quiet kindness in his grave firm voice. "Think of me as one to whom a long experience has been granted, which may enable him to help you."

In rather broken sentences, and with some effort, at first, but soon with the greater ease that came from a sense of relief in the confidence, Maggie told the brief story of a struggle that must be the beginning of a long sorrow. Only the day before, Dr. Kenn had been made acquainted with the contents of Stephen's letter, and he had believed them at once, without the confirmation of Maggie's statement. That involuntary plaint of hers, *"O, I must go,"* had remained with him as the sign that she was undergoing some inward conflict.

Maggie dwelt the longest on the feeling which had made her come back to her mother and brother, which made her cling to all the memories of the past. When she had ended, Dr. Kenn was silent for some minutes: there was a difficulty on his mind. He rose, and walked up and down the hearth with his hands behind him. At last he seated himself again, and said, looking at Maggie—

"Your prompting to go to your nearest friends—to remain where all the ties of your life have been formed—is a true prompting, to which the Church in its original constitution and discipline responds—opening its arms to the penitent—watching over its children to the last—never abandoning them until they are hopelessly reprobate. And the Church ought to represent the feeling of the community, so that every parish should be a family knit together by Christian brotherhood under a spiritual father. But the ideas of discipline and Christian fraternity are entirely relaxed—they can hardly be said to exist in the public mind: they hardly survive except in the partial, contradictory form they have taken in the narrow communities of schismatics; and if I were not supported by the firm faith that the Church must ultimately recover the full force of that constitution which is alone fitted to human needs, I should often lose heart at observing the want of fellowship and sense of mutual responsibility among my own flock. At present everything seems tending towards the relaxation of ties—towards the substitution of wayward choice for the adherence to obligation, which has its roots in the past. Your conscience and your heart have given you true light on this point, Miss Tulliver; and I have said all this that you may know what my wish about you—what my advice to you—would be, if they sprang from my own feeling and opinion unmodified by counteracting circumstances."

Dr. Kenn paused a little while. There was an entire absence of effusive benevolence in his manner; there was something almost cold in the gravity of his look and voice. If Maggie had not known that his benevolence was persevering in proportion to its reserve, she might have been chilled and frightened. As it was, she listened expectantly, quite sure that there would be some effective help in his words. He went on.

"Your inexperience of the world, Miss Tulliver, prevents you from anticipating fully the very unjust conceptions that will probably be formed concerning your conduct—conceptions which will have a baneful effect, even in spite of known evidence to disprove them."

"O, I do—I begin to see," said Maggie, unable to repress this utterance of her recent pain. "I know I shall be insulted: I shall be thought worse than I am."

"You perhaps do not yet know," said Dr. Kenn, with a touch of more personal pity, "that a letter is come which ought to satisfy every one who has known anything of you, that you chose the steep and difficult path of a return to the right, at the moment when that return was most of all difficult."

"O—where is he?" said poor Maggie, with a flush and tremor that no presence could have hindered.

"He is gone abroad: he has written of all that passed to his father. He has vindicated you to the utmost; and I hope the communication of that letter to your cousin will have a beneficial effect on her."

Dr. Kenn waited for her to get calm again before he went on.

"That letter, as I said, ought to suffice to prevent false impressions concerning you. But I am bound to tell you, Miss Tulliver, that not only the experience of my whole life, but my observation within the last three days, makes me fear that there is hardly any evidence which will save you from the painful effect of false imputations. The persons who are the most incapable of a conscientious struggle such as yours, are precisely those who will be likely to shrink from you; because they will not believe in your struggle. I fear your life here will be attended not only with much pain, but with many obstructions. For this reason—and for this only—I ask you to consider whether it will not perhaps be better for you to take a situation at a distance, according to your former intention. I will exert myself at once to obtain one for you."

"O, if I could but stop here!" said Maggie. "I have no heart to begin a strange life again. I should have no stay. I should feel like a lonely wanderer—cut off from the past. I have written to the lady who offered me a situation to excuse myself. If I remained here, I could perhaps atone in some way to Lucy—to others: I could convince them that I'm sorry. And," she added, with some of the old proud fire flashing out, "I will not go away because people say false things of me. They shall learn to retract them. If I must go away at last, because—because others wish it, I will not go now."

"Well," said Dr. Kenn, after some consideration, "if you determine on that, Miss Tulliver, you may rely on all the influence my position gives me. I am bound to aid and countenance you, by the very duties of my office as a parish priest. I will add, that personally I have a deep interest in your peace of mind and welfare."

"The only thing I want is some occupation that will enable me to get my bread and be independent," said Maggie. "I shall not want much. I can go on lodging where I am."

"I must think over the subject maturely," said Dr. Kenn, "and in a few days I shall be better able to ascertain the general feeling. I shall come to see you: I shall bear you constantly in mind."

When Maggie had left him, Dr. Kenn stood ruminating with his hands behind him, and his eyes fixed on the carpet, under a painful sense of doubt and difficulty. The tone of Stephen's letter, which he had read, and the actual relations of all the persons concerned, forced upon him powerfully the idea of an ultimate marriage between Stephen and Maggie as the least evil; and the impossibility of their proximity in St. Ogg's on any other supposition, until after years of separation, threw an insurmountable prospective difficulty over Maggie's stay there. On the other hand, he entered with all the comprehension of a man who had known spiritual conflict, and lived through years of devoted service to his fellow-men, into that state of Maggie's heart and conscience which made the consent to the marriage a desecration to her: her conscience must not be tampered with: the principle on which she had acted was a safer guide than any balancing of consequences. His experience told him that intervention was too dubious a responsibility to be lightly incurred: the possible issue either of an endeavour to restore the former relations with Lucy and Philip, or of counselling submission to this irruption of a new feeling, was hidden in a darkness all the more impenetrable because each immediate step was clogged with evil.

The great problem of the shifting relation between passion and duty is clear to no man who is capable of apprehending it: the question, whether the moment has come in which a man has fallen below the possibility of a renunciation that will carry any efficacy, and must accept the sway of a passion against which he had struggled as a trespass, is one for which we have no master key that will fit all cases. The casuists have become a by-word of reproach; but their perverted spirit of minute discrimination was the shadow of a truth to which eyes and hearts are too often fatally sealed: the truth, that moral judgments must remain false and hollow, unless they are checked and enlightened by a perpetual reference to the special circumstances that mark the individual lot.

All people of broad, strong sense have an instinctive repugnance to the men of maxims; because such people early discern that the mysterious complexity of our life is not to be embraced by maxims, and that to lace ourselves up in formulas of that sort is to repress all the divine promptings and inspirations that spring from growing insight and sympathy. And the man of maxims is the popular representative of the minds that are guided in their moral judgment solely by general rules, thinking that these will lead them to justice by a ready-made patent method, without the trouble of exerting patience, discrimination, impartiality—without any care to assure themselves whether they have the insight that comes from a hardly-earned estimate of temptation, or from a life vivid and intense enough to have created a wide fellow-feeling with all that is human.

CHAPTER III

SHOWING THAT OLD ACQUAINTANCES ARE CAPABLE OF SURPRISING US

WHEN Maggie was at home again, her mother brought her news of an unexpected line of conduct in aunt Glegg. As long as Maggie had not been heard of, Mrs. Glegg had half-closed her shutters and drawn down her blinds: she felt assured that Maggie was drowned: that was far more probable than that her niece and legatee should have done anything to wound the family honour in the tenderest point. When, at last, she learned from Tom that Maggie had come home, and gathered from him what was her explanation of her absence, she burst forth in severe reproof of Tom for admitting the worst of his sister until he was compelled. If you were not to stand by your "kin" as long as there was a shred of honour attributable to them, pray what were you to stand by? Lightly to admit conduct in one of your own family that would force you to alter your will, had never been the way of the Dodsons; and though Mrs. Glegg had always augured ill of Maggie's future at a time when other people were perhaps less clear-sighted, yet fair-play was a jewel, and it was not for her own friends to help to rob the girl of her fair fame, and to cast her out from family shelter to the scorn of the outer world, until she had become unequivocally a family disgrace. The circumstances were unprecedented in Mrs. Glegg's experience—nothing of that kind had happened among the Dodsons before; but it was a case in which her hereditary rectitude and personal strength of character found a common channel along with her fundamental ideas of clanship, as they did in her life-long regard to equity in money matters. She quarrelled with Mr. Glegg, whose kindness, flowing entirely into compassion for Lucy, made him as hard in his judgment of Maggie as Mr. Deane himself was; and, fuming against her sister Tulliver because she did not at once come to her for advice and help, shut herself up in her own room with "Baxter's Saint's Rest" from morning till night, denying herself to all visitors, till Mr. Glegg brought from Mr. Deane the news of Stephen's letter. Then Mrs. Glegg felt that she had adequate fighting-ground—then she laid aside Baxter, and was ready to meet all comers. While Mrs. Pullet could do nothing but shake her head and cry, and wish that cousin Abbot had died, or any number of funerals had happened rather than this, which had never happened before, so that there was no knowing how to act, and Mrs. Pullet could never enter St. Ogg's again, because "acquaintances" knew of it all,— Mrs. Glegg only hoped that Mrs. Wooll, or any one else, would come to her with their false tales about her own niece, and she would know what to say to that ill-advised person!

Again she had a scene of remonstrance with Tom, all the more severe, in proportion to the greater strength of her present position. But Tom, like other immovable things, seemed only the more rigidly fixed under that attempt to shake him. Poor Tom! he judged by what he had been able to see; and the judgment was painful enough to himself. He thought he had the demonstration of facts observed through years by his own eyes which gave no warning of their imperfection, that Maggie's nature was utterly untrustworthy, and too strongly marked with evil tendencies to be safely treated with leniency: he would act on that demonstration at any cost; but the thought of it made his days bitter to him. Tom, like every one of us, was imprisoned within the limits of his own nature, and his education had simply glided over him, leaving a slight deposit of polish: if you are inclined to be severe on his severity, remember that the responsibility of tolerance lies with those who have the wider vision. There had arisen in Tom a repulsion towards Maggie that derived its very intensity from their early childish love in the time when they had clasped tiny fingers together, and their later sense of nearness in a common duty and a common sorrow: the sight of her, as he had told her, was hateful to him. In this branch of the Dodson family aunt Glegg found a stronger nature than her own—a nature in which family feeling had lost the character of clanship, in taking on a doubly deep dye of personal pride. Mrs. Glegg allowed that Maggie ought to be punished—she was not a woman to deny that—she knew what conduct was; but punished in proportion to the misdeeds proved against her, not to those which were cast upon her by people outside her own family, who might wish to show that their own kin were better.

"Your aunt Glegg scolded me so as niver was, my dear," said poor Mrs. Tulliver, when she came back to Maggie, "as I didn't go to her before—she said it wasn't for her to come to me first. But she spoke like a sister, too: *having* she allays was, and hard to please—O dear!—but she's said the kindest word as has ever been spoke by you yet, my child. For she says, for all she's been so set again' having one extry in the house, and making extry spoons and things, and putting her about in her ways, you shall have a shelter in her house, if you'll go to her dutiful, and she'll uphold you against folks as say harm of you when they've no call. And I told her I thought you couldn't bear to see nobody but me, you was so beat down with trouble; but she said, 'I won't throw ill words at her—there's them out o' th' family 'ull be ready enough to do that. But I'll give her good advice; an' she must be humble.' It's wonderful o' Jane; for I'm sure she used to throw everything I did wrong at me—if it was the raisin wine as turned out bad, or the pies too hot—or whativer it was."

"O, mother," said poor Maggie, shrinking from the thought of all the contact her bruised mind would have to bear, "tell her I'm very grateful—I'll go to see her as soon as I can; but I can't see any one just yet, except Dr. Kenn. I've been to him—he will advise me, and help me to get some occupation. I can't live with any one, or be dependent on them, tell aunt Glegg; I must get my own bread. But did you hear nothing of Philip—Philip Wakem? Have you never seen any one that has mentioned him?"

"No, my dear: but I've been to Lucy's, and I saw your uncle, and he says they got her to listen to the letter, and she took notice o' Miss Guest, and asked questions, and the doctor thinks she's on the turn to be better. What a world this is—what trouble, O dear! The law was the first beginning, an' it's gone from bad to worse all of a sudden, just when the luck seemed on the turn." This was the first lamentation that Mrs. Tulliver had let slip to Maggie, but old habit had been revived by the interview with sister Glegg.

"My poor, poor mother!" Maggie burst out, cut to the heart with pity and compunction, and throwing her arms round her mother's neck, "I was always naughty and troublesome to you. And now you might have been happy if it hadn't been for me."

"Eh, my dear," said Mrs. Tulliver, leaning towards the warm young cheek; "I must put up wi' my children—I shall never have no more; and if they bring me bad luck, I must be fond on it—there's nothing else much to be fond on, for my furnitur' went long ago. And you'd got to be very good once; I can't think how it's turned out the wrong way so!"

Still two or three more days passed, and Maggie heard nothing of Philip; anxiety about him was becoming her predominant trouble, and she summoned courage at last to inquire about him of Dr. Kenn. on his next visit to her. He did not even know if Philip was at home. The elder Wakem was made moody by an accumulation of annoyance: the disappointment in this young Jetsome, to whom, apparently, he was a good deal attached, had been followed close by the catastrophe to his son's hopes after he had conceded his feelings to them, and incautiously mentioned this concession in St. Ogg's,—and he was almost fierce in his brusqueness when any one asked him a question about his son. But Philip could hardly have been ill, or it would have been known through the calling-in of the medical man; it was probable that he was gone out of the town for a little while. Maggie sickened under this suspense, and her imagination began to live more and more persistently in what Philip was enduring. What did he believe about her?

At last Bob brought her a letter, without a post-mark, directed in a hand which she knew familiarly in the letters of her own name—a hand in which her name had been written long ago, in a pocket Shakespeare which she possessed. Her mother was in the room, and Maggie, in violent agitation, hurried up-stairs, that she might read the letter in solitude. She read it with a throbbing brow.

"MAGGIE,—I believe in you—I know you never meant to deceive me—I know you tried to keep faith to me, and to all. I believed this before I had any other evidence of it than your own nature. The night after I last parted from you I suffered torments. I had seen what convinced me that you were not free; that there was another whose presence had a power over you which mine never possessed; but through all the suggestions—almost murderous suggestions—of rage and jealousy, my mind made its way to belief in your truthfulness. I was sure that you meant to cleave to me, as you had said; that you had rejected him; that you struggled to renounce him, for Lucy's sake and for mine. But I could see no issue that was not fatal for *you;* and that dread shut out the very thought of resignation. I foresaw that he would not relinquish you, and I believed then, as I believe now, that the strong attraction which drew you together proceeded only from one side of your characters, and belonged to that partial, divided action of our nature which makes half the tragedy of the human lot. I have felt the vibration of chords in your nature, that I have continually felt the want of in his. But perhaps I am wrong; perhaps I feel about you as the artist does about the scene over which his soul has brooded with love: he would tremble to see it confided to other hands; he would never believe that it could bear for another all the meaning and the beauty it bears for him.

"I dared not trust myself to see you that morning; I was filled with selfish passion; I was shattered by a night of conscious delirium. I told you long ago that I had never been resigned even to the mediocrity of my powers: how could I be resigned to the loss of the one thing which had ever come to me on earth, with the promise of such deep joy as would give a new and blessed meaning to the foregoing pain,—the promise of another self that would lift my aching affection into the divine rapture of an ever-springing, ever-satisfied want?

"But the miseries of that night had prepared me for what came before the next. It was no surprise to me. I was certain that he had prevailed on you to sacrifice everything to him, and I waited with equal certainty to hear of your marriage. I measured your love and his by my own. But I was wrong, Maggie. There is something stronger in you than your love for him.

"I will not tell you what I went through in that interval. But even in its utmost agony—even in those terrible throes that love must suffer before it can be disembodied of selfish desire—my love for you sufficed to withhold me from suicide, without the aid of any other motive. In the midst of my egoism, I yet could not bear to come like a death-shadow across the feast of your joy. I could not bear to forsake the world in which you still lived and might need me; it was part of the faith I had vowed to you—to wait and endure. Maggie, that is a proof of what I write now to assure you of—that no anguish I have had to bear on your account has been too heavy a price to pay for the new life into which I have entered in loving you. I want you to put aside all grief because of the grief you have caused me. I was nurtured in the sense of privation; I never expected happiness; and in knowing you, in loving you, I have had, and still have, what reconciles me to life. You have been to my affections what light, what colour is to my eyes —what music is to the inward ear; you have raised a dim unrest into a vivid consciousness. The new life I have found in caring for your joy and sorrow more than for what is directly my own, has transformed the spirit of rebellious murmuring into that willing endurance which is the birth of strong sympathy. I think nothing but such complete and intense love could have initiated me into that enlarged life which grows and grows by appropriating the life of others; for before, I was always dragged back from it by ever-present painful self-consciousness. I even think sometimes that this gift of transferred life which has come to me in loving you, may be a new power to me.

"Then—dear one—in spite of all, you have been the blessing of my life. Let no self-reproach weigh on you because of me. It is I who should rather reproach myself for having urged my feelings upon you, and hurried you into words that you have felt as fetters. You meant to be true to those words; you *have* been true. I can measure your sacrifice by what I have known in only one half-hour of your presence with me, when I dreamed that you might love me best. But, Maggie, I have no just claim on you for more than affectionate remembrance.

"For some time I have shrunk from writing to you, because I have shrunk even from the appearance of wishing to thrust myself before you, and so repeating my original error. But you will not misconstrue me. I know that we must keep apart for a long while; cruel tongues would force us apart, if nothing else did. But I shall not go away. The place where you are is the one where my mind must live, wherever I might travel. And remember that I am unchangeably yours: yours —not with selfish wishes—but with a devotion that excludes such wishes.

"God comfort you,—my loving, large-souled Maggie. If every one else has misconceived you, remember that you have never been doubted by him whose heart recognised you ten years ago.

"Do not believe any one who says I am ill, because I am not seen out of doors. I have only had nervous headaches—no worse than I have sometimes had them before. But the overpowering heat inclines me to be perfectly quiescent in the daytime. I am strong enough to obey any word which shall tell me that I can serve you by word or deed.

"Yours, to the last,
"PHILIP WAKEM."

As Maggie knelt by the bed sobbing, with that letter pressed under her, her feelings again and again gathered themselves in a whispered cry, always in the same words:

"O, God, is there any happiness in love that could make me forget *their* pain?"

CHAPTER IV

MAGGIE AND LUCY

By the end of the week Dr. Kenn had made up his mind that there was only one way in which he could secure to Maggie a suitable living at St. Ogg's. Even with his twenty years' experience as a parish priest, he was aghast at the obstinate continuance of imputations against her in the face of evidence. Hitherto he had been rather more adored and appealed to than was quite agreeable to him; but now, in attempting to open the ears of women to reason, and their consciences to justice, on behalf of Maggie Tulliver, he suddenly found himself as powerless as he was aware he would have been if he had attempted to influence the shape of bonnets. Dr. Kenn could not be contradicted; he was listened to in silence; but when he left the room, a comparison of opinions among his hearers yielded much the same result as before. Miss Tulliver had undeniably acted in a blamable manner; even Dr. Kenn did not deny that: how, then, could he think so lightly of her as to put that favourable interpretation on everything she had done? Even on the supposition that required the utmost stretch of belief—namely, that none of the things said about Miss Tulliver were true—still, since they *had* been said about her, they had cast an odour round her which must cause her to be shrunk from by every woman who had to take care of her own reputation—and of Society. To have taken Maggie by the hand and said, "I will not believe unproved evil of you: my lips shall not utter it; my ears shall be closed against it: I, too, am an erring mortal, liable to stumble, apt to come short of my most earnest efforts; your lot has been harder than mine, your temptation greater; let us help each other to stand and walk without more falling;"—to have done this would have demanded courage, deep pity, self-knowledge, generous trust—would have demanded a mind that tasted no piquancy in evil-speaking, that felt no self-exaltation in condemning, that cheated itself with no large words into the belief that life can have any moral end, any high religion, which excludes the striving after perfect truth, justice, and love towards the individual men and women who come across our own path. The ladies of St. Ogg's were not beguiled by any wide speculative conceptions; but they had their favourite abstraction, called Society, which served to make their consciences perfectly easy in doing what satisfied their own egoism—thinking and speaking the worst of Maggie Tulliver, and turning their backs upon her. It was naturally disappointing to Dr. Kenn, after two years of superfluous incense from his feminine parishioners, to find them suddenly maintaining their views in opposition to his; but then, they maintained them in opposition to a Higher Authority, which they had venerated longer. That Authority had furnished a very explicit answer to persons who might inquire where their social duties began, and might be inclined to take wide views as to the starting-point. The answer had not turned on the ultimate good of Society, but on "a certain man" who was found in trouble by the wayside.

Not that St. Ogg's was empty of women with some tenderness of heart and conscience: probably it had as fair a proportion of human goodness in it as any other small trading town of that day. But until every good man is brave, we must expect to find many good women timid: too timid even to believe in the correctness of their own best promptings, when these would place them in a minority. And the men at St. Ogg's were not all brave by any means: some of them were even fond of scandal—and to an extent that might have given their conversation an effeminate character, if it had not been distinguished by masculine jokes, and by an occasional shrug of the shoulders at the mutual hatred of women. It was the general feeling of the masculine mind at St. Ogg's that women were not to be interfered with in their treatment of each other.

And thus every direction in which Dr. Kenn had turned in the hope of procuring some kind recognition and some employment for Maggie, proved a disappointment to him. Mrs. James Torry could not think of taking Maggie as a nursery governess, even temporarily—a young woman about whom "such things had been said," and about whom "gentlemen joked;" and Miss Kirke, who had a spinal complaint, and wanted a reader and companion, felt quite sure that Maggie's mind must be of a quality with which she, for her part, could not risk *any* contact. Why did not Miss Tulliver accept the shelter offered her by her aunt Glegg?—it did not become a girl like her to refuse it. Or else, why did she not go out of the neighbourhood, and get a situation where she was not known? (It was not, apparently, of so much importance that she should carry her dangerous tendencies into strange families unknown at St. Ogg's.) She must be very bold and hardened to wish to stay in a parish where she was so much stared at and whispered about.

Dr. Kenn, having great natural firmness, began, in the presence of this opposition, as every firm man would have done, to contract a certain strength of determination over and above what would have been called forth by the end in view. He himself wanted a daily governess for his younger children; and though he had hesitated in the first instance to offer this position to Maggie, the resolution to protest with the utmost force of his personal and priestly character against her being crushed and driven away by slander, was now decisive. Maggie gratefully accepted an employment that gave her duties as well as a support: her days would be filled now, and solitary evenings would be a welcome rest. She no longer needed the sacrifice her mother made in staying with her, and Mrs. Tulliver was persuaded to go back to the Mill.

But now it began to be discovered that Dr. Kenn, exemplary as he had hitherto appeared, had his crotchets,—possibly his weaknesses. The masculine mind of St. Ogg's smiled pleasantly, and did not wonder that Kenn liked to see a fine pair of eyes daily, or that he was inclined to take so lenient a view of the past; the feminine mind, regarded at that period as less powerful, took a more melancholy view of the case. If Dr. Kenn should be beguiled into marrying that Miss Tulliver! It was not safe to be too confident even about the best of men: an apostle had fallen, and wept bitterly afterwards; and though Peter's denial was not a close precedent, his repentance was likely to be.

Maggie had not taken her daily walks to the Rectory for many weeks, before the dreadful possibility of her some time or other becoming the Rector's wife had been talked of so often in confidence, that ladies were beginning to discuss how they should behave to her in that position. For Dr. Kenn, it had been understood, had sat in the schoolroom half an hour one morning, when Miss Tulliver was giving her lessons; nay, he had sat there every morning: he had once walked home with her—he almost *always* walked home with her—and if not, he went to see her in the evening. What an artful creature she was! What a *mother* for those children! It was enough to make poor Mrs. Kenn turn in her grave, that they should be put under the care of this girl only a few weeks after her death. Would he be so lost to propriety as to marry her before the year was out? The masculine mind was sarcastic, and thought *not*.

The Miss Guests saw an alleviation to the sorrow of witnessing a folly in their Rector: at least their brother would be safe; and their knowledge of Stephen's tenacity was a constant ground of alarm to them, lest he should come back and marry Maggie. They were not among those who disbelieved their brother's letter; but they had no confidence in Maggie's adherence to her renunciation of him; they suspected that she had shrunk rather from the elopement than from the marriage, and that she lingered in St. Ogg's, relying on his return to her. They had always thought her disagreeable; they now thought her artful and proud; having quite as good grounds for that judgment as you and I probably have for many strong opinions of the same kind. Formerly they had not altogether delighted in the contemplated match with Lucy, but now their dread of a marriage between Stephen and Maggie added its momentum to their genuine pity and indignation on behalf of the gentle forsaken girl, in making them desire that he should return to her. As soon as Lucy was able to leave home, she was to seek relief from the oppressive heat of this August by going to the coast with the Miss Guests; and it was in their plans that Stephen should be induced to join them. On the very first hint of gossip concerning Maggie and Dr. Kenn, the report was conveyed in Miss Guest's letter to her brother.

Maggie had frequent tidings through her mother, or aunt Glegg, or Dr. Kenn, of Lucy's gradual progress towards recovery, and her thoughts tended continually towards her uncle Deane's house: she hungered for an interview with Lucy, if it were only for five minutes—to utter a word of penitence, to be assured by Lucy's own eyes and lips that she did not believe in the willing treachery of those whom she had loved and trusted. But she knew that even if her uncle's indignation had not closed his house against her, the agitation of such an interview would have been forbidden to Lucy. Only to have seen her without speaking, would have been some relief; for Maggie was haunted by a face cruel in its very gentleness: a face that had been turned on hers with glad sweet looks of trust and love from the twilight time of memory: changed now to a sad and weary face by a first heart-stroke. And as the days passed on, that pale image became more and more distinct —the picture grew and grew into more speaking definiteness under the avenging hand of remorse; the soft hazel eyes, in their look of pain, were bent for ever on Maggie, and pierced her the more because she could see no anger in them. But Lucy was not yet able to go to church, or any place where Maggie could see her; and even the hope of that departed, when the news was told her by aunt Glegg, that Lucy was really going away in a few days to Scarborough with the Miss Guests, who had been heard to say that they expected their brother to meet them there.

Only those who have known what hardest inward conflict is, can know what Maggie felt as she sat in her loneliness the evening after hearing that news from Mrs. Glegg,—only those who have known what it is to dread their own selfish desires as the watching mother would dread the sleeping-potion that was to still her own pain.

She sat without candle in the twilight, with the window wide open towards the river; the sense of oppressive heat adding itself undistinguishably to the burthen of her lot. Seated on a chair against the window, with her arm on the window-sill, she was looking blankly at the flowing river, swift with the advancing tide,—struggling to see still the sweet face in its unreproaching sadness, that seemed now from moment to moment to sink away and be hidden behind a form that thrust itself between, and made darkness. Hearing the door open, she thought Mrs. Jakin was coming in with her supper, as usual; and with that

repugnance to trivial speech which comes with languor and wretchedness, she shrank from turning round and saying she wanted nothing:
good little Mrs. Jakin would be sure to make some well-meant remarks.
But the next moment, without her having discerned the sound of a
footstep, she felt a light hand on her shoulder, and heard a voice close
to her saying, "Maggie!"

The face was there—changed, but all the sweeter: the hazel eyes
were there, with their heart-piercing tenderness.

"Maggie!" the soft voice said. "Lucy!" answered a voice with a
sharp ring of anguish in it; and Lucy threw her arms round Maggie's
neck, and leaned her pale cheek against the burning brow.

"I stole out," said Lucy, almost in a whisper, while she sat down
close to Maggie and held her hand, "when papa and the rest were away.
Alice is come with me. I asked her to help me. But I must only stay a
little while, because it is so late."

It was easier to say that at first than to say anything else. They sat
looking at each other. It seemed as if the interview must end without
more speech, for speech was very difficult. Each felt that there would be
something scorching in the words that would recall the irretrievable
wrong. But soon, as Maggie looked, every distinct thought began to be
overflowed by a wave of loving penitence, and words burst forth with
a sob.

"God bless you for coming, Lucy."

The sobs came thick on each other after that.

"Maggie, dear, be comforted," said Lucy now, putting her cheek
against Maggie's again. "Don't grieve." And she sat still, hoping to
soothe Maggie with that gentle caress.

"I didn't mean to deceive you, Lucy," said Maggie, as soon as she
could speak. "It always made me wretched that I felt what I didn't like
you to know. . . . It was because I thought it would all be conquered,
and you might never see anything to wound you."

"I know, dear," said Lucy. "I know you never meant to make me
unhappy. . . . It is a trouble that has come on us all:—you have more
to bear than I have—and you gave him up, when . . . you did what it
must have been very hard to do."

They were silent again a little while, sitting with clasped hands, and
cheeks leaned together.

"Lucy," Maggie began again, "*he* struggled too. He wanted to be
true to you. He will come back to you. Forgive him—he will be happy
then. . . ."

These words were wrung forth from Maggie's deepest soul, with an
effort like the convulsed clutch of a drowning man. Lucy trembled and
was silent.

A gentle knock came at the door. It was Alice, the maid, who entered
and said—

"I daredn't stay any longer, Miss Deane. They'll find it out, and
there'll be such anger at your coming out so late."

Lucy rose and said, "Very well, Alice—in a minute."

"I'm to go away on Friday, Maggie," she added, when Alice had closed the door again. "When I come back, and am strong, they will let me do as I like. I shall come to you when I please then."

"Lucy," said Maggie, with another great effort, "I pray to God continually that I may never be the cause of sorrow to you any more."

She pressed the little hand that she held between hers, and looked up into the face that was bent over hers. Lucy never forgot that look.

"Maggie," she said in a low voice, that had the solemnity of confession in it, "you are better than I am. I can't. . . ."

She broke off there, and said no more. But they clasped each other again in a last embrace.

CHAPTER V

THE LAST CONFLICT

In the second week of September, Maggie was again sitting in her lonely room, battling with the old shadowy enemies that were for ever slain and rising again. It was past midnight, and the rain was beating heavily against the window, driven with fitful force by the rushing, loud-moaning wind. For, the day after Lucy's visit there had been a sudden change in the weather: the heat and drought had given way to cold variable winds, and heavy falls of rain at intervals; and she had been forbidden to risk the contemplated journey until the weather should become more settled. In the counties higher up the Floss, the rains had been continuous, and the completion of the harvest had been arrested. And now, for the last two days, the rains on this lower course of the river had been incessant, so that the old men had shaken their heads and talked of sixty years ago, when the same sort of weather, happening about the equinox, brought on the great floods, which swept the bridge away, and reduced the town to great misery. But the younger generation, who had seen several small floods, thought lightly of these sombre recollections and forebodings, and Bob Jakin, naturally prone to take a hopeful view of his own luck, laughed at his mother when she regretted their having taken a house by the river-side; observing that but for that they would have had no boats, which were the most lucky of possessions in case of a flood that obliged them to go to a distance for food.

But the careless and the fearful were alike sleeping in their beds now. There was hope that the rain would abate, by the morrow; threatenings of a worse kind, from sudden thaws after falls of snow, had often passed off in the experience of the younger ones; and at the very worst, the banks would be sure to break lower down the river when the tide came in with violence, and so the waters would be carried off, without causing more than temporary inconvenience, and losses that would be felt only by the poorer sort, whom charity would relieve.

All were in their beds now, for it was past midnight: all, except some solitary watchers such as Maggie. She was seated in her little parlour towards the river with one candle, that left everything dim in the room, except a letter which lay before her on the table. That letter, which had come to her to-day, was one of the causes that had kept her up far on into the night—unconscious how the hours were going— careless of seeking rest—with no image of rest coming across her mind, except of that far, far off rest, from which there would be no more waking for her into this struggling earthly life.

Two days before Maggie received that letter, she had been to the Rectory for the last time. The heavy rain would have prevented her from going since; but there was another reason. Dr. Kenn, at first enlightened only by a few hints as to the new turn which gossip and slander had taken in relation to Maggie, had recently been made more fully aware of it by an earnest remonstrance from one of his male parishioners against the indiscretion of persisting in the attempt to overcome the prevalent feeling in the parish by a course of resistance. Dr. Kenn, having a conscience void of offence in the matter, was still inclined to persevere—was still averse to give way before a public sentiment that was odious and contemptible; but he was finally wrought upon by the consideration of the peculiar responsibility attached to his office, of avoiding the appearance of evil—an "appearance" that is always dependent on the average quality of surrounding minds. Where these minds are low and gross, the area of that "appearance" is proportionately widened. Perhaps he was in danger of acting from obstinacy; perhaps it was his duty to succumb: conscientious people are apt to see their duty in that which is the most painful course; and to recede was always painful to Dr. Kenn. He made up his mind that he must advise Maggie to go away from St. Ogg's for a time; and he performed that difficult task with as much delicacy as he could, only stating in vague terms that he found his attempt to countenance her stay was a source of discord between himself and his parishioners, that was likely to obstruct his usefulness as a clergyman. He begged her to allow him to write to a clerical friend of his, who might possibly take her into his own family, as governess; and, if not, would probably know of some other available position for a young woman in whose welfare Dr. Kenn felt a strong interest.

Poor Maggie listened with a trembling lip: she could say nothing but a faint "Thank you—I shall be grateful;" and she walked back to her lodgings, through the driving rain, with a new sense of desolation. She must be a lonely wanderer; she must go out among fresh faces, that would look at her wonderingly, because the days did not seem joyful to her; she must begin a new life, in which she would have to rouse herself to receive new impressions—and she was so unspeakably, sickeningly weary! There was no home, no help for the erring: even those who pitied, were constrained to hardness. But ought she to complain? Ought she to shrink in this way from the long penance of life, which was all the possibility she had of lightening the load to some other sufferers, and so changing that passionate error into a new force of unselfish human love? All the next day she sat in her lonely room, with a window darkened by the cloud and the driving rain, thinking of that future, and wrestling for patience:—for what repose could poor Maggie ever win except by wrestling?

And on the third day—this day of which she had just sat out the close—the letter had come which was lying on the table before her.

The letter was from Stephen. He was come back from Holland: he was at Mudport again, unknown to any of his friends; and had written to her from that place, enclosing the letter to a person whom he trusted in St. Ogg's. From beginning to end, it was a passionate cry of reproach: an appeal against her useless sacrifice of him—of herself: against that perverted notion of right which led her to crush all his hopes, for the sake of a mere idea, and not any substantial good—*his* hopes, whom she loved, and who loved her with that single overpowering passion, that worship, which a man never gives to a woman more than once in his life.

"They have written to me that you are to marry Kenn. As if I should believe that! Perhaps they have told you some such fables about me. Perhaps they tell you I have been 'travelling.' My body has been dragged about somewhere; but *I* have never travelled from the hideous place where you left me—where I started up from the stupor of helpless rage to find you gone.

"Maggie! whose pain can have been like mine? Whose injury is like mine? Who besides me has met that long look of love that has burnt itself into my soul, so that no other image can come there? Maggie, call me back to you!—call me back to life and goodness! I am banished from both now. I have no motives: I am indifferent to everything. Two months have only deepened the certainty that I can never care for life without you. Write me one word—say, 'Come!' In two days I should be with you. Maggie—have you forgotten what it was to be together?— to be within reach of a look—to be within hearing of each other's voice?"

When Maggie first read this letter she felt as if her real temptation had only just begun. At the entrance of the chill dark cavern, we turn with unworn courage from the warm light; but how, when we have trodden far in the damp darkness, and have begun to be faint and weary—how, if there is a sudden opening above us, and we are invited back again to the life-nourishing day? The leap of natural longing from under the pressure of pain is so strong, that all less immediate motives are likely to be forgotten—till the pain has been escaped from.

For hours Maggie felt as if her struggle had been in vain. For hours every other thought that she strove to summon was thrust aside by the image of Stephen waiting for the single word that would bring him to her. She did not *read* the letter: she heard him uttering it, and the voice shook her with its old strange power. All the day before she had been filled with the vision of a lonely future through which she must carry the burthen of regret, upheld only by clinging faith. And here—close within her reach—urging itself upon her even as a claim—was another future, in which hard endurance and effort were to be exchanged for easy delicious leaning on another's loving strength! And yet that promise of joy in the place of sadness did not make the dire force of the temptation to Maggie. It was Stephen's tone of misery,—it was the doubt in the justice of her own resolve, that made the balance tremble, and made her once start from her seat to reach the pen and paper, and write "Come!"

But close upon that decisive act, her mind recoiled; and the sense of contradiction with her past self in her moments of strength and clearness, came upon her like a pang of conscious degradation. No—she must wait—she must pray—the light that had forsaken her would come again: she should feel again what she had felt, when she had fled away, under an inspiration strong enough to conquer agony—to conquer love: she should feel again what she had felt when Lucy stood by her, when Philip's letter had stirred all the fibres that bound her to the calmer past.

She sat quite still, far on into the night: with no impulse to change her attitude, without active force enough even for the mental act of prayer: only waiting for the light that would surely come again. It came with the memories that no passion could long quench: the long past came back to her, and with it the fountains of self-renouncing pity and affection, of faithfulness and resolve. The words that were marked by the quiet hand in the little old book that she had long ago learned by heart, rushed even to her lips, and found a vent for themselves in a low murmur that was quite lost in the loud driving of the rain against the window and the loud moan and roar of the wind: "I have received the Cross, I have received it from Thy hand; I will bear it, and bear it till death, as Thou hast laid it upon me."

But soon other words rose that could find no utterance but in a sob: "Forgive me, Stephen! It will pass away. You will come back to her."

She took up the letter, held it to the candle, and let it burn slowly on the hearth. To-morrow she would write to him the last word of parting.

"I will bear it, and bear it till death. . . . But how long it will be before death comes! I am so young, so healthy. How shall I have patience and strength? Am I to struggle and fall and repent again?— has life other trials as hard for me still?" With that cry of self-despair, Maggie fell on her knees against the table, and buried her sorrow-stricken face. Her soul went out to the Unseen Pity that would be with her to the end. Surely there was something being taught her by this experience of great need; and she must be learning a secret of human tenderness and long-suffering, that the less erring could hardly know? "O, God, if my life is to be long, let me live to bless and comfort——"

At that moment Maggie felt a startling sensation of sudden cold about her knees and feet: it was water flowing under her. She started up: the stream was flowing under the door that led into the passage. She was not bewildered for an instant—she knew it was the flood!

The tumult of emotion she had been enduring for the last twelve hours seemed to have left a great calm in her: without screaming, she hurried with the candle up-stairs to Bob Jakin's bedroom. The door was ajar; she went in and shook him by the shoulder.

"Bob, the flood is come! it is in the house! let us see if we can make the boats safe."

She lighted his candle, while the poor wife, snatching up her baby, burst into screams; and then she hurried down again to see if the waters were rising fast. There was a step down into the room at the door leading from the staircase: she saw that the water was already on a level with the step. While she was looking, something came with a tremendous crash against the window, and sent the leaded panes and the old wooden framework inwards in shivers,—the water pouring in after it.

"It is the boat!" cried Maggie. "Bob, come down to get the boats!"

And without a moment's shudder of fear, she plunged through the water, which was rising fast to her knees, and by the glimmering light of the candle she had left on the stairs, she mounted on to the window-sill, and crept into the boat, which was left with the prow lodging and protruding through the window. Bob was not long after her, hurrying without shoes or stockings, but with the lanthorn in his hand.

"Why, they're both here—both the boats," said Bob, as he got into the one where Maggie was. "It's wonderful this fastening isn't broke too, as well as the mooring."

In the excitement of getting into the other boat, unfastening it and mastering an oar, Bob was not struck with the danger Maggie incurred. We are not apt to fear for the fearless, when we are companions in their danger, and Bob's mind was absorbed in possible expedients for the safety of the helpless in-doors. The fact that Maggie had been up, had waked him, and had taken the lead in activity, gave Bob a vague impression of her as one who would help to protect, not need to be protected. She too had got possession of an oar, and had pushed off, so as to release the boat from the over-hanging window-frame.

"The water's rising so fast," said Bob, "I doubt it'll be in at the chambers before long—th' house is so low. I've more mind to get Prissy and the child and the mother into the boat, if I could, and trusten to the water—for th' old house is none so safe. And if I let go the boat . . . but *you*," he exclaimed, suddenly lifting the light of his lanthorn on Maggie, as she stood in the rain with the oar in her hand and her black hair streaming.

Maggie had no time to answer, for a new tidal current swept along the line of the houses, and drove both the boats out on to the wide water, with a force that carried them far past the meeting current of the river.

In the first moments Maggie felt nothing, thought of nothing, but that she had suddenly passed away from that life which she had been

dreading: it was the transition of death, without its agony—and she
was alone in the darkness with God.

The whole thing had been so rapid—so dreamlike—that the threads
of ordinary association were broken: she sank down on the seat clutching the oar mechanically, and for a long while had no distinct conception of her position. The first thing that waked her to fuller consciousness, was the cessation of the rain, and a perception that the darkness
was divided by the faintest light, which parted the overhanging gloom
from the immeasurable watery level below. She was driven out upon
the flood:—that awful visitation of God which her father used to talk
of—which had made the nightmare of her childish dreams. And with
that thought there rushed in the vision of the old home—and Tom—and
her mother—they had all listened together.

"O, God, where am I? Which is the way home?" she cried out, in
the dim loneliness.

What was happening to them at the Mill? The flood had once nearly
destroyed it. They might be in danger—in distress: her mother and her
brother, alone there, beyond reach of help! Her whole soul was strained
now on that thought; and she saw the long-loved faces looking for
help into the darkness, and finding none.

She was floating in smooth water now—perhaps far on the over-
flooded fields. There was no sense of present danger to check the out-
going of her mind to the old home; and she strained her eyes against
the curtain of gloom that she might seize the first sight of her whereabout—that she might catch some faint suggestion of the spot towards
which all her anxieties tended.

O, how welcome, the widening of that dismal watery level—the
gradual uplifting of the cloudy firmament—the slowly defining blackness of objects above the glassy dark! Yes—she must be out on the
fields—those were the tops of hedgerow trees. Which way did the river
lie? Looking behind her, she saw the lines of black trees: looking before
her there were none: then, the river lay before her. She seized an oar
and began to paddle the boat forward with the energy of wakening
hope: the dawning seemed to advance more swiftly, now she was in
action; and she could soon see the poor dumb beasts crowding piteously
on a mound where they had taken refuge. Onward she paddled and
rowed by turns in the growing twilight: her wet clothes clung round
her, and her streaming hair was dashed about by the wind, but she was
hardly conscious of any bodily sensations—except a sensation of
strength, inspired by mighty emotion. Along with the sense of danger
and possible rescue for those long-remembered beings at the old home,
there was an undefined sense of reconcilement with her brother: what
quarrel, what harshness, what unbelief in each other can subsist in the
presence of a great calamity, when all the artificial vesture of our life
is gone, and we are all one with each other in primitive mortal needs?
Vaguely, Maggie felt this;—in the strong resurgent love towards her

brother that swept away all the later impressions of hard, cruel offence and misunderstanding, and left only the deep, underlying, unshakable memories of early union.

But now there was a large dark mass in the distance, and near to her Maggie could discern the current of the river. The dark mass must be— yes, it was—St. Ogg's. Ah, now she knew which way to look for the first glimpse of the well-known trees—the grey willows, the now yellow-ing chestnuts—and above them the old roof! But there was no colour, no shape yet: all was faint and dim. More and more strongly the ener-gies seemed to come and put themselves forth, as if her life were a stored-up force that was being spent in this hour, unneeded for any future.

She must get her boat into the current of the Floss, else she would never be able to pass the Ripple, and approach the house: this was the thought that occurred to her, as she imagined with more and more vividness the state of things round the old home. But then she might be carried very far down, and be unable to guide her boat out of the current again. For the first time distinct ideas of danger began to press upon her; but there was no choice of courses, no room for hesitation, and she floated into the current. Swiftly she went now, without effort; more and more clearly in the lessening distance and the growing light she began to discern the objects that she knew must be the well-known trees and roofs; nay, she was not far off a rushing muddy current that must be the strangely altered Ripple.

Great God! there were floating masses in it, that might dash against her boat as she passed, and cause her to perish too soon. What were those masses?

For the first time Maggie's heart began to beat in an agony of dread. She sat helpless—dimly conscious that she was being floated along— more intensely conscious of the anticipated clash. But the horror was transient: it passed away before the oncoming warehouses of St. Ogg's: she had passed the mouth of the Ripple, then: *now*, she must use all her skill and power to manage the boat and get it if possible out of the current. She could see now that the bridge was broken down: she could see the masts of a stranded vessel far out over the watery field. But no boats were to be seen moving on the river—such as had been laid hands on were employed in the flooded streets.

With new resolution, Maggie seized her oar, and stood up again to paddle; but the now ebbing tide added to the swiftness of the river, and she was carried along beyond the bridge. She could hear shouts from the windows overlooking the river, as if the people there were calling to her. It was not till she had passed on nearly to Tofton that she could get the boat clear of the current. Then with one yearning look towards her uncle Deane's house that lay farther down the river, she took to both her oars and rowed with all her might across the watery fields, back towards the Mill. Colour was beginning to awake now, and as she approached the Dorlcote fields, she could discern the tints of the trees—could see the old Scotch firs far to the right, and the home chestnuts—O! how deep they lay in the water: deeper than the trees on this side the hill. And the roof of the Mill—where was it? Those heavy fragments hurrying down the Ripple—what had they meant? But it was not the house—the house stood firm: drowned up to the first story, but still firm—or was it broken in at the end towards the Mill?

With panting joy that she was there at last—joy that overcame all distress, Maggie neared the front of the house. At first she heard no sound: she saw no object moving. Her boat was on a level with the up-stairs windows. She called out in a loud piercing voice,

"Tom, where are you? Mother, where are you? Here is Maggie!"

Soon, from the window of the attic in the central gable, she heard Tom's voice:

"Who is it? Have you brought a boat?"

"It is I, Tom—Maggie. Where is mother?"

"She is not here: she went to Garum, the day before yesterday. I'll come down to the lower window."

"Alone, Maggie?" said Tom, in a voice of deep astonishment, as he opened the middle window on a level with the boat.

"Yes, Tom: God has taken care of me, to bring me to you. Get in quickly. Is there no one else?"

"No," said Tom, stepping into the boat, "I fear the man is drowned: he was carried down the Ripple, I think, when part of the mill fell with the crash of trees and stones against it: I've shouted again and again, and there has been no answer. Give me the oars, Maggie."

It was not till Tom had pushed off and they were on the wide water—he face to face with Maggie—that the full meaning of what had happened rushed upon his mind. It came with so overpowering a force—it was such a new revelation to his spirit, of the depths in life, that had lain beyond his vision which he had fancied so keen and clear—that he was unable to ask a question. They sat mutely gazing at each other: Maggie with eyes of intense life looking out from a weary, beaten face—Tom pale with a certain awe and humiliation. Thought was busy though the lips were silent: and though he could ask no question, he guessed a story of almost miraculous divinely-protected effort. But at last a mist gathered over the blue-grey eyes, and the lips found a word they could utter: the old childish—"Magsie!"

Maggie could make no answer but a long deep sob of that mysterious wondrous happiness that is one with pain.

As soon as she could speak, she said, "We will go to Lucy, Tom: we'll go and see if she is safe, and then we can help the rest."

Tom rowed with untired vigour, and with a different speed from poor Maggie's. The boat was soon in the current of the river again, and soon they would be at Tofton.

"Park House stands high up out of the flood," said Maggie. "Perhaps they have got Lucy there."

Nothing else was said; a new danger was being carried towards them by the river. Some wooden machinery had just given way on one of the wharves, and huge fragments were being floated along. The sun was rising now, and the wide area of watery desolation was spread out in dreadful clearness around them—in dreadful clearness floated onwards the hurrying, threatening masses. A large company in a boat that was working its way along under the Tofton houses, observed their danger, and shouted, "Get out of the current!"

But that could not be done at once, and Tom, looking before him, saw death rushing on them. Huge fragments, clinging together in fatal fellowship, made one wide mass across the stream.

"It is coming, Maggie!" Tom said, in a deep hoarse voice, loosing the oars, and clasping her.

The next instant the boat was no longer seen upon the water—and the huge mass was hurrying on in hideous triumph.

But soon the keel of the boat reappeared, a black speck on the golden water.

The boat reappeared—but brother and sister had gone down in an embrace never to be parted: living through again in one supreme moment, the days when they had clasped their little hands in love, and roamed the daisied fields together.

CONCLUSION

NATURE repairs her ravages—repairs them with her sunshine, and with human labour. The desolation wrought by that flood, had left little visible trace on the face of the earth, five years after. The fifth autumn was rich in golden corn-stacks, rising in thick clusters among the distant hedgerows; the wharves and warehouses on the Floss were busy again, with echoes of eager voices, with hopeful lading and unlading.

And every man and woman mentioned in this history was still living —except those whose end we know.

Nature repairs her ravages—but not all. The uptorn trees are not rooted again; the parted hills are left scarred: if there is a new growth, the trees are not the same as the old, and the hills underneath their green vesture bear the marks of the past rending. To the eyes that have dwelt on the past, there is no thorough repair.

Dorlcote Mill was rebuilt. And Dorlcote church-yard,—where the brick grave that held a father whom we know, was found with the stone laid prostrate upon it after the flood,—had recovered all its grassy order and decent quiet.

Near that brick grave there was a tomb erected, very soon after the flood, for two bodies that were found in close embrace; and it was visited at different moments by two men who both felt that their keenest joy and keenest sorrow were for ever buried there.

One of them visited the tomb again with a sweet face beside him—but that was years after.

The other was always solitary. His great companionship was among the trees of the Red Deeps, where the buried joy seemed still to hover—like a revisiting spirit.

The tomb bore the names of Tom and Maggie Tulliver, and below the names it was written—

"In their death they were not divided."

SILAS MARNER:

THE WEAVER OF RAVELOE.

"A child, more than all other gifts
That earth can offer to declining man,
Brings hope with it, and forward-looking thoughts."

WORDSWORTH.

PART ONE

★

CHAPTER I

IN the days when the spinning-wheels hummed busily in the farm-houses—and even great ladies, clothed in silk and thread-lace, had their toy spinning-wheels of polished oak—there might be seen in districts far away among the lanes, or deep in the bosom of the hills, certain pallid undersized men, who, by the side of the brawny country-folk, looked like the remnants of a disinherited race. The shepherd's dog barked fiercely when one of these alien-looking men appeared on the upland, dark against the early winter sunset; for what dog likes a figure bent under a heavy bag?—and these pale men rarely stirred abroad without that mysterious burden. The shepherd himself, though he had good reason to believe that the bag held nothing but flaxen thread, or else the long rolls of strong linen spun from that thread, was not quite sure that this trade of weaving, indispensable though it was, could be carried on entirely without the help of the Evil One. In that far-off time superstition clung easily round every person or thing that was at all unwonted, or even intermittent and occasional merely, like the visits of the peddler or the knife-grinder. No one knew where wandering men had their homes or their origin; and how was a man to be explained unless you at least knew somebody who knew his father and mother? To the peasants of old times, the world outside their own direct experience was a region of vagueness and mystery: to their un-travelled thought a state of wandering was a conception as dim as the winter life of the swallows that came back with the spring; and even a settler, if he came from distant parts, hardly ever ceased to be viewed with a remnant of distrust, which would have prevented any surprise if a long course of inoffensive conduct on his part had ended in the commission of a crime; especially if he had any reputation for knowledge, or showed any skill in handicraft. All cleverness, whether in the rapid use of that difficult instrument the tongue, or in some other art unfamiliar to villagers, was in itself suspicious: honest folks, born and bred in a visible manner, were mostly not over-wise or clever—at least not beyond such a matter as knowing the signs of the weather; and the process by which rapidity and dexterity of any kind were acquired was so wholly hidden, that they partook of the nature of conjuring. In this way it came to pass that those scattered linen-weavers—emigrants from the town into the country—were to the last regarded as aliens by their rustic neighbors, and usually contracted the eccentric habits which belong to a state of loneliness.

In the early years of this century, such a linen-weaver, named Silas Marner, worked at his vocation in a stone cottage that stood among the nutty hedgerows near the village of Raveloe, and not far from the edge of a deserted stone-pit. The questionable sound of Silas's loom, so unlike the natural cheerful trotting of the winnowing machine, or the simpler rhythm of the flail, had a half-fearful fascination for the Raveloe boys, who would often leave off their nutting or birds'-nesting to peep in at the window of the stone cottage, counterbalancing a certain awe at the mysterious action of the loom, by a pleasant sense of scornful superiority, drawn from the mockery of its alternating noises, along with the bent, tread-mill attitude of the weaver. But sometimes it happened that Marner, pausing to adjust an irregularity in his thread, became aware of the small scoundrels, and, though chary of his time, he liked their intrusion so ill that he would descend from his loom, and, opening the door, would fix on them a gaze that was always enough to make them take to their legs in terror. For how was it possible to believe that those large brown protuberant eyes in Silas Marner's pale face really saw nothing very distinctly that was not close to them and not rather that their dreadful stare could dart cramp, or rickets, or a wry mouth at any boy who happened to be in the rear? They had, perhaps, heard their fathers and mothers hint that Silas Marner could cure folks' rheumatism if he had a mind, and add, still more darkly, that if you could only speak the devil fair enough, he might save you the cost of the doctor. Such strange lingering echoes of the old demon-worship might perhaps even now be caught by the diligent listener among the grey-haired peasantry; for the rude mind with difficulty associates the ideas of power and benignity. A shadowy conception of power that by much persuasion can be induced to refrain from inflicting harm, is the shape most easily taken by the sense of the Invisible in the minds of men who have always been pressed close by primitive wants, and to whom a life of hard toil has never been illuminated by any enthusiastic religious faith. To them pain and mishap present a far wider range of possibilities than gladness and enjoyment: their imagination is almost barren of the images that feed desire and hope, but is all overgrown by recollections that are a perpetual pasture to fear. "Is there any thing you can fancy that you would like to eat?" I once said to an old laboring man, who was in his last illness, and who had refused all the food his wife had offered him. "No," he answered, "I've never been used to nothing but common victual, and I can't eat that." Experience had bred no fancies in him that could raise the phantasm of appetite.

And Raveloe was a village where many of the old echoes lingered, undrowned by new voices. Not that it was one of those barren parishes lying on the outskirts of civilization—inhabited by meagre sheep and thinly-scattered shepherds: on the contrary, it lay in the rich central plain of what we are pleased to call Merry England, and held farms which, speaking from a spiritual point of view, paid highly-desirable tithes. But it was nestled in a snug well-wooded hollow, quite an hour's journey on horseback from any turnpike, where it was never reached by the vibrations of the coach-horn, or of public opinion. It was an important-looking village, with a fine old church and large churchyard in the heart of it, and two or three large brick-and-stone homesteads, with well-walled orchards and ornamental weather-cocks, standing close upon the road, and lifting more imposing fronts than the rectory, which peeped from among the trees on the other side of the churchyard; a village which showed at once the summits of its social life, and told the practised eye that there was no great park and manor-house in the vicinity, but that there were several chiefs in Raveloe who could farm badly quite at their ease, drawing enough money from their bad farming, in those war times, to live in a rollicking fashion, and keep a jolly Christmas, Whitsun, and Easter tide.

It was fifteen years since Silas Marner had first come to Raveloe; he was then simply a pallid young man, with prominent, short-sighted brown eyes, whose appearance would have had nothing strange for people of average culture and experience, but for the villagers near whom he had come to settle it had mysterious peculiarities which corresponded with the exceptional nature of his occupation, and his advent from an unknown region called "North'ard." So had his way of life: he invited no comer to step across his door-sill, and he never strolled into the village to drink a pint at the Rainbow, or to gossip at the wheelwright's: he sought no man or woman, save for the purposes of his calling, or in order to supply himself with necessaries; and it was soon clear to the Raveloe lasses that he would never urge one of them to accept him against her will—quite as if he had heard them declare that they would never marry a dead man come to life again. This view of Marner's personality was not without another ground than his pale face and unexampled eyes; for Jem Rodney, the mole-catcher, averred that, one evening as he was returning homeward, he saw Silas Marner leaning against a stile with a heavy bag on his back, instead of resting the bag on the stile as a man in his senses would have done; and that, on coming up to him, he saw that Marner's eyes were set like a dead man's, and he spoke to him, and shook him, and his limbs were stiff, and his hands clutched the bag as if they'd been made of iron; but just as he had made up his mind that the weaver was dead, he came all right again, like, as you might say, in the winking of an eye, and said "Good-night," and walked off. All this Jem swore he had seen, more by token that it was the very day he had been mole-catching on Squire Cass's land, down by the old saw-pit. Some said Marner must have been in a "fit," a word which seemed to explain things otherwise incredible; but the argumentative Mr. Macey, clerk of the parish, shook his head, and asked if any body was ever known to go off in a fit and not fall down. A fit was a stroke, wasn't it? and it was in the nature of a stroke to partly take away the use of a man's limbs and throw him on the parish, if

he'd got no children to look to. No, no; it was no stroke that would
let a man stand on his legs, like a horse between the shafts, and then
walk off as soon as you can say "Gee!" But there might be such a
thing as a man's soul being loose from his body, and going out and in,
like a bird out of its nest and back; and that was how folks got over-
wise, for they went to school in this shell-less state to those who could
teach them more than their neighbors could learn with their five senses
and the parson. And where did Master Marner get his knowledge of
herbs from—and charms too, if he liked to give them away? Jem
Rodney's story was no more than what might have been expected by
any body who had seen how Marner had cured Sally Oates, and made
her sleep like a baby, when her heart had been beating enough to burst
her body, for two months and more, while she had been under the
doctor's care. He might cure more folks if he would; but he was worth
speaking fair, if it was only to keep him from doing you a mischief.

It was partly to this vague fear that Marner was indebted for protecting him from the persecution that his singularities might have
drawn upon him, but still more to the fact that, the old linen-weaver in
the neighboring parish of Tarley being dead, his handicraft made him
a highly welcome settler to the richer housewives of the district, and
even to the more provident cottagers, who had their little stock of yarn
at the year's end; and their sense of his usefulness would have counteracted any repugnance or suspicion which was not confirmed by a deficiency in the quality or the tale of the cloth he wove for them. And
the years had rolled on without producing any change in the impressions of the neighbors concerning Marner, except the change from
novelty to habit. At the end of fifteen years the Raveloe men said just
the same things about Silas Marner as at the beginning: they did not
say them quite so often, but they believed them much more strongly
when they did say them. There was only one important addition which
the years had brought: it was, that Master Marner had laid by a fine
sight of money somewhere, and that he could buy up "bigger men"
than himself.

But while opinion concerning him had remained nearly stationary,
and his daily habits had presented scarcely any visible change, Marner's
inward life had been a history and a metamorphosis, as that of every
fervid nature must be when it has fled, or been condemned to solitude.
His life, before he came to Raveloe, had been filled with the movement,
the mental activity, and the close fellowship which, in that day as in
this, marked the life of an artisan early incorporated in a narrow religious sect, where the poorest layman has the chance of distinguishing
himself by gifts of speech, and has, at the very least, the weight of a
silent voter in the government of his community. Marner was highly
thought of in that little hidden world, known to itself as the church
assembling in Lantern Yard; he was believed to be a young man of
exemplary life and ardent faith; and a peculiar interest had been

centred in him ever since he had fallen, at a prayer-meeting, into a
mysterious rigidity and suspension of consciousness, which, lasting for
an hour or more, had been mistaken for death. To have sought a medical explanation for this phenomenon would have been held by Silas
himself, as well as by his minister and fellow-members, a wilful self-
exclusion from the spiritual significance that might lie therein. Silas
was evidently a brother selected for a peculiar discipline, and though
the effort to interpret this discipline was discouraged by the absence, on
his part, of any spiritual vision during his outward trance, yet it was
believed by himself and others that its effect was seen in an accession of
light and fervor. A less truthful man than him might have been tempted
into the subsequent creation of a vision in the form of resurgent memory; a less sane man might have believed in such a creation; but Silas
was both sane and honest, though, as with many honest and fervent
men, culture had not defined any channels for his sense of mystery, and
so it spread itself over the proper pathway of inquiry and knowledge.
He had inherited from his mother some acquaintance with medicinal
herbs and their preparation—a little store of wisdom which she had
imparted to him as a solemn bequest—but of late years he had had
doubts about the lawfulness of applying this knowledge, believing that
herbs could have no efficacy without prayer, and that prayer might
suffice without herbs; so that the inherited delight he had in wandering
in the fields in search of foxglove and dandelion and coltsfoot, began to
wear to him the character of a temptation.

Among the members of his church there was one young man, a little
older than himself, with whom he had long lived in such close friendship that it was the custom of their Lantern Yard brethren to call them
David and Jonathan. The real name of the friend was William Dane,
and he, too, was regarded as a shining instance of youthful piety,
though somewhat given to over-severity towards weaker brethren, and
to be so dazzled by his own light as to hold himself wiser than his
teachers. But whatever blemishes others might discern in William, to
his friend's mind he was faultless; for Marner had one of those impressible self-doubting natures which, at an inexperienced age, admire
imperativeness and lean on contradiction. The expression of trusting
simplicity in Marner's face, heightened by that absence of special observation, that defenseless, deer-like gaze which belongs to large prominent eyes, was strongly contrasted by the self-complacent suppression
of inward triumph that lurked in the narrow slanting eyes and compressed lips of William Dane. One of the most frequent topics of conversation between the two friends was Assurance of Salvation: Silas
confessed that he could never arrive at any thing higher than hope
mingled with fear, and listened with longing wonder when William declared that he had possessed unshaken assurance ever since, in the
period of his conversion, he had dreamed that he saw the words "calling
and election sure" standing by themselves on a white page in the open

Bible. Such colloquies have occupied many a pair of pale-faced weavers, whose unnurtured souls have been like young winged things, fluttering forsaken in the twilight.

It had seemed to the unsuspecting Silas that the friendship had suffered no chill even from his formation of another attachment of a closer kind. For some months he had been engaged to a young servant-woman, waiting only for a little increase to their mutual savings in order to their marriage; and it was a great delight to him that Sarah did not object to William's occasional presence in their Sunday interviews. It was at this point in their history that Silas's cataleptic fit occurred during the prayer-meeting; and amidst the various queries and expressions of interest addressed to him by his fellow-members, William's suggestion alone jarred with the general sympathy towards a brother thus singled out for special dealings. He observed that, to him, this trance looked more like a visitation of Satan than a proof of divine favour, and exhorted his friend to see that he hid no accursed thing within his soul. Silas, feeling bound to accept rebuke and admonition as a brotherly office, felt no resentment, but only pain, at his friend's doubts concerning him; and to this was soon added some anxiety at the perception that Sarah's manner towards him began to exhibit a strange fluctuation between an effort at an increased manifestation of regard and involuntary signs of shrinking and dislike. He asked her if she wished to break off their engagement; but she denied this: their engagement was known to the church, and had been recognized in the prayer-meetings; it could not be broken off without strict investigation, and Sarah could render no reason that would be sanctioned by the feeling of the community. At this time the senior deacon was taken dangerously ill, and, being a childless widower, he was tended night and day by some of the younger brethren or sisters. Silas frequently took his turn in the night-watching with William, the one relieving the other at two in the morning. The old man, contrary to expectation, seemed to be on the way to recovery, when one night Silas, sitting up by his bedside, observed that his usual audible breathing had ceased. The candle was burning low, and he had to lift it to see the patient's face distinctly. Examination convinced him that the deacon was dead—had been dead some time, for the limbs were rigid. Silas asked himself if he had been asleep, and looked at the clock: it was already four in the morning. How was it that William had not come? In much anxiety he went to seek for help, and soon there were several friends assembled in the house, the minister among them, while Silas went away to his work, wishing he could have met William to know the reason of his non-appearance. But at six o'clock, as he was thinking of going to seek his friend, William came, and with him the minister. They came to summon him to Lantern Yard, to meet the church members there; and to his inquiry concerning the cause of the summons the only reply was, "You will hear." Nothing further was said until Silas was seated in the vestry, in front of the minister, with the eyes of those who to him represented God's people fixed solemnly upon him. Then the minister, taking out a pocket-knife, showed it to Silas, and asked him if he knew where he had left that knife? Silas said, he did not know that he had left it anywhere out of his own pocket—but he was trembling at this strange interrogation. He was then exhorted not to hide his sin, but to confess and repent. The knife had been found in the bureau by the departed deacon's bedside—found in the place where the little bag of church money had lain, which the minister himself had seen the day before. Some hand had removed that bag; and whose hand could it be, if not that of the man to whom the knife belonged? For some time Silas was mute with astonishment: then he said, "God will clear me: I know nothing about the knife being there, or the money being gone. Search me and my dwelling; you will find nothing but three pound five of my own savings, which William Dane knows I have had these six months." At this William groaned, but the minister said, "The proof is heavy against you, brother Marner. The money was taken in the night last past, and no man was with our departed brother but you, for William Dane declares to us that he was hindered by sudden sickness from going to take his place as usual, and you yourself said that he had not come; and, moreover, you neglected the dead body."

"I must have slept," said Silas. Then, after a pause, he added, "Or I must have had another visitation like that which you have all seen me under, so that the thief must have come and gone while I was not in the body, but out of the body. But, I say again, search me and my dwelling, for I have been nowhere else."

The search was made, and it ended—in William Dane's finding the well-known bag, empty, tucked behind the chest of drawers in Silas's chamber! On this William exhorted his friend to confess, and not to hide his sin any longer. Silas turned a look of keen reproach on him, and said, "William, for nine years that we have gone in and out together, have you ever known me tell a lie? But God will clear me."

"Brother," said William, "how do I know what you may have done in the secret chambers of your heart, to give Satan an advantage over you?"

Silas was still looking at his friend. Suddenly a deep flush came over his face, and he was about to speak impetuously, when he seemed checked again by some inward shock, that sent the flush back and made him tremble. But at last he spoke feebly, looking at William.

"I remember now—the knife wasn't in my pocket."

William said, "I know nothing of what you mean." The other persons present, however, began to inquire where Silas meant to say that the knife was, but he would give no further explanation: he only said, "I am sore stricken; I can say nothing. God will clear me."

On their return to the vestry there was further deliberation. Any resort to legal measures for ascertaining the culprit was contrary to the principles of the Church: prosecution was held by them to be forbidden to Christians, even if it had been a case in which there was no scandal to the community. But they were bound to take other measures for finding out the truth, and they resolved on praying and drawing lots. This resolution can be a ground of surprise only to those who are unacquainted with that obscure religious life which has gone on in the alleys of our towns. Silas knelt with his brethren, relying on his own innocence being certified by immediate divine interference, but feeling that there was sorrow and mourning behind for him even then—that his trust in man had been cruelly bruised. *The lots declared that Silas Marner was guilty.* He was solemnly suspended from church-membership, and called upon to render up the stolen money: only on confession, as the sign of repentance, could he be received once more within the fold of the church. Marner listened in silence. At last, when every one rose to depart, he went towards William Dane and said, in a voice shaken by agitation—

"The last time I remember using my knife, was when I took it out to cut a strap for you. I don't remember putting it in my pocket again. *You* stole the money, and you have woven a plot to lay the sin at my door. But you may prosper, for all that: there is no just God that governs the earth righteously, but a God of lies, that bears witness against the innocent."

There was a general shudder at this blasphemy.

William said meekly, "I leave our brethren to judge whether this is the voice of Satan or not. I can do nothing but pray for you, Silas."

Poor Marner went out with that despair in his soul—that shaken trust in God and man, which is little short of madness to a loving nature. In the bitterness of his wounded spirit, he said to himself, "*She* will cast me off too." And he reflected that, if she did not believe the testimony against him, her whole faith must be upset as his was. To people accustomed to reason about the forms in which their religious feeling has incorporated itself, it is difficult to enter into that simple, untaught state of mind in which the form and the feeling have never been severed by an act of reflection. We are apt to think it inevitable that a man in Marner's position should have begun to question the validity of an appeal to the divine judgment by drawing lots; but to him this would have been an effort of independent thought such as he had never known; and he must have made the effort at a moment when all his energies were turned into the anguish of disappointed faith. If there is an angel who records the sorrows of men as well as their sins, he knows how many and deep are the sorrows that spring from false ideas for which no man is culpable.

Marner went home, and for a whole day sat alone, stunned by despair, without any impulse to go to Sarah and attempt to win her belief in his innocence. The second day he took refuge from benumbing unbelief, by getting into his loom and working away as usual; and before many hours were past, the minister and one of the deacons came to him with the message from Sarah, that she held her engagement to him at an end. Silas received the message mutely, and then turned away from the messengers to work at his loom again. In little more than a month from that time, Sarah was married to William Dane; and not long afterwards it was known to the brethren in Lantern Yard that Silas Marner had departed from the town.

CHAPTER II

EVEN people whose lives have been made various by learning, sometimes find it hard to keep a fast hold on their habitual views of life, on their faith in the Invisible—nay, on the sense that their past joys and sorrows are a real experience, when they are suddenly transported to a new land, where the beings around them know nothing of their history, and share none of their ideas—where their mother earth shows another lap, and human life has other forms than those on which their souls have been nourished. Minds that have been unhinged from their old faith and love, have perhaps sought this Lethean influence of exile, in which the past becomes dreamy because its symbols have all vanished, and the present too is dreamy because it is linked with no memories. But even *their* experience may hardly enable them thoroughly to imagine what was the effect on a simple weaver like Silas Marner, when he left his own country and people and came to settle in Raveloe. Nothing could be more unlike his native town, set within sight of the wide-spread hillsides, than this low, wooded region, where he felt hidden even from the heavens by the screening trees and hedgerows. There was nothing here, when he rose in the deep morning quiet and looked out on the dewy brambles and rank tufted grass, that seemed to have any relation with that life centring in Lantern Yard, which had once been to him the altar-place of high dispensations. The white-washed walls; the little pews where well-known figures entered with a subdued rustling, and where first one well-known voice and then another, pitched in a peculiar key of petition, uttered phrases at once occult and familiar, like the amulet worn on the heart; the pulpit where the minister delivered unquestioned doctrine, and swayed to and fro, and handled the book in a long accustomed manner; the very pauses between the couplets of the hymn, as it was given out, and the recurrent swell of voices in song; these things had been the channel of divine influences to Marner—they were the fostering home of his religious emotions—they were Christianity and God's kingdom upon earth. A weaver who finds hard words in his hymn-book knows nothing of abstractions; as the little child knows nothing of parental love, but only knows one face and one lap towards which it stretches its arms for refuge and nurture.

And what could be more unlike that Lantern Yard world than the world in Raveloe?—orchards looking lazy with neglected plenty; the large church in the wide churchyard, which men gazed at lounging at their own doors in service-time; the purple-faced farmers jogging along the lanes or turning in at the Rainbow; homesteads, where men supped heavily and slept in the light of the evening hearth, and where women seemed to be laying up a stock of linen for the life to come. There were no lips in Raveloe from which a word could fall that would stir Silas Marner's benumbed faith to a sense of pain. In the early ages of the world, we know, it was believed that each territory was inhabited and ruled by its own divinities, so that a man could cross the bordering heights and be out of the reach of his native gods, whose presence was confined to the streams and the groves and the hills among which he had lived from his birth. And poor Silas was vaguely conscious of something not unlike the feeling of primitive men, when they fled thus, in fear or in sullenness, from the face of an unpropitious deity. It seemed to him that the Power in which he had vainly trusted among the streets and in the prayer-meetings, was very far away from this land in which he had taken refuge, where men lived in careless abundance, knowing and needing nothing of that trust, which, for him, had been turned to bitterness. The little light he possessed spread its beams so narrowly, that frustrated belief was a curtain broad enough to create for him the blackness of night.

His first movement after the shock had been to work in his loom; and he went on with this unremittingly, never asking himself why, now he was come to Raveloe, he worked far on into the night to finish the tale of Mrs. Osgood's table-linen sooner than she expected—without contemplating beforehand the money she would put into his hand for the work. He seemed to weave, like the spider, from pure impulse, without reflection. Every man's work, pursued steadily, tends in this way to become an end in itself, and so to bridge over the loveless chasms of his life. Silas's hand satisfied itself with throwing the shuttle, and his eye with seeing the little squares in the cloth complete themselves under his effort. Then there were the calls of hunger; and Silas, in his solitude, had to provide his own breakfast, dinner, and supper, to fetch his own water from the well, and put his own kettle on the fire; and all these immediate promptings helped, along with the weaving, to reduce his life to the unquestioning activity of a spinning insect. He hated the thought of the past; there was nothing that called out his love and fellowship towards the strangers he had come amongst; and the future was all dark, for there was no Unseen Love that cared for him. Thought was arrested by utter bewilderment, now its old narrow pathway was closed, and affection seemed to have died under the bruise that had fallen on its keenest nerves.

But at last Mrs. Osgood's table-linen was finished, and Silas was paid in gold. His earnings in his native town, where he worked for a wholesale dealer, had been after a lower rate; he had been paid weekly, and of his weekly earnings a large proportion had gone to objects of piety and charity. Now, for the first time in his life, he had five bright guineas put into his hand; no man expected a share of them, and he loved no man that he should offer him a share. But what were the guineas to him who saw no vista beyond countless days of weaving? It was needless for him to ask that, for it was pleasant to him to feel them in his palm, and look at their bright faces, which were all his own: it was another element of life, like the weaving and the satisfaction of hunger, subsisting quite aloof from the life of belief and love from which he had been cut off. The weaver's hand had known the touch of hard-won money even before the palm had grown to its full breadth; for twenty years, mysterious money had stood to him as the symbol of earthly good, and the immediate object of toil. He had seemed to love it little in the years when every penny had its purpose for him; for he loved the *purpose* then. But now, when all purpose was gone, that habit of looking towards the money and grasping it with a sense of fulfilled effort made a loam that was deep enough for the seeds of desire; and as Silas walked homeward across the fields in the twilight, he drew out the money, and thought it was brighter in the gathering gloom.

About this time an incident happened which seemed to open a possibility of some fellowship with his neighbors. One day, taking a pair of shoes to be mended, he saw the cobbler's wife seated by the fire, suffering from the terrible symptoms of heart-disease and dropsy, which he had witnessed as the precursors of his mother's death. He felt a rush of pity at the mingled sight and remembrance, and, recalling the relief his mother had found from a simple preparation of foxglove, he promised Sally Oates to bring her something that would ease her, since the doctor did her no good. In this office of charity, Silas felt, for the first time since he had come to Raveloe, a sense of unity between his past and present life, which might have been the beginning of his rescue from the insect-like existence into which his nature had shrunk. But Sally Oates's disease had raised her into a personage of much interest and importance among the neighbors, and the fact of her having found relief from drinking Silas Marner's "stuff" became a matter of general discourse. When Doctor Kimble gave physic, it was natural that it should have an effect; but when a weaver, who came from nobody knew where, worked wonders with a bottle of brown waters, the occult character of the process was evident. Such a sort of thing had not been known since the Wise Woman at Tarley died; and she had charms as well as "stuff:" every body went to her when their children had fits. Silas Marner must be a person of the same sort, for how did he know what would bring back Sally Oates's breath, if he didn't know a fine sight more than that? The Wise Woman had words that she muttered to herself, so that you couldn't hear what they were, and if she tied a bit of red thread round the child's toe the while, it would keep off the water in the head. There were women in Raveloe, at that present time, who had worn one of the Wise Woman's little bags round their necks, and, in consequence, had never had an idiot child, as Ann Coulter had. Silas Marner could very likely do as much, and more; and now it was all clear how he should have come from unknown parts, and be so "comical-looking." But Sally Oates must mind and not tell the doctor, for he would be sure to set his

face against Marner; he was always angry about the Wise Woman, and
used to threaten those who went to her that they should have none of
his help any more.

Silas now found himself and his cottage suddenly beset by mothers
who wanted him to charm away the whooping-cough, or bring back the
milk, and by men who wanted stuff against the rheumatics or the knots
in the hands; and, to secure themselves against a refusal, the applicants
brought silver in their palms. Silas might have driven a profitable trade
in charms as well as in his small list of drugs; but money on this condition was no temptation to him: he had never known an impulse towards falsity, and he drove one after another away with growing irritation, for the news of him as a wise man had spread even to Tarley, and
it was long before people ceased to take long walks for the sake of asking his aid. But the hope in his wisdom was at length changed into dread,
for no one believed him when he said he knew no charms and could
work no cures, and every man and woman who had an accident or a
new attack after applying to him, set the misfortune down to Master
Marner's ill-will and irritated glances. Thus it came to pass that his
movement of pity towards Sally Oates, which had given him a transient
sense of brotherhood, heightened the repulsion between him and his
neighbors, and made his isolation more complete.

Gradually the guineas, the crowns, and the half-crowns, grew to a
heap, and Marner drew less and less for his own wants, trying to solve
the problem of keeping himself strong enough to work sixteen hours a
day on as small an outlay as possible. Have not men, shut up in solitary
imprisonment, found an interest in marking the moments by straight
strokes of a certain length on the wall, until the growth of the sum of
straight strokes, arranged in triangles, has become a mastering purpose?
Do we not while away moments of inanity or fatigued waiting by repeating some trivial movement or sound, until the repetition has bred
a want, which is incipient habit? That will help us to understand how
the love of accumulating money grows an absorbing passion in men
whose imaginations, even in the very beginning of their hoard, showed
them no purpose beyond it. Marner wanted the heaps of ten to grow into
a square, and then into a larger square; and every added guinea, while
it was itself a satisfaction, bred a new desire. In this strange world, made
a hopeless riddle to him, he might, if he had had a less intense nature,
have sat weaving, weaving—looking towards the end of his pattern, or
towards the end of his web, till he forgot the riddle, and every thing else
but his immediate sensations: but the money had come to mark off his
weaving into periods, and the money not only grew, but it remained
with him. He began to think it was conscious of him, as his loom was,
and he would on no account have exchanged those coins, which had become his familiars, for other coins with unknown faces. He handled
them, he counted them, till their form and colour were like the satisfaction of a thirst to him: but it was only in the night, when his work was
done, that he drew them out to enjoy their companionship. He had

taken up some bricks in his floor underneath his loom, and here he had made a hole in which he set the iron pot that contained his guineas and silver coins, covering the bricks with sand whenever he replaced them. Not that the idea of being robbed presented itself often or strongly to his mind: hoarding was common in country districts in those days; there were old laborers in the parish of Raveloe who were known to have their savings by them, probably inside their flock-beds; but their rustic neighbors, though not all of them as honest as their ancestors in the days of King Alfred, had not imaginations bold enough to lay a plan of burglary. How could they have spent the money in their own village without betraying themselves? They would be obliged to "run away"— a course as dark and dubious as a balloon journey.

So, year after year, Silas Marner had lived in this solitude, his guineas rising in the iron pot, and his life narrowing and hardening itself more and more into a mere pulsation of desire and satisfaction that had no relation to any other being. His life had reduced itself to the mere functions of weaving and hoarding, without any contemplation of an end towards which the functions tended. The same sort of process has perhaps been undergone by wiser men, when they have been cut off from faith and love—only, instead of a loom and a heap of guineas, they have had some erudite research, some ingenious project, or some well-knit theory. Strangely Marner's face and figure shrank and bent themselves into a constant mechanical relation to the objects of his life, so that he produced the same sort of impression as a handle or a crooked tube, which has no meaning standing apart. The prominent eyes that used to look trusting and dreamy, now looked as if they had been made to see only one kind of thing that was very small, like tiny grain, for which they hunted everywhere: and he was so withered and yellow, that, though he was not yet forty, the children always called him "Old Master Marner."

Yet even in this stage of withering a little incident happened which showed that the sap of affection was not all gone. It was one of his daily tasks to fetch his water from a well a couple of fields off, and for this purpose, ever since he came to Raveloe, he had had a brown earthenware pot, which he held as his most precious utensil, among the very few conveniences he had granted himself. It had been his companion for twelve years, always standing on the same spot, always lending its handle to him in the early morning, so that its form had an expression for him of willing helpfulness, and the impress of its handle on his palm gave a satisfaction mingled with that of having the fresh clear water. One day as he was returning from the well, he stumbled against the step of the stile, and his brown pot, falling with force against the stones that overarched the ditch below him, was broken in three pieces. Silas picked up the pieces and carried them home with grief in his heart. The brown pot could never be of use to him any more, but he stuck the bits together and propped the ruin in its old place for a memorial.

This is the history of Silas Marner until the fifteenth year after he came to Raveloe. The livelong day he sat in his loom, his ear filled with its monotony, his eyes bent close down on the slow growth of sameness in the brownish web, his muscles moving with such even repetition that their pause seemed almost as much a constraint as the holding of his breath. But at night came his revelry; at night he closed his shutters, and made fast his doors, and drew out his gold. Long ago the heap of coins had become too large for the iron pot to hold them, and he had made for them two thick leather bags, which wasted no room in their resting-place, but lent themselves flexibly to every corner. How the guineas shone as they came pouring out of the dark leather mouths! The silver bore no large proportion in amount to the gold, because the long pieces of linen which formed his chief work were always partly paid for in gold, and out of the silver he supplied his own bodily wants, choosing always the shillings and sixpences to spend in this way. He loved the guineas best, but he would not change the silver—the crowns and half-crowns that were his own earnings, begotten by his labour; he loved them all. He spread them out in heaps and bathed his hands in them; then he counted them and set them up in regular piles, and felt their rounded outline between his thumb and fingers, and thought fondly of the guineas that were only half-earned by the work in his loom, as if they had been unborn children—thought of the guineas that were coming slowly through the coming years, through all his life, which spread far away before him, the end quite hidden by countless days of weaving. No wonder his thoughts were still with his loom and his money when he made his journeys through the fields and the lanes to fetch and carry home his work, so that his steps never wandered to the hedge-banks and the lane-side in search of the once familiar herbs: these too belonged to the past, from which his life had shrunk away, like a rivulet that has sunk far down from the grassy fringe of its old breadth into a little shivering thread, that cuts a groove for itself in the barren sand.

But about the Christmas of that fifteenth year, a second great change came over Marner's life, and his history became blent in a singular manner with the life of his neighbours.

CHAPTER III

THE greatest man in Raveloe was Squire Cass, who lived in the large red house with the handsome flight of stone steps in front and the high stables behind it, nearly opposite the church. He was only one among several landed parishioners, but he alone was honored with the title of Squire: for though Mr. Osgood's family was also understood to be of timeless origin—the Raveloe imagination having never ventured back to that fearful blank when there were no Osgoods—still, he merely owned the farm he occupied; whereas Squire Cass had a tenant or two, who complained of the game to him quite as if he had been a lord.

It was still that glorious war-time which was felt to be a peculiar favor of Providence towards the landed interest, and the fall of prices had not yet come to carry the race of small squires and yeomen down that road to ruin for which extravagant habits and bad husbandry were plentifully anointing their wheels. I am speaking now in relation to Raveloe and the parishes that resembled it; for our old-fashioned country life had many different aspects, as all life must have when it is spread over a various surface, and breathed on variously by multitudinous currents, from the winds of heaven to the thoughts of men, which are forever moving and crossing each other with incalculable results. Raveloe lay low among the bushy trees and the rutted lanes, aloof from the currents of industrial energy and Puritan earnestness; the rich ate and drank freely, and accepted gout and apoplexy as things that ran mysteriously in respectable families, and the poor thought that the rich were entirely in the right of it to lead a jolly life; besides, their feasting caused a multiplication of orts, which were the heirlooms of the poor. Betty Jay scented the boiling of Squire Cass's hams, but her longing was arrested by the unctuous liquor in which they were boiled; and when the seasons brought round the great merry-makings, they were regarded on all hands as a fine thing for the poor. For the Raveloe feasts were like the rounds of beef and the barrels of ale—they were on a large scale, and lasted a good while, especially in the winter-time. After ladies had packed up their best gowns and top-knots in bandboxes, and had incurred the risk of fording streams on pillions with the precious burden in rainy or snowy weather, when there was no knowing how high the water would rise, it was not to be supposed that they looked forward to a brief pleasure. On this ground it was always contrived in the dark seasons, when there was little work to be done, and the hours were long, that several neighbours should keep open house in succession. So soon as Squire Cass's standing dishes diminished in plenty and freshness, his guests had nothing to do but to walk a little higher up the village to Mr. Osgood's, at the Orchards, and they found hams and chines uncut, pork-pies with the scent of the fire in them, spun butter in all its freshness—everything, in fact, that appetites at leisure could desire, in perhaps greater perfection, though not in greater abundance, than at Squire Cass's.

For the Squire's wife had died long ago, and the Red House was without that presence of the wife and mother which is the fountain of wholesome love and fear in parlour and kitchen; and this helped to account not only for there being more profusion than finished excellence in the holiday provisions, but also for the frequency with which the proud Squire condescended to preside in the parlour of the Rainbow rather than under the shadow of his own dark wainscot; perhaps, also, for the fact that his sons had turned out rather ill. Raveloe was not a place where moral censure was severe, but it was thought a weakness in the Squire that he had kept all his sons at home in idleness; and though some license was to be allowed to young men whose fathers could afford it, people shook their heads at the courses of the second son, Dunstan, commonly called Dunsey Cass, whose taste for swopping and betting might turn out to be a sowing of something worse than wild oats. To be sure, the neighbors said, it was no matter what became of Dunsey—a spiteful jeering fellow, who seemed to enjoy his drink the more when other people went dry—always provided that his doings did not bring trouble on a family like Squire Cass's, with a monument in the church and tankards older than King George. But it would be a thousand pities if Mr. Godfrey, the eldest, a fine, open-faced, good-natured young man, who was to come into the land some day, should take to going along the same road as his brother, as he had seemed to do of late. If he went on in that way, he would lose Miss Nancy Lammeter; for it was well-known that she had looked very shyly on him ever since last Whitsuntide twelvemonth, when there was so much talk about his being away from home days and days together. There was something wrong, more than common—that was quite clear; for Mr. Godfrey didn't look half so fresh-coloured and open as he used to do. At one time everybody was saying what a handsome couple he and Miss Nancy Lammeter would make! and if she could come to be mistress at the Red House, there would be a fine change, for the Lammeters had been brought up in that way, that they never suffered a pinch of salt to be wasted, and yet everybody in their household had of the best, according to his place. Such a daughter-in-law would be a saving to the old Squire, if she never brought a penny to her fortune, for it was to be feared that, notwithstanding his incomings, there were more holes in his pocket than the one where he put his own hand in. But if Mr. Godfrey didn't turn over a new leaf, he might say "Good-by" to Miss Nancy Lammeter.

It was the once hopeful Godfrey who was standing, with his hands in his side-pockets and his back to the fire, in the dark wainscoted parlor, one late November afternoon, in that fifteenth year of Silas Marner's life at Raveloe. The fading gray light fell dimly on the walls decorated with guns, whips, and foxes' brushes, on coats and hats flung on the chairs, on tankards sending forth a scent of flat ale, and on a half-choked fire, with pipes propped up in the chimney-corners: signs of a domestic life destitute of any hallowing charm, with which the look of gloomy vexation on Godfrey's blond face was in sad accordance. He seemed to be waiting and listening for some one's approach, and presently the sound of a heavy step, with an accompanying whistle, was heard across the large empty entrance-hall.

The door opened, and a thick-set, heavy-looking young man entered, with the flushed face and the gratuitously elated bearing which mark the first stage of intoxication. It was Dunsey, and at the sight of him Godfrey's face parted with some of its gloom to take on the more active expression of hatred. The handsome brown spaniel that lay on the hearth retreated under the chair in the chimney-corner.

"Well, Master Godfrey, what do you want with me?" said Dunsey, in a mocking tone. "You're my elders and betters, you know; I was obliged to come when you sent for me."

"Why, this is what I want—and just shake yourself sober and listen, will you?" said Godfrey, savagely. He had himself been drinking more than was good for him, trying to turn his gloom into uncalculating anger. "I want to tell you, I must hand over that rent of Fowler's to the Squire, or else tell him I gave it you; for he's threatening to distrain for it, and it'll all be out soon, whether I tell him or not. He said just now, before he went out, he should send word to Cox to distrain, if Fowler didn't come and pay up his arrears this week. The Squire's short o' cash, and in no humour to stand any nonsense; and you know what he threatened, if ever he found you making away with his money again. So, see and get the money, and pretty quickly, will you?"

"Oh!" said Dunsey, sneeringly, coming nearer to his brother, and looking in his face. "Suppose, now, you get the money yourself, and save me the trouble, eh? Since you was so kind as to hand it over to me, you'll not refuse me the kindness to pay it back for me: it was your brotherly love made you do it, you know."

Godfrey bit his lips and clenched his fist. "Don't come near me with that look, else I'll knock you down."

"Oh, no, you won't," said Dunsey, turning away on his heel, however. "Because I'm such a good-natured brother, you know. I might get you turned out of house and home, and cut off with a shilling any day. I might tell the Squire how his handsome son was married to that nice young woman, Molly Farran, and was very unhappy because he couldn't live with his drunken wife, and I should slip into your place as comfortable as could be. But you see, I don't do it—I'm so easy and good-natured. You'll take any trouble for me. You'll get the hundred pounds for me—I know you will."

"How can I get the money?" said Godfrey, quivering. "I haven't a shilling to bless myself with. And it's a lie that you'd slip into my place: you'd get yourself turned out too, that's all. For if you begin telling tales I'll follow. Bob's my father's favorite—you know that very well. He'd only think himself well rid of you."

"Never mind," said Dunsey, nodding his head sideways as he looked out of the window. "It 'ud be very pleasant to me to go in your company—you're such a handsome brother, and we've always been so fond of quarrelling with one another I shouldn't know what to do without you. But you'd like better for us both to stay at home together; I know you would. So you'll manage to get that little sum o' money, and I'll bid you good-by, though I'm sorry to part."

Dunstan was moving off, but Godfrey rushed after him and seized him by the arm, saying, with an oath,

"I tell you I have no money: I can get no money."

"Borrow of old Kimble."

"I tell you, he won't lend me any more, and I sha'n't ask him."

"Well then, sell Wildfire."

"Yes, that's easy talking. I must have the money directly."

"Well, you've only got to ride him to the hunt to-morrow. There'll be Bryce and Keating there, for sure. You'll get more bids than one."

"I dare say, and get back home at eight o'clock, splashed up to the chin. I'm going to Mrs. Osgood's birthday dance."

"Oho!" said Dunsey, turning his head on one side, and trying to speak in a small mincing treble. "And there's sweet Miss Nancy coming; and we shall dance with her and promise never to be naughty again, and be taken into favour, and—"

"Hold your tongue about Miss Nancy, you fool," said Godfrey, turning very red, "else I'll throttle you."

"What for?" said Dunsey, still in an artificial tone, but taking a whip from the table and beating the butt-end of it on his palm. "You've a very good chance. I'd advise you to creep up her sleeve again: it 'ud be saving time, if Molly should happen to take a drop too much laudanum some day, and make a widower of you. Miss Nancy wouldn't mind being a second, if she didn't know it. And you've got a good-natured brother, who'll keep your secret well, because you'll be so very obliging to him."

"I'll tell you what it is," said Godfrey, quivering, and pale again. "My patience is pretty near at an end. If you'd a little more sharpness in you, you might know that you may urge a man a bit too far, and make one leap as easy as another. I don't know but what it is so now: I may as well tell the Squire everything myself—I should get you off my back, if I got nothing else. And, after all, he'll know some time. She's been threatening to come herself and tell him. So, don't flatter yourself that your secrecy's worth any price you choose to ask. You drain me of money till I have got nothing to pacify *her* with, and she'll do as she threatens some day. It's all one. I'll tell my father everything myself, and you may go to the devil."

Dunsey perceived that he had overshot his mark, and that there was a point at which even the hesitating Godfrey might be driven into decision. But he said with an air of unconcern,

"As you please; but I'll have a draught of ale first." And ringing the bell, he threw himself across two chairs, and began to rap the window-seat with the handle of his whip.

Godfrey stood still with his back to the fire, uneasily moving his fingers among the contents of his side-pockets, and looking at the floor. That big muscular frame of his held plenty of animal courage, but helped him to no decision when the dangers to be braved were such as could neither be knocked down nor throttled. His natural irresolution and moral cowardice were exaggerated by a position in which dreaded consequences seemed to press equally on all sides, and his irritation had no sooner provoked him to defy Dunstan and anticipate all possible betrayals, than the miseries he must bring on himself by such a step seemed more unendurable to him than the present evil. The results of confession were not contingent, they were certain; whereas betrayal was not certain. From the near vision of that certainty he fell back on suspense and vacillation with a sense of repose. The disinherited son of a small squire, equally disinclined to dig and to beg, was almost as help-less as an uprooted tree, which, by the favor of earth and sky, has grown to a handsome bulk on the spot where it first shot upward. Perhaps it would have been possible to think of digging with some cheerfulness if Nancy Lammeter were to be won on those terms; but since he must irrevocably lose *her* as well as the inheritance, and must break every tie but the one that degraded him and left him without motive for trying to recover his better self, he could imagine no future for himself on the other side of confession but that of " 'listing for a soldier"—the most desperate step short of suicide, in the eyes of respectable families. No! he would rather trust to casualties than to his own resolve—rather go on sitting at the feast and sipping the wine he loved, though with the sword hanging over him and terror in his heart, than rush away into the cold darkness where there was no pleasure left. The utmost conces-sion to Dunstan about the horse began to seem easy, compared with the fulfillment of his own threat. But his pride would not let him recom-mence the conversation otherwise than by continuing the quarrel. Dun-stan was waiting for this, and took his ale in shorter draughts than usual.

"It's just like you," Godfrey burst out in a bitter tone, "to talk about my selling Wildfire in that cool way—the last thing I've got to call my own, and the best bit of horse-flesh I ever had in my life. And if you'd got a spark of pride in you, you'd be ashamed to see the stables emptied, and everybody sneering about it. But it's my belief you'd sell yourself, if it was only for the pleasure of making somebody feel he'd got a bad bargain."

"Ay, ay," said Dunstan, very placably, "you do me justice, I see. You know I'm a jewel for 'ticing people into bargains. For which reason I advise you to let *me* sell Wildfire. I'd ride him to the hunt to-morrow for you with pleasure. I shouldn't look so handsome as you in the saddle, but it's the horse they'll bid for, and not the rider."

"Yes, I dare say—trust my horse to you!"

"As you please," said Dunstan, rapping the window-seat again with an air of great unconcern. "It's *you* have got to pay Fowler's money; it's none of my business. You received the money from him when you went to Bramcote, and *you* told the Squire it wasn't paid. I'd nothing to do with that; you chose to be so obliging as give it me, that was all. If you don't want to pay the money, let it alone; it's all one to me. But I was willing to accommodate you by undertaking to sell the horse, see-ing it's not convenient to you to go so far to-morrow."

Godfrey was silent for some moments. He would have liked to spring on Dunstan, wrench the whip from his hand, and flog him within an inch of his life; and no bodily fear could have deterred him; but he was mastered by another sort of fear, which was fed by feelings stronger even than his resentment. When he spoke again, it was in a half-con-ciliatory tone.

"Well, you mean no nonsense about the horse, eh? You'll sell him all fair, and hand over the money? If you don't, you know, everything 'ull go to smash, for I've got nothing else to trust to. And you'll have less pleasure in pulling the house over my head, when your own skull's to be broken too."

"Ay, ay," said Dunstan, rising, "all right. I thought you'd come round. I'm the fellow to bring old Bryce up to the scratch. I'll get you a hundred and twenty for him, if I get you a penny."

"But it'll perhaps rain cats and dogs to-morrow, as it did yesterday, and then you can't go," said Godfrey, hardly knowing whether he wished for that obstacle or not.

"Not *it*," said Dunstan. "I'm always lucky in my weather. It might rain if you wanted to go yourself. You never hold trumps, you know— I always do. You've got the beauty, you see, and I've got the luck, so you must keep me by you for your crooked sixpence; you'll *ne*-ver get along without me."

"Confound you, hold your tongue!" said Godfrey, impetuously. "And take care to keep sober to-morrow, else you'll get pitched on your head coming home, and Wildfire might be the worse for it."

"Make your tender heart easy," said Dunstan, opening the door. "You never knew me see double when I'd got a bargain to make; it 'ud spoil the fun. Besides, whenever I fall, I'm warranted to fall on my legs."

With that, Dunstan slammed the door behind him, and left Godfrey to that bitter rumination on his personal circumstances which was now unbroken from day to day save by the excitement of sporting, drinking, card-playing, or the rarer and less oblivious pleasure of seeing Miss Nancy Lammeter. The subtle and varied pains springing from the higher sensibility that accompanies higher culture are perhaps less pitiable than that dreary absence of impersonal enjoyment and consolation which leaves ruder minds to the perpetual urgent companionship of their own griefs and discontents. The lives of those rural forefathers, whom we are apt to think very prosaic figures—men whose only work was to ride round their land, getting heavier and heavier in their saddles, and who passed the rest of their days in the half-listless gratification of senses dulled by monotony—had a certain pathos in them nevertheless. Calamities came to *them* too, and their early errors carried hard consequences: perhaps the love of some sweet maiden, the image of purity, order, and calm, had opened their eyes to the vision of a life in which the days would not seem too long, even without rioting; but the maiden was lost, and the vision passed away, and then what was left to them, especially when they had become too heavy for the hunt, or for carrying a gun over the furrows, but to drink and get merry, or to drink and get angry, so that they might be independent of variety, and say over again with eager emphasis the things they had said already any time that twelve-month? Assuredly, among these flushed and dull-eyed men there were some whom—thanks to their native human kindness— even riot could never drive into brutality; men who, when their cheeks were fresh, had felt the keen point of sorrow or remorse, had been

pierced by the reeds they leaned on, or had lightly put their limbs in
fetters from which no struggle could loose them; and under these sad
circumstances, common to us all, their thoughts could find no resting-
place outside the ever-trodden round of their own petty history.

That, at least, was the condition of Godfrey Cass in this six-and-
twentieth year of his life. A movement of compunction, helped by those
small indefinable influences which every personal relation exerts on a
pliant nature, had urged him into a secret marriage, which was a blight
on his life. It was an ugly story of low passion, delusion, and waking
from delusion, which needs not to be dragged from the privacy of Godfrey's bitter memory. He had long known that the delusion was partly
due to a trap laid for him by Dunstan, who saw in his brother's degrading marriage the means of gratifying at once his jealous hate and his
cupidity. And if Godfrey could have felt himself simply a victim, the
iron bit that destiny had put into his mouth would have chafed him less
intolerably. If the curses he muttered half aloud when he was alone had
had no other object than Dunstan's diabolical cunning, he might have
shrunk less from the consequences of avowal. But he had something
else to curse—his own vicious folly, which now seemed as mad and unaccountable to him as almost all our follies and vices do when their
promptings have long passed away. For four years he had thought of
Nancy Lammeter, and wooed her with tacit, patient worship, as the
woman who made him think of the future with joy: she would be his
wife, and would make home lovely to him, as his father's home had
never been; and it would be easy, when she was always near, to shake
off those foolish habits that were no pleasures, but only a feverish way
of annulling vacancy. Godfrey's was an essentially domestic nature,
bred up in a home where the hearth had no smiles, and where the daily
habits were not chastised by the presence of household order; his easy
disposition made him fall in unresistingly with the family courses, but
the need of some tender, permanent affection, the longing for some influence that would make the good he preferred easy to pursue, caused
the neatness, purity, and liberal orderliness of the Lammeter household,
sunned by the smile of Nancy, to seem like those fresh bright hours of
the morning, when temptations go to sleep, and leave the ear open to
the voice of the good angel, inviting to industry, sobriety, and peace.
And yet the hope of this paradise had not been enough to save him from
a course which shut him out of it forever. Instead of keeping fast hold
of the strong silken rope by which Nancy would have drawn him safe
to the green banks, where it was easy to step firmly, he had let himself
be dragged back into mud and slime, in which it was useless to struggle.
He had made ties for himself which robbed him of all wholesome motive,
and were a constant exasperation.

Still, there was one position worse than the present; it was the position he would be in when the ugly secret was disclosed; and the desire
that continually triumphed over every other was that of warding off
the evil day, when he would have to bear the consequences of his father's

violent resentment for the wound inflicted on his family pride—would have, perhaps, to turn his back on that hereditary ease and dignity which, after all, was a sort of reason for living, and would carry with him the certainty that he was banished forever from the sight and esteem of Nancy Lammeter. The longer the interval, the more chance there was of deliverance from some, at least, of the hateful consequences to which he had sold himself—the more opportunities remained for him to snatch the strange gratification of seeing Nancy, and gathering some faint indications of her lingering regard. Towards this gratification he was impelled fitfully, every now and then, after having passed weeks in which he had avoided her as the far-off bright-winged prize, that only made him spring forward, and find his chain all the more galling. One of those fits of yearning was on him now, and it would have been strong enough to have persuaded him to trust Wildfire to Dunstan rather than disappoint the yearning, even if he had not had another reason for his disinclination towards the morrow's hunt. That other reason was the fact that the morning's meet was near Batherley, the market-town where the unhappy woman lived, whose image became more odious to him every day; and to his thought the whole vicinage was haunted by her. The yoke a man creates for himself by wrong-doing will breed hate in the kindliest nature; and the good-humoured, affectionate-hearted Godfrey Cass was fast becoming a bitter man, visited by cruel wishes, that seemed to enter, and depart, and enter again, like demons who had found in him a ready-garnished home.

What was he to do this evening to pass the time? He might as well go to the Rainbow, and hear the talk about the cock-fighting: everybody was there, and what else was there to be done? Though, for his own part, he did not care a button for cock-fighting. Snuff, the brown spaniel, who had placed herself in front of him, and had been watching him for some time, now jumped up in impatience for the expected caress. But Godfrey thrust her away without looking at her, and left the room, followed humbly by the unresenting Snuff—perhaps because she saw no other career open to her.

CHAPTER IV

DUNSTAN CASS, setting off in the raw morning, at the judiciously quiet pace of a man who is obliged to ride to cover on his hunter, had to take his way along the lane which, at its farther extremity, passed by the piece of unenclosed ground called the Stone-pits, where stood the cottage, once a stone-cutter's shed, now for fifteen years inhabited by Silas Marner. The spot looked very dreary at this season, with the moist trodden clay about it, and the red muddy water high up in the deserted quarry. That was Dunstan's first thought as he approached it; the second was, that the old fool of a weaver, whose loom he heard rattling already, had a great deal of money hidden somewhere. How was it that he, Dunstan

Cass, who had often heard talk of Marner's miserliness, had never thought of suggesting to Godfrey that he should frighten or persuade the old fellow into lending the money on the excellent security of the young Squire's prospects? The resource occurred to him now as so easy and agreeable, especially as Marner's hoard was likely to be large enough to leave Godfrey a handsome surplus beyond his immediate needs, and enable him to accommodate his faithful brother, that he had almost turned the horse's head towards home again. Godfrey would be ready enough to accept the suggestion: he would snatch eagerly at a plan that might save him from parting with Wildfire. But when Dunstan's meditation reached this point, the inclination to go on grew strong and prevailed. He didn't want to give Godfrey that pleasure: he preferred that Master Godfrey should be vexed. Moreover, Dunstan enjoyed the self-important consciousness of having a horse to sell, and the opportunity of driving a bargain, swaggering, and, possibly, taking somebody in. He might have all the satisfaction attendant on selling his brother's horse, and not the less have the further satisfaction of setting Godfrey to borrow Marner's money. So he rode on to cover.

Bryce and Keating were there, as Dunstan was quite sure they would be—he was such a lucky fellow.

"Hey-day," said Bryce, who had long had his eye on Wildfire, "you're on your brother's horse to-day; how's that?"

"Oh, I've swapped with him," said Dunstan, whose delight in lying, grandly independent of utility, was not to be diminished by the likelihood that his hearer would not believe him—"Wildfire's mine now."

"What! has he swopped with you for that big-boned hack of yours?" said Bryce, quite aware that he should get another lie in answer.

"Oh, there was a little account between us," said Dunstan, carelessly, "and Wildfire made it even. I accommodated him by taking the horse, though it was against my will, for I'd got an itch for a mare o' Jortin's—as rare a bit o' blood as ever you threw your leg across. But I shall keep Wildfire, now I've got him, though I'd a bid of a hundred and fifty for him the other day from a man over at Flitton—he's buying for Lord Cromleck—a fellow with a cast in his eye, and a green waistcoat. But I mean to stick to Wildfire: I sha'n't get a better at a fence in a hurry. The mare's got more blood, but she's a bit too weak in the hind quarters."

Bryce of course divined that Dunstan wanted to sell the horse, and Dunstan knew that he divined it (horse-dealing is only one of many human transactions carried on in this ingenious manner); and they both considered that the bargain was in its first stage, when Bryce replied ironically—

"I wonder at that now; I wonder you mean to keep him; for I never heard of a man who didn't want to sell his horse getting a bid of half as much again as the horse was worth. You'll be lucky if you get a hundred."

Keating rode up now, and the transaction became more complicated.

It ended in the purchase of the horse by Bryce for a hundred and twenty, to be paid on the delivery of Wildfire, safe and sound, at the Batherley stables. It did occur to Dunsey that it might be wise for him to give up the day's hunting, proceed at once to Batherley, and, having waited for Bryce's return, hire a horse to carry him home with the money in his pocket. But the inclination for a run, encouraged by confidence in his luck, and by a draught of brandy from his pocket-pistol at the conclusion of the bargain, was not easy to overcome, especially with a horse under him that would take the fences to the admiration of the field. Dunstan, however, took one fence too many, and "staked" his horse. His own ill-favoured person, which was quite unmarketable, escaped without injury, but poor Wildfire, unconscious of his price, turned on his flank, and painfully panted his last. It happened that Dunstan, a short time before, having had to get down to arrange his stirrup, had muttered a good many curses at this interruption, which had thrown him in the rear of the hunt near the moment of glory, and under this exasperation had taken the fences more blindly. He would soon have been up with the hounds again, when the fatal accident happened; and hence he was between eager riders in advance, not troubling themselves about what happened behind them, and far-off stragglers, who were as likely as not to pass quite aloof from the line of road in which Wildfire had fallen. Dunstan, whose nature it was to care more for immediate annoyances than for remote consequences, no sooner recovered his legs, and saw that it was all over with Wildfire, than he felt a satisfaction at the absence of witnesses to a position which no swaggering could make enviable. Reinforcing himself, after his shake, with a little brandy and much swearing, he walked as fast as he could to a coppice on his right hand, through which it occurred to him that he could make his way to Batherley without danger of encountering any member of the hunt. His first intention was to hire a horse there and ride home forthwith, for to walk many miles without a gun in his hand, and along an ordinary road, was as much out of the question to him as to other spirited young men of his kind. He did not much mind about taking the bad news to Godfrey, for he had to offer him at the same time the resource of Marner's money; and if Godfrey kicked, as he always did, at the notion of making a fresh debt, from which he himself got the smallest share of advantage, why, he wouldn't kick long: Dunstan felt sure he could worry Godfrey into anything. The idea of Marner's money kept growing in vividness, now the want of it had become immediate; the prospect of having to make his appearance with the muddy boots of a pedestrian at Batherley, and encounter the grinning queries of stablemen, stood unpleasantly in the way of his impatience to be back at Raveloe and carry out his felicitous plan; and a casual visitation of his waistcoat-pocket, as he was ruminating, awakened his memory to the fact that the two or three small coins his fore-finger encountered there were of too pale a colour to cover that small debt, without payment of which Jennings had declared he would never do any more business with Dunsey Cass. After all, according to the direction in which the run had brought him, he was not so very much farther from home than he was from Batherley; but Dunsey, not being remarkable for clearness of head, was only led to this conclusion by the gradual perception that there were other reasons for choosing the unprecedented course of walking home. It was now nearly four o'clock, and a mist was gathering: the sooner he got into the road the better. He remembered having crossed the road and seen the finger-post only a little while before Wildfire broke down; so, buttoning his coat, twisting the lash of his hunting-whip compactly round the handle, and rapping the tops of his boots with a self-possessed air, as if to assure himself that he was not at all taken by surprise, he set off with the sense that he was undertaking a remarkable feat of bodily exertion, which somehow, and at some time, he should be able to dress up and magnify to the admiration of a select circle at the Rainbow. When a young gentleman like Dunsey is reduced to so exceptional a mode of locomotion as walking, a whip in his hand is a desirable corrective to a too bewildering dreamy sense of unwontedness in his position; and Dunstan, as he went along through the gathering mist, was always rapping his whip somewhere. It was Godfrey's whip, which he had chosen to take without leave because it had a gold handle; of course no one could see, when Dunstan held it, that the name *Godfrey Cass* was cut in deep letters on that gold handle—they could only see that it was a very handsome whip. Dunsey was not without fear that he might meet some acquaintance in whose eyes he would cut a pitiable figure, for mist is no screen where people get close to each other; but when he at last found himself in the well-known Raveloe lanes without having met a soul, he silently remarked that that was part of his usual good-luck. But now the mist, helped by the evening darkness, was more of a screen than he desired, for it hid the ruts into which his feet were liable to slip—hid every thing, so that he had to guide his steps by dragging his whip along the low bushes in advance of the hedgerow. He must soon, he thought, be getting near the opening at the Stone-pits: he should find it out by the break in the hedgerow. He found it out, however, by another circumstance which he had not expected—namely, by certain gleams of light, which he presently guessed to proceed from Silas Marner's cottage. That cottage and the money hidden within it had been in his mind continually during his walk, and he had been imagining ways of cajoling and tempting the weaver to part with the immediate possession of his money for the sake of receiving interest. Dunstan felt as if there must be a little frightening added to the cajolery, for his own arithmetical convictions were not clear enough to afford him any forcible demonstration as to the advantages of interest; and as for security, he regarded it vaguely as a means of cheating a man, by making him believe that he would be paid. Altogether, the operation on the miser's mind was a task that Godfrey would be sure to hand over to his more daring and cunning brother: Dunstan had made up his mind to that; and by the time he saw the light gleaming through the chinks of Marner's shutters, the idea of a dialogue with the weaver had become so familiar to him, that it occurred to him as quite a natural thing to make the acquaintance forthwith. There might be several conveniences attending this course; the weaver had possibly got a lantern, and Dunstan was tired of feeling his way. He was still nearly three-quarters of a mile from home, and the lane was becoming unpleasantly slippery, for the mist was passing into rain. He turned up the bank, not without some fear lest he might miss the right way, since he was not certain whether the light were in front or on the side of the cottage. But he felt the ground before him cautiously with his whip-handle, and at last arrived safely at the door. He knocked loudly, rather enjoying the idea that the old fellow would be frightened at the sudden noise. He heard no movement in reply: all was silence in the cottage. Was the weaver gone to bed, then? If so, why had he left a light? That was a strange forgetfulness in a miser. Dunstan knocked still more loudly, and, without pausing for a reply, pushed his fingers through the latch-hole, intending to shake the door and pull the latch-string up and down, not doubting that the door was fastened. But, to his surprise, at this double motion the door opened, and he found himself in front of a bright fire, which lit up every corner of the cottage —the bed, the loom, the three chairs, and the table—and showed him that Marner was not there.

Nothing at that moment could be much more inviting to Dunsey than the bright fire on the brick hearth; he walked in and seated himself by it at once. There was something in front of the fire, too, that would have been inviting to a hungry man, if it had been in a different stage of cooking. It was a small bit of pork suspended from the kettle-hanger by a string passed through a large door-key, in a way known to primitive housekeepers unpossessed of jacks. But the pork had been hung at the farthest extremity of the hanger, apparently to prevent the roasting from proceeding too rapidly during the owner's absence. The old staring simpleton had hot meat for his supper, then? thought Dunstan. People had always said he lived on mouldy bread, on purpose to check his appetite. But where could he be at this time, and on such an evening, leaving his supper in this stage of preparation, and his door unfastened? Dunstan's own recent difficulty in making his way suggested to him that the weaver had perhaps gone outside his cottage to fetch in fuel, or for some such brief purpose, and had slipped into the stone-pit. That was an interesting idea to Dunstan, carrying consequences of entire novelty. If the weaver was dead, who had a right to his money? Who would know where his money was hidden? *Who would know that any body had come to take it away?* He went no farther into the subleties of evidence: the pressing question, "Where *is* the money?" now took such entire possession of him as to make him quite forget that the weaver's death was not a certainty. A dull mind, once arriving at an inference that flatters a desire, is rarely able to retain the impression that the notion from which the inference started was purely problematic. And Dunstan's mind was as dull as the mind of a possible felon usually is. There were only three hiding-places where he had ever heard of cottagers' hoards being found; the thatch, the bed, and a hole in the floor. Marner's cottage had no thatch; and Dunstan's first act, after a train of thought made rapid by the stimulus of cupidity, was to go up to the bed; but while he did so, his eyes travelled eagerly over the floor, where the bricks, distinct in the fire-light, were discernible under the sprinkling of sand. But not everywhere; for there was one spot, and one only, which was quite covered with sand, and sand showing the marks of fingers, which had apparently been careful to spread it over a given space. It was near the treddles of the loom. In an instant Dunstan darted to that spot, swept away the sand with his whip, and, inserting the thin end of the hook between the bricks, found that they were loose. In haste he lifted up two bricks, and saw what he had no doubt was the object of his search; for what could there be but money in those two leathern bags? And, from their weight, they must be filled with guineas. Dunstan felt round the hole, to be certain that it held no more; then hastily replaced the bricks, and spread the sand over them. Hardly more than five minutes had passed since he entered the cottage, but it seemed to Dunstan like a long while; and though he was without any distinct recognition of the possibility that Marner might be alive, and might re-enter the cottage at any moment, he felt an undefinable dread laying hold on him, as he rose to his feet with the bags in his hand. He would hasten out into the darkness, and then consider what he should do with the bags. He closed the door behind him immediately, that he might shut in the stream of light; a few steps would be enough to carry him beyond betrayal by the gleams from the shutter-chinks and the latch-hole. The rain and darkness had got thicker, and he was glad of it; though it was awkward walking with both hands filled, so that it was as much as he could do to grasp his whip along with one of the bags. But when he had gone a yard or two, he might take his time. So he stepped forward into the darkness.

CHAPTER V

WHEN Dunstan Cass turned his back on the cottage, Silas Marner was not more than a hundred yards away from it, plodding along from the village with a sack thrown round his shoulders as an over-coat, and with a horn lantern in his hand. His legs were weary, but his mind was at ease, free from the presentiment of change. The sense of security more frequently springs from habit than from conviction, and for this reason it often subsists after such a change in the conditions as might have been expected to suggest alarm. The lapse of time during which a given event has not happened, is, in this logic of habit, constantly alleged as a reason why the event should never happen, even when the lapse of time is precisely the added condition which makes the event imminent. A man will tell you that he has worked in a mine for forty years unhurt by an accident as a reason why he should apprehend no danger, though the roof is beginning to sink; and it is often observable, that the older a man gets, the more difficult it is to him to retain a believing conception of his own death. This influence of habit was necessarily strong in a man whose life was so monotonous as Marner's—who saw no new people and heard of no new events to keep alive in him the idea of the unexpected and the changeful; and it explains, simply enough, why his mind could be at ease, though he had left his house and his treasure more defenseless than usual. Silas was thinking with double complacency of his supper: first, because it would be hot and savoury; and secondly, because it would cost him nothing. For the little bit of pork was a present from that excellent housewife, Miss Priscilla Lammeter, to whom he had this day carried home a handsome piece of linen; and it was only on occasion of a present like this, that Silas indulged himself with roast-meat. Supper was his favourite meal, because it came at his time of revelry, when his heart warmed over his gold; whenever he had roast-meat, he always chose to have it for supper. But this evening, he had no sooner ingeniously knotted his string fast round his bit of pork, twisted the string according to rule over his door-key, passed it through the handle, and made it fast on the hanger, than he remembered that a piece of very fine twine was indispensable to his "setting up" a new piece of work in his loom early in the morning. It had slipped his memory, because, in coming from Mr. Lammeter's, he had not had to pass through the village; but to lose time by going on errands in the morning was out of the question. It was a nasty fog to turn out into, but there were things Silas loved better than his own comfort; so, drawing his pork to the extremity of the hanger, and arming himself with his lantern and his old sack, he set out on what, in ordinary weather, would have been a twenty minutes' errand. He could not have locked his door without undoing his well-knotted string and retarding his supper; it was not worth his while to make that sacrifice. What thief would find his way to the Stone-pits on such a night as this? and why should he come on this particular night, when he had never come through all the fifteen years before? These questions were not distinctly present in Silas's mind; they merely serve to represent the vaguely-felt foundation of his freedom from anxiety.

He reached his door in much satisfaction that his errand was done: he opened it, and to his short-sighted eyes everything remained as he had left it, except that the fire sent out a welcome increase of heat. He trod about the floor while putting by his lantern and throwing aside his hat and sack, so as to merge the marks of Dunstan's feet on the sand in the marks of his own nailed boots. Then he moved his pork nearer to the fire, and sat down to the agreeable business of tending the meat and warming himself at the same time.

Any one who had looked at him as the red light shone upon his pale face, strange straining eyes, and meagre form, would perhaps have understood the mixture of contemptuous pity, dread, and suspicion with which he was regarded by his neighbors in Raveloe. Yet few men could be more harmless than poor Marner. In his truthful simple soul, not even the growing greed and worship of gold could beget any vice directly injurious to others. The light of his faith quite put out, and his affections made desolate, he had clung with all the force of his nature to his work and his money; and like all objects to which a man devotes himself, they had fashioned him into correspondence with themselves. His loom, as he wrought in it without ceasing, had in its turn wrought on him, and confirmed more and more the monotonous craving for its monotonous response. His gold, as he hung over it and saw it grow, gathered his power of loving together into a hard isolation like its own.

As soon as he was warm he began to think it would be a long while to wait till after supper before he drew out his guineas, and it would be pleasant to see them on the table before him as he ate his unwonted feast. For joy is the best of wine, and Silas's guineas were a golden wine of that sort.

He rose and placed his candle unsuspectingly on the floor near his loom, swept away the sand without noticing any change, and removed the bricks. The sight of the empty hole made his heart leap violently, but the belief that his gold was gone could not come at once—only terror, and the eager effort to put an end to the terror. He passed his trembling hand all about the hole, trying to think it possible that his eyes had deceived him; then he held the candle in the hole and examined it curiously, trembling more and more. At last he shook so violently that he let fall the candle, and lifted his hands to his head, trying to steady himself, that he might think. Had he put his gold somewhere else, by a sudden resolution last night, and then forgotten it? A man falling into dark waters seeks a momentary footing even on sliding stones; and Silas, by acting as if he believed in false hopes, warded off the moment of despair. He searched in every corner, he turned his bed over, and shook it, and kneaded it; he looked in his brick oven where he laid his sticks. When there was no other place to be searched, he kneeled down again and felt once more all round the hole. There was no untried refuge left for a moment's shelter from the terrible truth.

Yes, there was a sort of refuge which always comes with the prostration of thought under an overpowering passion: it was that expectation of impossibilities, that belief in contradictory images, which is still distinct from madness, because it is capable of being dissipated by the external fact. Silas got up from his knees trembling, and looked round at the table: didn't the gold lie there after all? The table was bare. Then he turned and looked behind him—looked all round his dwelling, seeming to strain his brown eyes after some possible appearance of the bags where he had already sought them in vain. He could see every object in his cottage—and his gold was not there.

Again he put his trembling hands to his head, and gave a wild ringing scream, the cry of desolation. For a few moments after, he stood motionless; but the cry had relieved him from the first maddening pressure of the truth. He turned, and tottered towards his loom, and got into the seat where he worked, instinctively seeking this as the strongest assurance of reality.

And now that all the false hopes had vanished, and the first shock of certainty was past, the idea of a thief began to present itself, and he entertained it eagerly, because a thief might be caught and made to restore the gold. The thought brought some new strength with it, and he started from his loom to the door. As he opened it the rain beat in upon him, for it was falling more and more heavily. There were no footsteps to be tracked on such a night—footsteps? When had the thief come? During Silas's absence in the day-time the door had been locked, and there had been no marks of any inroad on his return by day-light. And in the evening, too, he said to himself, everything was the same as when he had left it. The sand and bricks looked as if they had not been moved. *Was* it a thief who had taken the bags? or was it a cruel power that no hands could reach, which had delighted in making him a second time desolate? He shrank from this vaguer dread, and fixed his mind with struggling effort on the robber with hands, who could be reached by hands. His thoughts glanced at all the neighbors who had made any remarks, or asked any questions which he might now regard as a ground of suspicion. There was Jem Rodney, a known poacher, and otherwise disreputable: he had often met Marner in his journeys across the fields, and had said something jestingly about the weaver's money; nay, he had once irritated Marner, by lingering at the fire when he called to light his pipe, instead of going about his business. Jem Rodney was the man —there was ease in the thought. Jem could be found and made to restore the money: Marner did not want to punish him but only to get back his gold which had gone from him, and left his soul like a forlorn traveller on an unknown desert. The robber must be laid hold of. Marner's ideas of legal authority were confused, but he felt that he must go and proclaim his loss; and the great people in the village—the clergyman, the constable, and Squire Cass—would make Jem Rodney, or somebody else, deliver up the stolen money. He rushed out in the rain, under the stimulus of this hope, forgetting to cover his head, not caring to fasten his door; for he felt as if he had nothing left to lose. He ran swiftly, till want of breath compelled him to slacken his pace as he was entering the village at the turning close to the Rainbow.

The Rainbow, in Marner's view, was a place of luxurious resort for rich and stout husbands, whose wives had superfluous stores of linen; it was the place where he was likely to find the powers and dignities of Raveloe, and where he could most speedily make his loss public. He lifted the latch, and turned into the bright bar or kitchen on the right hand, where the less lofty customers of the house were in the habit of assembling, the parlour on the left being reserved for the more select society in which Squire Cass frequently enjoyed the double pleasure of conviviality and condescension. But the parlour was dark to-night, the chief personages who ornamented its circle being all at Mrs. Osgood's birthday dance, as Godfrey Cass was. And in consequence of this, the party on the high-screened seats in the kitchen was more numerous than usual; several personages, who would otherwise have been admitted in to the parlour and enlarged the opportunity of hectoring and condescension for their betters, being content this evening to vary their enjoyment by taking their spirits-and-water where they could themselves hector and condescend in company that called for beer.

CHAPTER VI

THE conversation, which was at a high pitch of animation when Silas approached the door of the Rainbow, had, as usual, been slow and intermittent when the company first assembled. The pipes began to be puffed in a silence which had an air of severity; the more important customers, who drank spirits and sat nearest the fire, staring at each other as if a bet were depending on the first man who winked; while the beer-drinkers, chiefly men in fustian jackets and smock-frocks, kept their eyelids down and rubbed their hands across their mouths, as if their draughts of beer were a funeral duty attended with embarrassing sadness. At last, Mr. Snell, the landlord, a man of a neutral disposition, accustomed to stand aloof from human differences, as those of beings who were all alike in need of liquor, broke silence, by saying in a doubtful tone to his cousin the butcher—

"Some folks 'ud say that was a fine beast you druv in yesterday, Bob?"

The butcher, a jolly, smiling, red-haired man, was not disposed to answer rashly. He gave a few puffs before he spat and replied, "And they wouldn't be fur wrong, John."

After this feeble delusive thaw, the silence set in as severely as before.

"Was it a red Durham?" said the farrier, taking up the thread of discourse after the lapse of a few minutes.

The farrier looked at the landlord, and the landlord looked at the butcher, as the person who must take the responsibility of answering

"Red it was," said the butcher, in his good-humored husky treble— "and a Durham it was."

"Then you needn't tell *me* who you bought it of," said the farrier, looking round with some triumph; "I know who it is has got the red Durhams o' this country-side. And she'd a white star on her brow, I'll bet a penny?" The farrier leaned forward with his hands on his knees as he put this question, and his eyes twinkled knowingly.

"Well; yes—she might," said the butcher, slowly, considering that he was giving a decided affirmative. "I don't say contrairy."

"I knew that very well," said the farrier, throwing himself backward again, and speaking defiantly; "if *I* don't know Mr. Lammeter's cows,

I should like to know who does—that's all. And as for the cow you've bought, bargain or no bargain, I've been at the drenching of her—contradick me who will."

The farrier looked fierce, and the mild butcher's conversational spirit was roused a little.

"I'm not for contradicking no man," he said; "I'm for peace and quietness. Some are for cutting long ribs—I'm for cutting 'em short myself; but *I* don't quarrel with 'em. All I say is, it's a lovely carkiss—and anybody as was reasonable, it 'ud bring tears into their eyes to look at it."

"Well, it's the cow as I drenched, whatever it is," pursued the farrier, angrily; "and it was Mr. Lammeter's cow, else you told a lie when you said it was a red Durham."

"I tell no lies," said the butcher, with the same mild huskiness as before, "and I contradick none—not if a man was to swear himself black: he's no meat o' mine, or none o' my bargains. All I say is, it's a lovely carkiss. And what I say I'll stick to; but I'll quarrel wi' no man."

"No," said the farrier, with bitter sarcasm, looking at the company generally; "and p'raps you aren't pig-headed; and p'raps you didn't say the cow was a red Durham; and p'raps you didn't say she'd got a star on her brow—stick to that, now you're at it."

"Come, come," said the landlord; "let the cow alone. The truth lies atween you: you're both right and both wrong, as I allays say. And as for the cow's being Mr. Lammeter's, I say nothing to that; but this I say, as the Rainbow's the Rainbow. And for the matter o' that, if the talk is to be o' the Lammeters, *you* know the most upo' that head, eh, Mr. Macey? You remember when first Mr. Lammeter's father came into these parts, and took the Warrens?"

Mr. Macey, tailor and parish-clerk, the latter of which functions rheumatism had of late obliged him to share with a small-featured young man who sat opposite him, held his white head on one side, and twirled his thumbs with an air of complacency, slightly seasoned with criticism. He smiled pityingly, in answer to the landlord's appeal, and said—

"Ay, ay; I know, I know; but I let other folks talk. I've laid by now, and gev up to the young uns. Ask them as have been to school at Tarley: they've learnt pernouncing; that's come up since my day."

"If you're pointing at me, Mr. Macey," said the deputy-clerk, with an air of anxious propriety, "I'm nowise a man to speak out of my place. As the psalm says—

> 'I know what's right, nor only so,
> But also practise what I know.'"

"Well, then, I wish you'd keep hold o' the tune, when it's set for you; if you're for prac*tis*ing, I wish you'd prac*tise* that," said a large jocose-looking man, an excellent wheelwright in his week-day capacity, but on Sundays leader of the choir. He winked, as he spoke, at two of the company, who were known officially as the "bassoon" and the "key-bugle," in the confidence that he was expressing the sense of the musical profession in Raveloe.

Mr. Tookey, the deputy-clerk, who shared the unpopularity common to deputies, turned very red, but replied, with careful moderation—"Mr. Winthrop, if you'll bring me any proof as I'm in the wrong, I'm not the man to say I won't alter. But there's people set up their own ears for a standard, and expect the whole choir to follow 'em. There may be two opinions, I hope."

"Ay, ay," said Mr. Macey, who felt very well satisfied with this attack on youthful presumption; "you're right there, Tookey: there's allays two 'pinions; there's the 'pinion a man has of himsen, and there's the 'pinion other folks have on him. There'd be two 'pinions about a cracked bell, if the bell could hear itself."

"Well, Mr. Macey," said poor Tookey, serious amidst the general laughter, "I undertook to partially fill up the office of parish-clerk by Mr. Crackenthorp's desire, whenever your infirmities should make you unfitting; and it's one of the rights thereof to sing in the choir—else why have you done the same yourself?"

"Ah! but the old gentleman and you are two folks," said Ben Winthrop. "The old gentleman's got a gift. Why, the Squire used to invite him to take a glass, only to hear him sing the 'Red Rovier;' didn't he, Mr. Macey? It's a nat'ral gift. There's my little lad Aaron, he's got a gift—he can sing a tune off straight, like a throstle. But as for you, Master Tookey, you'd better stick to your 'Amens:' your voice is well enough when you keep it up in your nose. It's your inside as isn't right made for music: it's no better nor a hollow stalk."

This kind of unflinching frankness was the most piquant form of joke to the company at the Rainbow, and Ben Winthrop's insult was felt by everybody to have capped Mr. Macey's epigram.

"I see what it is plain enough," said Mr. Tookey, unable to keep cool any longer. "There's a conspiracy to turn me out o' the choir, as I shouldn't share the Christmas money—that's where it is. But I shall speak to Mr. Crackenthorp; I'll not be put upon by no man."

"Nay, nay, Tookey," said Ben Winthrop. "We'll pay you your share to keep out of it—that's what we'll do. There's things folks 'ud pay to be rid on, besides varmin."

"Come, come," said the landlord, who felt that paying people for their absence was a principle dangerous to society; "a joke's a joke. We're all good friends here, I hope. We must give and take. You're both right and you're both wrong, as I say. I agree with Mr. Macey here, as there's two opinions; and if mine was asked, I should say they're both right. Tookey's right and Winthrop's right, and they've only got to split the difference and make themselves even."

The farrier was puffing his pipe rather fiercely, in some contempt at this trivial discussion. He had no ear for music himself, and never went to church, as being of the medical profession, and likely to be in requisition for delicate cows. But the butcher, having music in his soul, had listened with a divided desire for Tookey's defeat, and for the preservation of the peace.

"To be sure," he said, following up the landlord's conciliatory view, "we're fond of our old clerk; it's nat'ral, and him used to be such a singer, and got a brother as is known for the first fiddler in this country-side. Eh, it's a pity but what Solomon lived in our village, and could give us a tune when we liked; eh, Mr. Macey? I'd keep him in liver and lights for nothing—that I would."

"Ay, ay," said Mr. Macey, in the height of complacency; "our family's been known for musicianers as far back as any body can tell. But them things are dying out, as I tell Solomon every time he comes round; there's no voices like what there used to be, and there's nobody remembers what we remember, if it isn't the old crows."

"Ay, you remember when first Mr. Lammeter's father come into these parts, don't you, Mr. Macey?" said the landlord.

"I should think I did," said the old man, who had now gone through that complimentary process necessary to bring him up to the point of narration; "and a fine old gentleman he was—as fine, and finer nor the Mr. Lammeter as now is. He came from a bit north'ard, so far as I could ever make out. But there's nobody rightly knows about those parts: only it couldn't be far north'ard, nor much different from this country, for he brought a fine breed o' sheep with him, so there must be pastures there, and everything reasonable. We heared tell as he'd sold his own land to come and take the Warrens, and that seemed odd for a man as had land of his own, to come and rent a farm in a strange place. But they said it was along of his wife's dying; though there's reasons in things as nobody knows on—that's pretty much what I've made out; though some folks are so wise, they'll find you fifty reasons straight off, and all the while the real reason's winking at 'em in the corner, and they niver see't. Howsomever, it was soon seen as we'd got a new parish'ner as know'd the rights and customs o' things, and kep a good house, and was well looked on by everybody. And the young man—that's the Mr. Lammeter as now is, for he'd niver a sister—soon begun to court Miss Osgood, that's the sister o' the Mr. Osgood as now is, and a fine handsome lass she was—eh, you can't think—they pretend this young lass is like her, but that's the way wi' people as don't know what come before 'em. *I* should know, for I helped the old rector, Mr. Drumlow as was, I helped him marry 'em."

Here Mr. Macey paused; he always gave his narrative in instalments, expecting to be questioned according to precedent.

"Ay, and a partic'lar thing happened, didn't it, Mr. Macey, so as you were likely to remember that marriage?" said the landlord, in a congratulatory tone.

"I should think there did—a *very* partic'lar thing," said Mr. Macey, nodding sideways. "For Mr. Drumlow—poor old gentleman, I was fond on him, though he'd got a bit confused in his head, what wi' age and wi' taking a drop o' summat warm when the service come of a cold morning. And young Mr. Lammeter, he'd have no way but he must be married in Janiwary, which, to be sure, 's a unreasonable time to be married in, for it isn't like a christening or a burying, as you can't help; and so Mr. Drumlow—poor old gentleman, I was fond on him—but when he come to put the questions, he put 'em by the rule o' contrary, like, and he says, 'Wilt thou have this man to thy wedded wife?' says he, and then he says, 'Wilt thou have this woman to thy wedded husband?' says he. But the partic'larest thing of all is, as nobody took any notice on it but me, and they answered straight off 'yes' like as if it had been me saying 'Amen' i' the right place, without listening to what went before."

"But *you* knew what was going on well enough, didn't you, Mr. Macey? You were live enough, eh?" said the butcher.

"Lor bless you!" said Mr. Macey, pausing, and smiling in pity at the impotence of his hearer's imagination—"why, I was all of a tremble; it was as if I'd been a coat pulled by the two tails, like; for I couldn't stop the parson, I couldn't take upon me to do that; and yet I said to myself, I says, 'Suppose they shouldn't be fast married, 'cause the words are contrary?' and my head went working like a mill, for I was allays uncommon for turning things over and seeing all round 'em; and I says to myself, 'Is't the meanin' or the words as makes folks fast i' wedlock?' For the parson meant right, and the bride and bridegroom meant right. But then, when I come to think on it, meanin' goes but a little way i' most things, for you may mean to stick things together and your glue may be bad, and then where are you? And so I says to mysen, 'It isn't the meanin', it's the glue.' And I was worreted as if I'd got three bells to pull at once, when we got into the vestry, and they begun to sign their names. But where's the use o' talking? you can't think what goes on in a 'cute man's inside."

"But you held in, for all that, didn't you, Mr. Macey?" said the landlord.

"Ay, I held in tight till I was by mysen wi' Mr. Drumlow, and then I out wi' every thing, but respectful, as I allays did. And he made light on it, and he says, 'Pooh, pooh, Macey, make yourself easy,' he says; 'it's neither the meaning nor the words—it's the re*ges*ter does it—that's the glue.' So you see he settled it easy; for parsons and doctors know everything by heart, like, so as they aren't worreted wi' thinking what's the rights and wrongs o' things, as I'n been many and many's the time. And sure enough the wedding turned out all right, on'y poor Mrs. Lammeter—that's Miss Osgood as was—died afore the lasses were growed up; but for prosperity and everything respectable, there's no family more looked on."

Every one of Mr. Macey's audience had heard this story many times, but it was listened to as if it had been a favorite tune, and at certain points the puffing of the pipes was momentarily suspended, that the listeners might give their whole minds to the expected words. But there was more to come; and Mr. Snell, the landlord, duly put the leading question.

"Why, old Mr. Lammeter had a pretty fortin, didn't they say, when he come into these parts?"

"Well, yes," said Mr. Macey; "but I dare say it's as much as this Mr. Lammeter has done to keep it whole. For there was allays a talk as nobody could get rich on the Warrens: though he holds it cheap, for it's what they call Charity Land."

"Ay, and there's few folks know so well as you how it come to be Charity Land, eh, Mr. Macey?" said the butcher.

"How should they?" said the old clerk, with some contempt. "Why, my grandfather made the grooms' livery for that Mr. Cliff as came and built the big stables at the Warrens. Why, they're stables four times as big as Squire Cass's, for he thought o' nothing but hosses and hunting, Cliff didn't—a Lunnon tailor, some folks said, as had gone mad wi' cheating. For he couldn't ride; lor bless you! they said he'd got no more grip o' the hoss than if his legs had been cross sticks; my grandfather heared old Squire Cass say so many and many a time. But ride he would as if Old Harry had been a-driving him; and he'd a son, a lad o' sixteen; and nothing would his father have him do, but he must ride and ride—though the lad was frighted, they said. And it was a common saying as the father wanted to ride the tailor out o' the lad, and make a gentleman on him—not but what I'm a tailor myself, but in respect as God made me such, I'm proud on it, for 'Macey, tailor,' 's been wrote up over our door since afore the Queen's heads went out on the shillings. But Cliff, he was ashamed o' being called a tailor, and he was sore vexed as his riding was laughed at, and nobody o' the gentlefolks hereabouts could abide him. Howsomever, the poor lad got sickly and died, and the father didn't live long after him, for he got queerer nor ever, and they said he used to go out i' the dead o' the night, wi' a lantern in his hand, to the stables, and set a lot o' lights burning, for he got as he couldn't sleep; and there he'd stand, cracking his whip and looking at his hosses; and they said it was a mercy as the stables didn't get burnt down wi' the poor dumb creaturs in 'em. But at last he died raving, and they found as he'd left all his property, Warrens and all, to a Lunnon Charity, and that's how the Warrens come to be Charity Land; though, as for the stables, Mr. Lammeter never uses 'em—they're out o' all chariter—lor bless you! if you was to set the doors a-banging in 'em, it 'ud sound like thunder half o'er the parish."

"Ay, but there's more going on in the stables than what folks see by daylight, eh, Mr. Macey?" said the landlord.

"Ay, ay; go that way of a dark night, that's all," said Mr. Macey, winking mysteriously, "and then make believe, if you like, as you didn't see lights i' the stables, nor hear the stamping o' the hosses, nor the cracking o' the whips, and howling, too, if it's tow'rt daybreak. 'Cliff's Holiday' has been the name of it ever sin' I were a boy; that's to say some said as it was the holiday Old Harry gev him from roasting, like. That's what my father told me, and he was a reasonable man, though there's folks nowadays know what happened afore they were born better nor they know their own business."

"What do you say to that, eh, Dowlas?" said the landlord, turning to the farrier, who was swelling with impatience for his cue. "There's a nut for *you* to crack."

Mr. Dowlas was the negative spirit in the company, and was proud of his position.

"Say? I say what a man *should* say as doesn't shut his eyes to look at a finger-post. I say, as I'm ready to wager any man ten pound, if he'll stand out wi' me any dry night in the pasture before the Warren stables, as we shall neither see lights nor hear noises, if it isn't the blowing of our own noses. That's what I say, and I've said it many a time; but there's nobody 'ull ventur a ten-pun' note on their ghos'es as they make so sure of."

"Why, Dowlas, that's easy betting, that is," said Ben Winthrop. "You might as well bet a man as he wouldn't catch the rheumatise if he stood up to 's neck in the pool of a frosty night. It 'ud be fine fun for a man to win his bet as he'd catch the rheumatise. Folks as believe in Cliff's Holiday aren't a-going to ventur near it for a matter o' ten pound."

"If Master Dowlas wants to know the truth on it," said Mr. Macey, with a sarcastic smile, tapping his thumbs together, "he's no call to lay any bet—let him go and stan' by himself—there's nobody 'ull hinder him; and then he can let the parish'ners know if they're wrong."

"Thank you! I'm obliged to you," said the farrier, with a snort of scorn. "If folks are fools, it's no business o' mine. *I* don't want to make out the truth about ghos'es: I know it a'ready. But I'm not against a bet—everything fair and open. Let any man bet me ten pound as I shall see Cliff's Holiday, and I'll go and stand by myself. I want no company. I'd as lief do it as I'd fill this pipe."

"Ah, but who's to watch you, Dowlas, and see you do it? That's no fair bet," said the butcher.

"No fair bet?" replied Mr. Dowlas, angrily. "I should like to hear any man stand up and say I want to bet unfair. Come now, Master Lundy, I should like to hear you say it."

"Very like you would," said the butcher. "But it's no business o' mine. You're none o' my bargains, and I aren't agoing to try and 'bate your price. If anybody'll bid for you at your own vallying, let him. I'm for peace and quietness, I am."

"Yes, that's what every yapping cur is, when you hold a stick up at him," said the farrier. "But I'm afraid o' neither man nor ghost, and I'm ready to lay a fair bet—*I* aren't a turn-tail cur."

"Ay, but there's this in it, Dowlas," said the landlord, speaking in a tone of much candor and tolerance. "There's folks, i' my opinion, they can't see ghos'es, not if they stood as plain as a pike-staff before 'em.

And there's reason i' that. For there's my wife now, can't smell, not if she'd the strongest o' cheese under her nose. I never see'd a ghost myself; but then I says to myself, 'Very like I haven't got the smell for 'em.' I mean, putting a ghost for a smell, or else contrairiways. And so, I'm for holding with both sides; for, as I say, the truth lies between 'em. And if Dowlas was to go and stand, and say he'd never seen a wink o' Cliff's Holiday all the night through, I'd back him; and if anybody said as Cliff's Holiday was certain sure for all that, I'd back *him* too. For the smell's what I go by."

The landlord's analogical argument was not well received by the farrier—a man intensely opposed to compromise.

"Tut, tut," he said, setting down his glass with refreshed irritation; "what's the smell got to do with it? Did ever a ghost give a man a black eye? That's what I should like to know. If ghos'es want me to believe in 'em, let 'em leave off skulking i' the dark and i' lone places—let 'em come where there's company and candles."

"As if ghos'es 'ud want to be believed in by anybody so ignirant!" said Mr. Macey, in deep disgust at the farrier's crass incompetence to apprehend the conditions of ghostly phenomena.

CHAPTER VII

YET the next moment there seemed to be some evidence that ghosts had a more condescending disposition than Mr. Macey attributed to them; for the pale thin figure of Silas Marner was suddenly seen standing in the warm light, uttering no word, but looking round at the company with his strange unearthly eyes. The long pipes gave a simultaneous movement, like the antennæ of startled insects, and every man present, not excepting even the skeptical farrier, had an impression that he saw, not Silas Marner in the flesh, but an apparition; for the door by which Silas had entered was hidden by the high-screened seats, and no one had noticed his approach. Mr. Macey, sitting a long way off the ghost, might be supposed to have felt an argumentative triumph, which would tend to neutralize his share of the general alarm. Had he not always said that when Silas Marner was in that strange trance of his, his soul went loose from his body? Here was the demonstration: nevertheless, on the whole, he would have been as well contented without it. For a few moments there was a dead silence, Marner's want of breath and agitation not allowing him to speak. The landlord, under the habitual sense that he was bound to keep his house open to all company, and confident in the protection of his unbroken neutrality, at last took on himself the task of adjuring the ghost.

"Master Marner," he said, in a conciliatory tone, "what's lacking to you? What's your business here?"

"Robbed!" said Silas, gaspingly. "I've been robbed! I want the constable—and the Justice—and Squire Cass—and Mr. Crackenthorp."

"Lay hold on him, Jem Rodney," said the landlord, the idea of a ghost subsiding; "he's off his head, I doubt. He's wet through."

Jem Rodney was the outermost man, and sat conveniently near Marner's standing-place; but he declined to give his services.

"Come and lay hold on him yourself, Mr. Snell, if you've a mind," said Jem, rather sullenly. "He's been robbed, and murdered too, for what I know," he added, in a muttering tone.

"Jem Rodney!" said Silas, turning and fixing his strange eyes on the suspected man.

"Ay, Master Marner, what do ye want wi' me?" said Jem, trembling a little, and seizing his drinking-can as a defensive weapon.

"If it was you stole my money," said Silas, clasping his hands entreatingly, and raising his voice to a cry, "give it me back,—and I won't meddle with you. I won't set the constable on you. Give it me back, and I'll let you—I'll let you have a guinea."

"Me stole your money!" said Jem, angrily. "I'll pitch this can at your eye if you talk o' *my* stealing your money."

"Come, come, Master Marner," said the landlord, now rising resolutely, and seizing Marner by the shoulder, "if you've got any information to lay, speak it out sensible, and show as you're in your right mind, if you expect any body to listen to you. You're as wet as a drownded rat. Sit down and dry yourself, and speak straight forrard."

"Ah, to be sure, man," said the farrier, who began to feel that he had not been quite on a par with himself and the occasion. "Let's have no more staring and screaming, else we'll have you strapped for a madman. That was why I didn't speak at the first—thinks I, the man's run mad."

"Ay, ay, make him sit down," said several voices at once, well pleased that the reality of ghosts remained still an open question.

The landlord forced Marner to take off his coat, and then to sit down on a chair aloof from every one else in the centre of the circle, and in the direct rays of the fire. The weaver, too feeble to have any distinct purpose beyond that of getting help to recover his money, submitted unresistingly. The transient fears of the company were now forgotten in their strong curiosity, and all faces were turned towards Silas, when the landlord, having seated himself again, said—

"Now then, Master Marner, what's this you've got to say, as you've been robbed? Speak out."

"He'd better not say again as it was me robbed him," cried Jem Rodney, hastily. "What could I ha' done with his money? I could as easy steal the parson's surplice, and wear it."

"Hold your tongue, Jem, and let's hear what he's got to say," said the landlord. "Now then, Master Marner."

Silas now told his story under frequent questioning, as the mysterious character of the robbery became evident.

This strangely novel situation of opening his trouble to his Raveloe neighbors, of sitting in the warmth of a hearth not his own, and feeling the presence of faces and voices which were his nearest promise of help, had doubtless its influence on Marner, in spite of his passionate preoccupation with his loss. Our consciousness rarely registers the beginning of a growth within us any more than without us: there have been many circulations of the sap before we detect the smallest sign of the bud.

The slight suspicion with which his hearers at first listened to him, gradually melted away before the convincing simplicity of his distress: it was impossible for the neighbors to doubt that Marner was telling the truth, not because they were capable of arguing at once from the nature of his statements to the absence of any motive for making them falsely, but because, as Mr. Macey observed, "Folks as had the devil to back 'em were not likely to be so mushed" as poor Silas was. Rather, from the strange fact that the robber had left no traces, and had happened to know the nick of time, utterly incalculable by mortal agents, when Silas would go away from home without locking his door, the more probable conclusion seemed to be that his disreputable intimacy in that quarter, if it ever existed, had been broken up, and that, in consequence, this ill turn had been done to Marner by somebody it was quite in vain to set the constable after. Why this preternatural felon should be obliged to wait till the door was left unlocked, was a question which did not present itself.

"It isn't Jem Rodney as has done this work, Master Marner," said the landlord. "You mustn't be a-casting your eye at poor Jem. There may be a bit of a reckoning against Jem for the matter of a hare or so, if anybody was bound to keep their eyes staring open, and niver to wink —but Jem's been a-sitting here drinking his can, like the decentest man i' the parish, since before you left your house, Master Marner, by your own account."

"Ay, ay," said Mr. Macey; "let's have no accusing o' the innicent. That isn't the law. There must be folks to swear again' a man before he can be ta'en up. Let's have no accusing o' the innicent, Master Marner."

Memory was not so utterly torpid in Silas that it could not be wakened by these words. With a movement of compunction as new and strange to him as everything else within the last hour, he started from his chair and went close up to Jem, looking at him as if he wanted to assure himself of the expression in his face.

"I was wrong," he said—"yes, yes—I ought to have thought. There's nothing to witness against you, Jem. Only you'd been into my house oftener than anybody else, and so you came into my head. I don't accuse you—I won't accuse anybody—only," he added, lifting up his hands to his head, and turning away with bewildered misery, "I try—I try to think where my money can be."

"Ay, ay, they're gone where it's hot enough to melt 'em, I doubt," said Mr. Macey.

"Tchuh!" said the farrier. And then he asked, with a cross-examining air. "How much money might there be in the bags, Master Marner?"

"Two hundred and seventy-two pounds, twelve and six-pence, last night when I counted it," said Silas, seating himself again, with a groan.

"Pooh! why, they'd be none so heavy to carry. Some tramp's been in, that's all; and as for the no footmarks, and the bricks and the sand being all right—why, your eyes are pretty much like a insect's, Master Marner; they're obliged to look so close, you can't see much at a time. It's my opinion as, if I'd been you, or you'd been me—for it comes to the same thing—you wouldn't have thought you'd found everything as you left it. But what I vote is, as two of the sensiblest o' the company should go with you to Master Kench, the constable's—he's ill i' bed, I know that much—and get him to appoint one of us his deppity; for that's the law, and I don't think any body 'ull take upon him to contradick me there. It isn't much of a walk to Kench's; and then if it's me as is deppity, I'll go back with you, Master Marner, and examine your primises; and if any body's got any fault to find with that, I'll thank him to stand up and say it out like a man."

By this pregnant speech the farrier had re-established his self-complacency, and waited with confidence to hear himself named as one of the superlatively sensible men.

"Let us see how the night is, though," said the landlord, who also considered himself personally concerned in this proposition. "Why, it rains heavy still," he said, returning from the door.

"Well, I'm not the man to be afraid o' the rain," said the farrier. "For it'll look bad when Justice Malam hears as respectable men like us had a information laid before 'em and took no steps."

The landlord agreed with this view, and after taking the sense of the company, and duly rehearsing a small ceremony known in high ecclesiastical life as the *nolo episcopari,* he consented to take on himself the chill dignity of going to Kench's. But to the farrier's strong disgust, Mr. Macey now started an objection to his proposing himself as a deputy-constable; for that oracular old gentleman, claiming to know the law, stated, as a fact delivered to him by his father, that no doctor could be a constable.

"And you're a doctor, I reckon, though you're only a cow-doctor—for a fly's a fly, though it may be a hoss-fly," concluded Mr. Macey, wondering a little at his own " 'cuteness."

There was a hot debate upon this, the farrier being of course indisposed to renounce the quality of doctor, but contending that a doctor could be a constable if he liked—the law meant, he needn't be one if he didn't like. Mr. Macey thought this was nonsense, since the law was not likely to be fonder of doctors more than of other folks. Moreover, if it was in the nature of doctors more than of other men not to like being constables, how came Mr. Dowlas to be so eager to act in that capacity?

"*I* don't want to act the constable," said the farrier, driven into a corner by this merciless reasoning; "and there's no man can say it of me, if he'd tell the truth. But if there's to be any jealousy and envying about going to Kench's in the rain, let them go as like it—you won't get me to go, I can tell you."

By the landlord's intervention, however, the dispute was accommodated. Mr. Dowlas consented to go as a second person disinclined to act officially; and so poor Silas, furnished with some old coverings, turned out with his two companions into the rain again, thinking of the long night-hours before him, not as those do who long to rest, but as those who expect to "watch for the morning."

CHAPTER VIII

WHEN Godfrey Cass returned from Mrs. Osgood's party at midnight, he was not much surprised to learn that Dunsey had not come home. Perhaps he had not sold Wildfire, and was waiting for another chance— perhaps, on that foggy afternoon, he had preferred housing himself at the Red Lion at Batherley for the night, if the run had kept him in that neighborhood; for he was not likely to feel much concern about leaving his brother in suspense. Godfrey's mind was too full of Nancy Lammeter's looks and behavior, too full of the exasperation against himself and his lot, which the sight of her always produced in him, for him to give much thought to Wildfire, or to the probabilities of Dunstan's conduct.

The next morning the whole village was excited by the story of the robbery, and Godfrey, like every one else, was occupied in gathering and discussing news about it, and in visiting the Stone-pits. The rain had washed away all possibility of distinguishing footmarks, but a close investigation of the spot had disclosed, in the direction opposite to the village, a tinder-box, with a flint and steel, half sunk in the mud. It was not Silas's tinder-box, for the only one he had ever had was still standing on his shelf; and the inference generally accepted was, that the tinder-box in the ditch was somehow connected with the robbery. A small minority shook their heads, and intimated their opinion that it was not a robbery to have much light thrown on it by tinder-boxes, that Master Marner's tale had a queer look with it, and that such things had been known as a man's doing himself a mischief, and then setting the justice to look for the doer. But when questioned closely as to their grounds for this opinion, and what Master Marner had to gain by such false pretenses, they only shook their heads as before, and observed that there was no knowing what some folks counted gain; moreover, that everybody had a right to their own opinions, grounds or no grounds, and that the weaver, as everybody knew, was partly crazy. Mr. Macey, though he joined in the defense of Marner against all suspicions of deceit, also pooh-poohed the tinder-box; indeed, repudiated it as a rather impious suggestion, tending to imply that everything must be done by human hands, and that there was no power which could make away with the guineas without moving the bricks. Nevertheless, he turned round rather sharply on Mr. Tookey, when the zealous deputy, feeling that this was a view of the case peculiarly suited to a parish-clerk, carried it still farther, and doubted whether it was right to inquire into a robbery at all when the circumstances were so mysterious.

"As if," concluded Mr. Tookey—"as if there was nothing but what could be made out by justices and constables."

"Now, don't you be for overshooting the mark, Tookey," said Mr. Macey, nodding his head aside admonishingly. "That's what your allays at; if I throw a stone and hit, you think there's summat better than hitting, and you try to throw a stone beyond. What I said was against the tinder-box: I said nothing against justices and constables, for they're o' King George's making, and it 'ud be ill-becoming a man in a parish office to fly out again' King George."

While these discussions were going on amongst the group outside the Rainbow, a higher consultation was being carried on within, under the presidency of Mr. Crackenthorp, the rector, assisted by Squire Cass, and other substantial parishioners. It had just occurred to Mr. Snell, the landlord—he being, as he observed, a man accustomed to put two and two together—to connect with the tinder-box, which, as deputy constable, he himself had had the honorable distinction of finding, certain recollections of a peddler who had called to drink at the house about a month before, and had actually stated that he carried a tinder-box about with him to light his pipe. Here, surely, was a clue to be followed out. And as memory, when duly impregnated with ascertained facts, is sometimes surprisingly fertile, Mr. Snell gradually recovered a vivid impression of the effect produced on him by the peddler's countenance and conversation. He had a "look with his eye" which fell unpleasantly on Mr. Snell's sensitive organism. To be sure, he didn't say anything particular—no, except that about the tinder-box—but it isn't what a man says, it's the way he says it. Moreover, he had a swarthy foreignness of complexion, which boded little honesty.

"Did he wear ear-rings?" Mr. Crackenthorp wished to know, having some acquaintance with foreign customs.

"Well—stay—let me see," said Mr. Snell, like a docile clairvoyante, who would really not make a mistake if she could help it. After stretching the corners of his mouth and contracting his eyes, as if he were trying to see the ear-rings, he appeared to give up the effort, and said, "Well, he'd got ear-rings in his box to sell, so it's nat'ral to suppose he might wear 'em. But he called at every house, a'most, in the village: there's somebody else, mayhap, saw 'em in his ears, though I can't take upon me rightly to say."

Mr. Snell was correct in his surmise, that somebody else would remember the peddler's ear-rings. For, on the spread of inquiry among the villagers, it was stated with gathering emphasis, that the parson had wanted to know whether the peddler wore ear-rings in his ears, and an impression was created that a great deal depended on the eliciting of this fact. Of course, every one who heard the question, not having any distinct image of the peddler as *without* ear-rings, immediately had an image of him *with* ear-rings, larger or smaller, as the case might be; and the image was presently taken for a vivid recollection, so that the glazier's wife, a well-intentioned woman, not given to lying, and whose house was among the cleanest in the village, was ready to declare, as sure as ever she meant to take the sacrament the very next Christmas that was ever coming, that she had seen big ear-rings, in the shape of the young moon, in the peddler's two ears; while Jinny Oates, the cobbler's daughter, being a more imaginative person, stated not only that she had seen them too, but that they had made her blood creep, as it did at that very moment while there she stood.

Also, by way of throwing further light on this clue of the tinder-box, a collection was made of all the articles purchased from the peddler at various houses, and carried to the Rainbow to be exhibited there. In fact, there was a general feeling in the village, that for the clearing-up of this robbery there must be a great deal done at the Rainbow, and that no man need offer his wife an excuse for going there while it was the scene of severe public duties.

Some disappointment was felt, and perhaps a little indignation also, when it became known that Silas Marner, on being questioned by the Squire and the parson, had retained no other recollection of the peddler than that he had called at his door, but had not entered his house, having turned away at once when Silas, holding the door ajar, had said that he wanted nothing. This had been Silas's testimony, though he clutched strongly at the idea of the peddler's being the culprit, if only because it gave him a definite image of a whereabout for his gold, after it had been taken away from its hiding-place: he could see it now in the peddler's box. But it was observed with some irritation in the village, that anybody but a "blind creatur" like Marner would have seen the man prowling about, for how came he to leave his tinder-box in the ditch close by, if he hadn't been lingering there? Doubtless, he had made his observations when he saw Marner at the door. Anybody might know—and only look at him—that the weaver was a half-crazy miser. It was a wonder the peddler hadn't murdered him; men of that sort, with rings in their ears, had been known for murderers often and often; there had been one tried at the 'sizes, not so long ago but what there were people living who remembered it.

Godfrey Cass, indeed, entering the Rainbow during one of Mr. Snell's frequently repeated recitals of his testimony, had treated it lightly, stating that he himself had bought a penknife of the peddler, and thought him a merry grinning fellow enough; it was all nonsense, he said, about the man's evil looks. But this was spoken of in the village as the random talk of youth, "as if it was only Mr. Snell who had seen something odd about the peddler!" On the contrary, there were at least half a dozen who were ready to go before Justice Malam, and give in much more striking testimony than any the landlord could furnish. It was to be hoped Mr. Godfrey would not go to Tarley and throw cold water on what Mr. Snell said there, and so prevent the justice from drawing up a warrant. He was suspected of intending this, when, after mid-day, he was seen setting off on horseback in the direction of Tarley.

But by this time Godfrey's interest in the robbery had faded before his growing anxiety about Dunstan and Wildfire, and he was going, not to Tarley, but to Batherley, unable to rest in uncertainty about them any longer. The possibility that Dunstan had played him the ugly trick of riding away with Wildfire, to return at the end of a month, when he had gambled away or otherwise squandered the price of the horse, was a fear that urged itself upon him more, even, than the thought of an accidental injury; and now that the dance at Mrs. Osgood's was past, he was irritated with himself that he had trusted his horse to Dunstan. Instead of trying to still his fears, he encouraged them, with that superstitious impression which clings to us all, that if we expect evil very strongly it is the less likely to come; and when he heard a horse approaching at a trot, and saw a hat rising above a hedge beyond an angle of the lane, he felt as if his conjuration had succeeded. But no sooner did the horse come within sight, than his heart sank again. It was not Wildfire; and in a few moments more he discerned that the rider was not Dunstan, but Bryce, who pulled up to speak, with a face that implied something disagreeable.

"Well, Mr. Godfrey, that's a lucky brother of yours, that Master Dunsey, isn't he?"

"What do you mean?" said Godfrey, hastily.

"Why, hasn't he been home yet?" said Bryce.

"Home? No. What has happened? Be quick. What has he done with my horse?"

"Ah, I thought it was yours, though he pretended you had parted with it to him."

"Has he thrown him down and broken his knees?" said Godfrey, flushed with exasperation.

"Worse than that," said Bryce. "You see, I'd made a bargain with him to buy the horse for a hundred and twenty—a swinging price, but I always liked the horse. And what does he do but go and stake him— fly at a hedge with stakes in it, atop of a bank with a ditch before it. The horse had been dead a pretty good while when he was found. So he hasn't been home since, has he?"

"Home? No," said Godfrey, "and he'd better keep away. Confound me for a fool! I might have known this would be the end of it."

"Well, to tell you the truth," said Bryce, "after I'd bargained for the horse, it did come into my head that he might be riding and selling the horse without your knowledge, for I didn't believe it was his own. I knew Master Dunsey was up to his tricks sometimes. But where can he be gone? He's never been seen at Batherley. He couldn't have been hurt, for he must have walked off."

"Hurt?" said Godfrey, bitterly. "He'll never be hurt—he's made to hurt other people."

"And so you *did* give him leave to sell the horse, eh?" said Bryce.

"Yes; I wanted to part with the horse—he was always a little too hard in the mouth for me," said Godfrey; his pride making him wince under the idea that Bryce guessed the sale to be a matter of necessity. "I was going to see after him—I thought some mischief had happened. I'll go back now," he added, turning the horse's head, and wishing he could get rid of Bryce; for he felt that the long-dreaded crisis in his life was close upon him. "You're coming on to Raveloe, aren't you?"

"Well, no, not now," said Bryce. "I *was* coming round there, for I had to go to Flitton, and I thought I might as well take you in my way, and just let you know all I knew myself about the horse. I suppose Master Dunsey didn't like to show himself till the ill news had blown over a bit. He's perhaps gone to pay a visit at the Three Crowns, by Whitbridge—I know he's fond of the house."

"Perhaps he is," said Godfrey, rather absently. Then rousing himself, he said, with an effort at carelessness, "We shall hear of him soon enough, I'll be bound."

"Well, here's my turning," said Bryce, not surprised to perceive that Godfrey was rather 'down;' "so I'll bid you good-day, and wish I may bring you better news another time."

Godfrey rode along slowly, representing to himself the scene of confession to his father from which he felt that there was now no longer any escape. The revelation about the money must be made the very next morning; and if he withheld the rest, Dunstan would be sure to come back shortly, and, finding that he must bear the brunt of his father's anger, would tell the whole story out of spite, even though he had nothing to gain by it. There was one step, perhaps, by which he might still win Dunstan's silence and put off the evil day: he might tell his father that he had himself spent the money paid to him by Fowler; and as he had never been guilty of such an offense before, the affair would blow over after a little storming. But Godfrey could not bend himself to this. He felt that in letting Dunstan have the money, he had already been guilty of a breach of trust hardly less culpable than that of spending the money directly for his own behoof; and yet there was a distinction between the two acts which made him feel that the one was so much more blackening than the other as to be intolerable to him.

"I don't pretend to be a good fellow," he said to himself; "but I'm not a scoundrel—at least, I'll stop short somewhere. I'll bear the consequences of what I *have* done, sooner than make believe I've done what I never would have done. I'd never have spent the money for my own pleasure—I was tortured into it."

Through the remainder of this day Godfrey, with only occasional fluctuations, kept his will bent in the direction of a complete avowal to his father, and he withheld the story of Wildfire's loss till the next morning, that it might serve him as an introduction to heavier matter. The old Squire was accustomed to his son's frequent absence from home, and thought neither Dunstan's nor Wildfire's non-appearance a matter calling for remark. Godfrey said to himself again and again, that if he let slip this one opportunity of confession, he might never have another; the revelation might be made even in a more odious way than by Dunstan's malignity: *she* might come as she had threatened to do. And then he tried to make the scene easier to himself by rehearsal: he made up his mind how he would pass from the admission of his weakness in letting Dunstan have the money to the fact that Dunstan had a hold on him which he had been unable to shake off, and how he would work up his father to expect something very bad before he told him the fact. The old Squire was an implacable man: he made resolutions in violent anger, but he was not to be moved from them after his anger had subsided—as fiery volcanic matters cool and harden into rock. Like many violent and implacable men, he allowed evils to grow under favor of his own heedlessness, till they pressed upon him with exasperating force, and then he turned round with fierce severity and became unrelentingly hard. This was his system with his tenants: he allowed them to get into arrears, neglect their fences, reduce their stock, sell their straw, and otherwise go the wrong way,—and then, when he became short of money in consequence of this indulgence, he took the hardest measures and would listen to no appeal. Godfrey knew all this, and felt it with the greater force because he had constantly suffered annoyance from witnessing his father's sudden fits of unrelentingness, for which his own habitual irresolution deprived him of all sympathy. (He was not critical on the faulty indulgence which preceded these fits; *that* seemed to him natural enough.) Still there was just the chance, Godfrey thought, that his father's pride might see this marriage in a light that would induce him to hush it up, rather than turn his son out and make the family the talk of the country for ten miles round.

This was the view of the case that Godfrey managed to keep before him pretty closely till midnight, and he went to sleep thinking that he had done with inward debating. But when he awoke in the still morning darkness he found it impossible to re-awaken his evening thoughts; it was as if they had been tired out and were not to be roused to further work. Instead of arguments for confession, he could now feel the presence of nothing but its evil consequences: the old dread of disgrace came back—the old shrinking from the thought of raising a hopeless barrier between himself and Nancy—the old disposition to rely on chances which might be favorable to him, and save him from betrayal. Why, after all, should he cut off the hope of them by his own act? He had seen the matter in a wrong light yesterday. He had been in a rage with Dunstan, and had thought of nothing but a thorough break-up of their mutual understanding; but what it would be really wisest for him to do, was to try and soften his father's anger against Dunsey, and keep things as nearly as possible in their old condition. If Dunsey did not come back for a few days (and Godfrey did not know but that the rascal had enough money in his pocket to enable him to keep away still longer), everything might blow over.

CHAPTER IX

GODFREY rose and took his own breakfast earlier than usual, but lingered
in the wainscoted parlor till his younger brothers had finished their meal
and gone out, awaiting his father, who always went out and had a walk
with his managing-man before breakfast. Every one breakfasted at a
different hour in the Red House, and the Squire was always the latest,
giving a long chance to a rather feeble morning appetite before he
tried it. The table had been spread with substantial eatables nearly two
hours before he presented himself—a tall, stout man of sixty, with a
face in which the knit brow and rather hard glance seemed contradicted
by the slack and feeble mouth. His person showed marks of habitual
neglect, his dress was slovenly; and yet there was something in the
presence of the old Squire distinguishable from that of the ordinary
farmers in the parish, who were perhaps every whit as refined as he,
but, having slouched their way through life with a consciousness of being in the vicinity of their "betters," wanted that self-possession and
authoritativeness of voice and carriage which belonged to a man who
thought of superiors as remote existences, with whom he had personally
little more to do than with America or the stars. The Squire had been
used to parish homage all his life, used to the presupposition that his
family, his tankards, and everything that was his, were the oldest and
best; and as he never associated with any gentry higher than himself,
his opinion was not disturbed by comparison.

He glanced at his son as he entered the room, and said, "What, sir!
haven't *you* had your breakfast yet?" but there was no pleasant morning greeting between them; not because of any unfriendliness, but because the sweet flower of courtesy is not a growth of such homes as the
Red House.

"Yes, sir," said Godfrey, "I've had my breakfast, but I was waiting to
speak to you."

"Ah! well," said the Squire, throwing himself indifferently into his
chair, and speaking in a ponderous coughing fashion, which was felt in
Raveloe to be a sort of privilege of his rank, while he cut a piece of
beef, and held it up before the deer-hound that had come in with him.
"Ring the bell for my ale, will you? You youngsters' business is your
own pleasure, mostly. There's no hurry about it for anybody but yourselves."

The Squire's life was quite as idle as his sons', but it was a fiction
kept up by himself and his contemporaries in Raveloe that youth was
exclusively the period of folly, and that their aged wisdom was constantly in a state of endurance mitigated by sarcasm. Godfrey waited,
before he spoke again, until the ale had been brought and the door
closed—an interval during which Fleet, the deer-hound, had consumed
enough bits of beef to make a poor man's holiday dinner.

"There's been a cursed piece of ill-luck with Wildfire," he began; "happened the day before yesterday."

"What! broke his knees?" said the Squire, after taking a draught of ale. "I thought you knew how to ride better than that, sir. I never threw a horse down in my life. If I had, I might ha' whistled for another, for *my* father wasn't quite so ready to unstring as some other fathers I know of. But they must turn over a new leaf—*they* must. What with mortgages and arrears, I'm as short o' cash as a roadside pauper. And that fool Kimble says the newspaper's talking about peace. Why, the country wouldn't have a leg to stand on. Prices 'ud run down like a jack, and I should never get my arrears, not if I sold all the fellows up. And there's that damned Fowler, I won't put up with him any longer; I've told Winthrop to go to Cox this very day. The lying scoundrel told me he'd be sure to pay me a hundred last month. He takes advantage because he's on that outlying farm, and thinks I shall forget him."

The squire had delivered this speech in a coughing and interrupted manner, but with no pause long enough for Godfrey to make it a pretext for taking up the word again. He felt that his father meant to ward off any request for money on the ground of the misfortune with Wildfire, and that the emphasis he had thus been led to lay on his shortness of cash and his arrears was likely to produce an attitude of mind the most unfavorable for his own disclosure. But he must go on, now he had begun.

"It's worse than breaking the horse's knees—he's been staked and killed," he said, as soon as his father was silent, and had begun to cut his meat. "But I wasn't thinking of asking you to buy me another horse; I was only thinking I'd lost the means of paying you with the price of Wildfire, as I'd meant to do. Dunsey took him to the hunt to sell him for me the other day, and after he'd made a bargain for a hundred and twenty with Bryce, he went after the hounds, and took some fool's leap or other, that did for the horse at once. If it hadn't been for that, I should have paid you a hundred pounds this morning."

The Squire had laid down his knife and fork, and was staring at his son in amazement, not being sufficiently quick of brain to form a probable guess as to what could have caused so strange an inversion of the paternal and filial relations as this proposition of his son to pay him a hundred pounds.

"The truth is, sir—I'm very sorry—I was quite to blame," said Godfrey. "Fowler did pay that hundred pounds. He paid it to me, when I was over there one day last month. And Dunsey bothered me for the money, and I let him have it, because I hoped I should be able to pay it you before this."

The Squire was purple with anger before his son had done speaking, and found utterance difficult. "You let Dunsey have it, sir? And how long have you been so thick with Dunsey that you must *collogue* with him to embezzle my money? Are you turning out a scamp? I tell you

I won't have it. I'll turn the whole pack of you out of the house together, and marry again. I'd have you to remember, sir, my property's
got no entail on it;—since my grandfather's time the Casses can do as
they like with their land. Remember that, sir. Let Dunsey have the
money! Why should you let Dunsey have the money? There's some
lie at the bottom of it."

"There's no lie, sir," said Godfrey. "I wouldn't have spent the money
myself, but Dunsey bothered me, and I was a fool, and let him have
it. But I meant to pay it, whether he did or not. That's the whole
story. I never meant to embezzle money, and I'm not the man to do
it. You never knew me do a dishonest trick, sir."

"Where's Dunsey, then? What do you stand talking there for? Go
and fetch Dunsey, as I tell you, and let him give account of what he
wanted the money for, and what he's done with it. He shall repent it.
I'll turn him out. I said I would, and I'll do it. He shan't brave me.
Go and fetch him."

"Dunsey isn't come back, sir."

"What! did he break his own neck, then?" said the Squire, with
some disgust at the idea that, in that case, he could not fulfil his threat.

"No, he wasn't hurt, I believe, for the horse was found dead, and
Dunsey must have walked off. I dare say we shall see him again by-
and-by. I don't know where he is."

"And what must you be letting him have my money for? Answer me
that," said the Squire, attacking Godfrey again, since Dunsey was not
within reach.

"Well, sir, I don't know," said Godfrey hesitatingly. That was a
feeble evasion, but Godfrey was not fond of lying, and, not being
sufficiently aware that no sort of duplicity can long flourish without the
help of vocal falsehoods, he was quite unprepared with invented motives.

"You don't know? I tell you what it is, sir. You've been up to some
trick, and you've been bribing him not to tell," said the Squire, with a
sudden acuteness which startled Godfrey, who felt his heart beat
violently at the nearness of his father's guess. The sudden alarm pushed
him on to take the next step—a very slight impulse suffices for that
on a downward road.

"Why, sir," he said, trying to speak with careless ease, "it was a
little affair between me and Dunsey; it's no matter to anybody else.
It's hardly worth while to pry into young men's fooleries: it wouldn't
have made any difference to you, sir, if I'd not had the bad luck to
lose Wildfire. I should have paid you the money."

"Fooleries! Pshaw! it's time you'd done with fooleries. And I'd have
you know, sir, you *must* ha' done with 'em," said the Squire, frowning
and casting an angry glance at his son. "Your goings-on are not what
I shall find money for any longer. There's my grandfather had his
stables full o' horses, and kept a good house, too, and in worse times,
by what I can make out; and so might I, if I hadn't four good-for-

nothing fellows to hang on me like horse-leeches. I've been too good a father to you all—that's what it is. But I shall pull up, sir."

Godfrey was silent. He was not likely to be very penetrating in his judgments, but he had always had a sense that his father's indulgence had not been kindness, and had had a vague looking for some discipline that would have checked his own errant weakness, and helped his better will. The Squire ate his bread and meat hastily, took a deep draught of ale, then turned his chair from the table, and began to speak again.

"It'll be all the worse for you, you know—you'd need try and help me keep things together."

"Well, sir, I've often offered to take the management of things, but you know you've taken it ill always, and seemed to think I wanted to push you out of your place."

"I know nothing o' your offering or o' my taking it ill," said the Squire, whose memory consisted in certain strong impressions unmodified by detail; "but I know, one while you seemed to be thinking o' marrying, and I didn't offer to put any obstacles in your way, as some fathers would. I'd as lieve you married Lammeter's daughter as anybody. I suppose, if I'd said you nay you'd ha' kept on with it; but, for want o' contradiction, you've changed your mind. You're a shilly-shally fellow: you take after your poor mother. She never had a will of her own; a woman has no call for one, if she's got a proper man for a husband. But *your* wife had need have one, for you hardly know your own mind enough to make both your legs walk one way. The lass hasn't said downright she won't have you, has she?"

"No," said Godfrey, feeling very hot and uncomfortable; "but I don't think she will."

"Think! why haven't you the courage to ask her? Do you stick to it, you want to have *her*—that's the thing?"

"There's no other woman I want to marry," said Godfrey, evasively.

"Well, then, let me make the offer for you, that's all, if you haven't the pluck to do it yourself. Lammeter isn't likely to be loath for his daughter to marry into *my* family, I should think. And as for the pretty lass, she wouldn't have her cousin—and there's nobody else, as I see, could ha' stood in your way."

"I'd rather let it be, please sir, at present," said Godfrey, in alarm. "I think she's a little offended with me just now, and I should like to speak for myself. A man must manage these things for himself."

"Well, speak, then, and manage it, and see if you can't turn over a new leaf. That's what a man must do when he thinks o' marrying."

"I don't see how I can think of it at present, sir. You wouldn't like to settle me on one of the farms, I suppose, and I don't think she'd come to live in this house with all my brothers. It's a different sort of life to what she's been used to."

"Not come to live in this house? Don't tell me. You ask her, that's all," said the Squire, with a short, scornful laugh.

"I'd rather let the thing be, at present, sir," said Godfrey. "I hope you won't try to hurry it on by saying any thing."

"I shall do what I choose," said the Squire, "and I shall let you know I'm master; else you may turn out, and find an estate to drop into somewhere else. Go out and tell Winthrop not to go to Cox's, but wait for me. And tell 'em to get my horse saddled. And stop: look out and get that hack o' Dunsey's sold, and hand me the money, will you? He'll keep no more hacks at my expense. And if you know where he's sneaking—I dare say you do—you may tell him to spare himself the journey o' coming back home. Let him turn ostler, and keep himself. He shan't hang on me any more."

"I don't know where he is, sir; and if I did, it isn't my place to tell him to keep away," said Godfrey, moving towards the door.

"Confound it, sir, don't stay arguing, but go and order my horse," said the Squire, taking up a pipe.

Godfrey left the room, hardly knowing whether he were more relieved by the sense that the interview was ended without having made any change in his position, or more uneasy that he had entangled himself still further in prevarication and deceit. What had passed about his proposing to Nancy had raised a new alarm, lest by some after-dinner words of his father's to Mr. Lammeter he should be thrown into the embarrassment of being obliged absolutely to decline her when she seemed to be within his reach. He fled to his usual refuge, that of hoping for some unforeseen turn of fortune, some favorable chance which would save him from unpleasant consequences—perhaps even justify his insincerity by manifesting its prudence. And in this point of trusting to some throw of fortune's dice, Godfrey can hardly be called specially old-fashioned. Favourable Chance, I fancy, is the god of all men who follow their own devices instead of obeying a law they believe in. Let even a polished man of these days get into a position he is ashamed to avow, and his mind will be bent on all the possible issues that may deliver him from the calculable results of that position. Let him live outside his income, or shirk the resolute honest work that brings wages, and he will presently find himself dreaming of a possible benefactor, a possible simpleton who may be cajoled into using his interest, a possible state of mind in some possible person not yet forthcoming. Let him neglect the responsibilities of his office, and he will inevitably anchor himself on the chance that the thing left undone may turn out not to be of the supposed importance. Let him betray his friend's confidence, and he will adore that same cunning complexity called Chance, which gives him the hope that his friend will never know. Let him forsake a decent craft that he may pursue the gentilities of a profession to which nature never called him, and his religion will infallibly be the worship of blessed Chance, which he will believe in as the mighty creator of success. The evil principle deprecated in that religion, is the orderly sequence by which the seed brings forth a crop after its kind.

CHAPTER X

JUSTICE MALAM was naturally regarded in Tarley and Raveloe as a man of capacious mind, seeing that he could draw much wider conclusions without evidence than could be expected of his neighbors who were not on the Commission of the Peace. Such a man was not likely to neglect the clue of the tinder-box, and an inquiry was set on foot concerning a peddler, name unknown, with curly black hair and a foreign complexion, carrying a box of cutlery and jewelry, and wearing large rings in his ears. But either because inquiry was too slow-footed to overtake him, or because the description applied to so many peddlers that inquiry did not know how to choose among them, weeks passed away, and there was no other result concerning the robbery than a gradual cessation of the excitement it had caused in Raveloe. Dunstan Cass's absence was hardly a subject of remark: he had once before had a quarrel with his father, and had gone off, nobody knew whither, to return at the end of six weeks, take up his old quarters unforbidden, and swagger as usual. His own family, who equally expected this issue, with the sole difference that the Squire was determined this time to forbid him the old quarters, never mentioned his absence; and when his uncle Kimble or Mr. Osgood noticed it, the story of his having killed Wildfire, and committed some offense against his father, was enough to prevent surprise. To connect the fact of Dunsey's disappearance with that of the robbery occurring on the same day, lay quite away from the track of every one's thought—even Godfrey's, who had better reason than any one else to know what his brother was capable of. He remembered no mention of the weaver between them since the time, twelve years ago, when it was their boyish sport to deride him; and, besides, his imagination constantly created an *alibi* for Dunstan: he saw him continually in some congenial haunt, to which he had walked off on leaving Wildfire—saw him sponging on chance acquaintances, and meditating a return home to the old amusement of tormenting his elder brother. Even if any brain in Raveloe had put the said two facts together, I doubt whether a combination so injurious to the prescriptive respectability of a family with a mural monument and venerable tankards, would not have been suppressed as of unsound tendency. But Christmas puddings, brawn, and abundance of spirituous liquors, throwing the mental originality into the channel of nightmare, are great preservatives against a dangerous spontaneity of waking thought.

When the robbery was talked of at the Rainbow and elsewhere, in good company, the balance continued to waver between the rational explanation founded on the tinder-box, and the theory of an impenetrable mystery that mocked investigation. The advocates of the tinder-box-and-peddler view considered the other side a muddle-headed and credulous set, who, because they themselves were wall-eyed, supposed everybody else to have the same blank outlook; and the adherents of the inexplicable more than hinted that their antagonists were animals inclined to crow before they had found any corn—mere skimming-dishes in point of depth—whose clear-sightedness consisted in supposing there was nothing behind a barn-door because they couldn't see through it; so that, though their controversy did not serve to elicit the fact concerning the robbery, it elicited some true opinions of collateral importance.

But while poor Silas's loss served thus to brush the slow current of Raveloe conversation, Silas himself was feeling the withering desolation of that bereavement, about which his neighbors were arguing at their ease. To any one who had observed him before he lost his gold, it might have seemed that so withered and shrunken a life as his could hardly be susceptible of a bruise, could hardly endure any subtraction but such as would put an end to it altogether. But in reality it had been an eager life, filled with immediate purpose, which fenced him in from the wide, cheerless unknown. It had been a clinging life; and though the object round which its fibres had clung was a dead disrupted thing, it satisfied the need for clinging. But now the fence was broken down—the support was snatched away. Marner's thoughts could no longer move in their old round, and were baffled by a blank like that which meets a plodding ant when the earth has broken away on its homeward path. The loom was there, and the weaving, and the growing pattern in the cloth; but the bright treasure in the hole under his feet was gone; the prospect of handling and counting it was gone: the evening had no phantasm of delight to still the poor soul's craving. The thought of the money he would get by his actual work could bring no joy, for its meagre image was only a fresh reminder of his loss; and hope was too heavily crushed by the sudden blow for his imagination to dwell on the growth of a new hoard from that small beginning.

He filled up the blank with grief. As he sat weaving, he every now and then moaned low, like one in pain: it was the sign that his thoughts had come round again to the sudden chasm—to the empty evening time. And all the evening, as he sat in his loneliness by his dull fire, he leaned his elbows on his knees, and clasped his head with his hands, and moaned very low—not as one who seeks to be heard.

And yet he was not utterly forsaken in his trouble. The repulsion Marner had always created in his neighbors was partly dissipated by the new light in which this misfortune had shown him. Instead of a man who had more cunning than honest folks could come by, and, what was worse, had not the inclination to use that cunning in a neighborly way, it was now apparent that Silas had not cunning enough to keep his own. He was generally spoken of as a "poor mushed creatur;" and that avoidance of his neighbours, which had before been referred to his ill-will, and to a probable addiction to worse company, was now considered mere craziness.

This change to a kindlier feeling was shown in various ways. The odour of Christmas cooking being on the wind, it was the season when superfluous pork and black puddings are suggestive of charity in well-to-do families; and Silas's misfortune had brought him uppermost in the memory of housekeepers like Mrs. Osgood. Mr. Crackenthorp, too, while he admonished Silas that his money had probably been taken from him because he thought too much of it, and never came to church, enforced the doctrine by a present of pigs' pettitoes, well calculated to dissipate unfounded prejudices against the clerical character. Neighbours, who had nothing but verbal consolation to give, showed a disposition not only to greet Silas, and discuss his misfortune at some length when they encountered him in the village, but also to take the trouble of calling at his cottage, and getting him to repeat all the details on the very spot; and then they would try to cheer him by saying, "Well, Master Marner, you're no worse off nor other poor folks, after all; and if you was to be crippled, the parish 'ud give you a 'lowance."

I suppose one reason why we are seldom able to comfort our neighbors with our words is, that our good-will gets adulterated, in spite of ourselves, before it can pass our lips. We can send black puddings and pettitoes without giving them a flavour of our own egoism; but language is a stream that is almost sure to smack of a mingled soil. There was a fair proportion of kindness in Raveloe; but it was often of a beery and bungling sort, and took the shape least allied to the complimentary and hypocritical.

Mr. Macey, for example, coming one evening expressly to let Silas know that recent events had given him the advantage of standing more favourably in the opinion of a man whose judgment was not formed lightly, opened the conversation by saying, as soon as he had seated himself and adjusted his thumbs—

"Come, Master Marner, why, you've no call to sit a-moaning. You're a deal better off to ha' lost your money, nor to ha' kep it by foul means. I used to think, when you first come into these parts, as you were no better nor you should be; you were younger a deal than what you are now; but you were allays a staring, white-faced creatur, partly like a bald-faced calf, as I may say. But there's no knowing; it isn't every queer-looked thing as Old Harry's had the making of—I mean, speaking o' toads and such; for they're often harmless, and useful against varmin. And it's pretty much the same wi' you, as fur as I can see. Though as to the yarbs and stuff to cure the breathing, if you brought that sort o' knowledge from distant parts, you might ha' been a bit freer of it. And if the knowledge wasn't well come by, why, you might ha' made up for it by coming to church reg'lar; for, as for the children as the Wise Woman charmed, I've been at the christening of 'em again and again, and they took the water just as well. And that's reasonable; for if Old Harry's a mind to do a bit o' kindness for a holiday, like, who's got anything against it? That's my thinking; and I've been clerk o' this parish forty year, and I know, when the parson and me

does the cussing of a Ash Wednesday, there's no cussing o' folks as have
a mind to be cured without a doctor, let Kimble say what he will. And
so, Master Marner, as I was saying—for there's windings i' things as
they may carry you to the fur end o' the prayer-book afore you get
back to 'em—my advice is, as you keep up your sperrits; for as for
thinking you're a deep un, and ha' got more inside you nor 'ull bear
daylight, I'm not o' that opinion at all, and so I tell the neighbours.
For, says I, you talk o' Master Marner making out a tale—why, it's
nonsense, that is: it 'ud take a 'cute man to make a tale like that; and,
says I, he looked as scared as a rabbit."

During this discursive address Silas had continued motionless in his
previous attitude, leaning his elbows on his knees, and pressing his hands
against his head. Mr. Macey, not doubting that he had been listened
to, paused, in the expectation of some appreciatory reply, but Marner
remained silent. He had a sense that the old man meant to be good-
natured and neighbourly; but the kindness fell on him as sunshine falls
on the wretched—he had no heart to taste it, and felt that it was very
far off him.

"Come, Master Marner, have you got nothing to say to that?" said
Mr. Macey, at last, with a slight accent of impatience.

"Oh," said Marner, slowly, shaking his head between his hands, "I
thank you—thank you—kindly."

"Ay, ay, to be sure: I thought you would," said Mr. Macey; "and
my advice is—have you got a Sunday suit?"

"No," said Marner.

"I doubted it was so," said Mr. Macey. "Now, let me advise you to
get a Sunday suit: there's Tookey, he's a poor creatur, but he's got my
tailoring business, and some o' my money in it, and he shall make a
suit at a low price, and give you trust, and then you can come to church,
and be a bit neighborly. Why, you've never heared me say 'Amen' since
you come into these parts, and I recommend you to lose no time, for
it'll be poor work when Tookey has it all to himself, for I mayn't be
equil to stand i' the desk at all, come another winter." Here Mr. Macey
paused, perhaps expecting some sign of emotion in his hearer; but not
observing any, he went on. "And as for the money for the suit o' clothes,
why, you get a matter of a pound a-week at your weaving, Master
Marner, and you're a young man, eh, for all you look so mushed. Why,
you couldn't ha' been five-and-twenty when you come into these parts,
eh?"

Silas started a little at the change to a questioning tone, and answered
mildly, "I don't know; I can't rightly say—it's a long while since."

After receiving such an answer as this, it is not surprising that Mr.
Macey observed, later on in the evening at the Rainbow, that Marner's
head was "all of a muddle," and that it was to be doubted if he ever
knew when Sunday came around, which showed him a worse heathen
than many a dog.

Another of Silas's comforters, besides Mr. Macey, came to him with a mind highly charged on the same topic. This was Mrs. Winthrop, the wheelwright's wife. The inhabitants of Raveloe were not severely regular in their church-going, and perhaps there was hardly a person in the parish who would not have held that to go to church every Sunday in the calendar would have shown a greedy desire to stand well with Heaven, and get an undue advantage over their neighbours—a wish to be better than the "common run," that would have implied a reflection on those who had had godfathers and godmothers as well as themselves, and had an equal right to the burying-service. At the same time, it was understood to be requisite for all who were not household servants, or young men, to take the sacrament at one of the great festivals: Squire Cass himself took it on Christmas-day; while those who were held to be "good livers" went to church with greater, though still with moderate, frequency.

Mrs. Winthrop was one of these: she was in all respects a woman of scrupulous conscience, so eager for duties, that life seemed to offer them too scantily unless she rose at half-past four, though this threw a scarcity of work over the more advanced hours of the morning, which it was a constant problem with her to remove. Yet she had not the vixenish temper which is sometimes supposed to be a necessary condition of such habits: she was a very mild, patient woman, whose nature it was to seek out all the sadder and more serious elements of life, and pasture her mind upon them. She was the person always first thought of in Raveloe when there was illness or death in a family, when leeches were to be applied, or there was a sudden disappointment in a monthly nurse. She was a "comfortable woman"—good-looking, fresh-complexioned, having her lips always slightly screwed, as if she felt herself in a sick-room with the doctor or the clergyman present. But she was never whimpering; no one had seen her shed tears; she was simply grave and inclined to shake her head and sigh, almost imperceptibly, like a funereal mourner who is not a relation. It seemed surprising that Ben Winthrop, who loved his quart-pot and his joke, got along so well with Dolly; but she took her husband's jokes and joviality as patiently as everything else, considering that "men *would* be so," and viewing the stronger sex in the light of animals whom it had pleased Heaven to make naturally troublesome, like bulls and turkey-cocks.

This good wholesome woman could hardly fail to have her mind drawn strongly towards Silas Marner, now that he appeared in the light of a sufferer; and one Sunday afternoon she took her little boy Aaron with her, and went to call on Silas, carrying in her hand some small lard-cakes, flat paste-like articles, much esteemed in Raveloe. Aaron, an apple-cheeked youngster of seven, with a clean starched frill, which looked like a plate for the apples, needed all his adventurous curiosity to embolden him against the possibility that the big-eyed weaver might do him some bodily injury; and his dubiety was much increased when, on arriving at the Stone-pits, they heard the mysterious sound of the loom.

"Ah, it is as I thought," said Mrs. Winthrop, sadly.

They had to knock loudly before Silas heard them; but when he did come to the door, he showed no impatience, as he would once have done, at a visit that had been unasked for and unexpected. Formerly, his heart had been as a locked casket with its treasure inside; but now the casket was empty, and the lock was broken. Left groping in darkness, with his prop utterly gone, Silas had inevitably a sense, though a dull and half-despairing one, that if any help came to him it must come from without; and there was a slight stirring of expectation at the sight of his fellow-men, a faint consciousness of dependence on their goodwill. He opened the door wide to admit Dolly, but without otherwise returning her greeting than by moving the arm-chair a few inches as a sign that she was to sit down in it. Dolly, as soon as she was seated, removed the white cloth that covered her lard-cakes, and said in her gravest way—

"I'd a baking yesterday, Master Marner, and the lard-cakes turned out better nor common, and I'd ha' asked you to accept some, if you'd thought well. I don't eat such things myself, for a bit o' bread's what I like from one year's end to the other; but men's stomichs are made so comical, they want a change—they do, I know, God help 'em."

Dolly sighed gently as she held out the cakes to Silas, who thanked her kindly, and looked very close at them, absently, being accustomed to look so at everything he took into his hand—eyed all the while by the wondering bright orbs of the small Aaron, who had made an outwork of his mother's chair, and was peeping round from behind it.

"There's letters pricked on 'em," said Dolly. "I can't read 'em myself, and there's nobody, not Mr. Macey himself, rightly knows what they mean; but they've a good meaning, for they're the same as is on the pulpit-cloth at church. What are they, Aaron, my dear?"

Aaron retreated completely behind his outwork.

"Oh, go, that's naughty," said his mother, mildly. "Well, whativer the letters are, they've a good meaning; and it's a stamp as has been in our house, Ben says, ever since he was a little un, and his mother used to put it on the cakes, and I've allays put it on too; for if there's any good, we've need of it i' this world."

"It's I. H. S.," said Silas, at which proof of learning Aaron peeped round the chair again.

"Well, to be sure, you can read 'em off," said Dolly "Ben's read 'em to me many and many a time, but they slip out o' my mind again; the more's the pity, for they're good letters, else they wouldn't be in the church; and so I prick 'em on all the loaves and all the cakes, though sometimes they won't hold, because o' the rising—for, as I said, if there's any good to be got, we've need on it i' this world—that we have; and I hope they'll bring good to you, Master Marner, for it's wi' that will I brought you the cakes; and you see the letters have held better nor common."

Silas was as unable to interpret the letters as Dolly, but there was no possibility of misunderstanding the desire to give comfort that made itself heard in her quiet tones. He said, with more feeling than before— "Thank you—thank you kindly." But he laid down the cakes and seated himself absently- -drearily unconscious of any distinct benefit towards which the cakes and the letters, or even Dolly's kindness, could tend for him.

"Ah, if there's good anywhere, we've need of it," repeated Dolly, who did not lightly forsake a serviceable phrase. She looked at Silas pityingly as she went on. "But you didn't hear the church-bells this morning, Master Marner? I doubt you didn't know it was Sunday. Living so lone here, you lose your count, I dare say; and then, when your loom makes a noise, you can't hear the bells, more partic'lar now the frost kills the sound."

"Yes, I did; I heard 'em," said Silas, to whom Sunday bells were a mere accident of the day, and not part of its sacredness. There had been no bells in Lantern Yard.

"Dear heart!" said Dolly, pausing before she spoke again. "But what a pity it is you should work of a Sunday, and not clean yourself— if you *didn't* go to church; for if you'd a roasting bit, it might be as you couldn't leave it, being a lone man. But there's the bakehus, if you could make up your mind to spend a twopence on the oven now and then, not every week, in course—I shouldn't like to do that myself,— you might carry your bit o' dinner there, for it's nothing but right to have a bit o' summat hot of a Sunday, and not to make it as you can't know your dinner from Saturday. But now, upo' Christmas-day, this blessed Christmas as is ever coming, if you was to take your dinner to the bakehus, and go to church, and see the holly and the yew, and hear the anthim, and then take the sacramen', you'd be a deal the bet- ter, and you'd know which end you stood on, and you could put your trust i' Them as knows better nor we do, seein' you'd ha' done what it lies on us all to do."

Dolly's exhortation, which was an unusually long effort of speech for her, was uttered in the soothing persuasive tone with which she would have tried to prevail on a sick man to take his medicine, or a basin of gruel for which he had no appetite. Silas had never before been closely urged on the point of his absence from church, which had only been thought of as a part of his general queerness; and he was too direct and simple to evade Dolly's appeal.

"Nay, nay," he said, "I know nothing o' church. I've never been to church."

"No!" said Dolly, in a low tone of wonderment. Then bethinking herself of Silas's advent from an unknown country, she said, "Could it ha' been as they'd no church where you was born?"

"Oh, yes," said Silas, meditatively, sitting in his usual posture of lean- ing on his knees, and supporting his head. "There was churches—a many—it was a big town. But I knew nothing of 'em—I went to chapel."

Dolly was much puzzled at this new word, but she was rather afraid

of inquiring further, lest "chapel" might mean some haunt of wickedness. After a little thought, she said—

"Well, Master Marner, it's niver too late to turn over a new leaf,
and if you've never had no church, there's no telling the good it'll do
you. For I feel so set up and comfortable as niver was, when I've been
and heard the prayers, and the singing to the praise and glory o' God,
as Mr. Macey gives out—and Mr. Crackenthorp saying good words, and
more partic'ler on Sacramen' Day; and if a bit o' trouble comes, I feel
as I can put up wi' it, for I've looked for help i' the right quarter, and
gev myself up to Them as we must all give ourselves up to at the last;
and if we'n done our part, it isn't to be believed as Them as are above
us 'ull be worse nor we are, and come short o' Theirn."

Poor Dolly's exposition of her simple Raveloe theology fell rather
unmeaningly on Silas's ears, for there was no word in it that could rouse
a memory of what he had known as religion, and his comprehension
was quite baffled by the plural pronoun, which was no heresy of Dolly's,
but only her way of avoiding a presumptuous familiarity. He remained
silent, not feeling inclined to assent to the part of Dolly's speech which
he fully understood—her recommendation that he should go to church.
Indeed, Silas was so unaccustomed to talk beyond the brief questions
and answers necessary for the transaction of his simple business, that
words did not easily come to him without the urgency of a distinct
purpose.

But now, little Aaron, having become used to the weaver's awful
presence, had advanced to his mother's side, and Silas, seeming to notice
him for the first time, tried to return Dolly's signs of good-will by
offering the lad a bit of lard-cake. Aaron shrank back a little, and
rubbed his head against his mother's shoulder, but still thought the
piece of cake worth the risk of putting his hand out for it.

"Oh, for shame, Aaron," said his mother, taking him on her lap, however; "why, you don't want cake again yet awhile. He's wonderful
hearty," she went on, with a little sigh—"that he is, God knows. He's
my youngest, and we spoil him sadly, for either me or the father must
allays hev him in our sight—that we must."

She stroked Aaron's brown head, and thought it must do Master
Marner good to see such a "pictur of a child." But Marner, on the
other side of the hearth, saw the neat-featured rosy face as a mere dim
round, with two dark spots in it.

"And he's got a voice like a bird—you wouldn't think," Dolly went
on; "he can sing a Christmas carril as his father's taught him: and I
take it for a token as he'll come to good, as he can learn the good tunes
so quick. Come, Aaron, stan' up and sing the carril to Master Marner,
come."

Aaron replied by rubbing his forehead against his mother's shoulder.

"Oh, that's naughty," said Dolly, gently. "Stan' up, when mother
tells you, and let me hold the cake till you've done."

Aaron was not indisposed to display his talents, even to an ogre, under protecting circumstances; and after a few more signs of coyness, consisting chiefly in rubbing the backs of his hands over his eyes, and then peeping between them at Master Marner, to see if he looked anxious for the "carril," he at length allowed his head to be duly adjusted, and standing behind the table, which let him appear above it only as far as his broad frill, so that he looked like a cherubic head untroubled with a body, he began with a clear chirp, and in a melody that had the ryhthm of an industrious hammer,—

"God rest you, merry gentlemen,
Let nothing you dismay,
For Jesus Christ our Saviour
Was born on Christmas-day."

Dolly listened with a devout look, glancing at Marner in some confidence that this strain would help to allure him to church.

"That's Christmas music," she said, when Aaron had ended, and had secured his piece of cake again. "There's no other music equil to the Christmas music—'Hark the erol angils sing.' And you may judge what it is at church, Master Marner, with the bassoon and the voices, as you can't help thinking you've got to a better place a'ready—for I wouldn't speak ill o' this world, seeing as Them put us in it as knows best; but what wi' the drink, and the quarrelling, and the bad illnesses, and the hard dying, as I've seen times and times, one's thankful to hear of a better. The boy sings pretty, don't he, Master Marner?"

"Yes," said Silas, absently, "very pretty."

The Christmas carol, with its hammer-like rhythm, had fallen on his ears as strange music, quite unlike a hymn, and could have none of the effect Dolly contemplated. But he wanted to show her that he was grateful, and the only mode that occurred to him was to offer Aaron a bit more cake.

"Oh, no, thank you, Master Marner," said Dolly, holding down Aaron's willing hands. "We must be going home now. And so I wish you good-by, Master Marner; and if you ever feel anyways bad in your inside, as you can't fend for yourself, I'll come and clean up for you, and get you a bit o' victual, and willing. But I beg and pray of you to leave off weaving of a Sunday, for it's bad for soul and body—and the money as comes i' that way 'ull be a bad bed to lie down on at the last, if it doesn't fly away, nobody knows where like the white frost. And you'll excuse me being that free with you, Master Marner, for I wish you well—I do. Make your bow, Aaron."

Silas said "Good-by, and thank you kindly," as he opened the door for Dolly, but he couldn't help feeling relieved when she was gone—relieved that he might weave again and moan at his ease. Her simple view of life and its comforts, by which she had tried to cheer him, was only like a report of unknown objects, which his imagination could not fashion. The fountains of human love and divine faith had not yet been unlocked, and his soul was still the shrunken rivulet, with only this difference, that its little groove of sand was blocked up, and it wandered confusedly against dark obstruction.

And so, notwithstanding the honest persuasions of Mr. Macey and Dolly Winthrop, Silas spent his Christmas-day in loneliness, eating his meat in sadness of heart, though the meat had come to him as a neighbourly present. In the morning he looked out on the black frost that seemed to press cruelly on every blade of grass, while the half-icy red pool shivered under the bitter wind; but towards evening the snow began to fall, and curtained from him even that dreary outlook, shutting him close up with his narrow grief. And he sat in his robbed home through the livelong evening, not caring to close his shutters or lock his door, pressing his head between his hands and moaning, till the cold grasped him and told him that his fire was gray.

Nobody in this world but himself knew that he was the same Silas Marner who had once loved his fellow with tender love, and trusted in an unseen goodness. Even to himself that past experience had become dim.

But in Raveloe village the bells rang merrily, and the church was fuller than all through the rest of the year, with red faces among the abundant dark-green boughs—faces prepared for a longer service than usual by an odorous breakfast of toast and ale. Those green boughs, the hymn and anthem never heard but at Christmas—even the Athanasian Creed, which was discriminated from the others only as being longer and of exceptional virtue, since it was only read on rare occasions— brought a vague exulting sense, for which the grown men could as little have found words as the children, that something great and mysterious had been done for them in heaven above, and in earth below, which they were appropriating by their presence. And then the red faces made their way through the black biting frost to their own homes, feeling themselves free for the rest of the day to eat, drink, and be merry, and using that Christian freedom without diffidence.

At Squire Cass's family party that day nobody mentioned Dunstan —nobody was sorry for his absence, or feared it would be too long. The doctor and his wife, uncle and aunt Kimble, were there, and the annual Christmas talk was carried through without any omissions, rising to the climax of Mr. Kimble's experience when he walked the London hospitals thirty years back, together with striking professional anecdotes then gathered. Whereupon cards followed, with Aunt Kimble's annual failure to follow suit, and Uncle Kimble's irascibility concerning the odd trick which was rarely explicable to him, when it was not on his side, without a general visitation of tricks to see that they were formed on sound principles: the whole being accompanied by a strong steaming odour of spirits-and-water.

But the party on Christmas-day, being a strictly family party, was not the pre-eminently brilliant celebration of the season at the Red House. It was the great dance on New Year's Eve that made the glory of Squire Cass's hospitality, as of his forefathers', time out of mind.

This was the occasion when all the society of Raveloe and Tarley, whether old acquaintances separated by long rutty distances, or cooled acquaintances separated by misunderstandings concerning run-away calves, or acquaintances founded on intermittent condescension, counted on meeting and on comporting themselves with mutual appropriateness. This was the occasion on which fair dames who came on pillions sent their bandboxes before them, supplied with more than their evening costume; for the feast was not to end with a single evening, like a paltry town entertainment, where the whole supply of eatables is put on the table at once, and bedding is scanty. The Red House was provisioned as if for a siege; and as for the spare feather-beds ready to be laid on floors, they were as plentiful as might naturally be expected in a family that had killed its own geese for many generations.

Godfrey Cass was looking forward to this New Year's Eve with a foolish reckless longing, that made him half deaf to his importunate companion, Anxiety.

"Dunsey will be coming home soon: there will be a great blow-up, and how will you bribe his spite to silence?" said Anxiety.

"Oh, he won't come home before New Year's Eve, perhaps," said Godfrey; "and I shall sit by Nancy then, and dance with her, and get a kind look from her in spite of herself."

"But money is wanted in another quarter," said Anxiety, in a louder voice, "and how will you get it without selling your mother's diamond pin? And if you don't get it. . . ?"

"Well, but something may happen to make things easier. At any rate, there's one pleasure for me close at hand: Nancy is coming."

"Yes, and suppose your father should bring matters to a pass that will oblige you to decline marrying her—and to give your reasons?"

"Hold your tongue, and don't worry me. I can see Nancy's eyes, just as they will look at me, and feel her hand in mine already."

But Anxiety went on, though in noisy Christmas company; refusing to be utterly quieted even by much drinking.

CHAPTER XI

SOME women, I grant, would not appear to advantage seated on a pillion, and attired in a drab joseph and a drab beaver-bonnet, with a crown resembling a small stew-pan; for a garment suggesting a coachman's great-coat, cut out under an exiguity of cloth that would only allow of miniature capes, is not well adapted to conceal deficiencies of contour, nor is drab a color that will throw sallow cheeks into lively contrast. It was all the greater triumph to Miss Nancy Lammeter's beauty that she looked thoroughly bewitching in that costume, as, seated on the pillion behind her tall, erect father, she held one arm round him, and looked down, with open-eyed anxiety, at the treacherous snow-covered pools and puddles, which sent up formidable splashings of mud under the stamp of Dobbin's foot. A painter would, perhaps, have preferred her in those moments when she was free from self-consciousness; but certainly the bloom on her cheeks was at its highest point of contrast with the surrounding drab when she arrived at the door of the Red House, and saw Mr. Godfrey Cass ready to lift her from the pillion. She wished her sister Priscilla had come up at the same time with the servant, for then she would have contrived that Mr. Godfrey should have lifted off Priscilla first, and, in the meantime, she would have persuaded her father to go round to the horse-block instead of alighting at the door-steps. It was very painful, when you had made it quite clear to a young man that you were determined not to marry him, however much he might wish it, that he would still continue to pay you marked attentions; besides, why didn't he always show the same attentions, if he meant them sincerely, instead of being so strange as Mr. Godfrey Cass was, sometimes behaving as if he didn't want to speak to her, and taking no notice of her for weeks and weeks, and then, all on a sudden, almost making love again? Moreover, it was quite plain he had no real love for her, else he would not let people have *that* to say of him which they did say. Did he suppose that Miss Nancy Lammeter was to be won by any man, squire or no squire, who led a bad life? That was not what she had been used to see in her own father, who was the soberest and best man in that country-side, only a little hot and hasty now and then, if things were not done to the minute.

All these thoughts rushed through Miss Nancy's mind, in their habitual succession, in the moments between her first sight of Mr. Godfrey Cass standing at the door and her own arrival there. Happily, the Squire came out too, and gave a loud greeting to her father, so that, somehow, under cover of this noise, she seemed to find concealment for her confusion and neglect of any suitably formal behaviour, while she was being lifted from the pillion by strong arms, which seemed to find her ridiculously small and light. And there was the best reason for hastening into the house at once, since the snow was beginning to fall again, threatening an unpleasant journey for such guests as were still on the road. These were a small minority; for already the afternoon was beginning to decline, and there would not be too much time for the ladies who came from a distance to attire themselves in readiness for the early tea which was to inspirit them for the dance.

There was a buzz of voices through the house, as Miss Nancy entered, mingled with the scrape of a fiddle preluding in the kitchen; but the Lammeters were guests whose arrival had evidently been thought of so much that it had been watched for from the windows, for Mrs. Kimble, who did the honors at the Red House on these great occasions, came forward to meet Miss Nancy in the hall, and conduct her up-stairs. Mrs. Kimble was the Squire's sister, as well as the doctor's wife—a double dignity, with which her diameter was in direct proportion; so that, a journey up-stairs being rather fatiguing to her, she did not oppose Miss Nancy's request to be allowed to find her way alone to the Blue

Room, where the Miss Lammeters' bandboxes had been deposited on their arrival in the morning.

There was hardly a bedroom in the house where feminine compli-ments were not passing and feminine toilettes going forward, in various stages, in space made scanty by extra beds spread upon the floor; and Miss Nancy, as she entered the Blue Room, had to make her little formal courtesy to a group of six. On the one hand, there were ladies no less important than the two Miss Gunns, the wine merchant's daugh-ters from Lytherly, dressed in the height of fashion, with the tightest skirts and the shortest waists, and gazed at by Miss Ladbrook (of the Old Pastures) with a shyness not unsustained by inward criticism. Partly, Miss Ladbrook felt that her own skirt must be regarded as unduly lax by the Miss Gunns, and partly, that it was a pity the Miss Gunns did not show that judgment which she herself would show if she were in their place, by stopping a little on this side of the fashion. On the other hand, Mrs. Ladbrook was standing in skull-cap and front, with her turban in her hand, courtesying and smiling blandly and saying, "After you, ma'am," to another lady in similar circumstances, who had politely offered the precedence at the looking-glass.

But Miss Nancy had no sooner made her courtesy than an elderly lady came forward, whose full white muslin kerchief, and mob-cap round her curls of smooth gray hair, were in daring contrast with the puffed yellow satins and top-knotted caps of her neighbors. She ap-proached Miss Nancy with much primness, and said, with a slow, treble suavity,

"Niece, I hope I see you well in health." Miss Nancy kissed her aunt's cheek dutifully, and answered, with the same sort of amiable primness, "Quite well, I thank you, aunt; and I hope I see you the same."

"Thank you, niece; I keep my health for the present. And how is my brother-in-law?"

These dutiful questions and answers were continued until it was ascertained in detail that the Lammeters were all as well as usual, and the Osgoods likewise, also that niece Priscilla, must certainly arrive shortly, and that travelling on pillions in snowy weather was unpleas-ant, though a joseph was a great protection. Then Nancy was formally introduced to her aunt's visitors, the Miss Gunns, as being the daugh-ters of a mother known to *their* mother, though now for the first time induced to make a journey in these parts; and these ladies were so taken by surprise at finding such a lovely face and figure in an out-of-the-way country place, that they began to feel some curiosity about the dress she would put on when she took off her joseph. Miss Nancy, whose thoughts were always conducted with the propriety and modera-tion conspicuous in her manners, remarked to herself that the Miss Gunns were rather hard-featured than otherwise, and that such very low dresses as they wore might have been attributed to vanity if their shoulders had been pretty, but that, being as they were, it was not reasonable to suppose that they showed their necks from a love of display, but rather from some obligation not inconsistent with sense and modesty. She felt convinced, as she opened her box, that this must be her aunt Osgood's opinion, for Miss Nancy's mind resembled her aunt's to a degree that everybody said was surprising, considering the kinship was on Mr. Osgood's side; and though you might not have supposed it from the formality of their greeting, there was a devoted attachment and mutual admiration between aunt and niece. Even Miss Nancy's refusal of her cousin Gilbert Osgood (on the ground solely that he was her cousin), though it had grieved her aunt greatly, had not in the least cooled the preference which had determined her to leave Nancy several of her hereditary ornaments, let Gilbert's future wife be whom she might.

Three of the ladies quickly retired, but the Miss Gunns were quite content that Mrs. Osgood's inclination to remain with her niece gave them also a reason for staying to see the rustic beauty's toilette. And it was really a pleasure—from the first opening of the bandbox, where everything smelt of lavender and rose-leaves, to the clasping of the small coral necklace that fitted closely round her little white neck. Everything belonging to Miss Nancy was of delicate purity and nattiness: not a crease was where it had no business to be, not a bit of her linen professed whiteness without fulfilling its profession; the very pins on her pincushion were stuck in after a pattern from which she was careful to allow no aberration; and as for her own person, it gave the same idea of perfect unvarying neatness as the body of a little bird. It is true that her light-brown hair was cropped behind like a boy's, and was dressed in front in a number of flat rings, that lay quite away from her face; but there was no sort of coiffure that could make Miss Nancy's cheek and neck look otherwise than pretty; and when at last she stood complete in her silvery twilled silk, her lace tucker, her coral necklace, and coral ear-drops, the Miss Gunns could see nothing to criticise except her hands, which bore the traces of butter-making, cheese-crushing, and even still coarser work. But Miss Nancy was not ashamed of that, for while she was dressing she narrated to her aunt how she and Priscilla had packed their boxes yesterday, because this morning was baking morning, and since they were leaving home, it was desirable to make a good supply of meat-pies for the kitchen; and as she concluded this judicious remark, she turned to the Miss Gunns that she might not commit the rudeness of not including them in the conversation. The Miss Gunns smiled stiffly, and thought what a pity it was that these rich country people, who could afford to buy such good clothes (really Miss Nancy's lace and silk were very costly), should be brought up in utter ignorance and vulgarity. She actually said "mate" for "meat," "'appen" for "perhaps," and "oss" for "horse," which, to young ladies living in good Lytherly society, who habitually said 'orse, even in domestic privacy, and only said 'appen on the right occasions, was necessarily shocking. Miss Nancy, indeed, had never been to any school higher than Dame Tedman's: her acquaintance with profane literature hardly went beyond the rhymes she had worked in her large sampler under the lamb and the shepherdess; and in order to balance an account, she was obliged to effect her subtraction by removing visible metallic shillings and sixpences from a visible metallic total. There is hardly a servant-maid in these days who is not better informed than Miss Nancy; yet she had the essential attributes of a lady—high veracity, delicate honor in her dealings, deference to others, and refined personal habits,—and lest these should not suffice to convince grammatical fair ones that her feelings can at all resemble theirs, I will add that she was slightly proud and exacting, and as constant in her affection towards a baseless opinion as towards an erring lover.

The anxiety about sister Priscilla, which had grown rather active by the time the coral necklace was clasped, was happily ended by the entrance of that cheerful-looking lady herself, with a face made blowsy by cold and damp. After the first questions and greetings, she turned to Nancy, and surveyed her from head to foot—then wheeled her round, to ascertain that the back view was equally faultless.

"What do you think o' *these* gowns, aunt Osgood?" said Priscilla, while Nancy helped her to unrobe.

"Very handsome indeed, niece," said Mrs. Osgood, with a slight increase of formality. She always thought niece Priscilla too rough.

"I'm obliged to have the same as Nancy, you know, for all I'm five years older, and it makes me look yellow; for she never *will* have any thing without I have mine just like it, because she wants us to look like sisters. And I tell her, folks 'ull think it's my weakness makes me fancy as I shall look pretty in what she looks pretty in. For I *am* ugly—there's no denying that: I feature my father's family. But, law! I don't mind, do you?" Priscilla here turned to the Miss Gunns, rattling on in too much preoccupation with the delight of talking, to notice that her candor was not appreciated. "The pretty uns do for fly-catchers—they keep the men off us. I've no opinion o' the men, Miss Gunn—I don't know what *you* have. And as for fretting and stewing about what *they*'ll think of you from morning till night, and making your life uneasy about what they're doing when they're out o' your sight—as I tell Nancy, it's a folly no woman need be guilty of, if she's got a good father and a good home: let her leave it to them as have got no fortin, and can't help themselves. As I say, Mr. Have-your-own-way is the best husband, and the only one I'd ever promise to obey. I know it isn't pleasant, when you've been used to living in a big way, and managing hogsheads and all that, to go and put your nose in by somebody's else's fireside, or to sit down by yourself to a scrag or a knuckle; but, thank God! my father's a sober man and likely to live; and if you've got a man by the chimney-corner, it doesn't matter if he's childish—the business needn't be broke up."

The delicate process of getting her narrow gown over her head without injury to her smooth curls, obliged Miss Priscilla to pause in this

rapid survey of life, and Mrs. Osgood seized the opportunity of rising
and saying,

"Well, niece, you'll follow us. The Miss Gunns will like to go down."

"Sister," said Nancy, when they were alone, "you've offended the
Miss Gunns, I'm sure."

"What have I done, child?" said Priscilla, in some alarm.

"Why, you asked them if they minded about being ugly—you're so
very blunt."

"Law, did I? Well, it popped out: it's a mercy I said no more, for
I'm a bad un to live with folks when they don't like the truth. But as
for being ugly, look at me, child, in this silver-coloured silk—I told you
how it 'ud be—I look as yellow as a daffodil. Anybody 'ud say you
wanted to make a mawkin of me."

"No, Priscy, don't say so. I begged and prayed of you not to let us
have this silk if you'd like another better. I was willing to have *your*
choice, you know I was," said Nancy, in anxious self-vindication.

"Nonsense, child, you know you'd set your heart on this: and reason
good, for you're the colour o' cream. It 'ud be fine doings for you to
dress yourself to suit *my* skin. What I find fault with, is that notion o'
yours as I must dress myself just like you. But you do as you like with
me—you always did, from when first you begun to walk. If you wanted
to go the field's length, the field's length you'd go; and there was no
whipping you, for you looked as prim and innicent as a daisy all the
while."

"Priscy," said Nancy, gently, as she fastened a coral necklace,
exactly like her own, round Priscilla's neck, which was very far from
being like her own, "I'm sure I'm willing to give way as far as is right,
but who shouldn't dress alike if it isn't sisters? Would you have us go
about looking as if we were no kin to one another—us that have got no
mother and not another sister in the world? I'd do what was right, if I
dressed in a gown dyed with cheese-colouring; and I'd rather you'd
choose, and let me wear what pleases you."

"There you go again! You'd come round to the same thing if one
talked to you from Saturday night till Saturday morning. It will be
fine fun to see how you'll master your husband and never raise your
voice above the singing o' the kettle all the whole. I like to see the men
mastered!"

"Don't talk *so*, Priscy," said Nancy, blushing. "You know I don't
mean ever to be married."

"Oh, you never mean a fiddlestick's end!" said Priscilla, as she arranged her discarded dress, and closed her bandbox. "Who shall *I* have
to work for when father's gone, if you are to go and take notions in
your head and be an old maid, because some folks are no better than
they should be? I haven't a bit o' patience with you—sitting on an
addled egg forever, as if there was never a fresh un in the world. One
old maid's enough out o' two sisters; and I shall do credit to a single
life, for God A'mighty meant me for it. Come, we can go down now. I'm

as ready as a mawkin *can* be—there's nothing awanting to frighten the crows, now I've got my ear-droppers in."

As the two Miss Lammeters walked into the large parlour together, any one who did not know the character of both, might certainly have supposed that the reason why the square-shouldered, clumsy, high-featured Priscilla wore a dress the fac-simile of her pretty sister's, was either the mistaken vanity of the one, or the malicious contrivance of the other in order to set off her own rare beauty. But the good-natured self-forgetful cheeriness and common-sense of Priscilla would soon have dissipated the one suspicion; and the modest calm of Nancy's speech and manners told clearly of a mind free from all disavowed devices.

Places of honour had been kept for the Miss Lammeters near the head of the principal tea-table in the wainscoted parlour, now looking fresh and pleasant with handsome branches of holly, yew, and laurel, from the abundant growths of the old garden; and Nancy felt an inward flutter, that no firmness of purpose could prevent, when she saw Mr. Godfrey Cass advancing to lead her to a seat between himself and Mr. Crackenthorp, while Priscilla was called to the opposite side between her father and the Squire. It certainly did make some difference to Nancy that the lover she had given up was the young man of quite the highest consequence in the parish—at home in a venerable and unique parlour, which was the extremity of grandeur in her experience, a parlour where *she* might one day have been mistress, with the consciousness that she was spoken of as "Madam Cass," the Squire's wife. These circumstances exalted her inward drama in her own eyes, and deepened the emphasis with which she declared to herself that not the most dazzling rank should induce her to marry a man whose conduct showed him careless of his character, but that, "love once, love always," was the motto of a true and pure woman, and no man should ever have any right over her which would be a call on her to destroy the dried flowers that she treasured, and always would treasure, for Godfrey Cass's sake. And Nancy was capable of keeping her word to herself under very trying conditions. Nothing but a becoming blush betrayed the moving thoughts that urged themselves upon her as she accepted the seat next to Mr. Crackenthorp; for she was so instinctively neat and adroit in all her actions, and her pretty lips met each other with such quiet firmness, that it would have been difficult for her to appear agitated.

It was not the rector's practice to let a charming blush pass without an appropriate compliment. He was not in the least lofty or aristocratic, but simply a merry-eyed, small-featured, grey-haired man, with his chin propped by an ample, many-creased white neckcloth, which seemed to predominate over every other point in his person, and somehow to impress its peculiar character on his remarks; so that to have considered his amenities apart from his cravat, would have been a severe, and perhaps a dangerous, effort of abstraction.

"Ha, Miss Nancy," he said, turning his head within his cravat, and smiling down pleasantly upon her, "when anybody pretends this has

been a severe winter, I shall tell them I saw the roses blooming on New
Year's Eve—eh, Godfrey, what do *you* say?"

Godfrey made no reply, and avoided looking at Nancy very markedly; for though these complimentary personalities were held to be in
excellent taste in old-fashioned Raveloe society, reverent love has a
politeness of its own which it teaches to men otherwise of small schooling. But the Squire was rather impatient at Godfrey's showing himself
a dull spark in this way. By this advanced hour of the day, the Squire
was always in higher spirits than we have seen him in at the breakfast-
table, and felt it quite pleasant to fulfil the hereditary duty of being
noisily jovial and patronizing: the large silver snuff-box was in active
service, and was offered without fail to all neighbours from time to time,
however often they might have declined the favour. At present the
Squire had only given an express welcome to the heads of families as
they appeared; but always as the evening deepened, his hospitality
rayed out more widely, till he had tapped the youngest guests on the
back, and shown a peculiar fondness for their presence, in the full belief that they must feel their lives made happy by their belonging to a
parish where there was such a hearty man as Squire Cass to invite them
and wish them well. Even in this early stage of the jovial mood, it
was natural that he should wish to supply his son's deficiencies by
looking and speaking for him.

"Ay, ay," he began, offering his snuff-box to Mr. Lammeter, who for
the second time bowed his head and waved his hand in stiff rejection
of the offer, "us old fellows may wish ourselves young to-night, when
we see the mistletoe-bough in the White Parlor. It's true, most things are
gone back'ard in these last thirty years—the country's going down
since the old king fell ill. But when I look at Miss Nancy here, I begin
to think the lasses keep up their quality;—ding me if I remember a
sample to match here, not when I was a fine young fellow, and thought
a deal about my pigtail. No offense to you, madam," he added, bending
to Mrs. Crackenthorp, who sat by him, "I didn't know *you* when you
were as young as Miss Nancy here."

Mrs. Crackenthorp—a small blinking woman, who fidgeted incessantly with her lace, ribbons, and gold chain, turning her head about
and making subdued noises, very much like a guinea-pig, that twitches
its nose and soliloquizes in all company indiscriminately—now blinked
and fidgeted towards the Squire, and said, "Oh, no—no offense."

This emphatic compliment of the Squire's to Nancy was felt by
others besides Godfrey to have a diplomatic significance; and her father
gave a slight additional erectness to his back, as he looked across the
table at her with complacent gravity. That grave and orderly senior
was not going to bate a jot of his dignity by seeming elated at the notion of a match between his family and the Squire's: he was gratified
by any honour paid to his daughter; but he must see an alteration in
several ways before his consent would be vouchsafed. His spare but
healthy person, and high-featured, firm face, that looked as if it had

never been flushed by excess, was in strong contrast, not only with the Squire's, but with the appearance of the Raveloe farmers generally—in accordance with a favorite saying of his own, that "breed was stronger than pasture."

"Miss Nancy's wonderful like what her mother was, though; isn't she, Kimble?" said the stout lady of that name, looking round for her husband.

But Doctor Kimble (country apothecaries in old days enjoyed that title without authority of diploma), being a thin and agile man, was flitting about the room with his hands in his pockets, making himself agreeable to his feminine patients, with medical impartiality, and being welcomed everywhere as a doctor by hereditary right—not one of those miserable apothecaries who canvass for practice in strange neighbour-hoods, and spend all their income in starving their one horse, but a man of substance, able to keep an extravagant table like the best of his patients. Time out of mind the Raveloe doctor had been a Kimble; Kimble was inherently a doctor's name; and it was difficult to con-template firmly the melancholy fact that the actual Kimble had no son, so that his practice might one day be handed over to a successor, with the incongruous name of Taylor or Johnson. But in that case the wiser people in Raveloe would employ Dr. Blick of Flitton—as less unnatural.

"Did you speak to me, my dear?" said the authentic doctor, coming quickly to his wife's side; but, as if foreseeing that she would be too much out of breath to repeat her remark, he went on immediately—"Ha, Miss Priscilla, the sight of you revives the taste of that super-excellent work-pie. I hope the batch isn't near an end."

"Yes, indeed, it is, doctor," said Priscilla; "but I'll answer for it the next shall be as good. My pork-pies don't turn out well by chance."

"Not as your doctoring does, eh, Kimble?—because folks forget to take your physic, eh?" said the Squire, who regarded physic and doc-tors as many loyal churchmen regard the church and the clergy—tasting a joke against them when he was in health, but impatiently eager for their aid when anything was the matter with him. He tapped his box, and looked round with a triumphant laugh.

"Ah, she has a quick wit, my friend Priscilla has," said the doctor, choosing to attribute the epigram to a lady rather than allow a brother-in-law that advantage over him. "She saves a little pepper to sprinkle over her talk—that's the reason why she never puts too much into her pies. There's my wife, now, she never has an answer at her tongue's end; but if I offend her, she's sure to scarify my throat with black pep-per the next day, or else give me the colic with watery greens. That's an awful tit-for-tat." Here the vivacious doctor made a pathetic grimace.

"Did you ever hear the like?" said Mrs. Kimble, laughing above her double chin with much good-humour, aside to Mrs. Crackenthorp, who blinked and nodded, and seemed to intend a smile, which, by the cor-relation of forces, went off in small twitchings and noises.

"I suppose that's the sort of tit-for-tat adopted in your profession, Kimble, if you've a grudge against a patient," said the rector.

"Never do have a grudge against our patients," said Mr. Kimble, "except when they leave us: and then, you see, we haven't a chance of prescribing for 'em. Ha, Miss Nancy," he continued, suddenly skipping to Nancy's side, "you won't forget your promise? You're to save a dance for me, you know."

"Come, come, Kimble, don't you be too for'ard," said the Squire. "Give the young uns fair-play. There's my son Godfrey 'll be wanting to have a round with you if you run off with Miss Nancy. He's bespoke her for the first dance, I'll be bound. Eh, sir! what do you say?" he continued throwing himself backward, and looking at Godfrey. "Haven't you asked Miss Nancy to open the dance with you?"

Godfrey, sorely uncomfortable under this significant insistance about Nancy, and afraid to think where it would end by the time his father had set his usual hospitable example of drinking before and after supper, saw no course open but to turn to Nancy and say, with as little awkwardness as possible—

"No; I've not asked her yet, but I hope she'll consent—if somebody else hasn't been before me."

"No, I've not engaged myself," said Nancy, quietly, though blushingly. (If Mr. Godfrey founded any hopes on her consenting to dance with him, he would soon be undeceived; but there was no need for her to be uncivil.)

"Then I hope you've no objections to dancing with me," said Godfrey, beginning to lose the sense that there was anything uncomfortable in this arrangement.

"No, no objections," said Nancy, in a cold tone.

"Ah, well, you're a lucky fellow, Godfrey," said uncle Kimble; "but you're my godson, so I won't stand in your way. Else I'm not so very old, eh, my dear?" he went on, skipping to his wife's side again. "You wouldn't mind my having a second after you were gone—not if I cried a good deal first."

"Come, come, take a cup o' tea and stop your tongue, do," said good-humoured Mrs. Kimble, feeling some pride in a husband who must be regarded as so clever and amusing by the company generally. If he had only not been irritable at cards!

While safe, well-tested personalities were enlivening the tea in this way, the sound of the fiddle approaching within a distance at which it could be heard distinctly, made the young people look at each other with sympathetic impatience for the end of the meal.

"Why, there's Solomon in the hall," said the Squire, "and playing my fav'rite tune, I believe—'The flaxen-headed plough-boy'—he's for giving us a hint as we aren't enough in a hurry to hear him play. Bob," he called out to his third long-legged son, who was at the other end of the room, "open the door, and tell Solomon to come in. He shall give us a tune here."

Bob obeyed, and Solomon walked in, fiddling as he walked, for he would on no account break off in the middle of a tune.

"Here, Solomon," said the Squire with loud patronage. "Round here, my man. Ah, I knew it was 'The flaxen-headed plough-boy:' there's no finer tune."

Solomon Macey, a small, hale old man with an abundant crop of long white hair reaching nearly to his shoulders, advanced to the indicated spot, bowing reverently while he fiddled, as much as to say that he respected the company, though he respected the key-note more. As soon as he had repeated the tune and lowered his fiddle, he bowed again to the Squire and the rector, and said, "I hope I see your honour and your reverence well, and wishing you health and long life and a happy New Year. And wishing the same to you, Mr. Lammeter, sir; and to the other gentlemen, and the madams, and the young lasses."

As Solomon uttered the last words, he bowed in all directions solicitously, lest he should be wanting in due respect. But thereupon he immediately began to prelude, and fell into the tune which he knew would be taken as a special compliment by Mr. Lammeter.

"Thank ye, Solomon, thank ye," said Mr. Lammeter when the fiddle paused again. "That's 'Over the hills and far away,' that is. My father used say to me, whenever we heard that tune, 'Ah, lad, *I* come from over the hills and far away.' There's a many tunes I don't make head or tail of; but that speaks to me like the blackbird's whistle. I suppose it's the name: there's a deal in the name of a tune."

But Solomon was already impatient to prelude again, and presently broke with much spirit into "Sir Roger de Coverley," at which there was a sound of chairs pushed back, and laughing voices.

"Ay, ay, Solomon, we know what that means," said the Squire, rising. "It's time to begin the dance, eh? Lead the way, then, and we'll all follow you."

So Solomon, holding his white head on one side, and playing vigorously, marched forward at the head of the gay procession into the White Parlour, where the mistletoe-bough was hung, and multitudinous tallow candles made rather a brilliant effect, gleaming from among the berried holly-boughs, and reflected in the old-fashioned oval mirrors fastened in the panels of the white wainscot. A quaint procession: Old Solomon, in his seedy clothes and long white locks, seemed to be luring that decent company by the magic scream of his fiddle—luring discreet matrons in turban-shaped caps, nay, Mrs. Crackenthorp herself, the summit of whose perpendicular feather was on a level with the Squire's shoulder—luring fair lasses complacently conscious of very short waists and skirts blameless of front folds—luring burly fathers in large variegated waistcoats, and ruddy sons, for the most part shy and sheepish, in short nether garments and very long coat-tails.

Already Mr. Macey and a few other privileged villagers, who were allowed to be spectators on these great occasions, were seated on benches placed for them near the door; and great was the admiration and satisfaction in that quarter when the couples had formed themselves for the dance, and the Squire led off with Mrs. Crackenthorp, joining hands with the rector and Mrs. Osgood. That was as it should be—that was what everybody had been used to—and the charter of Raveloe seemed to be renewed by the ceremony. It was not thought of as an unbecoming levity for the old and middle-aged people to dance a little before sitting down to cards, but rather as part of their social duties. For what were these if not to be merry at appropriate times, interchanging visits and poultry with due frequency, paying each other old-established compliments in sound traditional phrases, passing well-tried personal jokes, urging your guests to eat and drink too much out of hospitality, and eating and drinking too much in your neighbor's house to show that you liked your cheer? And the parson naturally set an example in these social duties. For it would not have been possible for the Raveloe mind, without a peculiar revelation, to know that a clergyman should be a pale-faced memento of solemnities, instead of a reasonably faulty man, whose exclusive authority to read prayers and preach, to christen, marry, and bury you, necessarily co-existed with the right to sell you the ground to be buried in, and to take tithe in kind; on which last point, of course, there was a little grumbling, but not to the extent of irreligion—not of deeper significance than the grumbling at the rain, which was by no means accompanied with a spirit of impious defiance, but with a desire that the prayer for fine weather might be read forthwith.

There was no reason, then, why the rector's dancing should not be received as part of the fitness of things quite as much as the Squire's, or why, on the other hand, Mr. Macey's official respect should restrain him from subjecting the parson's performance to that criticism with which minds of extraordinary acuteness must necessarily contemplate the doings of their fallible fellow-men.

"The Squire's pretty springy, considering his weight," said Mr. Macey, "and he stamps uncommon well. But Mr. Lammeter beats 'em all for shapes: you see he holds his head like a sodger, and he isn't so cushiony as most o' the oldish gentle-folks—they run fat in general; and he's got a fine leg. The parson's nimble enough, but he hasn't got much of a leg: it's a bit too thick down'ard, and his knees might be a bit nearer wi'out damage; but he might do worse, he might do worse. Though he hasn't that grand way o' waving his hand as the Squire has."

"Talk o' nimbleness, look at Mrs. Osgood," said Ben Winthrop, who was holding his son Aaron between his knees. "She trips along with her little steps, so as nobody can see how she goes—it's like as if she had little wheels to her feet. She doesn't look a day older nor last year: she's the finest-made woman as is, let the next be where she will."

"I don't heed how the women are made," said Mr. Macey, with some contempt. "They wear nayther coat nor breeches you can't make much out o' their shapes."

"Fayder," said Aaron, whose feet were busy beating out the tune, "how does that big cock's-feather stick in Mrs. Crackenthorp's yead? Is there a little hole for it, like in my shuttlecock?"

"Hush, lad, hush; that's the way the ladies dress their selves, that is," said the father, adding, however, in an undertone to Mr. Macey, "It does make her look funny, though—partly like a short-necked bottle wi' a long quill in it. Hey, by jingo, there's the young Squire leading off now, wi' Miss Nancy for partners. There's a lass for you!—like a pink-and-white posy—there's nobody 'ud think as anybody could be so pritty. I shouldn't wonder if she's Madam Cass some day, arter all —and nobody more rightfuller, for they'd make a fine match. You can find nothing against Master Godfrey's shapes, Macey, *I*'ll bet a penny."

Mr. Macey screwed up his mouth, leaned his head farther on one side, and twirled his thumbs with a presto movement as his eyes followed Godfrey up the dance. At last he summed up his opinion.

"Pretty well down'ard, but a bit too round i' the shoulder-blades. And as for them coats as he gets from the Flitton tailor, they're a poor cut to pay double money for."

"Ah, Mr. Macey, you and me are two folks," said Ben, slightly indignant at this carping. "When I've got a pot of good ale, I like to swaller it, and do my inside good, i'stead o' smelling and staring at it to see if I can't find faut wi' the brewing. I should like you to pick me out a finer-limbed young fellow nor Master Godfrey—one as 'ud knock you down easier, or's more pleasanter looksed when he's piert and merry."

"Tchuh!" said Mr. Macey, provoked to increased severity, "he isn't come to his right color yet; he's partly like a slack-baked pie. And I doubt he's got a soft place in his head, else why should he be turned round the finger by that offal Dunsey as nobody's seen o' late, and let him kill that fine hunting hoss as was the talk o' the country? And one while he was allays after Miss Nancy, and then it all went off again, like a smell o' hot porridge, as I may say. That wasn't my way when *I* went a-coorting."

"Ah, but mayhap, Miss Nancy hung off, like, and your lass didn't," said Ben.

"I should say she didn't," said Mr. Macey, significantly. "Before I said 'sniff,' I took care to know as she'd say 'snaff,' and pretty quick too. I wasn't a-going to open *my* mouth, like a dog at a fly, and snap it to again, wi' nothing to swaller."

"Well, I think Miss Nancy's a-coming round again," said Ben, "for Master Godfrey doesn't look so down-hearted to-night. And I see he's for taking her away to sit down, now they're at the end o' the dance: that looks like sweethearting, that does."

The reason why Godfrey and Nancy had left the dance was not so tender as Ben imagined. In the close press of couples a slight accident had happened to Nancy's dress, which, while it was short enough to show her neat ankle in front, was long enough behind to be caught under the stately stamp of the Squire's foot, so as to rend certain stitches at the waist, and cause much sisterly agitation in Priscilla's mind, as well as serious concern in Nancy's. One's thoughts may be much occupied with love-struggles, but hardly so as to be insensible to a disorder in the general framework of things. Nancy had no sooner completed her duty in the figure they were dancing than she said to Godfrey, with a deep blush, that she must go and sit down till Priscilla could come to her; for the sisters had already exchanged a short whisper and an open-eyed glance full of meaning. No reason less urgent than this could have prevailed on Nancy to give Godfrey this opportunity of sitting apart with her. As for Godfrey, he was feeling so happy and oblivious under the long charm of the country-dance with Nancy, that he got rather bold on the strength of her confusion, and was capable of leading her straight away, without leave asked, into the adjoining small parlour, where the card-tables were set.

"Oh, no, thank you," said Nancy, coldly, as soon as she perceived where he was going, "not in there. I'll wait here till Priscilla's ready to come to me. I'm sorry to bring you out of the dance and make myself troublesome."

"Why, you'll be more comfortable here by yourself," said the artful Godfrey: "I'll leave you here till your sister can come." He spoke in an indifferent tone.

That was an agreeable proposition, and just what Nancy desired; why, then, was she a little hurt that Mr. Godfrey should make it? They entered, and she seated herself on a chair against one of the card-tables, as the stiffest and most unapproachable position she could choose.

"Thank you, sir," she said immediately. "I needn't give you any more trouble. I'm sorry you've had such an unlucky partner."

"That's very ill-natured of you," said Godfrey, standing by her without any sign of intended departure, "to be sorry you've danced with me."

"Oh, no, sir, I don't mean to say what's ill-natured at all," said Nancy, looking distractingly prim and pretty. "When gentlemen have so many pleasures, one dance can matter but very little."

"You know that isn't true. You know one dance with you matters more to me than all the other pleasures in the world."

It was a long, long while since Godfrey had said anything so direct as that, and Nancy was startled. But her instinctive dignity and repugnance to any show of emotion made her sit perfectly still, and only throw a little more decision into her voice as she said—

"No, indeed, Mr. Godfrey, that's not known to me, and I have very good reasons for thinking different. But if it's true, I don't wish to hear it."

"Would you never forgive me, then, Nancy—never think well of me, let what would happen—would you never think the present made amends for the past? Not if I turned a good fellow, and gave up everything you didn't like?"

Godfrey was half conscious that this sudden opportunity of speaking to Nancy alone had driven him beside himself, but blind feeling had got the mastery of his tongue. Nancy really felt much agitated by the possibility Godfrey's words suggested, but this very pressure of emotion that she was in danger of finding too strong for her, roused all her power of self-command.

"I should be glad to see a good change in anybody, Mr. Godfrey," she answered, with the slightest discernible difference of tone, "but i⁴ 'ud be better if no change was wanted."

"You're very hard-hearted, Nancy," said Godfrey, pettishly. "You might encourage me to be a better fellow. I'm very miserable—but you've no feeling."

"I think those have the least feeling that act wrong, to begin with," said Nancy, sending out a flash in spite of herself. Godfrey was delighted with that little flash, and would have liked to go on and make her quarrel with him; Nancy was so exasperatingly quiet and firm. But she was not indifferent to him *yet*.

The entrance of Priscilla, bustling forward and saying, "Dear heart alive, child, let us look at this gown," cut off Godfrey's hopes of a quarrel.

"I suppose I must go now," he said to Priscilla.

"It's no matter to me whether you go or stay," said that frank lady, searching for something in her pocket, with a preoccupied brow.

"Do *you* want me to go?" said Godfrey, looking at Nancy, who was now standing up by Priscilla's order.

"As you like," said Nancy, trying to recover all her former coldness, and looking down carefully at the hem of her gown.

"Then I like to stay," said Godfrey, with a reckless determination to get as much of this joy as he could to-night, and think nothing of the morrow.

CHAPTER XII

WHILE Godfrey Cass was taking draughts of forgetfulness from the sweet presence of Nancy, willingly losing all sense of that hidden bond which at other moments galled and fretted him so as to mingle irritation with the very sunshine, Godfrey's wife was walking with slow, uncertain steps through the snow-covered Raveloe lanes, carrying her child in her arms.

This journey on New Year's Eve was a premeditated act of vengeance which she had kept in her heart ever since Godfrey, in a fit of passion, had told her he would sooner die than acknowledge her as his wife. There would be a great party at the Red House on New Year's Eve, she knew: her husband would be smiling and smiled upon, hiding *her* existence in the darkest corner of his heart. But she would mar his pleasure: she would go in her dingy rags, with her faded face, once as handsome as the best, with her little child that had its father's hair and eyes, and disclose herself to the Squire as his eldest son's wife. It is seldom that the miserable can help regarding their misery as a wrong inflicted by those who are less miserable. Molly knew that the cause of her dingy rags was not her husband's neglect, but the demon Opium to whom she was enslaved, body and soul, except in the lingering mother's tenderness that refused to give him her hungry child. She knew this well; and yet, in the moments of wretched unbenumbed consciousness, the sense of her want and degradation transformed itself continually into bitterness towards Godfrey. *He* was well off; and if she had her rights she would be well off too. The belief that he repented his marriage, and suffered from it, only aggravated her vindictiveness. Just and self-reproving thoughts do not come to us too thickly, even in the purest air, and with the best lessons of heaven and earth; how should those white winged delicate messengers make their way to Molly's poisoned chamber, inhabited by no higher memories than those of a bar-maid's paradise of pink ribbons and gentlemen's jokes?

She had set out at an early hour, but had lingered on the road, inclined by her indolence to believe that if she waited under a warm shed the snow would cease to fall. She had waited longer than she knew, and now that she found herself belated in the snow-hidden ruggedness of the long lanes, even the animation of a vindictive purpose could not keep her spirit from failing. It was seven o'clock, and by this time she was not very far from Raveloe, but she was not familiar enough with those monotonous lanes to know how near she was to her journey's end. She needed comfort, and she knew but one comforter—the familiar demon in her bosom; but she hesitated a moment, after drawing out the black remnant, before she raised it to her lips. In that moment the mother's love pleaded for painful consciousness rather than oblivion— pleaded to be left in aching weariness, rather than to have the encircling arms benumbed so that they could not feel the dear burden. In another moment Molly had flung something away, but it was not the black remnant—it was an empty vial. And she walked on again under the breaking cloud, from which there came now and then the light of a quickly-veiled star, for a freezing wind had sprung up since the snowing had ceased. But she walked always more and more drowsily, and clutched more and more automatically the sleeping child at her bosom.

Slowly the demon was working his will, and cold and weariness were his helpers. Soon she felt nothing but a supreme immediate longing that curtained off all futurity—the longing to lie down and sleep. She had arrived at a spot where her footsteps were no longer checked by a hedgerow, and she had wandered vaguely, unable to distinguish any objects, notwithstanding the wide whiteness around her, and the growing starlight. She sank down against a straggling furze bush, an easy pillow enough; and the bed of snow, too, was soft. She did not feel that the bed was cold, and did not heed whether the child would wake and cry for her. But her arms had not yet relaxed their instinctive clutch;

and the little one slumbered on as gently as if it had been rocked in a lace-trimmed cradle.

But the complete torpor came at last: the fingers lost their tension, the arms unbent; then the little head fell away from the bosom, and the blue eyes opened wide on the cold starlight. At first there was a little peevish cry of "mammy," and an effort to regain the pillowing arm and bosom; but mammy's ear was deaf, and the pillow seemed to be slipping away backward. Suddenly, as the child rolled downward on its mother's knees, all wet with snow, its eyes were caught by a bright glancing light on the white ground, and, with the ready transition of infancy, it was immediately absorbed in watching the bright living thing running towards it, yet never arriving. That bright living thing must be caught; and in an instant the child had slipped on all fours, and held out one little hand to catch the gleam. But the gleam would not be caught in that way, and now the head was held up to see where the cunning gleam came from. It came from a very bright place; and the little one, rising on its legs, toddled through the snow, the old grimy shawl in which it was wrapped trailing behind it, and the queer little bonnet dangling at its back—toddled on to the open door of Silas Marner's cottage, and right up to the warm hearth, where there was a bright fire of logs and sticks, which had thoroughly warmed the old sack (Silas's great-coat) spread out on the bricks to dry. The little one, accustomed to be left to itself for long hours without notice from its mother, squatted down on the sack, and spread its tiny hands towards the blaze, in perfect contentment, gurgling and making many inarticulate communications to the cheerful fire, like a new-hatched gosling beginning to find itself comfortable. But presently the warmth had a lulling effect, and the little golden head sank down on the old sack, and the blue eyes were veiled by their delicate half-transparent lids.

But where was Silas Marner while this strange visitor had come to his hearth? He was in the cottage, but he did not see the child. During the last few weeks, since he had lost his money, he had contracted the habit of opening his door and looking out from time to time, as if he thought that his money might be somehow coming back to him, or that some trace, some news of it, might be mysteriously on the road, and be caught by the listening ear or the straining eye. It was chiefly at night, when he was not occupied in his loom, that he fell into this repetition of an act for which he could have assigned no definite purpose, and which can hardly be understood except by those who have undergone a bewildering separation from a supremely loved object. In the evening twilight, and later whenever the night was not dark, Silas looked out on that narrow prospect round the Stone-pits, listening and gazing, not with hope, but with mere yearning and unrest.

This morning he had been told by some of his neighbors that it was New Year's Eve, and that he must sit up and hear the old year rung out and the new rung in, because that was good-luck, and might bring his money back again. This was only a friendly Raveloe-way of jesting with the half-crazy oddities of a miser, but it had perhaps helped to throw Silas into a more than usually excited state. Since the on-coming of twilight he had opened his door again and again, though only to shut it immediately at seeing all distance veiled by the falling snow. But the last time he opened it the snow had ceased, and the clouds were parting here and there. He stood and listened, and gazed for a long while—there was really something on the road coming towards him then, but he caught no sign of it; and the stillness and the wide track-less snow seemed to narrow his solitude, and touched his yearning with the chill of despair. He went in again, and put his right hand on the latch of the door to close it—but he did not close it: he was arrested, as he had been already since his loss, by the invisible wand of catalepsy, and stood like a graven image, with wide but sightless eyes, holding open his door, powerless to resist either the good or evil that might enter there.

When Marner's sensibility returned, he continued the action which had been arrested, and closed his door, unaware of the chasm in his consciousness, unaware of any intermediate change, except that the light had grown dim, and that he was chilled and faint. He thought he had been too long standing at the door and looking out. Turning towards the hearth, where the two logs had fallen apart, and sent forth only a red uncertain glimmer, he seated himself on his fireside chair, and was stooping to push his logs together, when, to his blurred vision, it seemed as if there were gold on the floor in front of the hearth. Gold!—his own gold—brought back to him as mysteriously as it had been taken away! He felt his heart begin to beat violently, and for a few moments he was unable to stretch out his hand and grasp the restored treasure. The heap of gold seemed to glow and get larger beneath his agitated gaze. He leaned forward at last, and stretched forth his hand; but in-stead of the hard coin with the familiar resisting outline, his fingers encountered soft warm curls. In utter amazement, Silas fell on his knees and bent his head low to examine the marvel: it was a sleeping child— a round, fair thing, with soft yellow rings all over its head. Could this be his little sister come back to him in a dream—his little sister whom he had carried about in his arms for a year before she died, when he was a small boy without shoes or stockings? That was the first thought that darted across Silas's blank wonderment. *Was* it a dream? He rose to his feet again, pushed his logs together, and, throwing on some dried leaves and sticks, raised a flame; but the flame did not disperse the vision—it only lit up more distinctly the little round form of the child, and its shabby clothing. It was very much like his little sister. Silas sank into his chair powerless, under the double presence of an inex-plicable surprise and a hurrying influx of memories. How and when had the child come in without his knowledge? He had never been beyond the door. But along with that question, and almost thrusting it away, there was a vision of the old home and the old streets leading to Lantern

Yard—and within that vision another, of the thoughts which had been present with him in those far-off scenes. The thoughts were strange to him now, like old friendships impossible to revive; and yet he had a dreamy feeling that this child was somehow a message come to him from that far-off life: it stirred fibres that had never been moved in Raveloe—old quiverings of tenderness—old impressions of awe at the presentiment of some Power presiding over his life; for his imagination had not yet extricated itself from the sense of mystery in the child's sudden presence, and had formed no conjectures of ordinary natural means by which the event could have been brought about.

But there was a cry on the hearth: the child had awaked, and Marner stooped to lift it on his knee. It clung round his neck, and burst louder and louder into that mingling of inarticulate cries with "mammy" by which little children express the bewilderment of waking. Silas pressed it to him, and almost unconsciously uttered sounds of hushing tenderness, while he bethought himself that some of his porridge, which had got cool by the dying fire, would do to feed the child with if it were only warmed up a little.

He had plenty to do through the next hour. The porridge, sweetened with some dry brown sugar from an old store which he had refrained from using for himself, stopped the cries of the little one, and made her lift her blue eyes with a wide quiet gaze at Silas, as he put the spoon into her mouth. Presently she slipped from his knee and began to toddle about, but with a pretty stagger that made Silas jump up and follow her lest she should fall against any thing that would hurt her. But she only fell in a sitting posture on the ground, and began to pull at her boots, looking up at him with a crying face as if the boots hurt her. He took her on his knee again, but it was some time before it occurred to Silas's dull bachelor mind that the wet boots were the grievance, pressing on her warm ankles. He got them off with difficulty, and baby was at once happily occupied with the primary mystery of her own toes, inviting Silas, with much chuckling, to consider the mystery too. But the wet boots had at last suggested to Silas that the child had been walking on the snow, and this roused him from his entire oblivion of any ordinary means by which it could have entered or been brought into his house. Under the prompting of this new idea, and without waiting to form conjectures, he raised the child in his arms, and went to the door. As soon as he had opened it, there was the cry of "mammy" again, which Silas had not heard since the child's first hungry waking. Bending forward, he could just discern the marks made by the little feet on the virgin snow, and he followed their track to the furze bushes. "Mammy!" the little one cried again and again, stretching itself forward so as almost to escape from Silas's arms, before he himself was aware that there was something more than the bush before him—that there was a human body, with the head sunk low in the furze, and half-covered with the shaken snow.

CHAPTER XIII

IT was after the early supper-time at the Red House, and the entertainment was in that stage when bashfulness itself had passed into easy
jollity, when gentlemen, conscious of unusual accomplishments, could
at length be prevailed on to dance a hornpipe, and when the Squire preferred talking loudly, scattering snuff, and patting his visitors' backs, to
sitting longer at the whist-table—a choice exasperating to uncle Kimble,
who, being always volatile in sober business hours, became intense and
bitter over cards and brandy, shuffled before his adversary's deal with a
glare of suspicion, and turned up a mean trump-card with an air of
inexpressible disgust, as if in a world where such things could happen
one might as well enter on a course of reckless profligacy. When the
evening had advanced to this pitch of freedom and enjoyment, it was
usual for the servants, the heavy duties of supper being well over, to
get their share of amusement by coming to look on at the dancing; so
that the back regions of the house were left in solitude.

There were two doors by which the White Parlour was entered from
the hall, and they were both standing open for the sake of air; but the
lower one was crowded with the servants and villagers, and only the
upper doorway was left free. Bob Cass was figuring in a hornpipe, and
his father, very proud of this lithe son, whom he repeatedly declared to
be just like himself in his young days, in a tone that implied this to be
the very highest stamp of juvenile merit, was the centre of a group who
had placed themselves opposite the performer, not far from the upper
door. Godfrey was standing a little way off, not to admire his brother's
dancing, but to keep sight of Nancy, who was seated in the group, near
her father. He stood aloof, because he wished to avoid suggesting himself as a subject for the Squire's fatherly jokes in connection with matrimony and Miss Nancy Lammeter's beauty, which were likely to become more and more explicit. But he had the prospect of dancing with
her again when the hornpipe was concluded, and in the meanwhile it
was very pleasant to get long glances at her quite unobserved.

But when Godfrey was lifting his eyes from one of those long glances,
they encountered an object as startling to him at that moment as if it
had been an apparition from the dead. It *was* an apparition from that
hidden life which lies, like a dark by-street, behind the goodly ornamented façade that meets the sunlight and the gaze of respectable admirers. It was his own child carried in Silas Marner's arms. That was
his instantaneous impression, unaccompanied by doubt, though he had
not seen the child for months past; and when the hope was rising that
he might possibly be mistaken, Mr. Crackenthorp and Mr. Lammeter
had already advanced to Silas, in astonishment at this strange advent.
Godfrey joined them immediately, unable to rest without hearing every

word—trying to control himself, but conscious that if any one noticed him, they must see that he was white-lipped and trembling.

But now all eyes at that end of the room were bent on Silas Marner; the Squire himself had risen, and asked angrily, "How's this?—what's this?—what do you do coming in here in this way?"

"I'm come for the doctor—I want the doctor," Silas had said, in the first moment, to Mr. Crackenthorp.

"Why, what's the matter, Marner?" said the rector. "The doctor's here; but say quietly what you want him for."

"It's a woman," said Silas, speaking low, and half-breathlessly, just as Godfrey came up. "She's dead, I think—dead in the snow at the Stone-pits—not far from my door."

Godfrey felt a great throb: there was one terror in his mind at that moment: it was, that the woman might *not* be dead. That was an evil terror—an ugly inmate to have found a nestling-place in Godfrey's kindly disposition; but no disposition is a security from evil wishes to a man whose happiness hangs on duplicity.

"Hush, hush!" said Mr. Crackenthorp. "Go out into the hall there. I'll fetch the doctor to you. Found a woman in the snow—and thinks she's dead," he added, speaking low, to the Squire. "Better say as little about it as possible: it will shock the ladies. Just tell them a poor woman is ill from cold and hunger. I'll go and fetch Kimble."

By this time, however, the ladies had pressed forward, curious to know what could have brought the solitary linen-weaver there under such strange circumstances, and interested in the pretty child, who, half alarmed and half attracted by the brightness and the numerous company, now frowned and hid her face, now lifted up her head again and looked round placably, until a touch or a coaxing word brought back the frown, and made her bury her face with new determination.

"What child is it?" said several ladies at once, and, among the rest, Nancy Lammeter, addressing Godfrey.

"I don't know—some poor woman's who has been found in the snow, I believe," was the answer Godfrey wrung from himself with a terrible effort. ("After all, *am* I certain?" he hastened to add, silently, in anticipation of his own conscience.)

"Why, you'd better leave the child here, then, Master Marner," said good-natured Mrs. Kimble, hesitating, however, to take those dingy clothes into contact with her own ornamented satin boddice. "I'll tell one o' the girls to fetch it."

"No—no—I can't part with it, I can't let it go," said Silas, abruptly. "It's come to me—I've a right to keep it."

The proposition to take the child from him had come to Silas quite unexpectedly, and his speech, uttered under a strong sudden impulse, was almost like a revelation to himself: a minute before, he had no distinct intention about the child.

"Did you ever hear the like?" said Mrs. Kimble, in mild surprise to her neighbor.

"Now, ladies, I must trouble you to stand aside," said Mr. Kimble, coming from the card-room in some bitterness at the interruption, but drilled by the long habit of his profession into obedience to unpleasant calls, even when he was hardly sober.

"It's a nasty business turning out now, eh, Kimble?" said the Squire. "He might ha' gone for your young fellow—the 'prentice there—what's his name?"

"Might? ay—what's the use of talking about might?" growled uncle Kimble, hastening out with Marner, and followed by Mr. Crackenthorp and Godfrey. "Get me a pair of thick boots, Godfrey, will you? And stay, let somebody run to Winthrop's and fetch Dolly—she's the best woman to get. Ben was here himself before supper: is he gone?"

"Yes, sir, I met him," said Marner; "but I couldn't stop to tell him anything, only I said I was going for the doctor, and he said the doctor was at the Squire's. And I made haste and ran, and there was nobody to be seen at the back o' the house, and so I went in to where the company was."

The child, no longer distracted by the bright light and the smiling women's faces, began to cry and call for "mammy," though always clinging to Marner, who had apparently won her thorough confidence. Godfrey had come back with the boots, and felt the cry as if some fibre were drawn tight within him.

"I'll go," he said, hastily, eager for some movement; "I'll go and fetch the woman—Mrs. Winthrop."

"Oh, pooh—send somebody else," said uncle Kimble, hurrying away with Marner.

"You'll let me know if I can be of any use, Kimble," said Mr. Crackenthorp. But the doctor was out of hearing.

Godfrey, too, had disappeared: he was gone to snatch his hat and coat, having just reflection enough to remember that he must not look like a madman; but he rushed out of the house into the snow without heeding his thin shoes.

In a few minutes he was on his rapid way to the Stone-pits by the side of Dolly, who, though feeling that she was entirely in her place in encountering cold and snow on an errand of mercy, was much concerned at a young gentleman's getting his feet wet under a like impulse.

"You'd a deal better go back, sir," said Dolly, with respectful compassion. "You've no call to catch cold; and I'd ask you if you'd be so good as tell my husband to come, on your way back—he's at the Rainbow, I doubt—if you found him any way sober enough to be o' use. Or else, there's Mrs. Snell 'ud happen send the boy up to fetch and carry, for there may be things wanted from the doctor's."

"No, I'll stay, now I'm once out—I'll stay outside here," said Godfrey, when they came opposite Marner's cottage. "You can come and tell me if I can do anything."

"Well, sir, you're very good: you've a tender heart," said Dolly, going to the door.

Godfrey was too painfully preoccupied to feel a twinge of self-reproach at this undeserved praise. He walked up and down, unconscious that he was plunging ankle-deep in snow, unconscious of every thing but trembling suspense about what was going on in the cottage, and the effect of each alternative on his future lot. No, not quite unconscious of every thing else. Deeper down, and half-smothered by passionate desire and dread, there was the sense that he ought not to be waiting on these alternatives; that he ought to accept the consequences of his deeds, own the miserable wife, and fulfil the claims of the helpless child But he had not moral courage enough to contemplate that active renunciation of Nancy as possible for him: he had only conscience and heart enough to make him forever uneasy under the weakness that forbade the renunciation. And at this moment his mind leaped away from all restraint towards the sudden prospect of deliverance from his long bondage.

"Is she dead?" said the voice that predominated over every other within him. "If she is, I may marry Nancy; and then I shall be a good fellow in future, and have no secrets, and the child—shall be taken care of somehow." But across that vision came the other possibility—"She may live, and then it's all up with me."

Godfrey never knew how long it was before the door of the cottage opened and Mr. Kimble came out. He went forward to meet his uncle, prepared to suppress the agitation he must feel, whatever news he was to hear.

"I waited for you, as I'd come so far," he said, speaking first.

"Pooh, it was nonsense for you to come out: why didn't you send one of the men? There's nothing to be done. She's dead—has been dead for hours, I should say."

"What sort of a woman is she?" said Godfrey, feeling the blood rush to his face.

"A young woman, but emaciated, with long black hair. Some vagrant —quite in rags. She's got a wedding-ring on, however. They must fetch her away to the workhouse to-morrow. Come, come along."

"I want to look at her," said Godfrey. "I think I saw such a woman yesterday. I'll overtake you in a minute or two."

Mr. Kimble went on, and Godfrey turned back to the cottage. He cast only one glance at the dead face on the pillow, which Dolly had smoothed with decent care; but he remembered that last look at his unhappy hated wife so well, that at the end of sixteen years every line in the worn face was present to him when he told the full story of this night.

He turned immediately towards the hearth, where Silas Marner sat lulling the child. She was perfectly quiet now, but not asleep—only soothed by sweet porridge and warmth into that wide-gazing calm which makes us older human beings, with our inward turmoil, feel a certain awe in the presence of a little child, such as we feel before some quiet majesty or beauty in the earth or sky—before a steady glowing planet, or a full-flowered eglantine, or the bending trees over a silent pathway.

The wide-open blue eyes looked up at Godfrey's without any uneasiness or sign of recognition: the child could make no visible audible claim on its father; and the father felt a strange mixture of feelings, a conflict of regret and joy, that the pulse of that little heart had no response for the half-jealous yearning of his own, when the blue eyes turned away from him slowly, and fixed themselves on the weaver's queer face, which was bent low down to look at them, while the small hand began to pull Marner's withered cheek with loving disfiguration.

"You'll take the child to the parish to-morrow?" asked Godfrey, speaking as indifferently as he could.

"Who says so?" said Marner, sharply. "Will they make me take her?"

"Why, you wouldn't like to keep her, should you—an old bachelor like you?"

"Till anybody shows they've a right to take her away from me," said Marner. "The mother's dead, and I reckon it's got no father: it's a lone thing—and I'm a lone thing. My money's gone, I don't know where —and this is come from I don't know where. I know nothing—I'm partly mazed."

"Poor little thing!" said Godfrey. "Let me give something towards finding it clothes."

He had put his hand in his pocket and found half a guinea, and, thrusting it into Silas's hand, he hurried out of the cottage to overtake Mr. Kimble.

"Ah, I see it's not the same woman I saw," he said, as he came up. "It's a pretty little child: the old fellow seems to want to keep it; that's strange for a miser like him. But I gave him a trifle to help him out: the parish isn't likely to quarrel with him for the right to keep the child."

"No; but I've seen the time when I might have quarrelled with him for it myself. It's too late now, though. If the child ran into the fire, your aunt's too fat to overtake it: she could only sit and grunt like an alarmed sow. But what a fool you are, Godfrey, to come out in your dancing shoes and stockings in this way—and you one of the beaux of the evening, and at your own house! What do you mean by such freaks, young fellow? Has Miss Nancy been cruel, and do you want to spite her by spoiling your pumps?"

"Oh, everything has been disagreeable to-night. I was tired to death of jigging and gallanting, and that bother about the hornpipes. And I'd got to dance with the other Miss Gunn," said Godfrey, glad of the subterfuge his uncle had suggested to him.

The prevarication and white lies which a mind that keeps itself ambitiously pure is as uneasy under as a great artist under the false touches that no eye detects but his own, are worn as lightly as mere trimmings when once the actions have become a lie.

Godfrey reappeared in the White Parlour with dry feet, and, since the truth must be told, with a sense of relief and gladness that was too strong for painful thoughts to struggle with. For could he not venture now, whenever opportunity offered, to say the tenderest things to Nancy

Lammeter—to promise her and himself that he would always be just what she would desire to see him? There was no danger that his dead wife would be recognized: those were not days of active inquiry and wide report; and as for the registry of their marriage, that was a long way off, buried in unturned pages, away from every one's interest but his own. Dunsey might betray him if he came back; but Dunsey might be won to silence.

And when events turn out so much better for a man than he has had reason to dread, is it not a proof that his conduct has been less foolish and blameworthy than it might otherwise have appeared? When we are treated well, we naturally begin to think that we are not altogether un-meritorious, and that it is only just we should treat ourselves well, and not mar our own good fortune. Where, after all, would be the use of his confessing the past to Nancy Lammeter, and throwing away his happiness?—nay, hers? for he felt some confidence that she loved him. As for the child, he would see that it was cared for: he would never forsake it; he would do everything but own it. Perhaps it would be just as happy in life without being owned by its father, seeing that nobody could tell how things would turn out, and that—is there any other reason wanted?—well, then, that the father would be much happier without owning the child.

CHAPTER XIV

THERE was a pauper's burial that week in Raveloe, and up Kench Yard at Batherley it was known that the dark-haired woman with the fair child, who had lately come to lodge there, was gone away again. That was all the express note taken that Molly had disappeared from the eyes of men. But the unwept death which, to the general lot, seemed as trivial as the summer-shed leaf, was charged with the force of destiny to certain human lives that we know of, shaping their joys and sorrows even to the end.

Silas Marner's determination to keep the "tramp's child" was matter of hardly less surprise and iterated talk in the village than the robbery of his money. That softening of feeling towards him which dated from his misfortune, that merging of suspicion and dislike in a rather contemptuous pity for him as lone and crazy, was now accompanied with a more active sympathy, especially amongst the women. Notable mothers, who knew what it was to keep children "whole and sweet;" lazy mothers, who knew what it was to be interrupted in folding their arms and scratching their elbows by the mischievous propensities of children just firm on their legs, were equally interested in conjecturing how a lone man would manage with a two-year-old child on his hands, and were equally ready with their suggestions; the notable chiefly telling him what he had better do, and the lazy ones being emphatic in telling him what he would never be able to do.

Among the notable mothers, Dolly Winthrop was the one whose neigh-bourly offices were the most acceptable to Marner, for they were ren-dered without any show of bustling instruction. Silas had shown her the half guinea given to him by Godfrey, and had asked her what he should do about getting some clothes for the child.

"Eh, Master Marner," said Dolly, "there's no call to buy, no more nor a pair o' shoes; for I've got the little petticoats as Aaron wore five years ago, and it's ill spending the money on them baby-clothes, for the child 'ull grow like grass i' May, bless it—that it will."

And the same day Dolly brought her bundle, and displayed to Marner, one by one, the tiny garments in their due order of succession, most of them patched and darned, but clean and neat as fresh-sprung herbs. This was the introduction to a great ceremony with soap and water, from which baby came out in new beauty, and sat on Dolly's knee, handling her toes and chuckling and patting her palms together with an air of having made several discoveries about herself, which she comm-nicated by alternate sounds of "gug-gug-gug," and "mammy." The "mammy" was not a cry of need or uneasiness; Baby had been used to utter it without expecting either tender sound or touch to follow.

"Anybody 'ud think the angils in heaven couldn't be prettier," said Dolly, rubbing the golden curls and kissing them. "And to think of its being covered wi' them dirty rags—and the poor mother—froze to death; but there's Them as took care of it, and brought it to your door, Master Marner. The door was open, and it walked in over the snow, like as if it had been a little starved robin. Didn't you say the door was open?"

"Yes," said Silas, meditatively. "Yes—the door was open. The mon-ey's gone I don't know where, and this is come from I don't know where."

He had not mentioned to any one his unconsciousness of the child's entrance, shrinking from questions which might lead to the fact he him-self suspected—namely, that he had been in one of his trances.

"Ah," said Dolly, with soothing gravity, "it's like the night and the morning, and the sleeping and the waking, and the rain and the harvest —one goes and the other comes, and we know nothing how nor where. We may strive and scrat and fend, but it's little we can do arter all— the big things come and go wi' no striving o' our'n—they do, that they do; and I think you're in the right on it to keep the little un, Master Marner, seeing as it's been sent to you, though there's folks as thinks different. You'll happen be a bit moithered with it while it's so little; but I'll come, and welcome, and see to it for you: I've a bit o' time to spare most days, for when one gets up betimes i' the morning, the clock seems to stan' still tow'rt ten, afore it's time to go about the victual. So, as I say, I'll come and see to the child for you, and welcome."

"Thank you . . . kindly," said Silas, hesitating a little. "I'll be glad if you'll tell me things. But," he added, uneasily, leaning forward to look at baby with some jealousy, as she was resting her head backward against Dolly's arm, and eying him contentedly from a distance—"But

I want to do things for it myself, else it may get fond o' somebody else, and not fond o' me. I've been used to fending for myself in the house— I can learn, I can learn."

"Eh, to be sure," said Dolly, gently. "I've seen men as are wonderful handy wi' children. The men are awk'ard and contrary mostly, God help 'em—but when the drink's out of 'em, they aren't unsensible, though they're bad for leeching and bandaging—so fiery and impatient. You see this goes first, next the skin," proceeded Dolly, taking up the little shirt, and putting it on.

"Yes," said Marner, docilely, bringing his eyes very close, that they might be initiated in the mysteries; whereupon Baby seized his head with both her small arms, and put her lips against his face with purring noises.

"See there," said Dolly, with a woman's tender tact, "she's fondest o' you. She want's to go o' your lap, I'll be bound. Go, then: take her, Master Marner; you can put the things on, and then you can say as you've done for her from the first of her coming to you."

Marner took her on his lap, trembling with an emotion mysterious to himself, at something unknown dawning on his life. Thought and feeling were so confused within him, that if he had tried to give them utterance, he could only have said that the child was come instead of the gold— that the gold had turned into the child. He took the garments from Dolly, and put them on under her teaching; interrupted, of course, by Baby's gymnastics.

"There, then! why, you take to it quite easy, Master Marner," said Dolly; "but what shall you do when you're forced to sit in your loom? For she'll get busier and mischievouser every day—she will, bless her. It's lucky as you've got that high hearth i'stead of a grate, for that keeps the fire more out of her reach: but if you've got anything as can be split or broke, or as is fit to cut her fingers off, she'll be at it—and it is but right you should know."

Silas meditated a little while in some perplexity. "I'll tie her to the leg o' the loom," he said at last—"tie her with a good long strip o' something."

"Well, mayhap that'll do, as it's a little gell, for they're easier persuaded to sit i' one place nor the lads. I know what the lads are; for I've had four—four I've had, God knows—and if you was to take and tie 'em up, they'd make a fighting and a crying as if you was ringing the pigs. But I'll bring you my little chair, and some bits o' red rag and things for her to play wi'; an' she'll sit and chatter to 'em as if they was alive. Eh, if it wasn't a sin to the lads to wish 'em made different, bless 'em, I should ha' been glad for one of 'em to be a little gell; and to think as I could ha' taught her to scour, and mend, and the knitting, and every thing. But I can teach 'em this little un, Master Marner, when she gets old enough."

"But she'll be *my* little un," said Marner, rather hastily. "She'll be nobody else's."

"No, to be sure; you'll have a right to her, if you're a father to her, and bring her up according. But," added Dolly, coming to a point which she had determined beforehand to touch upon, "you must bring her up like christened folks's children, and take her to church, and let her learn her catechise, as my little Aaron can say off—the 'I believe,' and every thing, and 'hurt nobody by word or deed,'—as well as if he was the clerk. That's what you must do, Master Marner, if you'd do the right thing by the orphan child."

Marner's pale face flushed suddenly under a new anxiety. His mind was too busy trying to give some definite bearing to Dolly's words for him to think of answering her.

"And it's my belief," she went on, "as the poor little creature has never been christened, and it's nothing but right as the parson should be spoke to; and if you was noways unwilling, I'd talk to Mr. Macey about it this very day. For if the child ever went anyways wrong, and you hadn't done your part by it, Master Marner—'noculation, and every-thing to save it from harm—it 'ud be a thorn i' your bed forever o' this side the grave; and I can't think as it 'ud be easy lying down for any body when they'd got to another world, if they hadn't done their part by the helpless children as come wi'out their own asking."

Dolly herself was disposed to be silent for some time now, for she had spoken from the depths of her own simple belief, and was much con-cerned to know whether her words would produce the desired effect on Silas. He was puzzled and anxious, for Dolly's word "christened" con-veyed no distinct meaning to him. He had only heard of baptism, and had only seen the baptism of grown-up men and women.

"What is it as you mean by 'christened?' " he said at last, timidly. "Won't folks be good to her without it?"

"Dear, dear! Master Marner," said Dolly, with gentle distress and compassion. "Had you never no father nor mother as taught you to say your prayers, and as there's good words and good things to keep us from harm?"

"Yes," said Silas, in a low voice; "I know a deal about that—used to, used to. But your ways are different: my country was a good way off." He paused a few moments, and then added, more decidedly, "But I want to do everything as can be done for the child. And whatever's right for it i' this country, and you think 'ull do it good, I'll act accord-ing, if you'll tell me."

"Well, then, Master Marner," said Dolly, inwardly rejoiced, "I'll ask Mr. Macey to speak to the parson about it; and you must fix on a name for it, because it must have a name giv' it when it's christened."

"My mother's name was Hephzibah," said Silas, "and my little sister was named after her."

"Eh, that's a hard name," said Dolly. "I partly think it isn't a christened name."

"It's a Bible name," said Silas, old ideas recurring.

"Then I've no call to speak again' it," said Dolly, rather startled by

Silas's knowledge on this head; "but you see I'm no scholard, and I'm slow at catching the words. My husband says I'm allays like as if I was putting the haft for the handle—that's what he says—for he's very sharp, God help him. But it was awk'ard calling your little sister by such a hard name, when you'd got nothing big to say, like—wasn't it, Master Marner?"

"We called her Eppie," said Silas.

"Well, if it was noways wrong to shorten the name, it 'ud be a deal handier. And so I'll go now, Master Marner, and I'll speak about the christening afore dark; and I wish you the best o' luck, and it's my be- lief as it'll come to you, if you do what's right by the orphan child;— and there's the 'noculation to be seen to; and as to washing its bits o' things, you need look to nobody but me, for I can do 'em wi' one hand when I've got my suds about. Eh, the blessed angil! You'll let me bring my Aaron one o' these days, and he'll show her his little cart as his father's made for him, and the black-and-white pup as he's got a-rear- ing."

Baby *was* christened, the rector deciding that a double baptism was the lesser risk to incur; and on this occasion Silas, making himself as clean and tidy as he could, appeared for the first time within the church, and shared in the observances held sacred by his neighbors. He was quite unable, by means of anything he heard or saw, to identify the Raveloe religion with his old faith; if he could at any time in his previous life have done so, it must have been by the aid of a strong feel- ing ready to vibrate with sympathy, rather than by a comparison of phrases and ideas: and now for long years that feeling had been dor- mant. He had no distinct idea about the baptism and the church-going, except that Dolly had said it was for the good of the child; and in this way, as the weeks grew to months, the child created fresh and fresh links between his life and the lives from which he had hitherto shrunk continually into narrower isolation. Unlike the gold which needed noth- ing, and must be worshipped in close-locked solitude—which was hid- den away from the daylight, was deaf to the song of birds, and started to no human tones—Eppie was a creature of endless claims and ever- growing desires, seeking and loving sunshine, and living sounds, and living movements; making trial of everything, with trust in new joy, and stirring the human kindness in all eyes that looked on her. The gold had kept his thoughts in an ever-repeated circle, leading to nothing be- yond itself; but Eppie was an object compacted of changes and hopes that forced his thoughts onward, and carried them far away from their old eager pacing towards the same blank limit—carried them away to the new things that would come with the coming years, when Eppie would have learned to understand how her father Silas cared for her; and made him look for images of that time in the ties and charities that bound together the families of his neighbors. The gold had asked that he should sit weaving longer and longer, deafened and blinded more and more to all things except the monotony of his loom and the repetition of his web; but Eppie called him away from his weaving, and made him think all its pauses a holiday, re-awakening his senses with her fresh life, even to the old winter-flies that came crawling forth in the early spring sunshine, and warming him into joy because *she* had joy.

And when the sunshine grew strong and lasting, so that the butter-cups were thick in the meadows, Silas might be seen in the sunny mid·day, or in the late afternoon when the shadows were lengthening under the hedgerows, strolling out with uncovered head to carry Eppie beyond the Stone-pits to where the flowers grew, till they reached some favorite bank where he could sit down, while Eppie toddled to pluck the flowers, and make remarks to the winged things that murmured happily above the bright petals, calling "Dad-dad's" attention continually by bringing him the flowers. Then she would turn her ear to some sudden bird-note, and Silas learned to please her by making signs of hushed stillness, that they might listen for the note to come again: so that when it came, she set up her small back and laughed with gurgling triumph. Sitting on the banks in this way, Silas began to look for the once familiar herbs again; and as the leaves, with their unchanged outline and markings, lay on his palm, there was a sense of crowding remembrances from which he turned away timidly, taking refuge in Eppie's little world, that lay lightly on his enfeebled spirit.

As the child's mind was growing into knowledge, his mind was grow-ing into memory: as her life unfolded, his soul, long stupefied in a cold, narrow prison, was unfolding too, and trembling gradually into full consciousness.

It was an influence which must gather force with every new year: the tones that stirred Silas's heart grew articulate, and called for more distinct answers; shapes and sounds grew clearer for Eppie's eyes and ears, and there was more that "Dad-dad" was imperatively required to notice and account for. Also, by the time Eppie was three years old, she developed a fine capacity for mischief, and for devising ingenious ways of being troublesome, which found much exercise, not only for Silas's patience, but for his watchfulness and penetration. Sorely was poor Silas puzzled on such occasions by the incompatible demands of love. Dolly Winthrop told him punishment was good for Eppie, and that, as for rearing a child without making it tingle a little in soft and safe places now and then, it was not to be done.

"To be sure, there's another thing you might do, Master Marner," added Dolly, meditatively: "you might shut her up once i' the coal-hole. That was what I did wi' Aaron; for I was that silly wi' the youngest lad, as I could never bear to smack him. Not as I could find i' my heart to let him stay i' the coal-hole more nor a minute, but it was enough to colly him all over, so as he must be new washed and dressed, and it was as good as a rod to him—that was. But I put it upo' your conscience, Master Marner, as there's one of 'em you must choose—ayther smack-ing or the coal-hole—else she'll get so masterful, there'll be no holding her."

Silas was impressed with the melancholy truth of this last remark; but his force of mind failed before the only two penal methods open to him, not only because it was painful to him to hurt Eppie, but because he trembled at a moment's contention with her, lest she should love him the less for it. Let even an affectionate Goliath get himself tied to a small tender thing, dreading to hurt it by pulling, and dreading still more to snap the cord, and which of the two, pray, will be master? It was clear that Eppie, with her short toddling steps, must lead father Silas a pretty dance on any fine morning when circumstances favored mischief.

For example. He had wisely chosen a broad strip of linen as a means of fastening her to his loom when he was busy: it made a broad belt round her waist, and was long enough to allow of her reaching the truckle-bed and sitting down on it, but not long enough for her to attempt any dangerous climbing. One bright summer's morning Silas had been more engrossed than usual in "setting up" a new piece of work, an occasion on which his scissors were in requisition. These scissors, owing to an especial warning of Dolly's, had been kept carefully out of Eppie's reach; but the click of them had had a peculiar attraction for her ear, and, watching the results of that click, she had derived the philosophic lesson that the same cause would produce the same effect. Silas had seated himself in his loom, and the noise of weaving had begun; but he had left his scissors on a ledge which Eppie's arm was long enough to reach; and now, like a small mouse, watching her opportunity, she stole quietly from her corner, secured the scissors, and toddled to the bed again, setting up her back as a mode of concealing the fact. She had a distinct intention as to the use of the scissors; and having cut the linen strip in a jagged but effectual manner, in two moments she had run out at the open door where the sunshine was inviting her, while poor Silas believed her to be a better child than usual. It was not until he happened to need his scissors that the terrible fact burst upon him: Eppie had run out by herself—had perhaps fallen into the stone-pit. Silas, shaken by the worst fear that could have befallen him, rushed out, calling "Eppie!" and ran eagerly about the unenclosed space, exploring the dry cavities into which she might have fallen, and then gazing with questioning dread at the smooth red surface of the water. The cold drops stood on his brow. How long had she been out? There was one hope—that she had crept through the stile and got into the fields, where he habitually took her to stroll. But the grass was high in the meadow, and there was no descrying her, if she were there, except by a close search that would be a trespass on Mr. Osgood's crop. Still, that misdemeanour must be committed; and poor Silas, after peering all round the hedgerows, traversed the grass, beginning with perturbed vision to see Eppie behind every group of red sorrel, and to see her moving always farther off as he approached. The meadow was searched in vain; and he got over the stile into the next field, looking with dying hope towards a small pond which was now reduced to its summer shallowness, so as to leave a wide margin of good adhesive mud. Here, however, sat Eppie, discoursing cheerfully to her own small boot, which she was using as a bucket to convey the water into a deep hoof-mark, while her little naked foot was planted comfortably on a cushion of olive-green mud. A red-headed calf was observing her with alarmed doubt through the opposite hedge.

Here was clearly a case of aberration in a christened child which demanded severe treatment; but Silas, overcome with convulsive joy at finding his treasure again, could do nothing but snatch her up, and cover her with half-sobbing kisses. It was not until he had carried her home, and had begun to think of the necessary washing, that he recollected the need that he should punish Eppie, and "make her remember." The idea that she might run away again and come to harm, gave him unusual resolution, and for the first time he determined to try the coal-hole—a small closet near the hearth.

"Naughty, naughty Eppie," he suddenly began, holding her on his knee, and pointing to her muddy feet and clothes—"naughty to cut with the scissors and run away. Eppie must go into the coal-hole for being naughty. Daddy must put her in the coal-hole."

He half expected that this would be shock enough, and that Eppie would begin to cry. But instead of that, she began to shake herself on his knee, as if the proposition opened a pleasing novelty. Seeing that he must proceed to extremities, he put her into the coal-hole, and held the door closed, with a trembling sense that he was using a strong measure. For a moment there was silence, but then came a little cry, "Opy, opy!" and Silas let her out again, saying, "Now Eppie 'ull never be naughty again, else she must go in the coal-hole—a black naughty place."

The weaving must stand still a long while this morning, for now Eppie must be washed, and have clean clothes on; but it was to be hoped that this punishment would have a lasting effect, and save time in future—though, perhaps, it would have been better if Eppie had cried more.

In half an hour she was clean again, and Silas having turned his back to see what he could do with the linen band, threw it down again, with the reflection that Eppie would be good without fastening for the rest of the morning. He turned round again, and was going to place her in her little chair near the loom, when she peeped out at him with black face and hands again, and said, "Eppie in de toal-hole!"

This total failure of the coal-hole discipline shook Silas's belief in the efficacy of punishment. "She'd take it all for fun," he observed to Dolly, "if I didn't hurt her, and that I can't do, Mrs. Winthrop. If she makes me a bit o' trouble, I can bear it. And she's got no tricks but what she'll grow out of."

"Well, that's partly true, Master Marner," said Dolly, sympathetically; "and if you can't bring your mind to frighten her off touching things, you must do what you can to keep 'em out of her way. That's what I do wi' the pups as the lads are allays a-rearing. They *will* worry and gnaw—worry and gnaw they will, if it was one's Sunday cap as hung anywhere so as they could drag it. They know no difference, God help 'em: it's the pushing o' the teeth as sets 'em on, that's what it is."

So Eppie was reared without punishment, the burden of her misdeeds being borne vicariously by father Silas. The stone hut was made a soft nest for her, lined with downy patience: and also in the world that lay beyond the stone hut she knew nothing of frowns and denials.

Notwithstanding the difficulty of carrying her and his yarn or linen at the same time, Silas took her with him in most of his journeys to the farm-houses, unwilling to leave her behind at Dolly Winthrop's, who was always ready to take care of her: and little curly-headed Eppie, the weaver's child, became an object of interest at several outlying home-steads, as well as in the village. Hitherto he had been treated very much as if he had been a useful gnome or brownie—a queer and unaccountable creature, who must necessarily be looked at with wondering curiosity and repulsion, and with whom one would be glad to make all greetings and bargains as brief as possible, but who must be dealt with in a pro-pitiatory way, and occasionally have a present of pork or garden-stuff to carry home with him, seeing that without him there was no getting the yarn woven. But now Silas met with open smiling faces and cheerful questionings, as a person whose satisfactions and difficulties could be understood. Everywhere he must sit a little and talk about the child, and words of interest were always ready for him: "Ah, Master Marner, you'll be lucky if she takes the measles soon and easy!"—or, "Why, there isn't many lone men 'ud ha' been wishing to take up with a little un like that: but I reckon the weaving makes you handier than men as do out-door work—you're partly as handy as a woman, for weaving comes next to spinning." Elderly masters and mistresses, seated observantly in large kitchen arm-chairs, shook their heads over the difficulties attend-ant on rearing children, felt Eppie's round arms and legs, and pro-nounced them remarkably firm, and told Silas that, if she turned out well (which, however, there was no telling), it would be a fine thing for him to have a steady lass to do for him when he got helpless. Servant maidens were fond of carrying her out to look at the hens and chickens, or to see if any cherries could be shaken down in the orchard; and the small boys and girls approached her slowly, with cautious movement and steady gaze, like little dogs face to face with one of their own kind, till attraction had reached the point at which the soft lips were put out for a kiss. No child was afraid of approaching Silas when Eppie was near him: there was no repulsion around him now, either for young or old; for the little child had come to link him once more with the whole world. There was love between him and the child that blent them into one, and there was love between the child and the world—from men and women with parental looks and tones, to the red lady-birds and the round pebbles.

Silas began now to think of Raveloe life entirely in relation to Eppie: she must have everything that was a good in Raveloe; and he listened docilely, that he might come to understand better what this life was, from which, for fifteen years, he had stood aloof as from a strange thing,

wherewith he could have no communion: as some man who hast a precious plant to which he would give a nurturing home in a new soil, thinks
of the rain, and the sunshine, and all influences, in relation to his nurs-
ling, and asks industriously for all knowledge that will help him to
satisfy the wants of the searching roots, or to guard leaf and bud from
invading harm. The disposition to hoard had been utterly crushed at the
very first by the loss of his long-stored gold: the coins he earned afterwards seemed as irrelevant as stones brought to complete a house suddenly buried by an earthquake; the sense of bereavement was too heavy
upon him for the old thrill of satisfaction to rise again at the touch of
the newly-earned coin. And now something had come to replace his
hoard which gave a growing purpose to the earnings, drawing his hope
and joy continually onward beyond the money.

In old days there were angels who came and took men by the hand
and led them away from the city of destruction. We see no white-winged
angels now. But yet men are led away from threatening destruction: a
hand is put into theirs, which leads them forth gently towards a calm
and bright land, so that they look no more backward; and the hand may
be a little child's.

CHAPTER XV

THERE was one person, as you will believe, who watched with keener
though more hidden interest than any other, the prosperous growth of
Eppie under the weaver's care. He dared not do any thing that would
imply a stronger interest in a poor man's adopted child than could be
expected from the kindliness of the young Squire, when a chance meeting suggested a little present to a simple old fellow whom others noticed
with good-will; but he told himself that the time would come when he
might do something towards furthering the welfare of his daughter without incurring suspicions. Was he very uneasy in the meantime at his
inability to give his daughter her birthright? I can not say that he was.
The child was being taken care of, and would very likely be happy, as
people in humble stations often were—happier, perhaps, than those who
are brought up in luxury.

That famous ring that pricked its owner when he forgot duty and
followed desire—I wonder if it pricked very hard when he set out on
the chase, or whether it pricked but lightly then, and only pierced to
the quick when the chase had long been ended, and hope, folding her
wings, looked backward and became regret?

Godfrey Cass's cheek and eye were brighter than ever now. He was
so undivided in his aims, that he seemed like a man of firmness. No
Dunsey had come back: people had made up their minds that he was
gone for a soldier or gone "out of the country," and no one cared to be
specific in their inquiries on a subject delicate to a respectable family.
Godfrey had ceased to see the shadow of Dunsey across his path; and

the path now lay straight forward to the accomplishment of his best, longest-cherished wishes. Everybody said Mr. Godfrey had taken the right turn; and it was pretty clear what would be the end of things, for there were not many days in the week that he was not seen riding to the Warrens. Godfrey himself, when he was asked jocosely if the day had been fixed, smiled with the pleasant consciousness of a lover who could say "yes," if he liked. He felt a reformed man, delivered from temptation; and the vision of his future life seemed to him as a promised land for which he had no cause to fight. He saw himself with all his happiness centred on his own hearth, while Nancy would smile on him as he played with the children.

And that other child not on the hearth—he would not forget it; he would see that it was well provided for. That was a father's duty.

PART TWO

★

CHAPTER XVI

It was a bright autumn Sunday, sixteen years after Silas Marner had found his new treasure on the hearth. The bells of the old Raveloe church were ringing the cheerful peal which told that the morning service was ended; and out of the arched doorway in the tower came slowly, retarded by friendly greetings and questions, the richer parishioners who had chosen this bright Sunday morning as eligible for church-going. It was the rural fashion of that time for the more important members of the congregation to depart first, while their humbler neighbours waited and looked on, stroking their bent heads or dropping their courtesies to any large ratepayer who turned to notice them.

Foremost among these advancing groups of well-clad people, there are some whom we shall recognize, in spite of Time, who has laid his hand on them all. The tall blond man of forty is not much changed in feature from the Godfrey Cass of six-and-twenty: he is only fuller in flesh, and has only lost the indefinable look of youth—a loss which is marked even when the eye is undulled and the wrinkles are not yet come. Perhaps the pretty woman, not much younger than he, who is leaning on his arm, is more changed than her husband: the lovely bloom that used to be always on her cheek now comes but fitfully, with the fresh morning air or with some strong surprise; yet to all who love human faces best for what they tell of human experience, Nancy's beauty has a heightened interest. Often the soul is ripened into fuller goodness while age has spread an ugly film, so that mere glances can never divine the preciousness of the fruit. But the years have not been so cruel to Nancy. The firm yet placid mouth, the clear veracious glance of the brown eyes, speak now of a nature that has been tested and has kept its highest qualities; and even the costume, with its dainty neatness and purity, has more significance now the coquetries of youth can have nothing to do with it.

Mr. and Mrs. Godfrey Cass (any higher title has died away from Raveloe lips since the old Squire was gathered to his fathers and his inheritance was divided) have turned round to look for the tall aged man and the plainly dressed woman who are a little behind—Nancy having observed that they must wait for "father and Priscilla"—and now they all turn into a narrower path leading across the churchyard to a small gate opposite the Red House. We will not follow them now; for may there not be some others in this departing congregation whom we should like to see again—some of those who are not likely to be handsomely clad, and whom we may not recognize so easily as the master and mistress of the Red House?

But it is impossible to mistake Silas Marner. His large brown eyes seem to have gathered a longer vision, as is the way with eyes that have been short-sighted in early life, and they have a less vague, a more answering look; but in everything else one sees signs of a frame much enfeebled by the lapse of the sixteen years. The weaver's bent shoulders and white hair give him almost the look of advanced age, though he is not more than five-and-fifty; but there is the freshest blossom of youth close by his side—a blonde dimpled girl of eighteen, who has vainly tried to chastise her curly auburn hair into smoothness under her brown bonnet: the hair ripples as obstinately as a brooklet under the March breeze, and the little ringlets burst away from the restraining comb behind and show themselves below the bonnet-crown. Eppie can not help being rather vexed about her hair, for there is no other girl in Raveloe who has hair at all like it, and she thinks hair ought to be smooth. She does not like to be blameworthy even in small things: you see how neatly her prayer-book is folded in her spotted handkerchief.

That good-looking young fellow, in a new fustian suit, who walks behind her, is not quite sure upon the question of hair in the abstract, when Eppie puts it to him, and thinks that perhaps straight hair is the best in general, but he doesn't want Eppie's hair to be different. She surely divines that there is some one behind her who is thinking about her very particularly, and mustering courage to come to her side as soon as they are out in the lane, else why should she look rather shy, and take care not to turn away her head from her father Silas, to whom she keeps murmuring little sentences as to who was at church, and who was not at church, and how pretty the red mountain-ash is over the Rectory wall?

"I wish we had a little garden, father, with double daisies in, like Mrs. Winthrop's," said Eppie, when they were out in the lane; "only they say it 'ud take a deal of digging and bringing fresh soil—and you couldn't do that, could you, father? Anyhow, I shouldn't like you to do it, for it 'ud be too hard work for you."

"Yes, I could do it, child, if you want a bit o' garden: these long evenings, I could work at taking in a little bit o' the waste, just enough for a root or two o' flowers for you; and again, i' the morning, I could have a turn wi' the spade before I sat down to the loom. Why didn't you tell me before as you wanted a bit o' garden?"

"I can dig it for you, Master Marner," said the young man in fustian, who was now by Eppie's side, entering into the conversation without the trouble of formalities. "It'll be play to me after I've done my day's work, or any odd bits o' time when the work's slack. And I'll bring you some soil from Mr. Cass's garden—he'll let me, and willing."

"Eh, Aaron, my lad, are you there?" said Silas; "I wasn't aware of you; for when Eppie's talking o' things, I see nothing but what she's a-saying. Well, if you could help me with the digging, we might get her a bit o' garden all the sooner."

"Then if you think well and good," said Aaron, "I'll come to the Stone-pits this afternoon, and we'll settle what land's to be taken in, and I'll get up an hour earlier i' the morning, and begin on it."

"But not if you don't promise me not to work at the hard digging, father," said Eppie. "For I shouldn't ha' said any thing about it," she added, half-bashfully, half-roguishly, "only Mrs. Winthrop said as Aaron 'ud be so good, and—"

"And you might ha' known it without mother telling you," said Aaron. "And Master Marner knows too, I hope, as I'm able and willing to do a turn o' work for him, and he won't do me the unkindness to anyways take it out o' my hands."

"There now, father, you won't work in it till it's all easy," said Eppie, "and you and me can mark out the beds, and make holes and plant the roots. It'll be a deal livelier at the Stone-pits when we've got some flowers, for I always think the flowers can see us and know what we're talking about. And I'll have a bit o' rosemary, and bergamot, and thyme, because they're so sweet-smelling; but there's no lavender only in the gentlefolks' gardens, I think."

"That's no reason why you shouldn't have some," said Aaron, "for I can bring you slips of anything; I'm forced to cut no end of 'em when I'm gardening, and throw 'em away mostly. There's a big bed o' lavender at the Red House: the missis is very fond of it."

"Well," said Silas, gravely, "so as you don't make free for us, or ask for anything as is worth much at the Red House: for Mr. Cass's been so good to us, and built us up the new end o' the cottage, and given us beds and things, as I couldn't abide to be imposin' for garden-stuff or anything else."

"No, no, there's no imposin'," said Aaron; "there's never a garden in all the parish but what there's endless waste in it for want o' somebody as could use everything up. It's what I think to myself sometimes, as there need nobody run short o' victuals if the land was made the most on, and there was never a morsel but what could find its way to a mouth. It sets one thinking o' that—gardening does. But I must go back now, else mother 'ull be in trouble as I aren't there."

"Bring her with you this afternoon, Aaron," said Eppie; "I shouldn't like to fix about the garden, and her not know every thing from the first —should *you*, father?"

"Ay, bring her if you can, Aaron," said Silas; "she's sure to have a word to say as'll help us to set things on their right end."

Aaron turned back up the village, while Silas and Eppie went on up the lonely sheltered lane.

"Oh, daddy!" she began, when they were in privacy, clasping and squeezing Silas's arm, and skipping round to give him an energetic kiss. "My little old daddy! I'm so glad. I don't think I shall want any thing else when we've got a little garden; and I knew Aaron would dig it for us," she went on with roguish triumph—"I knew that very well."

"You're a deep little puss, you are," said Silas, with the mild passive happiness of love-crowned age in his face; "but you'll make yourself fine and beholden to Aaron."

"Oh no, I sha'n't," said Eppie, laughing and frisking; "he likes it."

"Come, come, let me carry your prayer-book, else you'll be dropping it, jumping i' that way."

Eppie was now aware that her behaviour was under observation, but it was only the observation of a friendly donkey, browsing with a log fastened to his foot—a meek donkey, not scornfully critical of human trivialities, but thankful to share in them, if possible, by getting his nose scratched; and Eppie did not fail to gratify him with her usual notice, through it was attended with the inconvenience of his following them, painfully, up to the very door of their home.

But the sound of a sharp bark inside, as Eppie put the key in the door, modified the donkey's views, and he limped away again without bidding. The sharp bark was the sign of an excited welcome that was awaiting them from a knowing brown terrier, who, after dancing at their legs in an hysterical manner, rushed with a worrying noise at a tortoise-shell kitten under the loom, and then rushed back with a sharp bark again, as much as to say, "I have done my duty by this feeble creature, you perceive;" while the lady-mother of the kitten sat sunning her white bosom in the window, and looked round with a sleepy air of expecting caresses, though she was not going to take any trouble for them.

The presence of this happy animal life was not the only change which had come over the interior of the stone cottage. There was no bed now in the living-room, and the small space was well filled with decent furniture, all bright and clean enough to satisfy Dolly Winthrop's eye. The oaken table and three-cornered oaken chair were hardly what was likely to be seen in so poor a cottage: they had come, with the beds and other things, from the Red House; for Mr. Godfrey Cass, as every one said in the village, did very kindly by the weaver; and it was nothing but right a man should be looked on and helped by those who could afford it, when he had brought up an orphan child, and been father and mother to her—and had lost his money too, so as he had nothing but what he worked for week by week, and when the weaving was going down too —for there was less and less flax spun—and Master Marner was none so young. Nobody was jealous of the weaver, for he was regarded as an exceptional person, whose claims on neighbourly help were not to be matched in Raveloe. Any superstition that remained concerning him had taken an entirely new colour; and Mr. Macey, now a very feeble old man of fourscore and six, never seen except in his chimney-corner or sitting in the sunshine at his door-sill, was of opinion that when a man had done what Silas had done by an orphan child, it was a sign that his money would come to light again, or leastwise that the robber would be made to answer for it—for, as Mr. Macey observed of himself, his faculties were as strong as ever.

Silas sat down now and watched Eppie with a satisfied gaze as she spread the clean cloth, and set on it the potato-pie, warmed up slowly in a safe Sunday fashion, by being put into a dry pot over a slowly-dying fire, as the best substitute for an oven. For Silas would not consent to have a grate and oven added to his conveniences: he loved the old brick hearth as he had loved his brown pot—and was it not there when he had found Eppie? The gods of the hearth exist for us still; and let all new faith be tolerant of that fetishism, lest it bruise its own roots.

Silas ate his dinner more silently than usual, soon laying down his knife and fork, and watching half-abstractedly Eppie's play with Snap and the cat, by which her own dining was made rather a lengthy business. Yet it was a sight that might well arrest wandering thoughts: Eppie, with the rippling radiance of her hair and the whiteness of her rounded chin and throat set off by the dark-blue cotton gown, laughing merrily as the kitten held on with her four claws to one shoulder, like a design for a jug-handle, while Snap on the right hand and Puss on the other put up their paws towards a morsel which she held out of the reach of both—Snap occasionally desisting in order to remonstrate with the cat by a cogent worrying growl on the greediness and futility of her conduct; till Eppie relented, caressed them both, and divided the morsel between them.

But at last Eppie, glancing at the clock, checked the play, and said, "Oh, daddy, you're wanting to go into the sunshine to smoke your pipe. But I must clear away first, so as the house may be tidy when godmother comes. I'll make haste—I won't be long."

Silas had taken to smoking a pipe daily during the last two years, having been strongly urged to it by the sages of Raveloe, as a practice "good for the fits;" and this advice was sanctioned by Dr. Kimble, on the ground that it was as well to try what could do no harm—a principle which was made to answer for a great deal of work in that gentleman's medical practice. Silas did not highly enjoy smoking, and often wondered how his neighbors could be so fond of it; but a humble sort of acquiescence in what was held to be good, had become a strong habit of that new self which had been developed in him since he had found Eppie on his hearth: it had been the only clue his bewildered mind could hold by in cherishing this young life that had been sent to him out of the darkness into which his gold had departed. By seeking what was needful for Eppie, by sharing the effect that everything produced on her, he had himself come to appropriate the forms of custom and belief which were the mould of Raveloe life; and as, with re-awakening sensibilities, memory also reawakened, he had begun to ponder over the elements of his old faith, and blend them with his new impressions, till he recovered a consciousness of unity between his past and present. The sense of presiding goodness and the human trust which come with all pure peace and joy, had given him a dim impression that there had been some error, some mistake, which had thrown that dark shadow over the days of his best years; and as it grew more and more easy to him to open his mind to Dolly Winthrop, he gradually communicated to her all he could describe of his early life. The communication was necessarily a slow and difficult process, for Silas's meagre power of explanation was not aided by any readiness of interpretation in Dolly, whose narrow outward experience gave her no key to strange customs, and made every novelty a source of wonder that arrested them at every step of the narrative. It was only by fragments, and at intervals which left Dolly time to revolve what she had heard till it acquired some familiarity for her, that Silas at last arrived at the climax of the sad story —the drawing of lots, and its false testimony concerning him; and this had to be repeated in several interviews, under new questions on her part as to the nature of this plan for detecting the guilty and clearing the innocent.

"And yourn's the same Bible, you're sure o' that, Master Marner— the Bible as you brought wi' you from that country—it's the same as what they've got at church, and what Eppie's a-learning to read in?"

"Yes," said Silas, "every bit the same; and there's drawing o' lots in the Bible, mind you," he added in a lower tone.

"Oh dear, dear," said Dolly in a grieved voice, as if she were hearing an unfavourable report of a sick man's case. She was silent for some minutes; at last she said—

"There's wise folks, happen, as know how it all is; the parson knows, I'll be bound; but it takes big words to tell them things, and such as poor folks can't make much out on. I can never rightly know the meaning o' what I hear at church, only a bit here and there, but I know it's good words—I do. But what lies upo' your mind—it's this, Master Marner: as, if Them above had done the right thing by you, They'd never ha' let you be turned out for a wicked thief when you was innicent."

"Ah!" said Silas, who had now come to understand Dolly's phraseology, "that was what fell on me like as if it had been red-hot iron; because, you see, there was nobody as cared for me or clave to me above nor below. And him as I'd gone out and in wi' for ten year and more, since when we was lads and went halves—mine own famil'ar friend, in whom I trusted, and lifted up his heel again' me, and worked to ruin me."

"Eh, but he was a bad un—I can't think as there's another such," said Dolly. "But I'm o'ercome, Master Marner; I'm like as if I'd waked and didn't know whether it was night or morning. I feel somehow as sure as I do when I've laid something up though I can't justly put my hand on it, as there was a rights in what happened to you, if one could but make it out; and you'd no call to lose heart as you did. But we'll talk on it again; for sometimes things come into my head when I'm leeching or poulticing, or such, as I could never think on when I was sitting still."

Dolly was too useful a woman not to have many opportunities of illumination of the kind she alluded to, and she was not long before she recurred to the subject.

"Master Marner," she said, one day that she came to bring home Eppie's washing, "I've been sore puzzled for a good bit wi' that trouble o' yourn and the drawing o' lots; and it got twisted back'ards and for'ards, as I didn't know which end to lay hold on. But it come to me all clear like, that night when I was sitting up wi' poor Bessy Fawkes, as is dead and left her children behind, God help 'em—it come to me as clear as daylight: but whether I've got hold on it now, or can anyways bring it to my tongue's end, that I don't know. For I've often a deal inside me as 'll niver come out; and for what you talk o' your folks in your old country niver saying prayers by heart nor saying 'em out of a book, they must be wonderful cliver; for if I didn't know 'Our Father,' and little bits o' good words as I can carry out o' church wi' me, I might down o' my knees every night, but nothing could I say."

"But you can mostly say something as I can make sense on, Mrs. Winthrop," said Silas.

"Well, then, Master Marner, it come to me summat like this: I can make nothing o' the drawing o' lots and the answer coming wrong; it 'ud mayhap take the parson to tell that, and he could only tell us i' big words. But what come to me as clear as the daylight, it was when I was troubling over poor Bessy Fawkes, and it allays comes into my head when I'm sorry for folks, and feel as I can't do a power to help 'em, not if I was to get up i' the middle o' the night—it comes into my head as Them above has got a deal tenderer heart nor what I've got—for I can't be anyways better nor Them as made me; and if anything looks hard to me, it's because there's things I don't know on; and for the matter o' that, there may be plenty o' things I don't know on, for it's little as I know—that it is. And so, while I was thinking o' that, you come into my mind, Master Marner, and it all come pouring in:— if I felt i' my inside what was the right and just thing by you, and them as prayed and drawed the lots, all but that wicked un, if they'd ha' done the right thing by you if they could, isn't there Them as was at the making on us, and knows better and has a better will? And that's all as ever I can be sure on, and everything else is a big puzzle to me when I think on it. For there was the fever come and took off them as were full-growed, and left the helpless children; and there's the breaking o' limbs; and them as 'ud do right and be sober have to suffer by them as are contrary—eh, there's trouble i' this world, and there's things as we can niver make out the rights on. And all as we've got to do is to trusten, Master Marner—to do the right thing as fur as we know, and to trusten. For if us as knows so little can see a bit o' good and rights, we may be sure as there's a good and a rights bigger nor what we can know—I feel it i' my own inside as it must be so. And if you could but ha' gone on trustening, Master Marner, you wouldn't ha' run away from your fellow-creaturs and been so lone."

"Ah, but that 'ud ha' been hard," said Silas, in an undertone; "it 'ud ha' been hard to trusten then."

"And so it would," said Dolly, almost with compunction; "them things are easier said nor done; and I'm partly ashamed o' talking."

"Nay, nay," said Silas, "you're i' the right, Mrs. Winthrop—you're i' the right. There's good i' this world—I've a feeling o' that now; and it makes a man feel as there's a good more nor he can see, i' spite o' the trouble and the wickedness. That drawing o' the lots is dark; but the child was sent to me: there's dealings with us—there's dealings."

This dialogue took place in Eppie's earlier years, when Silas had to part with her for two hours every day, that she might learn to read at the dame school, after he had vainly tried himself to guide her in that first step to learning. Now that she was grown up, Silas had often been led, in those moments of quiet outpouring which come to people who live together in perfect love, to talk with *her* too of the past, and how and why he had lived a lonely man until she had been sent to him. For it would have been impossible for him to hide from Eppie that she was not his own child: even if the most delicate reticence on the point could have been expected from Raveloe gossips in her presence, her own questions about her mother could not have been parried, as she grew up, without that complete shrouding of the past which would have made a painful barrier between their minds. So Eppie had long known how her mother had died on the snowy ground, and how she herself had been found on the hearth by father Silas, who had taken her golden curls for his lost guineas brought back to him. The tender and peculiar love with which Silas had reared her in almost inseparable companionship with himself, aided by the seclusion of their dwelling, had preserved her from the lowering influences of the village talk and habits, and had kept her mind in that freshness which is sometimes falsely supposed to be an invariable attribute of rusticity. Perfect love has a breath of poetry which can exalt the relations of the least-instructed human beings; and this breath of poetry had surrounded Eppie from the time when she had followed the bright gleam that beckoned her to Silas's hearth; so that it is not surprising if, in other things besides her delicate prettiness, she was not quite a common village maiden, but had a touch of refinement and fervor which came from no other teaching than that of tenderly-nurtured unvitiated feeling. She was too childish and simple for her imagination to rove into questions about her unknown father; for a long while it did not even occur to her that she must have had a father; and the first time that the idea of her mother having had a husband presented itself to her, was when Silas showed her the wedding-ring which had been taken from the wasted finger, and had been carefully preserved by him in a little lacquered box shaped like a shoe. He delivered this box into Eppie's charge when she had grown up, and she often opened it to look at the ring: but still she thought hardly at all about the father of whom it was the symbol. Had she not a father very close to her, who loved her better than any real fathers in the village seemed to love their daughters? On the contrary, who her mother was, and how she came to die in that forlornness, were questions that often pressed on Eppie's mind. Her knowledge of Mrs. Winthrop, who was her nearest friend next to Silas, made her feel that a mother must be very precious; and she had again and again asked Silas to tell her how her mother looked, whom she was like, and how he had found her against the furze-bush, led towards it by the little footsteps and the outstretched arms. The furze-bush was there still; and this afternoon, when Eppie came out with Silas into the sunshine, it was the first object that arrested her eyes and thoughts.

"Father," she said, in a tone of gentle gravity, which sometimes came like a sadder, slower cadence across her playfulness, "we shall take the furze-bush into the garden; it'll come into the corner, and just against it I'll put snowdrops and crocuses, 'cause Aaron says they won't die out, but'll always get more and more."

"Ah, child," said Silas, always ready to talk when he had his pipe in his hand, apparently enjoying the pauses more than the puffs, "it wouldn't do to leave out the furze-bush; and there's nothing prettier, to my thinking, when it's yallow with flowers. But it's just come into my head what we're to do for a fence—mayhap Aaron can help us to a thought; but a fence we must have, else the donkeys and things 'ull come and trample everything down. And fencing's hard to be got at, by what I can make out."

"Oh, I'll tell you, daddy," said Eppie, clasping her hands suddenly, after a minute's thought. "There's lots o' loose stones about, some of 'em not big, and we might lay 'em atop of one another, and make a wall. You and me could carry the smallest, and Aaron 'ud carry the rest—I know he would."

"Eh, my precious 'un," said Silas, "there isn't enough stones to go all round; and as for you carrying, wi' your little arms you couldn't carry a stone no bigger than a turnip. You're dillicate made, my dear," he added, with a tender intonation—"that's what Mrs. Winthrop says."

"Oh, I'm stronger than you think, daddy," said Eppie; "and if there wasn't stones enough to go all round, why, they'll go part o' the way, and then it'll be easier to get sticks and things for the rest. See here, round the big pit, what a many stones!"

She skipped forward to the pit, meaning to lift one of the stones and exhibit her strength, but she started back in surprise.

"Oh, father, just come and look here," she exclaimed—"come and see how the water's gone down since yesterday. Why, yesterday the pit was ever so full!"

"Well, to be sure," said Silas, coming to her side. "Why, that's the draining they've begun on, since harvest, i' Mr. Osgood's fields, I reckon. The foreman said to me the other day, when I passed by 'em, 'Master Marner,' he said, 'I shouldn't wonder if we lay your bit o' waste as dry as a bone.' It was Mr. Godfrey Cass, he said, had gone into the draining: he'd been taking these fields o' Mr. Osgood."

"How odd it'll seem to have the old pit dried up!" said Eppie, turning away, and stooping to lift rather a large stone. "See, daddy, I can carry this quite well," she said, going along with much energy for a few steps, but presently letting it fall.

"Ah, you're fine and strong, arn't you?" said Silas, while Eppie shook her aching arms and laughed. "Come, come, let us go and sit down on the bank against the stile there, and have no more lifting. You might hurt yourself, child. You'd need have somebody to work for you—and my arm isn't over strong."

Silas uttered the last sentence slowly, as if it implied more than met the ear; and Eppie, when they sat down on the bank, nestled close to his side, and, taking hold caressingly of the arm that was not over strong, held it on her lap, while Silas puffed again dutifully at the pipe, which occupied his other arm. An ash in the hedgerow behind made a fretted screen from the sun, and threw happy playful shadows all about them.

"Father," said Eppie, very gently, after they had been sitting in silence a little while, "if I was to be married, ought I to be married with my mother's ring?"

Silas gave an almost imperceptible start, though the question fell in with the under-current of thought in his own mind, and then said, in a subdued tone, "Why, Eppie, have you been a-thinking on it?"

"Only this last week, father," said Eppie, ingenuously, "since Aaron talked to me about it."

"And what did he say?" said Silas, still in the same subdued way, as if he were anxious lest he should fall into the slightest tone that was not for Eppie's good.

"He said he should like to be married, because he was a-going in four-and-twenty, and had got a deal of gardening work, now Mr. Mott's given up; and he goes twice a-week regular to Mr. Cass's and once to Mr. Osgood's, and they're going to take him on at the Rectory."

"And who is it as he's wanting to marry?" said Silas, with rather a sad smile.

"Why, me, to be sure, daddy," said Eppie, with dimpling laughter, kissing her father's cheeks; "as if he'd want to marry anybody else!"

"And you mean to have him, do you?" said Silas.

"Yes, some time," said Eppie, "I don't know when. Everybody's married some time, Aaron says. But I told him that wasn't true: for, I said, look at father—he's never been married."

"No, child," said Silas, "your father was a lone man till you was sent to him."

"But you'll never be lone again, father," said Eppie tenderly. "That was what Aaron said—'I could never think o' taking you away from Master Marner, Eppie.' And I said, 'It 'ud be no use if you did, Aaron.' And he wants us all to live together, so as you needn't work a bit, father, only what's for your own pleasure; and he'd be as good as a son to you—that was what he said."

"And should you like that, Eppie?" said Silas, looking at her.

"I shouldn't mind it, father," said Eppie, quite simply. "And I should like things to be so as you needn't work much. But if it wasn't for that, I'd sooner things didn't change. I'm very happy: I like Aaron to be fond of me, and come and see us often, and behave pretty to you—he always *does* behave pretty to you, doesn't he, father?"

"Yes, child, nobody could behave better," said Silas, emphatically. "He's his mother's lad."

"But I don't want any change," said Eppie. "I should like to go on a long, long while, just as we are. Only Aaron does want a change: and he made me cry a bit—only a bit—because he said I didn't care for him, for if I cared for him I should want us to be married, as he did."

"Eh, my blessed child," said Silas, laying down his pipe as if it were useless to pretend to smoke any longer, "you're o'er young to be married. We'll ask Mrs. Winthrop—we'll ask Aaron's mother what *she* thinks; if there's a right thing to do, she'll come at it. But there's this to be thought on, Eppie: things *will* change, whether we like it or no; things won't go on for a long while just as they are and no difference. I shall get older and helplesser, and be a burden on you, belike, if I don't go away from you altogether. Not as I mean you'd think me a burden—I know you wouldn't—but it 'ud be hard upon you; and when I look for'ard to that, I like to think as you'd have somebody else besides me—somebody young and strong, as'll outlast your own life, and take care on you to the end." Silas paused, and, resting his wrists on his knees, lifted his hands up and down meditatively as he looked on the ground.

"Then, would you like me to be married, father?" said Eppie, with a little trembling in her voice.

"I'll not be the man to say no, Eppie," said Silas, emphatically; "but we'll ask your godmother. She'll wish the right thing by you and her son too."

"There they come, then," said Eppie. "Let us go and meet 'em. Oh, the pipe! won't you have it lit again, father?" said Eppie, lifting that medicinal appliance from the ground.

"Nay, child," said Silas, "I've done enough for to-day. I think, mayhap, a little of it does me more good than so much at once."

CHAPTER XVII

WHILE Silas and Eppie were seated on the bank discoursing in the fleckered shade of the ash-tree, Miss Priscilla Lammeter was resisting her sister's arguments, that it would be better to stay tea at the Red House, and let her father have a long nap, than drive home to the Warrens so soon after dinner. The family party (of four only) were seated round the table in the dark wainscoted parlour, with the Sunday dessert before them, of fresh filberts, apples, and pears, duly ornamented with leaves by Nancy's own hand before the bells had rung for church.

A great change has come over the dark wainscoted parlour since we saw it in Godfrey's bachelor days, and under the wifeless reign of the old Squire. Now all is polish, on which no yesterday's dust is ever allowed to rest, from the yard's width of oaken boards round the carpet, to the old Squire's gun and whips and walking-sticks, ranged on the stag's antlers above the mantel-piece. All other signs of sporting and out-door occupation Nancy has removed to another room; but she has brought into the Red House the habit of filial reverence, and preserves sacredly in a place of honour these relics of her husband's departed father. The tankards are on the side-table still, but the bossed silver is undimmed by handling, and there are no dregs to send forth unpleasant suggestions: the only prevailing scent is of the lavender and rose-leaves that fill the vases of Derbyshire spar. All is purity and order in this once dreary room, for fifteen years ago, it was entered by a new presiding spirit.

"Now, father," said Nancy, "*is* there any call for you to go home to tea? Mayn't you just as well stay with us?—such a beautiful evening as it's likely to be."

The old gentleman had been talking with Godfrey about the increasing poor-rate and the ruinous times, and had not heard the dialogue between his daughters.

"My dear, you must ask Priscilla," he said, in the once firm voice, now become rather broken. "She manages me and the farm too."

"And reason good as I should manage you, father," said Priscilla, "else you'd be giving yourself your death with rheumatism. And as for the farm, if anything turns out wrong, as it can't but do in these times, there's nothing kills a man so soon as having nobody to find fault with but himself. It's a deal the best way o' being master, to let somebody else do the ordering, and keep the blaming in your own hands. It 'ud save many a man a stroke, *I* believe."

"Well, well, my dear," said her father, with a quiet laugh, "I didn't say you don't manage for everybody's good."

"Then manage so as you may stay tea, Priscilla," said Nancy, putting her hand on her sister's arm affectionately. "Come now; and we'll go round the garden while father has his nap."

"My dear child, he'll have a beautiful nap in the gig, for I shall drive. And as for staying tea, I can't hear of it; for there's this dairymaid, now she knows she's to be married, turned Michaelmas, she'd as lief pour the new milk into the pig-trough as into the pans. That's the way with 'em all: it's as if they thought the world 'ud be new-made because they're to be married. So come and let me put my bonnet on, and there'll be time for us to walk round the garden while the horse is being put in."

When the sisters were treading the neatly swept garden-walks, between the bright turf that contrasted pleasantly with the dark cones and arches and wall-like hedges of yew, Priscilla said—

"I'm as glad as any thing at your husband's making that exchange o' land with cousin Osgood, and beginning the dairying. It's a thousand pities you didn't do it before; for it'll give you something to fill your mind. There's nothing like a dairy if folks want a bit o' worrit to make the days pass. For as for rubbing furniture, when you can once see your face in a table there's nothing else to look for; but there's always something fresh with the dairy; for even in the depths o' winter there's some pleasure in conquering the butter, and making it come whether or no. My dear," added Priscilla, pressing her sister's hand affectionately as they walked side by side, "you'll never be low when you've got a dairy."

"Ah, Priscilla," said Nancy, returning the pressure with a grateful glance of her clear eyes, "but it won't make up to Godfrey: a dairy's not so much to a man. And it's only what he cares for that ever makes me low. I'm contented with the blessings we have, if he could be contented."

"It drives me past patience," said Priscilla, impetuously, "that way o' the men—always wanting and wanting, and never easy with what they've got: they can't sit comfortable in their chairs when they've neither ache nor pain, but either they must stick a pipe in their mouths, to make 'em better than well, or else they must be swallowing something strong, though they're forced to make haste before the next meal comes in. But joyful be it spoken, our father was never that sort o' man. And if it had pleased God to make you ugly, like me, so as the men wouldn't ha' run after you, we might have kept to our own family, and had nothing to do with folks as have got uneasy blood in their veins."

"Oh, don't say so, Priscilla," said Nancy, repenting that she had called forth this outburst; "nobody has any occasion to find fault with Godfrey. It's natural he should be disappointed at not having any children: every man likes to have somebody to work for and lay by for, and he always counted so on making a fuss with them when they were little. There's many another man 'ud hanker more than he does. He's the best of husbands."

"Oh, I know," said Priscilla, smiling sarcastically, "I know the way o' wives; they set one on to abuse their husbands, and then they turn round on one and praise 'em as if they wanted to sell 'em. But father'll be waiting for me; we must turn now."

The large gig with the steady old gray was at the front door, and Mr. Lammeter was already on the stone steps, passing the time in recalling to Godfrey what very fine points Speckle had when his master used to ride him.

"I always *would* have a good horse, you know," said the old gentleman, not liking that spirited time to be quite effaced from the memory of his juniors.

"Mind you bring Nancy to the Warrens before the week's out, Mr. Cass," was Priscilla's parting injunction, as she took the reins, and shook them gently, by way of friendly incitement to Speckle.

"I shall just take a turn to the fields against the Stone-pits, Nancy, and look at the draining," said Godfrey.

"You'll be in again by tea-time, dear?"

"Oh, yes, I shall be back in an hour."

It was Godfrey's custom on a Sunday afternoon to do a little contemplative farming in a leisurely walk. Nancy seldom accompanied him; for the women of her generation—unless, like Priscilla, they took to out-door management—were not given to much walking beyond their own house and garden, finding sufficient exercise in domestic duties. So, when Priscilla was not with her, she usually sat with Mant's Bible before her, and after following the text with her eyes for a little while, she would gradually permit them to wander as her thoughts had already insisted on wandering.

But Nancy's Sunday thoughts were rarely quite out of keeping with the devout and reverential intention implied by the book spread open before her. She was not theologically instructed enough to discern very clearly the relation between the sacred documents of the past which she opened without method, and her own obscure, simple life; but the spirit of rectitude, and the sense of responsibility for the effect of her conduct on others, which were strong elements in Nancy's character, had made it a habit with her to scrutinize her past feelings and actions with self-questioning solicitude. Her mind not being courted by a great variety of subjects, she filled the vacant moments by living inwardly, again and again, through all her remembered experience, especially through the fifteen years of her married time, in which her life and its significance had been doubled. She recalled the small details, the words, tones, and looks, in the critical scenes which had opened a new epoch for her, by giving her a deeper insight into the relations and trials of life, or which had called on her for some little effort of forbearance, or of painful adherence to an imagined or real duty—asking herself continually whether she had been in any respect blamable. This excessive rumination and self-questioning is perhaps a morbid habit inevitable to a mind of much moral sensibility when shut out from its due share of outward activity and of practical claims on its affections—inevitable to a noble-hearted, childless woman, when her lot is narrow. "I can do so little—have I done it all well?" is the perpetually recurring thought; and there are no voices calling her away from that soliloquy, no peremptory demands to divert energy from vain regret or superfluous scruple.

There was one main thread of painful experience in Nancy's married life, and on it hung certain deeply-felt scenes, which were the oftenest revived in retrospect. The short dialogue with Priscilla in the garden had determined the current of retrospect in that frequent direction this particular Sunday afternoon. The first wandering of her thought from the text, which she still attempted dutifully to follow with her eyes and silent lips, was into an imaginary enlargement of the defense she had set up for her husband against Priscilla's implied blame. The vindication of the loved object is the best balm affection can find for its wounds: —"A man must have so much on his mind," is the belief by which a wife often supports a cheerful face under rough answers and unfeeling words. And Nancy's deepest wounds had all come from the perception

that the absence of children from their hearth was dwelt on in her husband's mind as a privation to which he could not reconcile himself.

Yet sweet Nancy might have been expected to feel still more keenly
the denial of a blessing to which she had looked forward with all the
varied expectations and preparations, solemn and prettily trivial, which
fill the mind of a loving woman when she expects to become a mother.
Was there not a drawer filled with the neat work of her hands, all unworn and untouched, just as she had arranged it there fourteen years
ago—just, but for one little dress, which had been made the burial-dress?
But under this immediate personal trial Nancy was so firmly unmur-
muring, that years ago she had suddenly renounced the habit of visiting
this drawer, lest she should in this way be cherishing a longing for what
was not given.

Perhaps it was this very severity towards any indulgence of what
she held to be sinful regret in herself, that made her shrink from applying her own standard to her husband. "It was very different—it was
much worse for a man to be disappointed in that way; a woman could
always be satisfied with devoting herself to her husband, but a man
wanted something that would make him look forward more—and sitting by the fire was so much duller to him than to a woman." And always, when Nancy reached this point in her meditations—trying, with
predetermined sympathy, to see every thing as Godfrey saw it—there
came a renewal of self-questioning. *Had* she done every thing in her
power to lighten Godfrey's privation? Had she really been right in the
resistance which had cost her so much pain six years ago, and again
four years ago—the resistance to her husband's wish that they should
adopt a child? Adoption was more remote from the ideas and habits of
that time than of our own; still Nancy had her opinion on it. It was
as necessary to her mind to have an opinion on all topics, not exclusively
masculine, that had come under her notice, as for her to have a precisely
marked place for every article of her personal property: and her opinions
were always principles to be unwaveringly acted on. They were firm,
not because of their basis, but because she held them with a tenacity
inseparable from her mental action. On all the duties and proprieties
of life, from filial behavior to the arrangements of the evening toilette,
pretty Nancy Lammeter, by the time she was three-and-twenty, had
her unalterable little code, and had formed every one of her habits in
strict accordance with that code. She carried these decided judgments
within her in the most unobtrusive way: they rooted themselves in her
mind, and grew there as quietly as grass. Years ago, we know, she insisted on dressing like Priscilla, because "it was right for sisters to dress
alike," and because "she would do what was right if she wore a gown
dyed with cheese-coloring." That was a trivial but typical instance of
the mode in which Nancy's life was regulated.

It was one of those rigid principles, and no petty egoistic feeling, which
had been the ground of Nancy's difficult resistance to her husband's
wish. To adopt a child, because children of your own had been denied

you, was to try and choose your lot in spite of Providence: the adopted child, she was convinced, would never turn out well, and would be a curse to those who had wilfully and rebelliously sought what it was clear that, for some high reason, they were better without. When you saw a thing was not meant to be, said Nancy, it was a bounden duty to leave off so much as wishing for it. And so far, perhaps, the wisest of men could scarcely make more than a verbal improvement in her principle. But the conditions under which she held it apparent that a thing was not meant to be, depended on a more peculiar mode of thinking. She would have given up making a purchase at a particular place if, on three successive times, rain, or some other cause of Heaven's sending, had formed an obstacle; and she would have anticipated a broken limb or other heavy misfortune to any one who persisted in spite of such indications.

"But why should you think the child would turn out ill?" said Godfrey, in his remonstrances. "She has thriven as well as child can do with the weaver; and *he* adopted her. There isn't such a pretty little girl anywhere else in the parish, or one fitter for the station we could give her. Where can be the likelihood or her being a curse to anybody?"

"Yes, my dear Godfrey," said Nancy, who was sitting with her hands tightly clasped together, and with yearning, regretful affection in her eyes. "The child may not turn out ill with the weaver. But, then, he didn't go to seek her, as we should be doing. It will be wrong: I feel sure it will. Don't you remember what that lady we met at the Royston Baths told us about the child her sister adopted? That was the only adoption I ever heard of: and the child was transported when it was twenty-three. Dear Godfrey, don't ask me to do what I know is wrong: I should never be happy again. I know it's very hard for *you*—it's easier for me—but it's the will of Providence."

It might seem singular that Nancy—with her religious theory pieced together out of narrow social traditions, fragments of church doctrine imperfectly understood, and girlish reasonings on her small experience—should have arrived by herself at a way of thinking so nearly akin to that of many devout people, whose beliefs are held in the shape of a system quite remote from her knowledge—singular, if we did not know that human beliefs, like all other natural growths, elude the barriers of system.

Godfrey had from the first specified Eppie, then about twelve years old, as a child suitable for them to adopt. It had never occurred to him that Silas would rather part with his life than with Eppie. Surely the weaver would wish the best to the child he had taken so much trouble with, and would be glad that such good fortune should happen to her: she would always be very grateful to him, and he would be well provided for to the end of his life—provided for as the excellent part he had done by the child deserved. Was it not an appropriate thing for people in a higher station to take a charge off the hands of a man in a lower? It seemed an eminently appropriate thing to Godfrey, for reasons that were known only to himself; and, by a common fallacy, he imagined the measure would be easy because he had private motives for desiring it. This was rather a coarse mode of estimating Silas's relation to Eppie; but we must remember that many of the impressions which Godfrey was likely to gather concerning the laboring people around him would favor the idea that deep affections can hardly go along with callous palms and scant means; and he had not had the opportunity, even if he had had the power, of entering intimately into all that was exceptional in the weaver's experience. It was only the want of adequate knowledge that could have made it possible for Godfrey deliberately to entertain an unfeeling project; his natural kindness had outlived that blighting time of cruel wishes, and Nancy's praise of him as a husband was not founded entirely on a wilful illusion.

"I was right," she said to herself, when she had recalled all their scenes of discussion—"I feel I was right to say him nay, though it hurt me more than anything; but how good Godfrey has been about it? Many men would have been very angry with me for standing out against their wishes; and they might have thrown out that they'd had ill-luck in marrying me; but Godfrey has never been the man to say me an unkind word. It's only what he can't hide; everything seems so blank to him, I know; and the land—what a difference it 'ud make to him, when he goes to see after things, if he'd children growing up that he was doing it all for! But I won't murmur; and perhaps if he'd married a woman who'd have had children, she'd have vexed him in other ways."

This possibility was Nancy's chief comfort; and to give it greater strength, she laboured to make it impossible that any other wife should have had more perfect tenderness. She had been *forced* to vex him by that one denial. Godfrey was not insensible to her loving effort, and did Nancy no injustice as to the motives of her obstinacy. It was impossible to have lived with her fifteen years and not be aware that an unselfish clinging to the right, and a sincerity clear as the flower-born dew, were her main characteristics; indeed, Godfrey felt this so strongly, that his own more wavering nature, too averse to facing difficulty to be unvaryingly simple and truthful, was kept in a certain awe of this gentle wife who watched his looks with a yearning to obey them. It seemed to him impossible that he should ever confess to her the truth about Eppie: she would never recover from the repulsion the story of his earlier marriage would create, told to her now, after that long concealment. And the child, too, he thought, must become an object of repulsion: the very sight of her would be painful. The shock to Nancy's mingled pride and ignorance of the world's evil might be even too much for her delicate frame. Since he had married her with that secret on his heart, he must keep it there to the last. Whatever else he did, he could not make an irreparable breach between himself and this long-loved wife.

Meanwhile, why could he not make up his mind to the absence of children from the hearth brightened by such a wife? Why did his mind fly uneasily to that void, as if it were the sole reason why life was not thoroughly joyous to him? I suppose it is the way with all men and women who reach middle age without the clear perception that life never *can* be thoroughly joyous: under the vague dullness of the gray hours, dissatisfaction seeks a definite object, and finds it in the privation of an untried good. Dissatisfaction, seated musingly on a childless hearth, thinks with envy of the father whose return is greeted by young voices—seated at the meal where the little heads rise one above the other like nursery plants, it sees a black care hovering behind every one of them, and thinks the impulses by which men abandon freedom, and seek for ties, are surely nothing but a brief madness. In Godfrey's case there were further reasons why his thoughts should be continually solicited by this one point in his lot: his conscience, never thoroughly easy about Eppie, now gave his childless home the aspect of a retribution; and as the time passed on, under Nancy's refusal to adopt her, any retrieval of his error became more and more difficult.

On this Sunday afternoon it was already four years since there had been any allusion to the subject between them, and Nancy supposed that it was forever buried.

"I wonder if he'll mind it less or more as he gets older," she thought; "I'm afraid more. Aged people feel the miss of children: what would father do without Priscilla? And if I die, Godfrey will be very lonely—not holding together with his brothers much. But I won't be over-anxious, and trying to make things out beforehand: I must do my best for the present."

With that last thought Nancy roused herself from her reverie, and turned her eyes again towards the forsaken page. It had been forsaken longer than she imagined, for she was presently surprised by the appearance of the servant with the tea-things. It was, in fact, a little before the usual time for tea; but Jane had her reasons.

"Is your master come into the yard, Jane?"

"No 'm, he isn't," said Jane, with a slight emphasis, of which, however, her mistress took no notice.

"I don't know whether you've seen 'em, 'm," continued Jane, after a pause, "but there's folks making haste all one way, afore the front window. I doubt something's happened. There's niver a man to be seen i' the yard, else I'd send and see. I've been up into the top attic, but there's no seeing anything for trees. I hope nobody's hurt, that's all."

"Oh, no, I daresay there's nothing much the matter," said Nancy. It's perhaps Mr. Snell's bull got out again, as he did before."

"I wish he mayn't gore any body, then, that's all," said Jane, not altogether despising an hypothesis which covered a few imaginary calamities.

"That girl is always terrifying me," thought Nancy; "I wish Godfrey would come in."

She went to the front window and looked as far as she could see along the road, with an uneasiness which she felt to be childish, for there were now no such signs of excitement as Jane had spoken of, and Godfrey would not be likely to return by the village road, but by the fields. She continued to stand, however, looking at the placid churchyard with the long shadows of the gravestones across the bright green hillocks, and at the glowing autumn colors of the Rectory trees beyond. Before such calm external beauty the presence of a vague fear is more distinctly felt—like a raven flapping its slow wing across the sunny air. Nancy wished more and more that Godfrey would come in.

CHAPTER XVIII

SOME one opened the door at the other end of the room, and Nancy felt that it was her husband. She turned from the window with gladness in her eyes, for the wife's chief dread was stilled.

"Dear, I'm so thankful you're come," she said, going towards him. "I began to get—"

She paused abruptly, for Godfrey was laying down his hat with trembling hands, and turned towards her with a pale face and a strange unanswering glance, as if he saw her indeed, but saw her as part of a scene invisible to herself. She laid her hand on his arm, not daring to speak again; but he left the touch unnoticed, and threw himself into his chair.

Jane was already at the door with the hissing urn. "Tell her to keep away, will you?" said Godfrey; and when the door was closed again he exerted himself to speak more distinctly.

"Sit down, Nancy—there," he said, pointing to a chair opposite him. "I came back as soon as I could, to hinder anybody's telling you but me. I've had a great shock—but I care most about the shock it'll be to you."

"It isn't father and Priscilla?" said Nancy, with quivering lips, clasping her hands together tightly on her lap.

"No, it's nobody living," said Godfrey, unequal to the considerate skill with which he would have wished to make his revelation. "It's Dunstan—my brother Dunstan, that we lost sight of sixteen years ago. We've found him—found his body—his skeleton."

The deep dread Godfrey's look had created in Nancy made her feel these words a relief. She sat in comparative calmness to hear what else he had to tell. He went on:

"The Stone-pit has gone dry suddenly—from the draining, I suppose; and there he lies—has lain for sixteen years, wedged between two great stones. There's his watch and seals, and there's my gold-handled hunting-whip, with my name on: he took it away, without my knowing, the day he went hunting on Wildfire, the last time he was seen."

Godfrey paused: it was not so easy to say what came next. "Do you think he drowned himself?" said Nancy, almost wondering that her husband should be so deeply shaken by what had happened all those years ago to an unloved brother, of whom worse things had been augured.

"No, he fell in," said Godfrey, in a low but distinct voice, as if he felt some deep meaning in the fact. Presently he added: "Dunstan was the man that robbed Silas Marner."

The blood rushed to Nancy's face and neck at this surprise and shame, for she had been bred up to regard even a distant kinship with crime as a dishonour.

"Oh, Godfrey!" she said, with compassion in her tone, for she had immediately reflected that the dishonour must be felt still more keenly by her husband.

"There was the money in the pit," he continued—"all the weaver's money. Everything's been gathered up, and they're taking the skeleton to the Rainbow. But I came back to tell you: there was no hindering it; you must know."

He was silent, looking on the ground for two long minutes. Nancy would have said some words of comfort under this disgrace, but she refrained, from an instinctive sense that there was something behind— that Godfrey had something else to tell her. Presently he lifted his eyes to her face, and kept them fixed on her, as he said—

"Everything comes to light, Nancy, sooner or later. When God Almighty wills it, our secrets are found out. I've lived with a secret on my mind, but I'll keep it from you no longer. I wouldn't have you know it by somebody else, and not by me—I wouldn't have you find it out after I'm dead. I'll tell you now. It's been 'I will' and 'I won't' with me all my life—I'll make sure of myself now."

Nancy's utmost dread had returned. The eyes of the husband and wife met with awe in them, as at a crisis which suspended affection.

"Nancy," said Godfrey, slowly, "when I married you, I hid something from you—something I ought to have told you. That woman Marner found dead in the snow—Eppie's mother—that wretched woman—was my wife: Eppie is my child."

He paused, dreading the effect of his confession. But Nancy sat quite still, only that her eyes dropped and ceased to meet his. She was pale and quiet as a meditative statue, clasping her hands on her lap.

"You'll never think the same of me again," said Godfrey, after a little while, with some tremor in his voice.

She was silent.

"I oughtn't to have left the child unowned: I oughtn't to have kept it from you. But I couldn't bear to give you up, Nancy. I was led away into marrying her—I suffered for it."

Still Nancy was silent, looking down; and he almost expected that she would presently get up and say she would go to her father's. How could she have any mercy for faults that must seem so black to her, with her simple, severe notions?

But at last she lifted up her eyes to his again and spoke. There was no indignation in her voice—only deep regret.

"Godfrey, if you had but told me this six years ago, we could have done some of our duty by the child. Do you think I'd have refused to take her in, if I'd known she was yours?"

At that moment Godfrey felt all the bitterness of an error that was not simply futile, but had defeated its own end. He had not measured this wife with whom he had lived so long. But she spoke again, with more agitation.

"And—Oh, Godfrey—if we'd had her from the first, if you'd taken to her as you ought, she'd have loved me for her mother—and you'd have been happier with me: I could better have bore my little baby dying, and our life might have been more like what we used to think it 'ud be."

The tears fell, and Nancy ceased to speak.

"But you wouldn't have married me then, Nancy, if I'd told you," said Godfrey, urged, in the bitterness of his self-reproach, to prove to himself that his conduct had not been utter folly. "You may think you would now, but you wouldn't then. With your pride and your father's, you'd have hated having any thing to do with me after the talk there'd have been."

"I can't say what I should have done about that, Godfrey. I should never have married anybody else. But I wasn't worth doing wrong for —nothing is in this world. Nothing is so good as it seems beforehand— not even our marrying wasn't, you see." There was a faint sad smile on Nancy's face as she said the last words.

"I'm a worse man than you thought I was, Nancy," said Godfrey, rather tremulously. "Can you forgive me ever?"

"The wrong to me is but little, Godfrey: you've made it up to me— you've been good to me for fifteen years. It's another you did the wrong to; and I doubt it can never be all made up for."

"But we can take Eppie now," said Godfrey. "I won't mind the world knowing at last. I'll be plain and open for the rest o' my life."

"It'll be different coming to us, now she's grown up," said Nancy, shaking her head sadly. "But it's your duty to acknowledge her and provide for her; and I'll do my part by her, and pray to God Almighty to make her love me."

"Then we'll go together to Silas Marner's this very night, as soon as everything's quiet at the Stone-pits."

CHAPTER XIX

BETWEEN eight and nine o'clock that evening, Eppie and Silas were seated alone in the cottage. After the great excitement the weaver had undergone from the events of the afternoon, he had felt a longing for this quietude, and had even begged Mrs. Winthrop and Aaron, who had naturally lingered behind every one else, to leave him alone with his child. The excitement had not passed away: it had only reached the stage when the keenness of the susceptibility makes external stimulus intolerable—when there is no sense of weariness, but rather an intensity of inward life, under which sleep is an impossibility. Any one who has watched such moments in other men remembers the brightness of the eyes and the strange definiteness that comes over coarse features from that transient influence. It is as if a new fineness of ear for all spiritual voices had sent wonder-working vibrations through the heavy mortal frame—as if "beauty born of murmuring sound" had passed into the face of the listener.

Silas's face showed that sort of transfiguration, as he sat in his arm-chair and looked at Eppie. She had drawn her own chair towards his knees, and leaned forward, holding both his hands, while she looked up at him. On the table near them, lit by a candle, lay the recovered gold —the old long-loved gold, ranged in orderly heaps, as Silas used to range it in the days when it was his only joy. He had been telling her how he used to count it every night, and how his soul was utterly desolate till she was sent to him.

"At first, I'd a sort o' feeling come across me now and then," he was saying in a subdued tone, "as if you might be changed into the gold again; for sometimes, turn my head which way I would, I seemed to see the gold; and I thought I should be glad if I could feel, it, and find it was come back. But that didn't last long. After a bit, I should have thought it was a curse come again, if it had drove you from me, for I'd got to feel the need o' your looks and your voice and the touch o' your little fingers. You didn't know then, Eppie, when you were such a little un—you didn't know what your old father Silas felt for you."

"But I know now, father," said Eppie. "If it hadn't been for you, they'd have taken me to the workhouse, and there'd have been nobody to love me."

"Eh, my precious child, the blessing was mine. If you hadn't been sent to save me, I should ha' gone to the grave in my misery. The memory was taken away from me in time; and you see it's been kept—kept till it was wanted for you. It's wonderful—our life is wonderful."

Silas sat in silence a few minutes, looking at the money. "It takes no hold of me now," he said, ponderingly—"the money doesn't. I wonder if it ever could again—I doubt it might, if I lost you, Eppie. I might come to think I was forsaken again, and lose the feeling that God was good to me."

At that moment there was a knocking at the door; and Eppie was obliged to rise without answering Silas. Beautiful she looked, with the tenderness of gathering tears in her eyes and a slight flush on her cheeks, as she stepped to open the door. The flush deepened when she saw Mr. and Mrs. Godfrey Cass. She made her little rustic courtesy, and held the door wide for them to enter.

"We're disturbing you very late, my dear," said Mrs. Cass, taking Eppie's hand, and looking in her face with an expression of anxious interest and admiration. Nancy herself was pale and tremulous.

Eppie, after placing chairs for Mr. and Mrs. Cass, went to stand against Silas, opposite to them.

"Well, Marner," said Godfrey, trying to speak with perfect firmness, "it's a great comfort to me to see you with your money again, that you've been deprived of so many years. It was one of my family did you the wrong—the more grief to me—and I feel bound to make up to you for it in every way. Whatever I can do for you will be nothing but paying a debt, even if I looked no farther than the robbery. But there are other things I'm beholden—shall be beholden to you for, Marner."

Godfrey checked himself. It had been agreed between him and his wife that the subject of his fatherhood should be approached very carefully, and that, if possible, the disclosure should be reserved for the future, so that it might be made to Eppie gradually. Nancy had urged this, because she felt strongly the painful light in which Eppie must inevitably see the relation between her father and mother.

Silas, always ill at ease when he was being spoken to by "betters," such as Mr. Cass—tall, powerful, florid men, seen chiefly on horseback —answered with some constraint,

"Sir, I've a deal to thank you for a'ready. As for the robbery, I count it no loss to me. And if I did, you couldn't help it: you aren't answerable for it."

"You may look at it in that way, Marner, but I never can: and I hope you'll let me act according to my own feeling of what's just. I know you're easily contented: you've been a hard-working man all your life."

"Yes, sir, yes," said Marner, meditatively. "I should ha' been bad off without my work: it was what I held by when every thing else was gone from me."

"Ah," said Godfrey, applying Marner's words simply to his bodily wants, "it was a good trade for you in this country, because there's been a great deal of linen-weaving to be done. But you're getting rather past such close work, Marner: it's time you laid by and had some rest. You look a good deal pulled down, though you're not an old man, *are* you?"

"Fifty-five, as near as I can say, sir," said Silas.

"Oh, why, you may live thirty years longer—look at old Macey! And that money on the table, after all, is but little. It won't go far either way—whether it's put out to interest, or you were to live on it as long as it would last: it wouldn't go far if you'd nobody to keep but yourself, and you've had two to keep for a good many years now."

"Eh, sir," said Silas, unaffected by any thing Godfrey was saying, "I'm in no fear o' want. We shall do very well—Eppie and me 'ull do well enough. There's few working-folks have got so much laid by as that. I don't know what it is to gentlefolks, but I look upon it as a deal —almost too much. And as for us, it's little we want."

"Only the garden, father," said Eppie, blushing up to the ears the moment after.

"You love a garden, do you my dear?" said Nancy, thinking that this turn in the point of view might help her husband. "We should agree in that: I give a deal of time to the garden."

"Ah, there's plenty of gardening at the Red House," said Godfrey, surprised at the difficulty he found in approaching a proposition which had seemed so easy to him in the distance. "You've done a good part by Eppie, Marner, for sixteen years. It 'ud be a great comfort to you to see her well provided for, wouldn't it? She looks blooming and healthy, but not fit for any hardships: she doesn't look like a strapping girl come of working parents. You'd like to see her taken care of by those who can leave her well off, and make a lady of her; she's more fit for it than for a rough life, such as she might come to have in a few years' time."

A slight flush came over Marner's face, and disappeared like a passing gleam. Eppie was simply wondering Mr. Cass should talk so about things that seemed to have nothing to do with reality; but Silas was hurt and uneasy.

"I don't take your meaning, sir," he answered, not having words at command to express the mingled feelings with which he had heard Mr. Cass's words.

"Well, my meaning is this, Marner," said Godfrey, determined to come to the point. "Mrs. Cass and I, you know, have no children— nobody to benefit by our good home and everything else we have— more than enough for ourselves. And we should like to have somebody in the place of a daughter to us—we should like to have Eppie, and treat her in every way as our own child. It would be a great comfort to you in your old age, I hope, to see her fortune made in that way, after you have been at the trouble of bringing her up so well. And it's right you should have every reward for that. And Eppie, I'm sure, will always love you and be grateful to you: she'd come and see you very often, and we should all be on the look-out to do everything we could towards making you comfortable."

A plain man like Godfrey Cass, speaking under some embarrassment, necessarily blunders on words that are coarser than his intentions, and that are likely to fall gratingly on susceptible feelings. While he had been speaking, Eppie had quietly passed her arm behind Silas's head, and let her hand rest against it caressingly; she felt him trembling violently. He was silent for some moments when Mr. Cass had ended —powerless under the conflict of emotions, all alike painful. Eppie's heart was swelling at the sense that her father was in distress; and she was just going to lean down and speak to him, when one struggling dread at last gained the mastery over every other in Silas, and he said, faintly—

"Eppie, my child, speak. I won't stand in your way. Thank Mr. and Mrs. Cass."

Eppie took her hand from her father's head, and came forward a step. Her cheeks were flushed, but not with shyness this time: the sense that her father was in doubt and suffering banished that sort of self-consciousness. She dropped a low courtesy, first to Mrs. Cass and then to Mr Cass, and said—

"Thank you, ma'am—thank you, sir. But I can't leave my father, nor own anybody nearer than him. And I don't want to be a lady— thank you all the same" (here Eppie dropped another courtesy). "I couldn't give up the folks I've been used to."

Eppie's lip began to tremble a little at the last words. She retreated to her father's chair again, and held him round the neck: while Silas, with a subdued sob, put up his hand to grasp hers.

The tears were in Nancy's eyes, but her sympathy with Eppie was, naturally, divided with distress on her husband's account. She dared not speak, wondering what was going on in her husband's mind.

Godfrey felt an irritation inevitable to almost all of us when we encounter an unexpected obstacle. He had been full of his own penitence and resolution to retrieve his error as far as the time was left to him; he was possessed with all-important feelings, that were to lead to a pre-determined course of action which he had fixed on as the right, and he was not prepared to enter with lively appreciation into other people's feelings counteracting his virtuous resolves. The agitation with which he spoke again was not quite unmixed with anger.

"But I have a claim on you, Eppie—the strongest of all claims. It is my duty, Marner, to own Eppie as my child, and provide for her. She is my own child—her mother was my wife. I have a natural claim on her that must stand before every other."

Eppie had given a violent start, and turned quite pale. Silas, on the contrary, who had been relieved, by Eppie's answer, from the dread lest his mind should be in opposition to hers, felt the spirit of resistance in him set free, not without a touch of parental fierceness. "Then, sir," he answered, with an accent of bitterness that had been silent in him since the memorable day when his youthful hope had perished—"then, sir, why didn't you say so sixteen year ago, and claim her before I'd come to love her, i'stead o' coming to take her from me now, when you might as well take the heart out o' my body? God gave her to me because you turned your back upon her, and He looks upon her as mine: you've no right to her! When a man turns a blessing from his door it falls to them as take it in."

"I know that, Marner. I was wrong. I've repented of my conduct in that matter," said Godfrey, who could not help feeling the edge of Silas's words.

"I'm glad to hear it, sir," said Marner, with gathering excitement; "but repentance doesn't alter what's been going on for sixteen year. Your coming now and saying 'I'm her father' doesn't alter the feelings inside us. It's me she's been calling her father ever since she could say the word."

"But I think you might look at the thing more reasonably, Marner," said Godfrey, unexpectedly awed by the weaver's direct truth-speaking. "It isn't as if she was to be taken quite away from you, so that you'd never see her again. She'll be very near you, and come to see you very often. She'll feel just the same towards you."

"Just the same?" said Marner, more bitterly than ever. "How'll she feel just the same for me as she does now, when we eat o' the same bit, and drink o' the same cup, and think o' the same things from one day's end to another? Just the same? that's idle talk. You'd cut us i' two."

Godfrey, unqualified by experience to discern the pregnancy of Marner's simple words, felt rather angry again. It seemed to him that the weaver was very selfish (a judgment readily passed by those who have never tested their own power of sacrifice) to oppose what was undoubtedly for Eppie's welfare; and he felt himself called upon, for her sake, to assert his authority.

"I should have thought, Marner," he said, severely—"I should have thought your affection for Eppie would have made you rejoice in what was for her good, even if it did call upon you to give up something. You ought to remember that your own life is uncertain, and that she's at an age now when her lot may soon be fixed in a way very different from what it would be in her father's home: she may marry some low working-man, and then, whatever I might do for her, I couldn't make her well-off. You're putting yourself in the way of her welfare; and though I'm sorry to hurt you after what you've done, and what I've left undone, I feel now it's my duty to insist on taking care of my own daughter. I want to do my duty."

It would be difficult to say whether it were Silas or Eppie that was most deeply stirred by this last speech of Godfrey's. Thought had been very busy in Eppie as she listened to the contest between her old long-loved father and this new unfamiliar father who had suddenly come to fill the place of that black featureless shadow which had held the ring and placed it on her mother's finger. Her imagination had darted backward in conjectures, and forward in previsions, of what this revealed fatherhood implied: and there were words in Godfrey's last speech which helped to make the previsions especially definite. Not that these thoughts, either of past or future, determined her resolution—that was determined by the feelings which vibrated to every word Silas had uttered; but they raised, even apart from these feelings, a repulsion towards the offered lot and the newly-revealed father.

Silas, on the other hand, was again stricken in conscience, and alarmed lest Godfrey's accusation should be true—lest he should be raising his own will as an obstacle to Eppie's good. For many moments he was mute, struggling for the self-conquest necessary to the uttering of the difficult words. They came out tremulously.

"I'll say no more. Let it be as you will. Speak to the child. I'll hinder nothing."

Even Nancy, with all the acute sensibility of her own affections, shared her husband's view, that Marner was not justifiable in his wish to retain Eppie, after her real father had avowed himself. She felt that it was a very hard trial for the poor weaver, but her code allowed no question that a father by blood must have a claim above that of any foster-father. Besides, Nancy, used all her life to plenteous circumstances and the privileges of "respectability," could not enter into the pleasures which early nurture and habit connect with all the little aims and efforts of the poor who are born poor: to her mind, Eppie, in being restored to her birthright, was entering on a too-long withheld but unquestionable good. Hence she heard Silas's last words with relief, and thought, as Godfrey did, that their wish was achieved.

"Eppie, my dear," said Godfrey, looking at his daughter, not without some embarrassment, under the sense that she was old enough to judge him, "it'll always be our wish that you should show your love and gratitude to one who has been a father to you so many years, and we shall want to help you to make him comfortable in every way. But we hope you'll come to love us as well; and though I haven't been what a father should have been to you all these years, I wish to do the utmost in my power for you for the rest of my life, and provide for you as my only child. And you'll have the best of mothers in my wife—that'll be a blessing you haven't known since you were old enough to know it."

"My dear, you'll be a treasure to me," said Nancy, in her gentle voice. "We shall want for nothing when we have our daughter."

Eppie did not come forward and courtesy, as she had done before. She held Silas's hand in hers, and grasped it firmly—it was a weaver's hand, with a palm and finger-tips that were sensitive to such pressure—while she spoke with colder decision than before.

"Thank you, ma'am—thank you, sir, for your offers—they're very great, and far above my wish. For I should have no delight i' life any more if I was forced to go away from my father, and knew he was sitting at home a-thinking of me and feeling lone. We've been used to be happy together every day, and I can't think o' no happiness without him. And he says he'd nobody i' the world till I was sent to him, and he'd have nothing when I was gone. And he's took care of me and loved me from the first, and I'll cleave to him as long as he lives, and nobody shall ever come between him and me."

"But you must make sure, Eppie," said Silas, in a low voice—"you must make sure as you won't ever be sorry, because you've made your choice to stay among poor folks, and with poor clothes and things, when you might ha' had every thing o' the best."

His sensitiveness on this point had increased as he listened to Eppie's words of faithful affection.

"I can never be sorry, father," said Eppie. "I shouldn't know what to think on or to wish for with fine things about me, as I haven't been used to. And it 'ud be poor work for me to put on things, and ride in a gig, and sit in a place at church, as 'ud make them as I'm fond of think me unfitting company for 'em. What could I care for then?"

Nancy looked at Godfrey with a pained questioning glance. But his eyes were fixed on the floor, where he was moving the end of his stick, as if he were pondering on something absently. She thought there was a word which might perhaps come better from her lips than from his.

"What you say is natural, my dear child—it's natural you should cling to those who've brought you up," she said mildly; "but there's a duty you owe to your lawful father. There's perhaps something to be given up on more sides than one. When your father opens his home to you, I think it's right you shouldn't turn your back on it."

"I can't feel as I've got any father but one," said Eppie, impetuously, while the tears gathered. "I've always thought of a little home where he'd sit i' the corner, and I should fend and do everything for him: I can't think o' no other home. I wasn't brought up to be a lady, and I can't turn my mind to it. I like the working-folks, and their victuals, and their ways. And," she ended passionately, while the tears fell, "I'm promised to marry a working-man, as 'll live with father, and help me to take care of him."

Godfrey looked up at Nancy with a flushed face and a smarting dilation of the eyes. This frustration of a purpose towards which he had set out under the exalted consciousness that he was about to compensate in some degree for the greatest demerit of his life, made him feel the air of the room stifling.

"Let us go," he said, in an under-tone.

"We won't talk of this any longer now," said Nancy, rising. "We're your well-wishers, my dear—and yours too, Marner. We shall come and see you again. It's getting late now."

In this way she covered her husband's abrupt departure, for Godfrey had gone straight to the door, unable to say more.

CHAPTER XX

NANCY and Godfrey walked home under the starlight in silence. When they entered the oaken parlour, Godfrey threw himself into his chair, while Nancy laid down her bonnet and shawl, and stood on the hearth near her husband, unwilling to leave him even for a few minutes, and yet fearing to utter any word lest it might jar on his feeling. At last Godfrey turned his head towards her, and their eyes met, dwelling in that meeting without any movement on either side. That quiet mutual gaze of a trusting husband and wife is like the first moment of rest or refuge from a great weariness or a great danger—not to be interfered with by speech or action which would distract the sensations from the fresh enjoyment of repose.

But presently he put out his hand, and as Nancy placed hers within it, he drew her towards him, and said,

"That's ended!"

She bent to kiss him, and then said, as she stood by his side, "Yes,

I'm afraid we must give up the hope of having her for a daughter. It wouldn't be right to want to force her to come to us against her will. We can't alter her bringing up and what's come of it."

"No," said Godfrey, with a keen decisiveness of tone, in contrast with his usually careless and unemphatic speech—"there's debts we can't pay like money debts, by paying extra for the years that have slipped by. While I've been putting off and putting off, the trees have been growing—it's too late now. Marner was in the right in what he said about a man's turning away a blessing from his door: it falls to somebody else. I wanted to pass for childless once, Nancy—I shall pass for childless now against my wish."

Nancy did not speak immediately, but after a little while she asked —"You won't make it known, then, about Eppie's being your daughter?"

"No—where would be the good to anybody? Only harm. I must do what I can for her in the state of life she chooses. I must see who it is she's thinking of marrying."

"If it won't do any good to make the thing known," said Nancy, who thought she might now allow herself the relief of entertaining a feeling which she had tried to silence before, "I should be very thankful for father and Priscilla never to be troubled with knowing what was done in the past, more than about Dunsey: it can't be helped, their knowing that."

"I shall put it in my will—I think I shall put it in my will. I shouldn't like to leave anything to be found out, like this of Dunsey," said Godfrey, meditatively. "But I can't see anything but difficulties that 'ud come from telling it now. I must do what I can to make her happy in her own way. I've a notion," he added, after a moment's pause, "it's Aaron Winthrop she meant she was engaged to. I remember seeing him with her and Marner going away from church."

"Well, he's very sober and industrious," said Nancy, trying to view the matter as cheerfully as possible.

Godfrey fell into thoughtfulness again. Presently he looked up at Nancy sorrowfully, and said,

"She's a very pretty, nice girl, isn't she, Nancy?"

"Yes, dear; and with just your hair and eyes: I wondered it had never struck me before."

"I think she took a dislike to me at the thought of my being her father: I could see a change in her manner after that."

"She couldn't bear to think of not looking on Marner as her father," said Nancy, not wishing to confirm her husband's painful impression.

"She thinks I did wrong by her mother as well as by her. She thinks me worse than I am. But she *must* think it: she can never know all. It's part of my punishment, Nancy, for my daughter to dislike me. I should never have got into that trouble if I'd been true to you—if I hadn't been a fool. I'd no right to expect anything but evil could come of that marriage—and when I shirked doing a father's part, too."

Nancy was silent; her spirit of rectitude would not let her try to soften the edge of what she felt to be a just compunction. He spoke again after a little while, but the tone was rather changed: there was tenderness mingled with the previous self-reproach.

"And I got *you*, Nancy, in spite of all; and yet I've been grumbling and uneasy because I hadn't something else—as if I deserved it."

"You've never been wanting to me, Godfrey," said Nancy, with quiet sincerity. "My only trouble would be gone if you resigned yourself to the lot that's been given us."

"Well, perhaps it isn't too late to amend a bit there. Though it *is* too late to mend some things, say what they will."

CHAPTER XXI

THE next morning, when Silas and Eppie were seated at their breakfast, he said to her,

"Eppie, there's a thing I've had on my mind to do this two year, and now the money's been brought back to us, we can do it. I've been turning it over and over in the night, and I think we'll set out to-morrow, while the fine days last. We'll leave the house and everything for your godmother to take care on, and we'll make a little bundle o' things and set out."

"Where to go, daddy?" said Eppie, in much surprise.

"To my old country—to the town where I was born—up Lantern Yard. I want to see Mr. Paston, the minister: something may ha' come out to make 'em know I was innicent o' the robbery. And Mr. Paston was a man with a deal o' light—I want to speak to him about the drawing o' the lots. And I should like to talk to him about the religion of this country-side, for I partly think he doesn't know on it."

Eppie was very joyful, for there was the prospect not only of wonder and delight at seeing a strange country, but also of coming back to tell Aaron all about it. Aaron was so much wiser than she was about most things—it would be rather pleasant to have this little advantage over him. Mrs. Winthrop, though possessed with a dim fear of dangers attendant on so long a journey, and requiring many assurances that it would not take them out of the region of carriers' carts and slow wagons, was nevertheless well pleased that Silas should revisit his own country, and find out if he had been cleared from that false accusation.

"You'd be easier in your mind for the rest o' your life, Master Marner," said Dolly—"that you would. And if there's any light to be got up the yard as you talk on, we've need of it i' this world, and I'd be glad on it myself, if you could bring it back."

So on the fourth day from that time, Silas and Eppie, in their Sunday clothes, with a small bundle tied in a blue linen handkerchief, were making their way through the streets of a great manufacturing town. Silas, bewildered by the changes thirty years had brought over his native place, had stopped several persons in succession to ask them the name of this town, that he might be sure he was not under a mistake about it.

"Ask for Lantern Yard, father—ask this gentleman with the tassels on his shoulders a-standing at the shop door; he isn't in a hurry like the rest," said Eppie, in some distress at her father's bewilderment, and ill at ease, besides, amidst the noise, the movement, and the multitude of strange indifferent faces.

"Eh, my child, he won't know anything about it," said Silas; "gentlefolks didn't ever go up to the Yard. But happen somebody can tell me which is the way to Prison Street, where the jail is. I know the way out o' that as if I'd seen it yesterday."

With some difficulty, after many turnings and new inquiries, they reached Prison Street; and the grim walls of the jail, the first object that answered to any image in Silas's memory, cheered him with the certitude, which no assurance of the town's name had hitherto given him, that he was in his native place.

"Ah," he said, drawing a long breath, "there's the jail, Eppie; that's just the same: I aren't afraid now. It's the third turning on the left hand from the jail doors, that's the way we must go."

"Oh, what a dark, ugly place!" said Eppie. "How it hides the sky! It's worse than the Workhouse. I'm glad you don't live in this town now, father. Is Lantern Yard like this street?"

"My precious child," said Silas, smiling, "it isn't a big street like this. I never was easy i' this street myself, but I was fond o' Lantern Yard. The shops here are all altered, I think—I can't make 'em out; but I shall know the turning, because it's the third."

"Here it is," he said, in a tone of satisfaction, as they came to a narrow alley. "And then we must go to the left again, and then straight for'ard for a bit, up Shoe Lane: and then we shall be at the entry next to the o'erhanging window, where there's the nick in the road for the water to run. Eh, I can see it all."

"Oh, father, I'm like as if I was stifled," said Eppie. "I couldn't ha' thought as any folks lived i' this way, so close together. How pretty the Stone-pits 'ull look when we get back!"

"It looks comical to *me*, child, now—and smells bad. I can't think as it usened to smell so."

Here and there a sallow, begrimed face looked out from a gloomy doorway at the strangers, and increased Eppie's uneasiness, so that it was a longed-for relief when they issued from the alleys into Shoe Lane, where there was a broader strip of sky.

"Dear heart!" said Silas, "why, there's people coming out o' the Yard as if they'd been to chapel at this time o' day—a weekday noon!"

Suddenly he started and stood still with a look of distressed amazement, that alarmed Eppie. They were before an opening in front of a large factory, from which men and women were streaming for their mid-day meal.

"Father," said Eppie, clasping his arm, "what's the matter?"

But she had to speak again and again before Silas could answer her.

"It's gone, child," he said, at last, in strong agitation,—"Lantern Yard's gone. It must ha' been here, because here's the house with the o'erhanging window—I know that—it's just the same; but they've made this new opening; and see that big factory! It's all gone—chapel and all."

"Come into that little brush-shop and sit down, father—they'll let you sit down," said Eppie, always on the watch lest one of her father's strange attacks should come on. "Perhaps the people can tell you all about it."

But neither from the brush-maker, who had come to Shoe Lane only ten years ago, when the factory was already built, nor from any other source within his reach, could Silas learn any thing of the old Lantern Yard friends, or of Mr. Paston, the minister.

"The old place is all swep' away," Silas said to Dolly Winthrop on the night of his return—"the little graveyard and every thing. The old home's gone; I've no home but this now. I shall never know whether they got at the truth o' the robbery, nor whether Mr. Paston could ha' given me any light about the drawing o' the lots. It's dark to me, Mrs. Winthrop, that is; I doubt it'll be dark to the last."

"Well, yes, Master Marner," said Dolly, who sat with a placid listening face, now bordered by gray hairs; "I doubt it may. It's the will o' Them above as a many things should be dark to us; but there's some things as I've never felt i' the dark about, and they're mostly what comes i' the day's work. You were hard done by that once, Master Marner, and it seems as you'll never know the rights of it; but that doesn't hinder there *being* a rights, Master Marner, for all it's dark to you and me."

"No," said Silas, "no: that doesn't hinder. Since the time the child was sent to me, and I've come to love her as myself, I've had light enough to trusten by; and now she says she'll never leave me, I think I shall trusten till I die."

CONCLUSION

THERE was one time of the year which was held in Raveloe to be especially suitable for a wedding. It was when the great lilacs and laburnums in the old-fashioned gardens showed their golden and purple wealth above the lichen-tinted walls, and when there were calves still young enough to want bucketfuls of fragrant milk. People were not so busy then as they must become when the full cheese-making and the mowing had set in; and besides, it was a time when a light bridal dress could be worn with comfort and seen to advantage.

Happily the sunshine fell more warmly than usual on the lilac tufts the morning that Eppie was married, for her dress was a very light one. She had often thought, though with a feeling of renunciation, that the perfection of a wedding-dress would be a white cotton, with the tiniest pink sprig at wide intervals; so that when Mrs. Godfrey Cass begged to provide one, and asked Eppie to choose what it should be, previous meditation had enabled her to give a decided answer at once.

Seen at a little distance as she walked across the churchyard and down the village, she seemed to be attired in pure white, and her hair looked like the dash of gold on a lily. One hand was on her husband's arm, and with the other she clasped the hand of her father Silas.

"You won't be giving me away, father," she had said before they went to church; "you'll only be taking Aaron to be a son to you."

Dolly Winthrop walked behind with her husband; and there ended the little bridal procession.

There were many eyes to look at it, and Miss Priscilla Lammeter was glad that she and her father had happened to drive up to the door of the Red House just in time to see this pretty sight. They had come to keep Nancy company to-day, because Mr. Cass had had to go away to Lytherley, for special reasons. That seemed to be a pity, for otherwise he might have gone, as Mr. Crackentorp and Mr. Osgood certainly would, to look on at the wedding-feast which he had ordered at the Rainbow, naturally feeling a great interest in the weaver who had been wronged by one of his own family.

"I could ha' wished Nancy had had the luck to find a child like that and bring her up," said Priscilla to her father, as they sat in the gig; "I should ha' had something young to think of then, besides the lambs and the calves."

"Yes, my dear, yes," said Mr. Lammeter; "one feels that as one gets older. Things look dim to old folks: they'd need have some young eyes about 'em, to let 'em know the world's the same as it used to be."

Nancy came out now to welcome her father and sister, and the wedding group had passed on beyond the Red House to the humbler part of the village.

Dolly Winthrop was the first to divine that old Mr. Macey, who had been set in his arm-chair outside his own door, would expect some special notice as they passed, since he was too old to be at the wedding-feast.

"Mr. Macey's looking for a word from us," said Dolly; "he'll be hurt if we pass him and say nothing—and him so racked with rheumatiz."

So they turned aside to shake hands with the old man. He had looked forward to the occasion, and had his premeditated speech.

"Well, Master Marner," he said, in a voice that quavered a good deal, "I've lived to see my words come true. I was the first to say there was no harm in you, though your looks might be again' you; and I was the first to say you'd get your money back. And it's nothing but rightful as you should. And I'd ha' said the 'Amens,' and willing, at the holy matrimony; but Tookey's done it a good while now, and I hope you'll have none the worse luck."

In the open yard before the Rainbow the party of guests were already assembled, though it was still nearly an hour before the appointed feast-time. But by this means they could not only enjoy the slow advent of their pleasure; they had also ample leisure to talk of Silas Marner's strange history, and arrive by due degrees at the conclusion that he had brought a blessing on himself by acting like a father to a lone motherless child. Even the farrier did not negative this sentiment: on the contrary, he took it up as peculiarly his own, and invited any hardy person present to contradict him. But he met with no contradiction; and all differences among the company were merged in a general agreement with Mr. Snell's sentiment, that when a man had deserved his good luck, it was the part of his neighbours to wish him joy.

As the bridal group approached, a hearty cheer was raised in the Rainbow yard; and Ben Winthrop, whose jokes had retained their acceptable flavor, found it agreeable to turn in there and receive congratulations; not requiring the proposed interval of quiet at the Stone-pits before joining the company.

Eppie had a larger garden than she had ever expected there now; and in other ways there had been alterations at the expense of Mr. Cass, the landlord, to suit Silas's larger family. For he and Eppie had declared that they would rather stay at the Stone-pits than go to any new home. The garden was fenced with stones on two sides, but in front there was an open fence, through which the flowers shone with answering gladness, as the four united people came within sight of them.

"Oh, father," said Eppie, "what a pretty home ours is! I think nobody could be happier than we are."

ROMOLA

CONTENTS

★

BOOK THREE

CONTENTS

PROEM

MORE than three centuries and a half ago, in the mid-springtime of 1492, we are sure that the angel of the dawn, as he travelled with broad slow wing from the Levant to the Pillars of Hercules, and from the summits of the Caucasus across all the snowy Alpine ridges to the dark nakedness of the Western isles, saw nearly the same outline of firm land and unstable sea,—saw the same great mountain shadows on the same valleys as he has seen to-day,—saw olive mounts, and pine forests, and the broad plains green with young corn or rain-freshened grass,—saw the domes and spires of cities rising by the river-sides or mingled with the sedge-like masts on the many-curved sea-coast, in the same spots where they rise to-day. And as the faint light of his course pierced into the dwellings of men, it fell, as now, on the rosy warmth of nestling children; on the haggard waking of sorrow and sickness; on the hasty uprising of the hard-handed labourer; and on the late sleep of the night-student, who had been questioning the stars or the sages or his own soul, for that hidden knowledge which would break through the barrier of man's brief life, and show its dark path, that seemed to bend nowhither, to be an arc in an immeasurable circle of light and glory. The great river-courses which have shaped the lives of men have hardly changed; and those other streams, the life-currents that ebb and flow in human hearts, pulsate to the same great needs, the same great loves and terrors. As our thought follows close in the slow wake of the dawn, we are impressed with the broad sameness of the human lot, which never alters in the main headings of its history,—hunger and labour, seed-time and harvest, love and death.

Even if, instead of following the dim daybreak, our imagination pauses on a certain historical spot and awaits the fuller morning, we may see a world-famous city, which has hardly changed its outline since the days of Columbus, seeming to stand as an almost unviolated symbol, amidst the flux of human things, to remind us that we still resemble the men of the past more than we differ from them, as the great mechanical principles on which those domes and towers were raised must make a likeness in human building that will be broader and deeper than all possible change. And doubtless, if the spirit of a Florentine citizen, whose eyes were closed for the last time while Columbus was still waiting and arguing for the three poor vessels with which he was to set sail from the port of Palos, could return from the shades and pause where our thought is pausing, he would believe that there must still be fellowship and understanding for him among the inheritors of his birthplace.

Let us suppose that such a shade has been permitted to revisit the

925

glimpses of the golden morning, and is standing once more on the famous hill of San Miniato, which overlooks Florence from the south. The Spirit is clothed in his habit as he lived: the folds of his well-lined black silk garment, or *lucco*,[1] hang in grave unbroken lines from neck to ankle; his plain cloth cap, with its *becchetto*, or long hanging strip of drapery, to serve as a scarf in case of need, surmounts a penetrating face, not perhaps very handsome, but with a firm, well-cut mouth, kept distinctly human by a close-shaven lip and chin. It is a face charged with memories of a keen and various life passed below there on the banks of the gleaming river; and as he looks at the scene before him, the sense of familiarity is so much stronger than the perception of change that he thinks it might be possible to descend once more among the streets, and take up that busy life where he left it. For it is not only the mountains and the westward-bending river that he recognizes; not only the dark sides of Mount Morello opposite to him, and the long valley of the Arno that seems to stretch its gray low-tufted luxuriance to the far-off ridges of Carrara; and the steep height of Fiesole, with its crown of monastic walls and cypresses; and all the green and grey slopes sprinkled with villas which he can name as he looks at them. He sees other familiar objects much closer to his daily walks. For though he misses the seventy or more towers that once surmounted the walls, and encircled the city as with a regal diadem, his eyes will not dwell on that blank; they are drawn irresistibly to the unique tower springing, like a tall flower-stem drawn towards the sun, from the square-turreted mass of the Old Palace in the very heart of the city,—the tower that looks none the worse for the four centuries that have passed since he used to walk under it. The great dome, too, greatest in the world, which in his early boyhood had been only a daring thought in the mind of a small, quick-eyed man,—there it raises its large curves still, eclipsing the hills. And the well-known bell-towers,— Giotto's, with its distant hint of rich colour, and the graceful-spired Badia, and the rest,—he looked at them all from the shoulder of his nurse.

"Surely," he thinks, "Florence can still ring her bells with the solemn hammer-sound that used to beat on the hearts of her citizens and strike out the fire there. And here, on the right, stands the long dark mass of Santa Croce, where we buried our famous dead, laying the laurel on their cold brows and fanning them with the breath of praise and of banners. But Santa Croce had no spire then: we Florentines were too full of great building projects to carry them all out in stone and marble; we had our frescos and our shrines to pay for, not to speak of rapacious condottieri, bribed royalty, and purchased territories, and our façades

---

[1] The *lucco* was not necessarily always made of silk, but sometimes of cloth. In Florence and in Lucca the material chiefly used was rose-coloured cloth; it was the dress of magistrates and of citizens admitted to public offices, and this explains the words of Cosimo the Elder, quoted by Machiavelli in Book VII of his History, "Two yards of rose-coloured cloth make a gentleman."—EDITOR.

and spires must needs wait. But what architect can the Frati Minori [2] have employed to build that spire for them? If it had been built in my day, Filippo Brunelleschi or Michelozzo would have devised something of another fashion than that,—something worthy to crown the church of Arnolfo."

At this the Spirit, with a sigh, lets his eyes travel on to the city walls, and now he dwells on the change there with wonder at these modern times. Why have five out of the eleven convenient gates been closed? And why, above all, should the towers have been levelled that were once a glory and defence? Is the world become so peaceful, then, and do Florentines dwell in such harmony, that there are no longer conspiracies to bring ambitious exiles home again with armed bands at their back? These are difficult questions; it is easier and pleasanter to recognize the old than to account for the new. And there flows Arno, with its bridges just where they used to be,—the Ponte Vecchio, least like other bridges in the world, laden with the same quaint shops where our Spirit remembers lingering a little on his way perhaps to look at the progress of that great palace which Messer Luca Pitti had set a-building with huge stones got from the Hill of Bogoli [3] close behind, or perhaps to transact a little business with the cloth-dressers in Oltrarno. The exorbitant line of the Pitti roof is hidden from San Miniato; but the yearning of the old Florentine is not to see Messer Luca's too ambitious palace which he built unto himself; it is to be down among those narrow streets and busy humming Piazze where he inherited the eager life of his fathers. Is not the anxious voting with black and white beans still going on down there? Who are the Priori in these months, eating soberly regulated official dinners in the Palazzo Vecchio, with removes of tripe and boiled partridges, seasoned by practical jokes against the ill-fated butt among those potent signors? Are not the significant banners still hung from the windows,—still distributed with decent pomp under Orcagna's Loggia every two months?

Life had its zest for the old Florentine when he, too, trod the marble steps and shared in those dignities. His politics had an area as wide as his trade, which stretched from Syria to Britain; but they had also the passionate intensity and the detailed practical interest which could belong only to a narrow scene of corporate action,—only to the members of a community shut in close by the hills and by walls of six miles'

[2] The tower of Santa Croce was built by the architect Gaetano Baccani, who was responsible for several unfortunate "restorations" in the Florentine churches. It was completed in 1844 and is the best of all Baccani's achievements. Until the year 1855 there existed at the left side of the façade of Arnolfo's church the beginnings of a quadrangular tower which had been intended to serve as a belfry and which is believed to have been built from designs by Francesco Giuliano da S. Gallo about the year 1550.—EDITOR.

[3] The Boboli Hill, which formed the Garden of the Pitti, "adjoining the Palace and extending as far as that part of the city wall between the Gates of S. Pier Gattolino and San Giorgio," as described by Benedetto Varchi in Book IX of his History of Florence, was formerly called Bogoli, g having been changed to b, probably after an old family named Borgoli who held property there.—EDITOR.

circuit, where men knew each other as they passed in the street, set their eyes every day on the memorials of their commonwealth, and were conscious of having not simply the right to vote, but the chance of being voted for. He loved his honours and his gains, the business of his counting-house, of his guild, of the public council-chamber; he loved his enmities, too, and fingered the white bean which was to keep a hated name out of the *borsa* with more complacency than if it had been a golden florin. He loved to strengthen his family by a good alliance, and went home with a triumphant light in his eyes after concluding a satisfactory marriage for his son or daughter under his favourite loggia in the evening cool; he loved his game at chess under that same loggia, and his biting jest, and even his coarse joke, as not beneath the dignity of a man eligible for the highest magistracy. He had gained an insight into all sorts of affairs at home and abroad: he had been of the "Ten" who managed the war department, of the "Eight" who attended to home discipline, of the Priori or Signori who were the heads of the executive government; he had even risen to the supreme office of Gonfaloniere; he had made one in embassies to the Pope and to the Venetians; and he had been commissary to the hired army of the Republic, directing the inglorious, bloodless battles in which no man died of brave breast-wounds,—*virtuosi colpi,*—but only of casual falls and tramplings. And in this way he had learned to distrust men without bitterness; looking on life mainly as a game of skill, but not dead to traditions of heroism and clean-handed honour. For the human soul is hospitable, and will entertain conflicting sentiments and contradictory opinions with much impartiality. It was his pride, besides, that he was duly tinctured with the learning of his age, and judged not altogether with the vulgar, but in harmony with the ancients; he, too, in his prime, had been eager for the most correct manuscripts, and had paid many florins for antique vases and for disinterred busts of the ancient immortals,—some, perhaps, *truncis naribus,* wanting as to the nose, but not the less authentic; and in his old age he had made haste to look at the first sheets of that fine Homer which was among the early glories of the Florentine press. But he had not, for all that, neglected to hang up a waxen image or double of himself under the protection of the Madonna Annunziata, or to do penance for his sins in large gifts to the shrines of saints whose lives had not been modelled on the study of the classics; he had not even neglected making liberal bequests towards buildings for the Frati, against whom he had levelled many a jest.

For the Unseen Powers were mighty. Who knew—who was sure—that there was *any* name given to them behind which there was no angry force to be appeased, no intercessory pity to be won? Were not gems medicinal, though they only pressed the finger? Were not all things charged with occult virtues? Lucretius might be right,—he was an ancient, and a great poet; Luigi Pulci, too, who was suspected of not believing anything from the roof upward (*dal tetto in su*) had very much the air of being right over the supper-table, when the wine and *riboboli*[4] were circulating fast, though he was only a poet in the vulgar tongue. There were even learned personages who maintained that Aristotle, wisest of men (unless, indeed, Plato were wiser?), was a thoroughly irreligious philosopher; and a liberal scholar must entertain all speculations. But the negatives might, after all, prove false; nay, seemed manifestly false, as the circling hours swept past him, and turned round with graver faces. For had not the world become Christian? Had he not been baptized in San Giovanni, where the dome is awful with the symbols of coming judgment, and where the altar bears a crucified Image disturbing to perfect complacency in one's self and the world? Our resuscitated Spirit was not a pagan philosopher, nor a philosophizing pagan poet, but a man of the fifteenth century, inheriting its strange web of belief and unbelief; of Epicurean levity and fetichistic dread; of pedantic impossible ethics uttered by rote, and crude passions acted out with childish impulsiveness; of inclination towards a self-indulgent paganism, and inevitable subjection to that human conscience which, in the unrest of a new growth, was filling the air with strange prophecies and presentiments.

He had smiled, perhaps, and shaken his head dubiously, as he heard simple folk talk of a Pope Angelico, who was to come by-and-by and bring in a new order of things, to purify the Church from simony, and the lives of the clergy from scandal,—a state of affairs too different from what existed under Innocent the Eighth for a shrewd merchant and politician to regard the prospect as worthy of entering into his calculations. But he felt the evils of the time, nevertheless; for he was a man of public spirit, and public spirit can never be wholly immoral, since its essence is care for a common good. That very Quaresima, or Lent, of 1492 in which he died, still in his erect old age, he had listened in San Lorenzo, not without a mixture of satisfaction, to the preaching of a Dominican Friar, named Girolamo Savonarola, who denounced with a rare boldness the worldliness and vicious habits of the clergy, and insisted on the duty of Christian men not to live for their own ease when wrong was triumphing in high places, and not to spend their wealth in outward pomp even in the churches, when their fellow-citizens were suffering from want and sickness. The Frate carried his doctrine rather too far for elderly ears; yet it was a memorable thing to see a preacher move his audience to such a pitch that the women even took off their ornaments, and delivered them up to be sold for the benefit of the needy.

"He was a noteworthy man, that Prior of San Marco," thinks our Spirit; "somewhat arrogant and extreme, perhaps, especially in his

---

[4] *Ribobolo* is a pun, or saying expressed in few words, just as a song or a speech is a saying expressed in many words. It is almost the same as a proverb, except that a proverb is a short saying in general use, whilst a *ribobolo* is something original said by one person. (Giovammaria Cecchi, "Raccolta ed esplicazione dei proverbi.") —EDITOR.

denunciations of speedy vengeance. Ah, *Iddio non paga il Sabato*— the wages of men's sins often linger in their payment, and I myself saw much established wickedness of long-standing prosperity. But a Frate Predicatore who wanted to move the people,—how could he be moderate? He might have been a little less defiant and curt, though, to Lorenzo de' Medici, whose family had been the very makers of San Marco: was that quarrel ever made up? And our Lorenzo himself, with the dim outward eyes and the subtle inward vision, did he get over that illness at Careggi? It was but a sad, uneasy-looking face that he would carry out of the world which had given him so much, and there were strong suspicions that his handsome son would play the part of Rehoboam. How has it all turned out? Which party is likely to be banished and have its houses sacked just now? Is there any successor of the incomparable Lorenzo, to whom the great Turk is so gracious as to send over presents of rare animals, rare relics, rare manuscripts, or fugitive enemies, suited to the tastes of a Christian Magnifico who is at once lettered and devout,—and also slightly vindictive? And what famous scholar is dictating the Latin letters of the Republic,—what fiery philosopher is lecturing on Dante in the Duomo, and going home to write bitter invectives against the father and mother of the bad critic who may have found fault with his classical spelling? Are our wiser heads leaning towards alliance with the Pope and the Regno, or are they rather inclining their ears to the orators of France and of Milan?

"There is knowledge of these things to be had in the streets below, on the beloved *marmi* in front of the churches, and under the sheltering Loggie, where surely our citizens have still their gossip and debates, their bitter and merry jests as of old. For are not the well-remembered buildings all there? The changes have not been so great in those uncounted years. I will go down and hear,—I will tread the familiar pavement, and hear once again the speech of Florentines."

Go not down, good Spirit! for the changes are great, and the speech of Florentines would sound as a riddle in your ears. Or, if you go, mingle with no politicians on the *marmi* or elsewhere; ask no questions about trade in the Calimara; confuse yourself with no inquiries into scholarship, official or monastic. Only look at the sunlight and shadows on the grand walls that were built solidly, and have endured in their grandeur; look at the faces of the little children, making another sunlight amid the shadows of age; look, if you will, into the churches, and hear the same chants, see the same images as of old,—the images of willing anguish for a great end, of beneficent love and ascending glory; see upturned living faces, and lips moving to the old prayers for help. These things have not changed. The sunlight and shadows bring their old beauty and waken the old heart-strains at morning, noon, and eventide; the little children are still the symbol of the eternal marriage between love and duty; and men still yearn for the reign of peace and righteousness,—still own *that* life to be the highest which is a conscious voluntary sacrifice. For the Pope Angelico is not come yet.

BOOK ONE

★

CHAPTER I

THE SHIPWRECKED STRANGER

THE Loggia de' Cerchi stood in the heart of old Florence, within a labyrinth of narrow streets behind the Badia, now rarely threaded by the stranger, unless in a dubious search for a certain severely simple door-place, bearing this inscription:

QUI NACQUE IL DIVINO POETA.

To the ear of Dante the same streets rang with the shout and clash of fierce battle between rival families; but in the fifteenth century they were only noisy with the unhistorical quarrels and broad jests of wool-carders in the cloth-producing quarters of San Martino and Garbo.[1]

Under this loggia, in the early morning of the 9th of April, 1492, two men had their eyes fixed on each other: one was stooping slightly, and looking downward with the scrutiny of curiosity; the other, lying on the pavement, was looking upward with the startled gaze of a suddenly awakened dreamer.

The standing figure was the first to speak. He was a grey-haired,

[1] The so-called quarters of San Martino and Garbo were not properly quarters, but merely certain lengths of streets. The Via del Garbo corresponded to that portion of the present Via della Condotta between the Via Calzaiuoli and the Piazzetta delle Farine. Via della Condotta was so called because in the houses belonging to the della Tosa family, adjoining the Convent of the Badia, resided the officials of the Condotta, who engaged and controlled the soldiery in the service of the Republic. In olden language *condotta* signified an "Agreement whereby a man hired himself out for the service of others, in particular an agreement between soldiers and the government."

In Via del Garbo woollen cloth was manufactured, which was of finer quality than that made round San Martino.

At the reforming of the Government in 1342, after the expulsion of the Duke of Athens, the city was divided into four quarters, namely *Oltrarno*, or Santo Spirito, *Santa Croce*, *Santa Maria Novella*, and *San Giovanni*. Previously it had been divided into six *sestieri* or districts, respectively *Oltrarno* (the arms of that district being a scarlet bridge on a white field), *San Pier Scheraggio* (arms, a blue cart-wheel, because there was a marble wheel in front of the church of that name), *Borgo SS. Apostoli* (a black ram on a white field, because this was the butchers' district), *San Pancrazio* (a scarlet lion's paw on a white field, because the old Florentine pronounced it Brancazio and supposed the name to be an allusion to a *branca* or paw), *the Duomo* or *San Giovanni* (the church on a white field), and *S. Pier Maggiore* (crimson keys on a white field).—EDITOR.

931

broad-shouldered man, of the type which, in Tuscan phrase, is moulded with the fist and polished with the pickaxe; but the self-important gravity which had written itself out in the deep lines about his brow and mouth seemed intended to correct any contemptuous inferences from the hasty workmanship which Nature had bestowed on his exterior. He had deposited a large well-filled bag, make of skins, on the pavement, and before him hung a peddler's basket, garnished partly with small woman's-ware, such as thread and pins, and partly with fragments of glass, which had probably been taken in exchange for those commodities.

"Young man," he said, pointing to a ring on the finger of the reclining figure, "when your chin has got a stiffer crop on it, you'll know better than to take your nap in street corners with a ring like that on your forefinger. By the holy 'vangels! if it had been anybody but me standing over you two minutes ago—but Bratti Ferravecchi is not the man to steal. The cat couldn't eat her mouse if she didn't catch it alive, and Bratti couldn't relish gain if it had no taste of a bargain. Why, young man, one San Giovanni, three years ago, the Saint sent a dead body in my way,—a blind beggar, with his cap well lined with pieces,— but, if you'll believe me, my stomach turned against the *testoni*[2] I'd never bargained for, till it came into my head that San Giovanni owed me the pieces for what I spend yearly at the Festa; besides, I buried the body and paid for a mass,—and so I saw it was a fair bargain. But how comes a young man like you, with the face of Messer San Michele, to be sleeping on a stone bed with the wind for a curtain?"

The deep guttural sounds of the speaker were scarcely intelligible to the newly waked, bewildered listener; but he understood the action of pointing to his ring. He looked down at it, and with a half-automatic obedience to the warning, took it off and thrust it within his doublet, rising at the same time and stretching himself.

"Your tunic and hose match ill with that jewel, young man," said Bratti, deliberately. "Anybody might say the saints had sent *you* a dead body; but if you took the jewels, I hope you buried him,—and you can afford a mass or two for him into the bargain."

Something like a painful thrill appeared to dart through the frame of the listener, and arrest the careless stretching of his arms and chest. For an instant he turned on Bratti with a sharp frown; but he immediately recovered an air of indifference, took off the red Levantine cap which hung like a great purse over his left ear, pushed back his long dark-brown curls, and glancing at his dress, said smilingly,—

"You speak truth, friend: my garments are as weather-stained as an old sail, and they are not old either, only, like an old sail, they have

---

[2] *Testoni* were not yet in existence at the end of the fifteenth century. They were silver coins of the value of three *giuli*, or pauls, and were thus called because they bore the impression of a large head of Cosimo I, Grand Duke of Tuscany (1569).—EDITOR.

had a sprinkling of the sea as well as the rain. The fact is, I'm a stranger in Florence, and when I came in footsore last night, I preferred flinging myself in a corner of this hospitable porch to hunting any longer for a chance hostelry, which might turn out to be a nest of blood-suckers of more sorts than one."

"A stranger, in good sooth," said Bratti, "for the words come all melting out of your throat, so that a Christian and a Florentine can't tell a hook from a hanger. But you're not from Genoa? More likely from Venice, by the cut of your clothes?"

"At this present moment," said the stranger, smiling, "it is of less importance where I come from than where I can go to for a mouthful of breakfast. This city of yours turns a grim look on me just here: can you show me the way to a more lively quarter, where I can get a meal and a lodging?"

"That I can," said Bratti; "and it is your good fortune, young man, that I have happened to be walking in from Rovezzano this morning, and turned out of my way to Mercato Vecchio to say an Ave at the Badia. That, I say, is your good fortune. But it remains to be seen what is *my* profit in the matter. Nothing for nothing, young man. If I show you the way to Mercato Vecchio, you'll swear by your patron saint to let me have the bidding for that stained suit of yours, when you set up a better,—as doubtless you will."

"Agreed, by San Niccolò," said the other, laughing. "But now let us set off to this said Mercato, for I feel the want of a better lining to this doublet of mine which you are coveting."

"Coveting? Nay," said Bratti, heaving his bag on his back and setting out. But he broke off in his reply, and burst out in loud, harsh tones, not unlike the creaking and grating of a cart-wheel: *"Chi ab-baratta—baratta—b'ratta—chi abbaratta cenci e vetri—b'ratta ferri vecchi?"*

"It's worth but little," he said presently, relapsing into his conversational tone. "Hose and altogether, your clothes are worth but little. Still, if you've a mind to set yourself up with a lute worth more than any new one, or with a sword that's been worn by a Ridolfi, or with a paternoster of the best mode, I could let you have a great bargain, by making an allowance for the clothes; for, simple as I stand here, I've got the best-furnished shop in the Ferravecchi, and it's close by the Mercato. The Virgin be praised! it's not a pumpkin I carry on my shoulders. But I don't stay caged in my shop all day: I've got a wife and a raven to stay at home and mind the stock. *Chi abbaratta—baratta—b'ratta?* . . . And now, young man, where do you come from, and what's your business in Florence?"

"I thought you liked nothing that came to you without a bargain," said the stranger. "You've offered me nothing yet in exchange for that information."

"Well, well; a Florentine doesn't mind bidding a fair price for news;

it stays the stomach a little though he may win no hose by it. If I take
you to the prettiest damsel in the Mercato to get a cup of milk,—that
will be a fair bargain."

"Nay; I can find her myself, if she be really in the Mercato; for
pretty heads are apt to look forth of doors and windows. No, no.
Besides, a sharp trader like you ought to know that he who bids for
nuts and news, may chance to find them hollow."

"Ah! young man," said Bratti, with a side-way glance of some admiration, "you were not born of a Sunday,—the salt-shops were open
when you came into the world. You're not a Hebrew, eh?—come from
Spain or Naples, eh? Let me tell you the Frati Minori are trying to
make Florence as hot as Spain for those dogs of hell that want to get
all the profit of usury to themselves and leave none for Christians; and
when you walk the Calimara with a piece of yellow cloth in your cap, it
will spoil your beauty more than a sword-cut across that smooth olive
cheek of yours.—*Abbaratta, baratta—chi abbaratta?*—I tell you, young
man, grey cloth is against yellow cloth; and there's as much grey cloth
in Florence as would make a gown and cowl for the Duomo, and there's
not so much yellow cloth as would make hose for Saint Christopher—
blessed be his name, and send me a sight of him this day!—*Abbaratta,
baratta b'ratta—chi abbaratta?*"

"All that is very amusing information you are parting with for nothing," said the stranger, rather scornfully; "but it happens not to concern me. I am no Hebrew."

"See, now!" said Bratti, triumphantly; "I've made a good bargain
with mere words. I've made you tell me something, young man, though
you're as hard to hold as a lamprey. San Giovanni be praised! a blind
Florentine is a match for two one-eyed men. But here we are in the
Mercato."

They had now emerged from the narrow streets into a broad piazza,
known to the elder Florentine writers as the Mercato Vecchio, or the
Old Market. This piazza, though it had been the scene of a provision-
market from time immemorial, and may perhaps, says fond imagination, be the very spot to which the Fesulean ancestors of the Florentines
descended from their high fastness to traffic with the rustic population
of the valley, had not been shunned as a place of residence by Florentine wealth. In the early decades of the fifteenth century, which was
now near its end, the Medici and other powerful families of the *popolani
grassi,* or commercial nobility, had their houses there, not perhaps finding their ears much offended by the loud roar of mingled dialects, or
their eyes much shocked by the butchers' stalls, which the old poet
Antonio Pucci accounts a chief glory, or *dignità,* of a market that, in
his esteem, eclipsed the markets of all the earth beside. But the glory of
mutton and veal (well attested to be the flesh of the right animals; for
were not the skins, with the heads attached, duly displayed, according
to the decree of the Signoria?) was just now wanting to the Mercato,
the time of Lent not being yet over. The proud corporation, or "Art," of

butchers was in abeyance, and it was the great harvest-time of the
market-gardeners, the cheese-mongers, the venders of macaroni, corn,
eggs, milk, and dried fruits,—a change which was apt to make the
women's voices predominant in the chorus. But in all seasons there was
the experimental ringing of pots and pans, the chinking of the money-
changers, the tempting offers of cheapness at the old-clothes stalls, the
challenges of the dicers, the vaunting of new linens and woollens, of
excellent wooden-ware, kettles, and frying-pans; there was the choking
of the narrow inlets with mules and carts, together with much uncomplimentary remonstrance in terms remarkably identical with the insults
in use by the gentler sex of the present day, under the same imbrowning
and heating circumstances. Ladies and gentlemen who came to market
looked on at a larger amount of amateur fighting than could easily be
seen in these later times, and beheld more revolting rags, beggary, and
rascaldom than modern householders could well picture to themselves.
As the day wore on, the hideous drama of the gaming-house might be
seen here by any chance open-air spectator,—the quivering eagerness,
the blank despair, the sobs, the blasphemy, and the blows:—

"E vedesi chi perde con gran soffi,
E bestemmiar colla mano alla mascella,
E ricever e dar dimolti ingoffi."

But still there was the relief of prettier sights: there were brood-rab-
bits, not less innocent and astonished than those of our own period;
there were doves and singing-birds to be bought as presents for the
children; there were even kittens for sale, and here and there a handsome *gattuccio*, or "Tom," with the highest character for mousing; and,
better than all, there were young, softly rounded cheeks and bright
eyes, freshened by the start from the far-off castello at daybreak, not
to speak of older faces with the unfading charm of honest good-will in
them, such as are never quite wanting in scenes of human industry. And
high on a pillar in the centre of the place,—a venerable pillar, fetched
from the church of San Giovanni,—stood Donatello's stone statue of
Plenty, with a fountain near it, where, says old Pucci, the good wives
of the market freshened their utensils, and their throats also; not because they were unable to buy wine, but because they wished to save
the money for their husbands.

But on this particular morning a sudden change seemed to have come
over the face of the market. The *deschi*, or stalls, were indeed partly
dressed with their various commodities, and already there were purchasers assembled, on the alert to secure the finest, freshest vegetables
and the most unexceptionable butter. But when Bratti and his companion entered the piazza, it appeared that some common preoccupation
had for the moment distracted the attention both of buyers and sellers
from their proper business. Most of the traders had turned their backs
on their goods, and had joined the knots of talkers who were concentrating themselves at different points in the piazza. A vender of old

clothes, in the act of hanging out a pair of long hose, had distractedly hung them round his neck in his eagerness to join the nearest group; an oratorical cheese-monger, with a piece of cheese in one hand and a knife in the other, was incautiously making notes of his emphatic pauses on that excellent specimen of *marzolino;* and elderly market-women, with their egg-baskets in a dangerously oblique position, contributed a wailing fugue of invocation.

In this general distraction the Florentine boys, who were never wanting in any street scene, and were of an especially mischievous sort,—as who should say, very sour crabs indeed,—saw a great opportunity. Some made a rush at the nuts and dried figs, other preferred the farinaceous delicacies at the cooked-provision stalls,—delicacies to which certain four-footed dogs also, who had learned to take kindly to Lenten fare, applied a discriminating nostril, and then disappeared with much rapidity under the nearest shelter; while the mules, not without some kicking and plunging among impeding baskets, were stretching their muzzles towards the aromatic green-meat.

"Diavolo!" said Bratti, as he and his companion came, quite unnoticed, upon the noisy scene; "the Mercato is gone as mad as if the most Holy Father had excommunicated us again. I must know what this is. But never fear: it seems a thousand years to you till you see the pretty Tessa and get your cup of milk; but keep hold of me, and I'll hold to my bargain. Remember, I'm to have the first bid for your suit, specially for the hose, which, with all their stains, are the best *panno di garbo,*—as good as ruined, though, with mud and weather stains."

"Olà, Monna Trecca," Bratti proceeded, turning towards an old woman on the outside of the nearest group, who for the moment had suspended her wail to listen, and shouting close in her ear, "here are the mules upsetting all your bunches of parsley: is the world coming to an end, then?"

"Monna Trecca" (equivalent to "Dame Greengrocer") turned round at this unexpected trumpeting in her right ear, with a half-fierce, half-bewildered look, first at the speaker, then at her disarranged commodities, and then at the speaker again.

"A bad Easter and a bad year to you, and may you die by the sword!" she burst out, rushing towards her stall, but directing this first volley of her wrath against Bratti, who, without heeding the malediction, quietly slipped into her place, within hearing of the narrative which had been absorbing her attention; making a sign at the same time to the younger stranger to keep near him.

"I tell you I saw it myself," said a fat man, with a bunch of newly purchased leeks in his hand. "I was in Santa Maria Novella, and saw it myself. The woman started up and threw out her arms, and cried out and said she saw a big bull with fiery horns coming down on the church to crush it. I saw it myself."

"Saw what, Goro?" said a man of slim figure, whose eye twinkled rather roguishly. He wore a close jerkin, a skull-cap lodged carelessly over his left ear as if it had fallen there by chance, a delicate linen apron tucked up on one side, and a razor stuck in his belt. "Saw the bull, or only the woman?"

"Why, the woman, to be sure; but it's all one, *mi pare:* it doesn't alter the meaning—*va!*" answered the fat man, with some contempt.

"Meaning? No, no; that's clear enough," said several voices at once, and then followed a confusion of tongues, in which "Light shooting over San Lorenzo for three nights together"—"Thunder in the clear starlight"—"Lantern of the Duomo struck with the sword of Saint Michael"—"*Palle*"—"All smashed"—"Lions tearing each other to pieces"—"Ah! and they might well"—"*Boto caduto in Santissima Nunziata!*"—"Died like the best of Christians"—"God will have pardoned him"—were often repeated phrases, which shot across each other like storm-driven hailstones, each speaker feeling rather the necessity of utterance than of finding a listener. Perhaps the only silent members of the group were Bratti, who, as a newcomer, was busy in mentally piecing together the flying fragments of information; the man of the razor; and a thin-lipped, eager-looking personage in spectacles, wearing a pen-and-ink case at his belt.

"*Ebbene*, Nello," said Bratti, skirting the group till he was within hearing of the barber. "It appears the Magnifico is dead—rest his soul! —and the price of wax will rise?"

"Even as you say," answered Nello; and then added, with an air of extra gravity but with marvellous rapidity, "and his waxen image in the Nunziata fell at the same moment, they say; or at some other time, whenever it pleases the Frati Serviti, who know best. And several cows and women have had still-born calves this Quaresima; and for the bad eggs that have been broken since the Carnival, nobody has counted them. Ah! a great man,—a great politician,—a greater poet than Dante. And yet the cupola didn't fall, only the lantern. *Che miracolo!*"

A sharp and lengthened "Pst!" was suddenly heard darting across the pelting storm of gutturals. It came from the pale man in spectacles, and had the effect he intended; for the noise ceased, and all eyes in the group were fixed on him with a look of expectation.

" 'Tis well said you Florentines are blind," he began, in an incisive high voice. "It appears to me you need nothing but a diet of hay to make cattle of you. What! do you think the death of Lorenzo is the scourge God has prepared for Florence? Go! you are sparrows chattering praise over the dead hawk. What! a man who was trying to slip a noose over every neck in the Republic, that he might tighten it at his pleasure! You like that; you like to have the election of your magistrates turned into closet-work, and no man to use the rights of a citizen unless he is a Medicean. That is what is meant by qualification now: *netto di specchio* no longer means that a man pays his dues to the Republic; it means that he'll wink at robbery of the people's money,— at robbery of their daughters' dowries; that he'll play the chamberer and the philosopher by turns,—listen to bawdy songs at the Carnival

and cry 'Bellissimi!'—and listen to sacred lauds and cry again 'Bellissimi!' But this is what you love: you grumble and raise a riot over
your *quattrini bianchi* [white farthings]; but you take no notice when
the public treasury has got a hole in the bottom for the gold to run
into Lorenzo's drains. You like to pay for footmen to walk before and
behind one of your citizens, that he may be affable and condescending
to you. 'See, what a tall Pisan we keep,' say you, 'to march before him
with the drawn sword flashing in our eyes!—and yet Lorenzo smiles at
us. What goodness!' And you think the death of a man who would soon
have saddled and bridled you as the Sforza has saddled and bridled
Milan—you think his death is the scourge God is warning you of by
portents. I tell you there is another sort of scourge in the air."

"Nay, nay, Ser Cioni, keep astride your politics, and never mount
your prophecy; politics is the better horse," said Nello.

"But if you talk of portents, what portent can be greater than a
pious notary? Balaam's ass was nothing to it."

"Ay, but a notary out of work, with his ink-bottle dry," said another
by-stander, very much out at elbows. "Better don a cowl at once, Ser
Cioni; everybody will believe in your fasting."

The notary turned, and left the group with a look of indignant contempt, disclosing, as he did so, the sallow but mild face of a short man
who had been standing behind him, and whose bent shoulders told of
some sedentary occupation.

"By San Giovanni, though," said the fat purchaser of leeks, with the
air of a person rather shaken in his theories, "I am not sure there isn't
some truth in what Ser Cioni says. For I know I have good reason to
find fault with the *quattrini bianchi* myself. Grumble, did he say? Suffocation! I should think we do grumble; and, let anybody say the
word, I'll turn out into the piazza with the readiest, sooner than have
our money altered in our hands as if the magistracy were so many
necromancers. And it's true Lorenzo might have hindered such work if
he would,—and for the bull with the flaming horns, why, as Ser Cioni
says, there may be many meanings to it, for the matter of that; it may
have more to do with the taxes than we think. For when God above
sends a sign, it's not to be supposed he'd have only one meaning."

"Spoken like an oracle, Goro!" said the barber. "Why, when we poor
mortals can pack two or three meanings into one sentence, it were mere
blasphemy not to believe that your miraculous bull means everything
that any man in Florence likes it to mean."

"Thou art pleased to scoff, Nello," said the sallow, round-shouldered
man, no longer eclipsed by the notary; "but it is not the less true that
every revelation, whether by visions, dreams, portents, or the written
word, has many meanings, which it is given to the illuminated only
to unfold."

"Assuredly," answered Nello. "Haven't I been to hear the Frate in
San Lorenzo? But then, I've been to hear Fra Menico in the Duomo

too; and according to him, your Fra Girolamo, with his visions and interpretations, is running after the wind of Mongibello, and those who
follow him are like to have the fate of certain swine that ran headlong
into the sea,—or some hotter place. With San Domenico roaring *è vero*
in one ear, and San Francisco screaming *è falso* in the other, what is a
poor barber to do—unless he were illuminated? But it's plain our Goro
here is beginning to be illuminated; for he already sees that the bull
with the flaming horns means first himself, and secondly all the other
aggrieved taxpayers of Florence, who are determined to gore the magistracy on the first opportunity."

"Goro is a fool!" said a bass voice, with a note that dropped like the
sound of a great bell in the midst of much tinkling. "Let him carry
home his leeks and shake his flanks over his wool-beating. He'll mend
matters more that way than by showing his tun-shaped body in the
piazza, as if everybody might measure his grievances by the size of
his paunch. The burdens that harm him most are his heavy carcass and
his idleness."

The speaker had joined the group only in time to hear the conclusion of Nello's speech; but he was one of those figures for whom all
the world instinctively makes way, as it would for a battering-ram. He
was not much above the middle height; but the impression of enormous
force which was conveyed by his capacious chest and brawny arms
bared to the shoulder, was deepened by the keen sense and quiet resolution expressed in his glance and in every furrow of his cheek and
brow. He had often been an unconscious model to Domenico Ghirlandajo, when that great painter was making the walls of the churches reflect the life of Florence, and translating pale aerial traditions into the
deep colour and strong lines of the faces he knew. The naturally dark
tint of his skin was additionally bronzed by the same powdery deposit
that gave a polished black surface to his leathern apron,—a deposit
which habit had probably made a necessary condition of perfect ease,
for it was not washed off with punctilious regularity.

Goro turned his fat cheek and glassy eye on the frank speaker with a
look of deprecation rather than of resentment.

"Why, Niccolò," he said, in an injured tone, "I've heard you sing
to another tune than that, often enough, when you've been laying down
the law at San Gallo on a festa. I've heard you say yourself that a man
wasn't a mill-wheel, to be on the grind, grind, as long as he was driven,
and then stick in his place without stirring when the water was low.
And you're as fond of your vote as any man in Florence,—ay, and I've
heard you say, if Lorenzo—"

"Yes, yes," said Niccolò. "Don't you be bringing up my speeches
again after you've swallowed them, and handing them about as if they
were none the worse. I vote and I speak when there's any use in it: if
there's hot metal on the anvil, I lose no time before I strike; but I
don't spend good hours in tinkling on cold iron, or in standing on the

pavement as thou dost, Goro, with snout upward, like a pig under an oak-tree. And as for Lorenzo,—dead and gone before his time,—he was a man who had an eye for curious ironwork; and if anybody says he wanted to make himself a tyrant, I say, '*Sia;* I'll not deny which way the wind blows when every man can see the weathercock.' But that only means that Lorenzo was a crested hawk, and there are plenty of hawks without crests whose claws and beaks are as good for tearing. Though if there was any chance of a real reform, so that Marzocco might shake his mane and roar again, instead of dipping his head to lick the feet of anybody that will mount and ride him, I'd strike a good blow for it."

"And that reform is not far off, Niccolò," said the sallow, mild-faced man, seizing his opportunity like a missionary among the too light-minded heathens; "for a time of tribulation is coming, and the scourge is at hand. And when the Church is purged of cardinals and prelates who traffic in her inheritance that their hands may be full to pay the price of blood and to satisfy their own lusts, the State will be purged too,—and Florence will be purged of men who love to see avarice and lechery under the red hat and the mitre because it gives them the screen of a more hellish vice than their own."

"Ay, as Goro's broad body would be a screen for my narrow person in case of missiles," said Nello; "but if that excellent screen happened to fall, I were stifled under it surely enough. That is no bad image of thine, Nanni,—or, rather, of the Frate's; for I fancy there is no room in the small cup of thy understanding for any other liquor than what he pours into it."

"And it were well for thee, Nello," replied Nanni, "if thou couldst empty thyself of thy scoffs and thy jests, and take in that liquor too. The warning is ringing in the ears of all men; and it's no new story; for the Abbot Joachim prophesied of the coming time three hundred years ago, and now Fra Girolamo has got the message afresh. He has seen it in a vision, even as the prophets of old; he has seen the sword hanging from the sky."

"Ay, and thou wilt see it thyself, Nanni, if thou wilt stare upward long enough," said Niccolò; "for that pitiable tailor's work of thine makes thy noddle so overhang thy legs that thy eyeballs can see nought above the stitching-board but the roof of thy own skull."

The honest tailor bore the jest without bitterness, bent on convincing his hearers of his doctrine rather than of his dignity. But Niccolò gave him no opportunity for replying; for he turned away to the pursuit of his market business, probably considering further dialogue as a tinkling on cold iron.

"*Ebbene,*" said the man with the hose round his neck, who had lately migrated from another knot of talkers, "they are safest who cross themselves and jest at nobody. Do you know that the Magnifico sent for the Frate at the last, and couldn't die without his blessing?"

"Was it so,—in truth?" said several voices. "Yes, yes,—God will have pardoned him." "He died like the best of Christians." "Never took his eyes from the holy crucifix." "And the Frate will have given him his blessing?"

"Well, I know no more," said he of the hosen: "only Guccio there met a footman going back to Careggi, and he told him the Frate had been sent for yesternight, after the Magnifico had confessed and had the holy sacraments."

"It's likely enough the Frate will tell the people something about it in his sermon this morning; is it not true, Nanni?" said Goro. "What do you think?"

But Nanni had already turned his back on Goro, and the group was rapidly thinning; some being stirred by the impulse to go and hear "new things" from the Frate ("new things" were the nectar of Florentines); others by the sense that it was time to attend to their private business. In this general movement Bratti got close to the barber, and said,—

"Nello, you've a ready tongue of your own, and are used to worming secrets out of people when you've once got them well lathered. I picked up a stranger this morning as I was coming in from Rovezzano, and I can spell him out no better than I can the letters on that scarf I bought from the French cavalier. It isn't my wits are at fault,—I want no man to help me tell peas from Paternosters,—but when you come to foreign fashions, a fool may happen to know more than a wise man."

"Ay, thou hast the wisdom of Midas, who could turn rags and rusty nails into gold, even as thou dost," said Nello; "and he had also something of the ass about him. But where is thy bird of strange plumage?"

Bratti was looking round with an air of disappointment.

"Diavolo!" he said, with some vexation. "The bird's flown. It's true he was hungry, and I forgot him. But we shall find him in the Mercato, within scent of bread and savours, I'll answer for him."

"Let us make the round of the Mercato, then," said Nello.

"It isn't his feathers that puzzle me," continued Bratti, as they pushed their way together. "There isn't much in the way of cut and cloth on this side the Holy Sepulchre that can puzzle a Florentine."

"Or frighten him either," said Nello, "after he has seen an Englander or a German."

"No, no," said Bratti, cordially; "one may never lose sight of the cupola and yet know the world, I hope. Besides, this stranger's clothes are good Italian merchandise, and the hose he wears were dyed in Ognissanti before ever they were dyed with salt water, as he says. But the riddle about him is—"

Here Bratti's explanation was interrupted by some jostling as they reached one of the entrances of the piazza; and before he could resume it they had caught sight of the enigmatical object they were in search of.

CHAPTER II

BREAKFAST FOR LOVE

AFTER Bratti had joined the knot of talkers, the young stranger, hopeless of learning what was the cause of the general agitation, and not much caring to know what was probably of little interest to any but born Florentines, soon became tired of waiting for Bratti's escort, and chose to stroll round the piazza, looking out for some vender of eatables who might happen to have less than the average curiosity about public news. But as if at the suggestion of a sudden thought, he thrust his hand into a purse or wallet that hung at his waist, and explored it again and again with a look of frustration.

"Not an obolus, by Jupiter!" he murmured, in a language which was not Tuscan or even Italian. "I thought I had one poor piece left. I must get my breakfast for love, then!"

He had not gone many steps farther before it seemed likely that he had found a quarter of the market where that medium of exchange might not be rejected.

In a corner, away from any group of talkers, two mules were standing, well adorned with red tassels and collars. One of them carried wooden milk-vessels, the other a pair of panniers filled with herbs and salads. Resting her elbow on the neck of the mule that carried the milk, there leaned a young girl, apparently not more than sixteen, with a red hood surrounding her face, which was all the more baby-like in its prettiness from the entire concealment of her hair. The poor child, perhaps, was weary after her labour in the morning twilight in preparation for her walk to market from some castello three or four miles off, for she seemed to have gone to sleep in that half-standing, half-leaning posture. Nevertheless, our stranger had no compunction in awaking her; but the means he chose were so gentle that it seemed to the damsel in her dream as if a little sprig of thyme had touched her lips while she was stooping to gather the herbs. The dream was broken, however; for she opened her blue baby-eyes, and started up with astonishment and confusion to see the young stranger standing close before her. She heard him speaking to her in a voice which seemed so strange and soft that even if she had been more collected she would have taken it for granted that he said something hopelessly unintelligible to her, and her first movement was to turn her head a little away, and lift up a corner of her green serge mantle as a screen. He repeated his words,—

"Forgive me, pretty one, for awaking you. I'm dying with hunger, and the scent of milk makes breakfast seem more desirable than ever."

He had chosen the words *muoio di fame*, because he knew they would be familiar to her ears; and he had uttered them playfully, with the intonation of a mendicant. This time he was understood; the corner of the mantle was dropped, and in a few moments a large cup of fragrant milk was held out to him. He paid no further compliments before raising it to his lips, and while he was drinking, the little maiden found courage to look up at the long dark curls of this singular-voiced stranger who had asked for food in the tones of a beggar, but who, though his clothes were much damaged, was unlike any beggar she had ever seen.

While this process of survey was going on, there was another current of feeling that carried her hand into a bag which hung by the side of the mule; and when the stranger set down his cup, he saw a large piece of bread held out towards him, and caught a glance of the blue eyes that seemed intended as an encouragement to him to take this additional gift.

"But perhaps that is your own breakfast," he said. "No, I have had enough without payment. A thousand thanks, my gentle one."

There was no rejoinder in words; but the piece of bread was pushed a little nearer to him, as if in impatience at his refusal; and as the long dark eyes of the stranger rested on the baby-face, it seemed to be gathering more and more courage to look up and meet them.

"Ah, then, if I must take the bread," he said, laying his hand on it, "I shall get bolder still, and beg for another kiss to make the bread sweeter."

His speech was getting wonderfully intelligible in spite of the strange voice, which had at first almost seemed a thing to make her cross herself. She blushed deeply, and lifted up a corner of her mantle to her mouth again. But just as the too presumptuous stranger was leaning forward, and had his fingers on the arm that held up the screening mantle, he was startled by a harsh voice close upon his ear.

"Who are *you*—with a murrain to you? No honest buyer, I'll warrant, but a hanger-on of the dicers—or something worse. Go! dance off, and find fitter company, or I'll give you a tune to a little quicker time than you'll like."

The young stranger drew back and looked at the speaker with a glance provokingly free from alarm and deprecation, and his slight expression of saucy amusement broke into a broad beaming smile as he surveyed the figure of his threatener. She was a stout but brawny woman, with a man's jerkin slipped over her green serge gamurra, or gown, and the peaked hood of some departed mantle fastened round her sunburnt face, which, under all its coarseness and premature wrinkles, showed a half-sad, half-ludicrous maternal resemblance to the tender baby-face of the little maiden,—the sort of resemblance which often seems a more croaking, shudder-creating prophecy than that of the death's-head.

There was something irresistibly propitiating in that bright young smile; but Monna Ghita was not a woman to betray any weakness, and she went on speaking, apparently with heightened exasperation.

"Yes, yes, you can grin as well as other monkeys in cap and jerkin. You're a minstrel or a mountebank, I'll be sworn; you look for all the world as silly as a tumbler when he's been upside-down and has got on his heels again. And what fool's tricks hast thou been after, Tessa?" she added, turning to her daughter, whose frightened face was more inviting to abuse. "Giving away the milk and victuals, it seems; ay, ay, thou'dst carry water in thy ears for any idle vagabond that didn't like to stoop for it, thou silly staring rabbit! Turn thy back, and lift the herbs out of the panniers, else I'll make thee say a few Aves without counting."

"Nay, Madonna," said the stranger, with a pleading smile, "don't be angry with your pretty Tessa for taking pity on a hungry traveller, who found himself unexpectedly without a quattrino. Your handsome face looks so well when it frowns, that I long to see it illuminated by a smile."

"*Va via!* I know what paste you are made of. You may tickle me with that straw a good long while before I shall laugh, I can tell you. Get along, with a bad Easter! else I'll make a beauty-spot or two on that face of yours that shall spoil your kissing on this side Advent."

As Monna Ghita lifted her formidable talons by way of complying with the first and last requisite of eloquence, Bratti, who had come up a minute or two before, had been saying to his companion, "What think you of this pretty parrot, Nello? Doesn't his tongue smack of Venice?"

"Nay, Bratti," said the barber, in an undertone, "thy wisdom has much of the ass in it, as I told thee just now; especially about the ears. This stranger is a Greek, else I'm not the barber who has had the sole and exclusive shaving of the excellent Demetrio, and drawn more than one sorry tooth from his learned jaw. And this youth might be taken to have come straight from Olympus,—at least when he has had a touch of my razor."

"*Orsù!* Monna Ghita!" continued Nello, not sorry to see some sport; "what has happened to cause such a thunder-storm? Has this young stranger been misbehaving himself?"

"By San Giovanni!" said the cautious Bratti, who had not shaken off his original suspicions concerning the shabbily-clad possessor of jewels, "he did right to run away from *me*, if he meant to get into mischief. I can swear that I found him under the Loggia de' Cerchi, with a ring on his finger such as I've seen worn by Bernardo Rucellai himself. Not another rusty nail's worth do I know about him."

"The fact is," said Nello, eying the stranger good-humouredly, "this *bello giovane* has been a little too presumptuous in admiring the charms of Monna Ghita, and has attempted to kiss her while her daughter's back is turned; for I observe that the pretty Tessa is too busy to look this way at present. Was it not so, Messer?" Nello concluded, in a tone of courtesy.

"You have divined the offence like a soothsayer," said the stranger, laughingly. "Only that I had not the good fortune to find Monna Ghita here at first. I begged a cup of milk from her daughter, and had accepted this gift of bread, for which I was making a humble offering of gratitude, before I had the higher pleasure of being face to face with these riper charms which I was perhaps too bold in admiring."

"*Va, va!* be off, every one of you, and stay in purgatory till I pay to get you out, will you?" said Monna Ghita, fiercely, elbowing Nello, and leading forward her mule so as to compel the stranger to jump aside. "Tessa, thou simpleton, bring forward thy mule a bit; the cart will be upon us."

As Tessa turned to take the mule's bridle, she cast one timid glance at the stranger, who was now moving with Nello out of the way of an approaching market-cart; and the glance was just long enough to seize the beckoning movement of his hand, which indicated that he had been watching for this opportunity of an adieu.

"*Ebbene*," said Bratti, raising his voice to speak across the cart; "I leave you with Nello, young man, for there's no pushing my bag and basket any farther, and I have business at home. But you'll remember our bargain, because if you found Tessa without me, it was not my fault. Nello will show you my shop in the Ferravecchi, and I'll not turn my back on you."

"A thousand thanks, friend!" said the stranger, laughing, and then turned away with Nello up the narrow street which led most directly to the Piazza del Duomo.

CHAPTER III

THE BARBER'S SHOP

"To tell you the truth," said the young stranger to Nello, as they got a little clearer of the entangled vehicles and mules, "I am not sorry to be handed over by that patron of mine to one who has a less barbarous accent and a less enigmatical business. Is it a common thing among you Florentines for an itinerant trafficker in broken glass and rags to talk of a shop where he sells lutes and swords?"

"Common? No; our Bratti is not a common man. He has a theory, and lives up to it, which is more than I can say for any philosopher I have the honour of shaving," answered Nello, whose loquacity, like an over-full bottle, could never pour forth a small dose. "Bratti means to extract the utmost possible amount of pleasure, that is to say, of hard bargaining, out of this life; winding it up with a bargain for the easiest possible passage through purgatory, by giving Holy Church his winnings when the game is over. He has had his will made to that effect on the cheapest terms a notary could be got for. But I have often said to him, 'Bratti, thy bargain is a limping one, and thou art on the lame side of it. Does it not make thee a little sad to look at the pictures of the Paradiso? Thou wilt never be able there to chaffer for rags and rusty nails: the saints and angels want neither pins nor tinder; and except with San Bartolommeo, who carries his skin about in an inconvenient manner, I see no chance of thy making a bargain for second-hand clothing.' But, God pardon me," added Nello, changing his tone, and crossing himself, "this light talk ill beseems a morning when Lorenzo lies dead, and the Muses are tearing their hair,—always a painful thought to a barber; and you yourself, Messere, are probably under a cloud, for when a man of your speech and presence takes up with so sorry a night's lodging, it argues some misfortune to have befallen him."

"What Lorenzo is that whose death you speak of?" said the stranger, appearing to have dwelt with too anxious an interest on this point to have noticed the indirect inquiry that followed it.

"What Lorenzo? There is but one Lorenzo, I imagine, whose death could throw the Mercato into an uproar, set the lantern of the Duomo leaping in desperation, and cause the lions of the Republic to feel under an immediate necessity to devour one another. I mean Lorenzo de' Medici, the Pericles of our Athens,—if I may make such a comparison in the ear of a Greek."

"Why not?" said the other, laughingly; "for I doubt whether Athens, even in the days of Pericles, could have produced so learned a barber."

"Yes, yes; I thought I could not be mistaken," said the rapid Nello, "else I have shaved the venerable Demetrio Calcondila to little purpose; but pardon me, I am lost in wonder: your Italian is better than his, though he has been in Italy forty years,—better even than that of the accomplished Marullo, who may be said to have married the Italic Muse in more senses than one, since he has married our learned and lovely Alessandra Scala."

"It will lighten your wonder to know that I come of a Greek stock planted in Italian soil much longer than the mulberry-trees which have taken so kindly to it. I was born at Bari, and my—I mean I was brought up by an Italian—and, in fact, I am a Greek, very much as your peaches are Persian. The Greek dye was subdued in me, I suppose, till I had been dipped over again by long abode and much travel in the land of gods and heroes. And, to confess something of my private affairs to you, this same Greek dye, with a few ancient gems I have about me, is the only fortune shipwreck has left me. But—when the towers fall, you know it is an ill business for the small nest-builders—the death of your Pericles makes me wish I had rather turned my steps towards Rome, as I should have done but for a fallacious Minerva in the shape of an Augustinian monk. 'At Rome,' he said, 'you will be lost in a crowd of hungry scholars; but at Florence, every corner is penetrated by the sunshine of Lorenzo's patronage: Florence is the best market in Italy for such commodities as yours.'"

"*Gnaffè*, and so it will remain, I hope," said Nello. "Lorenzo was not the only patron and judge of learning in our city,—Heaven forbid! Because he was a large melon, every other Florentine is not a pumpkin, I suppose. Have we not Bernardo Rucellai, and Alamanno Rinuccini, and plenty more? And if you want to be informed on such matters, I,

Nello, am your man. It seems to me a thousand years till I can be of service to a *bel erudito* like yourself. And, first of all, in the matter of your hair. That beard, my fine young man, must be parted with, were it as dear to you as the nymph of your dreams. Here at Florence we love not to see a man with his nose projecting over a cascade of hair. But remember, you will have passed the Rubicon when once you have been shaven: if you repent, and let your beard grow after it has acquired stoutness by a struggle with the razor, your mouth will by and by show no longer what Messer Angelo calls the divine prerogative of lips, but will appear like a dark cavern fringed with horrent brambles."

"That is a terrible prophecy," said the Greek, "especially if your Florentine maidens are many of them as pretty as the little Tessa I stole a kiss from this morning."

"Tessa? She is a rough-handed contadina; you will rise into the favour of dames who bring no scent of the mule-stables with them. But to that end, you must not have the air of a *sgherro*, or a man of evil repute; you must look like a courtier, and a scholar of the more polished sort, such as our Pietro Crinito,—like one who sins among well-bred, well-fed people, and not one who sucks down vile *vino di sotto* in a chance tavern."

"With all my heart," said the stranger. "If the Florentine Graces demand it, I am willing to give up this small matter of my beard; but—"

"Yes, yes," interrupted Nello; "I know what you would say. It is the *bella zazzera*, the hyacinthine locks, you do not choose to part with; and there is no need. Just a little pruning—*ecco!*—and you will look not unlike the illustrious prince Pico di Mirandola in his prime. And here we are in good time in the Piazza San Giovanni, and at the door of my shop. But you are pausing, I see; naturally, you want to look at our wonder of the world, our Duomo, our Santa Maria del Fiore. Well, well, a mere glance; but I beseech you to leave a closer survey till you have been shaved: I am quivering with the inspiration of my art even to the very edge of my razor. Ah, then, come round this way."

The mercurial barber seized the arm of the stranger, and led him to a point, on the south side of the piazza, from which he could see at once the huge dark shell of the cupola, the slender soaring grace of Giotto's campanile, and the quaint octagon of San Giovanni in front of them, showing its unique gates of storied bronze, which still bore the somewhat dimmed glory of their original gilding. The inlaid marbles were then fresher in their pink and white and purple than they are now, when the winters of four centuries have turned their white to the rich ochre of well-mellowed meerschaum; the façade of the cathedral did not stand ignominious in faded stucco, but had upon it the magnificent promise of the half-completed marble in laying and statued niches, which Giotto had devised a hundred and fifty years before; and as the campanile in all its harmonious variety of colour and form led the eyes upward, high into the clear air of this April morning, it seemed a prophetic symbol, telling that human life must somehow and sometime shape itself into accord with that pure, aspiring beauty.

But this was not the impression it appeared to produce on the Greek. His eyes were irresistibly led upward; but as he stood with his arms folded and his curls falling backward, there was a slight touch of scorn on his lip, and when his eyes fell again they glanced round with a scanning coolness which was rather piquing to Nello's Florentine spirit.

"Well, my fine young man," he said, with some impatience, "you seem to make as little of our cathedral as if you were the angel Gabriel come straight from Paradise. I should like to know if you have ever seen finer work than our Giotto's tower, or any cupola that would not look a mere mushroom by the side of Brunelleschi's there, or any marbles finer or more cunningly wrought than these that our Signoria got from far-off quarries, at a price that would buy a dukedom. Come, now, have you ever seen anything to equal them?"

"If you asked me that question with a cimeter at my throat, after the Turkish fashion, or even your own razor," said the young Greek, smiling gayly, and moving on towards the gates of the Baptistery, "I dare say you might get a confession of the true faith from me. But with my throat free from peril, I venture to tell you that your buildings smack too much of Christian barbarism for my taste. I have a shuddering sense of what there is inside,—hideous smoked Madonnas; fleshless saints in mosaic, staring down idiotic astonishment and rebuke from the apse; skin-clad skeletons hanging on crosses, or stuck all over with arrows, or stretched on gridirons; women and monks with heads aside in perpetual lamentation. I have seen enough of those wry-necked favourites of heaven at Constantinople. But what is this bronze door rough with imagery? These women's figures seem moulded in a different spirit from those starved and staring saints I spoke of; these heads in high relief speak of a human mind within them, instead of looking like an index to perpetual spasms and colic."

"Yes, yes," said Nello, with some triumph. "I think we shall show you by-and-by that our Florentine art is not in a state of barbarism. These gates, my fine young man, were moulded half a century ago, by our Lorenzo Ghiberti, when he counted hardly so many years as you do."

"Ah, I remember," said the stranger, turning away, like one whose appetite for contemplation was soon satisfied. "I have heard that your Tuscan sculptors and painters have been studying the antique a little. But with monks for models, and the legends of mad hermits and martyrs for subjects, the vision of Olympus itself would be of small use to them."

"I understand," said Nello, with a significant shrug, as they walked along. "You are of the same mind as Michele Marullo, ay, and as Angelo Poliziano himself, in spite of his canonicate, when he relaxes himself a little in my shop after his lectures, and talks of the gods awaking from their long sleep and making the woods and streams vital once more. But he rails against the Roman scholars who want to make us all talk Latin again: 'My ears,' he says, 'are sufficiently flayed by the barbarisms of the learned, and if the vulgar are to talk Latin I would as soon have been in Florence the day they took to beating all the kettles in the city because the bells were not enough to stay the wrath of the saints.' Ah, Messer Greco, if you want to know the flavour of our scholarship, you must frequent my shop: it is the focus of Florentine intellect, and in that sense the navel of the earth,—as my great predecessor, Burchiello, said of *his* shop, on the more frivolous pretension that his street of the Calimara was the centre of our city. And here we are at the sign of 'Apollo and the Razor.' Apollo, you see, is bestowing the razor on the Triptolemus of our craft, the first reaper of beards, the sublime *Anonimo,* whose mysterious identity is indicated by a shadowy hand."

"I see thou hast had custom already, Sandro," continued Nello, addressing a solemn-looking dark-eyed youth, who made way for them on the threshold. "And now make all clear for this signor to sit down. And prepare the finest-scented lather, for he has a learned and a handsome chin."

"You have a pleasant little adytum there, I see," said the stranger, looking through a latticed screen which divided the shop from a room of about equal size, opening into a still smaller walled enclosure, where a few bays and laurels surrounded a stone Hermes. "I suppose your conclave of *eruditi* meets there?"

"There, and not less in my shop," said Nello, leading the way into the inner room, in which were some benches, a table, with one book in manuscript and one printed in capitals lying open upon it, a lute, a few oil sketches, and a model or two of hands and ancient masks. "For my shop is a no less fitting haunt of the Muses, as you will acknowledge when you feel the sudden illumination of understanding and the serene vigour of inspiration that will come to you with a clear chin. Ah! you can make that lute discourse, I perceive. I, too, have some skill that way, though the serenata is useless when daylight discloses a visage like mine, looking no fresher than an apple that has stood the winter. But look at that sketch; it is a fancy of Piero di Cosimo's, a strange freakish painter, who says he saw it by long looking at a mouldy wall."

The sketch Nello pointed to represented three masks,—one a drunken, laughing Satyr, another a sorrowing Magdalen, and the third, which lay between them, the rigid cold face of a Stoic; the masks rested obliquely on the lap of a little child, whose cherub features rose above them with something of the supernal promise in the gaze which painters had by that time learned to give to the Divine Infant.

"A symbolical picture, I see," said the young Greek, touching the lute while he spoke, so as to bring out a slight musical murmur. "The child, perhaps, is the Golden Age, wanting neither worship nor philosophy. And the Golden Age can always come back as long as men are born in the form of babies, and don't come into the world in cassock or furred mantle. Or the child may mean the wise philosophy of Epicurus, removed alike from the gross, the sad, and the severe."

"Ah! everybody has his own interpretation for that picture," said Nello; "and if you ask Piero himself what he meant by it, he says his pictures are an appendix which Messer Domeneddio has been pleased to make to the universe, and if any man is in doubt what they mean, he had better inquire of Holy Church. He has been asked to paint a picture after the sketch, but he puts his fingers to his ears and shakes his head at that; the fancy is past, he says,—a strange animal, our Piero. But now all is ready for your initiation into the mysteries of the razor."

"Mysteries they may well be called," continued the barber, with rising spirits at the prospect of a long monologue, as he imprisoned the young Greek in the shroud-like shaving-cloth; "mysteries of Minerva and the Graces. I get the flower of men's thoughts, because I seize them in the first moment after shaving. (Ah! you wince a little at the lather: it tickles the outlying limits of the nose, I admit.) And that is what makes the peculiar fitness of a barber's shop to become a resort of wit and learning. For, look now at a druggist's shop: there is a dull conclave at the sign of 'The Moor,' that pretends to rival mine; but what sort of inspiration, I beseech you, can be got from the scent of nauseous vegetable decoctions?—to say nothing of the fact that you no sooner pass the threshold than you see a doctor of physic, like a gigantic spider disguised in fur and scarlet, waiting for his prey; or even see him blocking up the doorway seated on a bony hack, inspecting saliva. (Your chin a little elevated, if it please you: contemplate that angel who is blowing the trumpet at you from the ceiling. I had it painted expressly for the regulation of my clients' chins.) Besides, your druggist, who herborizes and decocts, is a man of prejudices: he has poisoned people according to a system, and is obliged to stand up for his system to justify the consequences. Now, a barber can be dispassionate; the only thing he necessarily stands by is the razor, always providing he is not an author. That was the flaw in my great predecessor Burchiello: he was a poet, and had consequently a prejudice about his own poetry. I have escaped that; I saw very early that authorship is a narrowing business, in conflict with the liberal art of the razor, which demands an impartial affection for all men's chins. Ecco, Messer! the outline of your chin and lip is as clear as a maiden's; and now fix your mind on a knotty question,—ask yourself whether you are bound to spell Virgil with an *i* or an *e*, and say if you do not feel an unwonted clearness on the point. Only, if you decide for the *i,* keep it to yourself till your fortune is made, for the *e* hath the stronger following in Florence. Ah! I think I see a gleam of still quicker wit in your eye. I have it on the authority of our young Niccolò Macchiavelli, himself keen enough to discern *il pelo nell' uovo,* as we say, and a great lover of delicate shaving, though his beard is hardly of two years' date, that no sooner do the hairs begin to push themselves, than he perceives a certain grossness of apprehension creeping over him."

"Suppose you let me look at myself," said the stranger, laughing. "The happy effect on my intellect is perhaps obstructed by a little doubt as to the effect on my appearance."

"Behold yourself in this mirror, then; it is a Venetian mirror from Murano, the true *nosce teipsum*, as I have named it, compared with which the finest mirror of steel or silver is mere darkness. See now, how by diligent shaving the nether region of your face may preserve its human outline, instead of presenting no distinction from the physiognomy of a bearded owl or a Barbary ape. I have seen men whose beards have so invaded their cheeks that one might have pitied them as the victims of a sad, brutalizing chastisement befitting our Dante's Inferno, if they had not seemed to strut with a strange triumph in their extravagant hairiness."

"It seems to me," said the Greek, still looking into the mirror, "that you have taken away some of my capital with your razor,—I mean a year or two of age, which might have won me more ready credit for my learning. Under the inspection of a patron whose vision has grown somewhat dim, I shall have a perilous resemblance to a maiden of eighteen in the disguise of hose and jerkin."

"Not at all," said Nello, proceeding to clip the too extravagant curls; "your proportions are not those of a maiden. And for your age, I myself remember seeing Angelo Poliziano begin his lectures on the Latin language when he had a younger beard than yours; and between ourselves, his juvenile ugliness was not less signal than his precocious scholarship. Whereas you—no, no, your age is not against you; but between ourselves, let me hint to you that your being a Greek, though it be only an Apulian Greek, is not in your favour. Certain of our scholars hold that your Greek learning is but a wayside degenerate plant until it has been transplanted into Italian brains, and that now there is such a plentiful crop of the superior quality, your native teachers are mere propagators of degeneracy. Ecco! your curls are now of the right proportion to neck and shoulders; rise, Messer, and I will free you from the incumbrance of this cloth. *Gnaffè!* I almost advise you to retain the faded jerkin and hose a little longer; they give you the air of a fallen prince."

"But the question is," said the young Greek, leaning against the high back of a chair, and returning Nello's contemplative admiration with a look of inquiring anxiety,—"the question is, in what quarter I am to carry my princely air, so as to rise from the said fallen condition. If your Florentine patrons of learning share this scholarly hostility to the Greeks, I see not how your city can be a hospitable refuge for me, as you seemed to say just now."

"*Pian piano*—not so fast," said Nello, sticking his thumbs into his belt and nodding to Sandro to restore order. "I will not conceal from you that there is a prejudice against Greeks among us; and though, as a barber unsnared by authorship, I share no prejudices, I must admit that the Greeks are not always such pretty youngsters as yourself; their erudition is often of an uncombed, unmannerly aspect, and incrusted with a barbarous utterance of Italian, that makes their converse hardly more euphonious than that of a Tedesco in a state of vinous loquacity. And then, again, excuse me—we Florentines have liberal ideas about speech, and consider that an instrument which can flatter and promise so cleverly as the tongue, must have been partly made for those purposes; and that truth is a riddle for eyes and wit to discover, which it were a mere spoiling of sport for the tongue to betray. Still, we have our limits beyond which we call dissimulation treachery. But it is said of the Greeks that their honesty begins at what is the hanging-point with us, and that since the old Furies went to sleep, your Christian Greek is of so easy a conscience that he would make a stepping-stone of his father's corpse."

The flush on the stranger's face indicated what seemed so natural a movement of resentment, that the good-natured Nello hastened to atone for his want of reticence.

"Be not offended, *bel giovane;* I am but repeating what I hear in my shop; as you may perceive, my eloquence is simply the cream which I skim off my clients' talk. Heaven forbid I should fetter my impartiality by entertaining an opinion. And for that same scholarly objection to the Greeks," added Nello, in a more mocking tone, and with a significant grimace, "the fact is, you are heretics, Messer; jealousy has nothing to do with it: if you would just change your opinion about leaven, and alter your Doxology a little, our Italian scholars would think it a thousand years till they could give up their chairs to you. Yes, yes; it is chiefly religious scruple, and partly also the authority of a great classic,—Juvenal, is it not? He, I gather, had his bile as much stirred by the swarm of Greeks as our Messer Angelo, who is fond of quoting some passage about their incorrigible impudence,—*audacia perdita.*"

"Pooh! the passage is a compliment," said the Greek, who had recovered himself, and seemed wise enough to take the matter gayly,—

"'Ingenium velox, audacia perdita, sermo
Promptus, et Isæo torrentior.'

A rapid intellect and ready eloquence may carry off a little impudence."

"Assuredly," said Nello. "And since, as I see, you know Latin literature as well as Greek, you will not fall into the mistake of Giovanni Argiropulo, who ran full tilt against Cicero, and pronounced him all but a pumpkin-head. For, let me give you one bit of advice, young man—trust a barber who has shaved the best chins, and kept his eyes and ears open for twenty years—oil your tongue well when you talk of the ancient Latin writers, and give it an extra dip when you talk of the modern. A wise Greek may win favour among us; witness our excellent Demetrio, who is loved by many, and not hated immoderately even by the most renowned scholars."

"I discern the wisdom of your advice so clearly," said the Greek, with the bright smile which was continually lighting up the fine form and colour of his young face, "that I will ask you for a little more. Who now, for example, would be the most likely patron for me? Is there a son of Lorenzo who inherits his taste? Or is there any other wealthy Florentine specially addicted to purchasing antique gems? I have a fine Cleopatra cut in sardonyx, and one or two other intaglios and cameos, both curious and beautiful, worthy of being added to the cabinet of a prince. Happily, I had taken the precaution of fastening them within the lining of my doublet before I set out on my voyage. Moreover, I should like to raise a small sum for my present need on this ring of mine" (here he took out the ring and replaced it on his finger), "if you could recommend me to any honest trafficker."

"Let us see, let us see," said Nello, perusing the floor, and walking up and down the length of his shop. "This is no time to apply to Piero de' Medici, though he has the will to make such purchases if he could always spare the money; but I think it is another sort of Cleopatra that he covets most. . . . Yes, yes, I have it. What you want is a man of wealth and influence and scholarly tastes,—not one of your learned porcupines, bristling all over with critical tests, but one whose Greek and Latin are of a comfortable laxity. And that man is Bartolommeo Scala, the secretary of our Republic. He came to Florence as a poor adventurer himself,—a miller's son,—a 'branny monster,' as he has been nicknamed by our honey-lipped Poliziano, who agrees with him as well as my teeth agree with lemon-juice. And, by the by, that may be a reason why the secretary may be the more ready to do a good turn to a strange scholar. For, between you and me, *bel giovane*—trust a barber who has shaved the best scholars—friendliness is much such a steed as Ser Benghi's: it will hardly show much alacrity unless it has got the thistle of hatred under its tail. However, the secretary is a man who'll keep his word to you, even to the halving of a fennel-seed; and he is not unlikely to buy some of your gems."

"But how am I to get at this great man?" said the Greek, rather impatiently.

"I was coming to that," said Nello. "Just now everybody of any public importance will be full of Lorenzo's death, and a stranger may find it difficult to get any notice. But in the meantime I could take you to a man who, if he has a mind, can help you to a chance of a favourable interview with Scala sooner than anybody else in Florence,—worth seeing for his own sake too, to say nothing of his collections, or of his daughter Romola, who is as fair as the Florentine lily before it got quarrelsome and turned red."

"But if this father of the beautiful Romola makes collections, why should he not like to buy some of my gems himself?"

Nello shrugged his shoulders. "For two good reasons,—want of sight to look at the gems, and want of money to pay for them. Our old Bardo de' Bardi is so blind that he can see no more of his daughter than, as he says, a glimmering of something bright when she comes very near him: doubtless her golden hair, which, as Messer Luigi Pulci says of his

Meridiana's, *'raggia come stella per sereno.'* Ah, here come some clients of mine, and I shouldn't wonder if one of them could serve your turn about that ring."

CHAPTER IV

FIRST IMPRESSIONS

"Good-day, Messer Domenico," said Nello to the foremost of the two visitors who entered the shop, while he nodded silently to the other. "You come as opportunely as cheese on macaroni.[1] Ah! you are in haste —wish to be shaved without delay—ecco! And this is a morning when every one has grave matter on his mind. Florence orphaned—the very pivot of Italy snatched away—heaven itself at a loss what to do next. *Oimè!* Well, well; the sun is nevertheless travelling on towards dinner-time again; and, as I was saying, you come like cheese ready grated. For this young stranger was wishing for an honourable trader who would advance him a sum on a certain ring of value, and if I had counted every goldsmith and money-lender in Florence on my fingers I couldn't have found a better name than Menico Cennini. Besides, he hath other ware in which you deal,—Greek learning and young eyes,—a double implement which you printers are always in need of."

The grave elderly man, son of that Bernardo Cennini who twenty years before, having heard of the new process of printing carried on by Germans, had cast his own types in Florence, remained necessarily in lathered silence and passivity while Nello showered this talk in his ears, but turned a slow sideway gaze on the stranger.

"This fine young man has unlimited Greek, Latin, or Italian at your service," continued Nello, fond of interpreting by very ample paraphrase. "He is as great a wonder of juvenile learning as Francesco Filelfo or our own incomparable Poliziano. A second Guarino, too, for he has had the misfortune to be shipwrecked, and has doubtless lost a store of precious manuscripts that might have contributed some correctness even to your correct editions, Domenico. Fortunately, he has rescued a few gems of rare value. His name is—you said your name, Messer, was—"

"Tito Melema," said the stranger, slipping the ring from his finger and presenting it to Cennini, whom Nello, not less rapid with his razor than with his tongue, had now released from the shaving-cloth.

Meanwhile the man who had entered the shop in company with the goldsmith—a tall figure, about fifty, with a short-trimmed beard, wearing an old felt hat and a threadbare mantle—had kept his eye fixed on the Greek, and now said abruptly,—

"Young man, I am painting a picture of Simon deceiving old Priam,

---

[1] This proverb is older than one would suppose, although there are no instances of ancient quotations. But macaroni was already a favoured dish in Boccaccio's tales, and even then was usually eaten with grated cheese; so that the proverb must have been in use also at that time.—Editor.

and I should be glad of your face for my Simon, if you'd give me a sitting."

Tito Melema started and looked round with a pale astonishment in his face, as if at a sudden accusation; but Nello left him no time to feel at a loss for an answer: "Piero," said the barber, "thou art the most extraordinary compound of humours and fancies ever packed into a human skin. What trick wilt thou play with the fine visage of this young scholar to make it suit thy traitor? Ask him rather to turn his eyes upward, and thou mayst make a Saint Sebastian of him that will draw troops of devout women; or, if thou art in a classical vein, put myrtle about his curls and make him a young Bacchus, or say rather a Phœbus Apollo, for his face is as warm and bright as a summer morning; it made me his friend in the space of a 'credo.'"

"Ay, Nello," said the painter, speaking with abrupt pauses; "and if thy tongue can leave off its everlasting chirping long enough for thy understanding to consider the matter, thou mayst see that thou hast just shown the reason why the face of Messere will suit my traitor. A perfect traitor should have a face which vice can write no marks on, —lips that will lie with a dimpled smile,—eyes of such agate-like brightness and depth that no infamy can dull them,—cheeks that will rise from a murder and not look haggard. I say not this young man is a traitor: I mean, he has a face that would make him the more perfect traitor if he had the heart of one, which is saying neither more nor less than that he has a beautiful face, informed with rich young blood, that will be nourished enough by food, and keep its colour without much help of virtue. He may have the heart of a hero along with it; I aver nothing to the contrary. Ask Domenico there if the lapidaries can always tell a gem by the sight alone. And now I'm going to put the tow in my ears, for thy chatter and the bells together are more than I can endure: so say no more to me, but trim my beard."

With these last words Piero (called "di Cosimo," from his master, Cosimo Rosselli) drew out two bits of tow, stuffed them in his ears, and placed himself in the chair before Nello, who shrugged his shoulders and cast a grimacing look of intelligence at the Greek, as much as to say, "A whimsical fellow, you perceive! Everybody holds his speeches as mere jokes."

Tito, who had stood transfixed, with his long dark eyes resting on the unknown man who had addressed him so equivocally, seemed recalled to his self-command by Piero's change of position, and apparently satisfied with his explanation, was again giving his attention to Cennini, who presently said,—

"This is a curious and valuable ring, young man. This intaglio of the fish with the crested serpent above it, in the black stratum of the onyx, or rather nicolo, is well shown by the surrounding blue of the upper stratum. The ring has doubtless a history?" added Cennini, looking up keenly at the young stranger.

"Yes, indeed," said Tito, meeting the scrutiny very frankly. "The ring was found in Sicily, and I have understood from those who busy themselves with gems and sigils, that both the stone and intaglio are of virtue to make the wearer fortunate, especially at sea, and also to restore to him whatever he may have lost. But," he continued, smiling, "though I have worn it constantly since I quitted Greece, it has not made me altogether fortunate at sea, you perceive, unless I am to count escape from drowning as a sufficient proof of its virtue. It remains to be seen whether my lost chests will come to light; but to lose no chance of such a result, Messer, I will pray you only to hold the ring for a short space as pledge for a small sum far beneath its value, and I will redeem it as soon as I can dispose of certain other gems which are secured within my doublet, or indeed as soon as I can earn something by any scholarly employment, if I may be so fortunate as to meet with such."

"That may be seen, young man, if you will come with me," said Cennini. "My brother Pietro, who is a better judge of scholarship than I, will perhaps be able to supply you with a task that may test your capabilities. Meanwhile, take back your ring until I can hand you the necessary florins, and, if it please you, come along with me."

"Yes, yes," said Nello, "go with Messer Domenico; you cannot go in better company; he was born under the constellation that gives a man skill, riches, and integrity, whatever that constellation may be, which is of the less consequence because babies can't choose their own horoscopes, and, indeed, if they could, there might be an inconvenient rush of babies at particular epochs. Besides, our phœnix, the incomparable Pico, has shown that your horoscopes are all a nonsensical dream,—which is the less troublesome opinion. *Addio! bel giovane!* don't forget to come back to me."

"No fear of that," said Tito, beckoning a farewell, as he turned round his bright face at the door. "You are to do me a great service,—that is the most positive security for your seeing me again."

"Say what thou wilt, Piero," said Nello, as the young stranger disappeared, "I shall never look at such an outside as that without taking it as a sign of a lovable nature. Why, thou wilt say next that Lionardo, whom thou art always raving about, ought to have made his Judas as beautiful as Saint John! But thou art as deaf as the top of Mount Morello with that accursed tow in thy ears. Well, well: I'll get a little more of this young man's history from him before I take him to Bardo Bardi."

CHAPTER V

THE BLIND SCHOLAR AND HIS DAUGHTER

THE Via de' Bardi, a street noted in the history of Florence, lies in Oltrarno, or that portion of the city which clothes the southern bank of the river. It extends from the Ponte Vecchio to the Piazza de' Mozzi at the head of the Ponte alle Grazie; its right-hand line of houses and walls being backed by the rather steep ascent which in the fifteenth century was known as the Hill of Bogoli, the famous stone-quarry whence the city got its pavement—of dangerously unstable consistence when penetrated by rains; its left-hand buildings flanking the river and making on their northern side a length of quaint, irregularly pierced façade, of which the waters give a softened loving reflection as the sun begins to decline towards the western heights. But quaint as these buildings are, some of them seem to the historical memory a too modern substitute for the famous houses of the Bardi family, destroyed by popular rage in the middle of the fourteenth century.

They were a proud and energetic stock, these Bardi; conspicuous among those who clutched the sword in the earliest world-famous quarrels of Florentines with Florentines, when the narrow streets were darkened with the high towers of the nobles, and when the old tutelar god Mars, as he saw the gutters reddened with neighbours' blood, might well have smiled at the centuries of lip-service paid to his rival, the Baptist. But the Bardi hands were of the sort that not only clutch the sword-hilt with vigour, but love the more delicate pleasure of fingering minted metal: they were matched, too, with true Florentine eyes, capable of discerning that power was to be won by other means than by rending and riving, and by the middle of the fourteenth century we find them risen from their original condition of *popolani* to be possessors, by purchase, of lands and strongholds, and the feudal dignity of Counts of Vernio, disturbing to the jealousy of their republican fellow-citizens. These lordly purchases are explained by our seeing the Bardi disastrously signalized only a few years later as standing in the very front of European commerce—the Christian Rothschilds of that time—undertaking to furnish specie for the wars of our Edward the Third, and having revenues "in kind" made over to them; especially in wool, most precious of freights for Florentine galleys. Their august debtor left them with an august deficit, and alarmed Sicilian creditors made a too sudden demand for the payment of deposits, causing a ruinous shock to the credit of the Bardi and of associated houses, which was felt as a commercial calamity along all the coasts of the Mediterranean. But, like more modern bankrupts, they did not, for all that, hide their heads in humiliation; on the contrary, they seemed to have held them higher than ever, and to have been among the most arrogant of those grandees who under certain noteworthy circumstances, open to all who will read the honest pages of Giovanni Villani, drew upon themselves the exasperation of the armed people in 1343. The Bardi, who had made themselves fast in their street between the two bridges, kept these narrow inlets, like panthers at bay, against the oncoming gonfalons of the people, and were only made to give way by an assault from the hill behind them. Their houses by the river, to the number of twenty-two (*palagi e case grandi*), were sacked and burned, and many among the chief of those who bore the Bardi name were driven from the city. But an old Florentine family was many-rooted, and we find the Bardi maintaining importance and rising again and again to the surface of Florentine affairs in a more or less creditable manner, implying an untold family history that would have included even more vicissitudes and contrasts of dignity and disgrace, of wealth and poverty, than are usually seen on the background of wide kinship. But the Bardi never resumed their proprietorship in the old street on the banks of the river, which in 1492 had long been associated with other names of mark, and especially with the Neri, who possessed a considerable range of houses on the side towards the hill. In one of these Neri houses there lived, however, a descendant of the Bardi, and of that very branch which a century and a half before had become Counts of Vernio: a descendant who had inherited the old family pride and energy, the old love of pre-eminence, the old desire to leave a lasting track of his footsteps on the fast-whirling earth. But the family passions lived on in him under altered conditions: this descendant of the Bardi was not a man swift in street warfare, or one who loved to play the signor, fortifying strongholds and asserting the right to hang vassals, or a merchant and usurer of keen daring, who delighted in the generalship of wide commercial schemes: he was a man with a deep-veined hand cramped by much copying of manuscripts, who ate sparing dinners, and wore threadbare clothes, at first from choice and at last from necessity; who sat among his books and his marble fragments of the past, and saw them only by the light of those far-off younger days which still shone in his memory: he was a moneyless, blind old scholar—the Bardo de' Bardi to whom Nello, the barber, had promised to introduce the young Greek, Tito Melema.

The house in which Bardo lived was situated on the side of the street nearest the hill, and was one of those large sombre masses of stone building pierced by comparatively small windows, and surmounted by what may be called a roofed terrace or loggia, of which there are many examples still to be seen in the venerable city. Grim doors, with conspicuous scrolled hinges, having high up on each side of them a small window defended by iron bars, opened on a groined entrance-court, empty of everything but a massive lamp-iron suspended from the centre of the groin. A smaller grim door on the left hand admitted to the stone staircase and the rooms on the ground floor. These last were used as a warehouse by the proprietor; so was the first floor; and both were filled with precious stores, destined to be carried, some perhaps to the banks of the Scheldt, some to the shores of Africa, some to the Isles of the Ægean or to the banks of the Euxine. Maso, the old serving-man, when he returned from the Mercato with the stock of cheap vegetables, had to make his slow way up to the second story before he reached the door of his master, Bardo, through which we are about to enter only a few mornings after Nello's conversation with the Greek.

We follow Maso across the antechamber to the door on the left hand, through which we pass as he opens it. He merely looks in and nods, while a clear young voice says, "Ah, you are come back, Maso. It is well. We have wanted nothing."

The voice came from the farther end of a long, spacious room, surrounded with shelves, on which books and antiquities were arranged in scrupulous order. Here and there, on separate stands in front of the shelves, were placed a beautiful feminine torso; a headless statue, with an uplifted muscular arm wielding a bladeless sword; rounded, dimpled, infantine limbs severed from the trunk, inviting the lips to kiss the cold marble; some well-preserved Roman busts; and two or three vases from Magna Græcia. A large table in the centre was covered with antique bronze lamps and small vessels in dark pottery. The colour of these objects was chiefly pale or sombre; the vellum bindings, with their deep-ridged backs, gave little relief to the marble, livid with long burial; the once splendid patch of carpet at the farther end of the room had long been worn to dimness; the dark bronzes wanted sunlight upon them to bring out their tinge of green, and the sun was not yet high enough to send gleams of brightness through the narrow windows that looked on the Via de' Bardi.

The only spot of bright colour in the room was made by the hair of a tall maiden of seventeen or eighteen, who was standing before a carved *leggio,* or reading-desk, such as is often seen in the choirs of Italian churches. The hair was of a reddish gold colour, enriched by an unbroken small ripple such as may be seen in the sunset clouds on grandest autumnal evenings. It was confined by a black fillet above her small ears, from which it rippled forward again, and made a natural veil for her neck above her square-cut gown of black *rascia,* or serge. Her eyes were bent on a large volume placed before her: one long white hand rested on the reading-desk, and the other clasped the back of her father's chair.

The blind father sat with head uplifted and turned a little aside towards his daughter, as if he were looking at her. His delicate paleness, set off by the black velvet cap which surmounted his drooping white hair, made all the more perceptible the likeness between his aged features and those of the young maiden, whose cheeks were also without any tinge of the rose. There was the same refinement of brow and nostril in both, counterbalanced by a full though firm mouth and powerful chin, which gave an expression of proud tenacity and latent impetuousness: an expression carried out in the backward poise of the girl's head, and the grand line of her neck and shoulders. It was a type of face of which one could not venture to say whether it would inspire love or only that unwilling admiration which is mixed with dread: the question must be decided by the eyes, which often seem charged with a more direct message from the soul. But the eyes of the father had long been silent, and the eyes of the daughter were bent on the Latin pages of Politian's "Miscellanea," from which she was reading aloud at the eightieth chapter, to the following effect:—

"There was a certain nymph of Thebes named Chariclo, especially dear to Pallas; and this nymph was the mother of Teiresias. But once when in the heat of summer, Pallas, in company with Chariclo, was bathing her disrobed limbs in the Heliconian Hippocrene, it happened that Teiresias coming as a hunter to quench his thirst at the same fountain, inadvertently beheld Minerva unveiled, and immediately became blind. For it is declared in the Saturnian laws, that he who beholds the gods against their will, shall atone for it by a heavy penalty. . . . When Teiresias had fallen into this calamity, Pallas, moved by the tears of Chariclo, endowed him with prophecy and length of days, and even caused his prudence and wisdom to continue after he had entered among the shades, so that an oracle spake from his tomb; and she gave him a staff, wherewith, as by a guide, he might walk without stumbling. . . . And hence, Nonnus, in the fifth book of the 'Dionysiaca,' introduces Actæon exclaiming that he calls Teiresias happy, since, without dying, and with the loss of his eyesight merely, he had beheld Minerva unveiled, and thus, though blind, could forevermore carry her image in his soul."

At this point in the reading, the daughter's hand slipped from the back of the chair and met her father's, which he had that moment uplifted; but she had not looked round, and was going on, though with a voice a little altered by some suppressed feeling, to read the Greek quotation from Nonnus, when the old man said,—

"Stay, Romola; reach me my own copy of Nonnus. It is a more correct copy than any in Poliziano's hands, for I made emendations in it which have not yet been communicated to any man. I finished it in 1477, when my sight was fast failing me."

Romola walked to the farther end of the room, with the queenly step which was the simple action of her tall, finely wrought frame, without the slightest conscious adjustment of herself.

"Is it in the right place, Romola?" asked Bardo, who was perpetually seeking the assurance that the outward fact continued to correspond with the image which lived to the minutest detail in his mind.

"Yes, father; at the west end of the room, on the third shelf from the bottom, behind the bust of Hadrian, above Apollonius Rhodius and Callimachus, and below Lucan and Silius Italicus."

As Romola said this, a fine ear would have detected in her clear voice and distinct utterance a faint suggestion of weariness struggling with habitual patience. But as she approached her father and saw his arms stretched out a little with nervous excitement to seize the volume, her hazel eyes filled with pity; she hastened to lay the book on his lap, and kneeled down by him, looking up at him as if she believed that the love in her face must surely make its way through the dark obstruction that shut out everything else. At that moment the doubtful attractiveness of Romola's face, in which pride and passion seemed to be quivering in the balance with native refinement and intelligence, was transfigured to the most lovable womanliness by mingled pity and affection: it was evident that the deepest fount of feeling within her had not yet wrought its way to the less changeful features, and only found its outlet through her eyes.

But the father, unconscious of that soft radiance, looked flushed and agitated as his hand explored the edges and back of the large book.

"The vellum is yellowed in these thirteen years, Romola?"

"Yes, father," said Romola, gently; "but your letters at the back are dark and plain still,—fine Roman letters; and the Greek character," she continued, laying the book open on her father's knee, "is more beautiful than that of any of your bought manuscripts."

"Assuredly, child," said Bardo, passing his finger across the page, as if he hoped to discriminate line and margin. "What hired amanuensis can be equal to the scribe who loves the words that grow under his hand, and to whom an error or indistinctness in the text is more painful than a sudden darkness or obstacle across his path? And even these mechanical printers who threaten to make learning a base and vulgar thing,— even they must depend on the manuscript over which we scholars have bent with that insight into the poet's meaning which is closely akin to the *mens divinior* of the poet himself, unless they would flood the world with grammatical falsities and inexplicable anomalies that would turn the very fountain of Parnassus into a deluge of poisonous mud. But find the passage in the fifth book to which Poliziano refers. I know it very well."

Seating herself on a low stool, close to her father's knee, Romola took the book on her lap and read the four verses containing the exclamation of Actæon.

"It is true, Romola," said Bardo, when she had finished; "it is a true conception of the poet; for what is that grosser, narrower light by which men behold merely the petty scene around them, compared with that far-stretching, lasting light which spreads over centuries of thought, and over the life of nations, and makes clear to us the minds of the immortals who have reaped the great harvest and left us to glean in their furrows? For me, Romola, even when I could see, it was with the great dead that I lived; while the living often seemed to me mere spectres,—shadows dispossessed of true feeling and intelligence; and unlike those Lamiæ to whom Poliziano, with that superficial ingenuity which I do not deny to him, compares our inquisitive Florentines, because they put on their eyes when they went abroad, and took them off when they got home again, I have returned from the converse of the streets as from a forgotten dream, and have sat down among my books, saying with Petrarca, the modern who is least unworthy to be named after the ancients, 'Libri medullitus delectant, colloquuntur, consulunt, et viva quadam nobis atque arguta familiaritate junguntur.' "

"And in one thing you are happier than your favourite Petrarca, father," said Romola, affectionately humouring the old man's disposition to dilate in this way; "for he used to look at his copy of Homer and think sadly that the Greek was a dead letter to him: so far he had the inward blindness that you feel is worse than your outward blindness."

"True, child; for I carry within me the fruits of that fervid study which I gave to the Greek tongue under the teaching of the younger Crisolora, and Filelfo, and Argiropulo; though that great work in which I had desired to gather, as into a firm web, all the threads that my research had laboriously disentangled, and which would have been the vintage of my life, was cut off by the failure of my sight and my want of a fitting coadjutor. For the sustained zeal and unconquerable patience demanded from those who would tread the unbeaten paths of knowledge are still less reconcilable with the wandering, vagrant propensity of the feminine mind than with the feeble powers of the feminine body."

"Father," said Romola, with a sudden flush and in an injured tone, "I read anything you wish me to read; and I will look out any passages for you, and make whatever notes you want."

Bardo shook his head, and smiled with a bitter sort of pity. "As well try to be a pentathlos and perform all the five feats of the palæstra with the limbs of a nymph. Have I forgotten thy fainting in the mere search for the references I needed to explain a single passage of Callimachus?"

"But, father, it was the weight of the books, and Maso can help me; it was not want of attention and patience."

Bardo shook his head again. "It is not mere bodily organs that I want: it is the sharp edge of a young mind to pierce the way for my somewhat blunted faculties. For blindness acts like a dam, sending the streams of thought backward along the already-travelled channels and hindering the course onward. If my son had not forsaken me, deluded by debasing fanatical dreams, worthy only of an energumen whose dwelling is among tombs, I might have gone on and seen my path broadening to the end of my life; for he was a youth of great promise. . . . But it has closed in now," the old man continued, after a short pause; "it has closed in now,—all but the narrow track he has left me to tread— alone, in my blindness."

Romola started from her seat, and carried away the large volume to its place again, stung too acutely by her father's last words to remain motionless as well as silent; and when she turned away from the shelf again, she remained standing at some distance from him, stretching her arms downward and clasping her fingers tightly as she looked with a sad dreariness in her young face at the lifeless objects around her,—the parchment backs, the unchanging mutilated marble, the bits of obsolete bronze and clay.

Bardo, though usually susceptible to Romola's movements and eager to trace them, was now too entirely preoccupied by the pain of rankling memories to notice her departure from his side.

"Yes," he went on, "with my son to aid me, I might have had my due share in the triumphs of this century: the names of the Bardi, father and son, might have been held reverently on the lips of scholars in the ages to come; not on account of frivolous verses or philosophical treatises, which are superfluous and presumptuous attempts to imitate the inimitable, such as allure vain men like Panhormita, and from which even the admirable Poggio did not keep himself sufficiently free; but because we should have given a lamp whereby men might have studied the supreme productions of the past. For why is a young man like Poliziano (who was not yet born when I was already held worthy to maintain a discussion with Thomas of Sarzana) to have a glorious memory as a commentator on the Pandects,—why is Ficino, whose Latin is an offence to me, and who wanders purblind among the superstitious fancies that marked the decline at once of art, literature, and philosophy, to descend to posterity as the very high-priest of Platonism; while I, who am more than their equal, have not effected anything but scattered work, which will be appropriated by other men? Why? but because my son, whom I had brought up to replenish my ripe learning with young enterprise, left me and all liberal pursuits that he might lash himself and howl at midnight with besotted friars,—that he might go wandering on pilgrimages befitting men who know of no past older than the missal and the crucifix?—left me when the night was already beginning to fall on me?"

In these last words the old man's voice, which had risen high in indignant protest, fell into a tone of reproach so tremulous and plaintive that Romola, turning her eyes again towards the blind aged face, felt her heart swell with forgiving pity. She seated herself by her father again, and placed her hand on his knee,—too proud to obtrude consolation in words that might seem like a vindication of her own value, yet wishing to comfort him by some sign of her presence.

"Yes, Romola," said Bardo, automatically letting his left hand, with its massive prophylactic rings, fall a little too heavily on the delicate blue-veined back of the girl's right, so that she bit her lip to prevent herself from starting. "If even Florence only is to remember me, it can but be on the same ground that it will remember Niccolò Niccoli,—because I forsook the vulgar pursuit of wealth in commerce that I might devote myself to collecting the precious remains of ancient art and wisdom, and leave them, after the example of the munificent Romans, for an everlasting possession to my fellow-citizens. But why do I say Florence only? If Florence remembers me, will not the world remember me? . . . Yet," added Bardo, after a short pause, his voice falling again into a saddened key, "Lorenzo's untimely death has raised a new difficulty. I had his promise—I should have had his bond—that my collection should always bear my name and should never be sold, though the harpies might clutch everything else; but there is enough for them— there is more than enough—and for thee, too, Romola, there will be enough. Besides, thou wilt marry; Bernardo reproaches me that I do not seek a fitting *parentado* for thee, and we will delay no longer, we will think about it."

"No, no, father; what could you do? Besides, it is useless: wait till some one seeks me," said Romola, hastily.

"Nay, my child, that is not the paternal duty. It was not so held by the ancients, and in this respect Florentines have not degenerated from their ancestral customs."

"But I will study diligently," said Romola, her eyes dilating with anxiety. "I will become as learned as Cassandra Fedele: I will try and be as useful to you as if I had been a boy, and then perhaps some great scholar will want to marry me, and will not mind about a dowry; and he will like to come and live with you, and he will be to you in place of my brother . . . and you will not be sorry that I was a daughter."

There was a rising sob in Romola's voice as she said the last words, which touched the fatherly fibre in Bardo. He stretched his hand upward a little in search of her golden hair, and as she placed her head under his hand, he gently stroked it, leaning towards her as if his eyes discerned some glimmer there.

"Nay, Romola mia, I said not so; if I have pronounced an anathema on a degenerate and ungrateful son, I said not that I could wish thee other than the sweet daughter thou hast been to me. For what son could have tended me so gently in the frequent sickness I have had of late? And even in learning thou art not, according to thy measure, contemptible. Something perhaps were to be wished in thy capacity of attention and memory, not incompatible even with the feminine mind. But as Calcondila bore testimony, when he aided me to teach thee, thou hast a ready apprehension, and even a wide-glancing intelligence. And thou hast a man's nobility of soul: thou hast never fretted me with thy petty desires as thy mother did. It is true, I have been careful to keep thee aloof from the debasing influence of thy own sex, with their sparrow-like frivolity and their enslaving superstition, except, indeed, from that of our cousin Brigida, who may well serve as a scarecrow and a warning. And though—since I agree with the divine Petrarca, when he declares, quoting the 'Aulularia' of Plautus, who again was indebted for the truth to the supreme Greek intellect, 'Optimam fœminam nullam esse, alia licet alia pejor sit,'—I cannot boast that thou art entirely lifted out of that lower category to which Nature assigned thee, nor even that in erudition thou art on a par with the more learned women of this age; thou art, nevertheless—yes, Romola mia," said the old man, his pedantry again melting into tenderness, "thou art my sweet daughter, and thy voice is as the lower notes of the flute, 'dulcis, durabilis, clara, pura, secans aëra et auribus sedens,' according to the choice words of Quintilian; and Bernardo tells me thou art fair, and thy hair is like the brightness of the morning, and indeed it seems to me that I discern some radiance from thee. Ah! I know how all else looks in this room, but thy form I only guess at. Thou art no longer the little woman six years old, that faded for me into darkness; thou art tall, and thy arm is but little below mine. Let us walk together."

The old man rose; and Romola, soothed by these beams of tenderness, looked happy again as she drew his arm within hers, and placed in his right hand the stick which rested at the side of his chair. While Bardo had been sitting, he had seemed hardly more than sixty: his face, though pale, had that refined texture in which wrinkles and lines are never deep; but now that he began to walk he looked as old as he really was,—rather more than seventy; for his tall spare frame had the student's stoop of the shoulders, and he stepped with the undecided gait of the blind.

"No, Romola," he said, pausing against the bust of Hadrian, and passing his stick from the right to the left that he might explore the familiar outline with a "seeing hand." "There will be nothing else to preserve my memory and carry down my name as a member of the great republic of letters,—nothing but my library and my collection of antiquities. And they are choice," continued Bardo, pressing the bust and speaking in a tone of insistence. "The collections of Niccolò, I know, were larger; but take any collection which is the work of a single man,—that of the great Boccaccio even,—mine will surpass it. That of Poggio was contemptible compared with mine. It will be a great gift to unborn scholars. And there is nothing else. For even if I were to yield to the wish of Aldo Manuzio when he sets up his press at Venice, and give him the aid of my annotated manuscripts, I know well what would be the result: some other scholar's name would stand on the titlepage of the edition,—some scholar who would have fed on my honey, and then declared in his preface that he had gathered it all himself fresh from Hymettus. Else, why have I refused the loan of many an annotated codex? why have I refused to make public any of my translations?— why? but because scholarship is a system of licensed robbery, and your man in scarlet and furred robe who sits in judgment on thieves, is him-self a thief of the thoughts and the fame that belong to his fellows. But against that robbery Bardo de' Bardi shall struggle,—though blind and forsaken, he shall struggle. I too have a right to be remembered,— as great a right as Pontanus or Merula, whose names will be foremost on the lips of posterity, because they sought patronage and found it; because they had tongues that could flatter, and blood that was used to be nourished from the client's basket. I have a right to be remembered."

The old man's voice had become at once loud and tremulous, and a pink flush overspread his proud, delicately cut features, while the hab-itually raised attitude of his head gave the idea that behind the curtain of his blindness he saw some imaginary high tribunal to which he was appealing against the injustice of Fame.

Romola was moved with sympathetic indignation, for in her nature too there lay the same large claims, and the same spirit of struggle against their denial. She tried to calm her father by a still prouder word than his.

"Nevertheless, father, it is a great gift of the gods to be born with a hatred and contempt of all injustice and meanness. Yours is a higher lot, never to have lied and truckled, than to have shared honours won by dishonour. There is strength in scorn, as there was in the martial fury by which men became insensible to wounds."

"It is well said, Romola. It is a Promethean word thou hast uttered," answered Bardo, after a little interval, in which he had begun to lean on his stick again, and to walk on. "And I indeed am not to be pierced by the shafts of Fortune. My armour is the *œs triplex* of a clear con-science, and a mind nourished by the precepts of philosophy. 'For men,' says Epictetus, 'are disturbed not by things themselves, but by their opinions or thoughts concerning those things.' And again, 'Whosoever will be free, let him not desire or dread that which it is in the power of others either to deny or inflict: otherwise, he is a slave.' And of all such gifts as are dependent on the caprice of fortune or of men, I have long ago learned to say, with Horace,—who, however, is too wavering in his philosophy, vacillating between the precepts of Zeno and the less worthy maxims of Epicurus, and attempting, as we say, 'duabus sellis sedere,' —concerning such accidents, I say, with the pregnant brevity of the poet,—

'Sunt qui non habeant, est qui non curat habere.'

He is referring to gems, and purple, and other insignia of wealth; but I may apply his words not less justly to the tributes men pay us with their lips and their pens, which are also matters of purchase, and often with base coin. Yes, *'inanis'*—hollow, empty—is the epithet justly bestowed on Fame."

They made the tour of the room in silence after this; but Bardo's lip-born maxims were as powerless over the passion which had been moving him, as if they had been written on parchment and hung round his neck in a sealed bag; and he presently broke forth again in a new tone of insistence.

"*Inanis?* yes, if it is a lying fame; but not if it is the just meed of labour and a great purpose. I claim my right: it is not fair that the work of my brain and my hands should not be a monument to me,—it is not just that my labour should bear the name of another man. It is but little to ask," the old man went on bitterly, "that my name should be over the door,—that men should own themselves debtors to the Bardi Library in Florence. They will speak coldly of me, perhaps: 'a diligent collector and transcriber,' they will say, 'and also of some critical ingenuity, but one who could hardly be conspicuous in an age so fruitful in illustrious scholars. Yet he merits our pity, for in the latter years of his life he was blind, and his only son, to whose education he had devoted his best years—' Nevertheless my name will be remembered, and men will honour me: not with the breath of flattery, purchased by mean bribes, but because I have laboured, and because my labours will remain. Debts! I know there are debts; and there is thy dowry, Romola, to be paid. But there must be enough—or, at least, there can lack but a small sum, such as the Signoria might well provide. And if Lorenzo had not died, all would have been secured and settled. But now—"

At this moment Maso opened the door, and advancing to his master, announced that Nello, the barber, had desired him to say that he was come with the Greek scholar whom he had asked leave to introduce.

"It is well," said the old man. "Bring them in."

Bardo, conscious that he looked more dependent when he was walking, liked always to be seated in the presence of strangers; and Romola, without needing to be told, conducted him to his chair. She was standing by him at her full height, in quiet majestic self-possession, when the visitors entered; and the most penetrating observer would hardly have divined that this proud pale face, at the slightest touch on the fibres of affection or pity, could become passionate with tenderness, or that this woman, who imposed a certain awe on those who approached her, was in a state of girlish simplicity and ignorance concerning the world outside her father's books.

CHAPTER VI

DAWNING HOPES

WHEN Maso opened the door again, and ushered in the two visitors, Nello, first making a deep reverence to Romola, gently pushed Tito before him, and advanced with him towards her father.

"Messer Bardo," he said, in a more measured and respectful tone than was usual with him, "I have the honour of presenting to you the Greek scholar, who has been eager to have speech of you, not less from the report I have made to him of your learning and your priceless collections, than because of the furtherance your patronage may give him under the transient need to which he has been reduced by shipwreck. His name is Tito Melema, at your service."

Romola's astonishment could hardly have been greater if the stranger had worn a panther-skin and carried a thyrsus; for the cunning barber had said nothing of the Greek's age or appearance; and among her father's scholarly visitors, she had hardly ever seen any but middle-aged or grey-headed men. There was only one masculine face, at once youthful and beautiful, the image of which remained deeply impressed on her mind: it was that of her brother, who long years ago had taken her on his knee, kissed her, and never come back again: a fair face, with sunny hair, like her own. But the habitual attitude of her mind towards strangers,—a proud self-dependence and determination to ask for nothing even by a smile,—confirmed in her by her father's complaints against the world's injustice, was like a snowy embankment hemming in the rush of admiring surprise. Tito's bright face showed its rich-tinted beauty without any rivalry of color above his black *sajo* or tunic reaching to the knees. It seemed like a wreath of spring, dropped suddenly in Romola's young but wintry life, which had inherited nothing but memories,—memories of a dead mother, of a lost brother, of a blind father's happier time,—memories of far-off light, love, and beauty, that lay embedded in dark mines of books, and could hardly give out their brightness again until they were kindled for her by the torch of some known joy. Nevertheless, she returned Tito's bow, made to her on entering, with the same pale proud face as ever; but as he approached, the snow melted, and when he ventured to look towards her again, while Nello was speaking, a pink flush overspread her face, to vanish again almost immediately, as if her imperious will had recalled it. Tito's glance, on the contrary, had that gentle, beseeching admiration in it which is the

most propitiating of appeals to a proud, shy woman, and is perhaps the
only atonement a man can make for being too handsome. The finished
fascination of his air came chiefly from the absence of demand and as-
sumption. It was that of a fleet, soft-coated, dark-eyed animal that delights you by not bounding away in indifference from you, and unexpectedly pillows its chin on your palm, and looks up at you desiring to
be stroked—as if it loved you.

"Messere, I give you welcome," said Bardo, with some condescension;
"misfortune wedded to learning, and especially to Greek learning, is a
letter of credit that should win the ear of every instructed Florentine;
for, as you are doubtless aware, since the period when your countryman,
Manuelo Crisolora, diffused the light of his teaching in the chief cities
of Italy, now nearly a century ago, no man is held worthy of the name
of scholar who has acquired merely the transplanted and derivative
literature of the Latins; rather, such inert students are stigmatized as
opici or barbarians according to the phrase of the Romans themselves,
who frankly replenished their urns at the fountain-head. I am, as you
perceive, and as Nello has doubtless forewarned you, totally blind,—
a calamity to which we Florentines are held especially liable, whether
owing to the cold winds which rush upon us in spring from the passes
of the Apennines, or to that sudden transition from the cool gloom of
our houses to the dazzling brightness of our summer sun, by which the
lippi are said to have been made so numerous among the ancient Romans; or, in fine, to some occult cause which eludes our superficial sur-
mises. But I pray you be seated: Nello, my friend, be seated."

Bardo paused until his fine ear had assured him that the visitors were
seating themselves, and that Romola was taking her usual chair at his
right hand. Then he said,—

"From what part of Greece do you come, Messere? I had thought
that your unhappy country had been almost exhausted of those sons
who could cherish in their minds any image of her original glory, though
indeed the barbarous Sultans have of late shown themselves not indisposed to ingraft on their wild stock the precious vine which their own
fierce bands have hewn down and trampled under foot. From what part
of Greece do you come?"

"I sailed last from Nauplia," said Tito; "but I have resided both at
Constantinople and Thessalonica, and have travelled in various parts
little visited by Western Christians since the triumph of the Turkish
arms. I should tell you, however, Messere, that I was not born in Greece,
but at Bari. I spent the first sixteen years of my life in Southern Italy
and Sicily."

While Tito was speaking, some emotion passed, like a breath on the
waters, across Bardo's delicate features; he leaned forward, put out his
right hand towards Romola, and turned his head as if about to speak
to her; but then, correcting himself, turned away again, and said in a
subdued voice,—

"Excuse me; is it not true—you are young?"

"I am three-and-twenty," said Tito.

"Ah," said Bardo, still in a tone of subdued excitement, "and you had, doubtless, a father who cared for your early instruction,—who, perhaps, was himself a scholar?"

There was a slight pause before Tito's answer came to the ear of Bardo; but for Romola and Nello it began with a slight shock that seemed to pass through him, and cause a momentary quivering of the lip; doubtless at the revival of a supremely painful remembrance.

"Yes," he replied; "at least a father by adoption. He was a Neapolitan, and of accomplished scholarship, both Latin and Greek. But," added Tito, after another slight pause, "he is lost to me,—was lost on a voyage he too rashly undertook to Delos."

Bardo sank backward again, too delicate to ask another question that might probe a sorrow which he divined to be recent. Romola, who knew well what were the fibres that Tito's voice had stirred in her father, felt that this new acquaintance had with wonderful suddenness got within the barrier that lay between them and the alien world. Nello, thinking that the evident check given to the conversation offered a graceful opportunity for relieving himself from silence, said,—

"In truth, it is as clear as Venetian glass that this fine young man has had the best training; for the two Cennini have set him to work at their Greek sheets already, and it seems to me they are not men to begin cutting before they have felt the edge of their tools; they tested him well beforehand, we may be sure, and if there are two things not to be hidden—love and a cough—I say there is a third, and that is ignorance, when once a man is obliged to do something besides wagging his head. The *tonsor inequalis* is inevitably betrayed when he takes the shears in his hand; is it not true, Messer Bardo? I speak after the fashion of a barber, but, as Luigi Pulci says,—

'Perdonimi s'io fallo: chi m'ascolta
Intenda il mio volgar col suo latino.' "

"Nay, my good Nello," said Bardo, with an air of friendly severity, "you are not altogether illiterate, and might doubtless have made a more respectable progress in learning if you had abstained somewhat from the *cicalata* and gossip of the street-corner, to which our Florentines are excessively addicted; but still more if you had not clogged your memory with those frivolous productions of which Luigi Pulci has furnished the most peccant exemplar,—a compendium of extravagances and incongruities the farthest removed from the models of a pure age, and resembling rather the *grylli*, or conceits of a period when mystic meaning was held a warrant for monstrosity of form; with this difference, that while the monstrosity is retained, the mystic meaning is absent; in contemptible contrast with the great poem of Virgil, who, as I long held with Filelfo, before Laudino had taken upon him to expound the same opinion, embodied the deepest lessons of philosophy in a graceful and well-knit fable. And I cannot but regard the multiplication of these babbling, lawless productions, albeit countenanced by the patronage, and in some degree the example of Lorenzo himself, otherwise a friend to true learning, as a sign that the glorious hopes of this century are to be quenched in gloom; nay, that they have been the delusive prologue to an age worse than that of iron,—the age of tinsel and gossamer, in which no thought has substance enough to be moulded into consistent and lasting form."

"Once more, pardon," said Nello, opening his palms outwards, and shrugging his shoulders; "I find myself knowing so many things in good Tuscan before I have time to think of the Latin for them; and Messer Luigi's rhymes are always slipping off the lips of my customers,—that is what corrupts me. And, indeed, talking of customers, I have left my shop and my reputation too long in the custody of my slow Sandro, who does not deserve even to be called a *tonsor inequalis,* but rather to be pronounced simply a bungler in the vulgar tongue. So with your permission, Messer Bardo, I will take my leave,—well understood that I am at your service whenever Maso calls upon me. It seems a thousand years till I dress and perfume the damigella's hair, which deserves to shine in the heavens as a constellation, though indeed it were a pity for it ever to go so far out of reach."

Three voices made a fugue of friendly farewells to Nello, as he retreated with a bow to Romola and a beck to Tito. The acute barber saw that the pretty youngster, who had crept into his liking by some strong magic, was well launched in Bardo's favourable regard; and satisfied that his introduction had not miscarried so far, he felt the propriety of retiring.

The little burst of wrath, called forth by Nello's unlucky quotation, had diverted Bardo's mind from the feelings which had just before been hemming in further speech, and he now addressed Tito again with his ordinary calmness.

"Ah! young man, you are happy in having been able to unite the advantages of travel with those of study, and you will be welcome among us as a bringer of fresh tidings from a land which has become sadly strange to us, except through the agents of a now restricted commerce and the reports of hasty pilgrims. For those days are in the far distance which I myself witnessed, when men like Aurispa and Guarino went out to Greece as to a storehouse, and came back laden with manuscripts which every scholar was eager to borrow,—and, be it owned with shame, not always willing to restore; nay, even the days when erudite Greeks flocked to our shores for a refuge, seem far off now,—farther off than the oncoming of my blindness. But doubtless, young man, research after the treasures of antiquity was not alien to the purpose of your travels?"

"Assuredly not," said Tito. "On the contrary, my companion—my father—was willing to risk his life in his zeal for the discovery of inscriptions and other traces of ancient civilization."

"And I trust there is a record of his researches and their results," said Bardo, eagerly, "since they must be even more precious than those of Ciriaco, which I have diligently availed myself of, though they are not always illuminated by adequate learning."

"There *was* such a record," said Tito; "but it was lost, like everything else, in the shipwreck I suffered below Ancona. The only record left is such as remains in our—in my memory."

"You must lose no time in committing it to paper, young man," said Bardo, with growing interest. "Doubtless you remember much, if you aided in transcription; for when I was your age, words wrought themselves into my mind as if they had been fixed by the tool of the graver; wherefore I constantly marvel at the capriciousness of my daughter's memory which grasps certain objects with tenacity, and lets fall all those minutiæ whereon depends accuracy, the very soul of scholarship. But I apprehend no such danger with you, young man, if your will has seconded the advantages of your training."

When Bardo made this reference to his daughter, Tito ventured to turn his eyes towards her, and at the accusation against her memory his face broke into its brightest smile, which was reflected as inevitably as sudden sunbeams in Romola's. Conceive the soothing delight of that smile to her! Romola had never dreamed that there was a scholar in the world who would smile at a deficiency for which she was constantly made to feel herself a culprit. It was like the dawn of a new sense to her, —the sense of comradeship. They did not look away from each other immediately, as if the smile had been a stolen one; they looked and smiled with frank enjoyment.

"She is not really so cold and proud," thought Tito.

"Does *he* forget too, I wonder?" thought Romola. "Yet I hope not, else he will vex my father."

But Tito was obliged to turn away, and answer Bardo's question.

"I have had much practice in transcription," he said; "but in the case of inscriptions copied in memorable scenes, rendered doubly impressive by the sense of risk and adventure, it may have happened that my retention of written characters has been weakened. On the plain of the Eurotas, or among the gigantic stones of Mycenæ and Tyrins—especially when the fear of the Turk hovers over one like a vulture—the mind wanders even though the hand writes faithfully what the eye dictates. But something doubtless I have retained," added Tito, with a modesty which was not false, though he was conscious that it was politic; "something that might be of service if illustrated and corrected by a wider learning than my own."

"That is well spoken, young man," said Bardo, delighted. "And I will not withhold from you such aid as I can give, if you like to communicate with me concerning your recollections. I foresee a work which will be a useful supplement to the 'Isolario' of Christoforo Buondelmonte, and which may take rank with the 'Itineraria' of Ciriaco and the admirable Ambrogio Traversari. But we must prepare ourselves for calumny, young man," Bardo went on with energy, as if the work were already growing so fast that the time of trial was near; "if your book contains novelties you will be charged with forgery; if my elucidations should clash with any principles of interpretation adopted by another scholar, our personal characters will be attacked, we shall be impeached with foul actions; you must prepare yourself to be told that your mother was a fishwoman, and that your father was a renegade priest or a hanged malefactor. I myself, for having shown error in a single proposition, had an invective written against me wherein I was taxed with treachery, fraud, indecency, and even hideous crimes. Such, my young friend,—such are the flowers with which the glorious path of scholarship is strewed! But tell me, then: I have learned much concerning Byzantium and Thessalonica long ago from Demetrio Calcondila, who has but lately departed from Florence; but you, it seems, have visited less familiar scenes?"

"Yes; we made what I may call a pilgrimage full of danger, for the sake of visiting places which have almost died out of the memory of the West, for they lie away from the track of pilgrims; and my father used to say that scholars themselves hardly imagine them to have any existence out of books. He was of opinion that a new and more glorious era would open for learning when men should begin to look for their commentaries on the ancient writers in the remains of cities and temples, nay, in the paths of the rivers, and on the face of the valleys and the mountains."

"Ah!" said Bardo, fervidly, "your father, then, was not a common man. Was he fortunate, may I ask? Had he many friends?" These last words were uttered in a tone charged with meaning.

"No; he made enemies,—chiefly, I believe, by a certain impetuous candour; and they hindered his advancement, so that he lived in obscurity. And he would never stoop to conciliate: he could never forget an injury."

"Ah!" said Bardo again, with a long, deep intonation.

"Among our hazardous expeditions," continued Tito, willing to prevent further questions on a point so personal, "I remember with particular vividness a hastily snatched visit to Athens. Our hurry, and the double danger of being seized as prisoners by the Turks, and of our galley raising anchor before we could return, made it seem like a fevered vision of the night,—the wide plain, the girdling mountains, the ruined porticos and columns, either standing far aloof, as if receding from our hurried footsteps, or else jammed in confusedly among the dwellings of Christians degraded into servitude, or among the forts and turrets of their Moslem conquerors, who have their stronghold on the Acropolis."

"You fill me with surprise," said Bardo. "Athens, then, is not utterly destroyed and swept away, as I had imagined?"

"No wonder you should be under that mistake, for few even of the Greeks themselves, who live beyond the mountain boundary of Attica, know anything about the present condition of Athens, or *Setine*, as the sailors call it. I remember, as we were rounding the promontory of Sunium, the Greek pilot we had on board our Venetian galley pointed to the mighty columns that stand on the summit of the rock,—the remains, as you know well, of the great temple erected to the goddess Athena, who looked down from that high shrine with triumph at her conquered rival Poseidon;—well, our Greek pilot, pointing to those columns, said, 'That was the school of the great philosopher Aristotle.' And at Athens itself, the monk who acted as our guide in the hasty view we snatched, insisted most on showing us the spot where St. Philip baptized the Ethiopian eunuch, or some such legend."

"Talk not of monks and their legends, young man!" said Bardo, interrupting Tito impetuously. "It is enough to overlay human hope and enterprise with an eternal frost, to think that the ground which was trodden by philosophers and poets is crawled over by those insect-swarms of besotted fanatics or howling hypocrites."

"*Perdio*, I have no affection for them," said Tito, with a shrug; "servitude agrees well with a religion like theirs, which lies in the renunciation of all that makes life precious to other men. And they carry the yoke that befits them: their matin chant is drowned by the voice of the muezzin, who, from the gallery of the high tower on the Acropolis, calls every Mussulman to his prayers. That tower springs from the Parthenon itself; and every time we paused and directed our eyes toward it, our guide set up a wail, that a temple which had once been won from the diabolical uses of the Pagans to become the temple of another virgin than Pallas—the Virgin-Mother of God—was now again perverted to the accursed ends of the Moslem. It was the sight of those walls of the Acropolis, which disclosed themselves in the distance as we leaned over the side of our galley when it was forced by contrary winds to anchor in the Piræus, that fired my father's mind with the determination to see Athens at all risks, and in spite of the sailors' warnings that if we lingered till a change of wind, they would depart without us: but, after all, it was impossible for us to venture near the Acropolis, for the sight of men eager in examining 'old stones' raised the suspicion that we were Venetian spies, and we had to hurry back to the harbour."

"We will talk more of these things," said Bardo, eagerly. "You must recall everything, to the minutest trace left in your memory. You will win the gratitude of after-times by leaving a record of the aspect Greece bore while yet the barbarians had not swept away every trace of the structures that Pausanias and Pliny described: you will take those great writers as your models; and such contribution of criticism and suggestion as my riper mind can supply shall not be wanting to you. There will be much to tell; for you have travelled, you said, in the Peloponnesus?"

"Yes; and in Bœotia also: I have rested in the groves of Helicon, and tasted of the fountain Hippocrene. But on every memorable spot in Greece conquest after conquest has set its seal, till there is a confusion of ownership even in ruins, that only close study and comparison could unravel. High over every fastness, from the plains of Lacedæmon to the

Straits of Thermopylæ, there towers some huge Frankish fortress, once
inhabited by a French or Italian marquis, now either abandoned or held
by Turkish bands."

"Stay!" cried Bardo, whose mind was now too thoroughly preoccupied
by the idea of the future book to attend to Tito's further narration.
"Do you think of writing in Latin or Greek? Doubtless Greek is the
more ready clothing for your thoughts, and it is the nobler language.
But, on the other hand, Latin is the tongue in which we shall measure
ourselves with the larger and more famous number of modern rivals.
And if you are less at ease in it, I will aid you,—yes, I will spend on
you that long-accumulated study which was to have been thrown into
the channel of another work,—a work in which I myself was to have
had a helpmate."

Bardo paused a moment, and then added,—

"But who knows whether that work may not be executed yet? For
you, too, young man, have been brought up by a father who poured into
your mind all the long-gathered stream of his knowledge and experience.
Our aid might be mutual."

Romola, who had watched her father's growing excitement, and
divined well the invisible currents of feeling that determined every question and remark, felt herself in a glow of strange anxiety: she turned
her eyes on Tito continually, to watch the impression her father's words
made on him, afraid lest he should be inclined to dispel these visions
of co-operation which were lighting up her father's face with a new hope.
But no! He looked so bright and gentle: he must feel, as she did, that
in this eagerness of blind age there was piteousness enough to call forth
inexhaustible patience. How much more strongly he would feel this if
he knew about her brother! A girl of eighteen imagines the feelings behind the face that has moved her with its sympathetic youth, as easily
as primitive people imagined the humours of the gods in fair weather:
what is she to believe in, if not in this vision woven from within?

And Tito was really very far from feeling impatient. He delighted in
sitting there with the sense that Romola's attention was fixed on him,
and that he could occasionally look at her. He was pleased that Bardo
should take an interest in him; and he did not dwell with enough seriousness on the prospect of the work in which he was to be aided, to feel
moved by it to anything else than that easy good-humoured acquiescence
which was natural to him.

"I shall be proud and happy," he said, in answer to Bardo's last
words, "if my services can be held a meet offering to the matured scholarship of Messere. But doubtless"—here he looked towards Romola—
"the lovely damigella, your daughter, makes all other aid superfluous;
for I have learned from Nello that she has been nourished on the highest studies from her earliest years."

"You are mistaken," said Romola; "I am by no means sufficient to
my father: I have not the gifts that are necessary for scholarship."

Romola did not make this self-depreciatory statement in a tone of anxious humility, but with a proud gravity.

"Nay, my Romola," said her father, not willing that the stranger should have too low a conception of his daughter's powers; "thou art not destitute of gifts; rather, thou art endowed beyond the measure of women; but thou hast withal the woman's delicate frame, which ever craves repose and variety, and so begets a wandering imagination. My daughter"—turning to Tito—"has been very precious to me, filling up to the best of her power the place of a son. For I had once a son—"

Bardo checked himself: he did not wish to assume an attitude of complaint in the presence of a stranger, and he remembered that this young man, in whom he had unexpectedly become so much interested, was still a stranger, towards whom it became him rather to keep the position of a patron. His pride was roused to double activity by the fear that he had forgotten his dignity.

"But," he resumed, in his original tone of condescension, "we are departing from what I believe is to you the most important business. Nello informed me that you had certain gems which you would fain dispose of, and that you desired a passport to some man of wealth and taste who would be likely to become a purchaser."

"It is true; for, though I have obtained employment as a corrector with the Cennini, my payment leaves little margin beyond the provision of necessaries, and would leave less but that my good friend Nello insists on my hiring a lodging from him, and saying nothing about the rent till better days."

"Nello is a good-hearted prodigal," said Bardo; "and though, with that ready ear and ready tongue of his, he is too much like the ill-famed Margites,—knowing many things and knowing them all badly, as I hinted to him but now,—he is nevertheless 'abnormis sapiens,' after the manner of our born Florentines. But have you the gems with you? I would willingly know what they are—yet it is useless; no, it might only deepen regret. I cannot add to my store."

"I have one or two intaglios of much beauty," said Tito, proceeding to draw from his wallet a small case.

But Romola no sooner saw the movement than she looked at him with significant gravity, and placed her finger on her lips,

"Con viso che tacendo dicea, Taci."

If Bardo were made aware that the gems were within reach, she knew well he would want a minute description of them, and it would become pain to him that they should go away from him, even if he did not insist on some device for purchasing them in spite of poverty. But she had no sooner made this sign than she felt rather guilty and ashamed at having virtually confessed a weakness of her father's to a stranger. It seemed that she was destined to a sudden confidence and familiarity with this young Greek, strangely at variance with her deep-seated pride and reserve; and this consciousness again brought the unwonted colour to her cheeks.

Tito understood her look and sign, and immediately withdrew his hand from the case, saying in a careless tone, so as to make it appear that he was merely following up his last words: "But they are usually in the keeping of Messer Domenico Cennini, who has strong and safe places for these things. He estimates them as worth at least five hundred ducats."

"Ah, then, they are fine intagli," said Bardo. "Five hundred ducats! Ah, more than a man's ransom!"

Tito gave a slight, almost imperceptible start, and opened his long dark eyes with questioning surprise at Bardo's blind face, as if his words—a mere phrase of common parlance at a time when men were often being ransomed from slavery or imprisonment—had had some special meaning for him. But the next moment he looked towards Romola, as if her eyes must be her father's interpreters. She, intensely preoccupied with what related to her father, imagined that Tito was looking to her again for some guidance, and immediately spoke.

"Alessandra Scala delights in gems, you know, father; she calls them her winter flowers; and the Segretario would be almost sure to buy any gems that she wished for. Besides, he himself sets great store by rings and sigils, which he wears as a defence against pains in the joints."

"It is true," said Bardo. "Bartolommeo has overmuch confidence in the efficacy of gems,—a confidence wider than what is sanctioned by Pliny, who clearly shows that he regards many beliefs of that sort as idle superstitions; though not to the utter denial of medicinal virtues in gems. Wherefore I myself, as you observe, young man, wear certain rings, which the discreet Camillo Leonardi prescribed to me by letter when two years ago I had a certain infirmity of sudden numbness. But thou hast spoken well, Romola. I will dictate a letter to Bartolommeo, which Maso shall carry. But it were well that Messere should notify to thee what the gems are, together with the intagli they bear, as a warrant to Bartolommeo that they will be worthy of his attention."

"Nay, father," said Romola, whose dread lest a paroxysm of the collector's mania should seize her father gave her the courage to resist his proposal. "Your word will be sufficient that Messere is a scholar and has travelled much. The Segretario will need no further inducement to receive him."

"True, child," said Bardo, touched on a chord that was sure to respond. "I have no need to add proofs and arguments in confirmation of my word to Bartolommeo. And I doubt not that this young man's presence is in accord with the tones of his voice, so that, the door being once opened, he will be his own best advocate."

Bardo paused a few moments, but his silence was evidently charged with some idea that he was hesitating to express, for he once leaned forward a little as if he were going to speak, then turned his head aside towards Romola and sank backward again. At last, as if he had made up his mind, he said in a tone which might have become a prince giving the courteous signal of dismissal,—

"I am somewhat fatigued this morning, and shall prefer seeing you again to-morrow, when I shall be able to give you the secretary's answer, authorizing you to present yourself to him at some given time. But before you go"—here the old man, in spite of himself, fell into a more faltering tone,—"you will perhaps permit me to touch your hand? It is long since I touched the hand of a young man."

Bardo had stretched out his aged white hand, and Tito immediately placed his dark but delicate and supple fingers within it. Bardo's cramped fingers closed over them, and he held them for a few minutes in silence. Then he said,—

"Romola, has this young man the same complexion as thy brother,— fair and pale?"

"No, father," Romola answered, with determined composure, though her heart began to beat violently with mingled emotions. "The hair of Messere is dark,—his complexion is dark." Inwardly she said, "Will he mind it? will it be disagreeable? No; he looks so gentle and good-natured." Then aloud again,—

"Would Messere permit my father to touch his hair and face?"

Her eyes inevitably made a timid entreating appeal while she asked this, and Tito's met them with soft brightness as he said, "Assuredly;" and, leaning forward, raised Bardo's hand to his curls with a readiness of assent which was the greater relief to her because it was unaccompanied by any sign of embarrassment.

Bardo passed his hand again and again over the long curls and grasped them a little, as if their spiral resistance made his inward vision clearer; then he passed his hand over the brow and cheek, tracing the profile with the edge of his palm and fourth finger, and letting the breadth of his hand repose on the rich oval of the cheek.

"Ah!" he said, as his hand glided from the face and rested on the young man's shoulder. "He must be very unlike thy brother, Romola, and it is the better. You see no visions, I trust, my young friend?"

At this moment the door opened, and there entered, unannounced, a tall elderly man in a handsome black silk lucco, who, unwinding his becchetto from his neck and taking off his cap, disclosed a head as white as Bardo's. He cast a keen glance of surprise at the group before him,— the young stranger leaning in that filial attitude, while Bardo's hand rested on his shoulder, and Romola sitting near with eyes dilated by anxiety and agitation. But there was an instantaneous change: Bardo let fall his hand, Tito raised himself from his stooping posture, and Romola rose to meet the visitor with an alacrity which implied all the greater intimacy because it was unaccompanied by any smile.

"Well, god-daughter," said the stately man, as he touched Romola's shoulder; "Maso said you had a visitor, but I came in nevertheless."

"It is thou, Bernardo," said Bardo. "Thou art come at a fortunate moment. This, young man," he continued, while Tito rose and bowed, "is one of the chief citizens of Florence, Messer Bernardo del Nero, my oldest, I had almost said my only friend,—whose good opinion, if you can win it, may carry you far. He is but three-and-twenty, Bernardo, yet he can doubtless tell thee much which thou wilt care to hear; for though a scholar, he has already travelled far, and looked on other things besides the manuscripts for which thou hast too light an esteem."

"Ah, a Greek as I augur," said Bernardo, returning Tito's reverence but slightly, and surveying him with that sort of glance which seems almost to cut like fine steel. "Newly arrived in Florence, it appears. The name of Messere—or part of it, for it is doubtless a long one?"

"On the contrary," said Tito, with perfect good-humour, "it is most modestly free from polysyllabic pomp. My name is Tito Melema."

"Truly?" said Bernardo, rather scornfully, as he took a seat; "I had expected it to be at least as long as the name of a city, a river, a province, and an empire all put together. We Florentines mostly use names as we do prawns, and strip them of all flourishes before we trust them to our throats."

"Well, Bardo," he continued, as if the stranger were not worth further notice, and changing his tone of sarcastic suspicion for one of sadness, "we have buried him."

"Ah!" replied Bardo, with corresponding sadness, "and a new epoch has come for Florence,—a dark one, I fear. Lorenzo has left behind him an inheritance that is but like the alchemist's laboratory when the wisdom of the alchemist is gone."

"Not altogether so," said Bernardo. "Piero de' Medici has abundant intelligence; his faults are only the faults of hot blood. I love the lad,—lad he will always be to me, as I have always been 'little father' to him."

"Yet all who want a new order of things are likely to conceive new hopes," said Bardo. "We shall have the old strife of parties, I fear."

"If we could have a new order of things that was something else than knocking down one coat of arms to put up another," said Bernardo, "I should be ready to say, 'I belong to no party: I am a Florentine.' But as long as parties are in question, I am a Medicean and will be a Medicean till I die, I am of the same mind as Farinata degli Uberti: if any man asks me what is meant by siding with a party, I say, as he did, 'To wish ill or well, for the sake of past wrongs or kindnesses.' "

During this short dialogue Tito had been standing, and now took his leave.

"But come again at the same hour to-morrow," said Bardo, graciously, before Tito left the room, "that I may give you Bartolommeo's answer."

"From what quarter of the sky has this pretty Greek youngster alighted so close to thy chair, Bardo?" said Bernardo del Nero, as the door closed. He spoke with dry emphasis, evidently intended to convey something more to Bardo than was implied by the mere words.

"He is a scholar who has been shipwrecked and has saved a few gems, for which he wants to find a purchaser. I am going to send him to Bartolommeo Scala, for thou knowest it were more prudent in me to abstain from further purchases."

Bernardo shrugged his shoulders and said, "Romola, wilt thou see if my servant is without? I ordered him to wait for me here." Then, when Romola was at a sufficient distance, he leaned forward and said to Bardo in a low, emphatic tone,—

"Remember, Bardo, thou hast a rare gem of thy own; take care no one gets it who is not likely to pay a worthy price. That pretty Greek has a lithe sleekness about him, that seems marvellously fitted for slipping easily into any nest he fixes his mind on."

Bardo was startled: the association of Tito with the image of his lost son had excluded instead of suggesting the thought of Romola. But almost immediately there seemed to be a reaction which made him grasp the warning as if it had been a hope.

"But why not, Bernardo? If the young man approved himself worthy —he is a scholar—and—and there would be no difficulty about the dowry, which always makes thee gloomy."

CHAPTER VII

A LEARNED SQUABBLE

BARTOLOMMEO SCALA, secretary of the Florentine Republic, on whom Tito Melema had been thus led to anchor his hopes, lived in a handsome palace close to the Porta Pinti, now known as the Casa Gherardesca. His arms—an azure ladder transverse on a golden field, with the motto *Gradatim* placed over the entrance—told all comers that the miller's son held his ascent to honours by his own efforts a fact to be proclaimed without wincing. The secretary was a vain and pompous man, but he was also an honest one: he was sincerely convinced of his own merit, and could see no reason for feigning. The topmost round of his azure ladder had been reached by this time: he had held his secretaryship these twenty years,—had long since made his orations on the *ringhiera,* or platform of the Old Palace, as the custom was, in the presence of princely visitors, while Marzocco, the republican lion, wore his gold crown on the occasion, and all the people cried, "Viva Messer Bartolommeo!"—had been on an embassy to Rome, and had there been made titular Senator, Apostolical Secretary, Knight of the Golden Spur; and had, eight years ago, been Gonfaloniere,—last goal of the Florentine citizen's ambition. Meantime he had got richer and richer, and more and more gouty, after the manner of successful mortality; and the Knight of the Golden Spur had often to sit with helpless cushioned heel under the handsome loggia he had built for himself, overlooking the spacious gardens and lawn at the back of his palace.

He was in this position on the day when he had granted the desired interview to Tito Melema. The May afternoon sun was on the flowers and the grass beyond the pleasant shade of the loggia; the too stately silk lucco was cast aside, and the light loose mantle was thrown over his tunic; his beautiful daughter Alessandra and her husband, the Greek soldier-poet Marullo, were seated on one side of him; on the other, two friends not oppressively illustrious, and therefore the better listeners. Yet, to say nothing of the gout, Messer Bartolommeo's felicity was far from perfect; it was embittered by the contents of certain papers that lay before him, consisting chiefly of a correspondence between himself and Politian. It was a human foible at that period (incredible as it may seem) to recite quarrels, and favour scholarly visitors with the communication of an entire and lengthy correspondence; and this was neither the first nor the second time that Scala had asked the candid opinion of his friends as to the balance of right and wrong in some half-score Latin letters between himself and Politian, all springing out of certain epigrams written in the most playful tone in the world. It was the story of a very typical and pretty quarrel, in which we are interested, because it supplied precisely that thistle of hatred necessary, according to Nello, as a stimulus to the sluggish paces of the cautious steed, Friendship.

Politian, having been a rejected pretender to the love and the hand of Scala's daughter, kept a very sharp and learned tooth in readiness against the too prosperous and presumptuous secretary, who had declined the greatest scholar of the age for a son-in-law. Scala was a meritorious public servant, and moreover a lucky man,—naturally exasperating to an offended scholar; but then—oh, beautiful balance of things! —he had an itch for authorship, and was a bad writer—one of those excellent people who, sitting in gouty slippers, "penned poetical trifles" entirely for their own amusement, without any view to an audience, and consequently sent them to their friends in letters, which were the literary periodicals of the fifteenth century. Now Scala had abundance of friends who were ready to praise his writings,—friends like Ficino and Landino,—amiable browsers in the Medicean park along with himself, —who found his Latin prose style elegant and masculine; and the terrible Joseph Scaliger, who was to pronounce him totally ignorant of Latinity, was at a comfortable distance in the next century. But when was the fatal coquetry inherent in superfluous authorship ever quite contented with the ready praise of friends? That critical supercilious Politian—a fellow-browser, who was far from amiable—must be made aware that the solid secretary showed, in his leisure hours, a pleasant fertility in verses, which indicated pretty clearly how much he might do in that way if he were not a man of affairs.

Ineffable moment! when the man you secretly hate sends you a Latin epigram with a false gender,—hendeca-syllables with a questionable elision, at least a toe too much,—attempts at poetic figures which are manifest solecisms. That moment had come to Politian: the secretary had put forth his soft head from the official shell, and the terrible lurking crab was down upon him. Politian had used the freedom of a friend, and pleasantly, in the form of a Latin epigram, corrected the mistake of Scala in making the *culex* (an insect too well known on the banks of the Arno) of the inferior or feminine gender. Scala replied by a bad joke, in suitable Latin verses, referring to Politian's unsuccessful suit. Better and better. Politian found the verses very pretty and highly facetious: the more was the pity that they were seriously incorrect, and inasmuch as Scala had alleged that he had written them in imitation of a Greek epigram, Politian, being on such friendly terms, would enclose a Greek epigram of his own, on the same interesting insect,—not, we may presume, out of any wish to humble Scala, but rather to instruct him; said epigram containing a lively conceit about Venus, Cupid, and the *culex,* of a kind much tasted at that period, founded partly on the zoölogical fact, that the gnat, like Venus, was born from the waters. Scala, in reply, begged to say that his verses were never intended for a scholar with such delicate olfactories as Politian, nearest of all living men to the perfection of the ancients, and of a taste so fastidious that sturgeon itself must seem insipid to him; defended his own verses, nevertheless, though indeed they were written hastily, without correction, and intended as an agreeable distraction during the summer heat to himself and such friends as were satisfied with mediocrity, he, Scala, not being like some other people, who courted publicity through the booksellers. For the rest, he had barely enough Greek to make out the sense of the epigram so graciously sent him, to say nothing of tasting its elegances; but—the epigram was Politian's: what more need be said? Still, by way of postscript, he feared that his incomparable friend's comparison of the gnat to Venus, on account of its origin from the waters, was in many ways ticklish. On the one hand, Venus might be offended; and on the other, unless the poet intended an illusion to the doctrine of Thales, that cold and damp origin seemed doubtful to Scala in the case of a creature so fond of warmth; a fish were perhaps the better comparison, or, when the power of flying was in question, an eagle, or indeed, when the darkness was taken into consideration, a bat or an owl were a less obscure and more apposite parallel, etc., etc. Here was a great opportunity for Politian. He was not aware, he wrote, that when he had Scala's verses placed before him, there was any question of sturgeon, but rather of frogs and gudgeons; made short work with Scala's defence of his own Latin, and mangled him terribly on the score of the stupid criticisms he had ventured on the Greek epigram kindly forwarded to him as a model. Wretched cavils, indeed! for as to the damp origin of the gnat, there was the authority of Virgil himself, who had called it the "*alumnus* of the waters;" and as to what his dear dull friend had to say about the fish, the eagle, and the rest, it was "nihil ad rem;" for because the eagle could fly higher, it by no means followed that the gnat could not fly at all, etc., etc. He was ashamed, however, to dwell on such trivialities, and thus to swell a gnat into an elephant; but, for his own part, would only add that he had nothing deceitful or

double about him, neither was he to be caught when present by the false
blandishments of those who slandered him in his absence, agreeing
rather with a Homeric sentiment on that head,—which furnished a
Greek quotation to serve as powder to his bullet.

The quarrel could not end there. The logic could hardly get worse,
but the secretary got more pompously self-asserting and the scholarly
poet's temper more and more venomous. Politian had been generously
willing to hold up a mirror, by which the too-inflated secretary, beholding his own likeness, might be induced to cease setting up his ignorant defences of bad Latin agaainst ancient authorities whom the
consent of centuries had placed beyond question,—unless, indeed, he
had designed to sink in literature in proportion as he rose in honours,
that by a sort of compensation men of letters might feel themselves his
equals. In return, Politian was begged to examine Scala's writings;
nowhere would he find a more devout admiration of antiquity. The secretary was ashamed of the age in which he lived, and blushed for it.
Some, indeed, there were who wanted to have their own works praised
and exalted to a level with the divine monuments of antiquity; but he,
Scala, could not oblige them. And as to the honours which were offensive
to the envious, they had been well earned; witness his whole life since
he came in penury to Florence. The elegant scholar, in reply, was not
surprised that Scala found the Age distasteful to him, since he himself
was so distasteful to the Age; nay, it was with perfect accuracy that
he, the elegant scholar, had called Scala a branny monster, inasmuch
as he was formed from the offscourings of monsters, born amidst the
refuse of a mill, and eminently worthy the long-eared office of turning
the paternal millstones (*in pistrini sordibus natus et quidem pistrino
dignissimus*)!

It was not without reference to Tito's appointed visit that the papers
containing this correspondence were brought out to-day. Here was a
new Greek scholar whose accomplishments were to be tested; and on
nothing did Scala more desire a dispassionate opinion from persons of
superior knowledge than on that Greek epigram of Politian's. After
sufficient introductory talk concerning Tito's travels, after a survey
and discussion of the gems, and an easy passage from the mention of
the lamented Lorenzo's eagerness in collecting such specimens of ancient
art to the subject of classical tastes and studies in general, and their
present condition in Florence, it was inevitable to mention Politian, a
man of eminent ability indeed, but a little too arrogant,—assuming
to be a Hercules, whose office it was to destroy all the literary mon-
strosities of the age, and writing letters to his elders without signing
them, as if they were miraculous revelations that could only have one
source. And after all, were not his own criticisms often questionable and
his tastes perverse? He was fond of saying pungent things about the
men who thought they wrote like Cicero because they ended every sentence with "esse videtur:" but while he was boasting of his freedom from
servile imitation, did he not fall into the other extreme, running after

strange words and affected phrases? Even in his much-belauded "Mis·
cellanea," was every point tenable? And Tito, who had just been look··
ing into the "Miscellanea," found so much to say that was agreeable
to the secretary—he would have done so from the mere disposition to
please, without further motive—that he showed himself quite worthy
to be made a judge in the notable correspondence concerning the *culex*.
Here was the Greek epigram which Politian had doubtless thought the
finest in the world, though he had pretended to believe that the "trans-
marini," the Greeks themselves, would make light of it: had he not been
unintentionally speaking the truth in his false modesty?

Tito was ready, and scarified the epigram to Scala's content. O wise
young judge! He could doubtless appreciate satire even in the vulgar
tongue; and Scala—who, excellent man, not seeking publicity through
the booksellers, was never unprovided with "hasty uncorrected trifles,"
as a sort of sherbet for a visitor on a hot day, or, if the weather were
cold, why then as a cordial—had a few little matters in the shape of
Sonnets, turning on well-known foibles of Politian's, which he would
not like to go any farther, but which would, perhaps, amuse the company.

Enough: Tito took his leave under an urgent invitation to come again.
His gems were interesting; especially the agate, with the *lusus naturæ*
in it,—a most wonderful semblance of Cupid riding on the lion; and
the "Jew's stone," with the lion-headed serpent enchased in it; both of
which the secretary agreed to buy,—the latter as a reinforcement of
his preventives against the gout, which gave him such severe twinges
that it was plain enough how intolerable it would be if he were not well
supplied with rings of rare virtue, and with an amulet worn close under
the right breast. But Tito was assured that he himself was more interesting than his gems. He had won his way to the Scala Palace by the
recommendation of Bardo de' Bardi, who, to be sure, was Scala's old
acquaintance and a worthy scholar, in spite of his overvaluing himself
a little (a frequent foible in the secretary's friends); but he must come
again on the ground of his own manifest accomplishments.

The interview could hardly have ended more auspiciously for Tito;
and as he walked out at the Porta Pinti that he might laugh a little at
his ease over the affair of the *culex*, he felt that Fortune could hardly
mean to turn her back on him again at present. since she had taken him
by the hand in this decided way.

CHAPTER VIII

A FACE IN THE CROWD

It is easy to northern people to rise early on Midsummer morning, to
see the dew on the grassy edge of the dusty pathway, to notice the fresh
shoots among the darker green of the oak and fir in the coppice, and to

look over the gate at the shorn meadow, without recollecting that it is the Nativity of St. John the Baptist.

Not so to the Florentine,—still less to the Florentine of the fifteenth century: to him on that particular morning the brightness of the eastern sun on the Arno had something special in it; the ringing of the bells was articulate, and declared it to be the great summer festival of Florence, the day of San Giovanni.

San Giovanni had been the patron saint of Florence for at least eight hundred years,—ever since the time when the Lombard Queen Theodolinda had commanded her subjects to do him peculiar honour; nay, says old Villani, to the best of his knowledge, ever since the days of Constantine the Great and Pope Sylvester, when the Florentines deposed their idol Mars, whom they were nevertheless careful not to treat with contumely; for while they consecrated their beautiful and noble temple to the honour of God and of the "Beato Messere Santo Giovanni," they placed old Mars respectfully on a high tower near the river Arno, finding in certain ancient memorials that he had been elected as their tutelar deity under such astral influence that if he were broken, or otherwise treated with indignity, the city would suffer great damage and mutation. But in the fifteenth century that discreet regard to the feelings of the Man-destroyer had long vanished: the god of the spear and shield had ceased to frown by the side of the Arno, and the defences of the Republic were held to lie in its craft and its coffers. For spear and shield could be hired by gold florins, and on the gold florins there had always been the image of San Giovanni.

Much good had come to Florence since the dim time of struggle between the old patron and the new: some quarrelling and bloodshed, doubtless, between Guelf and Ghibelline, between Black and White, between orthodox sons of the Church and heretic Paterini; some floods, famine, and pestilence; but still much wealth and glory. Florence had achieved conquests over walled cities once mightier than itself, and especially over hated Pisa, whose marble buildings were too high and beautiful, whose masts were too much honoured on Greek and Italian coasts. The name of Florence had been growing prouder and prouder in all the courts of Europe, nay, in Africa itself, on the strength of purest gold coinage, finest dyes and textures, pre-eminent scholarship and poetic genius, and wits of the most serviceable sort for statesmanship and banking: it was a name so omnipresent that a Pope with a turn for epigram had called Florentines "the fifth element." And for this high destiny, though it might partly depend on the stars and Madonna dell' Impruneta, and certainly depended on other higher Powers less often named, the praise was greatly due to San Giovanni, whose image was on the fair gold florins.

Therefore it was fitting that the day of San Giovanni—that ancient Church festival already venerable in the days of St. Augustine—should be a day of peculiar rejoicing to Florence, and should be ushered in by a vigil duly kept in strict old Florentine fashion, with much dancing, with much street jesting, and perhaps with not a little stone-throwing and window-breaking, but emphatically with certain street sights such as could only be provided by a city which held in its service a clever Cecca, engineer and architect,[1] valuable alike in sieges and in shows. By the help of Cecca, the very saints, surrounded with their almond-shaped glory, and floating on clouds with their joyous companionship of winged cherubs, even as they may be seen to this day in the pictures of Perugino, seemed, on the eve of San Giovanni, to have brought their piece of the heavens down into the narrow streets, and to pass slowly through them; and, more wonderful still, saints of gigantic size, with attendant angels, might be seen, not seated, but moving in a slow mysterious manner along the streets, like a procession of colossal figures come down from the high domes and tribunes of the churches. The clouds were made of good woven stuff, the saints and cherubs were unglorified mortals supported by firm bars, and those mysterious giants were really men of very steady brain, balancing themselves on stilts, and enlarged, like Greek tragedians, by huge masks and stuffed shoulders; but he was a miserably unimaginative Florentine who thought only of that,—nay, somewhat impious, for in the images of sacred things was there not some of the virtue of sacred things themselves? And if, after that, there came a company of merry black demons well-armed with claws and thongs, and other implements of sport, ready to perform impromptu farces of bastinadoing and clothes-tearing, why, that was the demons' way of keeping a vigil, and they, too, might have descended from the domes and the tribunes. The Tuscan mind slipped from the devout to the burlesque as readily as water round an angle; and the saints had already had their turn, had gone their way, and made their due pause before the gates of San Giovanni, to do him honour on the eve of his *festa*. And on the morrow, the great day thus ushered in, it was fitting that the tributary symbols paid to Florence by all its dependent cities, districts, and villages, whether conquered, protected, or of immemorial possession, should be offered at the shrine of San Giovanni in the old octagonal church, once the cathedral, and now the baptistery, where every Florentine had had the sign of the Cross made with the anointing chrism on his brow; that all the city, from the white-haired man to the stripling, and from the matron to the lisping child, should be clothed in its best to do honour to the great day, and see the great sight; and that again, when the sun was sloping and the streets were cool, there should be the glorious race or Corso, when the

---

[1] Francesco d'Angelo, surnamed *la Cecca*, was at first a carpenter in the service of the Signoria of Florence, who employed him in various works, especially for the devices and machinery used at the festival of St. John and other similar ceremonies. He was born in 1447 and died May 4, 1488, of a wound in the head received at the taking by the Florentine army of the Castle of Piancaldoli, occupied by Count Girolamo Riario, Lord of Forli. During the last years of his life, Cecca was employed, together with Francioni his former master, as architect of civil and military works. An ample account of him is given by Giorgio Vasari in his "Lives."
—EDITOR.

unsaddled horses, clothed in rich trappings, should run right across the city, from the Porta al Prato on the northwest, through the Mercato Vecchio, to the Porta Santa Croce on the southeast, where the richest of *Palii,* or velvet and brocade banners with silk linings and fringe of gold, such as became a city that half clothed the well-dressed world, were mounted on a triumphal car awaiting the winner or winner's owner.

And thereafter followed more dancing; nay, through the whole day, says an old chronicler at the beginning of that century, there were weddings and the grandest gatherings, with so much piping, music, and song, with balls and feasts and gladness and ornament, that this earth might have been mistaken for Paradise!

In this year of 1492 it was, perhaps, a little less easy to make that mistake. Lorenzo the magnificent and subtle was dead, and an arrogant, incautious Piero was come in his room: an evil change for Florence, unless, indeed, the wise horse prefers the bad rider, as more easily thrown from the saddle; and already the regrets for Lorenzo were getting less predominant over the murmured desire for government on a broader basis, in which corruption might be arrested, and there might be that free play for everybody's jealousy and ambition which made the ideal liberty of the good old quarrelsome, struggling times, when Florence raised her great buildings, reared her own soldiers, drove out would-be tyrants at the sword's point, and was proud to keep faith at her own loss. Lorenzo was dead, Pope Innocent was dying, and a troublesome Neapolitan succession, with an intriguing, ambitious Milan, might set Italy by the ears before long: the times were likely to be difficult. Still, there was all the more reason that the Republic should keep its religious festivals.

And Midsummer morning, in this year 1492, was not less bright than usual. It was betimes in the morning that the symbolic offerings to be carried in grand procession were all assembled at their starting-point in the Piazza della Signoria,—that famous Piazza, where stood then, and stand now, the massive turreted Palace of the People, called the Palazzo Vecchio, and the spacious Loggia, built by Orcagna,—the scene of all grand State ceremonial. The sky made the fairest blue tent, and under it the bells swung so vigorously that every evil spirit with sense enough to be formidable must long since have taken his flight; windows and terraced roofs were alive with human faces; sombre stone houses were bright with hanging draperies; the boldly soaring palace tower, the yet older square tower of the Bargello, and the spire of the neighbouring Badia seemed to keep watch above; and below, on the broad polygonal flags of the piazza, was the glorious show of banners and horses with rich trappings, and gigantic *ceri,* or tapers, that were fitly called towers,—strangely aggrandized descendants of those torches by whose faint light the church worshipped in the catacombs. Betimes in the morning all processions had need to move under the Midsummer sky of Florence, where the shelter of the narrow streets must every now and then be exchanged for the glare of wide spaces; and the sun would be

that a city had won its independence? and by the blessing of San Giovanni this "beautiful sheepfold" of his had shown that token earliest among the Italian cities. Nevertheless, the annual function of representing the patron saint was not among the high prizes of public life; it was paid for with something like ten shillings, a cake weighing fourteen pounds, two bottles of wine, and a handsome supply of light eatables; the money being furnished by the magnificent Zecca, and the payment in kind being by peculiar "privilege" presented in a basket suspended on a pole from an upper window of a private house, whereupon the eidolon of the austere saint at once invigorated himself with a reasonable share of the sweets and wine, threw the remnants to the crowd, and embraced the mighty cake securely with his right arm through the remainder of his passage. This was the attitude in which the mimic San Giovanni presented himself as the tall car jerked and vibrated on its slow way round the piazza to the northern gate of the baptistery.

"There go the Masters of the Zecca, and there is my brother—you see him, Melema?" cried Cennini, with an agreeable stirring of pride at showing a stranger what was too familiar to be remarkable to fellow-citizens. "Behind come the members of the Corporation of Calimara, the dealers in foreign cloth, to which we have given our Florentine finish; men of ripe years, you see, who were matriculated before you were born; and then comes the famous Art of Money-changers."

"Many of them matriculated also to the noble art of usury before you were born," interrupted Francesco Cei, "as you may discern by a certain fitful glare of the eye and sharp curve of the nose which manifest their descent from the ancient harpies, whose portraits you saw supporting the arms of the Zecca. Shaking off old prejudices now, such a procession as that of some four hundred passably ugly men carrying their tapers in open daylight, Diogenes-fashion, as if they were looking for a lost quattrino, would make a merry spectacle for the Feast of Fools."

"Blaspheme not against the usages of our city," said Pietro Cennini, much offended. "There are new wits who think they see things more truly because they stand on their heads to look at them, like tumblers and mountebanks, instead of keeping the attitude of rational men. Doubtless it makes little difference to Maestro Vaiano's monkeys whether they see our Donatello's statue of Judith with their heads or their tails uppermost."

"Your solemnity will allow some quarter to playful fancy, I hope," said Cei, with a shrug, "else what becomes of the ancients, whose example you scholars are bound to revere, Messer Pietro? Life was never anything but a perpetual see-saw between gravity and jest."

"Keep your jest then till your end of the pole is uppermost," said Cennini, still angry; "and that is not when the great bond of our Republic is expressing itself in ancient symbols, without which the vulgar would be conscious of nothing beyond their own petty wants of back and stomach, and never rise to the sense of community in religion

and law. There has been no great people without processions, and the
man who thinks himself too wise to be moved by them to anything but
contempt, is like the puddle that was proud of standing alone while the
river rushed by."

No one said anything after this indignant burst of Cennini's till he
himself spoke again.

"Hark! the trumpets of the Signoria: now comes the last stage of
the show, Melema. That is our Gonfaloniere in the middle, in the starred
mantle, with the sword carried before him. Twenty years ago we used
to see our foreign Podestà, who was our judge in civil causes, walking
on his right hand; but our Republic has been over-doctored by clever
Medici. That is the Proposto of the Priori on the left; then come the
other seven Priori; then all the other magistracies and officials of our
Republic. You see your patron the Segretario?"

"There is Messer Bernardo del Nero also," said Tito; "his visage
is a fine and venerable one, though it has worn rather a petrifying look
towards me."

"Ah," said Nello, "he is the dragon that guards the remnant of old
Bardo's gold, which, I fancy, is chiefly that virgin gold that falls about
the fair Romola's head and shoulders; eh, my Apollino?" he added,
patting Tito's head.

Tito had the youthful grace of blushing, but he had also the adroît
and ready speech that prevents a blush from looking like embarrassment.
He replied at once,—

"And a very Pactolus it is,—a stream with golden ripples. If I were
an alchemist—"

He was saved from the need for further speech by the sudden fortis-
simo of drums and trumpets and fifes, bursting into the breadth of the
piazza in a grand storm of sound,—a roar, a blast, and a whistling, well
befitting a city famous for its musical instruments, and reducing the
members of the closest group to a state of deaf isolation.

During this interval Nello observed Tito's fingers moving in recognition of some one in the crowd below, but not seeing the direction of
his glance he failed to detect the object of this greeting—the sweet
round blue-eyed face under a white hood—immediately lost in the narrow border of heads, where there was a continual eclipse of round contadina cheeks by the harsh-lined features or bent shoulders of an old
spadesman, and where profiles turned as sharply from north to south
as weather-cocks under a shifting wind.

But when it was felt that the show was ended,—when the twelve prisoners released in honour of the day, and the very *barberi,* or race-horses,
with the arms of their owners embroidered on their cloths, had followed
up the Signoria, and been duly consecrated to San Giovanni, and every
one was moving from the window,—Nello, whose Florentine curiosity
was of that lively canine sort which thinks no trifle too despicable for
investigation, put his hand on Tito's shoulder and said,—

"What acquaintance was that you were making signals to, eh, *giovane mio?*"

"Some little contadina who probably mistook me for an acquaintance, for she had honoured me with a greeting."

"Or who wished to begin an acquaintance," said Nello. "But you are bound for the Via de' Bardi and the feast of the Muses: there is no counting on you for a frolic, else we might have gone in search of adventures together in the crowd, and had some pleasant fooling on honour of San Giovanni. But your high fortune has come on you too soon: I don't mean the professor's mantle,—*that* is roomy enough to hide a few stolen chickens, but—Messer Endymion minded his manners after that singular good fortune of his; and what says our Luigi Pulci?

> 'Da quel giorno in quà ch'amor m'accese
> Per lei son fatto e gentile e cortese.' "

"Nello, *amico mio*, thou hast an intolerable trick of making life stale by forestalling it with thy talk," said Tito, shrugging his shoulders, with a look of patient resignation, which was his nearest approach to anger; "not to mention that such ill-founded babbling would be held a great offence by that same goddess whose humble worshipper you are always professing yourself."

"I will be mute," said Nello, laying his finger on his lips, with a responding shrug. "But it is only under our four eyes that I talk any folly about her."

"Pardon! you were on the verge of it just now in the hearing of others. If you want to ruin me in the minds of Bardo and his daughter—"

"Enough, enough!" said Nello. "I am an absurd old barber. It all comes from that abstinence of mine, in not making bad verses in my youth: for want of letting my folly run out that way when I was eighteen, it runs out at my tongue's end now I am at the unseemly age of fifty. But Nello has not got his head muffled for all that; he can see a buffalo in the snow. *Addio, giovane mio!*"

CHAPTER IX

A MAN'S RANSOM

TITO was soon down among the crowd, and notwithstanding his indifferent reply to Nello's question about his chance acquaintance, he was not without a passing wish, as he made his way round the piazza to the Corso degli Adimari, that he might encounter the pair of blue eyes which had looked up towards him from under the square bit of white linen drapery that formed the ordinary hood of the contadina at festa time. He was perfectly well aware that that face was Tessa's; but he had not chosen to say so. What had Nello to do with the matter? Tito had an innate love of reticence—let us say a talent for it—which acted, as

other impulses do, without any conscious motive, and, like all people
to whom concealment is easy, he would now and then conceal something
which had as little the nature of a secret as the fact that he had seen
a flight of crows.

But the passing wish about pretty Tessa was almost immediately
eclipsed by the recurrent recollection of that friar whose face had some
irrecoverable association for him. Why should a sickly fanatic, worn
with fasting, have looked at *him* in particular, and where in all his
travels could he remember encountering that face before? Folly! such
vague memories hang about the mind like cobwebs, with tickling im-
portunity,—best to sweep them away at a dash; and Tito had pleasanter
occupation for his thoughts. By the time he was turning out of the Corso
degli Adimari into a side-street he was caring only that the sun was
high, and that the procession had kept him longer than he had intended
from his visit to that room in the Via de' Bardi, where his coming, he
knew, was anxiously awaited. He felt the scene of his entrance beforehand: the joy beaming diffusedly in the blind face like the light in a
semi-transparent lamp; the transient pink flush on Romola's face and
neck, which subtracted nothing from her majesty, but only gave it the
exquisite charm of womanly sensitiveness, heightened still more by
what seemed the paradoxical, boy-like frankness of her look and smile.
They were the best comrades in the world during the hours they passed
together round the blind man's chair: she was constantly appealing to
Tito, and he was informing her, yet he felt himself strangely in subjection to Romola with that simplicity of hers: he felt for the first time,
without defining it to himself, that loving awe in the presence of noble
womanhood, which is perhaps something like the worship paid of old
to a great nature-goddess, who was not all-knowing but whose life and
power were something deeper and more primordial than knowledge.
They had never been alone together, and he could frame to himself no
probable image of love-scenes between them: he could only fancy and
wish wildly—what he knew was impossible—that Romola would some
day tell him that she loved him. One day in Greece, as he was leaning
over a wall in the sunshine a little black-eyed peasant-girl, who had
rested her water-pot on the wall, crept gradually nearer and nearer to
him, and at last shyly asked him to kiss her, putting up her round olive
cheek very innocently. Tito was used to love that came in this unsought
fashion. But Romola's love would never come in that way: would it ever
come at all?—and yet it was that top-most apple on which he had set
his mind. He was in his fresh youth,—not passionate, but impressible:
it was as inevitable that he should feel lovingly towards Romola as that
the white irises should be reflected in the clear sunlit stream; but he
had no coxcombry, and he had an intimate sense that Romola was something very much above him. Many men have felt the same before a
large-eyed, simple child.

Nevertheless, Tito had had the rapid success which would have made
some men presuming, or would have warranted him in thinking that

there would be no great presumption in entertaining an agreeable confidence that he might one day be the husband of Romola,—nay, that her father himself was not without a vision of such a future for him. His first auspicious interview with Bartolommeo Scala had proved the commencement of a growing favour on the secretary's part, and had led to an issue which would have been enough to make Tito decide on Florence as the place in which to establish himself, even if it had held no other magnet. Politian was professor of Greek as well as Latin at Florence, professorial chairs being maintained there, although the university had been removed to Pisa;[1] but for a long time Demetrio Calcondila, one of the most eminent and respectable among the emigrant Greeks, had also held a Greek chair, simultaneously with the too predominant Italian. Calcondila was now gone to Milan, and there was no counterpoise or rival to Politian such as was desired for him by the friends who wished him to be taught a little propriety and humility. Scala was far from being the only friend of this class, and he found several who, if they were not among those thirsty admirers of mediocrity that were glad to be refreshed with his verses in hot weather, were yet quite willing to join him in doing that moral service to Politian. It was finally agreed that Tito should be supported in a Greek chair, as Demetrio Calcondila had been by Lorenzo himself, who, being at the same time the affectionate patron of Politian, had shown by precedent that there was nothing invidious in such a measure, but only a zeal for true learning and for the instruction of the Florentine youth.

Tito was thus sailing under the fairest breeze, and besides convincing fair judges that his talents squared with his good fortune, he wore that fortune so easily and unpretentiously that no one had yet been offended by it. He was not unlikely to get into the best Florentine society,—society where there was much more plate than the circle of enamelled silver in the centre of the brass dishes, and where it was not forbidden by the Signory to wear the richest brocade. For where could a handsome young scholar not be welcome when he could touch the lute and troll a gay song? That bright face, that easy smile, that liquid voice, seemed to give life a holiday aspect; just as a strain of gay music and the hoisting of colours make the work-worn and the sad rather ashamed of showing themselves. Here was a professor likely to render the Greek classics amiable to the sons of great houses.

And that was not the whole of Tito's good fortune; for he had sold all his jewels, except the ring he did not choose to part with, and he was master of full five hundred gold florins.

Yet the moment when he first had this sum in his possession was the crisis of the first serious struggle his facile, good-humoured nature had known. An importunate thought, of which he had till now refused to

---

[1] The University of Pisa having been re-established, in 1472 the seats of learning in Florence had been reduced to simple schools of belles-lettres, a status actually recognized later on under the Grand Duke Cosimo I, when the University of Pisa had larger endowments and a more definite organization.—EDITOR.

see more than the shadow as it dogged his footsteps, at last rushed upon him and grasped him: he was obliged to pause and decide whether he would surrender and obey, or whether he would give the refusal that must carry irrevocable consequences. It was in the room above Nello's shop, which Tito had now hired as a lodging, that the elder Cennini handed him the last quota of the sum on behalf of Bernardo Rucellai, the purchaser of the two most valuable gems.

"Ecco, giovane mio!" said the respectable printer and goldsmith, "you have now a pretty little fortune; and if you will take my advice, you will let me place your florins in a safe quarter, where they may increase and multiply, instead of slipping through your fingers for banquets and other follies which are rife among our Florentine youth. And it has been too much the fashion of scholars, especially when, like our Pietro Crinito, they think their scholarship needs to be scented and broidered, to squander with one hand till they have been fain to beg with the other. I have brought you the money, and you are free to make a wise choice or an unwise: I shall see on which side the balance dips. We Florentines hold no man a member of an Art till he has shown his skill and been matriculated; and no man is matriculated to the art of life till he has been well tempted. If you make up your mind to put your florins out to usury, you can let me know to-morrow. A scholar may marry, and should have something in readiness for the *morgen-cap.* Addio."

As Cennini closed the door behind him, Tito turned round with the smile dying out of his face, and fixed his eyes on the table where the florins lay. He made no other movement, but stood with his thumbs in his belt, looking down, in that transfixed state which accompanies the concentration of consciousness on some inward image.

"A man's ransom!"—who was it that had said five hundred florins was more than a man's ransom? If now, under this midday sun, on some hot coast far away, a man somewhat stricken in years,—a man not without high thoughts and with the most passionate heart,—a man who long years ago had rescued a little boy from a life of beggary, filth, and cruel wrong, had reared him tenderly, and been to him as a father,— if that man were now under this summer sun toiling as a slave, hewing wood and drawing water, perhaps being smitten and buffeted because he was not deft and active? If he were saying to himself, "Tito will find me: he had but to carry our manuscripts and gems to Venice; he will have raised money, and will never rest till he finds me out"? If that were certain, could he, Tito, see the price of the gems lying before him, and say, "I will stay at Florence, where I am fanned by soft airs of promised love and prosperity; I will not risk myself for his sake"? No, surely not, *if it were certain.* But nothing could be farther from certainty. The galley had been taken by a Turkish vessel on its way to Delos: *that* was known by the report of the companion galley, which had escaped. But there had been resistance, and probable bloodshed; a man had been seen falling overboard: who were the survivors, and what had befallen them among all the multitude of possibilities? Had not he, Tito, suffered shipwreck, and narrowly escaped drowning? He had good cause for feeling the omnipresence of casualties that threatened all projects with futility. The rumour that there were pirates who had a settlement in Delos was not to be depended on, or might be nothing to the purpose. What, probably enough, would be the result if he were to quit Florence and go to Venice; get authoritative letters,—yes, he knew that might be done,—and set out for the Archipelago? Why, that he should be himself seized, and spend all his florins on preliminaries, and be again a destitute wanderer,—with no more gems to sell.

Tito had a clearer vision of that result than of the possible moment when he might find his father again, and carry him deliverance. It would surely be an unfairness that he, in his full ripe youth, to whom life had hitherto had some of the stint and subjection of a school, should turn his back on promised love and distinction, and perhaps never be visited by that promise again. "And yet," he said to himself, "if I were certain that Baldassarre Calvo was alive, and that I could free him, by whatever exertions or perils, I would go now,—now I have the money: it was useless to debate the matter before. I would go now to Bardo and Bartolommeo Scala, and tell them the whole truth." Tito did not say to himself so distinctly that if those two men had known the whole truth he was aware there would have been no alternative for him but to go in search of his benefactor, who, if alive, was the rightful owner of the gems, and whom he had always equivocally spoken of as "lost;" he did not say to himself,—what he was not ignorant of,—that Greeks of distinction had made sacrifices, taken voyages again and again, and sought help from crowned and mitred heads for the sake of freeing relatives from slavery to the Turks. Public opinion did not regard this as exceptional virtue.

This was his first real colloquy with himself: he had gone on following the impulses of the moment, and one of those impulses had been to conceal half the fact, he had never considered this part of his conduct long enough to face the consciousness of his motives for the concealment. What was the use of telling the whole? It was true, the thought had crossed his mind several times since he had quitted Nauplia that, after all, it was a great relief to be quit of Baldassarre, and he would have liked to know *who* it was that had fallen overboard. But such thoughts spring inevitably out of a relation that is irksome. Baldassarre was exacting, and had got stranger as he got older: he was constantly scrutinizing Tito's mind to see whether it answered to his own exaggerated expectations; and age—the age of a thick-set, heavy-browed, bald man beyond sixty, whose intensity and eagerness in the grasp of ideas have long taken the character of monotony and repetition—may be looked at from many points of view without being found attractive. Such a man, stranded among new acquaintances, unless he had the philosopher's stone, would hardly find rank, youth, and beauty at his feet. The feelings that gather fervour from novelty will be of little help towards making the world a home for dimmed and faded human beings; and if there is any love of which they are not widowed, it must be the love that is rooted in memories and distils perpetually the sweet balms of fidelity and for-bearing tenderness.

But surely such memories were not absent from Tito's mind? Far in the backward vista of his remembered life, when he was only seven years old, Baldassarre had rescued him from blows, had taken him to a home that seemed like opened Paradise, where there was sweet food and sooth-ing caresses, all had on Baldassarre's knee; and from that time till the hour they had parted, Tito had been the one centre of Baldassarre's fatherly cares.

And he had been docile, pliable, quick of apprehension, ready to ac-quire: a very bright, lovely boy; a youth of even splendid grace, who seemed quite without vices, as if that beautiful form represented a vi-tality so exquisitely poised and balanced that it could know no uneasy desires, no unrest,—a radiant presence for a lonely man to have won for himself. If he were silent when his father expected some response, still he did not look moody; if he declined some labour,—why, he flung him-self down with such a charming, half-smiling, half-pleading air, that the pleasure of looking at him made amends to one who had watched his growth with a sense of claim and possession: the curves of Tito's mouth had ineffable good-humour in them. And then, the quick talent to which everything came readily, from philosophical systems to the rhymes of a street ballad caught up at a hearing! Would any one have said that Tito had not made a rich return to his benefactor, or that his gratitude and affection would fail on any great demand?

He did not admit that his gratitude had failed; but *it was not certain* that Baldassarre was in slavery, not certain that he was living.

"Do I not owe something to myself?" said Tito, inwardly, with a slight movement of his shoulders, the first he had made since he had turned to look down at the florins. "Before I quit everything, and incur again all the risks of which I am even now weary, I must at least have a reasonable hope. Am I to spend my life in a wandering search? *I be-lieve he is dead.* Cennini was right about my florins: I will place them in his hands to-morrow."

When, the next morning, Tito put this determination into act, he had chosen his colour in the game, and had given an inevitable bent to his wishes. He had made it impossible that he should not from henceforth desire it to be the truth that his father was dead; impossible that he should not be tempted to baseness rather than that the precise facts of his conduct should not remain forever concealed.

Under every guilty secret there is hidden a brood of guilty wishes, whose unwholesome infecting life is cherished by the darkness. The con-taminating effect of deeds often lies less in the commission than in the consequent adjustment of our desires,—the enlistment of our self-in-terest on the side of falsity; as, on the other hand, the purifying influ-ence of public confession springs from the fact that by it the hope in lies is forever swept away, and the soul recovers the noble attitude of simplicity.

Besides, in this first distinct colloquy with himself the ideas which had previously been scattered and interrupted had now concentrated themselves; the little rills of selfishness had united and made a channel, so that they could never again meet with the same resistance. Hitherto Tito had left in vague indecision the question whether, with the means in his power, he would not return, and ascertain his father's fate; he had now made a definite excuse to himself for not taking that course; he had avowed to himself a choice which he would have been ashamed to avow to others, and which would have made him ashamed in the resurgent presence of his father. But the inward shame, the reflex of that outward law which the great heart of mankind makes for every individual man, a reflex which will exist even in the absence of the sympathetic impulses that need no law, but rush to the deed of fidelity and pity as inevitably as the brute mother shields her young from the attack of the hereditary enemy,—that inward shame was showing its blushes in Tito's determined assertion to himself that his father was dead, or that at least search was hopeless.

CHAPTER X

UNDER THE PLANE-TREE

ON the day of San Giovanni it was already three weeks ago that Tito had handed his florins to Cennini, and we have seen that as he set out towards the Via de' Bardi he showed all the outward signs of a mind at ease. How should it be otherwise? He never jarred with what was immediately around him; and his nature was too joyous, too unapprehensive, for the hidden and the distant to grasp him in the shape of a dread. As he turned out of the hot sunshine into the shelter of a narrow street, took off the black cloth *berretta,* or simple cap with upturned lappet, which just crowned his brown curls, pushing his hair and tossing his head backward to court the cooler air, there was no brand of duplicity on his brow; neither was there any stamp of candour: it was simply a finely formed, square, smooth young brow; and the slow absent glance he cast around at the upper windows of the houses had neither more dissimulation in it nor more ingenuousness than belongs to a youthful well-opened eyelid with its unwearied breadth of gaze, to perfectly pellucid lenses, to the undimmed dark of a rich brown iris, and to a pure cerulean-tinted angle of whiteness streaked with the delicate shadows of long eyelashes. Was it that Tito's face attracted or repelled according to the mental attitude of the observer? Was it a cipher with more than one key? The strong, unmistakable expression in his whole air and person was a negative one, and it was perfectly veracious; it declared the absence of any uneasy claim, any restless vanity, and it made the admiration that followed him as he passed among the troop of holiday-makers a thoroughly willing tribute.

For by this time the stir of the Festa was felt even in the narrowest side-streets; the throng which had at one time been concentrated in the lines through which the procession had to pass, was now streaming out in all directions in pursuit of a new object. Such intervals of a Festa are precisely the moments when the vaguely active animal spirits of a crowd are likely to be the most petulant and most ready to sacrifice a stray individual to the greater happiness of the greater number. As Tito entered the neighbourhood of San Martino, he found the throng rather denser; and near the hostelry of the *Bertucce*, or Baboons, there was evidently some object which was arresting the passengers and forming them into a knot. It needed nothing of great interest to draw aside passengers unfreighted with a purpose, and Tito was preparing to turn aside into an adjoining street, when, amidst the loud laughter, his ear discerned a distressed childish voice crying, "Loose me! Holy Virgin, help me!" which at once determined him to push his way into the knot of gazers. He had just had time to perceive that the distressed voice came from a young contadina, whose white hood had fallen off in the struggle to get her hands free from the grasp of a man in the party-coloured dress of a *cerretano*, or conjurer, who was making laughing attempts to soothe and cajole her, evidently carrying with him the amused sympathy of the spectators. These, by a persuasive variety of words signifying simpleton, for which the Florentine dialect is rich in equivalents, seemed to be arguing with the contadina against her obstinacy. At the first moment the girl's face was turned away, and he saw only her light-brown hair plaited and fastened with a long silver pin; but in the next, the struggle brought her face opposite Tito's, and he saw the baby features of Tessa, her blue eyes filled with tears, and her under-lip quivering. Tessa, too, saw *him*, and through the mist of her swelling tears there beamed a sudden hope, like that in the face of a little child, when, held by a stranger against its will, it sees a familiar hand stretched out.

In an instant Tito had pushed his way through the barrier of by-standers, whose curiosity made them ready to turn aside at the sudden interference of this handsome young signor,[1] had grasped Tessa's waist, and had said, "Loose this child! What right have you to hold her against her will?"

The conjurer—a man with one of those faces in which the angles of the eyes and eyebrows, of the nostrils, mouth, and sharply defined jaw, all tend upward—showed his small regular teeth in an impish but not ill-natured grin, as he let go Tessa's hands and stretched out his own backward, shrugging his shoulders, and bending them forward a little in a half-apologetic, half-protesting manner.

"I meant the *ragazza* no evil in the world, Messere: ask this respectable company. I was only going to show them a few samples of my skill, in which this little damsel might have helped me the better be-

[1] The word should, in any case, be *signore*, without abbreviation. But the use of *Signore* for *messere*, as in this sentence, is quite modern.—EDITOR.

cause of her kitten face, which would have assured them of open dealing; and I had promised her a lapful of confetti as a reward. But what
then? Messer has doubtless better confetti at hand, and she knows it."

A general laugh among the by-standers accompanied these last words
of the conjurer, raised, probably, by the look of relief and confidence
with which Tessa clung to Tito's arm, as he drew it from her waist and
placed her hand within it. She only cared about the laugh as she might
have cared about the roar of wild beasts from which she was escaping,
not attaching any meaning to it; but Tito, who had no sooner got her
on his arm than he foresaw some embarrassment in the situation,
hastened to get clear of observers, who, having been despoiled of an
expected amusement, were sure to re-establish the balance by jests.

"See, see, little one! here is your hood," said the conjurer, throwing
the bit of white drapery over Tessa's head. "*Orsù,* bear me no malice;
come back to me when Messere can spare you."

"Ah! Maestro Vaiano, she'll come back presently, as the toad said
to the harrow," called out one of the spectators, seeing how Tessa
started and shrank at the action of the conjurer.

Tito pushed his way vigorously towards the corner of a side-street, a
little vexed at this delay in his progress to the Via de' Bardi, and intending to get rid of the poor little contadina as soon as possible. The
next street, too, had its passengers inclined to make holiday remarks
on so unusual a pair; but they had no sooner entered it than he said, in
a kind but hurried manner: "Now, little one, where were you going?
Are you come by yourself to the Festa?"

"Ah, no!" said Tessa, looking frightened and distressed again; "I
have lost my mother in the crowd,—her and my stepfather. They
will be angry,—he will beat me. It was in the crowd in San Pulinari,—
somebody pushed me along and I couldn't stop myself, so I got away
from them. Oh, I don't know where they're gone! Please, don't leave
me!"

Her eyes had been swelling with tears again, and she ended with a sob.

Tito hurried along again; the Church of the Badia was not far off.
They could enter it by the cloister that opened at the back, and in the
church he could talk to Tessa,—perhaps leave her. No! it was an hour
at which the church was not open; but they paused under the shelter
of the cloister, and he said, "Have you no cousin or friend in Florence,
my little Tessa, whose house you could find; or are you afraid of walking by yourself since you have been frightened by the conjurer? I am
in a hurry to get to Oltrarno; but if I could take you anywhere near—"

"Oh, I *am* frightened: he was the devil,—I know he was. And I don't
know where to go. I have nobody; and my mother meant to have her
dinner somewhere, and I don't know where. Holy Madonna! I shall be
beaten."

The corners of the pouting mouth went down piteously, and the poor
little bosom with the beads on it above the green serge gown heaved so
that there was no longer any help for it; a loud sob *would* come, and

the big tears fell as if they were making up for lost time. Here was a situation! It would have been brutal to leave her, and Tito's nature was all gentleness. He wished at that moment that he had not been expected in the Via de' Bardi. As he saw her lifting up her holiday apron to catch the hurrying tears, he laid his hand, too, on the apron, and rubbed one of the cheeks and kissed the baby-like roundness.

"My poor little Tessa! leave off crying. Let us see what can be done. Where is your home,—where do you live?"

There was no answer, but the sobs began to subside a little and the drops to fall less quickly.

"Come! I'll take you a little way, if you'll tell me where you want to go."

The apron fell, and Tessa's face began to look as contented as a cherub's budding from a cloud. The diabolical conjurer, the anger, and the beating seemed a long way off.

"I think I'll go home, if you'll take me," she said, in a half whisper, looking up at Tito with wide blue eyes, and with something sweeter than a smile,—with a childlike calm.

"Come, then, little one," said Tito, in a caressing tone, putting her arm within his again. "Which way is it?"

"Beyond Peretola,—where the large pear-tree is."

"Peretola? Out at which gate, pazzarella? I am a stranger, you must remember."

"Out at the Por del Prato,"[2] said Tessa, moving along with a very fast hold on Tito's arm.

He did not know all the turnings well enough to venture on an attempt at choosing the quietest streets; and besides, it occurred to him that where the passengers were most numerous there was, perhaps, the most chance of meeting with Monna Ghita and finding an end to his knight-errantship. So he made straight for Porto Rossa, and on to Ognissanti, showing his usual bright propitiatory face to the mixed observers who threw their jests at him and his little heavy-shod maiden with much liberality. Mingled with the more decent holiday-makers there were frolicsome apprentices, rather envious of his good fortune; bold-eyed women with the badge of the yellow veil; beggars who thrust forward their caps for alms, in derision at Tito's evident haste; dicers, sharpers, and loungers of the worst sort; boys whose tongues were used to wag in concert at the most brutal street games,—for the streets of Florence were not always a moral spectacle in those times, and Tessa's terror at being lost in the crowd was not wholly unreasonable.

When they reached the Piazzi d'Ognissanti, Tito slackened his pace;

---

[2] This is an error; it should be *Porta al Prato*. *Por* for *Porta* is only used in a single instance, *Por' Santa Maria*.

This gate was called *al Prato* because just within it was an immense triangular field, on the site of which is still to-day a large open space. Here the artisans of the city used to play games, and here took place the tiltings or tournaments of the *'Potenze,'* formed for the due celebration of certain festivals.—Editor.

they were both heated with their hurried walk, and here was a wider space where they could take breath. They sat down on one of the stone benches which were frequent against the walls of old Florentine houses.

"Holy Virgin!" said Tessa; "I am glad we have got away from those women and boys; but I was not frightened, because you could take care of me."

"Pretty little Tessa!" said Tito, smiling at her. "What makes you feel so safe with me?"

"Because you are so beautiful,--like the people going into Paradise: they are all good."

"It is a long while since you had your breakfast, Tessa," said Tito, seeing some stalls near, with fruit and sweetmeats upon them. "Are you hungry?"

"Yes, I think I am—if you will have some too."

Tito bought some apricots and cakes and comfits, and put them into her apron.

"Come," he said, "let us walk on to the Prato, and then perhaps you will not be afraid to go the rest of the way alone."

"But you will have some of the apricots and things," said Tessa, rising obediently and gathering up her apron as a bag for her store.

"We will see," said Tito, aloud; and to himself he said: "Here is a little contadina who might inspire a better idyl than Lorenzo de' Medici's 'Nencia da Barberino,' that Nello's friends rave about; if I were only a Theocritus, or had time to cultivate the necessary experience by unseasonable walks of this sort! However, the mischief is done now: I am so late already that another half-hour will make no difference. Pretty little pigeon!"

"We have a garden and plenty of pears," said Tessa, "and two cows, besides the mules; and I'm very fond of them. But my stepfather is a cross man: I wish my mother had not married him. I think he is wicked; he is very ugly."

"And does your mother let him beat you, poverina? You said you were afraid of being beaten."

"Ah, my mother herself scolds me: she loves my young sister better, and thinks I don't do work enough. Nobody speaks kindly to me, only the Pievano (parish priest) when I go to confession. And the men in the Mercato laugh at me and make fun of me. Nobody ever kissed me and spoke to me as you do; just as I talk to my little black-faced kid, because I'm very fond of it."

It seemed not to have entered Tessa's mind that there was any change in Tito's appearance since the morning he begged the milk from her, and that he looked now like a personage for whom she must summon her little stock of reverent words and signs. He had impressed her too differently from any human being who had ever come near her before, for her to make any comparison of details; she took no note of his dress; he was simply a voice and a face to her, something come from Paradise into a world where most things seemed hard and angry; and she prattled with as little restraint as if he had been an imaginary companion born of her own lovingness and sunshine.

They had now reached the Prato, which at that time was a large open space within the walls, where the Florentine youth played at their favourite *Calcio*,[3]—a peculiar kind of football,—and otherwise exercised themselves. At this mid-day time it was forsaken and quiet to the very gates, where a tent had been erected in preparation for the race. On the border of this wide meadow, Tito paused and said,—

"Now, Tessa, you will not be frightened if I leave you to walk the rest of the way by yourself. Addio! Shall I come and buy a cup of milk from you in the Mercato to-morrow morning, to see that you are quite safe?"

He added this question in a soothing tone, as he saw her eyes widening sorrowfully, and the corners of her mouth falling. She said nothing at first; she only opened her apron and looked down at her apricots and sweetmeats. Then she looked up at him again, and said complainingly,—

"I thought you would have some, and we could sit down under a tree outside the gate, and eat them together."

"Tessa, Tessa, you little siren, you would ruin me," said Tito, laughing, and kissing both her cheeks. "I ought to have been in the Via de' Bardi long ago. No! I must go back now; you are in no danger. There, —I'll take an apricot. Addio!"

He had already stepped two yards from her when he said the last word. Tessa could not have spoken,—she was pale, and a great sob was rising; but she turned round as if she felt there was no hope for her, and stepped on, holding her apron so forgetfully that the apricots began to roll out on the grass.

Tito could not help looking after her, and seeing her shoulders rise to the bursting sob, and the apricots fall, could not help going after her and picking them up. It was very hard upon him: he was a long way off the Via de' Bardi, and very near to Tessa.

"See, my silly one," he said, picking up the apricots. "Come, leave off crying; I will go with you, and we'll sit down under the tree. Come, I don't like to see you cry; but you know I must go back some time."

So it came to pass that they found a great plane-tree not far outside the gates, and they sat down under it, and all the feast was spread out on Tessa's lap, she leaning with her back against the trunk of the tree, and he stretched opposite to her, resting his elbows on the rough green growth cherished by the shade, while the sunlight stole through the boughs and played about them like a winged thing. Tessa's face was all contentment again, and the taste of the apricots and sweetmeats seemed very good.

[3] The *calcio*, which was a sort of football, was played in two ways. There was the simple game, without any elaborate outfit, played on the open space at the Porta al Prato, and there was the game *a livrea*, where each side wore a uniform device or costume, gold for one party, rose-colour for the other, and which was played on the Piazza of Santa Croce each year at Carnival time.—EDITOR.

"You pretty bird!" said Tito, looking at her as she sat eying the remains of the feast with an evident mental debate about saving them, since he had said he would not have any more. "To think of any one scolding you! What sins do you tell of at confession?"

"Oh, a great many. I am often naughty. I don't like work, and I can't help being idle, though I know I shall be beaten and scolded; and I give the mules the best fodder when nobody sees me, and then when the Madre is angry I say I didn't do it, and that makes me frightened at the devil. I think the conjurer was the devil. I am not so frightened after I've been to confession. And see, I've got a *Breve* here that a good father, who came to Prato preaching this Easter, blessed and gave us all." Here Tessa drew from her bosom a tiny bag carefully fastened up. "And I think the Holy Madonna will take care of me,—she looks as if she would; and perhaps if I wasn't idle, she wouldn't let me be beaten."

"If they are so cruel to you, Tessa, shouldn't you like to leave them, and go and live with a beautiful lady who would be kind to you, if she would have you to wait upon her?"

Tessa seemed to hold her breath for a moment or two. Then she said doubtfully, "I don't know."

"Then should you like to be *my* little servant, and live with me?" said Tito, smiling. He meant no more than to see what sort of pretty look and answer she would give.

There was a flush of joy immediately. "Will you take me with you now? Ah! I shouldn't go home and be beaten then." She paused a little while, and then added, more doubtfully, "But I should like to fetch my black-faced kid."

"Yes, you must go back to your kid, my Tessa," said Tito, rising, "and I must go the other way."

"By Jupiter!" he added, as he went from under the shade of the tree, "it is not a pleasant time of day to walk from here to the Via de' Bardi; I am more inclined to lie down and sleep in this shade."

It ended so. Tito had an unconquerable aversion to anything unpleasant, even when an object very much loved and desired was on the other side of it. He had risen early, had waited, had seen sights, and had been already walking in the sun; he was inclined for a siesta, and inclined all the more because little Tessa was there, and seemed to make the air softer. He lay down on the grass again, putting his cap under his head on a green tuft by the side of Tessa. That was not quite comfortable; so he moved again, and asked Tessa to let him rest his head against her lap; and in that way he soon fell asleep. Tessa sat quiet as a dove on its nest, just venturing, when he was fast asleep, to touch the wonderful dark curls, that fell backward from his ear. She was too happy to go to sleep,—too happy to think that Tito would wake up, and that then he would leave her, and she must go home. It takes very little water to make a perfect pool for a tiny fish, where it will find its world and Paradise all in one, and never have a presentiment of the dry bank. The fretted summer shade, and stillness, and the gentle breathing of some loved life near,—it would be Paradise to us all, if eager Thought, the strong angel with the implacable brow, had not long since closed the gates.

It really was a long while before the waking came,—before the long dark eyes opened at Tessa, first with a little surprise, and then with a smile, which was soon quenched by some preoccupying thought. Tito's deeper sleep had broken into a doze, in which he felt himself in the Via de' Bardi, explaining his failure to appear at the appointed time. The clear images of that doze urged him to start up at once to a sitting posture, and as he stretched his arms and shook his cap, he said,—

"Tessa, little one, you have let me sleep too long. My hunger and the shadows together tell me that the sun has done much travel since I fell asleep. I must lose no more time. Addio," he ended, patting her cheek with one hand, and settling his cap with the other.

She said nothing, but there were signs in her face which made him speak again in as serious and as chiding a tone as he could command,—

"Now, Tessa, you must not cry. I shall be angry; I shall not love you if you cry. You must go home to your black-faced kid, or if you like you may go back to the gate and see the horses start. But I can stay with you no longer, and if you cry, I shall think you are troublesome to me."

The rising tears were checked by terror at this change in Tito's voice. Tessa turned very pale, and sat in trembling silence, with her blue eyes widened by arrested tears.

"Look now," Tito went on soothingly, opening the wallet that hung at his belt, "here is a pretty charm that I have had a long while,—ever since I was in Sicily, a country a long way off."

His wallet had many little matters in it mingled with small coins, and he had the usual difficulty in laying his finger on the right thing. He unhooked his wallet, and turned out the contents on Tessa's lap. Among them was his onyx ring.

"Ah, my ring!" he exclaimed, slipping it on the forefinger of his right hand. "I forgot to put it on again this morning. Strange, I never missed it! See, Tessa," he added, as he spread out the smaller articles, and selected the one he was in search of. "See this pretty little pointed bit of red coral,—like your goat's horn, is it not?—and here is a hole in it, so you can put it on the cord round your neck along with your *Breve*,[4] and then the evil spirits can't hurt you: if you ever see them coming in the shadow round the corner, point this little coral horn at them, and they will run away. It is a 'buona fortuna,' and will keep you from harm when I am not with you. Come, undo the cord."

Tessa obeyed with a tranquillizing sense that life was going to be something quite new, and that Tito would be with her often. All who remember their childhood remember the strange vague sense, when

[4] A *breve* is a small packet or bag containing relics or prayers and worn round the neck as an act of devotion.—EDITOR.

some new experience came, that everything else was going to be changed, and that there would be no lapse into the old monotony. So the bit of coral was hung beside the tiny bag with the scrap of scrawled parchment in it, and Tessa felt braver.

"And now you will give me a kiss," said Tito, economizing time by speaking while he swept in the contents of the wallet and hung it at his waist again, "and look happy, like a good girl; and then—"

But Tessa had obediently put forward her lips in a moment, and kissed his cheek as he hung down his head.

"Oh, you pretty pigeon!" cried Tito, laughing, pressing her round cheeks with his hands, and crushing her features together so as to give them a general impartial kiss.

Then he started up and walked away, not looking round till he was ten yards from her, when he just turned and gave a parting beck. Tessa was looking after him, but he could see that she was making no signs of distress. It was enough for Tito if she did not cry while he was present. The softness of his nature required that all sorrow should be hidden away from him.

"I wonder when Romola will kiss my cheek in that way?" thought Tito, as he walked along. It seemed a tiresome distance now, and he almost wished he had not been so soft-hearted, or so tempted to linger in the shade. No other excuse was needed to Bardo and Romola than saying simply that he had been unexpectedly hindered; he felt confident their proud delicacy would inquire no farther. He lost no time in getting to Ognissanti, and hastily taking some food there, he crossed the Arno by the Ponte alla Carraja, and made his way as directly as possible towards the Via de' Bardi.

But it was the hour when all the world who meant to be in particularly good time to see the Corso were returning from the Borghi, or villages just outside the gates, where they had dined and reposed themselves; and the thoroughfares leading to the bridges were of course the issues towards which the stream of sight-seers tended. Just as Tito reached the Ponte Vecchio and the entrance of the Via de' Bardi, he was suddenly urged back towards the angle of the intersecting streets. A company on horseback, coming from the Via Guicciardini, and turning up the Via de' Bardi, had compelled the foot-passengers to recede hurriedly. Tito had been walking, as his manner was, with the thumb of his right hand resting in his belt; and as he was thus forced to pause, and was looking carelessly at the passing cavaliers, he felt a very thin cold hand laid on his. He started round, and saw the Dominican friar whose upturned face had so struck him in the morning. Seen closer, the face looked more evidently worn by sickness and not by age; and again it brought some strong but indefinite reminiscences to Tito.

"Pardon me, but—from your face and your ring," said the friar, in a faint voice,—is not your name Tito Melema?"

"Yes," said Tito, also speaking faintly, doubly jarred by the cold touch and the mystery. He was not apprehensive or timid through his imagination, but through his sensations and perceptions he could easily be made to shrink and turn pale like a maiden.

"Then I shall fulfil my commission."

The friar put his hand under his scapulary, and drawing out a small linen bag which hung round his neck, took from it a bit of parchment, doubled and stuck firmly together with some black adhesive substance, and placed it in Tito's hand. On the outside was written in Italian, in a small but distinct character,—

"Tito Melema, aged twenty-three, with a dark, beautiful face, long dark curls, the brightest smile, and a large onyx ring on his right forefinger."

Tito did not look at the friar, but tremblingly broke open the bit of parchment. Inside, the words were,—

"I am sold for a slave; I think they are going to take me to Antioch. The gems alone will serve to ransom me."

Tito looked round at the friar, but could only ask a question with his eyes.

"I had it at Corinth," the friar said, speaking with difficulty, like one whose small strength had been overtaxed,—"I had it from a man who was dying."

"He is dead, then?" said Tito, with a bounding of the heart.

"Not the writer. The man who gave it me was a pilgrim, like myself, to whom the writer had intrusted it, because he was journeying to Italy."

"You know the contents?"

"I do not know them, but I conjecture them. Your friend is in slavery: you will go and release him. But I am unable to talk now." The friar, whose voice had become feebler and feebler, sank down on the stone bench against the wall from which he had risen to touch Tito's hand, adding,—

"I am at San Marco; my name is Fra Luca."

CHAPTER XI

TITO'S DILEMMA

WHEN Fra Luca had ceased to speak, Tito still stood by him in irresolution, and it was not till, the pressure of the passengers being removed, the friar rose and walked slowly into the church of Santa Felicità, that Tito also went on his way along the Via de' Bardi.

"If this monk is a Florentine," he said to himself, "if he is going to remain at Florence, everything must be disclosed." He felt that a new crisis had come, but he was not, for all that, too evidently agitated to pay his visit to Bardo, and apologize for his previous non-appearance. Tito's talent for concealment was being fast developed into something less neutral. It was still possible,—perhaps it might be inevitable,—for

...im to accept frankly the altered conditions, and avow Baldassarre's existence; but hardly without casting an unpleasant light backward on his original reticence as studied equivocation in order to avoid the fulfilment of a secretly recognized claim, to say nothing of his quiet settlement of himself and investment of his florins, when, it would be clear, his benefactor's fate had not been certified. It was at least provisionally wise to act as if nothing had happened, and for the present he would suspend decisive thought; there was all the night for meditation, and no one would know the precise moment at which he had received the letter.

So he entered the room on the second story—where Romola and her father sat among the parchment and the marble, aloof from the life of the streets on holidays as well as on common days—with a face only a little less bright than usual, from regret at appearing so late,—a regret which wanted no testimony, since he had given up the sight of the Corso in order to express it; and then set himself to throw extra animation into the evening, though all the while his consciousness was at work like a machine with complex action, leaving deposits quite distinct from the line of talk; and by the time he descended the stone stairs and issued from the grim door in the starlight, his mind had really reached a new stage in its formation of a purpose.

And when, the next day, after he was free from his professional work, he turned up the Via del Cocomero towards the convent of San Marco, his purpose was fully shaped. He was going to ascertain from Fra Luca precisely how much he conjectured of the truth, and on what grounds he conjectured it; and, further, how long he was to remain at San Marco. And on that fuller knowledge he hoped to mould a statement which would in any case save him from the necessity of quitting Florence. Tito had never had occasion to fabricate an ingenious lie before: the occasion was come now,—the occasion which circumstance never fails to beget on tacit falsity; and his ingenuity was ready. For he had convinced himself that he was not bound to go in search of Baldassarre. He had once said that on a fair assurance of his father's existence and whereabout, he would unhesitatingly go after him. But, after all, *why* was he bound to go? What, looked at closely, was the end of all life, but to extract the utmost sum of pleasure? And was not his own blooming life a promise of incomparably more pleasure, not for himself only, but for others, than the withered wintry life of a man who was past the time of keen enjoyment, and whose ideas had stiffened into barren rigidity? Those ideas had all been sown in the fresh soil of Tito's mind, and were lively germs there: that was the proper order of things,—the order of Nature, which treats all maturity as a mere nidus for youth. Baldassarre had done his work, had had his draught of life: Tito said it was *his* turn now.

And the prospect was so vague: "I think they are going to take me to Antioch:" here was a vista! After a long voyage, to spend months, perhaps years, in a search for which even now there was no guarantee that it would not prove vain; and to leave behind at starting a life of distinction and love: and to find, if he found anything, the old exacting companionship which was known by rote beforehand. Certainly the gems and therefore the florins were, in a sense, Baldassarre's,—in the narrow sense by which the right of possession is determined in ordinary affairs; but in that large and more radically natural view by which the world belongs to youth and strength, they were rather his who could extract the most pleasure out of them. That, he was conscious, was not the sentiment which the complicated play of human feelings had engendered in society. The men around him would expect that he should immediately apply those florins to his benefactor's rescue. But what was the sentiment of society?—a mere tangle of anomalous traditions and opinions, which no wise man would take as a guide, except so far as his own comfort was concerned. Not that he cared for the florins, save, perhaps, for Romola's sake: he would give up the florins readily enough. It was the joy that was due to him and was close to his lips, which he felt he was not bound to thrust away from him and so travel on, thirsting. Any maxims that required a man to fling away the good that was needed to make existence sweet, were only the lining of human selfishness turned outward: they were made by men who wanted others to sacrifice themselves for their sake. He would rather that Baldassarre should not suffer: he liked no one to suffer; but could any philosophy prove to him that he was bound to care for another's suffering more than for his own? To do so, he must have loved Baldassarre devotedly, and he did *not* love him: was that his own fault? Gratitude! seen closely, it made no valid claim: his father's life would have been dreary without him: are we convicted of a debt to men for the pleasures they give themselves?

Having once begun to explain away Baldassarre's claim, Tito's thought showed itself as active as a virulent acid, eating its rapid way through all the tissues of sentiment. His mind was destitute of that dread which has been erroneously decried as if it were nothing higher than a man's animal care for his own skin: that awe of the Divine Nemesis which was felt by religious pagans, and, though it took a more positive form under Christianity, is still felt by the mass of mankind simply as a vague fear at anything which is called wrong-doing. Such terror of the unseen is so far above mere sensual cowardice that it will annihilate that cowardice; it is the initial recognition of a moral law restraining desire, and checks the hard bold scrutiny of imperfect thought into obligations which can never be proved to have any sanctity in the absence of feeling. "It is good," sing the old Eumenides, in Æschylus, "that fear should sit as the guardian of the soul, forcing it into wisdom,—good that men should carry a threatening shadow in their hearts under the full sunshine; else, how should they learn to revere the right?" That guardianship may become needless; but only when all outward law has become needless,—only when duty and love have united in one stream and made a common force.

At Tito entered the outer cloister of San Marco and inquired for Fra

Luca, there was no shadowy presentiment in his mind: he felt himself too cultured and sceptical for that: he had been nurtured in contempt for the tales of priests whose impudent lives were a proverb, and in erudite familiarity with disputes concerning the Chief Good, which had after all, he considered, left it a matter of taste. Yet fear was a strong element in Tito's nature,—the fear of what he believed or saw was likely to rob him of pleasure; and he had a definite fear that Fra Luca might be the means of driving him from Florence.

"Fra Luca? Ah, he is gone to Fiesole,—to the Dominican monastery there. He was taken on a litter in the cool of the morning. The poor Brother is very ill. Could you leave a message for him?"

This answer was given by a *fra converso*, or lay brother, whose accent told plainly that he was a raw contadino, and whose dull glance implied no curiosity.

"Thanks; my business can wait."

Tito turned away with a sense of relief. "This friar is not likely to live," he said to himself. "I saw he was worn to a shadow. And at Fiesole there will be nothing to recall me to his mind. Besides, if he should come back, my explanation will serve as well then as now. But I wish I knew what it was that his face recalled to me."

CHAPTER XII

THE PRIZE IS NEARLY GRASPED

TITO walked along with a light step, for the immediate fear had vanished; the usual joyousness of his disposition reassumed its predominance, and he was going to see Romola. Yet Romola's life seemed an image of that loving, pitying devotedness, that patient endurance of irksome tasks, from which he had shrunk and excused himself. But he was not out of love with goodness, or prepared to plunge into vice: he was in his fresh youth, with soft pulses for all charm and loveliness; he had still a healthy appetite for ordinary human joys, and the poison could only work by degrees. He had sold himself to evil, but at present life seemed so nearly the same to him that he was not conscious of the bond. He meant all things to go on as they had done before, both within and without him: he meant to win golden opinions by meritorious exertion, by ingenious learning, by amiable compliance: he was not going to do anything that would throw him out of harmony with the beings he cared for. And he cared supremely for Romola; he wished to have her for his beautiful and loving wife. There might be a wealthier alliance within the ultimate reach of successful accomplishments like his, but there was no woman in all Florence like Romola. When she was near him, and looked at him with her sincere hazel eyes, he was subdued by a delicious influence as strong and inevitable as those musical vibrations which take possession of us with a rhythmic empire that no sooner ceases than we desire it to begin again.

As he trod the stone stairs, when he was still outside the door, with no one but Maso near him, the influence seemed to have begun its work by the mere nearness of anticipation.

"Welcome, Tito mio," said the old man's voice, before Tito had spoken. There was a new vigour in the voice, a new cheerfulness in the blind face, since that first interview more than two months ago. "You have brought fresh manuscript, doubtless; but since we were talking last night I have had new ideas: we must take a wider scope,—we must go back upon our footsteps."

Tito, paying his homage to Romola as he advanced, went, as his custom was, straight to Bardo's chair, and put his hand in the palm that was held to receive it, placing himself on the cross-legged leather seat with scrolled ends, close to Bardo's elbow.

"Yes," he said, in his gentle way; "I have brought the new manuscript, but that can wait your pleasure. I have young limbs, you know, and can walk back up the hill without any difficulty."

He did not look at Romola as he said this, but he knew quite well that her eyes were fixed on him with delight.

"That is well said, my son." Bardo had already addressed Tito in this way once or twice of late. "And I perceive with gladness that you do not shrink from labour, without which, the poet has wisely said, life has given nothing to mortals. It is too often the 'palma sine pulvere,' the prize of glory without the dust of the race, that attracts young ambition. But what says the Greek? 'In the morning of life, work; in the mid-day give counsel; in the evening, pray.' It is true, I might be thought to have reached that helpless evening; but not so, while I have counsel within me which is yet unspoken. For my mind, as I have often said, was shut up as by a dam; the plenteous waters lay dark and motionless; but you, my Tito, have opened a duct for them, and they rush forward with a force that surprises myself. And now, what I want is that we should go over our preliminary ground again, with a wider scheme of comment and illustration: otherwise I may lose opportunities which I now see retrospectively, and which may never occur again. You mark what I am saying, Tito?"

He had just stooped to reach his manuscript, which had rolled down, and Bardo's jealous ear was alive to the slight movement.

Tito might have been excused for shrugging his shoulders at the prospect before him, but he was not naturally impatient; moreover, he had been bred up in that laborious erudition, at once minute and copious, which was the chief intellectual task of the age; and with Romola near, he was floated along by waves of agreeable sensation that made everything seem easy.

"Assuredly," he said; "you wish to enlarge your comments on certain passages we have cited."

"Not only so; I wish to introduce an occasional *excursus*, where we have noticed an author to whom I have given special study; for I may die too soon to achieve any separate work. And this is not a time for scholarly integrity and well-sifted learning to lie idle, when it is not only rash ignorance that we have to fear, but when there are men like Calderino,[1] who, as Poliziano has well shown, have recourse to impudent falsities of citation to serve the ends of their vanity and secure a triumph to their own mistakes. Wherefore, my Tito, I think it not well that we should let slip the occasion that lies under our hands. And now we will turn back to the point where we have cited the passage from Thucydides, and I wish you, by way of preliminary, to go with me through all my notes on the Latin translation made by Lorenzo Valla, for which the incomparable Pope Nicholas V.—with whose personal notice I was honoured while I was yet young, and when he was still Thomas of Sarzana—paid him (I say not unduly) the sum of five hundred gold scudi. But inasmuch as Valla, though otherwise of dubious fame, is held in high honour for his severe scholarship, whence the epigrammatist has jocosely said of him that since he went among the shades, Pluto himself has not dared to speak in the ancient languages, it is the more needful that his name should not be as a stamp warranting false wares; and therefore I would introduce an *excursus* on Thucydides, wherein my castigations of Valla's text may find a fitting place. My Romola, thou wilt reach the needful volumes—thou knowest them—on the fifth shelf of the cabinet."

Tito rose at the same moment with Romola, saying, "I will reach them, if you will point them out," and followed her hastily into the adjoining small room, where the walls were also covered with ranges of books in perfect order.

"There they are," said Romola, pointing upward; "every book is just where it was when my father ceased to see them."

Tito stood by her without hastening to reach the books. They had never been in this room together before.

"I hope," she continued, turning her eyes full on Tito, with a look of grave confidence,—"I hope he will not weary you; this work makes him so happy."

"And me too, Romola,—if you will only let me say I love you,—if you will only think me worth loving a little."

His speech was the softest murmur; and the dark beautiful face, nearer to hers than it had ever been before, was looking at her with beseeching tenderness.

"I do love you," murmured Romola; she looked at him with the same simple majesty as ever, but her voice had never in her life before

---

[1] Domizio Calderino, a clever and scholarly humanist, died in Rome in 1478, of the plague, when only thirty-two years old.

Angiolo Poliziano criticised him sharply in his "Miscellanies" (Chap. IX), although he wrote several years after Calderino's death. He depicted him as a man of great talent and equal learning, but too ready, in order to maintain the great reputation he bore, to write in defence of anything that came into his mind.

This criticism drew friendly reproaches from Jacopo Antiquario, to which Poliziano replied ("Polit. Epist.," Book 3, Ep. 18), with an acknowledgment, that Calderino had been a man of great genius.

sunk to that murmur. It seemed to them both that they were looking at each other a long while before her lips moved again; yet it was but a moment till she said, "I know *now* what it is to be happy."

The faces just met, and the dark curls mingled for an instant with the rippling gold. Quick as lightning after that, Tito set his foot on a projecting ledge of the book-shelves and reached down the needful volumes. They were both contented to be silent and separate, for that first blissful experience of mutual consciousness was all the more exquisite for being unperturbed by immediate sensation.

It had all been as rapid as the irreversible mingling of waters, for even the eager and jealous Bardo had not become impatient.

"You have the volumes, my Romola?" the old man said, as they came near him again. "And now you will get your pen ready; for as Tito marks off the scholia we determine on extracting, it will be well for you to copy them without delay,—numbering them carefully, mind, to correspond with the numbers in the text which he will write."

Romola always had some task which gave her a share in this joint work. Tito took his stand at the leggio, where he both wrote and read, and she placed herself at a table just in front of him, where she was ready to give into her father's hands anything that he might happen to want, or relieve him of a volume that he had done with. They had always been in that position since the work began; yet on this day it seemed new: it was so different now for them to be opposite each other; so different for Tito to take a book from her, as she lifted it from her father's knee. Yet there was no finesse to secure an additional look or touch. Each woman creates in her own likeness the love-tokens that are offered to her; and Romola's deep, calm happiness encompassed Tito like the rich but quiet evening light which dissipates all unrest.

They had been two hours at their work, and were just desisting because of the fading light, when the door opened, and there entered a figure strangely incongruous with the current of their thoughts and with the suggestions of every object around them. It was the figure of a short stout black-eyed woman, about fifty, wearing a black velvet berretta, or close cap, embroidered with pearls, under which surprisingly massive black braids surmounted the little bulging forehead, and fell in rich plaited curves over the ears, while an equally surprising carmine tint on the upper region of the fat cheeks contrasted with the surrounding sallowness. Three rows of pearls and a lower necklace of gold reposed on the horizontal cushion of her neck; the embroidered border of her trailing black velvet gown and her embroidered long-drooping sleeves of rose-coloured damask were slightly faded, but they conveyed to the initiated eye the satisfactory assurance that they were the splendid result of six months' labour by a skilled workman; and the rose-coloured petticoat, with its dimmed white fringe and seed-pearl arabesques, was duly exhibited in order to suggest a similar pleasing reflection. A handsome coral rosary hung from one side of an inferential belt which emerged into certainty with a large clasp of silver wrought in niello;

and, on the other side, where the belt again became inferential, hung a scarsella, or large purse, of crimson velvet, stitched with pearls. Her little fat right hand, which looked as if it had been made of paste, and had risen out of shape under partial baking, held a small book of devotions, also splendid with velvet, pearls, and silver.

The figure was already too familiar to Tito to be startling, for Monna Brigida was a frequent visitor at Bardo's, being excepted from the sentence of banishment passed on feminine triviality, on the ground of her cousinship to his dead wife and her early care for Romola, who now looked round at her with an affectionate smile, and rose to draw the leather seat to a due distance from her father's chair, that the coming gush of talk might not be too near his ear.

"*La cugina?*" said Bardo, interrogatively, detecting the short steps and the sweeping drapery.

"Yes, it is your cousin," said Monna Brigida, in an alert voice, raising her fingers smilingly at Tito, and the lifting up her face to be kissed by Romola. "Always the troublesome cousin breaking in on your wisdom," she went on, seating herself and beginning to fan herself with the white veil hanging over her arm. "Well, well; if I didn't bring you some news of the world now and then, I do believe you'd forget there was anything in life but these mouldy ancients, who want sprinkling with holy water if all I hear about them is true. Not but what the world is bad enough nowadays, for the scandals that turn up under one's nose at every corner,—I don't want to hear and see such things, but one can't go about with one's head in a bag; and it was only yesterday— Well, well, you needn't burst out at me, Bardo, I am not going to tell anything; if I'm not as wise as the three kings, I know how many legs go into one boot. But, nevertheless, Florence is a wicked city,—is it not true, Messer Tito? for you go into the world. Not but what one must sin a little,—Messer Domeneddio expects that of us, else what are the blessed sacraments for? And what I say is, we've got to reverence the saints, and not to set ourselves up as if we could be like them, else life would be unbearable; as it will be if things go on after this new fashion. For what do you think? I've been at the wedding to-day,—Dianora Acciajoli's with the young Albizzi that there has been so much talk of— and everybody wondered at its being to-day instead of yesterday; but, *cieli!*[2] such a wedding as it was might have been put off till the next Quaresima for a penance. For there was the bride looking like a white nun,—not so much as a pearl about her,—and the bridegroom as solemn as San Giuseppe. It's true! And half the people invited were *Piagnoni*— they call them *piagnoni* now, these new saints of Fra Girolamo's making. And to think of two families like the Albizzi and the Acciajoli taking up such notions, when they could afford to wear the best! Well, well, they invited me,—but they could do no other, seeing my husband

---

[2] *O ciel!* as an exclamation of surprise was not used in the fifteenth century. It is of later date and is only used melodramatically.—EDITOR.

was Luca Antonio's uncle by the mother's side,—and a pretty time I had of it while we waited under the canopy in front of the house, before they let us in. I couldn't stand in my clothes, it seemed, without giving offence; for there was Monna Berta, who has had worse secrets in her time than any I could tell of myself, looking askance at me from under her hood like a *pinzochera,* and telling me to read the Frate's book about widows, from which she had found great guidance. Holy Madonna! it seems as if widows had nothing to do now, but to buy their coffins, and think it a thousand years till they get into them, instead of enjoying themselves a little when they've got their hands free for the first time. And what do you think was the music we had, to make our dinner lively? A long discourse from Fra Domenico of San Marco, about the doctrines of their Blessed Fra Girolamo,—the three doctrines we are all to get by heart; and he kept marking them off on his fingers till he made my flesh creep: and the first is, Florence or the Church—I don't know which, for first he said one and then the other—shall be scourged; but if he means the pestilence, the Signory ought to put a stop to such preaching, for it's enough to raise the swelling under one's arms with fright; but then, after that, he says Florence is to be regenerated; but what will be the good of that when we're all dead of the plague, or something else? And then, the third thing, and what he said oftenest, is, that it's all to be in our days; and he marked that off on his thumb till he made me tremble like the very jelly before me. They had jellies, to be sure, with the arms of the Albizzi and the Acciajoli raised on them in all colours; they've not turned the world quite upside down yet. But all their talk is, that we are to go back to the old days; for up starts Francesco Valori, that I've danced with in the Via Larga when he was a bachelor and as fond of the Medici as anybody, and he makes a speech about the old times, before the Florentines had left off crying 'Popolo' and begun to cry 'Palle,'—as if that had anything to do with a wedding! —and how we ought to keep to the rules the Signory laid down Heaven knows when, that we were not to wear this and that, and not eat this and that,—and how our manners were corrupted and we read bad books; though he can't say that of *me*—"

"Stop, cousin!" said Bardo, in his imperious tone, for he had a remark to make, and only desperate measures could arrest the rattling lengthiness of Monna Brigida's discourse. But now she gave a little start, pursed up her mouth, and looked at him with round eyes.

"Francesco Valori is not altogether wrong," Bardo went on. "Bernardo, indeed, rates him not highly, and is rather of opinion that he christens private grudges by the name of public zeal; though I must admit that my good Bernardo is too slow of belief in that unalloyed patriotism which was found in all its lustre among the ancients. But it is true, Tito, that our manners have degenerated somewhat from that noble frugality which, as has been well seen in the public acts of our citizens, is the parent of true magnificence. For men, as I hear, will now spend on the transient show of a Giostra sums which would suffice to found a library, and confer a lasting possession on mankind. Still, I conceive, it remains true of us Florentines that we have more of that magnanimous sobriety which abhors a trivial lavishness that it may be grandly open-handed on grand occasions, than can be found in any other city of Italy; for I understand that the Neapolitan and Milanese courtiers laugh at the scarcity of our plate, and think scorn of our great families for borrowing from each other that furniture of the table at their entertainments. But in the vain laughter of folly wisdom hears half its applause."

"Laughter, indeed!" burst forth Monna Brigida again, the moment Bardo paused. "If anybody wanted to hear laughter at the wedding to-day they were disappointed, for when young Niccolò Macchiavelli tried to make a joke, and told stories out of Franco Sacchetti's book, how it was no use for the Signoria to make rules for us women, because we were cleverer than all the painters, and architects, and doctors of logic in the world, for we could make black look white, and yellow look pink, and crooked look straight, and, if anything was forbidden, we could find a new name for it,—Holy Virgin! the Piagnoni looked more dismal than before, and somebody said Sacchetti's book was wicked. Well, I don't read it,—they can't accuse *me* of reading anything. Save me from going to a wedding again, if that's to be the fashion; for all of us who were not Piagnoni were as comfortable as wet chickens. I was never caught in a worse trap but once before, and that was when I went to hear their precious Frate last Quaresima in San Lorenzo. Perhaps I never told you about it, Messer Tito?—it almost freezes my blood when I think of it. How he rated us poor women! and the men, too, to tell the truth, but I didn't mind that so much. He called us cows, and lumps of flesh, and wantons, and mischief-makers,—and I could just bear that, for there were plenty others more fleshy and spiteful than I was, though every now and then his voice shook the very bench under me like a trumpet; but then he came to the false hair, and, oh, misericordia! he made a picture—I see it now—of a young woman lying a pale corpse, and us light-minded widows,—of course he meant me as well as the rest, for I had my plaits on, for if one is getting old, one doesn't want to look as ugly as the Befana,—us widows rushing up to the corpse, like bare-pated vultures as we were, and cutting off its young dead hair to deck our old heads with. Oh, the dreams I had after that! And then he cried, and wrung his hands at us, and I cried too. And to go home, and to take off my jewels,—this very clasp and everything, and to make them into a packet, *fù tutt' uno;* and I was within a hair of sending them to the Good Men of St. Martin to give to the poor, but, by heaven's mercy, I bethought me of going first to my confessor, Fra Cristoforo, at Santa Croce, and he told me how it was all the work of the devil, this preaching and prophesying of their Fra Girolamo, and the Dominicans were trying to turn the world upside down, and I was never to go and hear him again, else I must do penance for it; for the great preachers Fra Mariano and Fra Menico had shown how Fra

Girolamo preached lies,—and that was true, for I heard them both in the Duomo,—and how the Pope's dream of San Francesco propping up the Church with his arms was being fulfilled still, and the Dominicans were beginning to pull it down. Well and good: I went away *con Dio,* and made myself easy. I am not going to be frightened by a Frate Predicatore again. And all I say is, I wish it hadn't been the Dominicans that poor Dino joined years ago, for then I should have been glad when I heard them say he was come back—"

"Silenzio!" said Bardo, in a loud agitated voice; while Romola half started from her chair, clasped her hands, and looked round at Tito, as if now she might appeal to him. Monna Brigida gave a little scream, and bit her lip.

"Donna!" said Bardo, again, "hear once more my will. Bring no reports about that name to this house; and thou, Romola, I forbid thee to ask. My son is dead."

Bardo's whole frame seemed vibrating with passion, and no one dared to break silence again. Monna Brigida lifted her shoulders and her hands in mute dismay; then she rose as quietly as possible, gave many significant nods to Tito and Romola, motioning to them that they were not to move, and stole out of the room like a culpable fat spaniel who has barked unseasonably.

Meanwhile Tito's quick mind had been combining ideas with lightning-like rapidity. Bardo's son was not really dead, then, as he had supposed; he was a monk; he was "come back:" and Fra Luca—yes! it was the likeness to Bardo and Romola that had made the face seem half-known to him. If he were only dead at Fiesole at that moment! This importunate selfish wish inevitably thrust itself before every other thought. It was true that Bardo's rigid will was a sufficient safeguard against any intercourse between Romola and her brother; but *not* against the betrayal of what he knew to others, especially when the subject was suggested by the coupling of Romola's name with that of the very Tito Melema whose description he had carried round his neck as an index. No! nothing but Fra Luca's death could remove all danger; but his death was highly probable, and after the momentary shock of the discovery, Tito let his mind fall back in repose on that confident hope.

They had sat in silence and in a deepening twilight for twenty minutes, when Romola ventured to say,—

"Shall I light the lamp, father, and shall we go on?"

"No, my Romola, we will work no more to-night. Tito, come and sit by me here."

Tito moved from the reading-desk, and seated himself on the other side of Bardo, close to his left elbow.

"Come nearer to me, figliuola mia," said Bardo again, after a moment's pause. And Romola seated herself on a low stool, and let her arm rest on her father's right knee, that he might lay his hand on her hair, as he was fond of doing.

"Tito, I never told you that I had once a son," said Bardo, forgetting what had fallen from him in the emotion raised by their first interview. The old man had been deeply shaken, and was forced to pour out his feelings in spite of pride. "But he left me,—he is dead to me. I have disowned him forever. He was a ready scholar, as you are, but more fervid and impatient, and yet sometimes rapt and self-absorbed, like a flame fed by some fitful source; showing a disposition from the very first to turn away his eyes from the clear lights of reason and philosophy, and to prostrate himself under the influences of a dim mysticism which eludes all rules of human duty as it eludes all argument. And so it ended. We will speak no more of him: he is dead to me. I wish his face could be blotted from that world of memory in which the distant seems to grow clearer and the near to fade."

Bardo paused, but neither Romola nor Tito dared to speak,—his voice was too tremulous, the poise of his feelings too doubtful. But he presently raised his hand and found Tito's shoulder to rest it on, while he went on speaking, with an effort to be calmer.

"But *you* have come to me, Tito,—not quite too late. I will lose no time in vain regret. When you are working by my side I seem to have found a son again."

The old man, preoccupied with the governing interest of his life, was only thinking of the much-meditated book which had quite thrust into the background the suggestion, raised by Bernardo del Nero's warning, of a possible marriage between Tito and Romola. But Tito could not allow the moment to pass unused.

"Will you let me be always and altogether your son? Will you let me take care of Romola,—be her husband? I think she will not deny me. She has said she loves me. I know I am not equal to her in birth,—in anything; but I am no longer a destitute stranger."

"Is it true, my Romola?" said Bardo, in a lower tone, an evident vibration passing through him and dissipating the saddened aspect of his features.

"Yes, father," said Romola, firmly. "I love Tito,—I wish to marry him, that we may both be your children and never part."

Tito's hand met hers in a strong clasp for the first time, while she was speaking, but their eyes were fixed anxiously on her father.

"Why should it not be?" said Bardo, as if arguing against any opposition to his assent, rather than assenting. "It would be a happiness to me; and thou, too, Romola, wouldst be the happier for it."

He stroked her long hair gently, and bent towards her.

"Ah, I have been apt to forget that thou needest some other love than mine. And thou wilt be a noble wife. Bernardo thinks I shall hardly find a husband fitting for thee. And he is perhaps right. For thou art not like the herd of thy sex: thou art such a woman as the immortal poets had a vision of when they sang the lives of the heroes,—tender but strong, like thy voice, which has been to me instead of the light in the years of my blindness. . . . And so thou lovest him?"

He sat upright again for a minute, and then said, in the same tone as before, "Why should it not be? I will think of it; I will talk with Bernardo."

Tito felt a disagreeable chill at this answer, for Bernardo del Nero's eyes had retained their keen suspicion whenever they looked at him, and the uneasy remembrance of Fra Luca converted all uncertainty into fear.

"Speak for me, Romola," he said pleadingly. "Messer Bernardo is sure to be against me."

"No, Tito," said Romola, "my godfather will not oppose what my father firmly wills. And it is your will that I should marry Tito,—is it not, father? Nothing has ever come to me before that I have wished for strongly: I did not think it possible that I could care so much for anything that could happen to myself."

It was a brief and simple plea; but it was the condensed story of Romola's self-repressing colourless young life, which had thrown all its passion into sympathy with aged sorrows, aged ambition, aged pride and indignation. It had never occurred to Romola that she should not speak as directly and emphatically of her love for Tito as of any other subject.

"Romola mia!" said her father fondly, pausing on the words, "it is true thou hast never urged on me any wishes of thy own. And I have no will to resist thine; rather, my heart met Tito's entreaty at its very first utterance. Nevertheless, I must talk with Bernardo about the measures needful to be observed. For we must not act in haste, or do anything unbeseeming my name. I am poor, and held of little account by the wealthy of our family,—nay, I may consider myself a lonely man,—but I must nevertheless remember that generous birth has its obligations. And I would not be reproached by my fellow-citizens for rash haste in bestowing my daughter. Bartolommeo Scala gave his Alessandra to the Greek Marullo, but Marullo's lineage was well known, and Scala himself is of no extraction. I know Bernardo will hold that we must take time: he will, perhaps, reproach me with want of due fore-thought. Be patient, my children: you are very young."

No more could be said, and Romola's heart was perfectly satisfied. Not so Tito's. If the subtle mixture of good and evil prepares suffering for human truth and purity, there is also suffering prepared for the wrong-doer by the same mingled conditions. As Tito kissed Romola on their parting that evening, the very strength of the thrill that moved his whole being at the sense that this woman, whose beauty it was hardly possible to think of as anything but the necessary consequence of her noble nature, loved him with all the tenderness that spoke in her clear eyes, brought a strong reaction of regret that he had not kept himself free from that first deceit which had dragged him into the danger of being disgraced before her. There was a spring of bitterness mingling with that fountain of sweets. Would the death of Fra Luca arrest it? He hoped it would.

CHAPTER XIII

THE SHADOW OF NEMESIS

It was the lazy afternoon time on the 7th of September, more than two months after the day on which Romola and Tito had confessed their love to each other.

Tito, just descended into Nello's shop, had found the barber stretched on the bench with his cap over his eyes; one leg was drawn up, and the other had slipped towards the ground, having apparently carried with it a manuscript volume of verse, which lay with its leaves crushed. In a corner sat Sandro playing a game at *mora* by himself, and watching the slow reply of his left fingers to the arithmetical demands of his right with solemn-eyed interest.

Treading with the gentlest step, Tito snatched up the lute, and bending over the barber, touched the strings lightly while he sang,—

> "Quant' è bella giovinezza,
> Che si fugge tuttavia!
> Chi vuol esser lieto sia,
> Di doman non c' è certezza."

Nello was as easily awaked as a bird. The cap was off his eyes in an instant, and he started up.

"Ah, my Apollino! I am somewhat late with my siesta on this hot day, it seems. That comes of not going to sleep in the natural way, but taking a potion of potent poesy. Hear you, how I am beginning to match my words by the initial letter, like a trovatore? That is one of my bad symptoms: I am sorely afraid that the good wine of my understanding is going to run off at the spigot of authorship, and I shall be left an empty cask with an odour of dregs, like many another incomparable genius of my acquaintance. What is it, my Orpheus?" Here Nello stretched out his arms to their full length, and then brought them round till his hands grasped Tito's curls, and drew them out playfully. "What is it you want of your well-tamed Nello? For I perceive a coaxing sound in that soft strain of yours. Let me see the very needle's eye of your desire, as the sublime poet says, that I may thread it."

"That is but a tailor's image of your sublime poet's," said Tito, still letting his fingers fall in a light dropping way on the strings. "But you have divined the reason of my affectionate impatience to see your eyes open. I want you to give me an extra touch of your art,—not on my chin, no; but on the *zazzera*, which is as tangled as your Florentine politics. You have an adroit way of inserting your comb, which flatters the skin, and stirs the animal spirits agreeably in that region; and a little of your most delicate orange-scent would not be amiss, for I am bound to the Scala Palace, and am to present myself in radiant company. The young Cardinal Giovanni de' Medici is to be there, and he brings with him a certain young Bernardo Dovizi of Bibbiena, whose wit is so rapid that I see no way of outrivalling it save by the scent of orange-blossoms."

Nello had already seized and flourished his comb, and pushed Tito gently backward into the chair, wrapping the cloth round him.

"Never talk of rivalry, bel giovane mio: Bernardo Dovizi is a keen youngster, who will never carry a net out to catch the wind; but he has something of the same sharp-muzzled look as his brother Ser Piero, the weasel that Piero de' Medici keeps at his beck to slip through small holes for him. No! you distance all rivals, and may soon touch the sky with your forefinger. They tell me you have even carried enough honey with you to sweeten the sour Messer Angelo; for he has pronounced you less of an ass than might have been expected, considering there is such ¬ good understanding between you and the Secretary."

"And between ourselves, Nello mio, that Messer Angelo has more genius and erudition than I can find in all the other Florentine scholars put together. It may answer very well for them to cry me up now, when Poliziano is beaten down with grief, or illness, or something else; I can try a flight with such a sparrow-hawk as Pietro Crinito; but for Poliziano, he is a large-beaked eagle who would swallow me, feathers and all, and not feel any difference."

"I will not contradict your modesty there, if you will have it so; but you don't expect us clever Florentines to keep saying the same things over again every day of our lives, as we must do if we always told the truth. We cry down Dante, and we cry up Francesco Cei, just for the sake of variety; and if we cry you up as a new Poliziano, heaven has taken care that it shall not be quite so great a lie as it might have been. And are you not a pattern of virtue in this wicked city? with your ears double waxed against all siren invitations that would lure you from the Via de' Bardi, and the great work which is to astonish posterity?"

"Posterity in good truth, whom it will probably astonish as the universe does, by the impossibility of seeing what was the plan of it."

"Yes, something like that was being prophesied here the other day. Cristoforo Landino said that the excellent Bardo was one of those scholars who lie overthrown in their learning, like cavaliers in heavy armour, and then get angry because they are overridden,—which pithy remark, it seems to me, was not an herb out of his own garden; for of all men, for feeding one with an empty spoon and gagging one with vain expectation by long discourse, Messer Cristoforo is the pearl. Ecco! you are perfect now." Here Nello drew away the cloth. "Impossible to add a grace more! But love is not always to be fed on learning, eh? I shall have to dress the *zazzera* for the betrothal before long,—is it not true?"

"Perhaps," said Tito, smiling, "unless Messer Bernardo should next recommend Bardo to require that I should yoke a lion and a wild boar to the car of the Zecca before I can win my Alcestis. But I confess he is right in holding me unworthy of Romola; she is a Pleiad that may grow dim by marrying any mortal."

"*Gnaffè,* your modesty is in the right place there. Yet Fate seems to have measured and chiselled you for the niche that was left empty by the old man's son, who, by the way, Cronaca was telling me, is now at San Marco. Did you know?"

A slight electric shock passed through Tito as he rose from the chair, but it was not outwardly perceptible, for he immediately stooped to pick up the fallen book, and busied his fingers with flattening the leaves, while he said,—

"No; he was at Fiesole, I thought. Are you sure he is come back to San Marco?"

"Cronaca is my authority," said Nello, with a shrug. "I don't frequent that sanctuary, but he does. Ah," he added, taking the book from Tito's hands, "my poor Nencia da Barberino! It jars your scholarly feelings to see the pages dog's-eared. I was lulled to sleep by the well-rhymed charms of that rustic maiden,—'prettier than the turnip-flower,' 'with a cheek more savoury than cheese.' But to get such a well-scented notion of the contadina, one must lie on velvet cushions in the Via Larga—not go to look at the Fierucoloni stumping in to the Piazza de la Nunziata this evening after sundown."

"And pray who are the Fierucoloni?" said Tito, indifferently, settling his cap.

"The contadine who came from the mountains of Pistoia, and the Casentino, and heaven knows where, to keep their vigil in the church of the Nunziata, and sell their yarn and dried mushrooms at the Fierucola,[1] as we call it. They make a queer show, with their paper lanterns, howling their hymns to the Virgin on this Eve of her Nativity,—if you had the leisure to see them. No?—well, I have had enough of it myself, for there is wild work in the Piazza. One may happen to get a stone or two about one's ears or shins without asking for it, and I was never fond of that pressing attention. Addio."

Tito carried a little uneasiness with him on his visit, which ended earlier than he had expected, the boy-cardinal Giovanni de' Medici, youngest of red-hatted fathers, who has since presented his broad dark cheek very conspicuously to posterity as Pope Leo the Tenth, having been detained at his favourite pastime of the chase, and having failed to appear. It still wanted half an hour of sunset as he left the door of the Scala Palace, with the intention of proceeding forthwith to the Via

---

[1] It is not certain that even in the fifteenth century the Festival of the *Fierucola* took place on the seventh of September, the Eve of the Nativity of the Virgin, when the peasant women come in to visit the Church of the Santissima Annunziata. According to some, the festival is held in remembrance of the taking of Siena under Cosimo I in 1555, which event took place at night by the light of lanterns and torches, as depicted by Vasari in the Salone del Cinquecento in the Palazzo Vecchio. Neither is it certain that the fair of the Annunziata was called *Fierucola;* but the name of *Fierucolone,* corrupted nowadays into *Rificolone,* is still given to the lanterns which are lighted for the Festival of the Madonna in September, and is also applied as a term of contempt to rough, uncouth peasants.—EDITOR.

de' Bardi; but he had not gone far when, to his astonishment, he saw Romola advancing towards him along the Borgo Pinti.

She wore a thick black veil and black mantle, but it was impossible to mistake her figure and her walk; and by her side was a short stout form, which he recognized as that of Monna Brigida, in spite of the unusual plainness of her attire. Romola had not been bred up to devotional observances, and the occasions on which she took the air elsewhere than under the loggia on the roof of the house were so rare and so much dwelt on beforehand, because of Bardo's dislike to be left without her, that Tito felt sure there must have been some sudden and urgent ground for an absence of which he had heard nothing the day before. She saw him through her veil, and hastened her steps.

"Romola, has anything happened?" said Tito, turning to walk by her side.

She did not answer at the first moment, and Monna Brigida broke in.

"Ah, Messer Tito, you do well to turn round, for we are in haste. And is it not a misfortune? We are obliged to go round by the walls and turn up the Via del Maglio, because of the Fair; for the contadine coming in block up the way by the Nunziata, which would have taken us to San Marco in half the time."

Tito's heart gave a great bound, and began to beat violently.

"Romola," he said in a lower tone, "are you going to San Marco?"

They were now out of the Borgo Pinti and were under the city walls, where they had wide gardens on their left hand, and all was quiet. Romola put aside her veil for the sake of breathing the air, and he could see the subdued agitation in her face.

"Yes, Tito mio," she said, looking directly at him with sad eyes. "For the first time I am doing something unknown to my father. It comforts me that I have met you, for at least I can tell *you*. But if you are going to him, it will be well for you not to say that you met me. He thinks I am only gone to my cousin, because she sent for me. I left my godfather with him: *he* knows where I am going, and why. You remember that evening when my brother's name was mentioned, and my father spoke of him to you?"

"Yes," said Tito, in a low tone. There was a strange complication in his mental state. His heart sank at the probability that a great change was coming over his prospects, while at the same time his thoughts were darting over a hundred details of the course he would take when the change had come, and yet he returned Romola's gaze with a hungry sense that it might be the last time she would ever bend it on him with full, unquestioning confidence.

"The *cugina* had heard that he was coming back, and the evening before—the evening of San Giovanni—as I afterwards found, he had been seen by our good Maso near the door of our house; but when Maso went to inquire at San Marco, Dino, that is, my brother,—he was christened Bernardino, after our godfather, but now he calls himself Fra Luca,—had been taken to the monastery at Fiesole, because he was ill. But this morning a message came to Maso, saying that he was come back to San Marco, and Maso went to him there. He is very ill, and he has adjured me to go and see him. I cannot refuse it, though I hold him guilty; I still remember how I loved him when I was a little girl, before I knew that he would forsake my father. And perhaps he has some word of penitence to send by me. It cost me a struggle to act in opposition to my father's feeling, which I have always held to be just. I am almost sure you will think I have chosen rightly, Tito, because I have noticed that your nature is less rigid than mine, and nothing makes you angry: it would cost you less to be forgiving; though, if you had seen your father forsaken by one to whom he had given his chief love,—by one in whom he had planted his labour and his hopes,—forsaken when his need was becoming greatest,—even you, Tito, would find it hard to forgive."

What could he say? He was not equal to the hypocrisy of telling Romola that such offences ought not to be pardoned; and he had not the courage to utter any words of dissuasion.

"You are right, my Romola; you are always right, except in thinking too well of me."

There was really some genuineness in those last words, and Tito looked very beautiful as he uttered them with an unusual pallor in his face, and a slight quivering of his lip. Romola, interpreting all things largely, like a mind prepossessed with high beliefs, had a tearful brightness in her eyes as she looked at him, touched with keen joy that he felt so strongly whatever she felt. But without pausing in her walk, she said,—

"And now, Tito, I wish you to leave me, for the *cugina* and I shall be less noticed if we enter the piazza alone."

"Yes, it were better you should leave us," said Monna Brigida; "for, to say the truth, Messer Tito, all eyes follow you, and let Romola muffle herself as she will, every one wants to see what there is under her veil, for she has that way of walking like a procession. Not that I find fault with her for it, only it doesn't suit my steps. And, indeed, I would rather not have us seen going to San Marco, and that's why I am dressed as if I were one of the Piagnoni themselves, and as old as Sant' Anna; for if it had been anybody but poor Dino, who ought to be forgiven if he's dying, for what's the use of having a grudge against dead people?—make them feel while they live, say I—"

No one made a scruple of interrupting Monna Brigida; and Tito, having just raised Romola's hand to his lips, and said, "I understand, I obey you," now turned away, lifting his cap,—a sign of reverence rarely made at that time by native Florentines, and which excited Bernardo del Nero's contempt for Tito as a fawning Greek; while to Romola, who loved homage, it gave him an exceptional grace.

He was half glad of the dismissal, half disposed to cling to Romola to the last moment in which she would love him without suspicion. For it seemed to him certain that this brother would before all things want to know, and that Romola would before all things confide to him, what was her father's position and her own after the years which must have brought so much change. She would tell him that she was soon to be publicly betrothed to a young scholar, who was to fill up the place left vacant long ago by a wandering son. He foresaw the impulse that would prompt Romola to dwell on that prospect, and what would follow on the mention of the future husband's name. Fra Luca would tell all he knew and conjectured, and Tito saw no possible falsity by which he could now ward off the worst consequences of his former dissimulation. It was all over with his prospects in Florence. There was Messer Bernardo del Nero, who would be delighted at seeing confirmed the wisdom of his advice about deferring the betrothal until Tito's character and position had been established by a longer residence; and the history of the young Greek professor, whose benefactor was in slavery, would be the talk under every loggia. For the first time in his life he felt too fevered and agitated to trust his power of self-command; he gave up his intended visit to Bardo, and walked up and down under the walls until the yellow light in the west had quite faded, when, without any distinct purpose, he took the first turning, which happened to be the Via San Sebastiano, leading him directly towards the Piazza dell' Annunziata.

He was at one of those lawless moments which comes to us all if we have no guide but desire, and if the pathway where desire leads us seems suddenly closed; he was ready to follow any beckoning that offered him an immediate purpose.

CHAPTER XIV

THE PEASANTS' FAIR

THE moving crowd and the strange mixture of noises that burst on him at the entrance of the piazza, reminded Tito of what Nello had said to him about the Fierucoloni, and he pushed his way into the crowd with a sort of pleasure in the hooting and elbowing which filled the empty moments, and dulled that calculation of the future which had so new a dreariness for him, as he foresaw himself wandering away solitary in pursuit of some unknown fortune, that his thought had even glanced towards going in search of Baldassarre after all.

At each of the opposite inlets he saw people struggling into the piazza, while above them paper lanterns, held aloft on sticks, were waving uncertainly to and fro. A rude monotonous chant made a distinctly traceable strand of noise, across which screams, whistles, gibing chants in piping boyish voices, the beating of drums, and the ringing of little bells, met each other in confused din. Every now and then one of the dim floating lights disappeared with a smash from a stone launched more or less vaguely in pursuit of mischief, followed by a scream and renewed shouts. But on the outskirts of the whirling tumult there were groups who were keeping this vigil of the Nativity of the Virgin in a more methodical manner than by fitful stone-throwing and gibing. Certain ragged men, darting a hard, sharp glance around them while their tongues rattled merrily, were inviting country people to game with them on fair and open-handed terms; two masquerading figures on stilts, who had snatched lanterns from the crowd, were swaying the lights to and fro in meteoric fashion, as they strode hither and thither; a sage trader was doing a profitable business at a small covered stall, in hot *berlingozzi*, a favourite farinaceous delicacy; one man standing on a barrel, with his back firmly planted against a pillar of the loggia in front of the Foundling Hospital (*Spedale degl' Innocenti*), was selling efficacious pills, invented by a doctor of Salerno, warranted to prevent toothache, and death by drowning; and not far off, against another pillar, a tumbler was showing off his tricks on a small platform; while a handful of 'prentices, despising the slack entertainment of guerilla stone-throwing, were having a private concentrated match of that favourite Florentine sport at the narrow entrance of the Via de' Febbrai.

Tito, obliged to make his way through chance openings in the crowd, found himself at one moment close to the trotting procession of barefooted, hard-heeled contadine, and could see their sun-dried, bronzed faces, and their strange, fragmentary garb, dim with hereditary dirt, and of obsolete stuffs and fashions, that made them look, in the eyes of the city people, like a wayworn ancestry returning from a pilgrimage on which they had set out a century ago. Just then it was the hardy, scant-feeding peasant-women from the mountains of Pistoia, who were entering with a year's labour in a moderate bundle of yarn on their backs, and in their hearts that meagre hope of good and that wide dim fear of harm, which were somehow to be cared for by the Blessed Virgin, whose miraculous image, painted by the angels, was to have the curtain drawn away from it on this Eve of her Nativity, that its potency might stream forth without obstruction.

At another moment he was forced away towards the boundary of the piazza, where the more stationary candidates for attention and small coin had judiciously placed themselves, in order to be safe in their rear. Among these Tito recognized his acquaintance Bratti, who stood with his back against a pillar, and his mouth pursed up in disdainful silence, eying every one who approached him with a cold glance of superiority, and keeping his hand fast on a serge covering which concealed the contents of the basket slung before him. Rather surprised at a deportment so unusual in an anxious trader, Tito went nearer and saw two women go up to Bratti's basket with a look of curiosity, whereupon the pedler drew the covering tighter, and looked another way. It was quite too provoking, and one of the women was fain to ask what there was in his basket.

"Before I answer that, Monna, I must know whether you mean to buy. I can't show such wares as mine in this fair for every fly to settle on and pay nothing. My goods are a little too choice for that. Besides, I've only two left, and I've no mind to sell them; for with the chances of the pestilence that wise men talk of, there is likelihood of their being worth their weight in gold. No, no: *andate con Dio*."

The two women looked at each other.

"And what may be the price?" said the second.

"Not within what you are likely to have in your purse, buona donna," said Bratti, in a compassionately supercilious tone. "I recommend you to trust in Messer Domeneddio and the saints: poor people can do no better for themselves."

"Not so poor!" said the second woman, indignantly, drawing out her money-bag. "Come, now! what do you say to a grosso?"

"I say you may get twenty-one quattrini for it," said Bratti, coolly; "but not of me, for I haven't got that small change."

"Come; two, then?" said the woman, getting exasperated, while her companion looked at her with some envy. "It will hardly be above two, I think."

After further bidding and further mercantile coquetry, Bratti put on an air of concession.

"Since you've set your mind on it," he said, slowly raising the cover, "I should be loath to do you a mischief; for Maestro Gabbadeo used to say, when a woman sets her mind on a thing and doesn't get it, she's in worse danger of the pestilence than before. Ecco! I have but two left; and let me tell you, the fellow to them is on the finger of Maestro Gabbadeo, who is gone to Bologna,—as wise a doctor as sits at any door."

The precious objects were two clumsy iron rings, beaten into the fashion of old Roman rings, such as were sometimes disinterred. The rust on them, and the entirely hidden character of their potency were so satisfactory that the grossi were paid without grumbling; and the first woman, destitute of those handsome coins, succeeded, after much show of reluctance on Bratti's part, in driving a bargain with some of her yarn, and carried off the remaining ring in triumph. Bratti covered up his basket, which was now filled with miscellanies, probably obtained under the same sort of circumstances as the yarn, and, moving from his pillar, came suddenly upon Tito, who, if he had had time, would have chosen to avoid recognition.

"By the head of San Giovanni, now," said Bratti, drawing Tito back to the pillar, "this is a piece of luck. For I was talking of you this morning, Messer Greco; but, I said, he is mounted up among the signori now,—and I'm glad of it, for I was at the bottom of his fortune,—but I can rarely get speech of him, for he's not to be caught lying on the stones now,—not he! But it's your luck, not mine, Messer Greco, save and except some small trifle to satisfy me for my trouble in the transaction."

"You speak in riddles, Bratti," said Tito. "Remember, I don't sharpen my wits, as you do, by driving hard bargains for iron rings: you must be plain."

"By the Holy 'Vangels! it was an easy bargain I gave them. If a Hebrew gets thirty-two per cent, I hope a Christian may get a little more. If I had not borne a conscience, I should have got twice the money and twice the yarn. But, talking of rings, it is your ring—that very ring you've got on your finger—that I could get you a purchaser for; ay, and a purchaser with a deep money-bag."

"Truly?" said Tito, looking at his ring and listening.

"A Genoese who is going straight away into Hungary, as I understand. He came and looked all over my shop to see if I had any old things I didn't know the price of; I warrant you, he thought I had a pumpkin on my shoulders. He had been rummaging all the shops in Florence. And he had a ring on,—not like yours, but something of the same fashion; and as he was talking of rings, I said I knew a fine young man, a particular acquaintance of mine, who had a ring of that sort. And he said, 'Who is he, pray? Tell him I'll give him his price for it.' And I thought of going after you to Nello's to-morrow; for it's my opinion of you, Messer Greco, that you're not one who'd see the Arno run broth, and stand by without dipping your finger."

Tito had lost no word of what Bratti had said, yet his mind had been very busy all the while. Why should he keep the ring? It had been a mere sentiment, a mere fancy, that had prevented him from selling it with the other gems; if he had been wiser and had sold it, he might perhaps have escaped that identification by Fra Luca. It was true that it had been taken from Baldassarre's finger and put on his own as soon as his young hand had grown to the needful size; but there was really no valid good to anybody in those superstitious scruples about inanimate objects. The ring had helped towards the recognition of him. Tito had begun to dislike recognition, which was a claim from the past. This foreigner's offer, if he would really give a good price, was an opportunity for getting rid of the ring without the trouble of seeking a purchaser.

"You speak with your usual wisdom, Bratti," said Tito. "I have no objection to hear what your Genoese will offer. But when and where shall I have speech of him?"

"To-morrow, at three hours after sunrise, he will be at my shop; and if your wits are of that sharpness I have always taken them to be, Messer Greco, you will ask him a heavy price; for he minds not money. It's my belief he's buying for somebody else, and not for himself,— perhaps for some great signor." [1]

"It is well," said Tito. "I will be at your shop, if nothing hinders."

"And you will doubtless deal nobly by me for old acquaintance' sake, Messer Greco, so I will not stay to fix the small sum you will give me in token of my service in the matter. It seems to me a thousand years now till I get out of the piazza, for a fair is a dull, not to say a wicked thing, when one has no more goods to sell."

Tito made a hasty sign of assent and adieu, and moving away from the pillar, again found himself pushed towards the middle of the piazza

[1] This is the modern *gran signore*. In the fifteenth century they said *gran mastro*. —EDITOR.

and back again, without the power of determining his own course. In this zigzag way he was carried along to the end of the piazza opposite the church, where, in a deep recess formed by an irregularity in the line of houses, an entertainment was going forward which seemed to be especially attractive to the crowd. Loud bursts of laughter interrupted a monologue which was sometimes slow and oratorical, at others rattling and buffoonish. Here a girl was being pushed forward into the inner circle with apparent reluctance, and there a loud laughing minx was finding a way with her own elbows. It was a strange light that was spread over the piazza. There was the pale stars breaking out above, and the dim waving lanterns below, leaving all objects indistinct except when they were seen close under the fitfully moving lights; but in this recess there was a stronger light, against which the heads of the encircling spectators stood in dark relief as Tito was gradually pushed towards them, while above them rose the head of a man wearing a white mitre with yellow cabalistic figures upon it.

"Behold, my children!" Tito heard him saying, "behold your opportunity! neglect not the holy sacrament of matrimony when it can be had for the small sum of a white quattrino,—the cheapest matrimony ever offered, and dissolved by special bull beforehand at every man's own will and pleasure. Behold the bull!" Here the speaker held up a piece of parchment with huge seals attached to it. "Behold the Indulgence granted by his Holiness Alexander the Sixth, who, being newly elected Pope for his peculiar piety, intends to reform and purify the Church, and wisely begins by abolishing that priestly abuse which keeps too large a share of this privileged matrimony to the clergy and stints the laity. Spit once, my sons, and pay a white quattrino! This is the whole and sole price of the indulgence. The quattrino is the only difference the Holy Father allows to be put any longer between us and the clergy,—who spit and pay nothing."

Tito thought he knew the voice, which had a peculiarly sharp ring, but the face was too much in shadow from the lights behind for him to be sure of the features. Stepping as near as he could, he saw within the circle behind the speaker an altar-like table raised on a small platform, and covered with a red drapery stitched all over with yellow cabalistical figures. Half a dozen thin tapers burned at the back of this table, which had a conjuring apparatus scattered over it, a large open book in the centre, and at one of the front angles a monkey fastened by a cord to a small ring and holding a small taper, which in his incessant fidgety movements fell more or less aslant, while an impish boy in a white surplice occupied himself chiefly in cuffing the monkey and adjusting the taper. The man in the mitre also wore a surplice, and over it a chasuble on which the signs of the zodiac were rudely marked in black upon a yellow ground. Tito was sure now that he recognized the sharp upward-tending angles of the face under the mitre: it was that of Maestro Vaiano, the mountebank, from whom he had rescued Tessa. Pretty little Tessa! Perhaps she too had come in among the troops of contadine.

"Come, my maidens! This is the time for the pretty who can have many chances, and for the ill-favoured who have few. Matrimony to be had,—hot, eaten, and done with as easily as *berlingozzi!* And see!" here the conjurer held up a cluster of tiny bags. "To every bride I give a *Breve* with a secret in it,—the secret alone worth the money you pay for the matrimony. The secret how to—No, no, I will not tell you what the secret is about, and that makes it a double secret. Hang it round your neck if you like, and never look at it; I don't say *that* will not be the best, for then you will see many things you don't expect: though if you open it you may break your leg, *è vero,* but you will know a secret! Something nobody knows but me! And mark,—I give you the *Breve,* I don't sell it, as many another holy man would: the quattrino is for the matrimony, and the *Breve* you get for nothing. *Orsù, giovanetti,* come like dutiful sons of the Church and buy the Indulgence of his Holiness Alexander the Sixth."

This buffoonery just fitted the taste of the audience; the Fierucola was but a small occasion, so the townsmen might be contented with jokes that were rather less indecent than those they were accustomed to hear at every carnival, put into easy rhyme by the magnifico and his poetic satellites; while the women, over and above any relish of the fun, really began to have an itch for the *Brevi.* Several couples had already gone through the ceremony, in which the conjurer's solemn gibberish and grimaces over the open book, the antics of the monkey, and even the preliminary spitting, had called forth peals of laughter; and now a well-looking, merry-eyed youth of seventeen, in a loose tunic and red cap, pushed forward, holding by the hand a plump brunette, whose scanty ragged dress displayed her round arms and legs very picturesquely.

"Fetter us without delay, maestro!" said the youth, "for I have got to take my bride home and paint her under the light of a lantern."

"Ha! Mariotto, my son, I commend your pious observance—" The conjurer was going on, when a loud chattering behind warned him that an unpleasant crisis had arisen with his monkey.

The temper of that imperfect acolyth was a little tried by the overactive discipline of his colleague in the surplice, and a sudden cuff administered as his taper fell to a horizontal position, caused him to leap back with a violence that proved too much for the slackened knot by which his cord was fastened. His first leap was to the other end of the table, from which position his remonstrances were so threatening that the imp in the surplice took up a wand by way of an equivalent threat, whereupon the monkey leaped on to the head of a tall woman in the foreground, dropping his taper by the way, and chattering with increased emphasis from that eminence. Great was the screaming and confusion, not a few of the spectators having a vague dread of the Maestro's monkey, as capable of more hidden mischief than mere teeth and claws could inflict; and the conjurer himself was in some alarm lest any harm should happen to his familiar. In the scuffle to seize the monkey's string, Tito got out of the circle, and, not caring to contend for his place again, he allowed himself to be gradually pushed towards the church of the Nunziata, and to enter among the worshippers.

The brilliant illumination within seemed to press upon his eyes with palpable force after the pale scattered lights and broad shadows of the piazza, and for the first minute or two he could see nothing distinctly. That yellow splendour was in itself something supernatural and heavenly to many of the peasant-women, for whom half the sky was hidden by mountains, and who went to bed in the twilight; and the uninterrupted chant from the choir was repose to the ear after the hellish hubbub of the crowd outside. Gradually the scene became clearer, though still there was a thin yellow haze from incense mingling with the breath of the multitude. In a chapel on the left hand of the nave, wreathed with silver lamps, was seen unveiled the miraculous fresco of the Annunciation, which, in Tito's oblique view of it from the right-hand side of the nave, seemed dark with the excess of light around it. The whole area of the great church was filled with peasant-women, some kneeling, some standing; the coarse bronzed skins, and the dingy clothing of the rougher dwellers on the mountains, contrasting with the softer-lined faces and white or red head-drapery of the well-to-do dwellers in the valley, who were scattered in irregular groups. And spreading high and far over the walls and ceiling there was another multitude, also pressing close against each other, that they might be nearer the potent Virgin. It was the crowd of votive waxen images, the effigies of great personages, clothed in their habit as they lived: Florentines of high name in their black silk lucco, as when they sat in council; popes, emperors, kings, cardinals, and famous condottieri with plumed morion seated on their chargers; all notable strangers who passed through Florence or had aught to do with its affairs—Mohammedans, even, in well-tolerated companionship with Christian cavaliers; some of them with faces blackened and robes tattered by the corroding breath of centuries, others fresh and bright in new red mantle or steel corselet, the exact doubles of the living. And wedged in with all these were detached arms, legs, and other members, with only here and there a gap where some image had been removed for public disgrace, or had fallen ominously, as Lorenzo's had done six months before. It was a perfect resurrection-swarm of remote mortals and fragments of mortals, reflecting, in their varying degrees of freshness, the sombre dinginess and sprinkled brightness of the crowd below.

Tito's glance wandered over the wild multitude in search of something. He had already thought of Tessa, and the white hoods suggested the possibility that he might detect her face under one of them. It was at least a thought to be courted, rather than the vision of Romola looking at him with changed eyes. But he searched in vain; and he was leaving the church, weary of a scene which had no variety, when, just against the doorway, he caught sight of Tessa, only two yards off him. She was kneeling with her back against the wall, behind a group of peasant-women, who were standing and looking for a spot nearer to the sacred image. Her head hung a little aside with a look of weariness, and her blue eyes were directed rather absently towards an altar-piece where the Archangel Michael stood in his armour, with young face and floating hair, among bearded and tonsured saints. Her right hand, holding a bunch of cocoons, fell by her side listlessly, and her round cheek was palid, either by the light or by the weariness that was expressed in her attitude: her lips were pressed poutingly together, and every now and then her eyelids half fell; she was a large image of a sweet sleepy child. Tito felt an irresistible desire to go up to her and get her pretty trusting looks and prattle: this creature, who was without moral judgment that could condemn him, whose little loving ignorant soul made a world apart, where he might feel in freedom from suspicions and exacting demands, had a new attraction for him now. She seemed a refuge from the threatened isolation that would come with disgrace. He glanced cautiously round, to assure himself that Monna Ghita was not near, and then, slipping quietly to her side, kneeled on one knee, and said, in the softest voice, "Tessa!"

She hardly started, any more than she would have started at a soft breeze that fanned her gently when she was needing it. She turned her head, and saw Tito's face close to her: it was very much more beautiful than the Archangel Michael's, who was so mighty and so good that he lived with the Madonna and all the saints and was prayed to along with them. She smiled in happy silence, for that nearness of Tito quite filled her mind.

"My little Tessa! you look very tired. How long have you been kneeling here?"

She seemed to be collecting her thoughts for a minute or two, and at last she said,—

"I'm very hungry."

"Come, then; come with me."

He lifted her from her knees, and led her out under the cloisters surrounding the atrium, which were then open, and not yet adorned with the frescos of Andrea del Sarto.

"How is it you are all by yourself, and so hungry, Tessa?"

"The Madre is ill; she has very bad pains in her legs, and sent me to bring these cocoons to the Santissima Nunziata, because they're so wonderful; see!"—she held up the bunch of cocoons, which were arranged with fortuitous regularity on a stem,—"and she had kept them to bring them herself, but she couldn't, and so she sent me, because she thinks the Holy Madonna may take away her pains; and somebody took my bag with the bread and chestnuts in it, and the people pushed me back, and I was so frightened coming in the crowd, and I couldn't get anywhere near the Holy Madonna, to give the cocoons to the Padre, but I must—oh, I must!"

"Yes, my little Tessa, you shall take them; but first come and let me give you some *berlingozzi*. There are some to be had not far off."

"Where did you come from?" said Tessa, a little bewildered. "I thought you would never come to me again, because you never came to the Mercata for milk any more. I set myself Aves to say, to see if they would bring you back, but I left off, because they didn't."

"You see I come when you want some one to take care of you, Tessa. Perhaps the Aves fetched me, only it took them a long while. But what shall you do if you are here all alone? Where shall you go?"

"Oh, I shall stay and sleep in the church—a great many of them do —in the church and all about here—I did once when I came with my mother; and the *patrigno* is coming with the mules in the morning."

They were out in the piazza now, where the crowd was rather less riotous than before, and the lights were fewer, the stream of pilgrims having ceased. Tessa clung fast to Tito's arm in satisfied silence, while he led her towards the stall where he remembered seeing the eatables. Their way was the easier because there was just now a great rush toward the middle of the piazza, where the masked figures on stilts had found space to execute a dance. It was very pretty to see the guileless thing giving her cocoons into Tito's hand, and then eating her *berlingozzi* with the relish of a hungry child. Tito had really come to take care of her, as he did before, and that wonderful happiness of being with him had begun again for her. Her hunger was soon appeased, all the sooner for the new stimulus of happiness that had roused her from her languor; and as they turned away from the stall, she said nothing about going into the church again, but looked round as if the sights in the piazza were not without attraction to her now she was safe under Tito's arm.

"How can they do that?" she exclaimed, looking up at the dancers on stilts. Then, after a minute's silence, "Do you think Saint Christopher helps them?"

"Perhaps. What do you think about it, Tessa?" said Tito, slipping his right arm round her, and looking down at her fondly.

"Because Saint Christopher is so very tall; and he is very good: if anybody looks at him, he takes care of them all day. He is on the wall of the church,—too tall to stand up there,—but I saw him walking through the streets one San Giovanni carrying the little Gesù."

"You pretty pigeon! Do you think anybody could help taking care of *you*, if you looked at them?"

"Shall you always come and take care of me?" said Tessa, turning her face up to him as he crushed her cheek with his left hand. "And shall you always be a long while first?"

Tito was conscious that some by-standers were laughing at them; and though the license of street fun, among artists and young men of the wealthier sort as well as among the populace, made few adventures exceptional, still less disreputable, he chose to move away towards the end of the piazza.

"Perhaps I shall come again to you very soon, Tessa," he answered, rather dreamily, when they had moved away. He was thinking that when all the rest had turned their backs upon him, it would be pleasant to have this little creature adoring him and nestling against him. The absence of presumptuous self-conceit in Tito made him feel all the more defenceless under prospective obloquy; he needed soft looks and caresses too much ever to be impudent.

"In the Mercato?" said Tessa. "Not to-morrow morning, because the *patrigno* will be there, and he is so cross. Oh! but you have money, and he will not be cross if you buy some salad. And there are some chestnuts. Do you like chestnuts?"

He said nothing, but continued to look down at her with a dreamy gentleness, and Tessa felt herself in a state of delicious wonder; everything seemed as new as if she were being carried on a chariot of clouds.

"Holy Virgin!" she exclaimed again presently; "there is a holy father like the Bishop I saw at Prato."

Tito looked up too, and saw that he had unconsciously advanced to within a few yards of the conjurer, Maestro Vaiano, who for the moment was forsaken by the crowd. His face was turned away from them, and he was occupied with the apparatus on his altar or table, preparing a new diversion by the time the interest in the dancing should be exhausted. The monkey was imprisoned under the red cloth, out of reach of mischief, and the youngster in the white surplice was holding a sort of dish or salver, from which his master was taking some ingredient. The altar-like table, with its gorgeous cloth, the row of tapers, the sham episcopal costume, the surpliced attendant, and even the movements of the mitred figure, as he alternately bent his head and then raised something before the lights, were a sufficiently near parody of sacred things to rouse poor little Tessa's veneration; and there was some additional awe produced by the mystery of their apparition in this spot, for when she had seen an altar in the street before, it had been on Corpus Christi Day, and there had been a procession to account for it. She crossed herself and looked up at Tito, but then, as if she had had time for reflection, said, "It is because of the Natività."

Meanwhile Vaiano had turned round, raising his hands to his mitre with the intention of changing his dress, when his quick eye recognized Tito and Tessa, who were both looking at him, their faces being shone upon by the light of his tapers, while his own was in shadow.

"Ha! my children!" he said instantly, stretching out his hands in a benedictory attitude, "you are come to be married. I commend your penitence,—the blessing of Holy Church can never come too late."

But while he was speaking he had taken in the whole meaning of Tessa's attitude and expression, and he discerned an opportunity for a new kind of joke which required him to be cautious and solemn.

"Should you like to be married to me, Tessa?" said Tito, softly, half enjoying the comedy, as he saw the pretty childish seriousness on her face, half prompted by hazy previsions which belonged to the intoxication of despair.

He felt her vibrating before she looked up at him and said timidly, "Will you let me?"

He answered only by a smile, and by leading her forward in front of the *cerretano,* who, seeing an excellent jest in Tessa's evident delusion, assumed a surpassing sacerdotal solemnity, and went through the mimic ceremony with a liberal expenditure of *lingua furbesca,* or thieves' Latin. But some symptoms of a new movement in the crowd urged him to bring it to a speedy conclusion, and dismiss them with hands outstretched in a benedictory attitude over their kneeling figures. Tito, disposed always to cultivate good-will, though it might be the least select, put a piece of four grossi into his hand, as he moved away, and was thanked by a look which, the conjurer felt sure, conveyed a perfect understanding of the whole affair.

But Tito himself was very far from that understanding, and did not, in fact, know whether, the next moment, he should tell Tessa of the joke and laugh at her for a little goose, or whether he should let her delusion last, and see what would come of it,—see what she would say and do next.

"Then you will not go away from me again," said Tessa, after they had walked a few steps, "and you will take me to where you live." She spoke meditatively, and not in a questioning tone. But presently she added, "I must go back once to the Madre,[2] though, to tell her I brought the cocoons, and that I am married, and shall not go back again."

Tito felt the necessity of speaking now; and in the rapid thought prompted by that necessity, he saw that by undeceiving Tessa he should be robbing himself of some at least of that pretty trustfulness which might by-and-by be his only haven from contempt. It would spoil Tessa to make her the least particle wiser or more suspicious.

"Yes, my little Tessa," he said caressingly, "you must go back to the Madre; but you must not tell her you are married,—you must keep that a secret from everybody; else some very great harm would happen to me, and you would never see me again."

She looked up at him with fear in her face.

"You must go back and feed your goats and mules, and do just as you have always done before, and say no word to any one about me."

The corners of her mouth fell a little.

"And then, perhaps, I shall come and take care of you again when you want me, as I did before. But you must do just what I tell you, else you will not see me again."

"Yes, I will, I will," she said in a loud whisper, frightened at that blank prospect.

They were silent a little while; and then Tessa, looking at her hand, said,—

"The Madre wears a betrothal ring. She went to church and had it put on, and then after that, another day, she was married. And so did the cousin Nannina. But then *she* married Gollo," added the poor little thing, entangled in the difficult comparison between her own case and others within her experience.

---

[2] This is not the correct word to use. In this case it should be the Italian *"Mamma,"* which corresponds to the English "mother"; but it might also be abbreviated, with the addition of the possessive pronoun *"a me' ma',"* which might be translated to "my mammy."—EDITOR.

"But you must not wear a betrothal ring, my Tessa, because no one must know you are married," said Tito, feeling some insistence necessary. "And the *buona fortuna* that I gave you did just as well for betrothal. Some people are betrothed with rings, and some are not."

"Yes, it is true, they would see the ring," said Tessa, trying to convince herself that a thing she would like very much was really not good for her.

They were now near the entrance of the church again, and she remembered her cocoons, which were still in Tito's hand.

"Ah, you must give me the *Boto*," she said; "and we must go in, and I must take it to the Padre, and I must tell the rest of my beads, because I was too tired before."

"Yes, you must go in, Tessa; but I will not go in. I must leave you now," said Tito, too feverish and weary to re-enter that stifling heat, and feeling that this was the least difficult way of parting with her.

"And not come back? Oh, where do you go?" Tessa's mind had never formed an image of his whereabout or his doings when she did not see him: he had vanished, and her thought, instead of following him, had stayed in the same spot where he was with her.

"I shall come back some time, Tessa," said Tito, taking her under the cloisters to the door of the church. "You must not cry,—you must go to sleep when you have said your beads. And here is money to buy your breakfast. Now kiss me, and look happy; else I shall not come again."

She made a great effort over herself as she put up her lips to kiss him, and submitted to be gently turned round, with her face towards the door of the church. Tito saw her enter; and then, with a shrug at his own resolution, leaned against a pillar, took off his cap, rubbed his hair backward, and wondered where Romola was now, and what she was thinking of him. Poor little Tessa had disappeared behind the curtain among the crowd of peasants; but the love which formed one web with all his worldly hopes, with the ambitions and pleasures that must make the solid part of his days,—the love that was identified with his larger self,—was not to be banished from his consciousness. Even to the man who presents the most elastic resistance to whatever is unpleasant, there will come moments when the pressure from without is too strong for him, and he must feel the smart and the bruise in spite of himself. Such a moment had come to Tito. There was no possible attitude of mind, no scheme of action, by which the uprooting of all his newly planted hopes could be made otherwise than painful.

CHAPTER XV

THE DYING MESSAGE

WHEN Romola arrived at the entrance of San Marco, she found one of the Frati waiting there in expectation of her arrival. Monna Brigida retired into the adjoining church, and Romola was conducted to the door of the chapter-house in the outer cloister, whither the invalid had been conveyed; no woman being allowed admission beyond this precinct.

When the door opened, the subdued external light blending with that of two tapers placed behind a truckle-bed, showed the emaciated face of Fra Luca, with the tonsured crown of golden hair above it, and with deep-sunken hazel eyes fixed on a small crucifix which he held before him. He was propped up into nearly a sitting posture; and Romola was just conscious, as she threw aside her veil, that there was another monk standing by the bed, with the black cowl drawn over his head, and that he moved towards the door as she entered; just conscious that in the background there was a crucified form rising high and pale on the frescoed wall, and pale faces of sorrow looking out from it below.

The next moment her eyes met Fra Luca's as they looked up at her from the crucifix, and she was absorbed in that pang of recognition which identified this monkish emaciated form with the image of her fair young brother.

"Dino!" she said, in a voice like a low cry of pain. But she did not bend towards him; she held herself erect, and paused at two yards' distance from him. There was an unconquerable repulsion for her in that monkish aspect; it seemed to her the brand of the dastardly undutifulness which had left her father desolate,—of the grovelling superstition which could give such undutifulness the name of piety. Her father, whose proud sincerity and simplicity of life had made him one of the few frank pagans of his time, had brought her up with a silent ignoring of any claims the Church could have to regulate the belief and action of beings with a cultivated reason. The Church, in her mind, belonged to that actual life of the mixed multitude from which they had always lived apart, and she had no ideas that could render her brother's course an object of any other feeling than incurious, indignant contempt. Yet the lovingness of Romola's soul had clung to that image in the past, and while she stood rigidly aloof, there was a yearning search in her eyes for something too faintly discernible.

But there was no corresponding emotion in the face of the monk. He looked at the little sister returned to him in her full womanly beauty, with the far-off gaze of a revisiting spirit.

"My sister!" he said, with a feeble and interrupted but yet distinct utterance, "it is well thou hast not longer delayed to come, for I have a message to deliver to thee, and my time is short."

Romola took a step nearer: the message, she thought, would be one of affectionate penitence to her father, and her heart began to open. Nothing could wipe out the long years of desertion; but the culprit, looking back on those years with the sense of irremediable wrong committed, would call forth pity. Now, at the last, there would be understanding and forgiveness. Dino would pour out some natural filial feeling; he would ask questions about his father's blindness,—how rapidly it had come on? how the long dark days had been filled? what the life was now in the home where he himself had been nourished?—and the last message from the dying lips would be one of tenderness and regret.

"Romola," Fra Luca began, "I have had a vision concerning thee. Thrice I have had it in the last two months: each time it has been clearer. Therefore I came from Fiesole, deeming it a message from heaven that I was bound to deliver. And I gather a promise of mercy to thee in this, that my breath is preserved in order to—"

The difficult breathing which continually interrupted him would not let him finish the sentence.

Romola had felt her heart chilling again. It was a vision, then, this message,—one of those visions she had so often heard her father allude to with bitterness. Her indignation rushed to her lips.

"Dino, I thought you had some words to send to my father. You forsook him when his sight was failing; you made his life very desolate. Have you never cared about that,—never repented? What is this religion of yours, that places visions before natural duties?"

The deep-sunken hazel eyes turned slowly towards her, and rested upon her in silence for some moments, as if he were meditating whether he should answer her.

"No," he said at last, speaking, as before, in a low passionless tone, as of some spirit not human, speaking through dying human organs,— "No; I have never repented fleeing from the stifling poison-breath of sin that was hot and thick around me, and threatened to steal over my senses like besotting wine. My father could not hear the voice that called me night and day; he knew nothing of the demon-tempters that tried to drag me back from following it. My father has lived amidst human sin and misery without believing in them: he has been like one busy picking shining stones in a mine, while there was a world dying of plague above him. I spoke, but he listened with scorn. I told him the studies he wished me to live for were either childish trifling,—dead toys,—or else they must be made warm and living by pulses that beat to worldly ambitions and fleshly lusts, for worldly ambitions and fleshly lusts made all the substance of the poetry and history he wanted me to bend my eyes on continually."

"Has not my father led a pure and noble life, then?" Romola burst forth, unable to hear in silence this implied accusation against her father. "He has sought no worldly honours; he has been truthful; he has denied himself all luxuries; he has lived like one of the ancient sages. He never wished you to live for worldly ambitions and fleshly lusts; he wished you to live as he himself has done, according to the purest maxims of philosophy in which he brought you up."

Romola spoke partly by rote, as all ardent and sympathetic young creatures do; but she spoke with intense belief. The pink flush was in her face, and she quivered from head to foot. Her brother was again slow to answer; looking at her passionate face with strange passionless eyes.

"What were the maxims of philosophy to me? They told me to be strong, when I felt myself weak; when I was ready, like the blessed Saint Benedict, to roll myself among thorns, and court smarting wounds as a deliverance from temptation. For the Divine love had sought me, and penetrated me, and created a great need in me; like a seed that wants room to grow. I had been brought up in carelessness of the true faith; I had not studied the doctrines of our religion; but it seemed to take possession of me like a rising flood. I felt that there was a life of perfect love and purity for the soul; in which there would be no uneasy hunger after pleasure, no tormenting questions, no fear of suffering. Before I knew the history of the saints, I had a foreshadowing of their ecstasy. For the same truth had penetrated even into pagan philosophy: that it is a bliss within the reach of man to die to mortal needs, and live in the life of God as the Unseen Perfectness. But to attain that I must forsake the world: I must have no affection, no hope, wedding me to that which passeth away; I must live with my fellow-beings only as human souls related to the eternal unseen life. That need was urging me continually: it came over me in visions when my mind fell away weary from the vain words which record the passions of dead men; it came over me after I had been tempted into sin and had turned away with loathing from the scent of the emptied cup. And in visions I saw the meaning of the Crucifix."

He paused, breathing hard for a minute or two; but Romola was not prompted to speak again. It was useless for her mind to attempt any contact with the mind of this unearthly brother,—as useless as for her hand to try and grasp a shadow. When he spoke again, his heaving chest was quieter.

"I felt whom I must follow; but I saw that even among the servants of the Cross who professed to have renounced the world, my soul would be stifled with the fumes of hypocrisy and lust and pride. God had not chosen me, as he chose Saint Dominic and Saint Francis, to wrestle with evil in the Church and in the world. He called upon me to flee: I took the sacred vows, and I fled,—fled to lands where danger and scorn and want bore me continually, like angels, to repose on the bosom of God. I have lived the life of a hermit, I have ministered to pilgrims; but my task has been short: the veil has worn very thin that divides me from my everlasting rest. I came back to Florence, that—"

"Dino, you *did* want to know if my father was alive," interrupted Romola, the picture of that suffering life touching her again with the desire for union and forgiveness.

"—that before I died I might urge others of our brethren to study the Eastern tongues, as I had not done, and go out to greater ends than I did; and I find them already bent on the work. And since I came, Romola, I have felt that I was sent partly to thee,—not to renew the bonds of earthly affection, but to deliver the heavenly warning conveyed in a vision. For I have had that vision thrice. And through all the years since first the Divine voice called me, while I was yet in the world,

I have been taught and guided by visions. For in the painful linking together of our waking thoughts we can never be sure that we have not mingled our own error with the light we have prayed for; but in visions and dreams we are passive, and our souls are as an instrument in the Divine hand. Therefore listen, and speak not again,—for the time is short."

Romola's mind recoiled strongly from listening to this vision. Her indignation had subsided, but it was only because she had felt the distance between her brother and herself widening. But while Fra Luca was speaking, the figure of another monk had entered, and again stood on the other side of the bed, with the cowl drawn over his head.

"Kneel, my daughter, for the Angel of Death is present, and waits while the message of heaven is delivered; bend thy pride before it is bent for thee by a yoke of iron," said a strong rich voice, startlingly in contrast with Fra Luca's.

The tone was not that of imperious command, but of quiet self-possession and assurance of the right, blended with benignity. Romola, vibrating to the sound, looked round at the figure on the opposite side of the bed. His face was hardly discernible under the shadow of the cowl; and her eyes fell at once on his hands, which were folded across his breast and lay in relief on the edge of his black mantle. They had a marked physiognomy which enforced the influence of the voice; they were very beautiful and almost of transparent delicacy. Romola's disposition to rebel against command, doubly active in the presence of monks, whom she had been taught to despise, would have fixed itself on any repulsive detail as a point of support. But the face was hidden, and the hands seemed to have an appeal in them against all hardness. The next moment the right hand took the crucifix to relieve the fatigued grasp of Fra Luca, and the left touched his lips with a wet sponge which lay near. In the act of bending, the cowl was pushed back, and the features of the monk had the full light of the tapers on them. They were very marked features, such as lend themselves to popular description. There was the high arched nose, the prominent under-lip, the coronet of thick dark hair above the brow, all seeming to tell of energy and passion; there were the blue-grey eyes, shining mildly under auburn eyelashes, seeming, like the hands, to tell of acute sensitiveness. Romola felt certain they were the features of Fra Girolamo Savonarola, the prior of San Marco, whom she had chiefly thought of as more offensive than other monks, because he was more noisy. Her rebellion was rising against the first impression, which had almost forced her to bend her knees.

"Kneel, my daughter," the penetrating voice said again; "the pride of the body is a barrier against the gifts that purify the soul."

He was looking at her with mild fixedness while he spoke, and again she felt that subtle mysterious influence of a personality by which it has been given to some rare men to move their fellows.

Slowly Romola fell on her knees, and in the very act a tremor came over her; in the renunciation of her proud erectness, her mental attitude seemed changed, and she found herself in a new state of passiveness. Her brother began to speak again:

"Romola, in the deep night, as I lay awake, I saw my father's room,— the library,—with all the books and the marbles and the leggio, where I used to stand and read; and I saw you,—you were revealed to me as I see you now, with fair long hair, sitting before my father's chair. And at the leggio stood a man whose face I could not see. I looked, and looked, and it was a blank to me, even as a painting effaced; and I saw him move and take thee, Romola, by the hand; and then I saw thee take my father by the hand; and you all three went down the stone steps into the streets, the man whose face was a blank to me leading the way. And you stood at the altar in Santa Croce, and the priest who married you had the face of death; and the graves opened, and the dead in their shrouds rose and followed you like a bridal train. And you passed on through the streets and the gates into the valley, and it seemed to me that he who led you hurried you more than you could bear, and the dead were weary of following you, and turned back to their graves. And at last you came to a stony place, where there was no water, and no trees or herbage; but instead of water, I saw written parchment unrolling itself everywhere, and instead of trees and herbage I saw men of bronze and marble springing up and crowding round you. And my father was faint for want of water, and fell to the ground; and the man whose face was a blank loosed thy hand and departed; and as he went I could see his face, and it was the face of the Great Tempter. And thou, Romola, didst wring thy hands and seek for water, and there was none. And the bronze and marble figures seemed to mock thee and hold out cups of water, and when thou didst grasp them and put them to my father's lips, they turned to parchment. And the bronze and marble figures seemed to turn into demons and snatch my father's body from thee, and the parchments shrivelled up, and blood ran everywhere instead of them, and fire upon the blood, till they all vanished, and the plain was bare and stony again, and thou wast alone in the midst of it. And then it seemed that the night fell and I saw no more.... Thrice I have had that vision, Romola. I believe it is a revelation meant for thee,—to warn thee against marriage as a temptation of the enemy; it calls upon thee to dedicate thyself—"

His pauses had gradually become longer and more frequent, and he was now compelled to cease by a severe fit of gasping, in which his eyes were turned on the crucifix as on a light that was vanishing. Presently he found strength to speak again, but in a feebler, scarcely audible tone.

"To renounce the vain philosophy and corrupt thoughts of the heathens: for in the hour of sorrow and death their pride will turn to mockery, and the unclean gods will—"

The words died away.

In spite of the thought that was at work in Romola, telling her that this vision was no more than a dream, fed by youthful memories and ideal convictions, a strange awe had come over her. Her mind was not apt to be assailed by sickly fancies; she had the vivid intellect and the healthy human passion, which are too keenly alive to the constant relations of things to have any morbid craving after the exceptional. Still the images of the vision she despised jarred and distressed her like painful and cruel cries. And it was the first time she had witnessed the struggle with approaching death: her young life had been sombre, but she had known nothing of the utmost human needs,—no acute suffering, no heart-cutting sorrow; and this brother, come back to her in his hour of supreme agony, was like a sudden awful apparition from an invisible world. The pale faces of sorrow in the fresco on the opposite wall seemed to have come nearer, and to make one company with the pale face of the bed.

"Frate," said the dying voice.

Fra Girolamo leaned down. But no other word came for some moments.

"Romola," it said next.

She leaned forward too; but again there was silence. The words were struggling in vain.

"Fra Girolamo, give her—"

"The crucifix," said the voice of Fra Girolamo.

No other sound came from the dying lips.

"Dino!" said Romola, with a low but piercing cry, as the certainty came upon her that the silence of misunderstanding could never be broken.

"Take the crucifix, my daughter," said Fra Girolamo, after a few minutes. "His eyes behold it no more."

Romola stretched out her hand to the crucifix, and this act appeared to relieve the tension of her mind. A great sob burst from her. She bowed her head by the side of her dead brother, and wept aloud.

It seemed to her as if this first vision of death must alter the daylight for her forevermore.

Fra Girolamo moved towards the door, and called in a lay Brother who was waiting outside. Then he went up to Romola, and said in a tone of gentle command, "Rise, my daughter, and be comforted. Our brother is with the blessed. He has left you the crucifix, in remembrance of the heavenly warning,—that it may be a beacon to you in the darkness."

She rose from her knees, trembling, folded her veil over her head, and hid the crucifix under her mantle. Fra Girolamo then led the way out into the cloistered court, lit now only by the stars and by a lantern which was held by some one near the entrance. Several other figures in the dress of the dignified laity were grouped about the same spot. They were some of the numerous frequenters of San Marco, who had come to visit the Prior, and having heard that he was in attendance on the dying brother in the chapter-house, had awaited him here.

Romola was dimly conscious of footsteps and rustling forms moving aside: she heard the voice of Fra Girolamo saying, in a low tone, "Our brother is departed;" she felt a hand laid on her arm. The next moment the door was opened, and she was out in the wide piazza of San Marco, with no one but Monna Brigida, and the servant carrying the lantern.

The fresh sense of space revived her, and helped her to recover her self-mastery. The scene which had just closed upon her was terribly distinct and vivid, but it began to narrow under the returning impressions of the life that lay outside it. She hastened her steps, with nervous anxiety to be again with her father—and with Tito; for were they not together in her absence? The images of that vision, while they clung about her like a hideous dream not yet to be shaken off, made her yearn all the more for the beloved faces and voices that would assure her of her waking life.

Tito, we know, was not with Bardo; his destiny was being shaped by a guilty consciousness, urging on him the despairing belief that by this time Romola possessed the knowledge which would lead to their final separation.

And the lips that could have conveyed that knowledge were forever closed. The prevision that Fra Luca's words had imparted to Romola had been such as comes from the shadowy region where human souls seek wisdom apart from the human sympathies which are the very life and substance of our wisdom; the revelation that might have come from the simple questions of filial and brotherly affection had been carried into irrevocable silence.

CHAPTER XVI

A FLORENTINE JOKE

EARLY the next morning Tito was returning from Bratti's shop in the narrow thoroughfare of the Ferravecchi. The Genoese stranger had carried away the onyx ring, and Tito was carrying away fifty florins. It did just cross his mind that if, after all, Fortune, by one of her able devices, saved him from the necessity of quitting Florence, it would be better for him not to have parted with his ring, since he had been understood to wear it for the sake of peculiar memories and predilections; still, it was a slight matter, not worth dwelling on with any emphasis, and in those moments he had lost his confidence in fortune. The feverish excitement of the first alarm which had impelled his mind to travel into the future had given place to a dull, regretful lassitude. He cared so much for the pleasures that could only come to him through the good opinion of his fellow-men, that he wished now he had never risked ignominy by shrinking from what his fellow-men called obligations.

But our deeds are like children that are born to us: they live and act apart from our own will. Nay, children may be strangled, but deeds never: they have an indestructible life both in and out of our consciousness; and that dreadful vitality of deeds was pressing hard on Tito for the first time.

He was going back to his lodgings in the Piazza di San Giovanni, but he avoided passing through the Mercato Vecchio, which was his nearest way, lest he should see Tessa. He was not in the humour to seek anything; he could only await the first sign of his altering lot.

The piazza with its sights of beauty was lit up by that warm morning sunlight under which the autumn dew still lingers, and which invites to an idlesse undulled by fatigue. It was a festival morning, too, when the soft warmth seems to steal over one with a special invitation to lounge and gaze. Here, too, the signs of the fair were present; in the spaces round the octagonal baptistery, stalls were being spread with fruit and flowers, and here and there laden mules were standing quietly absorbed in their nose-bags, while their drivers were perhaps gone through the hospitable sacred doors to kneel before the Blessed Virgin on this morning of her Nativity. On the broad marble steps of the Duomo there were scattered groups of beggars and gossipping talkers; here an old crone with white hair and hard sunburnt face encouraging a round-capped baby to try its tiny bare feet on the warmed marble, while a dog sitting near snuffed at the performance suspiciously; there a couple of shaggy-headed boys leaning to watch a small pale cripple who was cutting a face on a cherry-stone; and above them on the wide platform men were making changing knots in laughing desultory chat, or else were standing in close couples gesticulating eagerly.

But the largest and most important company of loungers was that toward which Tito had to direct his steps. It was the busiest time of the day with Nello, and in this warm season and at an hour when clients were numerous, most men preferred being shaved under the pretty red and white awning in front of the shop rather than within narrow walls. It is not a sublime attitude for a man to sit with lathered chin thrown backward, and have his nose made a handle of; but to be shaved was a fashion of Florentine respectability, and it is astonishing how gravely men look at each other when they are all in the fashion. It was the hour of the day, too, when yesterday's crop of gossip was freshest, and the barber's tongue was always in its glory when his razor was busy; the deft activity of those two instruments seemed to be set going by a common spring. Tito foresaw that it would be impossible for him to escape being drawn into the circle; he must smile and retort, and look perfectly at his ease. Well! it was but the ordeal of swallowing bread and cheese pills after all. The man who let the mere anticipation of discovery choke him was simply a man of weak nerves.

But just at that time Tito felt a hand laid on his shoulder, and no amount of previous resolution could prevent the very unpleasant sensation with which that sudden touch jarred him. His face, as he turned it round, betrayed the inward shock; but the owner of the hand that seemed to have such evil magic in it broke into a light laugh. He was a young man about Tito's own age, with keen features, small close-clipped head, and close-shaven lip and chin, giving the idea of a mind as little encumbered as possible with material that was not nervous. The keen eyes were bright with hope and friendliness, as so many other young eyes have been that have afterwards closed on the world in bitterness and disappointment; for at that time there were none but pleasant predictions about Niccolò Macchiavelli, as a young man of promise, who was expected to mend the broken fortunes of his ancient family.

"Why, Melema, what evil dream did you have last night, that you took my light grasp for that of a *sbirro* or something worse?"

"Ah, Messer Niccolò!" said Tito, recovering himself immediately; "it must have been an extra amount of dulness in my veins this morning that shuddered at the approach of your wit. But the fact is, I have had a bad night."

"That is unlucky, because you will be expected to shine without any obstructing fog to-day in the Rucellai Gardens. I take it for granted you are to be there."

"Messer Bernardo did me the honour to invite me," said Tito; "but I shall be engaged elsewhere."

"Ah! I remember, you are in love," said Macchiavelli, with a shrug, "else you would never have such inconvenient engagements. Why, we are to eat a peacock and ortolans under the loggia among Bernardo Rucellai's rare trees; there are to be the choicest spirits in Florence and the choicest wines. Only, as Piero de' Medici is to be there, the choice spirits may happen to be swamped in the capping of impromptu verses. I hate that game; it is a device for the triumph of small wits, who are always inspired the most by the smallest occasions."

"What is that you are saying about Piero de' Medici and small wits, Messer Niccolò?" said Nello, whose light figure was at that moment predominating over the Herculean frame of Niccolò Caparra.

That famous worker in iron, whom we saw last with bared muscular arms and leathern apron in the Mercato Vecchio, was this morning dressed in holiday suit, and as he sat submissively while Nello skipped round him, lathered him, seized him by the nose, and scraped him with magical quickness, he looked much as a lion might if it had donned linen and tunic and was preparing to go into society.

"A private secretary will never rise in the world if he couples great and small in that way," continued Nello. "When great men are not allowed to marry their sons and daughters as they like, small men must not expect to marry their words as they like. Have you heard the news Domenico Cennini, here, has been telling us? that Pagolantonio Soderini has given Ser Piero da Bibbiena a box on the ear for setting on Piero de' Medici to interfere with the marriage between young Tommaso Soderini and Fiammetta Strozzi, and is to be sent ambassador to Venice as a punishment?"

"I don't know which I envy him most," said Macchiavelli, "the offence or the punishment. The offence will make him the most popular man in all Florence, and the punishment will take him among the only people in Italy who have known how to manage their own affairs."

"Yes, if Soderini stays long enough at Venice," said Cennini, "he may chance to learn the Venetian fashion, and bring it home with him. The Soderini have been fast friends of the Medici; but what has hap-pened is likely to open Pagolantonio's eyes to the good of our old Flor-entine trick of choosing a new harness when the old one galls us,—if we have not quite lost the trick in these last fifty years."

"Not we," said Niccolò Caparra, who was rejoicing in the free use of his lips again. "Eat eggs in Lent and the snow will melt. That's what I say to our people when they get noisy over their cups at San Gallo, and talk of raising a *romor* [1] (insurrection): I say, never do you plan a *romor;* you may as well try to fill Arno with buckets. When there's water enough Arno will be full, and that will not be till the torrent is ready."

"Caparra, that oracular speech of yours is due to my excellent shav-ing," said Nello. "You could never have made it with that dark rust on your chin. Ecco, Messer Domenico, I am ready for you now. By the way, my bel erudito," continued Nello, as he saw Tito moving towards the door, "here has been old Maso seeking for you, but your nest was empty. He will come again presently. The old man looked mournful, and seemed in haste. I hope there is nothing wrong in the Via de' Bardi."

"Doubtless Messer Tito knows that Bardo's son is dead," said Cron-aca, who had just come up.

Tito's heart gave a leap,—had the death happened before Romola saw him?

"No, I had not heard it," he said, with no more discomposure than the occasion seemed to warrant, turning and leaning against the door-post, as if he had given up his intention of going away. "I knew that his sister had gone to see him. Did he die before she arrived?"

"No," said Cronaca; "I was in San Marco at the time, and saw her come out from the chapter-house with Fra Girolamo, who told us that the dying man's breath had been preserved as by a miracle, that he might make a disclosure to his sister."

Tito felt that his fate was decided. Again his mind rushed over all the circumstances of his departure from Florence, and he conceived a plan of getting back his money from Cennini before the disclosure had be-come public. If he once had his money, he need not stay long in endur-ance of scorching looks and biting words. He would wait now, and go away with Cennini and get the money from him at once. With that proj-ect in his mind he stood motionless,—his hands in his belt, his eyes fixed absently on the ground. Nello, glancing at him, felt sure that he was absorbed in anxiety about Romola, and thought him such a pretty image of self-forgetful sadness that he just perceptibly pointed his razor at him, and gave a challenging look at Piero di Cosimo, whom he had never forgiven for his refusal to see any prognostics of character in his favorite's handsome face. Piero, who was leaning against the other door-post, close to Tito, shrugged his shoulders: the frequent recurrence of

---

[1] *Romore* in old Italian meant a tumult or riot.—EDITOR.

such challenges from Nello had changed the painter's first declaration of neutrality into a positive inclination to believe ill of the much-praised Greek.

"So you have got your Fra Girolamo back again, Cronaca? I suppose we shall have him preaching again this next Advent," said Nello.

"And not before there is need," said Cronaca, gravely. "We have had the best testimony to his words since the last Quaresima; for even to the wicked wickedness has become a plague; and the ripeness of vice is turning to rottenness in the nostrils even of the vicious. There has not been a change since the Quaresima, either in Rome or at Florence, but has put a new seal on the Frate's words,—that the harvest of sin is ripe, and that God will reap it with a sword."

"I hope he has had a new vision, however," said Francesco Cei, sneeringly. "The old ones are somewhat stale. Can't your Frate get a poet to help out his imagination for him?"

"He has no lack of poets about him," said Cronaca, with quiet contempt, "but they are great poets and not little ones; so they are contented to be taught by him, and no more think the truth stale which God has given him to utter, than they think the light of the moon is stale. But perhaps certain high prelates and princes who dislike the Frate's denunciations might be pleased to hear that though Giovanni Pico, and Poliziano, and Marsilio Ficino, and most other men of mark in Florence, reverence Fra Girolamo, Messer Francesco Cei despises him."

"Poliziano?" said Cei with a scornful laugh. "Yes, doubtless he believes in your new Jonah; witness the fine orations he wrote for the envoys of Sienna, to tell Alexander the Sixth that the world and the Church were never so well off as since he became Pope."

"Nay, Francesco," said Macchiavelli, smiling, "a various scholar must have various opinions. And as for the Frate, whatever we may think of his saintliness, you judge his preaching too narrowly. The secret of oratory lies, not in saying new things, but in saying things with a certain power that moves the hearers,—without which, as old Filelfo has said, your speaker deserves to be called 'non *o*ratorem, sed *a*ratorem.' And, according to that test, Fra Girolamo is a great orator."

"That is true, Niccolò," said Cennini, speaking from the shaving-chair; "but part of the secret lies in the prophetic visions. Our people—no offence to you, Cronaca—will run after anything in the shape of a prophet, especially if he prophesies terrors and tribulations."

"Rather say, Cennini," answered Cronaca, "that the chief secret lies in the Frate's pure life and strong faith, which stamp him as a messenger of God."

"I admit it,—I admit it," said Cennini, opening his palms, as he rose from the chair. "His life is spotless; no man has impeached it."

"He is satisfied with the pleasant lust of arrogance," Cei burst out bitterly. "I can see it in that proud lip and satisfied eye of his. He hears the air filled with his own name,—Fra Girolamo Savonarola, of Ferrara;

the prophet, the saint, the mighty preacher, who frightens the very babies of Florence into laying down their wicked baubles."

"Come, come, Francesco, you are out of humour with waiting," said the conciliatory Nello. "Let me stop your mouth with a little lather. I must not have my friend Cronaca made angry: I have a regard for his chin; and his chin is in no respect altered since he became a Piagnone. And for my own part, I confess, when the Frate was preaching in the Duomo last Advent, I got into such a trick of slipping in to listen to him that I might have turned Piagnone too, if I had not been hindered by the liberal nature of my art; and also by the length of the sermons, which are sometimes a good while before they get to the moving point. But, as Messer Niccolò here says, the Frate lays hold of the people by some power over and above his prophetic visions. Monks and nuns who prophesy are not of that rareness. For what says Luigi Pulci? 'Dombruno's sharp-cutting cimeter had the fame of being enchanted; but,' says Luigi, 'I am rather of opinion that it cut sharp because it was of strongly tempered steel.' Yes, yes; Paternosters may shave clean, but they must be said over a good razor."

"See, Nello!" said Macchiavelli, "what doctor is this advancing on his Bucephalus? I thought your piazza was free from those furred and scarlet-robed lackeys of death. This man looks as if he had had some such night adventure as Boccaccio's Maestro Simone, and had his bonnet and mantle pickled a little in the gutter; though he himself is as sleek as a miller's rat."

"A-ah!" said Nello, with a low long-drawn intonation, as he looked up towards the advancing figure,—a round-headed, round-bodied personage, seated on a raw young horse, which held its nose out with an air of threatening obstinacy, and by a constant effort to back and go off in an oblique line showed free views about authority very much in advance of the age.

"And I have a few more adventures in pickle for him," continued Nello, in an undertone, "which I hope will drive his inquiring nostrils to another quarter of the city. He's a doctor from Padua; they say he has been at Prato for three months, and now he's come to Florence to see what he can net. But his great trick is making rounds among the contadini. And do you note those great saddle-bags he carries? They are to hold the fat capons and eggs and meal he levies on silly clowns with whom coin is scarce. He vends his own secret medicine, so he keeps away from the doors of the druggists; and for this last week he has taken to sitting in my piazza for two or three hours every day, and making it a resort for asthmas and squalling bambini. It stirs my gall to see the toad-faced quack fingering the greasy quattrini, or bagging a pigeon in exchange for his pills and powders. But I'll put a few thorns in his saddle, else I'm no Florentine. Laudamus! he is coming to be shaved; that is what I've waited for. Messer Domenico, go not away, wait; you shall see a rare bit of fooling, which I devised two days ago. Here, Sandro!"

Nello whispered in the ear of Sandro, who rolled his solemn eyes, nodded, and, following up these signs of understanding with a slow smile, took to his heels with surprising rapidity.

"How is it with you, Maestro Tacco?" said Nello, as the doctor, with difficulty, brought his horse's head round towards the barber's shop. "That is a fine young horse of yours, but something raw in the mouth, eh?"

"He is an accursed beast, the *vermocane* seize him!" said Maestro Tacco, with a burst of irritation, descending from his saddle and fastening the old bridle, mended with string, to an iron staple in the wall. "Nevertheless," he added, recollecting himself, "a sound beast and a valuable, for one who wanted to purchase, and get a profit by training him. I had him cheap."

"Rather too hard riding for a man who carries your weight of learning: eh, Maestro?" said Nello. "You seem hot."

"Truly, I am likely to be hot," said the doctor, taking off his bonnet, and giving to full view a bald low head and flat broad face, with high ears, wide lipless mouth, round eyes, and deep arched lines above the projecting eyebrows, which altogether made Nello's epithet "toad-faced" dubiously complimentary to the blameless batrachian. "Riding from Peretola, when the sun is high, is not the same thing as kicking your heels on a bench in the shade, like your Florence doctors. Moreover, I have had not a little pulling to get through the carts and mules into the Mercato, to find out the husband of a certain Monna Ghita, who had had a fatal seizure before I was called in; and if it had not been that I had to demand my fees—"

"Monna Ghita!" said Nello, as the perspiring doctor interrupted himself to rub his head and face. "Peace be with her angry soul! The Mercato will want a whip the more if her tongue is laid to rest."

Tito, who had roused himself from his abstraction, and was listening to the dialogue, felt a new rush of the vague half-formed ideas about Tessa which had passed through his mind the evening before: if Monna Ghita were really taken out of the way, it would be easier for him to see Tessa again,—whenever he wanted to see her.

"*Gnaffè*, Maestro," Nello went on, in a sympathizing tone, "you are the slave of rude mortals, who, but for you, would die like brutes, without help of pill or powder. It is pitiful to see your learned lymph oozing from your pores as if it were mere vulgar moisture. You think my shaving will cool and disencumber you? One moment and I have done with Messer Francesco here. It seems to me a thousand years till I wait upon a man who carries all the science of Arabia in his head and saddle-bag. Ecco!"

Nello held up the shaving-cloth with an air of invitation, and Maestro Tacco advanced and seated himself, under a pre-occupation with his heat and his self-importance which made him quite deaf to the irony conveyed in Nello's officiously polite speech.

"It is but fitting that a great medicus like you," said Nello, adjusting the cloth, "should be shaved by the same razor that has shaved the illustrious Antonio Benevieni, the greatest master of the chirurgic art."

"The chirurgic art!" interrupted the doctor, with an air of contemptuous disgust. "Is it your Florentine fashion to put the masters of the science of medicine on a level with men who do carpentry on broken limbs, and sew up wounds like tailors, and carve away excrescences as a butcher trims meat? *Via!* A manual art, such as any artificer might learn, and which has been practised by simple barbers like yourself,— on a level with the noble science of Hippocrates, Galen, and Avicenna, which penetrates into the occult influences of the stars and plants and gems!—a science locked up from the vulgar!"

"No, in truth, Maestro," said Nello, using his lather very deliberately, as if he wanted to prolong the operation to the utmost, "I never thought of placing them on a level: I know your science comes next to the miracles of Holy Church for mystery. But there, you see, is the pity of it,"—here Nello fell into a tone of regretful sympathy,—"your high science is sealed from the profane and the vulgar, and so you become an object of envy and slander. I grieve to say it, but there are low fellows in this city,—mere *sgherri,* who go about in nightcaps and long beards, and make it their business to sprinkle gall in every man's broth who is prospering. Let me tell you—for you are a stranger—this is a city where every man had need carry a large nail ready to fasten on the wheel of Fortune when his side happens to be uppermost. Already there are stories—mere fables doubtless—beginning to be buzzed about concerning you, that make me wish I could hear of your being well on your way to Arezzo. I would not have a man of your metal stoned; for though San Stefano was stoned, he was not great in medicine like San Cosmo and San Damiano—"

"What stories? what fables?" stammered Maestro Tacco. "What do you mean?"

"*Lasso!* I fear me you are come into the trap for your cheese, Maestro. The fact is, there is a company of evil youths who go prowling about the houses of our citizens carrying sharp tools in their pockets; no sort of door or window or shutter but they will pierce it. They are possessed with a diabolical patience to watch the doings of people who fancy themselves private. It must be they who have done it,—it must be they who have spread the stories about you and your medicines. Have you by chance detected any small aperture in your door or window-shutter? No? Well, I advise you to look; for it is now commonly talked of that you have been seen in your dwelling at the Canto di Paglia,[2] making your secret specifics by night: pounding dried toads in a mortar, compounding a salve out of mashed worms, and making your pills from the dried livers of rats which you mix with saliva emitted during the utterance of

---

[2] The *Canto alla Paglia,* or "Straw corner," so called from straw and hay being daily sold there, was at a corner of Borgo S. Lorenzo and Via dei Cerretani; this last part of which was called Via dei Marignolli.—EDITOR.

a blasphemous incantation,—which indeed these witnesses profess to repeat."

"It is a pack of lies!" exclaimed the doctor, struggling to get utterance, and then desisting in alarm at the approaching razor.

"It is not to me, or any of this respectable company, that you need to say that, doctor. *We* are not the heads to plant such carrots as those in. But what of that? What are a handful of reasonable men against a crowd with stones in their hands? There are those among us who think Cecco d'Ascoli was an innocent sage—and we all know how he was burnt alive for being wiser than his fellows. Ah, doctor, it is not by living at Padua that you can learn to know Florentines. My belief is, they would stone the Holy Father himself, if they could find a good excuse for it; and they are persuaded that you are a necromancer, who is trying to raise the pestilence by selling secret medicines—and I am told your specifics have in truth an evil smell."

"It is false!" burst out the doctor, as Nello moved away his razor; "it is false! I will show the pills and the powders to these honourable signori—and the salve—it has an excellent odour—an odour of—of salve." He started up with the lather on his chin, and the cloth round his neck, to search in his saddle-bag for the belied medicines; and Nello in an instant adroitly shifted the shaving-chair till it was in the close vicinity of the horse's head, while Sandro, who had now returned, at a sign from his master placed himself near the bridle.

"Behold, Messeri!" said the doctor, bringing a small box of medicines and opening it before them. "Let any signor apply this box to his nostrils and he will find an honest odour of medicaments,—not indeed of pounded gems, or rare vegetables from the East, or stones found in the bodies of birds; for I practise on the diseases of the vulgar, for whom heaven has provided cheaper and less powerful remedies according to their degree: and there are even remedies known to our science which are entirely free of cost,—as the new *tussis* may be counteracted in the poor, who can pay for no specifics, by a resolute holding of the breath. And here is a paste which is even of savoury odour, and is infallible against melancholia, being concocted under the conjunction of Jupiter and Venus; and I have seen it allay spasms."

"Stay, Maestro," said Nello, while the doctor had his lathered face turned towards the group near the door, eagerly holding out his box, and lifting out one specific after another; "here comes a crying contadina with her baby. Doubtless she is in search of you; it is perhaps an opportunity for you to show this honourable company a proof of your skill Here, buona donna! here is the famous doctor. Why, what is the matter with the sweet *bimbo?*"

This question was addressed to a sturdy-looking, broad-shouldered contadina, with her head-drapery folded about her face so that little was to be seen but a bronzed nose and a pair of dark eyes and eyebrows She carried her child packed up in the stiff mummy-shaped case in which Italian babies have been from time immemorial introduced into society turning its face a little towards her bosom, and making those sorrowful grimaces which women are in the habit of using as a sort of pulleys to draw down reluctant tears.

"Oh, for the love of the Holy Madonna!" said the woman in a wailing voice, "will you look at my poor bimbo? I know I can't pay you for it, but I took it in to the Nunziata last night, and it's turned a worse colour than before; it's the convulsions. But when I was holding it before the Santissima Nunziata, I remembered they said there was a new doctor come who cured everything; and so I thought it might be the will of the Holy Madonna that I should bring it to you."

"Sit down, Maestro, sit down," said Nello. "Here is an opportunity for you; here are honourable witnesses who will declare before the Magnificant Eight that they have seen you practising honestly and relieving a poor woman's child. And then if your life is in danger, the Magnificant Eight will put you in prison a little while just to insure your safety, and after that, their sbirri will conduct you out of Florence by night as they did the zealous Frate Minore, who preached against the Jews. What! our people are given to stone-throwing; but we have magistrates."

The doctor, unable to refuse, seated himself in the shaving-chair, trembling, half with fear and half with rage, and by this time quite unconscious of the lather which Nello had laid on with such profuseness. He deposited his medicine-case on his knees, took out his precious spectacles (wondrous Florentine device!) from his wallet, lodged them carefully above his flat nose and high ears, and lifting up his brows, turned towards the applicant.

"O Santiddio! look at him," said the woman, with a more piteous wail than ever, as she held out the small mummy, which had its head completely concealed by dingy drapery wound round the head of the portable cradle, but seemed to be struggling and crying in a demoniacal fashion under this imprisonment. "The fit is on him! *Ohimè!* I know what colour he is; it's the evil eye,—oh!"

The doctor, anxiously holding his knees together to support his box, bent his spectacles towards the baby, and said cautiously, "It may be a new disease! unwind these rags, Monna!"

The contadina, with sudden energy, snatched off the encircling linen, when out struggled—scratching, grinning, and screaming—what the doctor in his fright fully believed to be a demon, but what Tito recognized as Vaiano's monkey, made more formidable by an artificial blackness, such as might have come from a hasty rubbing up the chimney.

Up started the unfortunate doctor, letting his medicine-box fall, and away jumped the no less terrified and indignant monkey, finding the first resting-place for his claws on the horse's mane, which he used as a sort of rope-ladder till he had fairly found his equilibrium, when he continued to clutch it as a bridle. The horse wanted no spur under such a rider, and the already loosened bridle offering no resistance, darted off across the piazza, with the monkey clutching, grinning, and blinking, on his neck.

"*Il cavallo! Il Diavolo!*" was now shouted on all sides by the idle rascals who gathered from all quarters of the piazza, and was echoed in tones of alarm by the stall-keepers, whose vested interests seemed in some danger; while the doctor, out of his wits with confused terror at the Devil, the possible stoning, and the escape of his horse, took to his heels with spectacles on nose, lathered face, and the shaving-cloth about his neck, crying, "Stop him! stop him! for a powder,—a florin,—stop him for a florin!" while the lads, outstripping him, clapped their hands and shouted encouragement to the runaway.

The *cerretano*, who had not bargained for the flight of his monkey along with the horse, had caught up his petticoats with much celerity, had showed a pair of party-coloured hose above his contadina's shoes, far in advance of the doctor. And away went the grotesque race up the Corso degli Adimari,—the horse with the singular jockey, the contadina with the remarkable hose, and the doctor in lather and spectacles, with furred mantle outflying.

It was a scene such as Florentines loved, from the potent and reverend signor going to council in his lucco, down to the grinning youngster, who felt himself master of all situations when his bag was filled with smooth stones from the convenient dry bed of the torrent. The grey-headed Domenico Cennini laughed no less heartily than the younger men, and Nello was triumphantly secure of the general admiration.

"Aha!" he exclaimed, snapping his fingers when the first burst of laughter was subsiding, "I have cleared my piazza of that unsavoury fly-trap, *mi pare*. Maestro Tacco will no more come here again to sit for patients than he will take to licking marble for his dinner."

"You are going towards the Piazza della Signoria, Messer Domenico," said Macchiavelli. "I will go with you, and we shall perhaps see who has deserved the *palio* among these racers. Come, Melema, will you go too?"

It had been precisely Tito's intention to accompany Cennini; but before he had gone many steps, he was called back by Nello who saw Maso approaching.

Maso's message was from Romola. She wished Tito to go to the Via de' Bardi as soon as possible. She would see him under the loggia, at the top of the house, as she wished to speak to him alone.

CHAPTER XVII

UNDER THE LOGGIA

THE loggia at the top of Bardo's house rose above the buildings on each side of it, and formed a gallery round quadrangular walls. On the side towards the street the roof was supported by columns; but on the remaining sides, by a wall pierced with arched openings, so that at the back, looking over a crowd of irregular, poorly built dwellings towards the hill of Bogoli, Romola could at all times have a walk sheltered from observation. Near one of those arched openings, close to the door by which he had entered the loggia, Tito awaited her, with a sickening sense of the sunlight that slanted before him and mingled itself with the ruin of his hopes. He had never for a moment relied on Romola's passion for him as likely to be too strong for the repulsion created by the discovery of his secret; he had not the presumptuous vanity which might have hindered him from feeling that her love had the same root with her belief in him. But as he imagined her coming towards him in her radiant beauty, made so lovably mortal by her soft hazel eyes, he fell into wishing that she had been something lower, if it were only that she might let him clasp her and kiss her before they parted. He had no real caress from her,—nothing but now and then a long glance, a kiss, a pressure of the hand; and he had so often longed that they should be alone together. They were going to be alone now; but he saw her standing inexorably aloof from him. His heart gave a great throb as he saw the door move: Romola was there. It was all like a flash of lightning: he felt, rather than saw, the glory about her head, the tearful appealing eyes; he felt, rather than heard, the cry of love with which she said, "Tito!"

And in the same moment she was in his arms, and sobbing with her face against his.

How poor Romola had yearned through the watches of the night to see that bright face! The new image of death; the strange bewildering doubt infused into her by the story of a life removed from her understanding and sympathy; the haunting vision, which she seemed not only to hear uttered by the low gasping voice, but to live through, as if it had been her own dream, had made her more conscious than ever that it was Tito who had first brought the warm stream of hope and gladness into her life, and who had first turned away the keen edge of pain in the remembrance of her brother. She would tell Tito everything; there was no one else to whom she could tell it. She had been restraining herself in the presence of her father all the morning; but now that long-pent-up sob might come forth. Proud and self-controlled to all the world beside, Romola was as simple and unreserved as a child in her love for Tito. She had been quite contented with the days when they had only looked at each other; but now, when she felt the need of clinging to him, there was no thought that hindered her.

"My Romola! my goddess!" Tito murmured with passionate fondness, as he clasped her gently, and kissed the thick golden ripples on her neck. He was in paradise: disgrace, shame, parting,—there was no fear of them any longer. This happiness was too strong to be marred by the sense that Romola was deceived in him; nay, he could only rejoice in her delusion; for, after all, concealment had been wisdom. The only thing he could regret was his needless dread; if, indeed, the dread had not been worth suffering for the sake of this sudden rapture.

The sob had satisfied itself, and Romola raised her head. Neither of them spoke; they stood looking at each other's faces with that sweet wonder which belongs to young love,—she with her long white hands on the dark-brown curls, and he with his dark fingers bathed in the streaming gold. Each was so beautiful to the other; each was experiencing that undisturbed mutual consciousness for the first time. The cold pressure of a new sadness on Romola's heart made her linger the more in that silent soothing sense of nearness and love; and Tito could not even seek to press his lips to hers, because that would be change.

"Tito," she said at last, "it has been altogether painful, but I must tell you everything. Your strength will help me to resist the impressions that will not be shaken off by reason."

"I know, Romola,—I know he is dead," said Tito; and the long lustrous eyes told nothing of the many wishes that would have brought about that death long ago if there had been such potency in mere wishes. Romola only read her own pure thoughts in their dark depths, as we read letters in happy dreams.

"So changed, Tito! It pierced me to think that it was Dino. And so strangely hard: not a word to my father; nothing but a vision that he wanted to tell me. And yet it was so piteous,—the struggling breath, and the eyes that seemed to look towards the crucifix, and yet not to see it. I shall never forget it; it seems as if it would come between me and everything I shall look at."

Romola's heart swelled again, so that she was forced to break off. But the need she felt to disburden her mind to Tito urged her to repress the rising anguish. When she began to speak again, her thoughts had travelled a little.

"It was strange, Tito. The vision was about our marriage, and yet he knew nothing of you."

"What was it, my Romola? Sit down and tell me," said Tito, leading her to the bench that stood near. A fear had come across him lest the vision should somehow or other relate to Baldassarre; and this sudden change of feeling prompted him to seek a change of position.

Romola told him all that had passed, from her entrance into San Marco, hardly leaving out one of her brother's words, which had burnt themselves into her memory as they were spoken. But when she was at the end of the vision, she paused; the rest came too vividly before her to be uttered, and she sat looking at the distance, almost unconscious for the moment that Tito was near her. *His* mind was at ease now; that vague vision had passed over him like white mist, and left no mark. But he was silent, expecting her to speak again.

"I took it," she went on, as if Tito had been reading her thoughts,— "I took the crucifix; it is down below in my bedroom."

"And now, my Romola," said Tito entreatingly, "you will banish these ghastly thoughts. The vision was an ordinary monkish vision, bred of fasting and fanatical ideas. It surely has no weight with you."

"No, Tito, no. But poor Dino, *he* believed it was a Divine message. It is strange," she went on meditatively, "this life of men possessed with fervid beliefs that seem like madness to their fellow-beings. Dino was not a vulgar fanatic; and that Fra Girolamo, his very voice seems to have penetrated me with a sense that there is some truth in what moves them,—some truth of which I know nothing."

"It was only because your feelings were highly wrought, my Romola. Your brother's state of mind was no more than a form of that theosophy which has been the common disease of excitable, dreamy minds in all ages; the same ideas that your father's old antagonist, Marsilio Ficino, pores over in the New Platonists; only your brother's passionate nature drove him to act out what other men write and talk about. And for Fra Girolamo, he is simply a narrow-minded monk, with a gift of preaching and infusing terror into the multitude. Any words or any voice would have shaken you at that moment. When your mind has had a little repose, you will judge of such things as you have always done before."

"Not about poor Dino," said Romola. "I was angry with him; my heart seemed to close against him while he was speaking; but since then I have thought less of what was in my own mind and more of what was in his. Oh, Tito! it was very piteous to see his young life coming to an end in that way. That yearning look at the crucifix when he was gasping for breath,—I can never forget it. Last night I looked at the crucifix a long while, and tried to see that it would help him, until at last it seemed to me by the lamplight as if the suffering face shed pity."

"My Romola, promise me to resist such thoughts; they are fit for sickly nuns, not for my golden-tressed Aurora, who looks made to scatter all such twilight fantasies. Try not to think of them now; we shall not long be alone together."

The last words were uttered in a tone of tender beseeching, and he turned her face towards him with a gentle touch of his right hand.

Romola had had her eyes fixed absently on the arched opening, but she had not seen the distant hill; she had all the while been in the chapter-house, looking at the pale images of sorrow and death.

Tito's touch and beseeching voice recalled her; and now in the warm sunlight she saw that rich dark beauty which seemed to gather round it all images of joy,—purple vines festooned between the elms, the strong corn perfecting itself under the vibrating heat, bright-winged creatures hurrying and resting among the flowers, round limbs beating the earth in gladness with cymbals held aloft, light melodies chanted to the thrilling rhythm of strings,—all objects and all sounds that tell of Nature revelling in her force. Strange, bewildering transition from those pale images of sorrow and death to this bright youthfulness, as of a sun-god who knew nothing of night! What thought could reconcile that worn anguish in her brother's face—that straining after something invisible—with this satisfied strength and beauty, and making it intelligible that they belonged to the same world? Or was there never any reconciling of them, but only a blind worship of clashing deities, first in mad joy and then in wailing? Romola for the first time felt this questioning need like a sudden uneasy dizziness and want of something to grasp; it was an experience hardly longer than a sigh, for the eager theorizing of ages is compressed, as in a seed, in the momentary want of a single mind. But there was no answer to meet the need, and it vanished before the returning rush of young sympathy with the glad, loving beauty that beamed upon her in new radiance, like the dawn after we have looked away from it to the gray west.

"Your mind lingers apart from our love, my Romola," Tito said, with a soft reproachful murmur. "It seems a forgotten thing to you."

She looked at the beseeching eyes in silence, till the sadness all melted out of her own.

"My joy!" she said, in her full, clear voice.

"Do you really care for me enough, then, to banish those chill fancies, or shall you always be suspecting me as the Great Tempter?" said Tito, with his bright smile.

"How should I not care for you more than for everything else? Everything I had felt before in all my life—about my father and about my loneliness—was a preparation to love you. You would laugh at me, Tito, if you knew what sort of man I used to think I should marry,—some scholar with deep lines in his face, like Alamanno Rinuccini, and with rather gray hair, who would agree with my father in taking the side of the Aristotelians, and be willing to live with him. I used to think about the love I read of in the poets, but I never dreamed that anything like that could happen to me here in Florence in our old library. And then *you* came, Tito, and were so much to my father, and I began to believe that life could be happy for me too."

"My goddess! is there any woman like you?" said Tito, with a mixture of fondness and wondering admiration at the blended majesty and simplicity in her.

"But, dearest," he went on, rather timidly, "if you minded more about our marriage, you would persuade your father and Messer Bernardo not to think of any more delays. But you seem not to mind about it."

"Yes, Tito, I will, I do mind. But I am sure my godfather will urge more delay now, because of Dino's death. He has never agreed with my father about disowning Dino, and you know he has always said that we ought to wait until you had been at least a year in Florence. Do not think hardly of my godfather. I know he is prejudiced and narrow, but yet he is very noble. He has often said that it is folly in my father to want to keep his library apart, that it may bear his name; yet he would try to get my father's wish carried out. That seems to me very great and noble,—that power of respecting a feeling which he does not share or understand."

"I have no rancour against Messer Bernardo for thinking you too precious for me, my Romola," said Tito; and that was true. "But your father, then, knows of his son's death?"

"Yes, I told him,—I could not help it. I told him where I had been, and that I had seen Dino die; but nothing else, and he has commanded me not to speak of it again. But he has been very silent this morning, and has had those restless movements which always go to my heart; they look as if he were trying to get outside the prison of his blindness."

Let us go to him now. I had persuaded him to try to sleep, because he slept little in the night. Your voice will soothe him, Tito; it always does."

"And not one kiss? I have not had one," said Tito, in his gentle, reproachful tone, which gave him an air of dependence very charming in a creature with those rare gifts that seem to excuse presumption.

The sweet pink flush spread itself with the quickness of light over Romola's face and neck as she bent towards him. It seemed impossible that their kisses could ever become common things.

"Let us walk once round the loggia," said Romola, "before we go down."

"There is something grim and grave to me always about Florence," said Tito, as they paused in the front of the house, where they could see over the opposite roofs to the other side of the river, "and even in its merriment there is something shrill and hard,—biting rather than gay. I wish we lived in Southern Italy, where thought is broken, not by weariness, but by delicious languors such as never seem to come over the 'ingenia accerima Florentina.' I should like to see you under that southern sun, lying among the flowers, subdued into mere enjoyment, while I bent over you and touched the lute and sang to you some little unconscious strain that seemed all one with the light and warmth. You have never known that happiness of the nymphs, my Romola."

"No; but I have dreamed of it often since you came. I am very thirsty for a deep draught of joy,—for a life all bright like you. But we will not think of it now, Tito; it seems to me as if there would always be pale sad faces among the flowers, and eyes that look in vain. Let us go."

CHAPTER XVIII

THE PORTRAIT

WHEN Tito left the Via de' Bardi that day in exultant satisfaction at finding himself thoroughly free from the threatened peril, his thoughts, no longer claimed by the immediate presence of Romola and her father, recurred to those futile hours of dread in which he was conscious of having not only felt but acted as he would not have done if he had had a truer foresight. He would not have parted with his ring; for Romola, and others to whom it was a familiar object, would be a little struck with the apparent sordidness of parting with a gem he had professedly cherished, unless he feigned as a reason the desire to make some special gift with the purchase-money: and Tito had at that moment a nauseating weariness of simulation. He was well out of the possible consequences that might have fallen on him from that initial deception, and it was no longer a load on his mind; kind Fortune had brought him immunity, and he thought it was only fair that she should. Who was hurt by it? The results to Baldassarre were too problematical to be taken into account. But he wanted now to be free from any hidden shackles that would gall him, though ever so little, under his ties to Romola. He was not aware that that very delight in immunity which prompted resolutions not to entangle himself again, was deadening the sensibilities which alone could save him from entanglement.

But, after all, the sale of the ring was a slight matter. Was it also a slight matter that little Tessa was under a delusion which would doubtless fill her small head with expectations doomed to disappointment? Should he try to see the little thing alone again and undeceive her at once, or should he leave the disclosure to time and chance? Happy dreams are pleasant, and they easily come to an end with daylight and the stir of life. The sweet, pouting, innocent, round thing! It was impossible not to think of her. Tito thought he should like some time to take her a present that would please her, and just learn if her stepfather treated her more cruelly now her mother was dead. Or, should he at once undeceive Tessa, and then tell Romola about her, so that they might find some happier lot for the poor thing? No: that unfortunate little incident of the *cerretano* and the marriage, and his allowing Tessa to part from him in delusion, must never be known to Romola, and since no enlightenment could expel it from Tessa's mind, there would always be a risk of betrayal; besides, even little Tessa might have some gall in her when she found herself disappointed in her love,—yes, she *must* be a little in love with him, and that might make it well that he should not see her again. Yet it was a trifling adventure such as a country girl would perhaps ponder on till some ruddy *contadino* made acceptable love to her, when she would break her resolution of secrecy and get at the truth that she was free. *Dunque,*—good-by, Tessa! kindest wishes! Tito had made up his mind that the silly little affair of the *cerretano* should have no further consequences for himself; and people are apt to think that resolutions taken on their own behalf will be firm. As for the fifty-five florins, the purchase-money of the ring, Tito had made up his mind what to do with some of them; he would carry out a pretty, ingenious thought which would set him more at ease in accounting for the absence of his ring to Romola, and would also serve him as a means of guarding her mind from the recurrence of those monkish fancies which were especially repugnant to him; and with this thought in his mind, he went to the Via Gualfonda to find Piero di Cosimo,[1] the artist who at that time was pre-eminent in the fantastic mythological design which Tito's purpose required.

Entering the court on which Piero's dwelling opened, Tito found the heavy iron knocker on the door thickly bound round with wool and ingeniously fastened with cords. Remembering the painter's practice of stuffing his ears against obtrusive noises, Tito was not much surprised at this mode of defence against visitors' thunder, and betook himself first to tapping modestly with his knuckles, and then to a more im-

---

[1] The house of Piero di Cosimo, according to his own autographical declaration in the Rent-Rolls of 1498, preserved in the Royal State Archives of Florence, was not situated in Via *Gualfonda* or *Valfonda,* but in Via della Scala.—EDITOR.

portunate attempt to shake the door. In vain! Tito was moving away, blaming himself for wasting his time on this visit, instead of waiting till he saw the painter again at Nello's, when a little girl entered the court with a basket of eggs on her arm, went up to the door, and standing on tiptoe, pushed up a small iron plate that ran in grooves, and putting her mouth to the aperture thus disclosed, called out in a piping voice, "Messer Piero!"

In a few moments Tito heard the sound of bolts, the door opened, and Piero presented himself in a red nightcap and a loose brown serge tunic, with sleeves rolled up to the shoulder. He darted a look of surprise at Tito, but without further notice of him stretched out his hand to take the basket from the child, re-entered the house, and presently returning with the empty basket, said, "How much to pay?"

"Two grossoni, Messer Piero; they are already boiled, my mother says."

Piero took the coin out of the leather scarsella at his belt, and the little maiden trotted away, not without a few upward glances of awed admiration at the surprising young signor.

Piero's glance was much less complimentary as he said,—

"What do you want at my door, Messer Greco? I saw you this morning at Nello's; if you had asked me then, I could have told you that I see no man in this house without knowing his business and agreeing with him beforehand."

"Pardon, Messer Piero," said Tito, with his imperturbable good-humour: "I acted without sufficient reflection. I remembered nothing but your admirable skill in inventing pretty caprices, when a sudden desire for something of that sort prompted me to come to you."

The painter's manners were too notoriously odd to all the world for this reception to be held a special affront; but even if Tito had suspected any offensive intention, the impulse to resentment would have been less strong in him than the desire to conquer good-will.

Piero made a grimace which was habitual with him when he was spoken to with flattering suavity. He grinned, stretched out the corners of his mouth, and pressed down his brows, so as to defy any divination of his feelings under that kind of stroking.

"And what may that need be?" he said, after a moment's pause. In his heart he was tempted by the hinted opportunity of applying his invention.

"I want a very delicate miniature device taken from certain fables of the poets, which you will know how to combine for me. It must be painted on a wooden case,—I will show you the size,—in the form of a triptych. The inside may be simple gilding: it is on the outside I want the device. It is a favorite subject with you Florentines,—the triumph of Bacchus and Ariadne; but I want it treated in a new way. A story in Ovid will give you the necessary hints. The young Bacchus must be seated in a ship, his head bound with clusters of grapes, and a spear entwined with vine-leaves in his hand: dark-berried ivy must wind about the masts and sails, the oars must be thyrsi, and flowers must wreathe themselves about the poop; leopards and tigers must be crouching before him, and dolphins must be sporting round. But I want to have the fair-haired Ariadne with him, made immortal with her golden crown, —that is not in Ovid's story, but no matter, you will conceive it all,— and above there must be young Loves, such as you know how to paint, shooting with roses at the points of their arrows—"

"Say no more!" said Piero. "I have Ovid in the vulgar tongue. Find me the passage. I love not to be choked with other men's thoughts. You may come in."

Piero led the way through the first room, where a basket of eggs was deposited on the open hearth, near a heap of broken egg-shells and a bank of ashes. In strange keeping with that sordid litter, there was a low bedstead of carved ebony, covered carelessly with a piece of rich oriental carpet, that looked as if it had served to cover the steps to a Madonna's throne; and a carved *cassone,* or large chest, with painted devices on its sides and lid. There was hardly any other furniture in the large room, except casts, wooden steps, easels, and rough boxes, all festooned with cobwebs.

The next room was still larger, but it was also much more crowded. Apparently Piero was keeping the Festa, for the double door underneath the window which admitted the painter's light from above, was thrown open, and showed a garden, or rather thicket, in which fig-trees and vines grew in tangled trailing wildness among nettles and hemlocks, and a tall cypress lifted its dark head from a stifling mass of yellowish mulberry-leaves. It seemed as if that dank luxuriance had begun to penetrate even within the walls of the wide and lofty room; for in one corner, amidst a confused heap of carved marble fragments and rusty armour, tufts of long grass and dark feathery fennel had made their way, and a large stone vase, tilted on one side, seemed to be pouring out the ivy that streamed around. All about the walls hung pen and oil sketches of fantastic sea-monsters; dances of satyrs and mænads; Saint Margaret's resurrection out of the devouring dragon; Madonnas with the supernal light upon them; studies of plants and grotesque heads; and on irregular rough shelves a few books were scattered among great drooping bunches of corn, bullocks' horns, pieces of dried honeycomb, stones with patches of rare-coloured lichen, skulls and bones, peacocks' feathers, and large birds' wings. Rising from among the dirty litter of the floor were lay figures: one in the frock of a Vallombrosan monk, strangely surmounted by a helmet with barred visor, another smothered with brocade and skins hastily tossed over it. Among this heterogeneous still-life, several speckled and white pigeons were perched or strutting, too tame to fly at the entrance of men; three corpulent toads were crawling in an intimate friendly way near the door-stone; and a white rabbit, apparently the model for that which was frightening Cupid in the picture of Mars and Venus placed on the central easel, was twitching its nose with much content on a box full of bran.

"And now, Messer Greco," said Piero, making a sign to Tito that he might sit down on a low stool near the door, and then standing over him with folded arms, "don't be trying to see everything at once like Messer Domeneddio, but let me know how large you would have this same triptych."

Tito indicated the desired dimensions, and Piero marked them on a piece of paper.

"And now for the book," said Piero, reaching down a manuscript volume.

"There's nothing about the Ariadne there," said Tito, giving him the passage; "but you will remember I want the crowned Ariadne by the side of the young Bacchus; she must have golden hair."

"Ha!" said Piero abruptly, pursuing up his lips again. "And you want them to be likenesses, eh?" he added, looking down into Tito's face.

Tito laughed and blushed. "I know you are great at portraits, Messer Piero; but I could not ask Ariadne to sit for you, because the painting is a secret."

"There it is! I want her to sit to me. Giovanni Vespucci wants me to paint him a picture of Œdipus and Antigone at Colonos, as he has expounded it to me: I have a fancy for the subject, and I want Bardo and his daughter to sit for it. Now, you ask them; and then I'll put the likeness into Ariadne."

"Agreed, if I can prevail with them. And your price for the Bacchus and Ariadne?"

"*Baie!* If you get them to let me paint them, that will pay me. I'd rather not have your money: you may pay for the case."

"And when shall I sit for you?" said Tito; "for if we have one likeness, we must have two."

"I don't want *your* likeness; I've got it already," said Piero, "only I've made you look frightened. I must take the fright out of it for Bacchus."

As he was speaking, Piero laid down the book and went to look among some paintings, propped with their faces against the wall. He returned with an oil-sketch in his hand.

"I call this as good a bit of portrait as I ever did," he said, looking at it as he advanced. "Yours is a face that expresses fear well, because it's naturally a bright one. I noticed it the first time I saw you. The rest of the picture is hardly sketched; but I've painted *you* in thoroughly."

Piero turned the sketch and held it towards Tito's eyes. He saw himself with his right hand uplifted, holding a wine-cup, in the attitude of triumphant joy, but with his face turned away from the cup with an expression of such intense fear in the dilated eyes and pallid lips that he felt a cold stream through his veins, as if he were being thrown into sympathy with his imaged self.

"You are beginning to look like it already," said Piero, with a short laugh, moving the picture away again. "He's seeing a ghost,—that fine young man. I shall finish it some day, when I've settled what sort of ghost is the most terrible,—whether it should look solid like a dead man come to life, or half transparent like a mist."

Tito, rather ashamed of himself for a sudden sensitiveness strangely opposed to his usual easy self-command, said carelessly,—

"That is a subject after your own heart, Messer Piero,—a revel interrupted by a ghost. You seem to love the blending of the terrible with the gay. I suppose that is the reason your shelves are so well furnished with death's-heads, while you are painting those roguish Loves who are running away with the armour of Mars. I begin to think you are a Cynic philosopher in the pleasant disguise of a cunning painter."

"Not I, Messer Greco; a philosopher is the last sort of animal I should choose to resemble. I find it enough to live, without spinning lies to account for life. Fowls cackle, asses bray, women chatter, and philosophers spin false reasons,—that's the effect the sight of the world brings out of them. Well, I am an animal that paints instead of cackling, or braying, or spinning lies. And now, I think our business is done; you'll keep to your side of the bargain about the Œpidus and Antigone?"

"I will do my best," said Tito,—on this strong hint, immediately moving towards the door.

"And you'll let me know at Nello's. No need to come here again."

"I understand," said Tito laughingly, lifting his hand in sign of friendly parting.

CHAPTER XIX

THE OLD MAN'S HOPE

MESSER BERNARDO DEL NERO was as inexorable as Romola had expected in his advice that the marriage should be deferred till Easter; and in this matter Bardo was entirely under the ascendancy of his sagacious and practical friend. Nevertheless, Bernardo himself, though he was as far as ever from any susceptibility to the personal fascination in Tito which was felt by others, could not altogether resist that argument of success which is always powerful with men of the world. Tito was making his way rapidly in high quarters. He was especially growing in favour with the young Cardinal Giovanni de' Medici, who had even spoken of Tito's forming part of his learned retinue on an approaching journey to Rome; and the bright young Greek, who had a tongue that was always ready without ever being quarrelsome, was more and more wished for at gay suppers in the Via Larga, and in Florentine games in which he had no pretension to excel, and could admire the incomparable skill of Piero de' Medici in the most graceful manner in the world. By an unfailing sequence, Tito's reputation as an agreeable companion in "magnificent" society made his learning and talent appear more lustrous: and he was really accomplished enough to prevent an exaggerated estimate from being hazardous to him. Messer Bernardo had old prejudices and attachments which now began to argue down the newer and feebler prejudice against the young Greek stranger who was rather too supple. To the old Florentine it was impossible to despise the recommendation of standing well with the best Florentine families; and since Tito began to be thoroughly received into that circle whose views were the unquestioned standard of social value, it seemed irrational not to admit that there was no longer any check to satisfaction in the prospect of such a son-in-law for Bardo, and such a husband for Romola. It was undeniable that Tito's coming had been the dawn of a new life for both father and daughter, and the first promise had even been surpassed. The blind old scholar—whose proud truthfulness would never enter into that commerce of feigned and preposterous admiration which, varied by a corresponding measurelessness in vituperation, made the woof of all learned intercourse—had fallen into neglect even among his fellow-citizens, and when he was alluded to at all, it had long been usual to say that, though his blindness and the loss of his son were pitiable misfortunes, he was tiresome in contending for the value of his own labours; and that his discontent was a little inconsistent in a man who had been openly regardless of religious rites, and who in days past had refused offers made to him from various quarters, on the slight condition that he would take orders, without which it was not easy for patrons to provide for every scholar. But since Tito's coming there was no longer the same monotony in the thought that Bardo's name suggested; the old man, it was understood, had left off his plaints, and the fair daughter was no longer to be shut up in dowerless pride, waiting for a *parentado*. The winning manners and growing favour of the handsome Greek who was expected to enter into the double relation of son and husband helped to make the new interest a thoroughly friendly one, and it was no longer a rare occurrence when a visitor enlivened the quiet library. Elderly men came from that indefinite prompting to renew former intercourse which arises when an old acquaintance begins to be newly talked about; and young men whom Tito had asked leave to bring once, found it easy to go again when they overtook him on his way to the Via de' Bardi, and, resting their hands on his shoulder, fell into easy chat with him. For it was pleasant to look at Romola's beauty; to see her, like old Firenzuola's type of womanly majesty, "sitting with a certain grandeur, speaking with gravity, smiling with modesty, and casting around, as it were, an odour of queenliness;" and she seemed to unfold like a strong white lily under this genial breath of admiration and homage; it was all one to her with her new bright life in Tito's love.

Tito had even been the means of strengthening the hope in Bardo's mind that he might before his death receive the longed-for security concerning his library,—that it should not be merged in another collection; that it should not be transferred to a body of monks, and be called by the name of a monastery; but that it should remain forever the Bardi Library, for the use of Florentines. For the old habit of trusting in the Medici could not die out while their influence was still the strongest lever in the State; and Tito, once possessing the ear of the Cardinal Giovanni de' Medici, might do more even than Messer Bernardo towards winning the desired interest, for he could demonstrate to a learned audience the peculiar value of Bardo's collection. Tito himself talked sanguinely of such a result, willing to cheer the old man, and conscious that Romola repaid those gentle words to her father with a sort of adoration that no direct tribute to herself could have won from her.

This question of the library was the subject of more than one discussion with Bernardo del Nero when Christmas was turned and the prospect of the marriage was becoming near,—but always out of Bardo's hearing. For Bardo nursed a vague belief, which they dared not disturb, that his property, apart from the library, was adequate to meet all demands. He would not even, except under a momentary pressure of angry despondency, admit to himself that the will by which he had disinherited Dino would leave Romola the heir of nothing but debts; or that he needed anything from patronage beyond the security that a separate locality should be assigned to his library, in return for a deed of gift by which he made it over to the Florentine Republic.

"My opinion is," said Bernardo to Romola, in a consultation they had under the loggia, "that since you are to be married, and Messer Tito will have a competent income, we should begin to wind up the affairs, and ascertain exactly the sum that would be necessary to save the library from being touched, instead of letting the debts accumulate any longer. Your father needs nothing but his shred of mutton and his macaroni every day, and I think Messer Tito may engage to supply that for the years that remain; he can let it be in place of the *morgencap*."

"Tito has always known that my life is bound up with my father's," said Romola; "and he is better to my father than I am; he delights in making him happy."

"Ah, he's not made of the same clay as other men, is he?" said Bernardo, smiling. "Thy father has thought of shutting woman's folly out of thee by cramming thee with Greek and Latin; but thou hast been as ready to believe in the first pair of bright eyes and the first soft words that have come within reach of thee, as if thou couldst say nothing by heart but Paternosters, like other Christian men's daughters."

"Now, godfather," said Romola, shaking her head playfully, "as if it were only bright eyes and soft words that made me love Tito! You know better. You know I love my father and you because you are both good, and I love Tito too because he is so good. I see it, I feel it in everything he says and does. And if he is handsome, too, why should I not love him the better for that? It seems to me beauty is part of the finished language by which goodness speaks. You know *you* must have been a very handsome youth, godfather,"—she looked up with one of her happy loving smiles at the stately old man,—"you were about as tall as Tito, and you had very fine eyes; only you looked a little sterner and prouder, and—"

"And Romola likes to have all the pride to herself?" said Bernardo, not inaccessible to this pretty coaxing. "However, it is well that in one way Tito's demands are more modest than those of any Florentine husband of fitting rank that we should have been likely to find for you: he wants no dowry."

So it was settled in that way between Messer Bernardo del Nero, Romola, and Tito. Bardo assented with a wave of the hand when Bernardo told him that he thought it would be well now to begin to sell property and clear off debts; being accustomed to think of debts and property as a sort of thick wood that his imagination never even penetrated, still less got beyond. And Tito set about winning Messer Bernardo's respect by inquiring, with his ready faculty, into Florentine money-matters, the secrets of the *Monti* or public funds, the values of real property, and the profits of banking.

"You will soon forget that Tito is not a Florentine, godfather," said Romola. "See how he is learning everything about Florence."

"It seems to me he is one of the *demoni,* who are of no particular country, child," said Bernardo, smiling. "His mind is a little too nimble to be weighted with all the stuff we men carry about in our hearts."

Romola smiled, too, in happy confidence.

CHAPTER XX

THE DAY OF THE BETROTHAL

It was the last week of the Carnival, and the streets of Florence were at their fullest and noisiest: there were the masked processions, chanting songs, indispensable now they had once been introduced by Lorenzo the Magnificent; there was the favourite rigoletto, or round dance, footed "in piazza" under the blue frosty sky; there were practical jokes of all sorts, from throwing comfits to throwing stones,—especially stones. For the boys and striplings, always a strong element in Florentine crowds, became at the height of Carnival-time as loud and unmanageable as tree-crickets, and it was their immemorial privilege to bar the way with poles to all passengers, until a tribute had been paid towards furnishing those lovers of strong sensations with suppers and bonfires; to conclude with the standing entertainment of stone-throwing, which was not entirely monotonous, since the consequent maiming was various, and it was not always a single person who was killed. So that the pleasures of the Carnival were of a checkered kind, and if a painter were called upon to represent them truly, he would have to make a picture in which there would be so much grossness and barbarity that it must be turned with its face to the wall, except when it was taken down for the grave historical purpose of justifying a reforming zeal which, in ignorance of the facts, might be unfairly condemned for its narrowness. Still there was much of that more innocent picturesque merriment which is never wanting among a people with quick animal spirits and sensitive organs; there was not the heavy sottishness which belongs to the thicker northern blood, nor the stealthy fierceness which in the more southern regions of the peninsula makes the brawl lead to the dagger-thrust.

It was the high morning, but the merry spirits of the Carnival were still inclined to lounge and recapitulate the last night's jests, when Tito Melema was walking at a brisk pace on the way to the Via de' Bardi. Young Bernardo Dovizi, who now looks at us out of Raphael's portrait as the keen-eyed Cardinal da Bibbiena, was with him; and as they went, they held animated talk about some subject that had evidently no relation to the sights and sounds through which they were pushing their way along the Por' Santa Maria. Nevertheless, as they discussed, smiled, and gesticulated, they both, from time to time, cast quick glances around them, and at the turning towards the Lung' Arno, leading to the Ponte Rubaconte, Tito had become aware, in one of these rapid surveys, that there was some one not far off him by whom he very much desired not to be recognized at that moment. His time and thoughts were thoroughly preoccupied, for he was looking forward to a unique occasion in his life: he was preparing for his betrothal, which was to take place on the evening of this very day. The ceremony had been resolved upon rather suddenly; for although preparations towards the marriage had been going forward for some time,—chiefly in the application of Tito's florins to the fitting-up of rooms in Bardo's dwelling, which, the library excepted, had always been scantily furnished,—it had been intended to defer both the betrothal and the marriage until after Easter, when Tito's year of probation, insisted on by Bernardo del Nero, would have been complete. But when an express proposition had come that Tito should follow the Cardinal Giovanni to Rome to help Bernardo Dovizi with his superior knowledge of Greek in arranging a library, and there was no possibility of declining what lay so plainly on the road to advancement, he had become urgent in his entreaties that the betrothal might take place before his departure: there would be the less delay before the marriage on his return, and it would be less painful to part if he and Romola were outwardly as well as inwardly pledged to each other,—if he had a claim which defied Messer Bernardo or any one else to nullify it. For the betrothal, at which rings were exchanged and mutual contracts were signed, made more than half the legality of marriage, to be completed on a separate occasion by the nuptial benediction. Romola's feeling had met Tito's in this wish, and the consent of the elders had been won.

And now Tito was hastening, amidst arrangements for his departure the next day, to snatch a morning visit to Romola, to say and hear any last words that were needful to be said before their meeting for the betrothal in the evening. It was not a time when any recognition could be pleasant that was at all likely to detain him; still less a recognition by Tessa. And it was unmistakably Tessa whom he had caught sight of moving along, with a timid and forlorn look, towards that very turn of the Lung' Arno which he was just rounding. As he continued his talk with the young Dovizi, he had an uncomfortable undercurrent of consciousness which told him that Tessa had seen him and would certainly follow him; there was no escaping her along this direct road by the Arno, and over the Ponte Rubaconte. But she would not dare to speak to him or approach him while he was not alone, and he would continue to keep Dovizi with him till they reached Bardo's door. He quickened his pace, and took up new threads of talk; but all the while the sense that Tessa was behind him, though he had no physical evidence of the fact, grew stronger and stronger; it was very irritating,—perhaps all the more so because a certain tenderness and pity for the poor little thing made the determination to escape without any visible notice of her a not altogether agreeable resource. Yet Tito persevered, and carried his companion to the door, cleverly managing his "addio" without turning his face in a direction where it was possible for him to see an importunate pair of blue eyes; and as he went up the stone steps, he tried to get rid of unpleasant thoughts by saying to himself that, after all, Tessa might not have seen him, or, if she had, might not have followed him.

But—perhaps because that possibility could not be relied on strongly—when the visit was over, he came out of the doorway with a quick step and an air of unconsciousness as to anything that might be on his right hand or his left. Our eyes are so constructed, however, that they take in a wide angle without asking any leave of our will; and Tito knew that there was a little figure in a white hood standing near the doorway,—knew it quite well, before he felt a hand laid on his arm. It was a real grasp, and not a light timid touch; for poor Tessa, seeing his rapid step, had started forward with a desperate effort. But when he stopped and turned towards her, her face wore a frightened look, as if she dreaded the effect of her boldness.

"Tessa!" said Tito, with more sharpness in his voice than she had ever heard in it before. "Why are you here? You must not follow me,—you must not stand about door-places waiting for me."

Her blue eyes widened with tears, and she said nothing. Tito was afraid of something worse than ridicule, if he were seen in the Via de' Bardi with a girlish contadina looking pathetically at him. It was a street of high silent-looking dwellings, not of traffic; but Bernardo del Nero, or some one almost as dangerous, might come up at any moment. Even if it had not been the day of his betrothal, the incident would have been awkward and annoying. Yet it would be brutal—it was impossible—to drive Tessa away with harsh words. That accursed folly of his with the *cerretano*,—that it should have lain buried in a quiet way for months, and now start up before him as this unseasonable crop of vexation! He could not speak harshly, but he spoke hurriedly.

"Tessa, I cannot—must not talk to you here. I will go on to the bridge and wait for you there. Follow me slowly."

He turned and walked fast to the Ponte Rubaconte, and there leaned against the wall of one of the quaint little houses that rise at even distances on the bridge, looking towards the way by which Tessa would come. It would have softened a much harder heart than Tito's to see the little thing advancing with her round face much paled and saddened since he had parted from it at the door of the "Nunziata." Happily it was the least frequented of the bridges, and there were scarcely any passengers on it at this moment. He lost no time in speaking as soon as she came near him.

"Now, Tessa, I have very little time. You must not cry. Why did you follow me this morning? You must not do so again."

"I thought," said Tessa, speaking in a whisper, and struggling against a sob that *would* rise immediately at this new voice of Tito's,—"I thought you wouldn't be so long before you came to take care of me again. And the *patrigno* beats me, and I can't bear it any longer. And always when I come for a holiday I walk about to find you, and I can't. Oh, please don't send me away from you again! It has been so long, and I cry so now, because you never come to me. I can't help it, for the days are so long, and I don't mind about the goats and kids, or anything,— and I can't—"

The sobs came fast now, and the great tears. Tito felt that he could not do otherwise than comfort her. Send her away,—yes; that he *must* do at once. But it was all the more impossible to tell her anything that would leave her in a state of hopeless grief. He saw new trouble in the background; but the difficulty of the moment was too pressing for him to weigh distant consequences.

"Tessa, my little one," he said, in his old caressing tone, "you must not cry. Bear with the cross *patrigno* a little longer. I will come back to you. But I'm going now to Rome,—a long, long way off. I shall come back in a few weeks, and then I promise you to come and see you. Promise me to be good and wait for me."

It was the well-remembered voice again, and the mere sound was half enough to soothe Tessa. She looked up at him with trusting eyes, that still glittered with tears, sobbing all the while, in spite of her utmost efforts to obey him. Again he said in a gentle voice,

"Promise me, my Tessa."

"Yes," she whispered. "But you won't be long?"

"No, not long. But I must go now. And remember what I told you, Tessa. Nobody must know that you ever see me, else you will lose me forever. And now, when I have left you, go straight home, and never follow me again. Wait till I come to you. Good-by, my little Tessa: I *will* come."

There was no help for it; he must turn and leave her without looking behind him to see how she bore it, for he had no time to spare. When he did look round he was in the Via de' Benci, where there was no seeing what was happening on the bridge; but Tessa was too trusting and obedient not to do just what he had told her.

Yes, the difficulty was at an end for that day; yet this return of Tessa to him, at a moment when it was impossible for him to put an end to all difficulty with her by undeceiving her, was an unpleasant incident to carry in his memory. But Tito's mind was just now thoroughly penetrated with a hopeful first love, associated with all happy prospects flattering to his ambition; and that future necessity of grieving Tessa could be scarcely more to him than the far-off cry of some little suffering animal buried in the thicket, to a merry cavalcade in the sunny plain. When, for the second time that day, Tito was hastening across the Ponte Rubaconte, the thought of Tessa caused no perceptible diminution of his happiness. He was well muffled in his mantle, less, perhaps, to protect him from the cold than from the additional notice that would have been drawn upon him by his dainty apparel. He leaped up the stone steps by two at a time, and said hurriedly to Maso, who met him,—

"Where is the damigella?"

"In the library; she is quite ready, and Monna Brigida and Messer Bernardo are already there with Ser Braccio, but none of the rest of the company."

"Ask her to give me a few minutes alone; I will await her in the *salotto*."

Tito entered a room which had been fitted up in the utmost contrast with the half-pallid, half-sombre tints of the library. The walls were brightly frescoed with "caprices" of nymphs and loves sporting under the blue among flowers and birds. The only furniture besides the red leather seats and the central table were two tall white vases, and a young faun playing the flute, modelled by a promising youth named Michelangelo Buonarotti. It was a room that gave a sense of being in the sunny open air.

Tito kept his mantle round him, and looked towards the door. It was not long before Romola entered, all white and gold, more than ever like a tall lily. Her white silk garment was bound by a golden girdle, which fell with large tassels; and above that was the rippling gold of her hair, surmounted by the white mist of her long veil, which was fastened on her brow by a band of pearls, the gift of Bernardo del Nero, and was now parted off her face so that it all floated backward.

"Regina mia!" said Tito, as he took her hand and kissed it, still keeping his mantle round him. He could not help going backward to look at her again, while she stood in calm delight, with that exquisite self-consciousness which rises under the gaze of admiring love.

"Romola, will you show me the next room now?" said Tito, checking himself with the remembrance that the time might be short. "You said I should see it when you had arranged everything."

Without speaking, she led the way into a long narrow room, painted brightly like the other, but only with birds and flowers. The furniture in it was all old; there were old faded objects for feminine use or ornament, arranged in an open cabinet between the two narrow windows; above the cabinet was the portrait of Romola's mother; and below this, on the top of the cabinet, stood the crucifix which Romola had brought from San Marco.

"I have brought something under my mantle," said Tito, smiling; and throwing off the large loose garment, he showed the little tabernacle which had been painted by Piero di Cosimo. The painter had carried out Tito's intention charmingly, and so far had atoned for his long delay. "Do you know what this is for, my Romola?" added Tito, taking her by the hand, and leading her towards the cabinet. "It is a little shrine, which is to hide away from you forever that remembrancer of sadness. You have done with sadness now; and we will bury all images of it,—bury them in a tomb of joy. See!"

A slight quiver passed across Romola's face as Tito took hold of the crucifix. But she had no wish to prevent his purpose; on the contrary, she herself wished to subdue certain importunate memories and questionings which still flitted like unexplained shadows across her happier thought.

He opened the triptych and placed the crucifix within the central space; then closing it again, taking out the key, and setting the little tabernacle in the spot where the crucifix had stood, said,—

"Now, Romola, look and see if you are satisfied with the portraits old Piero has made of us. Is it not a dainty device? and the credit of choosing it is mine."

"Ah, it is you,—it is perfect!" said Romola, looking with moist joyful eyes at the miniature Bacchus, with his purple clusters. "And I am Ariadne, and you are crowning me! Yes, it is true, Tito; you have crowned my poor life."

They held each other's hands while she spoke, and both looked at their imaged selves. But the reality was far more beautiful; she all lily-white and golden, and he with his dark glowing beauty above the purple red-bordered tunic.

"And it was our good strange Piero who painted it?" said Romola. "Did you put it into his head to paint me as Antigone, that he might have my likeness for this?"

"No, it was he who made my getting leave for him to paint you and your father a condition of his doing this for me."

"Ah! I see now what it was you gave up your precious ring for. I perceived you had some cunning plan to give me pleasure."

Tito did not blench. Romola's little illusions about himself had long ceased to cause him anything but satisfaction. He only smiled and said,—

"I might have spared my ring; Piero will accept no money from me; he thinks himself paid by painting you. And now, while I am away, you will look every day at those pretty symbols of our life together,— the ship on the calm sea, and the ivy that never withers, and those Loves that have left off wounding us and shower soft petals that are like our kisses; and the leopards and tigers, they are the troubles of your life that are all quelled now; and the strange sea-monsters, with their merry eyes,—let us see,—they are the dull passages in the heavy books, which have begun to be amusing since we have sat by each other."

"Tito mio!" said Romola, in a half-laughing voice of love; "but you will give me the key?" she added, holding out her hand for it.

"Not at all!" said Tito, with playful decision, opening his scarsellar and dropping in the little key. "I shall drown it in the Arno."

"But if I ever wanted to look at the crucifix again?"

"Ah! for that very reason it is hidden,—hidden by these images of youth and joy."

He pressed a light kiss on her brow, and she said no more, ready to submit, like all strong souls, when she felt no valid reason for resistance.

And then they joined the waiting company, which made a dignified little procession as it passed along the Ponte Rubaconte towards Santa Croce. Slowly it passed, for Bardo, unaccustomed for years to leave his own house, walked with a more timid step than usual; and that slow pace suited well with the gouty dignity of Messer Bartolommeo Scala, who graced the occasion by his presence, along with his daughter Alessandra. It was customary to have very long troops of kindred and friends at the *sposalizio,* or betrothal, and it had even been found necessary in time past to limit the number by law to no more than *four hundred,*—two hundred on each side; for since the guests were all feasted after this initial ceremony, as well as after the *nozze,* or marriage, the very first stage of matrimony had become a ruinous expense, as that scholarly Benedict, Leonardo Bruno, complained in his own case. But Bardo who in his poverty had kept himself proudly free from any appearance of claiming the advantages attached to a powerful family name, would have no invitations given on the strength of mere friendship; and the modest procession of twenty that followed the *sposi* were, with three or four exceptions, friends of Bardo's and Tito's selected on personal grounds.

Bernardo del Nero walked as a vanguard before Bardo, who was led on the right by Tito, while Romola held her father's other hand. Bardo had himself been married at Santa Croce, and had insisted on Romola's being betrothed and married there, rather than in the little church of Santa Lucia close by their house, because he had a complete mental vision of the grand church where he hoped that a burial might be granted him among the Florentines who had deserved well. Happily the way was short and direct, and lay aloof from the loudest riot of the Carnival, if only they could return before any dances or shows began in the great piazza of Santa Croce. The west was red as they passed the bridge, and shed a mellow light on the pretty procession, which had a touch of solemnity in the presence of the blind father. But when the ceremony was over, and Tito and Romola came out on to the broad steps of the church, with the golden links of destiny on their fingers, the evening had deepened into struggling starlight, and the servants had their torches lit.

While they came out, a strange dreary chant, as of a *Miserere,* met their ears, and they saw that at the extreme end of the piazza there seemed to be a stream of people impelled by something approaching from the Borgo de' Greci.

"It is one of their masked processions, I suppose," said Tito, who was now alone with Romola, while Bernardo took charge of Bardo.

And as he spoke there came slowly into view, at a height far above the heads of the on-lookers, a huge and ghastly image of Winged Time with his scythe and hour-glass, surrounded by his winged children, the Hours. He was mounted on a high car completely covered with black, and the bullocks that drew the car were also covered with black, their horns alone standing out white above the gloom; so that in the sombre shadow of the houses it seemed to those at a distance as if Time and his children were apparitions floating through the air. And behind them came what looked like a troop of the sheeted dead gliding above blackness. And as they glided slowly, they chanted in a wailing strain.

A cold horror seized on Romola, for at the first moment it seemed as if her brother's vision, which could never be effaced from her mind, was being half fulfilled. She clung to Tito, who, divining what was in her thoughts, said,—

"What dismal fooling sometimes pleases your Florentines! Doubtless this is an invention of Piero di Cosimo, who loves such grim merriment."

"Tito, I wish it had not happened. It will deepen the images of that vision which I would fain be rid of."

"Nay, Romola, you will look only at the images of our happiness now. I have locked all sadness away from you."

"But it is still there,—it is only hidden," said Romola, in a low tone, hardly conscious that she spoke.

"See, they are all gone now!" said Tito. "You will forget this ghastly mummery when we are in the light, and can see each other's eyes. My Ariadne must never look backward now,—only forward to Easter, when she will triumph with her Care-dispeller."

BOOK TWO

★

CHAPTER I

FLORENCE EXPECTS A GUEST

IT was the 17th of November, 1494: more than eighteen months since Tito and Romola had been finally united in the joyous Easter time, and had had a rainbow-tinted shower of comfits thrown over them, after the ancient Greek fashion, in token that the heavens would shower sweets on them through all their double life.

Since that Easter a great change had come over the prospects of Florence; and as in the tree that bears a myriad of blossoms, each single bud with its fruit is dependent on the primary circulation of the sap, so the fortunes of Tito and Romola were dependent on certain grand political and social conditions which made an epoch in the history of Italy.

In this very November, little more than a week ago, the spirit of the old centuries seemed to have re-entered the breasts of Florentines. The great bell in the palace tower had rung out the hammer-sound of alarm, and the people had mustered with their rusty arms, their tools and impromptu cudgels, to drive out the Medici. The gate of San Gallo had been fairly shut on the arrogant, exasperating Piero, galloping away towards Bologna with his hired horsemen frightened behind him, and shut on his keener young brother, the cardinal, escaping in the disguise of a Franciscan monk: a price had been set on both their heads. After that, there had been some sacking of houses, according to old precedent; the ignominious images, painted on the public buildings, of the men who had conspired against the Medici in days gone by, were effaced; the exiled enemies of the Medici were invited home. The half-fledged tyrants were fairly out of their splendid nest in the Via Larga, and the Republic had recovered the use of its will again.

But now, a week later, the great palace in the Via Larga had been prepared for the reception of another tenant; and if drapery roofing the streets with unwonted colour, if banners and hangings pouring out of the windows, if carpets and tapestry stretched over all steps and pavement on which exceptional feet might tread, were an unquestionable proof of joy, Florence was very joyful in the expectation of its new guest. The stream of colour flowed from the palace in the Via Larga round by the cathedral, then by the great Piazza della Signoria, and across the Ponte Vecchio to the Porta San Frediano,—the gate that looks towards Pisa. There, near the gate, a platform and canopy had been erected for the Signoria; and Messer Luca Corsini, doctor of law, felt his heart palpitating a little with the sense that he had a Latin oration to read; and every chief elder in Florence had to make himself ready, with smooth chin and well-lined silk lucco, to walk in procession; and the well-born youths were looking at their rich new tunics after the French mode which was to impress the stranger as having a peculiar grace when worn by Florentines; and a large body of the clergy, from the archbishop in his effulgence to the train of monks, black, white, and gray, were consulting betimes in the morning how they should marshal themselves, with their burden of relics and sacred banners and consecrated jewels, that their movements might be adjusted to the expected arrival of the illustrious visitor, at three o'clock in the afternoon.

An unexampled visitor! For he had come through the passes of the Alps with such an army as Italy had not seen before: with thousands of terrible Swiss, well used to fight for love and hatred as well as for hire; with a host of gallant cavaliers proud of a name; with an unprecedented infantry, in which every man in a hundred carried an arquebus; nay, with cannon of bronze, shooting not stones but iron balls, drawn not by bullocks but by horses, and capable of firing a second time before a city could mend the breach made by the first ball. Some compared the newcomer to Charlemagne, reputed rebuilder of Florence, welcome conqueror of degenerate kings, regulator and benefactor of the Church: some preferred the comparison to Cyrus, liberator of the chosen people, restorer of the Temple. For he had come across the Alps with the most glorious projects: he was to march through Italy amid the jubilees of a grateful and admiring people; he was to satisfy all conflicting complaints at Rome; he was to take possession, by virtue of hereditary right and a little fighting, of the kingdom of Naples; and from that convenient starting-point he was to set out on the conquest of the Turks, who were partly to be cut to pieces and partly converted to the faith of Christ. It was a scheme that seemed to befit the Most Christian King, head of a nation which, thanks to the devices of a subtle Louis the Eleventh, who had died in much fright as to his personal prospects ten years before, had become the strongest of Christian monarchies; and this anti-type of Cyrus and Charlemagne was no other than the son of that subtle Louis,—the young Charles the Eighth of France.

Surely, on a general statement hardly anything could seem more grandiose, or fitter to revive in the breasts of men the memory of great dispensations by which new strata had been laid in the history of mankind. And there was a very widely spread conviction that the advent of the French king and his army into Italy was one of those events at which marble statues might well be believed to perspire, phantasmal fiery warriors to fight in the air, and quadrupeds to bring forth monstrous births,—that it did not belong to the usual order of Providence, but was in a peculiar sense the work of God. It was a conviction that rested less on the necessarily momentous character of a powerful foreign invasion than on certain moral emotions to which the aspect of the times gave the form of presentiments,—emotions which had found a very remarkable utterance in the voice of a single man.

That man was Fra Girolamo Savonarola, Prior of the Dominican convent of San Marco in Florence. On a September morning, when men's ears were ringing with the news that the French army had entered Italy, he had preached in the Cathedral of Florence from the text, "Behold I, even I, do bring a flood of waters upon the earth." He believed it was by supreme guidance that he had reached just so far in his exposition of Genesis the previous Lent; and he believed the "flood of water" —emblem at once of avenging wrath and purifying mercy—to be the divinely indicated symbol of the French army. His audience, some of whom were held to be among the choicest spirits of the age,—the most cultivated men in the most cultivated of Italian cities,—believed it too, and listened with shuddering awe. For this man had a power rarely paralleled, of impressing his beliefs on others, and of swaying very various minds. And as long as four years ago he had proclaimed from the chief pulpit of Florence that a scourge was about to descend on Italy, and that by this scourge the Church was to be purified. Savonarola appeared to believe, and his hearers more or less waveringly believed, that he had a mission like that of the Hebrew prophets, and that the Florentines among whom his message was delivered were in some sense a second chosen people. The idea of prophetic gifts was not a remote one in that age: seers of visions, circumstantial heralds of things to be, were far from uncommon either outside or inside the cloister; but this very fact made Savonarola stand out the more conspicuously as a grand exception. While in others the gift of prophecy was very much like a farthing candle illuminating small corners of human destiny with prophetic gossip, in Savonarola it was like a mighty beacon shining far out for the warning and guidance of men. And to some of the soberest minds the supernatural character of his insight into the future gathered a strong attestation from the peculiar conditions of the age.

At the close of 1492, the year in which Lorenzo de' Medici died and Tito Melema came as a wanderer to Florence, Italy was enjoying a peace and prosperity unthreatened by any near and definite danger. There was no fear of famine, for the seasons had been plenteous in corn and wine and oil; new palaces had been rising in all fair cities, new villas on pleasant slopes and summits; and the men who had more than their share of these good things were in no fear of the larger number who had less. For the citizens' armour was getting rusty, and populations seemed to have become tame, licking the hands of masters who paid for a ready-made army when they wanted it, as they paid for goods of Smyrna. Even the fear of the Turk had ceased to be active, and the Pope found it more immediately profitable to accept bribes from him for a little prospective poisoning than to form plans either for conquering or for converting him.

Altogether this world, with its partitioned empire and its roomy universal Church, seemed to be a handsome establishment for the few who were lucky or wise enough to reap the advantages of human folly,—a world in which lust and obscenity, lying and treachery, oppression and murder, were pleasant, useful, and when properly managed, not dangerous. And as a sort of fringe or adornment to the substantial delights of tyranny, avarice, and lasciviousness, there was the patronage of polite learning and the fine arts, so that flattery could always be had in the choicest Latin to be commanded at that time, and sublime artists were at hand to paint the holy and the unclean with impartial skill. The Church, it was said, had never been so disgraced in its head, had never shown so few signs of renovating, vital belief in its lower members; nevertheless it was much more prosperous than in some past days. The heavens were fair and smiling above; and below there were no signs of earthquake.

Yet at that time, as we have seen, there was a man in Florence who for two years and more had been preaching that a scourge was at hand; that the world was certainly not framed for the lasting convenience of hypocrites, libertines, and oppressors. From the midst of those smiling heavens he had seen a sword hanging—the sword of God's justice—which was speedily to descend with purifying punishment on the Church and the world. In brilliant Ferrara, seventeen years before, the contradiction between men's lives and their professed beliefs had pressed upon him with a force that had been enough to destroy his appetite for the world, and at the age of twenty-three had driven him into the cloister. He believed that God had committed to the Church the sacred lamp of truth for the guidance and salvation of men, and he saw that the Church, in its corruption, had become a sepulchre to hide the lamp. As the years went on scandals increased and multiplied, and hypocrisy seemed to have given place to impudence. Had the world, then, ceased to have a righteous Ruler? Was the Church finally forsaken? No, assuredly: in the Sacred Book there was a record of the past in which might be seen as in a glass what would be in the days to come, and the book showed that when the wickedness of the chosen people, type of the Christian Church, had become crying, the judgments of God had descended on them. Nay, reason itself declared that vengeance was imminent, for what else would suffice to turn men from their obstinacy in evil? And unless the Church were reclaimed, how could the promises be fulfilled, that the heathens should be converted and the whole world become subject to the one true law? He had seen his belief reflected in visions,—a mode of seeing which had been frequent with him from his youth up.

But the real force of demonstration for Girolamo Savonarola lay in his own burning indignation at the sight of wrong; in his fervent belief in an Unseen Justice that would put an end to the wrong, and in an Unseen Purity, to which lying and uncleanness were an abomination.

To his ardent, power-loving soul, believing in great ends, and longing to achieve those ends by the exertion of its own strong will, the faith in a supreme and righteous Ruler became one with the faith in a speedy divine interposition that would punish and reclaim.

Meanwhile, under that splendid masquerade of dignities sacred and secular which seemed to make the life of lucky Churchmen and princely families so luxurious and amusing, there were certain conditions at work which slowly tended to disturb the general festivity. Ludovico Sforza,—copious in gallantry, splendid patron of an incomparable Leonardo da Vinci,—holding the ducal crown of Milan in his grasp, and wanting to put it on his own head rather than let it rest on that of a feeble nephew who would take very little to poison him, was much afraid of the Spanish-born old King Ferdinand and the Crown Prince Alfonso of Naples, who, not liking cruelty and treachery which were useless to themselves, objected to the poisoning of a near relative for the advantage of a Lombard usurper; the royalties of Naples again were afraid of their suzerain, Pope Alexander Borgia; all three were anxiously watching Florence, lest with its midway territory it should determine the game by underhand backing; and all four, with every small state in Italy, were afraid of Venice,—Venice the cautious, the stable, and the strong, that wanted to stretch its arms not only along both sides of the Adriatic but across to the ports of the western coast.

Lorenzo de' Medici, it was thought, did much to prevent the fatal outbreak of such jealousies, keeping up the old Florentine alliance with Naples and the Pope, and yet persuading Milan that the alliance was for the general advantage. But young Piero de' Medici's rash vanity had quickly nullified the effect of his father's wary policy, and Lodovico Sforza, roused to suspicion of a league against him, thought of a move which would checkmate his adversaries: he determined to invite the French king to march into Italy, and as heir of the house of Anjou, take possession of Naples. Ambassadors—"orators," as they were called in those haranguing times—went and came; a recusant cardinal, determined not to acknowledge a Pope elected by bribery (and his own particular enemy), went and came also, and seconded the invitation with hot rhetoric; and the young king seemed to lend a willing ear. So that in 1493 the rumour spread and became louder and louder that Charles the Eighth of France was about to cross the Alps with a mighty army; and the Italian populations, accustomed, since Italy had ceased to be the heart of the Roman empire, to look for an arbitrator from afar, began vaguely to regard his coming as a means of avenging their wrongs and redressing their grievances.

And in that rumour Savonarola had heard the assurance that his prophecy was being verified. What was it that filled the ears of the prophets of old but the distant tread of foreign armies, coming to do the work of justice? He no longer looked vaguely to the horizon for the coming storm: he pointed to the rising cloud. The French army was that new deluge which was to purify the earth from iniquity; the French king, Charles the Eighth, was the instrument elected by God, as Cyrus had been of old, and all men who desired good rather than evil were to rejoice in his coming. For the scourge would fall destructively on the impenitent alone. Let any city of Italy, let Florence above all,—Florence beloved of God, since to its ear the warning voice had been specially sent,—repent and turn from its ways, like Nineveh of old, and the storm-cloud would roll over it and leave only refreshing raindrops.

Fra Girolamo's word was powerful; yet now that the new Cyrus had already been three months in Italy, and was not far from the gates of Florence, his presence was expected there with mixed feelings, in which fear and distrust certainly predominated. At present it was not understood that he had redressed any grievances; and the Florentines clearly had nothing to thank him for. He held their strong frontier fortresses, which Piero de' Medici had given up to him without securing any honourable terms in return; he had done nothing to quell the alarming revolt of Pisa, which had been encouraged by his presence to throw off the Florentine yoke; and "orators," even with a prophet at their head, could win no assurance from him, except that he would settle everything when he was once within the walls of Florence. Still, there was the satisfaction of knowing that the exasperating Piero de' Medici had been fairly pelted out for the ignominious surrender of the fortresses, and in that act of energy the spirit of the Republic had recovered some of its old fire.

The preparations for the equivocal guest were not entirely those of a city resigned to submission. Behind the bright drapery and banners symbolical of joy, there were preparations of another sort made with common accord by government and people. Well hidden within walls there were hired soldiers of the Republic, hastily called in from the surrounding districts; there were old arms duly furbished, and sharp tools and heavy cudgels laid carefully at hand, to be snatched up on short notice; there were excellent boards and stakes to form barricades upon occasion, and a good supply of stones to make a surprising hail from the upper windows. Above all, there were people very strongly in the humour for fighting any personage who might be supposed to have designs of hectoring over them, they having lately tasted that new pleasure with much relish. This humour was not diminished by the sight of occasional parties of Frenchmen, coming beforehand to choose their quarters, with a hawk, perhaps, on their left wrist, and, metaphorically speaking, a piece of chalk in their right hand to mark Italian doors withal; especially as creditable historians imply that many sons of France were at that time characterized by something approaching to a swagger, which must have whetted the Florentine appetite for a little stone-throwing.

And this was the temper of Florence on the morning of the 17th of November, 1494.

CHAPTER II

THE PRISONERS

THE sky was grey, but that made little difference in the Piazza del Duomo, which was covered with its holiday sky of blue drapery, and its constellations of yellow lilies and coats of arms. The sheaves of banners were unfurled at the angles of the baptistery, but there was no carpet yet on the steps of the Duomo, for the marble was being trodden by numerous feet that were not at all exceptional. It was the hour of the Advent sermons, and the very same reasons which had flushed the streets with holiday colour were reasons why the preaching in the Duomo could least of all be dispensed with.

But not all the feet in the piazza were hastening towards the steps. People of high and low degree were moving to and fro with the brisk pace of men who had errands before them; groups of talkers were thickly scattered, some willing to be late for the sermon, and others content not to hear it at all.

The expression on the faces of these apparent loungers was not that of men who are enjoying the pleasant laziness of an opening holiday. Some were in close and eager discussion; others were listening with keen interest to a single spokesman, and yet from time to time turned round with a scanning glance at any new passer-by. At the corner, looking towards the Via de' Cerretani—just where the artificial rainbow light of the piazza ceased, and the grey morning fell on the sombre stone houses—there was a remarkable cluster of the working people, most of them bearing on their dress or persons the signs of their daily labour, and almost all of them carrying some weapon, or some tool which might serve as a weapon upon occasion. Standing in the grey light of the street, with bare brawny arms and soiled garments, they made all the more striking the transition from the brightness of the piazza. They were listening to the thin notary, Ser Cioni, who had just paused on his way to the Duomo. His biting words could get only a contemptuous reception two years and a half before in the Mercato, but now he spoke with the more complacent humour of a man whose party is uppermost, and who is conscious of some influence with the people.

"Never talk to me," he was saying, in his incisive voice, "never talk to me of bloodthirsty Swiss or fierce French infantry: they might as well be in the narrow passes of the mountains as in our streets; and peasants have destroyed the finest armies of our condottieri in time past, when they had once got them between steep precipices. I tell you, Florentines need be afraid of no army in their own streets."

"That's true, Ser Cioni," said a man whose arms and hands were discoloured by crimson dye, which looked like blood-stains, and who had a small hatchet stuck in his belt; "and those French cavaliers, who came in squaring themselves in their smart doublets the other day, saw a sample of the dinner we could serve up for them. I was carrying my cloth in Ognissanti, when I saw my fine Messeri going by, looking round as if they thought the houses of the Vespucci and the Agli a poor pick of lodgings for them, and eying us Florentines, like top-knotted cocks as they are, as if they pitied us because we didn't know how to strut. 'Yes, my fine *Galli*,' says I, 'stick out your stomachs; I've got a meat-axe in my belt that will go inside you all the easier;' when presently the old cow lowed, and I knew something had happened—no matter what. So I threw my cloth in at the first doorway, and took hold of my meat-axe and ran after my fine cavaliers towards the Vigna Nuova. And 'What is it, Guccio?' said I, when he came up with me. 'I think it's the Medici coming back,' said Guccio. *Bembè!* I expected so! And up we reared a barricade, and the Frenchmen looked behind and saw themselves in a trap; and up comes a good swarm of our *Ciompi,* and one of them with a big scythe he had in his hand mowed off one of the fine cavalier's feathers: it's true! And the lasses peppered a few stones down to frighten them. However, Piero de' Medici wasn't come after all; and it was a pity, for we'd have left him neither legs nor wings to go away with again."

"Well spoken, Oddo," said a young butcher, with his knife at his belt; "and it's my belief Piero will be a good while before he wants to come back, for he looked as frightened as a hunted chicken, when we hustled and pelted him in the piazza. He's a coward, else he might have made a better stand when he'd got his horsemen. But we'll swallow no Medici any more, whatever else the French king wants to make us swallow."

"But I like not those French cannon they talk of," said Goro, none the less fat for two years' additional grievances. "San Giovanni defend us! If Messer Domeneddio means so well by us as your Frate says he does, Ser Cioni, why shouldn't he have sent the French another way to Naples?"

"Ay, Goro," said the dyer; "that's a question worth putting. Thou art not such a pumpkin-head as I took thee for. Why, they might have gone to Naples by Bologna, eh, Ser Cioni? or if they'd gone to Arezzo— we wouldn't have minded their going to Arezzo."

"Fools! It will be for the good and glory of Florence," Ser Cioni began. But he was interrupted by the exclamation, "Look there!" which burst from several voices at once, while the faces were all turned to a party who were advancing along the Via de' Cerretani.

"It's Lorenzo Tornabuoni, and one of the French noblemen who are in his house," said Ser Cioni, in some contempt at this interruption. "He pretends to look well satisfied,—that deep Tornabuoni,—but he's a Medicean in his heart: mind that."

The advancing party was rather a brilliant one, for there was not only the distinguished presence of Lorenzo Tornabuoni, and the splendid costume of the Frenchman with his elaborately displayed white linen and gorgeous embroidery; there were two other Florentines of high birth in handsome dresses donned for the coming procession, and on the left hand of the Frenchman was a figure that was not to be eclipsed by any amount of intention or brocade,—a figure we have often seen before. He wore nothing but black, for he was in mourning; but the black was presently to be covered by a red mantle, for he too was to walk in procession as Latin Secretary to the Ten. Tito Melema had become conspicuously serviceable in the intercourse with the French guests, from his familiarity with Southern Italy, and his readiness in the French tongue, which he had spoken in his early youth; and he had paid more than one visit to the French camp at Signa. The lustre of good fortune was upon him; he was smiling, listening, and explaining, with his usual graceful unpretentious ease, and only a very keen eye bent on studying him could have marked a certain amount of change in him which was not to be accounted for by the lapse of eighteen months. It was that change which comes from the final departure of moral youthfulness,—from the distinct self-conscious adoption of a part in life. The lincs of the face were as soft as ever, the eyes as pellucid; but something was gone,—something as indefinable as the changes in the morning twilight.

The Frenchman was gathering instructions concerning ceremonial before riding back to Signa, and now he was going to have a final survey of the Piazza del Duomo, where the royal procession was to pause for religious purposes. The distinguished party attracted the notice of all eyes as it entered the piazza, but the gaze was not entirely cordial and admiring; there were remarks not altogether allusive and mysterious to the Frenchman's hoof-shaped shoes,—delicate flattery of royal superfluity in toes; and there was no care that certain snarlings at "Mediceans" should be strictly inaudible. But Lorenzo Tornabuoni possessed that power of dissembling annoyance which is demanded in a man who courts popularity; and Tito, besides his natural disposition to overcome ill-will by good-humour, had the unimpassioned feeling of the alien towards names and details that move the deepest passions of the native.

Arrived where they could get a good oblique view of the Duomo, the party paused. The festoons and devices placed over the central doorway excited some demur, and Tornabuoni beckoned to Piero di Cosimo, who, as was usual with him at this hour, was lounging in front of Nello's shop. There was soon an animated discussion, and it became highly amusing from the Frenchman's astonishment at Piero's odd pungency of statement, which Tito translated literally. Even snarling on-lookers became curious, and their faces began to wear the half-smiling, half-humiliated expression of people who are not within hearing of the joke which is producing infectious laughter. It was a delightful moment for Tito, for he was the only one of the party who could have made so amusing an interpreter; and without any disposition to triumphant self-gratulation he revelled in the sense that he was an object of liking,—he basked in approving glances. The rainbow light fell about the laughing group, and the grave church-goers had all disappeared within the walls. It seemed as if the piazza had been decorated for a real Florentine holiday.

Meanwhile in the grey light of the unadorned streets there were on-comers who made no show of linen and brocade, and whose humour was far from merry. Here, too, the French dress and hoofed shoes were conspicuous, but they were being pressed upon by a larger and larger number of non-admiring Florentines. In the van of the crowd were three men in scanty clothing; each had his hands bound together by a cord, and a rope was fastened round his neck and body, in such a way that he who held the extremity of the rope might easily check any rebellious movement by the threat of throttling. The men who held the ropes were French soldiers, and by broken Italian phrases and strokes from the knotted end of the rope, they from time to time stimulated their prisoners to beg. Two of them were obedient, and to every Florentine they had encountered had held out their bound hands and said in piteous tones,—

"For the love of God and the Holy Madonna, give us something towards our ransom! We are Tuscans: we were made prisoners in Lunigiana."

But the third man remained obstinately silent under all the strokes from the knotted cord. He was very different in aspect from his two fellow-prisoners. They were young and hardy, and, in the scant clothing which the avarice of their captors had left them, looked like vulgar, sturdy mendicants. But he had passed the boundary of old age, and could hardly be less than four or five and sixty. His beard, which had grown long in neglect, and the hair which fell thick and straight round his baldness, were nearly white. His thick-set figure was still firm and upright, though emaciated, and seemed to express energy in spite of age,—an expression that was partly carried out in the dark eyes and strong dark eyebrows, which had a strangely isolated intensity of colour in the midst of his yellow, bloodless, deep-wrinkled face with its lank gray hairs. And yet there was something fitful in the eyes which contradicted the occasional flash of energy; after looking round with quick fierceness at windows and faces, they fell again with a lost and wandering look. But his lips were motionless, and he held his hands resolutely down. He would not beg.

This sight had been witnessed by the Florentines with growing exasperation. Many standing at their doors or passing quietly along had at once given money,—some in half-automatic response to an appeal in the name of God, others in that unquestioning awe of the French soldiery which had been created by the reports of their cruel warfare, and on which the French themselves counted as a guarantee of immunity in their acts of insolence. But as the group had proceeded farther into the heart of the city, that compliance had gradually disappeared, and the soldiers found themselves escorted by a gathering troop of men and boys, who kept up a chorus of exclamations sufficiently intelligible to foreign ears without any interpreter. The soldiers themselves began to dislike their position, for, with a strong inclination to use their weapons, they were checked by the necessity for keeping a secure hold on their prisoners, and they were now hurrying along in the hope of finding shelter in a hostelry.

"French dogs!" "Bullock-feet!" "Snatch their pikes from them!" "Cut the cords and make them run for their prisoners. They'll run as fast as geese,—don't you see they're web-footed!" These were the cries which the soldiers vaguely understood to be jeers, and probably threats. But every one seemed disposed to give invitations of this spirited kind rather than to act upon them.

"Santiddio! here's a sight!" said the dyer, as soon as he had divined the meaning of the advancing tumult, "and the fools do nothing but hoot. Come along!" he added, snatching his axe from his belt, and running to join the crowd, followed by the butcher and all the rest of his companions, except Goro, who hastily retreated up a narrow passage.

The sight of the dyer, running forward with blood-red arms and axe uplifted, and with his cluster of rough companions behind him, had a stimulating effect on the crowd. Not that he did anything else than pass beyond the soldiers and thrust himself well among his fellow-citizens, flourishing his axe; but he served as a stirring symbol of street-fighting, like the waving of a well-known gonfalon. And the first sign that fire was ready to burst out was something as rapid as a little leaping tongue of flame: it was an act of the conjurer's impish lad Lollo, who was dancing and jeering in front of the ingenious boys that made the majority of the crowd. Lollo had no great compassion for the prisoners, but being conscious of an excellent knife which was his unfailing companion, it had seemed to him from the first that to jump forward, cut a rope, and leap back again before the soldier who held it could use his weapon, would be an amusing and dexterous piece of mischief. And now, when the people began to hoot and jostle more vigorously, Lollo felt that his moment was come,—he was close to the eldest prisoner: in an instant he had cut the cord.

"Run, old one!" he piped in the prisoner's ear, as soon as the cord was in two; and himself set the example of running as if he were helped along with wings, like a scared fowl.

The prisoner's sensations were not too slow for him to seize the opportunity: the idea of escape had been continually present with him, and he had gathered fresh hope from the temper of the crowd. He ran at once; but his speed would hardly have sufficed for him if the

Florentines had not instantaneously rushed between him and his captor. He ran on into the piazza; but he quickly heard the tramp of feet behind him, for the other two prisoners had been released, and the soldiers were struggling and fighting their way after them, in such tardigrade fashion as their hoof-shaped shoes would allow,—impeded, but not very resolutely attacked, by the people. One of the two younger prisoners turned up the Borgo di San Lorenzo, and thus made a partial diversion of the hubbub; but the main struggle was still towards the piazza, where all eyes were turned on it with alarmed curiosity. The cause could not be precisely guessed, for the French dress was screened by the impeding crowd.

"An escape of prisoners," said Lorenzo Tornabuoni, as he and his party turned round just against the steps of the Duomo, and saw a prisoner rushing by them. "The people are not content with having emptied the Bargello the other day. If there is no other authority in sight they must fall on the *sbirri* and secure freedom to thieves. Ah! there is a French soldier: that is more serious."

The soldier he saw was struggling along on the north side of the piazza, but the object of his pursuit had taken the other direction. That object was the eldest prisoner, who had wheeled round the baptistery and was running towards the Duomo, determined to take refuge in that sanctuary rather than trust to his speed. But in mounting the steps his foot received a shock; he was precipitated towards the group of signori, whose backs were turned to him, and was only able to recover his balance as he clutched one of them by the arm.

It was Tito Melema who felt that clutch. He turned his head, and saw the face of his adoptive father, Baldassarre Calvo, close to his own.

The two men looked at each other, silent as death: Baldassarre, with dark fierceness and a tightening grip of the soiled worn hands on the velvet-clad arm; Tito, with cheeks and lips all bloodless, fascinated by terror. It seemed a long while to them,—it was but a moment.

The first sound Tito heard was the short laugh of Piero di Cosimo, who stood close by him, and was the only person that could see his face.

"Ha, ha! I know what a ghost should be now."

"This is another escaped prisoner," said Lorenzo Tornabuoni. "Who is he, I wonder?"

"*Some madman, surely,*" said Tito.

He hardly knew how the words had come to his lips: there are moments when our passions speak and decide for us, and we seem to stand by and wonder. They carry in them an inspiration of crime, that in one instant does the work of long premeditation.

The two men had not taken their eyes off each other, and it seemed to Tito, when he had spoken, that some magical poison had darted from Baldassarre's eyes, and that he felt it rushing through his veins. But the next instant the grasp on his arm had relaxed, and Baldassarre had disappeared within the church.

CHAPTER III

AFTER-THOUGHTS

"You are easily frightened, though," said Piero, with another scornful laugh. "My portrait is not as good as the original. But the old fellow *had* a tiger look: I must go into the Duomo and see him again."

"It is not pleasant to be laid hold of by a madman, if madman he be," said Lorenzo Tornabuoni, in polite excuse of Tito: "but perhaps he is only a ruffian. We shall hear. I think we must see if we have authority enough to stop this disturbance between our people and your countrymen," he added, addressing the Frenchman.

They advanced towards the crowd with their swords drawn, all the quiet spectators making an escort for them. Tito went too: it was necessary that he should know what others knew about Baldassarre, and the first palsy of terror was being succeeded by the rapid devices to which mortal danger will stimulate the timid.

The rabble of men and boys, more inclined to hoot at the soldier and torment him than to receive or inflict any serious wounds, gave way at the approach of signori with drawn swords, and the French soldier was interrogated. He and his companions had simply brought their prisoners into the city, that they might beg money for their ransom: two of the prisoners were Tuscan soldiers taken in Lunigiana; the other, an elderly man, was with a party of Genoese, with whom the French foragers had come to blows near Fivizzano. He might be mad, but he was harmless. The soldier knew no more, being unable to understand a word the old man said. Tito heard so far, but he was deaf to everything else till he was specially addressed. It was Tornabuoni who spoke.

"Will you go back with us, Melema? Or since Messere is going off to Signa now, will you wisely follow the fashion of the times and go to hear the Frate, who will be like the torrent at its height this morning? It's what we must all do, you know, if we are to save our Medicean skins. *I* should go if I had the leisure."

Tito's face had recovered its colour now, and he could make an effort to speak with gayety.

"Of course I am among the admirers of the inspired orator," he said smilingly; "but, unfortunately, I shall be occupied with the Segretario till the time of the procession."

"*I* am going into the Duomo to look at that savage old man again," said Piero.

"Then have the charity to show him to one of the hospitals for travellers, Piero mio," said Tornabuoni. "The monks may find out whether he wants putting into a cage."

The party separated, and Tito took his way to the Palazzo Vecchio, where he was to find Bartolommeo Scala. It was not a long walk, but, for Tito, it was stretched out like the minutes of our morning dreams:

the short spaces of street and piazza held memories and previsions and torturing fears that might have made the history of months. He felt as if a serpent had begun to coil round his limbs. Baldassarre living and in Florence was a living revenge, which would no more rest than a winding serpent would rest until it had crushed its prey. It was not in the nature of that man to let an injury pass unavenged: his love and his hatred were of that passionate fervour which subjugates all the rest of the being, and makes a man sacrifice himself to his passion as if it were a deity to be worshipped with self-destruction. Baldassarre had relaxed his hold, and had disappeared. Tito knew well how to interpret that: it meant that the vengeance was to be studied that it might be sure. If he had not uttered those decisive words, "He is a madman,"—if he could have summoned up the state of mind, the courage, necessary for avowing his recognition of Baldassarre,—would not the risk have been less? He might have declared himself to have had what he believed to be positive evidence of Baldassarre's death; and the only persons who could ever have had positive knowledge to contradict him, were Fra Luca, who was dead, and the crew of the companion galley, who had brought him the news of the encounter with the pirates. The chances were infinite against Baldassarre's having met again with any one of that crew, and Tito thought with bitterness that a timely, well-devised falsehood might have saved him from any fatal consequences. But to have told that falsehood would have required perfect self-command in the moment of a convulsive shock: he seemed to have spoken without any preconception: the words had leaped forth like a sudden birth that had been begotten and nourished in the darkness.

Tito was experiencing that inexorable law of human souls that we prepare ourselves for sudden deeds by the reiterated choice of good or evil which gradually determines character.

There was but one chance for him now; the chance of Baldassarre's failure in finding his revenge. And—Tito grasped at a thought more actively cruel than any he had ever encouraged before: might not his own unpremeditated words have some truth in them? Enough truth, at least, to bear him out in his denial of any declaration Baldassarre might make about him? The old man looked strange and wild; with his eager heart and brain, suffering was likely enough to have produced madness. If it were so, the vengeance that strove to inflict disgrace might be baffled.

But there was another form of vengeance not to be baffled by ingenious lying. Baldassarre belonged to a race to whom the thrust of the dagger seems almost as natural an impulse as the outleap of the tiger's talons. Tito shrank with shuddering dread from disgrace; but he had also that physical dread which is inseparable from a soft pleasure-loving nature, and which prevents a man from meeting wounds and death as a welcome relief from disgrace. His thoughts flew at once to some hidden defensive armour that might save him from a vengeance which no subtlety could parry.

He wondered at the power of the passionate fear that possessed him. It was as if he had been smitten with a blighting disease that had suddenly turned the joyous sense of young life into pain.

There was still one resource open to Tito. He might have turned back, sought Baldassarre again, confessed everything to him—to Romola—to all the world. But he never thought of that. The repentance which cuts off all moorings to evil, demands something more than selfish fear. He had no sense that there was strength and safety in truth; the only strength he trusted to lay in his ingenuity and dissimulation. Now that the first shock, which had called up the traitorous signs of fear, was well past, he hoped to be prepared for all emergencies by cool deceit— and defensive armour.

It was a characteristic fact in Tito's experience at this crisis, that no direct measures for ridding himself of Baldassarre ever occurred to him. All other possibilities passed through his mind, even to his own flight from Florence; but he never thought of any scheme for removing his enemy. His dread generated no active malignity, and he would still have been glad not to give pain to any mortal. He had simply chosen to make life easy to himself—to carry his human lot, if possible, in such a way that it should pinch him nowhere; and the choice had, at various times, landed him in unexpected positions. The question now was, not whether he should divide the common pressure of destiny with his suffering fellow-men; it was whether all the resources of lying would save him from being crushed by the consequences of that habitual choice.

CHAPTER IV

INSIDE THE DUOMO

WHEN Baldassarre, with his hands bound together, and the rope round his neck and body, pushed his way behind the curtain, and saw the interior of the Duomo before him, he gave a start of astonishment, and stood still against the doorway. He had expected to see a vast nave empty of everything but lifeless emblems,—side altars with candles unlit, dim pictures, pale and rigid statues,—with perhaps a few worshippers in the distant choir following a monotonous chant. That was the ordinary aspect of churches to a man who never went into them with any religious purpose.

And he saw, instead, a vast multitude of warm, living faces, upturned in breathless silence towards the pulpit, at the angle between the nave and the choir. The multitude was of all ranks, from magistrates and dames of gentle nurture to coarsely clad artisans and country people. In the pulpit was a Dominican friar, with strong features and dark hair, preaching with the crucifix in his hand.

For the first few minutes Baldassarre noted nothing of his preaching. Silent as his entrance had been, some eyes near the doorway had been turned on him with surprise and suspicion. The rope indicated plainly enough that he was an escaped prisoner, but in that case the church was a sanctuary which he had a right to claim; his advanced years and look of wild misery were fitted to excite pity rather than alarm; and as he stood motionless, with eyes that soon wandered absently from the wide scene before him to the pavement at his feet, those who had observed his entrance presently ceased to regard him, and became absorbed again in the stronger interest of listening to the sermon.

Among the eyes that had been turned towards him were Romola's: she had entered late through one of the side doors, and was so placed that she had a full view of the main entrance. She had looked long and attentively at Baldassarre, for grey hairs made a peculiar appeal to her, and the stamp of some unwonted suffering in the face, confirmed by the cord round his neck, stirred in her those sensibilities towards the sorrows of age, which her whole life had tended to develop. She fancied that his eyes had met hers in their first wandering gaze; but Baldassarre had not, in reality, noted her; he had only had a startled consciousness of the general scene, and the consciousness was a mere flash that made no perceptible break in the fierce tumult of emotion which the encounter with Tito had created. Images from the past kept urging themselves upon him like delirious visions strangely blended with thirst and anguish. No distinct thought for the future could shape itself in the midst of that fiery passion: the nearest approach to such thought was the bitter sense of enfeebled powers, and a vague determination to universal distrust and suspicion. Suddenly he felt himself vibrating to loud tones, which seemed like the thundering echo of his own passion. A voice that penetrated his very marrow with its accent of triumphant certitude was saying,—"The day of vengeance is at hand!"

Baldassarre quivered and looked up. He was too distant to see more than the general aspect of the preacher standing, with his right arm outstretched, lifting up the crucifix; but he panted for the threatening voice again as if it had been a promise of bliss. There was a pause before the preacher spoke again. He gradually lowered his arm. He deposited the crucifix on the edge of the pulpit, and crossed his arms over his breast, looking round at the multitude as if he would meet the glance of every individual face.

"All ye in Florence are my witnesses, for I spoke not in a corner. Ye are my witnesses, that four years ago, when there were yet no signs of war and tribulation, I preached the coming of the scourge. I lifted up my voice as a trumpet to the prelates and princes and people of Italy, and said, 'The cup of your iniquity is full. Behold, the thunder of the Lord is gathering, and it shall fall and break the cup, and your iniquity, which seems to you as pleasant wine, shall be poured out upon you, and shall be as molten lead.' And you, O priests, who say, Ha, ha! there is no Presence in the sanctuary—the Shechinah is naught—the Mercy-seat is bare: we may sin behind the veil, and who shall punish us? To you, I said, the presence of God shall be revealed in his temple as a consuming fire, and your sacred garments shall become a winding-sheet of flame, and for sweet music there shall be shrieks and hissing, and for soft couches there shall be thorns, and for the breath of wantons shall come the pestilence. Trust not in your gold and silver, trust not in your high fortresses; for, though the walls were of iron, and the fortresses of adamant, the Most High shall put terror into your hearts and weakness into your councils, so that you shall be confounded and flee like women. He shall break in pieces mighty men without number, and put others in their stead. For God will no longer endure the pollution of his sanctuary; he will thoroughly purge his Church.

"And forasmuch as it is written that God will do nothing but he revealeth it to his servants the prophets, he has chosen me, his unworthy servant, and made his purpose present to my soul in the living word of the Scriptures, and in the deeds of his providence; and by the ministry of angels he has revealed it to me in visions. And his word possesses me so that I am but as the branch of the forest when the wind of heaven penetrates it, and it is not in me to keep silence, even though I may be a derision to the scorner. And for four years I have preached in obedience to the Divine will: in the face of scoffing I have preached three things, which the Lord has delivered to me: that *in these times God will regenerate his Church,* and that *before the regeneration must come the scourge over all Italy,* and that *these things will come quickly.*

"But hypocrites who cloak their hatred of the truth with a show of love have said to me, 'Come now, Frate, leave your prophesyings: it is enough to teach virtue.' To these I answer: 'Yes, you say in your hearts, God lives afar off, and his word is as a parchment written by dead men, and he deals not as in the days of old, rebuking the nations, and punishing the oppressors, and smiting the unholy priests as he smote the sons of Eli. But I cry again in your ears: God is near and not afar off; his judgments change not. He is the God of armies; the strong men who go up to battle are his ministers, even as the storm, and fire, and pestilence. He drives them by the breath of his angels, and they come upon the chosen land which has forsaken the covenant. And thou, O Italy, art the chosen land; has not God placed his sanctuary within thee, and thou hast polluted it? Behold, the ministers of his wrath are upon thee,—they are at thy very doors!' "

Savonarola's voice had been rising in impassioned force up to this point, when he became suddenly silent, let his hands fall and clasped them quietly before him. His silence, instead of being the signal for small movements among his audience, seemed to be as strong a spell to them as his voice. Through the vast area of the cathedral men and women sat with faces upturned, like breathing statues, till the voice was heard again in clear low tones.

"Yet there is a pause—even as in the days when Jerusalem was destroyed there was a pause that the children of God might flee from it. There is a stillness before the storm: lo, there is blackness above, but not a leaf quakes: the winds are stayed, that the voice of God's warning may be heard. Hear it now, O Florence, chosen city in the chosen land! Repent and forsake evil: do justice: love mercy: put away all uncleanness from among you, that the spirit of truth and holiness may fill your souls and breathe through all your streets and habitations, and then the pestilence shall not enter, and the sword shall pass over you and leave you unhurt.

"For the sword is hanging from the sky; it is quivering; it is about to fall! *The sword of God upon the earth, swift and sudden!* Did I not tell you, years ago, that I had beheld the vision and heard the voice? And behold, it is fulfilled! Is there not a king with his army at your gates? Does not the earth shake with the tread of horses and the wheels of swift cannon? Is there not a fierce multitude that can lay bare the land as with a sharp razor? I tell you the French king with his army is the minister of God: God shall guide him as the hand guides a sharp sickle, and the joints of the wicked shall melt before him, and they shall be mown down as stubble: he that fleeth of them shall not flee away, and he that escapeth of them shall not be delivered. And the tyrants who have made to themselves a throne out of the vices of the multitude, and the unbelieving priests who traffic in the souls of men and fill the very sanctuary with fornication, shall be hurled from their soft couches into burning hell; and the pagans and they who sinned under the old covenant shall stand aloof and say: 'Lo, these men have brought the stench of a new wickedness into the everlasting fire.'

"But thou, O Florence, take the offered mercy. See! the Cross is held out to you: come and be healed. Which among the nations of Italy has had a token like unto yours? The tyrant is driven out from among you: the men who held a bribe in their left hand and a rod in the right are gone forth, and no blood has been spilled. And now put away every other abomination from among you, and you shall be strong in the strength of the living God. Wash yourselves from the black pitch of your vices, which have made you even as the heathens: put away the envy and hatred that have made your city as a nest of wolves. And there shall no harm happen to you; and the passage of armies shall be to you as a flight of birds, and rebellious Pisa shall be given to you again, and famine and pestilence shall be far from your gates, and you shall be as a beacon among the nations. But, mark! while you suffer the accursed thing to lie in the camp, you shall be afflicted and tormented, even though a remnant among you may be saved."

These admonitions and promises had been spoken in an incisive tone of authority; but in the next sentence the preacher's voice melted into a strain of entreaty.

"Listen, O people, over whom my heart yearns, as the heart of a mother over the children she has travailed for! God is my witness that but for your sakes I would willingly live as a turtle in the depths of the forest, singing low to my Beloved, who is mine and I am his. For you I toil, for you I languish, for you my nights are spent in watching, and my soul melteth away for very heaviness. O Lord, thou knowest

I am willing—I am ready. Take me, stretch me on thy Cross: let the wicked who delight in blood, and rob the poor, and defile the temple of their bodies, and harden themselves against thy mercy,—let them wag their heads and shoot out the lip at me: let the thorns press upon my brow, and let my sweat be anguish,—I desire to be made like thee in thy great love. But let me see the fruit of my travail,—let this people be saved! Let me see them clothed in purity; let me hear their voices rise in concord as the voices of the angels: let them see no wisdom but in thy eternal law, no beauty but in holiness. Then they shall lead the way before the nations, and the people from the four winds shall follow them, and be gathered into the fold of the blessed. For it is thy will, O God, that the earth shall be converted unto thy law: it is thy will that wickedness shall cease and love shall reign. Come, O blessed promise; and behold, I am willing,—lay me on the altar: let my blood flow and the fire consume me; but let my witness be remembered among men, that iniquity shall not prosper forever."

During the last appeal Savonarola had stretched out his arms and lifted up his eyes to heaven; his strong voice had alternately trembled with emotion and risen again in renewed energy; but the passion with which he offered himself as a victim became at last too strong to allow of further speech, and he ended in a sob. Every changing tone, vibrating through the audience, shook them into answering emotion. There were plenty among them who had very moderate faith in the Frate's prophetic mission, and who in their cooler moments loved him little; nevertheless, they too were carried along by the great wave of feeling which gathered its force from sympathies that lay deeper than all theory. A loud responding sob rose at once from the wide multitude, while Savonarola had fallen on his knees and buried his face in his mantle. He felt in that moment the rapture and glory of martyrdom without its agony.

In that great sob of the multitude Baldassarre's had mingled. Among all the human beings present, there was perhaps not one whose frame vibrated more strongly than his to the tones and words of the preacher; but it had vibrated like a harp of which all the strings had been wrenched away except one. That threat of a fiery inexorable vengeance —of a future into which the hated sinner might be pursued and held by the avenger in an eternal grapple—had come to him like the promise of an unquenchable fountain to unquenchable thirst. The doctrines of the sages, the old contempt for priestly superstitions, had fallen away from his soul like a forgotten language; if he could have remembered them, what answer could they have given to his great need like the answer given by this voice of energetic conviction? The thunder of denunciation fell on his passion-wrought nerves with all the force of self-evidence: his thought never went beyond it into questions,—he was possessed by it as the war-horse is possessed by the clash of sounds. No word that was not a threat touched his consciousness; he had no fibre to be thrilled by it. But the fierce exultant delight to which he was moved by the idea of perpetual vengeance found at once a climax and a

relieving outburst in the preacher's words of self-sacrifice. To Baldassarre those words only brought the vague triumphant sense that he too
was devoting himself—signing with his own blood the deed by which he
gave himself over to an unending fire, that would seem but coolness to
his burning hatred.

"I rescued him—I cherished him—if I might clutch his heart-strings
forever! Come, O blessed promise! Let my blood flow; let the fire consume me!"

The one chord vibrated to its utmost. Baldassarre clutched his own
palms, driving his long nails into them, and burst into a sob with the
rest.

CHAPTER V

OUTSIDE THE DUOMO

WHILE Baldassarre was possessed by the voice of Savonarola, he had
not noticed that another man had entered through the doorway behind
him, and stood not far off observing him. It was Piero di Cosimo who
took no heed of the preaching, having come solely to look at the escaped
prisoner. During the pause, in which the preacher and his audience had
given themselves up to inarticulate emotion, the new-comer advanced
and touched Baldassarre on the arm. He looked round with the tears
still slowly rolling down his face, but with a vigorous sigh, as if he had
done with that outburst. The painter spoke to him in a low tone,—

"Shall I cut your cords for you? I have heard how you were made
prisoner."

Baldassarre did not reply immediately; he glanced suspiciously at
the officious stranger. At last he said, "If you will."

"Better come outside," said Piero.

Baldassarre again looked at him suspiciously; and Piero, partly
guessing his thought, smiled, took out a knife, and cut the cords. He
began to think that the idea of the prisoner's madness was not improbable, there was something so peculiar in the expression of his face.
"Well," he thought, "if he does any mischief, he'll soon get tied up
again. The poor devil shall have a chance at least."

"You are afraid of me," he said again in an undertone; "you don't
want to tell me anything about yourself."

Baldassarre was folding his arms in enjoyment of the long-absent
muscular sensation. He answered Piero with a less suspicious look and a
tone which had some quiet decision in it.

"No, I have nothing to tell."

"As you please," said Piero, "but perhaps you want shelter, and
may not know how hospitable we Florentines are to visitors with torn
doublets and empty stomachs. There's an hospital for poor travellers
outside all our gates, and, if you liked, I could put you in the way to
one. There's no danger from your French soldier. He has been sent off."

Baldassarre nodded, and turned in silent acceptance of the offer, and he and Piero left the church together.

"You wouldn't like to sit to me for your portrait, should you?" said Piero, as they went along the Via dell' Oriuolo, on the way to the gate of Santa Croce. "I am a painter: I would give you money to get your portrait."

The suspicion returned into Baldassarre's glance, as he looked at Piero, and said decidedly, "No."

"Ah!" said the painter, curtly. "Well, go straight on and you'll find the Porta Santa Croce, and outside it there's an hospital for travellers. So you'll not accept any service from me?"

"I give you thanks for what you have done already. I need no more."

"It is well," said Piero, with a shrug; and they turned away from each other.

"A mysterious old tiger!" thought the artist, "well worth painting. Ugly—with deep lines—looking as if the plough and the harrow had gone over his heart. A fine contrast to my bland and smiling Messer Greco—my *Bacco trionfante,* who has married the fair Antigone in contradiction to all history and fitness. Aha! his scholar's blood curdled uncomfortably at the old fellow's clutch!"

When Piero re-entered the Piazza del Duomo the multitude who had been listening to Fra Girolamo were pouring out from all the doors, and the haste they made to go on their several ways was a proof how important they held the preaching which had detained them from the other occupations of the day. The artist leaned against an angle of the baptistery and watched the departing crowd, delighting in the variety of the garb and of the keen characteristic faces,—faces such as Masaccio had painted more than fifty years before, such as Domenico Ghirlandajo had not yet quite left off painting.

This morning was a peculiar occasion; and the Frate's audience, always multifarious, had represented even more completely than usual the various classes and political parties of Florence. There were men of high birth, accustomed to public charges at home and abroad, who had become newly conspicuous not only as enemies of the Medici and friends of popular government, but as thorough Piagnoni, espousing to the utmost the doctrines and practical teaching of the Frate, and frequenting San Marco as the seat of another Samuel: some of them, men of authoritative and handsome presence, like Francesco Valori, and perhaps also of a hot and arrogant temper, very much gratified by an immediate divine authority for bringing about freedom in their own way; others, like Soderini, with less of the ardent Piagnone, and more of the wise politician. There were men, also of family, like Piero Capponi, simply brave undoctrinal lovers of a sober republican liberty, who preferred fighting to arguing, and had no particular reasons for thinking any ideas false that kept out the Medici and made room for public spirit. At their elbows were doctors of law whose studies of Accursius and his brethren had not so entirely consumed their ardour as to prevent them from becoming enthusiastic Piagnoni: Messer Luca Corsini himself, for example, who on a memorable occasion yet to come was to raise his learned arms in street stone-throwing for the cause of religion, freedom, and the Frate. And among the dignities who carried their black lucco or furred mantle with an air of habitual authority, there was an abundant sprinkling of men with more contemplative and sensitive faces: scholars inheriting such high names as Strozzi and Acciajoli, who were already minded to take the cowl and join the community of San Marco; artists, wrought to a new and higher ambition by the teaching of Savonarola, like that young painter who had lately surpassed himself in his fresco of the divine child on the wall of the Frate's bare cell—unconscious yet that he would one day himself wear the tonsure and the cowl, and be called Fra Bartolommeo. There was the mystic poet Girolamo Benevieni hastening, perhaps, to carry tidings of the beloved Frate's speedy coming to his friend Pico della Mirandola, who was never to see the light of another morning. There were wellborn women attired with such scrupulous plainness that their more refined grace was the chief distinction between them and their less aristocratic sisters. There was a predominant proportion of the genuine *popolani*, or middle class, belonging both to the Major and Minor Arts, conscious of purses threatened by war-taxes. And more striking and various, perhaps, than all the other classes of the Frate's disciples, there was the long stream of poorer tradesmen and artisans, whose faith and hope in his Divine message varied from the rude and undiscriminating trust in him as the friend of the poor and the enemy of the luxurious oppressive rich, to that eager tasting of all the subtleties of biblical interpretation which takes a peculiarly strong hold on the sedentary artisan, illuminating the long dim spaces beyond the board where he stitches, with a pale flame that seems to him the light of Divine science.

But among these various disciples of the Frate were scattered many who were not in the least his disciples. Some were Mediceans who had already, from motives of fear and policy, begun to show the presiding spirit of the popular party a feigned deference. Others were sincere advocates of a free government, but regarded Savonarola simply as an ambitious monk—half sagacious, half fanatical—who had made himself a powerful instrument with the people, and must be accepted as an important social fact. There were even some of his bitter enemies: members of the old aristocratic anti-Medicean party,—determined to try and get the reins once more tight in the hands of certain chief families; or else licentious young men, who detested him as the kill-joy of Florence. For the sermons in the Duomo had already become political incidents, attracting the ears of curiosity and malice, as well as of faith. The men of ideas, like young Niccolò Macchiavelli, went to observe and write reports to friends away in country villas; the men of appetites, like Dolfo Spini, bent on hunting down the Frate, as a public nuisance who made game scare, went to feed their hatred and lie in wait for grounds of accusation.

Perhaps, while no preacher ever had a more massive influence than Savonarola, no preacher ever had more heterogeneous materials to work upon. And one secret of the massive influence lay in the highly mixed character of his preaching. Baldassarre, wrought into an ecstasy of self-martyring revenge, was only an extreme case among the partial and narrow sympathies of that audience. In Savonarola's preaching there were strains that appealed to the very finest susceptibilities of men's natures, and there were elements that gratified low egoism, tickled gossiping curiosity, and fascinated timorous superstition. His need of personal predominance, his labyrinthine allegorical interpretations of the Scriptures, his enigmatic visions, and his false certitude about the Divine intentions, never ceased, in his own large soul, to be ennobled by that fervid piety, that passionate sense of the infinite, that active sympathy, that clear-sighted demand for the subjection of selfish interests to the general good, which he had in common with the greatest of mankind. But for the mass of his audience all the pregnancy of his preaching lay in his strong assertion of supernatural claims, in his denunciatory visions, in the false certitude which gave his sermons the interest of a political bulletin; and having once held that audience in his mastery, it was necessary to his nature—it was necessary for their welfare—that he should *keep* the mastery. The effect was inevitable. No man ever struggled to retain power over a mixed multitude without suffering vitiation; his standard must be their lower needs and not his own best insight.

The mysteries of human character have seldom been presented in a way more fitted to check the judgments of facile knowingness than in Girolamo Savonarola; but we can give him a reverence that needs no shutting of the eyes to fact, if we regard his life as a drama in which there were great inward modifications accompanying the outward changes. And up to this period, when his more direct action on political affairs had only just begun, it is probable that his imperious need of ascendency had burned undiscernibly in the strong flame of his zeal for God and man.

It was the fashion of old, when an ox was led out for sacrifice to Jupiter, to chalk the dark spots, and give the offering a false show of unblemished whiteness. Let us fling away the chalk, and boldly say,— the victim is spotted, but it is not therefore in vain that his mighty heart is laid on the altar of men's highest hopes.

CHAPTER VI

THE GARMENT OF FEAR

AT six o'clock that evening most people in Florence were glad the entrance of the new Charlemagne was fairly over. Doubtless when the roll of drums, the blast of trumpets, and the tramp of horses along the Pisan road began to mingle with the pealing of the excited bells, it was a grand moment for those who were stationed on turreted roofs and could see the long-winding terrible pomp on the background of the green hills and valley. There was no sunshine to light up the splendour of banners, and spears, and plumes, and silken surcoats; but there was no thick cloud of dust to hide it, and as the picked troops advanced into close view, they could be seen all the more distinctly for the absence of dancing glitter. Tall and tough Scotch archers, Swiss halberdiers fierce and ponderous, nimble Gascons ready to wheel and climb, cavalry in which each man looked like a knight-errant with his indomitable spear and charger,—it was satisfactory to be assured that they would injure nobody but the enemies of God! With that confidence at heart it was a less dubious pleasure to look at the array of strength and splendour in nobles and knights, and youthful pages of choice lineage,—at the bossed and jewelled sword-hilts, at the satin scarfs embroidered with strange symbolical devices of pious or gallant meaning, at the gold chains and jewelled aigrettes, at the gorgeous horse-trappings and brocaded mantles, and at the transcendent canopy carried by select youths above the head of the Most Christian King. To sum up with an old diarist, whose spelling and diction halted a little behind the wonders of this royal visit —*"fù gran magnificenza."*

But for the Signoria, who had been waiting on their platform against the gates, and had to march out at the right moment, with their orator in front of them, to meet the mighty guest, the grandeur of the scene had been somewhat screened by unpleasant sensations. If Messer Luca Corsini could have had a brief Latin welcome depending from his mouth in legible characters, it would have been less confusing when the rain came on, and created an impatience in men and horses that broke off the delivery of his well-studied periods, and reduced the representatives of the scholarly city to offer a make-shift welcome in impromptu French. But that sudden confusion had created a great opportunity for Tito. As one of the secretaries he was among the officials who were stationed behind the Signoria, and with whom these highest dignities were promiscuously thrown when pressed upon by the horses.

"Somebody step forward and say a few words in French," said Soderini. But no one of high importance chose to risk a second failure. "You, Francesco Gaddi,—you can speak." But Gaddi, distrusting his own promptness, hung back, and pushing Tito, said, "You, Melema."

Tito stepped forward in an instant, and, with the air of profound deference that came as naturally to him as walking, said the few needful words in the name of the Signoria; then gave way gracefully, and let the king pass on. His presence of mind, which had failed him in the terrible crisis of the morning, had been a ready instrument this time. It was an excellent livery servant that never forsook him when danger was not visible. But when he was complimented on his opportune service, he laughed it off as a thing of no moment, and to those who had not witnessed it, let Gaddi have the credit of the improvised welcome. No wonder Tito was popular: the touchstone by which men try us is most often their own vanity.

Other things besides the oratorical welcome had turned out rather worse than had been expected. If everything had happened according to ingenious preconceptions, the Florentine procession of clergy and laity would not have found their way choked up and been obliged to take a make-shift course through the back streets, so as to meet the king at the cathedral only. Also, if the young monarch under the canopy, seated on his charger with his lance upon his thigh, had looked more like a Charlemagne and less like a hastily modelled grotesque, the imagination of his admirers would have been much assisted. It might have been wished that the scourge of Italian wickedness and "Champion of the honour of women" had had a less miserable leg, and only the normal sum of toes; that his mouth had been of a less reptilian width of slit, his nose and head of a less exorbitant outline. But the thin leg rested on cloth of gold and pearls, and the face was only an interruption of a few square inches in the midst of black velvet and gold, and the blaze of rubies, and the brilliant tints of the embroidered and bepearled canopy, —"*fù gran magnificenza.*"

And the people had cried *Francia, Francia!* with an enthusiasm proportioned to the splendour of the canopy which they had torn to pieces as their spoil according to immemorial custom; royal lips had duly kissed the altar; and after all mischances the royal person and retinue were lodged in the Palace of the Via Larga, the rest of the nobles and gentry were dispersed among the great houses of Florence, and the terrible soldiery were encamped in the Prato and other open quarters. The business of the day was ended.

But the streets still presented a surprising aspect, such as Florentines had not seen before under the November stars. Instead of a gloom unbroken except by a lamp burning feebly here and there before a saintly image at the street corners, or by a stream of redder light from an open doorway, there were lamps suspended at the windows of all houses, so that men could walk along no less securely and commodiously than by day,—"*fù gran magnificenza.*"

Along those illuminated streets Tito Melema was walking about eight o'clock in the evening, on his way homeward. He had been exerting himself throughout the day under the pressure of hidden anxieties, and had at last made his escape unnoticed from the midst of after-supper gayety. Once at leisure thoroughly to face and consider his circumstances, he hoped that he could so adjust himself to them and to all probabilities as to get rid of his childish fear. If he had only not been wanting in the presence of mind necessary to recognize Baldassarre under that surprise!—it would have been happier for him on all accounts; for he still winced under the sense that he was deliberately inflicting suffering on his father: he would very much have preferred that

Baldassarre should be prosperous and happy. But he had left himself
no second path now: there could be no conflict any longer: the only
thing he had to do was to take care of himself.

While these thoughts were in his mind he was advancing from the
Piazza di Santa Croce along the Via dei Benci, and as he neared the
angle turning into the Borgo Santa Croce his ear was struck by a music
which was not that of evening revelry, but of vigorous labour,—the
music of the anvil. Tito gave a slight start and quickened his pace, for
the sounds had suggested a welcome thought. He knew that they came
from the workshop of Niccolò Caparra, famous resort of all Florentines who cared for curious and beautiful iron-work.

"What makes the giant at work so late?" thought Tito. "But so much
the better for me. I can do that little bit of business to-night instead of
to-morrow morning."

Preoccupied as he was, he could not help pausing a moment in admiration as he came in front of the workshop. The wide doorway,
standing at the truncated angle of a great block or "isle" of houses, was
surmounted by a loggia roofed with fluted tiles, and supported by stone
columns with roughly carved capitals. Against the red light framed in
by the outline of the fluted tiles and columns stood in black relief the
grand figure of Niccolò, with his huge arms in rhythmic rise and fall,
first hiding and then disclosing the profile of his firm mouth and powerful brow. Two slighter ebony figures—one at the anvil, the other at the
bellows—served to set off his superior massiveness.

Tito darkened the doorway with a very different outline, standing in
silence, since it was useless to speak until Niccolò should deign to
pause and notice him. That was not until the smith had beaten the
head of an axe to the due sharpness of edge and dismissed it from his
anvil. But in the mean time Tito had satisfied himself by a glance
round the shop that the object of which he was in search had not disappeared.

Niccolò gave an unceremonious but good-humoured nod as he turned
from the anvil and rested his hammer on his hip.

"What is it, Messer Tito? Business?"

"Assuredly, Niccolò; else I should not have ventured to interrupt
you when you are working out of hours, since I take that as a sign that
your work is pressing."

"I've been at the same work all day,—making axes and spear-heads.
And every fool that has passed my shop has put his pumpkin-head in to
say, 'Niccolò, wilt thou not come and see the King of France and his
soldiers?' and I've answered, 'No: I don't want to see their faces,—I
want to see their backs.' "

"Are you making arms for the citizens, then, Niccolò, that they may
have something better than rusty scythes and spits in case of an
uproar?"

"We shall see. Arms are good, and Florence is likely to want them. The Frate tells us we shall get Pisa again, and I hold with the Frate; but I should be glad to know how the promise is to be fulfilled, if we don't get plenty of good weapons forged. The Frate sees a long way before him; that I believe. But he doesn't see birds caught with winking at them, as some of our people try to make out. He sees sense, and not nonsense. But you're a bit of a Medicean, Messer Tito Melema. Ebbene! so I've been myself in my time, before the cask began to run sour. What's your business?"

"Simply to know the price of that fine coat of mail I saw hanging up here the other day. I want to buy it for a certain personage who needs a protection of that sort under his doublet."

"Let him come and buy it himself, then," said Niccolò, bluntly. "I'm rather nice about what I sell, and whom I sell to. I like to know who's my customer."

"I know your scruples, Niccolò. But that is only defensive armour: it can hurt nobody."

"True; but it may make the man who wears it feel himself all the safer if he should want to hurt somebody. No, no; it's not my own work; but it's fine work of Maso of Brescia; I should be loath for it to cover the heart of a scoundrel. I must know who is to wear it."

"Well, then, to be plain with you, Niccolò mio, I want it myself," said Tito, knowing it was useless to try persuasion. "The fact is, I am likely to have a journey to take,—and you know what journeying is in these times. You don't suspect *me* of treason against the Republic?"

"No, I know no harm of you," said Niccolò, in his blunt way again. "But have you the money to pay for the coat? For you've passed my shop often enough to know my sign: you've seen the burning account-books. I trust nobody. The price is twenty florins, and that's because it's second hand. You're not likely to have so much money with you. Let it be till to-morrow."

"I happen to have the money," said Tito, who had been winning at play the day before, and had not emptied his purse. "I'll carry the armour home with me."

Niccolò reached down the finely wrought coat, which fell together into little more than two handfuls.

"There, then," he said, when the florins had been told down on his palm. "Take the coat. It's made to cheat sword, or poniard, or arrow. But, for my part, I would never put such a thing on. It's like carrying fear about with one."

Niccolò's words had an unpleasant intensity of meaning for Tito. But he smiled and said,—

"Ah, Niccolò, we scholars are all cowards. Handling the pen doesn't thicken the arm as your hammer-wielding does. Addio!"

He folded the armour under his mantle, and hastened across the Ponte Rubaconte.

CHAPTER VII

THE YOUNG WIFE

WHILE Tito was hastening across the bridge with the new-bought armour under his mantle, Romola was pacing up and down the old library, thinking of him and longing for his return.

It was but a few fair faces that had not looked forth from windows that day to see the entrance of the French king and his nobles. One of the few was Romola's. She had been present at no festivities since her father had died,—died quite suddenly in his chair, three months before. "Is not Tito coming to write?" he had said, when the bell had long ago sounded the usual hour in the evening. He had not asked before, from dread of a negative; but Romola had seen by his listening face and restless movements that nothing else was in his mind.

"No, father, he had to go to a supper at the cardinal's: you know he is wanted so much by every one," she answered, in a tone of gentle excuse.

"Ah! then perhaps he will bring some positive word about the library; the cardinal promised last week," said Bardo, apparently pacified by this hope.

He was silent a little while; then, suddenly flushing, he said,—

"I must go on without him, Romola. Get the pen. He has brought me no new text to comment on; but I must say what I want to say about the New Platonists. I shall die and nothing will have been done. Make haste, my Romola."

"I am ready, father," she said, the next minute, holding the pen in her hand.

But there was silence. Romola took no note of this for a little while, accustomed to pauses in dictation; and when at last she looked round inquiringly, there was no change of attitude.

"I am quite ready, father!"

Still Bardo was silent, and his silence was never again broken.

Romola looked back on that hour with some indignation against herself, because even with the first outburst of her sorrow there had mingled the irrepressible thought, "Perhaps my life with Tito will be more perfect now."

For the dream of a triple life with an undivided sum of happiness had not been quite fulfilled. The rainbow-tinted shower of sweets, to have been perfectly typical, should have had some invisible seeds of bitterness mingled with them; the crowned Ariadne, under the snowing roses, had felt more and more the presence of unexpected thorns. It was not Tito's fault, Romola had continually assured herself. He was still all gentleness to her, and to her father also. But it was in the nature of things,—she saw it clearly now,—it was in the nature of things that no one but herself could go on month after month, and year after year, fulfilling patiently all her father's monotonous, exacting demands. Even she, whose sympathy with her father had made all the passion and religion of her young years, had not always been patient, had been inwardly very rebellious. It was true that before their marriage, and even for some time after, Tito had seemed more unwearying than herself; but then, of course, the effort had the ease of novelty. We assume a load with confident readiness, and up to a certain point the growing irksomeness of pressure is tolerable; but at last the desire for relief can no longer be resisted. Romola said to herself that she had been very foolish and ignorant in her girlish time: she was wiser now, and would make no unfair demands on the man to whom she had given her best woman's love and worship. The breath of sadness that still cleaved to her lot while she saw her father month after month sink from elation into new disappointment as Tito gave him less and less of his time, and made bland excuses for not continuing his own share of the joint work. —that sadness was no fault of Tito's, she said, but rather of their inevitable destiny. If he stayed less and less with her, why, that was because they could hardly ever be alone. His caresses were no less tender: if she pleaded timidly on any one evening that he should stay with her father instead of going to another engagement which was not peremptory, he excused himself with such charming gayety, he seemed to linger about her with such fond playfulness before he could quit her, that she could only feel a little heartache in the midst of her love, and then go to her father and try to soften his vexation and disappointment. But all the while inwardly her imagination was busy trying to see how Tito could be as good as she had thought he was, and yet find it impossible to sacrifice those pleasures of society which were necessarily more vivid to a bright creature like him than to the common run of men. She herself would have liked more gayety, more admiration: it was true, she gave it up willingly for her father's sake,—she would have given up much more than that for the sake even of a slight wish on Tito's part. It was clear that their natures differed widely; but perhaps it was no more than the inherent difference between man and woman, that made her affections more absorbing. If there were any other difference, she tried to persuade herself that the inferiority was on her side. Tito was really kinder than she was, better tempered, less proud and resentful; he had no angry retorts, he met all complaints with perfect sweetness; he only escaped as quietly as he could from things that were unpleasant.

It belongs to every large nature, when it is not under the immediate power of some strong unquestioning emotion, to suspect itself, and doubt the truth of its own impressions, conscious of possibilities beyond its own horizon. And Romola was urged to doubt herself the more by the necessity of interpreting her disappointment in her life with Tito so as to satisfy at once her love and her pride. Disappointment? Yes there was no other milder word that would tell the truth. Perhaps all women had to suffer the disappointment of ignorant hopes, if she only knew their experience. Still, there had been something peculiar in her lot: her relation to her father had claimed unusual sacrifices from her husband. Tito had once thought that his love would make those sacrifices easy; his love had not been great enough for that. She was not justified in resenting a self-delusion. No! resentment must not rise: all endurance seemed easy to Romola rather than a state of mind in which she would admit to herself that Tito acted unworthily. If she had felt a new heartache in the solitary hours with her father through the last months of his life, it had been by no inexcusable fault of her husband's; and now—it was a hope that would make its presence felt even in the first moments when her father's place was empty—there was no longer any importunate claim to divide her from Tito; their young lives would flow in one current, and their true marriage would begin.

But the sense of something like guilt towards her father in a hope that grew out of his death, gave all the more force to the anxiety with which she dwelt on the means of fulfilling his supreme wish. That piety towards his memory was all the atonement she could make now for a thought that seemed akin to joy at his loss. The laborious simple life, pure from vulgar corrupting ambitions, embittered by the frustration of the dearest hopes, imprisoned at last in total darkness,—a long seed-time without a harvest,—was at an end now, and all that remained of it besides the tablet in Santa Croce and the unfinished commentary on Tito's text, was the collection of manuscripts and antiquities, the fruit of half a century's toil and frugality. The fulfilment of her father's life-long ambition about this library was a sacramental obligation for Romola.

The precious relic was safe from creditors, for when the deficit to-wards their payment had been ascertained, Bernardo del Nero, though he was far from being among the wealthiest Florentines, had advanced the necessary sum of about a thousand florins,—a large sum in those days,—accepting a lien on the collection as a security.

"The State will repay me," he had said to Romola, making light of the service, which had really cost him some inconvenience. "If the cardinal finds a building, as he seems to say he will, our Signoria may consent to do the rest. I have no children, I can afford the risk."

But within the last ten days all hopes in the Medici had come to an end; and the famous Medicean collections in the Via Larga were them-selves in danger of dispersion. French agents had already begun to see that such very fine antique gems as Lorenzo had collected belonged by right to the first nation in Europe; and the Florentine State, which had got possession of the Medicean library, was likely to be glad of a cus-tomer for it. With a war to recover Pisa hanging over it, and with the certainty of having to pay large subsidies to the French king, the State was likely to prefer money to manuscripts.

To Romola these grave political changes had gathered their chief interest from their bearing on the fulfilment of her father's wish. She had been brought up in learned seclusion from the interests of actual life, and had been accustomed to think of heroic deeds and great principles as something antithetic to the vulgar present, of the Pnyx and the Forum as something more worthy of attention than the councils of living Florentine men. And now the expulsion of the Medici meant little more for her than the extinction of her best hope about her father's library. The times, she knew, were unpleasant for friends of the Medici, like her godfather and Tito: superstitious shopkeepers and the stupid rabble were full of suspicions; but her new keen interest in public events, in the outbreak of war, in the issue of the French king's visit, in the changes that were likely to happen in the State, was kindled solely by the sense of love and duty to her father's memory. All Romola's ardour had been concentrated in her affections. Her share in her father's learned pursuits had been for her little more than a toil which was borne for his sake; and Tito's airy brilliant faculty had no attraction for her that was not merged in the deeper sympathies that belong to young love and trust. Romola had had contact with no mind that could stir the larger possibilities of her nature: they lay folded and crushed like embryonic wings, making no element in her consciousness beyond an occasional vague uneasiness.

But this new personal interest of hers in public affairs had made her care at last to understand precisely what influence Fra Girolamo's preaching was likely to have on the turn of events. Changes in the form of the State were talked of, and all she could learn from Tito, whose secretaryship and serviceable talents carried him into the heart of public business, made her only the more eager to fill out her lonely day by going to hear for herself what it was that was just now leading all Florence by the ears. This morning, for the first time, she had been to hear one of the Advent sermons in the Duomo. When Tito had left her, she had formed a sudden resolution, and after visiting the spot where her father was buried in Santa Croce, had walked on to the Duomo. The memory of that last scene with Dino was still vivid within her whenever she recalled it, but it had receded behind the experience and anxieties of her married life. The new sensibilities and questions which it had half awakened in her were quieted again by that subjection to her husband's mind which is felt by every wife who loves her husband with passionate devotedness and full reliance. She remembered the effect of Fra Girolamo's voice and presence on her as a ground for expecting that his sermon might move her in spite of his being a narrow-minded monk. But the sermon did no more than slightly deepen her previous impression, that this fanatical preacher of tribulations was after all a man towards whom it might be possible for her to feel personal regard and reverence. The denunciations and exhortations simply arrested her attention. She felt no terror, no pangs of conscience: it was the roll of distant thunder, that seemed grand, but could not shake her. But when she heard Savonarola invoke martyrdom, she sobbed with the rest; she felt herself penetrated with a new sensation,—a strange sympathy with something apart from all the definable interests of her life. It was not altogether unlike the thrill which had accompanied certain rare heroic touches in history and poetry; but the resemblance was as that between the memory of music, and the sense of being possessed by actual vibrating harmonies.

But that transient emotion, strong as it was, seemed to lie quite outside the inner chamber and sanctuary of her life. She was not thinking of Fra Girolamo now; she was listening anxiously for the step of her husband. During these three months of their double solitude she had thought of each day as an epoch in which their union might begin to be more perfect. She was conscious of being sometimes a little too sad or too urgent about what concerned her father's memory,—a little too critical or coldly silent when Tito narrated the things that were said and done in the world he frequented,—a little too hasty in suggesting that by living quite simply, as her father had done, they might become rich enough to pay Bernardo del Nero, and reduce the difficulties about the library. It was not possible that Tito could feel so strongly on this last point as she did, and it was asking a great deal from him to give up luxuries for which he really laboured. The next time Tito came home she would be careful to suppress all those promptings that seemed to isolate her from him. Romola was labouring, as a loving woman must, to subdue her nature to her husband's. The great need of her heart compelled her to strangle, with desperate resolution, every rising impulse of suspicion, pride, and resentment; she felt equal to any self-infliction that would save her from ceasing to love. That would have been like the hideous nightmare in which the world had seemed to break away all round her, and leave her feet overhanging the darkness. Romola had never distinctly imagined such a future for herself; she was only beginning to feel the presence of effort in that clinging trust which had once been mere repose.

She waited and listened long, for Tito had not come straight home after leaving Niccolò Caparra, and it was more than two hours after the time when he was crossing the Ponte Rubaconte that Romola heard the great door of the court turning on its hinges, and hastened to the head of the stone steps. There was a lamp hanging over the stairs, and they could see each other distinctly as he ascended. The eighteen months had produced a more definable change in Romola's face than in Tito's: the expression was more subdued, less cold, and more beseeching; and as the pink flush overspread her face now, in her joy that the long waiting was at an end, she was much lovelier than on the day when Tito had first seen her. On that day any on-looker would have said that Romola's nature was made to command, and Tito's to bend; yet now Romola's mouth was quivering a little, and there was some timidity in her glance.

He made an effort to smile, as she said,—

"My Tito, you are tired; it has been a fatiguing day: is it not true?"

Maso was there, and no more was said until they had crossed the antechamber and closed the door of the library behind them. The wood was burning brightly on the great dogs; that was one welcome for Tito, late as he was, and Romola's gentle voice was another.

He just turned and kissed her when she took off his mantle; then he went towards a high-backed chair placed for him near the fire, threw himself into it, and flung away his cap, saying, not peevishly, but in a fatigued tone of remonstrance, as he gave a slight shudder,—

"Romola, I wish you would give up sitting in this library. Surely our own rooms are pleasanter in this chill weather."

Romola felt hurt. She had never seen Tito so indifferent in his manner; he was usually full of lively solicitous attention. And she had thought so much of his return to her after the long day's absence! He must be very weary.

"I wonder you have forgotten, Tito," she answered, looking at him anxiously, as if she wanted to read an excuse for him in the signs of bodily fatigue. "You know I am making the catalogue on the new plan that my father wished for; you have not time to help me, so I must work at it closely."

Tito, instead of meeting Romola's glance, closed his eyes and rubbed his hands over his face and hair. He felt he was behaving unlike himself, but he would make amends to-morrow. The terrible resurrection of secret fears, which if Romola had known them would have alienated her from him forever, caused him to feel an alienation already begun between them,—caused him to feel a certain repulsion towards a woman from whose mind he was in danger. The feeling had taken hold of him unawares, and he was vexed with himself for behaving in this new cold way to her. He could not suddenly command any affectionate looks or words; he could only exert himself to say what might serve as an excuse.

"I am not well, Romola; you must not be surprised if I am peevish."

"Ah, you have had so much to tire you to-day," said Romola, kneeling down close to him, and laying her arm on his chest while she put his hair back caressingly.

Suddenly she drew her arm away with a start, and a gaze of alarmed inquiry.

"What have you got under your tunic, Tito? Something as hard as iron."

"It *is* iron,—it is chain-armour," he said at once. He was prepared for the surprise and the question, and he spoke quietly, as of something that he was not hurried to explain.

"There was some unexpected danger to-day, then?" said Romola, in a tone of conjecture. "You had it lent to you for the procession?"

"No; it is my own. I shall be obliged to wear it constantly for some time."

"What is it that threatens you, my Tito?" said Romola, looking terrified, and clinging to him again.

"Every one is threatened in these times, who is not a rabid enemy of the Medici. Don't look distressed, my Romola,—this armour will make me safe against covert attacks."

Tito put his hand on her neck and smiled. This little dialogue about the armour had broken through the new crust, and made a channel for the sweet habit of kindness.

"But my godfather, then," said Romola; "is not he, too, in danger? And he takes no precautions,—ought he not? since he must surely be in more danger than you, who have so little influence compared with him."

"It is just because I am less important that I am in more danger," said Tito, readily. "I am suspected constantly of being an envoy. And men like Messer Bernardo are protected by their position and their extensive family connections, which spread among all parties, while I am a Greek that nobody would avenge."

"But, Tito, is it a fear of some particular person, or only a vague sense of danger, that has made you think of wearing this?" Romola was unable to repel the idea of a degrading fear in Tito, which mingled itself with her anxiety.

"I have had special threats," said Tito, "but I must beg you to be silent on the subject, my Romola. I shall consider that you have broken my confidence, if you mention it to your godfather."

"Assuredly I will not mention it," said Romola, blushing, "if you wish it to be a secret. But, dearest Tito," she added, after a moment's pause, in a tone of loving anxiety, "it will make you very wretched."

"What will make me wretched?" he said, with a scarcely perceptible movement across his face, as from some darting sensation.

"This fear,—this heavy armour. I can't help shuddering as I feel it under my arm. I could fancy it a story of enchantment,—that some malignant fiend had changed your sensitive human skin into a hard shell. It seems so unlike my bright, light-hearted Tito!"

"Then you would rather have your husband exposed to danger, when he leaves you?" said Tito, smiling. "If you don't mind my being poniarded or shot, why need I mind? I will give up the armour,—shall I?"

"No, Tito, no. I am fanciful. Do not heed what I have said. But such crimes are surely not common in Florence? I have always heard my father and godfather say so. Have they become frequent lately?"

"It is not unlikely they will become frequent, with the bitter hatreds that are being bred continually."

Romola was silent a few moments. She shrank from insisting further on the subject of the armour. She tried to shake it off.

"Tell me what has happened to-day," she said, in a cheerful tone. "Has all gone off well?"

"Excellently well. First of all, the rain came and put an end to Luca Corsini's oration, which nobody wanted to hear, and a ready-tongued personage—some say it was Gaddi, some say it was Melema, but really it was done so quickly no one knows who it was—had the honour of giving the Cristianissimo the briefest possible welcome in bad French."

"Tito, it was you, I know," said Romola, smiling brightly and kissing him. "How is it you never care about claiming anything? And after that?"

"Oh! after that, there was a shower of armour and jewels, and trappings, such as you saw at the last Florentine *giostra*, only a great deal more of them. There was strutting, and prancing, and confusion, and scrambling, and the people shouted, and the Christianissimo smiled from ear to ear. And after that there was a great deal of flattery, and eating, and play. I was at Tornabuoni's. I will tell you about it to-morrow."

"Yes, dearest, never mind now. But is there any more hope that things will end peaceably for Florence, that the Republic will not get into fresh troubles?"

Tito gave a shrug. "Florence will have no peace but what it pays well for; that is clear."

Romola's face saddened, but she checked herself, and said cheerfully: "You would not guess where I went to-day, Tito. I went to the Duomo, to hear Fra Girolamo."

Tito looked startled,—he had immediately thought of Baldassarre's entrance into the Duomo; but Romola gave his look another meaning.

"You are surprised, are you not? It was a sudden thought. I want to know all about the public affairs now, and I determined to hear for myself what the Frate promised the people about this French invasion."

"Well, and what did you think of the prophet?"

"He certainly has a very mysterious power, that man. A great deal of his sermon was what I expected; but once I was strangely moved,—I sobbed with the rest."

"Take care, Romola," said Tito, playfully, feeling relieved that she had said nothing about Baldassarre; "you have a touch of fanaticism in you. I shall have you seeing visions, like your brother."

"No; it was the same with every one else. He carried them all with him; unless it were that gross Dolfo Spini, whom I saw there making grimaces. There was even a wretched-looking man, with a rope around his neck,—an escaped prisoner, I should think, who had run in for shelter,—a very wild-eyed old man: I saw him with great tears rolling down his cheeks, as he looked and listened quite eagerly."

There was a slight pause before Tito spoke.

"I saw the man," he said,—"the prisoner. I was outside the Duomo with Lorenzo Tornabuoni when he ran in. He had escaped from a French soldier. Did you see him when you came out?"

"No, he went out with our good old Piero di Cosimo. I saw Piero come in and cut off his rope, and take him out of the church. But you want rest, Tito? You feel ill?"

"Yes," said Tito, rising. The horrible sense that he must live in continual dread of what Baldassarre had said or done pressed upon him like a cold weight.

CHAPTER VIII

THE PAINTED RECORD

FOUR days later, Romola was on the way to the house of Piero di Cosimo, in the Via Gualfonda. Some of the streets through which she had to pass were lined with Frenchmen who were gazing at Florence, and with Florentines who were gazing at the French, and the gaze was not on either side entirely friendly and admiring. The first nation in Europe, of necessity finding itself, when out of its own country, in the presence of general inferiority, naturally assumed an air of conscious pre-eminence; and the Florentines, who had taken such pains to play the host amiably, were getting into the worst humour with their too superior guests.

For after the first smiling compliments and festivities were over,— after wondrous Mysteries with unrivalled machinery of floating clouds and angels had been presented in churches,—after the royal guest had honoured Florentine dames with much of his Most Christian ogling at balls and suppers, and business had begun to be talked of,—it appeared that the new Charlemagne regarded Florence as a conquered city, inasmuch as he had entered it with his lance in rest, talked of leaving his viceroy behind him, and had thoughts of bringing back the Medici. Singular logic this appeared to be on the part of an elect instrument of God! since the policy of Piero de' Medici, disowned by the people, had been the only offence of Florence against the majesty of France. And Florence was determined not to submit. The determination was being expressed very strongly in consultations of citizens inside the Old Palace, and it was beginning to show itself on the broad flags of the streets and piazza wherever there was an opportunity of flouting an insolent Frenchman. Under these circumstances the streets were not altogether a pleasant promenade for well-born women; but Romola, shrouded in her black veil and mantle, and with old Maso by her side, felt secure enough from impertinent observation.

And she was impatient to visit Piero di Cosimo. A copy of her father's portrait as Œdipus, which he had long ago undertaken to make for her, was not yet finished; and Piero was so uncertain in his work—sometimes, when the demand was not peremptory, laying aside a picture for months; sometimes thrusting it into a corner or coffer, where it was likely to be utterly forgotten—that she felt it necessary to watch over his progress. She was a favourite with the painter, and he was inclined to fulfil any wish of hers, but no general inclination could be trusted as a safeguard against his sudden whims. He had told her the week before that the picture would perhaps be finished by this time; and Romola was nervously anxious to have in her possession a copy of the only portrait existing of her father in the days of his blindness, lest his image should grow dim in her mind. The sense of defect in her devotedness to him made her cling with all the force of compunction as well as affection to the duties of memory. Love does not aim simply at the conscious good of the beloved object: it is not satisfied without perfect loyalty of heart; it aims at its own completeness.

Romola, by special favour, was allowed to intrude upon the painter without previous notice. She lifted the iron slide and called Piero in a flute-like tone, as the little maiden with the eggs had done in Tito's presence. Piero was quick in answering, but when he opened the door he accounted for his quickness in a manner that was not complimentary.

"Ah, Madonna Romola, is it you? I thought my eggs were come; I wanted them."

"I have brought you something better than hard eggs, Piero. Maso has got a little basket full of cakes and *confetti* for you," said Romola, smiling, as she put back her veil. She took the basket from Maso, and stepping into the house, said,—

"I know you like these things when you can have them without trouble. Confess you do."

"Yes, when they come to me as easily as the light does," said Piero, folding his arms and looking down at the sweetmeats as Romola un covered them and glanced at him archly.

"And they're come along with the light now," he added, lifting his eyes to her face and hair with a painter's admiration, as her hood, dragged by the weight of her veil, fell backward.

"But I know what the sweetmeats are for," he went on; "they are to stop my mouth while you scold me. Well, go on into the next room, and you will see I've done something to the picture since you saw it, though it's not finished yet. But I didn't promise, you know: I take care not to promise:

'Chi promette e non mantiene
L'anima sua non va mai bene.' "

The door opening on the wild garden was closed now, and the painter was at work. Not at Romola's picture, however. That was standing on the floor, propped against the wall; and Piero stooped to lift it, that he might carry it into the proper light. But in lifting away this picture, he had disclosed another,—the oil-sketch of Tito, to which he had made an important addition within the last few days. It was so much smaller than the other picture, that it stood far within it; and Piero, apt to forget where he had placed anything, was not aware of what he had revealed as, peering at some detail in the painting which he held in his hands, he went to place it on an easel. But Romola exclaimed, flushing with astonishment,—

"That is Tito!"

Piero looked round, and gave a silent shrug. He was vexed at his own forgetfulness.

She was still looking at the sketch in astonishment; but presently she turned towards the painter and said with puzzled alarm,—

"What a strange picture! When did you paint it? What does it mean?"

"A mere fancy of mine," said Piero, lifting off his skull-cap, scratching his head, and making the usual grimace by which he avoided the betrayal of any feeling. "I wanted a handsome young face for it, and your husband's was just the thing."

He went forward, stooped down to the picture, and lifting it away with its back to Romola, pretended to be giving it a passing examination, before putting it aside as a thing not good enough to show.

But Romola who had the fact of the armour in her mind, and was penetrated by this strange coincidence of things which associated Tito with the idea of fear, went to his elbow and said,—

"Don't put it away; let me look again. That man with the rope round his neck—I saw him—I saw you come to him in the Duomo. What was it that made you put him into a picture with Tito?"

Piero saw no better resource than to tell part of the truth.

"It was a mere accident. The man was running away,—running up the steps, and caught hold of your husband: I suppose he had stumbled. I happened to be there, and saw it, and I thought the savage-looking old fellow was a good subject. But it's worth nothing,—it's only a freakish daub of mine." Piero ended contemptuously, moving the sketch away with an air of decision, and putting it on a high shelf. "Come and look at the Œdipus."

He had shown a little too much anxiety in putting the sketch out of her sight, and had produced the very impression he had sought to prevent,—that there was really something unpleasant, something disadvantageous to Tito, in the circumstances out of which the picture arose. But this impression silenced her: her pride and delicacy shrank from questioning further, where questions might seem to imply that she could entertain even a slight suspicion against her husband. She merely said, in as quiet a tone as she could,—

"He was a strange, piteous-looking man, that prisoner. Do you know anything more of him?"

"No more: I showed him the way to the hospital, that's all. See, now, the face of Œdipus is pretty nearly finished; tell me what you think of it."

Romola now gave her whole attention to her father's portrait, standing in long silence before it.

"Ah," she said at last, "you have done what I wanted. You have given it more of the listening look. My good Piero,"—she turned towards him with bright moist eyes,—"I am very grateful to you."

"Now that's what I can't bear in you women," said Piero, turning impatiently, and kicking aside the objects that littered the floor,—"you are always pouring out feelings where there's no call for them. Why should you be grateful to me for a picture you pay me for, especially when I make you wait for it? And if I paint a picture, I suppose it's for my own pleasure and credit to paint it well, eh? Are you to thank a

man for not being a rogue or a noodle? It's enough if he himself thanks
Messer Domeneddio, who has made him neither the one nor the other.
But women think walls are held together with honey."

"You crusty Piero! I forgot how snappish you are. Here, put this
nice sweetmeat in your mouth," said Romola, smiling through her tears,
and taking something very crisp and sweet from the little basket.

Piero accepted it very much as that proverbial bear that dreams of
pears might accept an exceedingly mellow "swan-egg,"—really liking
the gift, but accustomed to have his pleasures and pains concealed under
a shaggy coat.

"It's good, Madonna Antigone," said Piero, putting his fingers in the
basket for another. He had eaten nothing but hard eggs for a fortnight.
Romola stood opposite him, feeling her new anxiety suspended for a
little while by the sight of his *naïve* enjoyment.

"Good-by, Piero," she said presently, setting down the basket. "I
promise not to thank you if you finish the portrait soon and well. I will
tell you, you were bound to do it for your own credit."

"Good," said Piero, curtly, helping her with much deftness to fold
her mantle and veil round her.

"I'm glad she asked no more questions about that sketch," he thought,
when he had closed the door behind her. "I should be sorry for her to
guess that I thought her fine husband a good model for a coward. But
I made light of it; she'll not think of it again."

Piero was too sanguine, as open-hearted men are apt to be when they
attempt a little clever simulation. The thought of the picture pressed
more and more on Romola as she walked homeward. She could not help
putting together the two facts of the chain-armour and the encounter
mentioned by Piero between her husband and the prisoner, which had
happened on the morning of the day when the armour was adopted.
That look of terror which the painter had given Tito, had he seen it?
What could it all mean?

"It means nothing," she tried to assure herself. "It was a mere coincidence. Shall I ask Tito about it?" Her mind said at last, "No: I will
not question him about anything he did not tell me spontaneously. It
is an offence against the trust I owe him." Her heart said, "I dare not
ask him."

There was a terrible flaw in the trust: she was afraid of any hasty
movement, as men are who hold something precious and want to believe
that it is not broken.

CHAPTER IX

A MOMENT OF TRIUMPH

"THE old fellow has vanished; went on towards Arezzo the next morning;
not liking the smell of the French, I suppose, after being their prisoner.

I went to the hospital to inquire after him; I wanted to know if those broth-making monks had found out whether he was in his right mind or not. However, they said he showed no signs of madness,—only no notice of questions, and seemed to be planting a vine twenty miles off. He was a mysterious old tiger. I should have liked to know something more about him."

It was in Nello's shop that Piero di Cosimo was speaking, on the 24th of November, just a week after the entrance of the French. There was a party of six or seven assembled at the rather unusual hour of three in the afternoon; for it was a day on which all Florence was excited by the prospect of some decisive political event. Every lounging-place was full, and every shopkeeper who had no wife or deputy to leave in charge, stood at his door with his thumbs in his belt; while the streets were constantly sprinkled with artisans pausing or passing lazily like floating splinters, ready to rush forward impetuously if any object attracted them.

Nello had been thrumming the lute as he half sat on the board against the shop-window, and kept an outlook towards the piazza.

"Ah," he said, laying down the lute, with emphasis, "I would not for a gold florin have missed that sight of the French soldiers waddling in their broad shoes after their runaway prisoners! That comes of leaving my shop to shave magnificent chins. It is always so: if ever I quit this navel of the earth, something takes the opportunity of happening in my piazza."

"Yes, you ought to have been there," said Piero, in his biting way, "just to see your favourite Greek look as frightened as if Satanasso had laid hold of him. I like to see your ready-smiling Messeri caught in a sudden wind and obliged to show their lining in spite of themselves. What colour do you think a man's liver is, who looks like a bleached deer as soon as a chance stranger lays hold of him suddenly?"

"Piero, keep that vinegar of thine as sauce to thine own eggs! What is it against my *bel erudito* that he looked startled when he felt a pair of claws upon him and saw an unchained madman at his elbow? Your scholar is not like those beastly Swiss and Germans, whose heads are only fit for battering-rams, and who have such large appetites that they think nothing of taking a cannon-ball before breakfast. We Florentines count some other qualities in a man besides that vulgar stuff called bravery, which is to be got by hiring dunderheads at so much per dozen. I tell you, as soon as men found out that they had more brains than oxen, they set the oxen to draw for them; and when we Florentines found out that we had more brains than other men, we set them to fight for us."

"Treason, Nello!" a voice called out from the inner sanctum; "that is not the doctrine of the State. Florence is grinding its weapons; and the last well-authenticated vision announced by the Frate was Mars standing on the Palazzo Vecchio with his arm on the shoulder of San Giovanni Battista, who was offering him a piece of honeycomb."

"It is well, Francesco," said Nello. "Florence has a few thicker skulls that may do to bombard Pisa with; there will still be the finer spirits left at home to do the thinking and the shaving. And as for our Piero here, if he makes such a point of valour, let him carry his biggest brush for a weapon and his palette for a shield, and challenge the widest-mouthed Swiss he can see in the Prato to a single combat."

"*Va*, Nello," growled Piero, "thy tongue runs on as usual, like a mill when the Arno's full,—whether there's grist or not."

"Excellent grist, I tell thee. For it would be as reasonable to expect a grizzled painter like thee to be fond of getting a javelin inside thee as to expect a man whose wits have been sharpened on the classics to like having his handsome face clawed by a wild beast."

"There you go, supposing you'll get people to put their legs into a sack because you call it a pair of hosen," said Piero. "Who said anything about a wild beast, or about an unarmed man rushing on battle? Fighting is a trade, and it's not my trade. I should be a fool to run after danger, but I could face it if it came to me."

"How is it you're so afraid of the thunder, then, my Piero?" said Nello, determined to chase down the accuser. "You ought to be able to understand why one man is shaken by a thing that seems a trifle to others,—you who hide yourself with the rats as soon as the storm comes on."

"That is because I have a particular sensibility to loud sounds; it has nothing to do with my courage or my conscience."

"Well, and Tito Melema may have a peculiar sensibility to being laid hold of unexpectedly by prisoners who have run away from French soldiers. Men are born with antipathies; I myself can't abide the smell of mint. Tito was born with an antipathy to old prisoners who stumble and clutch. Ecco!"

There was a general laugh at Nello's defence, and it was clear that Piero's disinclination towards Tito was not shared by the company. The painter, with his undecipherable grimace, took the tow from his scarsella, and stuffed his ears in indignant contempt, while Nello went on triumphantly,—

"No, my Piero, I can't afford to have my *bel erudito* decried; and Florence can't afford it either, with her scholars moulting off at the early age of forty. Our Phœnix Pico just gone straight to Paradise, as the Frate has informed us: and the incomparable Poliziano, not two months since, gone to—well, well, let us hope he is not gone to the eminent scholars in the Malebolge."

"By the way," said Francesco Cei, "have you heard that Camilla Rucellai has outdone the Frate in her prophecies? She prophesied two years ago that Pico would die in the time of lilies. He has died in November. 'Not at all the time of lilies,' said the scorners. 'Go to!' says Camilla; 'it is the lilies of France I meant, and it seems to me they are close enough under your nostrils.' I say, 'Euge, Camilla!' If the Frate can prove that any one of his visions has been as well fulfilled, I'll declare myself a Piagnone to-morrow."

"You are something too flippant about the Frate, Francesco," said Pietro Cennini, the scholarly. "We are all indebted to him in these weeks for preaching peace and quietness, and the laying aside of party quarrels. They are men of small discernment who would be glad to see the people slipping the Frate's leash just now. And if the Most Christian King is obstinate about the treaty to-day, and will not sign what is fair and honourable to Florence, Fra Girolamo is the man we must trust in to bring him to reason."

"You speak truth, Messer Pietro," said Nello, "the Frate is one of the firmest nails Florence has to hang on,—at least, that is the opinion of the most respectable chins I have the honour of shaving. But young Messer Niccolò was saying here the other morning—and doubtless Francesco means the same thing—there is as wonderful a power of stretching in the meaning of visions as in Dido's bull's hide. It seems to me a dream may mean whatever comes after it. As our Franco Sacchetti says, a woman dreams over night of a serpent biting her, breaks a drinking-cup the next day, and cries out, 'Look you, I thought something would happen,—it's plain now what the serpent meant.'"

"But the Frate's visions are not of that sort," said Cronaca. "He not only says what will happen,—that the Church will be scourged and renovated, and the heathens converted,—he says it shall happen quickly. He is no slippery pretender who provides loopholes for himself; he is—"

"What is this? what is this?" exclaimed Nello, jumping off the board, and putting his head out at the door. "Here are people streaming into the piazza, and shouting. Something must have happened in the Via Larga. Aha!" he burst forth with delighted astonishment, stepping out laughing and waving his cap.

All the rest of the company hastened to the door. News from the Via Larga was just what they had been waiting for. But if the news had come into the piazza, they were not a little surprised at the form of its advent. Carried above the shoulders of the people, on a bench apparently snatched up in the street, sat Tito Melema, in smiling amusement at the compulsion he was under. His cap had slipped off his head, and hung by the becchetto which was wound loosely round his neck; and as he saw the group at Nello's door, he lifted up his fingers in beckoning recognition. The next minute he had leaped from the bench on to a cart filled with bales, that stood in the broad space between the baptistery and the steps of the Duomo, while the people swarmed round him with the noisy eagerness of poultry expecting to be fed. But there was silence when he began to speak in his clear mellow voice,—

"Citizens of Florence! I have no warrant to tell the news except your will. But the news is good, and will harm no man in the telling. The Most Christian King is signing a treaty that is honourable to Florence. But you owe it to one of your citizens who spoke a word worthy of the ancient Romans,—you owe it to Piero Capponi!"

Immediately there was a roar of voices. "Capponi! Capponi! What said our Piero?" "Ah! he wouldn't stand being sent from Herod to Pilate!" "We knew Piero!" "*Orsù!* Tell us, what did he say?"

When the roar of insistence had subsided a little, Tito began again: "The Most Christian King demanded a little too much,—was obstinate, —said at last, 'I shall order my trumpets to sound.' Then, Florentine citizens! your Piero Capponi, speaking with the voice of a free city, said, 'If you sound your trumpets, we will ring our bells!' He snatched the copy of the dishonouring conditions from the hands of the secretary, tore it in pieces, and turned to leave the royal presence."

Again there were loud shouts, and again impatient demands for more. "Then, Florentines, the high majesty of France felt, perhaps for the first time, all the majesty of a free city. And the Most Christian King himself hastened from his place to call Piero Capponi back. The great spirit of your Florentine city did its work by a great word, without need of the great actions that lay ready behind it. And the King has consented to sign the treaty, which preserves the honour as well as the safety of Florence. The banner of France will float over every Florentine galley in sign of amity and common privilege, but above that banner will be written the word 'Liberty!'

"That is all the news I have to tell; is it not enough?—since it is for the glory of every one of you, citizens of Florence, that you have a fellow-citizen who knows how to speak your will."

As the shouts rose again, Tito looked round with inward amusement at the various crowd, each of whom was elated with the notion that Piero Capponi had somehow represented him,—that he was the mind of which Capponi was the mouthpiece. He enjoyed the humour of the incident, which had suddenly transformed him, an alien, and a friend of the Medici, into an orator who tickled the ears of the people blatant for some unknown good which they called liberty. He felt quite glad that he had been laid hold of and hurried along by the crowd as he was coming out of the palace in the Via Larga with a commission to the Signoria. It was very easy, very pleasant, this exercise of speaking to the general satisfaction: a man who knew how to persuade need never be in danger from any party; he could convince each that he was feigning with all the others. The gestures and faces of weavers and dyers were certainly amusing when looked at from above in this way.

Tito was beginning to get easier in his armour, and at this moment was quite unconscious of it. He stood with one hand holding his recovered cap, and with the other at his belt, the light of a complacent smile in his long lustrous eyes, as he made a parting reverence to his audience, before springing down from the bales,—when suddenly his glance met that of a man who had not at all the amusing aspect of the exulting weavers, dyers, and wool-carders. The face of this man was clean-shaven, his hair close-clipped, and he wore a decent felt hat. A single glance would hardly have sufficed to assure any one but Tito, that this was the face of the escaped prisoner who had laid hold of him on the steps. But to Tito it came not simply as the face of the escaped prisoner, but as a face with which he had been familiar long years before.

It seemed all compressed into a second,—the sight of Baldassarre looking at him, the sensation shooting through him like a fiery arrow, and the act of leaping from the cart. He would have leaped down in the same instant, whether he had seen Baldassarre or not, for he was in a hurry to be gone to the Palazzo Vecchio: this time he had not betrayed himself by look or movement, and he said inwardly that he should not be taken by surprise again; he should be prepared to see this face rise up continually like the intermittent blotch that comes in diseased vision. But this reappearance of Baldassarre so much more in his own likeness tightened the pressure of dread: the idea of his madness lost its likelihood now he was shaven and clad like a decent though poor citizen. Certainly, there was a great change in his face; but how could it be otherwise? And yet, if he were perfectly sane, in possession of all his powers and all his learning, why was he lingering in this way before making known his identity? It must be for the sake of making his scheme of vengeance more complete. But he did linger: that at least gave an opportunity for flight. And Tito began to think that flight was his only resource.

But while he, with his back turned on the Piazza del Duomo, had lost the recollection of the new part he had been playing, and was no longer thinking of the many things which a ready brain and tongue made easy, but of a few things which destiny had somehow made very difficult, the enthusiasm which he had fed contemptuously was creating a scene in that piazza in grand contrast with the inward drama of self-centred fear which he had carried away from it.

The crowd, on Tito's disappearance, had begun to turn their faces towards the outlets of the piazza in the direction of the Via Larga, when the sight of *mazzieri,* or mace-bearers, entering from the Via de' Martelli, announced the approach of dignitaries. They must be the syndics, or commissioners charged with the effecting of the treaty; the treaty must be already signed, and they had come away from the royal presence. Piero Capponi was coming,—the brave heart that had known how to speak for Florence. The effect on the crowd was remarkable; they parted with softening, dropping voices, subsiding into silence,—and the silence became so perfect that the tread of the syndics on the broad pavement, and the rustle of their black silk garments could be heard, like rain in the night. There were four of them; but it was not the two learned doctors of law, Messer Guidantonio Vespucci and Messer Domenico Bonsi, that the crowd waited for; it was not Francesco Valori, popular as he had become in these late days. The moment belonged to another man of firm presence, as little inclined to humour the people as to humour any other unreasonable claimants,—loving order, like one who by force of fortune had been made a merchant, and by force of nature had become a soldier. It was not till he was seen at the entrance of the piazza that the silence was broken, and then one loud shout of "Capponi, Capponi! Well done, Capponi!" rang through the piazza. The simple resolute man looked round him with grave joy. His fellow-citizens gave him a great funeral two years later, when he had died in fight; there were torches carried by all the magistracy, and torches again, and trains of banners. But it is not known that he felt any joy in the oration that was delivered in his praise, as the banners waved over his bier. Let us be glad that he got some thanks and praise while he lived.

CHAPTER X

THE AVENGER'S SECRET

It was the first time that Baldassarre had been in the Piazza del Duomo since his escape. He had a strong desire to hear the remarkable monk preach again, but he had shrunk from reappearing in the same spot where he had been seen half naked, with neglected hair, with a rope round his neck,—in the same spot where he had been called a madman. The feeling, in its freshness, was too strong to be overcome by any trust he had in the change he had made in his appearance; for when the words "*Some madman, surely,*" had fallen from Tito's lips, it was not their baseness and cruelty only that had made their viper sting,—it was Baldassarre's instantaneous bitter consciousness that he might be unable to prove the words false. Along with the passionate desire for vengeance which possessed him had arisen the keen sense that his power of achieving the vengeance was doubtful. It was as if Tito had been helped by some diabolical prompter, who had whispered Baldassarre's saddest secret in the traitor's ear. He was not mad; for he carried within him that piteous stamp of sanity, the clear consciousness of shattered faculties; he measured his own feebleness. With the first movement of vindictive rage awoke a vague caution, like that of a wild beast that is fierce but feeble,—or like that of an insect whose little fragment of earth has given way, and made it pause in a palsy of distrust. It was this distrust, this determination to take no step which might betray anything concerning himself, that had made Baldassarre reject Piero di Cosimo's friendly advances.

He had been equally cautious at the hospital, only telling, in answer to the questions of the brethren there, that he had been made a prisoner by the French on his way from Genoa. But his age, and the indications in his speech and manner that he was of a different class from the ordinary mendicants and poor travellers who were entertained in the hospital, had induced the monks to offer him extra charity: a coarse woollen tunic to protect him from the cold, a pair of peasant's shoes, and a few *danari*, smallest of Florentine coins, to help him on his way. He had ᵛone on the road to Arezzo, early in the morning; but he had paused at

the first little town, and had used a couple of his *danari* to get himself
shaved, and to have his circle of hair clipped short, in his former fashion.
The barber there had a little hand-mirror of bright steel: it was a long
while, it was years since Baldassarre had looked at himself; and now, as
his eyes fell on that hand-mirror, a new thought shot through his mind.
"Was he so changed that Tito really did not know him?" The thought
was such a sudden arrest of impetuous currents that it was a painful
shock to him; his hand shook like a leaf, as he put away the barber's
arm and asked for the mirror. He wished to see himself before he was
shaved. The barber, noticing his tremulousness, held the mirror for him.

No, he was not so changed as that. He himself had known the wrinkles
as they had been three years ago; they were only deeper now; there was
the same rough, clumsy skin, making little superficial bosses on the
brow, like so many cipher marks: the skin was only yellower, only
looked more like a lifeless rind. That shaggy white beard,—it was no
disguise to eyes that had looked closely at him for sixteen years,—to
eyes that ought to have searched for him with the expectation of finding
him changed, as men search for the beloved among the bodies cast up by
the waters. There was something different in his glance, but it was a
difference that should only have made the recognition of him the more
startling; for is not a known voice all the more thrilling when it is
heard as a cry? But the doubt was folly: he had felt that Tito knew him.
He put out his hand and pushed the mirror away. The strong currents
were rushing on again, and the energies of hatred and vengeance were
active once more.

He went back on the way towards Florence again, but he did not wish
to enter the city till dusk; so he turned aside from the highroad, and
sat down by a little pool shadowed on one side by alder-bushes still
sprinkled with yellow leaves. It was a calm November day, and he no
sooner saw the pool than he thought its still surface might be a mirror
for him. He wanted to contemplate himself slowly, as he had not dared
to do in the presence of the barber. He sat down on the edge of the pool,
and bent forward to look earnestly at the image of himself.

Was there something wandering and imbecile in his face,—something
like what he felt in his mind?

Not now; not when he was examining himself with a look of eager
inquiry: on the contrary, there was an intense purpose in his eyes. But
at other times? Yes, it must be so: in the long hours when he had the
vague aching of an unremembered past within him,—when he seemed to
sit in dark loneliness, visited by whispers which died out mockingly as
he strained his ear after them, and by forms that seemed to approach
him and float away as he thrust out his hand to grasp them,—in those
hours, doubtless, there must be continual frustration and amazement in
his glance. And more horrible still, when the thick cloud parted for a
moment, and, as he sprang forward with hope, rolled together again, and
left him helpless as before; doubtless, there was then a blank confusion
in his face, as of a man suddenly smitten with blindness.

Could he prove anything? Could he even begin to allege anything, with the confidence that the links of thought would not break away? Would any believe that he had ever had a mind filled with rare knowledge, busy with close thoughts, ready with various speech? It had all slipped away from him,—that laboriously gathered store. Was it utterly and forever gone from him, like the waters from an urn lost in the wide ocean? Or was it still within him, imprisoned by some obstruction that might one day break asunder?

It might be so; he tried to keep his grasp on that hope. For, since the day when he had first walked feebly from his couch of straw, and had felt a new darkness within him under the sunlight, his mind had undergone changes, partly gradual and persistent, partly sudden and fleeting. As he had recovered his strength of body, he had recovered his self-command and the energy of his will; he had recovered the memory of all that part of his life which was closely enwrought with his emotions; and he had felt more and more constantly and painfully the uneasy sense of lost knowledge. But more than that—once or twice, when he had been strongly excited, he had seemed momentarily to be in entire possession of his past self, as old men doze for an instant and get back the consciousness of their youth: he seemed again to see Greek pages and understand them, again to feel his mind moving unbenumbed among familiar ideas. It had been but a flash, and the darkness closing in again seemed the more horrible; but might not the same thing happen again for longer periods? If it would only come and stay long enough for him to achieve a revenge,—devise an exquisite suffering, such as a mere right arm could never inflict!

He raised himself from his stooping attitude, and, folding his arms, attempted to concentrate all his mental force on the plan he must immediately pursue. He had to wait for knowledge and opportunity, and while he waited he must have the means of living without beggary. What he dreaded of all things now, was that any one should think him a foolish, helpless old man. No one must know that half his memory was gone: the lost strength might come again; and if it were only for a little while, *that* might be enough. He knew how to begin to get the information he wanted about Tito. He had repeated the words "Bratti Ferravecchi" so constantly after they had been uttered to him, that they never slipped from him for long together. A man at Genoa, on whose finger he had seen Tito's ring, had told him that he bought that ring at Florence, of a young Greek, well dressed, and with a handsome dark face, in the shop of a *rigattiere* called Bratti Ferravecchi, in a street also called Ferravecchi. This discovery had caused a violent agitation in Baldassarre. Until then he had clung with all the tenacity of his fervent nature to his faith in Tito, and had not for a moment believed himself to be wilfully forsaken. At first he had said, "My bit of parchment has never reached him; that is why I am still toiling at Antioch. But he is searching; he knows where I was lost: he will trace me out and find me at last." Then, when he was taken to Corinth, he induced his owners, by the assurance

that he should be sought out and ransomed, to provide securely against
the failure of any inquiries that might be made about him at Antioch;
and at Corinth he thought joyfully, "Here, at last, he must find me.
Here he is sure to touch, whichever way he goes." But before another
year had passed, the illness had come from which he had risen with body
and mind so shattered that he was worse than worthless to his owners,
except for the sake of the ransom that did not come. Then, as he sat
helpless in the morning sunlight, he began to think, "Tito has been
drowned, or they have made *him* a prisoner too. I shall see him no more.
He set out after me, but misfortune overtook him. I shall see his face
no more." Sitting in his new feebleness and despair, supporting his head
between his hands, with blank eyes and lips that moved uncertainly, he
looked so much like a hopelessly imbecile old man, that his owners were
contented to be rid of him, and allowed a Genoese merchant, who had
compassion on him as an Italian, to take him on board his galley. In a
voyage of many months in the Archipelago and along the seaboard of
Asia Minor, Baldassarre had recovered his bodily strength; but on landing at Genoa he had so weary a sense of his desolateness that he almost
wished he had died of that illness at Corinth. There was just one possibility that hindered the wish from being decided: it was that Tito
might not be dead, but living in a state of imprisonment or destitution;
and if he lived there was still a hope for Baldassarre—faint, perhaps,
and likely to be long deferred, but still a hope—that he might find his
child, his cherished son again; might yet again clasp hands and meet face
to face with the one being who remembered him as he had been before
his mind was broken.

In this state of feeling he had chanced to meet the stranger who wore
Tito's onyx ring; and though Baldassarre would have been unable to
describe the ring beforehand, the sight of it stirred the dormant fibres,
and he recognized it. That Tito nearly a year after his father had been
parted from him should have been living in apparent prosperity at Florence, selling the gem which he ought not to have sold till the last extremity, was a fact that Baldassarre shrank from trying to account for:
he was glad to be stunned and bewildered by it, rather than to have any
distinct thought; he tried to feel nothing but joy that he should behold
Tito again. Perhaps Tito had thought his father was dead; somehow the
mystery would be explained. "But at least I shall meet eyes that will
remember me. I am not alone in the world."

And now again Baldassarre said, "I am not alone in the world; I
shall never be alone, for my revenge is with me."

It was as the instrument of that revenge, as something merely external
and subservient to his true life, that he bent down again to examine
himself with hard curiosity,—not, he thought, because he had any care
for a withered, forsaken old man, whom nobody loved, whose soul was
like a deserted home, where the ashes were cold upon the hearth, and
the walls were bare of all but the marks of what had been. It is in the
nature of all human passion, the lowest as well as the highest, that there

is a point where it ceases to be properly egoistic, and is like a fire kindled within our being to which everything else in us is mere fuel.

He looked at the pale black-browed image in the water till he identified it with that self from which his revenge seemed to be a thing apart; and he felt as if the image too heard the silent language of his thought.

"I was a loving fool,—I worshipped a woman once, and believed she could care for me; and then I took a helpless child and fostered him; and I watched him as he grew, to see if he would care for me only a little, —care for *me* over and above the good he got from me. I would have torn open my breast to warm him with my life-blood if I could only have seen him care a little for the pain of my wound. I have laboured, I have strained to crush out of this hard life one drop of unselfish love. Fool! men love their own delights; there is no delight to be had in me. And yet I watched till I believed I saw what I watched for. When he was a child he lifted soft eyes towards me, and held my hand willingly; I thought, this boy will surely love me a little: because I give my life to him and strive that he shall know no sorrow, he will care a little when I am thirsty,—the drop he lays on my parched lips will be a joy to him. . . . Curses on him! I wish I may see him lie with those red lips white and dry as ashes, and when he looks for pity I wish he may see my face rejoicing in his pain. It is all a lie,—this world is a lie,—there is no goodness but in hate. Fool! not one drop of love came with all your striving: life has not given you one drop. But there are deep draughts in this world for hatred and revenge. I have memory left for that, and there is strength in my arm, there is strength in my will; and if I can do nothing but kill him—"

But Baldassarre's mind rejected the thought of that brief punishment. His whole soul had been thrilled into immediate unreasoning belief in that eternity of vengeance where he, an undying hate, might clutch forever an undying traitor, and hear that fair smiling hardness cry and moan with anguish. But the primary need and hope was to see a slow revenge under the same sky and on the same earth where he himself had been forsaken and had fainted with despair. And as soon as he tried to concentrate his mind on the means of attaining his end, the sense of his weakness pressed upon him like a frosty ache. This despised body, which was to be the instrument of a sublime vengeance, must be nourished and decently clad. If he had to wait, he must labour; and his labour must be of a humble sort, for he had no skill. He wondered whether the sight of written characters would so stimulate his faculties that he might venture to try and find work as a copyist: *that* might win him some credence for his past scholarship. But no! he dared trust neither hand nor brain. He must be content to do the work that was most like that of a beast of burden: in this mercantile city many porters must be wanted, and he could at least carry weights. Thanks to the justice that struggled in this confused world in behalf of vengeance, his limbs had got back some of their old sturdiness. He was stripped of all else that men would give coin for.

But the new urgency of this habitual thought brought a new suggestion. There was something hanging by a cord round his bare neck:
something apparently so paltry that the piety of Turks and Frenchmen
had spared it,—a tiny parchment bag blackened with age. It had hung
round his neck as a precious charm when he was a boy, and he had kept
it carefully on his breast, not believing that it contained anything but
a tiny scroll of parchment rolled up hard. He might long ago have thrown
it away as a relic of his dead mother's superstition; but he had thought
of it as a relic of her love, and had kept it. It was part of the piety associated with such *brevi*, that they should never be opened; and at any
previous moment in his life Baldassarre would have said that no sort
of thirst would prevail upon him to open this little bag for the chance
of finding that it contained, not parchment, but an engraved amulet
which would be worth money. But now a thirst had come like that which
makes men open their own veins to satisfy it, and the thought of the
possible amulet no sooner crossed Baldassarre's mind than with nervous
fingers he snatched the *breve* from his neck. It all rushed through his
mind,—the long years he had worn it, the far-off sunny balcony at
Naples looking towards the blue waters, where he had leaned against
his mother's knee; but it made no moment of hesitation: all piety now
was transmuted into a just revenge. He bit and tore till the doubles of
parchment were laid open, and then—it was a sight that made him
pant—there *was* an amulet. It was very small, but it was as blue as
those far-off waters; it was an engraved sapphire, which must be worth
some gold ducats. Baldassarre no sooner saw those possible ducats than
he saw some of them exchanged for a poniard. He did not want to use
the poniard yet, but he longed to possess it. If he could grasp its handle
and try its edge, that blank in his mind—that past which fell away continually—would not make him feel so cruelly helpless; the sharp steel
that despised talents and eluded strength would be at his side, as the
unfailing friend of feeble justice. There was a sparkling triumph under
Baldassarre's black eyebrows as he replaced the little sapphire inside
the bits of parchment and wound the string tightly round them.

It was nearly dusk now, and he rose to walk back towards Florence.
With his *danari* to buy him some bread, he felt rich: he could lie out in
the open air, as he found plenty more doing in all corners of Florence.
And in the next few days he had sold his sapphire, had added to his
clothing, had bought a bright dagger, and had still a pair of gold florins
left. But he meant to hoard that treasure carefully: his lodging was an
outhouse with a heap of straw in it, in a thinly inhabited part of Oltrarno, and he thought of looking about for work as a porter.

He had bought his dagger at Bratti's. Paying his meditated visit there
one evening at dusk, he had found that singular rag-merchant just returned from one of his rounds, emptying out his basketful of broken glass
and old iron among his handsome show of miscellaneous second-hand
goods. As Baldassarre entered the shop, and looked towards the smart
pieces of apparel, the musical instruments, and weapons, which were dis-

played in the broadest light of the window, his eye at once singled out a dagger hanging up high against a red scarf. By buying the dagger he could not only satisfy a strong desire, he could open his original errand in a more indirect manner than by speaking of the onyx ring. In the course of bargaining for the weapon, he let drop, with cautious carelessness, that he came from Genoa, and had been directed to Bratti's shop by an acquaintance in that city who had bought a very valuable ring here. Had the respectable trader any more such rings?

Whereupon Bratti had much to say as to the unlikelihood of such rings being within reach of many people, with much vaunting of his own rare connections, due to his known wisdom and honesty. It might be true that he was a peddler,—he chose to be a peddler: though he was rich enough to kick his heels in his shop all day. But those who thought they had said all that there was to be said about Bratti when they had called him a peddler, were a good deal further off the truth than the other side of Pisa. How was it that he could put that ring in a stranger's way? It was because he had a very particular knowledge of a handsome young signor, who did not look quite so fine a feathered bird when Bratti first set eyes on him as he did at the present time. And by a question or two Baldassarre extracted, without any trouble, such a rough and rambling account of Tito's life as the peddler could give, since the time when he had found him sleeping under the Loggia de' Cerchi. It never occurred to Bratti that the decent man (who was rather deaf apparently, asking him to say many things twice over) had any curiosity about Tito; the curiosity was doubtless about himself, as a truly remarkable peddler.

And Baldassarre left Bratti's shop, not only with the dagger at his side, but also with a general knowledge of Tito's conduct and position,— of his early sale of the jewels, his immediate quiet settlement of himself at Florence, his marriage, and his great prosperity.

"What story had he told about his previous life,—about his father?"

It would be difficult for Baldassarre to discover the answer to that question. Meanwhile he wanted to learn all he could about Florence. But he found, to his acute distress, that of the new details he learned he could only retain a few, and those only by continual repetition; and he began to be afraid of listening to any new discourse, lest it should obliterate what he was already striving to remember.

The day he was discerned by Tito in the Piazza del Duomo, he had the fresh anguish of this consciousness in his mind; and Tito's ready speech fell upon him like the mockery of a glib, defying demon.

As he went home to his heap of straw, and passed by the bookseller's shops in the Via del Garbo, he paused to look at the volumes spread open. Could he by long gazing at one of those books lay hold of the slippery threads of memory? Could he, by striving, get a firm grasp somewhere, and lift himself above these waters that flowed over him?

He was tempted, and bought the cheapest Greek book he could see. He carried it home and sat on his heap of straw, looking at the characters by the light of the small window; but no inward light arose on them. Soon the evening darkness came; but it made little difference to Baldassarre. His strained eyes seemed still to see the white pages with the unintelligible black marks upon them.

CHAPTER XI

FRUIT IS SEED

"My Romola," said Tito, the second morning after he had made his speech in the Piazza del Duomo, "I am to receive grand visitors to-day; the Milanese Count is coming again, and the Seneschal de Beaucaire, the great favourite of the Cristianissimo. I know you don't care to go through smiling ceremonies with these rustling magnates, whom we are not likely to see again; and as they will want to look at the antiquities and the library, perhaps you had better give up your work to-day, and go to see your cousin Brigida."

Romola discerned a wish in this intimation, and immediately assented. But presently, coming back in her hood and mantle, she said: "Oh, what a long breath Florence will take when the gates are flung open, and the last Frenchman is walking out of them! Even you are getting tired, with all your patience, my Tito; confess it. Ah, your head is hot."

He was leaning over his desk, writing, and she had laid her hand on his head, meaning to give a parting caress. The attitude had been a frequent one; and Tito was accustomed, when he felt her hand there, to raise his head, throw himself a little backward, and look up at her. But he felt now as unable to raise his head as if her hand had been a leaden cowl. He spoke instead, in a light tone, as his pen still ran along.

"The French are as ready to go from Florence as the wasps to leave a ripe pear when they have just fastened on it."

Romola, keenly sensitive to the absence of the usual response, took away her hand and said, "I am going, Tito."

"Farewell, my sweet one. I must wait at home. Take Maso with you."

Still Tito did not look up, and Romola went out without saying any more. Very slight things make epochs in married life, and this morning for the first time she admitted to herself not only that Tito had changed, but that he had changed towards her. Did the reason lie in herself? She might perhaps have thought so, if there had not been the facts of the armour and the picture to suggest some external event which was an entire mystery to her.

But Tito no sooner believed that Romola was out of the house than he laid down his pen and looked up, in delightful security from seeing anything else than parchment and broken marble. He was rather disgusted with himself that he had not been able to look up at Romola and behave to her just as usual. He would have chosen, if he could, to be even more than usually kind; but he could not, on a sudden, master an involuntary shrinking from her, which by a subtle relation depended on those very characteristics in him that made him desire not to fail in his marks of affection. He was about to take a step which he knew would arouse her deep indignation; he would have to encounter much that was unpleasant before he could win her forgiveness. And Tito could never find it easy to face displeasure and anger; his nature was one of those most remote from defiance or impudence, and all his inclinations leaned towards preserving Romola's tenderness. He was not tormented by sentimental scruples which, as he had demonstrated to himself by a very rapid course of argument, had no relation to solid utility; but his freedom from scruples did not release him from the dread of what was disagreeable. Unscrupulousness gets rid of much, but not of toothache, or wounded vanity, or the sense of loneliness, against which, as the world at present stands, there is no security but a thoroughly healthy jaw, and a just, loving soul. And Tito was feeling intensely at this moment that no devices could save him from pain in the impending collision with Romola; no persuasive blandness could cushion him against the shock towards which he was being driven like a timid animal urged to a desperate leap by the terror of the tooth and the claw that are close behind it.

The secret feeling he had previously had that the tenacious adherence to Bardo's wishes about the library had become under existing difficulties a piece of sentimental folly, which deprived himself and Romola of substantial advantages, might perhaps never have wrought itself into action but for the events of the past week, which had brought at once the pressure of a new motive and the outlet of a rare opportunity. Nay, it was not till his dread had been aggravated by the sight of Baldassarre looking more like his sane self, not until he had begun to feel that he might be compelled to flee from Florence, that he had brought himself to resolve on using his legal right to sell the library before the great opportunity offered by French and Milanese bidders slipped through his fingers. For if he had to leave Florence he did not want to leave it as a destitute wanderer. He had been used to an agreeable existence, and he wished to carry with him all the means at hand for retaining the same agreeable conditions. He wished among other things to carry Romola with him, and *not,* if possible, to carry any infamy. Success had given him a growing appetite for all the pleasures that depend on an advantageous social position, and at no moment could it look like a temptation to him, but only like a hideous alternative, to decamp under dishonour, even with a bag of diamonds, and incur the life of an adventurer. It was not possible for him to make himself independent even of those Florentines who only greeted him with regard; still less was it possible for him to make himself independent of Romola. She was the wife of his first love,—he loved her still; she belonged to that furniture of life which he shrank from parting with. He winced under her judgment, he felt uncertain how far the revulsion of her feeling towards him might go; and all that sense of power over a wife which makes a husband risk betrayals that a lover never ventures on, would not suffice to counteract Tito's uneasiness. This was the leaden weight which had been too strong for his will, and kept him from raising his head to meet her eyes. Their pure light brought too near him the prospect of a coming struggle. But it was not to be helped; if they had to leave Florence, they must have money; indeed Tito could not arrange life at all to his mind without a considerable sum of money. And that problem of arranging life to his mind had been the source of all his misdoing. He would have been equal to any sacrifice that was not unpleasant.

The rustling magnates came and went, the bargains had been concluded, and Romola returned home; but nothing grave was said that night. Tito was only gay and chatty, pouring forth to her, as he had not done before, stories and descriptions of what he had witnessed during the French visit. Romola thought she discerned an effort in his liveliness, and attributing it to the consciousness in him that she had been wounded in the morning, accepted the effort as an act of penitence, inwardly aching a little at that sign of growing distance between them,—that there was an offence about which neither of them dared to speak.

The next day Tito remained away from home until late at night. It was a marked day to Romola, for Piero di Cosimo, stimulated to greater industry on her behalf by the fear that he might have been the cause of pain to her in the past week, had sent home her father's portrait. She had propped it against the back of his old chair, and had been looking at it for some time, when the door opened behind her, and Bernardo del Nero came in.

"It is you, godfather! How I wish you had come sooner! it is getting a little dusk," said Romola, going towards him.

"I have just looked in to tell you the good news, for I know Tito has not come yet," said Bernardo. "The French king moves off to-morrow: not before it is high time. There has been another tussle between our people and his soldiers this morning. But there's a chance now of the city getting into order once more and trade going on."

"That is joyful," said Romola. "But it is sudden, is it not? Tito seemed to think yesterday that there was little prospect of the king's going soon."

"He has been well barked at; that's the reason," said Bernardo, smiling. "His own generals opened their throats pretty well, and at last our Signoria sent the mastiff of the city, Fra Girolamo. The Cristianissimo was frightened at that thunder, and has given the order to move. I'm afraid there'll be small agreement among us when he's gone; but, at any rate, all parties are agreed in being glad not to have Florence stifled with soldiery any longer, and the Frate has barked this time to some purpose. Ah, what is this?" he added, as Romola, clasping him by the arm, led him in front of the picture. "Let us see."

He began to unwind his long scarf while she placed a seat for him.

"Don't you want your spectacles, godfather?" said Romola, in anxiety that he should see just what she saw.

"No, child, no," said Bernardo, uncovering his gray head, as he seated himself with firm erectness. "For seeing at this distance, my old eyes are perhaps better than your young ones. Old men's eyes are like old men's memories; they are strongest for things a long way off."

"It is better than having no portrait," said Romola, apologetically, after Bernardo had been silent a little while. "It is less like him now than the image I have in my mind, but then that might fade with the years." She rested her arm on the old man's shoulder as she spoke, drawn towards him strongly by their common interest in the dead.

"I don't know," said Bernardo. "I almost think I see Bardo as he was when he was young, better than that picture shows him to me as he was when he was old. Your father had a great deal of fire in his eyes when he was young. It was what I could never understand, that he, with his fiery spirit, which seemed much more impatient than mine, could hang over the books and live with shadows all his life. However, he had put his heart into that."

Bernardo gave a slight shrug as he spoke the last words; but Romola discerned in his voice a feeling that accorded with her own.

"And he was disappointed to the last," she said involuntarily. But immediately fearing lest her words should be taken to imply an accusation against Tito, she went on almost hurriedly, "If we could only see his longest, dearest wish fulfilled just to his mind!"

"Well, so we may," said Bernardo, kindly, rising and putting on his cap. "The times are cloudy now, but fish are caught by waiting. Who knows? When the wheel has turned often enough, I may be Gonfaloniere yet before I die; and no creditor can touch these things." He looked round as he spoke; then, turning to her, and patting her cheek, said, "And you need not be afraid of my dying; my ghost will claim nothing. I've taken care of that in my will."

Romola seized the hand that was against her cheek, and put it to her lips in silence.

"Haven't you been scolding your husband for keeping away from home so much lately? I see him everywhere but here," said Bernardo, willing to change the subject.

She felt the flush spread over her neck and face as she said, "He has been very much wanted; you know he speaks so well. I am glad to know that his value is understood."

"You are contented then, Madonna Orgogliosa?" said Bernardo, smiling, as he moved to the door.

"Assuredly."

Poor Romola! There was one thing that would have made the pang of disappointment in her husband harder to bear; it was, that any one should know he gave her cause for disappointment. This might be a woman's weakness, but it is closely allied to a woman's nobleness. She who willingly lifts up the veil of her married life has profaned it from a sanctuary into a vulgar place.

CHAPTER XII

THE next day Romola, like every other Florentine, was excited about the departure of the French. Besides her other reasons for gladness, she had a dim hope, which she was conscious was half superstitious, that those new anxieties about Tito, having come with the burdensome guests, might perhaps vanish with them. The French had been in Florence hardly eleven days, but in that space she had felt more acute unhappiness than she had known in her life before. Tito had adopted the hateful armour on the day of their arrival; and though she could frame no distinct notion why their departure should remove the cause of his fear,—though, when she thought of that cause, the image of the prisoner grasping him, as she had seen it in Piero's sketch, urged itself before her and excluded every other,—still, when the French were gone, she would be rid of something that was strongly associated with her pain.

Wrapped in her mantle, she waited under the loggia at the top of the house, and watched for the glimpses of the troops and the royal retinue passing the bridges on their way to the Porta San Piero, that looks towards Siena and Rome. She even returned to her station when the gates had been closed, that she might feel herself vibrating with the great peal of the bells. It was dusk then; and when at last she descended into the library, she lit her lamp with the resolution that she would overcome the agitation which had made her idle all day, and sit down to work at her copying of the catalogue. Tito had left home early in the morning, and she did not expect him yet. Before he came she intended to leave the library, and sit in the pretty saloon, with the dancing nymphs and the birds. She had done so every evening since he had objected to the library as chill and gloomy.

To her great surprise, she had not been at work long before Tito entered. Her first thought was, how cheerless he would feel in the wide darkness of this great room, with one little oil-lamp burning at the further end, and the fire nearly out. She almost ran towards him.

"Tito, dearest, I did not know you would come so soon," she said nervously, putting up her white arms to unwind his becchetto.

"I am not welcome, then," he said, with one of his brightest smiles, clasping her, but playfully holding his head back from her.

"Tito!" She uttered the word in a tone of pretty, loving reproach; and then he kissed her fondly, stroked her hair, as his manner was, and seemed not to mind about taking off his mantle yet. Romola quivered with delight. All the emotions of the day had been preparing in her a keener sensitiveness to the return of this habitual manner. "It will come back," she was saying to herself; "the old happiness will perhaps come back. He is like himself again."

Tito was taking great pains to be like himself; his heart was palpitating with anxiety.

"If I had expected you so soon," said Romola, as she at last helped him to take off his wrappings, "I would have had a little festival prepared to this joyful ringing of the bells. I did not mean to be here in the library when you came home."

"Never mind, sweet," he said carelessly. "Do not think about the fire. Come,—come and sit down."

There was a low stool against Tito's chair, and that was Romola's habitual seat when they were talking together. She rested her arm on his knee, as she used to do on her father's, and looked up at him while he spoke. He had never yet noticed the presence of the portrait, and she had not mentioned it,—thinking of it all the more.

"I have been enjoying the clang of the bells for the first time, Tito," she began. "I like being shaken and deafened by them: I fancied I was something like a Bacchante possessed by a divine rage. Are not the people looking very joyful to-night?"

"Joyful after a sour and pious fashion," said Tito, with a shrug. "But in truth, those who are left behind in Florence have little cause to be joyful: it seems to me, the most reasonable ground of gladness would be to have got out of Florence."

Tito had sounded the desired key-note without any trouble, or appearance of premeditation. He spoke with no emphasis, but he looked grave enough to make Romola ask rather anxiously,—

"Why, Tito? Are there fresh troubles?"

"No need of fresh ones, my Romola. There are three strong parties in the city, all ready to fly at each other's throats. And if the Frate's party is strong enough to frighten the other two into silence, as seems most likely, life will be as pleasant and amusing as a funeral. They have the plan of a Great Council simmering already; and if they get it, the man who sings sacred Lauds the loudest will be the most eligible for office. And besides that, the city will be so drained by the payment of this great subsidy to the French king, and by the war to get back Pisa, that the prospect would be dismal enough without the rule of fanatics. On the whole, Florence will be a delightful place for those worthies who entertain themselves in the evening by going into crypts and lashing themselves; but for everything else, the exiles have the best of it. For my own part, I have been thinking seriously that we should be wise to quit Florence, my Romola."

She started. "Tito, how could we leave Florence? Surely you do not think I could leave it—at least, not yet—not for a long while." She had turned cold and trembling, and did not find it quite easy to speak. Tito must know the reasons she had in her mind.

"That is all a fabric of your own imagination, my sweet one. Your secluded life has made you lay such false stress on a few things. You know I used to tell you, before we were married, that I wished we were somewhere else than in Florence. If you had seen more places and more people, you would know what I mean when I say that there is something in the Florentines that reminds me of their cutting spring winds. I like people who take life less eagerly; and it would be good for my Romola, too, to see a new life. I should like to dip her a little in the soft waters of forgetfulness."

He leaned forward and kissed her brow, and laid his hand on her fair hair again; but she felt his caress no more than if he had kissed a mask. She was too much agitated by the sense of the distance between their minds to be conscious that his lips touched her.

"Tito, it is not because I suppose Florence is the pleasantest place in the world that I desire not to quit it. It is because I—because we have to see my father's wish fulfilled. My godfather is old,—he is seventy-one; we could not leave it to him."

"It is precisely those superstitions which hang about your mind like bedimming clouds, my Romola, that make one great reason why I could wish we were two hundred leagues from Florence. I am obliged to take care of you in opposition to your own will: if those dear eyes, that look so tender, see falsely, I must see for them, and save my wife from wasting her life in disappointing herself by impracticable dreams."

Romola sat silent and motionless: she could not blind herself to the direction in which Tito's words pointed: he wanted to persuade her that they might get the library deposited in some monastery, or take some other ready means to rid themselves of a task, and of a tie to Florence; and she was determined never to submit her mind to his judgment on this question of duty to her father; she was inwardly prepared to encounter any sort of pain in resistance. But the determination was kept latent in these first moments by the heart-crushing sense that now at last she and Tito must be confessedly divided in their wishes. He was glad of her silence; for, much as he had feared the strength of her feeling, it was impossible for him, shut up in the narrowness that hedges in all merely clever, unimpassioned men, not to overestimate the persuasiveness of his own arguments. His conduct did not look ugly to himself, and his imagination did not suffice to show him exactly how it would look to Romola. He went on in the same gentle, remonstrating tone.

"You know, dearest,—your own clear judgment always showed you, —that the notion of isolating a collection of books and antiquities, and attaching a single name to them forever, was one that had no valid, substantial good for its object: and yet more, one that was liable to be defeated in a thousand ways. See what has become of the Medici collections! And, for my part, I consider it even blameworthy to entertain those petty views of appropriation: why should any one be reasonably glad that Florence should possess the benefits of learned research and taste more than any other city? I understand your feeling about the

wishes of the dead; but wisdom puts a limit to these sentiments, else
lives might be continually wasted in that sort of futile devotion,—like
praising deaf gods forever. You gave your life to your father while he
lived; why should you demand more of yourself?"

"Because it was a trust," said Romola, in a low but distinct voice.
"He trusted me, he trusted you, Tito. I did not expect you to feel anything else about it,—to feel as I do,—but I did expect you to feel that."

"Yes, dearest, of course I should feel it on a point where your father's
real welfare or happiness was concerned; but there is no question of
that now. If we believed in purgatory, I should be as anxious as you to
have masses said; and if I believed it could now pain your father to see
his library preserved and used in a rather different way from what
he had set his mind on, I should share the strictness of your views. But
a little philosophy should teach us to rid ourselves of those air-woven
fetters that mortals hang round themselves, spending their lives in misery under the mere imagination of weight. Your mind, which seizes
ideas so readily, my Romola, is able to discriminate between substantial good and these brain-wrought fantasies. Ask yourself, dearest, what
possible good can these books and antiquities do, stowed together under
your father's name in Florence, more than they would do if they were
divided or carried elsewhere? Nay, is not the very dispersion of such
things in hands that know how to value them, one means of extending
their usefulness? This rivalry of Italian cities is very petty and illiberal.
The loss of Constantinople was the gain of the whole civilized world."

Romola was still too thoroughly under the painful pressure of the
new revelation Tito was making of himself for her resistance to find
any strong vent. As that fluent talk fell on her ears, there was a rising
contempt within her, which only made her more conscious of her bruised,
despairing love, her love for the Tito she had married and believed in.
Her nature, possessed with the energies of strong emotion, recoiled from
this hopelessly shallow readiness which professed to appropriate the
wildest sympathies and had no pulse for the nearest. She still spoke like
one who was restrained from showing all she felt. She had only drawn
away her arm from his knee, and sat with her hands clasped before her,
cold and motionless as locked waters.

"You talk of substantial good, Tito! Are faithfulness, and love, and
sweet grateful memories no good? Is it no good that we should keep
our silent promises on which others build because they believe in our
love and truth? Is it no good that a just life should be justly honoured?
Or, is it good that we should harden our hearts against all the wants
and hopes of those who have depended on us? What good can belong
to men who have such souls? To talk cleverly, perhaps, and find soft
couches for themselves, and live and die with their base selves as their
best companions."

Her voice had gradually risen till there was a ring of scorn in the last
words. She made a slight pause; but he saw there were other words
quivering on her lips, and he chose to let them come.

"I know of no good for cities or the world if they are to be made up of such beings. But I am not thinking of other Italian cities and the whole civilized world,—I am thinking of my father, and of my love and sorrow for him, and of his just claims on us. I would give up anything else, Tito,—I would leave Florence,—what else did I live for but for him and you? But I will not give up that duty. What have I to do with your arguments? It was a yearning of *his* heart, and therefore it is a yearning of mine."

Her voice, from having been tremulous, had become full and firm. She felt that she had been urged on to say all that it was needful for her to say. She thought, poor thing, there was nothing harder to come than this struggle against Tito's suggestions as against the meaner part of herself.

He had begun to see clearly that he could not persuade her into assent: he must take another course, and show her that the time for resistance was past. That, at least, would put an end to further struggle; and if the disclosure were not made by himself to-night, to-morrow it must be made in another way. This necessity nerved his courage; and his experience of her affectionateness and unexpected submissiveness, ever since their marriage until now, encouraged him to hope that, at last, she would accommodate herself to what had been his will.

"I am sorry to hear you speak in that spirit of blind persistence, my Romola," he said quietly, "because it obliges me to give you pain. But I partly foresaw your opposition, and as a prompt decision was necessary, I avoided that obstacle and decided without consulting you. The very care of a husband for his wife's interest compels him to that separate action sometimes,—even when he has such a wife as you, my Romola."

She turned her eyes on him in breathless inquiry.

"I mean," he said, answering her look, "that I have arranged for the transfer, both of the books and of the antiquities, where they will find the highest use and value. The books have been bought for the Duke of Milan, the marbles and bronzes and the rest are going to France; and both will be protected by the stability of a great Power, instead of remaining in a city which is exposed to ruin."

Before he had finished speaking, Romola had started from her seat, and stood up looking down at him, with tightened hands falling before her, and, for the first time in her life, with a flash of fierceness in her scorn and anger.

"You have *sold* them?" she asked, as if she distrusted her ears.

"I have," said Tito, quailing a little. The scene was unpleasant,—the descending scorn already scorched him.

"You are a treacherous man!" she said, with something grating in her voice, as she looked down at him.

She was silent for a minute; and he sat still, feeling that ingenuity was powerless just now. Suddenly she turned away, and said in an agitated tone: "It may be hindered,—I am going to my godfather."

In an instant Tito started up, went to the door, locked it, and took out the key. It was time for all the masculine predominance that was latent in him to show itself. But he was not angry; he only felt that the moment was eminently unpleasant, and that when this scene was at an end he should be glad to keep away from Romola for a little while. But it was absolutely necessary first that she should be reduced to passiveness.

"Try to calm yourself a little, Romola," he said, leaning in the easiest attitude possible against a pedestal under the bust of a grim old Roman. Not that he was inwardly easy: his heart palpitated with a moral dread, against which no chain-armour could be found. He had locked in his wife's anger and scorn, but he had been obliged to lock himself in with it; and his blood did not rise with contest,—his olive cheek was perceptibly paled.

Romola had paused and turned her eyes on him as she saw him take his stand and lodge the key in his scarsella. Her eyes were flashing, and her whole frame seemed to be possessed by impetuous force that wanted to leap out in some deed. All the crushing pain of disappointment in her husband, which had made the strongest part of her consciousness a few minutes before, was annihilated by the vehemence of her indignation. She could not care in this moment that the man she was despising as he leaned there in his loathsome beauty—she could not care that he was her husband; she could only feel that she despised him. The pride and fierceness of the old Bardo blood had been thoroughly awakened in her for the first time.

"Try at least to understand the fact," said Tito, "and do not seek to take futile steps which may be fatal. It is of no use for you to go to your godfather. Messer Bernardo cannot reverse what I have done. Only sit down. You would hardly wish, if you were quite yourself, to make known to any third person what passes between us in private."

Tito knew that he had touched the right fibre there. But she did not sit down; she was too unconscious of her body voluntarily to change her attitude.

"Why can it not be reversed?" she said after a pause. "Nothing is moved yet."

"Simply because the sale has been concluded by written agreement; the purchasers have left Florence, and I hold the bonds for the purchase-money."

"If my father had suspected you of being a faithless man," said Romola, in a tone of bitter scorn, which insisted on darting out before she could say anything else, "he would have placed the library safely out of your power. But death overtook him too soon, and when you were sure his ear was deaf, and his hand stiff, you robbed him." She paused an instant, and then said with gathered passion: "Have you robbed somebody else, who is not dead? Is that the reason you wear armour?"

Romola had been driven to utter the words as men are driven to use the lash of the horsewhip. At first Tito felt horribly cowed; it seemed to him that the disgrace he had been dreading would be worse than he had imagined it. But soon there was a reaction: such power of dislike and resistance as there was within him was beginning to rise against a wife whose voice seemed like the herald of a retributive fate. Her, at least, his quick mind told him that he might master.

"It is useless," he said coolly, "to answer the words of madness, Romola. Your peculiar feeling about your father has made you mad at this moment. Any rational person looking at the case from a due distance will see that I have taken the wisest course. Apart from the influence of your exaggerated feelings on him, I am convinced that Messer Bernardo would be of that opinion."

"He would not!" said Romola. "He lives in the hope of seeing my father's wish exactly fulfilled. We spoke of it together only yesterday. He will help me yet. Who are these men to whom you have sold my father's property?"

"There is no reason why you should not be told, except that it signifies little. The Count di San Severino and the Seneschal de Beaucaire are now on their way with the king to Siena."

"They may be overtaken and persuaded to give up their purchase," said Romola, eagerly, her anger beginning to be surmounted by anxious thought.

"No, they may not," said Tito, with cool decision.

"Why?"

"Because I do not choose that they should."

"But if you were paid the money?—we will pay you the money," said Romola.

No words could have disclosed more fully her sense of alienation from Tito; but they were spoken with less of bitterness than of anxious pleading. And he felt stronger, for he saw that the first impulse of fury was past.

"No, my Romola. Understand that such thoughts as these are impracticable. You would not, in a reasonable moment, ask your godfather to bury three thousand florins in addition to what he has already paid on the library. I think your pride and delicacy would shrink from that."

She began to tremble and turn cold again with discouragement, and sank down on the carved chest near which she was standing. He went on in a clear voice, under which she shuddered, as if it had been a narrow cold stream coursing over a hot cheek.

"Moreover, it is not my will that Messer Bernardo should advance the money, even if the project were not an utterly wild one. And I beg you to consider, before you take any step or utter any word on the subject, what will be the consequences of your placing yourself in opposition to me, and trying to exhibit your husband in the odious light which your own distempered feelings cast over him. What object will you serve by injuring me with Messer Bernardo? The event is irrevocable, the library is sold, and you are my wife."

Every word was spoken for the sake of a calculated effect, for his intellect was urged into the utmost activity by the danger of the crisis. He knew that Romola's mind would take in rapidly enough all the wide meaning of his speech. He waited and watched her in silence.

She had turned her eyes from him, and was looking on the ground, and in that way she sat for several minutes. When she spoke, her voice was quite altered,—it was quiet and cold.

"I have one thing to ask."

"Ask anything that I can do without injuring us both, Romola."

"That you will give me that portion of the money which belongs to my godfather, and let me pay him."

"I must have some assurance from you, first, of the attitude you intend to take towards me."

"Do you believe in assurances, Tito?" she said, with a tinge of returning bitterness.

"From you I do."

"I will do you no harm. I shall disclose nothing. I will say nothing to pain him or you. You say truly, the event is irrevocable."

"Then I will do what you desire to-morrow morning."

"To-night, if possible," said Romola, "that we may not speak of it again."

"It is possible," he said, moving towards the lamp, while she sat still, looking away from him with absent eyes.

Presently he came and bent down over her, to put a piece of paper into her hand. "You will receive something in return, you are aware, my Romola?" he said gently, not minding so much what had passed, now he was secure; and feeling able to try and propitiate her.

"Yes," she said, taking the paper, without looking at him, "I understand."

"And you will forgive me, my Romola, when you have had time to reflect." He just touched her brow with his lips; but she took no notice, and seemed really unconscious of the act.

She was aware that he unlocked the door and went out. She moved her head and listened. The great door of the court opened and shut again. She started up as if some sudden freedom had come, and going to her father's chair where his picture was propped, fell on her knees before it, and burst into sobs.

CHAPTER XIII

BALDASSARRE MAKES AN ACQUAINTANCE

WHEN Baldassarre was wandering about Florence in search of a spare outhouse where he might have the cheapest of sheltered beds, his steps had been attracted towards that sole portion of ground within the walls of the city which is not perfectly level, and where the spectator, lifted above the roofs of the houses, can see beyond the city to the protecting hills and far-stretching valley, otherwise shut out from his view except along the welcome opening made by the course of the Arno. Part of that ground has been already seen by us as the hill of Bogoli, at that time a great stone-quarry; but the side towards which Baldassarre directed his steps was the one that sloped down behind the Via de' Bardi, and was most commonly called the hill of San Giorgio. Bratti had told him that Tito's dwelling was in the Via de' Bardi; and after surveying that street, he turned up the slope of the hill which he had observed as he was crossing the bridge. If he could find a sheltering outhouse on that hill, he would be glad; he had now for some years been accustomed to live with a broad sky about him; and, moreover, the narrow passes of the streets, with their strip of sky above, and the unknown labyrinth around them, seemed to intensify his sense of loneliness and feeble memory.

The hill was sparsely inhabited, and covered chiefly by gardens; but in one spot was a piece of rough ground jagged with great stones, which had never been cultivated since a landslip had ruined some houses there towards the end of the thirteenth century. Just above the edge of this broken ground stood a queer little square building, looking like a truncated tower roofed in with fluted tiles; and close by was a small outhouse, apparently built up against a piece of ruined stonewall. Under a large half-dead mulberry tree that was now sending its last fluttering leaves in at the open doorways a shrivelled, hardy old woman was untying a goat with two kids, and Baldassarre could see that part of the outbuilding was occupied by live-stock; but the door of the other part was open, and it was empty of everything but some tools and straw. It was just the sort of place he wanted. He spoke to the old woman; but it was not till he got close to her and shouted in her ear, that he succeeded in making her understand his want of a lodging, and his readiness to pay for it. At first he could get no answer beyond shakes of the head and the words, "No—no lodging," uttered in the muffled tone of the deaf. But, by dint of persistence, he made clear to her that he was a poor stranger from a long way over seas, and could not afford to go to hostelries; that he only wanted to lie on the straw in the outhouse, and would pay her a quattrino or two a week for that shelter. She still looked at him dubiously, shaking her head and talking low to herself; but presently, as if a new thought occurred to her, she fetched a hatchet from the house and, showing him a chump that lay half covered with litter in a corner, asked him if he would chop that up for her; if he would, he might lie in the outhouse for one night. He agreed, and Monna Lisa stood with her arms akimbo to watch him, with a smile of gratified cunning, saying low to herself,—

"It's lain there ever since my old man died. What then? I might as well have put a stone on the fire. He chops very well, though he does speak with a foreign tongue, and looks odd. I couldn't have got it done cheaper. And if he only wants a bit of straw to lie on, I might make him do an errand or two up and down the hill. Who need know? And sin that's hidden's half forgiven.[1] He's a stranger: he'll take no notice of *her*. And I'll tell her to keep her tongue still."

The antecedent to these feminine pronouns had a pair of blue eyes, which at that moment were applied to a large round hole in the shutter of the upper window. The shutter was closed, not for any penal reasons, but because only the opposite window had the luxury of glass in it: the weather was not warm, and a round hole four inches in diameter served all the purposes of observation. The hole was, unfortunately, a little too high, and obliged the small observer to stand on a low stool of a rickety character; but Tessa would have stood a long while in a much more inconvenient position for the sake of seeing a little variety in her life. She had been drawn to the opening at the first loud tones of the strange voice speaking to Monna Lisa; and darting gently across her room every now and then to peep at something, she continued to stand there until the wood had been chopped, and she saw Baldassarre enter the outhouse, as the dusk was gathering, and seat himself on the straw.

A great temptation had laid hold of Tessa's mind; she would go and take that old man part of her supper and talk to him a little. He was not deaf like Monna Lisa, and besides she could say a great many things to him that it was no use to shout at Monna Lisa, who knew them already. And he was a stranger,—strangers came from a long way off and went away again, and lived nowhere in particular. It was naughty, she knew, for obedience made the largest part in Tessa's idea of duty; but it would be something to confess to the Padre next Pasqua, and there was nothing else to confess except going to sleep sometimes over her beads, and being a little cross with Monna Lisa because she was so deaf; for she had as much idleness as she liked now, and was never frightened into telling white lies. She turned away from her shutter with rather an excited expression in her childish face, which was as pretty and pouting as ever. Her garb was still that of a simple contadina, but of a contadina prepared for a festa: her gown of dark-green serge, with its red girdle, was very clean and neat; she had the string of red glass beads round her neck; and her brown hair, rough from curliness, was duly knotted up, and fastened with the silver pin. She had but one new ornament, and she was very proud of it, for it was a fine gold ring.

Tessa sat on a low stool, nursing her knees, for a minute or two, with her little soul poised in fluttering excitement on the edge of this pleasant transgression. It was quite irresistible. She had been commanded to make no acquaintances, and warned that if she did, all her new happy lot would vanish away, and be like a hidden treasure that turned to lead as soon as it was brought to the daylight; and she had been so obedient that when she had to go to church she had kept her face

[1] The Italian proverb "Peccato celato è mezzo perdonato" means that a hidden sin is more worthy of forgiveness than a sin which is known to others.—EDITOR.

shaded by her hood and had pursed up her lips quite tightly. It was
true, her obedience had been a little helped by her own dread lest the
alarming stepfather Nofri should turn up even in this quarter, so far
from the Por' del Prato, and beat her at least, if he did not drag her
back to work for him. But this old man was not an acquaintance; he
was a poor stranger going to sleep in the outhouse, and he probably
knew nothing of stepfather Nofri; and, besides, if she took him some
supper, he would like her, and not want to tell anything about her.
Monna Lisa would say she must not go and talk to him, therefore
Monna Lisa must not be consulted. It did not signify what she found
out after it had been done.

Supper was being prepared, she knew,—a mountain of macaroni
flavoured with cheese, fragrant enough to tame any stranger. So she
tripped downstairs with a mind full of deep designs, and first asking
with an innocent look what that noise of talking had been, without
waiting for an answer knit her brow with a peremptory air, something
like a kitten trying to be formidable, and sent the old woman upstairs;
saying, she chose to eat her supper down below. In three minutes Tessa,
with her lantern in one hand and a wooden bowl of macaroni in the
other, was kicking gently at the door of the outhouse; and Baldassarre,
roused from sad revery, doubted in the first moment whether he were
awake as he opened the door and saw this surprising little handmaid,
with delight in her wide eyes, breaking in on his dismal loneliness.

"I've brought you some supper," she said, lifting her mouth towards
his ear and shouting, as if he had been deaf like Monna Lisa. "Sit
down and eat it while I stay with you."

Surprise and distrust surmounted every other feeling in Baldassarre;
but though he had no smile or word of gratitude ready, there could not
be any impulse to push away this visitant, and he sank down passively
on his straw again, while Tessa placed herself close to him, put the
wooden bowl on his lap, and set down the lantern in front of them,
crossing her hands before her, and nodding at the bowl with a significant smile, as much as to say, "Yes, you may really eat it." For in the
excitement of carrying out her deed, she had forgotten her previous
thought that the stranger would not be deaf, and had fallen into her
habitual alternative of dumb show and shouting.

The invitation was not a disagreeable one, for he had been gnawing
a remnant of dry bread, which had left plenty of appetite for anything
warm and relishing. Tessa watched the disappearance of two or three
mouthfuls without speaking, for she had thought his eyes rather fierce
at first; but now she ventured to put her mouth to his ear again and
cry,—

"I like my supper, don't you?"

It was not a smile, but rather the milder look of a dog touched by
kindness, but unable to smile, that Baldassarre turned on this round
blue-eyed thing that was caring about him.

"Yes," he said; "but I can hear well,—I'm not deaf."

"It is true; I forgot," said Tessa, lifting her hands and clasping them. "But Monna Lisa is deaf and I live with her. She's a kind old woman, and I'm not frightened at her. And we live very well; we have plenty of nice things. I can have nuts if I like. And I'm not obliged to work now. I used to have to work, and I didn't like it; but I liked feeding the mules, and I should like to see poor Giannetta, the little mule, again. We've only got a goat and two kids, and I used to talk to the goat a good deal, because there was nobody else but Monna Lisa. But now I've got something else,—can you guess what it is?"

She drew her head back, and looked with a challenging smile at Baldassarre, as if she had proposed a difficult riddle to him.

"No," said he, putting aside his bowl, and looking at her dreamily. It seemed as if this young prattling thing were some memory come back out of his own youth.

"You like me to talk to you, don't you?" said Tessa; "but you must not tell anybody. Shall I fetch you a bit of cold sausage?"

He shook his head, but he looked so mild now that Tessa felt quite at her ease.

"Well, then, I've got a little baby. Such a pretty bambinetto, with little fingers and nails! Not old yet; it was born at the Nativitá, Monna Lisa says. I was married one Nativitá, a long, long while ago, and nobody knew. O Santa Madonna! I didn't mean to tell you that!"

Tessa set up her shoulders and bit her lip, looking at Baldassarre as if this betrayal of secrets must have an exciting effect on him too. But he seemed not to care much; and perhaps that was in the nature of strangers.

"Yes," she said, carrying on her thought aloud, "you are a stranger; you don't live anywhere or know anybody, do you?"

"No," said Baldassarre, also thinking aloud, rather than consciously answering; "I only know one man."

"His name is not Nofri, is it?" said Tessa, anxiously.

"No," said Baldassarre, noticing her look of fear. "Is that your husband's name?"

That mistaken supposition was very amusing to Tessa. She laughed and clapped her hands as she said,—

"No, indeed! But I must not tell you anything about my husband. You would never think what he is,—not at all like Nofri!"

She laughed again at the delightful incongruity between the name of Nofri—which was not separable from the idea of the cross-grained step-father,—and the idea of her husband.

"But I don't see him very often," she went on, more gravely. "And sometimes I pray to the Holy Madonna to send him oftener, and once she did. But I must go back to my bimbo now. I'll bring it to show you to-morrow. You would like to see it. Sometimes it cries and makes a face, but only when it's hungry, Monna Lisa says. You wouldn't think it, but Monna Lisa had babies once, and they are all dead old men. My husband says she will never die now, because she's so well dried. I'm glad of that, for I'm fond of her. You would like to stay here to-morrow, shouldn't you?"

"I should like to have this place to come and rest in, that's all," said Baldassarre. "I would pay for it, and harm nobody."

"No, indeed; I think you are not a bad old man. But you look sorry about something. Tell me, is there anything you shall cry about when I leave you by yourself? *I* used to cry once."

"No, child; I think I shall cry no more."

"That's right; and I'll bring you some breakfast, and show you the bimbo. Good-night."

Tessa took up her bowl and lantern, and closed the door behind her. The pretty loving apparition had been no more to Baldassarre than a faint rainbow on the blackness to the man who is wrestling in deep waters. He hardly thought of her again till his dreamy waking passed into the more vivid images of disturbed sleep.

But Tessa thought much of him. She had no sooner entered the house than she told Monna Lisa what she had done, and insisted that the stranger should be allowed to come and rest in the outhouse when he liked. The old woman, who had had her notions of making him a useful tenant, made a great show of reluctance, shook her head, and urged that Messer Naldo would be angry if she let any one come about the house. Tessa did not believe that. Naldo had said nothing against strangers who lived nowhere; and this old man knew nobody except one person, who was not Nofri.

"Well," conceded Monna Lisa at last, "if I let him stay for a while and carry things up the hill for me, thou must keep thy counsel and tell nobody."

"No," said Tessa, "I'll only tell the bimbo."

"And then," Monna Lisa went on, in her thick undertone, "God may love us well enough not to let Messer Naldo find out anything about it. For he never comes here but at dark; and as he was here two days ago, it's likely he'll never come at all till the old man's gone away again."

"Oh me! Monna," said Tessa, clasping her hands, "I wish Naldo had not to go such a long, long way sometimes before he comes back again."

"Ah, child! the world's big, they say. There are places behind the mountains, and if people go night and day, night and day, they get to Rome, and see the Holy Father."

Tessa looked submissive in the presence of this mystery, and began to rock her baby, and sing syllables of vague loving meaning, in tones that imitated a triple chime.

The next morning she was unusually industrious in the prospect of more dialogue, and of the pleasure she should give the poor old stranger by showing him her baby. But before she could get ready to take Baldassarre his breakfast, she found that Monna Lisa had been employing him as a drawer of water. She deferred her Paternosters, and hurried down to insist that Baldassarre should sit on his straw, so that she might come and sit by him again while he ate his breakfast. That attitude made the new companionship all the more delightful to Tessa, for she had been used to sitting on straw in old days along with her goats and mules.

"I will not let Monna Lisa give you too much work to do," she said, bringing him some steaming broth and soft bread. "I don't like much work, and I dare say you don't. I like sitting in the sunshine and feeding things. Monna Lisa says, work is good; but she does it all herself, so I don't mind. She's not a cross old woman; you needn't be afraid of her being cross. And now, you eat that, and I'll go and fetch my baby and show it you."

Presently she came back with the small mummy-case in her arms. The mummy looked very lively, having unusually large dark eyes, though no more than the usual indication of a future nose.

"This is my baby," said Tessa, seating herself close to Baldassarre. "You didn't think it was so pretty, did you? It is like the little Gesù, and I should think the Santa Madonna would be kinder to me now, is it not true? But I have not much to ask for, because I have everything now,—only that I should see my husband oftener. You may hold the bambino a little if you like, but I think you must not kiss him, because you might hurt him."

She spoke this prohibition in a tone of soothing excuse, and Baldassarre could not refuse to hold the small package. "Poor thing! poor thing!" he said in a deep voice which had something strangely threatening in its apparent pity. It did not seem to him as if this guileless loving little woman could reconcile him to the world at all, but rather that she was with him against the world, that she was a creature who would need to be avenged.

"Oh, don't you be sorry for me," she said; "for though I don't see him often, he is more beautiful and good than anybody else in the world. I say prayers to him when he's away. You couldn't think what he is!"

She looked at Baldassarre with a wide glance of mysterious meaning, taking the baby from him again, and almost wishing he would question her as if he wanted very much to know more. "Yes, I could," said Baldassarre, rather bitterly.

"No, I'm sure you never could," said Tessa, earnestly. "You thought he might be Nofri," she added, with a triumphant air of conclusiveness. "But never mind; you couldn't know. What is your name?"

He rubbed his hand over his knitted brow, then looked at her blankly and said, "Ah, child, what is it?"

It was not that he did not often remember his name well enough; and if he had had presence of mind now to remember it, he would have chosen not to tell it. But a sudden question appealing to his memory had a paralyzing effect, and in that moment he was conscious of nothing but helplessness.

Ignorant as Tessa was, the pity stirred in her by his blank look taught her to say,—

"Never mind: you are a stranger, it is no matter about your having

a name. Good-by now, because I want my breakfast. You will come
here and rest when you like; Monna Lisa says you may. And don't you
be unhappy, for we'll be good to you."

"Poor thing!" said Baldassarre again.

CHAPTER XIV

NO PLACE FOR REPENTANCE

MESSER NALDO came again sooner than was expected: he came on the
evening of the 28th of November, only eleven days after his previous
visit, proving that he had not gone far beyond the mountains; and a
scene which we have witnessed as it took place that evening in the Via
de' Bardi may help to explain the impulse which turned his steps towards the hill of San Giorgio.

When Tito had first found this home for Tessa, on his return from
Rome, more than a year and a half ago, he had acted, he persuaded
himself, simply under the constraint imposed on him by his own kindliness after the unlucky incident which had made foolish little Tessa
imagine him to be her husband. It was true that the kindness was
manifested towards a pretty trusting thing whom it was impossible to
be near without feeling inclined to caress and pet her; but it was not
less true that Tito had movements of kindness towards her apart from
any contemplated gain to himself. Otherwise, charming as her prettiness and prattle were in a lazy moment, he might have preferred to be
free from her; for he was not in love with Tessa,—he was in love for
the first time in his life with an entirely different woman, whom he
was not simply inclined to shower caresses on, but whose presence possessed him so that the simple sweep of her long tresses across his cheek
seemed to vibrate through the hours. All the young ideal passion he
had in him had been stirred by Romola, and his fibre was too fine, his
intellect too bright, for him to be tempted into the habits of a gross
pleasure-seeker. But he had spun a web about himself and Tessa, which
he felt incapable of breaking: in the first moments after the mimic
marriage he had been prompted to leave her under an illusion by a
distinct calculation of his own possible need, but since that critical
moment it seemed to him that the web had gone on spinning itself in
spite of him, like a growth over which he had no power. The elements
of kindness and self-indulgence are hard to distinguish in a soft nature
like Tito's; and the annoyance he had felt under Tessa's pursuit of
him on the day of his betrothal, the thorough intention of revealing
the truth to her with which he set out to fulfil his promise of seeing her
again, were a sufficiently strong argument to him that in ultimately
leaving Tessa under her illusion and providing a home for her, he had
been overcome by his own kindness. And in these days of his first devotion to Romola he needed a self-justifying argument. He had learned

to be glad that she was deceived about some things. But every strong
feeling makes to itself a conscience of its own,—has its own piety; just
as much as the feeling of the son towards the mother, which will sometimes survive amid the worst fumes of depravation; and Tito could not
yet be easy in committing a secret offence against his wedded love.
But he was all the more careful in taking precautions to preserve
the secrecy of the offence. Monna Lisa, who, like many of her class,
never left her habitation except to go to one or two particular shops,
and to confession once a year, knew nothing of his real name and whereabout: she only knew that he paid her so as to make her very comfortable, and minded little about the rest, save that she got fond of
Tessa, and found pleasure in the cares for which she was paid. There
was some mystery behind, clearly, since Tessa was a contadina, and
Messer Naldo was a signor[1]; but, for aught Monna Lisa knew, he might
be a real husband. For Tito had thoroughly frightened Tessa into silence
about the circumstances of their marriage, by telling her that if she
broke that silence she would never see him again; and Monna Lisa's
deafness, which made it impossible to say anything to her without some
premeditation, had saved Tessa from any incautious revelation to her,
such as had run off her tongue in talking with Baldassarre. For a long
while Tito's visits were so rare that it seemed likely enough he took
journeys between them. They were prompted chiefly by the desire to
see that all things were going on well with Tessa; and though he always
found his visit pleasanter than the prospect of it,—always felt anew
the charm of that pretty ignorant lovingness and trust,—he had not
yet any real need of it. But he was determined, if possible, to preserve
the simplicity on which the charm depended; to keep Tessa a genuine
contadina, and not place the small field-flower among conditions that
would rob it of its grace. He would have been shocked to see her in the
dress of any other rank than her own; the piquancy of her talk would
be all gone, if things began to have new relations for her, if her world
became wider, her pleasures less childish; and the squirrel-like enjoyment of nuts at discretion marked the standard of the luxuries he had
provided for her. By this means Tito saved Tessa's charm from being
sullied; and he also, by a convenient coincidence, saved himself from
aggravating expenses that were already rather importunate to a man
whose money was all required for his avowed habits of life.

This in brief had been the history of Tito's relation to Tessa up to
a very recent date. It is true that once or twice before Bardo's death,
the sense that there was Tessa up the hill, with whom it was possible
to pass an hour agreeably, had been an inducement to him to escape
from a little weariness of the old man, when, for lack of any positive
engagement, he might otherwise have borne the weariness patiently
and shared Romola's burden. But the moment when he had first felt a
real hunger for Tessa's ignorant lovingness and belief in him had not

[1] *Signore* used in this sense is modern. The authoress should have rather used
gentiluomo.—Editor.

come till quite lately, and it was distinctly marked out by circumstances as little to be forgotten as the oncoming of a malady that has permanently vitiated the sight and hearing. It was the day when he had first seen Baldassarre, and had bought the armour. Returning across the bridge that night, with the coat of mail in his hands, he had felt an unconquerable shrinking from an immediate encounter with Romola. She, too, knew little of the actual world; she, too, trusted him; but he had an uneasy consciousness that behind her frank eyes there was a nature that could judge him, and that any ill-founded trust of hers sprang not from pretty brute-like incapacity, but from a nobleness which might prove an alarming touchstone. He wanted a little ease, a little repose from self-control, after the agitation and exertions of the day; he wanted to be where he could adjust his mind to the morrow, without caring how he behaved at the present moment. And there was a sweet, adoring creature within reach whose presence was as safe and unconstraining as that of her own kids,—who would believe any fable, and remain quite unimpressed by public opinion. And so, on that evening, when Romola was waiting and listening for him, he turned his steps up the hill.

No wonder, then, that the steps took the same course on this evening, eleven days later, when he had had to recoil under Romola's first outburst of scorn. He could not wish Tessa in his wife's place, or refrain from wishing that his wife should be thoroughly reconciled to him; for it was Romola, and not Tessa, that belonged to the world where all the larger desires of a man who had ambition and effective faculties must necessarily lie. But he wanted a refuge from a standard disagreeably rigorous, of which he could not make himself independent simply by thinking it folly; and Tessa's little soul was that inviting refuge.

It was not much more than eight o'clock when he went up the stone steps to the door of Tessa's room. Usually she heard his entrance into the house, and ran to meet him, but not to-night; and when he opened the door he saw the reason. A single dim light was burning above the dying fire, and showed Tessa in a kneeling attitude by the head of the bed where the baby lay. Her head had fallen aside on the pillow, and her brown rosary, which usually hung above the pillow over the picture of the Madonna and the golden palm-branches, lay in the loose grasp of her right hand. She had gone fast asleep over her beads. Tito stepped lightly across the little room, and sat down close to her. She had probably heard the opening of the door as part of her dream, for he had not been looking at her two moments before she opened her eyes. She opened them without any start, and remained quite motionless looking at him, as if the sense that he was there smiling at her shut out any impulse which could disturb that happy passiveness. But when he put his hand under her chin, and stooped to kiss her, she said,—

"I dreamed it, and then I said it was dreaming,—and then I awoke, and it was true."

"Little sinner!" said Tito, pinching her chin, "you have not said half your prayers. I will punish you by not looking at your baby; it is ugly."

Tessa did not like those words, even though Tito was smiling. She had some pouting distress in her face, as she said, bending anxiously over the baby,—

"Ah, it is not true! He is prettier than anything. You do not think he is ugly. You will look at him. He is even prettier than when you saw him before,—only he's asleep, and you can't see his eyes or his tongue, and I can't show you his hair—and it grows—isn't that wonderful? Look at him! It's true his face is very much all alike when he's asleep, there is not so much to see as when he's awake. If you kiss him very gently, he won't wake: you want to kiss him, is it not true?"

He satisfied her by giving the small mummy a butterfly kiss, and then putting his hand on her shoulder and turning her face towards him, said,—

"You like looking at the baby better than looking at your husband, you false one."

She was still kneeling, and now rested her hands on his knee, looking up at him like one of Fra Lippo Lippi's round-cheeked adoring angels.

"No," she said, shaking her head; "I love you always best, only I want you to look at the bambino and love him. I used only to want you to love me."

"And did you expect me to come again so soon?" said Tito, inclined to make her prattle. He still felt the effects of the agitation he had undergone,—still felt like a man who has been violently jarred; and this was the easiest relief from silence and solitude.

"Ah, no," said Tessa, "I have counted the days—to-day I began at my right thumb again—since you put on the beautiful chain-coat that Messer San Michele gave you to take care of you on your journey. And you have got it on now," she said, peeping through the opening in the breast of his tunic. "Perhaps it made you come back sooner."

"Perhaps it did, Tessa," he said. "But don't mind the coat now. Tell me what has happened since I was here. Did you see the tents in the Prato, and the soldiers and horsemen when they passed the bridges,—did you hear the drums and trumpets?"

"Yes, and I was rather frightened, because I thought the soldiers might come up here. And Monna Lisa was a little afraid too, for she said they might carry our kids off; she said it was their business to do mischief. But the Holy Madonna took care of us, for we never saw one of them up here. But something has happened, only I hardly dare tell you, and that is what I was saying more Aves for."

"What do you mean, Tessa?" said Tito, rather anxiously. "Make haste and tell me."

"Yes, but will you let me sit on your knee? because then I think I shall not be so frightened."

He took her on his knee, and put his arm round her, but looked grave: it seemed that something unpleasant must pursue him even here.

"At first I didn't mean to tell you," said Tessa, speaking almost in a whisper, as if that would mitigate the offence; "because we thought the old man would be gone away before you came again, and it would be as if it had not been. But now he is there, and you are come, and I never did anything you told me not to do before. And I want to tell you, and then you will perhaps forgive me, for it is a long while before I go to confession."

"Yes, tell me everything, my Tessa." He began to hope it was, after all, a trivial matter.

"Oh, you will be sorry for him: I'm afraid he cries about something when I don't see him. But that was not the reason I went to him first; it was because I wanted to talk to him and show him my baby, and he was a stranger that lived nowhere, and I thought you wouldn't care so much about my talking to him. And I think he is not a bad old man, and he wanted to come and sleep on the straw next to the goats, and I made Monna Lisa say, 'Yes, he might,' and he's away all the day almost; but when he comes back I talk to him, and take him something to eat."

"Some beggar, I suppose. It was naughty of you, Tessa, and I am angry with Monna Lisa. I must have him sent away."

"No, I think he is not a beggar, for he wanted to pay Monna Lisa, only she asked him to do work for her instead. And he gets himself shaved, and his clothes are tidy: Monna Lisa says he is a decent man. But sometimes I think he is not in his right mind: Lupo, at Peretola, was not in his right mind, and he looks a little like Lupo sometimes, as if he didn't know where he was."

"What sort of face has he?" said Tito, his heart beginning to beat strangely. He was so haunted by the thought of Baldassarre, that it was already he whom he saw in imagination sitting on the straw not many yards from him. "Fetch your stool, my Tessa, and sit on it."

"Shall you not forgive me?" she said timidly, moving from his knee.

"Yes, I will not be angry,—only sit down, and tell me what sort of old man this is."

"I can't think how to tell you: he is not like my stepfather Nofri, or anybody. His face is yellow, and he has deep marks in it; and his hair is white, but there is none on the top of his head: and his eyebrows are black, and he looks from under them at me, and says, 'Poor thing!' to me, as if he thought I was beaten as I used to be; and that seems as if he couldn't be in his right mind, doesn't it? And I asked him his name once, but he couldn't tell me; yet everybody has a name,—is it not true? And he has a book now, and keeps looking at it ever so long, as if he were a Padre. But I think he is not saying prayers, for his lips never move;—ah, you are angry with me, or is it because you are sorry for the old man?"

Tito's eyes were still fixed on Tessa; but he had ceased to see her, and was only seeing the objects her words suggested. It was this absent glance which frightened her, and she could not help going to kneel at his side again. But he did not heed her, and she dared not touch him or speak to him: she knelt, trembling and wondering; and this state of mind suggesting her beads to her, she took them from the floor, and began to tell them again, her pretty lips moving silently, and her blue eyes wide with anxiety and struggling tears.

Tito was quite unconscious of her movements, unconscious of his own attitude; he was in that rapt state in which a man will grasp painful roughness, and press and press it closer, and never feel it. A new possibility had risen before him which might dissolve at once the wretched conditions of fear and suppression that were marring his life. Destiny had brought within his reach an opportunity of retrieving that moment on the steps of the Duomo, when the Past had grasped him with living quivering hands, and he had disowned it. A few steps, and he might be face to face with his father, with no witness by; he might seek forgiveness and reconciliation; and there was money now, from the sale of the library, to enable them to leave Florence without disclosure, and go into Southern Italy, where under the probable French rule he had already laid a foundation for patronage. Romola need never know the whole truth, for she could have no certain means of identifying that prisoner in the Duomo with Baldassarre, or of learning what had taken place on the steps, except from Baldassarre himself; and if his father forgave, he would also consent to bury that offence.

But with this possibility of relief, by an easy spring, from present evil, there rose the other possibility, that the fierce-hearted man might refuse to be propitiated. Well—and if he did, things would only be as they had been before; for there would be *no witness by*. It was not repentance with a white sheet round it and taper in hand, confessing its hated sin in the eyes of men, that Tito was preparing for: it was a repentance that would make all things pleasant again, and keep all past unpleasant things secret. And Tito's soft-heartedness, his indisposition to feel himself in harsh relations with any creature, was in strong activity towards his father, now his father was brought near to him. It would be a state of ease that his nature could not but desire, if the poisonous hatred in Baldassarre's glance could be replaced by something of the old affection and complacency.

Tito longed to have his world once again completely cushioned with good-will, and longed for it the more eagerly because of what he had just suffered from the collision with Romola. It was not difficult to him to smile pleadingly on those whom he had injured, and offer to do them much kindness: and no quickness of intellect could tell him exactly the taste of that honey on the lips of the injured. The opportunity was there, and it raised an inclination which hemmed in the calculating activity of his thought. He started up, and stepped towards the door; but Tessa's cry, as she dropped her beads, roused him from his absorption. He turned and said,—

"My Tessa, get me a lantern; and don't cry, little pigeon, I am not angry."

They went down the stairs, and Tessa was going to shout the need of the lantern in Monna Lisa's ear, when Tito, who had opened the door, said: "Stay, Tessa—no, I want no lantern: go upstairs again, and keep quiet, and say nothing to Monna Lisa."

In half a minute he stood before the closed door of the outhouse, where the moon was shining white on the old paintless wood.

In this last decisive moment Tito felt a tremor upon him,—a sudden instinctive shrinking from a possible tiger-glance, a possible tiger-leap. Yet why should he, a young man, be afraid of an old one? a young man with armour on, of an old man without a weapon? It was but a moment's hesitation, and Tito laid his hand on the door. Was his father asleep? Was there nothing else but the door that screened him from the voice and the glance which no magic could turn into ease?

Baldassarre was not asleep. There was a square opening high in the wall of the hovel, through which the moonbeams sent in a stream of pale light; and if Tito could have looked through the opening, he would have seen his father seated on the straw, with something that shone like a white star in his hand. Baldassarre was feeling the edge of his poniard, taking refuge in that sensation from a hopeless blank of thought that seemed to lie like a great gulf between his passion and its aim.

He was in one of his most wretched moments of conscious helplessness: he had been poring, while it was light, over the book that lay open beside him: then he had been trying to recall the names of his jewels, and the symbols engraved on them; and though at certain other times he had recovered some of those names and symbols, to-night they were all gone into darkness. And this effort at inward seeing had seemed to end in utter paralysis of memory. He was reduced to a sort of mad consciousness that he was a solitary pulse of just rage in a world filled with defiant baseness. He had clutched and unsheathed his dagger, and for a long while had been feeling its edge, his mind narrowed to one image, and the dream of one sensation,—the sensation of plunging that dagger into a base heart, which he was unable to pierce in any other way.

Tito had his hand on the door and was pulling it: it dragged against the ground, as such old doors often do; and Baldassarre, startled out of his dreamlike state, rose from his sitting posture in vague amazement, not knowing where he was. He had not yet risen to his feet, and was still kneeling on one knee, when the door came wide open, and he saw, dark against the moonlight, with the rays falling on one bright mass of curls and one rounded olive cheek, the image of his revery,—not shadowy,—close and real like water at the lips after the thirsty dream of it. No thought could come athwart that eager thirst. In one moment, before Tito could start back, the old man, with the preternatural force of rage in his limbs, had sprung forward, and the dagger had flashed out. In the next moment the dagger had snapped in two; and Baldassarre, under the parrying force of Tito's arm, had fallen back on the straw, clutching the hilt with its bit of broken blade. The pointed end lay shining against Tito's feet.

Tito had felt one great heart-leap of terror as he had staggered under the weight of the thrust: he felt now the triumph of deliverance and safety. His armour had been proved, and vengeance lay helpless before him. But the triumph raised no devilish impulse; on the contrary, the sight of his father close to him and unable to injure him made the effort at reconciliation easier. He was free from fear, but he had only the more unmixed and direct want to be free from the sense that he was hated. After they had looked at each other a little while, Baldassarre lying motionless in despairing rage, Tito said in his soft tones, just as they had sounded before the last parting on the shores of Greece,—

"Padre mio!" There was a pause after those words, but no movement or sound till he said,—

"I came to ask your forgiveness!"

Again he paused, that the healing balm of those words might have time to work. But there was no sign of change in Baldassarre: he lay as he had fallen, leaning on one arm: he was trembling, but it was from the shock that had thrown him down.

"I was taken by surprise that morning. I wish now to be a son to you again. I wish to make the rest of your life happy, that you may forget what you have suffered."

He paused again. He had used the clearest and strongest words he could think of. It was useless to say more, until he had some sign that Baldassarre understood him. Perhaps his mind was too distempered or too imbecile even for that; perhaps the shock of his fall and his disappointed rage might have quite suspended the use of his faculties.

Presently Baldassarre began to move. He threw away the broken dagger, and slowly and gradually, still trembling, began to raise himself from the ground. Tito put out his hand to help him; and so strangely quick are men's souls that in this moment, when he began to feel his atonement was accepted, he had a darting thought of the irksome efforts it entailed. Baldassarre clutched the hand that was held out, raised himself and clutched it still, going close up to Tito till their faces were not a foot off each other. Then he began to speak, in a deep trembling voice.

"I saved you—I nurtured you—I loved you. You forsook me—you robbed me—you denied me. What can you give me? You have made the world bitterness to me: but there is one draught of sweetness left,— *that you shall know agony.*"

He let fall Tito's hand, and going backwards a little, first rested his arm on a projecting stone in the wall, and then sank again in a sitting posture on the straw. The outleap of fury in the dagger-thrust had evidently exhausted him.

Tito stood silent. If it had been a deep yearning emotion which had brought him to ask his father's forgiveness, the denial of it might have caused him a pang which would have excluded the rushing train of thought that followed those decisive words. As it was, though the sentence of unchangeable hatred grated on him and jarred him terribly, his mind glanced round with a self-preserving instinct to see how far those words could have the force of a substantial threat. When he had come down to speak to Baldassarre, he had said to himself that if his effort at reconciliation failed, things would only be as they had been before. The first glance of his mind was backward to that thought again, but the future possibilities of danger that were conjured up along with it brought the perception that things were *not* as they had been before, and the perception came as a triumphant relief. There was not only the broken dagger, there was the certainty, from what Tessa had told him, that Baldassarre's mind was broken too, and had no edge that could reach him. Tito felt he had no choice now: he must defy Baldassarre as a mad, imbecile old man; and the chances were so strongly on his side that there was hardly room for fear. No; except the fear of having to do many unpleasant things in order to save himself from what was yet more unpleasant. And one of those unpleasant things must be done immediately: it was very difficult.

"Do you mean to stay here?" he said.

"No," said Baldassarre, bitterly, "you mean to turn me out."

"Not so," said Tito; "I only ask."

"I tell you, you have turned me out. If it is your straw, you turned me off it three years ago."

"Then you mean to leave this place?" said Tito, more anxious about this certainty than the ground of it.

"I have spoken," said Baldassarre.

Tito turned and re-entered the house. Monna Lisa was nodding; he went up to Tessa, and found her crying by the side of her baby.

"Tessa," he said, sitting down and taking her head between his hands; "leave off crying, little goose, and listen to me."

He lifted her chin upward, that she might look at him, while he spoke very distinctly and emphatically.

"You must never speak to that old man again. He is a mad old man, and he wants to kill me. Never speak to him or listen to him again."

Tessa's tears had ceased, and her lips were pale with fright.

"Is he gone away?" she whispered.

"He will go away. Remember what I have said to you."

"Yes; I will never speak to a stranger any more," said Tessa, with a sense of guilt.

He told her, to comfort her, that he would come again to-morrow; and then went down to Monna Lisa to rebuke her severely for letting a dangerous man come about the house.

Tito felt that these were odious tasks; they were very evil-tasted morsels, but they were forced upon him. He heard Monna Lisa fasten the door behind him, and turned away, without looking towards the open door of the hovel. He felt secure that Baldassarre would go, and he could not wait to see him go. Even *his* young frame and elastic spirit were shattered by the agitations that had been crowded into this single evening.

Baldassarre was still sitting on the straw when the shadow of Tito passed by. Before him lay the fragments of the broken dagger; beside him lay the open book, over which he had pored in vain. They looked like mocking symbols of his utter helplessness; and his body was still too trembling for him to rise and walk away.

But the next morning very early, when Tessa peeped anxiously through the hole in the shutter, the door of the hovel was open, and the strange old man was gone.

CHAPTER XV

WHAT FLORENCE WAS THINKING OF

FOR several days Tito saw little of Romola. He told her gently, the next morning, that it would be better for her to remove any small articles of her own from the library, as there would be agents coming to pack up the antiquities. Then, leaning to kiss her on the brow, he suggested that she should keep in her own room where the little painted tabernacle was, and where she was then sitting, so that she might be away from the noise of strange footsteps. Romola assented quietly, making no sign of emotion: the night had been one long waking to her, and, in spite of her healthy frame, sensation had become a dull continuous pain, as if she had been stunned and bruised. Tito divined that she felt ill, but he dared say no more; he only dared, perceiving that her hand and brow were stone cold, to fetch a furred mantle and throw it lightly round her. And in every brief interval that he returned to her, the scene was nearly the same: he tried to propitiate her by some unobtrusive act or word of tenderness, and she seemed to have lost the power of speaking to him, or of looking at him. "Patience!" he said to himself. "She will recover it, and forgive at last. The tie to me must still remain the strongest." When the stricken person is slow to recover and look as if nothing had happened, the striker easily glides into the position of the aggrieved party; he feels no bruise himself, and is strongly conscious of his own amiable behaviour since he inflicted the blow. But Tito was not naturally disposed to feel himself aggrieved; the constant bent of his mind was towards propitiation, and he would have submitted to much for the sake of feeling Romola's hand resting on his head again, as it did that morning when he first shrank from looking at her.

But he found it the less difficult to wait patiently for the return of his home happiness, because his life out of doors was more and more interesting to him. A course of action which is in strictness a slowly prepared outgrowth of the entire character, is yet almost always traceable to a single impression as its point of apparent origin; and since that moment in the Piazza del Duomo, when Tito, mounted on the bales, had tasted a keen pleasure in the consciousness of his ability to tickle the ears of men with any phrases that pleased them, his imagination had glanced continually towards a sort of political activity which the troubled public life of Florence was likely enough to find occasion for. But the fresh dread of Baldassarre, waked in the same moment, had lain like an immovable rocky obstruction across that path, and had urged him into the sale of the library, as a preparation for the possible necessity of leaving Florence, at the very time when he was beginning to feel that it had a new attraction for him. That dread was nearly removed now: he must wear his armour still, he must prepare himself for possible demands on his coolness and ingenuity, but he did not feel obliged to take the inconvenient step of leaving Florence and seeking new fortunes. His father had refused the offered atonement,—had forced him into defiance; and an old man in a strange place, with his memory gone, was weak enough to be defied.

Tito's implicit desires were working themselves out now in very explicit thoughts. As the freshness of young passion faded, life was taking more and more decidedly for him the aspect of a game in which there was an agreeable mingling of skill and chance.

And the game that might be played in Florence promised to be rapid and exciting; it was a game of revolutionary and party struggle, sure to include plenty of that unavowed action in which brilliant ingenuity, able to get rid of all inconvenient beliefs except that "ginger is hot in the mouth," is apt to see the path of superior wisdom.

No sooner were the French guests gone, than Florence was as agitated as a colony of ants when an alarming shadow has been removed, and the camp has to be repaired. "How are we to raise the money for the French king? How are we to manage the war with those obstinate Pisan rebels? Above all, how are we to mend our plan of government, so as to hit on the best way of getting our magistrates chosen and our laws voted?" Till those questions were well answered trade was in danger of standing still, and that large body of the workingmen who were not counted as citizens and had not so much as a vote to serve as an anodyne to their stomachs were likely to get impatient. Something must be done.

And first the great bell was sounded, to call the citizens to a parliament in the Piazza de' Signori; and when the crowd was wedged close, and hemmed in by armed men at all the outlets, the Signoria (or Gonfaloniere and eight Priors for the time being) came out and stood by the stone lion on the platform in front of the Old Palace, and proposed that twenty chief men of the city should have dictatorial authority given them, by force of which they should for one year choose all magistrates, and set the frame of government in order. And the people shouted their assent, and felt themselves the electors of the Twenty.

This kind of "Parliament" was a very old Florentine fashion, by which the will of the few was made to seem the choice of the many.

The shouting in the piazza was soon at an end, but not so the debating inside the palace: was Florence to have a Great Council after the Venetian mode, where all the officers of government might be elected, and all laws voted by a wide number of citizens of a certain age and of ascertained qualifications, without question of rank or party? or was it to be governed on a narrower and less popular scheme, in which the hereditary influence of good families would be less adulterated with the votes of shopkeepers? Doctors of law disputed day after day, and far into the night. Messer Pagolantonio Soderini alleged excellent reasons on the side of the popular scheme; Messer Guidantonio Vespucci alleged reasons equally excellent on the side of a more aristocratic form. It was a question of boiled or roast, which had been prejudged by the palates of the disputants; and the excellent arguing might have been protracted a long while without any other result than that of deferring the cooking. The majority of the men inside the palace, having power already in their hands, agreed with Vespucci, and thought change should be moderate; the majority outside the palace, conscious of little power and many grievances, were less afraid of change.

And there was a force outside the palace which was gradually tending to give the vague desires of that majority the character of a determinate will. That force was the preaching of Savonarola. Impelled partly by the spiritual necessity that was laid upon him to guide the people, and partly by the prompting of public men who could get no measures carried without his aid, he was rapidly passing in his daily sermons from the general to the special,—from telling his hearers that they must postpone their private passions and interests to the public good, to telling them precisely what sort of government they must have in order to promote that good,—from "Choose whatever is best for all," to "Choose the Great Council," and "The Great Council is the will of God."

To Savonarola these were as good as identical propositions. The Great Council was the only practicable plan for giving an expression to the public will large enough to counteract the vitiating influence of party interests: it was a plan that would make honest impartial public action at least possible. And the purer the government of Florence would become—the more secure from the designs of men who saw their own advantage in the moral debasement of their fellows—the nearer would the Florentine people approach the character of a pure community, worthy to lead the way in the renovation of the Church and the world. And Fra Girolamo's mind never stopped short of that sublimest end: the objects towards which he felt himself working had always the same moral magnificence. He had no private malice,—he sought no petty gratification. Even in the last terrible days, when ignominy, torture, and the fear of torture had laid bare every hidden weakness of his soul, he could say to his importunate judges: "Do not wonder if it seems to you that I have told but few things; for my purposes were few and great."

CHAPTER XVI

ARIADNE DISCROWNS HERSELF

IT was more than three weeks before the contents of the library were all packed and carried away. And Romola, instead of shutting her eyes and ears, had watched the process. The exhaustion consequent on violent emotion is apt to bring a dreamy disbelief in the reality of its cause; and in the evening, when the workmen were gone, Romola took her hand-lamp and walked slowly round among the confusion of straw and wooden cases, pausing at every vacant pedestal, every well-known object laid prostrate, with a sort of bitter desire to assure herself that there was a sufficient reason why her love was gone and the world was barren for her. And still, as the evenings came, she went and went again; no longer to assure herself, but because this vivifying of pain and despair about her father's memory was the strongest life left to her affections. On the 23d of December she knew that the last packages were going. She ran to the loggia at the top of the house, that she might not lose the last pang of seeing the slow wheels move across the bridge.

It was a cloudy day, and nearing dusk. Arno ran dark and shivering; the hills were mournful; and Florence with its girdling stone towers had that silent, tomb-like look, which unbroken shadow gives to a city seen from above. Santa Croce, where her father lay, was dark amidst that darkness; and slowly crawling over the bridge, and slowly vanishing up the narrow street, was the white load, like a cruel, deliberate Fate carrying away her father's lifelong hope to bury it in an unmarked grave. Romola felt less that she was seeing this herself than that her father was conscious of it as he lay helpless under the imprisoning stones, where her hand could not reach his to tell him that he was not alone.

She stood still even after the load had disappeared, heedless of the cold, and soothed by the gloom which seemed to cover her like a mourning garment and shut out the discord of joy—when suddenly the great bell in the palace-tower rang out a mighty peal; not the hammer-sound of alarm, but an agitated peal of triumph; and one after another every other bell in every other tower seemed to catch the vibration and join the chorus. And as the chorus swelled and swelled till the air seemed made of sound, little flames, vibrating too, as if the sound had caught fire, burst out between the turrets of the palace and on the girdling towers.

That sudden clang, that leaping light, fell on Romola like sharp wounds. They were the triumph of demons at the success of her husband's treachery, and the desolation of her life. Little more than three weeks ago she had been intoxicated with the sound of those very bells; and in the gladness of Florence she had heard a prophecy of her own gladness. But now the general joy seemed cruel to her: she stood aloof from that common life,—that Florence which was flinging out its loud exultation to stun the ears of sorrow and loneliness. She could never join hands with gladness again, but only with those whom it was in the hard nature of gladness to forget. And in her bitterness she felt that all rejoicing was mockery. Men shouted pæans with their souls full of heaviness, and then looked in their neighbours' faces to see if there was really such a thing as joy. Romola had lost her belief in the happiness she had once thirsted for: it was a hateful, smiling, soft-handed thing with a narrow, selfish heart.

She ran down from the loggia, with her hands pressed against her ears, and was hurrying across the antechamber, when she was startled by unexpectedly meeting her husband, who was coming to seek her.

His step was elastic, and there was a radiance of satisfaction about him not quite usual.

"What! the noise was a little too much for you?" he said; for Romola, as she started at the sight of him, had pressed her hands all the closer against her ears. He took her gently by the wrist, and drew her arm within his, leading her into the saloon surrounded with the dancing nymphs and fauns, and then went on speaking: "Florence is gone quite mad at getting its Great Council, which is to put an end to all the evils under the sun, especially to the vice of merriment. You may well look stunned, my Romola, and you are cold. You must not stay so late under that windy loggia without wrappings. I was coming to tell you that I am suddenly called to Rome about some learned business for Bernardo Rucellai. I am going away immediately, for I am to join my party at San Gaggio to-night, that we may start early in the morning. I need give you no trouble; I have had my packages made already. It will not be very long before I am back again."

He knew he had nothing to expect from her but quiet endurance of what he said and did. He could not even venture to kiss her brow this evening, but just pressed her hand to his lips, and left her. Tito felt that Romola was a more unforgiving woman than he had imagined; her love was not that sweet clinging instinct, stronger than all judgments, which, he began to see now, made the great charm of a wife. Still, this petrified coldness was better than a passionate, futile opposition. Her pride and capability of seeing where resistance was useless had their convenience.

But when the door had closed on Tito, Romola lost the look of cold immobility which came over her like an inevitable frost whenever he approached her. Inwardly she was very far from being in a state of quiet endurance, and the days that had passed since the scene which had divided her from Tito had been days of active planning and preparation for the fulfillment of a purpose.

The first thing she did now was to call old Maso to her.

"Maso," she said in a decided tone, "we take our journey to-morrow morning. We shall be able now to overtake that first convoy of cloth, while they are waiting at San Piero. See about the two mules to-night, and be ready to set off with them at break of day, and wait for me at Trespiano."

She meant to take Maso with her as far as Bologna, and then send him back with letters to her godfather and Tito, telling them that she was gone and never meant to return. She had planned her departure so that its secrecy might be perfect, and her broken love and life be hidden away unscanned by vulgar eyes. Bernardo del Nero had been absent at his villa, willing to escape from political suspicions to his favourite occupation of attending to his land, and she had paid him the debt without a personal interview. He did not even know that the library was sold, and was left to conjecture that some sudden piece of good fortune had enabled Tito to raise this sum of money. Maso had been taken into her confidence only so far that he knew her intended journey was a secret; and to do just what she told him was the thing he cared most for in his withered wintry age.

Romola did not mean to go to bed that night. When she had fastened the door, she took her taper to the carved and painted chest which contained her wedding-clothes. The white silk and gold lay there, the long white veil and the circlet of pearls. A great sob rose as she looked at them: they seemed the shroud of her dead happiness. In a tiny gold loop of the circlet a sugar-plum had lodged,—a pink hailstone from the shower of sweets: Tito had detected it first, and had said that it should always remain there. At certain moments—and this was one of them—Romola was carried, by a sudden wave of memory, back again into the time of perfect trust, and felt again the presence of the husband whose love made the world as fresh and wonderful to her as to a little child that sits in stillness among the sunny flowers: heard the gentle tones and saw the soft eyes without any lie in them, and breathed again that large freedom of the soul which comes from the faith that the being who is nearest to us is greater than ourselves. And in those brief moments the tears always rose: the woman's lovingness felt something akin to what the bereaved mother feels when the tiny fingers seem to lie warm on her bosom, and yet are marble to her lips as she bends over the silent bed.

But there was something else lying in the chest besides the wedding-clothes: it was something dark and coarse, rolled up in a close bundle. She turned away her eyes from the white and gold to the dark bundle; and as her hands touched the serge, her tears began to be checked. That coarse roughness recalled her fully to the present, from which love and delight were gone. She unfastened the thick white cord, and spread the bundle out on the table. It was the grey serge dress of a sister belonging to the third order of St. Francis, living in the world, but especially devoted to deeds of piety,—a personage whom the Florentines were accustomed to call a Pinzochera. Romola was going to put on this dress as a disguise; and she determined to put it on at once, so that, if she needed sleep before the morning, she might wake up in perfect readiness to be gone. She put off her black garment; and as she thrust her soft white arms into the harsh sleeves of the serge mantle, and felt the hard girdle of rope hurt her fingers as she tied it, she courted those rude sensations: they were in keeping with her new scorn of that thing called pleasure which made men base,—that dexterous contrivance for selfish ease, that shrinking from endurance and strain, when others were bowing beneath burdens too heavy for them, which now made one image with her husband. Then she gathered her long hair together, drew it away tight from her face, bound it in a great hard knot at the back of her head, and taking a square piece of black silk, tied it in the fashion of a kerchief close across her head and under her chin; and over that she drew the cowl. She lifted the candle to the mirror. Surely her disguise would be complete to any one who had not lived very near to her. To herself she looked strangely like her brother Dino: the full oval of the cheek had only to be wasted; the eyes, already sad, had only to become a little sunken. Was she getting more like him in anything else? Only in this, that she understood now how men could be prompted to rush away forever from earthly delights, how they could be prompted to dwell on images of sorrow rather than of beauty and joy.

But she did not linger at the mirror: she set about collecting and packing all the relics of her father and mother that were too large to be carried in her small travelling-wallet. They were all to be put in the chest along with her wedding-clothes, and the chest was to be committed to her godfather when she was safely gone. First she laid in the portraits; then one by one every little thing that had a sacred memory clinging to it was put into her wallet or into the chest. She paused. There was still something else to be stript away from her, belonging to that past on which she was going to turn her back forever. She put her thumb and her forefinger to her betrothal ring; but they rested there, without drawing it off. Romola's mind had been rushing with an impetuous current towards this act, for which she was preparing: the act of quitting a husband who had disappointed all her trust, the act of breaking an outward tie that no longer represented the inward bond of love. But that force of outward symbols by which our active life is knit together so as to make an inexorable external identity for us, not to be shaken by our wavering consciousness, gave a strange effect to this simple movement towards taking off her ring,—a movement which was but a small sequence of her energetic resolution. It brought a vague but arresting sense that she was somehow violently rending her life in two: a presentiment that the strong impulse which had seemed to exclude doubt and make her path clear might after all be blindness, and that there was something in human bonds which must prevent them from being broken with the breaking of illusions.

If that beloved Tito who had placed the betrothal ring on her finger was not in any valid sense the same Tito whom she had ceased to love, why should she return to him the sign of their union, and not rather retain it as a memorial? And this act, which came as a palpable demonstration of her own and his identity, had a power unexplained to herself, of shaking Romola. It is the way with half the truth amidst which we live, that it only haunts us and makes dull pulsations that are never born into sound. But there was a passionate voice speaking within her that presently nullified all such muffled murmurs.

"It cannot be! I cannot be subject to him. He is false. I shrink from him. I despise him!"

She snatched the ring from her finger, and laid it on the table against the pen with which she meant to write. Again she felt that there could be no law for her but the law of her affections. That tenderness and keen fellow-feeling for the near and the loved which are the main outgrowth of the affections, had made the religion of her life: they had made her patient in spite of natural impetuosity; they would have sufficed to make her heroic. But now all that strength was gone, or, rather, it was converted into the strength of repulsion. She had recoiled from Tito in proportion to the energy of that young belief and love which he had disappointed, of that lifelong devotion to her father against which he had commited an irredeemable offence. And it seemed as if all motive had slipped away from her, except the indignation and scorn that made her tear herself asunder from him.

She was not acting after any precedent, or obeying any adopted maxims. The grand severity of the stoical philosophy in which her father had taken care to instruct her, was familiar enough to her ears and lips, and its lofty spirit had raised certain echoes within her; but she had never used it, never needed it as a rule of life. She had endured and forborne because she loved: maxims which told her to feel less, and not to cling close lest the onward course of great Nature should jar her, had been as powerless on her tenderness as they had been on her father's yearning for just fame. She had appropriated no theories: she had simply felt strong in the strength of affection, and life without that energy came to her as an entirely new problem.

She was going to solve the problem in a way that seemed to her very simple. Her mind had never yet bowed to any obligation apart from personal love and reverence; she had no keen sense of any other human relations, and all she had to obey now was the instinct to sever herself from the man she loved no longer.

Yet the unswerving resolution was accompanied with continually varying phases of anguish. And now that the active preparation for her departure was almost finished, she lingered: she deferred writing the irrevocable words of parting from all her little world. The emotions of the past weeks seemed to rush in again with cruel hurry, and take possession even of her limbs. She was going to write, and her hand fell. Bitter tears came now at the delusion which had blighted her young years: tears very different from the sob of remembered happiness with which she had looked at the circlet of pearls and the pink hailstone. And now she felt a tingling shame at the words of ignominy she had cast at Tito,—"Have you robbed some one else who is *not* dead?" To have had such words wrung from her, to have uttered them to her husband, seemed a degradation of her whole life. Hard speech between those who have loved is hideous in the memory, like the sight of greatness and beauty sunk into vice and rags.

That heart-cutting comparison of the present with the past urged itself upon Romola till it even transformed itself into wretched sensations: she seemed benumbed to everything but inward throbbings, and began to feel the need of some hard contact. She drew her hands tight along the harsh knotted cord that hung from her waist. She started to her feet and seized the rough lid of the chest: there was nothing else to go in? No. She closed the lid, pressing her hand upon the rough carving, and locked it.

Then she remembered that she had still to complete her equipment as a Pinzochera. The large leather purse or scarsella, with small coin in it, had to be hung on the cord at her waist (her florins and small jewels, presents from her godfather and cousin Brigida, were safely fastened within her serge mantle), and on the other side must hang the rosary.

It did not occur to Romola, as she hung that rosary by her side, that something else besides the mere garb would perhaps be necessary to enable her to pass as a Pinzochera, and that her whole air and expression were as little as possible like those of a sister whose eyelids were used to be bent, and whose lips were used to move in silent iteration. Her inexperience prevented her from picturing distant details, and it helped her proud courage in shutting out any foreboding of danger and insult. She did not know that any Florentine woman had ever done exactly what she was going to do: unhappy wives often took refuge with their friends or in the cloister, she knew, but both those courses were impossible to her; she had invented a lot for herself,—to go to the most learned woman in the world, Cassandra Fedele, at Venice, and ask her how an instructed woman could support herself in a lonely life there.

She was not daunted by the practical difficulties in the way or the dark uncertainty at the end. Her life could never be happy any more, but it must not, could not, be ignoble. And by a pathetic mixture of childish romance with her woman's trials, the philosophy which had nothing to do with this great decisive deed of hers had its place in her imagination of the future: so far as she conceived her solitary loveless life at all, she saw it animated by a proud stoical heroism, and by an indistinct but strong purpose of labour, that she might be wise enough to write something which would rescue her father's name from oblivion.

After all, she was only a young girl,—this poor Romola, who had found herself at the end of her joys.

There were other things yet to be done. There was a small key in a casket on the table,—but now Romola perceived that her taper was dying out, and she had forgotten to provide herself with any other light. In a few moments the room was in total darkness. Feeling her way to the nearest chair, she sat down to wait for the morning.

Her purpose in seeking the key had called up certain memories which had come back upon her during the past week with the new vividness that remembered words always have for us when we have learned to give them a new meaning. Since the shock of the revelation which had seemed to divide her forever from Tito, that last interview with Dino had never been for many hours together out of her mind. And it solicited her all the more because while its remembered images pressed upon her almost with the imperious force of sensations, they raised struggling thoughts which resisted their influence. She could not prevent herself from hearing inwardly the dying prophetic voice saying again and again: "The man whose face was a blank loosed thy hand and departed; and as he went, I could see his face, and it was the face of the great Tempter. . . . And thou, Romola, didst wring thy hands and seek for water, and there was none . . . and the plain was bare and stony again, and thou wast alone in the midst of it. And then it seemed that the night fell, and I saw no more." She could not prevent herself from dwelling with a sort of agonized fascination on the wasted face, on the straining gaze at the crucifix, on the awe which had compelled her to kneel, on the last broken words, and then the unbroken silence,—on all the details of the death-scene, which had seemed like a sudden opening into a world apart from that of her lifelong knowledge.

But her mind was roused to resistance of impressions that, from being obvious phantoms, seemed to be getting solid in the daylight. As a strong body struggles against fumes with the more violence when they begin to be stifling, a strong soul struggles against fantasies with all the more alarmed energy when they threaten to govern in the place of thought.

What had the words of that vision to do with her real sorrows? That fitting of certain words was a mere chance; the rest was all vague,— nay, those words themselves were vague; they were determined by nothing but her brother's memories and beliefs. He believed there was something fatal in pagan learning; he believed that celibacy was more holy than marriage; he remembered their home, and all the objects in the library; and of these threads the vision was woven. What reasonable warrant could she have had for believing in such a vision and acting on it? None. True as the voice of foreboding had proved, Romola saw with unshaken conviction that to have renounced Tito in obedience to a warning like that would have been meagre-hearted folly. Her trust had been delusive, but she would have chosen over again to have acted on it rather than be a creature led by phantoms and disjointed whispers in a world where there was the large music of reasonable speech, and the warm grasp of living hands.

But the persistent presence of these memories, linking themselves in her imagination with her actual lot, gave her a glimpse of understanding into the lives which had before lain utterly aloof from her sympathy,— the lives of the men and women who were led by such inward images and voices.

"If they were only a little stronger in me," she said to herself, "I should lose the sense of what that vision really was, and take it for a prophetic light. I might in time get to be a seer of visions myself, like the Suora Maddalena, and Camilla Rucellai, and the rest."

Romola shuddered at the possibility. All the instruction, all the main influences of her life had gone to fortify her scorn of that sickly superstition which led men and women, with eyes too weak for the daylight, to sit in dark swamps and try to read human destiny by the chance flame of wandering vapours.

And yet she was conscious of something deeper than that coincidence of words which made the parting contact with her dying brother live anew in her mind, and gave a new sisterhood to the wasted face. If there were much more of such experience as his in the world, she would like to understand it,—would even like to learn the thoughts of men who sank in ecstasy before the pictured agonies of martyrdom. There seemed to be something more than madness in that supreme fellowship with suffering. The springs were all dried up around her; she wondered what other waters there were at which men drank and found strength in the desert. And those moments in the Duomo when she had sobbed with a mysterious mingling of rapture and pain, while Fra Girolamo offered himself a willing sacrifice for the people, came back to her as if they had been a transient taste of some such far-off fountain. But again she shrank from impressions that were alluring her within the sphere of visions and narrow fears which compelled men to outrage natural affections as Dino had done.

This was the tangled web that Romola had in her mind as she sat weary in the darkness. No radiant angel came across the gloom with a clear message for her. In those times, as now, there were human beings who never saw angels or heard perfectly clear messages. Such truth as came to them was brought confusedly in the voices and deeds of men not at all like the seraphs of unfailing wing and piercing vision,—men who believed falsities as well as truths, and did the wrong as well as the right. The helping hands stretched out to them were the hands of men who stumbled and often saw dimly, so that these beings unvisited by angels had no other choice than to grasp that stumbling guidance along the path of reliance and action which is the path of life, or else to pause in loneliness and disbelief, which is no path, but the arrest of inaction and death.

And so Romola, seeing no ray across the darkness, and heavy with conflict that changed nothing, sank at last to sleep.

CHAPTER XVII

ROMOLA was waked by a tap at the door. The cold light of early morning was in the room, and Maso was come for the travelling-wallet. The old man could not help starting when she opened the door, and showed him, instead of the graceful outline he had been used to, crowned with the brightness of her hair, the thick folds of the grey mantle and the pale face shadowed by the dark cowl.

"It is well, Maso," said Romola, trying to speak in the calmest voice, and make the old man easy. "Here is the wallet quite ready. You will go on quietly, and I shall not be far behind you. When you get out of the gates you may go more slowly, for I shall perhaps join you before you get to Trespiano."

She closed the door behind him, and then put her hand on the key which she had taken from the casket the last thing in the night. It was the original key of the little painted tabernacle: Tito had forgotten to drown it in the Arno, and it had lodged, as such small things will, in the corner of the embroidered scarsella which he wore with the purple tunic. One day, long after their marriage, Romola had found it there, and had put it by without using it, but with a sense of satisfaction that the key was within reach. The cabinet on which the tabernacle stood had been moved to the side of the room, close to one of the windows, where the pale morning light fell upon it so as to make the painted forms discernible enough to Romola, who knew them well,—the triumphant Bacchus, with his clusters and his vine-clad spear, clasping the crowned Ariadne; the Loves showering roses, the wreathed vessel, the cunning-eyed dolphins, and the rippled sea: all encircled by a flowery border, like a bower of paradise. Romola looked at the familiar images with new bitterness and repulsion: they seemed a more pitiable mockery than ever on this chill morning, when she had waked up to wander in loneliness. They had been no tomb of sorrow, but a lying screen. Foolish Ariadne! with her gaze of love, as if that bright face, with its hyacinthine curls like tendrils among the vines, held the deep secret of her life!

"Ariadne is wonderfully transformed," thought Romola. "She would look strange among the vines and the roses now."

She took up the mirror, and looked at herself once more. But the sight was so startling in this morning light that she laid it down again, with a sense of shrinking almost as strong as that with which she had turned from the joyous Ariadne. The recognition of her own face, with the cowl about it, brought back the dread lest she should be drawn at last into fellowship with some wretched superstition,—into the company of the howling fanatics and weeping nuns, who had been her contempt from childhood till now. She thrust the key into the tabernacle hurriedly:

hurriedly she opened it, and took out the crucifix, without looking at it; then, with trembling fingers, she passed a cord through the little ring, hung the crucifix round her neck, and hid it in the bosom of her mantle. "For Dino's sake," she said to herself.

Still there were the letters to be written which Maso was to carry back from Bologna. They were very brief. The first said,—

"Tito, my love for you is dead; and therefore, so far as I was yours, I too am dead. Do not try to put in force any laws for the sake of fetching me back: that would bring you no happiness. The Romola you married can never return. I need explain nothing to you after the words I uttered to you the last time we spoke long together. If you supposed them to be words of transient anger, you will know now that they were the sign of an irreversible change.

"I think you will fulfil my wish that my bridal chest should be sent to my godfather, who gave it me. It contains my wedding-clothes and the portraits and other relics of my father and mother."

She folded the ring inside this letter, and wrote Tito's name outside. The next letter was to Bernardo del Nero:—

DEAREST GODFATHER,—If I could have been any good to your life by staying, I would not have gone away to a distance. But now I am gone. Do not ask the reason; and if you love my father, try to prevent any one from seeking me. I could not bear my life at Florence. I cannot bear to tell any one why. Help to cover my lot in silence. I have asked that my bridal chest should be sent to you; when you open it, you will know the reason. Please to give all the things that were my mother's to my cousin Brigida, and ask her to forgive me for not saying any words of parting to her.

Farewell, my second father. The best thing I have in life is still to remember your goodness and be grateful to you.

ROMOLA.

Romola put the letters, along with the crucifix, within the bosom of her mantle, and then felt that everything was done. She was ready now to depart.

No one was stirring in the house, and she went almost as quietly as a gray phantom down the stairs and into the silent street. Her heart was palpitating violently, yet she enjoyed the sense of her firm tread on the broad flags,—of the swift movement, which was like a chained-up resolution set free at last. The anxiety to carry out her act, and the dread of any obstacle, averted sorrow; and as she reached the Ponte Rubaconte, she felt less that Santa Croce was in her sight than that the yellow streak of morning which parted the grey was getting broader and broader, and that, unless she hastened her steps, she should have to encounter faces.

Her simplest road was to go right on to the Borgo Pinti, and then along by the walls to the Porta San Gallo, from which she must leave the city; and this road carried her by the Piazza di Santa Croce. But she walked as steadily and rapidly as ever through the piazza, not trusting herself to look towards the church. The thought that any eyes might be turned on her with a look of curiosity and recognition, and that indifferent minds might be set speculating on her private sorrows, made Romola shrink physically as from the imagination of torture. She felt degraded even by that act of her husband from which she was helplessly suffering. But there was no sign that any eyes looked forth from windows to notice this tall grey sister, with the firm step, and proud attitude of the cowled head. Her road lay aloof from the stir of early traffic; and when she reached the Porta San Gallo, it was easy to pass while a dispute was going forward about the toll for panniers of eggs and market produce which were just entering.

Out! Once past the houses of the Borgo, she would be beyond the last fringe of Florence, the sky would be broad above her, and she would have entered on her new life,—a life of loneliness and endurance, but of freedom. She had been strong enough to snap asunder the bonds she had accepted in blind faith: whatever befell her, she would no more feel the breath of soft hated lips warm upon her cheek, no longer feel the breath of an odious mind stifling her own. The bare wintry morning, the chill air, were welcome in their severity: the leafless trees, the sombre hills, were not haunted by the gods of beauty and joy, whose worship she had forsaken forever.

But presently the light burst forth with sudden strength, and shadows were thrown across the road. It seemed that the sun was going to chase away the greyness. The light is perhaps never felt more strongly as a divine presence stirring all those inarticulate sensibilities which are our deepest life, than in these moments when it instantaneously awakens the shadows. A certain awe which inevitably accompanied this most momentous act of her life became a more conscious element in Romola's feeling as she found herself in the sudden presence of the impalpable golden glory and the long shadow of herself that was not to be escaped. Hitherto she had met no one but an occasional contadino with mules, and the many turnings of the road on the level prevented her from seeing that Maso was not very far ahead of her. But when she had passed Pietra and was on rising ground, she lifted up the hanging roof of her cowl and looked eagerly before her.

The cowl was dropped again immediately. She had seen, not Maso, but —two monks, who were approaching within a few yards of her. The edge of her cowl making a pent-house on her brow had shut out the objects above the level of her eyes, and for the last few moments she had been looking at nothing but the brightness on the path and at her own shadow tall and shrouded like a dread spectre.

She wished now that she had not looked up. Her disguise made her especially dislike to encounter monks: they might expect some pious pass-words of which she knew nothing, and she walked along with a careful appearance of unconsciousness till she had seen the skirts of the black mantles pass by her. The encounter had made her heart beat disagreeably, for Romola had an uneasiness in her religious disguise, a shame at this studied concealment, which was made more distinct by a special effort to appear unconscious under actual glances.

But the black skirts would be gone the faster because they were going down-hill; and seeing a great flat stone against a cypress that rose from a projecting green bank, she yielded to the desire which the slight shock had given her, to sit down and rest.

She turned her back on Florence, not meaning to look at it till the monks were quite out of sight; and raising the edge of her cowl again when she had seated herself, she discerned Maso and the mules at a distance where it was not hopeless for her to overtake them, as the old man would probably linger in expectation of her.

Meanwhile she might pause a little. She was free and alone.

CHAPTER XVIII

THE BLACK MARKS BECOME MAGICAL

THAT journey of Tito's to Rome, which had removed many difficulties from Romola's departure, had been resolved on quite suddenly, at a supper, only the evening before.

Tito had set out towards that supper with agreeable expectations. The meats were likely to be delicate, the wines choice, the company distinguished; for the place of entertainment was the Selva or Orto de' Rucellai, or, as we should say, the Rucellai Gardens; and the host, Bernardo Rucellai, was quite a typical Florentine grandee. Even his family name has a significance which is prettily symbolic: properly understood, it may bring before us a little lichen, popularly named *orcella* or *rocella,* which grows on the rocks of Greek isles and in the Canaries, and having drunk a great deal of light into its little stems and button-heads, will, under certain circumstances, give it out again as a reddish purple dye, very grateful to the eyes of men. By bringing the excellent secret of this dye, called *oricello,* from the Levant to Florence, a certain merchant, who lived nearly a hundred years before our Bernardo's time, won for himself and his descendants much wealth, and the pleasantly suggestive surname of Oricellari or Roccellari, which on Tuscan tongues speedily became Rucellai.

And our Bernardo, who stands out more prominently than the rest on this purple background, had added all sorts of distinction to the family name: he had married the sister of Lorenzo de' Medici, and had had the most splendid wedding in the memory of Florentine upholstery; and for these and other virtues he had been sent on embassies to France and Venice, and had been chosen Gonfaloniere; he had not only built himself a fine palace, but had finished putting the black and white marble façade to the church of Santa Maria Novella; he had planted a garden with rare trees, and had made it classic ground by receiving within it the meetings of the Platonic Academy, orphaned by the death of Lorenzo; he had written an excellent, learned book, of a new topographical sort, about ancient Rome; he had collected antiquities; he had a pure Latinity. The simplest account of him, one sees, reads like a laudatory epitaph at the end of which the Greek and Ausonian Muses might be confidently requested to tear their hair, and Nature to desist from any second attempt to combine so many virtues with one set of viscera.

His invitation had been conveyed to Tito through Lorenzo Tornabuoni, with an emphasis which would have suggested that the object of the gathering was political, even if the public questions of the time had been less absorbing. As it was, Tito felt sure that some party purposes were to be furthered by the excellent flavours of stewed fish and old Greek wine; for Bernardo Rucellai was not simply an influential personage, he was one of the elect Twenty who for three weeks had held the reins of Florence. This assurance put Tito in the best spirits as he made his way to the Via della Scala, where the classic garden was to be found: without it, he might have had some uneasy speculation as to whether the high company he would have the honour of meeting was likely to be dull as well as distinguished; for he had had experience of various dull suppers even in the Rucellai gardens, and especially of the dull philosophic sort, wherein he had not only been called upon to accept an entire scheme of the universe (which would have been easy to him), but to listen to an exposition of the same, from the origin of things to their complete ripeness in the tractate of the philosopher then speaking.

It was a dark evening, and it was only when Tito crossed the occasional light of a lamp suspended before an image of the Virgin, that the outline of his figure was discernible enough for recognition. At such moments any one caring to watch his passage from one of these lights to another might have observed that the tall and graceful personage with the mantle folded round him was followed constantly by a very different form, thick-set and elderly, in a serge tunic and felt hat. The conjunction might have been taken for mere chance, since there were many passengers along the streets at this hour. But when Tito stopped at the gate of the Rucellai gardens, the figure behind stopped too. The *sportello*, or smaller door of the gate, was already being held open by the servant, who in the distraction of attending to some question had not yet closed it since the last arrival, and Tito turned in rapidly, giving his name to the servant, and passing on between the evergreen bushes that shone like metal in the torchlight. The follower turned in too.

"Your name?" said the servant.

"Baldassarre Calvo," was the immediate answer.

"You are not a guest; the guests have all passed."

"I belong to Tito Melema, who has just gone in. I am to wait in the gardens."

The servant hesitated. "I had orders to admit only guests. Are you a servant of Messer Tito?"

"No, friend, I am not a servant; I am a scholar."

There are men to whom you need only say, "I am a buffalo," in a certain tone of quiet confidence, and they will let you pass. The porter gave way at once, Baldassarre entered, and heard the door closed and chained behind him, as he too disappeared among the shining bushes.

Those ready and firm answers argued a great change in Baldassarre since the last meeting face to face with Tito, when the dagger broke in two. The change had declared itself in a startling way.

At the moment when the shadow of Tito passed in front of the hovel as he departed homeward, Baldassarre was sitting in that state of after-tremor known to every one who is liable to great outbursts of passion,— a state in which physical powerlessness is sometimes accompanied by an exceptional lucidity of thought, as if that disengagement of excited passion had carried away a fire-mist and left clearness behind it. He felt unable to rise and walk away just yet; his limbs seemed benumbed; he was cold, and his hands shook. But in that bodily helplessness he sat surrounded, not by the habitual dimness and vanishing shadows, but by the clear images of the past; he was living again in an unbroken course through that life which seemed a long preparation for the taste of bitterness.

For some minutes he was too thoroughly absorbed by the images to reflect on the fact that he saw them, and note the fact as a change. But when that sudden clearness had travelled through the distance, and came at last to rest on the scene just gone by, he felt fully where he was: he remembered Monna Lisa and Tessa. Ah! *he* then was the mysterious husband; he who had another wife in Via de' Bardi. It was time to pick up the broken dagger and go,—go and leave no trace of himself; for to hide his feebleness seemed the thing most like power that was left to him. He leaned to take up the fragments of the dagger; then he turned towards the book which lay open at his side. It was a fine large manuscript, an odd volume of Pausanias. The moonlight was upon it, and he could see the large letters at the head of the page:

$$\text{ΜΕΣΣΗΝΙΚΑ. ΚΒ΄.}$$

In old days he had known Pausanias familiarly; yet an hour or two ago he had been looking hopelessly at that page, and it had suggested no more meaning to him than if the letters had been black weather-marks on a wall; but at this moment they were once more the magic signs that conjur up a world. That moonbeam falling on the letters had raised Messenia before him, and its struggle against the Spartan oppression.

He snatched up the book, but the light was too pale for him to read further by. No matter: he knew that chapter; he read inwardly. He saw the stoning of the traitor Aristocrates,—stoned by a whole people, who cast him out from their borders to lie unburied, and set up a pillar with verses upon it telling how Time had brought home justice to the unjust. The words arose within him, and stirred innumerable vibrations of memory. He forgot that he was old: he could almost have shouted. The light was come again, mother of knowledge and joy! In that exultation his limbs recovered their strength: he started up with his broken dagger and book, and went out under the broad moonlight.

It was a nipping frosty air, but Baldassarre could feel no chill,—he only felt the glow of conscious power. He walked about and paused on all the open spots of that high ground, and looked down on the domed and towered city sleeping darkly under its sleeping guardians the mountains, on the pale gleam of the river, on the valley vanishing towards the peaks of snow; and felt himself master of them all.

That sense of mental empire which belongs to us all in moments of exceptional clearness was intensified for him by the long days and nights in which memory had been little more than the consciousness of something gone. That city, which had been a weary labyrinth, was material that he could subdue to his purposes now: his mind glanced through its affairs with flashing conjecture; he was once more a man who knew cities, whose sense of vision was instructed with large experience, and who felt the keen delight of holding all things in the grasp of language. Names! Images!—his mind rushed through its wealth without pausing, like one who enters on a great inheritance.

But amidst all that rushing eagerness there was one End presiding in Baldassarre's consciousness,—a dark deity in the inmost cell, who only seemed forgotten while his hecatomb was being prepared. And when the first triumph in the certainty of recovered power had had its way, his thoughts centered themselves on Tito. That fair slippery viper could not escape him now; thanks to struggling justice, the heart that never quivered with tenderness for another had its sensitive selfish fibres that could be reached by the sharp point of anguish. The soul that bowed to no right bowed to the great lord of mortals, Pain.

He could search into every secret of Tito's life now: he knew some of the secrets already, and the failure of the broken dagger, which seemed like frustration, had been the beginning of achievement. Doubtless that sudden rage had shaken away the obstruction which stifled his soul. Twice before, when his memory had partially returned, it had been in consequence of sudden excitation,—once when he had had to defend himself from an enraged dog; once when he had been overtaken by the waves, and had had to scramble up a rock to save himself.

Yes; but if this time, as then, the light were to die out, and the dreary conscious blank come back again! This time the light was stronger and steadier; but what security was there that before the morrow the dark fog would not be round him again? Even the fear seemed like the beginning of feebleness: he thought with alarm that he might sink the faster for this excited vigil of his on the hill, which was expending his force; and after seeking anxiously for a sheltered corner where he might lie down, he nestled at last against a heap of warm garden straw, and so fell asleep.

When he opened his eyes again, it was daylight. The first moments were filled with strange bewilderment: he was a man with a double identity; to which had he awaked?—to the life of dim-sighted sensibilities like the sad heirship of some fallen greatness, or to the life of recovered power? Surely the last, for the events of the night all came back to him,—the recognition of the page in Pausanias, the crowding resurgence of facts and names, the sudden wide prospect which had given him such a moment as that of the Mænad in the glorious amaze of her morning waking on the mountain top.

He took up the book again, he read, he remembered without reading. He saw a name, and the images of deeds rose with it: he saw the mention of a deed, and he linked it with a name. There were stories of inexpiable crimes, but stories also of guilt that seemed successful. There were sanctuaries for swift-footed miscreants: baseness had its armour, and the weapons of justice sometimes broke against it. What then? If baseness triumphed everywhere else, if it could heap to itself all the goods of the world and even hold the keys of hell, it would never triumph over the hatred which it had itself awakened. It could devise no torture that would seem greater than the torture of submitting to its smile. Baldassarre felt the indestructible independent force of a supreme emotion, which knows no terror, and asks for no motive, which is itself an ever-burning motive, consuming all other desire. And now in this morning light, when the assurance came again that the fine fibres of association were active still, and that his recovered self had not departed, all his gladness was but the hope of vengeance.

From that time till the evening on which we have seen him enter the Rucellai gardens, he had been incessantly, but cautiously, inquiring into Tito's position and all his circumstances, and there was hardly a day on which he did not contrive to follow his movements. But he wished not to arouse any alarm in Tito: he wished to secure a moment when the hated favourite of blind fortune was at the summit of confident ease, surrounded by chief men on whose favour he depended. It was not any retributive payment or recognition of himself for his own behoof, on which Baldassarre's whole soul was bent: it was to find the sharpest edge of disgrace and shame by which a selfish smiler could be pierced: it was to send through his marrow the most sudden shock of dread. He was content to lie hard, and live stintedly,—he had spent the greater part of his remaining money in buying another poniard: his hunger and his thirst were after nothing exquisite but an exquisite vengeance. He had avoided addressing himself to any one whom he suspected of intimacy with Tito, lest an alarm raised in Tito's mind should urge him either to flight or to some other counteracting measure which hard-pressed ingenuity might devise. For this reason he had never entered Nello's shop, which he observed that Tito frequented, and he had turned aside to avoid meeting Piero di Cosimo.

The possibility of frustration gave added eagerness to his desire that the great opportunity he sought should not be deferred. The desire was eager in him on another ground: he trembled lest his memory should go again. Whether from the agitating presence of that fear, or from some other causes, he had twice felt a sort of mental dizziness, in which the inward sense or imagination seemed to be losing the distinct forms of things. Once he had attempted to enter the Palazza Vecchio and make his way into a council-chamber where Tito was, and had failed. But now, on this evening, he felt that his occasion was come.

CHAPTER XIX

A SUPPER IN THE RUCELLAI GARDENS

On entering the handsome pavilion, Tito's quick glance soon discerned in the selection of the guests the confirmation of his conjecture that the object of the gathering was political, though, perhaps, nothing more distinct than that strengthening of party which comes from good-fellowship. Good dishes and good wine were at that time believed to heighten the consciousness of political preferences, and in the inspired ease of after-supper talk it was supposed that people ascertained their own opinions with a clearness quite inaccessible to uninvited stomachs. The Florentines were a sober and frugal people; but wherever men have gathered wealth, Madonna della Gozzoviglia and San Buonvino have had their worshippers; and the Rucellai were among the few Florentine families who kept a great table and lived splendidly. It was not probable that on this evening there would be any attempt to apply high philosophic theories; and there could be no objection to the bust of Plato looking on, or even to the modest presence of the cardinal virtues in fresco on the walls.

That bust of Plato had been long used to look down on conviviality of a more transcendental sort, for it had been brought from Lorenzo's villa after his death, when the meetings of the Platonic Academy had been transferred to these gardens. Especially on every 13th of November, reputed anniversary of Plato's death, it had looked down from under laurel leaves on a picked company of scholars and philosophers, who met to eat and drink with moderation, and to discuss and admire, perhaps with less moderation, the doctrines of the great master,—on Pico della Mirandola, once a Quixotic young genius with long curls, astonished at his own powers and astonishing Rome with heterodox theses, afterwards a more humble student with a consuming passion for inward perfection, having come to find the universe more astonishing than his own cleverness; on innocent, laborious Marsilio Ficino, picked out young to be reared as a Platonic philosopher, and fed on Platonism in all its stages till his mind was perhaps a little pulpy from that too exclusive diet; on Angelo Poliziano, chief literary genius of that age, a born poet, and a scholar without dulness, whose phrases had blood in them and are alive still; or, further back, on Leon Battista Alberti, a reverend senior when those three were young, and of a much grander type than they, a robust universal mind, at once practical and theoretic, artist, man of science, inventor, poet; and on many more valiant workers whose names are not registered where every day we turn the leaf to read them, but whose labours make a part, though an unrecognized part, of our inheritance, like the ploughing and sowing of past generations.

Bernardo Rucellai was a man to hold a distinguished place in that

Academy even before he became its host and patron. He was still in the prime of life, not more than four and forty, with a somewhat haughty, cautiously dignified presence; conscious of an amazingly pure Latinity, but, says Erasmus, not to be caught speaking Latin,—no word of Latin to be sheared off him by the sharpest of Teutons. He welcomed Tito with more marked favour than usual, and gave him a place between Lorenzo Tornabuoni and Giannozzo Pucci, both of them accomplished young members of the Medicean party.

Of course the talk was the lightest in the world while the brass bowl filled with scented water was passing round, that the company might wash their hands, and rings flashed on white fingers under the wax-lights, and there was the pleasant fragrance of fresh white damask newly come from France. The tone of remark was a very common one in those times. Some one asked what Dante's pattern old Florentine would think if the life could come into him again under his leathern belt and bone clasp, and he could see silver forks on the table? And it was agreed on all hands that the habits of posterity would be very surprising to ancestors, if ancestors could only know them.

And while the silver forks were just dallying with the appetizing delicacies that introduced the more serious business of the supper,—such as morsels of liver, cooked to that exquisite point that they would melt in the mouth,—there was time to admire the designs on the enamelled silver centres of the brass service, and to say something, as usual, about the silver dish for confetti, a masterpiece of Antonio Pollajuolo, whom patronizing Popes had seduced from his native Florence to more gorgeous Rome.

"Ah, I remember," said Niccolò Ridolfi, a middle-aged man, with that negligent ease of manner which, seeming to claim nothing, is really based on the life-long consciousness of commanding rank,—"I remember our Antonio getting bitter about his chiselling and enamelling of these metal things, and taking in a fury to painting, because, said he, 'the artist who puts his work into gold and silver, puts his brains into the melting pot.'"

"And that is not unlikely to be a true foreboding of Antonio's," said Giannozzo Pucci. "If this pretty war with Pisa goes on, and the revolt only spreads a little to our other towns, it is not only our silver dishes that are likely to go; I doubt whether Antonio's silver saints round the altar of San Giovanni will not some day vanish from the eyes of the faithful to be worshipped more devoutly in the form of coin."

"The Frate is preparing us for that already," said Tornabuoni. "He is telling the people that God will not have silver crucifixes and starving stomachs; and that the church is best adorned with the gems of holiness and the fine gold of brotherly love."

"A very useful doctrine of war-finance, as many a Condottiere has found," said Bernardo Rucellai, dryly. "But politics come on after the confetti, Lorenzo, when we can drink wine enough to wash them down; they are too solid to be taken with roast and boiled."

"Yes, indeed," said Niccolò Ridolfi. "Our Luigi Pulci would have said this delicate boiled kid must be eaten with an impartial mind. I remember one day at Creggi, when Luigi was in his rattling vein he was maintaining that nothing perverted the palate like opinion. 'Opinion,' said he, 'corrupts the saliva,—that's why men took to pepper. Scepticism is the only philosophy that doesn't bring a taste in the mouth.' 'Nay,' says poor Lorenzo de' Medici, 'you must be out there, Luigi. Here is this untainted sceptic, Matteo Franco, who wants hotter sauce than any of us.' 'Because he has a strong opinion of *himself*,' flashes out Luigi, 'which is the original egg of all other opinion. *He* a sceptic? He believes in the immortality of his own verses. He is such a logician as that preaching friar who described the pavement of the bottomless pit.' Poor Luigi, his mind was like sharpest steel that can touch nothing without cutting."

"And yet a very gentle-hearted creature," said Giannozzo Pucci. "It seemed to me his talk was a mere blowing of soap-bubbles. What dithyrambs he went into about eating and drinking! and yet he was as temperate as a butterfly."

The light talk and the solid eatables were not soon at an end, for after the roast and boiled meats came the indispensable capon and game, and, crowning glory of a well-spread table, a peacock cooked according to the receipt of Apicius for cooking partridges, namely, with the feathers on, but not plucked afterwards, as that great authority ordered concerning his partridges; on the contrary, so disposed on the dish that it might look as much as possible like a live peacock taking its unboiled repose. Great was the skill required in that confidential servant who was the official carver, respectfully to turn the classical though insipid bird on its back, and expose the plucked breast from which he was to dispense a delicate slice to each of the honourable company, unless any one should be of so independent a mind as to decline that expensive toughness and prefer the vulgar digestibility of capon.

Hardly any one was so bold. Tito quoted Horace, and dispersed his slice in small particles over his plate; Bernardo Rucellai made a learned observation about the ancient price of peacock's eggs, but did not pretend to eat his slice; and Niccolò Ridolfi held a mouthful on his fork while he told a favourite story of Luigi Pulci's, about a man of Siena, who, wanting to give a splendid entertainment at moderate expense, bought a wild goose, cut off its beak and webbed feet, and boiled it in its feathers, to pass for a pea-hen.

In fact, very little peacock was eaten; but there was the satisfaction of sitting at a table where peacock was served up in a remarkable manner, and of knowing that such caprices were not within reach of any but those who supped with the very wealthiest men. And it would have been rashness to speak slightingly of peacock's flesh, or any other venerable institution, at a time when Fra Girolamo was teaching the disturbing doctrine that it was not the duty of the rich to be luxurious for the sake of the poor.

Meanwhile, in the chill obscurity that surrounded this centre of

warmth and light and savoury odours, the lonely disowned man was
walking in gradually narrowing circuits. He paused among the trees, and
looked in at the windows, which made brilliant pictures against the
gloom. He could hear the laughter; he could see Tito gesticulating with
careless grace, and hear his voice, now alone, now mingling in the merry
confusion of interlacing speeches. Baldassarre's mind was highly strung.
He was preparing himself for the moment when he could win his entrance into this brilliant company; and he had a savage satisfaction in
the sight of Tito's easy gayety, which seemed to be preparing the unconscious victim for more effective torture.

But the men seated among the branching tapers and the flashing cups
could know nothing of the pale fierce face that watched them from without. The light can be a curtain as well as the darkness.

And the talk went on with more eagerness as it became less discon-
nected and trivial. The sense of citizenship was just then strongly forced
even on the most indifferent minds. What the overmastering Fra Girolamo was saying and prompting was really uppermost in the thoughts
of every one at table; and before the stewed fish was removed, and
while the favourite sweets were yet to come, his name rose to the surface of the conversation, and, in spite of Rucellai's previous prohibition,
the talk again became political. At first, while the servants remained
present, it was mere gossip: what had been done in the Palazzo on the
first day's voting for the Great Council, how hot-tempered and domineering Francesco Valori was, as if he were to have everything his own
way by right of his austere virtue; and how it was clear to everybody
who heard Soderini's speeches in favour of the Great Council and also
heard the Frate's sermons, that they were both kneaded in the same
trough.

"My opinion is," said Niccolò Ridolfi, "that the Frate has a longer
head for public matters than Soderini or any Piagnone among them: you
may depend on it that Soderini is his mouthpiece more than he is Soderini's."

"No, Niccolò; there I differ from you," said Bernardo Rucellai: "the
Frate has an acute mind, and readily sees what will serve his own ends;
but it is not likely that Pagolantonio Soderini, who has had long experience of affairs, and has specially studied the Venetian Council,
should be much indebted to a monk for ideas on that subject. No, no;
Soderini loads the cannon; though, I grant you, Fra Girolamo brings the
powder and lights the match. He is master of the people, and the people
are getting master of us. Ecco!"

"Well," said Lorenzo Tornabuoni, presently, when the room was
clear of servants, and nothing but wine was passing round, "whether
Soderini is indebted or not, *we* are indebted to the Frate for the general amnesty which has gone along with the scheme of the Council. We
might have done without the fear of God and the reform of morals being passed by a majority of black beans; but that excellent proposition,
that our Medicean heads should be allowed to remain comfortably on

our shoulders, and that we should not be obliged to hand over our property in fines, has my warm approval, and it is my belief that nothing
but the Frate's predominance could have procured that for us. And you
may rely on it that Fra Girolamo is as firm as a rock on that point of
promoting peace. I have had an interview with him."

There was a murmur of surprise and curiosity at the farther end of
the table; but Bernardo Rucellai simply nodded, as if he knew what
Tornabuoni had to say, and wished him to go on.

"Yes," proceeded Tornabuoni, "I have been favoured with an interview in the Frate's own cell, which, let me tell you, is not a common
favour; for I have reason to believe that even Francesco Valori very
seldom sees him in private. However, I think he saw me the more willingly because I was not a ready-made follower, but had to be converted.
And, for my part, I see clearly enough that the only safe and wise policy
for us Mediceans to pursue is to throw our strength into the scale of
the Frate's party. We are not strong enough to make head on our own
behalf; and if the Frate and the popular party were upset, every one
who hears me knows perfectly well what other party would be uppermost just now: Nerli, Alberti, Pazzi, and the rest,—*Arrabbiati*, as somebody christened them the other day,—who instead of giving us an amnesty, would be inclined to fly at our throats like mad dogs, and not be
satisfied till they had banished half of us."

There were strong interjections of assent to this last sentence of Tornabuoni's, as he paused and looked round a moment.

"A wise dissimulation," he went on, "is the only course for moderate
rational men in times of violent party feeling. I need hardly tell this
company what are my real political attachments: I am not the only
man here who has strong personal ties to the banished family; but,
apart from any such ties, I agree with my more experienced friends,
who are allowing me to speak for them in their presence, that the only
lasting and peaceful state of things for Florence is the predominance of
some single family interest. This theory of the Frate's that we are to
have a popular government, in which every man is to strive only for
the general good, and know no party names, is a theory that may do for
some isle of Cristoforo Colombo's finding, but will never do for our fine
old quarrelsome Florence. A change must come before long, and with
patience and caution we have every chance of determining the change
in our favour. Meanwhile, the best thing we can do will be to keep the
Frate's flag flying; for if any other were to be hoisted just now, it would
be a black flag for us."

"It's true," said Niccolò Ridolfi, in a curt, decisive way. "What you
say is true, Lorenzo. For my own part, I am too old for anybody to believe that I have changed my feathers. And there are certain of us—our
old Bernardo del Nero for one—whom you would never persuade to borrow another man's shield. But we can lie still, like sleepy old dogs; and
it's clear enough that barking would be of no use just now. As for this

psalm-singing party, who vote for nothing but the glory of God, and want to make believe we can all love each other, and talk as if vice could be swept out with a besom by the Magnificent Eight, their day will not be a long one. After all the talk of scholars, there are but two sorts of government: one where men show their teeth at each other, and one where men show their tongues and lick the feet of the strongest. They'll get their Great Council finally voted to-morrow—that's certain enough —and they'll think they've found out a new plan of government; but as sure as there's a human skin under every lucco in the Council, their new plan will end like every other, in snarling or in licking. That's my view of things as a plain man. Not that I consider it becoming in men of family and following, who have got others depending on their constancy and on their sticking to their colours, to go a-hunting with a fine net to catch reasons in the air, like doctors of law. I say frankly that, as the head of my family, I shall be true to my old alliances; and I have never yet seen any chalk-mark on political reasons to tell me which is true and which is false. My friend Bernardo Rucellai here is a man of reasons, I know, and I have no objection to anybody's finding fine-spun reasons for me, so that they don't interfere with my actions as a man of family who has faith to keep with his connections."

"If that is an appeal to me, Niccolò," said Bernardo Rucellai, with a formal dignity, in amusing contrast with Ridolfi's curt and pithy ease, "I may take this opportunity of saying, that while my wishes are partly determined by long-standing personal relations, I cannot enter into any positive schemes with persons over whose actions I have no control. I myself might be content with a restoration of the old order of things; but with modifications,—with important modifications. And the one point on which I wish to declare my concurrence with Lorenzo Tornabuoni is, that the best policy to be pursued by our friends is, to throw the weight of their interest into the scale of the popular party. For myself, I condescend to no dissimulation; nor do I at present see the party or the scheme that commands my full assent. In all alike there is crudity and confusion of ideas, and of all the twenty men who are my colleagues in the present crisis, there is not one with whom I do not find myself in wide disagreement."

Niccolò Ridolfi shrugged his shoulders, and left it to some one else to take up the ball. As the wine went round, the talk became more and more frank and lively, and the desire of several at once to be the chief speaker, as usual, caused the company to break up into small knots of two and three.

It was a result which had been foreseen by Lorenzo Tornabuoni and Giannozzo Pucci, and they were among the first to turn aside from the highroad of general talk and enter into a special conversation with Tito, who sat between them; gradually pushing away their seats, and turning their backs on the table and wine.

"In truth, Melema," Tornabuoni was saying at this stage, laying one hose-clad leg across the knee of the other, and caressing his ankle, "I know of no man in Florence who can serve our party better than you. You see what most of our friends are,—men who can no more hide their prejudices than a dog can hide the natural tone of his bark, or else men whose political ties are so notorious that they must always be objects of suspicion. Giannozzo here, and I, I flatter myself, are able to over-come that suspicion; we have that power of concealment and finesse without which a rational cultivated man, instead of having any pre-rogative, is really at a disadvantage compared with a wild bull or a savage. But, except yourself, I know of no one else on whom we could rely for the necessary discretion."

"Yes," said Giannozzo Pucci, laying his hand on Tito's shoulder, "the fact is, Tito mio, you can help us better than if you were Ulysses him-self, for I am convinced that Ulysses often made himself disagreeable. To manage men one ought to have a sharp mind in a velvet sheath. And there is not a soul in Florence who could undertake a business like this journey to Rome, for example, with the same safety that you can. There is your scholarship, which may always be a pretext for such journeys; and what is better, there is your talent, which it would be harder to match than your scholarship. Niccolò Macchiavelli might have done for us if he had been on our side, but hardly so well. He is too much bitten with notions, and has not your power of fascination. All the worse for him. He has lost a great chance in life, and you have got it."

"Yes," said Tornabuoni, lowering his voice in a significant manner, "you have only to play your game well, Melema, and the future be-longs to you. For the Medici, you may rely upon it, will keep a foot in Rome as well as in Florence, and the time may not be far off when they will be able to make a finer career for their adherents even than they did in old days. Why shouldn't you take orders some day? There's a cardinal's hat at the end of that road, and you would not be the first Greek who has won that ornament."

Tito laughed gayly. He was too acute not to measure Tornabuoni's exaggerated flattery, but still the flattery had a pleasant flavour.

"My joints are not so stiff yet," he said, "that I can't be induced to run without such a high prize as that. I think the income of an abbey or two held 'in commendam,' without the trouble of getting my head shaved, would satisfy me at present."

"I was not joking," said Tornabuoni, with grave suavity; "I think a scholar would always be the better off for taking orders. But we'll talk of that another time. One of the objects to be first borne in mind is that you should win the confidence of the men who hang about San Marco; that is what Giannozzo and I shall do, but you may carry it farther than we can, because you are less observed. In that way you can get a thorough knowledge of their doings, and you will make a broader screen for your agency on our side. Nothing of course can be done before you start for Rome, because this bit of business between Piero de' Medici and the French nobles must be effected at once. I mean when you come back, of course; I need say no more. I believe you could make yourself the pet votary of San Marco, if you liked; but you are wise enough to know that effective dissimulation is never immoderate."

"If it were not that an adhesion to the popular side is necessary to your safety as an agent of our party, Tito mio," said Giannozzo Pucci, who was more fraternal and less patronizing in his manner than Tornabuoni, "I could have wished your skill to have been employed in another way, for which it is still better fitted. But now we must look out for some other man among us who will manage to get into the confidence of our sworn enemies, the Arrabbiati; we need to know their movements more than those of the Frate's party, who are strong enough to play above-board. Still, it would have been a difficult thing for you, from your known relations with the Medici a little while back, and that sort of kinship your wife has with Bernardo del Nero. We must find a man who has no distinguished connections, and who has not yet taken any side."

Tito was pushing his hair backward automatically, as his manner was, and looking straight at Pucci with a scarcely perceptible smile on his lips.

"No need to look out for any one else," he said promptly. "I can manage the whole business with perfect ease. I will engage to make myself the special confidant of that thick-headed Dolfo Spini, and know his projects before he knows them himself."

Tito seldom spoke so confidently of his own powers, but he was in a state of exultation at the sudden opening of a new path before him, where fortune seemed to have hung higher prizes than any he had thought of hitherto. Hitherto he had seen success only in the form of favour; it now flashed on him in the shape of power,—of such power as is possible to talent without traditional ties and without beliefs. Each party that thought of him as a tool might become dependent on him. His position as an alien, his indifference to the ideas or prejudices of the men among whom he moved, were suddenly transformed into advantages; he became newly conscious of his own adroitness in the presence of a game that he was called on to play. And all the motives which might have made Tito shrink from the triple deceit that came before him as a tempting game had been slowly strangled in him by the successive falsities of his life.

Our lives make a moral tradition for our individual selves, as the life of mankind at large makes a moral tradition for the race; and to have once acted nobly seems a reason why we should always be noble. But Tito was feeling the effect of an opposite tradition: he had won no memories of self-conquest and perfect faithfulness from which he could have a sense of falling.

The triple colloquy went on with growing spirit till it was interrupted by a call from the table. Probably the movement came from the listeners in the party, who were afraid lest the talkers should tire themselves. At all events it was agreed that there had been enough of gravity, and Rucellai had just ordered new flasks of Montepulciano.

"How many minstrels are there among us?" he said, when there had been a general rallying round the table. "Melema, I think you are the chief: Matteo will give you the lute."

"Ah, yes!" said Giannozzo Pucci, "lead the last chorus from Poliziano's 'Orfeo,' that you have found such an excellent measure for, and we will all fall in:—

> " 'Ciascun segua, o Bacco, te:
> Bacco, Bacco, evoè, evoè!' "

The servant put the lute into Tito's hands, and then said something in an undertone to his master. A little subdued questioning and answering went on between them, while Tito touched the lute in a preluding way to the strain of the chorus, and there was a confusion of speech and musical humming all round the table. Bernardo Rucellai had said, "Wait a moment, Melema;" but the words had been unheard by Tito, who was leaning towards Pucci, and singing low to him the phrases of the Mænad-chorus. He noticed nothing until the buzz round the table suddenly ceased, and the notes of his own voice, with its soft low-toned triumph, "Evoè, evoè!" fell in startling isolation.

It was a strange moment. Baldassarre had moved round the table till he was opposite Tito; and as the hum ceased, there might be seen for an instant Baldassarre's fierce dark eyes bent on Tito's bright, smiling unconsciousness, while the low notes of triumph dropped from his lips into the silence.

Tito looked up with a slight start, and his lips turned pale, but he seemed hardly more moved than Giannozzo Pucci, who had looked up at the same moment,—or even than several others round the table; for that sallow-lined face with the hatred in its eyes seemed a terrible apparition across the wax-lit ease and gayety. And Tito quickly recovered some self-command. "A mad old man,—he looks like it,—he *is* mad!" was the instantaneous thought that brought some courage with it; for he could conjecture no inward change in Baldassarre since they had met before. He just let his eyes fall and laid the lute on the table with apparent ease; but his fingers pinched the neck of the lute hard while he governed his head and his glance sufficiently to look with an air of quiet appeal towards Bernardo Rucellai, who said at once,—

"Good man, what is your business? What is the important declaration that you have to make?"

"Messer Bernardo Rucellai, I wish you and your honourable friends to know in what sort of company you are sitting. There is a traitor among you."

There was a general movement of alarm. Every one present, except Tito, thought of political danger and not of private injury.

Baldassarre began to speak as if he were thoroughly assured of what he had to say; but in spite of his long preparation for this moment, there was the tremor of over-mastering excitement in his voice. His passion shook him. He went on, but he did not say what he had meant to say. As he fixed his eyes on Tito again, the passionate words were like blows,—they defied premeditation.

"There is a man among you who is a scoundrel, a liar, a robber. I was a father to him. I took him from beggary when he was a child. I reared him, I cherished him, I taught him, I made him a scholar. My head has lain hard that his might have a pillow. And he left me in slavery; he sold the gems that were mine, and when I came again, he denied me."

The last words had been uttered with almost convulsed agitation; and Baldassarre paused, trembling. All glances were turned on Tito, who was now looking straight at Baldassarre. It was a moment of desperation that annihilated all feeling in him, except the determination to risk anything for the chance of escape. And he gathered confidence from the agitation by which Baldassarre was evidently shaken. He had ceased to pinch the neck of the lute, and had thrust his thumbs into his belt, while his lips had begun to assume a slight curl. He had never yet done an act of murderous cruelty even to the smallest animal that could utter a cry, but at that moment he would have been capable of treading the breath from a smiling child for the sake of his own safety.

"What does this mean, Melema?" said Bernardo Rucellai, in a tone of cautious surprise. He, as well as the rest of the company, felt relieved that the tenor of the accusation was not political.

"Messer Bernardo," said Tito, "I believe this man is mad. I did not recognize him the first time he encountered me in Florence, but I know now that he is the servant who years ago accompanied me and my adoptive father to Greece, and was dismissed on account of misdemeanours. His name is Jacopo di Nola. Even at that time I believed his mind was unhinged, for, without any reason, he had conceived a strange hatred towards me; and now I am convinced that he is laboring under a mania which causes him to mistake his identity. He has already attempted my life since he has been in Florence; and I am in constant danger from him. But he is an object of pity rather than of indignation. It is too certain that my father is dead. You have only my word for it; but I must leave it to your judgment how far it is probable that a man of intellect and learning would have been lurking about in dark corners for the last month with the purpose of assassinating me; or how far it is probable that if this man were my second father, I could have any motive for denying him. That story about my being rescued from beggary is the vision of a diseased brain. But it will be a satisfaction to me at least if you will demand from him proofs of his identity, lest any malignant person should choose to make this mad impeachment a reproach to me."

Tito had felt more and more confidence as he went on: the lie was not so difficult when it was once begun; and as the words fell easily from his lips, they gave him a sense of power such as men feel when they have begun a muscular feat successfully. In this way he acquired boldness enough to end with a challenge for proofs.

Baldassarre, while he had been walking in the gardens and afterwards waiting in an outer room of the pavilion with the servants, had been making anew the digest of the evidence he would bring to prove his identity and Tito's baseness, recalling the description and history of his gems, and assuring himself by rapid mental glances that he could attest his learning and his travels. It might be partly owing to this nervous strain that the new shock of rage he felt as Tito's lie fell on his ears brought a strange bodily effect with it: a cold stream seemed to rush over him, and the last words of the speech seemed to be drowned by ringing chimes. Thought gave way to a dizzy horror, as if the earth were slipping away from under him. Every one in the room was looking at him as Tito ended, and saw that the eyes which had had such fierce intensity only a few minutes before had now a vague fear in them. He clutched the back of a seat, and was silent.

Hardly any evidence could have been more in favour of Tito's assertion.

"Surely I have seen this man before, somewhere," said Tornabuoni.

"Certainly you have," said Tito, readily, in a low tone. "He is the escaped prisoner who clutched me on the steps of the Duomo. I did not recognize him then: he looks now more as he used to do, except that he has a more unmistakable air of mad imbecility."

"I cast no doubt on your word, Melema," said Bernardo Rucellai, with cautious gravity, "but you are right to desire some positive test of the fact." Then turning to Baldassarre, he said: "If you are the person you claim to be, you can doubtless give some description of the gems which were your property. I myself was the purchaser of more than one gem from Messer Tito,—the chief rings, I believe, in his collection. One of them is a fine sard, engraved with a subject from Homer. If, as you allege, you are a scholar, and the rightful owner of that ring, you can doubtless turn to the noted passage in Homer from which that subject is taken. Do you accept this test, Melema? or have you anything to allege against its validity? The Jacopo you speak of, was he a scholar?"

It was a fearful crisis for Tito. If he said "Yes," his quick mind told him that he would shake the credibility of his story; if he said "No," he risked everything on the uncertain extent of Baldassarre's imbecility. But there was no noticeable pause before he said, "No. I accept the test."

There was a dead silence while Rucellai moved towards the recess where the books were, and came back with the fine Florentine Homer in his hand. Baldassarre, when he was addressed, had turned his head towards the speaker, and Rucellai believed that he had understood him. But he chose to repeat what he had said, that there might be no mistake as to the test.

"The ring I possess," he said, "is a fine sard, engraved with a subject from Homer. There was no other at all resembling it in Messer Tito's collection. Will you turn to the passage in Homer from which that subject is taken? Seat yourself here," he added, laying the book on the table, and pointing to his own seat while he stood beside it.

Baldassarre had so far recovered from the first confused horror produced by the sensation of rushing coldness and chiming din in the ears as to be partly aware of what was said to him: he was aware that something was being demanded from him to prove his identity, but he formed no distinct idea of the details. The sight of the book recalled the habitual longing and faint hope that he could read and understand, and he moved towards the chair immediately.

The book was open before him, and he bent his head a little towards it, while everybody watched him eagerly. He turned no leaf. His eyes wandered over the pages that lay before him, and then fixed on them a straining gaze. This lasted for two or three minutes in dead silence. Then he lifted his hands to each side of his head, and said, in a low tone of despair, "Lost, lost!"

There was something so piteous in the wandering look and the low cry, that while they confirmed the belief in his madness they raised compassion. Nay, so distinct sometimes is the working of a double consciousness within us, that Tito himself, while he triumphed in the apparent verification of his lie, wished that he had never made the lie necessary to himself,—wished he had recognized his father on the steps, —wished he had gone to seek him,—wished everything had been different. But he had borrowed from the terrible usurer Falsehood, and the loan had mounted and mounted with the years, till he belonged to the usurer, body and soul.

The compassion excited in all the witnesses was not without its danger to Tito; for conjecture is constantly guided by feeling, and more than one person suddenly conceived that this man might have been a scholar and have lost his faculties. On the other hand, they had not present to their minds the motives which could have led Tito to the denial of his benefactor, and having no ill-will towards him, it would have been difficult to them to believe that he had been uttering the basest of lies. And the originally common type of Baldassarre's person, coarsened by years of hardship, told as a confirmation of Tito's lie. If Baldassarre, to begin with, could have uttered precisely the words he had premeditated, there might have been something in the form of his accusation which would have given it the stamp not only of true experience but of mental refinement. But there had been no such testimony in his impulsive agitated words; and there seemed the very opposite testimony in the rugged face and the coarse hands that trembled beside it, standing out in strong contrast in the midst of that velvet-clad, fair-handed company.

His next movement, while he was being watched in silence, told against him too. He took his hands from his head, and felt for something under his tunic. Every one guessed what that movement meant,—guessed that there was a weapon at his side. Glances were interchanged; and Bernardo Rucellai said, in a quiet tone, touching Baldassarre's shoulder,—

"My friend, this is an important business of yours. You shall have all justice. Follow me into a private room."

Baldassarre was still in that half-stunned state in which he was susceptible to any prompting, in the same way as an insect that forms no conception of what the prompting leads to. He rose from his seat, and followed Rucellai out of the room.

In two or three minutes Rucellai came back again, and said,—

"He is safe under lock and key. Piero Pitti, you are one of the Magnificent Eight, what do you think of our sending Matteo to the palace for a couple of sbirri, who may escort him to the Stinche? If there is any danger in him, as I think there is, he will be safe there; and we can inquire about him to-morrow."

Pitti assented, and the order was given.

"He is certainly an ill-looking fellow," said Tornabuoni. "And you say he has attempted your life already, Melema?"

And the talk turned on the various forms of madness, and the fierceness of the southern blood. If the seeds of conjecture unfavourable to Tito had been planted in the mind of any one present, they were hardly strong enough to grow without the aid of much daylight and ill-will. The common-looking, wild-eyed old man, clad in serge, might have won belief without very strong evidence, if he had accused a man who was envied and disliked. As it was, the only congruous and probable view of the case seemed to be the one that sent the unpleasant accuser safely out of sight, and left the pleasant serviceable Tito just where he was before.

The subject gradually floated away, and gave place to others, till a heavy tramp, and something like the struggling of a man who was being dragged away, were heard outside. The sounds soon died out, and the interruption seemed to make the last hour's conviviality more resolute and vigorous. Every one was willing to forget a disagreeable incident.

Tito's heart was palpitating, and the wine tasted no better to him than if it had been blood.

To-night he had paid a heavier price than ever to make himself safe. He did not like the price, and yet it was inevitable that he should be glad of the purchase.

And after all he led the chorus. He was in a state of excitement in which oppressive sensations, and the wretched consciousness of something hateful but irrevocable, were mingled with a feeling of triumph which seemed to assert itself as the feeling that would subsist and be master of the morrow.

And it *was* master. For on the morrow, as we saw, when he was about to start on his mission to Rome, he had the air of a man well satisfied with the world.

CHAPTER XX

AN ARRESTING VOICE

WHEN Romola sat down on the stone under the cypress, all things conspired to give her the sense of freedom and solitude,—her escape from the accustomed walls and streets; the widening distance from her husband, who was by this time riding towards Siena, while every hour would take her farther on the opposite way; the morning stillness; the great dip of ground on the roadside making a gulf between her and the sombre calm of the mountains. For the first time in her life she felt alone in the presence of the earth and sky, with no human presence interposing and making a law for her.

Suddenly a voice close to her said,—

"You are Romola de' Bardi, the wife of Tito Melema."

She knew the voice,—it had vibrated through her more than once before; and because she knew it, she did not turn round or look up. She sat shaken by awe, and yet inwardly rebelling against the awe. It was one of those black-skirted monks who was daring to speak to her, and interfere with her privacy: that was all. And yet she was shaken, as if that destiny which men thought of as a sceptred deity had come to her, and grasped her with fingers of flesh.

"You are fleeing from Florence in disguise. I have a command from God to stop you. You are not permitted to flee."

Romola's anger at the intrusion mounted higher at these imperative words. She would not turn round to look at the speaker, whose examining gaze she resented. Sitting quite motionless, she said,—

"What right have you to speak to me or to hinder me?"

"The right of a messenger. You have put on a religious garb, and you have no religious purpose. You have sought the garb as a disguise. But you were not suffered to pass me without being discerned. It was declared to me who you were: it is declared to me that you are seeking to escape from the lot God has laid upon you. You wish your true name and your true place in life to be hidden, that you may choose for yourself a new name and a new place, and have no rule but your own will. And I have a command to call you back. My daughter, you must return to your place."

Romola's mind rose in stronger rebellion with every sentence. She was the more determined not to show any sign of submission, because the consciousness of being inwardly shaken made her dread lest she should fall into irresolution. She spoke with more irritation than before.

"I will not return. I acknowledge no right of priests and monks to interfere with my actions. You have no power over me."

"I know—I know you have been brought up in scorn of obedience. But it is not the poor monk who claims to interfere with you: it is the truth that commands you. And you cannot escape it. Either you must obey it, and it will lead you; or you must disobey it, and it will hang on you with the weight of a chain which you will drag forever. But you will obey it, my daughter. Your old servant will return to you with the mules; my companion is gone to fetch him; and you will go back to Florence."

She started up with anger in her eyes, and faced the speaker. It was Fra Girolamo; she knew that well enough before. She was nearly as tall as he was, and their faces were almost on a level. She had started up with defiant words ready to burst from her lips, but they fell back again without utterance. She had met Fra Girolamo's calm glance, and the impression from it was so new to her that her anger sank ashamed as something irrelevant.

There was nothing transcendent in Savonarola's face. It was not beautiful. It was strong-featured, and owed all its refinement to habits of mind and rigid discipline of the body. The source of the impression his glance produced on Romola was the sense it conveyed to her of interest in her and care for her apart from any personal feeling. It was the first time she had encountered a gaze in which simple human fellowship expressed itself as a strongly felt bond. Such a glance is half the vocation of the priest or spiritual guide of men, and Romola felt it impossible again to question his authority to speak to her. She stood silent, looking at him. And he spoke again.

"You assert your freedom proudly, my daughter. But who is so base as the debtor that thinks himself free?"

There was a sting in those words, and Romola's countenance changed as if a subtle pale flash had gone over it.

"And you are flying from your debts,—the debt of a Florentine woman, the debt of a wife. You are turning your back on the lot that has been appointed for you; you are going to choose another. But can man or woman choose duties? No more than they can choose their birthplace or their father and mother. My daughter, you are fleeing from the presence of God into the wilderness."

As the anger melted from Romola's mind, it had given place to a new presentiment of the strength there might be in submission, if this man, at whom she was beginning to look with a vague reverence, had some valid law to show her. But no—it was impossible; he could not know what determined her. Yet she could not again simply refuse to be guided; she was constrained to plead; and in her new need to be reverent while she resisted, the title which she had never given him before came to her lips without forethought.

"My father, you cannot know the reasons which compel me to go. None can know them but myself. None can judge for me. I have been driven by great sorrow. I am resolved to go."

"I know enough, my daughter: my mind has been so far illuminated concerning you, that I know enough. You are not happy in your married life: but I am not a confessor, and I seek to know nothing that should be reserved for the seal of confession. I have a Divine warrant to stop you, which does not depend on such knowledge. You were warned by a message from heaven, delivered in my presence,—you were warned before marriage, when you might still have lawfully chosen to be free from the marriage-bond. But you chose the bond; and in wilfully breaking it—I speak to you as a pagan, if the holy mystery of matrimony is not sacred to you—you are breaking a pledge. Of what wrongs will you complain, my daughter, when you yourself are committing one of the greatest wrongs a woman and a citizen can be guilty of,—withdrawing in secrecy and disguise from a pledge which you have given in the face of God and your fellow-men? Of what wrongs will you complain, when you yourself are breaking the simplest law that lies at the foundation of the trust which binds man to man,—faithfulness to the spoken word? This, then, is the wisdom you have gained by scorning the mysteries of the Church?—not to see the bare duty of integrity, where the Church would have taught you to see, not integrity only, but religion."

The blood had rushed to Romola's face, and she shrank as if she had been stricken. "I would not have put on a disguise," she began; but she could not go on,—she was too much shaken by the suggestion in the Frate's words of a possible affinity between her own conduct and Tito's.

"And to break that pledge you fly from Florence,—Florence, where there are the only men and women in the world to whom you owe the debt of a fellow-citizen."

"I should never have quitted Florence," said Romola, tremulously, "as long as there was any hope of my fulfilling a duty to my father there."

"And do you owe no tie but that of a child to her father in the flesh? Your life has been spent in blindness, my daughter. You have lived with those who sit on a hill aloof, and look down on the life of their fellow-men. I know their vain discourse. It is of what has been in the times which they fill with their own fancied wisdom, while they scorn God's work in the present. And doubtless you were taught how there were pagan women who felt what it was to live for the Republic; yet you have never felt that you, a Florentine woman, should live for Florence. If your own people are wearing a yoke, will you slip from under it, instead of struggling with them to lighten it? There is hunger and misery in our streets; yet you say, 'I care not; I have my own sorrows; I will go away, if peradventure I can ease them.' The servants of God are struggling after a law of justice, peace, and charity, that the hundred thousand citizens among whom you were born may be governed righteously; but you think no more of this than if you were a bird, that may spread its wings and fly whither it will in search of food to its liking. And yet you have scorned the teaching of the Church, my daughter. As if you, a wilful wanderer, following your own blind choice, were not below the humblest Florentine woman who stretches forth her hands with her own people, and craves a blessing for them; and feels a close sisterhood with the neighbour who kneels beside her and is not of her

own blood; and thinks of the mighty purpose that God has for Florence;
and waits and endures because the promised work is great, and she feels
herself little."

"I was not going away to ease and self-indulgence," said Romola,
raising her head again, with a prompting to vindicate herself. "I was
going away to hardship. I expect no joy: it is gone from my life."

"You are seeking your own will, my daughter. You are seeking some
good other than the law you are bound to obey. But how will you find
good? it is not a thing of choice: it is a river that flows from the foot
of the Invisible Throne, and flows by the path of obedience. I say
again, man cannot choose his duties. You may choose to forsake your
duties, and choose not to have the sorrow they bring. But you will go
forth; and what will you find, my daughter? Sorrow without duty,—
bitter herbs, and no bread with them."

"But if you knew," said Romola, clasping her hands and pressing
them tight, as she looked pleadingly at Fra Girolamo,—"if you knew
what it was to me,—how impossible it seemed to me to bear it."

"My daughter," he said, pointing to the cord round Romola's neck,
"you carry something within your mantle; draw it forth, and look at it."

Romola gave a slight start, but her impulse now was to do just what
Savonarola told her. Her self-doubt was grappled by a stronger will and
a stronger conviction than her own. She drew forth the crucifix. Still
pointing towards it, he said,—

"There, my daughter, is the image of a Supreme Offering, made by
Supreme Love, because the need of man was great."

He paused, and she held the crucifix trembling,—trembling under a
sudden impression of the wide distance between her present and her
past self. What a length of road she had travelled through since she first
took that crucifix from the Frate's hands! Had life as many secrets before her still as it had for her then, in her young blindness? It was a
thought that helped all other subduing influences; and at the sound of
Fra Girolamo's voice again, Romola, with a quick involuntary movement pressed the crucifix against her mantle and looked at him with
more submission than before.

"Conform your life to that image, my daughter; make your sorrow
an offering: and when the fire of Divine charity burns within you, and
you behold the need of your fellow-men by the light of that flame, you
will not call your offering great. You have carried yourself proudly, as
one who held herself not of common blood or of common thoughts; but
you have been as one unborn to the true life of man. What! you say
your love for your father no longer tells you to stay in Florence? Then,
since that tie is snapped, you are without a law, without religion: you
are no better than a beast of the field when she is robbed of her young.
If the yearning of a fleshly love is gone, you are without love, without
obligation. See, then, my daughter, how you are below the life of the
believer who worships that image of the Supreme Offering, and feels the
glow of a common life with the lost multitude for whom that offering was

made, and beholds the history of the world as the history of a great re-
demption in which he is himself a fellow-worker, in his own place and
among his own people! If you held that faith, my beloved daughter, you
would not be a wanderer flying from suffering, and blindly seeking the
good of a freedom which is lawlessness. You would feel that Florence
was the home of your soul as well as your birthplace, because you would
see the work that was given you to do there. If you forsake your place,
who will fill it? You ought to be in your place now, helping in the great
work by which God will purify Florence, and raise it to be the guide
of the nations. What! the earth is full of iniquity, full of groans,—the
light is still struggling with a mighty darkness, and you say, 'I cannot
bear my bonds; I will burst them asunder; I will go where no man
claims me'? My daughter, every bond of your life is a debt: the right
lies in the payment of that debt; it can lie nowhere else. In vain will
you wander over the earth; you will be wandering forever away from
the right."

Romola was inwardly struggling with strong forces,—that immense
personal influence of Savonarola, which came from the energy of his
emotions and beliefs; and her consciousness, surmounting all prejudice,
that his words implied a higher law than any she had yet obeyed. But
the resisting thoughts were not yet overborne.

"How, then, could Dino be right? He broke ties; he forsook his place."

"That was a special vocation. He was constrained to depart, else he
could not have attained the higher life. It would have been stifled within
him."

"And I too," said Romola, raising her hands to her brow, and speaking in a tone of anguish, as if she were being dragged to some torture.
"Father, you may be wrong."

"Ask your conscience, my daughter. You have no vocation such as
your brother had. You are a wife. You seek to break your ties in self-
will and anger, not because the higher life calls upon you to renounce
them. The higher life begins for us, my daughter, when we renounce
our own will to bow before a Divine law. That seems hard to you. It
is the portal of wisdom and freedom and blessedness. And the symbol
of it hangs before you. That wisdom is the religion of the Cross. And
you stand aloof from it: you are a pagan; you have been taught to say,
'I am as the wise men who lived before the time when the Jew of Naz-
areth was crucified.' And that is your wisdom! To be as the dead whose
eyes are closed, and whose ear is deaf to the work of God that has been
since their time. What has your dead wisdom done for you, my daughter? It has left you without a heart for the neighbours among whom you
dwell, without care for the great work by which Florence is to be regenerated and the world made holy; it has left you without a share
in the Divine life which quenches the sense of suffering Self in the ardours of an ever-growing love. And now, when the sword has pierced
your soul, you say, 'I will go away; I cannot bear my sorrow.' And you
think nothing of the sorrow and the wrong that are within the walls of

the city where you dwell: you would leave your place empty, when it ought to be filled with your pity and your labour. If there is wickedness in the streets, your steps should shine with the light of purity; if there is a cry of anguish, you, my daughter, because you know the meaning of the cry, should be there to still it. My beloved daughter, sorrow has come to teach you a new worship: the sign of it hangs before you."

Romola's mind was still torn by conflict. She foresaw that she should obey Savonarola and go back: his words had come to her as if they were an interpretation of that revulsion from self-satisfied ease, and of that new fellowship with suffering, which had already been awakened in her. His arresting voice had brought a new condition into her life, which made it seem impossible to her that she could go on her way as if she had not heard it; yet she shrank as one who sees the path she must take, but sees, too, that the hot lava lies there. And the instinctive shrinking from a return to her husband brought doubts. She turned away her eyes from Fra Girolamo, and stood for a minute or two with her hands hanging clasped before her, like a statue. At last she spoke, as if the words were being wrung from her, still looking on the ground.

"My husband . . . he is not . . . my love is gone!"

"My daughter, there is the bond of a higher love. Marriage is not carnal only, made for selfish delight. See what that thought leads you to! It leads you to wander away in a false garb from all the obligations of your place and name. That would not have been, if you had learned that it is a sacramental vow, from which none but God can release you. My daughter, your life is not as a grain of sand, to be blown by the winds; it is a thing of flesh and blood, that dies if it be sundered. Your husband is not a malefactor?"

Romola started. "Heaven forbid! No; I accuse him of nothing."

"I did not suppose he was a malefactor. I meant that if he were a malefactor, your place would be in the prison beside him. My daughter, if the cross comes to you as a wife, you must carry it as a wife. You may say, 'I will forsake my husband,' but you cannot cease to be a wife."

"Yet if—oh, how could I bear—" Romola had involuntarily begun to say something which she sought to banish from her mind again.

"Make your marriage-sorrows an offering too, my daughter: an offering to the great work by which sin and sorrow are being made to cease. The end is sure, and is already beginning. Here in Florence it is beginning, and the eyes of faith behold it. And it may be our blessedness to die for it: to die daily by the crucifixion of our selfish will,—to die at last by laying our bodies on the altar. My daughter, you are a child of Florence; fulfil the duties of that great inheritance. Live for Florence,— for your own people, whom God is preparing to bless the earth. Bear the anguish and the smart. The iron is sharp—I know, I know—it rends the tender flesh. The draught is bitterness on the lips. But there is rapture in the cup,—there is the vision which makes all life below it dross forever. Come, my daughter, come back to your place!"

While Savonarola spoke with growing intensity, his arms tightly folded before him still, as they had been from the first, but his face alight as from an inward flame, Romola felt herself surrounded and possessed by the glow of his passionate faith. The chill doubts all melted away; she was subdued by the sense of something unspeakably great to which she was being called by a strong being who roused a new strength within herself. In a voice that was like a low, prayerful cry, she said,—

"Father, I will be guided. Teach me! I will go back."

Almost unconsciously she sank on her knees. Savonarola stretched out his hands over her; but feeling would no longer pass through the channel of speech, and he was silent.

CHAPTER XXI

COMING BACK

"RISE, my daughter," said Fra Girolamo, at last. "Your servant is waiting not far off with the mules. It is time that I should go onward to Florence."

Romola arose from her knees. That silent attitude had been a sort of sacrament to her, confirming the state of yearning passivity on which she had newly entered. By the one act of renouncing her resolve to quit her husband, her will seemed so utterly bruised that she felt the need of direction even in small things. She lifted up the edge of her cowl, and saw Maso and the second Dominican standing with their backs towards her on the edge of the hill about ten yards from her; but she looked at Savonarola again without speaking, as if the order to Maso to turn back must come from him and not from her.

"I will go and call them," he said, answering her glance of appeal; "and I will recommend you, my daughter, to the brother who is with me. You desire to put yourself under guidance, and to learn that wisdom which has been hitherto as foolishness to you. A chief gate of that wisdom is the sacrament of confession. You will need a confessor, my daughter, and I desire to put you under the care of Fra Salvestro, one of the brethren of San Marco, in whom I most confide."

"I would rather have no guidance but yours, father," said Romola, looking anxious.

"My daughter, I do not act as a confessor. The vocation I have withdraws me from offices that would force me into frequent contact with the laity, and interfere with my special duties."

"Then shall I not be able to speak to you in private? if I waver, if—" Romola broke off from rising agitation. She felt a sudden alarm lest her new strength in renunciation should vanish if the immediate personal influence of Savonarola vanished.

"My daughter, if your soul has need of the word in private from my lips, you will let me know it through Fra Salvestro, and I will see you in the sacristy or in the choir of San Marco. And I will not cease to watch over you. I will instruct my brother concerning you, that he may guide you into that path of labour for the suffering and the hungry to which you are called as a daughter of Florence in these times of hard need. I desire to behold you among the feebler and more ignorant sisters as the apple-tree among the trees of the forest, so that your fairness and all natural gifts may be but as a lamp through which the Divine light shines the more purely. I will go now and call your servant."

When Maso had been sent a little way in advance, Fra Salvestro came forward, and Savonarola led Romola towards him. She had beforehand felt an inward shrinking from a new guide who was a total stranger to her; but to have resisted Savonarola's advice would have been to assume an attitude of independence at a moment when all her strength must be drawn from the renunciation of independence. And the whole bent of her mind now was towards doing what was painful rather than what was easy. She bowed reverently to Fra Salvestro before looking directly at him; but when she raised her head and saw him fully, her reluctance became a palpitating doubt. There are men whose presence infuses trust and reverence; there are others to whom we have need to carry our trust and reverence ready-made; and that difference flashed on Romola as she ceased to have Savonarola before her, and saw in his stead Fra Salvestro Maruffi. It was not that there was anything manifestly repulsive in Fra Salvestro's face and manner, any air of hypocrisy, any tinge of coarseness; his face was handsomer than Fra Girolamo's, his person a little taller. He was the long-accepted confessor of many among the chief personages in Florence, and had therefore had large experience as a spiritual director. But his face had the vacillating expression of a mind unable to concentrate itself strongly in the channel of one great emotion or belief,—an expression which is fatal to influence over an ardent nature like Romola's. Such an expression is not the stamp of insincerity; it is the stamp simply of a shallow soul, which will often be found sincerely striving to fill a high vocation, sincerely composing its countenance to the utterance of sublime formulas, but finding the muscles twitch or relax in spite of belief, as prose insists on coming instead of poetry to the man who has not the divine frenzy. Fra Salvestro had a peculiar liability to visions, dependent apparently on a constitution given to somnambulism. Savonarola believed in the supernatural character of these visions, while Fra Salvestro himself had originally resisted such an interpretation of them, and had even rebuked Savonarola for his prophetic preaching,—another proof, if one were wanted, that the relative greatness of men is not to be gauged by their tendency to disbelieve the superstitions of their age; for of these two there can be no question which was the great man and which the small.

The difference between them was measured very accurately by the change in Romola's feeling as Fra Salvestro began to address her in words of exhortation and encouragement. After her first angry resistance of Savonarola had passed away, she had lost all remembrance of the old dread lest any influence should drag her within the circle of fanaticism and sour monkish piety. But now again, the chill breath of that dread stole over her. It could have no decisive effect against the impetus her mind had just received; it was only like the closing of the grey clouds over the sunrise, which made her returning path monotonous and sombre.

And perhaps of all sombre paths that on which we go back after treading it with a strong resolution is the one that most severely tests the fervour of renunciation. As they re-entered the city gates, the light snow-flakes fell about them; and as the grey sister walked hastily homeward from the Piazza di San Marco, and trod the bridge again, and turned in at the large door in the Via de' Bardi, her foot-steps were marked darkly on the thin carpet of snow, and her cowl fell laden and damp about her face.

She went up to her room, threw off her serge, destroyed the parting letters, replaced all her precious trifles, unbound her hair, and put on her usual black dress. Instead of taking a long exciting journey, she was to sit down in her usual place. The snow fell against the windows, and she was alone.

She felt the dreariness, yet her courage was high, like that of a seeker who has come on new signs of gold. She was going to thread life by a fresh clew. She had thrown all the energy of her will into renunciation. The empty tabernacle remained locked, and she placed Dino's crucifix outside it.

Nothing broke the outward monotony of her solitary home, till the night came like a white ghost at the windows. Yet it was the most memorable Christmas-eve in her life to Romola, this of 1494.

BOOK THREE

★

CHAPTER XXII

ROMOLA IN HER PLACE

It was the 30th of October, 1496. The sky that morning was clear enough, and there was a pleasant autumnal breeze. But the Florentines just then thought very little about the land breezes: they were thinking of the gales at sea, which seemed to be uniting with all other powers to disprove the Frate's declaration that Heaven took special care of Florence.

For those terrible gales had driven away from the coast of Leghorn certain ships from Marseilles, freighted with soldiery and corn; and Florence was in the direst need, first of food, and secondly of fighting men. Pale Famine was in her streets, and her territory was threatened on all its borders.

For the French king, that new Charlemagne, who had entered Italy in anticipatory triumph, and had conquered Naples without the least trouble, had gone away again fifteen months ago, and was even, it is feared in his grief for the loss of a new-born son, losing the languid intention of coming back again to redress grievances and set the Church in order. A league had been formed against him—a Holy League, with Pope Borgia at its head—to "drive out the barbarians," who still garrisoned the fortress of Naples. That had a patriotic sound; but, looked at more closely, the Holy League seemed very much like an agreement among certain wolves to drive away all other wolves, and then to see which among themselves could snatch the largest share of the prey. And there was a general disposition to regard Florence not as a fellow-wolf, but rather as a desirable carcass. Florence, therefore, of all the chief Italian States, had alone declined to join the League, adhering still to the French alliance.

She had declined at her peril. At this moment Pisa, still fighting savagely for liberty, was being encouraged not only by strong forces from Venice and Milan, but by the presence of the German Emperor Maximilian, who had been invited by the League, and was joining the Pisans with such troops as he had in the attempt to get possession of Leghorn, while the coast was invested by Venetian and Genoese ships. And if Leghorn should fall into the hands of the enemy, woe to Florence! For if that one outlet towards the sea were closed, hedged in as she was on the land by the bitter ill-will of the Pope and the jealousy of smaller States, how could succour reach her?

The government of Florence had shown a great heart in this urgent need, meeting losses and defeats with vigorous efforts, raising fresh money, raising fresh soldiers, but not neglecting the good old method of Italian defence,—conciliatory embassies. And while the scarcity of food was every day becoming greater, they had resolved, in opposition to old precedent, not to shut out the starving country people, and the mendicants driven from the gates of other cities, who came flocking to Florence like birds from a land of snow.

These acts of a government in which the disciples of Savonarola made the strongest element were not allowed to pass without criticism. The disaffected were plentiful, and they saw clearly that the government took the worst course for the public welfare. Florence ought to join the League and make common cause with the other great Italian States, instead of drawing down their hostility by a futile adherence to a foreign ally. Florence ought to take care of her own citizens, instead of opening her gates to famine and pestilence in the shape of starving contadini and alien mendicants.

Every day the distress became sharper: every day the murmurs became louder. And, to crown the difficulties of the government, for a month and more,—in obedience to a mandate from Rome,—Fra Girolamo had ceased to preach. But on the arrival of the terrible news that the ships from Marseilles had been driven back, and that no corn was coming, the need for the voice that could infuse faith and patience into the people became too imperative to be resisted. In defiance of the Papal mandate the Signoria requested Savonarola to preach. And two days ago he had mounted again the pulpit of the Duomo, and had told the people only to wait and be steadfast, and the Divine help would certainly come.

It was a bold sermon: he consented to have his frock stripped off him if, when Florence persevered in fulfilling the duties of piety and citizenship, God did not come to her rescue.

Yet, at present, on this morning of the 30th, there were no signs of rescue. Perhaps if the precious Tabernacle of the Madonna dell' Impruneta were brought into Florence and carried in devout procession to the Duomo, that Mother, rich in sorrows and therefore in mercy, would plead for the suffering city? For a century and a half there were records how the Florentines, suffering from drought, or flood, or famine, or pestilence, or the threat of wars, had fetched the potent image within their walls, and had found deliverance. And grateful honour had been done to her and her ancient church of L'Impruneta; the high house of Buondelmonti, patrons of the church, had to guard her hidden image with bare sword; wealth had been poured out for prayers at her shrine, for chantings and chapels and ever-burning lights; and lands had been added, till there was much quarreling for the privilege of serving her. The Florentines were deeply convinced of her graciousness to them, so that the sight of her tabernacle within their walls was like the parting of the cloud, and the proverb ran, that the Florentines had a Madonna who would do what they pleased.

When were they in more need of her pleading pity than now? And already, the evening before, the tabernacle containing the miraculous hidden image had been brought with high and reverend escort from L'Impruneta, the privileged spot six miles beyond the gate of San Piero that looks towards Rome, and had been deposited in the church of San Gaggio, outside the gate, whence it was to be fetched in solemn procession by all the fraternities, trades, and authorities of Florence.

But the Pitying Mother had not yet entered within the walls, and the morning arose on unchanged misery and despondency. Pestilence was hovering in the track of famine. Not only the hospitals were full, but the courtyards of private houses had been turned into refuges and infirmaries; and still there was unsheltered want. And early this morning, as usual, members of the various fraternities who made it part of their duty to bury the unfriended dead, were bearing away the corpses that had sunk by the wayside. As usual, sweet womanly forms, with the refined air and carriage of the well-born, but in the plainest garb, were moving about the streets on their daily errands of tending the sick and relieving the hungry.

One of these forms was easily distinguishable as Romola de' Bardi. Clad in the simplest garment of black serge, with a plain piece of black drapery drawn over her head, so as to hide all her hair, except the bands of gold that rippled apart on her brow, she was advancing from the Ponte Vecchio towards the Por' Santa Maria—the street in a direct line with the bridge,—when she found her way obstructed by the pausing of a bier, which was being carried by members of the company of San Jacopo del Popolo, in search for the unburied dead. The brethren at the head of the bier were stooping to examine something, while a group of idle workmen, with features paled and sharpened by hunger, were clustering around and all talking at once.

"He's dead, I tell you! Messer Domeneddio has loved him well enough to take him."

"Ah, and it would be well for us all if we could have our legs stretched out and go with our heads two or three *bracci* foremost! It's ill standing upright with hunger to prop you."

"Well, well, he's an old fellow. Death has got a poor bargain. Life's had the best of him."

"And no Florentine, ten to one! A beggar turned out of Siena. San Giovanni defend us! They've no need of soldiers to fight us. They send us an army of starving men."

"No, no! This man is one of the prisoners turned out of the Stinche. I know by the gray patch where the prison badge was."

"Keep quiet! Lend a hand! Don't you see the brethren are going to lift him on the bier?"

"It's likely he's alive enough if he could only look it. The soul may be inside him if it had only a drop of *vernaccia* to warm it."

"In truth, I think he is not dead," said one of the brethren, when they had lifted him on the bier. "He has perhaps only sunk down for want of food."

"Let me try to give him some wine," said Romola, coming forward. She loosened the small flask which she carried at her belt, and, leaning towards the prostrate body, with a deft hand she applied a small ivory implement between the teeth, and poured into the mouth a few drops of wine. The stimulus acted: the wine was evidently swallowed. She poured more, till the head was moved a little towards her, and the eyes of the old man opened full upon her with the vague look of returning consciousness.

Then for the first time a sense of complete recognition came over Romola. Those wild dark eyes opening in the sallow deep-lined face, with the white beard, which was now long again, were like an unmistakable signature to a remembered handwriting. The light of two summers had not made that image any fainter in Romola's memory: the image of the escaped prisoner, whom she had seen in the Duomo the day when Tito first wore the armour,—at whose grasp Tito was paled with terror in the strange sketch she had seen in Piero's studio. A wretched tremor and palpitation seized her. Now, at last, perhaps, she was going to know some secret which might be more bitter than all that had gone before. She felt an impulse to dart away as from a sight of horror; and again, a more imperious need to keep close by the side of this old man, whom, the divination of keen feeling told her, her husband had injured. In the very instant of this conflict she still leaned towards him and kept her right hand ready to administer more wine, while her left was passed under his neck. Her hands trembled, but their habit of soothing helpfulness would have served to guide them without the direction of her thought.

Baldassarre was looking at *her* for the first time. The close seclusion in which Romola's trouble had kept her in the weeks preceding her flight and his arrest had denied him the opportunity he had sought of seeing the Wife who lived in the Via de' Bardi; and at this moment the descriptions he had heard of the fair golden-haired woman were all gone, like yesterday's waves.

"Will it not be well to carry him to the steps of San Stefano?" said Romola. "We shall cease then to stop up the street, and you can go on your way with your bier."

They had only to move onward for about thirty yards before reaching the steps of San Stefano; and by this time Baldassarre was able himself to make some efforts towards getting off the bier, and propping himself on the steps against the church doorway. The charitable brethren passed on; but the group of interested spectators, who had nothing to do and much to say, had considerably increased. The feeling towards

the old man was not so entirely friendly now it was quite certain that
he was alive, but the respect inspired by Romola's presence caused the
passing remarks to be made in a rather more subdued tone than before.

"Ah, they gave him his morsel every day in the Stinche,—that's
why he can't do so well without it. You and I, Cecco, know better what
it is to go to bed fasting."

"*Gnaffè!* that's why the Magnificent Eight have turned out some of
the prisoners, that they may shelter honest people instead. But if every
thief is to be brought to life with good wine and wheaten bread, we
Ciompi had better go and fill ourselves in Arno while the water's plenty."

Romola had seated herself on the steps by Baldassarre, and was saying, "Can you eat a little bread now? perhaps by-and-by you will be
able, if I leave it with you. I must go on, because I have promised to be
at the hospital. But I will come back, if you will wait here, and then I
will take you to some shelter. Do you understand? Will you wait? I
will come back."

He looked dreamily at her, and repeated her words, "come back." It
was no wonder that his mind was enfeebled by his bodily exhaustion, but
she hoped that he apprehended her meaning. She opened her basket,
which was filled with pieces of soft bread, and put one of the pieces
into his hand.

"Do you keep your bread for those that can't swallow, madonna?"
said a rough-looking fellow, in a red nightcap, who had elbowed his
way into the inmost circle of spectators,—a circle that was pressing
rather closely on Romola.

"If anybody isn't hungry," said another, "I say, let him alone. He's
better off than people who've got craving stomachs and no breakfast."

"Yes, indeed; if a man's a mind to die, it's a time to encourage him,
instead of making him come back to life against his will. Dead men
want no trencher."

"Oh, you don't understand the Frate's charity," said a young man
in an excellent cloth tunic, whose face showed no signs of want. "The
Frate has been preaching to the birds, like Saint Anthony, and he's been
telling the hawks they were made to feed the sparrows, as every good
Florentine citizen was made to feed six starving beggarmen from Arezzo
or Bologna. Madonna, there, is a pious Piagnone; she's not going to
throw away her good bread on honest citizens who've got all the Frate's
prophecies to swallow."

"Come, madonna," said he of the red cap, "the old thief doesn't eat
the bread, you see; you'd better try *us*. We fast so much, we're half
saints already."

The circle had narrowed till the coarse men—most of them gaunt
from privation—had left hardly any margin round Romola. She had
been taking from her basket a small horn-cup, into which she put the
piece of bread and just moistened it with wine; and hitherto she had not
appeared to heed them. But now she rose to her feet, and looked round

at them. Instinctively the men who were nearest to her pushed backward a little, as if their rude nearness were the fault of those behind. Romola held out the basket of bread to the man in the nightcap, looking at him without any reproach in her glance, as she said,—

"Hunger is hard to bear, I know, and you have the power to take this bread if you will. It was saved for sick women and children. You are strong men; but if you do not choose to suffer because you are strong, you have the power to take everything from the weak. You can take the bread from this basket; but I shall watch by this old man; I shall resist your taking the bread from *him*."

For a few moments there was perfect silence, while Romola looked at the faces before her, and held out the basket of bread. Her own pale face had the slightly pinched look and the deepening of the eye-socket which indicates unusual fasting in the habitually temperate, and the large direct gaze of her hazel eyes was all the more impressive.

The man in the nightcap looked rather silly, and backed, thrusting his elbow into his neighbour's ribs with an air of moral rebuke. The backing was general, every one wishing to imply that he had been pushed forward against his will; and the young man in the fine cloth tunic had disappeared.

But at this moment the armed servitors of the Signoria, who had begun to patrol the line of streets through which the procession was to pass, came up to disperse the group which was obstructing the narrow street. The man addressed as Cecco retreated from a threatening mace up the church steps, and said to Romola, in a respectful tone,—

"Madonna, if you want to go on your errands, I'll take care of the old man."

Cecco was a wild-looking figure: a very ragged tunic, made shaggy and variegated by cloth-dust and clinging fragments of wool, gave relief to a pair of bare bony arms and a long sinewy neck: his square jaw shaded by a bristly black beard, his bridgeless nose and low forehead, made his face look as if it had been crushed down for purposes of packing, and a narrow piece of red rag tied over his ears seemed to assist in the compression. Romola looked at him with some hesitation.

"Don't distrust me, madonna," said Cecco, who understood her look perfectly; "I am not so pretty as you, but I've got an old mother who eats my porridge for me. What! there's a heart inside me, and I've bought a candle for the most Holy Virgin before now. Besides, see there, the old fellow is eating his sop. He's hale enough: he'll be on his legs as well as the best of us by-and-by."

"Thank you for offering to take care of him, friend," said Romola, rather penitent for her doubting glance. Then leaning to Baldassarre, she said, "Pray wait for me till I come again."

He assented with a slight movement of the head and hand; **and** Romola went on her way towards the hospital of San Matteo, **in the** Piazza di San Marco.

CHAPTER XXIII

THE UNSEEN MADONNA

In returning from the hospital, more than an hour later, Romola took a different road, making a wider circuit towards the river, which she reached at some distance from the Ponte Vecchio. She turned her steps towards that bridge, intending to hasten to San Stefano in search of Baldassarre. She dreaded to know more about him, yet she felt as if, in forsaking him, she would be forsaking some near claim upon her.

But when she approached the meeting of the roads where the Por' Santa Maria would be on her right hand and the Ponte Vecchio on her left, she found herself involved in a crowd who suddenly fell on their knees; and she immediately knelt with them. The Cross was passing,— the Great Cross of the Duomo—which headed the procession. Romola was later than she had expected to be, and now she must wait till the procession had passed. As she rose from her knees, when the Cross had disappeared, the return to a standing posture, with nothing to do but gaze, made her more conscious of her fatigue than she had been while she had been walking and occupied. A shopkeeper by her side said,—

"Madonna Romola, you will be weary of standing: Gian Fantoni will be glad to give you a seat in his house. Here is his door close at hand. Let me open it for you. What! he loves God and the Frate as we do. His house is yours."

Romola was accustomed now to be addressed in this fraternal way by ordinary citizens, whose faces were familiar to her from her having seen them constantly in the Duomo. The idea of home had come to be identified for her less with the house in the Via de' Bardi, where she sat in frequent loneliness, than with the towered circuit of Florence, where there was hardly a turn of the streets at which she was not greeted with looks of appeal or of friendliness. She was glad enough to pass through the open door on her right hand and be led by the fraternal hose-vender to an upstairs window where a stout woman with three children, all in the plain garb of Piagnoni, made a place for her with much reverence above the bright hanging draperies. From this corner station she could see not only the procession pouring in solemn slowness between the lines of houses on the Ponte Vecchio, but also the river and the Lung' Arno on towards the bridge of the Santa Trinità.

In sadness and in stillness came the slow procession. Not even a wailing chant broke the silent appeal for mercy; there was only the tramp of footsteps, and the faint sweep of woollen garments. They were young footsteps that were passing when Romola first looked from the window,—a long train of the Florentine youth, bearing high in the midst of them the white image of the youthful Jesus, with a golden glory above his head, standing by the tall cross where the thorns and the nails lay ready.

After that train of fresh beardless faces came the mysterious-looking Companies of Discipline, bound by secret rules to self-chastisement, and devout praise, and special acts of piety; all wearing a garb which concealed the whole head and face except the eyes. Every one knew that these mysterious forms were Florentine citizens of various ranks, who might be seen at ordinary times going about the business of the shop, the counting-house, or the State; but no member now was discernible as son, husband, or father. They had dropped their personality, and walked as symbols of a common vow. Each company had its colour and its badge; but the garb of all was a complete shroud, and left no expression but that of fellowship.

In comparison with them, the multitude of monks seemed to be strongly distinguished individuals, in spite of the common tonsure and the common frock. First came a white stream of reformed Benedictines; and then a much longer stream of the Frati Minori, or Franciscans, in that age all clad in grey, with the knotted cord round their waists, and some of them with the *zoccoli*, or wooden sandals, below their bare feet; —perhaps the most numerous order in Florence, owning many zealous members who loved mankind and hated the Dominicans. And after the grey came the black of the Augustinians of San Spirito, with more cultured human faces above it,—men who had inherited the library of Boccaccio, and had made the most learned company in Florence when learning was rarer; then the white over dark of the Carmelites; and then again the unmixed black of the Servites, that famous Florentine order founded by seven merchants who forsook their gains to adore the Divine Mother.

And now the hearts of all on-lookers began to beat a little faster, either with hatred or with love, for there was a stream of black and white coming over the bridge,—of black mantles over white scapularies; and every one knew that the Dominicans were coming. Those of Fiesole passed first. One black mantle parted by white after another, one tonsured head after another, and still expectation was suspended. They were very coarse mantles, all of them, and many were threadbare, if not ragged; for the Prior of San Marco had reduced the fraternities under his rule to the strictest poverty and discipline. But in the long line of black and white there was at last singled out a mantle only a little more worn than the rest, with a tonsured head above it which might not have appeared supremely remarkable to a stranger who had not seen it on bronze medals, with the sword of God as its obverse; or surrounded by an armed guard on the way to the Duomo; or transfigured by the inward flame of the orator as it looked round on a rapt multitude.

As the approach of Savonarola was discerned, none dared conspicuously to break the stillness by a sound which would rise above the solemn tramp of footsteps and the faint sweep of garments; nevertheless his ear, as well as other ears, caught a mingled sound of slow hissing that longed to be curses, and murmurs that longed to be blessings. Perhaps it was the sense that the hissing predominated which made two or three of his disciples in the foreground of the crowd, at the meeting of the roads, fall on their knees, as if something divine were passing. The movement of silent homage spread: it went along the sides of the streets like a subtle shock, leaving some unmoved, while it made the most bend the knee and bow the head. But the hatred, too, gathered a more intense expression; and as Savonarola passed up the Por' Santa Maria, Romola could see that some one at an upper window spat upon him.

Monks again—Frati Umiliati, or Humbled Brethren, from Ognissanti, with a glorious tradition of being the earliest workers in the wool-trade; and again more monks—Vallombrosan and other varieties of Benedictines, reminding the instructed eye by niceties of form and colour that in ages of abuse, long ago, reformers had arisen who had marked a change of spirit by a change of garb; till at last the shaven crowns were at an end, and there came the train of untonsured secular priests.

Then followed the twenty-one incorporated Arts of Florence in long array, with their banners floating above them in proud declaration that the bearers had their distinct functions from the bakers of bread to the judges and notaries. And then all the secondary officers of State, beginning with the less and going on to the greater, till the line of secularities was broken by the Canons of the Duomo, carrying a sacred relic,—the very head, enclosed in silver, of San Zenobio, immortal bishop of Florence, whose virtues were held to have saved the city perhaps a thousand years before.

Here was the nucleus of the procession. Behind the relic came the archbishop in gorgeous cope, with canopy held above him; and after him the mysterious hidden Image,—hidden first by rich curtains of brocade enclosing an outer painted tabernacle, but within this, by the more ancient tabernacle which had never been opened in the memory of living men, or the fathers of living men. In that inner shrine was the image of the Pitying Mother, found ages ago in the soil of L'Impruneta, uttering a cry as the spade struck it. Hitherto the unseen Image had hardly ever been carried to the Duomo without having rich gifts borne before it. There was no reciting the list of precious offerings made by emulous men and communities, especially of veils and curtains and mantles. But the richest of all these, it was said, had been given by a poor abbess and her nuns, who, having no money to buy materials, wove a mantle of gold brocade with their prayers, embroidered it and adorned it with their prayers, and, finally, saw their work presented to the Blessed Virgin in the great piazza by two beautiful youths who spread out white wings and vanished in the blue.

But to-day there were no gifts carried before the tabernacle: no donations were to be given to-day except to the poor. That had been the advice of Fra Girolamo, whose preaching never insisted on gifts to the invisible powers, but only on help to visible need; and altars had been raised at various points in front of the churches, on which the oblations for the poor were deposited. Not even a torch was carried. Surely the hidden Mother cared less for torches and brocade than for the wail of the hungry people. Florence was in extremity: she had done her utmost, and could only wait for something divine that was not in her own power.

The Frate in the torn mantle had said that help would certainly come, and many of the faint-hearted were clinging more to their faith in the Frate's word, than to their faith in the virtues of the unseen Image. But there were not a few of the fierce-hearted who thought with secret rejoicing that the Frate's word might be proved false.

Slowly the tabernacle moved forward, and knees were bent. There was profound stillness; for the train of priests and chaplains from L'Impruneta stirred no passion in the on-lookers. The procession was about to close with the Priors and the Gonfaloniere: the long train of companies and symbols which have their silent music and stir the mind as a chorus stirs it, was passing out of sight, and now a faint yearning hope was all that struggled with the accustomed despondency.

Romola, whose heart had been swelling, half with foreboding, half with that enthusiasm of fellowship which the life of the last two years had made as habitual to her as the consciousness of costume to a vain and idle woman, gave a deep sigh, as at the end of some long mental tension, and remained on her knees for very languor; when suddenly there flashed from between the houses on to the distant bridge something bright-coloured. In the instant Romola started up and stretched out her arms, leaning from the window, while the black drapery fell from her head, and the golden gleam of her hair and the flush in her face seemed the effect of one illumination. A shout arose in the same instant; the last troops of the procession paused, and all faces were turned towards the distant bridge.

But the bridge was passed now: the horseman was pressing at full gallop along by the Arno; the sides of his bay horse, just streaked with foam, looked all white from swiftness: his cap was flying loose by his red becchetto, and he waved an olive-branch in his hand. It was a messenger,—a messenger of good tidings! The blessed olive-branch spoke afar off. But the impatient people could not wait. They rushed to meet the on-comer, and seized his horse's rein, pushing and trampling.

And now Romola could see that the horseman was her husband, who had been sent to Pisa a few days before on a private embassy. The recognition brought no new flash of joy into her eyes. She had checked her first impulsive attitude of expectation; but her governing anxiety was still to know what news of relief had come for Florence.

"Good news!" "Best news!" "News to be paid with hose (*novelle da calze*)!" [1] were the vague answers with which Tito met the importunities

---

[1] It was an ancient custom to give a pair of long trunk hose to the messenger who first brought a welcome piece of news.--EDITOR.

of the crowd, until he had succeeded in pushing on his horse to the spot at the meeting of the ways where the Gonfaloniere and the Priors were awaiting him. There he paused, and bowing low, said,—

"Magnificent Signori! I have to deliver to you the joyful news that the galleys from France, laden with corn and men, have arrived safely in the port of Leghorn, by favour of a strong wind, which kept the enemy's fleet at a distance."

The words had no sooner left Tito's lips than they seemed to vibrate up the streets. A great shout rang through the air, and rushed along the river; and then another, and another; and the shouts were heard spreading along the line of the procession towards the Duomo; and then there were fainter answering shouts, like the intermediate plash of distant waves in a great lake whose waters obey one impulse.

For some minutes there was no attempt to speak further: the Signoria themselves lifted up their caps, and stood bareheaded in the presence of a rescue which had come from outside the limit of their own power, —from that region of trust and resignation which has been in all ages called divine.

At last, as the signal was given to move forward, Tito said, with a smile,—

"I ought to say that any hose to be bestowed by the Magnificent Signoria in reward of these tidings are due, not to me, but to another man who had ridden hard to bring them, and would have been here in my place if his horse had not broken down just before he reached Signa. Meo di Sasso will doubtless be here in an hour or two, and may all the more justly claim the glory of the messenger, because he has had the chief labour and has lost the chief delight."

It was a graceful way of putting a necessary statement; and after a word of reply from the *Proposto*, or spokesman of the Signoria, this dignified extremity of the procession passed on, and Tito turned his horse's head to follow in its train, while the great bell of the Palazzo Vecchio was already beginning to swing, and give a louder voice to the people's joy.

In that moment, when Tito's attention had ceased to be imperatively directed, it might have been expected that he would look round and recognize Romola; but he was apparently engaged with his cap, which, now the eager people were leading his horse, he was able to seize and place on his head, while his right hand was still encumbered by the olive-branch. He had a becoming air of lassitude after his exertions; and Romola, instead of making any effort to be recognized by him, threw her black drapery over her head again, and remained perfectly quiet. Yet she felt almost sure that Tito had seen her; he had the power of seeing everything without seeming to see it.

CHAPTER XXIV

THE VISIBLE MADONNA

THE crowd had no sooner passed onward than Romola descended to the street, and hastened to the steps of San Stefano. Cecco had been attracted with the rest towards the piazza, and she found Baldassarre standing alone against the church door, with the horn-cup in his hand, waiting for her. There was a striking change in him: the blank, dreamy glance of a half-returned consciousness had given place to a fierceness which, as she advanced and spoke to him, flashed upon her as if she had been its object. It was the glance of caged fury that sees its prey passing safe beyond the bars.

Romola started as the glance was turned on her, and her immediate thought was that he had seen Tito. And as she felt the look of hatred grating on her, something like a hope arose that this man might be the criminal, and that her husband might not have been guilty towards him. If she could learn that now, by bringing Tito face to face with him, and have her mind set at rest!

"If you will come with me," she said, "I can give you shelter and food until you are quite rested and strong. Will you come?"

"Yes," said Baldassarre, "I shall be glad to get my strength. I want to get my strength," he repeated, as if he were muttering to himself rather than speaking to her.

"Come!" she said, inviting him to walk by her side, and taking the way by the Arno towards the Ponte Rubaconte as the more private road.

"I think you are not a Florentine," she said presently, as they turned on to the bridge.

He looked round at her without speaking. His suspicious caution was more strongly upon him than usual, just now that the fog of confusion and oblivion was made denser by bodily feebleness. But she was looking at him too, and there was something in her gentle eyes which at last compelled him to answer her. But he answered cautiously,—

"No, I am no Florentine; I am a lonely man."

She observed his reluctance to speak to her, and dared not question him further, lest he should desire to quit her. As she glanced at him from time to time, her mind was busy with thoughts which quenched the faint hope that there was nothing painful to be revealed about her husband. If this old man had been in the wrong, where was the cause for dread and secrecy?

They walked on in silence till they reached the entrance into the Via de' Bardi, and Romola noticed that he turned and looked at her with a sudden movement as if some shock had passed through him. A few moments after, she paused at the half-open door of the court and turned towards him.

"Ah!" he said, not waiting for her to speak, "you are his wife."

"Whose wife?" said Romola.

It would have been impossible for Baldassarre to recall any name at that moment. The very force with which the image of Tito pressed upon him seemed to expel any verbal sign. He made no answer, but looked at her with strange fixedness.

She opened the door wide, and showed the court covered with straw, on which lay four or five sick people, while some little children crawled or sat on it at their ease,—tiny pale creatures, biting straws and gurgling.

"If you will come in," said Romola, tremulously, "I will find you a comfortable place, and bring you some more food."

"No, I will not come in," said Baldassarre. But he stood still, arrested by the burden of impressions under which his mind was too confused to choose a course.

"Can I do nothing for you?" said Romola. "Let me give you some money, that you may buy food. It will be more plentiful soon."

She had put her hand into her scarsella as she spoke, and held out her palm with several *grossi* [1] in it. She purposely offered him more than she would have given to any other man in the same circumstances. He looked at the coins at little while, and then said,—

"Yes, I will take them."

She poured the coins into his palm, and he grasped them tightly.

"Tell me," said Romola, almost beseechingly, "What shall you—"

But Baldassarre had turned away from her, and was walking again towards the bridge. Passing from it, straight on up the Via del Fosso, he came upon the shop of Niccolò Caparra, and turned towards it without a pause, as if it had been the very object of his search. Niccolò was at that moment in procession with the armourers of Florence, and there was only one apprentice in the shop. But there were all sorts of weapons in abundance hanging there, and Baldassarre's eyes discerned what he was more hungry for than for bread. Niccolò himself would probably have refused to sell anything that might serve as a weapon to this man with signs of the prison on him; but the apprentice, less observant and scrupulous, took three *grossi* for a sharp hunting-knife without any hesitation. It was a conveniently small weapon, which Baldassarre could easily thrust within the breast of his tunic; and he walked on, feeling stronger. That sharp edge might give deadliness to the thrust of an aged arm: at least it was a companion, it was a power in league with him, even if it failed. It would break against armour, but was the armour sure to be always there? In those long months while vengeance had lain in prison, baseness had perhaps become forgetful and secure. The knife had been bought with the traitor's own money. That was just. Before he took the money, he had felt what he should do with it,—buy a weapon. Yes, and if possible, food too,—food to nourish

[1] *Grosso*, or *grossone*, was a small coin of old Florentine money of the value of twenty-one Tuscan quattrini, about twenty-nine centesimi of modern money.— EDITOR.

the arm that would grasp the weapon, food to nourish the body which was the temple of vengeance. When he had had enough bread, he should be able to think and act,—to think first how he could hide himself, lest Tito should have him dragged away again.

With that idea of hiding in his mind, Baldassarre turned up the narrowest streets, bought himself some meat and bread, and sat down under the first loggia to eat. The bells that swung out louder and louder peals of joy, laying hold of him and making him vibrate along with all the air, seemed to him simply part of that strong world which was against him.

Romola had watched Baldassarre until he had disappeared round the turning into the Piazza de' Mozzi, half feeling that his departure was a relief, half reproaching herself for not seeking with more decision to know the truth about him, for not assuring herself whether there were any guiltless misery in his lot which she was not helpless to relieve. Yet what could she have done if the truth had proved to be the burden of some painful secret about her husband, in addition to the anxieties that already weighed upon her? Surely a wife was permitted to desire ignorance of a husband's wrong-doing, since she alone must not protest and warn men against him. But that thought stirred too many intricate fibres of feeling to be pursued now in her weariness. It was a time to rejoice, since help had come to Florence; and she turned into the court to tell the good news to her patients on their straw beds.

She closed the door after her, lest the bells should drown her voice, and then throwing the black drapery from her head, that the women might see her better, she stood in the midst and told them that corn was coming, and that the bells were ringing for gladness at the news. They all sat up to listen, while the children trotted or crawled towards her, and pulled her black skirts, as if they were impatient at being all that long way off her face. She yielded to them, weary as she was, and sat down on the straw, while the little pale things peeped into her basket and pulled her hair down, and the feeble voices around her said, "The Holy Virgin be praised!" "It was the procession!" "The Mother of God has had pity on us!"

At last Romola rose from the heap of straw, too tired to try and smile any longer, saying as she turned up the stone steps,—

"I will come by-and-by, to bring you your dinner."

"Bless you, madonna! bless you!" said the faint chorus, in much the same tone as that in which they had a few minutes before praised and thanked the unseen Madonna.

Romola cared a great deal for that music. She had no innate taste for tending the sick and clothing the ragged, like some women to whom the details of such work are welcome in themselves, simply as an occupation. Her early training had kept her aloof from such womanly labours; and if she had not brought to them the inspiration of her deepest feelings, they would have been irksome to her. But they had come to be the one unshaken resting-place of her mind, the one narrow pathway on which the light fell clear. If the gulf between herself and Tito which only gathered a more perceptible wideness from her attempts to bridge it by submission, brought a doubt whether, after all, the bond to which she had laboured to be true might not itself be false,—if she came away from her confessor, Fra Salvestro, or from some contact with the disciples of Savonarola among whom she worshipped, with a sickening sense that these people were miserably narrow, and with an almost impetuous reaction towards her old contempt for their superstition,—she found herself recovering a firm footing in her works of womanly sympathy. Whatever else made her doubt, the help she gave to her fellow-citizens made her sure that Fra Girolamo had been right to call her back. According to his unforgotten words, her place had not been empty: it had been filled with her love and her labour. Florence had had need of her, and the more her own sorrow pressed upon her, the more gladness she felt in the memories, stretching through the two long years of hours and moments in which she had lightened the burden of life to others. All that ardour of her nature which could no longer spend itself in the woman's tenderness for father and husband, had transformed itself into an enthusiasm of sympathy with the general life. She had ceased to think that her own lot could be happy,—had ceased to think of happiness at all: the one end of her life seemed to her to be the diminishing of sorrow.

Her enthusiasm was continually stirred to fresh vigour by the influence of Savonarola. In spite of the wearisome visions and allegories from which she recoiled in disgust when they came as stale repetitions from other lips than his, her strong affinity for his passionate sympathy and the splendour of his aims had lost none of its power. His burning indignation against the abuses and oppression that made the daily story of the Church and of States had kindled the ready fire in her too. His special care for liberty and purity of government in Florence, with his constant reference of this immediate object to the wider end of a universal regeneration, had created in her a new consciousness of the great drama of human existence in which her life was a part; and through her daily helpful contact with the less fortunate of her fellow-citizens this new consciousness became something stronger than a vague sentiment; it grew into a more and more definite motive of self-denying practice. She thought little about dogmas, and shrank from reflecting closely on the Frate's prophecies of the immediate scourge and closely following regeneration. She had submitted her mind to his, and had entered into communion with the Church, because in this way she had found an immediate satisfaction for moral needs which all the previous culture and experience of her life had left hungering. Fra Girolamo's voice had waked in her mind a reason for living, apart from personal enjoyment and personal affection; but it was a reason that seemed to need feeding with greater forces than she possessed within herself, and her submissive use of all offices of the Church was simply a watching and waiting if by any means fresh strength might come. The pressing problem for Romola just then was not to settle questions of controversy, but to keep alive that flame of unselfish emotion by which a life of sadness might still be a life of active love.

Her trust in Savonarola's nature as greater than her own made a large part of the strength she had found. And the trust was not to be lightly shaken. It is not force of intellect which causes ready repulsion from the aberration and eccentricities of greatness, any more than it is force of vision that causes the eye to explore the warts on a face bright with human expression; it is simply the negation of high sensibilities. Romola was so deeply moved by the grand energies of Savonarola's nature, that she found herself listening patiently to all dogmas and prophecies, when they came in the vehicle of his ardent faith and believing utterance.

No soul is desolate as long as there is a human being for whom it can feel trust and reverence. Romola's trust in Savonarola was something like a rope suspended securely by her path, making her step elastic while she grasped it: if it were suddenly removed, no firmness of the ground she trod could save her from staggering, or perhaps from falling.

CHAPTER XXV

AT THE BARBER'S SHOP

AFTER that welcome appearance as the messenger with the olive-branch, which was an unpromised favour of fortune, Tito had other commissions to fulfil of a more premeditated character. He paused at the Palazza Vecchio, and awaited there the return of the Ten, who managed external and war affairs, that he might duly deliver to them the results of his private mission to Pisa, intended as a preliminary to an avowed embassy of which Bernardo Rucellai was to be the head, with the object of coming, if possible, to a pacific understanding with the Emperor Maximilian and the League.

Tito's talents for diplomatic work had been well ascertained; and as he gave with fulness and precision the results of his inquiries and interviews, Bernardo del Nero, who was at that time one of the Ten, could not withhold his admiration. He would have withheld it if he could; for his original dislike of Tito had returned, and become stronger, since the sale of the library. Romola had never uttered a word to her godfather on the circumstances of the sale, and Bernardo had understood her silence as a prohibition to him to enter on the subject; but he felt sure that the breach of her father's wish had been a blighting grief to her, and the old man's observant eyes discerned other indications that her married life was not happy.

"Ah," he said inwardly, "that doubtless is the reason she has taken to listening to Fra Girolamo, and going among the Piagnoni, which I never expected from her. These women, if they are not happy, and

have no children, must either take to folly or to some overstrained religion that makes them think they've got all heaven's work on their
shoulders. And as for my poor child Romola, it is as I always said,—
the cramming with Latin and Greek has left her as much a woman as if
she had done nothing all day but prick her fingers with the needle. And
this husband of hers, who gets employed everywhere, because he's a
tool with a smooth handle, I wish Tornabuoni and the rest may not
find their fingers cut. Well, well, *solco torto, sacco dritto,*—many a full
sack comes from a crooked furrow; and he who will be captain of none
but honest men will have small hire to pay."

With this long-established conviction that there could be no moral
sifting of political agents, the old Florentine abstained from all interference in Tito's disfavour. Apart from what must be kept sacred and
private for Romola's sake, Bernardo had nothing direct to allege against
the useful Greek, except that he was a Greek, and that he, Bernardo,
did not like him; for the doubleness of feigning attachment to the popular government, while at heart a Medicean, was common to Tito with
more than half of the Medicean party. He only feigned with more skill
than the rest: that was all. So Bernardo was simply cold to Tito, who
returned the coldness with a scrupulous, distant respect. And it was
still the notion in Florence that the old tie between Bernardo and
Bardo made any service done to Romola's husband an acceptable homage to her godfather.

After delivering himself of his charge at the Old Palace, Tito felt
that the avowed official work of the day was done. He was tired and
adust with long riding; but he did not go home. There were certain
things in his scarsella and on his mind from which he wished to free
himself as soon as possible, but the opportunities must be found so
skilfully that they must not seem to be sought. He walked from the
Palazzo in a sauntering fashion towards the Piazza del Duomo. The
procession was at an end now, but the bells were still ringing, and the
people were moving about the streets restlessly, longing for some more
definite vent to their joy. If the Frate could have stood up in the great
piazza and preached to them, they might have been satisfied; but now,
in spite of the new discipline which declared Christ to be the special
King of the Florentines, and required all pleasures to be of a Christian
sort, there was a secret longing in many of the youngsters who shouted
"Viva Gesù!" for a little vigorous stone-throwing in sign of thankfulness.

Tito, as he passed along, could not escape being recognized by some
as the welcome bearer of the olive-branch, and could only rid himself
of an inconvenient ovation, chiefly in the form of eager questions, by
telling those who pressed on him that Meo di Sasso, the true messenger
from Leghorn, must now be entering, and might certainly be met towards the Porta San Frediano. He could tell much more than Tito knew.

Freeing himself from importunities in this adroit manner, he made his
way to the Piazza del Duomo, casting his long eyes round the space with
an air of the utmost carelessness, but really seeking to detect some pres-

ence which might furnish him with one of his desired opportunities. The fact of the procession having terminated at the Duomo made it probable that there would be more than the usual concentration of loungers and talkers in the piazza and round Nello's shop. It was as he expected. There was a group leaning against the rails near the north gates of the baptistery,[1] so exactly what he sought that he looked more indifferent than ever, and seemed to recognize the tallest member of the group entirely by chance as he had half passed him, just turning his head to give him a slight greeting, while he tossed the end of his *becchetto* over his left shoulder.

Yet the tall, broad-shouldered personage greeted in that slight way looked like one who had considerable claims. He wore a richly embroidered tunic, with a great show of linen, after the newest French mode, and at his belt there hung a sword and poniard of fine workmanship. His hat, with a red plume in it, seemed a scornful protest against the gravity of Florentine costume, which had been exaggerated to the utmost under the influence of the Piagnoni. Certain undefinable indications of youth made the breadth of his face and the large diameter of his waist appear the more emphatically a stamp of coarseness, and his eyes had that rude desecrating stare at all men and things which to a refined mind is as intolerable as a bad odour or a flaring light.

He and his companions, also young men dressed expensively and wearing arms, were exchanging jokes with that sort of ostentatious laughter which implies a desire to prove that the laughter is not mortified, though some people might suspect it. There were good reasons for such a suspicion; for this broad-shouldered man with the red feather was Dolfo Spini, leader of the Compagnacci, or Evil Companions,—that is to say, of all the dissolute young men belonging to the old aristocratic party, enemies of the Mediceans, enemies of the popular government, but still more bitter enemies of Savonarola. Dolfo Spini, heir of the great house with the loggia, over the bridge of the Santa Trinità, had organized these young men into an armed band, as sworn champions of extravagant suppers and all the pleasant sins of the flesh, against reforming pietists who threatened to make the world chaste and temperate to so intolerable a degree that there would soon be no reason for living, except the extreme unpleasantness of the alternative. Up to this very morning he had been loudly declaring that Florence was given up to famine and ruin entirely through its blind adherence to the advice of the Frate, and that there could be no salvation for Florence but in joining the League and driving the Frate out of the city,—sending him to Rome, in fact, whither he ought to have gone long ago in obedience to the summons of the Pope. It was suspected, therefore, that Messer Dolfo Spini's heart was not aglow with pure joy at the unexpected succours which had come in apparent fulfilment of the Frate's prediction; and the laughter, which was ringing out afresh as Tito joined the group at Nello's door, did not serve to dissipate the suspicion. For leaning

[1] The rails in front of S. Giovanni did not exist at this period.—EDITOR.

against the door-post in the centre of the group was a close-shaven, keen-eyed personage, named Niccolò Macchiavelli, who, young as he was, had penetrated all the small secrets of egoism.

"Messer Dolfo's head," he was saying, "is more of a pumpkin than I thought. I measure men's dulness by the devices they trust in for deceiving others. Your dullest animal of all is he who grins and says he doesn't mind just after he has had his shins kicked. If I were a trifle duller, now," he went on, smiling as the circle opened to admit Tito, "I should pretend to be fond of this Melema, who has got a secretary-ship that would exactly suit me,—as if Latin ill-paid could love better Latin that's better paid! Melema, you are a pestiferously clever fellow, very much in my way, and I'm sorry to hear you've had another piece of good-luck to-day."

"Questionable luck, Niccolò," said Tito, touching him on the shoulder in a friendly way; "I have got nothing by it yet but being laid hold of and breathed upon by wool-beaters, when I am as soiled and battered with riding as a *tabellario* (letter-carrier) from Bologna."

"Ah! you want a touch of my art, Messer Oratore," said Nello, who had come forward at the sound of Tito's voice; "your chin, I perceive, has yesterday's crop upon it. Come, come,—consign yourself to the priest of all the Muses. Sandro, quick with the lather!"

"In truth, Nello, that is just what I most desire at this moment," said Tito, seating himself; "and that was why I turned my steps towards thy shop, instead of going home at once, when I had done my business at the Palazzo."

"Yes, indeed, it is not fitting that you should present yourself to Madonna Romola with a rusty chin and a tangled *zazzera*. Nothing that is not dainty ought to approach the Florentine lily; though I see her constantly going about like a sunbeam among the rags that line our corners,—if indeed she is not more like a moonbeam now, for I thought yesterday, when I met her, that she looked as pale and worn as that fainting Madonna of Fra Giovanni's. You must see to it, my bel erudito: she keeps too many fasts and vigils in your absence."

Tito gave a melancholy shrug. "It is too true, Nello. She has been depriving herself of half her proper food every day during this famine. But what can I do? Her mind has been set all aflame. A husband's influence is powerless against the Frate's."

"As every other influence is likely to be, that of the Holy Father included," said Domenico Cennini, one of the group at the door, who had turned in with Tito. "I don't know whether you have gathered anything at Pisa about the way the wind sits at Rome, Melema?"

"Secrets of the council chamber, Messer Domenico!" said Tito, smiling and opening his palms in a deprecatory manner. "An envoy must be as dumb as a father confessor."

"Certainly, certainly," said Cennini. "I ask for no breach of that rule. Well, my belief is, that if his Holiness were to drive Fra Girolamo to extremity, the Frate would move heaven and earth to get a General

Council of the Church,—ay, and would get it too; and I, for one, should not be sorry, though I am no Piagnone."

"With leave of your greater experience, Messer Domenico," said Macchiavelli, "I must differ from you,—not in your wish to see a General Council which might reform the Church, but in your belief that the Frate will checkmate his Holiness. The Frate's game is an impossible one. If he had contented himself with preaching against the vices of Rome, and with prophesying that in some way, not mentioned, Italy would be scourged, depend upon it Pope Alexander would have allowed him to spend his breath in that way as long as he could find hearers. Such spiritual blasts as those knock no walls down. But the Frate wants to be something more than a spiritual trumpet: he wants to be a lever, and what is more, he *is* a lever. He wants to spread the doctrine of Christ by maintaining a popular government in Florence, and the Pope, as I know, on the best authority, has private views to the contrary."

"Then Florence will stand by the Frate," Cennini broke in, with some fervour. "I myself should prefer that he would let his prophesying alone; but if our freedom to choose our own government is to be attacked—I am an obedient son of the Church, but I would vote for resisting Pope Alexander the Sixth, as our forefathers resisted Pope Gregory the Eleventh."

"But pardon me, Messer Domenico," said Macchiavelli, sticking his thumbs into his belt, and speaking with that cool enjoyment of exposition which surmounts every other force in discussion. "Have you correctly seized the Frate's position? How is it that he has become a lever, and made himself worth attacking by an acute man like his Holiness? Because he has got the ear of the people: because he gives them threats and promises, which they believe come straight from God, not only about hell, purgatory, and paradise, but about Pisa and our Great Council. But let events go against him, so as to shake the people's faith, and the cause of his power will be the cause of his fall. He is accumulating three sorts of hatred on his head,—the hatred of average mankind against every one who wants to lay on them a strict yoke of virtue; the hatred of the stronger powers in Italy who want to farm Florence for their own purposes; and the hatred of the people, to whom he has ventured to promise good in this world, instead of confining his promises to the next. If a prophet is to keep his power, he must be a prophet like Mahomet, with an army at his back, that when the people's faith is fainting it may be frightened into life again."

"Rather sum up the three sorts of hatred in one," said Francesco Cei, impetuously, "and say he has won the hatred of all men who have sense and honesty, by inventing hypocritical lies. His proper place is among the false prophets in the Inferno, who walk with their heads turned hindforemost."

"You are too angry, my Francesco," said Macchiavelli, smiling; "you poets are apt to cut the clouds in your wrath. I am no votary of the Frate's, and would not lay down my little finger for his veracity. But

veracity is a plant of paradise, and the seeds have never flourished
beyond the walls. You yourself, my Francesco, tell poetical lies only;
partly compelled by the poet's fervour, partly to please your audience;
but you object to lies in prose. Well, the Frate differs from you as to
the boundary of poetry, that is all. When he gets into the pulpit of the
Duomo, he has the fervour within him, and without him he has the
audience to please. Ecco!"

"You are somewhat lax there, Niccolò," said Cennini, gravely. "I
myself believe in the Frate's integrity, though I don't believe in his
prophecies; and as long as his integrity is not disproved, we have a
popular party strong enough to protect him and resist foreign interference."

"A party that seems strong enough," said Macchiavelli, with a shrug,
and an almost imperceptible glance towards Tito, who was abandoning
himself with much enjoyment to Nello's combing and scenting. "But
how many Mediceans are there among you? How many who will not
be turned round by a private grudge?"

"As to the Mediceans," said Cennini, "I believe there is very little
genuine feeling left on behalf of the Medici. Who would risk much for
Piero de' Medici? A few old stanch friends, perhaps, like Bernardo del
Nero; but even some of those most connected with the family are hearty
friends of the popular government, and would exert themselves for the
Frate. I was talking to Giannozzo Pucci only a little while ago, and I
am convinced there's nothing he would set his face against more than
against any attempt to alter the new order of things."

"You are right there, Messer Domenico," said Tito, with a laughing
meaning in his eyes, as he rose from the shaving-chair; "and I fancy the
tender passion came in aid of hard theory there. I am persuaded there
was some jealousy at the bottom of Giannozzo's alienation from Piero
de' Medici; else so amiable a creature as he would never feel the bitterness he sometimes allows to escape him in that quarter. He was in the
procession with you, I suppose?"

"No," said Cennini; "he is at his villa,—went there three days ago."

Tito was settling his cap and glancing down at his splashed hose as if
he hardly heeded the answer. In reality he had obtained a much-desired
piece of information. He had at that moment in his scarsella a crushed
gold ring which he had engaged to deliver to Giannozzo Pucci. He had
received it from an envoy of Piero de' Medici, whom he had ridden out
of his way to meet at Certaldo on the Siena road. Since Pucci was not
in the town, he would send the ring by Fra Michele, a Carthusian lay
Brother in the service of the Mediceans; and the receipt of that sign
would bring Pucci back to hear the verbal part of Tito's mission.

"Behold him!" said Nello, flourishing his comb and pointing it at
Tito, "the handsomest scholar in the world or in the worlds, now he has
passed through my hands! A trifle thinner in the face, though, than
when he came in his first bloom to Florence,—eh? and, I vow, there are
some lines just faintly hinting themselves about your mouth, Messer

Oratore! Ah, mind is an enemy to beauty! I myself was thought beautiful by the women at one time,—when I was in my swaddling-bands. But now—oimè! I carry my unwritten poems in cipher on my face!"

Tito, laughing with the rest as Nello looked at himself tragically in the hand-mirror, made a sign of farewell to the company generally, and took his departure.

"I'm of our old Piero di Cosimo's mind," said Francesco Cei. "I don't half like Melema. That trick of smiling gets stronger than ever,—no wonder he has lines about the mouth."

"He's too successful," said Macchiavelli, playfully. "I'm sure there's something wrong about him, else he wouldn't have that secretaryship."

"He's an able man," said Cennini, in a tone of judicial fairness. "I and my brother have always found him useful with our Greek sheets, and he gives great satisfaction to the Ten. I like to see a young man work his way upward by merit. And the secretary Scala, who befriended him from the first, thinks highly of him still, I know."

"Doubtless," said a notary in the background. "He writes Scala's official letters for him, or corrects them, and gets well paid for it too."

"I wish Messer Bartolommeo would pay *me* to doctor his gouty Latin," said Macchiavelli, with a shrug. "Did *he* tell you about the pay, Ser Ceccone, or was it Melema himself?" he added, looking at the notary with a face ironically innocent.

"Melema? No, indeed," answered Ser Ceccone. "He is as close as a nut. He never brags. That's why he's employed everywhere. They say he's getting rich with doing all sorts of underhand work."

"It *is* a little too bad," said Macchiavelli, "and so many able notaries out of employment!"

"Well, I must say I thought that was a nasty story a year or two ago about the man who said he had stolen jewels," said Cei. "It got hushed up somehow; but I remember Piero di Cosimo said, at the time, he believed there was something in it, for he saw Melema's face when the man laid hold of him, and he never saw a visage so 'painted with fear,' as our sour old Dante says."

"Come, spit no more of that venom, Francesco," said Nello, getting indignant, "else I shall consider it a public duty to cut your hair awry the next time I get you under my scissors. That story of the stolen jewels was a lie. Bernardo Rucellai and the Magnificent Eight knew all about it. The man was a dangerous madman, and he was very properly kept out of mischief in prison. As for our Piero di Cosimo, his wits are running after the wind of Mongibello: he has such an extravagant fancy that he would take a lizard for a crocodile. No: that story has been dead and buried too long,—our noses object to it."

"It is true," said Macchiavelli. "You forget the danger of the precedent, Francesco. The next mad beggarman may accuse you of stealing his verses, or me, God help me! of stealing his coppers. Ah!" he went on, turning towards the door, "Dolfo Spini has carried his red feather out of the piazza. That captain of swaggerers would like the Republic to lose Pisa just for the chance of seeing the people tear the frock off the Frate's back. With your pardon, Francesco,—I know he is a friend of yours,—there are few things I should like better than to see him play the part of Capo d'Oca, who went out to the tournament blowing his trumpets and returned with them in a bag."

CHAPTER XXVI

BY A STREET LAMP

THAT evening, when it was dark and threatening rain, Romola, returning with Maso and the lantern by her side, from the hospital of San Matteo, which she had visited after vespers, encountered her husband just issuing from the monastery of San Marco. Tito, who had gone out again shortly after his arrival in the Via de' Bardi, and had seen little of Romola during the day, immediately proposed to accompany her home, dismissing Maso, whose short steps annoyed him. It was only usual for him to pay her such an official attention when it was obviously demanded from him. Tito and Romola never jarred, never remonstrated with each other. They were too hopelessly alienated in their inner life ever to have that contest which is an effort towards agreement. They talked of all affairs, public and private, with careful adherence to an adopted course. If Tito wanted a supper prepared in the old library, now pleasantly furnished as a banqueting-room, Romola assented, and saw that everything needful was done; and Tito, on his side, left her entirely uncontrolled in her daily habits, accepting the help she offered him in transcribing or making digests, and in return meeting her conjectured want of supplies for her charities. Yet he constantly, as on this very morning, avoided exchanging glances with her; affected to believe that she was out of the house, in order to avoid seeking her in her own room; and playfully attributed to her a perpetual preference of solitude to his society.

In the first ardour of her self-conquest, after she had renounced her resolution of flight, Romola had made many timid efforts towards the return of a frank relation between them. But to her such a relation could only come by open speech about their differences, and the attempt to arrive at a moral understanding; while Tito could only be saved from alienation from her by such a recovery of her effusive tenderness as would have presupposed oblivion of their differences. He cared for no explanation between them; he felt any thorough explanation impossible: he would have cared to have Romola fond again, and to her, fondness was impossible. She could be submissive and gentle, she could repress any sign of repulsion; but tenderness was not to be feigned. She was helplessly conscious of the result: her husband was alienated from her.

It was an additional reason why she should be carefully kept outside of secrets which he would in no case have chosen to communicate to her. With regard to his political action he sought to convince her that he considered the cause of the Medici hopeless; and that on that practical ground, as well as in theory, he heartily served the popular government, in which she had now a warm interest. But impressions subtle as odours made her uneasy about his relations with San Marco. She was painfully divided between the dread of seeing any evidence to arouse her suspicions, and the impulse to watch lest any harm should come that she might have arrested.

As they walked together this evening, Tito said: "The business of the day is not yet quite ended for me. I shall conduct you to our door, my Romola, and then I must fulfil another commission, which will take me an hour, perhaps, before I can return and rest, as I very much need to do."

And then he talked amusingly of what he had seen at Pisa, until they were close upon a loggia, near which there hung a lamp before a picture of the Virgin. The street was a quiet one, and hitherto they had passed few people; but now there was a sound of many approaching footsteps and confused voices.

"We shall not get home without a wetting, unless we take shelter under this convenient loggia," Tito said hastily, hurrying Romola, with a slightly startled movement, up the step of the loggia.

"Surely it is useless to wait for this small drizzling rain," said Romola, in surprise.

"No; I felt it becoming heavier. Let us wait a little." With that wakefulness to the faintest indication which belongs to a mind habitually in a state of caution, Tito had detected by the glimmer of the lamp that the leader of the advancing group wore a red feather and a glittering sword-hilt,—in fact, was almost the last person in the world he would have chosen to meet at this hour with Romola by his side. He had already during the day had one momentous interview with Dolfo Spini, and the business he had spoken of to Romola as yet to be done was a second interview with that personage, a sequence of the visit he had paid at San Marco. Tito, by a long-preconcerted plan, had been the bearer of letters to Savonarola,—carefully forged letters; one of them, by a stratagem, bearing the very signature and seal of the Cardinal of Naples, who of all the Sacred College had most exerted his influence at Rome in favour of the Frate. The purport of the letters was to state that the Cardinal was on his progress from Pisa, and, unwilling for strong reasons to enter Florence, yet desirous of taking counsel with Savonarola at this difficult juncture, intended to pause this very day at San Casciano, about ten miles from the city, whence he would ride out the next morning in the plain garb of a priest, and meet Savonarola, as if casually, five miles on the Florence road, two hours after sunrise. The plot, of which these forged letters were the initial step, was that Dolfo Spini with a band of his Compagnacci was to be posted in ambush on the road, at a lonely spot about five miles from the gates; that he was to seize Savonarola with the Dominican brother who would accompany him according to rule, and deliver him over to a small detachment of Milanese horse in readiness near San Casciano, by whom he was to be carried into the Roman territory.

There was a strong chance that the penetrating Frate would suspect a trap, and decline to incur the risk, which he had for some time avoided, of going beyond the city walls. Even when he preached, his friends held it necessary that he should be attended by an armed guard; and here he was called on to commit himself to a solitary road, with no other attendant than a fellow-monk. On this ground the minimum of time had been given him for decision, and the chance in favour of his acting on the letters was that the eagerness with which his mind was set on the combining of interests within and without the Church towards the procuring of a General Council, and also the expectation of immediate service from the Cardinal in the actual juncture of his contest with the Pope, would triumph over his shrewdness and caution in the brief space allowed for deliberation.

Tito had had an audience of Savonarola, having declined to put the letters into any hands but his, and with consummate art had admitted that incidentally, and by inference, he was able so far to conjecture their purport as to believe they referred to a rendezvous outside the gates, in which case he urged that the Frate should seek an armed guard from the Signoria, and offered his services in carrying the request with the utmost privacy. Savonarola had replied briefly that this was impossible: an armed guard was incompatible with privacy. He spoke with a flashing eye, and Tito felt convinced that he meant to incur the risk.

Tito himself did not much care for the result. He managed his affairs so cleverly that all results, he considered, must turn to his advantage. Whichever party came uppermost, he was secure of favour and money. That is an indecorously naked statement; the fact, clothed as Tito habitually clothed it, was that his acute mind, discerning the equal hollowness of all parties, took the only rational course in making them subservient to his own interest.

If Savonarola fell into the snare, there were diamonds in question and papal patronage; if not, Tito's adroit agency had strengthened his position with Savonarola and with Spini, while any confidences he obtained from them made him the more valuable as an agent of the Mediceans.

But Spini was an inconvenient colleague. He had cunning enough to delight in plots, but not the ability or self-command necessary to so complex an effect as secrecy. He frequently got excited with drinking for even sober Florence had its *Beoni*, or topers, both lay and clerical, who became loud at taverns and private banquets; and in spite of the agreement between him and Tito, that their public recognition of each other should invariably be of the coolest sort, there was always the possibility that on an evening encounter he would be suddenly blurting and affectionate. The delicate sign of casting the becchetto over the left shoulder was understood in the morning, but the strongest hint short of a threat might not suffice to keep off a fraternal grasp of the shoulder in the evening.

Tito's chief hope now was that Dolfo Spini had not caught sight of him, and the hope would have been well founded if Spini had had no clearer view of him than he had caught of Spini. But, himself in shadow, he had seen Tito illuminated for an instant by the direct rays of the lamp, and Tito in his way was as strongly marked a personage as the captain of the Compagnacci. Romola's black-shrouded figure had escaped notice, and she now stood behind her husband's shoulder in the corner of the loggia. Tito was not left to hope long.

"Ha! my carrier-pigeon," grated Spini's harsh voice, in what he meant to be an undertone, while his hand grasped Tito's shoulder; "what did you run into hiding for? You didn't know it was comrades who were coming. It's well I caught sight of you; it saves time. What of the chase to-morrow morning? Will the bald-headed game rise? Are the falcons to be got ready?"

If it had been in Tito's nature to feel an access of rage, he would have felt it against this bull-faced accomplice, unfit either for a leader or a tool. His lips turned white, but his excitement came from the pressing difficulty of choosing a safe device. If he attempted to hush Spini, that would only deepen Romola's suspicion, and he knew her well enough to know that if some strong alarm were roused in her, she was neither to be silenced nor hoodwinked; on the other hand, if he repelled Spini angrily, the wine-breathing Compagnaccio might become savage, being more ready at resentment than at the divination of motives. He adopted a third course, which proved that Romola retained one sort of power over him,—the power of dread.

He pressed her hand, as if intending a hint to her, and said in a good-humoured tone of comradeship,—

"Yes, my Dolfo, you may prepare in all security. But take no trumpets with you."

"Don't be afraid," said Spini, a little piqued. "No need to play Ser Saccante with me. I know where the devil keeps his tail as well as you do. What! he swallowed the bait whole? The prophetic nose didn't scent the hook at all?" he went on, lowering his tone a little, with a blundering sense of secrecy.

"The brute will not be satisfied till he has emptied the bag," thought Tito; but aloud he said: "Swallowed all as easily as you swallow a cup of Trebbiano. Ha! I see torches: there must be a dead body coming. The pestilence has been spreading, I hear."

"Santiddio! I hate the sight of those biers. Good-night," said Spini, hastily moving off.

The torches were really coming, but they preceded a church dignitary who was returning homeward; the suggestion of the dead body and the pestilence was Tito's device for getting rid of Spini without telling him to go. The moment he had moved away, Tito turned to Romola, and said quietly,—

"Do not be alarmed by anything that *bestia* has said, my Romola. We will go on now: I think the rain has not increased."

She was quivering with indignant resolution; it was of no use for Tito to speak in that unconcerned way. She distrusted every word he could utter.

"I will not go on," she said. "I will not move nearer home until I have some security against this treachery being perpetrated."

"Wait, at least, until these torches have passed," said Tito, with perfect self-command, but with a new rising of dislike to a wife who this time, he foresaw, might have the power of thwarting him in spite of the husband's predominance.

The torches passed, with the Vicario dell' Arcivescovo, and due reverence was done by Tito, but Romola saw nothing outward. If for the defeat of this treachery, in which she believed with all the force of long presentiment, it had been necessary at that moment for her to spring on her husband and hurl herself with him down a precipice, she felt as if she could have done it. Union with this man! At that moment the self-quelling discipline of two years seemed to be nullified: she felt nothing but that they were divided.

They were nearly in darkness again, and could only see each other's faces dimly.

"Tell me the truth, Tito,—this time tell me the truth," said Romola, in a low, quivering voice. "It will be safer for you."

"Why should I desire to tell you anything else, my angry saint?" said Tito, with a slight touch of contempt, which was the vent of his annoyance; "since the truth is precisely that over which you have most reason to rejoice,—namely, that my knowing a plot of Spini's enables me to secure the Frate from falling a victim to it."

"What is the plot?"

"That I decline to tell," said Tito. "It is enough that the Frate's safety will be secured."

"It is a plot for drawing him outside the gates, that Spini may murder him."

"There has been no intention of murder. It is simply a plot for compelling him to obey the Pope's summons to Rome. But as I serve the popular government, and think the Frate's presence here is a necessary means of maintaining it at present, I choose to prevent his departure. You may go to sleep with entire ease of mind to-night."

For a moment Romola was silent. Then she said, in a voice of anguish, "Tito, it is of no use: I have no belief in you."

She could just discern his action as he shrugged his shoulders, and spread out his palms in silence. That cold dislike which is the anger of unimpassioned beings was hardening within him.

"If the Frate leaves the city,—if any harm happens to him," said Romola, after a slight pause, in a new tone of indignant resolution,—"I will declare what I have heard to the Signoria, and you will be disgraced. What if I am your wife?" she went on impetuously; "I will be disgraced with you. If we are united, I am that part of you that will save you from crime. Others shall not be betrayed."

"I am quite aware of what you would be likely to do, *anima mia*," said Tito, in the coolest of his liquid tones; "therefore if you have a small amount of reasoning at your disposal just now, consider that if you believe me in nothing else, you may believe me when I say I will take care of myself, and not put it in your power to ruin me."

"Then you assure me that the Frate is warned,—he will not go beyond the gates?"

"He shall not go beyond the gates."

There was a moment's pause, but distrust was not to be expelled.

"I will go back to San Marco now and find out," Romola said, making a movement forward.

"You shall not!" said Tito, in a bitter whisper, seizing her wrists with all his masculine force. "I am master of you. You shall not set yourself in opposition to me."

There were passers-by approaching. Tito had heard them, and that was why he spoke in a whisper. Romola was too conscious of being mastered to have struggled, even if she had remained unconscious that witnesses were at hand. But she was aware now of footsteps and voices, and her habitual sense of personal dignity made her at once yield to Tito's movement towards leading her from the loggia.

They walked on in silence for some time, under the small drizzling rain. The first rush of indignation and alarm in Romola had begun to give way to more complicated feelings, which rendered speech and action difficult. In that simpler state of vehemence, open opposition to the husband from whom she felt her soul revolting had had the aspect of temptation for her; it seemed the easiest of all courses. But now, habits of self-questioning, memories of impulse subdued, and that proud reserve which all discipline had left unmodified, began to emerge from the flood of passion. The grasp of her wrists, which asserted her husband's physical predominance, instead of arousing a new fierceness in her, as it might have done if her impetuosity had been of a more vulgar kind, had given her a momentary shuddering horror at this form of contest with him. It was the first time they had been in declared hostility to each other since her flight and return, and the check given to her ardent resolution then, retained the power to arrest her now. In this altered condition her mind began to dwell on the probabilities that would save her from any desperate course: Tito would not risk betrayal by her; whatever had been his original intention, he must be determined now by the fact that she knew of the plot. She was not bound now to do anything else than to hang over him that certainty,—that if

he deceived her, her lips would not be closed. And then, it was possible
—yes, she must cling to that possibility till it was disproved—that Tito
had never meant to aid in the betrayal of the Frate.

Tito, on his side, was busy with thoughts, and did not speak again
till they were near home. Then he said,—

"Well, Romola, have you now had time to recover calmness? If so,
you can supply your want of belief in me by a little rational inference:
you can see, I presume, that if I had had any intention of furthering
Spini's plot, I should now be aware that the possession of a fair Piagnone for my wife, who knows the secret of the plot, would be a serious
obstacle in my way."

Tito assumed the tone which was just then the easiest to him, conjecturing that in Romola's present mood persuasive deprecation would
be lost upon her.

"Yes, Tito," she said in a low voice, "I think you believe that I
would guard the Republic from further treachery. You are right to believe it: if the Frate is betrayed, I will denounce you." She paused a
moment, and then said with an effort: "But it was not so. I have perhaps
spoken too hastily,—you never meant it. Only, why will you seem to
be that man's comrade?"

"Such relations are inevitable to practical men, my Romola," said
Tito, gratified by discerning the struggle within her. "You fair creatures
live in the clouds. Pray go to rest with an easy heart," he added, opening the door for her.

CHAPTER XXVII

CHECK

Tito's clever arrangements had been unpleasantly frustrated by trivial
incidents which could not enter into a clever man's calculations. It was
very seldom that he walked with Romola in the evening, yet he had
happened to be walking with her precisely on this evening when her
presence was supremely inconvenient. Life was so complicated a game
that the devices of skill were liable to be defeated at every turn by air-
blown chances, incalculable as the descent of thistle-down.

It was not that he minded about the failure of Spini's plot, but he
felt an awkward difficulty in so adjusting his warning to Savonarola on
the one hand, and to Spini on the other, as not to incur suspicion. Suspicion roused in the popular party might be fatal to his reputation and
ostensible position in Florence: suspicion roused in Dolfo Spini might
be as disagreeable in its effects as the hatred of a fierce dog not to be
chained.

If Tito went forthwith to the monastery to warn Savonarola before
the monks went to rest, his warning would follow so closely on his delivery of the forged letters that he could not escape unfavourable sur-

mises. He could not warn Spini at once without telling him the true reason, since he could not immediately allege the discovery that Savonarola had changed his purpose; and he knew Spini well enough to know that his understanding would discern nothing but that Tito had "turned round" and frustrated the plot. On the other hand, by deferring his warning to Savonarola until the morning, he would be almost sure to lose the opportunity of warning Spini that the Frate had changed his mind; and the band of Compagnacci would come back in all the rage of disappointment. This last, however, was the risk he chose, trusting to his power of soothing Spini by assuring him that the failure was due only to the Frate's caution.

Tito was annoyed. If he had had to smile, it would have been an unusual effort to him. He was determined not to encounter Romola again, and he did not go home that night.

She watched through the night, and never took off her clothes. She heard the rain become heavier and heavier. She liked to hear the rain; the stormy heavens seemed a safeguard against men's devices, compelling them to inaction. And Romola's mind was again assailed, not only by the utmost doubt of her husband, but by doubt as to her own conduct. What lie might he not have told her? What project might he not have, of which she was still ignorant? Every one who trusted Tito was in danger; it was useless to try and persuade herself of the contrary. And was not she selfishly listening to the promptings of her own pride, when she shrank from warning men against him? "If her husband was a malefactor, her place was in the prison by his side"—that might be; she was contented to fulfil that claim. But was she, a wife, to allow a husband to inflict the injuries that would make him a malefactor, when it might be in her power to prevent them? Prayer seemed impossible to her. The activity of her thought excluded a mental state of which the essence is expectant passivity.

The excitement became stronger and stronger. Her imagination, in a state of morbid activity, conjured up possible schemes by which, after all, Tito would have eluded her threat; and towards daybreak the rain became less violent, till at last it ceased, the breeze rose again and dispersed the clouds, and the morning fell clear on all the objects around her. It made her uneasiness all the less endurable. She wrapped her mantle round her, and ran up to the loggia, as if there could be anything in the wide landscape that might determine her action; as if there could be anything but roofs hiding the line of street along which Savonarola might be walking towards betrayal.

If she went to her godfather, might she not induce him, without any specific revelation, to take measures for preventing Fra Girolamo from passing the gates? But that might be too late. Romola thought, with new distress, that she had failed to learn any guiding details from Tito, and it was already long past seven. She must go to San Marco: there was nothing else to be done.

She hurried down the stairs, she went out into the street without

looking at her sick people, and walked at a swift pace along the Via de'
Bardi towards the Ponte Vecchio. She would go through the heart of
the city; it was the most direct road, and, besides, in the great piazza
there was a chance of encountering her husband, who, by some possibility to which she still clung, might satisfy her of the Frate's safety, and
leave no need for her to go to San Marco. When she arrived in front
of the Palazzo Vecchio, she looked eagerly into the pillared court; then
her eyes swept the piazza; but the well-known figure, once painted in
her heart by young love, and now branded there by eating pain, was
nowhere to be seen. She hurried straight on to the Piazza del Duomo.
It was already full of movement: there were worshippers passing up
and down the marble steps, there were men pausing for chat, and there
were market-people carrying their burdens. Between those moving figures Romola caught a glimpse of her husband. On his way from San
Marco he had turned into Nello's shop, and was now leaning against
the door-post. As Romola approached she could see that he was standing and talking, with the easiest air in the world, holding his cap in
his hand, and shaking back his freshly combed hair. The contrast of
this ease with the bitter anxieties he had created convulsed her with
indignation: the new vision of his hardness heightened her dread. She
recognized Cronaca and two other frequenters of San Marco standing
near her husband. It flashed through her mind,—"I will compel him
to speak before those men." And her light step brought her close upon
him before he had time to move, while Cronaca was saying, "Here comes
Madonna Romola."

A slight shock passed through Tito's frame as he felt himself face to
face with his wife. She was haggard with her anxious watching, but there
was a flash of something else than anxiety in her eyes as she said,—

"Is the Frate gone beyond the gates?"

"No," said Tito, feeling completely helpless before this woman, and
needing all the self-command he possessed to preserve a countenance
in which there should seem to be nothing stronger than surprise.

"And you are certain that he is not going?" she insisted.

"I am certain that he is not going."

"That is enough," said Romola; and she turned up the steps, to take
refuge in the Duomo till she could recover from her agitation.

Tito never had a feeling so near hatred as that with which his eyes
followed Romola retreating up the steps.

There were present not only genuine followers of the Frate, but Ser
Ceccone, the notary, who at that time, like Tito himself, was secretly
an agent of the Mediceans.

Ser Francesco di Ser Barone, more briefly known to infamy as Ser
Ceccone, was not learned, not handsome, not successful, and the reverse
of generous. He was a traitor without charm. It followed that he was
not fond of Tito Melema.

CHAPTER XXVIII

COUNTER-CHECK

It was late in the afternoon when Tito returned home. Romola, seated opposite the cabinet in her narrow room, copying documents, was about to desist from her work because the light was getting dim, when her husband entered. He had come straight to this room to seek her, with a thoroughly defined intention; and there was something new to Romola in his manner and expression as he looked at her silently on entering, and, without taking off his cap and mantle, leaned one elbow on the cabinet, and stood directly in front of her.

Romola, fully assured during the day of the Frate's safety, was feeling the reaction of some penitence for the access of distrust and indignation which had impelled her to address her husband publicly on a matter that she knew he wished to be private. She told herself that she had probably been wrong. The scheming duplicity which she had heard even her godfather allude to as inseparable from party tactics might be sufficient to account for the connection with Spini, without the supposition that Tito had ever meant to further the plot. She wanted to atone for her impetuosity by confessing that she had been too hasty, and for some hours her mind had been dwelling on the possibility that this confession of hers might lead to other frank words breaking the two years' silence of their hearts. The silence had been so complete that Tito was ignorant of her having fled from him and come back again; they had never approached an avowal of that past which, both in its young love and in the shock that shattered the love, lay locked away from them like a banquet-room where death had once broken the feast.

She looked up at him with that submission in her glance which belonged to her state of self-reproof; but the subtle change in his face and manner arrested her speech. For a few moments they remained silent, looking at each other.

Tito himself felt that a crisis was come in his married life. The husband's determination to mastery, which lay deep below all blandness and beseechingness, had risen permanently to the surface now, and seemed to alter his face, as a face is altered by a hidden muscular tension with which a man is secretly throttling or stamping out the life from something feeble, yet dangerous.

"Romola," he began, in the cool liquid tone that made her shiver, "it is time that we should understand each other." He paused.

"That is what I most desire, Tito," she said faintly. Her sweet pale face, with all its anger gone and nothing but the timidity of self-doubt in it, seemed to give a marked predominance to her husband's dark strength.

"You took a step this morning," Tito went on, "which you must now yourself perceive to have been useless,—which exposed you to remark and may involve me in serious practical difficulties."

"I acknowledge that I was too hasty; I am sorry for any injustice I may have done you." Romola spoke these words in a fuller and firmer tone; Tito, she hoped, would look less hard when she had expressed her regret, and then she could say other things.

"I wish you once for all to understand," he said, without any change of voice, "that such collisions are incompatible with our position as husband and wife. I wish you to reflect on the mode in which you were led to that step, that the process may not be repeated."

"That depends chiefly on you, Tito," said Romola, taking fire slightly. It was not at all what she had thought of saying, but we see a very little way before us in mutual speech.

"You would say, I suppose," answered Tito, "that nothing is to occur in future which can excite your unreasonable suspicions. You were frank enough to say last night that you have no belief in me. I am not surprised at any exaggerated conclusion you may draw from slight premises, but I wish to point out to you what is likely to be the fruit of your making such exaggerated conclusions a ground for interfering in affairs of which you are ignorant. Your attention is thoroughly awake to what I am saying?"

He paused for a reply.

"Yes," said Romola, flushing in irrepressible resentment at this cold tone of superiority.

"Well, then, it may possibly not be very long before some other chance words or incidents set your imagination at work devising crimes for me, and you may perhaps rush to the Palazzo Vecchio to alarm the Signoria and set the city in an uproar. Shall I tell you what may be the result? Not simply the disgrace of your husband, to which you look forward with so much courage, but the arrest and ruin of many among the chief men in Florence, including Messer Bernardo del Nero."

Tito had meditated a decisive move, and he had made it. The flush died out of Romola's face, and her very lips were pale,—an unusual effect with her, for she was little subject to fear. Tito perceived his success.

"You would perhaps flatter yourself," he went on, "that you were performing a heroic deed of deliverance; you might as well try to turn locks with fine words as apply such notions to the politics of Florence. The question now is, not whether you can have any belief in me, but whether, now you have been warned, you will dare to rush, like a blind man with a torch in his hand, among intricate affairs of which you know nothing."

Romola felt as if her mind were held in a vice by Tito's: the possibilities he had indicated were rising before her with terrible clearness.

"I am too rash," she said. "I will try not to be rash."

"Remember," said Tito, with unsparing insistence, "that your act of distrust towards me this morning might, for aught you knew, have had more fatal effects than that sacrifice of your husband which you have learned to contemplate without flinching."

"Tito, it is not so," Romola burst forth in a pleading tone, rising and going nearer to him, with a desperate resolution to speak out. "It is false that I would willingly sacrifice you. It has been the greatest effort of my life to cling to you. I went away in my anger two years ago, and I came back again because I was more bound to you than to anything else on earth. But it is useless. You shut me out from your mind. You affect to think of me as a being too unreasonable to share in the knowledge of your affairs. You will be open with me about nothing."

She looked like his good angel pleading with him, as she bent her face towards him with dilated eyes, and laid her hand upon his arm. But Romola's touch and glance no longer stirred any fibre of tenderness in her husband. The good-humoured, tolerant Tito, incapable of hatred, incapable almost of impatience, disposed always to be gentle towards the rest of the world, felt himself becoming strangely hard towards this wife whose presence had once been the strongest influence he had known. With all his softness of disposition, he had a masculine effectiveness of intellect and purpose which, like sharpness of edge, is itself an energy, working its way without any strong momentum. Romola had an energy of her own which thwarted his; and no man, who is not exceptionally feeble, will endure being thwarted by his wife. Marriage must be a relation either of sympathy or of conquest.

No emotion darted across his face as he heard Romola for the first time speak of having gone away from him. His lips only looked a little harder as he smiled slightly and said,—

"My Romola, when certain conditions are ascertained, we must make up our minds to them. No amount of wishing will fill the Arno, as your people say, or turn a plum into an orange. I have not observed even that prayers have much efficacy that way. You are so constituted as to have certain strong impressions inaccessible to reason; I cannot share those impressions, and you have withdrawn all trust from me in consequence. You have changed towards me; it has followed that I have changed towards you. It is useless to take any retrospect. We have simply to adapt ourselves to altered conditions."

"Tito, it would not be useless for us to speak openly," said Romola, with the sort of exasperation that comes from using living muscle against some lifeless, insurmountable resistance. "It was the sense of deception in you that changed me, and that has kept us apart. And it is not true that I changed first. You changed towards me the night you first wore that chain-armour. You had some secret from me—it was about that old man—and I saw him again yesterday. Tito," she went on, in a tone of agonized entreaty, "if you would once tell me everything, let it be what it may—I would not mind pain—that there might be no wall between us! Is it not possible that we could begin a new life?"

This time there was a flash of emotion across Tito's face. He stood perfectly still; but the flash seemed to have whitened him. He took no notice of Romola's appeal, but after a moment's pause said quietly,—

"Your impetuosity about trifles, Romola, has a freezing influence that would cool the baths of Nero." At these cutting words Romola shrank, and drew herself up into her usual self-sustained attitude. Tito went on: "If by 'that old man' you mean the mad Jacopo di Nola who attempted my life and made a strange accusation against me, of which I told you nothing because it would have alarmed you to no purpose, he, poor wretch, has died in prison. I saw his name in the list of dead."

"I know nothing about his accusation," said Romola; "but I know he is the man whom I saw with the rope round his neck in the Duomo, —the man whose portrait Piero di Cosimo painted, grasping your arm as he saw him grasp it the day the French entered, the day you first wore the armour."

"And where is he now, pray?" said Tito, still pale, but governing himself.

"He was lying lifeless in the street from starvation," said Romola. "I revived him with bread and wine. I brought him to our door, but he refused to come in. Then I gave him some money, and he went away without telling me anything. But he had found out that I was your wife. *Who* is he?"

"A man, half mad, half imbecile, who was once my father's servant in Greece, and who has a rancorous hatred towards me because I got him dismissed for theft. Now you have the whole mystery, and the further satisfaction of knowing that I am again in danger of assassination. The fact of my wearing the armour, about which you seem to have thought so much, must have led you to infer that I was in danger from this man. Was that the reason you chose to cultivate his acquaintance and invite him into the house?"

Romola was mute. To speak was only like rushing with bare breast against a shield.

Tito moved from his leaning posture, slowly took off his cap and mantle, and pushed back his hair. He was collecting himself for some final words. And Romola stood upright, looking at him as she might have looked at some on-coming deadly force, to be met only by silent endurance.

"We need not refer to these matters again, Romola," he said, precisely in the same tone as that in which he had spoken at first. "It is enough if you will remember that the next time your generous ardour leads you to interfere in political affairs, you are likely, not to save any one from danger, but to be raising scaffolds and setting houses on fire. You are not yet a sufficiently ardent Piagnone to believe that Messer Bernardo del Nero is the prince of darkness, and Messer Francesco Valori the archangel Michael. I think I need demand no promise from you?"

"I have understood you too well, Tito."

"It is enough," he said, leaving the room.

Romola turned around with despair in her face, and sank into her seat. "O God, I have tried—I cannot help it. We shall always be divided." Those words passed silently through her mind. "Unless," she said aloud, as if some sudden vision had startled her into speech,—"unless misery should come and join us!"

Tito, too, had a new thought in his mind after he had closed the door behind him. With the project of leaving Florence as soon as his life there had become a high enough stepping-stone to a life elsewhere, perhaps at Rome or Milan, there was now for the first time associated a desire to be free from Romola, and to leave her behind him. She had ceased to belong to the desirable furniture of his life; there was no possibility of an easy relation between them without genuineness on his part. Genuineness implied confession of the past, and confession involved a change of purpose. But Tito had as little bent that way as a leopard has to lap milk when its teeth are grown. From all relations that were not easy and agreeable, we know that Tito shrank: why should he cling to them?

And Romola had made his relations difficult with others besides herself. He had had a troublesome interview with Dolfo Spini, who had come back in a rage after an ineffectual soaking with rain and long waiting in ambush; and that scene between Romola and himself at Nello's door, once reported in Spini's ear, might be a seed of something more unmanageable than suspicion. But now, at least, he believed that he had mastered Romola by a terror which appealed to the strongest forces of her nature. He had alarmed her affection and her conscience by the shadowy image of consequences; he had arrested her intellect by hanging before it the idea of a hopeless complexity in affairs which defined any moral judgment.

Yet Tito was not at ease. The world was not yet quite cushioned with velvet, and, if it had been, he could not have abandoned himself to that softness with thorough enjoyment; for before he went out again this evening, he put on his coat of chain-armour.

CHAPTER XXIX

THE PYRAMID OF VANITIES

THE wintry days passed for Romola as the white ships pass one who is standing lonely on the shore,—passing in silence and sameness, yet each bearing a hidden burden of coming change. Tito's hint had mingled so much dread with her interest in the progress of public affairs that she had begun to court ignorance rather than knowledge. The threatening German Emperor was gone again; and, in other ways besides, the position of Florence was alleviated; but so much distress remained that Romola's active duties were hardly diminished, and in these, as usual, her mind found a refuge from its doubt.

She dared not rejoice that the relief which had come in extremity and had appeared to justify the policy of the Frate's party was making that party so triumphant that Francesco Valori, hot-tempered chieftain of the Piagnoni, had been elected Gonfaloniere at the beginning of the year, and was making haste to have as much of his own liberal way as possible during his two months of power. That seemed for the moment like a strengthening of the party most attached to freedom, and a rein-forcement of protection to Savonarola; but Romola was now alive to every suggestion likely to deepen her foreboding that whatever the present might be, it was only an unconscious brooding over the mixed germs of change which might any day become tragic. And already by Carnival time, a little after mid-February, her presentiment was con-firmed by the signs of a very decided change: the Mediceans had ceased to be passive, and were openly exerting themselves to procure the elec-tion of Bernardo del Nero as the new Gonfaloniere.

On the last day of the Carnival, between ten and eleven in the morn-ing, Romola walked out, according to promise, towards the Corso degli Albizzi, to fetch her cousin Brigida, that they might both be ready to start from the Via de' Bardi early in the afternoon, and take their places at a window which Tito had had reserved for them in the Piazza della Signoria, where there was to be a scene of so new and striking a sort that all Florentine eyes must desire to see it. For the Piagnoni were having their own way thoroughly about the mode of keeping the Car-nival. In vain Dolfo Spini and his companions had struggled to get up the dear old masks and practical jokes, well spiced with indecency. Such things were not to be in a city where Christ had been declared king.

Romola set out in that languid state of mind with which every one enters on a long day of sight-seeing purely for the sake of gratifying a child or some dear childish friend. The day was certainly an epoch in carnival-keeping; but this phase of reform had not touched her enthusi-asm: and she did not know that it was an epoch in her own life when *another* lot would begin to be no longer secretly but visibly entwined with her own.

She chose to go through the great piazza that she might take a first survey of the unparalleled sight there while she was still alone. Entering it from the south, she saw something monstrous and many-coloured in the shape of a pyramid, or, rather, like a huge fir-tree, sixty feet high, with shelves on the branches, widening and widening towards the base till they reached a circumference of eighty yards. The piazza was full of life: slight young figures, in white garments, with olive wreaths on their heads, were moving to and fro about the base of the pyramidal tree, carrying baskets full of bright-coloured things; and maturer forms, some in the monastic frock, some in the loose tunics and dark-red caps of artists, were helping and examining, or else retreating to various points in the distance to survey the wondrous whole; while a consider-able group. among whom Romola recognized Piero di Cosimo, standing on the marble steps of Orgagna's Loggia, seemed to be keeping aloof in discontent and scorn.

Approaching nearer, she paused to look at the multifarious objects ranged in gradation from the base to the summit of the pyramid. There were tapestries and brocades of immodest design, pictures and sculptures held too likely to incite to vice; there were boards and tables for all sorts of games, playing-cards along with the blocks for printing them, dice, and other apparatus for gambling; there were worldly music-books, and musical instruments in all the pretty varieties of lute, drum, cymbal, and trumpet; there were masks and masquerading-dresses used in the old Carnival shows; there were handsome copies of Ovid, Boccaccio, Petrarca, Pulci, and other books of a vain or impure sort; there were all the implements of feminine vanity,—rouge-pots, false hair, mirrors, perfumes, powders, and transparent veils intended to provoke inquisitive glances; lastly, at the very summit, there was the unflattering effigy of a probably mythical Venetian merchant, who was understood to have offered a heavy sum for this collection of marketable abominations, and, soaring above him in surpassing ugliness, the symbolic figure of the old debauched Carnival.

This was the preparation for a new sort of bonfire,—the Burning of Vanities. Hidden in the interior of the pyramid was a plentiful store of dry fuel and gunpowder; and on this last day of the festival, at evening, the pile of vanities was to be set ablaze to the sound of trumpets, and the ugly old Carnival was to tumble into the flames amid the songs of reforming triumph.

This crowning act of the new festivities could hardly have been prepared but for a peculiar organization which had been started by Savonarola two years before. The mass of the Florentine boyhood and youth was no longer left to its own genial promptings towards street mischief and crude dissoluteness. Under the training of Fra Domenico, a sort of lieutenant to Savonarola, lads and striplings, the hope of Florence, were to have none but pure words on their lips, were to have a zeal for Unseen Good that should put to shame the lukewarmness of their elders, and were to know no pleasures save of an angelic sort,—singing Divine praises and walking in white robes. It was for them that the ranges of seats had been raised high against the walls of the Duomo; and they had been used to hear Savonarola appeal to them as the future glory of a city specially appointed to do the work of God.

These fresh-cheeked troops were the chief agents in the regenerated merriment of the new Carnival, which was a sort of sacred parody of the old. Had there been bonfires in the old time? There was to be a bonfire now, consuming impurity from off the earth. Had there been symbolic processions? There were to be processions now, but the symbols were to be white robes and red crosses and olive wreaths,—emblems of peace and innocent gladness,—and the banners and images held aloft were to tell the triumphs of goodness. Had there been dancing in a ring under the open sky of the piazza, to the sound of choral voices chanting loose songs? There was to be dancing in a ring now, but dancing of monks and laity in fraternal love and divine joy, and the music was to be the music of hymns. As for the collections from street passengers, they were to be greater than ever,—not for gross and superfluous suppers, but for the benefit of the hungry and needy; and, besides, there was the collecting of the *Anathema,* or the Vanities to be laid on the great pyramidal bonfire.

Troops of young inquisitors went from house to house on this exciting business of asking that the Anathema should be given up to them. Perhaps, after the more avowed vanities had been surrendered, Madonna, at the head of the household, had still certain little reddened balls brought from the Levant, intended to produce on a sallow cheek a sudden bloom of the most ingenuous falsity? If so, let her bring them down and cast them into the basket of doom. Or, perhaps, she had ringlets and coils of "dead hair"? If so, let her bring them to the street-door, not on her head, but in her hands, and publicly renounce the Anathema which hid the respectable signs of age under a ghastly mockery of youth. And, in reward, she would hear fresh young voices pronounce a blessing on her and her house.

The beardless inquisitors, organized into little regiments, doubtless took to their work very willingly. To coerce people by shame, or other spiritual pelting, into the giving up of things it will probably vex them to part with, is a form of piety to which the boyish mind is most readily converted; and if some obstinately wicked men got enraged and threatened the whip or the cudgel, this also was exciting. Savonarola himself evidently felt about the training of these boys the difficulty weighing on all minds with noble yearnings towards great ends, yet with that imperfect perception of means which forces a resort to some supernatural constraining influence as the only sure hope. The Florentine youth had had very evil habits and foul tongues: it seemed at first an unmixed blessing when they were got to shout, *"Viva Gesù!"* But Savonarola was forced at last to say from the pulpit, "There is a little too much shouting of *'Viva Gesù!'* This constant utterance of sacred words brings them into contempt. Let me have no more of that shouting till the next Festa."

Nevertheless, as the long stream of white-robed youthfulness, with its little red crosses and olive wreaths, had gone to the Duomo at dawn this morning to receive the communion from the hands of Savonarola, it was a sight of beauty; and, doubtless, many of those young souls were laying up memories of hope and awe that might save them from ever resting in a merely vulgar view of their work as men and citizens. There is no kind of conscious obedience that is not an advance on lawlessness, and these boys became the generation of men who fought greatly and endured greatly in the last struggle of their Republic. Now, in the intermediate hours between the early communion and dinner-time, they were making their last perambulations to collect alms and vanities, and this was why Romola saw the slim white figures moving to and fro about the base of the great pyramid.

"What think you of this folly, Madonna Romola?" said a brusque voice close to her ear. "Your Piagnoni will make *l'inferno* a pleasant prospect to us, if they are to carry things their own way on earth. It's enough to fetch a cudgel over the mountains to see painters, like Lorenzo di Credi and young Baccio there, helping to burn colour out of life in this fashion."

"My good Piero," said Romola, looking up and smiling at the grim man, "even you must be glad to see some of these things burnt. Look at those gewgaws and wigs and rouge-pots: I have heard you talk as indignantly against those things as Fra Girolamo himself."

"What then?" said Piero, turning round on her sharply. "I never said a woman should make a black patch of herself against the background. Va! Madonna Antigone, it's a shame for a woman with your hair and shoulders to run into such nonsense,—leave it to women who are not worth painting. What! the most holy Virgin herself has always been dressed well; that's the doctrine of the Church:—talk of heresy, indeed! And I should like to know what the excellent Messer Bardo would have said to the burning of the divine poets by these Frati, who are no better an imitation of men than if they were onions with the bulbs uppermost. Look at that Petrarca sticking up beside a rouge-pot: do the idiots pretend that the heavenly Laura was a painted harridan? And Boccaccio, now: do you mean to say, Madonna Romola,—you who are fit to be a model for a wise Saint Catherine of Egypt,—do you mean to say you have never read the stories of the immortal Messer Giovanni?"

"It is true I have read them, Piero," said Romola. "Some of them a great many times over, when I was a little girl. I used to get the book down when my father was asleep, so that I could read to myself."

"*Ebbene?*" said Piero, in a fiercely challenging tone.

"There are some things in them I do not want ever to forget," said Romola; "but you must confess, Piero, that a great many of those stories are only about low deceit for the lowest ends. Men do not want books to make them think lightly of vice, as if life were a vulgar joke. And I cannot blame Fra Girolamo for teaching that we owe our time to something better."

"Yes, yes, it's very well to say so now you've read them," said Piero, bitterly, turning on his heel and walking away from her.

Romola, too, walked on, smiling at Piero's innuendo, with a sort of tenderness towards the old painter's anger, because she knew that her father would have felt something like it. For herself, she was conscious of no inward collision with the strict and sombre view of pleasure which tended to repress poetry in the attempt to repress vice. Sorrow and joy have each their peculiar narrowness; and a religious enthusiasm like Savonarola's which ultimately blesses mankind by giving the soul a strong propulsion towards sympathy with pain, indignation against

wrong, and the subjugation of sensual desire, must always incur the reproach of a great negation. Romola's life had given her an affinity for
sadness which inevitably made her unjust towards merriment. That
subtle result of culture which we call Taste was subdued by the need
for deeper motive; just as the nicer demands of the palate are annihilated by urgent hunger. Moving habitually among scenes of suffering,
and carrying woman's heaviest disappointment in her heart, the severity which allied itself with self-renouncing beneficent strength had no
dissonance for her.

CHAPTER XXX

TESSA ABROAD AND AT HOME

ANOTHER figure easily recognized by us—a figure not clad in black, but
in the old red, green, and white—was approaching the piazza that morning to see the Carnival. She came from an opposite point, for Tessa no
longer lived on the hill of San Giorgio. After what had happened there
with Baldassarre, Tito had thought it best for that and other reasons to
find her a new home, but still in a quiet airy quarter, in a house bordering on the wide garden grounds north of the Porta Santa Croce.

Tessa was not come out sight-seeing without special leave. Tito had
been with her the evening before, and she had kept back the entreaty
which she felt to be swelling her heart and throat until she saw him in
a state of radiant ease, with one arm round the sturdy Lillo, and the
other resting gently on her own shoulder as she tried to make the tiny
Ninna steady on her legs. She was sure then that the weariness with
which he had come in and flung himself into his chair had quite melted
away from his brow and lips. Tessa had not been slow at learning a few
small stratagems by which she might avoid vexing Naldo and yet have a
little of her own way. She could read nothing else, but she had learned to
read a good deal in her husband's face.

And certainly the charm of that bright, gentle-humoured Tito who
woke up under the Loggia de' Cerchi on a Lenten morning five years
before, not having yet given any hostages to deceit, never returned so
nearly as in the person of Naldo, seated in that straight-backed, carved
arm-chair which he had provided for his comfort when he came to see
Tessa and the children. Tito himself was surprised at the growing sense
of relief which he felt in these moments. No guile was needed towards
Tessa: she was too ignorant and too innocent to suspect him of anything. And the little voices calling him "Babbo" were very sweet in his
ears for the short while that he heard them. When he thought of leaving
Florence, he never thought of leaving Tessa and the little ones behind.
He was very fond of these round-cheeked, wide-eyed human things that
clung about him and knew no evil of him. And wherever affection can
spring, it is like the green leaf and the blossom,—pure, and breathing

purity, whatever soil it may grow in. Poor Romola, with all her self-sacrificing effort, was really helping to harden Tito's nature by chilling it with a positive dislike which had beforehand seemed impossible in him; but Tessa kept open the fountains of kindness.

"Ninna is very good without me now," began Tessa, feeling her request rising very high in her throat, and letting Ninna seat herself on the floor. "I can leave her with Monna Lisa any time; and if she is in the cradle and cries, Lillo is as sensible as can be,—he goes and thumps Monna Lisa."

Lillo, whose great dark eyes looked all the darker because his curls were of a light brown like his mother's, jumped off Babbo's knee, and went forthwith to attest his intelligence by thumping Monna Lisa, who was shaking her head slowly over her spinning at the other end of the room.

"A wonderful boy!" said Tito, laughing.

"Isn't he?" said Tessa, eagerly, getting a little closer to him; "and I might go and see the Carnival to-morrow, just for an hour or two, mightn't I?"

"Oh, you wicked pigeon!" said Tito, pinching her cheek; "those are your longings, are they? What have you to do with carnivals now you are an old woman with two children?"

"But old women like to see things," said Tessa, her lower lip hanging a little. "Monna Lisa said she should like to go, only she's so deaf she can't hear what is behind her, and she thinks we couldn't take care of both the children."

"No, indeed, Tessa," said Tito, looking rather grave, "you must not think of taking the children into the crowded streets, else I shall be angry."

"But I have never been into the piazza without leave," said Tessa, in a frightened, pleading tone, "since the Holy Saturday, and I think Nofri is dead, for you know the poor *madre* died; and I shall never forget the Carnival I saw once: it was so pretty—all roses and a king and queen under them—and singing. I liked it better than the San Giovanni."

"But there's nothing like that now, my Tessa. They are going to make a bonfire in the piazza,—that's all. But I cannot let you go out by yourself in the evening."

"Oh, no, no! I don't want to go in the evening. I only want to go and see the procession by daylight. There *will* be a procession,—is it not true?"

"Yes, after a sort," said Tito, "as lively as a flight of cranes. You must not expect roses and glittering kings and queens, my Tessa. However, I suppose any string of people to be called a procession will please your blue eyes. And there's a thing they have raised in the Piazza de' Signori for the bonfire. You may like to see that. But come home early, and look like a grave little old woman; and if you see any men with feathers and swords, keep out of their way: they are very fierce, and like to cut old women's heads off."

"Santa Madonna! where do they come from? Ah! you are laughing; it is not so bad. But I will keep away from them. Only," Tessa went on in a whisper, putting her lips near Naldo's ear, "if I might take Lillo with me! He is very sensible."

"But who will thump Monna Lisa then, if she doesn't hear?" said Tito, finding it difficult not to laugh, but thinking it necessary to look serious. "No, Tessa, you could not take care of Lillo if you got into a crowd, and he's too heavy for you to carry him."

"It is true," said Tessa, rather sadly, "and he likes to run away. I forgot that. Then I will go alone. But now look at Ninna,—you have not looked at her enough."

Ninna was a blue-eyed thing, at the tottering, tumbling age,—a fair solid, which, like a loaded die, found its base with a constancy that warranted prediction. Tessa went to snatch her up, and when Babbo was paying due attention to the recent teeth and other marvels, she said, in a whisper, "And shall I buy some confetti for the children?"

Tito drew some small coins from his scarsella, and poured them into her palm.

"That will buy no end," said Tessa, delighted at this abundance. "I shall not mind going without Lillo so much, if I bring him something."

So Tessa set out in the morning towards the great piazza where the bonfire was to be. She did not think the February breeze cold enough to demand further covering than her green woollen dress. A mantle would have been oppressive, for it would have hidden a new necklace and a new clasp, mounted with silver, the only ornamental presents Tito had ever made her. Tessa did not think at all of showing her figure, for no one had ever told her it was pretty; but she was quite sure that her necklace and clasp were of the prettiest sort ever worn by the richest contadina, and she arranged her white hood over her head so that the front of her necklace might be well displayed. These ornaments, she considered, must inspire respect for her as the wife of some one who could afford to buy them.

She tripped along very cheerily in the February sunshine, thinking much of the purchases for the little ones with which she was to fill her small basket, and not thinking at all of any one who might be observing her. Yet her descent from her upper story into the street had been watched, and she was being kept in sight as she walked by a person who had often waited in vain to see if it were not Tessa who lived in that house to which he had more than once dogged Tito. Baldassarre was carrying a package of yarn: he was constantly employed in that way, as a means of earning his scanty bread, and keeping the sacred fire of vengeance alive; and he had come out of his way this morning, as he had often done before, that he might pass by the house to which he had followed Tito in the evening. His long imprisonment had so intensified his timid suspicion and his belief in some diabolic fortune favouring Tito, that he had not dared to pursue him, except under cover of a crowd or of the darkness; he felt, with instinctive horror, that if Tito's eyes fell upon him, he should again be held up to obloquy, again be dragged away; his weapon would be taken from him, and he should be cast helpless into a prison-cell. His fierce purpose had become as stealthy as a serpent's, which depends for its prey on one dart of the fang. Justice was weak and unfriended; and he could not hear again the voice that pealed the promise of vengeance in the Duomo; he had been there again and again, but that voice, too, had apparently been stifled by cunning strong-armed wickedness. For a long while Baldassarre's ruling thought was to ascertain whether Tito still wore the armour, for now at last his fainting hope would have been contented with a successful stab on this side the grave; but he would never risk his precious knife again. It was a weary time he had had to wait for the chance of answering this question by touching Tito's back in the press of the street. Since then, the knowledge that the sharp steel was useless, and that he had no hope but in some new device, had fallen with leaden weight on his enfeebled mind. A dim vision of winning one of those two wives to aid him came before him continually, and continually slid away. The wife who had lived on the hill was no longer there. If he could find her again, he might grasp some thread of a project, and work his way to more clearness.

And this morning he had succeeded. He was quite certain now where this wife lived, and as he walked, bent a little under his burden of yarn, yet keeping the green and white figure in sight, his mind was dwelling upon her and her circumstances as feeble eyes dwell on lines and colours, trying to interpret them into consistent significance.

Tessa had to pass through various long streets without seeing any other sign of the Carnival than unusual groups of the country people in their best garments, and that disposition in everybody to chat and loiter which marks the early hours of a holiday, before the spectacle has begun. Presently, in her disappointed search for remarkable objects, her eyes fell on a man with a peddler's basket before him, who seemed to be selling nothing but little red crosses to all the passengers. A little red cross would be pretty to hang up over her bed; it would also help to keep off harm, and would perhaps make Ninna stronger. Tessa went to the other side of the street, that she might ask the peddler the price of the crosses, fearing that they would cost a little too much for her to spare from her purchase of sweets. The peddler's back had been turned towards her hitherto, but when she came near him she recognized an old acquaintance of the Mercato Bratti Ferravecchi, and, accustomed to feel that she was to avoid old acquaintances, she turned away again and passed to the other side of the street. But Bratti's eye was too well practised in looking out at the corner after possible customers, for her movement to have escaped him, and she was presently arrested by a tap on the arm from one of the red crosses.

"Young woman," said Bratti, as she unwillingly turned her head, "you come from some castello a good way off, it seems to me, else you'd never think of walking about, this blessed Carnival, without a red cross in your hand. Santa Madonna! Four white quattrini is a small price to pay for your soul,—prices rise in purgatory, let me tell you."

"Oh, I should like one," said Tessa, hastily, "but I couldn't spare four white quattrini."

Bratti had at first regarded Tessa too abstractedly as a mere customer to look at her with any scrutiny, but when she began to speak he exclaimed: "By the head of San Giovanni, it must be the little Tessa, and looking as fresh as a ripe apple! What! you've done none the worse, then, for running away from father Nofri? You were in the right of it, for he goes on crutches now, and a crabbed fellow with crutches is dangerous; he can reach across the house and beat a woman as he sits."

"I'm married," said Tessa, rather demurely, remembering Naldo's command that she should behave with gravity; "and my husband takes great care of me."

"Ah, then you've fallen on your feet! Nofri said you were good-for-nothing vermin; but what then? An ass may bray a good while before he shakes the stars down. I always said you did well to run away, and it isn't often Bratti's in the wrong. Well, and so you've got a husband and plenty of money? Then you'll never think much of giving four white quattrini for a red cross. I get no profit; but what with the famine and the new religion, all other merchandise is gone down. You live in the country where the chestnuts are plenty, eh? You've never wanted for polenta, I can see."

"No, I've never wanted anything," said Tessa, still on her guard.

"Then you can afford to buy a cross. I got a Padre to bless them, and you get blessing and all for four quattrini. It isn't for the profit; I hardly get a danaro by the whole lot. But then they're holy wares, and it's getting harder and harder work to see your way to Paradise: the very Carnival is like Holy Week, and the least you can do to keep the Devil from getting the upper hand is to buy a cross. God guard you! think what the Devil's tooth is! You've seen him biting the man in San Giovanni, I should hope?"

Tessa felt much teased and frightened. "Oh, Bratti," she said, with a discomposed face, "I want to buy a great many confetti: I've got little Lillo and Ninna at home. And nice coloured sweet things cost a great deal. And they will not like the cross so well, though I know it would be good to have it."

"Come, then," said Bratti, fond of laying up a store of merits by imagining possible extortions and then heroically renouncing them, "since you're an old acquaintance, you shall have it for two quattrini. It's making you a present of the cross, to say nothing of the blessing."

Tessa was reaching out her two quattrini with trembling hesitation, when Bratti said abruptly, "Stop a bit! Where do you live?"

"Oh, a long way off," she answered, almost automatically, being pre-occupied with her quattrini; "beyond San Ambrogio, in the Via Piccola, at the top of the house where the wood is stacked below."

"Very good," said Bratti, in a patronizing tone; "then I'll let you have the cross on trust, and call for the money. So you live inside the gates? Well, well, I shall be passing."

"No, no!" said Tessa, frightened lest Naldo should be angry at this revival of an old acquaintance. "I can spare the money. Take it now."

"No," said Bratti, resolutely; "I'm not a hard-hearted peddler. I'll call and see if you've got any rags, and you shall make a bargain. See, here's the cross; and there's Pippo's shop not far behind you: you can go and fill your basket, and I must go and get mine empty. *Addio, piccina.*"

Bratti went on his way, and Tessa, stimulated to change her money into confetti before further accident, went into Pippo's shop, a little fluttered by the thought that she had let Bratti know more about her than her husband would approve. There were certainly more dangers in coming to see the Carnival than in staying at home; and she would have felt this more strongly if she had known that the wicked old man who had wanted to kill her husband on the hill was still keeping her in sight. But she had not noticed the man with the burden on his back.

The consciousness of having a small basketful of things to make the children glad dispersed her anxiety, and as she entered the Via de' Libraj her face had its usual expression of childlike content. And now she thought there was really a procession coming, for she saw white robes and a banner, and her heart began to palpitate with expectation. She stood a little aside, but in that narrow street there was the pleasure of being obliged to look very close. The banner was pretty: it was the Holy Mother with the Babe, whose love for her Tessa had believed in more and more since she had had her babies; and the figures in white had not only green wreaths on their heads, but little red crosses by their side, which caused her some satisfaction that she also had her red cross. Certainly they looked as beautiful as the angels on the clouds; and to Tessa's mind they, too, had a background of cloud, like everything else that came to her in life. How and whence did they come? She did not mind much about knowing. But one thing surprised her as newer than wreaths and crosses; it was that some of the white figures carried baskets between them. What could the baskets be for?

But now they were very near, and, to her astonishment, they wheeled aside and came straight up to her. She trembled as she would have done if Saint Michael in the picture had shaken his head at her, and was conscious of nothing but terrified wonder till she saw close to her a round, boyish face, lower than her own, and heard a treble voice saying, "Sister, you carry the Anathema about you. Yield it up to the blessed Gesù, and He will adorn you with the gems of His grace."

Tessa was only more frightened, understanding nothing. Her first conjecture settled on her basket of sweets. They wanted that, these alarming angels. Oh, dear, dear! She looked down at it.

"No, sister," said a taller youth, pointing to her necklace and the clasp of her belt, "it is those vanities that are the Anathema. Take off that necklace and unclasp that belt, that they may be burned in the holy Bonfire of Vanities, and save *you* from burning."

"It is the truth, my sister," said a still taller youth, evidently the archangel of this band. "Listen to these voices speaking the divine message. You already carry a red cross: let that be your only adornment. Yield up your necklace and belt, and you shall obtain grace."

This was too much. Tessa, overcome with awe, dared not say "no," but she was equally unable to render up her beloved necklace and clasp. Her pouting lips were quivering, the tears rushed to her eyes, and a great drop fell. For a moment she ceased to see anything; she felt nothing but confused terror and misery. Suddenly a gentle hand was laid on her arm, and a soft, wonderful voice, as if the Holy Madonna were speaking, said, "Do not be afraid; no one shall harm you."

Tessa looked up and saw a lady in black, with a young heavenly face and loving hazel eyes. She had never seen any one like this lady before, and under other circumstances might have had awestruck thoughts about her; but now everything else was overcome by the sense that loving protection was near her. The tears only fell the faster, relieving her swelling heart, as she looked up at the heavenly face, and, putting her hand to her necklace, said sobbingly,—

"I can't give them to be burnt. My husband—he bought them for me —and they are so pretty—and Ninna—oh, I wish I'd never come."

"Do not ask her for them," said Romola, speaking to the white-robed boys in a tone of mild authority. "It answers no good end for people to give up such things against their will. That is not what Fra Girolamo approves: he would have such things given up freely."

Madonna Romola's word was not to be resisted, and the white train moved on. They even moved with haste, as if some new object had caught their eyes; and Tessa felt with bliss that they were gone, and that her necklace and clasp were still with her.

"Oh, I will go back to the house," she said, still agitated; "I will go nowhere else. But if I should meet them again, and you not be there?" she added, expecting everything from this heavenly lady.

"Stay a little," said Romola. "Come with me under this doorway, and we will hide the necklace and clasp, and then you will be in no danger."

She led Tessa under the archway, and said, "Now, can we find room for your necklace and belt in your basket? Ah! your basket is full of crisp things that will break: let us be careful, and lay the heavy necklace under them."

It was like a change in a dream to Tessa—the escape from nightmare into floating safety and joy—to find herself taken care of by this lady, so lovely and powerful and gentle. She let Romola unfasten her necklace and clasp, while she herself did nothing but look up at the face that bent over her.

"They are sweets for Lillo and Ninna," she said, as Romola carefully lifted up the light parcels in the basket, and placed the ornaments below them.

"Those are your children?" said Romola, smiling. "And you would rather go home to them than to see any more of the Carnival? Else you have not far to go to the Piazza de' Signori, and there you would see the pile for the great bonfire."

"No, oh, no!" said Tessa, eagerly; "I shall never like bonfires again, I will go back."

"You live at some castello, doubtless," said Romola, not waiting for an answer. "Towards which gate do you go?"

"Towards Por' Santa Croce."

"Come, then," said Romola, taking her by the hand and leading her to the corner of a street nearly opposite. "If you go down there," she said, pausing, "you will soon be in a straight road. And I must leave you now, because some one else expects me. You will not be frightened. Your pretty things are quite safe now. Addio."

"Addio, Madonna," said Tessa, almost in a whisper, not knowing what else it would be right to say; and in an instant the heavenly lady was gone. Tessa turned to catch a last glimpse, but she only saw the tall gliding figure vanish round the projecting stonework. So she went on her way in wonder, longing to be once more safely housed with Monna Lisa, undesirous of carnivals forevermore.

Baldassarre had kept Tessa in sight till the moment of her parting with Romola; then he went away with his bundle of yarn. It seemed to him that he had discerned a clue which might guide him if he could only grasp the necessary details firmly enough. He had seen the two wives together, and the sight had brought to his conceptions that vividness which had been wanting before. His power of imagining facts needed to be reinforced continually by the senses. The tall wife was the noble and rightful wife; she had the blood in her that would be readily kindled to resentment; she would know what scholarship was, and how it might lie locked in by the obstructions of the stricken body, like a treasure buried by earthquake. She could believe him: she would be *inclined* to believe him, if he proved to her that her husband was unfaithful. Women cared about that: they would take vengeance for that. If this wife of Tito's loved him, she would have a sense of injury which Baldassarre's mind dwelt on with keen longing, as if it would be the strength of another Will added to his own, the strength of another mind to form devices.

Both these wives had been kind to Baldassarre, and their acts toward him, being bound up with the very image of them, had not vanished from his memory; yet the thought of their pain could not present itself to him as a check. To him it seemed that pain was the order of the world for all except the hard and base. If any were innocent, if any were noble, where could the utmost gladness lie for them? Where it lay for him,—in unconquerable hatred and triumphant vengeance. But he must be cautious: he must watch this wife in the Via de' Bardi, and learn more of her; for even here frustration was possible. There was no power for him now but in patience.

CHAPTER XXXI

WHEN Romola said that some one else expected her, she meant her cousin Brigida, but she was far from suspecting how much that good kinswoman was in need of her. Returning together towards the piazza, they had descried the company of youths coming to a stand before Tessa, and when Romola, having approached near enough to see the simple little contadina's distress, said, "Wait for me a moment, Cousin," Monna Brigida said hastily, "Ah, I will not go on: come for me to Boni's shop, —I shall go back there."

The truth was, Monna Brigida had a consciousness on the one hand of certain "vanities" carried on her person, and on the other of a growing alarm lest the Piagnoni should be right in holding that rouge and false hair and pearl embroidery endamaged the soul. Their serious view of things filled the air like an odour; nothing seemed to have exactly the same flavour as it used to have; and there was the dear child Romola, in her youth and beauty, leading a life that was uncomfortably suggestive of rigorous demands on woman. A widow at fifty-five whose satisfaction has been largely drawn from what she thinks of her own person, and what she believes others think of it, requires a great fund of imagination to keep her spirits buoyant. And Monna Brigida had begun to have frequent struggles at her toilet. If her soul would prosper better without them, was it really worth while to put on the rouge and the braids? But when she lifted up the hand-mirror and saw a sallow face with baggy cheeks, and crows'-feet that were not to be dissimulated by any simpering of the lips,—when she parted her grey hair, and let it lie in simple Piagnone fashion round her face, her courage failed. Monna Berta would certainly burst out laughing at her, and call her an old hag; and as Monna Berta was really only fifty-two, she had a superiority which would make the observation cutting. Every woman who was not a Piagnone would give a shrug at the sight of her, and the men would accost her as if she were their grandmother. Whereas at fifty-five a woman was not so very old,—she only required making up a little. So the rouge and the braids and the embroidered berretta went on again, and Monna Brigida was satisfied with the accustomed effect; as for her neck, if she covered it up, people might suppose it was too old to show, and, on the contrary, with the necklaces round it, it looked better than Monna Berta's. This very day, when she was preparing for the Piagnone Carnival, such a struggle had occurred; and the conflicting fears and longings which caused the struggle, caused her to turn back and seek refuge in the druggist's shop rather than encounter the collectors of the Anathema when Romola was not by her side. But Monna Brigida was not quite rapid enough in her retreat. She had been descried, even before she turned away, by the white-robed boys in the rear of those who wheeled round towards Tessa; and the willingness with which Tessa was given up was, perhaps, slightly due to the fact that part of the troop had already accosted a personage carrying more markedly upon her the dangerous weight of the Anathema. It happened that several of this troop were at the youngest age taken into peculiar training; and a small fellow of ten, his olive wreath resting above cherubic cheeks and wide brown eyes, his imagination really possessed with a hovering awe at existence as something in which great consequences impended on being good or bad, his longings nevertheless running in the direction of mastery and mischief, was the first to reach Monna Brigida and place himself across her path. She felt angry, and looked for an open door; but there was not one at hand, and by attempting to escape now, she would only make things worse. But it was not the cherubic-faced young one who first addressed her; it was a youth of fifteen, who held one handle of a wide basket.

"Venerable mother!" he began, "the blessed Jesus commands you to give up the Anathema which you carry upon you. That cap embroidered with pearls, those jewels that fasten up your false hair,—let them be given up and sold for the poor; and cast the hair itself away from you, as a lie that is only fit for burning. Doubtless, too, you have other jewels under your silk mantle."

"Yes, lady," said the youth at the other handle, who had many of Fra Girolamo's phrases by heart, "they are too heavy for you: they are heavier than a millstone, and are weighting you for perdition. Will you adorn yourself with the hunger of the poor, and be proud to carry God's curse upon your head?"

"In truth you are old, buona madre," said the cherubic boy, in a sweet soprano. "You look very ugly with the red on your cheeks, and that black glistening hair, and those fine things. It is only Satan who can like to see you. Your Angel is sorry. He wants you to rub away the red."

The little fellow snatched a soft silk scarf from the basket, and held it towards Monna Brigida, that she might use it as her guardian angel desired. Her anger and mortification were fast giving way to spiritual alarm. Monna Berta and that cloud of witnesses, highly dressed society in general, were not looking at her, and she was surrounded by young monitors, whose white robes, and wreaths, and red crosses, and dreadful candour had something awful in their unusualness. Her Franciscan confessor, Fra Cristoforo, of Santa Croce, was not at hand to reinforce her distrust of Dominican teaching, and she was helplessly possessed and shaken by a vague sense that a supreme warning was come to her. Unvisited by the least suggestion of any other course that was open to her, she took the scarf that was held out, and rubbed her cheeks, with trembling submissiveness.

"It is well, madonna," said the second youth. "It is a holy beginning. And when you have taken those vanities from your head, the dew of heavenly grace will descend on it." The infusion of mischief was getting stronger, and putting his hand to one of the jewelled pins that fastened

her braids to the berretta, he drew it out. The heavy black plait fell
down over Monna Brigida's face, and dragged the rest of the head-gear
forward. It was a new reason for not hesitating: she put up her hands
hastily, undid the other fastenings, and flung down into the basket of
doom her beloved crimson-velvet berretta, with all its unsurpassed embroidery of seed-pearls, and stood an unrouged woman, with grey hair
pushed backward from a face where certain deep lines of age had triumphed over *embonpoint*.

But the berretta was not allowed to lie in the basket. With impish zeal
the youngsters lifted it, and held it up pitilessly, with the false hair
dangling.

"See, venerable mother," said the taller youth, "what ugly lies you
have delivered yourself from! And now you look like the blessed Saint
Anna, the mother of the Holy Virgin."

Thoughts of going into a convent forthwith, and never showing herself
in the world again, were rushing through Monna Brigida's mind. There
was nothing possible for her but to take care of her soul. Of course,
there were spectators laughing: she had no need to look round to assure
herself of that. Well! it would, perhaps, be better to be forced to think
more of Paradise. But at the thought that the dear accustomed world
was no longer in her choice, there gathered some of those hard tears
which just moisten elderly eyes, and she could see but dimly a large
rough hand holding a red cross, which was suddenly thrust before her
over the shoulders of the boys, while a strong guttural voice said,—

"Only four quattrini, madonna, blessing and all! Buy it. You'll find
a comfort in it now your wig's gone. Deh! what are we sinners doing
all our lives? Making soup in a basket, and getting nothing but the
scum for our stomachs. Better buy a blessing, madonna! Only four quattrini; the profit is not so much as the smell of a danaro, and it goes to
the poor."

Monna Brigida, in dim-eyed confusion, was proceeding to the further
submission of reaching money from her embroidered scarsella, at present
hidden by her silk mantle, when the group round her, which she had not
yet entertained the idea of escaping, opened before a figure as welcome
as an angel loosing prison-bolts.

"Romola, look at me!" said Monna Brigida, in a piteous tone, putting
out both her hands.

The white troop was already moving away, with a slight consciousness
that its zeal about the head-gear had been superabundant enough to
afford a dispensation from any further demand for penitential offerings.

"Dear cousin, don't be distressed," said Romola, smitten with pity,
yet hardly able to help smiling at the sudden apparition of her kinswoman in a genuine, natural guise, strangely contrasted with all memories of her. She took the black drapery from her own head, and threw
it over Monna Brigida's. "There," she went on soothingly, "no one will
remark you now. We will turn down the Via del Palagio and go straight
to our house."

They hastened away, Monna Brigida grasping Romola's hand tightly, as if to get a stronger assurance of her being actually there.

"Ah, my Romola, my dear child!" said the short fat woman, hurrying with frequent steps to keep pace with the majestic young figure beside her; "what an old scarecrow I am! I must be good,—I mean to be good!"

"Yes, yes; buy a cross!" said the guttural voice, while the rough hand was thrust once more before Monna Brigida: for Bratti was not to be abashed by Romola's presence into renouncing a probable customer, and had quietly followed up their retreat. "Only four quattrini, blessing and all,—and if there was any profit, it would all go to the poor."

Monna Brigida would have been compelled to pause, even if she had been in a less submissive mood. She put up one hand deprecatingly to arrest Romola's remonstrance, and with the other reached out a grosso, worth many white quattrini, saying, in an entreating tone,—

"Take it, good man, and begone."

"You're in the right, madonna," said Bratti, taking the coin quickly, and thrusting the cross into her hand: "I'll not offer you change, for I might as well rob you of a mass. What! we must all be scorched a little, but you will come off the easier: better fall from the window than the roof. A good Easter and a good year to you!"

"Well, Romola," cried Monna Brigida, pathetically, as Bratti left them, "if I'm to be a Piagnone, it's no matter how I look!"

"Dear cousin," said Romola, smiling at her affectionately, "you don't know how much better you look than you ever did before. I see now how good-natured your face is, like yourself. That red and finery seemed to thrust themselves forward and hide expression. Ask our Piero or any other painter if he would not rather paint your portrait now than before. I think all lines of the human face have something either touching or grand, unless they seem to come from low passions. How fine old men are, like my godfather! Why should not old women look grand and simple?"

"Yes, when one gets to be sixty, my Romola," said Brigida, relapsing a little; "but I'm only fifty-five, and Monna Berta, and everybody— But it's no use: I will be good, like you. Your mother, if she'd been alive, would have been as old as I am; we were cousins together. One must either die or get old. But it doesn't matter about being old, if one's a Piagnone."

CHAPTER XXXII

A PROPHETESS

THE incidents of that Carnival day seemed to Romola to carry no other personal consequences to her than the new care of supporting poor Cousin Brigida in her fluctuating resignation to age and grey hairs; but they introduced a Lenten time in which she was kept at a high pitch of mental excitement and active effort.

Bernardo del Nero had been elected Gonfaloniere. By great exertions, the Medicean party had so far triumphed, and that triumph had deepened Romola's presentiment of some secretly prepared scheme likely to ripen either into success or betrayal during these two months of her godfather's authority. Every morning the dim daybreak as it peered into her room seemed to be that haunting fear coming back to her. Every morning the fear went with her as she passed through the streets on her way to the early sermon in the Duomo; but there she gradually lost the sense of its chill presence, as men lose the dread of death in the clash of battle.

In the Duomo she felt herself sharing in a passionate conflict which had wider relations than any enclosed within the walls of Florence. For Savonarola was preaching,—preaching the last course of Lenten sermons he was ever allowed to finish in the Duomo: he knew that excommunication was imminent, and he had reached the point of defying it. He held up the condition of the Church in the terrible mirror of his unflinching speech, which called things by their right names and dealt in no polite periphrases; he proclaimed with heightening confidence the advent of renovation,—of a moment when there would be a general revolt against corruption. As to his own destiny, he seemed to have a double and alternating prevision: sometimes he saw himself taking a glorious part in that revolt, sending forth a voice that would be heard through all Christendom, and making the dead body of the Church tremble into new life, as the body of Lazarus trembled when the Divine voice pierced the sepulchre; sometimes he saw no prospect for himself but persecution and martyrdom,—this life for him was only a vigil, and only after death would come the dawn.

The position was one which must have had its impressiveness for all minds that were not of the dullest order, even if they were inclined, as Macchiavelli was, to interpret the Frate's character by a key that presupposed no loftiness. To Romola, whose kindred ardour gave her a firm belief in Savonarola's genuine greatness of purpose, the crisis was as stirring as if it had been part of her personal lot. It blent itself as an exalting memory with all her daily labours; and those labours were calling not only for difficult perseverance, but for new courage. Famine had never yet taken its flight from Florence, and all distress, by its long continuance, was getting harder to bear; disease was spreading in the crowded city, and the Plague was expected. As Romola walked, often in weariness, among the sick, the hungry, and the murmuring, she felt it good to be inspired by something more than her pity,—by the belief in a heroism struggling for sublime ends, towards which the daily action of her pity could only tend feebly, as the dews that freshen the weedy ground to-day tend to prepare an unseen harvest in the years to come.

But that mighty music which stirred her in the Duomo was not without its jarring notes. Since those first days of glowing hope when the

Frate, seeing the near triumph of good in the reform of the Republic and the coming of the French deliverer, had preached peace, charity, and oblivion of political differences, there had been a marked change of conditions: political intrigue had been too obstinate to allow of the desired oblivion; the belief in the French deliverer, who had turned his back on his high mission, seemed to have wrought harm; and hostility, both on a petty and on a grand scale, was attacking the Prophet with new weapons and new determination.

It followed that the spirit of contention and self-vindication pierced more and more conspicuously in his sermons; that he was urged to meet the popular demands not only by increased insistence and detail concerning visions and private revelations, but by a tone of defiant confidence against objectors; and from having denounced the desire for the miraculous, and declared that miracles had no relation to true faith, he had come to assert that at the right moment the Divine power would attest the truth of his prophetic preaching by a miracle. And continually, in the rapid transitions of excited feeling, as the vision of triumphant good receded behind the actual predominance of evil, the threats of coming vengeance against vicious tyrants and corrupt priests gathered some impetus from personal exasperation as well as from indignant zeal.

In the career of a great public orator who yields himself to the inspiration of the moment, that conflict of selfish and unselfish emotion which in most men is hidden in the chamber of the soul, is brought into terrible evidence: the language of the inner voices is written out in letters of fire.

But if the tones of exasperation jarred on Romola, there was often another member of Fra Girolamo's audience to whom they were the only thrilling tones, like the vibration of deep bass notes to the deaf. Baldassarre had found out that the wonderful Frate was preaching again, and as often as he could, he went to hear the Lenten sermon, that he might drink in the threats of a voice which seemed like a power on the side of justice. He went the more because he had seen that Romola went too; for he was waiting and watching for a time when not only outward circumstances, but his own varying mental state, would mark the right moment for seeking an interview with her. Twice Romola had caught sight of his face in the Duomo,—once when its dark glance was fixed on hers. She wished not to see it again, and yet she looked for it, as men look for the reappearance of a portent. But any revelation that might be yet to come about this old man was a subordinate fear now: it referred, she thought, only to the past, and her anxiety was almost absorbed by the present.

Yet the stirring Lent passed by; April, the second and final month of her godfather's supreme authority, was near its close; and nothing had occurred to fulfil her presentiment. In the public mind, too, there had been fears, and rumours had spread from Rome of a menacing activity on the part of Piero de' Medici, but in a few days the suspected Bernardo would go out of power.

Romola was trying to gather some courage from the review of her futile fears, when on the 27th, as she was walking out on her usual errands of mercy in the afternoon, she was met by a messenger from Camilla Rucellai, chief among the feminine seers of Florence, desiring her presence forthwith on matters of the highest moment. Romola, who shrank with unconquerable repulsion from the shrill volubility of those illuminated women, and had just now a special repugnance towards Camilla because of a report that she had announced revelations hostile to Bernardo del Nero, was at first inclined to send back a flat refusal. Camilla's message might refer to public affairs, and Romola's immediate prompting was to close her ears against knowledge that might only make her mental burden heavier. But it had become so thoroughly her habit to reject her impulsive choice, and to obey passively the guidance of outward claims, that, reproving herself for allowing her presentiments to make her cowardly and selfish, she ended by compliance, and went straight to Camilla.

She found the nervous grey-haired woman in a chamber arranged as much as possible like a convent cell. The thin fingers clutching Romola as she sat, and the eager voice addressing her at first in a loud whisper, caused her a physical shrinking that made it difficult for her to keep her seat.

Camilla had a vision to communicate,—a vision in which it had been revealed to her by Romola's Angel, that Romola knew certain secrets concerning her godfather, Bernardo del Nero, which, if disclosed, might save the Republic from peril. Camilla's voice rose louder and higher as she narrated her vision, and ended by exhorting Romola to obey the command of her Angel, and separate herself from the enemy of God.

Romola's impetuosity was that of a massive nature, and, except in moments when she was deeply stirred, her manner was calm and self-controlled. She had a constitutional disgust for the shallow excitability of women like Camilla, whose faculties seemed all wrought up into fantasies, leaving nothing for emotion and thought. The exhortation was not yet ended when she started up and attempted to wrench her arm from Camilla's tightening grasp. It was of no use. The prophetess kept her hold like a crab, and, only incited to more eager exhortation by Romola's resistance, was carried beyond her own intention into a shrill statement of other visions which were to corroborate this. Christ himself had appeared to her and ordered her to send his commands to certain citizens in office that they should throw Bernardo del Nero from the window of the Palazzo Vecchio. Fra Girolamo himself knew of it, and had not dared this time to say that the vision was not of Divine authority.

"And since then," said Camilla, in her excited treble, straining upward with wild eyes towards Romola's face, "the Blessed Infant has come to me and laid a wafer of sweetness on my tongue in token of his pleasure that I had done his will."

"Let me go!" said Romola, in a deep voice of anger. "God grant you are mad! else you are detestably wicked!"

The violence of her effort to be free was too strong for Camilla now. She wrenched away her arm and rushed out of the room, not pausing till she had hurriedly gone far along the street, and found herself close to the church of the Badia. She had but to pass behind the curtain under the old stone arch, and she would find a sanctuary shut in from the noise and hurry of the street, where all objects and all uses suggested the thought of an eternal peace subsisting in the midst of turmoil.

She turned in, and sinking down on the step of the altar in front of Filippino Lippi's serene Virgin appearing to Saint Bernard,[1] she waited in hope that the inward tumult which agitated her would by and by subside.

The thought which pressed on her the most acutely was that Camilla could allege Savonarola's countenance of her wicked folly. Romola did not for a moment believe that he had sanctioned the throwing of Bernardo del Nero from the window as a Divine suggestion; she felt certain that there was falsehood or mistake in that allegation. Savonarola had become more and more severe in his views of resistance to malcontents; but the ideas of strict law and order were fundamental to all his political teaching. Still, since he knew the possibly fatal effects of visions like Camilla's, since he had a marked distrust of such spirit-seeing women, and kept aloof from them as much as possible, why, with his readiness to denounce wrong from the pulpit, did he not publicly denounce these pretended revelations which brought new darkness instead of light across the conception of a Supreme Will? Why? The answer came with painful clearness: he was fettered inwardly by the consciousness that such revelations were not, in their basis, distinctly separable from his own visions; he was fettered outwardly by the foreseen consequence of raising a cry against himself even among members of his own party, as one who would suppress all Divine inspiration of which he himself was not the vehicle,—he or his confidential and supplementary seer of visions, Fra Salvestro.

Romola, kneeling with buried face on the altar-step, was enduring one of those sickening moments, when the enthusiasm which had come to her as the only energy strong enough to make life worthy, seemed to be inevitably bound up with vain dreams and wilful eye-shutting. Her mind rushed back with a new attraction towards the strong worldly sense, the dignified prudence, the untheoretic virtues of her godfather, who was to be treated as a sort of Agag because he held that a more restricted form of government was better than the Great Council, and because he would not pretend to forget old ties to the banished family.

But with this last thought rose the presentiment of some plot to restore

---

[1] The picture by Filippino Lippi, representing the appearance of the Virgin surrounded by angels to San Bernard as he sits writing in a wood, was at that time in the Chapel belonging to Francesco del Pugliese at *le Campora*, a convent of the Badia monks outside the city. It remained there until the Seige of 1529, when it was removed for safety to the sacristy of the Badia. Francesco del Pugliese paid Filippino Lippi 250 ducats for the picture.—EDITOR.

the Medici; and then again she felt that the popular party was half justified in its fierce suspicion. Again she felt that to keep the Government
of Florence pure, and to keep out a vicious rule, was a sacred cause; the
Frate was right there, and had carried her understanding irrevocably
with him. But at this moment the assent of her understanding went
alone; it was given unwillingly. Her heart was recoiling from a right
allied to so much narrowness; a right apparently entailing that hard
systematic judgment of men which measures them by assents and denials
quite superficial to the manhood within them. Her affection and respect
were clinging with new tenacity to her godfather, and with him to those
memories of her father which were in the same opposition to the division
of men into sheep and goats by the easy mark of some political or religious symbol.

After all has been said that can be said about the widening influence
of ideas, it remains true that they would hardly be such strong agents
unless they were taken in a solvent of feeling. The great world-struggle
of developing thought is continually foreshadowed in the struggle of the
affections, seeking a justification for love and hope.

If Romola's intellect had been less capable of discerning the com-
plexities in human things, all the early loving associations of her life
would have forbidden her to accept implicitly the denunciatory exclusiveness of Savonarola. She had simply felt that his mind had suggested
deeper and more efficacious truth to her than any other, and the large
breathing-room she found in his grand view of human duties had made
her patient towards that part of his teaching which she could not absorb, so long as its practical effect came into collision with no strong force
in her. But now a sudden insurrection of feeling had brought about that
collision. Her indignation, once roused by Camilla's visions, could not
pause there, but ran like an illuminating fire over all the kindred facts
in Savonarola's teaching, and for the moment she felt what was true in
the scornful sarcasms she heard continually flung against him, more
keenly than she felt what was false.

But it was an illumination that made all life look ghastly to her.
Where were the beings to whom she could cling, with whom she could
work and endure, with the belief that she was working for the right?
On the side from which moral energy came, lay a fanaticism from which
she was shrinking with newly startled repulsion; on the side to which
she was drawn by affection and memory, there was the presentiment of
some secret plotting, which her judgment told her would not be unfairly
called crime. And still surmounting every other thought was the dread
inspired by Tito's hints, lest that presentiment should be converted into
knowledge, in such a way that she would be torn by irreconcilable claims.

Calmness would not come even on the altar-steps; it would not come
from looking at the serene picture where the saint, writing in the rocky
solitude, was being visited by faces with celestial peace in them. Romola
was in the hard press of human difficulties, and that rocky solitude was
too far off. She rose from her knees that she might hasten to her sick

people in the courtyard, and by some immediate beneficent action revive
that sense of worth in life which at this moment was unfed by any wider
faith. But when she turned round, she found herself face to face with a
man who was standing only two yards off her. The man was Baldassarre.

CHAPTER XXXIII

ON SAN MINIATO

"I would speak with you," said Baldassarre, as Romola looked at him
in silent expectation. It was plain that he had followed her, and had been
waiting for her. She was going at last to know the secret about him.

"Yes," she said, with the same sort of submission that she might have
shown under an imposed penance. "But you wish to go where no one can
hear us?"

"Where *he* will not come upon us," said Baldassarre, turning and
glancing behind him timidly. "Out—in the air,—away from the streets."

"I sometimes go to San Miniato at this hour," said Romola. "If you
like, I will go now, and you can follow me. It is far, but we can be solitary
there."

He nodded assent, and Romola set out. To some women it might have
seemed an alarming risk to go to a comparatively solitary spot with
a man who had some of the outward signs of that madness which Tito
attributed to him. But Romola was not given to personal fears, and she
was glad of the distance that interposed some delay before another blow
fell on her. The afternoon was far advanced, and the sun was already
low in the west, when she paused on some rough ground in the shadow
of the cypress-trunks, and looked round for Baldassarre. He was not
far off, but when he reached her, he was glad to sink down on an edge
of stony earth. His thick-set frame had no longer the sturdy vigour
which belonged to it when he first appeared with the rope round him in
the Duomo; and under the transient tremor caused by the exertion of
walking up the hill, his eyes seemed to have a more helpless vagueness.

"The hill is steep," said Romola, with compassionate gentleness, seating herself by him. "And I fear you have been weakened by want?"

He turned his head and fixed his eyes on her in silence, unable, now
the moment of speech was come, to seize the words that would convey
the thought he wanted to utter; and she remained as motionless as she
could, lest he should suppose her impatient. He looked like nothing
higher than a common-bred, neglected old man; but she was used now
to be very near to such people, and to think a great deal about their
troubles. Gradually his glance gathered a more definite expression, and
at last he said with abrupt emphasis,—

"Ah! you would have been my daughter!"

The swift flush came in Romola's face and went back again as swiftly,
leaving her with white lips a little apart, like a marble image of horror.

For her mind, the revelation was made. She divined the facts that lay behind that single word, and in the first moment there could be no check to the impulsive belief which sprang from her keen experience of Tito's nature. The sensitive response of her face was a stimulus to Baldassarre; for the first time his words had wrought their right effect. He went on with gathering eagerness and firmness, laying his hand on her arm.

"You are a woman of proud blood,—is it not true? You go to hear the preacher; you hate baseness,—baseness that smiles and triumphs. You hate your husband?"

"Oh, God! were you really his father?" said Romola, in a low voice, too entirely possessed by the images of the past to take any note of Baldassarre's question. "Or was it as he said? Did you take him when he was little?"

"Ah, you believe me,—you know what he is!" said Baldassarre, exultingly, tightening the pressure on her arm, as if the contact gave him power. "You will help me?"

"Yes," said Romola, not interpreting the words as he meant them. She laid her palm gently on the rough hand that grasped her arm, and the tears came to her eyes as she looked at him. "Oh, it is piteous! Tell me,—you were a great scholar; you taught him. *How* is it?"

She broke off. Tito's allegation of this man's madness had come across her; and where were the signs even of past refinement? But she had the self-command not to move her hand. She sat perfectly still, waiting to listen with new caution.

"It is gone!—it is all gone!" said Baldassarre, "and they would not believe me, because he lied, and said I was mad; and they had me dragged to prison. And I am old,—my mind will not come back. And the world is against me."

He paused a moment, and his eyes sank as if he were under a wave of despondency. Then he looked up at her again, and said with renewed eagerness,—

"But *you* are not against me. He made you love him, and he has been false to you; and you hate him. Yes, he made *me* love him: he was beautiful and gentle, and I was a lonely man. I took him when they were beating him. He slept in my bosom when he was little, and I watched him as he grew, and gave him all my knowledge, and everything that was mine I meant to be his. I had many things,—money and books and gems. He had my gems,—he sold them; and he left me in slavery. He never came to seek me; and when I came back poor and in misery, he denied me. He said I was a madman."

"He told us his father was dead,—was drowned," said Romola, faintly. "Surely he must have believed it then. Oh! he could not have been so base *then!*"

A vision had risen of what Tito was to her in those first days when she thought no more of wrong in him than a child thinks of poison in flowers. The yearning regret that lay in that memory brought some relife from the tension of horror. With one great sob the tears rushed forth.

"Ah, you are young, and the tears come easily," said Baldassarre, with some impatience. "But tears are no good; they only put out the fire within, and it is the fire that works. Tears will hinder us. Listen to me."

Romola turned towards him with a slight start. Again the possibility of his madness had darted through her mind, and checked the rush of belief. If, after all, this man were only a mad assassin? But her deep belief in this story still lay behind, and it was more in sympathy than in fear that she avoided the risk of paining him by any show of doubt.

"Tell me," she said, as gently as she could, "how did you lose your memory,—your scholarship?"

"I was ill. I can't tell how long,—it was a blank. I remember nothing, only at last I was sitting in the sun among the stones, and everything else was darkness. And slowly, and by degrees, I felt something besides that: a longing for something,—I did not know what,—that never came. And when I was in the ship on the waters I began to know what I longed for; it was for the Boy to come back,—it was to find all my thoughts again, for I was locked away outside them all. And I am outside now. I feel nothing but a wall and darkness."

Baldassarre had become dreamy again, and sank into silence, resting his head between his hands: and again Romola's belief in him had submerged all cautioning doubts. The pity with which she dwelt on his words seemed like the revival of an old pang. Had she not daily seen how her father missed Dino and the future he had dreamed of in that son?

"It all came back once," Baldassarre went on presently. "I was master of everything. I saw all the world again, and my gems, and my books; and I thought I had him in my power, and I went to expose him where —where the lights were and the trees; and he lied again, and said I was mad, and they dragged me away to prison. . . . Wickedness is strong; and he wears armour."

The fierceness had flamed up again. He spoke with his former intensity, and again he grasped Romola's arm.

"But you will help me? He has been false to you too. He has another wife, and she has children. He makes her believe he is her husband, and she is a foolish, helpless thing. I will show you where she lives."

The first shock that passed through Romola was visibly one of anger. The woman's sense of indignity was inevitably foremost. Baldassarre instinctively felt her in sympathy with him.

"You hate him," he went on. "Is it not true? There is no love between you; I know that. I know women can hate; and you have proud blood. You hate falseness, and you can love revenge."

Romola sat paralyzed by the shock of conflicting feelings. She was not conscious of the grasp that was bruising her tender arm.

"You shall contrive it," said Baldassarre, presently, in an eager whisper. "I have learned by heart that you are his rightful wife. You are a noble woman. You go to hear the preacher of vengeance; you will help justice. But you will think for me. My mind goes—everything goes sometimes—all but the fire. The fire is God: it is justice; it will not die. You believe that,—is it not true? If they will not hang him for robbing me, you will take away his armour,—you will make him go without it, and I will stab him. I have a knife, and my arm is still strong enough."

He put his hand under his tunic, and reached out the hidden knife, feeling the edge abstractedly, as if he needed the sensation to keep alive his ideas.

It seemed to Romola as if every fresh hour of her life were to become more difficult than the last. Her judgment was too vigorous and rapid for her to fall into the mistake of using futile deprecatory words to a man in Baldassarre's state of mind. She chose not to answer his last speech. She would win time for his excitement to allay itself by asking something else that she cared to know. She spoke rather tremulously,—

"You say she is foolish and helpless,—that other wife,—and believes him to be her real husband. Perhaps he is: perhaps he married her before he married me."

"I cannot tell," said Baldassarre, pausing in that action of feeling the knife, and looking bewildered. "I can remember no more. I only know where she lives. You shall see her. I will take you; but not now," he added hurriedly, "*he* may be there. The night is coming on."

"It is true," said Romola, starting up with a sudden consciousness that the sun had set and the hills were darkening; "but you will come and take me—when?"

"In the morning," said Baldassarre, dreaming that she, too, wanted to hurry to her vengeance.

"Come to me, then, where you came to me to-day, in the church. I will be there at ten; and if you are not there, I will go again towards mid-day. Can you remember?"

"Mid-day," said Baldassarre,—"only mid-day. The same place, and mid-day. And, after that," he added, rising and grasping her arm again with his left hand, while he held the knife in his right, "we will have our revenge. He shall feel the sharp edge of justice. The world is against me, but you will help me."

"I would help you in other ways," said Romola, making a first, timid effort to dispel his illusion about her. "I fear you are in want; you have to labour, and get little. I should like to bring you comforts, and make you feel again that there is some one who cares for you."

"Talk no more about that," said Baldassarre, fiercely. "I will have nothing else. Help me to wring one drop of vengeance on this side of the grave. I have nothing but my knife. It is sharp; but there is a moment after the thrust when men see the face of death,—and it shall be *my* face that he will see."

He loosed his hold, and sank down again in a sitting posture. Romola felt helpless: she must defer all intentions till the morrow.

"Mid-day, then," she said, in a distinct voice.

"Yes," he answered, with an air of exhaustion. "Go; I will rest here."

She hastened away. Turning at the last spot whence he was likely to be in sight, she saw him seated still.

CHAPTER XXXIV

THE EVENING AND THE MORNING

ROMOLA had a purpose in her mind as she was hastening away,—a purpose which had been growing through the afternoon hours like a side-stream, rising higher and higher along with the main current. It was less a resolve than a necessity of her feeling. Heedless of the darkening streets, and not caring to call for Maso's slow escort, she hurried across the bridge where the river showed itself black before the distant dying red, and took the most direct way to the Old Palace.[1] She might encounter her husband there. No matter. She could not weigh probabilities; she must discharge her heart. She did not know what she passed in the pillared court or up the wide stairs; she only knew that she asked an usher for the Gonfaloniere, giving her name, and begging to be shown into a private room.

She was not left long alone with the frescoed figures and the newly lit tapers. Soon the door opened, and Bernardo del Nero entered, still carrying his white head erect above his silk lucco.

"Romola, my child, what is this?" he said, in a tone of anxious surprise as he closed the door.

She had uncovered her head and went towards him without speaking. He laid his hand on her shoulder, and held her a little way from him that he might see her better. Her face was haggard from fatigue and long agitation, her hair had rolled down in disorder; but there was an excitement in her eyes that seemed to have triumphed over the bodily consciousness.

"What has he done?" said Bernardo, abruptly. "Tell me everything, child; throw away pride. I am your father."

"It is not about myself,—nothing about myself," said Romola, hastily. "Dearest godfather, it is about you. I have heard things,—some I cannot tell you. But you are in danger in the palace; you are in danger everywhere. There are fanatical men who would harm you, and—and there are traitors. Trust nobody. If you trust, you will be betrayed."

Bernardo smiled.

"Have you worked yourself up into this agitation, my poor child,"

[1] *The Palazzo del Popolo,* dei *Signori,* or della *Signoria* (not to be confused with the *Palagio del Comune,* which corresponded to the *Palagio del Podestà,* or *Bargello*) could not, at the end of the fifteenth century, yet be called the *Palazzo Vecchio,* or the Old Palace, because at that time there was no other for which it could be mistaken. It was only called *Palazzo Vecchio* when Cosimo I, in 1550, established the Grand Ducal residence in the palace he had bought from the Pitti family and had had embellished by Bartolommeo Ammannati.—EDITOR.

he said, raising his hand to her head and patting it gently, "to tell such old truth as that to an old man like me?"

"Oh, no, no! they are not old truths that I mean," said Romola, pressing her clasped hands painfully together, as if that action would help her to suppress what must not be told. "They are fresh things that I know, but cannot tell. Dearest godfather, you know I am not foolish. I would not come to you without reason. Is it too late to warn you against any one, *every* one who seems to be working on your side? Is it too late to say, 'Go to your villa and keep away in the country when these three more days of office are over'? Oh, God! perhaps it is too late! and if any harm comes to you, it will be as if I had done it!"

The last words had burst from Romola involuntarily: a long-stifled feeling had found spasmodic utterance. But she herself was startled and arrested.

"I mean," she added hesitatingly, "I know nothing positive. I only know what fills me with fears."

"Poor child!" said Bernardo, looking at her with quiet penetration for a moment or two. Then he said: "Go, Romola,—go home and rest. These fears may be only big ugly shadows of something very little and harmless. Even traitors must see their interest in betraying; the rats will run where they smell the cheese, and there is no knowing yet which way the scent will come."

He paused, and turned away his eyes from her with an air of abstraction, till, with a slow shrug, he added,—

"As for warnings, they are of no use to me, child. I enter into no plots, but I never forsake my colours. If I march abreast with obstinate men, who will rush on guns and pikes, I must share the consequences. Let us say no more about that. I have not many years left at the bottom of my sack for them to rob me of. Go, child; go home and rest."

He put his hand on her head again caressingly, and she could not help clinging to his arm, and pressing her brow against his shoulder. Her godfather's caress seemed the last thing that was left to her out of that young filial life, which now looked so happy to her even in its troubles, for they were troubles untainted by anything hateful.

"Is silence best, my Romola?" said the old man.

"Yes, now; but I cannot tell whether it always will be," she answered hesitatingly, raising her head with an appealing look.

"Well, you have a father's ear while I am above ground,"—he lifted the black drapery and folded it round her head, adding—"and a father's home; remember that." Then opening the door, he said: "There, hasten away. You are like a black ghost; you will be safe enough."

When Romola fell asleep that night, she slept deep. Agitation had reached its limits; she must gather strength before she could suffer more; and, in spite of rigid habit, she slept on far beyond sunrise.

When she awoke, it was to the sound of guns. Piero de' Medici, with thirteen hundred men at his back, was before the gate that looks towards Rome.

So much Romola learned from Maso, with many circumstantial additions of dubious quality. A countryman had come in and alarmed the Signoria before it was light, else the city would have been taken by surprise. His master was not in the house, having been summoned to the Palazzo long ago. She sent out the old man again, that he might gather news, while she went up to the loggia from time to time to try and discern any signs of the dreaded entrance having been made, or of its having been effectively repelled. Maso brought her word that the great piazza was full of armed men, and that many of the chief citizens suspected as friends of the Medici had been summoned to the palace and detained there. Some of the people seemed not to mind whether Piero got in or not, and some said the Signoria itself had invited him; but however that might be, they were giving him an ugly welcome; and the soldiers from Pisa were coming against him.

In her memory of those morning hours, there were not many things that Romola could distinguish as actual external experiences standing markedly out above the tumultuous waves of retrospect and anticipation. She knew that she had really walked to the Badia by the appointed time in spite of street alarms; she knew that she had waited there in vain. And the scene she had witnessed when she came out of the church, and stood watching on the steps while the doors were being closed behind her for the afternoon interval, always came back to her like a remembered waking.

There was a change in the faces and tones of the people, armed and unarmed, who were pausing or hurrying along the streets. The guns were firing again, but the sound only provoked laughter. She soon knew the cause of the change. Piero de' Medici and his horsemen had turned their backs on Florence, and were galloping as fast as they could along the Siena road. She learned this from a substantial shopkeeping Piagnone, who had not yet laid down his pike.

"It is true," he ended, with a certain bitterness in his emphasis. "Piero is gone, but there are those left behind who were in the secret of his coming,—we all know that; and if the new Signoria does its duty, we shall soon know *who* they are."

The words darted through Romola like a sharp spasm; but the evil they foreshadowed was not yet close upon her, and as she entered her home again, her most pressing anxiety was the possibility that she had lost sight for a long while of Baldassarre.

CHAPTER XXXV

WAITING

THE lengthening sunny days went on without bringing either what Romola most desired or what she most dreaded. They brought no sign from Baldassarre, and, in spite of special watch on the part of the government, no revelation of the suspected conspiracy. But they brought other things which touched her closely, and bridged the phantom-crowded space of anxiety with active sympathy in immediate trial. They brought the spreading Plague and the Excommunication of Savonarola.

Both these events tended to arrest her incipient alienation from the Frate, and to rivet again her attachment to the man who had opened to her the new life of duty, and who seemed now to be worsted in the fight for principle against profligacy. For Romola could not carry from day to day into the abodes of pestilence and misery the sublime excitement of a gladness that, since such anguish existed, she too existed to make some of the anguish less bitter, without remembering that she owed this transcendant moral life to Fra Girolamo. She could not witness the silencing and excommunication of a man whose distinction from the great mass of the clergy lay, not in any heretical belief, not in his superstitions, but in the energy with which he sought to make the Christian life a reality, without feeling herself drawn strongly to his side.

Far on in the hot days of June the Excommunication, for some weeks arrived from Rome, was solemnly published in the Duomo. Romola went to witness the scene, that the resistance it inspired might invigorate that sympathy with Savonarola which was one source of her strength. It was in memorable contrast with the scene she had been accustomed to witness there.

Instead of upturned citizen-faces filling the vast area under the morning light, the youngest rising amphitheatre-wise towards the walls, and making a garland of hope around the memories of age,—instead of the mighty voice thrilling all hearts with the sense of great things, visible and invisible, to be struggled for,—there were the bare walls at evening made more sombre by the glimmer of tapers; there was the black and gray flock of monks and secular clergy with bent, unexpectant faces; there was the occasional tinkling of little bells in the pauses of a monotonous voice reading a sentence which had already been long hanging up in the churches; and at last there was the extinction of the tapers, and the slow, shuffling tread of monkish feet departing in the dim silence.

Romola's ardour on the side of the Frate was doubly strengthened by the gleeful triumph she saw in hard and coarse faces, and by the fear-stricken confusion in the faces and speech of many among his strongly attached friends. The question where the duty of obedience ends, and the duty of resistance begins, could in no case be an easy one; but it was made overwhelmingly difficult by the belief that the Church was— not a compromise of parties to secure a more or less approximate justice in the appropriation of funds, but—a living organism, instinct with Divine power to bless and to curse. To most of the pious Florentines, who had hitherto felt no doubt in their adherence to the Frate, that belief in the Divine potency of the Church was not an embraced opinion, it was an inalienable impression, like the concavity of the blue firmament; and the boldness of Savonarola's written arguments that the Excommunication was unjust, and that, being unjust, it was not valid, only made them tremble the more, as a defiance cast at a mystic image, against whose subtle immeasurable power there was neither weapon nor defence.

But Romola, whose mind had not been allowed to draw its early nourishment from the traditional associations of the Christian community in which her father had lived a life apart, felt her relation to the Church only through Savonarola; his moral force had been the only authority to which she had bowed; and in his excommunication she only saw the menace of hostile vice: on one side she saw a man whose life was devoted to the ends of public virtue and spiritual purity, and on the other the assault of alarmed selfishness, headed by a lustful, greedy, lying, and murderous old man, once called Rodrigo Borgia, and now lifted to the pinnacle of infamy as Pope Alexander the Sixth. The finer shades of fact which soften the edge of such antitheses are not apt to be seen except by neutrals, who are not distressed to discern some folly in martyrs and some judiciousness in the men who burnt them.

But Romola required a strength that neutrality could not give; and this Excommunication, which simplified and ennobled the resistant position of Savonarola by bringing into prominence its wider relations, seemed to come to her like a rescue from the threatening isolation of criticism and doubt. The Frate was now withdrawn from that smaller antagonism against Florentine enemies into which he continually fell in the unchecked excitement of the pulpit, and presented himself simply as appealing to the Christian world against a vicious exercise of ecclesiastical power. He was a standard-bearer leaping into the breach. Life never seems so clear and easy as when the heart is beating faster at the sight of some generous self-risking deed. We feel no doubt then what is the highest prize the soul can win; we almost believe in our own power to attain it. By a new current of such enthusiasm Romola was helped through these difficult summer days. She had ventured on no words to Tito that would apprise him of her late interview with Baldassarre, and the revelation he had made to her. What would such agitating, difficult words win from him? No admission of the truth; nothing, probably, but a cool sarcasm about her sympathy with his assassin. Baldassarre was evidently helpless: the thing to be feared was, not that he should injure Tito, but that Tito, coming upon his traces, should carry out some new scheme for ridding himself of the injured man who was a haunting dread to him. Romola felt that she could do nothing decisive until she had seen Baldassarre again, and learned the full truth about that "other wife,"—learned whether she were the wife to whom Tito was first bound.

The possibilities about that other wife, which involved the worst wound to her hereditary pride, mingled themselves as a newly embittering suspicion with the earliest memories of her illusory love, eating away the lingering associations of tenderness with the past image of her husband; and her irresistible belief in the rest of Baldassarre's revelation made her shrink from Tito with a horror which would perhaps have urged some passionate speech in spite of herself if he had not been more than usually absent from home. Like many of the wealthier citizens in that time of pestilence, he spent the intervals of business chiefly in the country: the agreeable Melema was welcome at many villas, and since Romola had refused to leave the city, he had no need to provide a country residence of his own.

But at last, in the later days of July, the alleviation of those public troubles which had absorbed her activity and much of her thought, left Romola to a less counteracted sense of her personal lot. The Plague had almost disappeared, and the position of Savonarola was made more hopeful by a favourable magistracy, who were writing urgent vindicatory letters to Rome on his behalf, entreating the withdrawal of the Excommunication.

Romola's healthy and vigorous frame was undergoing the reaction of languor inevitable after continuous excitement and over-exertion; but her mental restlessness would not allow her to remain at home without peremptory occupation, except during the sultry hours. In the cool of the morning and evening she walked out constantly, varying her direction as much as possible, with the vague hope that if Baldassarre were still alive she might encounter him. Perhaps some illness had brought a new paralysis of memory, and he had forgotten where she lived,—forgotten even her existence. That was her most sanguine explanation of his non-appearance. The explanation she felt to be most probable was, that he had died of the Plague.

CHAPTER XXXVI

THE OTHER WIFE

THE morning warmth was already beginning to be rather oppressive to Romola, when, after a walk along by the walls on her way from San Marco, she turned towards the intersecting streets again at the gate of Santa Croce.

The Borgo La Croce was so still that she listened to her own footsteps on the pavement in the sunny silence, until, on approaching a bend in the street, she saw, a few yards before her, a little child not more than three years old, with no other clothing than his white shirt, pause from a waddling run and look around him. In the first moment of coming nearer she could only see his back,—a boy's back, square and sturdy, with a cloud of reddish-brown curls above it; but in the next he turned towards her, and she could see his dark eyes wide with tears, and his lower lip pushed up and trembling, while his fat brown fists clutched his shirt helplessly. The glimpse of a tall black figure sending a shadow over him brought his bewildered fear to a climax, and a loud crying sob sent the big tears rolling.

Romola, with the ready maternal instinct which was one hidden source of her passionate tenderness, instantly uncovered her head, and, stooping down on the pavement, put her arms round him, and her cheeks against his, while she spoke to him in caressing tones. At first his sobs were only the louder, but he made no effort to get away, and presently the outburst ceased with that strange abruptness which belongs to childish joys and griefs: his face lost its distortion, and was fixed in an openmouthed gaze at Romola.

"You have lost yourself, little one," she said, kissing him. "Never mind! we will find the house again. Perhaps mamma will meet us."

She divined that he had made his escape at a moment when the mother's eyes were turned away from him, and thought it likely that he would soon be followed.

"Oh, what a heavy, heavy boy!" she said, trying to lift him. "I cannot carry you. Come, then, you must toddle back by my side."

The parted lips remained motionless in awed silence, and one brown fist still clutched the shirt with as much tenacity as ever; but the other yielded itself quite willingly to the wonderful white hand, strong but soft.

"You *have* a mamma?" said Romola, as they set out, looking down at the boy with a certain yearning. But he was mute. A girl under those circumstances might perhaps have chirped abundantly; not so this square-shouldered little man with the big cloud of curls.

He was awake to the first sign of his whereabout, however. At the turning by the front of San Ambrogio he dragged Romola towards it, looking up at her.

"Ah, that is the way home, is it?" she said, smiling at him. He only thrust his head forward and pulled, as an admonition that they should go faster.

There was still another turning that he had a decided opinion about, and then Romola found herself in a short street leading to open garden ground. It was in front of a house at the end of this street that the little fellow paused, pulling her towards some stone stairs. He had evidently no wish for her to loose his hand, and she would not have been willing to leave him without being sure that she was delivering him to his friends. They mounted the stairs, seeing but dimly in that sudden withdrawal from the sunlight, till, at the final landing-place, an extra stream of light came from an open doorway. Passing through a small lobby, they came to another open door, and there Romola paused. Her approach had not been heard.

On a low chair at the farther end of the room, opposite the light, sat Tessa, with one hand on the edge of the cradle, and her head hanging a little on one side, fast asleep. Near one of the windows, with her back turned towards the door, sat Monna Lisa at her work of preparing salad, in deaf unconsciousness. There was only an instant for Romola's eyes to take in that still scene; for Lillo snatched his hand away from her and ran up to his mother's side, not making any direct effort to wake

her, but only leaning his head back against her arm, and surveying
Romola seriously from that distance.

As Lillo pushed against her, Tessa opened her eyes, and looked up
in bewilderment; but her glance had no sooner rested on the figure at
the opposite doorway than she started up, blushed deeply, and began
to tremble a little, neither speaking nor moving forward.

"Ah! we have seen each other before," said Romola, smiling, and
coming forward. "I am glad it was *your* little boy. He was crying in the
street; I suppose he had run away. So we walked together a little way,
and then he knew where he was, and brought me here. But you had not
missed him? That is well, else you would have been frightened."

The shock of finding that Lillo had run away overcame every other
feeling in Tessa for the moment. Her colour went again, and, seizing
Lillo's arm, she ran with him to Monna Lisa, saying, with a half sob,
loud in the old woman's ear,—

"Oh, Lisa, you are wicked! Why will you stand with your back to the
door? Lillo ran away ever so far into the street."

"Holy Mother!" said Monna Lisa, in her meek, thick tone, letting the
spoon fall from her hands. "Where were *you* then? I thought you were
there and had an eye on him."

"But you *know* I go to sleep when I am rocking," said Tessa, in pettish remonstrance.

"Well, well, we must keep the outer door shut, or else tie him up,"
said Monna Lisa, "for he'll be as cunning as Satan before long, and
that's the holy truth. But how came he back, then?"

This question recalled Tessa to the consciousness of Romola's presence. Without answering, she turned towards her, blushing and timid
again, and Monna Lisa's eyes followed her movement. The old woman
made a low reverence, and said,—

"Doubtless the most noble lady brought him back." Then, advancing a little nearer to Romola, she added: "It's my shame for him to have
been found with only his shirt on; but he kicked, and wouldn't have
his other clothes on this morning, and the mother, poor thing, will never
hear of his being beaten. But what's an old woman to do without a stick
when the lad's legs get so strong? Let your nobleness look at his legs."

Lillo, conscious that his legs were in question, pulled his shirt up a
little higher, and looked down at their olive roundness with a dispassionate and curious air. Romola laughed, and stooped to give him a
caressing shake and a kiss, and this action helped the reassurance that
Tessa had already gathered from Monna Lisa's address to Romola. For
when Naldo had been told about the adventure of the Carnival, and
Tessa had asked him who the heavenly lady that had come just when
she was wanted, and had vanished so soon, was likely to be,—whether
she could be the Holy Madonna herself?—he had answered, "Not exactly, my Tessa; only one of the saints," and had not chosen to say
more. So that in the dreamlike combination of small experience which

made up Tessa's thought, Romola had remained confusedly associated
with the pictures in the churches, and when she reappeared, the grateful remembrance of her protection was slightly tinctured with religious
awe,—not deeply, for Tessa's dread was chiefly of ugly and evil beings.
It seemed unlikely that good beings would be angry and punish her, as
it was the nature of Nofri and the devil to do. And now that Monna Lisa
had spoken freely about Lillo's legs and Romola had laughed, Tessa
was more at her ease.

"Ninna's in the cradle," she said. "*She's* pretty too."

Romola went to look at the sleeping Ninna; and Monna Lisa, one of
the exceptionally meek deaf, who never expect to be spoken to, returned
to her salad.

"Ah! she is waking: she has opened her blue eyes," said Romola.
"You must take her up, and I will sit down in this chair—may I?—and
nurse Lillo. Come, Lillo!"

She sat down in Tito's chair, and put out her arms towards the lad,
whose eyes had followed her. He hesitated; and, pointing his small fingers at her with a half-puzzled, half-angry feeling, said, "That's Babbo's
chair," not seeing his way out of the difficulty if Babbo came and found
Romola in his place.

"But Babbo is not here, and I shall go soon. Come, let me nurse you
as he does," said Romola, wondering to herself for the first time what
sort of Babbo he was whose wife was dressed in contadina fashion, but
had a certain daintiness about her person that indicated idleness and
plenty. Lillo consented to be lifted up, and, finding the lap exceedingly
comfortable, began to explore her dress and hands, to see if there were
any ornaments beside the rosary.

Tessa, who had hitherto been occupied in coaxing Ninna out of her
waking peevishness, now sat down in her low chair, near Romola's knee,
arranging Ninna's tiny person to advantage, jealous that the strange
lady, too, seemed to notice the boy most, as Naldo did.

"Lillo was going to be angry with me, because I sat in Babbo's
chair," said Romola, as she bent forward to kiss Ninna's little foot.
"Will he come soon and want it?"

"Ah, no!" said Tessa, "you can sit in it a long while. I shall be sorry
when you go. When you first came to take care of me at the Carnival,
I thought it was wonderful; you came and went away again so fast.
And Naldo said, perhaps you were a saint, and that made me tremble
a little though the saints are very good, I know; and you were good to
me, and now you have taken care of Lillo. Perhaps you will always
come and take care of me. That was how Naldo did a long while ago;
he came and took care of me when I was frightened, one San Giovanni.
I couldn't think where he came from,—he was so beautiful and good.
And so are you," ended Tessa, looking up at Romola with devout admiration.

"Naldo is your husband. His eyes are like Lillo's," said Romola, looking at the boy's darkly pencilled eyebrows, unusual at his age. She did not speak interrogatively, but with a quiet certainty of inference which was necessarily mysterious to Tessa.

"Ah! you know him!" she said, pausing a little in wonder. "Perhaps you know Nofri and Peretola, and our house on the hill, and everything. Yes, like Lillo's; but not his hair. His hair is dark and long," she went on, getting rather excited. "Ah! if you know it, ecco!"

She had put her hand to a thin red silk cord that hung round her neck, and drew from her bosom the tiny old parchment *breve,* the horn of red coral, and a long dark curl carefully tied at one end and suspended with those mystic treasures. She held them towards Romola, away from Ninna's snatching hand.

"It is a fresh one. I cut it lately. See how bright it is!" she said, laying it against the white background of Romola's fingers. "They get dim, and then he lets me cut another when his hair is grown; and I put it with the *breve,* because sometimes he is away a long while, and then I think it helps to take care of me."

A slight shiver passed through Romola as the curl was laid across her fingers. At Tessa's first mention of her husband as having come mysteriously she knew not whence, a possibility had risen before Romola that made her heart beat faster; for to one who is anxiously in search of a certain object the faintest suggestions have a peculiar significance. And when the curl was held towards her, it seemed for an instant like a mocking phantasm of the lock she herself had cut to wind with one of her own five years ago. But she preserved her outward calmness, bent not only on knowing the truth, but also on coming to that knowledge in a way that would not pain this poor, trusting, ignorant thing, with the child's mind in the woman's body. "Foolish and helpless:" yes; so far she corresponded to Baldassarre's account.

"It is a beautiful curl," she said, resisting the impulse to withdraw her hand. "Lillo's curls will be like it, perhaps, for *his* cheek, too, is dark. And you never know where your husband goes to when he leaves you?"

"No," said Tessa, putting back her treasures out of the children's way. "But I know Messer San Michele takes care of him, for he gave him a beautiful coat, all made of little chains; and if he puts that on, nobody can kill him. And perhaps, if—" Tessa hesitated a little, under a recurrence of that original dreamy wonder about Romola which had been expelled by chatting contact,—"if you *were* a saint, you would take care of him, too, because you have taken care of me and Lillo."

An agitated flush came over Romola's face in the first moment of certainty, but she had bent her cheek against Lillo's head. The feeling that leaped out in that flush was something like exultation at the thought that the wife's burden might be about to slip from her overladen shoulders; that this little ignorant creature might prove to be Tito's lawful wife. A strange exultation for a proud and high-born woman to have been brought to! But it seemed to Romola as if that were the only issue that would make duty anything else for her than an insoluble problem. Yet she was not deaf to Tessa's last appealing words; she raised her head, and said in her clearest tones,—

"I will always take care of you if I see you need me. But that beautiful coat? your husband did not wear it when you were first married? Perhaps he used not to be so long away from you then?"

"Ah, yes! he was. Much—much longer. So long, I thought he would never come back. I used to cry. Oh me! I was beaten then; a long, long while ago at Peretola, where we had the goats and mules."

"And how long had you been married before your husband had that chain coat?" said Romola, her heart beating faster and faster.

Tessa looked meditative, and began to count on her fingers, and Romola watched the fingers as if they would tell the secret of her destiny.

"The chestnuts were ripe when we were married," said Tessa, marking off her thumb and fingers again as she spoke; "and then again they were ripe at Peretola before he came back, and then again, after that, on the hill. And soon the soldiers came, and we heard the trumpets, and then Naldo had the coat."

"You had been married more than two years. In which church were you married?" said Romola, too entirely absorbed by one thought to put any question that was less direct. Perhaps before the next morning she might go to her godfather and say that she was not Tito Melema's lawful wife,—that the vows which had bound her to strive after an impossible union had been made void beforehand.

Tessa gave a slight start at Romola's new tone of inquiry, and looked up at her with a hesitating expression. Hitherto she had prattled on without consciousness that she was making revelations, any more than when she said old things over and over again to Monna Lisa.

"Naldo said I was never to tell about that," she said doubtfully. "Do you think he would not be angry if I told you?"

"It is right that you should tell me. Tell me everything," said Romola, looking at her with mild authority.

If the impression from Naldo's command had been much more recent than it was, the constraining effect of Romola's mysterious authority would have overcome it. But the sense that she was telling what she had never told before made her begin with a lowered voice.

"It was not in a church,—it was at the Natività, when there was a fair, and all the people went over-night to see the Madonna in the Nunziata, and my mother was ill and couldn't go, and I took the bunch of cocoons for her; and then he came to me in the church, and I heard him say, 'Tessa!' I knew him because he had taken care of me at the San Giovanni, and then we went into the piazza where the fair was, and I had some *berlingozzi,* for I was hungry and he was very good to me; and at the end of the piazza there was a holy father, and an altar like what they have at the processions outside the churches. So he married us, and then Naldo took me back into the church and left me; and I went home, and my mother died, and Nofri began to beat me more, and Naldo never came back. And I used to cry, and once at the Carnival I

saw him and followed him, and he was angry, and said he would come
some time, I must wait. So I went and waited; but oh! it was a long
while before he came; but he would have come if he could, for he was
good; and then he took me away, because I cried and said I could not
bear to stay with Nofri. And, oh! I was so glad, and since then I have
been always happy, for I don't mind about the goats and mules, because I have Lillo and Ninna now; and Naldo is never angry, only I
think he doesn't love Ninna so well as Lillo, and she *is* pretty."

Quite forgetting that she had thought her speech rather momentous
at the beginning, Tessa fell to devouring Ninna with kisses, while Romola sat in silence with absent eyes. It was inevitable that in this moment she should think of the three beings before her chiefly in their relation to her own lot, and she was feeling the chill of disappointment
that her difficulties were not to be solved by external law. She had relaxed her hold of Lillo, and was leaning her cheek against her hand, seeing nothing of the scene around her. Lillo was quick in perceiving a
change that was not agreeable to him; he had not yet made any return
to her caresses, but he objected to their withdrawal, and putting up
both his brown arms to pull her head towards him, he said, "play with
me again!"

Romola, roused from her self-absorption, clasped the lad anew, and
looked from him to Tessa, who had now paused from her shower of
kisses, and seemed to have returned to the more placid delight of contemplating the heavenly lady's face. That face was undergoing a subtle
change, like the gradual oncoming of a warmer, softer light. Presently
Romola took her scissors from her scarsella, and cut off one of her long
wavy locks, while the three pair of wide eyes followed her movements
with kitten-like observation.

"I must go away from you now," she said, "but I will leave this lock
of hair that it may remind you of me, because if you are ever in trouble
you can think that perhaps God will send me to take care of you again.
I cannot tell you where to find me, but if I ever know that you want me,
I will come to you. Addio!"

She had set down Lillo hurriedly, and held out her hand to Tessa, who
kissed it with a mixture of awe and sorrow at this parting. Romola's
mind was oppressed with thoughts; she needed to be alone as soon as
possible, but with her habitual care for the least fortunate, she turned
aside to put her hand in a friendly way on Monna Lisa's shoulder and
make her a farewell sign. Before the old woman had finished her deep
reverence, Romola had disappeared.

Monna Lisa and Tessa moved towards each other by simultaneous
impulses, while the two children stood clinging to their mother's skirts
as if they, too, felt the atmosphere of awe.

"Do you think she *was* a saint?" said Tessa, in Lisa's ear, showing
her the lock.

Lisa rejected that notion very decidedly by a backward movement of
her fingers, and then stroking the rippled gold, said,—

"She's a great and noble lady. I saw such in my youth."

Romola went home and sat alone through the sultry hours of that day
with the heavy certainty that her lot was unchanged. She was thrown
back again on the conflict between the demands of an outward law,
which she recognized as a widely ramifying obligation, and the demands
of inner moral facts which were becoming more and more peremptory.
She had drunk in deeply the spirit of that teaching by which Savonarola
had urged her to return to her place. She felt that the sanctity attached
to all close relations, and, therefore, pre-eminently to the closest, was
but the expression in outward law of that result towards which all human goodness and nobleness must spontaneously tend; that the light
abandonment of ties, whether inherited or voluntary, because they had
ceased to be pleasant, was the uprooting of social and personal virtue.
What else had Tito's crime towards Baldassarre been but that abandonment working itself out to the most hideous extreme of falsity and
ingratitude?

And the inspiring consciousness breathed into her by Savonarola's influence that her lot was vitally united with the general lot had exalted
even the minor details of obligation into religion. She was marching with
a great army; she was feeling the stress of a common life. If victims
were needed, and it was uncertain on whom the lot might fall, she would
stand ready to answer to her name. She had stood long; she had striven
hard to fulfil the bond, but she had seen all the conditions which made
the fulfilment possible gradually forsaking her. The one effect of her
marriage-tie seemed to be the stifling predominance over her of a nature that she despised. All her efforts at union had only made its impossibility more palpable, and the relation had become for her simply a
degrading servitude. The law was sacred. Yes, but rebellion might be
sacred too. It flashed upon her mind that the problem before her was
essentially the same as that which had lain before Savonarola,—the problem where the sacredness of obedience ended, and where the sacredness
of rebellion began. To her, as to him, there had come one of those moments in life when the soul must dare to act on its own warrant, not
only without external law to appeal to, but in the face of a law which is
not unarmed with Divine lightnings,—lightnings that may yet fall if
the warrant has been false.

Before the sun had gone down she had adopted a resolve. She would
ask no counsel of her godfather or of Savonarola until she had made
one determined effort to speak freely with Tito and obtain his consent
that she should live apart from him. She desired not to leave him clandestinely again, or to forsake Florence. She would tell him that if he
ever felt a real need of her, she would come back to him. Was not that
the utmost faithfulness to her bond that could be required of her? A
shuddering anticipation came over her that he would clothe a refusal in
a sneering suggestion that she should enter a convent as the only mode
of quitting him that would not be scandalous. He knew well that her
mind revolted from that means of escape, not only because of her own

repugnance to a narrow rule, but because all the cherished memories of her father forbade that she should adopt a mode of life which was associated with his deepest griefs and his bitterest dislike.

Tito had announced his intention of coming home this evening. She would wait for him, and say what she had to say at once, for it was difficult to get his ear during the day. If he had the slightest suspicion that personal words were coming, he slipped away with an appearance of unpremeditated ease. When she sent for Maso to tell him that she would wait for his master, she observed that the old man looked at her and lingered with a mixture of hesitation and wondering anxiety; but finding that she asked him no question, he slowly turned away. Why should she ask questions? Perhaps Maso only knew or guessed something of what she knew already.

It was late before Tito came. Romola had been pacing up and down the long room which had once been the library, with the windows open, and a loose white linen robe on instead of her usual black garment. She was glad of that change after the long hours of heat and motionless meditation; but the coolness and exercise made her more intensely wakeful, and as she went with the lamp in her hand to open the door for Tito, he might well have been startled by the vividness of her eyes and the expression of painful resolution, which was in contrast with her usual self-restrained quiescence before him. But it seemed that this excitement was just what he expected.

"Ah! it is you, Romola. Maso is gone to bed," he said, in a grave, quiet tone, interposing to close the door for her. Then, turning round, he said, looking at her more fully than he was wont, "You have heard it all, I see."

Romola quivered. *He* then was inclined to take the initiative. He had been to Tessa. She led the way through the nearest door, set down her lamp, and turned towards him again.

"You must not think despairingly of the consequences," said Tito, in a tone of soothing encouragement, at which Romola stood wondering, until he added, "The accused have too many family ties with all parties not to escape; and Messer Bernardo del Nero has other things in his favour besides his age."

Romola started, and gave a cry as if she had been suddenly stricken by a sharp weapon.

"What! you did not know it?" said Tito, putting his hand under her arm that he might lead her to a seat; but she seemed to be unaware of his touch.

"Tell me," she said hastily,—"tell me what it is."

"A man, whose name you may forget,—Lamberto dell' Antella,—who was banished, has been seized within the territory: a letter has been found on him of very dangerous import to the chief Mediceans; and the scoundrel, who was once a favourite hound of Piero de' Medici, is ready now to swear what any one pleases against him or his friends. Some have made their escape, but five are now in prison."

"My godfather?" said Romola, scarcely above a whisper, as Tito made a slight pause.

"Yes; I grieve to say it. But along with him there are three, at least, whose names have a commanding interest even among the popular party, —Niccolò Ridolfi, Lorenzo Tornabuoni, and Giannozzo Pucci."

The tide of Romola's feelings had been violently turned into a new channel. In the tumult of that moment there could be no check to the words which came as the impulsive utterance of her long-accumulating horror. When Tito had named the men of whom she felt certain he was the confederate, she said, with a recoiling gesture and low-toned bitterness,—

"And *you*—you are safe?"

"You are certainly an amiable wife, my Romola," said Tito, with the coldest irony. "Yes; I am safe."

They turned away from each other in silence.

CHAPTER XXXVII

WHY TITO WAS SAFE

TITO had good reasons for saying that he was safe. In the last three months, during which he had foreseen the discovery of the Medicean conspirators as a probable event, he had had plenty of time to provide himself with resources. He had been strengthening his influence at Rome and at Milan, by being the medium of secret information and indirect measures against the Frate and the popular party; he had cultivated more assiduously than ever the regard of this party, by showing subtle evidence that his political convictions were entirely on their side; and all the while, instead of withdrawing his agency from the Mediceans, he had sought to be more actively employed and exclusively trusted by them. It was easy to him to keep up this triple game. The principle of duplicity admitted by the Mediceans on their own behalf deprived them of any standard by which they could measure the trustworthiness of a colleague who had not, like themselves, hereditary interests, alliances, and prejudices which were intensely Medicean. In their minds, to deceive the opposite party was fair stratagem; to deceive their own party was a baseness to which they felt no temptation; and in using Tito's facile ability, they were not keenly awake to the fact that the absence of traditional attachments which made him a convenient agent was also the absence of what among themselves was the chief guarantee of mutual honour. Again, the Roman and Milanese friends of the aristocratic party, or Arrabbiati, who were the bitterest enemies of Savonarola, carried on a system of underhand correspondence and espionage, in which the deepest hypocrisy was the best service, and demanded the heaviest pay; so that to suspect an agent because he played a part strongly would have been an absurd want of logic. On the other hand, the Piagnoni of the popular party, who had the directness that belongs to energetic conviction, were the more inclined to credit Tito with sincerity in his political adhesion to them, because he affected no religious sympathies.

By virtue of these conditions, the last three months had been a time of flattering success to Tito. The result he most cared for was the securing of a future position for himself at Rome or at Milan; for he had a growing determination, when the favourable moment should come, to quit Florence for one of those great capitals where life was easier, and the rewards of talent and learning were more splendid. At present, the scale dipped in favour of Milan; and if within the year he could render certain services to Duke Ludovico Sforza, he had the prospect of a place at the Milanese court which outweighed the advantages of Rome.

The revelation of the Medicean conspiracy, then, had been a subject of forethought to Tito; but he had not been able to foresee the mode in which it would be brought about. The arrest of Lamberto dell' Antella with a tell-tale letter on his person, and a bitter rancour against the Medici in his heart, was an incalculable event. It was not possible, in spite of the careful pretexts with which his agency had been guarded, that Tito should escape implication: he had never expected this in case of any wide discovery concerning the Medicean plots. But his quick mind had soon traced out the course that would secure his own safety with the fewest unpleasant concomitants. It is agreeable to keep a whole skin; but the skin still remains an organ sensitive to the atmosphere.

His reckoning had not deceived him. That night, before he returned home, he had secured the three results for which he most cared: he was to be freed from all proceedings against him on account of complicity with the Mediceans; he was to retain his secretaryship for another year, unless he previously resigned it; and, lastly, the price by which he had obtained these guarantees was to be kept as a State secret. The price would have been thought heavy by most men; and Tito himself would rather not have paid it.

He had applied himself first to win the mind of Francesco Valori, who was not only one of the Ten under whom he immediately held his secretaryship, but one of the Special Council appointed to investigate the evidence of the plot. Francesco Valori, as we have seen, was the head of the Piagnoni, a man with certain fine qualities that were not incompatible with violent partisanship, with an arrogant temper that alienated his friends, nor with bitter personal animosities,—one of the bitterest being directed against Bernardo del Nero. To him, in a brief private interview, after obtaining a pledge of secrecy, Tito avowed his own agency for the Mediceans,—an agency induced by motives about which he was very frank, declaring at the same time that he had always believed their efforts futile, and that he sincerely preferred the maintenance of the popular government; affected to confide to Valori, as a secret, his own personal dislike for Bernardo del Nero; and, after this preparation, came to the important statement that there was another Medicean plot, of which, if he obtained certain conditions from the government, he could, by a journey to Siena and into Romagna, where Piero de' Medici was again trying to gather forces, obtain documentary evidence to lay before the council. To this end it was essential that his character as a Medicean agent should be unshaken for all Mediceans, and hence the fact that he had been a source of information to the authorities must be wrapped in profound secrecy. Still, some odour of the facts might escape in spite of precaution, and before Tito could incur the unpleasant consequences of acting against his friends, he must be assured of immunity from any prosecution as a Medicean, and from deprivation of office for a year to come.

These propositions did not sound in the ear of Francesco Valori precisely as they sound to us. Valori's mind was not intensely bent on the estimation of Tito's conduct; and it *was* intensely bent on procuring an extreme sentence against the five prisoners. There were sure to be immense efforts to save them; and it was to be wished (on public grounds) that the evidence against them should be of the strongest, so as to alarm all well-affected men at the dangers of clemency. The character of legal proceedings at that time implied that evidence was one of those desirable things which could only be come at by foul means. To catch a few people and torture them into confessing everybody's guilt was one step towards justice; and it was not always easy to see the next, unless a traitor turned up. Lamberto dell' Antella had been tortured in aid of his previous willingness to tell more than he knew; nevertheless, additional and stronger facts were desirable, especially against Bernardo del Nero, who, so far as appeared hitherto, had simply refrained from betraying the late plot after having tried in vain to discourage it; for the welfare of Florence demanded that the guilt of Bernardo del Nero should be put in the strongest light. So Francesco Valori zealously believed; and perhaps he was not himself aware that the strength of his zeal was determined by his hatred. He decided that Tito's proposition ought to be accepted, laid it before his colleagues without disclosing Tito's name, and won them over to his opinion. Late in the day, Tito was admitted to an audience of the Special Council, and produced a deep sensation among them by revealing another plot for insuring the mastery of Florence to Piero de' Medici, which was to have been carried into execution in the middle of this very month of August. Documentary evidence of this subject would do more than anything else to make the right course clear. He received a commission to start for Siena by break of day: and, besides this, he carried away with him from the council chamber a written guarantee of his immunity and of his retention of office.

Among the twenty Florentines who bent their grave eyes on Tito, as he stood gracefully before them, speaking of startling things with easy periphrasis, and with that apparently unaffected admission of being actuated by motives short of the highest, which is often the intensest affectation, there were several whose minds were not too entirely pre-occupied to pass a new judgment on him in these new circumstances; they silently concluded that this ingenious and serviceable Greek was in future rather to be used for public needs than for private intimacy. Unprincipled men were useful, enabling those who had more scruples to keep their hands tolerably clean in a world where there was much dirty work to be done. Indeed, it was not clear to respectable Florentine brains, unless they held the Frate's extravagant belief in a possible pur-ity and loftiness to be striven for on this earth, how life was to be car-ried on in any department without human instruments whom it would not be unbecoming to kick or to spit upon in the act of handing them their wages. Some of these very men who passed a tacit judgment on Tito were shortly to be engaged in a memorable transaction that could by no means have been carried through without the use of an unscru-pulousness as decided as his; but as their own bright poet Pulci had said for them, it is one thing to love the fruits of treachery, and another thing to love traitors,—

> "Il tradimento a molti piace assai,
> Ma il traditore a gnun non piacque mai."

The same society has had a gibbet for the murderer and a gibbet for the martyr, an execrating hiss for a dastardly act, and as loud a hiss for many a word of generous truthfulness or just insight: a mixed con-dition of things which is the sign, not of hopeless confusion, but of strug-gling order.

For Tito himself, he was not unaware that he had sunk a little in the estimate of the men who had accepted his services. He had that degree of self-contemplation which necessarily accompanies the habit of acting on well-considered reasons, of whatever quality; and if he could have chosen, he would have declined to see himself disapproved by men of the world. He had never meant to be disapproved; he had meant always to conduct himself so ably that if he acted in opposition to the standard of other men they should not be aware of it; and the barrier between himself and Romola had been raised by the impossibility of such concealment with her. He shrank from condemnatory judgments as from a climate to which he could not adapt himself. But things were not so plastic in the hands of cleverness as could be wished, and events had turned out inconveniently. He had really no rancour against Messer Bernardo del Nero; he had a personal liking for Lorenzo Tornabuoni and Giannozzo Pucci. He had served them very ably, and in such a way that if their party had been winners he would have merited high reward; but was he to relinquish all the agreeable fruits of life because their party had failed? His proffer of a little additional proof against them would probably have no influence on their fate; in fact, he felt convinced they would escape any extreme consequences; but if he had not given it, his own fortunes, which made a promising fabric, would have been utterly ruined. And what motive could any man really have, except his own interest? Florentines whose passions were engaged in their petty and precarious political schemes might have no self-interest separable from family pride and tenacity in old hatreds and attachments; a modern simpleton who swallowed whole one of the old systems of philosophy, and took the indigestion it occasioned for the signs of a divine afflux or the voice of an inward monitor, might see his interest in a form of self-conceit which he called self-rewarding virtue; fanatics who believed in the coming Scourge and Renovation might see their own interest in a future palm-branch and white robe: but no man of clear intellect allowed his course to be determined by such puerile impulses or questionable inward fumes. Did not Pontanus, poet and philosopher of unrivalled Latinity, make the finest possible oration at Naples to welcome the French king, who had come to dethrone the learned orator's royal friend and patron? and still Pontanus held up his head and prospered. Men did not really care about these things, except when their personal spleen was touched. It was weakness only that was despised; power of any sort carried its immunity; and no man, unless by very rare good fortune, could mount high in the world without incurring a few unpleasant necessities which laid him open to enmity, and perhaps to a little hissing, when enmity wanted a pretext.

It was a faint prognostic of that hissing, gathered by Tito from certain indications when he was before the council, which gave his present conduct the character of an epoch to him, and made him dwell on it with argumentative vindication. It was not that he was taking a deeper step in wrong-doing, for it was not possible that he should feel any tie to the Mediceans to be stronger than the tie to his father; but his conduct to his father had been hidden by successful lying: his present act did not admit of total concealment,—in its very nature it was a revelation. And Tito winced under his new liability to disesteem.

Well! a little patience, and in another year, or perhaps in half a year, he might turn his back on these hard, eager Florentines, with their futile quarrels and sinking fortunes. His brilliant success at Florence had had some ugly flaws in it: he had fallen in love with the wrong woman, and Baldassarre had come back under incalculable circumstances. But as Tito galloped with a loose rein towards Siena, he saw a future before him in which he would no longer be haunted by those mistakes. He had much money safe out of Florence already; he was in the fresh ripeness of eight-and-twenty; he was conscious of well-tried skill. Could he not strip himself of the past, as of rehearsal clothing, and throw away the old bundle, to robe himself for the real scene?

It did not enter into Tito's meditations on the future, that, on issuing from the council chamber and descending the stairs, he had brushed against a man whose face he had not stayed to recognize in the lamplight. The man was Ser Ceccone,—also willing to serve the State by giving information against unsuccessful employers.

CHAPTER XXXVIII

A FINAL UNDERSTANDING

Tito soon returned from Siena, but almost immediately set out on another journey, from which he did not return till the 17th of August. Nearly a fortnight had passed since the arrest of the accused, and still they were in prison, still their fate was uncertain. Romola had felt during this interval as if all cares were suspended for her, other than watching the fluctuating probabilities concerning that fate. Sometimes they seemed strongly in favour of the prisoners; for the chances of effective interest on their behalf were heightened by delay, and an indefinite prospect of delay was opened by the reluctance of all persons in authority to incur the odium attendant on any decision. On the one side there was a loud cry that the Republic was in danger, and that lenity to the prisoners would be the signal of attack for all its enemies; on the other, there was a certainty that a sentence of death and confiscation of property passed on five citizens of distinguished name, would entail the rancorous hatred of their relatives on all who were conspicuously instrumental to such a sentence.

The final judgment properly lay with the Eight, who presided over the administration of criminal justice; and the sentence depended on a majority of six votes. But the Eight shrank from their onerous responsibility, and asked in this exceptional case to have it shared by the Signoria (or the Gonfaloniere and the eight Priors). The Signoria in its turn shrugged its shoulders, and proposed the appeal to the Great Council. For, according to a law passed by the earnest persuasion of Savonarola nearly three years before, whenever a citizen was condemned to death by the fatal six votes (called the *sei fave* or *six beans,* beans being in more senses than one the political pulse of Florence), he had the right of appealing from that sentence to the Great Council.

But in this stage of the business, the friends of the accused resisted the appeal, determined chiefly by the wish to gain delay; and, in fact, strict legality required that sentence should have been passed prior to the appeal. Their resistance prevailed, and a middle course was taken; the sentence was referred to a large assembly convened on the 17th, consisting of all the higher magistracies, the smaller council or Senate of Eighty, and a select number of citizens.

On this day Romola, with anxiety heightened by the possibility that before its close her godfather's fate might be decided, had obtained leave to see him for the second time, but only in the presence of witnesses. She had returned to the Via de' Bardi in company with her cousin Brigida, still ignorant whether the council had come to any decisive issue; and Monna Brigida had gone out again to await the momentous news at the house of a friend belonging to one of the magistracies, that she might bring back authentic tidings as soon as they were to be had.

Romola had sunk on the first seat in the bright saloon, too much agitated, too sick at heart, to care about her place, or be conscious of discordance in the objects that surrounded her. She sat with her back to the door, resting her head on her hands. It seemed a long while since Monna Brigida had gone, and Romola was expecting her return. But when the door opened she knew it was not Monna Brigida who entered.

Since she had parted from Tito on that memorable night, she had had no external proof to warrant her belief that he had won his safety by treachery; on the contrary, she had had evidence that he was still trusted by the Mediceans, and was believed by them to be accomplishing certain errands of theirs in Romagna, under cover of fulfilling a commission of the government. For the obscurity in which the evidence concerning the conspirators was shrouded allowed it to be understood that Tito had escaped any implication.

But Romola's suspicion was not to be dissipated: her horror of his conduct towards Baldassarre projected itself over every conception of his acts; it was as if she had seen him committing a murder, and had had a diseased impression ever after that his hands were covered with fresh blood.

As she heard his step on the stone floor, a chill shudder passed through her; she could not turn round, she could not rise to give any greeting. He did not speak, but after an instant's pause took a seat on the other side of the table just opposite to her. Then she raised her eyes and looked at him; but she was mute. He did not show any irritation, but said coolly,—

"This meeting corresponds with our parting, Romola. But I understand that it is a moment of terrible suspense. I am come, however, if you will listen to me, to bring you the relief of hope."

She started, and altered her position, but looked at him dubiously.

"It will not be unwelcome to you to hear—even though it is I who tell it—that the council is prorogued till the 21st. The Eight have been frightened at last into passing a sentence of condemnation, but the demand has now been made on behalf of the condemned for the Appeal to the Great Council."

Romola's face lost its dubious expression; she asked eagerly,—

"And when is it to be made?"

"It has not yet been granted; but it *may* be granted. The Special Council is to meet again on the 21st to deliberate whether the Appeal shall be allowed or not. In the meantime there is an interval of three days, in which chances may occur in favour of the prisoners,—in which interest may be used on their behalf."

Romola started from her seat. The colour had risen to her face like a visible thought, and her hands trembled. In that moment her feeling towards Tito was forgotten.

"Possibly," said Tito, also rising, "your own intention may have anticipated what I was going to say. You are thinking of the Frate."

"I am," said Romola, looking at him with surprise. "Has he done anything? Is there anything to tell me?"

"Only this. It was Messer Francesco Valori's bitterness and violence which chiefly determined the course of things in the council to-day. Half the men who gave in their opinion against the prisoners were frightened into it, and there are numerous friends of Fra Girolamo both in this Special Council and out of it who are strongly opposed to the sentence of death,—Piero Guicciardini, for example, who is one member of the Signoria that made the stoutest resistance; and there is Giovan Battista Ridolfi, who, Piagnone as he is, will not lightly forgive the death of his brother Niccolò."

"But how can the Appeal be denied," said Romola, indignantly, "when it is the law,—when it was one of the chief glories of the popular government to have passed the law?"

"They call this an exceptional case. Of course there are ingenious arguments, but there is much more of loud bluster about the danger of the Republic. But, you see, no opposition could prevent the assembly from being prorogued, and a certain powerful influence rightly applied during the next three days might determine the wavering courage of those who desire that the Appeal should be granted, and might even give a check to the headlong enmity of Francesco Valori. It happens to have come to my knowledge that the Frate has so far interfered as to send a message to him in favour of Lorenzo Tornabuoni. I know you can sometimes have access to the Frate: it might at all events be worth while to use your privilege now."

"It is true," said Romola, with an air of abstraction. "I cannot believe that the Frate would approve denying the Appeal."

"I heard it said by more than one person in the court of the Palazzo before I came away, that it would be to the everlasting discredit of Fra Girolamo if he allowed a government which is almost entirely made up of his party, to deny the Appeal, without entering his protest, when he has been boasting in his books and sermons that it was he who got the law passed. But between ourselves, with all respect for your Frate's ability, my Romola, he has got into the practice of preaching that form of human sacrifices called killing tyrants and wicked malcontents, which some of his followers are likely to think inconsistent with lenity in the present case."

"I know, I know," said Romola, with a look and tone of pain. "But he is driven into those excesses of speech. It used to be different. I *will* ask for an interview. I cannot rest without it. I trust in the greatness of his heart."

She was not looking at Tito; her eyes were bent with a vague gaze towards the ground, and she had no distinct consciousness that the words she heard came from her husband.

"Better lose no time, then," said Tito, with unmixed suavity, moving his cap round in his hands as if he were about to put it on and depart. "And now, Romola, you will perhaps be able to see, in spite of prejudice, that my wishes go with yours in this matter. You will not regard the misfortune of my safety as an offence."

Something like an electric shock passed through Romola: it was the full consciousness of her husband's presence returning to her. She looked at him without speaking.

"At least," he added, in a slightly harder tone, "you will endeavour to base our intercourse on some other reasonings than that because an evil deed is possible, *I* have done it. Am I alone to be beyond the pale of your extensive charity?"

The feeling which had been driven back from Romola's lips a fortnight before rose again with the gathered force of a tidal wave. She spoke with a decision which told him that she was careless of consequences.

"It is too late, Tito. There is no killing the suspicion that deceit has once begotten. And now I know everything, I know who that old man was: he was your father, to whom you owe everything,—to whom you owe more than if you had been his own child. By the side of that, it is a small thing that you broke my trust and my father's. As long as you deny the truth about that old man, there is a horror rising between us: the law that should make us one can never be obeyed. I too am a human being. I have a soul of my own that abhors your actions. Our union is a pretence,—as if a perpetual lie could be a sacred marriage."

Tito did not answer immediately. When he did speak it was with a calculated caution that was stimulated by alarm.

"And you mean to carry out that independence by quitting me, I presume?"

"I desire to quit you," said Romola, impetuously.

"And supposing I do not submit to part with what the law gives me some security for retaining? You will then, of course, proclaim your reasons in the ear of all Florence. You will bring forward your mad assassin, who is doubtless ready to obey your call, and you will tell the world that you believe his testimony because he is so rational as to desire to assassinate me. You will first inform the Signoria that I am a Medicean conspirator, and then you will inform the Mediceans that I have betrayed them, and in both cases you will offer the excellent proof that you believe me capable in general of everything bad. It will certainly be a striking position for a wife to adopt. And if, on such evidence, you succeed in holding me up to infamy, you will have surpassed all the heroines of the Greek drama."

He paused a moment, but she stood mute. He went on with the sense of mastery.

"I believe you have no other grievance against me,—except that I have failed in fulfilling some lofty indefinite conditions on which you gave me your wifely affection, so that, by withdrawing it, you have gradually reduced me to the careful supply of your wants as a fair Piagnone of high condition and liberal charities. I think your success in gibbeting me is not certain. But doubtless you would begin by winning the ear of Messer Bernardo del Nero?"

"Why do I speak of anything?" cried Romola, in anguish, sinking on her chair again. "It is hateful in me to be thinking of myself."

She did not notice when Tito left the room, or know how long it was before the door opened to admit Monna Brigida. But in that instant she started up and said,—

"Cousin, we must go to San Marco directly. I must see my confessor, Fra Salvestro."

CHAPTER XXXIX

PLEADING

THE morning was in its early brightness when Romola was again on her way to San Marco, having obtained through Fra Salvestro, the evening before, the promise of an interview with Fra Girolamo in the chapter-house of the convent. The rigidity with which Savonarola guarded his life from all the pretexts of calumny made such interviews very rare, and whenever they were granted, they were kept free from any appearance of mystery. For this reason the hour chosen was one at which there were likely to be other visitors in the outer cloisters of San Marco.

She chose to pass through the heart of the city, that she might notice the signs of public feeling. Every loggia, every convenient corner of the piazza, every shop that made a rendezvous for gossips, was astir with the excitement of gratuitous debate; a languishing trade tended to make political discussion all the more vigorous. It was clear that the parties for and against the death of the conspirators were bent on making the fullest use of the three days' interval in order to determine the popular mood. Already handbills were in circulation; some presenting, in large print, the alternative of justice on the conspirators or ruin to the Republic; others in equally large print urging the observance of the law and the granting of the Appeal. Round these jutting islets of black capitals there were lakes of smaller characters setting forth arguments less necessary to be read: for it was an opinion entertained at that time (in the first flush of triumph at the discovery of printing), that there was no argument more widely convincing than question-begging phrases in large type.

Romola, however, cared especially to become acquainted with the arguments in smaller type, and, though obliged to hasten forward, she looked round anxiously as she went that she might miss no opportunity of securing copies. For a long way she saw none but such as were in the hands of eager readers, or else fixed on the walls from which in some places the sbirri were tearing them down. But at last, passing behind San Giovanni with a quickened pace that she might avoid the many acquaintances who frequented the piazza, she saw Bratti with a stock of handbills which he appeared to be exchanging for small coin with the passers-by. She was too familiar with the humble life of Florence for Bratti to be any stranger to her, and turning towards him she said, "Have you two sorts of handbills, Bratti? Let me have them quickly."

"Two sorts," said Bratti, separating the wet sheets with a slowness that tried Romola's patience. "There's 'Law' and there's 'Justice.' "

"Which sort do you sell most of?"

" 'Justice'—'Justice' goes the quickest,—so I raised the price, and made it two denari. But then I bethought me the 'Law' was good ware, too, and had as good a right to be charged for as 'Justice;' for people set no store by cheap things, and if I sold the 'Law' at one denaro, I should be doing it a wrong. And I'm a fair trader. 'Law' or 'Justice,' it's all one to me; they're good wares. I get 'em both for nothing, and I sell 'em at a fair profit. But you'll want more than one of a sort?"

"No, no; here's a white quattrino for the two," said Romola, folding up the bills and hurrying away.

She was soon in the outer cloisters of San Marco, where Fra Salvestro was awaiting her under the cloister, but did not notice the approach of her light step. He was chatting, according to his habit, with lay visitors; for under the auspices of a government friendly to the Frate, the timidity about frequenting San Marco, which had followed on the first shock of the Excommunication, had been gradually giving way. In one of these lay visitors she recognized a well-known satellite of Francesco Valori, named Andrea Cambini, who was narrating or expounding with emphatic gesticulation, while Fra Salvestro was listening with that air of trivial curiosity which tells that the listener cares very much about news and very little about its quality. This characteristic of her confessor, which was always repulsive to Romola, was made exasperating to her at this moment by the certainty she gathered, from the disjointed words which reached her ear, that Cambini was narrating something relative to the fate of the conspirators. She chose not to approach the group, but as soon as she saw that he had arrested Fra Salvestro's attention, she turned towards the door of the chapter-house, while he, making a sign of approval, disappeared within the inner cloister. A lay Brother stood ready to open the door of the chapter-house for her, and closed it behind her as she entered.

Once more looked at by those sad frescoed figures which had seemed to be mourning with her at the death of her brother Dino, it was inevitable that something of that scene should come back to her; but the intense occupation of her mind with the present made the remembrance less a retrospect than an indistinct recurrence of impressions which blended themselves with her agitating fears, as if her actual anxiety were a revival of the strong yearning she had once before brought to this spot—to be repelled by marble rigidity. She gave no space for the remembrance to become more definite, for she at once opened the handbills, thinking she should perhaps be able to read them in the interval

before Fra Girolamo appeared. But by the time she had read to the end
of the one that recommended the observance of the law, the door was
opening, and doubling up the papers she stood expectant.

When the Frate had entered she knelt, according to the usual practice of those who saw him in private; but as soon as he had uttered a
benedictory greeting, she rose and stood opposite to him at a few yards'
distance. Owing to his seclusion since he had been excommunicated, it
had been an unusually long while since she had seen him, and the late
months had visibly deepened in his face the marks of over-taxed mental
activity and bodily severities; and yet Romola was not so conscious of
this change as of another, which was less definable. Was it that the expression of serene elevation and pure human fellowship which had once
moved her was no longer present in the same force, or was it that the
sense of his being divided from her in her feeling about her godfather
roused the slumbering sources of alienation, and marred her own vision?
Perhaps both causes were at work. Our relations with our fellow-men
are most often determined by coincident currents of that sort; the inexcusable word or deed seldom comes until after affection or reverence has
been already enfeebled by the strain of repeated excuses.

It was true that Savonarola's glance at Romola had some of that hardness which is caused by an egotistic pre-possession. He divined that the
interview she had sought was to turn on the fate of the conspirators, a
subject on which he had already had to quell inner voices that might
become loud again when encouraged from without. Seated in his cell,
correcting the sheets of his "Triumph of the Cross," it was easier to
repose on a resolution of neutrality.

"It is a question of moment, doubtless, on which you wished to see
me, my daughter," he began, in a tone which was gentle rather from
self-control than from immediate inclination. "I know you are not wont
to lay stress on small matters."

"Father, you know what it is before I tell you," said Romola, forgetting everything else as soon as she began to pour forth her plea. "You
know what I am caring for,—it is for the life of the old man I love best
in the world. The thought of him has gone together with the thought
of my father as long as I remember the daylight. That is my warrant for
coming to you, even if my coming should have been needless. Perhaps
it is: perhaps you have already determined that your power over the
hearts of men shall be used to prevent them from denying to Florentines
a right which you yourself helped to earn for them."

"I meddle not with the functions of State, my daughter," said Fra
Girolamo, strongly disinclined to reopen externally a debate which he
had already gone through inwardly. "I have preached and laboured that
Florence should have a good government, for a good government is
needful to the perfecting of the Christian life; but I keep away my hands
from particular affairs which it is the office of experienced citizens to administer."

"Surely, father—" Romola broke off. She had uttered this first word almost impetuously, but she was checked by the counter-agitation of feeling herself in an attitude of remonstrance towards the man who had been the source of guidance and strength to her. In the act of rebelling she was bruising her own reverence.

Savonarola was too keen not to divine something of the conflict that was arresting her,—too noble deliberately to assume in calm speech that self-justifying evasiveness into which he was often hurried in public by the crowding impulses of the orator.

"Say what is in your heart; speak on, my daughter," he said, stand‑ ing with his arms laid one upon the other, and looking at her with quiet expectation.

"I was going to say, father, that this matter is surely of higher mo‑ ment than many about which I have heard you preach and exhort fer‑ vidly. If it belonged to you to urge that men condemned for offences against the State should have the right to appeal to the Great Council —if—" Romola was getting eager again—"if you count it a glory to have won that right for them, can it less belong to you to declare your‑ self against the right being denied to almost the first men who need it? Surely that touches the Christian life more closely than whether you knew beforehand that the Dauphin would die, or whether Pisa will be conquered."

There was a subtle movement, like a subdued sign of pain, in Savo‑ narola's strong lips, before he began to speak.

"My daughter, I speak as it is given me to speak,—I am not master of the times when I may become the vehicle of knowledge beyond the common lights of men. In this case I have no illumination beyond what wisdom may give to those who are charged with the safety to the State. As to the law of Appeal against the Six Votes, I laboured to have it passed, in order that no Florentine should be subject to loss of life and goods through the private hatred of a few who might happen to be in power; but these five men, who have desired to overthrow a free govern‑ ment and restore a corrupt tyrant, have been condemned with the assent of a large assembly of their fellow-citizens. They refused at first to have their cause brought before the Great Council. They have lost the right to the Appeal."

"How can they have lost it?" said Romola. "It is the right to appeal against condemnation, and they have never been condemned till now; and, forgive me, father, it *is* private hatred that would deny them the appeal; it *is* the violence of the few that frightens others; else why was the assembly divided again directly after it had seemed to agree? And if anything weighs against the observance of the law, let this weigh *for* it,—this, that you used to preach more earnestly than all else, that there should be no place given to hatred and bloodshed because of these party strifes, so that private ill-will should not find its opportunities in public acts. Father, you *know* that there is private hatred concerned here:

will it not dishonour you not to have interposed on the side of mercy, when there are many who hold that it is also the side of law and justice?"

"My daughter," said Fra Girolamo, with more visible emotion than before, "there is a mercy which is weakness, and even treason against the common good. The safety of Florence, which means even more than the welfare of Florentines, now demands severity, as it once demanded mercy. It is not only for a past plot that these men are condemned, but also for a plot which has not yet been executed; and the devices that were leading to its execution are not put an end to: the tyrant is still gathering his forces in Romagna, and the enemies of Florence, who sit in the highest places of Italy, are ready to hurl any stone that will crush her."

"What plot?" said Romola, reddening, and trembling with alarmed surprise.

"You carry papers in your hand, I see," said Fra Girolamo, pointing to the handbills. "One of them will, perhaps, tell you that the government has had new information."

Romola hastily opened the handbill she had not yet read, and saw that the government had now positive evidence of a second plot, which was to have been carried out in this August time. To her mind it was like reading a confirmation that Tito had won his safety by foul means; his pretence of wishing that the Frate should exert himself on behalf of the condemned only helped the wretched conviction. She crushed up the paper in her hand, and, turning to Savonarola, she said, with new passion, "Father, what safety can there be for Florence when the worst man can always escape? And," she went on, a sudden flash of remembrance coming from the thought about her husband, "have not you yourself encouraged this deception which corrupts the life of Florence, by wanting more favour to be shown to Lorenzo Tornabuoni, who has worn two faces, and flattered you with a show of affection, when my godfather has always been honest? Ask all Florence who of those five men has the truest heart, and there will not be many who will name any other name than Bernardo del Nero. You did interpose with Francesco Valori for the sake of one prisoner: you have *not* then been neutral; and you know that your word will be powerful."

"I do not desire the death of Bernardo," said Savonarola, colouring deeply. "It would be enough if he were sent out of the city."

"Then why do you not speak to save an old man of seventy-five from dying a death of ignominy,—to give him at least the fair chances of the law?" burst out Romola, the impetuosity of her nature so roused that she forgot everything but her indignation. "It is not that you feel bound to be neutral; else why did you speak for Lorenzo Tornabuoni? You spoke for him because he is more friendly to San Marco; my godfather feigns no friendship. It is not, then, as a Medicean that my godfather is to die; it is as a man you have no love for!"

When Romola paused, with cheeks glowing and with quivering lips, there was dead silence. As she saw Fra Girolamo standing motionless before her, she seemed to herself to be hearing her own words over again,—words that in this echo of consciousness were in strange, painful dissonance with the memories that made part of his presence to her. The moments of silence were expanded by gathering compunction and self-doubt. She had committed sacrilege in her passion. And even the sense that she could retract nothing of her plea, that her mind could not submit itself to Savonarola's negative, made it the more needful to her to satisfy those reverential memories. With a sudden movement towards him she said,—

"Forgive me, father; it is pain to me to have spoken those words,—yet I cannot help speaking. I am little and feeble compared with you; you brought me light and strength. But I submitted because I felt the proffered strength,—because I saw the light. *Now* I cannot see it. Father, you yourself declare that there comes a moment when the soul must have no guide but the voice within it, to tell whether the consecrated thing has sacred virtue. And therefore I must speak."

Savonarola had that readily roused resentment towards opposition, hardly separable from a power-loving and powerful nature, accustomed to seek great ends that cast a reflected grandeur on the means by which they are sought. His sermons have much of that red flame in them. And if he had been a meaner man, his susceptibility might have shown itself in irritation at Romola's accusatory freedom, which was in strong contrast with the deference he habitually received from his disciples. But at this moment such feelings were nullified by that hard struggle which made half the tragedy of his life,—the struggle of a mind possessed by a never-silent hunger after purity and simplicity, yet caught in a tangle of egoistic demands, false ideas, and difficult outward conditions, that made simplicity impossible. Keenly alive to all the suggestions of Romola's remonstrating words, he was rapidly surveying, as he had done before, the courses of action that were open to him, and their probable results. But it was a question on which arguments could seem decisive only in proportion as they were charged with feeling, and he had received no impulse that could alter his bias. He looked at Romola and said,—

"You have full pardon for your frankness, my daughter. You speak, I know, out of the fulness of your family affections. But these affections must give way to the needs of the Republic. If those men who have a close acquaintance with the affairs of the State believe, as I understand they do, that the public safety requires the extreme punishment of the law to fall on the five conspirators, I cannot control their opinion, seeing that I stand aloof from such affairs."

"Then you desire that they should die? You desire that the Appeal should be denied them?" said Romola, feeling anew repelled by a vindication which seemed to her to have the nature of a subterfuge.

"I have said that I do not desire their death."

"Then," said Romola, her indignation rising again, "you can be in-

different that Florentines should inflict death which you do not desire,
when you might have protested against it,—when you might have
helped to hinder it, by urging the observance of a law which you held
it good to get passed. Father, you used not to stand aloof: you used
not to shrink from protesting. Do not say you cannot protest where the
lives of men are concerned; say rather, you desire their death. Say
rather, you hold it good for Florence that there shall be more blood
and more hatred. Will the death of five Mediceans put an end to parties
in Florence? Will the death of a noble old man like Bernardo del Nero
save a city that holds such men as Dolfo Spini?"

"My daughter, it is enough. The cause of freedom, which is the cause
of God's kingdom upon earth, is often most injured by the enemies
who carry within them the power of certain human virtues. The wicked-
est man is often not the most insurmountable obstacle to the triumph
of good."

"Then why do you say again, that you do not desire my godfather's
death?" said Romola, in mingled anger and despair. "Rather, you hold
it the more needful he should die because he is the better man. I cannot
unravel your thoughts, father; I cannot hear the real voice of your
judgment and conscience."

There was a moment's pause. Then Savonarola said, with keener
emotion than he had yet shown,—

"Be thankful, my daughter, if your own soul has been spared perplexity; and judge not those to whom a harder lot has been given. *You*
see one ground of action in this matter. I see many. I have to choose
that which will further the work intrusted to me. The end I seek is
one to which minor respects must be sacrificed. The death of five men
—were they less guilty than these—is a light matter weighed against
the withstanding of the vicious tyrannies which stifle the life of Italy,
and foster the corruption of the Church; a light matter weighed against
the furthering of God's kingdom upon earth, the end for which I live
and am willing myself to die."

Under any other circumstances, Romola would have been sensitive
to the appeal at the beginning of Savonarola's speech; but at this moment she was so utterly in antagonism with him, that what he called
perplexity seemed to her sophistry and doubleness; and as he went on,
his words only fed that flame of indignation which now again, more
fully than ever before, lit up the memory of all his mistakes, and made
her trust in him seem to have been a purblind delusion. She spoke
almost with bitterness.

"Do you, then, know so well what will further the coming of God's
kingdom, father, that you will dare to despise the plea of mercy,—of
justice,—of faithfulness to your own teaching? Has the French king,
then, brought renovation to Italy? Take care, father, lest your enemies
have some reason when they say that in your visions of what will further God's kingdom you see only what will strengthen your own party."

"And that is true!" said Savonarola, with flashing eyes. Romola's voice had seemed to him in that moment the voice of his enemies. "The cause of my party *is* the cause of God's kingdom."

"I do not believe it!" said Romola, her whole frame shaken with passionate repugnance. "God's kingdom is something wider,—else, let me stand outside it with the beings that I love."

The two faces were lit up, each with an opposite emotion, each with an opposite certitude. Further words were impossible. Romola hastily covered her head and went out in silence.

CHAPTER XL

THE SCAFFOLD

THREE days later the moon that was just surmounting the buildings of the piazza in front of the Old Palace within the hour of midnight, did not make the usual broad lights and shadows on the pavement. Not a hand's-breadth of pavement was to be seen, but only the heads of an eager struggling multitude. And instead of that background of silence in which the pattering footsteps and buzzing voices, the lute-thrumming or rapid scampering of the many night-wanderers of Florence stood out in obtrusive distinctness, there was the background of a roar from mingled shouts and imprecations, tramplings and pushings, and accidental clashing of weapons, across which nothing was distinguishable but a darting shriek, or the heavy dropping toll of a bell.

Almost all who could call themselves the public of Florence were awake at that hour, and either enclosed within the limits of that piazza or struggling to enter it. Within the palace were still assembled in the council chamber all the chief magistracies, the eighty members of the senate, and the other select citizens who had been in hot debate through long hours of daylight and torchlight whether the Appeal should be granted or whether the sentence of death should be executed on the prisoners forthwith, to forestall the dangerous chances of delay. And the debate had been so much like fierce quarrel that the noise from the council chamber had reached the crowd outside. Only within the last hour had the question been decided: the Signoria had remained divided, four of them standing out resolutely for the Appeal in spite of the strong argument that if they did not give way their houses should be sacked, until Francesco Valori, in brief and furious speech, made the determination of his party more ominously distinct by declaring that if the Signoria would not defend the liberties of the Florentine people by executing those five perfidious citizens, there would not be wanting others who would take that cause in hand to the peril of all who opposed it. The Florentine Cato triumphed. When the votes were counted again, the four obstinate white beans no longer appeared; the whole nine were of the fatal affirmative black, deciding the death of the five prisoners without delay,—deciding also, only tacitly and with much more delay, the death of Francesco Valori.

And now, while the judicial Eight were gone to the Bargello to prepare for the execution, the five condemned men were being led barefoot and in irons through the midst of the council. It was their friends who had contrived this: would not Florentines be moved by the visible association of such cruel ignominy with two venerable men like Bernardo del Nero and Niccolò Ridolfi, who had taken their bias long before the new order of things had come to make Mediceanism retrograde,—with two brilliant popular young men like Tornabuoni and Pucci, whose absence would be felt as a haunting vacancy wherever there was a meeting of chief Florentines? It was useless: such pity as could be awakened now was of that hopeless sort which leads not to rescue, but to the tardier action of revenge.

While this scene was passing upstairs Romola stood below against one of the massive pillars in the court of the palace, expecting the moment when her godfather would appear, on his way to execution. By the use of strong interest she had gained permission to visit him in the evening of this day, and remain with him until the result of the council should be determined. And now she was waiting with his confessor to follow the guard that would lead him to the Bargello. Her heart was bent on clinging to the presence of the childless old man to the last moment, as her father would have done; and she had overpowered all remonstrances. Giovan Battista Ridolfi, a disciple of Savonarola, who was going in bitterness to behold the death of his elder brother Niccolò, had promised that she should be guarded, and now stood by her side.

Tito, too, was in the palace; but Romola had not seen him. Since the evening of the 17th they had avoided each other, and Tito only knew by inference from the report of the Frate's neutrality that her pleading had failed. He was now surrounded with official and other personages, both Florentine and foreign, who had been awaiting the issue of the long-protracted council, maintaining, except when he was directly addressed, the subdued air and grave silence of a man whom actual events are placing in a painful state of strife between public and private feeling. When an allusion was made to his wife in relation to those events, he implied that, owing to the violent excitement of her mind, the mere fact of his continuing to hold office under a government concerned in her godfather's condemnation, roused in her a diseased hostility towards him; so that for her sake he felt it best not to approach her.

"Ah, the old Bardi blood!" said Cennini, with a shrug. "I shall not be surprised if this business shakes *her* loose from the Frate, as well as some others I could name."

"It is excusable in a woman, who is doubtless beautiful, since she is the wife of Messer Tito," said a young French envoy, smiling and bowing to Tito, "to think that her affections must overrule the good of the State, and that nobody is to be beheaded who is anybody's cousin;

but such a view is not to be encouraged in the male population. It seems to me your Florentine polity is much weakened by it."

"That is true," said Niccolò Macchiavelli; "but where personal ties are strong, the hostilities they raise must be taken due account of. Many of these half-way severities are mere hot-headed blundering. The only safe blows to be inflicted on men and parties are the blows that are too heavy to be avenged."

"Niccolò," said Cennini, "there is a clever wickedness in thy talk sometimes that makes me mistrust thy pleasant young face as if it were a mask of Satan."

"Not at all, my good Domenico," said Macchiavelli, smiling, and laying his hand on the elder's shoulder. "Satan was a blunderer, an introducer of *novità*, who made a stupendous failure. If he had succeeded, we should all have been worshipping him, and his portrait would have been more flattered."

"Well, well," said Cennini, "I say not thy doctrine is not too clever for Satan: I only say it is wicked enough for him."

"I tell you," said Macchiavelli, "my doctrine is the doctrine of all men who seek an end a little farther off than their own noses. Ask our Frate, our prophet, how his universal renovation is to be brought about: he will tell you, first, by getting a free and pure government; and since it appears that this cannot be done by making all Florentines love each other, it must be done by cutting off every head that happens to be obstinately in the way. Only if a man incurs odium by sanctioning a severity that is not thorough enough to be final, he commits a blunder. And something like that blunder, I suspect, the Frate has committed. It was an occasion on which he might have won some lustre by exerting himself to maintain the Appeal; instead of that, he has lost lustre, and has gained no strength."

Before any one else could speak, there came the expected announcement that the prisoners were about to leave the council chamber; and the majority of those who were present hurried towards the door, intent on securing the freest passage to the Bargello in the rear of the prisoners' guard; for the scene of the execution was one that drew alike those who were moved by the deepest passions and those who were moved by the coldest curiosity.

Tito was one of those who remained behind. He had a native repugnance to sights of death and pain, and five days ago whenever he had thought of this execution as a possibility he had hoped that it would not take place, and that the utmost sentence would be exile: his own safety demanded no more. But now he felt that it would be a welcome guarantee of his security when he had learned that Bernardo del Nero's head was off the shoulders. The new knowledge and new attitude towards him disclosed by Romola on the day of his return, had given him a new dread of the power she possessed to make his position insecure. If any act of hers only succeeded in making him an object of suspicion and odium, he foresaw not only frustration, but frustration under un pleasant circumstances. Her belief in Baldassarre had clearly determined her wavering feelings against further submission, and if her godfather lived she would win him to share her belief without much trouble. Romola seemed more than ever an unmanageable fact in his destiny. But if Bernardo del Nero were dead, the difficulties that would beset her in placing herself in opposition to her husband would probably be insurmountable to her shrinking pride. Therefore Tito had felt easier when he knew that the Eight had gone to the Bargello to order the instant erection of the scaffold. Four other men—his intimates and confederates—were to die, besides Bernardo del Nero. But a man's own safety is a god that sometimes makes very grim demands. Tito felt them to be grim: even in the pursuit of what was agreeable, this paradoxical life forced upon him the desire for what was disagreeable. But he had had other experience of this sort, and as he heard through the open doorway the shuffle of many feet and the clanking of metal on the stairs, he was able to answer the questions of the young French envoy without showing signs of any other feeling than that of sad resignation to State necessities.

Those sounds fell on Romola as if her power of hearing had been exalted along with every other sensibility of her nature. She needed no arm to support her; she shed no tears. She felt that intensity of life which seems to transcend both grief and joy,—in which the mind seems to itself akin to elder forces that wrought out existence before the birth of pleasure and pain. Since her godfather's fate had been decided, the previous struggle of feeling in her had given way to an identification of herself with him in these supreme moments: she was inwardly asserting for him that if he suffered the punishment of treason, he did not deserve the name of traitor: he was the victim to a collision between two kinds of faithfulness. It was not given him to die for the noblest cause, and yet he died because of his nobleness. He might have been a meaner man and found it easier not to incur this guilt. Romola was feeling the full force of that sympathy with the individual lot that is continually opposing itself to the formulæ by which actions and parties are judged. She was treading the way with her second father to the scaffold, and nerving herself to defy ignominy by the consciousness that it was not deserved.

The way was fenced in by three hundred armed men, who had been placed as a guard by the orders of Francesco Valori; for among the apparent contradictions that belonged to this event, not the least striking was the alleged alarm on the one hand at the popular rage against the conspirators, and the alleged alarm on the other lest there should be an attempt to rescue them in the midst of a hostile crowd. When they had arrived within the court of the Bargello, Romola was allowed to approach Bernardo with his confessor for a moment of farewell. Many eyes were bent on them even in that struggle of an agitated throng, as the aged man, forgetting that his hands were bound with irons, lifted them towards the golden head that was bent towards him, and then, checking that movement, leaned to kiss her. She seized the fettered hands that were hung down again, and kissed them as if they had been sacred things.

"My poor Romola," said Bernardo, in a low voice, "I have only to die, but thou hast to live—and I shall not be there to help thee."

"Yes," said Romola, hurriedly, "you *will* help me—always—because I shall remember you."

She was taken away and conducted up the flight of steps that led to the loggia surrounding the grand old court. She took her place there, determined to look till the moment when her godfather laid his head on the block. Now while the prisoners were allowed a brief interval with their confessor, the spectators were pressing into court until the crowd became dense around the black scaffold, and the torches fixed in iron rings against the pillars threw a varying startling light at one moment on passionless stone carvings, at another on some pale face agitated with suppressed rage or suppressed grief,—the face of one among the many near relatives of the condemned, who were presently to receive their dead and carry them home.

Romola's face looked like a marble image against the dark arch as she stood watching for the moment when her godfather would appear at the foot of the scaffold. He was to suffer first; and Battista Ridolfi, who was by her side, had promised to take her away through a door behind them when she would have seen the last look of the man who alone in all the world had shared her pitying love for her father. And still, in the background of her thought, there was the possibility striving to be a hope, that some rescue might yet come, something that would keep that scaffold unstained by blood.

For a long while there was constant movement, lights flickering, heads swaying to and fro, confused voices within the court, rushing waves of sound through the entrance from without. It seemed to Romola as if she were in the midst of a storm-troubled sea, caring nothing about the storm, caring only to hold out a signal till the eyes that looked for it could seek it no more.

Suddenly there was stillness, and the very tapers seemed to tremble into quiet. The executioner was ready on the scaffold, and Bernardo del Nero was seen ascending it with a slow firm step. Romola made no visible movement, uttered not even a suppressed sound: she stood more firmly, caring for *his* firmness. She saw him pause, saw the white head kept erect, while he said in a voice distinctly audible,—

"It is but a short space of life that my fellow-citizens have taken from me."

She perceived that he was gazing slowly round him as he spoke. She felt that his eyes were resting on her, and that she was stretching out her arms towards him. Then she saw no more till—a long while after, as it seemed—a voice said, "My daughter, all is peace now. I can conduct you to your house."

She uncovered her head and saw her godfather's confessor standing by
her, in a room where there were other grave men talking in subdued
tones.

"I am ready," she said, starting up. "Let us lose no time."

She thought all clinging was at an end for her: all her strength now
should be given to escape from a grasp under which she shuddered.

CHAPTER XLI

DRIFTING AWAY

On the eighth day from that memorable night Romola was standing on
the brink of the Mediterranean, watching the gentle summer pulse of
the sea just above what was then the little fishing-village of Viareggio.

Again she had fled from Florence, and this time no arresting voice had
called her back. Again she wore the grey religious dress; and this time,
in her heart-sickness, she did not care that it was a disguise. A new
rebellion had risen within her, a new despair. Why should she care
about wearing one badge more than another, or about being called by
her own name? She despaired of finding any consistent duty belonging
to that name. What force was there to create for her that supremely
hallowed motive which men call duty, but which can have no inward
constraining existence save through some form of believing love?

The bonds of all strong affection were snapped. In her marriage, the
highest bond of all, she had ceased to see the mystic union which is its
own guarantee of indissolubleness, had ceased even to see the obligation of a voluntary pledge: had she not proved that the things to which
she had pledged herself were impossible? The impulse to set herself
free had risen again with overmastering force; yet the freedom could
only be an exchange of calamity. There is no compensation for the
woman who feels that the chief relation of her life has been no more
than a mistake. She has lost her crown. The deepest secret of human
blessedness has half whispered itself to her, and then forever passed
her by.

And now Romola's best support under that supreme woman's sorrow
had slipped away from her. The vision of any great purpose, any end
of existence which could ennoble endurance and exalt the common
deeds of a dusty life with divine ardours, was utterly eclipsed for her
now by the sense of a confusion in human things which made all effort
a mere dragging at tangled threads; all fellowship, either for resistance or advocacy, mere unfairness and exclusiveness. What, after
all, was the man who had represented for her the highest heroism,—the
heroism not of hard, self-contained endurance, but of willing, self-offer-
ing love? What was the cause he was struggling for? Romola had lost
her trust in Savonarola, had lost that fervour of admiration which had
made her unmindful of his aberrations, and attentive only to the grand

curve of his orbit. And now that her keen feeling for her godfather had thrown her into antagonism with the Frate, she saw all the repulsive and inconsistent details in his teaching with a painful lucidity which exaggerated their proportions. In the bitterness of her disappointment she said that his striving after the renovation of the Church and the world was a striving after a mere name which told no more than the title of a book: a name that had come to mean practically the measures that would strengthen his own position in Florence; nay, often questionable deeds and words, for the sake of saving his influence from suffering by his own errors. And that political reform which had once made a new interest in her life seemed now to reduce itself to narrow devices for the safety of Florence, in contemptible contradiction with the alternating professions of blind trust in the Divine care.

It was inevitable that she should judge the Frate unfairly on a question of individual suffering, at which *she* looked with the eyes of personal tenderness, and *he* with the eyes of theoretic conviction. In that declaration of his, that the cause of his party was the cause of God's kingdom, she heard only the ring of egoism. Perhaps such words have rarely been uttered without that meaner ring in them; yet they are the implicit formula of all energetic belief. And if such energetic belief, pursuing a grand and remote end, is often in danger of becoming a demon-worship, in which the votary lets his son and daughter pass through the fire with a readiness that hardly looks like sacrifice; tender fellow-feeling for the nearest has its danger too, and is apt to be timid and sceptical towards the larger aims without which life cannot rise into religion. In this way poor Romola was being blinded by her tears.

No one who has ever known what it is thus to lose faith in a fellow-man whom he has profoundly loved and reverenced, will lightly say that the shock can leave the faith in the Invisible Goodness unshaken. With the sinking of high human trust, the dignity of life sinks too; we cease to believe in our own better self, since that also is part of the common nature which is degraded in our thought; and all the finer impulses of the soul are dulled. Romola felt even the springs of her once active pity drying up, and leaving her to barren egoistic complaining. Had not *she* had her sorrows too? And few had cared for her, while she had cared for many. She had done enough; she had striven after the impossible, and was weary of this stifling crowded life. She longed for that repose in mere sensation which she had sometimes dreamed of in the sultry afternoons of her early girlhood, when she had fancied herself floating naiad-like in the waters.

The clear waves seemed to invite her: she wished she could lie down to sleep on them and pass from sleep into death. But Romola could not directly seek death; the fulness of young life in her forbade that. She could only wish that death would come.

At the spot where she had paused there was a deep bend in the shore, and a small boat with a sail was moored there. In her longing to glide over the waters that were getting golden with the level sun-rays,

she thought of a story which had been one of the things she had loved
to dwell on in Boccaccio, when her father fell asleep and she glided
from her stool to sit on the floor and read the "Decamerone." It was the
story of that fair Gostanza who in her lovelornness desired to live no
longer, but not having the courage to attack her young life, had put
herself into a boat and pushed off to sea; then, lying down in the boat,
had wrapped her mantle round her head, hoping to be wrecked, so that
her fear would be helpless to flee from death. The memory had remained a mere thought in Romola's mind, without budding into any
distinct wish; but now, as she paused again in her walking to and fro,
she saw gliding black against the red gold another boat with one man in
it, making towards the bend where the first and smaller boat was
moored. Walking on again, she at length saw the man land, pull his boat
ashore and begin to unlade something from it. He was perhaps the
owner of the smaller boat also: he would be going away soon, and her
opportunity would be gone with him,—her opportunity of buying that
smaller boat. She had not yet admitted to herself that she meant to use
it, but she felt a sudden eagerness to secure the possibility of using it,
which disclosed the half-unconscious growth of a thought into a desire.

"Is that little boat yours also?" she said to the fisherman, who had
looked up, a little startled by the tall grey figure, and had made a reverence to this holy sister wandering thus mysteriously in the evening
solitude.

It *was* his boat; an old one, hardly seaworthy, yet worth repairing
to any man who would buy it. By the blessing of San Antonio, whose
chapel was in the village yonder, his fishing had prospered, and he had
now a better boat, which had once been Gianni's who died. But he had
not yet sold the old one. Romola asked him how much it was worth,
and then, while he was busy, thrust the price into a little satchel lying
on the ground and containing the remnant of his dinner. After that,
she watched him furling his sail and asked him how he should set it if
he wanted to go out to sea, and then pacing up and down again, waited
to see him depart.

The imagination of herself gliding away in that boat on the darkening waters was growing more and more into a longing, as the thought of
a cool brook in sultriness becomes a painful thirst. To be freed from
the burden of choice when all motive was bruised, to commit herself,
sleeping, to destiny which would either bring death or else new necessities that might rouse a new life in her!—it was a thought that beckoned her the more because the soft evening air made her long to rest
in the still solitude, instead of going back to the noise and heat of the
village.

At last the slow fisherman had gathered up all his movables and was
walking away. Soon the gold was shrinking and getting duskier in sea
and sky, and there was no living thing in sight, no sound but the lulling
monotony of the lapping waves. In this sea there was no tide that
would help to carry her away if she waited for its ebb; but Romola

thought the breeze from the land was rising a little. She got into the boat, unfurled the sail, and fastened it as she had learned in that first brief lesson. She saw that it caught the light breeze, and this was all she cared for. Then she loosed the boat from its moorings, and tried to urge it with an oar, till she was far out from the land, till the sea was dark even to the west, and the stars were disclosing themselves like a palpitating life over the wide heavens. Resting at last, she threw back her cowl, and taking off the kerchief underneath, which confined her hair, she doubled them both under her head for a pillow on one of the boat's ribs. The fair head was still very young, and could bear a hard pillow.

And so she lay, with the soft night air breathing on her while she glided on the water and watched the deepening quiet of the sky. She was alone now: she had freed herself from all claims, she had freed herself even from that burden of choice which presses with heavier and heavier weight when claims have loosed their guiding hold.

Had she found anything like the dream of her girlhood? No. Memories hung upon her like the weight of broken wings that could never be lifted,—memories of human sympathy which even in its pain leaves a thirst that the Great Mother has no milk to still. Romola felt orphaned in those wide spaces of sea and sky. She read no message of love for her in that far-off symbolic writing of the heavens, and with a great sob she wished that she might be gliding into death.

She drew the cowl over her head again and covered her face, choosing darkness rather than the light of the stars, which seemed to her like the hard light of eyes that looked at her without seeing her. Presently she felt that she was in the grave, but not resting there: she was touching the hands of the beloved dead beside her, and trying to wake them.

CHAPTER XLII

THE BENEDICTION

ABOUT ten o'clock on the morning of the 27th of February the currents of passengers along the Florentine streets set decidedly towards San Marco. It was the last morning of the Carnival, and every one knew there was a second Bonfire of Vanities being prepared in front of the Old Palace; but at this hour it was evident that the centre of popular interest lay elsewhere.

The Piazza di San Marco was filled by a multitude who showed no other movement than that which proceeded from the pressure of new-comers trying to force their way forward from all the openings: but the front ranks were already close-serried and resisted the pressure. Those ranks were ranged around a semicircular barrier in front of the church, and within this barrier were already assembling the Dominican Brethren of San Marco.

But the temporary wooden pulpit erected over the church-door was still empty. It was presently to be entered by the man whom the Pope's command had banished from the pulpit of the Duomo, whom the other eccleciastics of Florence had been forbidden to consort with, whom the citizens had been forbidden to hear on pain of excommunication. This man had said, "A wicked, unbelieving Pope who has gained the pontifical chair by bribery is not Christ's Vicar. His curses are broken swords: he grasps a hilt without a blade. His commands are contrary to the Christian life: it is lawful to disobey them,—nay, *it is not lawful to obey them.*" And the people still flocked to hear him as he preached in his own church of San Marco, though the Pope was hanging terrible threats over Florence if it did not renounce the pestilential schismatic and send him to Rome to be "converted,"—still, as on this very morning, accepted the Communion from his excommunicated hands. For how if this Frate had really more command over the Divine lightnings than that official successor of Saint Peter? It was a momentous question, which for the mass of citizens could never be decided by the Frate's ultimate test; namely, what was and what was not accordant with the highest spiritual law. No; in such a case as this, if God had chosen the Frate as his prophet to rebuke the High Priest who carried the mystic raiment unworthily, he would attest his choice by some unmistakable sign. As long as the belief in the Prophet carried no threat of outward calamity, but rather the confident hope of exceptional safety, no sign was needed: his preaching was a music to which the people felt themselves marching along the way they wished to go; but now that belief meant an immediate blow to their commerce, the shaking of their position among the Italian States, and an interdict on their city, there inevitably came the question, "What miracle showest thou?" Slowly at first, then faster and faster, that fatal demand had been swelling in Savonarola's ear, provoking a response, outwardly in the declaration that at the fitting time the miracle would come; inwardly in the faith,—not unwavering, for what faith is so?—that if the need for miracle became urgent, the work he had before him was too great for the Divine power to leave it halting. His faith wavered, but not his speech: it is the lot of every man who has to speak for the satisfaction of the crowd, that he must often speak in virtue of yesterday's faith, hoping it will come back to-morrow.

It was in preparation for a scene which was really a response to the popular impatience for some supernatural guarantee of the Prophet's mission, that the wooden pulpit had been erected above the church-door. But while the ordinary Frati in black mantles were entering and arranging themselves, the faces of the multitude were not yet eagerly directed towards the pulpit: it was felt that Savonarola would not appear just yet, and there was some interest in singling out the various monks, some of them belonging to high Florentine families, many of them having fathers, brothers, or cousins among the artisans and shopkeepers who made the majority of the crowd. It was not till the tale of monks was complete, not till they had fluttered their books and had begun to chant, that people said to each other, "Fra Girolamo must be coming now."

That expectation rather than any spell from the accustomed wail of psalmody was what made silence and expectation seem to spread like a paling solemn light over the multitude of upturned faces, all now directed towards the empty pulpit.

The next instant the pulpit was no longer empty. A figure covered from head to foot in black cowl and mantle had entered it, and was kneeling with bent head and with face turned away. It seemed a weary time to the eager people while the black figure knelt and the monks chanted. But the stillness was not broken, for the Frate's audiences with Heaven were yet charged with electric awe for that mixed multitude, so that those who had already the will to stone him felt their arms unnerved.

At last there was a vibration among the multitude, each seeming to give his neighbor a momentary aspen-like touch, as when men who have been watching for something in the heavens see the expected presence silently disclosing itself. The Frate had risen, turned towards the people, and partly pushed back his cowl. The monotonous wail of psalmody had ceased, and to those who stood near the pulpit, it was as if the sounds which had just been filling their ears had suddenly merged themselves in the force of Savonarola's flashing glance, as he looked round him in the silence. Then he stretched out his hands, which in their exquisite delicacy seemed transfigured from an animal organ for grasping into vehicles of sensibility too acute to need any gross contact,— hands that came like an appealing speech from that part of his soul which was masked by his strong passionate face, written on now with deeper lines about the mouth and brow than are made by forty-four years of ordinary life.

At the first stretching out of the hands some of the crowd in the front ranks fell on their knees, and here and there a devout disciple farther off; but the great majority stood firm, some resisting the impulse to kneel before this excommunicated man (might not a great judgment fall upon him even in this act of blessing?)—others jarred with scorn and hatred of the ambitious deceiver who was getting up this new comedy, before which, nevertheless, they felt themselves impotent, as before the triumph of a fashion.

But then came the voice, clear and low at first, uttering the words of absolution,—"*Misereatur vestri,*"—and more fell on their knees; and as it rose higher and yet clearer, the erect heads became fewer and fewer, till, at the words *"Benedicat vos omnipotens Deus,"* it rose to a masculine cry, as if protesting its power to bless under the clutch of a demon that wanted to stifle it: it rang like a trumpet to the extremities of the piazza, and under it every head was bowed.

After the utterance of that blessing, Savonarola himself fell on his knees and hid his face in temporary exhaustion. Those great jets of emotion were a necessary part of his life; he himself had said to the people long ago, "Without preaching I cannot live." But it was a life that shattered him.

In a few minutes more, some had risen to their feet, but a larger number remained kneeling, and all faces were intently watching him. He had taken into his hands a crystal vessel, containing the consecrated Host, and was about to address the people.

"You remember, my children, three days ago I besought you, when I should hold this Sacrament in my hand in the face of you all, to pray fervently to the Most High that if this work of mine does not come from Him, He will send a fire and consume me, that I may vanish into the eternal darkness away from His light which I have hidden with my falsity. Again I beseech you to make that prayer, and to make it *now*."

It was a breathless moment: perhaps no man really prayed, if some in a spirit of devout obedience made the effort to pray. Every consciousness was chiefly possessed by the sense that Savonarola was praying, in a voice not loud, but distinctly audible in the wide stillness.

"Lord, if I have not wrought in sincerity of soul, if my word cometh not from Thee, strike me in this moment with Thy thunder, and let the fires of Thy wrath enclose me."

He ceased to speak, and stood motionless, with the consecrated mystery in his hand, with eyes uplifted and a quivering excitement in his whole aspect. Every one else was motionless and silent too, while the sunlight, which for the last quarter of an hour had here and there been piercing the greyness, made fitful streaks across the convent wall, causing some awe-stricken spectators to start timidly. But soon there was a wider parting, and with a gentle quickness, like a smile, a stream of brightness poured itself on the crystal vase, and then spread itself over Savonarola's face with mild glorification.

An instantaneous shout rang through the piazza, "Behold the answer!"

The warm radiance thrilled through Savonarola's frame, and so did the shout. It was his last moment of untroubled triumph, and in its rapturous confidence he felt carried to a grander scene yet to come, before an audience that would represent all Christendom, in whose presence he should again be sealed as the messenger of the supreme righteousness, and feel himself full charged with Divine strength. It was but a moment that expanded itself in that prevision. While the shout was still ringing in his ears he turned away within the church, feeling the strain too great for him to bear it longer.

But when the Frate had disappeared, and the sunlight seemed no longer to have anything special in its illumination, but was spreading itself impartially over all things clean and unclean, there began, along with the general movement of the crowd, a confusion of voices in which certain strong discords and varying scales of laughter made it evident that, in the previous silence and universal kneeling, hostility and scorn had only submitted unwillingly to a momentary spell.

"It seems to me the plaudits are giving way to criticism," said Tito, who had been watching the scene attentively from an upper loggia in one of the houses opposite the church. "Nevertheless it was a striking moment, eh, Messer Pietro? Fra Girolamo is a man to make one understand that there was a time when the monk's frock was a symbol of power over men's minds rather than over the keys of women's cupboards."

"Assuredly," said Pietro Cennini. "And until I have seen proof that Fra Girolamo has much less faith in God's judgments than the common run of men, instead of having considerably more, I shall not believe that he would brave Heaven in this way if his soul were laden with a conscious lie."

CHAPTER XLIII

RIPENING SCHEMES

A MONTH after that Carnival, one morning near the end of March, Tito descended the marble steps of the Old Palace, bound on a pregnant errand to San Marco. For some reason he did not choose to take the direct road, which was but a slightly bent line from the Old Palace; he chose rather to make a circuit by the Piazza di Santa Croce, where the people would be pouring out of the church after the early sermon.

It was in the grand church of Santa Croce that the daily Lenten sermon had of late had the largest audience. For Savonarola's voice had ceased to be heard even in his own church of San Marco, a hostile Signoria having imposed silence on him in obedience to a new letter from the Pope, threatening the city with an immediate interdict if this "wretched worm" and "monstrous idol" were not forbidden to preach, and sent to demand pardon at Rome. And next to hearing Fra Girolamo himself, the most exciting Lenten occupation was to hear him argued against the villified. This excitement was to be had in Santa Croce, where the Franciscan appointed to preach the Quaresimal sermons had offered to clench his arguments by walking through the fire with Fra Girolamo. Had not that schismatical Dominican said that his prophetic doctrine would be proved by a miracle at the fitting time? Here, then, was the fitting time. Let Savonarola walk through the fire, and if he came out unhurt, the Divine origin of his doctrine would be demonstrated; but if the fire consumed him, his falsity would be manifest; and that he might have no excuse for evading the test, the Franciscan declared himself willing to be a victim to this high logic, and to be burned for the sake of securing the necessary minor premise.

Savonarola, according to his habit, had taken no notice of these pulpit attacks. But it happened that the zealous preacher of Santa Croce was no other than the Fra Francesco di Puglia, who at Prato the year before had been engaged in a like challenge with Savonarola's fervent follower Fra Domenico, but had been called home by his superiors while the heat was simply oratorical. Honest Fra Domenico, then, who was preaching Lenten sermons to the women in the Via del Cocomero, no sooner heard of this new challenge than he took up the gauntlet for his master, and declared himself ready to walk through the fire with Fra Francesco. Already the people were beginning to take a strong interest in what seemed to them a short and easy method of argument (for those who were to be convinced), when Savonarola, keenly alive to the dangers that lay in the mere discussion of the case, commanded Fra Domenico to withdraw his acceptance of the challenge and secede from the affair. The Franciscan declared himself content; he had not directed his challenge to any subaltern, but to Fra Girolamo himself.

After that, the popular interest in the Lenten sermons had flagged a little. But this morning, when Tito entered the Piazza di Santa Croce, he found, as he expected, that the people were pouring from the church in large numbers. Instead of dispersing, many of them concentrated themselves towards a particular spot near the entrance of the Franciscan monastery, and Tito took the same direction, threading the crowd with a careless and leisurely air, but keeping careful watch on that monastic entrance, as if he expected some object of interest to issue from it.

It was no such expectation that occupied the crowd. The object they were caring about was already visible to them in the shape of a large placard, affixed by order of the Signoria, and covered with very legible official handwriting. But curiosity was somewhat balked by the fact that the manuscript was chiefly in Latin, and though nearly every man knew beforehand approximately what the placard contained, he had an appetite for more exact knowledge, which gave him an irritating sense of his neighbour's ignorance in not being able to interpret the learned tongue. For that aural acquaintance with Latin phrases which the unlearned might pick up from pulpit quotations constantly interpreted by the preacher could help them little when they saw written Latin; the spelling even of the modern language being in an unorganized and scrambling condition for the mass of people who could read and write, while the majority of those assembled nearest to the placard were not in the dangerous predicament of possessing that little knowledge.

"It's the Frate's doctrines that he's to prove by being burned," said that large public character Goro, who happened to be among the foremost gazers. "The Signoria has taken it in hand, and the writing is to let us know. It's what the Padre has been telling us about in his sermon."

"Nay, Goro," said a sleek shopkeeper, compassionately, "thou hast got thy legs into twisted hose there. The Frate has to prove his doctrines by *not* being burned: he is to walk through the fire, and come out on the other side sound and whole."

"Yes, yes," said a young sculptor, who wore his white-streaked cap and tunic with a jaunty air. "But Fra Girolamo objects to walking through the fire. Being sound and whole already, he sees no reason why he should walk through the fire to come out in just the same condition. He leaves such odds and ends of work to Fra Domenico."

"Then I say he flinches like a coward," said Goro, in a wheezy treble. "Suffocation! that was what he did at the Carnival. He had us all in the piazza to see the lightning strike him, and nothing came of it."

"Stop that bleating," said a tall shoemaker, who had stepped in to hear part of the sermon, with bunches of slippers hanging over his shoulders. "It seems to me, friend, that you are about as wise as a calf with water on its brain. The Frate will flinch from nothing: he'll say nothing beforehand, perhaps, but when the moment comes he'll walk through the fire without asking any grey-frock to keep him company. But I would give a shoestring to know what this Latin all is."

"There's so much of it," said the shopkeeper, "else I'm pretty good at guessing. Is there no scholar to be seen?" he added, with a slight expression of disgust.

There was a general turning of heads, which caused the talkers to descry Tito approaching in their rear.

"Here is one," said the young sculptor, smiling and raising his cap.

"It is the secretary of the Ten: he is going to the convent, doubtless; make way for him," said the shopkeeper, also doffing, though that mark of respect was rarely shown by Florentines except to the highest officials. The exceptional reverence was really exacted by the splendour and grace of Tito's appearance, which made his black mantle, with its gold fibula, look like a regal robe, and his ordinary black velvet cap like an entirely exceptional head-dress. The hardening of his cheeks and mouth, which was the chief change in his face since he came to Florence, seemed to a superficial glance only to give his beauty a more masculine character. He raised his own cap immediately, and said,—

"Thanks, my friend, I merely wished, as you did, to see what is at the foot of this placard,—ah, it is as I expected. I had been informed that the government permits any one who will, to subscribe his name as a candidate to enter the fire,—which is an act of liberality worthy of the magnificent Signoria,—reserving of course the right to make a selection. And doubtless many believers will be eager to subscribe their names. For what is it to enter the fire, to one whose faith is firm? A man is afraid of the fire, because he believes it will burn him; but if he believes the contrary?"—here Tito lifted his shoulders and made an oratorical pause,—"for which reason I have never been one to disbelieve the Frate, when he has said that he would enter the fire to prove his doctrine. For in his place, if you believed the fire would not burn you, which of you, my friends, would not enter it as readily as you would walk along the dry bed of the Mugnone?"

As Tito looked round him during this appeal, there was a change in some of his audience very much like the change in an eager dog when he is invited to smell something pungent. Since the question of burning was becoming practical, it was not every one who would rashly commit himself to any general view of the relation between faith and fire. The scene might have been too much for a gravity less under command than Tito's.

"Then, Messer Segretario," said the young sculptor, "it seems to me Fra Francesco is the greater hero, for he offers to enter the fire for the truth, though he is sure the fire will burn him."

"I do not deny it," said Tito, blandly. "But if it turns out that Fra Francesco is mistaken, he will have been burned for the wrong side, and the Church has never reckoned such victims to be martyrs. We must suspend our judgment until the trial has really taken place."

"It is true, Messer Segretario," said the shopkeeper, with subdued impatience. "But will you favour us by interpreting the Latin?"

"Assuredly," said Tito. "It does but express the conclusions or doctrines which the Frate specially teaches, and which the trial by fire is to prove true or false. They are doubtless familiar to you. First, that Florence—"

"Let us have the Latin bit by bit, and then tell us what it means," said the shoemaker, who had been a frequent hearer of Fra Girolamo.

"Willingly," said Tito, smiling. "You will then judge if I give you the right meaning."

"Yes, yes; that's fair," said Goro.

"*Ecclesia Dei indiget renovatione;* that is, the Church of God needs purifying or regenerating."

"It is true," said several voices at once.

"That means, the priests ought to lead better lives; there needs no miracle to prove that. That's what the Frate has always been saying," said the shoemaker.

"*Flagellabitur,*" Tito went on. "That is, it will be scourged. *Renovabitur:* it will be purified. *Florentia quoque post flagellam renovabitur et prosperabitur:* Florence also, after the scourging, shall be purified and shall prosper."

"That means we are to get Pisa again," said the shopkeeper.

"And get the wool from England as we used to do, I should hope," said an elderly man, in an old-fashioned berretta, who had been silent till now. "There's been scourging enough with the sinking of the trade."

At this moment a tall personage, surmounted by a red feather, issued from the door of the convent, and exchanged an indifferent glance with Tito; who, tossing his becchetto carelessly over his left shoulder, turned to his reading again, while the bystanders, with more timidity than respect, shrank to make a passage for Messer Dolfo Spini.

"*Infideles convertentur ad Christum,*" Tito went on. "That is, the infidels shall be converted to Christ."

"Those are the Turks and the Moors. Well, I've nothing to say against that," said the shopkeeper, dispassionately.

"*Hæc autem omnia erunt temporibus nostris:* and all these things shall happen in our times."

"Why, what use would they be else?" said Goro.

"*Excommunicatio nuper lata contra Reverendum Patrem nostrum Fratrem Hieronymum nulla est:* the excommunication lately pronounced against our reverend father, Fra Girolamo, is null. *Non observantes eam non peccant:* those who disregard it are not committing a sin."

"I shall know better what to say to that when we have had the Trial by Fire," said the shopkeeper.

"Which doubtless will clear up everything," said Tito. "That is all the Latin,—all the conclusions that are to be proved true or false by the trial. The rest you can perceive is simply a proclamation of the Signoria in good Tuscan, calling on such as are eager to walk through the fire, to come to the Palazzo and subscribe their names. Can I serve you further? If not—"

Tito, as he turned away, raised his cap and bent slightly, with so easy an air that the movement seemed a natural prompting of deference.

He quickened his pace as he left the piazza, and after two or three turnings he paused in a quiet street before a door at which he gave a light and peculiar knock. It was opened by a young woman whom he chucked under the chin as he asked her if the Padrone was within; and he then passed, without further ceremony, through another door which stood ajar on his right hand. It admitted him into a handsome but untidy room, where Dolfo Spini sat playing with a fine stag-hound which alternately snuffed at a basket of pups and licked his hands with that affectionate disregard of her master's morals sometimes held to be one of the most agreeable attributes of her sex. He just looked up as Tito entered, but continued his play, simply from that disposition to persistence in some irrelevant action, by which slow-witted sensual people seem to be continually counteracting their own purposes. Tito was patient.

"A handsome *bracca* that," he said quietly, standing with his thumbs in his belt. Presently he added, in that cool liquid tone which seemed mild, but compelled attention: "When you have finished such caresses as cannot possibly be deferred, my Dolfo, we will talk of business, if you please. My time, which I could wish to be eternity at your service, is not entirely my own this morning."

"Down, Mischief, down!" said Spini, with sudden roughness. "Malediction!" he added, still more gruffly, pushing the dog aside; then, starting from his seat, he stood close to Tito, and put a hand on his shoulder as he spoke.

"I hope your sharp wits see all the ins and outs of this business, my fine necromancer, for it seems to me no clearer than the bottom of a sack."

"What is your difficulty, my cavalier?"

"These accursed Frati Minori at Santa Croce. They are drawing back now. Fra Francesco himself seems afraid of sticking to his challenge; talks of the Prophet being likely to use magic to get up a false miracle, —thinks he himself might be dragged into the fire and burned, and the Prophet might come out whole by magic, and the Church be none the better. And then, after all our talking, there's not so much as a blessed lay brother who will offer himself to pair with that pious sheep Fra Domenico."

"It is the peculiar stupidity of the tonsured skull that prevents them from seeing of how little consequence it is whether they are burned or not," said Tito. "Have you sworn well to them that they shall be in no danger of entering the fire?"

"No," said Spini, looking puzzled; "because one of them will be obliged to go in with Fra Domenico, who thinks it a thousand years till the fagots are ready."

"Not at all. Fra Domenico himself is not likely to go in. I have told you before, my Dolfo, only your powerful mind is not to be impressed without more repetition than suffices for the vulgar,—I have told you that now you have got the Signoria to take up this affair and prevent it from being hushed up by Fra Girolamo, nothing is necessary but that on a given day the fuel should be prepared in the piazza, and the people got together with the expectation of seeing something prodigious. If, after that, the Prophet quits the piazza without any appearance of a miracle on his side, he is ruined with the people: they will be ready to pelt him out of the city, the Signoria will find it easy to banish him from the territory, and his Holiness may do as he likes with him. Therefore, my Alicibiades, swear to the Franciscans that their grey frocks shall not come within singeing distance of the fire."

Spini rubbed the back of his head with one hand, and tapped his sword against his leg with the other, to stimulate his power of seeing these intangible combinations.

"But," he said presently, looking up again, "unless we fall on him in the piazza, when the people are in a rage, and make an end of him and his lies then and there, Valori and the Salviati and the Albizzi will take up arms and raise a fight for him. I know that was talked of when there was the hubbub on Ascension Sunday. And the people may turn round again: there may be a story raised of the French king coming again, or some other cursed chance in the hypocrite's favour. The city will never be safe till he's out of it."

"He *will* be out of it before long, without your giving yourself any further trouble than this little comedy of the Trial by Fire. The wine and the sun will make vinegar without any shouting to help them, as your Florentine sages would say. You will have the satisfaction of delivering your city from an incubus by an able stratagem, instead of risking blunders with sword-thrusts."

"But suppose he *did* get magic and the devil to help him, and walk through the fire after all?" said Spini, with a grimace intended to hide a certain shyness in trenching on this speculative ground. "How do you know there's nothing in those things? Plenty of scholars believe in them, and this Frate is bad enough for anything."

"Oh, of course there are such things," said Tito, with a shrug: "but I have particular reasons for knowing that the Frate is not on such terms with the devil as can give him any confidence in this affair. The only magic he relies on is his own ability."

"Ability!" said Spini. "Do you call it ability to be setting Florence at loggerheads with the Pope and all the powers of Italy,—all to keep beckoning at the French king who never comes? You may call him able, but I call him a hypocrite, who wants to be master of everybody, and get himself made Pope."

"You judge with your usual penetration, my captain, but our opinions do not clash. The Frate, wanting to be master, and to carry out his projects against the Pope, requires the lever of a foreign power, and requires Florence as a fulcrum. I used to think him a narrow-minded bigot; but now I think him a shrewd ambitious man who knows what he is aiming at, and directs his aim as skilfully as you direct a ball when you are playing at *maglio*."

"Yes, yes," said Spini, cordially, "I can aim a ball."

"It is true," said Tito, with bland gravity; "and I should not have troubled you with my trivial remark on the Frate's ability, but that you may see how this will heighten the credit of your success against him at Rome and at Milan, which is sure to serve you in good stead when the city comes to change its policy."

"Well, thou art a good little demon, and shalt have good pay," said Spini, patronizingly; whereupon he thought it only natural that the useful Greek adventurer should smile with gratification as he said,—

"Of course, any advantage to me depends entirely on your—"

"We shall have our supper at my palace to-night," interrupted Spini, with a significant nod and an affectionate pat on Tito's shoulder, "and I shall expound the new scheme to them all."

"Pardon, my magnificent patron," said Tito; "the scheme has been the same from the first,—it has never varied except in your memory. Are you sure you have fast hold of it now?"

Spini rehearsed.

"One thing more," he said, as Tito was hastening away. "There is that sharp-nosed notary, Ser Ceccone; he has been handy of late. Tell me, you who can see a man wink when you're behind him, do you think I may go on making use of him?"

Tito dared not say, "No." He knew his companion too well to trust him with advice when all Spini's vanity and self-interest were not engaged in concealing the adviser.

"Doubtless," he answered, promptly. "I have nothing to say against Ceccone."

That suggestion of the notary's intimate access to Spini caused Tito a passing twinge, interrupting his amused satisfaction in the success with which he made a tool of the man who fancied himself a patron. For he had been rather afraid of Ser Ceccone. Tito's nature made him peculiarly alive to circumstances that might be turned to his disadvantage; his memory was much haunted by such possibilities, stimulating him to contrivances by which he might ward them off. And it was not likely that he should forget that October morning more than a year ago, when Romola had appeared suddenly before him at the door of Nello's shop, and had compelled him to declare his certainty that Fra Girolamo was not going outside the gates. The fact that Ser Ceccone had been a witness of that scene, together with Tito's perception that for some reason or other he was an object of dislike to the notary, had received a new importance from the recent turn of events. For after having been implicated in the Medicean plots, and having found it advisable in consequence to retire into the country for some time, Ser Ceccone had of late, since his reappearance in the city, attached himself to the Arrabbiati, and cultivated the patronage of Dolfo Spini. Now that captain of the Compagnacci was much given, when in the company of intimates, to confidential narrative about his own doings; and if Ser Ceccone's powers of combination were sharpened by enmity, he might gather some knowledge which he could use against Tito with very unpleasant results.

It would be pitiable to be balked in well-conducted schemes by an insignificant notary; to be lamed by the sting of an insect whom he had offended unawares. "But," Tito said to himself, "the man's dislike to me can be nothing deeper than the ill-humour of a dinnerless dog; I shall conquer it if I can make him prosperous." And he had been very glad of an opportunity which had presented itself of providing the notary with a temporary post as an extra *cancelliere* or registering secretary under the Ten, believing that with this sop and the expectation of more, the waspish cur must be quite cured of the disposition to bite him.

But perfect scheming demands omniscience, and the notary's envy had been stimulated into hatred by causes of which Tito knew nothing. That evening when Tito, returning from his critical audience with the Special Council, had brushed by Ser Ceccone on the stairs, the notary, who had only just returned from Pistoja, and learned the arrest of the conspirators, was bound on an errand which bore a humble resemblance to Tito's. He also, without giving up a show of popular zeal, had been putting in the Medicean lottery. He also had been privy to the unexecuted plot, and was willing to tell what he knew, but knew much less to tell. He also would have been willing to go on treacherous errands, but a more eligible agent had forestalled him. His propositions were received coldly; the council, he was told, was already in possession of the needed information, and since he had been thus busy in sedition, it would be well for him to retire out of the way of mischief, otherwise the government might be obliged to take note of him. Ser Ceccone wanted no evidence to make him attribute his failure to Tito, and his spite was the more bitter because the nature of the case compelled him to hold his peace about it. Nor was this the whole of his grudge against the flourishing Melema. On issuing from his hiding-place, and attaching himself to the Arrabbiati, he had earned some pay as one of the spies who reported information on Florentine affairs to the Milanese court; but his pay had been small, notwithstanding his pains to write full letters, and he had lately been apprised that his news was seldom more than a late and imperfect edition of what was known already. Now Ser Ceccone had no positive knowledge that Tito had an underhand connection with the Arrabbiati and the Court of Milan, but he had a suspicion of which he chewed the cud with as strong a sense of flavour as if it had been a certainty.

This fine-grown vigorous hatred could swallow the feeble opiate of Tito's favours, and be as lively as ever after it. Why should Ser Ceccone like Melema any the better for doing him favours? Doubtless the suave secretary had his own ends to serve; and what right had he to the superior position which made it possible for him to show favour? But since he had turned his voice to flattery, Ser Ceccone would pitch his in the same key, and it remained to be seen who would win at the game of outwitting.

To have a mind well oiled with that sort of argument which prevents any claim from grasping it seems eminently convenient sometimes: only the oil becomes objectionable when we find it anointing other minds on which we want to establish a hold.

Tito, however, not being quite omniscient, felt now no more than a passing twinge of uneasiness at the suggestion of Ser Ceccone's power to hurt him. It was only for a little while that he cared greatly about keeping clear of suspicions and hostility. He was now playing his final game in Florence, and the skill he was conscious of applying gave him a pleasure in it even apart from the expected winnings. The errand on which he was bent to San Marco was a stroke in which he felt so much confidence that he had already given notice to the Ten of his desire to resign his office at an indefinite period within the next month or two, and had obtained permission to make that resignation suddenly, if his affairs needed it, with the understanding that Niccolò Macchiavelli was to be his provisional substitute, if not his successor. He was acting on hypothetic grounds, but this was the sort of action that had the keenest interest for his diplomatic mind. From a combination of general knowledge concerning Savonarola's purposes with diligently observed details he had framed a conjecture which he was about to verify by this visit to San Marco. If he proved to be right, his game would be won, and he might soon turn his back on Florence. He looked eagerly towards that consummation, for many circumstances besides his own weariness of the place told him that it was time to be gone.

CHAPTER XLIV

THE PROPHET IN HIS CELL

TITO's visit to San Marco had been announced beforehand, and he was at once conducted by Fra Niccolò, Savonarola's secretary, up the spiral staircase into the long corridors lined with cells,—corridors where Fra Angelico's frescoes, delicate as the rainbow on the melting cloud, startled the unaccustomed eye here and there, as if they had been sudden reflections cast from an ethereal world, where the Madonna sat crowned in her radiant glory, and the Divine infant looked forth with perpetual promise.

It was an hour of relaxation in the monastery, and most of the cells were empty. The light through the narrow windows looked in on nothing but bare walls, and the hard pallet and the crucifix. And even behind that door at the end of a long corridor, in the inner cell opening from an antechamber where the Prior usually sat at his desk or received private visitors, the high jet of light fell on only one more object that looked quite as common a monastic sight as the bare walls and hard pallet. It was but the back of a figure in the long white Dominican tunic and scapulary, kneeling with bowed head before a crucifix. It might have been any ordinary Fra Girolamo, who had nothing worse to confess than thinking of wrong things when he was singing *in coro*, or feeling a spiteful joy when Fra Benedetto dropped the ink over his own miniatures in the breviary he was illuminating,—who had no higher thought than that of climbing safely into Paradise up the narrow ladder of prayer, fasting, and obedience. But under this particular white tunic there was a heart beating with a consciousness inconceivable to the average monk, and perhaps hard to be conceived by any man who has not arrived at self-knowledge through a tumultuous inner life; a consciousness in which irrevocable errors and lapses from veracity were so entwined with noble purposes and sincere beliefs, in which self-justifying expediency was so inwoven with the tissue of a great work which the whole being seemed as unable to abandon as the body was unable to abandon glowing and trembling before the objects of hope and fear, that it was perhaps impossible, whatever course might be adopted, for the conscience to find perfect repose.

Savonarola was not only in the attitude of prayer, there were Latin words of prayer on his lips; and yet he was not praying. He had entered his cell, had fallen on his knees, and burst into words of supplication, seeking in this way for an influx of calmness which would be a warrant to him that the resolutions urged on him by crowding thoughts and passions were not wresting him away from the Divine support; but the previsions and impulses which had been at work within him for the last hour were too imperious; and while he pressed his hands against his face, and while his lips were uttering audibly, *"Cor mundum crea in me,"* his mind was still filled with the images of the snare his enemies had prepared for him, was still busy with the arguments by which he could justify himself against their taunts and accusations.

And it was not only against his opponents that Savonarola had to defend himself. This morning he had had new proof that his friends and followers were as much inclined to urge on the Trial by Fire as his enemies: desiring and tacitly expecting that he himself would at last accept the challenge and evoke the long-expected miracle which was to dissipate doubt and triumph over malignity. Had he not said that God would declare himself at the fitting time? And to the understanding of plain Florentines, eager to get party questions settled, it seemed that no time could be more fitting than this. Certainly, if Fra Domenico walked through the fire unhurt, *that* would be a miracle, and the faith and ardour of that good brother were felt to be a cheering augury; but Savonarola was acutely conscious that the secret longing of his followers to see him accept the challenge had not been dissipated by any reasons he had given for his refusal.

Yet it was impossible to him to satisfy them; and with bitter distress he saw now that it was impossible for him any longer to resist the prosecution of the trial in Fra Domenico's case. Not that Savonarola had uttered and written a falsity when he declared his belief in a future supernatural attestation of his work; but his mind was so constituted that while it was easy for him to believe in a miracle which, being distant and undefined, was screened behind the strong reasons he saw for its occurrence, and yet easier for him to have a belief in inward miracles such as his own prophetic inspiration and divinely wrought intuitions; it was at the same time insurmountably difficult to him to believe in the probability of a miracle which, like this of being carried unhurt through the fire, pressed in all its details on his imagination and involved a demand not only for belief but for exceptional action.

Savonarola's nature was one of those in which opposing tendencies co-exist in almost equal strength: the passionate sensibility which, impatient of definite thought, floods every idea with emotion and tends towards contemplative ecstasy, alternated in him with a keen perception of outward facts and a vigorous practical judgment of men and things. And in this case of the Trial by Fire, the latter characteristics were stimulated into unusual activity by an acute physical sensitiveness which gives overpowering force to the conception of pain and destruction as a necessary sequence of facts which have already been causes of pain in our experience. The promptitude with which men will consent to touch red-hot iron with a wet finger is not to be measured by their theoretic acceptance of the impossibility that the iron will burn them: practical belief depends on what is most strongly represented in the mind at a given moment. And with the Frate's constitution, when the Trial by Fire was urged on his imagination as an immediate demand, it was impossible for him to believe that he or any other man could walk through the flames unhurt,—impossible for him to believe that even if he resolved to offer himself, he would not shrink at the last moment.

But the Florentines were not likely to make these fine distinctions. To the common run of mankind it has always seemed a proof of mental vigour to find moral questions easy, and judge conduct according to concise alternatives. And nothing was likely to seem plainer than that a man who at one time declared that God would not leave him without the guarantee of a miracle, and yet drew back when it was proposed to test his declaration, had said what he did not believe. Were not Fra Domenico and Fra Mariano, and scores of Piagnoni besides, ready to enter the fire? What was the cause of their superior courage, if it was not their superior faith? Savonarola could not have explained his conduct satisfactorily to his friends, even if he had been able to explain it thoroughly to himself. And he was not. Our naked feelings make haste to clothe themselves in propositions which lie at hand among our store of opinions, and to give a true account of what passes within us something else is necessary besides sincerity, even when sincerity is unmixed. In these very moments, when Savonarola was kneeling in audible prayer, he had ceased to hear the words on his lips. They were drowned by argumentative voices with him that shaped their reasons more and more for an outward audience.

"To appeal to heaven for a miracle by a rash acceptance of a challenge, which is a mere snare prepared for me by ignoble foes, would be a tempting of God, and the appeal would not be responded to. Let the Pope's legate come, let the ambassadors of all the great Powers come and promise that the calling of a General Council and the reform of the Church shall hang on the miracle, and I will enter the flames, trusting that God will not withhold His seal from that great work. Until then I reserve myself for higher duties which are directly laid upon me: it is not permitted to me to leap from the chariot for the sake of wrestling with every loud vaunter. But Fra Domenico's invincible zeal to enter into the trial may be the sign of a Divine vocation, may be a pledge that the miracle—"

But no! when Savonarola brought his mind close to the threatened scene in the piazza, and imagined a human body entering the fire, his belief recoiled again. It was not an event that his imagination could simply see: he felt it with shuddering vibrations to the extremities of his sensitive fingers. The miracle could not be. Nay, the trial itself was not to happen: he was warranted in doing all in his power to hinder it. The fuel might be got ready in the piazza, the people might be assembled, the preparatory formalities might be gone through: all this was perhaps inevitable now, and he could no longer resist it without bringing dishonour on—himself? Yes, and therefore on the cause of God. But it was not really intended that the Franciscan should enter the fire, and while *he* hung back there would be the means of preventing Fra Domenico's entrance. At the very worst, if Fra Domenico were compelled to enter, he should carry the consecrated Host with him, and with that Mystery in his hand, there might be a warrant for expecting that the ordinary effects of fire would be stayed; or, more probably, this demand would be resisted, and might thus be a final obstacle to the trial.

But these intentions could not be avowed: he must appear frankly to await the trial, and to trust in its issue. That dissidence between inward reality and outward seeming was not the Christian simplicity after which he had striven through years of his youth and prime, and which he had preached as a chief fruit of the Divine life. In the stress and heat of the day, with cheeks burning, with shouts ringing in the ears, who is so blest as to remember the yearnings he had in the cool and silent morning and know that he has not belied them?

"O God, it is for the sake of the people,—because they are blind,—because their faith depends on me. If I put on sackcloth and cast myself among the ashes, who will take up the standard and head the battle? Have I not been led by a way which I knew not to the work that lies before me?"

The conflict was one that could not end, and in the effort at prayerful pleading the uneasy mind laved its smart continually in thoughts of the greatness of that task which there was no man else to fulfil if he forsook it. It was not a thing of every day that a man should be inspired with the vision and the daring that made a sacred rebel.

Even the words of prayer had died away. He continued to kneel, but his mind was filled with the images of results to be felt through all Europe; and the sense of immediate difficulties was being lost in the glow of that vision, when the knocking at the door announced the expected visit.

Savonarola drew on his mantle before he left his cell, as was his custom when he received visitors; and with that immediate response to any appeal from without which belongs to a power-loving nature accustomed to make its power felt by speech, he met Tito with a glance as self-possessed and strong as if he had risen from resolution instead of conflict.

Tito did not kneel, but simply made a greeting of profound deference, which Savonarola received quietly without any sacerdotal words, and then desiring him to be seated, said at once,—

"Your business is something of weight, my son, that could not be conveyed through others?"

"Assuredly, father, else I should not have presumed to ask it. I will not trespass on your time by any proem. I gathered from a remark of Messer Domenico Mazzinghi that you might be glad to make use of the next special courier who is sent to France with despatches from the Ten. I must entreat you to pardon me if I have been too officious; but inasmuch as Messer Domenico is at this moment away at his villa, I wished to apprise you that a courier carrying important letters is about to depart for Lyons at daybreak to-morrow."

The muscles of Fra Girolamo's face were eminently under command, as must be the case with all men whose personality is powerful, and in deliberate speech he was habitually cautious, confiding his intentions to none without necessity. But under any strong mental stimulus, his eyes were liable to a dilatation and added brilliancy that no strength of will could control. He looked steadily at Tito, and did not answer immediately, as if he had to consider whether the information he had just heard met any purpose of his.

Tito, whose glance never seemed observant, but rarely let anything escape it, had expected precisely that dilatation and flash of Savonarola's eyes which he had noted on other occasions. He saw it, and then immediately busied himself in adjusting his gold fibula, which had got wrong; seeming to imply that he awaited an answer patiently.

The fact was that Savonarola had expected to receive this intimation from Domenico Mazzinghi, one of the Ten, an ardent disciple of his whom he had already employed to write a private letter to the Florentine ambassador in France, to prepare the way for a letter to the French king himself in Savonarola's handwriting, which now lay ready in the desk at his side. It was a letter calling on the king to assist in summoning a General Council, that might reform the abuses of the Church, and begin by deposing Pope Alexander, who was not rightfully Pope, being a vicious unbeliever, elected by corruption and governing by simony.

This fact was not what Tito knew, but what his constructive talent, guided by subtle indications, had led him to guess and hope.

"It is true, my son," said Savonarola, quietly,—"it is true I have letters which I would gladly send by safe conveyance under cover to our ambassador. Our community of San Marco, as you know, has affairs in France, being, among other things, responsible for a debt to that singularly wise and experienced Frenchman, Signor Philippe de Comines, on the library of the Medici, which we purchased; but I apprehend that Domenico Mazzinghi himself may return to the city before evening, and I should gain more time for preparation of the letters if I waited to deposit them in his hands."

"Assuredly, reverend father, that might be better on all grounds, except one, namely, that if anything occurred to hinder Messer Domenico's return, the despatch of the letters would require either that I should come to San Marco again at a late hour, or that you should send them to me by your secretary; and I am aware that you wish to guard against the false inferences which might be drawn from a too frequent communication between yourself and any officer of the government." In throwing out this difficulty Tito felt that the more unwillingness the Frate showed to trust him, the more certain he would be of his conjecture.

Savonarola was silent; but while he kept his mouth firm, a slight glow rose in his face with the suppressed excitement that was growing within him. It would be a critical moment,—that in which he delivered the letter out of his own hands.

"It is most probable that Messer Domenico will return in time," said Tito, affecting to consider the Frate's determination settled, and rising from his chair as he spoke. "With your permission, I will take my leave, father, not to trespass on your time when my errand is done; but as I may not be favoured with another interview, I venture to confide to you—what is not yet known to others, except to the magnificent Ten —that I contemplate resigning my secretaryship, and leaving Florence

shortly. Am I presuming too much on your interest in stating what re-
lates chiefly to myself?"

"Speak on, my son," said the Frate; "I desire to know your prospects."

"I find, then, that I have mistaken my real vocation in forsaking the
career of pure letters, for which I was brought up. The politics of Florence, father, are worthy to occupy the greatest mind—to occupy yours
—when a man is in a position to execute his own ideas; but when, like
me, he can only hope to be the mere instrument of changing schemes, he
requires to be animated by the minor attachments of a born Florentine:
also, my wife's unhappy alienation from a Florentine residence since the
painful events of August naturally influences me. I wish to join her."

Savonarola inclined his head approvingly.

"I intend, then, soon to leave Florence, to visit the chief courts of
Europe, and to widen my acquaintance with the men of letters in the
various universities. I shall go first to the court of Hungary, where
scholars are eminently welcome; and I shall probably start in a week
or ten days. I have not concealed from you, father, that I am no religious enthusiast; I have not my wife's ardour; but religious enthusiasm, as I conceive, is not necessary in order to appreciate the
grandeur and justice of your views concerning the government of nations
and the Church. And if you condescend to intrust me with any commission that will further the relations you wish to establish, I shall feel
honoured. May I now take my leave?"

"Stay, my son. When you depart from Florence I will send a letter
to your wife, of whose spiritual welfare I would fain be assured, for
she left me in anger. As for the letters to France, such as I have ready—"

Savonarola rose and turned to his desk as he spoke. He took from it
a letter on which Tito could see, but not read, an address in the Frate's
own minute and exquisite handwriting, still to be seen covering the
margins of his Bibles. He took a large sheet of paper, enclosed the
letter, and sealed it.

"Pardon me, father," said Tito, before Savonarola had time to speak,
"unless it were your decided wish, I would rather not incur the responsibility of carrying away the letter. Messer Domenico Mazzinghi will
doubtless return, or, if not, Fra Niccolò can convey it to me at the
second hour of the evening, when I shall place the other despatches in
the courier's hands."

"At present, my son," said the Frate, waiving that point, "I wish you
to address this packet to our ambassador in your own handwriting,
which is preferable to my secretary's."

Tito sat down to write the address, while the Frate stood by him with
folded arms, the glow mounting in his cheek, and his lip at last quivering. Tito rose and was about to move away, when Savonarola said
abruptly: "Take it, my son. There is no use in waiting. It does not
please me that Fra Niccolò should have needless errands to the Palazzo."

As Tito took the letter, Savonarola stood in suppressed excitement that forbade further speech. There seems to be a subtle emanation from passionate natures like his, making their mental states tell immediately on others; when they are absentminded and inwardly excited, there is silence in the air.

Tito made a deep reverence, and went out with the letter under his mantle.

The letter was duly delivered to the courier and carried out of Florence. But before that happened another messenger, privately employed by Tito, had conveyed information in cipher, which was carried by a series of relays to armed agents of Ludovico Sforza, Duke of Milan, on the watch for the very purpose of intercepting despatches on the borders of the Milanese territory.

CHAPTER XLV

THE TRIAL BY FIRE

LITTLE more than a week after, on the 7th of April, the great Piazza della Signoria presented a stranger spectacle even than the famous Bonfire of Vanities; and a greater multitude had assembled to see it than had ever before tried to find place for themselves in the wide piazza, even on the day of San Giovanni.

It was near midday, and since the early morning there had been a gradual swarming of the people at every coign of vantage or disadvantage offered by the façades and roofs of the houses, and such spaces of the pavement as were free to the public. Men were seated on iron rods that made a sharp angle with the rising wall, were clutching slim pillars with arms and legs, were astride on the necks of the rough statuary that here and there surmounted the entrances of the grander houses, were finding a palm's-breadth of seat on a bit of architrave, and a footing on the rough projections of the rustic stonework, while they clutched the strong iron rings or staples driven into the walls beside them.

For they were come to see a Miracle: cramped limbs and abraded flesh seemed slight inconveniences with that prospect close at hand. It is the ordinary lot of mankind to hear of miracles, and more or less to believe in them; but now the Florentines were going to see one. At the very least they would see half a miracle; for if the monk did not come whole out of the fire, they would see him enter it, and infer that he was burned in the middle.

There could be no reasonable doubt, it seemed, that the fire would be kindled, and that the monks would enter it. For there, before their eyes, was the long platform, eight feet broad, and twenty yards long, with a grove of fuel heaped up terribly, great branches of dry oak as a foundation, crackling thorns above, and well-anointed tow and rags, known to make fine flames in Florentine illuminations. The platform began at the corner of the marble terrace in front of the Old Palace, close to Marzocco, the stone lion, whose aged visage looked frowningly along the grove of fuel that stretched obliquely across the piazza.

Besides that, there were three large bodies of armed men: five hundred hired soldiers of the Signoria stationed before the palace; five hundred Compagnacci under Dolfo Spini, far off on the opposite side of the piazza; and three hundred armed citizens of another sort, under Marco Salviati, Savonarola's friend, in front of Orgagna's Loggia, where the Franciscans and Dominicans were to be placed with their champions.

Here had been much expense of money and labour, and high dignities were concerned. There could be no reasonable doubt that something great was about to happen; and it would certainly be a great thing if the two monks were simply burned, for in that case too God would have spoken, and said very plainly that Fra Girolamo was not His prophet.

And there was not much longer to wait, for it was now near midday. Half the monks were already at their post, and that half of the Loggia that lies towards the Palace was already filled with gray mantles; but the other half, divided off by boards, was still empty of everything except a small altar. The Franciscans had entered and taken their places in silence. But now, at the other side of the piazza was heard loud chanting from two hundred voices, and there was general satisfaction, if not in the chanting, at least in the evidence that the Dominicans were come. That loud chanting repetition of the prayer, "Let God arise, and let His enemies be scattered," was unpleasantly suggestive to some impartial ears of a desire to vaunt confidence and excite dismay; and so was the flame-coloured velvet cope in which Fra Domenico was arrayed as he headed the procession, cross in hand, his simple mind really exalted with faith, and with the genuine intention to enter the flames for the glory of God and Fra Girolamo. Behind him came Savonarola in the white vestment of a priest, carrying in his hands a vessel containing the consecrated Host. He, too, was chanting loudly; he, too, looked firm and confident, and as all eyes were turned eagerly on him, either in anxiety, curiosity, or malignity, from the moment when he entered the piazza till he mounted the steps of the Loggia and deposited the Sacrament on the altar, there was an intensifying flash and energy in his countenance responding to that scrutiny.

We are so made, almost all of us, that the false seeming which we have thought of with painful shrinking when beforehand in our solitude it has urged itself on us as a necessity, will possess our muscles and move our lips as if nothing but that were easy when once we have come under the stimulus of expectant eyes and ears. And the strength of that stimulus to Savonarola can hardly be measured by the experience of ordinary lives. Perhaps no man has ever had a mighty influence over his fellows without having the innate need to dominate, and this need usually becomes the more imperious in proportion as the complications of life make Self inseparable from a purpose which is not selfish. In this way it came to pass that on the day of the Trial by Fire, the doubleness which is the pressing temptation in every public career, whether of priest, orator, or statesman, was more strongly defined in Savonarola's consciousness as the acting of a part, than at any other period in his life. He was struggling not against impending martyrdom, but against impending ruin.

Therefore he looked and acted as if he were thoroughly confident, when all the while foreboding was pressing with leaden weight on his heart, not only because of the probable issues of this trial, but because of another event already past,—an event which was spreading a sunny satisfaction through the mind of a man who was looking down at the passion-worn prophet from a window of the Old Palace. It was a common turning-point towards which those widely sundered lives had been converging, that two evenings ago the news had come that the Florentine courier of the Ten had been arrested and robbed of all his despatches, so that Savonarola's letter was already in the hands of the Duke of Milan, and would soon be in the hands of the Pope, not only heightening rage, but giving a new justification to extreme measures. There was no malignity in Tito Melema's satisfaction: it was the mild self-gratulation of a man who has won a game that has employed hypothetic skill, not a game that has stirred the muscles and heated the blood. Of course that bundle of desires and contrivances called human nature, when moulded into the form of a plain-feature Frate Predicatore, more or less of an impostor, could not be a pathetic object to a brilliant-minded scholar who understood everything. Yet this tonsured Girolamo with the high nose and large under-lip was an immensely clever Frate, mixing with his absurd superstitions or fabrications very remarkable notions about government; no babbler, but a man who could keep his secrets. Tito had no more spite against him than against Saint Dominic. On the contrary, Fra Girolamo's existence had been highly convenient to Tito Melema, furnishing him with that round of the ladder from which he was about to leap on to a new and smooth footing very much to his heart's content. And everything now was in forward preparation for that leap; let one more sun rise and set, and Tito hoped to quit Florence. He had been so industrious that he felt at full leisure to amuse himself with to-day's comedy, which the thick-headed Dolfo Spini could never have brought about for him.

Not yet did the loud chanting cease, but rather swelled to a deafening roar, being taken up in all parts of the piazza by the Piagnoni, who carried their little red crosses as a badge, and, most of them, chanted the prayer for the confusion of God's enemies with the expectation of an answer to be given through the medium of a more signal personage than Fra Domenico. This good Frate in his flame-coloured cope was now kneeling before the little altar on which the Sacrament was deposited, awaiting his summons.

On the Franciscan side of the Loggia there was no chanting and no flame-colour; only silence and greyness. But there was this counter-balancing difference, that the Franciscans had two champions: a certain Fra Giuliano was to pair with Fra Domenico, while the original champion, Fra Francesco, confided his challenge to Savonarola.

"Surely," thought the men perched uneasily on the rods and pillars, "all must be ready now. This chanting might stop, and we should see better when the Frati are moving towards the platform."

But the Frati were not to be seen moving yet. Pale Franciscan faces were looking uneasily over the boarding at that flame-coloured cope. It had an evil look and might be enchanted, so that a false miracle would be wrought by magic. Your monk may come whole out of the fire, and yet it may be the work of the devil.

And now there was passing to and fro between the Loggia and the marble terrace of the Palazzo, and the roar of chanting became a little quieter, for every one at a distance was beginning to watch more eagerly. But it soon appeared that the new movement was not a be-ginning, but an obstacle to beginning. The dignified Florentines ap-pointed to preside over this affair as moderators on each side, went in and out of the Palace, and there was much debate with the Franciscans. But at last it was clear that Fra Domenico, conspicuous in his flame-colour, was being fetched towards the Palace. Probably the fire had already been kindled,—it was difficult to see at a distance,—and the miracle was going to begin.

Not at all. The flame-coloured cope disappeared within the Palace; then another Dominican was fetched away; and for a long while every-thing went on as before,—the tiresome chanting, which was not miracu-lous, and Fra Girolamo in his white vestment standing just in the same place. But at last something happened: Fra Domenico was seen com-ing out of the Palace again, and returning to his brethren. He had changed all his clothes with a brother monk, but he was guarded on each flank by a Franciscan, lest coming into the vicinity of Savonarola he should be enchanted again.

"Ah, then," thought the distant spectators, a little less conscious of cramped limbs and hunger, "Fra Domenico is not going to enter the fire. It is Fra Girolamo who offers himself, after all. We shall see him move presently, and if he comes out of the flames we shall have a fine view of him!"

But Fra Girolamo did not move, except with the ordinary action accompanying speech. The speech was bold and firm, perhaps some-what ironically remonstrant, like that of Elijah to the priests of Baal, demanding the cessation of these trivial delays. But speech is the most irritating kind of argument for those who are out of hearing, cramped in the limbs, and empty in the stomach. And what need was there for speech? If the miracle did not begin, it could be no one's fault but Fra Girolamo's, who might put an end to all difficulties by offering himself now the fire was ready, as he had been forward enough to do when there was no fuel in sight.

More movement to and fro, more discussion; and the afternoon seemed to be slipping away all the faster because the clouds had gathered, and changed the light on everything, and sent a chill through the spectators, hungry in mind and body.

Now it was the crucifix which Fra Domenico wanted to carry into the fire and must not be allowed to profane in that manner. After some little resistance Savonarola gave way to this objection, and thus had the advantage of making one more concession; but he immediately placed in Fra Domenico's hands the vessel containing the consecrated Host. The idea that the presence of the sacred Mystery might in the worst extremity avert the ordinary effects of fire hovered in his mind as a possibility; but the issue on which he counted was of a more positive kind. In taking up the Host he said quietly, as if he were only doing what had been presupposed from the first,—

"Since they are not willing that you should enter with the crucifix, my brother, enter simply with the Sacrament."

New horror in the Franciscans; new firmness in Savonarola. "It was impious presumption to carry the Sacrament into the fire: if it were burned the scandal would be great in the minds of the weak and ignorant." "Not at all: even if it were burned, the Accidents only would be consumed, the Substance would remain." Here was a question that might be argued till set of sun and remain as elastic as ever; and no one could propose settling it by proceeding to the trial, since it was essentially a preliminary question. It was only necessary that both sides should remain firm,—that the Franciscans should persist in not permitting the Host to be carried into the fire, and that Fra Domenico should persist in refusing to enter without it.

Meanwhile the clouds were getting darker, the air chiller. Even the chanting was missed now it had given way to inaudible argument; and the confused sounds of talk from all points of the piazza, showing that expectation was everywhere relaxing, contributed to the irritating presentiment that nothing decisive would be done. Here and there a dropping shout was heard; then, more frequent shouts in a rising scale of scorn.

"Light the fire and drive them in!" "Let us have a smell of roast,— we want our dinner!" "Come, Prophet, let us know whether anything is to happen before the twenty-four hours are over!" "Yes, yes, what's your last vision?" "Oh, he's got a dozen in his inside; they're the small change for a miracle!" "Olà, Frate, where are you? Never mind wasting the fuel!"

Still the same movement to and fro between the Loggia and the Palace; still the same debate, slow and unintelligible to the multitude as the colloquies of insects that touch antennæ to no other apparent effect than that of going and coming. But an interpretation was not long wanting to unheard debates in which Fra Girolamo was constantly a speaker: it was he who was hindering the trial; everybody was appealing to him now, and he was hanging back.

Soon the shouts ceased to be distinguishable, and were lost in an uproar not simply of voices, but of clashing metal and trampling feet. The suggestions of the irritated people had stimulated old impulses in Dolfo Spini and his band of Compagnacci; it seemed an opportunity not to be lost for putting an end to Florentine difficulties by getting possession of the arch-hypocrite's person; and there was a vigorous rush of the armed men towards the Loggia, thrusting the people aside, or driving them on to the file of soldiery stationed in front of the Palace. At this movement everything was suspended, both with monks and embarrassed magistrates, except the palpitating watch to see what would come of the struggle.

But the Loggia was well guarded by the band under the brave Salviati; the soldiers of the Signoria assisted in the repulse; and the trampling and rushing were all backward again towards the Tetto de' Pisani, when the blackness of the heavens seemed to intensify in this moment of utter confusion; and the rain, which had already been felt in scattered drops, began to fall with rapidly growing violence, wetting the fuel, and running in streams off the platform, wetting the weary hungry people to the skin, and driving every man's disgust and rage inwards to ferment there in the damp darkness.

Everybody knew now that the Trial by Fire was not to happen. The Signoria was doubtless glad of the rain, as an obvious reason, better than any pretext, for declaring that both parties might go home. It was the issue which Savonarola had expected and desired; yet it would be an ill description of what he felt to say that he was glad. As that rain fell, and plashed on the edge of the Loggia, and sent spray over the altar and all garments and faces, the Frate knew that the demand for him to enter the fire was at an end. But he knew, too, with a certainty as irresistible as the damp chill that had taken possession of his frame, that the design of his enemies was fulfilled, and that his honour was not saved. He knew that he should have to make his way to San Marco again through the enraged crowd, and that the hearts of many friends who would once have defended him with their lives would now be turned against him.

When the rain had ceased, he asked for a guard from the Signoria, and it was given him. Had he said that he was willing to die for the work of his life? Yes, and he had not spoken falsely. But to die in dishonour,—held up to scorn as a hypocrite and a false prophet? "O God! *that* is not martyrdom! It is the blotting out of a life that has been a protest against wrong. Let me die because of the worth that is in me, not because of my weakness."

The rain had ceased, and the light from the breaking clouds fell on Savonarola as he left the Loggia in the midst of his guard, walking as he

had come, with the Sacrament in his hand. But there seemed no glory in
the light that fell on him now, no smile of heaven: it was only that light
which shines on, patiently and impartially, justifying or condemning
by simply showing all things in the slow history of their ripening. He
heard no blessing, no tones of pity, but only taunts and threats. He
knew this was a foretaste of coming bitterness; yet his courage mounted
under all moral attack, and he showed no sign of dismay.

"Well parried, Frate!" said Tito, as Savonarola descended the steps
of the Loggia. "But I fear your career at Florence is ended. What say
you, my Niccolò?"

"It is a pity his falsehoods were not all of a wise sort," said Macchiavelli, with a melancholy shrug. "With the times so much on his side as
they are about Church affairs, he might have done something great."

CHAPTER XLVI

A MASQUE OF THE FURIES

THE next day was Palm Sunday, or Olive Sunday, as it was chiefly
called in the olive-growing Valdarno; and the morning sun shone with
a more delicious clearness for the yesterday's rain. Once more Savonarola mounted the pulpit in San Marco, and saw a flock around him
whose faith in him was still unshaken; and this morning in calm and
sad sincerity he declared himself ready to die: in front of all visions he
saw his own doom. Once more he uttered the benediction, and saw the
faces of men and women lifted towards him in venerating love. Then he
descended the steps of the pulpit and turned away from that sight
forever.

For before the sun had set Florence was in an uproar. The passions
which had been roused the day before had been smouldering through
that quiet morning, and had now burst out again with a fury not unassisted by design, and not without official connivance. The uproar had
begun at the Duomo in an attempt of some Compagnacci to hinder the
evening sermon, which the Piagnoni had assembled to hear. But no
sooner had men's blood mounted and the disturbances had become an
affray than the cry arose, "To San Marco! the fire to San Marco!"

And long before the daylight had died, both the church and convent
were being besieged by an enraged and continually increasing multitude.
Not without resistance. For the monks, long conscious of growing hostility without, had arms within their walls, and some of them fought as
vigorously in their long white tunics as if they had been Knights
Templars. Even the command of Savonarola could not prevail against
the impulse to self-defence in arms that were still muscular under the
Dominican serge. There were laymen too who had not chosen to depart,
and some of them fought fiercely; there was firing from the high altar
close by the great crucifix, there was pouring of stones and hot embers

from the convent roof, there was close fighting with swords in the cloisters. Notwithstanding the force of the assailants, the attack lasted till deep night.

The demonstrations of the government had all been against the convent; early in the attack guards had been sent for, not to disperse the assailants, but to command all within the convent to lay down their arms, all laymen to depart from it, and Savonarola himself to quit the Florentine territory within twelve hours. Had Savonarola quitted the convent then, he could hardly have escaped being torn to pieces; he was willing to go, but his friends hindered him. It was felt to be a great risk even for some laymen of high name to depart by the garden wall; but among those who had chosen to do so was Francesco Valori, who hoped to raise rescue from without.

And now when it was deep night—when the struggle could hardly have lasted much longer, and the Compagnacci might soon have carried their swords into the library, where Savonarola was praying with the Brethren who had either not taken up arms or had laid them down at his command—there came a second body of guards, commissioned by the Signoria to demand the persons of Fra Girolamo and his two coadjutors, Fra Domenico and Fra Salvestro.

Loud was the roar of triumphant hate when the light of lanterns showed the Frate issuing from the door of the convent with a guard who promised him no other safety than that of the prison. The struggle now was, who should get first in the stream that rushed up the narrow street to see the Prophet carried back in ignominy to the piazza where he had braved it yesterday,—who should be in the best place for reaching his ear with insult, nay, if possible, for smiting him and kicking him. This was not difficult for some of the armed Compagnacci who were not prevented from mixing themselves with the guards.

When Savonarola felt himself dragged and pushed along in the midst of that hooting multitude; when lanterns were lifted to show him deriding faces; when he felt himself spit upon, smitten and kicked with grossest words of insult, it seemed to him that the worst bitterness of life was past. If men judged him guilty, and were bent on having his blood, it was only death that awaited him. But the worst drop of bitterness can never be wrung on to our lips from without: the lowest depth of resignation is not to be found in martyrdom; it is only to be found when we have covered our heads in silence and felt, "I am not worthy to be a martyr; the Truth shall prosper, but not by me."

But that brief imperfect triumph of insulting the Frate, who had soon disappeared under the doorway of the Old Palace, was only like the taste of blood to the tiger. Were there not the houses of the hypocrite's friends to be sacked? Already one half of the armed multitude, too much in the rear to share greatly in the siege of the convent, had been employed in the more profitable work of attacking rich houses, not with planless desire for plunder, but with that discriminating selection of such as belonged to chief Piagnoni, which showed that the riot was under guidance, and that the rabble with clubs and staves was well officered by sword-girt Compagnacci. Was there not—next criminal after the Frate—the ambitious Francesco Valori, suspected of wanting with the Frate's help, to make himself a Doge or Gonfaloniere for life? And the grey-haired man who eight months ago had lifted his arm and his voice in such ferocious demand for justice on five of his fellow-citizens, only escaped from San Marco to experience what *others* called justice,—to see his house surrounded by an angry, greedy multitude, to see his wife shot dead with an arrow, and to be himself murdered, as he was on his way to answer a summons to the Palazzo, by the swords of men named Ridolfi and Tornabuoni.

In this way that Masque of the Furies, called Riot, was played on in Florence through the hours of night and early morning.

But the chief director was not visible: he had his reasons for issuing his orders from a private retreat, being of rather too high a name to let his red feather be seen waving among all the work that was to be done before the dawn. The retreat was the same house and the same room in a quiet street between Santa Croce and San Marco, where we have seen Tito paying a secret visit to Dolfo Spini. Here the Captain of the Compagnacci sat through this memorable night, receiving visitors who came and went, and went and came, some of them in the guise of armed Compagnacci, others dressed obscurely and without visible arms. There was abundant wine on the table, with drinking-cups for chance comers; and though Spini was on his guard against excessive drinking, he took enough from time to time to heighten the excitement produced by the news that was being brought to him continually.

Among the obscurely dressed visitors Ser Ceccone was one of the most frequent; and as the hours advanced towards the morning twilight he had remained as Spini's constant companion, together with Francesco Cei, who was then in rather careless hiding in Florence, expecting to have his banishment revoked when the Frate's fall had been accomplished.

The tapers had burnt themselves into low shapeless masses, and holes in the shutters were just marked by a sombre outward light, when Spini, who had started from his seat and walked up and down with an angry flush on his face at some talk that had been going forward with those two unmilitary companions, burst out,—

"The devil spit him! he shall pay for it, though! Ha, ha! the claws shall be down on him when he little thinks of them. So *he* was to be the great man, after all! He's been pretending to chuck everything towards my cap, as if I were a blind beggarman, and all the while he's been winking and filling his own scarsella. I should like to hang skins about him and set my hounds on him! And he's got that fine ruby of mine, I was fool enough to give him yesterday. Malediction! And he was laughing at me in his sleeve two years ago, and spoiling the best plan that ever was laid. I was a fool for trusting myself with a

parture; and in all delay he had an uneasy sense that there was danger, Falsehood had prospered and waxed strong; but it had nourished the twin life, Fear. He no longer wore his armour, he was no longer afraid of Baldassarre; but from the corpse of that dead fear a spirit had risen,—the undying *habit* of fear. He felt he should not be safe till he was out of this fierce, turbid Florence; and now he was ready to go. Maso was to deliver up his house to the new tenant; his horses and mules were awaiting him in San Gallo; Tessa and the children had been lodged for the night in the Borgo outside the gate, and would be dressed in readiness to mount the mules and join him. He descended the stone steps into the courtyard, he passed through the great doorway, not the same Tito, but nearly as brilliant as on the day when he had first entered that house and made the mistake of falling in love with Romola. The mistake was remedied now; the old life was cast off, and was soon to be far behind him.

He turned with rapid steps towards the Piazza dei Mozzi, intending to pass over the Ponte Rubaconte; but as he went along certain sounds came upon his ears that made him turn round and walk yet more quickly in the opposite direction. Was the mob coming into Oltrarno? It was a vexation, for he would have preferred the more private road. He must now go by the Ponte Vecchio; and unpleasant sensations made him draw his mantle close round him, and walk at his utmost speed. There was no one to see him in that grey twilight. But before he reached the end of the Via de' Bardi, like sounds fell on his ear again, and this time they were much louder and nearer. Could he have been deceived before? The mob must be coming over the Ponte Vecchio. Again he turned, from an impulse of fear that was stronger than reflection; but it was only to be assured that the mob was actually entering the street from the opposite end. He chose not to go back to his house: after all, they would not attack *him*. Still, he had some valuables about him; and all things except reason and order are possible with a mob. But necessity does the work of courage. He went on towards the Ponte Vecchio, the rush and the trampling and the confused voices getting so loud before him that he had ceased to hear them behind.

For he had reached the end of the street, and the crowd pouring from the bridge met him at the turning and hemmed in his way. He had not time to wonder at a sudden shout before he felt himself surrounded, not, in the first instance, by an unarmed rabble, but by armed Compagnacci; the next sensation was that his cap fell off, and that he was thrust violently forward among the rabble, along the narrow passage of the bridge. Then he distinguished the shouts, "Piagnone! Medicean! Piagnone! Throw him over the bridge!"

His mantle was being torn off him with strong pulls that would have throttled him if the fibula had not given way. Then his scarsella was snatched at; but all the while he was being hustled and dragged; and the snatch failed,—his scarsella still hung at his side. Shouting, yelling, half motiveless execration rang stunningly in his ears, spreading even among those who had not yet seen him, and only knew there was a man to be reviled. Tito's horrible dread was that he should be struck down or trampled on before he reached the open arches that surmount the centre of the bridge. There was one hope for him, that they might throw him over before they had wounded him or beaten the strength out of him; and his whole soul was absorbed in that one hope and its obverse terror.

Yes,—they *were* at the arches. In that moment Tito, with bloodless face and eyes dilated, had one of the self-preserving inspirations that come in extremity. With a sudden desperate effort he mastered the clasp of his belt, and flung belt and scarsella forward towards a yard of clear space against the parapet, crying in a ringing voice,—

"There are diamonds! there is gold!"

In the instant the hold on him was relaxed, and there was a rush toward the scarsella. He threw himself on the parapet with a desperate leap, and the next moment plunged,—plunged with a great plash into the dark river far below.

It was his chance of salvation; and it was a good chance. His life had been saved once before by his fine swimming, and as he rose to the surface again after his long dive he had a sense of deliverance. He struck out with all the energy of his strong prime, and the current helped him. If he could only swim beyond the Ponte alla Carrara, he might land in a remote part of the city, and even yet reach San Gallo. Life was still before him. And the idiot mob, shouting and bellowing on the bridge there, would think he was drowned.

They did think so. Peering over the parapet along the dark stream, they could not see afar off the moving blackness of the floating hair, and the velvet tunic-sleeves.

It was only from the other way that a pale olive face could be seen looking white above the dark water,—a face not easy even for the indifferent to forget, with its square forehead, the long low arch of the eyebrows, and the long lustrous agate-like eyes. Onward the face went on the dark current, with inflated quivering nostrils, with the blue veins distended on the temples. One bridge was passed,—the bridge of Santa Trinità. Should he risk landing now rather than trust to his strength? No. He heard, or fancied he heard, yells and cries pursuing him. Terror pressed him most from the side of his fellow-men: he was less afraid of indefinite chances, and he swam on, panting and straining. He was not so fresh as he would have been if he had passed the night in sleep.

Yet the next bridge—the last bridge—was passed. He was conscious of it; but in the tumult of his blood, he could only feel vaguely that he was safe and might land. But where? The current was having its way with him: he hardly knew where he was; exhaustion as bringing on the dreamy state that precedes unconsciousness.

But now there were eyes that discerned him,—aged eyes, strong

for the distance. Baldassarre, looking up blankly from the search in
the runlet that brought him nothing, had seen a white object coming
along the broader stream. Could that be any fortunate chance for *him?*
He looked and looked till the object gathered form; then he leaned forward with a start as he sat among the rank green stems, and his eyes
seemed to be filled with a new light. Yet he only watched,—motionless. Something was being brought to him.

The next instant a man's body was cast violently on the grass two
yards from him, and he started forward like a panther, clutching the
velvet tunic as he fell forward on the body and flashed a look in the
man's face.

Dead,—was he dead? The eyes were rigid. But no, it could not be.
—Justice had brought him. Men looked dead sometimes, and yet the
life came back into them. Baldassarre did not feel feeble in that moment. He knew just what he could do. He got his large fingers within
the neck of the tunic and held them there, kneeling on one knee beside
the body and watching the face. There was a fierce hope in his heart.
but it was mixed with trembling. In his eyes there was only fierceness;
all the slow-burning remnant of life within him seemed to have leaped
into flame.

Rigid,—rigid still. Those eyes with the half-hidden lids were locked
against vengeance. *Could* it be that he was dead? There was nothing
to measure the time; it seemed long enough for hope to freeze into
despair.

Surely at last the eyelids were quivering; the eyes were no longer
rigid. There was a vibrating light in them; they opened wide.

"Ah, yes! You see me,—you know me."

Tito knew him; but he did not know whether it was life or death
that had brought him into the presence of his injured father. It might
be death,—and death might mean this chill gloom with the face of the
hideous past hanging over him forever.

But now Baldassarre's only dread was lest the young limbs should
escape him. He pressed his knuckles against the round throat, and
knelt upon the chest with all the force of his aged frame. Let death
come now!

Again he kept his watch on the face; and when the eyes were rigid
again, he dared not trust them. He would never loose his hold till some
one came and found them. Justice would send some witness; and then
he, Baldassarre, would declare that he had killed this traitor, to whom
he had once been a father. They would perhaps believe him now, and
then he would be content with the struggle of justice on earth,—then
he would desire to die with his hold on this body, and follow the traitor
to hell that he might clutch him there.

And so he knelt, and so he pressed his knuckles against the round
throat, without trusting to the seeming death, till the light got strong
and he could kneel no longer. Then he sat on the body, still clutching
the neck of the tunic. But the hours went on, and no witness came.

No eyes descried afar off the two human bodies among the tall grass by the river-side. Florence was busy with greater affairs, and the preparation of a deeper tragedy.

Not long after those two bodies were lying in the grass, Savonarola was being tortured, and crying out in his agony, "I will confess!"

It was not until the sun was westward that a wagon drawn by a mild gray ox came to the edge of the grassy margin, and as the man who led it was leaning to gather up the round stones that lay heaped in readiness to be carried away, he detected some startling object in the grass. The aged man had fallen forward, and his dead clutch was on the garment of the other. It was not possible to separate them; nay, it was better to put them into the wagon and carry them as they were into the great piazza, that notice might be given to the Eight.

As the wagon entered the frequented streets, there was a growing crowd escorting it with its strange burden. No one knew the bodies for a long while, for the aged face had fallen forward, half hiding the younger. But before they had been moved out of sight, they had been recognized.

"I know that old man," Piero di Cosimo had testified. "I painted his likeness once. He is the prisoner who clutched Melema on the steps of the Duomo."

"He is perhaps the same old man who appeared at supper in my gardens," said Bernardo Ruccellai, one of the Eight. "I had forgotten him. I thought he had died in prison. But there is no knowing the truth now."

Who shall put his finger on the work of justice and say, "It is there"? Justice is like the Kingdom of God,—it is not without us as a fact, it is within us as a great yearning.

CHAPTER XLVIII

ROMOLA'S WAKING

ROMOLA in her boat passed from dreaming into long deep sleep, and then again from deep sleep into busy dreaming, till at last she felt herself stretching out her arms in the court of the Bargello, where the flickering flames of the tapers seemed to get stronger and stronger till the dark scene was blotted out with light. Her eyes opened, and she saw it was the light of morning. Her boat was lying still in a little creek; on her right hand lay the speckless sapphire-blue of the Mediterranean; on her left one of those scenes which were and still are repeated again and again like a sweet rhythm, on the shores of that loveliest sea.

In a deep curve of the mountains lay a breadth of green land, curtained by gentle tree-shadowed slopes leaning towards the rocky heights. Up these slopes might be seen here and there, gleaming between the tree-tops, a pathway leading to a little irregular mass of building that seemed to have clambered in a hasty way up the mountain-side, and taken a difficult stand there for the sake of showing the tall belfry as a sight of beauty to the scattered and clustered houses of the village below. The rays of the newly risen sun fell obliquely on the westward horn of this crescent-shaped nook; all else lay in dewy shadow. No sound came across the stillness; the very waters seemed to have curved themselves there for rest.

The delicious sun-rays fell on Romola, and thrilled her gently like a caress. She lay motionless, hardly watching the scene; rather, feeling simply the presence of peace and beauty. While we are still in our youth there can always come, in our early waking, moments when mere passive existence is itself a Lethe, when the exquisiteness of subtle indefinite sensation creates a bliss which is without memory and without desire. As the soft warmth penetrated Romola's young limbs, as her eyes rested on this sequestered luxuriance, it seemed that the agitating past had glided away like that dark scene in the Bargello, and that the after-noon dreams of her girlhood had really come back to her. For a min-ute or two the oblivion was untroubled; she did not even think that she could rest here forever, she only felt that she rested. Then she became distinctly conscious that she was lying in the boat which had been bearing her over the waters all through the night. Instead of bringing her to death, it had been the gently lulling cradle of a new life. And in spite of her evening despair she was glad that the morning had come to her again: glad to think that she was resting in the familiar sunlight rather than in the unknown regions of death. *Could* she not rest here? No sound from Florence would reach her. Already oblivion was troubled; from behind the golden haze were piercing domes and towers and walls, parted by a river and enclosed by the green hills.

She rose from her reclining posture and sat up in the boat, willing, if she could, to resist the rush of thoughts that urged themselves along with the conjecture how far the boat had carried her. Why need she mind? This was a sheltered nook where there were simple villagers who would not harm her. For a little while, at least, she might rest and resolve on nothing. Presently she would go and get some bread and milk, and then she would nestle in the green quiet, and feel that there was a pause in her life. She turned to watch the crescent-shaped valley, that she might get back the soothing sense of peace and beauty which she had felt in her first waking.

She had not been in this attitude of contemplation more than a few minutes when across the stillness there came a piercing cry; not a brief cry, but continuous and more and more intense. Romola felt sure it was the cry of a little child in distress that no one came to help. She started up and put one foot on the side of the boat ready to leap on to the beach; but she paused there and listened: the mother of the child must be near, the cry must soon cease. But it went on, and drew Rom-ola so irresistibly, seeming the more piteous to her for the sense of peace which had preceded it. that she jumped on to the beach and walked many paces before she knew what direction she would take. The cry, she thought, came from some rough garden growth many yards on her right hand, where she saw a half-ruined hovel. She climbed over a low broken stone fence and made her way across patches of weedy green crops and ripe but neglected corn. The cry grew plainer, and convinced that she was right she hastened towards the hovel; but even in that hurried walk she felt an oppressive change in the air as she left the sea behind. Was there some taint lurking among the green luxuriance that had seemed such an inviting shelter from the heat of the coming day? She could see the opening into the hovel now, and the cry was darting through her like a pain. The next moment her foot was within the doorway, but the sight she beheld in the sombre light arrested her with a shock of awe and horror. On the straw, with which the floor was scattered, lay three dead bodies, one of a tall man, one of a girl about eight years old, and one of a young woman whose long black hair was being clutched and pulled by a living child,—the child that was sending forth the piercing cry. Romola's experience in the haunts of death and disease made thought and action prompt: she lifted the little living child, and in trying to soothe it on her bosom, still bent to look at the bodies and see if they were really dead. The strongly marked type of race in their features, and their peculiar garb made her conjecture that they were Spanish or Portuguese Jews, who had perhaps been put ashore and abandoned there by rapacious sailors, to whom their property remained as a prey. Such things were happening continually to Jews compelled to abandon their homes by the Inquisition: the cruelty of greed thrust them from the sea, and the cruelty of superstition thrust them back to it.

"But, surely," thought Romola, "I shall find some woman in the village whose mother's heart will not let her refuse to tend this helpless child,—if the real mother is indeed dead."

This doubt remained, because while the man and girl looked emaciated and also showed signs of having been long dead, the woman seemed to have been hardier, and had not quite lost the robustness of her form. Romola, kneeling, was about to lay her hand on her heart; but as she lifted the piece of yellow woollen drapery that lay across the bosom, she saw the purple spots which marked the familiar pestilence. Then it struck her that if the villagers knew of this, she might have more difficulty than she had expected in getting help from them; they would perhaps shrink from her with that child in her arms. But she had money to offer them, and they would not refuse to give her some goat's milk in exchange for it.

She set out at once towards the village, her mind filled now with the effort to soothe the little dark creature, and with wondering how she should win some woman to be good to it. She could not help hoping a little in a certain awe she had observed herself to inspire, when she appeared, unknown and unexpected, in her religious dress. As she passed across a breadth of cultivated ground, she noticed, with wonder, that little patches of corn mingled with the other crops had been left to over-ripeness untouched by the sickle, and that golden apples and dark figs lay rotting on the weedy earth. There were grassy spaces within sight, but no cow, or sheep, or goat.

The stillness began to have something fearful in it to Romola; she hurried along towards the thickest cluster of houses, where there would be the most life to appeal to on behalf of the helpless life she carried in her arms. But she had picked up two figs, and bit little pieces from the sweet pulp to still the child with.

She entered between two lines of dwellings. It was time that villagers should have been stirring long ago, but not a soul was in sight. The air was becoming more and more oppressive, laden, it seemed, with some horrible impurity. There was a door open; she looked in, and saw grim emptiness. Another open door; and through that she saw a man lying dead with all his garments on, his head lying athwart a spade handle, and an earthenware cruse in his hand, as if he had fallen suddenly.

Romola felt horror taking possession of her. Was she in a village of the unburied dead? She wanted to listen if there were any faint sound, but the child cried out afresh when she ceased to feed it, and the cry filled her ears. At last she saw a figure crawling slowly out of a house, and soon sinking back in a sitting posture against the wall. She hastened towards the figure; it was a young woman in fevered anguish, and she, too, held a pitcher in her hand. As Romola approached her, she did not start; the one need was too absorbing for any other idea to impress itself on her.

"Water! get me water!" she said, with a moaning utterance.

Romola stooped to take the pitcher, and said gently in her ear, "You shall have water; can you point towards the well?"

The hand was lifted towards the more distant end of the little street, and Romola set off at once with as much speed as she could use under the difficulty of carrying the pitcher as well as feeding the child. But the little one was getting more content as the morsels of sweet pulp were repeated, and ceased to distress her with its cry, so that she could give a less distracted attention to the objects around her.

The well lay twenty yards or more beyond the end of the street; and as Romola was approaching it, her eyes were directed to the opposite green slope immediately below the church. High up, on a patch of grass between the trees, she had descried a cow and a couple of goats, and she tried to trace a line of path that would lead her close to that cheering sight, when once she had done her errand to the well. Occupied in this way, she was not aware that she was very near the well, and that some one approaching it on the other side had fixed a pair of astonished eyes upon her.

Romola certainly presented a sight which at that moment and in that place could hardly have been seen without some pausing and palpitation. With her gaze fixed intently on the distant slope, the long lines of her thick grey garment giving a gliding character to her rapid walk, her hair rolling backward and illuminated on the left side by the sun-rays, the little olive baby on her right arm now looking out with jet-black eyes, she might well startle that youth of fifteen, accustomed to swing the censer in the presence of a Madonna less fair and marvellous than this.

"She carries a pitcher in her hand,—to fetch water for the sick. It is the Holy Mother, come to take care of the people who have the pesti-lence."

It was a sight of awe: she would, perhaps, be angry with those who fetched water for themselves only. The youth flung down his vessel in terror; and Romola, aware now of some one near her, saw the black and white figure fly as if for dear life towards the slope she had just been contemplating. But remembering the parched sufferer, she half filled her pitcher quickly and hastened back.

Entering the house to look for a small cup, she saw salt meat and meal: there were no signs of want in the dwelling. With nimble move-ment she seated baby on the ground, and lifted a cup of water to the sufferer, who drank eagerly and then closed her eyes and leaned her head backward, seeming to give herself up to the sense of relief. Pres-ently she opened her eyes, and, looking at Romola, said languidly,—

"Who are you?"

"I came over the sea," said Romola. "I only came this morning. Are all the people dead in these houses?"

"I think they are all ill now,—all that are not dead. My father and my sister lie dead upstairs, and there is no one to bury them; and soon I shall die."

"Not so, I hope," said Romola. "I am come to take care of you. I am used to the pestilence; I am not afraid. But there must be some left who are not ill. I saw a youth running towards the mountain when I went to the well."

"I cannot tell. When the pestilence came, a great many people went away, and drove off the cows and goats. Give me more water!"

Romola, suspecting that if she followed the direction of the youth's flight, she should find some men and women who were still healthy and able, determined to seek them out at once, that she might at least win them to take care of the child, and leave her free to come back and see how many living needed help, and how many dead needed burial. She trusted to her powers of persuasion to conquer the aid of the timorous, when once she knew what was to be done.

Promising the sick woman to come back to her, she lifted the dark bantling again, and set off towards the slope. She felt no burden of choice on her now, no longing for death. She was thinking how she would go to the other sufferers, as she had gone to that fevered woman.

But, with the child on her arm, it was not so easy to her as usual to walk up a slope, and it seemed a long while before the winding path took her near the cow and the goats. She was beginning herself to feel faint from heat, hunger, and thirst, and as she reached a double turning, she paused to consider whether she would not wait near the cow, which some one was likely to come and milk soon, rather than toil up to the church before she had taken any rest. Raising her eyes to measure the steep distance, she saw peeping between the boughs, not more than five yards off, a broad round face, watching her attentively, and lower down the black skirt of a priest's garment, and a hand grasping a bucket. She stood mutely observing, and the face, too, remained motionless. Romola had often witnessed the overpowering force of dread in cases of pestilence, and she was cautious.

Raising her voice in a tone of gentle pleading, she said, "I came over the sea. I am hungry, and so is the child. Will you not give us some milk?"

Romola had divined part of the truth, but she had not divined that preoccupation of the priest's mind which charged her words with a strange significance. Only a little while ago, the young acolyte had brought word to the Padre that he had seen the Holy Mother with the Babe, fetching water for the sick: she was as tall as the cypresses, and had a light about her head, and she looked up at the church. The pievano had not listened with entire belief: he had been more than fifty years in the world without having any vision of the Madonna, and he thought the boy might have misinterpreted the unexpected appearance of a villager. But he had been made uneasy, and before venturing to come down and milk his cow, he had repeated many Aves. The pievano's conscience tormented him a little: he trembled at the pestilence, but he also trembled at the thought of the mild-faced Mother, conscious that that Invisible Mercy might demand something more of him than prayers and "Hails." In this state of mind—unable to banish the image the boy had raised of the Mother with the glory about her tending the sick—the pievano had come down to milk his cow, and had suddenly caught sight of Romola pausing at the parted way. Her pleading words, with their strange refinement of tone and accent, instead of being explanatory, had a preternatural sound for him. Yet he did not quite believe he saw the Holy Mother: he was in a state of alarmed hesitation. If anything miraculous were happening, he felt there was no strong presumption that the miracle would be in his favour. He dared not run away; he dared not advance.

"Come down," said Romola, after a pause. "Do not fear. Fear rather to deny food to the hungry when they ask you."

A moment after, the boughs were parted, and the complete figure of a thick-set priest with a broad, harmless face, his black frock much worn and soiled, stood, bucket in hand, looking at her timidly, and still keeping aloof as he took the path towards the cow in silence.

Romola followed him and watched him without speaking again, as he seated himself against the tethered cow, and, when he had nervously drawn some milk, gave it to her in a brass cup he carried with him in the bucket. As Romola put the cup to the lips of the eager child, and afterwards drank some milk herself, the Padre observed her from his wooden stool with a timidity that changed its character a little. He recognized the Hebrew baby, he was certain that he had a substantial woman before him; but there was still something strange and unaccountable in Romola's presence in this spot, and the Padre had a presentiment that things were going to change with him. Moreover, that Hebrew baby was terribly associated with the dread of pestilence.

Nevertheless, when Romola smiled at the little one sucking its own milky lips, and stretched out the brass cup again, saying, "Give us more, good father," he obeyed less nervously than before.

Romola on her side was not unobservant; and when the second supply of milk had been drunk, she looked down at the round-headed man, and said with mild decision,—

"And now tell me, father, how this pestilence came, and why you let your people die without the sacraments, and lie unburied. For I am come over the sea to help those who are left alive,—and you, too, will help them now."

He told her the story of the pestilence; and while he was telling it, the youth, who had fled before, had come peeping and advancing gradually, till at last he stood and watched the scene from behind a neighbouring bush.

Three families of Jews, twenty souls in all, had been put ashore many weeks ago, some of them already ill of the pestilence. The villagers, said the priest, had of course refused to give shelter to the miscreants, otherwise than in a distant hovel, and under heaps of straw. But when the strangers had died of the plague, and some of the people had thrown the bodies into the sea, the sea had brought them back again in a great storm, and everybody was smitten with terror. A grave was dug, and the bodies were buried; but then the pestilence attacked the Christians, and the greater number of the villagers went away over the mountain, driving away their few cattle, and carrying provisions. The priest had not fled; he had stayed and prayed for the people, and he had prevailed on the youth Jacopo to stay with him; but he confessed that a mortal terror of the plague had taken hold of him, and he had not dared to go down into the valley.

"You will fear no longer, father," said Romola, in a tone of encouraging authority; "you will come down with me, and we will see who is living, and we will look for the dead to bury them. I have walked about for months where the pestilence was, and see, I am strong. Jacopo will come with us," she added, motioning to the peeping lad, who came slowly from behind his defensive bush, as if invisible threads were dragging him.

"Come, Jacopo," said Romola again, smiling at him, "you will carry the child for me. See! your arms are strong, and I am tired."

That was a dreadful proposal to Jacopo, and to the priest also; but they were both under a peculiar influence forcing them to obey. The suspicion that Romola was a supernatural form was dissipated, but their minds were filled instead with the more effective sense that she was a human being whom God had sent over to sea to command them.

"Now we will carry down the milk," said Romola, "and see if any one wants it."

So they went all together down the slope, and that morning the sufferers saw help come to them in their despair. There were hardly more than a score alive in the whole valley; but all of these were comforted, most were saved, and the dead were buried.

In this way days, weeks, and months passed with Romola till the men were digging and sowing again, till the women smiled at her as they carried their great vases on their heads to the well, and the Hebrew baby was a tottering tumbling Christian, Benedetto by name, having been baptized in the church on the mountain-side. But by that time she herself was suffering from the fatigue and languor that must come after a continuous strain on mind and body. She had taken for her dwelling one of the houses abandoned by their owners, standing a little aloof from the village street; and here on a thick heap of clean straw,— a delicious bed for those who do not dream of down,—she felt glad to lie still through most of the daylight hours, taken care of along with the little Benedetto by a woman whom the pestilence had widowed.

Every day the Padre and Jacopo and the small flock of surviving villagers paid their visit to this cottage to see the blessed Lady, and to bring her of their best as an offering,—honey, fresh cakes, eggs, and polenta. It was a sight they could none of them forget, a sight they all told of in their old age,—how the sweet and sainted lady with her fair face, her golden hair, and her brown eyes that had a blessing in them, lay weary with her labours after she had been sent over the sea to help them in their extremity, and how the queer little black Benedetto used to crawl about the straw by her side and want everything that was brought to her, and she always gave him a bit of what she took, and told them if they loved her they must be good to Benedetto.

Many legends were afterwards told in that valley about the blessed Lady who came over the sea, but they were legends by which all who heard might know that in times gone by a woman had done beautiful loving deeds there, rescuing those who were ready to perish.

CHAPTER XLIX

HOMEWARD

IN those silent wintry hours when Romola lay resting from her weariness, her mind, travelling back over the past, and gazing across the undefined distance of the future, saw all objects from a new position. Her experience since the moment of her waking in the boat had come to her with as strong an effect as that of the fresh seal on the dissolving wax. She had felt herself without bonds, without motive; sinking in mere egoistic complaining that life could bring her no content; feeling a right to say, "I am tired of life, I want to die." That thought had sobbed within her as she fell asleep, but from the moment after her waking when the cry had drawn her, she had not even reflected, as she used to do in Florence, that she was glad to live because she could lighten sorrow,—she had simply lived, with so energetic an impulse to share the life around her, to answer the call of need and do the work which cried aloud to be done, that the reasons for living, enduring, labouring, never took the form of argument.

The experience was like a new baptism to Romola. In Florence the simpler relations of the human being to his fellow-men had been complicated for her with all the special ties of marriage, the State, and religious discipleship; and when these had disappointed her trust, the shock seemed to have shaken her aloof from life and stunned her sympathy. But now she said, "It was mere baseness in me to desire death. If everything else is doubtful, this suffering that I can help is certain; if the glory of the cross is an illusion, the sorrow is only the truer. While the strength is in my arm I will stretch it out to the fainting; while the light visits my eyes they shall seek the forsaken."

And then the past arose with a fresh appeal to her. Her work in this green valley was done, and the emotions that were disengaged from the people immediately around her rushed back into the old deep channels of use and affection. That rare possibility of self-contemplation which comes in any complete severance from our wonted life made her judge herself as she had never done before: the compunction which is inseparable from a sympathetic nature keenly alive to the possible experience of others, began to stir in her with growing force. She questioned the justness of her own conclusions, of her own deeds: she had been rash, arrogant, always dissatisfied that others were not good enough, while she herself had not been true to what her soul had once recognized as the best. She began to condemn her flight: after all, it had been cowardly self-care; the grounds on which Savonarola had once taken her back were truer, deeper than the grounds she had had for her second flight. How could she feel the needs of others and not feel, above all, the needs of the nearest?

But then came reaction against such self-reproach. The memory of her life with Tito, of the conditions which made their real union impossible, while their external union imposed a set of false duties on her which were essentially the concealment and sanctioning of what her mind revolted from, told her that flight had been her only resource. All minds, except such as are delivered from doubt by dulness of sensibility, must be subject to this recurring conflict where the many-twisted conditions of life have forbidden the fulfilment of a bond. For in strictness there is no replacing of relations: the presence of the new does not nullify the failure and breach of the old. Life has lost its perfection: it has been maimed; and until the wounds are quite scarred, conscience continually casts backward, doubting glances.

Romola shrank with dread from the renewal of her proximity to
Tito, and yet she was uneasy that she had put herself out of reach of
knowing what was his fate,—uneasy that the moment might yet come
when he would be in misery and need her. There was still a thread of
pain within her, testifying to those words of Fra Girolamo, that she
could not cease to be a wife. Could anything utterly cease for her that
had once mingled itself with the current of her heart's blood?

Florence, and all her life there, had come back to her like hunger;
her feelings could not go wandering after the possible and the vague:
their living fibre was fed with the memory of familiar things. And the
thought that she had divided herself from them forever became more
and more importunate in these hours that were unfilled with action.
What if Fra Girolamo had been wrong? What if the life of Florence
was a web of inconsistencies? Was she, then, something higher, that
she should shake the dust from off her feet, and say, "This world is not
good enough for me"? If she had been really higher, she would not so
easily have lost all her trust.

Her indignant grief for her godfather had no longer complete possession of her, and her sense of debt to Savonarola was recovering predominance. Nothing that had come, or was to come, could do away
with the fact that there had been a great inspiration in him which had
waked a new life in her. Who, in all her experience, could demand the
same gratitude from her as he? His errors,—might they not bring
calamities?

She could not rest. She hardly knew whether it was her strength
returning with the budding leaves that made her active again, or
whether it was her eager longing to get nearer Florence. She did not
imagine herself daring to enter Florence, but the desire to be near
enough to learn what was happening there urged itself with a strength
that excluded all other purposes.

And one March morning the people in the valley were gathered together to see the blessed Lady depart. Jacopo had fetched a mule for
her, and was going with her over the mountains. The Padre, too, was
going with her to the nearest town, that he might help her in learning
the safest way by which she might get to Pistoja. Her store of trinkets
and money, untouched in this valley, was abundant for her needs.

If Romola had been less drawn by the longing that was taking her
away, it would have been a hard moment for her when she walked
along the village street for the last time, while the Padre and Jacopo,
with the mule, were awaiting her near the well. Her steps were hindered by the wailing people, who knelt and kissed her hands, then
clung to her skirts and kissed the grey folds, crying, "Ah, why will
you go, when the good season is beginning and the crops will be plentiful? Why will you go?"

"Do not be sorry," said Romola; "you are well now, and I shall
remember you. I must go and see if my own people want me."

"Ah, yes, if they have the pestilence!"

"Look at us again, Madonna!"

"Yes, yes, we will be good to the little Benedetto!"

At last Romola mounted her mule; but a vigorous screaming from Benedetto as he saw her turn from him in this new position, was an excuse for all the people to follow her and insist that he must ride on the mule's neck to the foot of the slope.

The parting must come at last; but as Romola turned continually before she passed out of sight, she saw the little flock lingering to catch the last waving of her hand.

CHAPTER L

MEETING AGAIN

On the 14th of April Romola was once more within the walls of Florence. Unable to rest at Pistoja, where contradictory reports reached her about the Trial by Fire, she had gone on to Prato; and was beginning to think that she should be drawn on to Florence in spite of dread, when she encountered that monk of San Spirito who had been her godfather's confessor. From him she learned the full story of Savonarola's arrest and of her husband's death. This Augustinian monk had been in the stream of people who had followed the wagon with its awful burthen into the piazza, and he could tell her what was generally known in Florence,—that Tito had escaped from an assaulting mob by leaping into the Arno, but had been murdered on the bank by an old man who had long had an enmity against him. But Romola understood the catastrophe as no one else did. Of Savonarola the monk told her, in that tone of unfavourable prejudice which was usual in the Black Brethren (Frati Neri) towards the brother who showed white under his black, that he had confessed himself a deceiver of the people.

Romola paused no longer. That evening she was in Florence, sitting in agitated silence under the exclamations of joy and wailing, mingled with exuberant narrative, which were poured into her ears by Monna Brigida, who had backslidden into false hair in Romola's absence, but now drew it off again and declared she would not mind being grey, if her dear child would stay with her.

Romola was too deeply moved by the main events which she had known before coming to Florence, to be wrought upon by the doubtful gossiping details added in Brigida's narrative. The tragedy of her husband's death, of Fra Girolamo's confession of duplicity under the coercion of torture, left her hardly any power of apprehending minor circumstances. All the mental activity she could exert under that load of awe-stricken grief was absorbed by two purposes which must supersede every other,—to try and see Savonarola, and to learn what had become of Tessa and the children.

"Tell me, cousin," she said abruptly, when Monna Brigida's tongue had run quite away from troubles into projects of Romola's living with her, "has anything been seen or said since Tito's death of a young woman with two little children?"

Brigida started, rounded her eyes, and lifted up her hands.

"Cristo! no. What! was he so bad as that, my poor child? Ah, then, that was why you went away, and left me word only that you went of your own free will. Well, well; if I'd known that, I shouldn't have thought you so strange and flighty. For I did say to myself, though I didn't tell anybody else, 'What was she to go away from her husband for, leaving him to mischief, only because they cut poor Bernardo's head off? She's got her father's temper,' I said; 'that's what it is.' Well, well; never scold me, child: Bardo *was* fierce, you can't deny it. But if you had only told me the truth, that there was a young hussy and children, I should have understood it all. Anything seen or said of her? No; and the less the better. They say enough of ill about him without that. But since that was the reason you went—"

"No, dear cousin," said Romola, interrupting her earnestly, "pray do not talk so. I wish above all things to find that young woman and her children, and to take care of them. They are quite helpless. Say nothing against it; that is the thing I shall do first of all."

"Well," said Monna Brigida, shrugging her shoulders and lowering her voice with an air of puzzled discomfiture, "if that's being a Piagnone, I've been taking peas for Paternosters. Why, Fra Girolamo said as good as that widows ought not to marry again. Step in at the door and it's a sin and a shame, it seems; but come down the chimney and you're welcome. *Two* children—Santiddio!"

"Cousin, the poor thing has done no conscious wrong: she is ignorant of everything. I will tell you—but not now."

Early the next morning Romola's steps were directed to the house beyond San Ambrogio where she had once found Tessa; but it was as she had feared: Tessa was gone. Romola conjectured that Tito had sent her away beforehand to some spot where he had intended to join her, for she did not believe that he would willingly part with those children. It was a painful conjecture, because, if Tessa were out of Florence, there was hardly a chance of finding her, and Romola pictured the childish creature waiting and waiting at some wayside spot in wondering, helpless misery. Those who lived near could tell her nothing except that old deaf Lisa had gone away a week ago with her goods, but no one knew where Tessa had gone. Romola saw no further active search open to her; for she had no knowledge that could serve as a starting-point for inquiry, and not only her innate reserve but a more noble sensitiveness made her shrink from assuming an attitude of generosity in the eyes of others by publishing Tessa's relation to Tito, along with her own desire to find her. Many days passed in anxious inaction. Even under strong solicitation from other thoughts Romola found her heart palpitating if she caught sight of a pair of round brown legs, or of a short woman in the contadina dress.

She never for a moment told herself that it was heroism or exalted charity in her to seek these beings: she needed something that she was bound specially to care for; she yearned to clasp the children and to make them love her. This at least would be some sweet result, for others as well as herself, from all her past sorrow. It appeared there was much property of Tito's to which she had a claim; but she distrusted the cleanness of that money, and she had determined to make it all over to the State, except so much as was equal to the price of her father's library. This would be enough for the modest support of Tessa and the children. But Monna Brigida threw such planning into the background by clamourously insisting that Romola must live with her and never forsake her till she had seen her safe in Paradise—else why had she persuaded her to turn Piagnone?—and if Romola wanted to rear other people's children, she, Monna Brigida, must rear them too. Only they must be found first.

Romola felt the full force of that innuendo. But strong feeling unsatisfied is never without its superstition, either of hope or despair. Romola's was the superstition of hope: *somehow* she was to find that mother and the children. And at last another direction for active inquiry suggested itself. She learned that Tito had provided horses and mules to await him in San Gallo; he was therefore going to leave Florence by the gate of San Gallo, and she determined, though without much confidence in the issue, to try and ascertain from the gatekeepers if they had observed any one corresponding to the description of Tessa, with her children, to have passed the gates before the morning of the 9th of April. Walking along the Via San Gallo, and looking watchfully about her through her long widow's veil, lest she should miss any object that might aid her, she descried Bratti chaffering with a customer. That roaming man, she thought, might aid her: she would not mind talking of Tessa to *him*. But as she put aside her veil and crossed the street towards him, she saw something hanging from the corner of his basket which made her heart leap with a much stronger hope.

"Bratti, my friend," she said abruptly, "where did you get that necklace?"

"Your servant, Madonna," said Bratti, looking round at her very deliberately, his mind not being subject to surprise. "It's a necklace worth money, but I shall get little by it, for my heart's too tender for a trader's; I have promised to keep it in pledge."

"Pray tell me where you got it;—from a little woman named Tessa, is it not true?"

"Ah! if you know her," said Bratti, "and would redeem it of me at a small profit, and give it her again, you'd be doing a charity, for she cried at parting with it—you'd have thought she was running into a brook. It's a small profit I'll charge you. You shall have it for a florin, for I don't like to be hard-hearted."

"Where is she?" said Romola, giving him the money, and unclasping the necklace from the basket in joyful agitation.

"Outside the gate there, at the other end of the Borgo, at old Sibilla Manetti's: anybody will tell you which is the house."

Romola went along with winged feet, blessing that incident of the Carnival which had made her learn by heart the appearance of this necklace. Soon she was at the house she sought. The young woman and the children were in the inner room,—were to have been fetched away a fortnight ago and more,—had no money, only their clothes, to pay a poor widow with for their food and lodging. But since Madonna knew them—Romola waited to hear no more, but opened the door.

Tessa was seated on the low bed: her crying had passed into tearless sobs, and she was looking with sad blank eyes at the two children, who were playing in an opposite corner,—Lillo covering his head with his skirt and roaring at Ninna to frighten her, then peeping out again to see how she bore it. The door was a little behind Tessa, and she did not turn round when it opened, thinking it was only the old woman: expectation was no longer alive. Romola had thrown aside her veil and paused a moment, holding the necklace in sight. Then she said, in that pure voice that used to cheer her father,—

"Tessa!"

Tessa started to her feet and looked round.

"See," said Romola, clasping the beads on Tessa's neck, "God has sent me to you again."

The poor thing screamed and sobbed, and clung to the arms that fastened the necklace. She could not speak. The two children came from their corner, laid hold of their mother's skirts, and looked up with wide eyes at Romola.

That day they all went home to Monna Brigida's in the Borgo degli Albizzi. Romola had made known to Tessa, by gentle degrees, that Naldo could never come to her again,—not because he was cruel, but because he was dead.

"But be comforted, my Tessa," said Romola. "I am come to take care of you always. And we have got Lillo and Ninna."

Monna Brigida's mouth twitched in the struggle between her awe of Romola and the desire to speak unseasonably.

"Let be, for the present," she thought; "but it seems to me a thousand years till I tell this little contadina, who seems not to know how many fingers she's got on her hand, who Romola is. And I *will* tell her some day, else she'll never know her place. It's all very well for Romola;— nobody will call their souls their own when she's by; but if I'm to have this puss-faced minx living in my house, she must be humble to me."

However, Monna Brigida wanted to give the children too many sweets for their supper, and confessed to Romola, the last thing before going to bed, that it would be a shame not to take care of such cherubs.

"But you must give up to me a little, Romola, about their eating, and those things. For you have never had a baby, and I had twins, only they died as soon as they were born."

CHAPTER LI

THE CONFESSION

When Romola brought home Tessa and the children, April was already near its close, and the other great anxiety on her mind had been wrought to its highest pitch by the publication in print of Fra Girolamo's Trial, or rather of the confessions drawn from him by the sixteen Florentine citizens commissioned to interrogate him. The appearance of this document, issued by order of the Signoria, had called forth such strong expressions of public suspicion and discontent, that severe measures were immediately taken for recalling it. Of course there were copies accidentally mislaid; and a second edition, *not* by order of the Signoria, was soon in the hands of eager readers.

Romola, who began to despair of ever speaking with Fra Girolamo, read this evidence again and again, desiring to judge it by some clearer light than the contradictory impressions that were taking the form of assertions in the mouths of both partisans and enemies.

In the more devout followers of Savonarola his want of constancy under torture, and his retraction of prophetic claims, had produced a consternation too profound to be at once displaced as it ultimately was by the suspicion, which soon grew into a positive datum, that any reported words of his which were in inexplicable contradiction to their faith in him, had not come from the lips of the prophet, but from the falsifying pen of Ser Ceccone, that notary of evil repute, who had made the digest of the examination. But there were obvious facts that at once threw discredit on the printed document. Was not the list of sixteen examiners half made up of the prophet's bitterest enemies? Was not the notorious Dolfo Spini one of the new Eight prematurely elected, in order to load the dice against a man whose ruin had been determined on by the party in power? It was but a murder with slow formalities that was being transacted in the Old Palace. The Signoria had resolved to drive a good bargain with the Pope and the Duke of Milan, by extinguishing the man who was as great a molestation to vicious citizens and greedy foreign tyrants as to a corrupt clergy. The Frate had been doomed beforehand, and the only question that was pretended to exist now was, whether the Republic, in return for a permission to lay a tax on ecclesiastical property, should deliver him alive into the hands of the Pope, or whether the Pope should further concede to the Republic what its dignity demanded,—the privilege of hanging and burning its own prophet on its own piazza.

Who, under such circumstances, would give full credit to this so-called confession? If the Frate had denied his prophetic gift, the denial had only been wrenched from him by the agony of torture,—agony that, in his sensitive frame, must quickly produce raving. What if these wicked examiners declared that he had only had the torture of the rope and pulley thrice, and only on one day, and that his confessions had been made when he was under no bodily coercion,—was that to be believed? He had been tortured much more; he had been tortured in proportion to the distress his confessions had created in the hearts of those who loved him.

Other friends of Savonarola, who were less ardent partisans, did not doubt the substantial genuineness of the confession, however it might have been coloured by the transpositions and additions of the notary; but they argued indignantly that there was nothing which could warrant a condemnation to death, or even to grave punishment. It must be clear to all impartial men that if this examination represented the only evidence against the Frate, he would die, not for any crime, but because he had made himself inconvenient to the Pope, to the rapacious Italian States that wanted to dismember their Tuscan neighbour, and to those unworthy citizens who sought to gratify their private ambition in opposition to the common weal.

Not a shadow of political crime had been proved against him. Not one stain had been detected on his private conduct: his fellow-monks, including one who had formerly been his secretary for several years, and who, with more than the average culture of his companions, had a disposition to criticise Fra Girolamo's rule as Prior, bore testimony, even after the shock of his retractation, to an unimpeachable purity and consistency in his life, which had commanded their unsuspecting veneration. The Pope himself had not been able to raise a charge of heresy against the Frate, except on the ground of disobedience to a mandate, and disregard of the sentence of excommunication. It was difficult to justify that breach of discipline by argument, but there was a moral insurgence in the minds of grave men against the Court of Rome, which tended to confound the theoretic distinction between the Church and churchmen, and to lighten the scandal of disobedience.

Men of ordinary morality and public spirit felt that the triumph of the Frate's enemies was really the triumph of gross license. And keen Florentines like Soderini and Piero Guicciardini may well have had an angry smile on their lips at a severity which dispensed with all law in order to hang and burn a man in whom the seductions of a public career had warped the strictness of his veracity; may well have remarked that if the Frate had mixed a much deeper fraud with a zeal and ability less inconvenient to high personages, the fraud would have been regarded as an excellent oil for ecclesiastical and political wheels.

Nevertheless such shrewd men were forced to admit that, however poor a figure the Florentine government made in its clumsy pretence of a judicial warrant for what had in fact been predetermined as an act of policy, the measures of the Pope against Savonarola were necessary measures of self-defence. Not to try and rid himself of a man who wanted to stir up the Powers of Europe to summon a General Council and depose him, would have been adding ineptitude to iniquity. There was no denying that towards Alexander the Sixth Savonarola was a rebel, and, what was much more, a dangerous rebel. Florence had heard him say, and had well understood what he meant, that we would not *obey the devil*. It was inevitably a life-and-death struggle between the Frate and the Pope; but it was less inevitable that Florence should make itself the Pope's executioner.

Romola's ears were filled in this way with the suggestions of a faith still ardent under its wounds, and the suggestions of worldly discernment, judging things according to a very moderate standard of what is possible to human nature. She could be satisfied with neither. She brought to her long meditations over that printed document many painful observations, registered more or less consciously through the years of her discipleship, which whispered a presentiment that Savonarola's retractation of his prophetic claims was not merely a spasmodic effort to escape from torture. But, on the other hand, her soul cried out for some explanation of his lapses which would make it still possible for her to believe that the main striving of his life had been pure and grand. The recent memory of the selfish discontent which had come over her like a blighting wind along with the loss of her trust in the man who had been for her an incarnation of the highest motives, had produced a reaction which is known to many as a sort of faith that has sprung up to them out of the very depths of their despair. It was impossible, she said now, that the negative disbelieving thoughts which had made her soul arid of all good, could be founded in the truth of things: impossible that it had not been a living spirit, and no hollow pretence, which had once breathed in the Frate's words, and kindled a new life in her. Whatever falsehood there had been in him, had been a fall and not a purpose; a gradual entanglement in which he struggled, not a contrivance encouraged by success.

Looking at the printed confessions, she saw many sentences which bore the stamp of bungling fabrication: they had that emphasis and repetition in self-accusation which none but very low hypocrites use to their fellow-men. But the fact that these sentences were in striking opposition, not only to the character of Savonarola, but also to the general tone of the confessions, strengthened the impression that the rest of the text represented in the main what had really fallen from his lips. Hardly a word was dishonourable to him except what turned on his prophetic annunciations. He was unvarying in his statement of the ends he had pursued for Florence, the Church, and the world; and, apart from the mixture of falsity in that claim to special inspiration by which he sought to gain hold of men's minds, there was no admission of having used unworthy means. Even in this confession, and without expurgation of the notary's malign phrases, Fra Girolamo shone forth as a man who had sought his own glory indeed, but sought it by labouring for the very highest end,—the moral welfare of men,—not by vague exhortations, but by striving to turn beliefs into energies that would work in all the details of life.

"Everything that I have done," said one memorable passage, which may perhaps have had its erasures and interpolations, "I have done with the design of being forever famous in the present and in future ages, and that I might win credit in Florence, and that nothing of great import should be done without my sanction. And when I had thus established my position in Florence, I had it in my mind to do great things in Italy and beyond Italy, by means of those chief personages with whom I had contracted friendship and consulted on high matters, such as this of the General Council. And in proportion as my first efforts succeeded, I should have adopted further measures. Above all, when the General Council had once been brought about, I intended to rouse the princes of Christendom, and especially those beyond the borders of Italy, to subdue the infidels. It was not much in my thoughts to get myself made a Cardinal or Pope, for when I should have achieved the work I had in view, I should, without being Pope, have been the first man in the world in the authority I should have possessed, and the reverence that would have been paid me. If I had been made Pope, I would not have refused the office: but it seemed to me that to be the head of that work was a greater thing than to be Pope, because a man without virtue may be Pope; but *such a work as I contemplated demanded a man of excellent virtues."*

That blending of ambition with belief in the supremacy of goodness made no new tone to Romola, who had been used to hear it in the voice that rang through the Duomo. It was the habit of Savonarola's mind to conceive great things, and to feel that he was the man to do them. Iniquity should be brought low; the cause of justice, purity, and love should triumph; and it should triumph by his voice, by his work, by his blood. In moments of ecstatic contemplation, doubtless, the sense of self melted in the sense of the Unspeakable, and in that part of his experience lay the elements of genuine self-abasement; but in the presence of his fellow-men for whom he was to act, pre-eminence seemed a necessary condition of his life.

And perhaps this confession, even when it described a doubleness that was conscious and deliberate, really implied no more than that wavering of belief concerning his own impressions and motives which most human beings who have not a stupid inflexibility of self-confidence must be liable to under a marked change of external conditions. In a life where the experience was so tumultuously mixed as it must have been in the Frate's, what a possibility was opened for a change of self-judgment, when, instead of eyes that venerated and knees that knelt, instead of a great work on its way to accomplishment, and in its prosperity stamping the agent as a chosen instrument, there came the hooting and the spitting and the curses of the crowd; and then the hard faces of enemies made judges; and then the horrible torture, and with the torture the irrepressible cry, "It is true, what you would have me say: let me go: do not torture me again: yes, yes, I am guilty. O God! Thy Stroke has reached me!"

As Romola thought of the anguish that must have followed the confession,—whether, in the subsequent solitude of the prison, conscience retracted or confirmed the self-taxing words,—that anguish seemed to be pressing on her own heart and urging the slow bitter tears. Every vulgar self-ignorant person in Florence was glibly pronouncing on this man's demerits, while *he* was knowing a depth of sorrow which can only be known to the soul that has loved and sought the most perfect thing, and beholds itself fallen.

She had not then seen—what she saw afterwards—the evidence of the Frate's mental state after he had had thus to lay his mouth in the dust. As the days went by, the reports of new unpublished examinations, eliciting no change of confessions, ceased; Savonarola was left alone in his prison, and allowed pen and ink for a while, that, if he liked, he might use his poor bruised and strained right arm to write with. He wrote; but what he wrote was no vindication of his innocence, no protest against the proceedings used towards him: it was a continued colloquy with that Divine purity with which he sought complete reunion; it was the outpouring of self-abasement; it was one long cry for inward renovation. No lingering echoes of the old vehement self-assertion, "Look at my work, for it is good, and those who set their faces against it are the children of the devil!" The voice of Sadness tells him: "God placed thee in the midst of the people even as if thou hadst been one of the excellent. In this way thou hast taught others, and hast failed to learn thyself. Thou hast cured others; and thou thyself hast been still diseased. Thy heart was lifted up at the beauty of thy own deeds, and through this thou hast lost thy wisdom, and art become, and shalt be to all eternity, nothing. . . . After so many benefits with which God has honoured thee, thou art fallen into the depths of the sea; and after so many gifts bestowed on thee, thou, by thy pride and vainglory, hast scandalized all the world." And when Hope speaks and argues that the Divine love has not forsaken him, it says nothing now of a great work to be done, but only says, "Thou art not forsaken, else why is thy heart bowed in penitence? That too is a gift."

There is no jot of worthy evidence that from the time of his imprisonment to the supreme moment, Savonarola thought or spoke of himself as a martyr. The idea of martyrdom had been to him a passion dividing the dream of the future with the triumph of beholding his work achieved. And now, in place of both, had come a resignation which he called by no glorifying name.

But therefore he may the more fitly be called a martyr by his fellow-men to all time. For power rose against him not because of his sins, but because of his greatness,—not because he sought to deceive the world, but because he sought to make it noble. And through that greatness of his he endured a double agony,—not only the reviling and the torture and the death-throe, but the agony of sinking from the vision of glorious achievement into that deep shadow where he could only say, "I count as nothing; darkness encompasses me: yet the light I saw was the true light."

CHAPTER LII

THE LAST SILENCE

ROMOLA had seemed to hear, as if they had been a cry, the words repeated to her by many lips,—the words uttered by Savonarola when he took leave of those brethren of San Marco who had come to witness his signature of the confession: "Pray for me, for God has withdrawn from me the spirit of phophecy."

Those words had shaken her with new doubts as to the mode in which he looked back at the past in moments of complete self-possession; and the doubts were strengthened by more piteous things still, which soon reached her ears.

The 19th of May had come, and by that day's sunshine there had entered into Florence the two Papal Commissaries, charged with the completion of Savonarola's trial. They entered amid the acclamations of the people, calling for the death of the Frate. For now the popular cry was, "It is the Frate's deception that has brought on all our misfortunes; let him be burned, and all things right will be done, and our evils will cease."

The next day it is well certified that there was fresh and fresh torture of the shattered sensitive frame; and now, at the first sight of the horrible implements, Savonarola, in convulsed agitation, fell on his knees, and in brief passionate words *retracted his confession*, declared that he had spoken falsely in denying his prophetic gift, and that if he suffered, he would suffer for the truth,—"The things that I have spoken, I had them from God."

But not the less the torture was laid upon him; and when he was under it he was asked why he had uttered those retracting words. Men were not demons in those days, and yet nothing but confessions of guilt were held a reason for release from torture. The answer came: "I said it that I might seem good: tear me no more, I will tell you the truth."

There were Florentine assessors at this new trial, and those words of twofold retraction had soon spread. They filled Romola with dismayed uncertainty.

"But"—it flashed across her—"there will come a moment when he may speak. When there is no dread hanging over him but the dread of falsehood, when they have brought him into the presence of death, when he is lifted above the people, and looks on them for the last time, they cannot hinder him from speaking a last decisive word. I will be there."

Three days after, on the 23d of May, 1498, there was again a long narrow platform stretching across the great piazza, from the Palazzo Vecchio towards the Tetta de' Pisani. But there was no grove of fuel as before: instead of that, there was one great heap of fuel placed on the circular area which made the termination of the long narrow platform. And above this heap of fuel rose a gibbet with three halters on it; a gib-

bet which, having two arms, still looked so much like a cross as to make
some beholders uncomfortable, though one arm had been truncated to
avoid the resemblance.

On the marble terrace of the Palazzo were three tribunals,—one near
the door for the Bishop, who was to perform the ceremony of degradation
on Fra Girolamo and the two brethren who were to suffer as his followers and accomplices; another for the Papal Commissaries, who were to
pronounce them heretics and schismatics, and deliver them over to the
secular arm; and a third, close to Marzacco, at the corner of the terrace
where the platform began, for the Gonfaloniere, and the Eight who were
to pronounce the sentence of death.

Again the piazza was thronged with expectant faces; again there was
to be a great fire kindled. In the majority of the crowd that pressed
around the gibbet the expectation was that of ferocious hatred, or of
mere hard curiosity to behold a barbarous sight. But there were still
many spectators on the wide pavement, on the roofs, and at the windows, who, in the midst of their bitter grief and their own endurance of
insult as hypocritical Piagnoni, were not without a lingering hope, even
at this eleventh hour, that God would interpose, by some sign, to manifest their beloved prophet as His servant. And there were yet more who
looked forward with trembling eagerness, as Romola did, to that final
moment when Savonarola might say, "O people, I was innocent of
deceit."

Romola was at the window on the north side of the piazza, far away
from the marble terrace where the tribunals stood; and near her, also
looking on in painful doubt concerning the man who had won his early
reverence, was a young Florentine of two-and-twenty, named Jacopo
Nardi, afterwards to deserve honour as one of the very few who, feeling
Fra Girolamo's eminence, have written about him with the simple desire
to be veracious. He had said to Romola, with respectful gentleness, when
he saw the struggle in her between her shuddering horror of the scene
and her yearning to witness what might happen in the last moment,—

"Madonna, there is no need for you to look at these cruel things. I
will tell you when he comes out of the Palazzo. Trust to me; I know
what you would see."

Romola covered her face, but the hootings that seemed to make the
hideous scene still visible could not be shut out. At last her arm was
touched, and she heard the words, "He comes." She looked towards the
Palace, and could see Savonarola led out in his Dominican garb; could
see him standing before the Bishop, and being stripped of the black
mantle, the white scapulary, and long white tunic, till he stood in a
close woolen under-tunic, that told of no sacred office, no rank. He had
been degraded, and cut off from the Church Militant.

The baser part of the multitude delight in degradations, apart from
any hatred; it is the satire they best understand. There was a fresh hoot
of triumph as the three degraded brethren passed on to the tribunal of
the Papal Commissaries, who were to pronounce them schismatics and

heretics. Did not the prophet look like a schismatic and heretic now? It is easy to believe in the damnable state of a man who stands stripped and degraded.

Then the third tribunal was passed—that of the Florentine officials who were to pronounce sentence, and among whom, even at her distance, Romola could discern the odious figure of Dolfo Spini, indued in the grave black lucco, as one of the Eight.

Then the three figures, in their close white raiment, trod their way along the platform, amidst yells and grating tones of insult.

"Cover your eyes, Madonna," said Jacopo Nardi; "Fra Girolamo will be the last."

It was not long before she had to uncover them again. Savonarola was there. He was not far off her now. He had mounted the steps; she could see him look round on the multitude.

But in the same moment expectation died, and she only saw what he was seeing,—torches waving to kindle the fuel beneath his dead body, faces glaring with a yet worse light; she only heard what *he* was hearing, —gross jests, taunts, and curses.

The moment was past. Her face was covered again, and she only knew that Savonarola's voice had passed into eternal silence.

EPILOGUE

On the evening of the 22d of May, 1509, five persons, of whose history we have known something, were seated in a handsome upper room opening on to a loggia which, at its right-hand corner, looked all along the Borgo Pinti, and over the city gate towards Fiesole, and the solemn heights beyond it.

At one end of the room was an archway opening into a narrow inner room, hardly more than a recess, where the light fell from above on a small altar covered with fair white linen. Over the altar was a picture, discernible at the distance where the little party sat only as the small full-length portrait of a Dominican Brother. For it was shaded from the light above by overhanging branches and wreaths of flowers, and the fresh tapers below it were unlit. But it seemed that the decoration of the altar and its recess was not complete. For part of the floor was strewn with a confusion of flowers and green boughs, and among them sat a delicate blue-eyed girl of thirteen, tossing her long light-brown hair out of her eyes, as she made selections for the wreaths she was weaving, or looked up at her mother's work in the same kind, and told her how to do it with a little air of instruction.

For that mother was not very clever at weaving flowers or at any other work. Tessa's fingers had not become more adroit with the years, —only very much fatter. She got on slowly and turned her head about a good deal, and asked Ninna's opinion with much deference; for Tessa never ceased to be astonished at the wisdom of her children. She still wore her contadina gown: it was only broader than the old one; and there was the silver pin in her rough curly brown hair, and round her neck the memorable necklace, with a red cord under it, that ended mysteriously in her bosom. Her rounded face wore even a more perfect look of childish content than in her younger days: everybody was so good in the world, Tessa thought; even Monna Brigida never found fault with her now, and did little else than sleep, which was an amiable practice in everybody, and one that Tessa liked for herself.

Monna Brigida was asleep at this moment, in a straight-backed arm-chair, a couple of yards off. Her hair, parting backward under her black hood, had that soft whiteness which is not like snow or anything else, but is simply the lovely whiteness of aged hair. Her chin had sunk on her bosom, and her hands rested on the elbow of her chair. She had not been weaving flowers or doing anything else; she had only been looking on as usual, and as usual had fallen asleep.

The other two figures were seated farther off, at the wide doorway that opened on to the loggia. Lillo sat on the ground with his back against the angle of the door-post, and his long legs stretched out, while he held a large book open on his knee, and occasionally made a dash with his hand at an inquisitive fly, with an air of interest stronger than that excited by the finely printed copy of Petrarch which he kept open at one place, as if he were learning something by heart.

Romola sat nearly opposite Lillo, but she was not observing him. Her hands were crossed on her lap, and her eyes were fixed absently on the distant mountains: she was evidently unconscious of anything around her. An eager life had left its marks upon her: the finely moulded cheek had sunk a little, the golden crown was less massive; but there was a placidity in Romola's face which had never belonged to it in youth. It is but once that we can know our worst sorrows, and Romola had known them while life was new.

Absorbed in this way, she was not at first aware that Lillo had ceased to look at his book, and was watching her with a slightly impatient air, which meant that he wanted to talk to her, but was not quite sure whether she would like that entertainment just now. But persevering looks make themselves felt at last. Romola did presently turn away her eyes from the distance, and met Lillo's impatient dark gaze with a brighter and brighter smile. He shuffled along the floor, still keeping the book on his lap, till he got close to her and lodged his chin on her knee.

"What is it, Lillo?" said Romola, pulling his hair back from his brow. Lillo was a handsome lad, but his features were turning out to be more massive and less regular than his father's. The blood of the Tuscan peasant was in his veins.

"Mamma Romola, what am I to be?" he said, well contented that there was a prospect of talking till it would be too late to con "Spirto gentil" any longer.

"What should you like to be, Lillo? You might be a scholar. My father was a scholar, you know, and taught me a great deal. That is the reason why I can teach you."

"Yes," said Lillo, rather hesitatingly. "But he is old and blind in the picture. Did he get a great deal of glory?"

"Not much, Lillo. The world was not always very kind to him, and he saw meaner men than himself put into higher places, because they could flatter and say what was false. And then his dear son thought it right to leave him and become a monk; and after that, my father, being blind and lonely, felt unable to do the things that would have made his learning of greater use to men, so that he might still have lived in his works after he was in his grave."

"I should not like that sort of life," said Lillo. "I should like to be something that would make me a great man, and very happy besides,—something that would not hinder me from having a good deal of pleasure."

"That is not easy, my Lillo. It is only a poor sort of happiness that could ever come by caring very much about our own narrow pleasures. We can only have the highest happiness, such as goes along with being a great man, by having wide thoughts, and much feeling for the rest of the world as well as ourselves; and this sort of happiness often brings so much pain with it that we can only tell it from pain by its being what we would choose before everything else, because our souls see it is good. There are so many things wrong and difficult in the world, that no man can be great—he can hardly keep himself from wickedness—unless he gives up thinking much about pleasure or rewards, and gets strength to endure what is hard and painful. My father had the greatness that belongs to integrity; he chose poverty and obscurity rather than falsehood. And there was Fra Girolamo,—you know why I keep to-morrow sacred: *he* had the greatness which belongs to a life spent in struggling against powerful wrong, and in trying to raise men to the highest deeds they are capable of. And so, my Lillo, if you mean to act nobly and seek to know the best things God has put within reach of men, you must learn to fix your mind on that end, and not on what will happen to you because of it. And remember, if you were to choose something lower, and make it the rule of your life to seek your own pleasure and escape from what is disagreeable, calamity might come just the same; and it would be a calamity falling on a base mind, which is the one form of sorrow that has no balm in it, and that may well make a man say, 'It would have been better for me if I had never been born.' I will tell you something, Lillo."

Romola paused for a moment. She had taken Lillo's cheeks between her hands, and his young eyes were meeting hers.

"There was a man to whom I was very near, so that I could see a great deal of his life, who made almost every one fond of him, for he was young and clever and beautiful, and his manners to all were gentle and kind. I believe, when I first knew him, he never thought of anything cruel or base. But because he tried to slip away from everything that was unpleasant, and cared for nothing else so much as his own safety, he came at last to commit some of the basest deeds,—such as make men infamous. He denied his father, and left him to misery; he betrayed every trust that was reposed in him, that he might keep himself safe and get rich and prosperous. Yet calamity overtook him."

Again Romola paused. Her voice was unsteady, and Lillo was looking up at her with awed wonder.

"Another time, my Lillo,—I will tell you another time. See, there are our old Piero di Cosimo and Nello coming up the Borgo Pinti, bringing us their flowers. Let us go and wave our hands to them, that they may know we see them."

"How queer old Piero is!" said Lillo, as they stood at the corner of the loggia, watching the advancing figures. "He abuses you for dressing the altar and thinking so much of Fra Girolamo, and yet he brings you the flowers."

"Never mind," said Romola. "There are many good people who did not love Fra Girolamo. Perhaps I should never have learned to love him if he had not helped me when I was in great need."